Prai

"Okie perfectly captures the sweetness of falling in love with witty, sparkling prose. Searingly funny, heart-wrenchingly romantic, and painfully honest, *The Best Worst Thing* is a knockout debut."

—Kate Golden, *USA Today* bestselling author of *If Not for My Baby*

"*The Best Worst Thing* absolutely blew me away. It's sexy, complex, and raw—the perfect story of imperfect people in an impossible situation. Don't even get me started on the banter, which lands itself among the GREATS. Lauren Okie's writing is so ridiculously good that I had to put the book down a few times just to catch my breath. Consider me officially obsessed."

—Jessica Joyce, *USA Today* bestselling author of *The Ex Vows*

"*The Best Worst Thing* is so sharp, sexy, and real. Every character feels like someone messy and raw and perfectly human. It's a refreshing novel with plenty of twists you don't see coming. Highly recommend this beautiful and redemptive debut!"

—Jamie Varon, author of *Main Character Energy*

"*The Best Worst Thing* is a stop-you-in-your-tracks kind of story—dazing and illuminating, filled with real, messy people figuring out what they want and deserve in the most heart-wrenching of circumstances. I inhaled every gorgeous word of Lauren Okie's prose. Absurdly sexy, psychologically rich, and joyously hopeful, Nicole and Logan's life-affirming love story will take permanent residence in your heart, and you'll be much better for it."

—Katie Naymon, author of *You Between the Lines*

"Lauren Okie's *The Best Worst Thing* squeezed my heart in the best possible way. It's a tender, honest, and beautiful book."

—Amy T. Matthews, author of *Someone Else's Bucket List*

"A dynamic novel with so much heart, packed with adorable banter and very real and messy characters to root for; *The Best Worst Thing* has everything I love in a romance, and Lauren Okie's voice jumps off every page. A true delight of a read."

—Natalie Sue, author of *I Hope This Finds You Well*

"With resonant prose and a full-hearted, unforgettable romance, Okie weaves a life's worth of humor and heartbreak, happiness and honesty into these pages. *The Best Worst Thing* is the best thing that's been on our bookshelves in a while."

—Emily Wibberley and Austin Siegemund-Broka, authors of *The Roughest Draft*

"*The Best Worst Thing* is read-in-one-sitting brilliance! The perfect blend of California summer romance, emotional depth, years of unresolved longing, and the constant sense of teetering on the edge of heartbreak. I loved every second!"

—Meg Jones, author of *Clean Point*

THE BEST WORST THING

A Novel

LAUREN OKIE

AVON

An Imprint of HarperCollins*Publishers*

Without limiting the exclusive rights of any author, contributor or the publisher of this publication, any unauthorized use of this publication to train generative artificial intelligence (AI) technologies is expressly prohibited. HarperCollins also exercise their rights under Article 4(3) of the Digital Single Market Directive 2019/790 and expressly reserve this publication from the text and data mining exception.

This is a work of fiction. Names, characters, places, and incidents are products of the author's imagination or are used fictitiously and are not to be construed as real. Any resemblance to actual events, locales, organizations, or persons, living or dead, is entirely coincidental.

THE BEST WORST THING. Copyright © 2025 by Lauren Okie. All rights reserved. Printed in the United States of America. No part of this book may be used or reproduced in any manner whatsoever without written permission except in the case of brief quotations embodied in critical articles and reviews. For information, address HarperCollins Publishers, 195 Broadway, New York, NY 10007. In Europe, HarperCollins Publishers, Macken House, 39/40 Mayor Street Upper, Dublin 1, D01 C9W8, Ireland.

HarperCollins books may be purchased for educational, business, or sales promotional use. For information, please email the Special Markets Department at SPsales@harpercollins.com.

hc.com

Avon, Avon & logo, and Avon Books & logo are registered trademarks of HarperCollins Publishers in the United States of America and other countries.

FIRST EDITION

Designed by Diahann Sturge-Campbell

Library of Congress Cataloging-in-Publication Data

Names: Okie, Lauren author
Title: The best worst thing : a novel / Lauren Okie.
Description: First edition. | New York, NY : Avon, an imprint of
  HarperCollinsPublishers, 2025.
Identifiers: LCCN 2025020233 | ISBN 9780063432673 trade paperback | ISBN
  9780063432680 ebook
Subjects: LCGFT: Romance fiction | Fiction | Novels
Classification: LCC PS3615.K58 B47 2025 | DDC 813/.6--dc23/eng/20250603
LC record available at https://lccn.loc.gov/2025020233

ISBN 978-0-06-343267-3

25 26 27 28 29 LBC 5 4 3 2 1

For Ashley

"Time will explain."
Jane Austen, *Persuasion*

Author's Note

When I set out to write this novel, I did so in hopes of creating a love story that was, if nothing else, both tons of fun and brutally honest. And so, while *The Best Worst Thing* is teeming with banter, yearning, and ridiculously hot sex, please know it also touches on some serious themes, including infertility and pregnancy loss.

1

Pretty Infertile

"So," Gabe said, "tell them what's next."

"Okay," Nicole said, glancing at her note card, "well, tonight at midnight, we're doing the trigger shot. That gets the eggs mature, ready to be fertilized. And this time, my doctor wants me to inject it intramuscularly, so it's this giant needle, and it goes pretty much right in my ass, and—"

"It's really more your hip, babe."

"It's my ass. I would know. I sit on it all day, trying to make you an heir."

Gabe looked up from his microphone and grinned. Ten years later, he was still stupidly handsome. Tall and broad, with dark brown hair and ink-blue eyes and a strong, defined jaw. And while two years of hormones had left Nicole drained, Gabe had grown even more attractive as he aged, in that way the best-looking men always seemed to do in their late thirties.

"I know," he said, coffee mug in hand, "and thank you. But I'm the one who does the shot, and trust me, it's your hip."

"Whatever. Point is, we'll do the trigger, and then Sunday morning, we'll go to the clinic and they'll knock me out, which is easily the best part, and then they'll use another giant needle to pull out all my eggs—"

"And then I get to come in a cup!"

Nicole laughed, smiling up at him. He'd nailed that one.

Gabe wasn't always on the podcast. When Nicole had first

started her show—*Pretty Infertile*—a couple of years ago, he was a little bewildered by the whole thing. But lately, he'd begun recording with her once or twice a month. He'd set up her jokes and push her stories forward. And sure, it took a bit of begging to get Gabe behind the microphone, but it was well worth it. Because the episodes they did together always seemed to be the stickiest—to get the most attention, the most engagement.

"Oh!" Nicole said. "I meant to ask you! Did you pick your porn yet?"

"Mm . . . I'm torn. Teacher-student or girl-on-girl-on-girl."

"Seriously? How vanilla. Why not live a little?"

"Fine," he said. "You pick it out, then!"

Nicole grunted into her microphone, then rattled off a few choice fetishes while their goldendoodle, Nero, settled at her feet. Through the balcony doors off Nicole's upstairs office, the marine layer was just beginning to cast its cool, sleepy glow across Manhattan Beach, a coastal suburb of Los Angeles where nothing ever happened. July 1, and still—fog. Nicole had called the South Bay home for nine years, but she'd never quite gotten used to this.

How late the summers started. And then, how long they dragged.

"I mean, if we're talking about losing inhibitions," Gabe said, "let's revisit your first egg retrieval."

"Oh god. I was high as a kite."

"Just ridiculous." He turned to his next note card. "Like, Colie literally wakes up from the procedure, reaches for my hand, and screams at the top of her lungs, 'Gabe, wait, how was your ejaculation!? Was it powerful!?'"

"Dr. Williams said you should make it powerful! I was just checking!"

Nicole, weaving her toes into Nero's spine, thought back to her first cycle of in vitro fertilization, when she'd really believed things were going to be different. And why wouldn't they have been? She'd been only thirty, and she'd done everything right. Started getting nine hours of sleep. Quit running, quit hot yoga, quit drinking Diet Coke. Ate nothing but fatty fish, organic avocados, and Brazil nuts.

Had the goddamn surgery. Twice.

"I mean, Nicole's just putting on a show. I think every other patient in the surgery center could hear her. The nurses were giggling. An admin came and hushed us."

"So then Gabe asks our doctor, who'd stopped by to see how I was doing, if everyone made a fool of themselves or if it was just me. And she, like, gives me this pitiful-but-adoring look, pats my head, and goes, 'No, not usually, sweetheart. This is really something.'"

Nicole took a long sip of her coffee—decaf, of course, with a drop of almond milk—then glanced at her notes. They had a lot more to cover. And all joking aside, Sunday morning's procedure was a big deal. Because this was their last chance to make embryos for their gestational carrier, whose first two transfers had failed. Their contract, a boilerplate agreement, covered three. And after that, who knew?

Nicole would never admit it, but she was beginning to lose steam. She was tired of spending hours a week driving up and down the 405 for an ultrasound, a quick blood draw, a last-minute vial of Menopur. She was tired of needing a two-hour nap by noon just to make it through the day. And she was tired of skipping out on baby showers, of crying over due dates that came and went, of watching the other women in her IVF forum disappear into motherhood, leaving her behind.

"Anyway," she said, "the plan is—"

An alarm went off on Gabe's phone. Nicole winced, then paused the recording.

"Sorry, babe," he said, swiping through his email as he rose to his feet. "I have a nine thirty at the office. Can we finish tonight?"

"Oh, um, I guess so, sure . . . but then I really need you to come home on time, okay? Because I want to have everything done by tomorrow so I can rest after the retrieval, and making the graphics has been taking forever lately, and—"

"You're the best," he said, kissing the top of her head. Nicole nodded, nearly biting her tongue as Gabe disappeared down the hall. With her jaw still heavy, she began scrolling through the show's latest analytics. She hovered her cursor over a dip in last week's drop-off chart. She pinpointed the moment she'd lost too many listeners. She compared that time stamp to her monthly, quarterly, and year-to-date averages.

And then, when she finally heard the front door shut, Nicole Speyer stared into her computer screen a little harder and tried not to think too much about the way she used to go places, see people, do things.

About the way Gabe used to look at her.

About the way she used to beg for him to fuck her.

2

How Babies Are Made

That night, Nicole was lying on the off-white sectional in her living room, eating precut watermelon from a plastic container, when the front door unlocked. It was half past ten.

"Sorry, babe," Gabe said, tossing his keys onto the entryway console as Nero greeted him, tail wagging. "That due diligence came in late, and then Kyle wanted to grab a drink, talk it over. I tried to cut out early, but you know how he gets."

Nicole nodded. She knew exactly how Kyle got—and it wasn't worth the fight. It wasn't like there was anything she could do about him, or the fact that Gabe hadn't been home before nine all week.

"Well, we can just record tomorrow, I guess. After you get home from golf?"

"Definitely," Gabe said as he kicked off his dress shoes. He wandered into the open kitchen, poured himself a drink, grabbed his foil-covered plate, and then slid onto the couch next to Nicole. By the time he finished eating, he'd already told her all about his day—how he wasn't loving the numbers on that Irvine deal, how he might need to travel back and forth if he couldn't close it before they left for Colorado next month.

The Aspen trip was an August tradition for everyone who was anyone at Gabe's office. She and Gabe had first been invited a couple of years ago when Nicole stopped working, and they hadn't missed a season since. That said, attendance was, as far as completely optional vacations were concerned, thoroughly mandatory.

"Anyway." Gabe tossed Nero his last flake of salmon, then set his dish on the coffee table. "What's up with you? You talk to the agency at all?"

"Yeah." Nicole tugged one of Gabe's old sweatshirts over her stomach. Her ovaries, these past ten days, had swollen to the size of grapefruits. "We're still on track for a week from Monday. Valerie's got everything lined up with childcare too."

Valerie—Nicole and Gabe's gestational carrier, the same one Nicole had been texting for the past four hours—lived in Virginia. Five days after Nicole's egg retrieval, the clinic would perform genetic screening on the embryos, then overnight them across the country. It wasn't ideal, working with a surrogate on the East Coast. But wait times to match with a California-based carrier were unbelievably long, and Valerie had been, from day one, an absolute dream.

"You still going?" Gabe said.

"To Norfolk? Yeah. If nothing else, for Val. You should come. You should meet her, even if . . . She's just really great."

"I want to." Gabe's phone vibrated in his pocket. He silenced it, then took a long sip of his whiskey. "I really do. And I know you guys have gotten superclose. But you know how it is at the office. The guys don't understand this stuff. And I'm finally in Kyle's ear."

Nicole tugged at the tassel of a throw pillow. "I just wanted to do this last one together, that's all."

"I know," he said. "But it's a really tough month for me, okay? I'm sorry."

Nicole gave that tassel another tug, then rested her head on the thick, square arm of the sofa and stared straight into the TV screen. Gabe exhaled, then scrolled through his phone. And then, a few minutes later, just when Nero had fallen asleep underneath the coffee table and Nicole had sufficiently squashed whatever it was she really wished to say or do or scream, Gabe glanced up at the suddenly moaning television and raised an eyebrow.

"What on earth are you watching? Should this be my sperm-collection porn?"

She snickered. Gabe scooted closer, laughing, demanding details as he pulled her feet into his lap. Luckily for him, Nicole had seen this episode twice already.

Usually, when Gabe worked late, Nicole would dive into a new book or breeze through an old favorite. But lately, she hadn't had the energy. Besides, Valerie was doing a rewatch too, and it was nice, connecting over something mindless—something low stakes. Pretending their friendship was normal when, quite clearly, it was not.

"Okay, so," she said, just as Gabe's thumbs found her ankles. She reached for the watermelon, then passed him the container. "That's Fitz—he's actually president. And he's supposed to be at the inaugural ball. But he's just gonna rail her instead. Right there, on his desk."

Gabe smirked. "Must be nice."

Every muscle in Nicole's body clenched. "I . . ."

"I'm kidding, baby." He pulled her into his arms, then grabbed the remote and turned up the volume. "Let's just watch your ridiculous show, okay? I love you."

Nicole nodded, scrunching her eyes closed as he softly scratched her back and the television talked and talked until, finally, she drifted off to sleep. And then, just before midnight, Gabe tapped her awake, swiped her backside with an alcohol swab, and jabbed her with a three-millimeter syringe of Novarel right where her ass met her hip.

3

Independence Day

"Speyer, man!"

"Kyle, hey," Gabe said, flashing that million-dollar grin and extending his hand. "The pool deck looks great. House looks great."

Nicole smiled, then waved hello. Her egg retrieval was only yesterday, and truthfully, she belonged in bed. But that was never going to happen. This was Kyle McMahon's famous Fourth of July barbecue, and everyone from Gabe's office was here . . . with their big, beautiful families in tow.

And besides, the party was lovely. Nothing like the Fourth of July get-togethers Nicole had grown up going to, but there were still plenty of burgers and baked beans to go around. It was just, there were also two sushi chefs, a red-white-and-blue children's flower crown station, and dozens of very shiny, very thin women wearing thousand-dollar midi dresses. Oh, and cocaine. Upstairs, of course—and only upon request. This was a family-friendly affair.

"Well, you know Alexis," Kyle said, taking a sip of his beer. He was pushing fifty, balding, and standing there in boat shoes and a blue linen button-down. "Can't go a year without renovating something. God help me if the tennis court's next."

"No way," Gabe said. "Court looks great. Better than what I'm playing on at my club."

This went on for several light-years while Nicole politely studied the lemon wedge floating in her iced tea. Kyle got Gabe up to speed on which semidisgraced movie producer might buy the just-listed monstrosity next door, why so-and-so was totally going to get fucked by that securities fraud investigation, and just how much cash his wife's latest girls' trip to Tulum had cost him. Fascinating stuff, really.

Back in the day, when they'd first moved out to LA, Gabe would parade Nicole around these parties like she was some kind of trophy. She'd never felt quite comfortable in his world, but the way he rested a couple of fingers on her hip or arm or waist while she told a story, the way he lit up when she landed a joke, it had been easy to forget all that.

But that was then. This was now.

"So, tell me, Nicole," Kyle said, "how's that podcast of yours?"

"Oh, it's . . . it's good, actually."

"You still making your husband here late for work so he can talk about his feelings?"

Nicole swallowed. Gabe flinched, then slipped a hand onto the small of her back.

"Colie actually studied English in college, so she's really good with this stuff—with stories. It's kind of her thing."

"English, huh?" Kyle tipped back his beer, found a server to hand the empty bottle to, then signaled for another. "Didn't know that about you. Just remember you were in advertising for a few years there."

"I was, yeah."

"Well, maybe you'll write a book someday. You know, make something of all this."

Gabe began to open his mouth, then scratched the back of his neck and gulped his beer instead. Nicole, arms clamped around her elbows, smiled right on cue. And then, when she realized her husband wasn't going to say a goddamn word, she excused herself and disappeared into the house.

A moment later, Gabe was following her down the hall. His voice, hushed.

"Colie, wait, I—"

"I want to go home," she said.

"We can't. It just started, I . . ."

They were walking and talking, twisting and turning, until they'd stumbled into Kyle's son's computer room, all white oak and black matte and soft gray. Gabe shut the door.

That was when Nicole finally began to cry.

"You let me look like an idiot out there! You make me come to this thing. I look like shit. I feel like shit. And then you let him talk to me like my whole life is a joke! Like the things I do don't matter! How can you expect me to go spend a month with these fucking people? Seriously, Gabe. How?"

"I'm sorry, okay? But what am I supposed to do? What am I supposed to say? He's my boss."

"I don't know," Nicole said, poking at some *Star Wars* bobble-head on a floating shelf, her back turned. Her face, stinging. "Probably not that, though."

This continued for a few more minutes. A held-in-whispers screaming match they both knew would never be resolved. When there was nothing left to discuss, Nicole told Gabe she needed a little more time to get herself together. That she would be out soon.

Alone and waiting for her tears to trail off, she wandered toward a desk in the corner and ran her fingers across its smooth, clean wood. At once, a sleeping computer's screen came aglow. And that was when she saw it: *Dwarf Fortress*.

It had been years, but she'd have recognized those ridiculous graphics, those pixelated letters and shapes and symbols anywhere. She'd seen them countless times at her old agency, obscured by a pitch deck, a billboard mock-up, a live stream of a Mariners double-header . . .

"It's the most complex game ever made," he'd said to her one afternoon, polishing off a granola bar, then tearing open another. "Pure chaos."

Nicole rolled her eyes. He was like this most days by three or four o'clock. Hungry. Talkative. Barely working. She'd popped into his office to drop off a few last-minute costs for next week's pitch only to find him doing, well, this.

"No, seriously," he said. "The rules are so strange and specific that you have to study for a week just to learn how to build a hut. It's excruciating."

"And you play this . . . on purpose?"

"Yes, Pottery Barn. On purpose."

Nicole scoffed. She was really more of a Crate & Barrel girl, if anything. He swiveled his chair toward his computer screen, pulled up some obscure message board where people seemed to agree with him, and read a few posts aloud. As if they were real evidence. As if they strengthened his case.

"Okay, I think we're done here, I—"

"Wait! I haven't even explained cave adaptation to you! If you let the dwarves get too drunk, if you let them spend too much time inside, they'll just start vomiting the second they're exposed to sunlight and—"

"Holy shit, Logan. I cannot listen to this a second longer."

"Oh, come on." Now he was grinning like an idiot, running a few fingers through his hair. Closing out his game, getting back to work. "We both know that deep down, you're just as weird as—"

"Nicole?"

A cloying, mousy voice snapped the memory in half. It was Alexis McMahon—Kyle's wife.

"Do you need something, sweetie? What are you doing in here?"

"Oh, sorry . . . I'm just a little out of it today."

Alexis just stood there, smiling at her. A barely forty blond waif who was always draped in something effortlessly gorgeous. Today, an ivory slip dress that hung off her body just so.

"Come," she said, touching a few manicured fingers to Nicole's wrist, then nudging her toward the hallway. "The girls have been asking where you've been all summer. Come say hi."

And with that, Nicole shoved the memory back onto the very top shelf of her mind, slipped on her game face, and got on with it.

4

Smithereens

The transfer went smoothly.

Dr. Akhtar used a catheter and a tiny puff of air to push two genetically screened embryos—one boy, one girl—into Valerie's uterus, told her to sit with her legs up for an hour, then sent her home to do a whole bunch of nothing for two days.

"This one's going to stick," an eager nurse who'd never laid eyes on Nicole's medical records said as she wheeled a Valium-woozy Valerie through the parking lot. And Nicole, fully prepared to wrinkle her nose, didn't.

Instead, she decided to believe. She decided to let herself forget what her doctor had said after Valerie's second transfer failed. That she didn't know why Nicole and Gabe's embryos weren't working, but as a physician, she had an ethical responsibility to tell them it was time to stop. That it was time to maybe start exploring other options.

But Nicole and Gabe weren't in the business of taking no for an answer. And when they'd learned the only viable embryos from Nicole's latest cycle had received unfavorable grades, they decided to throw a Hail Mary. They decided to transfer both.

And so Nicole—buzzing, believing—drove Valerie home, set her up with another season of *Scandal*, gave her a very careful hug, then headed to the airport to catch an earlier flight out of Virginia. After all, a summer storm was set to batter the mid-Atlantic later that afternoon. But just when she'd reached across the check-in counter for her new boarding pass, Nicole's phone slipped through her jittery fingers and landed smack against the speckled linoleum, shattering the screen into smithereens.

And so, phoneless, Nicole settled into her newly assigned seat, closed her eyes, and let herself imagine, just for the afternoon, that in nine months, she'd have twins. Boy-girl twins. And as she touched down in Los Angeles, wandered through the airport parking garage, drove the mindless twenty minutes home, and opened the navy door to her big white house, she was still riding that high.

"Nero, boy?" she said, setting her weekender down in the foyer. At her feet, strewn across the blond oak, a lilac sweatshirt.

That must've belonged to Cassidy, the dog walker. She usually came twice a day when Nicole was traveling: once in the morning and then again in the afternoon. It was too hard for Gabe to predict whether he'd make it home in time to feed Nero dinner and take him for a quick stroll around the block.

Nicole folded the sweatshirt, placed it on the console, then called out for Nero again.

His bed in the living room, empty.

The rug beneath the dining table, bare.

The armchair in the den, vacant.

He must've been in her office, curled up in a comma, sunbathing in his little spot on the hardwood just where the afternoon light poured in. After all, the marine layer had finally burned off today. Summer was here.

So she headed up the stairwell. That was when a voice—soft and young and too familiar—called down from the loft.

"Gabe?" it said. "I'm upstairs."

Three little words, and that was it. The walls began to spin.

Nicole's lungs cracked.

Her heart howled.

Her world stopped.

She clutched onto the banister and begged her body to take a few more impossible steps toward the landing.

One . . .

Two . . .

Three . . .

Cassidy was just lying there, headphones in, bare feet propped up on the arm of Nicole's linen loveseat, Nero half asleep in her lap. Her wild blond hair, bronzed legs, and very pretty face—now frozen.

"I, um . . ." Cassidy pulled the blaring buds out of her ears. "I wasn't feeling well, I was just laying down, I . . ."

Nicole nodded. She just nodded, staring at this girl, forced to picture her warm, wet lips all over Gabe's mouth and ears and neck and throat and—

"I'll go," Cassidy said, pulling her ridden-up shirt over her perfect little stomach, then darting down the stairs, one long leg after another, until she'd finally disappeared. As if it made any difference. As if anything could stop the past ten years from unraveling now.

Nicole could still see him standing there—six foot three, ridiculous Patagonia vest—talking up her roommate at that dive on Waverly. He caught her rolling her eyes right at him, then grinned from across the windowless, brick-walled basement—an ocean of pool tables and barely legals and watered-down Blue Moons separating him from her. He parted the sea like it was nothing. All she saw was him.

The way he looked right before he'd first kissed her—his hands up her dress in the filthy bathroom of that Astor Place Kmart, smack in the middle of her reading day, a forgotten shopping basket filled to the brim with half-priced Easter candy between their twisted toes. How, that first week, he'd fucked her maybe twenty, thirty times. Nicole was in finals, and when she'd beg for a break to study, he'd frown, then go down on her instead.

The way he smirked when, together for two months, they'd first pulled up to his parents' house, three stories of cream stucco and Spanish tile and wrought iron carefully perched atop the peak of Manhattan Beach. It was the coldest home Nicole had ever entered, but in Gabe's old bedroom, it was just the two of them, sharing a plate of microwave nachos, watching *The Office* under the covers, then screwing like animals until they finally fell asleep.

All of it, bullshit.

All of it, a lie.

Gabe knew every inch of her. And she didn't know him at all. And Nicole—all the bits and pieces and broken parts of her—just stood there, frozen at the top of that stairwell, mocked by those oversize black-and-white wedding photos she'd begged him to hang for years.

You stupid idiot, they whispered. *You jobless, childless, nothing little fool.*

She scoured his closet.

She ransacked his office.

She hurled his tennis racket at his rowing machine.

And then she sat on the stoop of their starter home, folded her body in half, and waited for him. She just sat there and counted every last car that crawled by.

An Audi SUV, white.

A Range Rover, silver.

Another Audi—a hatchback, champagne.

And then, finally, a Tesla. Model S, black, and screeching into the driveway on a breathless diagonal.

"Nicole, I swear, nothing happened!"

"Whatever she told you, it's not true!"

"Whatever you're thinking, it's not that!"

Nicole just sat there, lifeless, listening to her husband lie to her. It came easy, didn't it? He was born to do this—to lie. Every one, more desperate than the last.

"She's trying to get a job in finance! I told her I would help!"

"She's obsessed with me! Please, you have to let me explain!"

"She's just trying to get between us! I'm telling you, she's fucking nuts!"

It was strange—an out-of-body experience, really—watching the man she'd loved since she was twenty-two scrape her insides out with his bare hands. But he was a natural. He just kept talking and pacing and pleading and lying until there was nothing left. Until he'd gutted her.

This couldn't be Gabe. This couldn't be the same Gabe she'd married.

Hadn't he held her? His fingers sealed around hers during that first dilation and curettage; Nicole in shock, headphones blaring to drown the noise of their itty-bitty baby—a clump of cells whose first birthday she'd already begun to plan—being removed from her good-for-nothing body with forceps? With a spoon? Hadn't he slid his black card against the ivory quartz countertop of that surrogacy agency, Nicole a ghost as she clutched onto an inch-thick folder of women ready, willing, and able to carry their baby to term? Hadn't he promised they could try forever? That he'd have picked her all the same even if he'd known, that Thursday at the bar, this would be the war of their lives?

Nicole didn't know what was real. Not anymore. But she knew those memories. She had lived them. They had lived them together. And yet, somehow, they amounted to nothing. Somehow, she was just another clueless wife.

And so, Nicole—looking at him, listening to him lie—couldn't even ask. *How long? How many times? How many different women? Do you tell them that we're over? Do you keep your ring on when you fuck them? Do they like that? Do you like that? Do your friends know? Does Kyle know? Does everybody know?*

All she could muster was this:

"How could you?"

Her words—low, quiet, cracked—hung in the air for an eternity.

Gabe's hands were in his pockets. His eyes were on the ground.

He knew. She knew.

The show was over.

"I'm so sorry," he said.

And Nicole, not sure what to do next, just sat on the stoop of her picture-perfect home, put her head in her hands, and let that first summer sun fry her broken heart like an egg.

5
Eagle Scout Hot

"Mari! Open up!" Minutes later, Nicole was banging on the front door of a downtown Manhattan Beach apartment, tears streaming down her face. "Mari, please!"

The door flung open. Mariana—a doe-eyed brunette a few years older than Nicole—was standing there in a lime-green pencil skirt, her heels in her hands and her face panicked.

"Nic? What's wrong? I just got home. Did I miss your call?"

"No, it's . . . It's Gabe."

"Gabe? What happened? Is he okay?"

"Yeah. No. I . . ." Nicole, shaking, took a deep breath. "He's cheating on me. He fucked the dog walker. And god knows who else."

"Holy shit, Nicole. Oh my god." Mari dropped an arm around Nicole's trembling body and pushed open the door. "Come in, okay? Come inside."

Nicole whimpered. Mari led her to a blush pink sectional where Nicole spent the next hour curled up in a ball, falling apart. She snotted onto a cashmere throw blanket. She clutched onto a brass objet d'art. She disappeared into the cracks of the cushions. And then, finally, she rolled over and stared at Mari, who'd been sitting at her feet the entire time, saying all the right things.

"Is this my fault?" Nicole said.

"What? No!"

Nicole shrunk back into the sofa, sifting through the supercut of her story with Gabe. Their last few years, coming into focus: The forced smiles. The late-night fights. The fact that, sometimes, when they got home from dinner or a date or a goddamn trip to Paris, the two of them would step into that big, beautiful house, and Nicole would, at once, fall completely and involuntarily silent.

"We stopped having sex," she said. "Every time he tried, I pushed him away. I never thought about what that felt like for him. I was so tired. I was so sad."

"Nicole, stop it. You dedicated your body to science for two years. Like, nonstop poking and prodding. He could have jerked off in the shower. He could have watched porn. This is not your fault. You did not do this."

Nicole grimaced as Mari walked over to a Lucite bar cart and pulled two oversize wineglasses off the top shelf.

"You want a drink?" Mari said.

Nicole nodded. She hadn't had a sip of alcohol in twenty-six months, not since she first started fertility treatment. And while she wasn't ready to admit it—or even think about it, really—those days were over, weren't they? Those days were long gone.

"Wine okay?"

Nicole had barely begun to shrug when Mari reached for a handle of tequila instead. She poured them each three fingers, then slid back onto the sofa with their glasses and told Nicole to drink up.

The two of them were drunk.

Delightfully, distractedly drunk.

Mari was twirling around on her string-lit terrace, telling Nicole that everything was going to be okay, that she was too good for

Gabe, all the usual reassurances, when she came to a halt. Her eyes lit up.

"You know who we should go see?"

Nicole rolled over on her lounge chair and took another swig. "Who?"

"Logan Milgram."

Nicole's body jolted. "Wh-what? Why?"

"Oh, come on. You know he had a thing for you."

"No way. We were just friends."

Mari glanced at her sidelong. "Yeah, no. I saw the way he looked at you. I sat right outside his office. He was like a little puppy dog, staring at you every time you walked by. Any dumb reason he could come up with to stroll over to your desk, he'd do it. He'd ask you for staples. I had staples. Darnell had staples. The mailroom had staples."

"No, really. We were just friends, okay? We just had the same sense of humor, that's all."

"Uh-huh."

Nicole glared at a smirking Mari, then lay there for a minute and watched the slightly spinning sun settle into a thick, peachy twilight. Very intently.

"Besides," Nicole said. "I bet he's, like, married by now."

"Nope. Still single. Trust me, I'd know. Every few months, he pops up on one of my apps and I kind of want to die. But objectively, he's as odd and funny and cute as ever."

"You think he's cute? Since when? You never told me that."

"Well, he's not my type," Mari said, taking a swig from her glass, then sinking into the lounge chair next to Nicole. "You know I don't do men with golden retriever energy. Also, he was my boss. And you and I were both married. But yeah, he definitely has something going for him. He's got a look, for sure."

Nicole's face was starting to warm. Although that was probably the alcohol, right?

"He's just a blond guy in his mid-to-late thirties. How is that a look?"

"I'm serious!" Mari said. "He's, like, summer camp hot, you know? Eagle Scout hot."

Nicole laughed while Mari rolled onto her elbows and cited several more ways her old boss could, for lack of a better term, get it. The two of them went back and forth like this for a while, drunkenly debating whether Logan was too quirky to date, why he never seemed to bring anyone to work parties, whether grown men who ate Frosted Flakes were even fuckable. And then Nicole buried her face into the green-and-white, cabana-striped cushion of the chaise and squawked.

"Was that a yes?" Mari said. "I've got his number right here."

"If you fucking call him, I swear to god . . ."

But Mari was already pacing around her patio, typing furiously into her phone, ignoring Nicole's increasingly dramatic protests.

"I found his address. He's still right by us—in Hermosa." Mari held up a map on her glowing screen. "Come on, let's go. Let's go get Gabe out of your system!"

"No."

"Puh-leeeease? It'll be fun! You never have fun!"

"Not happening."

Mari sat down next to Nicole and exhaled. Very emphatically. "Nic, I love you. And I'm a bit drunk. So I'm just going to tell it to you straight. Your life is about to get so complicated. Not just with

Gabe either. Like, I don't even know what would happen if the transfer—"

"Oh, that's not going to work. Our doctors said no chance."

"Wait, what?"

"I can't even go there right now," Nicole said, reaching for her drink. She took a giant gulp as Mari stared at her. "It's just over, okay?"

Nicole was doing everything she could to forget about the transfer. Her future. The fact that now, she'd probably never get to be a mother. How suddenly, she didn't even have a plan. Sure, the old plan had been complete and utter bullshit. But at least she'd had one. Now, she had nothing.

"Okay," Mari said. "Then, if that's really over, don't you just want to do something for yourself?"

Nicole's face twisted. It was one thing for her to delight in the highly specific retellings of Mari's awful first dates and absurd five-week flings. But to sit here and actually consider having one of her own? That was crazy. This morning, she'd been at a fertility clinic twenty-seven hundred miles away, texting her husband pictures of their crappy little embryos.

"It's been, like, two hours . . ."

"So? Who gives a shit? Haven't you spent enough time doing what everyone else thinks is best for you? Isn't there a tiny part of you that just wants to know what else is out there? Whether there was anything to that spark?"

"I'm still married . . ."

For a minute, neither of them said a word.

And then, something very strange happened. Nicole stood up, threw back the last of her tequila, and let her hair down.

"Fuck it," she said. "Let's go."

6

A Little Inkling

Nicole stumbled onto Logan Milgram's spinning stoop, then dragged her fuzzy fingertips along the chipped green paint of his front door. For, like, a very long time. Mari—still in her work clothes and chugging tequila out of a travel mug—poked her head out from behind a shrub.

"Ring the bell, Nic!"

Nicole shushed her, then closed her eyes. She breathed in, then breathed out. She begged her brain to tell her hand to press the button, but nothing happened. Her arm just hung there, hovering and heavy, a few inches from the rusting buzzer.

"Nicole! Just do it!"

"Stop rushing me! I'm thinking!"

Back at Mari's, this little caper had been the perfect distraction. It had been fun, really, rifling through the pile of Nicole's clothes that had accumulated at Mari's over the years, searching for the skimpiest pair of cutoffs they could find, then darting out the door, dying of laughter. But here? Now? Standing in front of Logan's apartment? This was batshit crazy. And sure, Nicole was wasted. But she wasn't drunk enough for this. This just wasn't her.

And so, swaying, she steadied her hand onto the edge of Logan's salt-roughened, slightly overflowing mailbox, took one last swirling glance at the wrought-iron "2" affixed to his front door, then clumsily began to turn away.

That was when it happened.

It happened so, so fast.

His keys tumbled to the concrete.

Her arms fell to her sides.

They just stood there, staring at each other.

Mouths open, bodies frozen.

Nicole's heart, racing.

Logan's eyes, wide.

His grip, suddenly slack against the handle of his suitcase.

"N-Nicole?"

She couldn't say a word.

She couldn't move a muscle.

"What are you doing here?" he said. "Are . . . are you okay?"

Nicole and Logan hadn't seen or spoken to each other in over two years. Not since her last day at Porter Sloane. It was where she'd met Mari too. But it was different with Logan. As chatty as he and Nicole had been, as friendly as they'd become, they had no relationship outside of work. Two years—two years and two months had gone by—and nothing. Nicole hadn't so much as taken a peek at his LinkedIn profile.

They were strangers.

Except now, Nicole was standing at his door, drunk. Still not a mother, and maybe not anyone's wife anymore.

Finally, she spoke.

"I kind of really have to pee."

He laughed, and that was all it took. He was, in an instant, exactly as she remembered him: raising an eyebrow and shaking his head, that signature smirk of his smacked across his scruffy face.

"Nicole Speyer, have you been drinking? On a school night?"

"Uh-huh."

"In excess?"

"It's been a while."

"Yeah." He came a couple of steps closer. Nicole's breath hitched. "I can see that."

She gulped. If she'd been sober, she'd have already run away. But she was not. So instead, she took him in very carefully—his navy trousers, his untucked dress shirt, his forearms—and started rambling.

"How was your trip? You're always traveling. Where'd you go? I like your plant."

"Um, Chicago?" He cocked his head, then briefly glanced at a half-dead fern that, upon further inspection, probably belonged to the unit next door. "Hey, do you, are you—"

"Oh, I love Chicago! It's so nice there. I don't know why more people don't live there. They should. It's really cold, though. It's the lakes, you know? And the snow is so cold. Can you believe people live north of there? There's a whole other country above it! It's . . ."

He looked at her—head still tilted, brow still raised—and scratched his neck. "Do you want to come in? Maybe have a cup of coffee?"

Nicole nodded. Made some sort of strange little yelp. Logan smirked a second time, then picked up his keys, unlocked the door, flicked on the lights, and pointed Nicole to the bathroom. By the time she wandered into his kitchen, he'd already put on a pot of coffee.

"Have a seat, you lush."

Nicole, again with the weird noise, climbed onto a counter stool while he rinsed out a mug at the sink.

Logan's place was nothing fancy. A town house, clean enough, but certainly not tidy. It was lived in, but by a childless adult who traveled four or five times a month. A bachelor pad, really. A scuffed-up coffee table, an old gray couch, a too-big TV. Creaky wood floors, carpeted stairs, a bright orange mountain bike in the hallway. Nicole decided she kind of liked it.

"Did you get to have any pizza?" she said.

"What?"

"In Chicago. The pizza is so good. I haven't eaten cheese in two years. Isn't that crazy? We should go sometime, just like, to eat . . ." The words kept coming out. They made no sense. And yet, Nicole continued to say them. "Just for fun or something. I mean, like, for pizza."

"All right," he said, pulling a rolled-up paper bag out of his freezer. It was possible he'd also blinked a few extra times, but who could say for sure? Everything was a bit upside down. "I think we should get you some toast. Immediately."

"I think I would like to die instead, please."

"Before or after our trip to Chicago?"

Nicole dropped her face into her hands and groaned. When she finally looked up, Logan's toaster was glowing, and he was grinning like an idiot, staring directly into his fridge.

"So." He pulled out a Red Stripe and cracked it open. "You get separated from the group at a bachelorette party? Get lost on the way home from your tennis club?"

"Is that what you think of me?"

"Obviously not."

Nicole—now folding a take-out menu she'd found on his cluttered countertop into a not-describable polygon—tried to figure out what he'd meant by that, but her brain wasn't really working tonight. By the time she'd formed half a coherent thought, Logan had already made a few minutes of small talk, poured her a cup of coffee, then slid a plate her way. On it, the strangest-looking bagel imaginable.

"Why is this purple? Is that mold?"

"It's blueberry! I gave you the best one!"

"No, that doesn't make any sense. Who would put fruit in a bagel? I mean, cinnamon raisin, fine, but even then, that's a dessert bagel! This is . . . how do you put lox on this? Where did you get this? Why would you ever serve this to a Jewish person?"

"Nicole," he said, pushing himself onto the counter a few feet away. His legs dangled as he nursed his beer. "I've been very sick. My pediatrician told me the Flintstones Vitamins weren't cutting it anymore, that I really needed to start eating better. This is how I get my fruit in, okay? Show some respect."

Nicole snickered, then took a sip of her coffee. It was terrible.

"What are you, four?"

"Thirty-nine, actually." He bit into his bagel. "Last week."

"Disgusting."

"Well, we can't all age like you, Miss Missouri."

Nicole could barely keep a straight face. God, had she missed this. Just talking about nothing. About left-handed scissors and Greek mythology and street meat.

"It was one pageant! It was the Midwest! I was seven! I didn't even place!"

"Probably the brown hair. And the attitude."

"I hate you," she said. "You're very stupid, and your coffee is bad, and I hate you."

Logan smiled right at her. Big, bright, ridiculous.

Nicole would never admit it, but he'd always looked good to her. Since day one. He was no Gabe, of course. Nobody was. But there was something about Logan. Tall, with dirty-blond hair—a few streaks almost platinum from too much sun. A smattering of freckles. Warm brown eyes. That easy, forgotten five o'clock shadow. A body kept long and lean from years of distance running. You know, summer camp hot. Eagle Scout hot.

"So," he said, fiddling with the rim of his beer bottle. "Now that I've got you talking, you want to tell me what you're doing here?"

"Nope."

"Seriously? You're not going to tell me anything? You're just going to sit here and eat my food and make fun of me until I throw you out?"

"Basically, yeah. That all right?"

He laughed, nodding, but then he looked at her again. He really, really looked at her. His smiling face grew serious. "You've really been doing nothing? For two years? You never . . . ?"

Nicole stared at her bagel. Logan winced.

"I'm sorry," he said. "I just assumed."

Nicole shrugged, poking at a petrified blueberry. When she finally glanced back up, he was staring right at her ring. It had lasted only a split second. Blink, and she'd have missed it. But she had not.

"I, um . . ."

Her jaw was heavy. She was fighting back tears. Usually, she was good at that. But she was so drunk. She was so tired. She really didn't want to fall apart in front of Logan. Last time she'd done that—in that hallway, what, almost three years ago?—had been one of the worst days of her life. He didn't need to see her like that again.

"Nicole?" he said. "What's going on? Why are you here? Is something wrong?"

Nicole was entirely ready to make up a ridiculous story. But instead, the truth tumbled out of her.

"I think my marriage ended tonight."

Logan's mouth fell open. For a moment, there was silence. And then he looked at her, and—like he always had, whenever anything bad happened—he hung his head.

"I'm so sorry."

They just sat there for a minute, doing nothing. Saying nothing. Nicole pushed her mug around. Logan peeled the label off his beer. Both of them, eyes down.

Eventually, Logan slid off the counter, asked Nicole if she was familiar with the time-honored tradition of eating her feelings, then tossed a pint of ice cream and a giant spoon her way. She laughed, digging right in as he articulated the many vulnerabilities of the Mariners bullpen, caught her up on all the latest office drama, and went on a very specific diatribe against cantaloupe.

And by the time Nicole had stumbled back into her big empty house and crawled into her cold, lonely bed, she had a little inkling that Mari was right.

That Logan Milgram was lying to her.

And that he wasn't sorry.

He wasn't sorry at all.

7

Room-Temperature Gatorade

The next morning, Nicole—head pounding—rolled over, acknowledged the blur that was her little sister, and held a hand over her eyes. Through the drawn curtains, a few too-bright streaks of daylight had snuck across the hardwood in hot, white slices.

It was, quite possibly, noon.

"Mari warned me this might happen," Paige said, twisting the cap off a bottle of lemon-lime Gatorade, then sitting on the edge of Nicole's bed. "Drink up."

Nicole tried—and failed—to take a sip as Paige began rifling through a giant canvas tote. Mari must've told Paige to book a flight out of San Francisco this morning, because here she was with her cool, ugly jeans and her cool, quirky hair, a receptacle full of your-husband-fucked-at-least-one-person-who-wasn't-you distractions in tow. Revealed so far: two matching pairs of fuzzy socks, a thick stack of trashy magazines, and a bag of Red Hot Riplets.

"I brought *Sense & Sensibility* too," she said, holding up a DVD. "The one with Emma Thompson. Director's cut, obviously. Also, weed, in case you decide to reinvent yourself."

Nicole nodded, attempted another half sip, then disappeared beneath her ivory duvet cover. Without a word, Paige loaded the DVD player that remained on Nicole's dresser for only this reason, then crawled under the sheets and pulled Nero into her arms. About halfway through the movie, Nicole sat up against the tufted linen of her headboard and frowned.

"They all go to London too much."

"What?"

"In *Sense & Sensibility*," Nicole said, rubbing her temples, trying to make the throbbing stop. When Mari had managed to throw a groveling, still-in-his-suit Gabe out of the house around three this morning, Nicole was still drunk. "All the men, Edward . . . They're just always going to London."

"Nicole . . ."

She collapsed back into bed. "I think I'm in shock."

"I mean, of course you are," Paige said, eyeing Gabe's nightstand, littered with his crap. His AirPods, half a bottle of water, a stack of books Nicole had picked out for him—*Billion Dollar Whale*, *Dark Matter*, *The Razor's Edge*—looking curiously crisp. "He never read any of them, did he?"

Nicole's heart sank as she disappeared underneath her pillow. She would've much rather discussed some silly plot device in a centuries-old regency romance than her dumpster fire of a real life.

She'd been sad last night, sure. Devastated. But more than anything, she'd been distracted. By Mari. By the alcohol. By the instantly permissible bagels and coffee and ice cream. By Logan Milgram.

But here? Now? Nicole was sobering up in a world, on a hill, in a house that had always belonged to Gabe. His scent was still all over their sheets, a suddenly repulsive blend of base notes and bullshit and bergamot. Her throat burned and her heart ached.

"What am I supposed to do?" Nicole said.

"I think you stay in bed and just . . . cry."

"More?"

Paige nodded. Nicole closed her eyes. It started slow: a whimper, a few tears. A quiet, respectable sob. Until finally, Nicole's jaw gave out.

She shattered.

The floodgates to her broken heart burst open, and whatever rushed out, she didn't try to stop it. She cried like a baby, and she didn't emerge for air until nightfall. And that was only because, around eight o'clock, her husband walked into the foyer.

✺

"Paige, come on! You have to let me talk to her!"

Nicole was standing in the loft, leaning against a wall just out of sight, shuddering at his every last syllable.

"What are you going to say to her that you can't say to me? You're sorry you screwed some girl whose parents still pay her phone bill? You're sorry you told her you couldn't go to Virginia because work was too busy, but you still found the time to rush home and rail someone that wasn't your wife? You're sorry you—"

"You don't know what you're talking about! You're always like this! You and Mari think you know everything! You don't, okay? This shit's between me and Nicole!"

Their voices were growing louder and louder, getting closer and closer. Nicole took a few more steps out of view.

"Is it, though? Because it seems to me you have no problem inviting other people into—"

"You don't know what we've been through! You don't know what it's been like! You haven't been here, you—"

"For once, Gabe, just shut the hell up!" Paige said as Nero scurried up the stairs and pushed open the door to Nicole's office with his nose. He didn't even notice Nicole standing there, trembling. "You blew your life up, okay? Nobody did this to you. You made your bed. Man up, and lay in it."

Nicole—still in some old T-shirt and a pair of sweatpants; eyes sunken and lips chapped—winced at the sound of Gabe's exhale. At the sound of his dress shoes, rushing up the stairs. She knew by the time he called out her name that she would have to face him.

"Colie! I'm begging you! Just let me come up, okay? Let me explain!"

Nicole inhaled slowly, then inched toward the stairs, one tiny tiptoe at a time, until she'd folded herself onto the top step of her landing. When she raised her hung head and her burning eyes met his pleading gaze, her insides wrenched. Gabe was standing there in that same suit and tie with his lips narrowed and his forehead creased and his eyes, sorry.

"Nicole," he said.

Gabe had always had one of those voices. Thick, warm, smooth. Everything he'd ever spoken, that first year, had gone down easy. He had, in the beginning, made this life she'd agreed to build with him sound so good.

"Please, baby, just talk to me," he said as Paige pushed her way past him and steadied a hand on Nicole's slumping shoulder. Nicole, without a word, nodded her sister off. Paige, scoffing directly at her brother-in-law, disappeared into the guest room off the hall.

When her door slammed shut, Gabe took two steps toward Nicole. At once, she stood up and took three back. It was all too much. His body, getting closer to hers. His words, stressed and cracking and strange.

"You have to know, Colie, how much I love you."

Nicole turned away. She was midpivot when she looked back at him. "I think I know exactly how much you love me."

Gabe cowered. Nicole shook her head, then finished dragging herself down the hall. Her body, thin and bent and folded—like a rejection letter, like a piece of junk mail. She was inches from her bedroom door when Gabe spoke again.

"Baby, I—"

"Please, just go," she said, closing her eyes as her fingers turned the doorknob. "Please."

"You have to let me fight for us! You have to let me try! I love you!"

"If you love me half as much as you claim to, you'll give me some space, okay? Just give me some fucking space."

And with that, Nicole stepped inside her bedroom and closed the door. She didn't bother to slam it. Come to think of it, she couldn't remember whether she'd even felt the doorknob in the palm of her hand.

Whether she'd truly felt anything, ever, at all.

∽

Wednesday was a bit better.

Nicole slept in while Paige worked downstairs, walked Nero, and dealt with Nicole's broken phone. By midafternoon, they were lying in bed watching literally every last thing on BritBox while Nicole drifted in and out of sleep, texted Valerie bullshit words of encouragement, and ignored her husband's calls. That evening, Mari stopped by and got stoned with Paige while Nicole picked at her dinner and stared off into space.

She didn't even think about the podcast.

On Thursday morning, Nicole's period arrived, calming her haywire hormones but reminding her of what she'd been desperately trying to forget. That her body didn't work, that her doomed embryos were nestled inside of a clueless, lovely Valerie, and that she'd done it all for a man who couldn't keep his promise. Who couldn't keep his dick in his pants.

By Friday, Nicole was showing signs of life, although she was still in bed, unshowered, and subsisting on nothing but graham crackers and the occasional piece of string cheese.

"I think we should text Mari," Paige said, looking up from her laptop, where she was fielding a dozen different work chats. Several of them, JavaScript, but at least two, simply GIFs of Elmo screaming. "We need to get you out of this house. Besides, it's my last night. We should do something fun."

"I don't know if I'm ready."

"You are," Paige said, staring at Nicole, who was now staring at her ring. "It's time."

8

The Appraisal

October, Four Years Ago

"Can you cover that thing up?" he said, already laughing. "I can't see in here!"

Nicole rolled her eyes. She'd been at Porter Sloane for five months and every day was kind of like this. Nicole, working on some report. Logan working on . . . nothing. He'd been on his way to the copy room, or maybe it was the kitchen, but had gotten a bit sidetracked.

"Logan, come on. I'm—"

"Eye health, Speyer." He slid on a pair of Ray-Bans and smirked. "You don't hear about it a lot, it's not sexy. But I'm a very careful man."

Nicole stared into her computer screen, trying not to laugh. "I'm literally in the middle of something. Isn't there anyone else here you can—"

"Come on," he said. "Let's see that thing."

She rolled her eyes again, then held out her hand. They'd played this game a dozen times. On Nicole's finger? A flawless, four-carat diamond. Princess cut, set atop a simple platinum band. He peered at it like a child playing detective.

"Subtle," he said. "I like it."

Nicole snickered, then pulled back her hand. Fingers to keys. Eyes to spreadsheet.

"So," he said. "Whatcha doing today?"

"Working. You should try it."

Logan did work, of course. He was SVP, New Business. If Porter Sloane had a chance to score a first-time client, Logan handled the courtship, the big pitch. But that was all he did. If there was no account to win, no chief marketing officer to woo, then there was no work. Unless Quentin—the agency's owner—felt like asking Logan a question. If he couldn't answer it over a two-minute phone call, Quentin would demand Logan come meet him for dinner in Monterey, or a seven-hour hike in Big Sur, or, once even, the entire back half of Burning Man.

"Me? Work? Never."

"Why do you get such a nice office, then?"

"Oh, for gaming purposes," he said, taking a seat on her filing cabinet, putzing around with a paper clip. "You should stop by later. I'll show you my SimFarm."

Nicole, who'd just taken a long sip of her soda, nearly spit it out. "Your what?"

"My simulated farm, obviously. Aren't you a wordsmith? Anyway, it's an old game—a classic, really. Very true-to-life. Droughts and pests and tractor depreciation and everything."

Nicole shook her head, double-checking a pricing table from her media buyer in LatAm while Logan just . . . loitered.

"Do you need something?" she said. "I'm trying to finish this thing."

"Yeah, actually. Brie said you were getting all the Buenos Aires numbers together? That ready yet? Need it for tomorrow."

"That's what I'm doing! I'm almost done. Go away and maybe I'll finish before sundown."

Logan twiddled the paper clip. "You know I can't promise that."

"I'm serious," Nicole said. "I'll never get out on time if you keep talking at me."

"Fine." He took the paper clip he'd stretched into a straight line and shoved it into his pocket. "I should probably be tending to my rutabagas anyway. Very harsh season."

She waved him off, tsking.

And then, once he'd retreated to his office, once she finally had her peace and quiet, Nicole stared a little more closely at her spreadsheet and tried to wipe the stupid smile off her face.

9

Girls' Night Out

By eight o'clock, Nicole, Paige, and Mari were at dinner. Mari had picked out some bougie rooftop on the Westside, all succulents and sleek white chairs and rattan pendant lights that dangled from the veranda like ivy. At every table, pretty little things thumbed through their phones, nursing twenty-dollar cocktails as the dusty sun melted into the twinkling hills. There was also a pool, because Los Angeles.

"Well, this is it," Paige said as the group behind them finished up their fourth very serious, very shameless photo shoot. "This is, hands down, the straightest, most basic thing I've ever done."

"First of all," Mari said, "it's a good life. I won't apologize for it. And where else were we going to go? Los Feliz? Silver Lake? Can you imagine Nicole there? She'd probably—"

"I'm right here, assholes. I'm depressed, not dead. And I would've been fine in Silver Lake! I would've gone to Silver Lake!"

"Nicole," Paige said. "When was the last time you were actually in Silver Lake?"

Nicole huffed. "Fine. I've never been. But I would go in theory."

The truth was, Nicole didn't go much of anywhere. But tonight, she'd insisted on leaving Manhattan Beach. Anything to get away from another reminder of Gabe. Who, for the record, had most definitely never been to Silver Lake either.

"Why don't you ask Logan to take you?" Mari said, reaching for a glorified sweet potato fry.

Nicole rolled her eyes. She'd hardly let herself think about Logan these past few days. She'd been busy bawling her eyes out, trying to do the right thing: grieve her failed marriage. Still, she couldn't totally help herself. From time to time, she'd dust off a memory of theirs. Give it a closer look. Decide if maybe it played back a little differently now that she could see it through a strange new lens.

"Wait," Paige said. "*Logan*, Logan? Like, work Logan?"

"Hold on a second," Mari said. "How do you know about Logan?"

"Nic's favorite person at work. Other than you, of course."

It was true that with Paige, Nicole had talked about Logan quite a bit. Not recently, of course—that would've been superweird. But back when she was still at Porter Sloane, Nicole would call Paige and tell her all about her day. Logan, it just so happened, seemed to play a starring role in Nicole's most colorful stories.

"Interesting." Mari raised an eyebrow—make that two—at Nicole, who was now shifting in her seat, fiddling with her empty glass. "Very interesting."

"I always thought the New York story was a little odd," Paige said.

"Huh?" Mari said. "What New York story?"

Now Nicole's cheeks were really starting to burn. "We can skip this, guys. Please."

"Wait a second," Mari said. "Weren't you and Logan both in New York? Right when we opened up the East Coast office?"

"It was a work trip. We—"

"Holy shit! You guys went out, didn't you?"

"It was my birthday!" Nicole's face was on fire. "He was just being nice!"

"This is a safe space, Nic." Mari caught their server's attention, then signaled for another round of drinks. "Nobody here liked Gabe. Like, at all."

Nicole glared at Mari, then at Paige. Both of whom were giggling, sucking down the bottoms of their drinks through very cute, tangerine-and-white-striped paper straws.

"Screw both of you," she said.

Paige hooked her arm around Nicole and pulled her in tight. "Just giving you a hard time. Although I am curious why we're even talking about this guy. Haven't heard that name in years."

"Wait," Mari said to Nicole. "You didn't tell her about Monday?"

Now Paige was glancing around the table. "Tell me what about Monday?"

"I . . ."

"I convinced her to go knock on his door the night she found out about Gabe. We were pretty drunk. She chickened out, but he caught her there anyway. She was inside for, like, two hours. He even walked her back to my place."

"And?" Paige said.

"And nothing!" Nicole said.

For a good ten minutes, this continued. Paige demanding the play-by-play. Nicole blushing, offering the bare minimum, protesting a bit too much. Mari chiming in with humiliating little details Nicole must've let slip after Logan dropped her off. By the end of it, Mari was pulling up Logan's headshot on her phone and Nicole was hiding her face in her hands.

"Okay, guys," Nicole said. "Enough, though, really. I need to be alone."

"Myth!" Mari turned to Paige. "Tell her it's a myth. Tell her you don't need to be alone after a breakup!"

"There is well-documented evidence," Paige said, dunking a now-soggy fry in the last of some heirloom tomato compote, "that you have to get under someone to get over someone."

"See!" Mari said. "And Paige would know. She's had sex with more than, what, four people in her lifetime?"

Paige snickered. Nicole, at this point, was just cracking up.

"Why are you guys so obsessed with me having rebound sex?"

"We're not obsessed with you having rebound sex," Mari said as their drinks arrived. "We're obsessed with you being happy *and* having rebound sex."

The server—a woman, maybe forty—gave the group a knowing glance. Nicole thanked her, then apologized on behalf of her very rowdy table.

"So you haven't heard from him?" Paige said.

"Oh, no, I did."

"Wait, what?" Paige said. "Read it to us!"

"It's nothing, it's—"

"Right now," Mari said. "You read it to us right now."

Nicole laughed, then pulled out her phone, wincing at the latest barrage of messages from Gabe. She opened up her text from Logan and handed over her phone.

> Really good to see you. Sorry things have been so hard. When you're sobered up and ready to see the light of day, let's run?

"Running?" Mari said as she and Paige peered at Nicole's screen. "Jesus Christ. The most Logan pass ever."

But it wasn't as dumb as Mari thought. Back in the day, Logan and Nicole would sometimes cross paths on the Greenbelt before work. She had mentioned to him on their walk from his place to Mari's the other night how much she missed getting out there.

"Well, are you going?" Paige said. "Did you call him or something? Did you say yes?"

"I . . . I haven't responded."

Nicole was telling the truth; she hadn't. But she failed to mention that she'd been drafting a reply for two days now, ever since she got her new phone.

"You have to text him back!" Mari said. "He's probably dying!"

Nicole shook her head. "This has been fun, guys. But I'm not ready to date. Or hook up or anything, okay?"

"Okay," Mari said, nodding. She put her hand on the table and leaned toward Nicole. "You're right. You should do whatever you want."

Nicole exhaled. She'd finally gotten Paige and Mari—especially Mari—to drop it.

But it wasn't that simple, was it? Because what Nicole really wanted wasn't to be alone. It wasn't to stay in bed and cry like a baby, ignoring Gabe's incessant calls. It was to text Logan back—to see him again. Just for, like, a run. Maybe a cup of coffee.

You know, as a friend.

10
The Reply

Nicole—sitting at her kitchen table in her pajamas—stared into her fully functional phone. She took a deep breath, then started typing.

> Could you link me to that *Dwarf Fortress* message board? I've done nothing but get drunk in a dark room for four days, and I'm pretty sure I have whatever syndrome you told me about. Cave adaptation?

There. She'd sent it.
Now, all she had to do was wait.

11

The Greenbelt

She didn't have to wait very long.

By noon, Nicole and Logan were sinking their sneakered feet into the warm, soft earth of the Greenbelt, a miles-long, tree-lined running path that connected their two towns. Logan was wearing some Tahoe Marathon shirt and these short, navy shorts, and Nicole could see how tan and long and lean his quads were, which was not something she was entirely prepared for, so she'd spent the past seventeen minutes focusing on her breathing instead. Which was probably a good thing. Because she needed all the help she could get.

"You okay, Missouri? You want to stop?"

"No," Nicole said between heaves. "I do not want to stop."

He came to a halt. Nicole, a half step later, dropped her hands onto her knees, wheezing.

"What are you doing?" she said. "I'm fine, I—"

"I actually hate running," he said. "It's completely pointless. Nihilistic and Sisyphean and anything else you can think of, it's definitely that too. Just a horrible sport, if you ask me. And I won't waste another minute engaged in this middle-aged performance art. I've had enough. I'm done."

Nicole—still catching her breath—rolled her eyes, rattling off every which way Logan was a full-fledged moron. He grinned the entire time, then motioned her down the trail and asked if she'd like to take a break from making fun of him for some lunch. Nicole nodded, and off they went, chatting about bread-and-butter pickles, professional table tennis, and whatever else was on Logan's mind while the midday sun beamed through the arching trees in rustling spots and streaks. As they headed south, the cresting hill curved, revealing long, wide stretches of the glistening Pacific until they'd finally arrived at Pier Avenue, a low-key string of cafés, surf shops, and yoga studios that sloped all the way down to the shore of Hermosa Beach.

They grabbed iced coffees, premade sandwiches, and a few half-priced pastries from a bakery Logan liked, then worked their way down to the water, where they kicked off their shoes and socks and twisted their toes into the warm white sand. With the sun beating down on their shoulders, Logan told Nicole all about Quentin's months-long retreat to Fez, the Nintendo 8-bit system his best friend had been restoring all week, and how his mom kept sending him newspaper cutouts of age-appropriate female journalists affixed with Post-its that said things like "What about her?" and "She seems nice!" But by the time they'd finished their picnic, the conversation had come back to Nicole and what she'd been doing the past couple of years.

"I don't know," she said, poking at an ice cube with her straw. "I mostly do this podcast thing? It's nothing, though. It's stupid."

"Wait, you have a podcast? That sounds really cool. Why is that stupid?"

"I don't know. I don't know why I said that."

But, of course, there were a million reasons to have said that. Because of what had happened at Kyle's party. Because the whole show was literally about getting pregnant with her cheating husband's baby. And because if Logan went home and listened, he'd realize within seconds that Nicole might be a mother by March. Because while Nicole knew there wasn't a chance in hell that transfer would work, she'd never shared that with anyone. Except for Mari, kind of, the other night. Because that—that, and what had happened with Gabe—were failures so definitive she wasn't quite sure how to broach them, let alone broadcast them.

"What's it about?" he said. "Can I listen?"

"Oh, no. Trust me, you'd hate it. It's mostly women's issues."

"I like women! I like issues!"

Nicole's fingers found a cracked, sand-crusted seashell at her feet. She traced its grooves for a moment, then tossed it aside. "It's about infertility. Please don't listen. I'm serious, okay?"

"Okay," he said, nodding once. Then he turned to her, sifted his fingers through the sand, and took a deep breath. "I was kind of surprised when I saw you . . . I just assumed . . ." Another inhale. "What I'm trying to say is, I know how much you wanted that. And I can't imagine how hard it's been for you."

Nicole wrinkled her nose. Who would've thought, of all the people on this planet, it'd be Logan who wasn't afraid to talk about this stuff? But then again, hadn't he always surprised her? Especially those last six months?

"I can't carry children," she said. "That's what I found out. That it's my fault, that—"

"It's not your fault."

Nicole buried her feet in the sand and stared out at the horizon.

"It is," she said. "If it weren't for me, if . . ."

She was crying. It just kind of happened. She was crying—right here, right next to Logan on a perfect July day, a crumpled-up bag of moderately stale baked goods between them. She pulled her legs into her chest and hid her face in her knees.

Logan began to say her name, then stopped himself.

He reached out his hand, then pulled it back.

"I'm sorry," she said, wiping her face with the hem of her shirt, half looking at him. "I don't even know why I'm telling you this. I talk about it every week, but it's not the same, I guess. The whole podcast is just . . . I don't know. It's kind of one big joke. And the truth is, I don't even know who I'm trying to make laugh."

"Well, you can tell me anything," he said. "I've got nowhere to be until . . . ever, actually. Maybe Atlanta midweek, but until then, nothing."

She kicked a little sand his way. "Why is your job so fake? What do you even do again?"

"Same as always, Nicole. I sell shit." He reached for her abandoned cinnamon roll and took a bite. "I sell shit, and I talk to you."

"You're really good at it."

"Yeah," he said. "I know."

And then, for a little while, they just sat there. Waves crashed. Children shrieked. Lifeguards whistled. Yet somehow, everything was perfectly quiet.

☙

Afternoon melted into evening. They wandered for hours, walking and talking and stopping for cones of vanilla soft serve that dripped down their rainbow-sprinkled wrists. They perused a farmers' market, rifled through a record store, then sneezed their way through a two-story antique shop teeming with moth-holed costumery nobody wished to buy.

By seven thirty, the California sky had softened into sherbet-colored brushstrokes of coral and lilac and rose; the slowly dipping sun, gold. They grabbed tacos from a hole in the wall on Fifth Street, then snatched the least wobbly table they could find and rolled their eyes at each other some more.

After dinner, they glided north across town, talking shit about creative directors while the finally setting sun cast that last, magical glow on the run-down bars and shuttered hardware supply stores that lined this strange little stretch of Pacific Coast Highway. And by the time the laid-back, paint-chipped tall-and-skinnies that filled Hermosa's steep, crowded streets had given way to the Hill Section of Manhattan Beach—where the trees were trimmed and the houses were huge and the views, limitless—night had fallen.

"I'm just a few more down," Nicole said.

Logan nodded. Every ten feet or so, he'd look around, eyes wide, and kind of shake his head. Nicole kept trying to think of something witty to say to keep the conversation going, but she couldn't. So they just wandered silently until she came to a stop. Logan smirked.

"Are you laughing at my house?" she said.

"No," he said. "I'm laughing *near* your house."

Nicole looked around, cheeks warm. Four thousand square feet of crisp white siding, careful stonework, and glossy black-framed picture windows stared back at her. A single forgotten light was on in her upstairs bedroom, revealing the sleeping silhouette of a bistro table and two chairs centered on an oversize balcony. Succulents burst from glazed planters, and above the front stoop, a statement pendant hung, oil-rubbed bronze and frosted glass.

"It's . . ."

"Subtle?" he said.

"It is subtle!"

"Totally," Logan said. They were both chuckling now, and almost at her front door. He eyed the SUV parked in the lavender-lined driveway. "Your car's white?"

"Um, yeah?"

Logan stifled another smirk.

"What?" she said. "Is my car funny now too?"

"Nothing, it's . . . Never mind."

They were standing on her stoop, shifting in their sneakers. The sky, ink. The air, dense. Their summer day, smudged across the bridge of his nose. His hands were in his pockets.

"Can we do this again next Saturday?" he said.

Nicole nodded. Logan's face lit up.

And then Nicole stepped inside her house, let Nero pee in the backyard, left the dishes for tomorrow, and just lay in her unmade bed, trying her best not to replay every single second of her day, over and over again.

She gave herself a C+, then finally fell asleep.

12

You'd Better Hope

The next morning, Nicole woke up to a missed call from Mari, eleven more from Gabe, and a trio of rambling text messages from Logan.

> Remember that fire drill gone wrong where I watched the entirety of *The Matrix* on my phone and you made fun of me the whole time?

> I was wondering, had you even seen it?

> Or did you just assume it was bad because of all the robots?

She'd just sent her ridiculously semicolon-rich reply—**I remember; I had not seen it; and yes, the robots**—when her stomach twisted into knots.

Six whole days had passed since Valerie's transfer. If she peed on a good enough pregnancy test, it'd almost certainly be accurate. And while it was going to be negative, Nicole needed to know that for sure. Even if it meant slamming the door on her only shot at motherhood, she needed closure. And so, she sat herself up in her messy bed, took a deep breath, and FaceTimed Valerie Lowell.

"Really? You made me promise I wouldn't!"

Valerie was pacing back and forth in her kitchen—all shaker cabinets and dinosaur lunchboxes and corkboard calendars—while her toddler and five-year-old screeched along to some deranged version of "Wheels on the Bus."

"I know," Nicole said. "But I can't wait any longer."

"You mean it? You're serious?"

"Yes." Nicole didn't even blink. "Please."

"Well, it's up to you," Valerie said, wandering down the hall and into her bathroom, then disappearing off-screen. Already, sounds of rummaging. "I'm sure I have a test around here somewhere."

Nicole had always asked Valerie to hold out for the official blood test. That was how Nicole liked to handle her two-week waits. She appreciated the certainty.

But that had been before. Back when she had known how to ride the wave: the glowing optimism that warmed her body from the inside out on day one, day two, day three; the sudden, scraping shift that seized her head and her heart on day five, when her body—or later, Valerie's body—knew the truth but she did not; and then, the sleepless crawl through days six, seven, and eight until finally, it was day nine. Test day.

"Found one!" Valerie came back into focus holding up a small foil pouch. She narrowed her eyes, her face twisting slightly as she looked at Nicole, who'd forgotten to respond. "You sure about this?"

"I need to know. Please?"

Valerie nodded, unwrapping the test. "Okay. Just let me pee, and I guess we'll see."

The screen was Valerie's ceiling, smooth and blank. Nicole

clutched her phone, pacing around her bedroom as Valerie's toilet flushed, her faucet ran, the water stopped.

"All right," Valerie said, the camera back on her soft blue eyes, her thick-rimmed glasses, her blond, hurried mom bun. "Now we wait. Three minutes."

"Three minutes," Nicole said as she bit back tears.

She hadn't thought about this, about saying goodbye to Valerie. Over the past hell of a year, they'd become unlikely friends, sending each other dinner ideas and holiday gifts and long-winded, late-night texts about the aches and pains of motherhood—the pursuit of it, the pressure of it. The first time Nicole had met Valerie, it had been over video, just like this. Their agency matched them, and Nicole was so anxious she could barely speak. What could she do or say or show to prove to a stranger she deserved this? That she was worthy of being made a mother?

But then she met Valerie, and all that fear melted away. She was an angel, she just glowed. Nicole had never met a person quite like that. So kind, so good. The second Valerie smiled, the second she said, "Nicole, I've been so nervous to meet you," Nicole just waved and said, "Hi, I'm . . . I'm shaking," and they both laughed and this strange, warm easiness stretched across Nicole's chest and she thought, *This woman is going to change my entire life*. It wouldn't be the first time she'd gotten something like that wrong.

"The control line's starting to show up," Valerie said. "Just waiting on the other one, okay?"

"Okay," Nicole said, heart racing.

Not like it did before, of course.

Not like it did in the beginning, when she'd first gotten off the pill. When she and Gabe would screw dutifully on all the right days, at all the right times. When it was still perfectly fun and safe and reasonable to test out the syllables of every possible baby name. To imagine falling in love with some chubby-thighed, milk-drunk blob in a dinosaur onesie or a floppy pink bow. To fantasize about watching said blob transform your work-obsessed, never-not-golfing-or-drinking-or-out-with-the-boys husband into the kind of man who came home from the office early, grilled on Sundays, and adored the woman who'd turned him into the father he'd never had.

And not like it did the past couple of years either. Once she already knew grief and panic and terror. Once she already knew hopelessness. When the only thing she could do, as her mind screamed and her body quaked, was wait for that late-afternoon call from the clinic. Beg Gabe to come home and hold her and wait for that call.

But all that—every chapter of that story—was over now. This, here, was it: the cruel, bitter end of a long and foolish war Nicole had waged against herself. She'd gone to battle against her own body and lost every last fight.

"You sure you don't want to patch in Gabe?" Valerie said.

"No, that's okay. He's in . . . Oregon."

"Oh." Valerie's lips curved into a smile. Nicole's throat went dry. "That's too bad."

Valerie held up the test.

Two little blue lines.

Dark, clear, unmistakable.

She was pregnant.

Pregnant.

This was all Nicole had ever wanted—all she'd chased for three years. And now, here it was. The best shot at a baby she'd ever had, and she couldn't blink. She couldn't breathe.

"It worked, Nicole! It worked! You guys are going to be parents! You're going to be a mama! You have to call Gabe right now! I'm just so excited for you guys! Tell me what's going through your mind! Tell me what you're feeling!"

"I can't believe it," Nicole said. "I don't even know what to say."

∽

The next few minutes were a blur.

She must've ended the conversation. She must've lugged her body across her bedroom. She must've unlocked her phone, traced his name, and pressed her shaking fingers to the screen. Because the next thing she knew, this:

"Colie? I've been—"

"Valerie's pregnant."

Silence.

She could hear him breathe.

"Nicole, I—"

"You'd better hope it's just one."

And then she hurled her phone against the wall, let out the loudest, loneliest cry of her life, and cleared her husband's nightstand in one irreversible strike, watching in silence as his books, his headphones, his lamp took flight.

She just stood there and watched the porcelain shatter, the shade spin, the light go out.

13

Century City

"This is just outstanding work. Your husband had an excellent lawyer, I—"

"Are you kidding me?" Mari said, glaring at some gawky attorney in wire-rimmed glasses and a suit that was, somehow, both ill-fitting and very expensive. He was also halfway through his second blueberry muffin. "This is not the *Yale Law Review*."

That seemed to do the trick.

Mitchell Winters, Esquire—one of the best divorce attorneys in Los Angeles, supposedly—put down his pastry and Nicole's prenuptial agreement, then glanced at his newest client. Nicole and Mari had been warned Mitch's bedside manner was not great, but nobody had expected he'd be quite this technical.

"Sorry, right," he said. "You understood what you signed, yes? When you agreed to this? No duress, no threats? And you selected your own counsel?"

"I knew exactly what I signed," Nicole said. "I used to read a hundred contracts a week at my old job."

"So you're aware, then, that your spousal support will be severely limited, and pay out for only half the duration of your marriage? And that the deed to the Manhattan Beach property is—"

"I know all about the alimony and all about the house. I know why his parents gifted it to him before the wedding. I know about the loopholes and separate property and why he bought the Aspen condo with cash he earned before he married me. I never cared. I didn't marry him for his money."

The attorney nodded. He also kind of smirked. Nicole could get like this sometimes. Especially when people made assumptions about her—and what she saw in Gabe.

"I just need a divorce," she said, pinning her hands to the edge of the conference room table. "Can you get me one, or not?"

She'd been up all night, reading articles and message boards and the Judicial Branch of California's *Interactive Guide to Divorce*, which was surprisingly intuitive and well-written for a government resource. Point is, she'd read everything. Most of it, twice. And Nicole knew, despite the prenup she'd signed nearly six years ago, that her case might be extracomplicated. After all, there could be custody to sort out, and California had tricky community property laws. There were a lot of assets in Gabe's name, and they were kind of just . . . everywhere.

Gabe made tons of money, and while he liked to spend it, what he really loved to do was invest it. Mostly with his financial adviser, but also by himself, late at night, when Nicole would curl up next to him in bed, reading or sleeping or giggling at his too-serious face. He'd just sit there—contacts out, glasses on—staring into his laptop, making his own trades on whatever markets were open like he was searching for flights or shopping for a new bathrobe.

"So," the attorney said, "there's a bit of a hurdle."

"I know I have to wait six months. That's fine. But can we just start today?"

Mitch shook his head. At once, a dull ache crept across Nicole's body. She quelled it with the same sentence she'd spent the whole night repeating: *People get divorced all the time.*

"Nicole, I spoke to Jasmine Clark earlier this morning."

Jasmine was Nicole and Gabe's surrogacy attorney in Virginia. Nicole had sent Mitch a copy of Valerie's contract, but she'd never thought much of it. After all, she'd sent him a lot of things. Yesterday evening, when Mari had finally peeled Nicole off her bedroom floor—and successfully banished Gabe yet again—the two of them sat in Nicole's office and scanned in every last document Mitch's assistant had asked for, from her car registration to the latest income statement for her suddenly dormant, barely profitable podcast.

"She's very concerned about your situation," he said. "Honestly, we both are."

"What? What do you mean?"

Mitch slid a sheet of paper across the glossed mahogany. When it landed a few inches from Nicole's now-trembling fingers, every single letter was out of focus. She stared at the sentences. She begged the words to rearrange into something she could interpret, into a language she could understand. But nothing helped.

"I'm sorry, Nicole, but you cannot file for divorce. It's not in your best interest."

"What?" Nicole had risen out of her chair. Somehow, she was already halfway across the room, hands on her head, pacing. Mari watched her carefully. "Why the hell not?"

"We've been on the phone all morning, trying to figure out whether any of this is enforceable. Whether a judge would ever revoke custody of—"

"Why would that even come up? That doesn't make any sense! What are you saying?"

"I understand you're upset," he said. "I understand you've been through a lot."

"You have no idea what I've been through!"

"Just explain it," Mari said, walking toward Nicole. "Don't tell her to calm down. Just give her an explanation, please. Now."

He sighed. "Virginia is a postbirth order state. As long as you're married, this process is quite simple. Halfway through your carrier's pregnancy, Jasmine will take your executed contract and a signed affidavit from the fertility clinic to family court in Norfolk. The judge will issue a postbirth order, no questions asked. Then, when Baby X is born in March or whenever, your attorney will head back to court next business day and have the birth certificate amended so that you, Nicole, are listed as—"

"I know all that!" Nicole threw her hands in the air. "Why does that matter? Why would anything change that? I'm the mom! It's my egg!"

Mitch swallowed, then attempted to lock eyes with Nicole. He could barely keep up with her circuits now. Her path had grown erratic. Her pace, unpredictable. She was everywhere.

"If you and your husband are not married when that baby is born," he said, "the court is compelled to take a closer look at whether you and Gabriel are suitable parents, whether—"

"Of course we are!"

"I'm not saying you're not. I'm just advising you that you're in uncharted territory here. That, in Virginia, a judge could decide not to grant you parental rights."

"And give them to who? This is insane!"

"They'd declare *prima facie*, most likely. They'd declare your carrier the baby's rightful mother."

"That doesn't make any sense! Valerie would never do that to me!"

"It's not about what your carrier wants," he said. "It's about what the court determines. Besides, most relationships between intended parents and surrogate mothers break down over time. It's a very tenuous arrangement. Who knows? By spring, you and your carrier might not even be on speaking terms."

Nicole winced. She would never, ever let that happen.

"The judge," he said, "could give your carrier the right to put the baby up for adoption. You could have to contend against her for custody. And not in a California court either. In Virginia. It could take years."

Nicole tried to breathe. She pressed her hands against the cool, thick glass—the heat of her skin at war with the floor-to-ceiling windows of a sky-high Century City conference room that, despite being freezing, despite being massive, was on fire. Was closing in on her.

"What the hell is she supposed to do, then?" Mari said.

"As long as she's willing to wait, everything is going to be fine."

Nicole whirled around. "I don't want to wait! I fucking hate him!"

"I understand this is difficult news. I really do." Mitch closed her file and looked at her from across the room. "And honestly, I think you're right. That the law is unfair. But your story—the podcast, the hotshot husband—it's hyperpalatable. It's prime time. It'd be all over the news. The national news. And I'd love nothing more than to help take your case all the way to the Supreme Court. But we'd lose. The lowest court in Virginia wouldn't hear our case.

Third-party reproduction, the laws haven't been tested. The truth is, if we make too much noise, if we push the limits of a system this fragile—all so you can leave an unfaithful spouse, an otherwise good provider who poses no real threat to you or your hypothetical child—we could wind up getting surrogacy banned in Virginia. Maybe even federally."

Nicole slumped against the window, then slid down the glass until she was seated on the cold, colorless tile. Behind her, Los Angeles—a sprawling city she barely knew—carried on.

"Nicole, please," Mitch said, rising from his chair. He was walking toward her to shake her goddamn hand. All this, business as usual. All this, another day's work.

It was just like IVF, wasn't it? Divorce? A whole cottage industry designed to make her feel like she had control of her life, like she could maybe have a second chance at it, when she did not. When she could not.

It was a business. A machine. And every time it chewed her up and spit her out, there'd be yet another woman—shit out of luck, with a little money to burn—waiting in line.

She was a patient again. A name on a schedule, a number to bill. This was her entire life, and to everyone else, she was just another hysterical woman. Crazy for wanting a baby. Crazy for wanting a husband who could love her all the way. Crazy for wanting the two very things the world had told her, for over three decades now, would make her life whole.

"Nicole," he said again, extending down his hand.

She just sat there, motionless. Her body, limp.

He turned to Mari instead. "She needs to cool off. She needs to do nothing. No new job, nothing like that. I think any judge, upon hearing why she left the workforce, would agree the spousal support provision is unconscionable. But to get that thrown out, she needs to stay in that house. She needs to keep living the life she's always lived. Here—in Los Angeles."

Mari nodded. Mitch walked back to the table, picked up Nicole's file, and turned to her.

"It's only a pause," he said. "A couple of years, if that. And when the ink dries on that amended birth certificate, when the baby is legally, officially yours, we will file. We will get started. We will get you everything you deserve, and we will get you that divorce."

Nicole closed her eyes.

"It might be two."

"Sorry, what? Two what?"

"Babies," Nicole said. Her eyes were still closed. "I think there might be two."

She opened them just in time to watch Mitch Winters—who was both completely right and totally fucking fired—flinch.

14

Mirrors

The drive home was silent.

For forty-five minutes, Mari stared ahead while Nicole slumped in the passenger seat and watched the world whirl by. They were in Nicole's driveway, the car still running—the sun a clock, announcing noon—when she finally spoke.

"Hey, Mari?"

"Yeah?"

Nicole unbuckled her seat belt. "Did you ever feel, when you were still with Lucas, that that's all you were? That you were just an extension of him?"

Mari shook her head. Nicole reached for the car door, her fingers lingering on the metal long after the lock had unlatched. Her gaze, elsewhere.

"When I look in the mirror," Nicole said, "he's all I see."

15

Hovering

For the next couple of days, Nicole did nothing.

Midweek, the clinic confirmed Valerie's pregnancy—news Nicole still hadn't shared with anyone but Gabe, Mari, and Paige. Her podcast, her very concerned mother, her need for real food and water? She ignored them all.

And every time Gabe called or texted or showed up after work with his tail between his legs, Nicole grew a little more numb. She could barely manage to brush her teeth or change her clothes or feed her dog. What was she supposed to do? Talk to her husband calmly, and face-to-face? Sift through the evidence of her failed marriage, of all the signs she'd missed? Sort through her finances? Come to terms with the fact that, according to a miscarriage odds calculator she'd found online, the likelihood she'd become a mother was hovering somewhere around seventy-five percent? Higher, really, when you factored in that the embryos they'd transferred had already been genetically screened? Search for a job she'd been warned not to take? Find another place to live when she'd been told to stay put? Figure out a way to support herself and start her life over, when that awful-but-spot-on attorney had been crystal clear that a premature attempt at independence would only screw Nicole and her maybe-babies over a million times more? When Mari's divorce attorney, a day later, practically recited the same counsel but in much kinder words?

No. Absolutely not. She was trapped, and all she could do was fall apart. All she could do was push Gabe—and the rest of the mess they'd made—very far away.

And so, by Wednesday evening, when Nicole had finally convinced her husband to disappear for good, she did just that. She crawled back into bed, stared at the half-empty bottles of whiskey and orange juice and wine on her nightstand, and cried. And then, when she ran out of tears, Nicole decided to torture herself a little bit more.

She rolled over, reached for her phone, and scrolled through her old text messages with Logan. Their plans for that coming Saturday, floating there, suspended between what Nicole had promised on her stoop last weekend and what she now knew to be true.

She closed her eyes for a moment, then sent this:

> Are you back in town? Can we maybe talk?

16

The Stoop

They sat on Nicole's front step in silence. The night was dark, lit only by a few humming sconces, that hanging porch light, and the glimmering glass panes that framed Nicole's front door. The rest of her street, a string of sleeping houses, illuminated just so.

"So, Atlanta?" she said.

"Atlanta," he said.

They were maybe a foot from each other, staring at their feet, studying their hands. Apparently, Logan had just touched down a couple of hours ago, a few minutes before Nicole texted him.

"Coca-Cola, right? Quentin will never give up on them, will he?"

"If there's one word I'd use to describe that man, it'd be relentless."

"What if you had two?"

He smirked. "Erratic toddler-king?"

"That's three."

"No. I hyphenated it. It's two."

Nicole laughed, and then . . . more quiet. They just sat there, doing nothing, saying nothing. Logan's phone buzzed. He pulled it out, ignored the call.

"Dave," he said, shoving it back into his pocket.

Nicole nodded.

She looked around.

She considered making a joke about Dave—Logan's best friend, whom she'd never met but who'd starred in so many of Logan's watercooler stories that sometimes, it felt like she had. And then she decided just to say it, to tell him the truth, to get it over with. But when she opened her mouth to recite the words—*I'm having a baby, I think. Maybe even two*—nothing came out. So instead, she went back to staring at her hands. She didn't even realize she was twirling her ring around her finger until she'd felt the unmistakable heat of Logan's eyes, watching her do it.

Her whole body tensed.

"This thing," she said, giving it another look. This time, through a lens she couldn't quite explain. Through a filter, thick and distorted.

"Shiny as ever," he said.

Nicole winced. "God, you too?"

"What?" Logan's head jerked back. "Wait, I didn't mean . . . You know I'm only—"

"I know you always saw my ring as this giant punch line. Guess you were right all along. Turns out my whole life's a fucking joke."

"That's not true. That's not—"

"But it is," she said, biting back a frown. "It really is."

"I promise you, Nicole. It's not."

She looked at him. She really, really looked. And what she saw—him, sitting there, trying to convince her that her life meant something, that she meant something, when it did not, when she did not—only made the truth that much harder to tell. Maybe that was why all she mustered was this:

"He fucked our dog walker."

Logan grimaced. "Holy shit. I'm so sorry."

"I met with a divorce attorney Monday." She paused for a moment, carefully weighed her words, then continued. "I don't know if there were others. But I'm pretty sure you don't start with a twenty-three-year-old, right? In your own home?"

Logan closed his eyes, then covered his mouth with his hands. When he exhaled, Nicole—who'd been sitting there, nearly unmoving—recoiled.

"What?" she said, pulling back another inch. "Did you know too?"

"Me? How would I have known?"

"But you could've guessed, right?" She stood up and began to pace behind him. He rose to his feet and faced her. "That he'd do this to me? That he'd cheat?"

"I barely knew Gabe, I—"

"You should've said something! That night, when we were in New York! Or before I left, or . . . If you knew, Logan, why didn't you say something? Why didn't you tell me?"

"I don't, I . . . You—"

"I *what?* I should've known?" she said, backing up until her shoulders were square against her front door. Logan just stood there, mouth open and hands up. "Is that how you see me? You think I signed up for this? That he was like this when I met him? That he was out of my league? That it was only a matter of time until a guy like him got tired of coming home to a girl like me?"

"No, Nicole! I don't! And you know it!"

Nicole looked at him.

Logan looked right back.

And then, she crumbled. She took a seat on her stoop and she fell apart while Logan watched on. He shuffled and stuttered and strained, and then he sat down next to her and hunched his shoulders, bowed his head, and let her cry. When her tears had slowed and she finally looked up, his hands were fists and his jaw was tight.

"That fucking piece of . . ." His eyes scrunched closed. "Fuck. I'm sorry. I really shouldn't have said that."

Nicole cracked a smile. "What? Were you, like, going to defend my honor?"

"I mean, I could." He was reanimating: his hands, his shoulders, his face. "I was overexposed to *The Princess Bride* as a kid and now I have this savior complex, but I'm working on it, because it's very outdated and it sends a bad message, not just to—"

"Do me a favor and never finish that sentence, okay? Like, ever. It's very dumb."

He glowered at her. "We could be in a full-on zombie apocalypse, and you'd literally stop running for your life to remind me I was an idiot, wouldn't you?"

"Making fun of you is my passion. You know that. It's my art. It sustains me."

Logan chuckled. Nicole wiped her face with the sleeve of her sweatshirt and exhaled.

"I'm sorry I yelled at you," she said.

"It was more . . . adjacent to me, if anything. I'll be all right."

She brushed a few grains of sand off the slate. "Why are you so nice to me?"

"I'm nice to everyone," he said. "You see, growing up, I was but a comically compliant farm boy in the always-misty, majestically verdant kingdom of Flor—"

"Logan! No!"

And then they both sat there, laughing some more, until the

twelve inches between them became six and then, once Logan had no more *Princess Bride* jokes to deliver, he told Nicole that sometimes, when he was sad or confused or couldn't sleep, he'd rank Pop-Tart flavors until the feelings passed, and Nicole told him there was no way that was true, but it sounded fun, and could they please do it anyway.

And so Logan pulled up the Kellogg's website on his phone, and Nicole leaned in a little closer, and he scrolled and she scrolled until the six inches between them became two and they'd settled on a toaster pastry hierarchy of their own. Logan lobbied hard for S'Mores, and Nicole made a solid case for Frosted Strawberry, and they both agreed nothing hit quite like a Brown Sugar Cinnamon.

And when night had dwindled into morning, when it was too late and cold and damp to continue, they said their goodbyes and Nicole walked Logan to his car and she apologized again and he told her not to worry about it, that it was okay, that he understood. She was almost to her stoop when he called out from the street.

"Hey, Nicole?"

She turned around.

"Just so we're clear," he said, "you're the one who's out of Gabe's league."

Nicole just stood there, staring at him.

And then, after a minute had passed, after she realized she was never going to think of a clever comeback to try and transform what he'd said into something else—into a joke, into nothing—she bit her bottom lip and looked at him a little longer. And then, when that became borderline ridiculous, she smiled, cracked open her front door, and slipped inside.

Three hours later, Nicole still hadn't fallen asleep.

She drew a long, hot bath. She read two pages of *All The Pretty Horses*. She stood in front of the open refrigerator until it beeped at her. But mostly, she just lay in her bed, thinking. Not about Gabe, and not even about the pregnancy, but about Logan. About how strange it felt, sitting there with him, struggling to get the truth off her chest. About how good it felt—once she'd stopped lashing out at him, once she'd let him in a little—to sit there and move on. To sit there and have some fun. To, for a moment, not take her dumpster fire of a life so seriously.

And sure, she'd only managed to tell him half the story, but it was a start, right? Now all she had to do was explain Valerie. And how hard could that be? Logan was a nice guy—and a real friend. It wasn't like he didn't know she'd been trying to have a kid for years.

What could she possibly have to lose?

17

Runner's High

November, Four Years Ago

"Oh, hey," Logan said, looking up from the espresso machine as Nicole walked into the break room. "Good run today?"

They'd bumped into each other on the Greenbelt earlier this morning. As usual, they'd chatted for a few minutes, then gone their separate ways.

"Not really," she said, rummaging through the dishwasher for her mug. "Lead legs again. You know, slow people problems."

"Oh, come on. Happens to the best of us."

"Yeah, right," she said. "You've run, what, a hundred marathons?"

"The trick," he said as he reached for his drink, then pulled the half-and-half out of the fridge, "is to save up enough intrusive thoughts that you never get bored. Also, foam rolling."

She shoved a pod in the machine. "You forgot the ability to run twenty-six point two miles. Which I cannot."

"Sure you could. You already run, have disposable income, are very organized, live in a temperate climate at sea level, are likely to take stretching and hydration seriously . . ."

Nicole rolled her eyes as he handed her the milk carton. Logan was just full of facts. He could talk about anything for as long as you'd let him. It was both very entertaining and a little concerning, how much he had to say about things that did not matter.

"But you ran in college, right? So you're, like, programmed to do this."

"Nope." He dropped an elbow onto the kitchen island. Above them, a maze of exposed pipes was coated in the agency's signature shade of cobalt blue. "I went to a D1 school, remember? And I run an eight-minute mile. What would they have done with me? Let me blow the little horn? Let me hand out orange slices?"

Nicole laughed. She forgot, sometimes, that other schools had actual sports programs. Not just rehabilitated child stars and people who didn't get into Brown putting on spontaneous reinterpretations of Lin-Manuel Miranda's earliest works.

"And you really don't get bored?" she said. "Even after an hour or two?"

"Lots of questions today, huh?"

"Sorry, I—"

"I'm kidding," he said as they moseyed down the corridor. "Honestly, it's just my thing. Plus, I really need the dopamine. Six days a week, I wake up and go. No phone, no music. Everything else in my life is so last minute, you know? But I guess I run when I'm traveling, or when I lose a deal, or when my mom's in town, or—"

"Your mom comes to town?"

"Yes, Nicole," he said. "People have mothers. Even me."

"I'd die to meet your mother."

"What?"

"Um, I . . . I didn't mean . . ."

But just when Nicole had decided to quit her job, change her name, and relocate to Panama City to live out the rest of her years in peace, Logan laughed.

"Oh, she'd adore you," he said. "You guys could just sit around and eat vegetables and talk about all the reasons I'm thirty-five and nobody loves me."

Nicole raised an eyebrow as they neared his office but make no mistake: Panama beckoned. "I mean, have you tried changing . . . everything?"

Logan glared at her, leaning against the edge of his propped-open glass door. Next to him, framed posters of the creative that had put Porter Sloane on the map. A print ad for a swanky hotel in Vegas. A couple of stills from a sixty-second BMW spot. A legitimately not-suitable-for-work triptych of bruised, misshapen, and highly sexualized pieces of fruit posing above taglines like *Come on, take a bite*; *Good enough to eat*; and *You never forget your first time*.

"So, what about you?" he said. "Why do you run?"

"I don't know, really. I guess, by the end of it, I just want to feel like I've had the shit kicked out of me."

Logan smirked, then took a long sip of his coffee.

"Funny," he said. "That's exactly why I go on dates."

Nicole laughed.

Logan laughed.

And then, for the rest of the day, they barely looked at each other.

18

The Bookshelf

Thursday evening, Nicole drove over to Logan's to tell him the rest of the truth. Instead, she ended up on his couch, eating microwave popcorn and watching *The Matrix*. Well, she was more watching Logan watch *The Matrix*, but still.

"You need a break or something?" he said. "I know how hard this must be for you."

"No, dingbat." She tossed a burnt kernel at him. "I do not need a break."

He paused the movie and smiled at her. Just this ridiculous, shameless smile. He was leaning back into the corner of his sofa—still in his work clothes, still in his dress socks, his stupid face growing scruffier with every passing scene.

"You sure about that? You keep . . . repositioning yourself."

Nicole, whose bare legs were currently in something of a lotus pose, scowled at him. When he raised an eyebrow, she pelted a bag of gummy worms at his chest. He caught it, then ate one.

He wasn't making this easy.

An hour ago, she'd had every intention of telling him about Valerie, the two embryos, and what the attorney had said. But then he answered the door like he'd just woken up from a nap—his face soft, his hair haywire—and made some stupid joke, scratched the back of his neck, and offered her a beer, and everything else got a little fuzzy and Nicole decided that a movie, a little bit of company, didn't sound half bad. And then, by the time she'd realized the movie was indeed very bad, it was too late. Because she didn't want to leave.

"I won't say no to actual food, though," she said. "You have anything like that?"

"I'm sure I could whip something up."

"Wait, like one of those gas station challenges? Are you going to roll string cheese in Cheeto dust? Will there be a Go-Gurt dipping sauce?"

Logan signaled her toward the kitchen. "Guess you're about to find out."

And then, for the next half hour, Nicole sat backward on a counter stool while Logan provided a painstakingly detailed oral history of Seattle's floating bridges. He also claimed to be cooking. When he was done, and the heat of his running oven had practically forced them outdoors, Logan directed an eyes-closed Nicole into a chair on the balcony off his living room.

"Okay," he said, slipping a paper plate into her hands. "Ruin me."

Nicole took one very careful bite, then nearly gagged. "Logan! What the fuck!"

"It's that awful? Really?"

She nodded, laughing. "It's like you took a shelf-stable jar of Alfredo sauce, frozen pita bread, and the cheapest deli meat available, then broiled it all for ten minutes too long."

When she opened her eyes, Logan had narrowed his. "That is . . . almost exactly what I did. Were you spying on me? Did you cheat?"

"Excuse me?" Nicole rocked back in her chair. It was the kind you'd buy at a CVS in some sort of strange, I-need-patio-furniture emergency. "I had a childhood too, you know. I've definitely played the taste test game."

"That game was banned in my house," Logan said. "Matty shoved a raw egg down my throat."

"What!?"

"I had to crack it with my teeth, I—"

"Why didn't you just spit it out!?"

"I don't know! I panicked!"

Nicole was losing it. She didn't know what visual was worse: ten-year-old Logan spitting out an entire egg, or biting into one, screaming as the shell cracked and his brothers howled.

"Please tell me you've never told that story on a date before," she said.

"Uh, it's the only story I tell on dates?"

"Because everybody leaves after?"

Logan glared at her. "I love that you think I'm the biggest bonehead to ever roam this planet. That you think I have zero game. Women love me! I know about things! Mesopotamia. The Space Race. Several wars . . ."

"Really? You are vaguely aware that there have been wars? And they haven't asked you to write a book yet?"

"Oh, no. They did." Logan helped himself to a bite of Nicole's pizza-sandwich thing. He flinched, then took another. "It's complete garbage, but I'm surprised you haven't gotten to it yet. You'd read anything."

"It's true," Nicole said, taking a sip of her beer. The evening sky was quiet and steady. Unremarkable, really, for July. A medium blue, fading almost imperceptibly into navy. "I'm just a disgusting book slut."

Logan snickered, then looked right at her. Nicole glanced back for a split second, then went off on some tangent about magical realism while Logan nodded intently, only interrupting her twice. Once, to ask if she wanted to order actual pizza, and then again a few minutes later, just to give her a hard time. The sky stayed perfectly still.

"Anyway, what about you?" she said. "You reading anything good these days? I've actually been in a bit of a slump."

Logan's cheeks turned the slightest bit pink. Nicole inched forward.

"What? What is it?"

"It's nothing."

"It's obviously not nothing. I've literally never seen you blush. And now I'll die if you don't tell me."

He tipped back his beer, then set the bottle on the table between them. His eyes, gleaming. It was that same look of his—the one he'd made nearly every day for two years. He was, without question, about to say something ridiculous.

"Rest in peace, Nicole Speyer." He bit his lip. "Very pretty. Very smart. Very fast and loose with literature."

"Logan Milgram." Nicole bit hers back. "Cute enough. Smart enough. Very bad at food."

He stopped his chair midrock. "Wait, you think I'm cute?"

Nicole rolled her eyes as Logan, grinning, caught her gaze again. This time, she didn't look away. She had no clue what she was doing here. And, strangest of all, she didn't care. Here, on this patio, there was no dog walker, half naked on her couch. No positive pregnancy test. No "pause" on her divorce. No house she didn't own or career she didn't have. No ten years down the goddamn drain.

There was only this.

There was only Nicole, demanding answers. There was only Logan, nursing his beer, pretending to hate it. Until, finally, he stood from his chair and nodded her inside.

"Fuck it," he said. "Come on. Come with me."

They headed upstairs, Logan a half step ahead as Nicole took it all in. The scuffed, bare walls of the stairwell; the wobbling, faded pine of the handrail; how the carpeted stairs gave way to a washer, a dryer, a couple of closed doors. One of them, ajar—a sliver of his bedroom.

The other, Logan announced as she stepped inside, was his office. Really, though, the whole place was more of a storage unit: an old pullout couch, a desk, a few dumbbells. A foam roller, camping gear. Shoeboxes—one, full of old race medals. The others, just empty. Just trash. There was also a framed print of Mount Rainier leaning against the wall that kind of made Nicole chuckle. She couldn't help but wonder how long he'd been meaning to hang it.

"Did you bring me up here to prove you're outdoorsy? Because I already know you drive a Subaru, and—"

"Nicole," he said. "Stop talking. Come here."

She swallowed, then took a few steps closer as Logan opened the rickety bifold doors of his closet and nodded toward the bottom shelf. Sandwiched between a dangling wetsuit and a red ski parka: two lidless boxes teeming with books. Hastily stacked, well-loved, crinkle-cornered books.

Nicole knelt down. She traced the fraying covers and peeling spines as Logan stood there, silent. *Beneath a Scarlet Sky. Franny and Zooey. Erasure. Men Without Women. White Teeth* . . . They were all there.

"I'm still working on your list," he said.

Nicole nodded. Her heart, racing. Her mind, spinning. She picked up a copy of *The Black Dahlia*, thumbed through its delightfully dog-eared pages, traced a few words, then set it down.

He'd read them. He'd actually read them.

"I know what you're thinking," Logan said.

"You do?"

"Yeah," he said. "That I need a Kindle."

∽

By the time Logan and Nicole were standing outside her car, it was nearly midnight. The navy sky; still dull, still dreamy. They'd said their goodbyes twenty minutes ago, but there were other things to discuss, like dim sum and *Duck Hunt* and what Logan had thought of *Three Nights in August* ("Fuck the Cubs!"); *Normal People* ("Fuck that whole year in Sweden!"); and *Bridge to Terabithia* ("Fuck you for making me read that again!").

Nicole could have done this forever.

"So, you think I should just skip *American Pastoral*?" he said, shoving his hands in his pockets as he shifted in place on the cool, cracked sidewalk. His dress shirt was untucked. Above him, a streetlight flickered, and the moon dangled like a crescent, fast asleep.

"Yeah, I mean, it's outstanding. You'll love all the LBJ stuff—the history. Watergate, Vietnam. But it's brutal. It's lonely. A guaranteed book hangover, you know? We'll have to get you right into a romance after that. Balance you back out."

"Is that how you do it, Missouri?"

"That's exactly how I do it," Nicole said, looking at him. Trying to forget the way it felt to hear him call her that. The way it felt to stand next to him on his empty street, at an ungodly hour, talking about nothing. Talking about books.

"Were you always like this?" he said.

"A dork? A reader?"

Logan nodded.

"I guess so," she said. "You know how when you read, you're just kind of floating? Like, you can feel your legs under the covers and your hands on the pages, but you're not quite there? You're halfway between your own bed and some other world, and everything blends together, and you kind of just . . . hover? You're kind of just . . . nowhere?"

Logan stared at her. "God, are you something."

"Yeah," Nicole said, yanking a loose thread from her sweatshirt. "A book slut."

"That's not exactly how I'd put it."

Nicole wrinkled her nose, reached for the handle of her car door, then turned to him.

"Hey, Logan?"

"What's up?"

She clutched her arms around her elbows. "There's something I want to talk to you about. From earlier."

"Is this about all the plot holes in *The Matrix*? Because everyone knows that dinner with Cypher and Agent Smith makes zero sense. No way Cypher gets access to the Matrix all by himself. You have to suspend disbelief, Nicole. You of all people should know that."

She tried not to laugh. "It's not about your dumb movie. It's important."

"Okay," he said, dropping his shoulders. "What's going on?"

She knew this version of Logan—the serious one. It'd always taken her by surprise how quickly he could morph into . . . this adult. This grown man. She'd seen him do it that first night in his kitchen, and again last Saturday on the beach. Yesterday, too, on her stoop. And then, of course, nearly three years ago, when he found her in the hallway at work, hunched over, frozen.

"I, um . . ."

He looked at her, waiting. She hugged her body tighter, then exhaled.

"I think you should add some citrus to your diet," she said. "You could get scurvy."

19

Napkin Studies

December, Four Years Ago

"They take away your Banana Republic credit card?"

Nicole—who'd been checking her phone, trying to get an update from a work-swamped, still-halfway-across-the-city Gabe—craned her neck, already rolling her eyes. Logan was standing there in a suit and tie and what could only be described as first-date hair, smirking at her.

"Very funny," she said.

They were at the agency's holiday party. Mari, who was around here somewhere, had mentioned the event was Quentin's favorite way to burn a few hundred bucks off everyone's December bonuses. This year, he'd chosen the Culver Hotel, an art deco, Old Hollywood hot spot that had played host to the likes of Greta Garbo and Clark Gable during the Roaring Twenties. A century later, the hotel still dripped in history. Scandal seeped through the lounge's dimly lit walls, swirling through the room and reflecting off every surface—black and white, mirrored and gilded.

Logan gripped a few fingers into the beveled edge of the bar. "I'm kidding. You look great. Very festive—like a Christmas tree! Reminds me of home."

"Gee, thanks." Nicole smoothed out the invisible creases of the skintight, emerald minidress Mari had made her buy last weekend.

For this party. With her husband. Who was not here. "Exactly what I was going for. Tree."

Logan rubbed his jaw. "Doing my best here, Speyer."

"That's your best? You just walk up to random women at bars and tell them they remind you of your weird hometown?"

"Well," he said, getting the bartender's attention. Nicole hesitated, then ordered a glass of white wine. Logan, an old-fashioned. "First, I tell them I have unlimited systemwide upgrades on American Airlines. And then, if that doesn't work, yes. I start describing the Pacific Northwest, leaf by leaf."

Nicole tsked. Logan was from Seattle—Issaquah, actually. She knew this because he talked about it almost constantly, rambling on and on about hiking and Puget Sound and how the 405 had nothing on Issaquah-Hobart Road come rush hour.

"You're going to be alone forever," she said. "You do realize that, right?"

"I have prospects! It's just, they're all . . ."

"Too normal for you?"

He laughed. "That's one way to put it."

The bartender, who Nicole could've sworn raised an eyebrow at them, slid their drinks across the onyx.

"To you," Logan said, raising his glass. Nicole did the same. "For never missing an opportunity to remind me I'm worse than a box of raisins on Halloween."

"To me. For seven months without murdering you."

Their glasses clinked.

Their gazes met.

He looked right at her.

But by the time she'd caught her breath, tried to read his eyes, tried to figure out exactly what they were trying to say, it was over. He'd taken a long sip of his drink and begun to examine the embossed edges of his cocktail napkin.

Nobody had ever looked at her like that, not even Gabe. But just a few moments later, Nicole couldn't say for sure whether she'd manufactured the whole thing. Whether he'd glanced at her at all.

She scratched her collarbone, he twisted his lips, and then they just stood there, sipping their drinks in this strange, synchronized silence. She was about to open her mouth and make some stupid joke about some stupid thing when a voice called out behind her.

"Hey, babe."

Nicole spun around.

Gabe. Here, finally, and folding a valet ticket into his suit pocket, ninety minutes too late.

Nicole steadied her voice as best she could.

"Oh, hey," she said. "You, uh, you made it."

"Yeah, sorry, I . . ." Gabe looked over Nicole's shoulder. Logan was leaning against the bar, still studying the grooves of that napkin. When their eyes met, Logan slipped it into his pocket, then lifted his glass and offered Gabe a quick, cordial nod.

"Sorry, man," Gabe said, extending his hand. Logan, with a smile, did the same. "Didn't notice you there for a second. It's Leland, right?"

The tendons in Logan's wrist tightened. Firm, stiff shake.

"Good to see you, Gabe. And it's Logan, actually."

Gabe pulled back his hand. "Oh, right. My bad."

Logan took a long sip of his drink. "Happens all the time. My parents were hippies. Gave us all these outrageous names. Even I can barely spell it."

Gabe snickered. He gave Logan another glance—this one, a little longer—then finally dropped an arm around Nicole, who was very busy counting the silver sequins on her shoes. Wondering whether it'd be weird if she bolted for the restroom and never, ever came back.

"Well," Gabe said. "Thanks for keeping Colie company. Holiday traffic, you know?"

"Sure do."

Gabe signaled for the bartender and ordered a whiskey neat. For the next few minutes, he and Logan made small talk about holding companies while Nicole fingered the rim of her wineglass and focused, pretty much, on only that. Were they ever going to stop talking? When was this party going to end? And where the fuck was Mari? The moon?

"You know," Gabe said, "this is exactly how I met"—a squeeze of her waist—"Colie here. She was standing at this NYU bar, just scowling at me. Wearing some tiny, little dress. Called me a finance bro to my face. Told me to go back to Goldman. But by the end of the night, I'm behind the bar, digging through receipts, trying to find her last na—"

"This story's only interesting to us, Gabe," Nicole said. But she'd had to stop him, right? This wasn't their wedding. They weren't at dinner with Gabe's friends, or even with Mari and her husband. Logan was legitimately Nicole's colleague. It was simply not a relevant anecdote.

Gabe smirked.

Logan scratched his neck.

And then it was over. Logan told Gabe and Nicole to enjoy the rest of their evening and disappeared into the crowd.

"Strange guy," Gabe said, his attention now on nobody but Nicole. He was rubbing the seams of her dress, his fingers tracing her ribs. His voice, low. "God, do you look good."

Nicole smiled as she peeled Gabe off her, reminding him her boss was here, her whole office was here. She turned him so they were facing away from the party and then lowered her voice.

"Hey, so, it kind of sucked that you weren't on time tonight," she said. "When we go to your work stuff, it's a huge deal. I come home early, I do my hair, I plan my whole day around it, and . . . I just wish you'd been here. I wish I didn't have to beg, or even be in the position I'm in now, where I'm hurt, and then I feel stupid about being hurt because I know my job isn't as big as yours, and . . . I don't know. It just sucked, okay?"

Gabe chewed on his bottom lip. He dropped his hands to the small of Nicole's back and drew her toward him so his forehead was nearly touching hers. "I didn't mean to, babe. I got caught up with Kyle, and then the freeway was completely insane. Let me make it up to you. We'll go to that diner on the way home. Get pancakes, milkshakes, whatever you want, okay?"

Nicole blinked the past couple of hours away. This was a work event, not their bedroom. What was she going to do? Cry about it? Make a scene? Slam a door?

"Okay," she said. "But I want hash browns too. More than necessary. Like, a truly ridiculous amount."

Gabe laughed, nodding, pulling her a little closer.

At the edge of the room, Logan was leaning against a velvet armchair; his phone, pressed against his ear with the help of a raised shoulder. It sure didn't look like business, whatever call he was taking. He was nursing his drink, his face soft and interested. He was laughing, glancing at his watch.

He looked up.

For a second, their eyes met.

And then he straightened his tie, hung up the phone, and walked out the door.

"Hey," Gabe said. Nicole startled. "We gonna try again tonight?"

"Oh, um . . . Yeah. Sorry—yes." Nicole put a few fingers on his chest, then took a sip of her drink. God, he was gorgeous, wasn't he? Gabe, of course. Her husband. "Wine's okay for now, right? Like, half a glass?"

Gabe nodded, his eyes still fixed on hers. And the way he smiled at her, the way she could see their future unfolding in front of them, it was just enough to forget all about that strange little moment with Logan . . . and the fact that he'd almost certainly left this party an hour early to charm some other girl.

20

Small Talk

"You sure you don't want to tell him?" Mari said.

"I don't know." Nicole poked at a cherry tomato. "I told him about Gabe Wednesday. And then last night, I went over, and we just . . . did nothing instead."

They were at lunch in downtown Manhattan Beach, tucked into a corner table of a mediocre cafe's ivy-drenched terrace. The afternoon sun bounced off the Pacific and back onto the sleepy storefronts of the swimsuit boutiques and optical shops that lined the stroller-filled, spotless sidewalks of Highland Avenue. Nicole had done her best to discuss Mari's work trip to Austin for as long as possible, but after twenty minutes of follow-up questions, Mari caught on.

"I mean, listen," Mari said. "The pregnancy is superearly. And he doesn't really need to know. It's not like you're the pregnant one. But what if he listened to your podcast? He'd find out about the transfer, and—"

"He doesn't. He won't. I asked him not to."

Mari smirked, taking a bite of her avocado toast.

"What?" Nicole said. "Why are you making that face?"

"It's just, it was so obvious to me he had a thing for you. I mean, from day one. And then when you left, it was like you never existed. I was there four more months, and he never asked about you again. Not even once."

"Because we were work friends. You know how those things go."

Mari stole a cucumber off Nicole's plate. "Right. Your work friend who takes you on extend-a-dates. Who you won't let listen to your podcast. Who you won't tell you're having a baby."

"Right," Nicole said, slurping down the last of her iced tea. Good thing Mari didn't know about the books sitting in Logan's closet. All fifty of them. "That's exactly right."

∽

After lunch, Nicole walked back up the hill, took Nero out to pee, then lay down on her kitchen floor like a completely normal thirty-two-year-old woman. Fifteen minutes later, she rolled over and called her surrogate.

Valerie caught Nicole up on all the drama at the clinic, within her subdivision, and on last night's *Real Housewives*. They reviewed the logistics Nicole already knew from her own IVF pregnancies: If results from this morning's second blood test showed Valerie's beta-hCG had doubled properly, they'd do a third and final draw Monday. If that one looked good, they'd schedule an ultrasound between seven and eight weeks—about twenty days from now. That was when they'd confirm the heartbeat. Or heartbeats.

"Do you and Gabe want to come out early?" Valerie said. "Maybe stay with us?"

Nicole flinched. Thank god she'd called and not videoed. "Oh, we'll probably come out separately. He's working on . . . this thing. But we won't miss the scan, okay? I promise."

It didn't feel good, lying to Valerie. But what choice did Nicole have? How could a woman like Valerie—a supermom, a military wife who ran a happy home with her eyes closed, a woman who'd let Nicole borrow her goddamn body—ever understand how Nicole had gotten herself into this mess?

"Well," Valerie said, "just let me know. The boys are really excited about the pregnancy, and I know they'd love to see you again. Maybe, even if Gabe can't, you could come a day or two early by yourself? Talk to him—see what works."

Nicole closed her eyes. Mitch Winters was right about the relationships between carriers and intended parents. They were tenuous. They were breakable. They weren't set in stone.

"No need," Nicole said. "I'll be there."

⚬

After she'd hung up, Nicole stepped into her shower, cranked the temperature valve so high the scalding water burned her skin, then stood there until she'd adequately boiled her conscience clean. She'd only just crawled under the covers when her pillow buzzed.

> Have you ever been to the Tar Pits?

She almost dropped her phone.

> No, because I'm not a fucking dinosaur.

> It's more of a woolly mammoth situation. For the record.

> Talking to you is like reading a deleted scene from *The 40-Year-Old Virgin*.

> I'm 39, remember?

Nicole laughed. Loud enough that Nero, who'd been snoozing on the foot of her bed, turned around and huffed. She shrugged at him, then decided to shoot her shot.

> Are you asking me to go? Or are you just sitting in your office, thinking about me?

The next response took a few seconds.

> Yes and . . . no?

This strange feeling came over her. She was, in an instant, both intensely giddy and unbearably lonely. It was the kind of feeling, she knew, that was pretty much impossible not to act on.

And she knew that because the last time she'd felt this way, she was curled up in some twin-extralong bed, texting Gabe Speyer—the very hot, kinda douchey guy she'd been talking to for a couple of days. The one from LA, the one who went to Vanderbilt, the one who was halfway through his MBA at Columbia. The one who'd spent the whole rest of the night they met tracking her down, then parked himself outside the entrance to her dorm, where he just stood there—gorgeous, grinning—asking if she'd give a "dumb-as-rocks Wall Street fuckboy" like him a chance to buy her another drink. Maybe even dinner.

Funny, wasn't it? How much she'd changed since then. And how much she'd stayed exactly the same. How, if she narrowed her line of sight enough, she was still that same girl: biting her lip, baking cookies with her roommates, hunting for an entry-level job in publishing and a decent apartment below Fourteenth Street.

> Bummer. I was kinda hoping you were.

Immediately, bubbles. She flexed her toes. Waited.

> Sorry, I should have been more clear. I am thinking about you. I'm just not in my office. I'm in the copy room, of all places.

The copy room? He remembered that night too? Her skin, suddenly, prickled. She had to bite her tongue and scrunch her face to stifle whatever strange little squeal was unraveling inside her. Whatever wild little thrill was coursing through her bloodstream. Once she was satisfied she'd suppressed it, she flopped face-first into her pillow and chucked her phone across the bed.

It landed with a thud where her husband used to sleep.

21

The Paper Jam

September, Three Years Ago

"Logan?" Nicole said. "What are you doing here? Are you okay?"

"No," he said, laughing through a wail as he turned to her, holding up a few sheets of crumpled-up paper. He was hovering over the massive, glowing printer, and his hands were covered in ink. "I'm going to die. Here. Tonight. And soon."

Nicole chuckled, taking another step into the copy room. It was nearly midnight, and she'd been working out of a conference room on the other side of the office for hours, not realizing anyone else was around. She and Gabe were headed to Santa Barbara tomorrow for a wedding, and she had a project to finish before she took the rest of the week off.

The plan, at least in Nicole's mind, had been for her and Gabe to spend the long weekend together. To maybe sleep in, walk on the beach, take some pressure off their relationship. The novelty of trying to get pregnant had worn off months ago, and with that came ovulation strips and basal body thermometers and a shift in the air of their home she could not quite put her finger on. But then Gabe booked two tee times with his buddies from high school, so Nicole dumped four new books and a face mask in her suitcase instead.

"Isn't this why you have a team?" she said. "To print shit for you?"

"Contrary to popular belief," he said, "I actually do work. The night before a big pitch, I lock myself in my office and make sure everything is just the way I want it."

"Wow. That's exactly what I would do."

Logan looked up from the printer's beeping notification screen and smirked. "Guess we have that one thing in common, then."

She rolled her eyes, then walked toward the printer to assess the damage herself. She and Logan were maybe a foot apart, just standing there, staring at the sputtering, squawking machine while the copy room kind of hummed. Nicole had been in here hundreds of times and never noticed it. And yet tonight, with the rest of the office so silent, the buzz was unmistakable. Probably just the air-conditioning, though. Or the overhead lights. Maybe that old paper shredder, idling in the corner.

"You know," she said as Logan raced through the touchscreen troubleshooter for the third time, "it helps if you actually read the instructions."

He turned to her, his eyes twinkling. They got like that sometimes when he was dicking around. So, all the time, basically. He was like this all the time.

"This is war," he said. "You're either with me, or you're with them."

"Who is 'them,' exactly? Technology?"

"Sure, Bradbury," he said before throwing his body on the floor, where—in a full stretch—he shoved his hands back into the paper drawer. Nicole was about to fire off a comeback about how surprised she was Logan had read any short story, ever, when he yelped.

"Fuck!" He pulled out his hand and shook it a few times. He was bleeding. "It fucking got me!"

"Do you want me to call an ambulance? Do you want me to call your mom?"

He pushed his face into the ground and let out another little scream. This one was more directed at Nicole, though.

"Sorry!" she said as she made her way toward the first aid kit mounted to the wall. She sifted through the ibuprofen and the antacids until she'd found a bandage. "It doesn't have to be your mom. We could call your Dungeon Master! I'm sure he could . . . cast a spell? That's how it works, right?"

Logan, still lying down, snatched the bandage with a scoff. "Wouldn't you like to know."

"No, actually, I—"

"Hey, you know what?" Logan rolled toward her as he secured the bandage around his index finger. He was on his back now, facing her. His hair, a mess. His untucked dress shirt, pushed up a few careless inches, revealing the sharp lines of his stomach and the hard edges of his hips. Nicole was not entirely sure this was information she required. "Can I borrow your little hands?"

"No way. That thing just ate you alive."

"Please?" he said. "I'm dying."

Nicole walked over to where Logan was lying down, picked up what she could of the endless pieces of bandage packaging he'd let fall to the floor, then tossed them in the trash.

"Fine," she said. "But only because I want to go home."

He smiled. "Better take that ring off, Speyer. You're going in the trenches."

Nicole laughed. And then she slid off her ring and lay down on the cold polished concrete, right next to him. They were inches from each other—their heads, shoulders, hips almost touching as together, they peered into the black hole that was the first paper tray of Porter Sloane's notoriously fickle printer.

With his phone, Logan spotlit a microscopic scrap of paper entrenched in the printer's thick plastic jaws. Nicole flexed her hand and reached. She tried. She really tried.

"Do you have it?" he said.

"Almost!" Her forefingers were stretching, searching. "I can't reach! It's right there, I can feel it, but it's—"

"You're doing it all wrong!" Logan slid an inch closer, squinting as he shined the flashlight on her hand. "Go to the left more!"

"I am left!"

"God, you're infuriating!" he said, grabbing her hand to push it farther into the drawer, to put it exactly where he believed it needed to go. But the moment his fingertips touched her wrist, they both froze.

A second passed, maybe two.

Logan's hand didn't move.

Nicole didn't pull hers back.

They just lay there, alone, suspended in some alternate reality. A windowless copy room that was a bright light in a sea of black— every other office, every other cubicle having called it a night. Having fallen fast asleep.

It was just them.

That was when she turned to him and saw it—that look. Dense, careful, reckless. Painful. Really, really painful.

But half a second later, it was over. Just like last time, it was gone.

He pulled back his hand.

"I . . . I'm sorry, I—"

"For what?" Nicole said, shaking her head. Shaking it off. Gathering herself and her things and her diamond ring. "For putting me in harm's way?"

Logan was still peering into the paper tray as Nicole walked toward the door.

"Yeah," he said. "You could've chipped a nail."

22

Heat Waves

On Saturday morning, a relentless heat wave—the first of the summer—crept over Los Angeles County, leaving almost every inch of it scalding. By midafternoon, the temperatures inland had reached triple digits. And that, of course, was precisely when Nicole Speyer found herself standing a few hundred yards off Wilshire Boulevard, a couple of feet from Logan Milgram, and way too close to a steaming reservoir of liquid asphalt.

"Okay, so," Nicole said, wiping the sweat off her forehead, "what, exactly, is the appeal of this place again?"

"I'm sorry. Are you bored? Are you complaining about our adventure? Would you like to find a nice tree to sit under and read?"

"Is that an option?"

Logan poked her with the pointy edge of a brochure about the Ice Age. "Open your mind, will you? Try one new thing."

"Sorry!" Nicole said. "It's just, I hate it."

"For now, you do," he said. "But the Tar Pits are more of an acquired taste. I promise, after I make you stand out here for five, six more hours, you'll really start to appreciate it. Plus, if we stick around after sundown, they'll maybe even fish out a dead body."

Nicole snickered as she pulled her hair—soaked at the scalp and stuck to the nape of her neck—into a topknot high off her skin. The heat clung to her like a film, thick and wet and close. Logan, almost mirroring Nicole, ran a few fingers through his hair, taming his flyaways with the sweat that had collected on his brow. When his hand reached the crown of his head, the hem of his shirt crept up a few inches. Nicole tried not to stare. Despite his steady diet of frosted animal crackers and microwaved chicken tenders, Logan looked . . . good.

He still looked really good, didn't he? Easy and rugged and kind of damp and—

"Eyes on the exhibit, Speyer."

"Screw you."

Logan raised an eyebrow at her, then went off on an unsolicited, fifteen-minute soliloquy about fossils and isotopes and radiometric dating that Nicole could only assume was accurate. Mostly because Logan was very convincing, but also because she had no intention of ever fact-checking a word he'd said. When he paused for questions, Nicole rolled her eyes.

"I used to wonder," she said, taking a sip of the iced coffee he'd bought her at some record-store-turned-noodle-shop tucked onto a backstreet nearby, "why you could never find a nice girl to settle down with. It's all so clear to me now. It's your brain."

Logan chuckled, then bit into his bottom lip. For a few minutes, they just stood there underneath the hazy, scorching sun, watching those filthy elemental pools of crude oil simmer. They just stood there and watched them stew.

"Logan?"

"Yeah?"

Nicole raked her forefingers along her collarbone, then stared into her nearly empty plastic cup. She sucked down the last few drops of melted ice.

"You're not actually a virgin, right?"

He glared at her. "No, Nicole. I am not a virgin."

She burst into laughter. "Just checking."

A second passed.

"Was—"

"Yes, Nicole." Now he was laughing too. Really laughing. "The sex was with real people. Sometimes, even more than once. Sometimes, for years."

Nicole was beet red. The heat made for a good cover, though. Maybe. Hopefully.

"When?" she said.

He turned to her, head tilted. "Are you drunk again? Am I under investigation?"

Nicole was stone-cold sober. A little dehydrated, sure. But really, it was simple. She'd never known a thing about Logan's love life. Yeah, they'd made jokes—almost always at his expense. And she knew he went to bars, to barbecues, to bachelor parties. And that, according to him, with no additional context provided, he'd once almost moved to Wisconsin for a woman. But how he swiped right or spent his Saturday nights or swept a girl off her feet? She never asked, and he never told.

That was, until today.

"Sorry," Nicole said. "I just . . . I don't know."

"You want me to tell you all the times I've had sex, ever?"

"No, um . . ."

"Oh." Logan was wearing sunglasses, but it didn't matter. He'd still found a way to narrow his eyes. "You're trying to ask me if I've been seeing anyone, aren't you? There were so many normal, inoffensive, straightforward ways for you to ask that question. And yet . . ."

Nicole peeled her shirt off her torso an inch, as if the motionless air could provide any relief. Sweat was dripping down her sternum in warm, wet beads. Everything was sticking to her. The heat, their day, this whole damn summer.

"Sorry, it's so nosy, I just—"

"There was Danielle," he said. He was just telling her. Like it was nothing. All she had to do was ask. "We were together for almost three years. We broke up, like, four years ago? Since then, there was Andrea. That lasted nine or ten months."

"And then what?" Nicole was fiddling with a glossy pamphlet. She studied the schedule of live excavations. If they hurried, they could catch the three o'clock at the Observation Pit. "You killed them?"

"That's exactly right." Logan pointed at a pulsing bubble of tar a few yards away. It gurgled right on cue. "That, over there, is Lena. They'll never find her."

"And you didn't want to . . . ?"

"Marry them?"

Nicole shrugged. "I'm sorry. I just always wondered. That's all."

"No, it's fine. And I don't know. I guess not, right?"

Logan motioned her toward a picnic table not far away. Nicole kept talking as they walked the twenty-five or so feet, knowing just how weird the whole thing was. The texts, the standing on each other's stoops, the seemingly pointless excursions. The bursts of conversation. The buzzy silences she kind of wished she could bottle up and save for later.

"What were they like? Before you killed them?"

"Honestly, they were great. Especially Andrea."

Nicole shoved the schedule in the pocket of her cutoffs, then took a seat on the hot concrete bench. Logan sat right next to her;

his body, twisted. Their knees, angled at each other's like arrows. His face, flushed. His hands, fidgeting. His lips and eyebrows and the tendons in his neck, tensing just a little when he talked or listened or laughed.

"What was her deal?" she said.

"She was a teacher. She lived in Santa Monica, she—"

"Wait, you drove to the Westside? For a girl?"

Logan shrugged. "Reverse commute."

"Disgusting."

He pricked her knee with the brochure. "Get your mind out of the gutter."

"Sorry! Sorry!" Nicole said, both hands up as Logan poked her with the pamphlet twice more. She was lucky he hadn't thrown her over his shoulder and tossed her into that radioactive lake or whatever the hell he'd said it was. "Seriously, tell me. What was she like?"

"You know—pretty, smart." He wiped his sunglasses with his shirt, then looked right at her. "Oh, and I almost forgot. She didn't talk back."

Nicole inhaled sharply. She begged her brain to breathe or make a joke or ask a follow-up question. Whatever a normal person would do, please.

"Why didn't it work out? With her? With any of them?"

"I don't know," he said, rolling his brochure into a tight little tube. "It just never did."

Nicole nodded. They were just sitting there, boiling on that bench. Full sun, 101 goddamn degrees. Nothing left to drink or eat or see or do. Their bodies, damp and hot and tired. Their little outing, quite obviously, coming to its natural end.

And still, they lingered.

23

Neutral Zone Infraction

The rest of Nicole's weekend was lazy and quiet. Back on the coast, the heat wave was actually kind of nice—a hot, dreamy reprieve from the climate-controlled, perpetually seventysomething days that made Manhattan Beach so aggressively pleasant.

On Sunday morning, Nicole walked her dog with her headphones blasting, ate two scoops of ice cream for breakfast, and ignored a few more calls from her husband. And then, when the afternoon sun began to slant, she lay in the warm, soft grass of her backyard and gave that Cormac McCarthy novel another go. From time to time, she'd roll over, smile at a dumb text from Logan, and send one right back. Apparently, he was spending the day with his friends, glitchless speedrunning *Kirby's Adventure*, whatever that meant.

> Are your buddies local children that you babysit? Or do you legitimately know other men your age who share your interests?

> The thing about dorks is we stick together. Mostly for gaming purposes, but also because it wards off jocks, gutter clowns, and other Stephen King–like threats.

She laughed, then fired off a response.

> Actually, Stephen King says the real monster is adverbs.

⁓

On Monday, temperatures cooled down, and Nicole stopped by Mari's new office in Playa del Rey. Mari, as usual, was multitasking: flagging every last inch of a pitch deck, guzzling an iced matcha latte, and picking apart Nicole's rather tepid recap of her literally hot date with Logan.

"I'm sorry, he took you where?"

"The Tar Pits?"

"And you just grilled him about his sex life? In broad daylight?"

"Essentially," Nicole said, collapsing deeper into a bright red womb chair. And then, because she wasn't a liar, and she would never withhold pertinent information from a friend, she offered up another little detail. "We also may have discussed why he never got married."

Mari raised an eyebrow. Nicole looked around.

Mari's office was nice—really nice. She'd only been working here since May, but already, she seemed right at home. Almost two years ago, when Mari realized that Logan was never going to leave Porter Sloane, she took another second-in-command job at a small, female-focused agency in Venice where she suspected she could rise to the top sooner. When that didn't pan out, she called every agency owner in town and asked for a meeting. Within six weeks, she had three offers to run her own show.

"Listen," Mari said, "I'm not going to pretend to understand how you two weirdos flirt. But whatever the hell you guys are doing, it's definitely not casual sex."

"It couldn't be more than that, anyway," Nicole said. "I'm the most entangled person on Earth."

Mari whirled around in her chair, propping her heels up on the coffee table. "If you really think it's nothing serious, why don't you just tell him? He's the nicest guy ever. And it's not like he's twenty-three. He's probably gone on a date with someone who has kids. It's kind of what happens in your thirties."

Nicole, now flipping through a coffee table book about white space, didn't know how to respond to that. The truth was, she didn't completely understand why she hadn't told Logan about the pregnancy. All she knew was she liked the way it felt when they were together. That she didn't want anything to change. That she didn't want him to see her any other way than exactly how he did on Saturday evening, when he drove her home, walked her to her front door, then got down on his hands and knees and let Nero lick him in the face.

Nicole knew Logan deserved the truth. And she would tell him, eventually. But not until she was sure. And yes, she knew the embryos were screened, that Valerie had carried both her previous pregnancies to term, that Friday's bloodwork looked great. None of that mattered. Before he told her to get lost, she had to be absolutely certain. She needed to hear that heartbeat. She needed proof that her life was going to irrevocably, irreversibly change. At least, that was what she kept telling herself every time he made her laugh or looked at her some kind of way.

"We're just having fun," Nicole said, flipping to the book's next page. Very carefully. "That's all. I swear."

Mari issued her a knowing glance. "Have you ever had casual sex, Nicole?"

"Yes. Well, no. Well, yes, but not on purpose? It was weird, and kind of an accident. But it's different with Logan, anyway. Because we were friends first, and because we've known each other so long, and—"

"Oh my god, girl." Mari tossed her phone into her bag and nodded Nicole toward the door. Mari had an afternoon meeting downtown, but they still had an hour to grab lunch before she left. "Do you want him, or not?"

"I . . . well . . . it's . . ."

Mari laughed in Nicole's face as they walked across the floor of the bustling agency—everyone typing or talking or handling this or checking on that—and stepped into the corridor.

Nicole frowned. "I don't know what I'm doing! Help me!"

"You're overthinking this," Mari said. "Take off the ring, for starters. That should help quite a bit. And then, just try and screw him. He slows you down, that's how you know you've got a problem on your hands."

"What, like some kind of truth serum? Why would I even need that?"

Mari called the elevator. "Because, Nicole, sleeping with someone for fun does not typically require this much . . . *talking*." Another knowing glance, which Nicole expertly averted. "When are you going to see him again, anyway?"

"I'm actually not sure. He's supposed to go to Chicago tomorrow.

And then he has a panel with Quentin at the end of the week, some conference in San Francisco, I think."

"Oh! I'm going to that!"

"Really? That's . . . that's amazing!" The elevator dinged. They stepped inside, and Nicole pricked the lobby button with her index finger, leaving it pressed against the warm plastic shell long after it'd begun to glow. "I'm really proud of you. It's so cool to see you like this."

"Come on, Nic. You're doing it too. Your podcast is—"

"What's good around here? Where should we go?"

"I mean it," Mari said, dropping her hand to Nicole's wrist. Nicole shook it off. "Your story is amazing. You built something, and people actually listen. You don't realize—"

"Please, can we not? Can we not pretend I didn't give up what I gave up? That my podcast is anything close to a legitimate career?"

Mari scratched the back of her neck, then exhaled. "There's a new place across the street that makes a decent Cobb. It's fast too."

Nicole agreed, and the elevator doors opened, and off they went to buy boring little salads, settle into a seldom-used, stark-white outdoor sectional, and shoot the shit. They talked about Mari's next pitch, whether she'd have time to meet Paige for a quick drink Friday, and if she should swipe left or right on this physical therapist who was very tall, dark, and handsome but also owned three parakeets. Nicole was midsentence, pontificating whether a grown-ass man caring for several expensive birds was a red flag or a green one, when Mari's phone rang.

"Sorry," she said, rising to her feet. "I have to take this. Give me, like, five, okay?"

Nicole nodded, and then she just sat there, watching Mari pace and laugh and work her magic from across the courtyard.

She just sat there and pretended she hadn't nearly had that too. That, when push came to shove, she hadn't been so quick to buy the dream Gabe was selling . . . and accidentally leave the rest of herself behind.

***

Later that afternoon, the clinic confirmed Valerie's betas had doubled perfectly again. They scheduled the seven-week ultrasound for two weeks from Friday. Nicole texted Gabe the appointment time and nothing else. And then, realizing she couldn't put it off any longer, she called her over-the-moon, utterly clueless parents with the good news. And when that was over, she FaceTimed Paige.

"When are you going to tell Mom what happened with Gabe?"

"Hopefully never."

"And what about the podcast? Shouldn't you put out a statement or something? Your listeners probably think you're dead."

"Aren't I, though?"

Once she'd hung up, Nicole went out for a run. When she hit her goal—thirty minutes, the longest she'd managed in years—she just kept going. Her lungs burned. The sky blurred. She ran anyway. And then, when she could no longer breathe, when she could no longer see, when the shit had finally, mercifully, been kicked out of her, she came to a sudden halt, wiped her stinging face with the sleeve of her shirt, and walked home.

She was sitting at her kitchen table, covered in sweat and dirt and tears, contemplating the shit show that was her life, when her phone dinged. Three times, in rapid succession.

> My meeting got moved.

> I may have spent the whole day reading *American Pastoral*.

> I am unwell.

Nicole snickered. She'd warned him, hadn't she?

> I prescribe *Pride & Prejudice*. The movie, not the book. This is dire.

> I'm very dumb. Want to come over and explain it to me?

Nicole laughed. And then she took a very thorough shower, inched into the shortest pair of bike shorts she owned, and slid that ridiculous diamond ring off her finger.

It wasn't like she needed it where she was going, anyway.

❦

By dinnertime, Nicole and Logan were tucked into their respective corners of Logan's couch; bodies twisted and knees bent so their feet fell only inches from each other's. That middle cushion—last week, uncharted territory and little more than a resting place for buzzing phones nobody bothered to answer—had become a neutral zone. A place to toe the line.

"You're loving this shit, aren't you?" he said.

"All my dreams are coming true," Nicole said, taking a long sip of an ice-cold glass of whole milk. Logan's fridge, all joking aside, was pretty fun. "I'm very pleased."

"Good."

He was just lying there, slumped into his sofa in a pair of gray sweatpants and an old Michigan T-shirt, watching *Pride & Prejudice* on purpose. Enjoying it, even, if the glimmer in his eye could be believed.

"About five minutes until the big moment, okay?" Nicole said.

Logan looked at her. And then, very quickly, her bare left hand. And then, again, at her. "How many times have you seen this movie, exactly?"

"Just, like, a really small, reasonable number." She reached over him for an Oreo. "Like, whatever that number is in your head, it's right around there."

Logan smirked. "So, twice?"

". . . a month?"

"Holy shit! And for years, we've been making fun of me? For just, like, a tiny bit of *Dungeons & Dragons*? A tiny, little bit of *Legend of Zelda*?"

"Excuse me, but only one person in this room broke their hand playing video games."

"That was a strain! No structural damage!"

She glared at him, laughing. He caught her gaze, then glanced at the TV screen.

"This still your favorite?" he said.

Nicole bit her lip.

Logan watched her do it.

"No, actually." She pulled some fleece Super Bowl blanket over her legs—his too. The windows were cracked, and the summer air had turned cool and damp. It was one of the best things about Logan's place. How his slider, his front door were always open, and California always seemed to creep through his screens. How, from time to time, in the distance, a car would start, a stranger would laugh, or a dog would bark. "It's *Persuasion* now."

"Really? Since when?"

On-screen, Elizabeth was already headed to the carriage. They didn't have much time.

"I don't know," she said. "It's grown on me, I guess. It's really good."

"Should I read it?"

Nicole studied him. She wasn't shy about it. She scanned him, head to toe. His ungovernable, dirty-blond hair. His scruffy, sun-kissed face. The curves of his hands, the lines in his arms, the way the seams of his shirt settled across his shoulders like he'd never felt a hint of stress his whole life. He looked really good, didn't he?

There was no use denying it anymore.

He looked good. He did then, and he did now.

"Yeah," she said, nodding like he hadn't just watched her eye all six feet of him, inch by inch. "It's hot."

Logan laughed, then started asking his requisite questions, but Nicole shushed him. And then they both watched Elizabeth Bennet wrap her pretty little hand around Fitzwilliam Darcy's fingers and Lizzy looked at Darcy and Darcy looked at Lizzy and Nicole looked at Logan and then Matthew MacFadyen flexed his damn hand and Logan yelped and Nicole squealed—even though she'd watched this scene a hundred times—because she'd known Logan was going to love it and she was right. He had.

"Holy shit!"

"I know! Iconic!" Nicole said, squeezing a pillow into her chest, beaming, and that was when it happened. Her socked foot, somewhere underneath that absurd Seahawks blanket, had found itself between his legs and she could feel the cotton of his sweatpants graze her bare shins and she could feel her legs start to want his hands to find her skin and she could feel something deep and heavy and unmistakable start to brew inside of her—a pound, it was a pound, and she wasn't sure when or how or where it started or how to stop it or whether she even wanted to—and he was looking right at her and she was looking right at him and then she pressed the edge of her right foot into the inside of his left one and he kind of bit his lip and she kind of gasped and that was it.

They were touching.

Logan scratched his neck—eyes on her—and Nicole nodded—eyes on him—and then, without a word, they began to rearrange their limbs in brilliant, blanketed silence as the movie blurred and blue light lapped the room and blood rushed between Nicole's legs. And then, like magic, the seams of their socks had found each other's and they just sat there—bodies, mirrors—and pressed their feet together and looked at each other and shook their heads and laughed.

It was happening.

They'd done it.

They continued their movie, grinning like idiots, toes tangled. They watched as Mr. Darcy barged into the Collinses' home, they watched as rain poured down on that botched proposal, they watched as Lizzy tore Darcy a new one. Every scene, sparks.

"I want to kiss you, Nicole," Logan said. Her whole body jolted. "You know that, right?"

She nodded. Every inch of her seized, and she just nodded.

"I had a feeling, yeah."

She pressed her foot against his a little harder. He pressed back.

"You just tell me when, then."

"Okay."

He smiled at her, and she smiled back, and then they just sat there—eating junk food, making small talk, watching Mr. Darcy get the girl—with their soles intertwined.

When the movie ended, they started another.

24

The Note

The next morning, Nicole was barely awake when she rolled over in her mess of a bed and reached for her phone. Which was about to die and roughly three inches from her face.

It had been one of those nights.

> Your next assignment is the Colin Firth *Pride & Prejudice*. Most people prefer it, but they're wrong. Don't be wrong.

> What about the one with all the zombies? Where does that rank for you?

And then, after ten more minutes of whatever the hell it was they were doing, Logan asked if he could stop by before he left for the airport.

Half an hour later, he showed up with two coffees and two not-blueberry bagels and his hair wet and combed and tidy—it was better wild, but this wasn't so bad either—and for a few minutes, they just stood there, staring at each other, talking about nothing while the morning sun warmed Nicole's street, her sidewalk, her stoop.

"Well, I'd better go," he said, eyeing his watch. "Promise you won't go to the Tar Pits without me?"

Nicole looked him up and down. An ivory Henley, a nice pair of jeans. His hands, clutched around a cup of coffee. Clutched around his car keys.

"What would you do to me, Logan? If I did?"

His head jerked back. Then he took a long sip of his coffee. "Turns out you're quite the flirt, aren't you?"

"Just genuinely curious," Nicole said, running a couple of fingers over her collarbone. She was barefoot, in her pajamas—a flimsy white tank top and a paper-thin pair of cotton shorts. Her hair, a mess. She'd made sure of that. "What you'd do to me."

Logan's eyes bulged. And then he just looked at her, shaking his head.

"Come on," Nicole said. "Just tell me."

He bit down on his bottom lip, gave her one last glance, then turned and walked away, laughing as he unlocked his car—a mossy, almost metallic-green hatchback with roof racks and a dusty windshield.

"Wait!" Nicole followed him a few steps across her driveway. He was nearly to his door. "You can't leave! You have to tell me!"

Logan spun around and grinned.

Eagle Scout hot, was it?

"I'll tell you what," he said, leaning against his door, eyes twinkling. "I'll write it down, and show you later. When I think you're ready. How's that sound?"

That sent Nicole leaping across the pavement. But by the time she'd made it to his car, he was already safe inside. She grabbed for the handle just in time for it to latch.

"Logan! Open the door!"

He was just sitting there, taking his sweet time, sifting through his center console, pulling out a bunch of random shit—half a granola bar, a sock, what appeared to be the remnants of a glow stick—until he'd found a scrap of paper and a crappy old pen. He held them both up toward the window like a game of show-and-tell. Nicole shrieked, trying the handle over and over as Logan laughed and licked his lips and looked right at her. And then, after she shouted at him a minute more, he shrugged a single shoulder at her, flattened his little sheet of paper against the dashboard, and clicked his pen.

"Logan! Don't you dare!"

He cracked his window open an inch. Nicole curled her fingers into the crevice, smooshed her face against the glass, and cursed his name. He pressed a single finger over his mouth.

"Quiet," he said. "I'm trying to think of the right words."

When he put pen to paper, Nicole screamed. He winked at her, then folded his left hand around the note, shielding it from view. And then, he began to write.

Nicole squawked and shouted and squeaked while Logan, relaxed as ever, just sat there, writing. His every etch, slow and thoughtful. From time to time, he'd pause to stroke his chin or tilt his head or look right up at Nicole and let his lips fall open just a bit. And then, after one final pause, after he'd taken a few extra seconds to reread his work and nod his head in approval and give Nicole a glimpse of what she was pretty sure were his fuck-me eyes, he pricked pen to paper one last time, like he was adding a period or dotting an i or something. A little finishing touch. For emphasis.

That was the final straw.

"Logan Milgram! Show me now! Or I'll never let you kiss me!"

He dropped his hand over the note, slid it off his dash, shoved it into his wallet, and tucked that into his pocket—all while Nicole, squealing, yanked at his door over and over again.

Until suddenly, it flung open.

He'd unlocked the car.

"Where is it, you dipshit!" Nicole said, wrapping her hands around his wrists, fighting his arms out of her way, forcing her fingers into his pockets, sliding her legs around his hips—oh god, her legs were locked around his hips; oh god, his hands were crawling up her bare ribs; oh god, he was hard, he was already so hard, and her shorts were so thin, and it felt so good, he felt so good, and his hands were so strong and so sure and so steady, and she was just pulling him into her, closer and closer and closer until finally, her forehead found his, his nose found hers, and her half-open mouth lingered a quarter inch from his parted lips.

She slipped her arms around his neck. He dragged his thumb across her bottom lip and looked right at her.

"Nicole," he said.

She nodded, and that was it. That was all it took.

He pulled her face into his, and they were kissing.

They were kissing.

Everything was spinning: the car, the sky, the two of them, fumbling for each other, rough and impatient and reckless. Nicole couldn't breathe; she didn't care. She just kept pushing herself onto him, pulling him into her; their bodies, pressed against each other's, tongues and teeth and skin and hair; his hands, flying up her legs, her ass, the bare skin of her back; her hands, racing up his jeans, his stomach, his chest—rushing to feel him, to touch him;

every inch of him, somehow, exactly what she'd hoped, and it just went on forever.

They kissed for an eternity.

Five, ten, fifteen minutes.

Logan had a flight to catch.

They both knew it. Nobody cared.

Nobody stopped.

They just kept going. Their hands and lips and fingertips, everywhere. They were everywhere. It was sloppy, almost—learning each other. A bit of a mess. Moans and groans and the occasional clunk, always followed by a laugh and a look and another kiss, harder and dumber and more desperate than the last. And then, after a few minutes more of that—of making out like teenagers, damp and noisy and stupid—Nicole sunk her teeth into Logan's bottom lip, curled a finger into his belt loop, and looked him right in the eye.

"Now you wanna tell me what you wrote down?"

He gulped. "You're not ready."

She kissed him again. "Maybe I'll surprise you."

Logan pulled back—it took a while, and he kept stopping himself to groan or grab Nicole by the neck or bury his face into her ear or her throat or the palm of her hand, anywhere he could get his mouth or teeth or tongue on—but eventually, he did retreat.

"Not like this," he said.

Nicole raked her fingernails down his forearms. He quivered. "Please?"

Logan laughed, then tucked her hair behind her ear.

"Saturday," he said, after a long exhale. Nicole was still moving her hips, still pulling him into her, and his hands were cupping her ass, helping her do it. "Dinner. You, me. Anywhere you'd like. And then, after that, if you still want me to, I'll kiss you again. Probably for hours."

Nicole interlocked their fingers.

"I hate you," she said.

"Yeah," he said, before kissing her one last time. "I can tell."

And then off he went, leaving a breathless, disheveled, and dazed Nicole Speyer in her driveway with nothing to do but watch his completely unremarkable car—which she'd decided, this morning, she liked quite a bit—disappear.

And once it did, Nicole just stood there a minute longer, trying not to think too hard about Mari's little litmus test. Because she'd just begged Logan Milgram to take her upstairs and screw her six ways from Sunday, and he'd flat-out refused. He'd turned her down.

Oh, and the kiss? Very good.

The kind you don't forget.

Maybe ever.

25

The Problem

She tried everything.
Cold shower.
Long walk.
More Cormac McCarthy.
When all that failed to cool her down, Nicole gave up and texted Mari.

> I think I have a Logan problem.

When Mari called her, immediately, Nicole didn't even know where to begin. How could she explain to her best friend that some guy—Mari's old boss, no less—had left her . . . like this? That her stupid body was suddenly so sure? That the rest of her was now dumb as rocks? Little more than a melted pile of mush?

She couldn't. So instead, she pretty much stuck to one-word answers.

"Did he talk about *Star Wars* the whole time?"

"Mari."

"Was he better than Gabe?"

"Mari."

"Do you remember how to use a condom?"

"Mari!"

Once that interrogation ended, Nicole poured herself a massive glass of wine, sent Paige a very niche Charlotte Brontë meme, and dumped Gabe's newest issue of *The Economist* straight into the recycling bin. She was about to head out on another aimless walk when her phone buzzed.

> My seatmate just told me I had bedhead.

Nicole shook her head. Her fingers fired back.

> Literally zero chance that happened.

> Oh, it did. We're friends now.

> He gave me his cashews.

She laughed. He was funny. He really was. In this dumb, perfect way that barely made sense.

> What did you tell him?

> That this crazy hot girl from work tried to have sex with me in her driveway, but I didn't do it.

Nicole inhaled sharply. This was a game, wasn't it? A game she had not forgotten how to play.

> Wow, that's wild. Why didn't you take her up on that?

His text bubble came and went, came and went. When the wait became untenable, Nicole flipped her phone over, held her breath, and walked in a circle around the kitchen island. Halfway through her fourth lap, Logan put her out of her misery.

> Because I wanted to take my time.

"Well, fuck," Nicole said. Possibly out loud.

She steadied her hands onto the cool marbled curve of the countertop. She closed her eyes, she clenched her fists, she straightened her toes. It didn't help. She was a mess. All she could think about was that morning. All she could think about was that kiss. His hands, his mouth, his teeth flying over her frenzied skin.

How hard he was.

How close he was.

How good he felt.

And every time she did anything—washed her hands, watered her basil, walked past a mirror—she could see it, feel it, taste it. The whole scene, playing on repeat. Backward and forward. Hard and soft. Fast and slow.

Their morning was all over her.

She was swimming in it.

And by nighttime, Nicole was a lost cause. She lay in bed, tossing and turning, her hands and legs and lips desperate and restless and lonely. She threw off her sheets. She dragged her forefingers down the sweat gathering on her throat, her sternum, her stomach. She closed her eyes, flexed her toes, and shoved her fist between her teeth.

Yeah, she had a Logan problem, all right.

A big one.

26

Silver Lake

Nicole asked Logan to take her to Silver Lake, and he planned the rest. And then, on Saturday evening at seven o'clock on the dot, he rang her doorbell in a blue-and-white-checked button-down and a nice pair of jeans and his hair, sadly, perfect.

He was also . . . holding a cactus?

"There was some confusion between me and the florist," he said. "I told her I wanted something that wasn't going to die, and then we started talking about xeriscaping, and I didn't want to be late, and I didn't want to show up empty-handed, and . . ."

"I love it," Nicole said, coaxing Nero back inside, then locking her front door. "It's very spiky."

Logan laughed. "You, uh, look amazing, by the way."

"Thanks," she said, like it was nothing. Like she hadn't spent the entire afternoon trying on every last thing she owned before settling on a white eyelet babydoll dress that was all ruffles and shoulders and legs. Especially legs.

Logan looked at her again, then nodded her toward his car. It was a little awkward, those next ten, fifteen steps. Was she supposed to kiss him, or wait for him to kiss her? Were they going to hold hands? Was she allowed to wrap her fingers around his forearm? Ask him, very nicely, to please throw her against a wall?

They'd spent the whole week texting. She'd spent the whole week waiting. But now that tonight was finally here? She didn't know what to do. And he didn't seem so sure either.

Logan opened the car door for her, then walked to the driver's side and sat himself down. He fiddled with the radio. He adjusted his rearview mirror. He fussed with the air-conditioning. And then, when he was done fine-tuning a car he'd definitely owned for years, he turned to Nicole, who was staring at the dashboard in silence.

"Hey," he said.

"Hey," she said.

And then she just looked at him, remembering how it felt to lock her legs around him, to pull him into her, to fall asleep wishing her hands were his—and that was when she realized she was still holding the cactus.

"I'll, uh . . . I'll be right back."

Logan just sat there, laughing, as Nicole—cracking up too—darted out of the car, placed the little pot on her welcome mat, then hopped back in. That broke the ice.

"You're so adorable," he said, leaning over his center console and, finally, kissing her. "It's ridiculous."

Nicole shrugged, wiping her lips. "I'm sure you say that to all your cactus girls."

"I definitely do not," he said, rubbing little shapes onto her wrist. "And you know it."

Nicole wrinkled her nose, then ruffled his too-tidy hair a bit, and off they went. On a date. A real one. It wasn't the quickest drive, because every chance he got, Logan grabbed Nicole by the neck and kissed her, but eventually, they did make it onto the freeway. By the time the 405 had become the 105, Logan's free hand had settled a few inches above Nicole's knee and the evening was melting into one of those perfect summer nights. Clouds stretched like cotton, and the sky went on forever—orange and pink and blue.

They talked about window seats and watering instructions for Nicole's new plant and whether corn was a vegetable, and then, when some obscure Dave Matthews song came on, Nicole twisted toward Logan a little more and narrowed her eyes.

"What the hell are we listening to? Is this, like, your sex playlist?"

"My understanding is that anything can be a sex playlist, if you try hard enough."

Nicole snickered while Logan, mouth quirking, squeezed her leg. She twisted her fingers into his, and then, for the next half hour, they whirled through a hundred different worlds. LA was like that—sprawling, full of hamlets. Each mile, something new. And with every passing exit sign, downtown grew bigger and bolder. Freeways fused, and through the haze, thick stacks of concrete and steel gripped the road—skyscrapers so close, you could reach out and touch them.

And then, like magic, the city was in the rearview. The 101 had melted into the mountains, and they were in the hills. Evening had turned to dusk, soft and purple, and tall and skinny palm trees formed a skyline of their own: sparse, willowy silhouettes that dotted the sweet, smoggy evening at random. Coffee bars, record stores, and gas-stations-turned-taco-shops flanked the clogged, winding curves of Sunset Boulevard.

"You ever been here?" Logan said, parking the car on a side street where houses piled onto the hill like mismatched blocks.

"Never," Nicole said as he opened her door. Streetlights were stapled with flyers for midnight shows, slam poetry readings, five-hundred-dollar rewards for rescue dogs that'd gone missing while hiking Griffith Park with their foster families.

"What do you think?"

"I think," she said, looping her arms around his neck, then tugging him back toward the car, "that we're not cool enough to be here. And that we should probably turn around."

He laughed, kissing her for a minute, then twirling her back to his side. "You know I am one hundred percent taking you to dinner, right? That we're going to do this one thing in order?"

"Yeah," Nicole said. "I've kinda figured that out by now."

Logan chuckled, and then off they went, holding hands, stopping from time to time to make out like idiots, until they'd reached a cute little French place where the tablecloths were checked, the walls were brick, and the art was crooked, charming, and warm. They opted to sit outside—the night, balmy and long—and from the awning, twinkle lights and greenery and copper pots and pans hung like stars. Everyone was chatting, drinking, in no rush at all, and Nicole just sat at their tiny table, twisting around a flickering tea candle, taking it all in. Logan locked her bare legs between his knees.

"God, are you pretty."

"Very original."

"I mean it," he said, topping off her glass of wine—some red the waiter had recommended. "I told my mom you were the prettiest girl I've ever seen."

Nicole flung a piece of bread at him. "You told your mom that? When? After you wrote down some deranged sexual fantasy of yours on a receipt for, like, Froot Loops and let me dry hump you in my driveway? At nine thirty a.m. on a Tuesday?"

Logan's eyes lit up as his hand found her knee underneath the table. "A bit before that, actually."

Nicole's stomach fluttered. She took a long sip of her wine. He didn't take his eyes off her.

"I always thought you were cute too," she said. "I mean, for a total moron."

This went on for a while. The teasing. The touching. The passing back and forth of a plate of very buttery, thyme-roasted carrots. They talked about their childhood pets and their prom dates and how, in Saint Louis, children are legitimately required to tell terrible jokes in exchange for a fistful of Halloween candy. And then, after Nicole begrudgingly performed a half-dozen poltergeist-laden puns for a very-amused, hand-halfway-up-her-leg Logan, he tilted his head and exhaled.

"I'm sorry, Nicole, about everything that's happened to you. I really am. But these past few weeks . . . I hope you're having as much fun as I am."

"Yeah." She put her hand on his, helping him up another inch. "This has been really fun."

He looked at her. Nicole looked right back. And then, their waiter—some actor who could not read the room—stumbled over to refill their half-full water carafe. They thanked him, and then he and Logan accidentally discussed rapidly changing bicycle culture in California for five minutes. By the time they'd finished up that fascinating conversation, dinner had arrived.

"You're too nice," Nicole said, swiping a fry from his plate. "You know that, right?"

"What can I say? I'm a man of the people."

"I feel like it's more of a you-don't-ever-shut-the-fuck-up situation."

"Well," he said, "it worked on you, didn't it?"

Nicole scoffed, and then they laughed and ate and talked some more. The night aged. The patio buzzed. People came, people went. They barely noticed. They just kept on talking. Their gazes, fixed. Their legs, locked. Their bodies, bait.

"Do you still love your job?" Nicole said, scraping her foot around his calf.

"I love what I do, sure. But I don't know if I love my job anymore."

"Doesn't it feel good, though? Doing something big? Having somewhere to be besides here?"

"Not lately," he said. His fingers, still climbing, and firm against her goose-bumped skin. She pulled her chair in and narrowed her eyes.

"What'd you write on that sheet of paper, Logan?"

"We're talking about my career, Nicole. How rude of you."

"It's butt stuff, isn't it?"

He bumped her knee under the table. "You're lucky you're cute."

"Sorry!" Nicole said, giggling. "I'm done now—I'm serious. Please explain to me how the captain of the Michigan debate team ended up anywhere but the state attorney's office."

And so Logan, after a little more knee knocking, told her everything. She'd known bits and pieces, but now she got the entire story, start to finish. How Quentin was the creative director at the agency where Logan worked in Boston right out of college, when he realized he had no desire to do what everyone else around him was doing: going to law school. How he stuck around Massachusetts for a few years until he found a cool opportunity in San Diego, and then another one back in Seattle, and then for a little while, New

York, until one day the phone rang and it was Quentin, asking if he'd like to head up New Business at an agency he was starting in Los Angeles.

"And then," Logan said, "nine years went by. They just kind of flew, you know?"

Nicole nodded, taking a sip of her wine. "And you've never thought about leaving?"

"No, I have. A lot, actually." He scratched his throat for a moment. "Sometimes, I think about starting my own thing. I know it's dumb, that everyone in advertising does that. But I've been saving up for a few years. I could get by for a while if I kept things really lean, I just . . ."

Nicole looked at him, so ready to tease him, to tear him to shreds. After all, when had Logan Milgram had reservations about anything, ever? But instead, she squeezed his hand.

"It's not dumb," she said. "I think a lot of people want something that's only theirs. If you can do it, I think you should try."

"Someday, maybe. It's a big risk, going out on your own. And it's just not the right time, I don't think."

Nicole nodded again, still squeezing his hand. He played with her fingers, stretching them, circling them.

"What about going somewhere new, then?" she said. "A bigger agency, maybe?"

"Working on that too," he said as Nicole slid his hand back onto her leg and guided him higher up her thigh. He leaned forward, his jaw twitching as his fingers found the napkin in her lap and slipped beneath it. "Not sure I love the details, though. Of what's out there."

Nicole nodded a third time, tightening her grip on his wrist, leading him to the hem of her dress, helping him get to know the skin below it. Her mouth was wet, and his hand was trembling. She knew he wouldn't go any farther than this. Not here, not now. But she kind of wished he would. She wanted his hands on her hips. She wanted him peeling back every inch of lace and cotton and denim that kept him from her. She wanted him figuring out how to make her fall apart. She wanted him, here and hard and now.

"What else have you been thinking about, Logan?"

"Are you trying to kill me?"

"The opposite, I think."

He looked at her, and then at their waiter, who was off somewhere, reading the menu from a very impractical chalkboard at the top of his lungs. And then, without taking his gaze off her, Logan shoved a wad of cash underneath that candle and nodded her toward the sidewalk.

"Car," he said. "Right now."

They scurried into the street; his arm around her waist, her hand in his back pocket, their steps, quick and brisk and in sync. They got all the way to that sleepy, residential street where they'd parked—a dark, sloping road that ended in a cul-de-sac at the base of the hill. Above them, power lines dangled like string lights.

But they didn't quite make it to the car. They were more, on it? Against it? Nicole was, anyway. Pinned there against his door, his hands up her dress, her mouth on his collar, both of them panting, pulling, pushing as Nicole's hands slid underneath Logan's shirt, as Logan's teeth met her ear, her neck, her shoulders. Nicole only pulled away—lips, swollen; her voice, a whisper—to plead with him.

"Please don't stop touching me."

Logan kissed her again. This time, differently. Softly. Slowly.

"Do you want me to take you home?" he said.

"Yeah."

He took a deep breath, then unlocked his car and helped her in. When she buckled her seat belt, Logan—already bent over—put his mouth on her knee. Nicole grabbed the hair at the nape of his neck and gasped.

"Your place, please," she said.

"Okay," he said. "Let's get you home."

∽

By the time Logan was fumbling for his house keys, Nicole had already locked her legs around his waist. She was glued to him—kissing his neck, unbuttoning his shirt, scraping her fingernails down his back—as he laughed and groaned and pulled her closer. He hoisted her against his front door with a single knee, twisted his key into the lock, used their bodies to force the door open, then spun her against the wall of his pitch-black entryway. She yelped.

"You're so fucking perfect," he said, throwing his keys to the floor. He sunk his teeth into her throat, her collarbone, her chest. His hands were all over her. "I've been thinking about you all week. I—"

"Kiss me," she said, grabbing his face, finding his mouth, sliding her tongue between his lips. She unbuckled his belt, then begged him to grab her harder, pull her closer, push her dress up sooner. He did as he was told.

"You're . . ." she said as his hands flew up her thighs, rushing to find the lace of her underwear. He yanked it down her arching hips, slowing himself only to drag a single finger across her now bare and sparking skin. She gasped, then tipped her head back and closed her eyes. "You're . . ."

"I'm what, Nicole?" he said, pushing his hands—still, under her dress—up her waist until she was in his arms, until she was over his shoulder, until he'd flung her onto that old couch of his. When she landed, laughing, her dress was already halfway up her stomach and her hair was everywhere.

Logan threw off his shoes, crawled on top of her, and kissed her hard. Nicole pushed herself up a couple of feet, tugged at the collar of his shirt, and finished unbuttoning it. She tossed it somewhere, anywhere, then collapsed back onto the cushion as Logan, still in his jeans, pressed himself harder between her legs. When she moaned, he did it again, then traced the nearly invisible links of her dainty little necklaces with his tongue.

"Tell me what I am," he said.

"You're really good at this," she said, between mutters. Between tiny gasps for air. "Why didn't we do this weeks ago?"

He chuckled, then pushed her dress up another inch, two inches, three inches, until it was off, until his mouth was sliding down her sternum, down her stomach, while he touched her, kissed her, tasted her, while she fumbled for the buttons on his jeans, the waistband of his boxer briefs. His hands were back on her hips, they were right there, right where she'd wanted them all night, right where she'd wanted them all week, and he was reaching for his wallet, touching her face, whispering "are you sure?" and then, just when she began to nod, just when she began to lick her lips, just when she began to reach for him, to pull him into her, she froze.

She couldn't breathe.

She couldn't move.

She couldn't see.

The truth flooded her body like a punishment. All at once—and ruthlessly. And every last thing she'd tried to hide or forget or bury these past few weeks began to surround her, sink her, drown her. Her cheating husband, her broken body, the divorce she couldn't have. The career she'd given up. The pregnancy she'd prayed for. The surrogate she couldn't stop lying to. All of it, engulfing her. Here, tonight, as her heart raced, her skin screamed, her body begged for someone else. Someone who barely knew her.

"Nicole? Are you—"

"I can't do this."

Logan peeled his hands off her. He sat up. He wiped his brow, rolled back his shoulders, then took a deep breath and nodded. "No problem."

"I'm so sorry," Nicole said, folding herself in half. She just sat there, pulling her knees into her chest and her head into her hands. "I don't know what happened."

"You don't owe me an explanation."

Nicole slumped. Through the darkness, Logan slid on his jeans and found his shirt. He offered it to her, but she shook her head.

"I didn't mean to lead you on," she said, closing her eyes. "I don't know what happened. I didn't mean to, I promise. I really wanted this."

"It's okay, Nicole," he said. "You don't have to worry. It is completely okay."

They were quiet for a minute. When she finally opened her eyes,

Logan was folding her dress and placing it on the edge of his coffee table, right beside her.

"Do you want to talk?" he said. "Do you want me to leave? Do you want me to take you home? You can stay as long as you'd like. Just tell me what you need, okay?"

She looked at him.

"I think I should probably just go home."

"Okay," he said.

Nicole got dressed. Logan looked away. When she was ready, they walked through the living room and down the hall. Nicole turned around for a second, just to take another glance, just to remember this place. That old couch and those cluttered kitchen counters and the bare, warm walls. And then it was over. The door was closed.

They dragged their bodies into Logan's car. The six-minute drive was long and swift and silent. The windows were cracked, and the night air was cold and damp and cruel.

He pulled into her driveway.

"I'll call you," she said.

"Anytime."

Nicole nodded, then opened the car door. She turned to him one last time. He was reaching for his seat belt—all this, and he still wanted to walk her to her door, didn't he?—but Nicole winced and he did too. He pursed his lips, put his hands back on his steering wheel, then looked at her and that was it.

They were strangers.

27

Rock Bottom

"Open the fucking door, Gabe!" Nicole was pounding her fists on the sleek wood door of some Beverly Hills hotel room, still in that dress, still in those sandals. Her knuckles, burning. Her voice, ablaze. She'd found the charges from this place plastered all over his credit card statement. "You want to talk? Let's fucking talk!"

The door cracked open.

"Nicole?" Gabe's rounded eyes squinted at the light that filled the hallway. He looked like shit. "Wh-what's wrong? Are you okay?"

"What's wrong? Are you kidding me? Everything is wrong! I fucking hate you!"

Gabe winced, then eyed a half-full luggage cart poking out from beyond the elevator bay. "Keep your voice down, okay? There's—"

"Don't tell me to calm down!" She clutched her keys. "You screwed a twenty-three-year-old in our own home! While I was across the country, trying to have a baby! You'd fuck her, and I'd Venmo her! So forgive me if I don't give a shit what that bellhop thinks about you or me or our marriage!"

Gabe's eyes scrunched closed again. "Will you please just come inside? I'm begging you, just get in here."

Nicole barged past him, smashed her palm onto the wall switch, and hurled her keys against the lacquered headboard of his unmade bed. A few beams of recessed light cast a too-stylish glow on the mess he'd made. Wrinkled clothes and empty bottles and loose credit cards and—

"Are you doing coke?" Nicole said.

"It's . . ."

"No! You don't get to do that, ever! Party's over! I talked to Valerie! She's throwing up! It's really happening! It's—"

"She is? You really think that?"

"Yep! You're going to be a dad! A shitty one, I'm sure, but I'm stuck with you, so if you could try not to die for the next eighteen years, that'd be great!"

"Stuck with me? What does that even mean?"

"Exactly what you think it means! How fucking high are you!?"

Gabe didn't answer. He was too busy studying Nicole, head to toe. The waves in her hair, the shimmer on her eyelids, the mascara running down her cheeks. The splotches on her shoulders. The creases in her dress. The tension in her fists.

"Where's your ring, Nicole?"

She laughed in his face. "In the safe. Don't worry, I didn't flush it down the toilet. Wouldn't want some judge in Virginia to think I'm unfit to be a mother."

"What judge? What the hell are you talking about? You're not making any sense."

"Holy shit! You don't even know, do you? You didn't even call a lawyer. That's how great you think you are. You thought I'd stay! What did you think was going to happen when you decided to start screwing people who weren't me? Does everyone else in your world actually get away with this shit? Am I really the first crazy wife to tell you to get the hell out? Because I never gave a shit about your money or your family or your weird fucking town? Which, by the way, is—"

"You don't like LA?"

Nicole howled, taking three steps toward him as Gabe took four back. "No! I hate it! I've always hated it! And it's not even LA! It's Pleasantville-by-the-sea and your mother stops by whenever she wants and I'm so small and I'm so bored and I did it for you! I did it all for you, and you repaid me by fucking literally anything you wanted for god knows how long, and I will never, ever forgive you!"

Gabe, standing near the foot of the bed, grimaced. Behind him, the television lulled. Mouths moved, stocks ticked.

"Please, baby," he said. "Just let me explain, okay?"

"Go right ahead! Help me understand how the guy I fell in love with in New York became whatever the hell it is you are now. Please, explain away!"

"Nicole, I'm still him, I swear!"

"You're not! I don't even know you! I was twenty-two! You whisked me away and you promised me forever and I believed you. I built my life around you. Now I've got nothing! No career. I can't have kids. I've got one friend. I can't even tell my parents what you did because they'll just tell me to forgive you. And that's it, that's my whole life. So nice work, Gabe! You sure put some spell on me!"

Gabe shuddered. He was backed into a corner now. All six feet, three inches of him, retreating into the rippled silk of the floor-to-ceiling curtains he'd drawn closed. Nicole took a step closer anyway.

"Why'd it have to be me?" she said.

"Colie, stop it."

"Why didn't you just fuck me and ghost me? You could've had

any girl you wanted. I had my own plans! I had my own life! Why'd it have to be me?"

Gabe gulped, pushing his palms against the wall, searching for an escape. His sweat clung to the stucco. Blood roared through Nicole's veins.

"Answer the question! Make my stupid life mean something! Make me love you again! Fix what you broke, you fucking asshole! Fix it now!"

"Colie, I still love you! I still—"

"No! Something real! Tell me why you ruined my life! Tell me why it had to be me!"

Gabe took a deep breath, then floated his hand toward her. "Come to Colorado," he said. "Come with me, okay? I'm leaving tomorrow, first thing. I bought that place for us—for you. We can spend the rest of the summer fixing this. We can drive out. We can—"

"No!" She threw her hands onto his chest. "You bought that place for Kyle! For your fucking job! So you could play ball at your stupid finance bro summer camp! None of that was ever about me! Nothing we've done, since the day we moved here, has been about me! So for once, stop lying, and tell me the truth! Tell me why you did it! Tell me why you broke us! Make it good!"

Gabe slammed his fists together. "Fine! You want the truth? I never thought it was going to stop! How's that? You happy now? There's your fucking answer! You were gone! You didn't give a shit about me! All you wanted was a baby! You were my best friend! I lost you! It was hard for me too!"

Nicole took a step back.

Blood rushed to her ears.

The whole room blurred.

Her sight was a tunnel.

There was only him. The man she could never rid herself of now.

"Hard for you? It was hard for you?"

"Colie, I didn't mean—"

"Tell me how fucking hard it was for you, Gabe. Did it hurt? When our babies died inside of me? When they fell out of my body? Blood and guts and tissue—four fucking times? Was that so hard? Did you stand up from your desk and feel it happen? Did you clutch your stomach while your body heaved out your dreams like an infection? Like a mistake? While you were at work? While you were trying to do your job? I couldn't even reach you! I called you a hundred times! Where were you?"

"Nicole—"

"Was it so hard? When I did every single thing the doctors said and nothing changed? When they just kept dying? When the surgeries only made it worse? When I drove to the Westside every day so they could inject crap into my veins and shut down my immune system, just in case? While you were in Hong Kong or Vegas or Osaka with Kyle, doing god knows what? Was that so hard for you? When I became a science experiment, and you missed half a day of work?"

Gabe's eyes were closed. He was crumbling.

"Was it hard for you, when the doctors finally told us I'd never carry, and I turned to you to comfort me, and all you could do was scream that they'd fucked up? That it was the surgeries that did this to me? What, you couldn't wrap your pretty little brain around the fact that inside, I was damaged goods? That I'd been this way since the day you met me, and you just didn't know it yet? What, did you think I tricked you? Do you think I knew?"

"No, baby, I—"

"You promised!" she said, hands back on his chest. "You told me you would've chosen me no matter what! That we could try forever! Now it's your excuse?"

"Everything changed, Nicole. I don't know what to say. I don't—"

"What changed for you? Other than I wasn't perfect anymore? Other than I couldn't give you the three kids you needed to impress your boss? Other than I wasn't just some thing you could mold into a trophy wife, or whatever the hell you had planned for me! What changed? Tell me!"

He threw his hands over his mouth. "You, Nicole! You changed!"

"Me?" She pulled her fists off him and flung them in the air. Somehow, she was halfway across the room. "All I ever wanted was to be enough for you! Nobody ever understood it, how you ended up with someone like me. And then, finally, I had this chance to give you the one thing you needed me for, and I couldn't do it! I gave up everything and it still wasn't enough! I was never, ever going to be enough!"

"Colie, you are! You really are!"

She stared at him. She studied his beady eyes and his sniffling nose and his trembling hands. She opened her mouth to keep going—to hurl whatever else was left at his perfect, pitiful face, but nothing came out.

She was empty.

The whole room, empty.

Their whole story, gutted.

They slumped onto the floor like children.

Gabe tipped his head back. He opened his mouth, then closed his eyes and changed his mind. Nicole didn't bother to move. They just sat there with their backs against the wall and their heads in their hands and their dumb, young hearts, cold and old and broken.

A few minutes passed. And then, when the silence was too much, Gabe reached out and pulled Nicole into his arms. She fell into him like a rag doll—her hot, wet face so ready to collapse into that perfect nook between his shoulder and his chest. The one that used to feel like forever. The one where, those first few years, she'd fallen asleep every night she could. But before her head could meet the creases of his T-shirt, before she could listen to his racing heart begin to calm, before he could anchor her drifting body with his careless hands, she recoiled.

"Nicole," he said, his half-opened eyes watching her stand up and begin to slip away. "Please don't go."

She found her keys, crossed the room, and turned to him.

"I'm already gone," she said.

And then she walked out the door.

28

Early August

The next ten days were quiet.

It took some time, but Nicole did settle into reality.

She developed a little routine. In the mornings, she'd walk Nero, read a book, and FaceTime Valerie. In the afternoons, she'd find something to do around the house: alphabetize her spices, replace a water filter, throw Gabe's shit in a box. In the evenings, she'd go for a run—north, of course, and never on the Greenbelt—until the cerulean sky turned white. After that, she'd take a screaming hot shower, crawl into her pajamas, and wander around the house until bedtime.

When Mari wasn't traveling, she'd stop by after work for dinner. While Nicole cooked, Mari would search for the fanciest bottle of white she could find in Gabe's wine room and pour them each a glass. They'd sit at Nicole's island or breakfast nook or dining table—the house, hushed and dim and lonely—and make small talk. From time to time, Mari would put down her fork and say, "What are you going to do, Nic?" and Nicole would push a tomato across her plate and say, "I don't know."

Because, honestly, other than getting on that plane to Virginia midmonth, she didn't know what she was supposed to do next.

And she didn't know, either, why it hurt so bad to let Logan go.

Why, when she lay in bed at night, she'd still toss and turn, waiting for the familiar ding of her phone. For him to text her some rambling, rapid-fire string of messages about bioluminescence or pet rocks or the morality of hedgehog cafés. For him to pound on her door, drop his keys to the floor, and pull her into him. For him to crawl into her bed and slide his hands up her legs and his nose down her spine. For him to put his mouth on her lips, to inch off whatever was left on their bodies, to give her another chance, to just push himself into her until all she felt was him.

All she knew was none of that mattered anymore. Those had been fantasies.

The kind you could never act on once someone really knew you.

29

Heartbeats

"You really don't have to do that," Valerie said from her living room sofa, where she was lying with her feet propped up on a few throw pillows. "They're just going to mess it up again in the morning."

"Oh, it's okay," Nicole said. She was on her hands and knees, stacking a few board books on the curiously sticky ottoman Valerie used as a coffee table. She placed an abandoned snack cup atop the books, then squished a blinking, LED-lit minifootball in the palm of her hand. "It kind of helps with all the . . ."

"Anxiety?"

"Yeah," Nicole said. "Something like that."

Tomorrow was the big day—the ultrasound. A milestone Nicole had never made it past. She'd been pregnant four times in the last few years, but every pregnancy had been marred from the start. There was always something: sluggish betas, blood clots, bed rest. And then, when seven weeks rolled around—or when the bleeding finally got bad enough that she could beg her doctors to see her sooner—Nicole would slide into a paper gown, sink into the examination chair, and wait for the words she already knew were coming. She'd just lie there, eyes half closed, as Gabe's grip on her trembling hand grew a little weaker and the doctor pushed on her stomach a little harder. They'd pause, they'd purse their lips, and then they'd turn the screen to Nicole and say, very quietly, that there was no baby to see. That there was no heartbeat to hear.

"It's going to be okay," Valerie said. "I really believe that everything bad that's going to happen to you has already happened."

Nicole forced a smile. "I sure hope so."

Valerie nodded, then glanced at her phone while Nicole headed into the kitchen to start the dinner dishes. From time to time, as Nicole wiped down the counters or hushed the whistling kettle, Valerie would call out from the couch for Nicole's opinion on crockpot chili or belt bags or melamine cereal bowls.

"Oh, don't let me forget," Nicole said, wandering back into the living room with their steaming mugs, then sitting at the foot of the sofa, sorting a bin of magnetic tiles by shape and color. "I promised Mason I'd do one last monster check before we went to bed."

Valerie, who was rewinding their episode of *Grey's Anatomy* to a few minutes before they'd nodded off last night, pressed play. "He's walking all over you, you know."

"Not at all," Nicole said, stacking a red triangle with its mates. "I get it. When I was a kid, Paige and I would stay up way too late reading *Goosebumps*, and then whenever someone would walk down the hall or the house creaked kind of weird, I'd jump into her bed with my eyes closed while she did a full inspection of our upstairs."

"Even though she was younger?"

"Yeah." Nicole snapped the lid onto the now-organized bin and pushed it under the boys' activity table. "Paige is fearless. She came out that way, I guess. Giving zero fucks."

Valerie laughed, then pointed Nicole—who was already covering her mouth—toward the swear jar on the kitchen counter. She got up and shoved another dollar in it. Since Nicole arrived yesterday afternoon, she'd already paid out six bucks to Valerie's church's after-school program.

"What about you?" Valerie said as Nicole finally holed up on the other side of the couch. "What were you like as a kid?"

"Kind of serious. I liked rules. I liked things being just so."

"Sounds like you two needed each other."

Nicole, nodding, reached for a throw blanket as they settled into their evening. They sipped Valerie's antinausea ginger tea, snacked on her antinausea ginger chews, and scrolled through their glowing phones. The television talked and the dishwasher hummed and from down the hall, Carson's white noise machine whirred. Inside Valerie's happy home, everything was quiet, cozy, and calm.

Things were fine. Good, even. For the past day or so, things were really okay.

After all, when Nicole had touched down in Norfolk, she'd had one goal: to make Valerie's life as easy as possible. And so far, she'd done just that. She made heart-shaped pancakes, she vacuumed an absurdly high-pile shag rug, she watched the first twenty minutes of *Cars* seven times. She did a Costco run, she finger painted, she took the boys to the very crowded, very humid Virginia Zoo. She folded laundry, she played hopscotch, she showed Valerie how to avoid turning her bathroom into a crime scene every time she injected herself with progesterone. She even ordered pizza with pineapple on it.

But inside, the truth clawed at Nicole's organs like a rake. And every time Valerie puked or her sons threw their sticky hands around Nicole's bug-sprayed legs or *Grey's Anatomy* showed another wide-lens shot of the goddamn Space Needle, her secrets scraped a little deeper.

"What do you think of these?" Valerie said, handing her phone to Nicole. "I thought the blue would look really nice on Gabe."

On Valerie's screen, a trio of smiling models donned heather-navy T-shirts with white lettering printed across the chest. *Mama. Dada. Pod.* Nicole's throat burned as she scrolled through the carousel images.

"I thought we could maybe wear them to the second ultrasound?" Valerie said. "When we graduate to my regular OB's office? The nurse coordinator—you remember Maria, she's so nice—said she'd take some pictures for us. I could do a letter board, that could be cute, or whatever you want. You guys could use it for a holiday card, or put it on Instagram, or we could just give it to the clinic, or even make a scrapbook, or . . ."

"Uh, totally. Yeah."

"What size is Gabe? Large, right? He looks so tall in pictures. Your baby, or babies, they're going to be so gorgeous. All my friends joke about it, how—"

"I need to tell you something," Nicole said.

Valerie cringed. "Oh my gosh. That was so selfish of me. I shouldn't be taking any of this pregnancy from you. This isn't even about me. This is your time, I know that. We don't have to get the shirts. We don't have to do anything. I don't have to be involved. I'm sure you have your own announcement planned, or something for the podcast. I know you took a break from recording, I—"

"It's not you. It's . . . about me. About me and Gabe."

"What? What do you mean?" Valerie fanned her face, then put a hand on her heart. "Is Gabe okay? Are you okay? Oh my gosh, I'm going to have a heart attack. What's wrong?"

Nicole closed her eyes. She could explain everything. She could tell her the whole story. How the night she'd laid eyes on Gabe, she knew exactly the kind of man he was. That when she approached him, it was only to tell him to leave her roommate alone. To tell him he was too old, too rich, too obnoxious to be here. She was a little drunk. Really drunk.

How he'd said, "Your accent is the hottest thing I've ever heard." How she said, "Are you exoticizing my Northern Cities Vowel Shift?" How he said, "Yeah, definitely," then bought her every drink the bartender could think of—because she was a kid, because she didn't have a drink yet—until she'd sipped them all and picked a favorite. How she settled on a Jack and Coke and he leaned into her a little more and said, "That's a very trashy drink order, Nicole," and she turned toward him another inch and said, "How many girls have you fucked this week?" and he fingered the rim of his whiskey and said, "Honestly, three," and Nicole narrowed her eyes and bit her lip and said, "Separately or all at once?" and he grinned and looked right at her and Nicole looked right back and she knew exactly what was standing there—a liar, a cheater, a status-obsessed, smooth-talking, money-hungry, beautiful piece of shit—and so she rolled her eyes and clutched her phone and found her friends and walked away.

And sure, she was a little giddy, and sure, she might've looked back and caught him staring right at her, but that was only natural. That was only because it felt good when a guy like that fixed his gaze on you, decided you were special. There was nothing more to it. It was just a little moment at a bar. Just a blitz of attention. Just a buzz of electricity, a few too-fast beats of her wide-eyed heart.

But then he found her. The next day, Gabe Speyer came and found her. Twenty-four hours later, she was putty in his hands.

"Nicole?"

"I . . ."

There was no easy way to say this. There was no backstory, no context, no perfect first year that could cushion the blow of the mess they'd made. Valerie deserved the truth. And Nicole was going to give it to her.

"Gabe's having an affair," she said.

Valerie's mouth fell open. "No, he's not."

Nicole hugged her elbows. "I'm so sorry. I didn't know how to tell you. I didn't know until after the transfer. I would've never put you in this position, I promise."

Valerie was pale. Her gaze, lost past the piles of toys and the tower of half-opened Target boxes and the semipetrified, make-your-own-slime experiment the boys had abandoned midafternoon. In the background, the television murmured, its melodrama playing on a loop as reality sunk its teeth into the world Valerie had welcomed Nicole into with open arms.

"Please don't hate me," Nicole said.

Valerie closed her eyes. Nicole's heart sank. Every time she thought it couldn't possibly break again—because what was left to shatter?—it found a way to surprise her.

It was a foolish organ, wasn't it?

So desperate, so hopeful.

So eager. So stupid.

Nicole put her head in her hands.

"I know I don't deserve this baby," she said. "I know we don't. You can tell me that we don't. I'll spend forever trying to make this right."

"Why are you apologizing?"

"Because I should've known," Nicole said. "I should've protected you. I should've told you the minute I found out. I didn't want you to think any less of us. Any less of Gabe."

"You don't need to clean up your husband's mess for me," Valerie said. "He can do that himself."

Nicole's frown, somehow, went slack. Did she miss the day at school when they passed out backbones? Or did everyone else grow them in their twenties, while she was already fused to Gabe?

"I understand if you don't want to see us anymore. We don't have to come to the appointments. The agency can update me."

"It's okay, Nicole," Valerie said. "You didn't do this. I'm angry for you, not at you. I just needed a moment, that's all. This is a lot, you know? I promise, I'm not mad. I'm just really sad for you. But this is not your fault. You're not the one who stepped out on their marriage. You're not the one sleeping with somebody else."

Nicole nodded. She ignored the yank in her ribs reminding her just how close she'd come. "I feel like such a failure. I wanted to be the kind of family you were proud to help. I don't want you to think you did this for nothing. For bad people."

Valerie put her hand on Nicole's wrist. "Nobody thinks that. I don't think that."

Nicole eyed the TV. "Gabe's mother does. She used to tell me maybe there was a reason I couldn't have kids."

Valerie's nostrils flared. "I'm sorry, she told you what?"

"She's a cruel woman. Never liked me. Never thought I was good enough for her firstborn son. But after a while, it's like, maybe she's right. If I were meant to be a mom, wouldn't it have been easier? It's hard not to think sometimes that maybe there was a reason it was so difficult."

Valerie swiped through her phone, then held out a video and hit play. It was a clip Nicole had sent that morning, when she took Valerie's kids to the drive-through car wash. In it, an off-camera Nicole shouted that the streamers of sherbet-colored soap sliding down the sides of Valerie's minivan were, in fact, unicorn droppings. The boys—screaming, cackling—covered their heads with board books while Nicole's free hand crept on-screen, tickling their crew-socked ankles while they squealed with delight.

Nicole sniffled. "I would say that to an adult. It really does look like unicorn shit."

Valerie shook her head. She didn't even nod Nicole toward the swear jar. "You know what I think? I think you got dealt a lousy hand. I really think it's that simple."

Nicole shrugged, then wiped her face with a tissue from the ottoman.

"I don't know if you remember this," Valerie said, "but it took my mom a few years to have me. She had a few losses too. That's why I'm an only."

Nicole nodded. Of course she remembered.

"It always felt like a lot, knowing how bad she wanted me. That's a lot to live up to, you know? And then when she died, I was still in middle school. All I have of her are memories. Of those first years, before she got sick. Doing this kind of stuff. Going to the zoo. Making breakfast. Driving through the car wash."

Nicole rolled her tissue into a wet little ball. "What was that like, for you and your dad?"

"He did his best," Valerie said, "but it wasn't perfect. The night I got my first period, I was thirteen. She was in hospice. I could hear him crying through the walls."

"I'm so sorry. I can't imagine."

Valerie pulled up a picture on her phone. In it, she was maybe six years old, sitting on a beaming woman's lap in a carpeted play gym, each of them in matching aqua bike shorts and tie-dyed T-shirts. Scrunchies and sparkly bracelets and two identical sets of twinkling blue eyes.

Nicole's voice choked. "You must miss her so much."

"I do." Valerie ran a few fingers over the screen. Over her mother's face. "But I'm okay, you know? Life gets bigger around the grief. You learn to love the life you have. The gifts you've got. My boys. My friends. Young Patrick Dempsey."

Nicole chuckled between a few tears as Valerie glanced at the photo again.

"Do you still feel her, ever?" Nicole said.

"I do. And I'm always trying to do things that bring me closer to her. Closer to God."

"Like what?"

Valerie pulled Nicole's hand onto her stomach and closed her eyes. "Like this."

∽

The exam room was dark, lit only by the flickering screen of a buzzing ultrasound machine. Beneath the barely visible laminate cabinetry that lined the far side of the room was all the usual fertility clinic accoutrement: medical jars stuffed with sanitary pads, box after box of single-ply tissues, and pictures of miracle babies dressed as puppies and pumpkins and pirates.

"You're going to feel a little pressure," Dr. Akhtar said, pushing her free hand onto Valerie's abdomen, then adjusting the angle of her wand from underneath the thin medical blanket covering Valerie's stirruped legs. The familiar crinkle of a paper gown sent a shudder down Nicole's spine. "Does that feel okay?"

"Yeah," Valerie said, nodding as she grabbed Nicole's hand. In the farthest corner of the room, Gabe watched on with his neck craned and his lips sealed. "Just cold."

"Okay then," Dr. Akhtar said. "Let's have a look."

Nicole's stomach churned. She'd forgotten, these past few weeks, how desperately she'd wanted this. She'd been so focused on the million things she'd thrown away for this moment that she lost sight of how much it might hurt to watch it slip through her fingers one last time. But just when she was about to close her eyes, Dr. Akhtar rotated the screen and smiled.

"See that little flicker, right there?" she said as Nicole gasped and Valerie squealed, squeezing Nicole's wrist. "That's the heartbeat, girls. Everything looks perfect."

Nicole left her body.

It wasn't hers. She couldn't speak or think or see.

"It's just one?" Valerie said, voice hazy.

"Yes," Dr. Akhtar said, words blurred. "It's just the one. I know that can be disappointing, I know twins are exciting, especially after years and years of trying. But this is better. We want one safe baby, one safe Valerie. We want an easy, full-term delivery."

Valerie gave Nicole another squeeze. Nicole—still somewhere else—nodded.

One baby.

One baby was good.

She could do one baby without Gabe, right?

Nicole turned to him just as he floated his hand a few inches toward her. He opened his lips, mouthed a few words, and tried to say something with his eyes. But none of it registered.

She could hardly remember how it felt to want this moment with him. To want all of it: the dirty diapers, the sleepless nights, the waking up at the crack of dawn to a tangle of blue-eyed toddlers demanding hugs and kisses and chocolate-chip pancakes. To want it all so badly she'd try anything, give up everything, become someone she barely knew. To want it all so badly that, just six weeks ago, she'd begged Gabe to fly across the country and watch a woman who—in every reasonable version of Nicole's universe—should've remained a stranger instead lend Nicole her body and bring this blinking, blueberry-size bundle of cells to life. But she must have, because here the two of them were, barely speaking and living under separate roofs and staring at the proof.

Dr. Akhtar followed Nicole's gaze to where Gabe stood in silence.

"Come on, Dad." She nodded him toward the group while she printed a few pictures. "You ready to hear the heartbeat? Get over here. We won't bite."

Gabe hesitated, then took a couple of steps closer. He was maybe five feet from Valerie when she turned her head and frowned at him. He flinched, then took a step back.

And that was when it filled the room.

Thump. Thump. Thump.

The unmistakable beat of a heart. Nicole's own baby's heart.

Three years of terror tore through Nicole's bloodstream like wildfire—fast and hot and then, gone. It left her body in a wail, a thousand days of hopelessness compressed into one final cry. All while Valerie tightened her grip on Nicole, Gabe bowed his head, and Nicole disintegrated. All while the baby's heartbeat played on. Sixty seconds, but it might as well have been forever.

"One hundred and seventy-two beats per minute," Dr. Akhtar said, beaming as she switched off the sound. "I couldn't feel better about this one."

Nicole clutched Valerie's hand again. Valerie wiped her face on the too-loose shoulder of her gown, then squeezed Nicole's hand back. Gabe—watching the two women with damp eyes and closed lips—clasped his hands behind his neck and studied the floor.

"I know it's been quite a road, Mom," Dr. Akhtar said as she handed Nicole an envelope full of photos. "Congratulations."

Nicole nodded, then pulled out a picture. This was it: the glossy piece of cardstock that was supposed to make her world whole. Except now, holding it between her trembling fingers, her pain didn't wash away. Her story didn't rewind. Her life didn't tidy itself up or put everything back where it belonged, back where it all seemed so perfect.

Instead, a sliver of her future flashed before her. The images played out like slides on a projector, fuzzy and oversaturated and far too bright, but there all the same. Board books and trips to the aquarium and a faceless, shrieking little thing chasing Nero around a living room Nicole did not yet recognize. Laughter. Raw cookie dough. Sand, absolutely everywhere. Bento boxes and boo-boos and birthday parties at unknown, grassy parks, and then, that was it. The glimpse dissolved.

It wasn't much, but it was enough.

Nicole tucked the picture back into the envelope, slipped it in her bag, and cracked a smile.

There was only one problem. Her husband followed her right down the hall.

30

New York Minute

"Colie, wait!" Gabe said, racing through the medical building's double doors and into the pouring rain. Over the past hour, a rumbling summer storm had blown into Norfolk, and from churning charcoal clouds, the torrent pummeled the steaming asphalt in hot, wild drops. The water, by now, was everywhere: surging through gutters, rushing across the pavement, and whipping back into the air with every gust of wind.

Nicole, already drenched, threw her bag over her head and darted toward Valerie's car without looking back. Clicking furiously at the keys as Gabe called her name again, she leaped into the driver's seat, pulled back her dripping wet hair, and started the engine. When she looked up, Gabe was standing right there with his hands on his head, his polo shirt soaked, and his frowning face ready to plead its case. Valerie's low beams, his spotlight.

"Nicole!" He leaped toward her window and threw his hands on the glass. "I have to make this right! You have to let me fix this!"

"Gabe, come on," she said, cracking the window. Rain flew sideways through the crevice. "Not today. It's too much. Valerie's going to be out soon. I'm supposed to be pulling the car around for her. Don't make a scene."

"Let's go home!" he said. "Let's just go back to California! Forget Aspen. We can drive up the coast—rent a place somewhere. Big Sur, Mendocino. It'll be a real vacation—no Kyle, none of the wives.

It'll be the way it should've been all along. Just you and me, having a summer. We can hike and swim, get ice cream. We can bring the dog, we—"

"No," Nicole said, as calmly as she could. "I don't want to go anywhere with you."

"But we can fix this! I know we can! We can stay up all night, just talking, like we used to. We can make a plan. I'll do anything you say. I'll quit drinking. I'll never see Tommy or Wyatt or Brandon or any of the guys, ever again. I'll spend every minute fixing what I broke. Just don't give up on me. Because everything's going to change, I swear! I just—"

"No," she said.

"Then I'll quit my job!" He flung his hands back onto the window as thunder roared. "I'm serious! I'll quit right now!"

"Gabe, stop." Lightning cracked. "Be an adult. It's too late."

"Let's go back to New York! We can get on a plane right now! We never have to go back to California. I'll live anywhere you want! Brooklyn? You love Brooklyn! Park Slope? The Upper West Side? Somewhere with parks and coffee shops and places to get pancakes in the middle of the night. Let's start over, okay? We can raise our kid in the city, where things were perfect, before anything was hard. No big job, no stupid parents, no dumb mistakes. It'll be just us again. You and me and our baby!"

"Please don't do this," she said. "Please don't ruin today for me."

"Our baby, Nicole!" He pressed his face against the window. His eyes, wet and wide. His hand, streaking down the fogged-up glass. His wedding band, still on. "We're finally having a baby! The hard part is over! We can do this! I know it's not too late. We can—"

"*Over!?* It's just beginning, Gabe! We have to raise a human! For the rest of our lives! Have you not realized that yet? Are you out of your fucking mind?"

"I didn't mean . . . I just . . ." Gabe smashed his forehead deeper against the glass and exhaled. His fists, loose and desperately clinging to the window's opening. Nicole fought back tears, trying to get her screaming pulse to calm. "All I meant was that we're a family now. That we have to start over. That we can still have everything."

Nicole took a long, deep breath. Every word, an exercise in self-control. "Please don't use the family card on me. It's not fair."

"Just give me a weekend! Two days to show you I can do this. That's all I'm asking for, okay? A chance to show you how different things are going to be. The city's empty. We can go anywhere you want. The library. The MoMA. That gross little hot dog cart you were obsessed with that first summer. Just give me one more chance. I can't lose you. I love you. Just give me—"

"I said no. Please stop making promises you don't know how to keep."

Gabe shuddered, grabbing his hair by the fistful. Nicole scrunched her eyes shut. It was too much—this day, these past few weeks. Gabe, standing there, putting on another show.

"I mean it, Nicole! I'll call Kyle right now! Fuck my job! Fuck this life! I'll work at a fucking wine shop! I don't care anymore! From now on, you come first. You and the baby. Nothing else matters!"

Nicole opened her eyes. Gabe was back in front of the car, pacing in the rain, his phone to his ear, his left hand clenching and releasing into a fist over and over again.

He wasn't bluffing.

Nicole leaped out of the driver's seat and into the storm. She snatched Gabe's phone just as Kyle's voice had begun to send a shiver up her spine.

"Don't quit your fucking job!"

Gabe threw his hands on his head. "Why not!?"

"Because it's too late! Because you love it! Because it wouldn't make a goddamn difference!"

"You don't know that!" His sopping wet shirt clung to his chest. Rain dripped down his warping brow, his pulsing neck. "Tell me why you won't let me fight for our family! Tell me why you won't even let me try!"

Nicole's arms flung open. "Because you're a fucking liar, Gabe! Because you're a fucking cheater, that's why!"

Gabe clenched his fists, wailing as he struck a rain-slicked parking block with his foot. His whole body jerked back. For a moment, he just stood there, thrashing, absorbing the shock. And then, finally, he fell apart. His neck bent and his shoulders slumped and he sank to the curb, knees to chest.

"I wanted to die in there," he said, voice breaking. He turned toward her. His eyes were red and his face had fallen. "I didn't know what to say, what to do. Watching you hear the heartbeat from across the room . . . It was the worst moment of my whole life. I was dying to hold you. To just be next to you. Fuck, Nicole. I don't know how to make this right. I don't know how to fix this. You won't answer my calls. You won't let me see you. I don't know what else to do to show you how sorry I am. How stupid I was. All I want is to be the father I never had. The husband you deserve. All I want is one more chance."

Nicole, standing a few feet behind him with her body bent and her heart wrenched, was silent for a minute. She closed her eyes and breathed.

Had there been two sides to this story? Could it have been true, what he'd said in his hotel room? That she'd changed? That she'd been a ghost—so caught up in the pursuit of some perfect baby that she'd forgotten to love him? That she'd been distant and cold and someone else for nearly three years now? That when he'd try to touch her, she'd recoil? That when he'd take her out to dinner, she'd stare into space and count down to a due date that had already slipped through their fingers?

Hadn't he, that first IVF cycle, measured and mixed her shots every night he could beat traffic home? Hadn't he, whenever she asked, sat down in her office and read straight off some absurd podcast script? Hadn't he driven to Redding the Sunday after her first miscarriage to charm his way to the very top of the waiting list for a chestnut-colored, standard-size goldendoodle? Hadn't he, around midnight, cracked open their bedroom door to find her lying there in tears, then climbed under the covers with a bewildered pipsqueak of a puppy and a pint of ice cream in his arms?

Did she really want to do this? Raise their baby alone? Ask this child—this itty-bitty clump of cells that was dividing against all odds, and only because Nicole had willed it into existence—to grow up without a father in the house just because they'd hit a rough patch? Just because they'd both fallen short? She could have been warmer. She could have been kinder. She could have loved him harder. She could have, at the very least, tried.

Maybe this past month had been good for them. Maybe, because of what'd happened this summer, Gabe would become the kind of father who came home early, took his baby out to breakfast while his wife slept in, and kept a stuffed platypus in his glove compartment and a picture of his family on his desk. Maybe, now, she'd get the old Gabe back. Get what she'd signed up for. What he'd promised her all those years ago.

Nicole sat down on the parking curb one spot over and wiped the rain off her forehead. The storm had hushed to a quiet drizzle.

"How many were there?" she said.

Gabe's shoulders rose for a split second. He took a long, careful breath. "It never meant a thing to me. I made a mistake. I—"

"I need a number."

Gabe was silent for a moment. He studied the puddled, murky pavement. When he looked back at Nicole, her eyes were wet, and her arms were clutched around her elbows.

"It will never happen again," he said. "That I can promise you. I swear on my life."

Nicole closed her eyes. "When did it start?"

"Nicole . . ."

"Before or after the first miscarriage?"

"Everything's going to change," he said. "We're a family now. All that matters is—"

"No," she said. "Tell me when it started. Tell me you weren't fucking anybody else before I lost the first baby. Tell me that when we started trying, there was nobody else. Tell me I didn't throw my life away for some piece of shit, Gabe. Swear on our baby that when you let me walk down that aisle, there was nobody else."

"Colie," he said, hands wrung behind his neck. "I love you. I have always loved you. You are the only one I've ever loved. It will always, always only be you."

Nicole nodded. She nodded furiously. And her heart—her foolish, naive little heart; the same one that had watched beautiful men lie to the women they loved since before she could tie her own shoes—didn't even bother to break. Instead, she rose to her feet.

"You," she said, "are exactly who I thought you were."

Gabe stood up at once. "I'm not! And I'm not going to give up on us! I'm not going to give up on our family without a fight! I'm not going to . . ."

But it didn't matter. What else he said, what else he promised. Because Nicole was already walking away. She turned to face him just before she arrived at the car, tears streaming down her face. Her jaw, aching.

"I'm taking Valerie to lunch," she said. "And then I'm going home. Please don't call me. Please don't text me. And please don't show up at the house. I mean it. I'm done."

"Nic—"

"Go to Colorado," she said. "Go get your shit together. I'll see you at the ten-week."

Gabe sank back onto the curb as Nicole climbed into Valerie's car and put her head in her hands. He reached for a random, jagged rock he'd found at his feet, closed his eyes, then hurled it across the flooded parking lot in one perfect, thoughtless pitch. He opened his eyes and watched it fly. He watched it land a few empty rows away in a navy lake of predictably wild summer rain. And then, as Nicole began to drive away, he watched the ripples it made stretch on and on and on.

31

Homeward Bound

Nicole spent the first half of her flight leaning against the window, wiping quiet tears from her tired eyes. And then, somewhere over the Continental Divide, when the world outside had turned a cold and blank sapphire and the rest of the whirring plane had fallen fast asleep, Nicole pulled out her phone and did what she did best. She made a list. She made a plan.

She needed to call Mari's attorney. She needed to ask Mari to sage her bedroom. She needed, on that note, a new smoke detector. She needed to learn CPR, and how to bolt furniture to the wall, and whether early exposure to peanut butter was recommended or frowned upon this year. She needed to research bottle feeding and determine whether Valerie's offer to pump and ship breast milk was more stress for everyone than it was worth. She needed to think about money, and the house, and how long she could possibly expect Gabe to let her live in it, and whether she could still be a stay-at-home mom, and whether she'd ever really wanted that, or if it'd just been something she convinced herself of because having a baby seemed so impossible, she thought she'd only be rewarded if she made motherhood—and the pursuit of it—her whole world.

She needed to put one foot in front of the other. She needed to do the next right thing, over and over, until the day that baby came. And she needed—more than she could've possibly imagined, even just twenty-four hours ago—to get back to California.

To get back home.

32

Tea Leaves

When Nicole landed later that night, she picked Nero up from his boarding kennel, took a long, hot shower, then sat down at her dining room table with a massive cup of chamomile tea and FaceTimed her sister. Paige was fumbling around her tiny, cluttered kitchen, gathering ingredients for a plant-based charcuterie board as Nicole caught her up on what had happened in Virginia.

"You actually think he'll stay in Colorado all month?" Paige said. "With everything that's going on?"

"Yeah," Nicole said. "He's not doing so great."

"Good. Fuck him."

Nicole shook her head. "I know this probably sounds weird, but when I saw the baby, and after our fight . . . It's just different now, I guess. I feel like I can finally start to focus on what's next."

Paige paused from butchering a salami-inspired cylinder of tempeh to look at her sister. Nicole, twirling her mug around in silence, looked back.

Only eighteen months separated them, and since before Nicole could remember, they'd shared everything from a bedroom full of princess costumes to a candy-themed bat mitzvah to whichever of their mother's steamy romance novels they could get their teenage hands on. Nicole's freshman year of college, Paige would sometimes fly all the way to New York for a long weekend just so they could bundle up in Nicole's bed, watch movies on her laptop, and eat raspberry sorbet straight from the pint.

A few years later, when Nicole first started bringing Gabe home to Missouri for holidays, Nicole and Gabe struck up a deal. She'd let him do anything he wanted to her—within reason, of course—and in exchange, Gabe would sleep in Nicole's little brother's room so she and Paige could have their sister time. Ethan was finishing up high school back then. Kind of a big man on campus as far as backup quarterbacks go, and certifiably obsessed with the fancy-pants, ten-years-his-senior investment banker sleeping on the deflated blowup mattress smushed between his cluttered desk and a rusting rack of dumbbells.

Gabe—quite satisfied, and rather amused by the childish high jinks of his new girlfriend and her quirky sister—would go right along with it. The two guys would watch hockey and talk about money and take turns shooting a tiny foam basketball through the sagging hoop drilled above Ethan's doorframe. Once, when Nicole wandered downstairs for a glass of water in the middle of the night, she found them in the garage, getting drunk underneath the Ping-Pong table. They were just sitting there in their boxers and sweatshirts, sharing a bottle of Nicole's dad's gin while Ethan cried over some girl he'd played it so cool with she decided he was an asshole and went to third base with his best friend instead.

But that was in the beginning. That first year, when everyone was still on their best behavior. When Nicole was still peeling back the layers of New York Gabe.

"Nicole," Paige said. "You gotta tell Mom."

Nicole nodded. It was strange, really, talking to Paige like an adult. These past few days, she'd started to feel it—her age. She wasn't a kid anymore, was she? She wasn't even close.

"I know. I already texted her to call me in the morning. Dad too."

"What are you going to say?"

"The shortest, least up-for-discussion version of the truth possible. I've been working on it all day."

On her flight home, Nicole had written maybe two dozen drafts of what she might tell her parents, tailoring each word to the life they'd lived. Now, with Paige's help, Nicole finessed the messaging until they'd settled on this: *Gabe cheated on me. I don't think we can fix our relationship. I understand you guys are going to be concerned about the baby. About me. I will figure it out. I need you to trust me.*

"They're going to give you a million reasons to stay," Paige said.

"I know," Nicole said. "I'll deal with it."

Paige sighed, ripping the seal off a jar of fig jam as her intercom buzzed. Nicole was already saying goodbye when Paige interrupted her.

"Nic, wait," she said. "I know this isn't how you wanted it, but I'm really happy for you. I think you were made to do this. I think it's going to be good. And now you'll be one of those hot moms who makes sandwiches that look like panda bears and says whatever's on her mind and wears tiny little dresses and answers to no one."

Nicole rolled her eyes. "That's just Mari, but with a kid. That doesn't sound like me at all."

Paige—whose friends' voices were beginning to fill her very crowded, very-fourth-floor walk-up—shook her head. "Maybe you don't remember it, but that's kind of who you became right when you were finishing college. You were really fucking cool."

Nicole wrinkled her nose, said goodbye for a second time, then walked across her kitchen in a daze trying to remember that version of herself. Trying to remember whether what Paige had said was true. Whether she really was on her way to becoming that kind of girl. That kind of woman.

By the time Nicole had snapped out of it, she was standing at her island, poking the tip of her finger against the spiky paddle of that cactus she'd placed on her counter nearly two weeks ago. The one she'd been so careful not to water, ever, at all. And then—because she was suddenly in the business of cleaning up her messes—Nicole unlocked her phone, pressed her index finger to the glass, and let it ring.

Logan Milgram picked right up.

33

Loose Ends

They agreed to meet at his favorite diner, a greasy spoon a block off PCH where the air swirled with the smell of bacon and breakfast potatoes and burnt coffee. On the far side of the restaurant, framed press clippings from long-gone local newspapers hung along a wall painted a muted shade of split-pea green. Rounded, retro countertops teemed with sugar canisters and napkin caddies. Forks clanked and cash registers dinged. And at a corner table by the window—where the hot morning sun beat through the glass, clear and bright—Nicole Speyer twirled around her coffee mug and tried to look Logan Milgram in the eye.

"So," she said, "how far did you run today?"

"Seventeen miles."

"Oh, wow. That's really far."

"Yeah," he said, scratching his neck. "And somehow, not far enough."

Nicole chuckled. "I get that."

Logan smirked, holding her gaze for a moment. Nicole ignored the flutter in her stomach, the heat in her hands. The fact that, five minutes ago, he'd walked in here looking better than ever—all scruffy and sun-kissed and scanning the restaurant, searching for her. He wore a fraying, navy Mariners ball cap, a pair of faded jeans, and a crisp white T-shirt that reminded Nicole of exactly what she'd put the brakes on.

"Logan, listen, I . . ."

Goddamnit. He was still looking right at her.

His morning—that long run—was still all over him. Sure, he'd showered off the sweat and the salt, but the distance showed. It was in the sunburn settling across his nose. In the lines of his forearms, all bronzed and taut and soft. There was a certain thoughtlessness, a certain lightness to him that he couldn't seem to shake, despite his hunched shoulders, his fidgeting fingers, his open ears.

He was exhausted, wasn't he? That was what it was. The run had worn him out in that quiet, delightful way—the kind that makes you want to crawl into bed and just . . . float. He'd probably spend the rest of the day half asleep on his couch, playing video games, nursing a gallon of Gatorade and a six-pack of Red Stripe while his dorky friends came and went. Maybe at night, he'd order a pizza or watch the ball game or . . .

Maybe he had a date. Maybe he was completely, totally fine.

Maybe he was just humoring her, like any nice guy would when the very-much-married girl he was half an inch from railing had a full-blown panic attack in his living room. Maybe he'd already realized what she'd known all along. That July had been a flash in the pan, an exercise in make-believe. Fun as hell, but a fool's errand. Nicole was here to tell Logan the truth, to clean up her side of the street. To make sure that when she ran into him two years from now at some grocery store with her toddler in tow, she'd only half want to dive behind a teetering display of Wheat Thins.

"Nicole?" he said. "What's going on?"

"Sorry." She stared at her menu. "I was just thinking about your run."

"For three minutes?"

"No . . . not, uh, not like that, I . . ."

He tapped his fingers on the table, then chuckled. "Well, this is almost as awkward as the last time I saw you, isn't it?"

She laughed, then took a deep breath. She could do this. She'd already done it twice this week—with Valerie, and then with her mom and dad. And sure, that second chat had gone about as poorly as expected, but Nicole was a grown-up now. At least, she was trying to be. She didn't need her parents' approval to walk away from an asshole or raise a baby alone. And if she could take that level of bullshit on the chin, then she could certainly handle this. She could certainly fess up to some guy she'd been fooling around with for, like, a week.

"Do you remember that day on the beach? When I told you I couldn't carry children?"

He nodded, lips narrowing. Face, straightening. "Yeah, of course."

"Well, a year ago, we found this carrier. You know, like a surrogate?" Another inhale. Another exhale. "Anyway, we transferred our embryos to her twice, but they didn't take. Then the third one, well, it was our last try. It wasn't supposed to work. The doctors, everyone, they all told us not to do it. But we did. And so when I found out about Gabe, I got drunk and I ended up at your door and I thought maybe we could . . . I don't know."

Logan's eyes were closed. Nicole swallowed the lump in her throat and kept talking. She needed to be more clear. She knew that.

"What I'm trying to say is, that night, when I came to see you, I was so confused. But I didn't think, not in a million years, that the transfer was going to work. Everything happened so fast. It was all the same day. The transfer, finding out about Gabe, seeing you."

Logan's face had fallen. He gripped his elbows, closed his shoulders, and nodded. He'd already figured it out. But Nicole knew she'd have to say the words out loud. That he needed to hear it from her. She took another deep breath and finished the job.

"I'm having a baby," she said. "My carrier is due in March."

Logan's chin dipped into a slow, gentle nod. Nicole tried not to read into his every twitch or blink or breath, but it wasn't that easy. Somehow, she managed to keep talking.

"I found out the day after our run, our beach day. I don't know why I didn't tell you. I had a million reasons. They all sucked."

He stroked his throat, then pressed his lips together and looked at her, his eyes distant but kind. Nicole's chest ached as her shoulders sank. She'd been so sure that coming clean would leave her feeling lighter, better, back in control. But already, something else--this old, familiar tug she'd felt from time to time—had begun to weigh her down and dull her senses.

"You could have told me," he said.

"I didn't want to tell anyone."

Logan clasped his hands together. The tendons in his forearms tightened. But when he looked back up at her a moment later, every inch of him had softened.

"Okay," he said. "I can understand that."

Nicole pushed her coffee mug around, then bit down on her tongue to keep a frown from unfolding across her face.

"After our date," she said, "when we were about to, well . . . I just didn't want to lie to you anymore. I'm sorry it was so sudden, and I'm sorry it took me so long to tell you. I just wanted to be sure about the baby. But the more I think about it, the more I know I was just being a liar. And I'm sorry. You didn't deserve that.

I'm sorry I led you on. And I'm sorry I gave you the wrong idea about . . . about me."

Logan pulled a half-closed fist to his mouth. He opened his lips to speak, but stopped himself. A sharp inhale later, he tried again.

"I'm sort of taking this all in," he said, fiddling with a pod of coffee creamer without breaking eye contact. "But we're good, okay? We were always good, and we're still good."

"You're not mad? You don't think I'm a fraud?"

"Nicole," he said. "I know you. I've known you for years. I don't know why you keep acting like I don't."

She crossed her arms over her body, hoping that might hush the stupid ache she felt tugging at the top of her ribs. She could never quite put her finger on it—where it came from, what it meant. And she could never quite figure out how to shut it up for good.

"I think you're a good person," he said. "I think you're going to be a great mother. I think you're loyal and smart and really funny. There's not much you could do to change my mind about that. And that includes not sleeping with me, okay?"

Nicole nodded, swallowing. She knew Logan made things sound good for a living, but nothing had quite prepared her to hear that. That was just a really nice thing to say. The kind of thing she'd have liked to remember long after he walked out the door. The kind of thing she somehow wished he'd sent in a text message, so she could read it over and over until the words didn't surprise her anymore.

"Thank you," she said. "For saying that. For always being so nice to me. For everything. This summer, and back at the office. It means a lot. It always has."

He took a long sip of his coffee. "You're welcome."

Nicole wasn't quite sure what to say next. Maybe he wasn't either, because for the next little while, nobody made a sound. She scratched her leg. He fiddled with his creamer pod. And then, after another thirty seconds or so of silence, he looked back up at Nicole.

"Is this why you didn't want me to listen to your podcast?"

"I just . . . I don't know. It's not very sexy, I guess. My past few years."

"Well, now that we're both totally clothed, feel free to fill me in."

And so Nicole finally told him everything. How after her first two miscarriages—those, Logan knew about—she'd gone to see the fanciest fertility doctor they could find because Nicole's regular OB still wasn't worried. How he was still telling her she was only thirty, that these things happen, that if she miscarried a third time, they'd take a closer look. How at the fertility clinic, there was no such wait. She had every test imaginable scheduled within a week. "A uterine septum," Dr. Williams told her. "A birth defect, but nothing we can't fix." With no desire to waste another seventeen months trying at home, they jumped right into surgery and IVF. "You'll be a mother in a year," the doctor said as Nicole signed an inch-thick stack of consent forms, hand shaking.

How that was not what happened at all. How the surgeries only made things worse. How scar tissue filled her womb like poison ivy, pesky and dense and impossible to cut back or keep at bay. How Nicole's first two egg retrievals yielded only three good embryos. And before both transfers, Nicole's body taunted her doctor like a game of Whack-a-Mole. Every day, some new obstacle: a too-thin uterine lining here, a pocket of fluid pooling at her cervix there. With every red flag, Dr. Williams whittled off another solution, each stranger than the last. The best reproductive endocrinologist money could buy, and Nicole would still drive home in tears, ready to tackle a to-do list whose tasks ranged from questionable medical advice to full-on quackery: daily acupuncture, Viagra suppositories, a massive orgasm, twenty minutes on an inversion table, a carefully brewed pot of tea made from wild raspberry leaves that had to be ordered over the phone, in cash, from the goddamn Netherlands. Anything to make her womb warm and flushed out and fertile. Anything to improve her odds.

How with both transfers, Nicole managed to get pregnant. How both times, she'd bled within a week. That was when they found Valerie. That was when everything was supposed to change. But nothing changed, of course. Not until the afternoon Nicole's entire life was turned upside down.

"So, yeah," she said, staring into her mug, "that's the whole story. That's what I've actually been up to."

Logan blew out a breath. "I had no idea what happened after you left. I'm so sorry."

"What's crazy is, it doesn't even sound that bad to me. Like, when I talk through it, it's just my life. It never felt like a choice. Every time something bad happened, I just pushed harder. I had to keep going, you know? Because if I slowed down, then I'd have to . . ."

"Feel something?"

Nicole flinched. "I . . ."

"I'm sorry," he said. "I just want to understand, that's all."

"No, it's okay. I like that you ask questions. It's just, nobody has ever really wanted to know about this part. People are quick to give you advice. Ask if you've tried exercising less or fucking more or wanting it a little less desperately. But they never want to know what it feels like. Nobody wants to hear about pain they can't make go away."

Logan squeezed his hand into a fist until that pod he'd been fidgeting with all morning burst open, sending a stream of milk down his stiffened wrist and onto the edge of their wobbling table. He wiped up the mess with a napkin, then pushed it aside.

"Do you want to tell me?" he said.

She nodded slowly while Logan refilled their coffees. Their server, who knew Logan by name, had left them a fresh pot over half an hour ago.

"It felt . . . hopeless." Nicole clanked a spoon against the side of her mug, searching for a way to say something she'd never really put into words. "Every time I thought it might be over, that was actually the worst part. Because deep down, I always knew it was only a matter of time. I'd finally get what I wanted, and then every morning, I'd wake up in terror. My body was a ticking time bomb. I'd just sit around, waiting for it to break my heart again."

Logan frowned.

God, did it feel good for someone to just listen to her. To just sit there and hold her pain and not tell her how to feel or what to do or how to channel that sadness into a new hobby like pottery or horseback riding or learning French. To just sit there and take her past few years for what they were.

"Thank you," she said. "I know I've said it a thousand times, but I really mean it. Thank you for never making me feel like an idiot."

He smirked. "Thank you for the exact opposite."

"For making you feel like an idiot?"

"Yeah," he said. "Every damn day, since the very beginning."

Nicole rolled her eyes while Logan slid her a menu.

"Come on," he said. "Let's just eat until nothing hurts anymore, okay?"

She nodded, chuckling. He laughed too, and then Nicole ordered a mushroom omelet and Logan ordered enough pancakes, bacon, and eggs to feed a small family, plus a hunk of coffee cake and a slice of chocolate peanut butter pie, just because. For the next hour, they talked and ate and talked some more. About Logan's big pitch at the end of the month, how happy he was to only have one trip on the books these next few weeks, and the race he was training for in Santa Barbara this fall.

When there was no more toast to pick at or lukewarm honeydew to push around their plates, they settled the check, dumped the dregs of their desserts into a couple of cardboard containers, then rose to their feet and walked out of the restaurant. As their eyes adjusted to the cloudless sky, they meandered through the alley and into the parking lot, making small talk about diner culture until they'd arrived at Nicole's car.

She reached for her door—and then she felt it again.

That tug. That ache.

She didn't want to say goodbye, did she? And the more they talked, the more she looked at him, the more she let herself unravel, the less she knew. About what she wanted. About what came next. About what was right.

"Thanks again for meeting me," she said, reaching for the handle of her car door. The hot metal burned her fingertips. "I'm glad we got to talk."

Logan just stood there, looking at her.

"Come on," he said, outstretching his arms. "Get over here."

Nicole inhaled, reminding herself of every last reason she had to drive away. But it didn't matter. It was too late. She'd already dropped her grip, taken the five steps toward him, burrowed her face into the soft, thick cotton of his T-shirt, and closed her eyes. He wrapped his arms around her, dropped his nose into her shoulder, and held her tight.

For a minute, they just stood there, connected.

Their chests, rising and falling.

Everything else, standing still.

She listened to his heart beat.

She breathed him in.

And then, right when she decided she wanted to hold on a little longer, she let him go. It just seemed like the thing to do.

"That was, um . . ." She rubbed the sleeves of her dress. The asphalt was cracked and faded beneath her feet. "That was really nice."

"Nicole," he said. "I don't want to stop seeing you."

"What?"

"You think I've never dated a woman with a kid before?"

"I don't know, I . . ."

"I'm thirty-nine years old," he said. "This is not a deal-breaker for me. Once, I even went on a date *with* a kid. There was a childcare mishap. We went mini-golfing. I let him win, and the little shit repaid me by eating all my ravioli."

This warm and fuzzy glow stretched across Nicole's chest. By the time she let out a laugh, it had made it all the way to her toes. She curled them, then raised an eyebrow. "I'm pretty sure if the mom wasn't there, you were babysitting. That's not a date, Logan."

He grinned. "The mom was there! Fuck you!"

Nicole bit her lip and took a step closer to him. Her stomach fluttered and her heart raced.

"Can I tell you something?" she said.

"Anything," he said.

"I think, maybe, I didn't tell you because I didn't want to stop."

34

Three Weeks' Notice

They spent the rest of the day driving around the county, stockpiling the last dozen pairs of Logan's favorite running shoes. Apparently, Brooks had changed the toe box on this year's model of his most-beloved neutral sneaker, and Logan—who'd been wearing it religiously for a decade—wasn't ready to search for a replacement just yet. Nicole did the driving, which was probably for the better, because Logan had spent the past few hours recapping some Ken Burns documentary about Yosemite, dozing off in Nicole's passenger seat, and downright staring at her legs. A handful of times, he'd nearly managed to do all three at once.

"So, you just get a new one of these every few years?" he said, dragging his forefingers along the soft beige leather of Nicole's dash. "You just pick a color, and that's that?"

She signaled to change lanes as the hot inland sun baked through her windshield. "Yeah, that's pretty much how car leases work."

"Interesting," he said. "Learn something new every day."

Nicole scoffed as Logan fiddled with the tab of his half-empty soda can for a few seconds, then leaned his head against the glass and just looked at her.

A minute passed, maybe two.

Nicole bit her lip, then kept driving. She drummed the steering wheel. She fussed with the stereo. She itched her leg. And then, finally, as she veered down the Ventura Boulevard off-ramp, she turned her head.

She'd caught him midstare.

He blinked twice, then glanced away, chuckling.

"What?" Nicole said. "What's so funny?"

"Nothing. It's just, usually Dave drives me around on my long run days. And you're much more fun to look at, that's all."

Dave and Logan had grown up together in Seattle, and their friendship was more than three decades old. After high school, Dave had gone to CalTech and never left Los Angeles. He was, much like Logan, a colossal nerd.

"Yeah, well, I feel like that's not very hard," Nicole said, turning into the parking lot of another strip mall anchored by a defunct pet store and a yogurt shop. "The image of Dave in my head is pretty much that wizard from the weird arcade game. Bonkers hair, navy cape with stars, a zillion years old . . ."

"Actually, Dave's very sexy. Like a Black James Bond, but with glasses."

Nicole put the car in park. "That's literally Idris Elba. If you know someone who looks like Idris Elba, you'd better tell me now."

Logan laughed, then hopped out of the car and opened her door while she tossed a few things in her bag. But as soon as she'd climbed out of her seat, he took a step back.

It had been like this all afternoon—since they'd driven off from the diner. Every time she'd catch him staring, he'd look away, then make some dumb joke. And every time he got too close to her, Nicole's body would begin to buzz, at once remembering the rush of his hands flying up her skin, the slick of his mouth sloping down her stomach, the heat of his shoulders hovering over her breathless body, and then, all of a sudden, he'd pull away.

He'd put space between them.

A foot, maybe two.

Not much—but enough.

"You hungry?" he said. "There's this dim sum place here that's pretty decent. We can put in a take-out order, grab it once we're done at the store."

Nicole just stood there, trying to not scan the parking lot for an oversize dumpster or any other larger-than-Logan object they could conceivably go and have sex behind.

"Speyer?"

"Sorry. What?"

"Food," he said. "Do you want food?"

"Oh." Nicole smoothed out her dress. "Sure, yeah. I like food."

Logan laughed, then nodded her across the parking lot toward a hole-in-the-wall where he ordered a week's worth of takeout, plus three extra trays of scallion pancakes, just in case. He tossed a can of Diet Coke at Nicole, who barely caught it because her mind was . . . elsewhere. And then, without a word, she followed him out the door and into their fifth and final store of the day.

The Runner's Emporium in Encino was nothing to write home about. The air smelled like rubber; every employee looked like a college student, a gazelle, or both; and decades-old one-hit wonders played so quietly you could hear the diagnostic treadmill in the corner screech. The place was exactly the same as every other mom-and-pop running shop they'd visited today.

Except here, things felt different. Except here, as they walked past the cash register, Nicole was sure it was about to happen. That this time, finally, Logan was going to reach out and touch her. After all, he was a step behind her, maybe less.

His eyes, fixed on the small of her back.

His hands, rubbing the cotton of her dress.

His fingers, slipping down her spine.

But no. Nothing.

She'd imagined it.

Nicole walked herself to the back of the store and sifted through a sale rack of fluorescent exercise garb. Logan, twenty feet away, stood by a wall of sneakers, lamenting the Great Crowded Toe Box Crisis to anyone who'd listen. From time to time, she'd stop her inspection of a highlighter-yellow sports bra to look him up and down. He could really wear a white T-shirt, couldn't he? It was the triceps. Also, the tan. That beat-up hat didn't hurt either.

Logan must've been seven minutes into his impassioned speech, waving that criminally narrow sneaker in disgust while two equally outraged employees nodded along, when he caught Nicole staring right at him.

His whole face lit up.

He tilted his head.

He bit his lip.

And then, without taking his eyes off Nicole, he said a few words to one of the sales guys, handed him a credit card, and walked right toward her.

Nicole's stomach somersaulted. The rest of the store blurred. And with his every step closer, she melted a little bit more. She knew it. He knew it. The smaller, younger, more brunet version of Logan ringing up Logan's shoes while watching them from across the floor knew it.

It was written all over Nicole's flushing face. Over her damp hands and her slightly parted lips and how she couldn't go thirty seconds without closing her eyes or touching her throat or running her fingers through her hair. How, by the time Logan was standing a few inches beside her, Nicole had to remind herself to breathe.

"Hey," he said.

"Hi," she said, barely. "Did you find your shoes?"

"I did," he said.

Nicole nodded. This time, she forgot to inhale.

Logan coiled his hand around the clothing rod a few inches from her fist, which was now clenched so firmly her knuckles had turned white. His grip tightened, revealing every muscle and tendon and vein along his forearm. Nicole wanted to put the whole thing in her mouth.

All he had to do was come a little bit closer.

All he had to do was drop his hand.

All he had to do was say her name.

Grab her by the elbow, jerk her into that dressing room, yank the curtain closed. Slam her against the mirror, hike up her dress, bite into her neck. Use one hand to cover her mouth and the other to shove hims—

"Have you suffered enough?" he said.

"Wh-what?"

"I meant with the grand tour of running stores in the Greater Los Angeles area. Not, uh . . ."

Nicole nodded again. Swallowed. Hard.

"You see anything you want?" he said. "You ready to get out of here?"

She closed her eyes, rubbed her throat, and tried to get her mouth to be less . . . wet. "I'm ready, yeah."

When she opened her eyes, Logan's hand was still glued to the clothing rod. He unfurled his grip, wiped his palm on the front of his jeans, then nodded Nicole toward the door.

"All right," he said. "Let's go then."

The store—a very traditional rectangle that led to one single, clearly marked exit—was a maze. They somehow made their way outside and to Nicole's car, each clutching a couple of shoeboxes while the late afternoon baked onto the steaming pavement.

Nicole started the engine, cleared her throat, and tried to remember which side of the road was the right one. Logan, for once, didn't have much to say. He put something on the radio. Nicole kept her eyes ahead. Neither bothered with the air-conditioning. Music blurred. Traffic tensed. They just drove home in this thick, sticky silence that made simple concepts like time, space, and small talk wilt. They did not remember that they had forgotten the dumplings.

And by the time they were off the freeway and around the block from Logan's place, Nicole was a lost cause. She jerked her car into his alley and slammed her gearshift into park.

"Will you just kiss me already?"

Logan startled, then crumpled up some receipt he'd been studying for the past few minutes. "Listen, we should talk about what happened. About—"

"We can talk later," she said, unbuckling her seat belt.

"Nicole," he said, but not very loudly. Not very convincingly.

"Do you have any idea how much I want you?"

Logan shook his head, mouth half open. Outside, the sun had given way to that late-summer twilight, long and blue. Nobody was around.

"Do you want me to show you?"

He made a strange noise. Nodded.

Nicole climbed over her center console, pinned him against his seat, then straddled his waist. Her left knee was jammed against the passenger door; her right one, bending into Logan's tensing hand. She pushed him back another inch, then ran her teeth down his throat. His head tipped back as he groaned, and his skin was rough and clean on her tongue.

"All I think about," she said, "is how you kiss me."

He pulled her closer as Nicole let the hem of her dress ride higher and higher up her waist. She yanked off his ball cap, twisted her fingers into his hair, and whispered again. This time, into his ear.

"All I've thought about," she said, "since that morning in your car, is how you put your hands on me. That night, against your wall, it was like you already knew how I liked it."

He nodded, jaw still dropping as his chest rose and his eyes closed and his hands crawled farther up her thighs. His fingertips slid beneath the lace on her hips as Nicole fumbled for the seat recliner.

"All I think about," she said, centering him between her legs, "is what it's going to feel like when you finally take me upstairs. When you're finally . . ."

He inhaled and nodded and muttered all at once.

"Open your eyes," she said.

"Nicole . . ."

"Yeah?" She parted her lips and locked his gaze and then, when she was sure he wouldn't miss it, lifted up his shirt and began sliding her mouth down his heaving chest so slowly every bit of him shuddered. Beneath her dress, his hands were wandering up her stomach, past her ribs, and toward the frilly beginning of her bralette. She helped him up another inch, another two inches, until he'd dug his fingers beneath the lace and she was soft in the palms of his hands. She groaned, pinned his fists behind his head, and teased her lips farther down his torso while he sunk deeper into his seat. She circled his erection, then unbuttoned his fly. His eyes bulged.

"What are you doing?"

Nicole inched down his jeans. "What does it look like I'm doing?"

Another odd noise.

"Logan," she said.

He was panting. "Yeah?"

"Tell me you still want me. Tell me you—"

He lunged forward and kissed her.

He kissed her harder than anyone had kissed her, ever before. Every ounce of it, filthy. Tongues and lips and teeth and throats, all so hard and sloppy and certain Nicole wondered if he wasn't going to shove himself inside her right then and there—just yank her underwear aside and bite down on her shoulder and make her scream his name until she couldn't take it any longer. Until she fell apart, half dressed and a complete mess in his arms.

"You're killing me," he said, jerking her closer, grabbing her harder. "You know how good you look. You know how good you sound. You know what you do to me."

Nicole moaned, then pushed him back against his seat and dropped her hands onto the waistband of his boxers. She traced the juts of his hip bones while he inhaled, fists clutched.

"Can I touch you?" she said.

He nodded. He was staring at her, watching her watch him as she finally began to feel him. To learn him. His jaw softened and his shoulders stiffened and his eyes rolled as he bent to her touch. She licked her lips, then slid onto the floor mat beneath him, gliding her tongue down his tensing stomach and kissing the twitching muscles along the way.

"Holy shit," he said.

Nicole looked up at him, teeth on his waistband as he throbbed in her hands. "Is this okay?"

He nodded. His chest, rising and falling. His hands, clenched onto either side of his seat as Nicole slipped her lips a little lower, kissed him a little closer, made him breathe a little louder.

"I want to take care of you," she said. "I want to make that whole night up to you. I—"

"Nicole, wait," he said, pulling back, peeling her off him. She froze. "We need to talk, okay?"

"Oh my god. I'm so sorry. I thought you said yes. I thought you wanted this."

"You didn't do anything wrong," he said, yanking up his jeans before lifting her onto his lap. She closed her eyes and tried to wriggle away, but he held her back. "I'm literally dying. There's not a bone in my body that doesn't want to say yes. To that, to you. To everything. I want all of you. I'm the dumbest man in the world. I'll never sleep again. I just—"

"I'm not going to change my mind. That's not going to happen, ever again. I promise."

"It's not that. It's . . ."

Nicole wrinkled her nose. Logan, after a long exhale, put his arms around her waist.

"Listen," he said. "When we do this, I want you to be completely sure. I want us to be on the same page. And I want you to understand that you don't owe me a thing."

"I am sure." She tried to look at him. "I won't ever be more sure. You have to believe me."

"I don't think it's a good idea," he said. "Not yet, okay?"

Nicole nodded, then tugged down her dress and again began climbing into her seat. Logan, at once, pulled her back into his arms and tucked a lock of hair behind her ear.

"Hey," he said. "I just want to slow things down. That's all. I promise."

"Because I freaked out after our date? Because of what I told you today? Because I'm going to be a mom?"

"It's not that simple. It's a lot of things. This is complicated, what we're doing. Now more than ever. And we didn't quite get it right the first time, you know?"

Nicole looked down, tracing her wrist. "I wanted to call you. After what happened. I wanted to call you every night."

"I wanted to call you too. I wanted to make sure you were okay. I didn't know what I was supposed to do."

"Me neither."

Logan took a deep breath. Outside, the hushed, narrow alley they'd been blocking had grown dark. For a few moments, Nicole just sat there. Her body, hot and cold and confused. Her mind, a mess. She wrung her hands together and closed her eyes.

"I like you," she said. "I like you so much. I'm not sure if adults still say that to each other. I don't know what I'm doing. I don't know what's cool or okay or how any of this is going to work. I just like you. And I just wanted to say that out loud, I think."

Nicole held her breath, waiting for a response. Too afraid to open her eyes. Too afraid to read his face. She just sat there, dented and desperate and his for the taking. But all Logan did was find her chin and tilt it toward his and wait for her to open her eyes. And when she finally did—even though her gaze remained fixed on her lap—he pressed his palms onto the tops of her tensed shoulders and dug his fingertips into the base of her neck.

"Dave's wife had to make me depression lasagna, you know."

A bit of warmth flickered between Nicole's ribs. "And what does that entail, exactly?"

"It's just regular lasagna," he said, kneading his fingers a little harder, a little lower. "But served to me on their couch in broad daylight while I watch *Lord of the Rings* on mute because I'm sad about a girl."

"Does she serve that often?"

"No," he said, kissing her wrists. "Only on special occasions."

Nicole looked up at him and smiled. At once, Logan beamed.

"You're such a dork," she said. "I don't know what we're going to do about it."

He laughed, then looked right at her. "This baby thing... I don't want to pretend it's nothing. It's a really big deal. But we have time, okay? We deserve a little time. Let's just slow down and see what we have here. I would really, really like to see what we have here."

Nicole nodded. Logan grabbed his phone and began swiping through his calendar.

"And on that note," he said, "what are you doing Labor Day Weekend?"

"Nothing, I think."

He typed for a few seconds. A moment later, Nicole's phone buzzed. She grabbed it from the cupholder.

"Is this a calendar invite to fuck you?"

"Sure is."

She peered at the screen. "I can't wait three weeks."

Logan slid his hands up her dress, yanked her back into him, and kissed her again.

"Three weeks is nothing," he said. "Trust me."

35

Not Quite Saint Barts

By quarter to eleven the next day, Nicole was dressed, sufficiently caffeinated, and hopping into Mari's passenger seat while Mari looked up from her phone, one eyebrow raised.

"Why are you glowing?"

"I am not glowing," Nicole said.

"You told me you guys were, like, grabbing breakfast. Breakfast doesn't make people glow."

Nicole tossed her bag in the back seat. "Maybe I'm really excited about grapefruit juice. Maybe I just discovered everything bagel seasoning. There could be any number of reasons—"

"You totally fucked him, didn't you?"

"I did not," Nicole said.

"But you're going to, right?"

"Drive the car, Mari."

Now Mari raised both eyebrows. "Oh god, you're, like, dating him, aren't you? What, are you waiting to have romantic sex that's emotionally vulnerable and thoroughly rooted in mutual respect or something gross and mature like that?"

Nicole, nodding, covered her burning face. "Just drive the fucking car, okay?"

Mari laughed, then giddily backed out of the driveway, pestering Nicole with questions. Once Nicole's blushing had subsided, she caught Mari up on her and Logan's very-chill, definitely-not-serious-at-all plan to take things slow. After that, she and Mari returned to their regularly scheduled Sunday programming: discussing every detail of Mari's third date with that physical therapist, then reviewing each of the dozen meetings she'd set up for her weeklong trip to the East Coast. Twenty minutes later, the two women were venturing through an untouched-since-the-nineties shopping mall and into a musty, dinosaur-themed toy store where virtually everything was earth-toned, unpriced, and covered in a decade's worth of grime.

"I feel like we're in a time machine," Nicole said, studying a shelf of stegosaurus figurines. They were shopping for Mari's eight-year-old nephew, whose birthday party was in a few hours. "Or some shop in the East Village run by a very mysterious, lonely old man."

"I know," Mari said. "But last year, I wrote Mateo a check for his 529 and he burst into tears in front of my entire family. So this year, he's getting a crappy toy *and* a check."

Nicole laughed, then meandered to the edge of the store, which was marked by an objectively terrible mural that spanned the back wall. She snapped a few pictures of a hastily painted, googly-eyed pterodactyl holding a bouquet of party balloons and had just begun to send them to a certain someone when Mari called out her name. Nicole found her a couple of aisles away, dusting off a DIY volcanic apocalypse kit.

"You think lava expires?" Mari said.

Nicole, who was still staring into her phone, shoved it into her back pocket, then ran her fingers over the active ingredients list. "Well, there's baking soda in here. That definitely won't react after a year or whatever. But I bet you could make your own at home with Alka-Seltzer or something. Do you have food coloring? Canola oil? We could probably use an egg too, or mustard? Something to emulsify . . ."

Mari stared at her, mouth open. "Don't take this the wrong way. But you're a giant fucking nerd."

"I am not a nerd! I just spent a lot of time at the Saint Louis Science Center growing up. Paige was a nerd. I was supporting her!"

"Yeah, no. You're a first-degree dork, and we both know it."

Nicole was beginning to prepare some smart-ass response when a bright yellow, shrink-wrapped box on a just-out-of-reach shelf caught her eye. She got on her tippy-toes and used the tail of a stuffed triceratops to send it tumbling into her arms. She was halfway through the blurb on the side panel when Mari walked over to her.

"Oh, that's perfect!" Mari said, nearly prying the box out of Nicole's hands. "Come on, let's go. There's a yogurt place here with good toppings."

Nicole pulled the package a little closer to her chest. "This one's for me."

Mari's whole face lit up. "Nicole Speyer, are you buying an ant farm? For a boy?"

"You're the one who started this! Leave me alone!"

Mari cocked her head at a beet-red Nicole, then used Nicole's dinosaur-tail trick to send a Jurassic-themed ant farm of her own sliding off the top shelf. Mari caught it, then nudged Nicole toward the cash register, laughing out loud when Nicole began asking the extremely stoned teenager ringing them up whether the manufacturer sold additional larva and cleaning kits online and, if so, whether those items shipped quickly.

"Can I say one more thing?" Mari said as they strolled back into the ready-to-be-condemned mall, packages tucked beneath their arms. The damp, skylit air; a blend of hot pretzels and orange chicken and black mold. Cell phone repair kiosks blinked. Massage chairs buzzed.

"Since when do you need permission to speak freely?"

"I just wanted to take a moment to discuss how you went from spending New Year's in Saint Barts to buying literal bugs at an indoor mall in deep Torrance," she said. "It's . . ."

Nicole rolled her eyes. "It's what?"

"It's going to be the best sex of your life," Mari said. "Trust me. The weird ones always surprise you."

36

Sunday Night Baseball

"Just tell me exactly what I'm supposed to do," Logan said, staring at a giant block of feta with a dented, decade-old paring knife in his hand.

"Cube it, you moron."

"Isn't it already a cube, though?"

Nicole flicked a cherry tomato at him. Logan, laughing, bumped her hip, then proceeded to slice the feta into not-quite-cubes and dump them into some giant bowl she'd found in the back of his oven. From the open window above his kitchen sink, summer evening slipped through the tattered screen, swirling with the cheers, boos, and called strikes of *Sunday Night Baseball*. Nicole was halfway through a fine chop of mint, parsley, and oregano when Logan stepped behind her, swooped his arms around her stomach, and rested his chin on her shoulder.

"I like watching you cook," he said.

"Why? Are you secretly harboring domestic fantasies about me?"

"Mm." He slid his mouth down the back of her neck. "Probably."

She chuckled, then muttered something unimportant as his hands began working their way beneath the waist of her shorts, fiddling with the hem of her underwear. When her breath caught, he pushed her against the counter, traced the curve of her shoulder with his tongue, and pressed himself between her legs as she blindly dropped a handful of herbs into the bowl.

"We're not going to make it until September," she said between shallow little inhales. "We're not even going to make it to the fourth inning."

He spun her around so her waist was in his hands and her fingers were clutched onto the edge of the countertop behind her. Her lips parted and her pulse raced.

"I didn't mean to turn you on," he said. "It's just, you taught me how to use a vegetable peeler, and I was so . . . moved. It's like my real life started today, like these first forty years—"

Nicole shut him up with a kiss. He seemed to enjoy that quite a bit.

"Oh!" She pulled back. "I almost forgot! I got you the dumbest thing ever! It made me think of you!"

"Did it now?" he said as Nicole tugged him toward the front door, where an oversize canvas tote bag lay beside her kicked-off sandals. She pulled out a neatly wrapped, blue-and-green polka-dotted box topped with a silver bow. Logan ripped it open like a toddler, hastily and scrappily and without strategy.

"An ant farm! Nic!"

Nicole's eyes crinkled as Logan pulled her into him.

"It comes with a voucher for larva and everything," she said, pressing a few fingers onto his chest as he turned the box over. "But I figured you wouldn't want to wait, so I went to the pet store and got you some ants that are ready to go. They're kind of in my purse." Nicole darted over to her bag, handed him a tube of critters, then settled back into his arms. "You can order more, if you want. Antports, too, so you can connect with another habitat later. There's a whole website with all these accessories and expansion kits. I'm a bit of an expert now."

"You're, like, comically thorough," he said. "It's amazing. No wonder Brie wanted Quentin to give you her job. I always . . ."

Logan didn't finish his sentence because Nicole—arms suddenly limp by her sides—had taken a step back.

"Hey," he said. "Where'd you go? What's wrong?"

"Nothing. It's nothing."

"You know I was just teasing, right?" He put down the box and insects, then reached for her hand. He settled instead for a few fingers around her lifeless wrist. "I'm sorry. I didn't know you were sensitive about that."

"I'm not," she said. "It's not like it's news to me that I blew up my career for nothing. I've had lots of time to let that sink in. I don't really care anymore."

"Nicole," he said. "We're not going to do that again, okay?"

"Do what?"

"Put up walls."

He led her into the kitchen, grabbed a bottle of wine from the fridge, then nodded toward his patio. Once they were outside, he poured Nicole a drink, did the same for himself, and looked over at her. She was staring out into the warm blue evening like her eyes were made of glass.

"Turning down that job was the dumbest thing I've ever done," she said. "Even dumber than marrying Gabe. You remember, you were there."

"Listen." He rocked his chair back an inch, then stopped it with his foot. "You did what you thought was best at the time. Nobody's judging you for that."

"Seriously? You're seriously telling me you didn't think what I did was dumb?"

"I didn't think it was my place to give you career advice. You had plenty of other people to bounce decisions off."

"Well, I kind of wish you had," she said, biting down on her tongue, trying not to think about those last few weeks at Porter Sloane. About that second miscarriage. About that Friday night fight with Gabe. About the Saturday her mother-in-law stopped by for a heart-to-heart. About the Sunday she decided to resign. It had all happened so fast.

"I meant what I told you," Logan said, "that night we were in New York."

Nicole felt that strange little tug again. Except this time, it was stronger. Hot and sharp and noisy. She ignored it, then took a swig of her drink and smirked. "That every time you check into a fancy hotel for work, you kind of wish it was a DoubleTree, because of the cookies?"

"Yes," he said, squeezing her knee. "But the other thing too. That there's nothing stupid about going after exactly what you want."

Nicole took a deep breath and let her mind, just for a moment, drift back to that night. Thick wool coats and shitty hot chocolate and the whole city, covered in snow. Of all the memories she'd stowed away, it was this one she'd placed on the very top shelf of her mind. But it didn't really make a difference, did it? Where she'd stored it. How much dust she'd let it collect. Because even now, two and a half years later, she could play back the whole thing perfectly. Some memories were like that. They stayed asleep until something roused them. They didn't haunt you until you were ready to look back.

"That job," she said, "meant so much to me. That promotion, all of it. I never loved what I did, at least not at the beginning.

It was never my dream—contracts, logistics, whatever. But I was getting really good at it. And people noticed, people knew it. It felt really nice, to be needed. To feel important. To have something that was . . ."

"Yours?" he said.

Nicole nodded. "I see you, Mari, Gabe, my sister . . . You guys all have these careers. Your lives keep getting bigger. Opportunity after opportunity. That job was the last thing in my life that belonged to me. And I didn't even fight for it. The minute things got hard, I just gave up. I just let it go.

"Even my podcast turned out to be bullshit. All it did was feed that obsession with getting pregnant. I'd work on it all day. Nine, ten hours. More, sometimes, if Gabe was out late. I'd hang on every comment, every new listener. It was supposed to be all mine, something that made my life mean something. But then, last month, I just stopped. Just like last time, I gave up. I can't even face it. I've barely stepped foot in my office. I've probably lost half my audience. I have one sponsor—they're gone, I'm sure."

"You're so hard on yourself. Why are you punishing yourself like this?"

"Because," she said, fingering the rim of her wineglass. They were quite nice—stemless, oversize. She made a mental note to ask which of his exes had bought them for him some other time when the mood was lighter. "I had this chance to prove I was more than some poor little rich girl, more than some finance guy's barren wife, and I got it all wrong. I got it wrong a hundred different times."

"Come on, Nicole. Nobody who actually cares about you thinks that. It is not a moral failing to want a child or trust your partner.

People make those choices all the time, and it doesn't define them. You are so much more than the guy you married. You are so much more than a girl who quit her job or couldn't get pregnant."

She closed her eyes. "I want to believe you. I know that you're probably right. But there's this voice inside my head that keeps telling me, if I was really more than that, wouldn't I have done something with my life? Wouldn't I not be in the position I'm in now, where divorce attorneys have to tell me point-blank not to fuck up my settlement by getting a job? Wouldn't I have something to show for myself besides an abandoned pet project?"

Logan put his drink down and looked right at her. "Can I just listen to this thing? Please?"

"It's really a lot of Gabe . . ."

"If you don't care," he said, "I don't care."

Nicole nodded, then took a long last sip of her wine and let Logan lead her upstairs into his extra bedroom. He opened his laptop, sat himself down in a rolling chair at a thick walnut desk littered with version after version of the same pitch deck, then pulled her onto his lap. He pushed his lips into the back of her shoulder, then draped his arm over hers, kissing her gently as she brought up her podcast's page.

"Which one are you most proud of?" he said.

Nicole ran her finger across the trackpad until the cursor landed on an episode she'd recorded after Valerie's second transfer failed. "This one, I think."

Logan grabbed a pair of headphones from his drawer, then picked Nicole up and set her down on the sofa. He opened his closet, grabbed a box of books, then dropped it beside her.

"You read," he said. "I'll listen. Then we'll regroup."

Nicole reached for a copy of *City of Thieves* and headed downstairs. Zero chance she could sit in that office and watch Logan kick his feet up while she talked about Gabe's sperm count for the whole world to hear. Forty-two minutes, three trips to Logan's junk food drawer, and five chapters later, he emerged with a smile on his face.

"You're so fucking funny," he said, padding down the stairs. "I don't know how you make bad news so entertaining. It's very cool."

"Thanks," she said, tucked into the corner of the same sofa he'd almost railed her on fifteen days ago. "I may have accidentally consumed all your candy."

He laughed from his bottom step, then plopped down next to her and pulled her into his arms, telling her there was no way they were eating that fancy salad, that they deserved real food. And then, for the next hour, they just lay there, drinking, discussing Nicole's podcast. What she loved about it and what she wished she'd done differently. What felt right and what felt wrong.

"I like that it's funny," she said. "I really do. But looking back, it was all to control the narrative. Every time something bad happened, I'd turn the whole thing into some drawn-out joke before anyone could beat me to the punch. I'm not sure that's something I want to do anymore."

"Then start over," he said. "Do it the way you want to do it. Figure out what that looks like for you and go for it."

Nicole sat up as Logan traced her arms, her shoulders, her spine. She'd been so sure she'd never see this place again. Now here she was, letting him in—but in this other, kind of extraordinary way. One that only came from taking your time. From keeping your hands to yourself. From telling the goddamn truth.

"On Thursday," she said, "when I was in Virginia for Valerie's ultrasound, we had this conversation that blew me away. We're really different, but we have this connection. Always have. And her perspective on motherhood is incredible. She's been through a lot. She lost her mom superyoung. She's raising two kids while her husband is deployed. Plus the whole having-a-baby-for-someone-else thing."

Logan nodded. He was still touching her. Just sitting there, listening. The night, dark. The ball game, hushed. His living room, aglow.

"I was thinking, what if she and I did it together? What if we started using all that humor and all the bad shit that's happened to us to have real conversations? To talk to other women? To start telling the truth? I mean, I don't know if she'd want to, if she'd even have the time or energy, but I think it could really work. That we could really scratch the surface of something."

Logan lit up. "Do it," he said, just as the doorbell buzzed. "Ask her."

He rose to his feet, grabbed their dinner off his stoop, then slid back onto the couch. The truth was, Nicole had come here tonight to make a dumb salad, give Logan some absurd gift, and see if maybe she could convince him to screw her a little sooner. Instead, she was fully clothed and inches from him, eating garlic naan, watching the Mariners blank the Rangers, and letting him begin to crack her heart right open.

37

The Box

November, Three Years Ago

"Nicole? Are you okay?"

She didn't answer him.

She just stood there.

Shaking, colorless, silent.

It was a Tuesday morning—early, quiet. Maybe half past nine. And from the strange internal maze that led Porter Sloane's hundred-or-so employees to restrooms, a too-small mailroom, and a storage closet that stocked little more than a couple of cases of expired craft beer, there wasn't even a hint of natural light. No sign of the cold, gray November sky. No sign of that first California rain. Just a few dozen yards of navy carpet, ad-bespeckled white walls, and a water fountain that never worked.

"What's going on?" Logan said, coming a step closer. "Are you okay?"

She closed her eyes and tried to speak.

"I . . . I don't think so."

He put his hand on her shoulder. Nicole barely felt it. She could barely feel a thing—except for the scraping, cramping howl that sliced from deep inside her stomach to straight between her legs. He placed a second hand on her shoulder. His folded face, a blur. The hallway, bright and dull and indistinct. The last ten minutes, surreal. The whole morning, not happening.

This wasn't happening.

Ten months of waiting. Two weeks of bliss.

And now, this.

"Please tell me what's going on," he said.

"I'm—" She grabbed her stomach and writhed in pain, an involuntary reflex that shut her eyes, clamped her jaw, and bent her body without warning. When the heave ended, the wad of paper towels she'd shoved into her underwear pooled with what she already knew was more blood.

"Nicole," he said, his eyes frantic. His brow, skewed. "You have to talk to me."

"I'm pregnant," she said.

He closed his eyes for a second, then nodded.

"Okay," he said. "And what's happening right now?"

Another cramp—deep and hot and painful. Nicole scrunched her face and threw her hands back on her stomach. As if it mattered now.

"I'm bleeding," she said. "It just started. I can't make it stop."

"Did you talk to your doctor? Is Gabe on his way?"

Nicole winced again. "I can't reach him. He's in a meeting, I think."

"Your doctor? Or Gabe?"

Nicole hugged her arms around her elbows. "Gabe."

"Okay," he said, pulling out his phone. "Do you want me to call Mari? She can come get you."

"She's getting ready for New York, she's—"

"I'll go to New York," Logan said.

Nicole shook her head. "That's crazy. I can just drive myself. Gabe will call soon. I'm fine."

"I have to go next week anyway," he said, swiping rapidly through his phone, then pressing it to his ear. He paced in place, keeping an eye on Nicole, who could barely hear it ring. "Might as well get it out of the way."

"No, really, I—"

"Hey," he said into the receiver. He leaned against the wall, one hand hooked behind his neck. She'd never seen him this serious. "Change of plans. Can you actually come to the office? Nicole needs you. It's, um . . . it's not about work."

He shook his head while Mari's voice—muffled, imperceptible—garbled back. "No big deal. Send me the schedule, and I'll find a flight, okay? I'll scout, and you can go next week and meet my top three. I trust you."

They each said a few more words, then Logan hung up and ushered Nicole down the hall, into the elevator, through the lobby, and across the breezeway. They sat on the curb of the parking lot in silence, the overhang above—an unfinished slab of concrete supported by two sleek steel beams—shielding them from the cold, unglamorous rain. The drops, gray and exhausted and confused, fell to the faded asphalt like they'd already given up. Like they already knew they weren't quite right for this town. Like they didn't really care anymore, whether they sloped or pooled or puddled.

Nicole tried Gabe a few more times.

Logan booked a flight on his phone.

"Mari should be here soon," he said. "Do you need anything? Do you want to wait inside?"

Nicole shook her head. They just sat in silence and watched the strange, bleary rain.

"You didn't have to do this, you know."

"It's really no problem," he said. "Mari will be here, in case you need her. And New York will be good. I'll get a giant pretzel. Go to the Olive Garden in Times Square. Maybe I'll stay for the weekend, see if my cousin will go to the M&M's experience store with me. I always try to sneak in something cultural when I'm in the city, you know?"

Nicole laughed through a few hot, wet tears.

"Thank you," she said.

He nodded, wringing his hands together. "I really hope everything's okay."

"It's not," Nicole said, studying the ground. She wasn't quite sure why she'd said that. To him, to anyone. She just needed to. "The nurse I talked to, she told me to calm down. That it might be nothing, to just put my feet up and come in for bloodwork. But I know my body. And it's not nothing. It's over. I can feel it."

Nicole, with that, put her head in her hands. For a minute, they were quiet. When Logan finally exhaled, she glanced over at him. He was looking right at her. His face, pained but kind.

"I'm really sorry," he said.

She shrugged, wiping her nose with the sleeve of her cardigan. He was more of a grown-up than she'd ever given him credit for, wasn't he? And there was this whole other side to him, she realized, that she would never really get to know. She'd met him a couple of years ago—right here, right in that coffee shop across the parking lot, rambling about *Dungeons & Dragons* with his phone to his shoulder and his dress shirt, untucked—and filled in all his blanks at once. She'd been so sure, in that moment, she knew exactly who he was.

But she'd been mistaken, hadn't she?

She did that sometimes. Made snap judgments. Got people wrong.

She'd done it with Gabe, that was for sure. She'd taken her first impression of him and stuck him in a box, then ended up falling in love with the man she watched cut open its seals and crawl out.

"I'm sorry too," she said, the tiniest smirk stretching across her stinging face. "Sounds like you're actually going to have to work this week. And I know how much you hate that."

He side-eyed her, chuckling. "Worst day of your life, and you still can't help yourself, can you?"

"What can I say?" she said. "Making fun of you is my passion."

38

Girl Talk

Around lunchtime Monday, Nicole pushed down her shoulders, opened the door to her sleeping office, pressed her forefingers to the cool plastic of the wall switch, and clicked on the lights.

She barely recognized the place.

In just a few weeks, a filter—fuzzy and foreign—had faded every inch of the room. All of it, distant and peculiar. The wide planks of oak slotted beneath a colorless, tasseled rug. The sorry-you-can't-get-pregnant self-help books that lined the shelves on the back wall, alphabetized and organized and pale pink or green or blue. The soft maple of her desk, still home to a dozen color-coded sticky notes, a few tidy stacks of note cards, and a single unfinished script, left to collect dust.

Nicole ran her fingers over the top page. *Episode 98: The Waiting Game.* She sifted through a few more lines, her index finger tracing chunks of dialogue that were no longer hers. Sure, she had written them. She had brought them to life. But now, they were meaningless. Every single word had been an artifice. Proof to the whole world, and to herself, that nothing mattered more than motherhood. Week after week of channeling all that pain and disappointment into a story that, when she inspected it now, looked a whole lot like armor.

She let out a short, sharp cry, then chucked the whole script in the trash. And then, when that felt surprisingly good, she kept going. She tore the place apart. The injection schedules. The social media calendars. The books that told her what to eat and how to sleep and when to fuck. A framed selfie of her and Gabe kissing—cheeks, pink—on the icy cobblestone outside their place in New York, a few months after she realized she'd gotten him all wrong. That deep down, he was a good one. That she was never going to let him go.

She threw it all away.

It was fast.

It was easy.

And when she was done—when the room had been sufficiently exorcised—Nicole pulled back the curtains, let the midday sun pour through the glass doors, and reached for her phone.

"I was going to call you earlier!" Valerie said as steam billowed around her freckled face. "But then I put on a movie for the boys, and then I fell asleep, and then I started ironing these little name tags into all these little T-shirts . . ."

Nicole, who was pacing, smiled. "I mean, I get that. Labeling is very soothing for me."

Valerie laughed, and the conversation, despite Nicole's knotted stomach, carried on. As much as she wanted to, Nicole couldn't just spit out her question. After all, her relationship with Valerie was different. It was inherently vulnerable. Fraught and imbalanced and, possibly, finite.

How many times had Nicole, in those online forums, watched an intended mother and her carrier start out as the best of friends? As two grown women, suddenly brought together by some strange and new commercial sisterhood? Each of them so eager to please, to play their part?

And how many times had she watched those bonds fall to pieces? Pregnancies, after all, were long. The feelings that first connected you—excitement, maternal instinct, the desire to post something cute on Instagram—grew complicated. At some point, the stress would surface. The panic, the trauma. The jealousy, the inadequacy. Every one of those big, ugly emotions you swore you'd leave out of this brighter path to motherhood would break through. What had brought you and your carrier together in the first place— the idea of some perfect baby who was finally going to heal your broken heart—lived in her now. It was, for those nine months, hers to keep safe, to care for, to remember not to feed room-temperature coleslaw or take on a roller coaster or bring along for a soak in a bacteria-ridden hot tub. By delivery day, that was simply more pressure than any woman, on either side, could take.

And so Nicole was polite. She was kind. She asked what the boys were up to today. How Valerie's husband was doing in Japan. Whether the medicine Dr. Akhtar had prescribed was helping with Valerie's morning sickness. And finally, when there were no more green smoothie hacks or home organization trends to discuss, when there were no more chances to prove she was a good person, that Valerie was so much more than an incubator, that what they had was real, Nicole's restless legs came to a halt. She wiped her palms on her shirt and steadied her voice.

"So, if you have a few minutes, I wanted to talk to you about my podcast?"

"Oh, okay, sure," Valerie said, wandering into her kitchen and beginning to prepare her usual afternoon snack of saltine crackers. In the background, her sons had started some sort of war revolving around a single baby carrot. Valerie did not seem concerned. "You know, I've been meaning to ask you about that. I figured with everything going on, maybe you weren't going to do it anymore. I felt bad bringing it up."

"I felt that way for a while too. But then I sort of, well, reconnected with an old friend of mine. We ended up talking about the podcast a lot. It made me realize how much I actually miss it. And that I don't want to just let it die."

Valerie nodded, nibbling the edge of a cracker very carefully as Nicole continued.

"I do want it to be different, though. I want to start talking about motherhood the way you and I always have, if that makes any sense. Just be superreal about the whole thing—about how it's not a sure thing. How it's kind of ugly and scary. Trying for it, deciding against it, being in it, losing it. How the whole thing is out of our control. How it's so different for everybody."

Nicole was walking in circles now. Quick ones. "I was wondering, and please don't feel like you need to say yes or answer right away or anything like that, if maybe you'd want to help me? Like, as a cohost? You can totally say no. I know you're so busy. And pregnant. But I thought you'd be perfect. Just you and me, telling stories. Talking to other women who've gone through something that's changed them. Who've been to hell and back."

Valerie's face had lit up. "Wow. I don't even know what to say. Are you sure I'm the right person? I'm not a writer or a reader or anything like that. I don't know if I'd be any good at it."

"Are you kidding?" Nicole had probably walked ten thousand steps at this point. Most of them, in place. "You're one of the most interesting people I've ever met. You're such a good mom. Your heart is enormous, and you're so warm and honest and vulnerable.

And you might not've realized this, but I've known it since the day we met. You're a storyteller. A good one."

Valerie beamed. Nicole did too. And then Valerie—who was pacing now herself—began to rattle off every question under the sun. How would they record? How long would it take? How would they handle the time difference? How would they pick guests? Choose topics? What if Valerie had a horrible radio voice? They talked it all through—eager, giddy—while Valerie deftly policed the Battle of the Last Carrot unfolding behind her.

"What about all the tech stuff?" Valerie said, plopping onto her sofa once her children had been sent to their rooms to look quietly at their books until their three-minute timers went off. "I can barely crop a photo on my phone."

"It's not as hard as it looks. I learned to record, edit, do everything myself. The marketing, the social media too. Once you get the hang of it, it's actually really fun. But even if you only had a little time to record, that would be okay. I could handle the rest."

Valerie nodded. "Would I need anything? Other than my laptop?"

"Oh!" Nicole zipped over to her desk, hastily unplugging a microphone and a pair of studio headphones. "I pretty much have two of everything, from before! I can ship it! Or I could even come out, if you wanted? I'm just really excited. We can try it out—you don't have to commit. Maybe we could start with your story? See how you like it? See how we sound?"

"Oh my gosh! Yes! Come!" Valerie's face had scrunched so deeply Nicole almost wanted to cry. "We start school in a week—the twenty-second. Let me double-check our calendar, but come! Stay with us, and stay until the ultrasound, okay? I can definitely sneak in a little work when the boys are sleeping or watching their shows these next few days, but once school starts, I'm all yours. Well, from nine thirty to two fifteen, Monday to Friday, anyway."

Nicole leaned against the balcony door and smiled straight into her phone. The hot glass warmed her tingling skin.

"Okay," she said. "Just let me know. I'll find a flight."

⁂

The next few days flew by.

In the mornings, Logan and Nicole would time their runs—his fast, eight miles; hers, slow and four—so they could sneak in fifteen or twenty minutes together before their days began. They'd meet up on the Greenbelt over on Logan's side of town, each of them damp and sweaty and smiling, then grab iced coffees, talk through their to-do lists, and take each other in as the hazy morning sun crept higher and higher up the hill.

Once Nicole got home, she'd fry an egg or grab a banana or toast a waffle, then take a quick shower and settle into her desk for the day. She'd put together a crash course for Valerie. She'd take notes. She'd organize thoughts, ideas, and inspiration. She'd search for potential guests everywhere she could find them—message boards, the comments sections of Facebook posts, the crowdfunding pages of women who didn't have the cash to pay for an adoption attorney. She'd replay interviews over and over, trying to put her finger on what made the great ones so good. The best hosts, it seemed, knew when to make small talk, when to press for more, and when to shut the hell up. When to sit back and just listen.

She and Valerie, Nicole realized, didn't have to do this show perfectly. There would be no script. Sure, they could prepare for every guest. Pore through questions, seek to understand. Edit masterfully.

Help moments crackle. But really, more than anything, what they needed to do—what Nicole needed to do—was lighten up. To be herself. To make space for the truth, then get out of the way.

It would be a change, but she could do it. That much she knew.

And so Nicole got lost in the work. In seeing the podcast through this new lens. Every morning was endless; hour after hour to uncover this or consider that. And then, seemingly out of nowhere, her office—sun-drenched and ivory and bright—would turn yellow, then peach, then red. Somehow, another day had dissolved. Somehow, it was seven. She'd rub her eyes and shut down her monitors and rise to her feet, gathering the half-empty yogurt cups and ripped-open bags of pita chips that littered her newly cluttered desk. And then, every night—before she darted downstairs to grab her keys and head over to Logan's for dinner—she'd pause.

She'd turn around, she'd put her hand on the wall switch, and just before she dimmed the lights, she'd take a few moments to breathe it all in.

39

Impossible Things

On Thursday evening, Nicole was at the grocery store grabbing a couple of things for dinner when Logan texted to say he was caught up at the office, but to let herself in with his hidden key—that he wouldn't be longer than an hour. And so, with a bag of stir-fry ingredients tucked under her arm, Nicole unlocked Logan's front door, helped herself to a handful of gummy worms, then wandered upstairs to find something to read. She was lying on the couch in his office with her legs kicked up, twenty swollen pages through his water-damaged copy of *The Man in the High Castle*, when she heard his screen door swing open.

Logan was talking to someone—on the phone, it seemed. And his voice sounded different.

"I don't know, man. The creative is great. The art is done, the deck is done. The pricing is all set. We're ready to go. I believe in it. Maya believes in it. It's a month of work—of great work. I don't think we can throw together anything that holds a candle to this. Not in two weeks, that's for sure. It's just too big of a campaign. Trust me, if I thought we could pitch anything better, I'd tell you. You know that."

Nicole stepped onto the landing and issued Logan—who was pacing around his living room with his AirPods in and his brow furrowed—a half wave. He smiled, then held up a single finger—that universal sign for one more minute. When he rolled his eyes and twirled his finger in a few wacky loops, she chuckled. That was the universal sign for one more minute on the phone with Quentin Porter.

"I don't think New York can do it either," he said as Nicole tiptoed down the stairs. "I think we run with what we've got. I think that gives us our best chance here."

Logan was still walking in circles as Nicole took her last couple of steps toward him. Just before she arrived, he closed his eyes and frowned. Nicole slung her arms around him. He put his hands on her waist.

Hey, he mouthed. *I'm so sorry.*

Nicole shook her head and kissed his neck as his hands crawled underneath her sweatshirt. While Quentin, it seemed, kept on talking.

"Okay," Logan said, his fingers tensing then releasing against Nicole's ribs as he exhaled. "We'll figure it out in the morning, then."

He yanked out his headphones and chucked them onto the sofa, eyes still glued to Nicole. Leaning against the back of the couch, he locked her legs around him and kissed her.

"Guess where I'm going tomorrow?" he said.

"Mm." She pressed her hands onto his chest, tugging down on his collar while he tightened his grip on her ass. "Discovery Zone? Colonial Williamsburg? The Museum of SPAM?"

He laughed, carrying her into the kitchen as she rattled off a dozen other obscure Loganesque destinations. The Ben & Jerry's Factory. Rancho Obi-Wan. Canada. Without letting go of Nicole, he grabbed a beer from his fridge, then propped her up on the counter and stood between her kicking legs. He slid his free hand up her thigh.

"One more guess."

"Space Camp?"

He smirked, shaking his head. "Fucking Monterey."

Nicole frowned. "For how long?"

"Fifteen minutes? Two days? The rest of my life?"

Logan reached for the bottle opener a foot or so behind where he'd parked Nicole, then cracked open his beer and sighed. Nicole unfastened the top few buttons of his shirt and ran her nose along his collarbone. He closed his eyes.

"Can I tell you something?" he said.

Nicole nodded. He took a sip of his beer, then exhaled.

"I fucking hate my job. I am so tired of Quentin. I am so tired of having a boss who only makes things harder. Who's so far removed from reality and from the everyday operations of his own business that he just disappears for months. And then, out of nowhere, when he realizes we're at the finish line for some eight-figure deal, decides to call me up in a total panic with a completely impossible idea and no time to execute it."

Nicole put her hands on his shoulders. Tried to do what he always did for her lately, when she was worked up or nervous or stressed. She touched him. She kneaded her fingers into his neck, his shoulders, his back and tried to listen to what he had to say.

"Our pitch is two weeks from today. The creative is brilliant. I am so, so sure about it. We're all so sure about it. Quentin hasn't written a line of copy, hasn't flown down to sit in his office, hasn't done a thing to help us win a client in five years. It's one thing to be out of touch. It's one thing to be a pain in the ass. But now, he's actually starting to get in the way. He's a fucking problem."

Nicole nodded. Logan slammed back the rest of his beer, then flung open the fridge door and grabbed another.

"We don't have another opportunity this big in our pipeline. People are going to lose their jobs. Our best talent is leaving. They're fed up. And he won't look at the numbers. He's in denial. He's trying to open this office in London, and I don't even know why. He's going to bleed the agency dry. We don't need thirty people in London. We just need him to shut up and let us do our jobs.

"But you know Quentin." Another swig. Another sigh. "It's all just prestige for him. He used to be the best around. And I know he's a creative. I know he's not an accounts guy. But he knows better. He knows agencies are only as good as the work they're doing right now. That nobody gives a shit that we were the coolest shop around seven Super Bowls ago. We need this account. We really do."

Logan stopped to shove a fistful of dry Fruity Pebbles in his mouth, then handed the giant box to Nicole, who was just sitting there, listening. She held out a second palm of rainbow-colored pellets for him, then set the carton aside.

"If he interferes here, I don't know what's going to happen. Except that he's going to ruin the agency's reputation—and mine. I can't go into this meeting and pitch shit. I won't do it. I'm not going to look like an idiot. And I'm not going to sit there and let him burn the whole place down. Not with me and my team there to watch."

Nicole was just nodding. Just taking him in. He kept going. Fifteen, twenty, thirty more minutes. He paced around the kitchen and he ate his weird children's cereal and he let it all out. When he was done—nearly out of breath and halfway through his third beer and kind of damp and red and drained—he settled back between Nicole's legs and closed his eyes.

"What do you think I should do?" he said.

"Me?"

"Yeah, you. You're, like, the smartest person I know. Well, other than Dave."

Nicole laughed, her legs still dangling around his hips. His hands, back to running up and down her thighs.

"Well, maybe you just take it one step at a time, you know? Figure out how to win this account, and do that. Quentin's an idiot, underneath it all. He's always needed you. So do what you have to do to make sure the pitch is perfect. Close the deal. And then, maybe after that, it's time to make a change. Maybe it's finally time to go."

He raised an eyebrow. "That's, like, legitimate advice. You didn't even make fun of me."

"Yeah, well, I'm starting to think you kinda know what you're doing."

He glared at her. She kissed him.

"I have this other idea too," she said, dropping her lips to his throat and her hands to his belt loops. He laughed, took a long, last swig of his drink, then picked her up and tossed her onto his couch. She lay there, giggling, biting into her bottom lip while he kicked off his shoes.

"Describe it to me," he said, crawling on top of her as she finished unbuttoning his shirt. "Spare no details. Use extra words."

Nicole rolled him over and kissed him hard. He licked his lips, then pulled off her sweatshirt as she outstretched her arms.

"Why don't you tell me what you want for a change?" she said.

"I want two things. Very badly."

"Yeah?" She ran a few fingers down his torso. His muscles tensed, and he was hard between her legs. "Tell me."

"I'd like to play shortstop for the Seattle Mariners. I understand I'm probably too old at this point, so I'm willing to settle for manager. Even first base coach would be fine."

"That's one," Nicole said, sliding her mouth onto his stomach. He craned his neck, watching her lips glide lower and lower. "If the second one's about the Seahawks, so help me god."

Logan laughed, shaking his head. "The truth," he said, "is the things I want are impossible. I can't quit my job without a better one lined up. And I can't take you upstairs and fuck the living daylights out of you. Which, to be completely honest, is pretty much all I think about, all day and all night, no matter where I am or what I'm supposed to be doing."

Nicole inhaled sharply, then sat up and straddled him. "You could absolutely take me upstairs," she said, unbuckling his belt. He closed his eyes and clenched his jaw. "You could do whatever you wanted to me. You just . . . won't."

Logan, chest heaving, peeled off Nicole's shirt, then unhooked her bra and pulled her down onto him, running his mouth over every inch of her bare skin. When he slowed down to circle his tongue over her pinched nipple, Nicole yanked him deeper between her legs, then tugged the hair at the crown of his head.

"We need to have sex," she said. "We do this every night. Push your plan to the limit, then go home and listen to each other breathe. Over the phone. In the dark. In our own beds. It's ridiculous. Neither of us can think straight. We're both adults. You know I'm ready. And I know you want to."

"September," he said, while stripping off her shorts. While sliding his hands down her quaking hips. While slipping his forefingers just beneath the frilly seams of her underwear and watching her eyes go wide. She had her hands down his unzipped pants and her half-opened mouth pressed against his ear.

"Take me upstairs," she said, "and show me what you wrote on that little sheet of paper."

He closed his eyes, then kissed her again.

"In any other universe," he said, "I would. But I can't get this wrong with you. And I'm not going to sleep with you for the first time because I'm sad or I'm angry or I hate my boss or anything like that. When we do this, you're going to know exactly how much I want you, exactly what I'm doing here, and exactly what kind of man I am. I don't want there to be any confusion about that, ever again."

Nicole nodded, then floated her hands to his open palms and exhaled as their fingers intertwined.

"Tell me the truth," she said. "You kind of love this, don't you? Making me wait? Driving me crazy?"

He laughed, then reached for the remote as she rolled over and curved her bare spine into his chest. The back of her head fell just beneath the front of his shoulder. He pulled a blanket over them, pushed up her hair to kiss the nape of her neck, then threaded his arms around her stomach.

"There are worse things," he said, "than listening to Nicole Speyer beg me to screw her brains out every night. I'll leave it at that."

40

The Ice Queen

On Saturday afternoon, Nicole was sunbathing in her backyard and nearly through the novel she'd snatched from Logan when her doorbell rang. Nero, who'd been napping in a hot tuft of grass with his backbone flush against Nicole's shin, let out a startled woof and darted toward the door, tail up. Nicole creased her page, tucked her book under her arm, then wandered through the open slider and straight toward the foyer.

Her stomach dropped.

Her chest grew heavy.

Her sun-warmed body went cold.

The glow of her whole day—that miles-long walk on the Strand with Mari; the thirty-minute FaceTime with Paige devoted almost entirely to internet stalking their little brother's newest girlfriend; the delightfully absurd, occasionally explicit texts she and Logan had been trading back and forth while he killed time at the Monterey Airport—was put out at once. Because from the windowpane that flanked the side of Nicole's front door, Cynthia Speyer—with her tight face and her tennis bracelets and her honey-colored bob, blown out just so—was staring at her daughter-in-law with pursed lips and a pair of ice-cold blue eyes.

Nicole swallowed the lump in her throat.

Cynthia flashed a careful, cordial smile, then tipped her head toward the door.

"Cynthia," Nicole said, barely opening it. Nero pushed his snout between Nicole's wobbling knees. "Gabe's . . . Gabe's not here. He's in Aspen."

"I know where my son is, sweetheart," Cynthia said, stepping inside. She placed her white Chanel flap bag on the entryway console and looked around, studying the half-drunk iced coffee cup sweating onto the bottom stair, the pair of cutoffs abandoned in the foyer, the trail of dirt and sand and summer that Nicole had let gather down the hall.

"Do you need something? I—"

"Did you let your person go?" Cynthia said, walking herself into the kitchen. She ran a few freshly manicured fingers along the veined marble of Nicole's cluttered island, then looked her up and down.

Nicole just stood there, holding her book over her stomach, wishing she was wearing more than an old bathing suit and a beat-up Cardinals cap. Wishing she was wearing a goddamn snowsuit, ten sizes too big. Wishing she didn't care that her husband's mother was inspecting every inch of her home, every inch of her body—every stretch mark and chipped nail and split end—to add to Nicole's decade-thick file of itty-bitty mistakes.

"I was going to head out soon. I'll—"

"Gabriel told me you have the only pictures of my grandchild. I would like to see them."

Nicole nodded, then walked across the kitchen to a writing desk opposite the pantry. Hunched over, she rifled through a stack of mail, a couple of shopping lists, and a few random podcast ideas scribbled onto old receipts. She found the envelope from the clinic, pulled out a glossy black-and-white square, and handed it over.

Cynthia peered at it for a few seconds. "You're finally going to be a mother, Nicole. After everything you put your body through. It's very exciting."

"It is."

Cynthia looked at the picture again, then back up at Nicole. "Are you going to offer me some tea?"

Nicole flinched. "I . . . I didn't realize you were staying." She fumbled over to her electric kettle and flicked it on without a second thought. "It'll just be a minute."

"Iced, Nicole. It's August."

Nicole just stood there. "I don't have any. I—"

"What if somebody stops by?"

"Nobody stops by."

Cynthia smirked, then placed the sonogram on the counter and pushed it a few inches toward Nicole, who shuddered as it slid across the marble.

"We both know that somebody's been stopping by, honey. And that it's not my son."

Nicole's pulse had quickened. She was rubbing her throat, and hot red splotches were spreading across her skin. "Why did you come here? What do you want from me?"

Cynthia tilted her head. "I've come to discuss my grandchild."

"You should do that with Gabe."

"My son is committed to his family. He is aware of his responsibility to you and this baby. There's nothing left to discuss with him. You, on the other hand, seem to have forgotten what you've signed up for."

Nicole clutched her sweating palms onto the edge of a counter stool and drew a long, steady breath. "I signed up to love him. The rest of the games your family plays, as far as—"

"I spoke to your mother, Nicole."

"You what?"

"I picked up the phone, and I called your mother. She's worried about you. She says you barely call, that you—"

"I'm thirty-two years old! Why on earth would you call my mother?"

"Because," Cynthia said, "your mother and I have quite a bit in common. We both had our firsts before we'd even turned twenty-five. And it changed us. We learned to put our families first. We dedicated ourselves to our children. We learned that our husbands were here to provide, and that we were here to hold the family together. That's what good mothers do, dear." Cynthia paused for a moment, looked around. "They make a house a home."

"You should go," Nicole said as the kettle began to howl. Cynthia shook her head, then walked over and stopped the noise herself. She pulled a water glass off the shelf, held it up to the light, and frowned before placing it in the crowded sink and turning to Nicole.

"You chose this life, you know. When you married him."

"I did not *choose this life*."

"But you did," Cynthia said. "When you moved to California. When you let him pay your rent. When you let him take you to Saint Tropez, to the Maldives, to Morocco. When you let us throw you that wedding. When you let us buy you this house. When you decided to stop working."

Nicole's whole body was burning. "That's not what happened! That's not what fucking happened, and you know it!"

"Of course that's what happened, sweetheart. You were so stressed. You were so desperate to prove yourself. It was so hard for me to see you like that. To see both of you like that. My son, working so hard, and for what? So his wife could slave away and lose sleep—lose her own babies—over a job that she didn't need? Oh, Nicole. I didn't think you needed to take on more stress. I didn't think you needed to work longer hours or travel across the country twice a month. I didn't think you needed to spend your nights at USC sitting in on a silly contract law class. But I would have never told you to quit. You did that. Nobody else—"

"I need you to leave."

"Nicole," Cynthia said. "I expect my son back in this house by the time my grandchild is born. Whatever's going on with you, get it out of your system. And quickly. Because when that baby is finally here, you'll realize it. That family comes first. That a mother will do anything for her child. That—"

"You don't know me," Nicole said. "And you don't have a clue what I would or wouldn't do for my child."

"But I do know you, Nicole." She lifted the sonogram off the counter. "So believe me when I tell you this, because the sooner you realize it, the better. You're the one who's calling the shots. You're the one with the ring on her finger. All those other girls—they don't matter. He's coming home to you. I just hope you realize that before you break up your family. That you'll never have a chance at a life like this again."

Nicole closed her eyes and gritted her teeth. "Get out of my house."

Cynthia smiled, then walked toward the foyer, sonogram in hand. She picked up her purse by its gold-knotted chain, then put her hand on the doorknob and turned to Nicole.

"It's not your house, sweetheart," she said. "Surely you know that by now."

41

Night Dive

An hour later, Nicole was standing on Logan's stoop.

After Cynthia had left, Nicole texted him to see if maybe she could stop by when he got home from his night out with his friends, that she knew he'd only just gotten back into town but she was having a really shitty day. A few minutes later, he'd called to make sure she was okay, clarify his plans were actually inside the home, remind her she was always welcome at his place, and tell her to practice her eye roll . . . because tonight was his *Dungeons & Dragons* game, and it was his turn to host.

And so Nicole—stomach fluttery and pulse a bit too quick—took a calming breath, relaxed her shoulders, and rang the doorbell. This, of course, was a formality. Logan's door was already propped wide open, and through his screen, laughter rose and chairs screeched over exactly the kind of music you'd throw on when you needed to get yourself in the mood to argue over imaginary swords and rations of ham. A moment later, Logan—neck craned back toward the raucous living room to shout that "maybe José should try being less of a heal slut, then"—padded down the hall in blue jeans and a pair of crew socks, beer in hand. He kicked open the screen and grinned. Something warm and easy stretched across Nicole's chest.

"Come on in, m'lady."

"Fuck you so much."

Neither of them could keep a straight face as Logan slipped an arm around Nicole's waist and kissed her. "You want to talk or anything? The guys can wait. We can go for a walk or whatever you need."

"No, I'm fine, really. I just wanted to see you for a minute, that's all. I can go, I—"

"You're not going anywhere," he said, tugging her back into him. He looked toward the ground, where Nicole had placed a case of sparkling rosé and a giant bag of grain-free tortilla chips she'd found in the back of her pantry. "Nobody's going to touch any of that shit, but come on. Come inside and meet my friends."

Nicole, legs a little wobbly again, nodded as Logan handed her his beer and held open the screen with his heel. Inside, he quickly tossed Nicole's provisions on his kitchen counter, then put his hand on the small of her back and ushered her into the living room.

It was unrecognizable.

Logan's dinner table was, somehow, sandwiched between his couch and a few dining chairs, with a couple of stacks of upside-down milk crates offering two additional seats. The table itself was a free-for-all, every inch of it covered in Twizzlers and tablets and scuffed-up three-ring binders teeming with printouts and paraphernalia. On the TV, a mirrored computer screen flashed a five-foot-wide, living, breathing map that positioned twitching-and-twirling avatars between thick, rustling forests; raging orange-red wildfires; and a charred, crumbling castle. Bathed in the map's glow, men in their midthirties to late forties swarmed the room, drinking and eating and sifting through their notes before beginning to settle into their seats.

"Hot, right?" Logan said, giving Nicole a squeeze. "Dave coded the whole thing himself. Took him a year. Did it on company time too, so don't take any pictures, okay? He could get sued."

"That's not going to be a problem. I would never document this."

Logan laughed, then walked Nicole toward the table, where a few of his friends had already glanced up and waved hello.

"Guys, this is Nicole." More nods and greetings. "Nicole, this is, well, everyone."

Nicole bit her lip, then smiled as Logan began to take her from seat to seat to meet each friend individually. He was good at this, of course: schmoozing. With every introduction, he offered up a silly anecdote or common ground for Nicole to work with.

"J.P.'s from Saint Louis too," Logan said as they arrived at friend number four. "J.P., Nicole's dad once did an emergency tooth filling for Albert Pujols."

"Before or after we burned his jersey?"

"Before," Nicole said. "When he signed with the Angels, he closed his practice for two days of mourning. Paid time off for everyone—bereavement. And when Kroenke moved the Rams to LA, I was already living here, and he wouldn't speak to me for, like, a month. He even removed me from our group text."

This continued for maybe ten more minutes. Nicole—now halfway through Logan's beer—worked the room. She shook hands, she talked about World War II, she teamed up with several of Logan's friends to make fun of Logan right to his delighted face. But by the time she'd arrived at the head of the table, where a handsome man in clear-rimmed glasses and an old Radiohead shirt stared into his laptop screen with narrowed lips and a tight jaw, time slowed down. The room, somehow, fell quiet. Nicole's noisy heart began to beat a bit too fast.

"Dave, this is—"

"Hey, Nicole," Dave said, pushing his laptop back a couple of inches. He smiled pleasantly, although the warmth never really reached his eyes. But Nicole couldn't read too much into that, right? After all, he seemed pretty busy Dungeon Mastering, whatever that meant.

"It's, um, it's so nice to finally meet you." The rest of Logan's friends had gotten back to their conversations, their IPAs, their pregame routines. "I've heard so much about you. Your map is very cool. I really like all the topography. My sister's a software engineer too. She works at Google . . . Anyway, I'm sorry to crash your game. I tried to bring snacks, but Logan told me they were too bougie and hid them in the kitchen."

"Well, the man does think Pop Rocks are a food group, so . . ."

Nicole chuckled. Dave, again, smiled politely, then twirled a mechanical pencil between his fingers and clicked its eraser a few times.

"You playing with Logan, then? Or just watching?"

"Nic's going to play herself," Logan said. "I want her to learn."

Dave rubbed his still-working jaw. He wore a wedding band, silver and slim. "We've got a lot to cover tonight, man. Probably no time to teach as we go. Why don't you guys just team up?"

"She's a quick study," Logan said, putting his arm around Nicole, who was suddenly very busy inspecting her bare feet. He gave her a little squeeze. "She's read a lot of medieval literature. If you get her tipsy enough, she'll recite the first twenty lines of *Beowulf*, for fun and for free."

"That's, unfortunately, completely true. I should not be overserved unless the crowd has been prescreened and only includes Seamus Heaney's ghost."

Dave smirked at both of them. "Just adorable," he said. "Come pick a player, then."

Logan nudged Nicole toward the table, then hunched over one of Dave's books and flipped through a few pages. "You should be one of these," he said, pointing at a horned creature with boobs and a giant tail. "They're called tieflings."

"Uh, why?"

"Because they're very hot. And extremely rude."

Nicole, cheeks burning, glared at him. Logan, eyes twinkling, lifted both shoulders. All while Dave, watching the two of them ogle each other like eighth graders at a school dance, shook his head and reached for his laptop. He assigned Nicole a periwinkle avatar and placed her on the outskirts of a dense forest just before the decrepit castle's broken gates.

"We play pretty fast," he said, handing her a blank character sheet and a massive textbook. "Most of us have kids, so we try to finish up by ten thirty or eleven if we can. Logan'll help you figure out the sheet before your first turn. The rest he can explain as we go. Try to decide what you want to do before we get to you. There's an element of groupthink here too, so whatever you do, make sure it serves the story."

Nicole nodded as Logan sat on the edge of the couch, then scooted over a few inches. She plopped next to him and sifted through her materials while Dave loosened the drawstring around a purple velvet pouch.

"All right, idiots." He dumped a handful of dice onto the table. "Let's play."

And so they did. The music hushed and the chatter dwindled

while Dave—between the occasional good-spirited interruption—recapped last week's events and began to set the stage for tonight's adventure. He spared no detail, even describing the dead ivy that covered the castle's withering walls as wooden cobwebs spun from splintered bark, gray as ash.

"The castle you've entered—despite warnings from good people along the way—groans ominously," Dave said, reaching for a few Sour Patch Kids. "Its stones, black; its skeleton, cold. And as its rotted doors slam shut behind you, a shiver runs up your spine. Then, as—"

"But I don't have a spine! Ian broke all my bones last week!"

"Sorry, man, but that weird half-prince dude told me I had to punish you because you looked at his sister's corpse wrong, and that he had a Gold Canary he would give me if I followed his orders, and . . ."

Once Dave was done painting the picture, and as Logan helped Nicole fine-tune her character within the oddly specific species and class-related constraints he seemed to know off the top of his head, the game really began. Every player took his turn—cross-referencing his skills and spells and strengths, then deciding whether to cower in a candlelit corridor, chase the glimmering green light that beamed from the window of the castle's tallest tower, or dare to force open the dungeon's nailed-shut, throbbing doors to fight whatever lurched below. After Nicole scrambled through her first turn with quite a bit of help from Logan, he pulled her closer and whispered in her ear.

"Don't worry about Dave," he said, drawing swirls on her wrist underneath the table. "He just takes a little time to warm up, that's all."

Nicole nodded, then flipped through the handbook some more while Logan leaned back, nursed his beer, and watched her study. The game carried on. Most of the guys headed downstairs to fight. Two of Logan's friends almost died, although José—who really was quite the healer—did everything he could to nurse them back to health. Logan, as his buddies dealt with the monster in the dungeon, raced to the top of the castle only to discover that those shimmering, verdant beams belonged not to the Orb of Dragonkind but the Orb of Slope Finding—a notoriously useless magic item that was, for all intents and purposes, a glorified picture hanging level. And Nicole—who had immediately researched that Golden Canary Figurine of Wondrous Power everyone kept talking about—spent her evening in the woods constructing a carriage with the remnants of an abandoned trailside pastry shop that, according to Logan, had been run by two beady-eyed orphans with nervous voices and a reputation for serving delicious, powerful pies that, one-third of the time, also killed you.

"What are you building that for?" he said, leaning into her.

She bumped his knee under the table. "I figure, if this place goes up in flames, we'd need a way through the forest. It's very dry, you know. Full of kindle—not a good situation, and Dave keeps reminding us, so feels like it could definitely happen. If things go south, I thought maybe we could get Ian to use his Canary and we could all Trojan horse it the hell out of here."

"You fucking nerd! You're a natural! You love it!"

"Screw you. I only like it very much."

By the time play had wound down—Miles in a coma, J.P. ransacking a vault, Glen bewitching that nine-eyed basement monster into a pony he could ride around the countryside until Dave told him otherwise—Nicole was a little tipsy, cozied up in Logan's lap, and waving her arms in the air, animatedly discussing C.S. Lewis with a few of Logan's lingering friends.

Near midnight, once the empty beer bottles had been cleared and the leftover boxes of pizza had been claimed and Logan's furniture was back where it belonged, the house was quiet. Nicole was standing in the kitchen, sealing shut half-eaten bags of potato chips with a giant roll of packing tape when Logan, who'd been taking out the trash, came in through the front door. He looked at her, and then, for a moment, his face fell. He said nothing. He just stood there until, eventually, his frown gave way to a weak and quiet smile. He walked toward her.

"I really like having you here," he said.

"At your *Game of Thrones* cosplay convention?"

Logan shook his head as Nicole settled into his arms. "Just . . . around. Just, I don't know."

She nodded, taking him in. Thirty-nine, and so charming, and so adorable, and so kind. And still, here he was, all alone. She was about to touch his face, ask him how this could've happened, how he, of all people, wound up the guy cleaning up by himself at the end of the night, and how many hearts he must've broken over the past twenty years, and who might've been dumb enough to have broken his, when he kissed her.

"You want to talk about what happened today?" he said.

Nicole shrugged, still in his embrace as he lifted her onto his counter. She shook off the residual daze of that little moment—of Logan, showing his hand. Showing her something that looked a whole lot like loneliness.

"Honestly," she said, shelving the thought. Filing the rest of it away for later. "There's nothing to talk about. Gabe's mom was horrible to me, that's all. I'm used to it. And it's over now. Really, I think I just needed to get out of my house and out of my head. So, thank you."

He nodded. "Hey, so listen. I think I have to go straight to New York on Monday night, after I'm done in Chicago."

"Really? I thought you were supposed to have a light month."

"Yeah, well, not anymore. I'll be there for at least a week. Quentin is making them run with his creative. My two-day visit to NorCal could've been an email that said no in giant red letters."

Nicole tightened her swinging legs around him. "You can't pitch this thing, though, right? It's a death wish, I thought."

"That's why I'm going," he said. "To make sure half our employees don't quit—and to make sure whatever campaign they throw together isn't strong enough to bring to that meeting."

"So you're flying all the way across the country to distract people?"

"Isn't that all you think I do, anyway?"

She laughed as he grabbed her hands.

"Why don't you come?" he said. "For a day or two, before you leave for Virginia? I can still do dinner—late, probably, but I've got to eat eventually. You can work during the day or do whatever you want. I've got a ton of miles."

"Next time, for sure," she said. "But if you're not coming back Monday, I think I'll just go to Val's early. She could really use the help around the house, and we have so much to do to get ready for our recording. Also, I'd need my own room. Because you won't fuck me. So there's that."

He raised an eyebrow, then pulled back the neck of her shirt to kiss her collarbone. When his mouth met her shoulder, he fingered the emerald strap of her bathing suit. His eyes went wide.

"What now?" she said.

"Put your shoes on," he said, scooping her off the counter. "We're going to end your bad day the best way I know how."

⁂

Logan Milgram jumped into the Pacific Ocean like it was a kiddie pool. That first shriek, pure joy.

"Speyer! Get in here!"

"No way!" she said, laughing, standing a few feet back from the shoreline. She dug her toes into the cool, soft sand as Logan dove under another crashing wave. When he emerged, he was maybe twenty feet out, bobbing up and down as the moonlight glimmered off the ocean's surface, noisy and navy and white-capped. His hair was soaked. His shoulders, perfect.

"Come on!" he said. "Once you get used to it, it'll feel amazing, I promise!"

"I've lived here for nine years, asshole! The Pacific has never been pleasant, not even once! Do not lie to me!"

He paddled halfway toward her, head above water, then stood up and pushed his sopping wet hair out of his eyes and over his forehead, which . . . Mari was right all along, wasn't she? He really was summer camp hot, just on a twenty-five-year delay.

"Let me get this straight," he said. "You'll risk getting us caught in a blizzard in New York City for no reason, but you won't go swimming with me? In Los Angeles? In August?"

"Sounds about right," Nicole said as she plopped onto one of the towels Logan had grabbed from his downstairs bathroom before they darted out the door. He'd also pulled on a pair of swim trunks that'd been hang-drying on his balcony since at least last weekend, when they picked this thing back up again.

"But I'm lonely!" he said.

"There are sharks!" she said.

Logan disappeared underwater for a bit. When he came up, he dramatically gasped for air. "Just checked!" Another ridiculous gasp. "No sharks!"

Nicole laughed, rising to her feet. She took a few tiny steps closer to him and let her toes skim the cool, silky shoreline. When a wave crashed up to her ankles, ice flew through her body, sending goose bumps across her shivering skin.

"Holy shit! It's so cold! It's even worse than I remembered!"

Logan scoffed, then paddled toward her, eyes wide. At once, she leaped backward, already squealing as he slunk through the ocean's shallowest edge on his hands and knees.

"Don't you fucking dare, Logan! Don't even touch me. I swear to god!"

"Oh, shut up," he said, standing now, and striding toward her. Water dripped down his body in clear, cold drops Nicole could taste from three or four feet away. "We both know you're going in."

And though she continued to protest, her every wail was in vain because Logan was already peeling off her shirt, yanking down her shorts, and wrapping his freezing arms around her thrashing body as she laughed and cursed and cried out his name. And then, after a brief pause to kiss her—his cold lips on her warm tongue—he carried her into the ocean like a rolled-up carpet, his every step bringing her that much closer to the Pacific's loud, icy surface.

"Logan! I hate it, I—"

"Then I'm sorry for what I'm about to do," he said, twisting her body in one swift motion until she was standing waist-deep in the freezing ocean, screaming bloody murder. Her skin prickled and her veins ached.

"Logan! Fuck!" She threw her arms around her chest. "It's horrible!"

He smiled, then pulled her under his arm and peered out at the sea. "Big one's coming. Hold your breath, close your eyes, and dive under it."

"Not happening."

He splashed her. She splashed him back. Also, yelled.

"It's not actually big," he said. "Maybe three feet. Just try it, okay? Trust me."

Nicole was about to protest—about to race back to the sand and steal both their towels and bundle herself up—when she decided that, at the very least, she could do this one silly thing. That, at the very least, she could shut her mouth and close her eyes and try to care a little less about the dumb, rigid rules that had never managed to keep her safe, anyway.

And so she did. She watched and she waited and she held her breath and she closed her eyes and she heard the wave roll itself back and roar itself forward and when it came for her, rough and loud and unstoppable, she simply slipped beneath it, and the whole world warped into a quiet, soft, dizzying nothingness—an endless sea of deep, wavy echoes that swirled from miles below the surface, flooding her floating limbs and her wild lungs and her wide open wounds. And for those ten-or-so fleeting, infinite seconds, she did not think or wonder or worry. She did not care or plan or panic.

She was—for the first time, maybe ever—weightless. And when she came up for air, at least for a little while longer, she stayed that way.

"How do you feel?" Logan said, pushing the hair out of her eyes as she hooked her legs around his waist. Her teeth, chattering. Her heart, racing. Every screaming inch of her, alive.

"Brand-new."

He smiled, then turned them so she was facing the shoreline.

God, it was beautiful, wasn't it? Los Angeles and its flickering, crowded hills—dense and old and new, sloping down toward an empty shore where the sand was cool and gray and the sky stretched on forever, a deep, dusty indigo dotted with twinkling stars. The moon, nearly full, hanging low and bright, illuminating what the city lights could not—hushed fishing piers, unmanned lifeguard stations, and this little slice of the California coast that, just for tonight, belonged only to them. How had she missed it? How had it taken her so long to love this stupid town?

"Logan?" she said.

He looked right at her. "Yeah?"

"What are we doing?"

He traced her cheekbone, then pulled her closer.

"Exactly what you think we're doing."

Nicole nodded and took a deep breath.

And then—still weightless—she kissed him.

42

Norfolk, Virginia

Nicole and Valerie didn't waste any time.

Every waking minute the boys were at school or asleep or lying on the living room floor, FaceTiming their father, the two women were hard at work. They locked down guests, they mapped out their next ten episodes, they pored over each other's notes from the week before. They scoured the comments sections of mom groups and message boards and magazines with similar missions to see what those mediums were getting right and where they were falling short. They identified look-alike audiences they could target across every platform imaginable. They took an hour-long call with Mari, who—from an airport lounge in Miami, where she'd just closed a deal with a start-up that sent very sexily packaged espresso pods to your door for less than a dollar a day—gave them a crash course in securing partnerships with D-list celebrities, momfluencers, and women-owned brands with money to burn and awareness to build. They wrote intros and outros. They designed a new logo. They begged Paige to debug the very glitchy contact form on their website on three separate occasions.

And then, on Friday morning, they recorded. They sat on the carpeted floor of Valerie's perfectly insulated walk-in closet—where smooshed maxi dresses and maternity overalls dangled from mismatched hangers like curtains—as Nicole's fingers pressed down on her trackpad in a long, careful click.

"What was your first memory of your mother?" Nicole said.

"I was four," Valerie said with a soft, distant chuckle. She tilted her head just a little, her gaze unfocused and her smile, slight. "I broke my wrist at school—it was Bike Day. She had to come and pick me up early. At first, I went back to my classroom with everyone else, but I wouldn't stop crying, so they brought me to the back office and gave me an extra Popsicle and a bag of ice, and then, finally, they called her."

Nicole raised an eyebrow, then held up her index finger. They'd practiced that—quietly signaling each other when to create little, conversational breaks in their stories. Nicole had assured Valerie that as their rapport grew stronger, they'd learn to anticipate the beats in their banter. After a week of nonstop practice, they were nearly there—but for now, the little gestures still helped.

"Wait, I'm sorry, but that's the most nineties thing I've ever heard. That your preschool just let you wander around all day with a dangling arm."

Valerie laughed into her microphone.

It was a real one: deep and warm and perfect.

"I know, right? And of course, the minute she got there, she knew it was broken. She drove me to the pediatrician and I got a pink cast and a sling and then we made Rice Krispies Treats. She let me stir the bowl with my good hand while my dad was still at work. We must have eaten half of it straight from the pot, just standing in the kitchen. I don't remember my arm even hurting now. Not after she came and got me, anyway. I just remember melting margarine, you know? Being too full for dinner. Being really, really happy."

Nicole smiled. She'd never heard this story before. They hadn't rehearsed this. "How do you feel about that day now, when you think back to it? Now that you're a mom? Now that . . . now that she's gone?"

Valerie closed her eyes for a moment.

"It's weird," she said, "because, looking back, I think she was already dying. She was so, so sick when they found the cancer. It was already everywhere. That was only a few years later too, so I just believe that. That it was already too late." Valerie dried her eyes with the hem of her tank top. Her stomach, all of a sudden, had curved. It hadn't been there yesterday. "But I don't think it would have changed a thing, even if she'd known. She was all in until the minute she couldn't be. That's how I remember her."

Something sharp cut through Nicole's ribs, then rose through her voice like an ache. "Do you know how amazing that is? To have someone in your life who's truly all in?"

"I do," Valerie said. "And sometimes, it almost makes me mad. Because I'm not as patient or kind or present as she was. And because sometimes it feels like, since my job is to stay home with the kids, I don't get to have bad days. Because she never did, you know? She was always happy. My husband says I'm just not remembering it right, because it's not actually possible that she was always on like that. Rose-colored glasses or something. But I swear, he's wrong. I swear, she was perfect. I think that's the way God planned it."

Nicole was quiet for a few seconds.

"What do you mean by that?"

"I know it sounds silly. But sometimes, I think maybe she knew. Maybe that's the real reason I was an only child. Maybe it was only supposed to be us. Maybe that's why she loved on me so hard.

Because she knew we didn't have forever. That we were only going to have each other for a little while."

∽

It was nearly midnight on Monday when Nicole—drained but buzzing from putting their first episode out into the world—crawled underneath the covers of Valerie's guest bed, pulled a floral print throw pillow between her knees, and grabbed her book off the nightstand.

Outside, Virginia was dark and still. Crickets chirped. Dew gathered on the windowpanes. A few garden lights flickered, revealing little hints of bluegrass, velvety and overgrown. Nicole was already twenty pages into a comfort reread of *Emma* when her phone dinged. She reached for it, wondering what absurd factoid or filthy one-liner Logan was going to open their chat with tonight.

It was . . . a picture of a hot dog?

Her eyes rolled as she flung back a response.

> Mari warned me that guys like to send these sometimes. Told me I should be prepared.

A bubble danced next to Logan's name.

> So you're saying I'm your first?

> Hot.

She laughed, turning onto her stomach and kicking her feet into the air. She only had another night here—tomorrow morning was the ultrasound, and then she'd take an eight p.m. flight out of Norfolk and head home.

> Please. You won't even show me your bedroom. Starting to think that's where you keep the bodies. That you're just trying to change the pH levels of my blood with stale Oreos or something before you put my head in a jar.

A second later, Nicole's phone rang.

"Yes?"

"The bodies are in the Tar Pits. I was clear with you about that from the start."

Nicole rolled over. "You're so weird."

"You are too," he said. "You know that, right?"

"It has been brought to my attention lately, yes," she said, imagining the smirk stretching across his face. In the background, the city clamored. He'd already told her he was taking his team out for sorry-you-had-to-work-seven-days-straight-to-cobble-together-a-pitch-I-never-intended-to-use drinks this evening, probably somewhere downtown. "Anyway, how was your last night? How's New York?"

"Oh, you know," he said as a horn honked, as tires screeched. "Hot. Dirty. Full of trash. But magical, for sure. Greatest city in the world. There's something in the water. Something in the air. If you can make it here, you can make it any—"

"Shut up. You know it's my favorite."

"I know," he said, his voice, suddenly, not so playful. His voice, suddenly, thick. "I'm on Jane Street, Nicole. I remember."

43

New York City

January, Two Years Ago

"You first," Logan said, nodding Nicole through the office building's revolving doors. She thanked him, then stepped outside where, at once, New York was ice on her nose, lips, and eyes.

The six o'clock sky was charcoal: a stretch of dark, damp clouds that cloaked Midtown's skyscrapers and streetlights in a low, thick haze. Over the past few hours, a winter storm had brewed over Manhattan, sending the city into a frenzy of honking horns on swollen avenues and rushing coats on cold, cracked concrete. Neon dulled and delis shuttered as steam slipped through the rusted grates of shaking, shimmering sidewalks, where too-full subway cars screeched below.

"So," he said, fumbling for his gloves. They were headed east on Fortieth Street, buttoning their coats and tying their scarves. "You doing anything fun tonight?"

"I'm pretty tired. I'll probably just clean up the new vendor list back at the hotel."

Logan raised an eyebrow. "On your thirtieth birthday?"

"How'd you know it was my birthday?"

"Oh, just, Mari mentioned it to me fifteen times during our four o'clock sync, that's all."

Nicole chuckled, her breath visible as they stopped at Fifth

Avenue's crowded curb. Strangers swarmed around them, bumping, nudging, desperate to get home.

"You don't have any friends out here from college or anything like that?" he said.

"Not really. We all kind of fell out of touch."

Logan rubbed his throat.

The walk sign turned white.

"You know what?" he said as they began crossing the street. He pulled his scarf—Watch plaid, navy and green and black—tighter around his neck. His cheeks were pink and his peacoat, gray. "We should do something. Dinner, a drink, anything you want. I've got Quentin's credit card. If we invite a client, we can go spend eight hundred dollars on raw fish sliced within ten yards of a disgraced celebrity chef. Mari's favorite thing to do when we're out here."

Nicole laughed, then dug her hands into her pockets. She hadn't had much fun these past couple of months. Since the miscarriage, everything had been sad and flat and all wrong. But this training trip—a last-minute thing for Nicole, whose boss had to put out a fire in LA—had given her a new energy. Something to do besides fall apart over a baby that'd been gone since autumn.

She could totally go to dinner, right? After all, that was what people did on business trips. Worked, then got something to eat. It'd be weird not to go. Besides, she and Logan were friends. Things had been different, sure, since September in that copy room, since November in that hallway, but they were still colleagues—still friends. And work friends ate work dinners on work trips.

"Actually, sure," Nicole said. "Doing something sounds kind of nice."

Logan, at once, yanked off a glove and began swiping through his phone. "Was that a yes on the shark-tasting menu? Because there's a ton of tables. Guess all the rich people here are afraid of a few feet of snow."

Nicole smiled. "Would you want to maybe just go for a walk or something?"

"It's"—he gestured broadly—"not exactly frolicking weather, Speyer."

"I know," she said. "But I love New York like this, right before that first big snow. It gets so quiet. It gets so still." She looked up at him. "Do I sound totally unhinged?"

"It's more . . . insufferable blizzard propagandist, if anything. But I'll allow it."

Nicole rolled her eyes and then, without bothering to make a plan, the two of them walked and talked and zigzagged south through Manhattan's narrowing streets as the city swirled by. They sipped crappy hot chocolates from an overpriced bodega near the Empire State Building, then barely noticed as Thirty-Second Street gave way to the Flatiron, to Union Square, and then to the Village—to the New York Nicole had always known. They discussed the unequivocally superior snack selection in the new office and the pros and cons of speculoos cookies and how strange it was to live in a place where it never, ever snowed. And then, at Thirteenth Street, Nicole's feet turned right.

It was instinct, really. It just happened.

"I used to live around here," she said as they wandered past the empty wine bars, bistros, and bookshops that lined the familiar sidewalks of her old walk home. By now, downtown was quiet, but for the occasional taxi, a few thirtysomethings taking tiny dogs in teeny coats on hurried walks, and a handful of doormen standing in warm yellow lobbies, arms crossed over their tired bodies as they watched the city slow from double-paned doors.

"In college?" he said. "Kind of fancy for a dorm."

"Oh, no. For a year, before I moved." She took a few more steps, her feet guiding her down Eighth Avenue. "There was this little hot dog cart, it's always open, on the corner of—"

"Jane Street."

Nicole itched her neck. "You know it? Did you live around here? How have we never talked about this?"

"Nope," he said. "I lived in StuyTown, as is required of all thirty-year-old men who are too lazy to come to New York and find an apartment themselves. I was only here, like, eight months—April or May to right before Christmas. That was six years ago now. Quentin poached me before I even understood the subway system. But my office was right by here, in Chelsea."

"Oh, wow," she said. "I left that June. We must've just missed each other."

"Guess so."

They walked in silence for another minute. They both knew the way. When they found the cart—there it was, like nothing had ever changed—they ordered a few hot dogs and settled onto someone else's stoop while snow began to fall in thick, soft flakes. She sat a step in front of him and a couple of feet to his left, beneath an awning that kept their bent bodies dry. The brownstone's glistening lobby, their backlight.

"So," he said, opening a bag of chips, "you one of those girls who makes liking New York their entire personality?"

"First of all, rude. Second of all, yes."

Logan snickered, then offered her a chip. She snatched the

whole bag and began unwrapping the foil around her dinner. The same one she'd shared with Gabe a hundred times, back when he'd spend his entire Saturday roaming around a botanical garden. Back when he'd ask her to final-eye his projects for school. Back when he'd happily salt the pasta water at the silly dinner parties her friends would throw in their shitty apartments. Back when he was just another fancy little fish in a New York–sized pond.

"What'd you love about it?" he said.

"I don't know. I just always have. I always wanted to move here. And then, when I did, it was even better than I'd imagined. It was so packed and crowded and gross and expensive, and still, I couldn't get enough of it. If I wanted to be energized, I stepped outside. If I wanted to be alone, I closed my door. But no matter what, I could always stare out the window and put my hand on the glass and take it all in. It always felt like a living, breathing thing to me." She looked over at him and cringed. "Sorry, does that make any sense? Do I sound totally nuts again?"

He nodded, smiling wryly. Nicole shook her head, cheeks warm.

"Why'd you leave, then?" he said. "Doesn't sound like you got tired of it."

"Gabe's from Manhattan Beach."

"Oh, right," he said. "You guys met here?"

Gabe had told Logan as much that night at the agency's holiday party, but that was over a year ago now. He must've not remembered.

"Yeah," she said. "And he had this really good job lined up in LA after he was done at Columbia, the kind you don't turn down. And I never really got the job I wanted here, so I was working in advertising, and he had this big career ahead of him and that was kind of that. Been in California ever since."

"You like it?"

"LA?" Nicole laughed as she reached for a napkin. "Not one bit."

Logan gave her a quick raise of his brow. Nicole cringed again.

"God," she said, "when I say it out loud, it sounds a little pathetic, doesn't it?"

"Oh, come on. Undesirable relocation is a rite of passage. We all do dumb shit for love. Believe me, I'd know. I almost moved to Milwaukee for a girl."

"Milwaukee? Seriously? It's like a colder, smaller Saint Louis, except everyone's obsessed with cheese."

"Tell me about it," he said. "But when you know, you know. And there's nothing stupid about going after exactly what you want."

Nicole wrinkled her nose. And then she handed him back his half-finished bag of chips and decided not to ask any follow-up questions about the mystery woman in Wisconsin who, from the sound of his voice, had almost certainly broken his heart.

"Anyway," he said. "What was the job you wanted?"

"Publishing. I wanted to edit books."

"You'd be good at that."

She yanked a loose thread from the sleeve of her coat. "Yeah, well, maybe in some other life."

"Right," Logan said, squishing a ketchup-sodden foil wrapper into his fist, then chucking it into an overflowing trash can a few yards away. He didn't miss. "Maybe in some other life."

They sat quietly for a few minutes.

Logan cracked open his soda.

Nicole scrolled through her phone.

Snow had blanketed the empty street.

"Hey, I just . . ." He fiddled with the tab on his can. "I've been meaning to ask you for a while now, if you're doing okay? With, you know, with everything? With what happened?"

Nicole found another loose thread to yank at.

What was she going to tell him? The truth? That some therapist with a pixie cut and black ballet flats and a broken Keurig in her waiting room had told Nicole she'd be her old self again in six weeks, but it had been ten, and every day was worse than the one before? That Gabe—fresh off a promotion—was working more than ever? Traveling twice as much? Having dinner with Kyle on the Westside three or four nights a week now? Or golfing, or in Vegas, or wherever else his awful boss told him to be at any given moment? That whenever Gabe actually managed to make it home before Nicole fell asleep, she'd walk around the house in a daze and he'd glance up from his laptop or his newspaper or his phone and scrunch his eyes and grit his teeth and say, "It'll happen, baby," or just click his tongue and look away?

What was she going to say? That the puppymoon had worn off? That the cutest, derpiest little fuzzbutt money could buy hadn't managed to fill the massive hole in her heart? That it wasn't even fun anymore, fucking the most beautiful man she'd ever seen? That she'd just lie there and stare at the ceiling and try not to cry while her gorgeous, distant husband came inside her like she was a task on a to-do list? That they had nothing in common anymore? That they'd been trying for thirteen months and she wasn't anything close to pregnant? That she was starting to panic? That the pathology from her D&C had revealed she'd been carrying a healthy baby boy? That even though her doctor had assured her not every miscarriage could be explained, Nicole knew, deep down, that something wasn't quite right inside her body, but nobody would listen?

That nobody believed her? That she felt like she was going crazy? That she'd never, ever felt this alone?

No, of course not.

She wasn't going to tell him—or anyone—any of that.

Not now. Not ever.

And so, instead, she said, "I'm fine."

Logan nodded, smiling weakly. But when he looked at her, he looked for a half second too long. Nicole's stomach ached.

He didn't believe her, did he? He could tell she was lying. And in that moment, Nicole knew it. That he saw her. That she could've told him the truth. That he would have listened. That he would have, somehow, understood.

But she couldn't do it. She couldn't say a single word.

He pressed a fist to his closed lips, then rose to his feet.

"All right, you." He pointed to a diner across the street. Its lights, glowing. Its empty booths, beckoning. "Come on, get up. You're not off the hook quite yet. This night isn't finished until I've sung you 'Happy Birthday' at the top of my lungs over a giant piece of cake that is, best-case scenario, three weeks old."

Nicole, now carefully adding her trash to the top of the too-full bin, chuckled as Logan darted backward into a snow-dusted Eighth Avenue without bothering to look both ways.

"Come on, Missouri! Live a little! Cross the street!"

"What do you think I'm doing?" she said as the glowing red hand of the crosslight kept the soles of her shoes glued to the sidewalk. Logan, meanwhile, stood in the middle of the intersection with his eyes bright and his scarf tight and his arms outstretched wide. Flurries swirled around him. He was grinning like an idiot. He kind of looked like a snowman.

"Being a bit uptight! To be honest!"

"People die like this!" she said, arms folded across her chest, but that was before she'd dropped them. That was before she'd skipped across the street, laughing; her laptop bag, banging against her hip as her suddenly thoughtless feet began to leave a second set of footprints—a second set of impossible divots—in the soft white snow.

They ducked through the diner's ding-a-linging doors, then huddled into a booth in the back of the restaurant—burnt hash browns, giant menus, maroon curtains faded from fifty years of sky-high rent—and inched out of their wet coats and scarves and hats. Outside, from the picture window that framed their table, snow swirled like confetti, floating every which way before softly settling onto the silent street.

"Well, what'll it be?" he said as Nicole considered the suspiciously well-stocked pastry case to her left for the third time. He'd already warned their weary-eyed server that they had a birthday girl on their hands—that she was a bit of an overoptimizer, that she wasn't usually his problem and tonight was a special treat.

"Carrot, please."

Logan, snickering, shook his head. "There we go. I knew you weren't perfect."

"What?"

"I'm kidding," he said, dumping a splash of creamer into his coffee as the now-smirking server disappeared into the kitchen. "So, tell me, what are your real plans for your birthday, once we get home? Anything good?"

Nicole bit her lip. "I'm not going home. Gabe's supposed to meet me."

"In New York?"

"At JFK," she said. "Tomorrow night, after work, assuming all the flights aren't canceled. We're going to Paris."

He tapped his fingers on the table. "You ever been?"

"Yeah, actually. We kind of go every year for my birthday."

Logan chuckled, pushing his mug around the laminate. "I think I picked the wrong career," he said. "Maybe that's my problem. Can't take girls to Paris enough."

Nicole tsked, and then the cake came—candle and all—and Logan sang as loud as he could and a couple of servers joined in and Nicole just sat there, cheeks burning as the flame flickered and the snow fluttered and her twenties compressed into a single, finished file.

"Make a wish," he said.

Nicole looked up at him. "I can't think of anything."

And she couldn't. Not tonight, anyway. Of course, there was the obvious stuff—getting a promotion, getting things back on track with Gabe, getting pregnant as soon as possible. But those weren't the kinds of things you were supposed to wish for. They were too ordinary. They were too tangible. And so Nicole, wishless, blew out the candles with her mind blank and dug into her very stale birthday cake while Logan stole at least a dozen deeply pained, overly dramatic forkfuls and ranked Australia's most common marsupials from sunniest disposition to least. Koalas, it turned out, weren't just remarkably frisky; they were rude little creatures too.

"How do you remember all this shit?"

"My brain's weird," he said. "Also, I majored in history. And—please don't google this, okay?—but I was a bit of a celebrity on the national debate circuit in high school. Point is, I've ingested way too much information, and now my mind is full of trash. But I'm very good at *Trivial Pursuit*, and it paid for college, so . . ."

"I am so totally googling you," she said, rescuing a smear of frosting from their plate and then licking her fork. "Did you like it, by the way? Michigan?"

"Loved it. Best four years of my life. Cold as shit, though. Why?"

"My little brother just got into business school there. I think he's going to go."

"Give him my number," he said. "I know a bunch of people in Ann Arbor. And I have a few friends who got MBAs there, too—mostly living in Chicago now. We all still go back once or twice a year for football games and that sort of stuff."

Nicole nodded. Logan smiled. And then, coffees refilled, they talked for another hour—nearly two. About Saint Louis and Seattle and the careers they'd wanted and the cities they'd visited and the million reasons why, according to Logan, carrots and walnuts and raisins did not belong in desserts, despite the fact that he'd polished off her slice of cake nearly all on his own and asked Nicole on four separate occasions whether she'd like some more. And then, when it was too late to continue, when Nicole's stomach ached from laughing and Logan's voice was hoarse from never not talking and snow had piled onto the street by the foot and there wasn't another soul around, they called it a night. Logan settled the check and the diner doors ding-a-linged again and they stepped back into the blizzard and New York was a snow globe—white and slow and small enough to hold in the palms of their hands—and Logan managed to hail a cab and they sat in the back seat and Nicole wasn't sure why, but she kind of wanted to cry.

They were quiet.

They stepped out of the taxi and into the hotel lobby, teeth chattering, noses pink. They hurried into the elevator, its doors so quick to open, so slow to close.

"What floor?" Logan said as Nicole stood in the back of the car, digging her freezing fingers into the pockets of her coat. Her heart was racing. Why was her heart racing?

"Seven, please."

Logan gulped, then pressed the button.

"Me too," he said.

Nicole nodded. Snow was melting on her shoes. There was a new scuff on her workbag. The elevator's permit would need to be renewed next month. The numbers on the tiny black screen changed from five to six to, finally, seven.

The doors slid open.

Nicole exhaled.

Logan—eyes ahead—waved her through, then walked a few steps behind her down the hall. The fifty feet to her room were an eternity, enough time to count every carpet fiber and wall sconce and nanosecond that slogged by. But eventually, they were standing outside her door.

"This is me," she said.

"This is you," he said.

She pressed her lips together, then reached for her key, almost expecting it to give her trouble, to make her try a dozen times before it worked, but it was effortless. One quick dip, and the light flickered green. She swallowed, then pushed the door ajar.

"Well, good night," she said. "Thanks again for the junk food."

"Least I could do. Nothing worse than a work birthday."

"It's actually the most fun I've had in months."

He closed his eyes for a moment, then smiled. "Good, then. I'm glad we did it."

Nicole nodded, and then, just when she'd begun to turn away and step into her cold, clean room, she twisted around to face him. Her pulse, pounding. Her shoulder blades, hard against the cracked-opened door.

"There's nothing wrong with you," she said. "Any girl would be lucky to have you. Just for the record or whatever. You should know that. You shouldn't change a thing."

Logan stared at her, frozen. And then, a second later, he smirked. He leaned against her doorframe, shook his head, and ran his fingers through his hair.

"Can you tell all your hot friends that?"

Nicole laughed.

He did too.

And something inside her—was it her chest? her ribs?—began to tug, began to ache.

She inhaled.

He did too.

He bit his lip.

She did too.

She leaned in an inch.

She didn't know why. It just happened.

But then, he did too.

His hands were wrapped around her doorframe. They were tense. They were clenched. They were glued to the edges.

And there it was—that same look. Clearer than anything she'd ever seen, ever before. Strange and dense and unmistakable. She studied him. His warm brown eyes, the freckles on the bridge of his nose, the way his lips settled across his face so effortlessly. How relaxed and easy and alive he seemed. How good it felt when she made him laugh. How quiet and simple and small the whole world was when they were alone. When it was just the two of them.

"Logan, I—"

"It's, um, it's really late." He peeled back his hands and looked at her again. This time, differently. This time, in the real world. "I'll see you in the morning. Happy birthday."

When he walked away, his knuckles were wrung around the nape of his neck, and his head was tipped to the ceiling. She could hear him exhale.

He didn't look back.

He didn't turn around to see Nicole stand there and watch him go.

44

Persuasion

"Nicole?" Logan was frozen at the top of his stoop. His workbag, dangling from his shoulder. His keys, jangling in his hand. His back foot, in midair. It was Tuesday evening in Los Angeles. "What are you doing here? I thought your flight didn't get in until—"

She kissed him.

She grabbed him by the jaw and she kissed him so hard his head jerked back and his breath hitched and his hands dropped to his sides, then softly, steadily began to float up her burning, billowing ribs.

"I'm ready," she said, blood roaring through her body, heart hammering through her throat. Tugging on the neck of his shirt, she inched them backward until she was flush against his front door, then pressed her shaking hands onto his heaving chest and pushed her forehead against his. Sunset whirled around them. "I don't want to wait another second. I don't—"

"Okay," he said.

"Okay?" Nicole stared at him. Her pulse, now, a mallet. She had expected pushback. She had expected a discussion. She had expected, at the very least, that he'd pour her an extremely stiff drink. "Really? Now? Like, right now?"

"Yeah," he said, taking a deep breath, then turning his keys in the door, locking it behind them, and carrying her upstairs and into his bedroom. With one hand, he flicked on a floor lamp, then set her down a few feet from the edge of his unmade bed and kissed her again. The walls spun. "Right now."

She swallowed, nodding, trying to steady herself, trying to see through the haze. Speechless, she took in what she could of the place in blurry, dimly lit bits and pieces—a basket of unfolded laundry here, an ant farm perched atop a stack of magazines there—while he shoved a half-opened suitcase into his closet, smoothed out his rumpled jersey sheets, then kicked whatever else remained directly underneath his bed. Smirking, he slid off his sneakers and looped his arms around her neck.

"Sorry about the mess," he said. "I wasn't expecting you up here until this weekend. I would've unpacked. I would've made the bed."

"No, it's . . . it's perfect," she said. "I like it up here. I like all your clutter. It suits you."

He laughed onto her neck; his lips, wet. His fingers, grazing the edges of her shirtdress—a gauzy, linen little thing already unbuttoned to her sternum—right where its soft, short hem skimmed her thighs. He began working the fabric up her hips ever so slightly, ever so slowly, ever so lightly, until Nicole's throat was hoarse and his fingertips were feathers on her tingling skin. Her mouth moistened and her stomach curled.

"Nicole," he said, her lips parting at the crack of his voice, at the sound of her name. A few streaks of dripping pink sky slipped through the drawn slats of his blinds. He pushed back her collar with his nose, then took slow, soft bites of the skin along her shoulder while his hands crawled higher and higher up her legs. "Every single time you have said my name or laughed at my dumb jokes or looked my way, I have wanted you. I have wanted this."

Nicole closed her eyes. He kissed her throat, her neck, her ear. He grazed her hip bones with his thumbs. He whispered all the ways he'd been dreaming of her into the waves of her hair.

"I have never wanted anyone," he said, "the way I want you."

"Me neither," she said between short, nothing little breaths. His tongue was tracing her wrist, and her fingers were skimming the curve of his jaw as he lifted her against him. Their hips met. Nicole inhaled. Logan let out a long, low groan, then pulled her closer. Blood rushed between her legs, leaving the rest of her lightheaded. "This whole summer. That first night."

"You don't know," he said, her fingers in his mouth; her hips, arching into his hands, clinging to him. Already, she was a magnet, shaking but sure. "You don't know what you do to me. When I finally kissed you, you could never understand . . ."

"I could," she said. "I think I could."

He shook his head, then took a few steps back toward his bed—a bit of a mess, but soft-looking and clean and so, so him. With steady hands, he lifted his shirt over his stomach, past his shoulders, and above his head until it was off and he was standing there, staring at her. His torso, tensing then releasing as a hot, wet ache flooded Nicole's already-boiling bloodstream. She tried to breathe.

"Come here," he said.

Nicole nodded, taking one, two, three silent tiptoes toward him. He stepped out of his jeans, then got onto his knees, pressed his mouth onto her ankle and began to kiss her, began to—slowly, so slowly—drag his warm, soft lips up her shins, her knees, her quads. He didn't miss an inch, moving from leg to leg, stopping to study her, to touch her, to tell her what he'd been dying to do to her.

She steadied her fists on his shoulders, kneading out the knots beneath his skin while his mouth moved higher and higher up her thighs and his forehead pushed her dress farther and farther up her hips. As he approached the delicate hem of her underwear, his kisses grew slower, sloppier, more sure. And the second his tongue slid over the stitching—slid onto her—she threw her knuckles into her mouth and let out a high, quick gasp.

"This okay?" he said, his hands wrapped around her ass, her dress hiked up around her waist, his mouth beginning to draw warm, slick circles over the open lacework of her nothing little thong—ivory and flimsy and, by this point, dripping wet.

"Yeah," she said. Her hands were twisted into his hair and her eyes were closed. "Just . . . yeah. Really good."

He let out a focused, satisfied groan, then kissed her again and again and again—an endless stretch of damp, deliberate mouthfuls that left her heart racing and her body bracing. And just when she'd finally dropped her shoulders and steadied her breathing, he slipped his tongue beneath the seam and began to tease her with long, soft swirls so close her eyes rolled to the back of her head. She tugged his hair by the fistful and moaned.

Logan—forehead, damp; eyes, wide—glanced up and grinned. And when he met her gaze, when he took in her burning cheeks and her shaking head and her sheepish glare, he simply floated his free hand up to hers, gave her a little squeeze, and disappeared back between her legs.

Nicole could barely breathe. Already, she was beginning to lose it. And when she let out her loudest gasp yet, Logan responded with a low, muffled growl, then grabbed the lace that lay on her heaving hips with his parted lips and slowly worked the fabric down her trembling thighs with nothing but his teeth and his tongue.

"You're still shaking," he said, his mouth on her calf, her thong dropped around her ankles.

"I'm just really nervous . . ."

He stood up and kissed her. "Do you want me to slow down? Do you want me to stop?"

"No, not at all. I just . . ." She took a deep breath. "There's nobody else, right?"

He pulled her tighter into his arms. "There's nobody else. You know that."

She nodded.

"This summer, Nicole. I had this whole plan. I wanted to change everything. I had this whole plan, and then . . ." His mouth was on her neck, and he was swollen against her dress. Nicole moved closer, dropping her hands to his waist and then beginning to trace him over the thin cotton of his boxers. His eyes broadened and his bottom lip twitched.

"And then?" she said.

"And then you showed up at my door," he said, easing her onto the edge of his bed, where he stood between her knees, harder than ever. "And everything changed."

She nodded, kissing his stomach as he massaged the nape of her neck. Her tongue, finding his waistband, then exploring the skin beneath it, soft and slow.

"That night," he said, his chest, rising and falling. She slid her underwear off the tops of her feet with her toes and stared at him, mouth wet. He cupped her face. "You turned my whole world upside down."

She muttered, then inched the elastic down his hips until he was throbbing in the palms of her hands, until he was in her mouth, until he'd closed his eyes and slid his fingers between her lips and let out a low, perfect groan.

"Holy shit," he said, over and over as she teased him, toyed with him, tasted him. He glided his hands up her thighs, softly nudging her hips back against his bed while she shook her head, fought him forward, and worked him harder. He exhaled again—a delightfully thick, head-rolling, neck-cracking release—then finally, after a few more minutes of letting her have her way, pulled himself back.

"Please," she said. "Let me—"

"Lay down," he said.

She lowered herself onto the mattress. He rolled back his shoulders, then climbed on top of her and kissed her. His hands began to unbutton her dress. His mouth began to slide down her sternum. Nicole, thoughts twisted and tongue tied, couldn't do a thing but reach for him as he peeled back the frilled edges of her bralette and traced the curves of her breasts with his tongue. He cradled her head with his left hand while his right skirted down her barely fastened dress, along the goose-bumped skin of her stomach, and then—slowly, carefully, curiously—between her tensing thighs.

"I've been dying to touch you," he said. "Every night, I think about this. About you. About taking my time. How you'll feel. How you'll sound."

Nicole whimpered, nodding. He licked his lips, kissed her neck, and then—like it was the most delicate, deliberate task he'd ever taken on—slipped a single finger alongside her and watched with irises wide as her eyes softened and her breathing slowed and her fingers tightened into clutched fists. She grabbed his pillow, bit into it, and moaned. It smelled just like him—simple and good; like August, like drugstore shampoo, like nothing fancy.

"This okay?"

"It's . . . yeah. Yes."

He started slow. Gentle, soft strokes that grew and built and bent to her, that explored her everywhere. And as her hips continued to rock and rise—as they synced to his touch and curved to his hands—he worked his mouth down her stirring skin, from her collarbone to her ribs to the slopes of her stomach, and then finally, to high between her legs, where another slew of impossibly light kisses sent Nicole's boiling body rolling away from him and onto her side, knees closed.

"Logan!"

"Where'd you go?" he said, laughing on all fours. "You okay up there?"

"No!" She crawled toward his headboard, giggling as he swam through his sheets after her. "You're, like, really good at this, and I have a lot of thoughts, and I don't know what to do with my hands, and I feel like you're going to want to do it forever, and . . ."

"Do you want me to do it forever?"

She nodded, squawking, covering her face. He grinned, then pinned her back down and parted her knees with his chin. Her inhale caught.

"I'm going to try to get away," she said. "I'm going to tell you to stop. But don't listen. Don't stop."

"That"—a smirk—"won't be a problem."

She groaned, kicking him in the shoulder. He swatted her foot away. And then, for the next five, ten, fifteen minutes—every time she wriggled or writhed or tried to worm her way out from under him—he held her down that much tighter, kissed her that much closer, and made her beg for him that much louder.

"Logan," she said, yanking at his hair, peeling him off her for the hundredth time. She couldn't keep her hips down or her hands to herself. She had to have him. She had to have him now. "Come up here and fuck me. Please, I can't take it anymore. It's too good, I won't last, I . . ."

"Nicole," he said. "I'm very busy. Please stop thinking. Relax."

"I can't!"

"Fine." He reached across her body to his bedside table, rifled through a drawer, then tossed a paperback at her. "Read a book for all I care."

"Logan Milgram! This is *Persuasion*!"

"We aim to please, Missouri."

"Logan!"

"You were right—a hot read, for sure." More kisses. More shrieking. "I particularly enjoyed all the sex."

"If you don't get up here right now," she said, "I'll murder you. I'm serious, okay? I need you. I'm ready. Please, I . . . I don't want to do this alone."

He nodded, then kissed her one last time before floating his body over hers, pulling her into his arms, and rolling them both onto their sides so they lay there, heads on pillows, foreheads touching, bodies intertwined. He tugged the sheets over their shoulders, then kissed her for a very long time.

"Hey, gorgeous."

"Hey, dingbat."

"You good?"

"I'm perfect," she said.

"You're perfect," he said, one, two, three more times. He tangled his hands in her hair. "You know that, right? You are exactly what I've always wanted."

"So are you," she said, pushing the hair out of his eyes. He peeled away what little was left on her body, and she did the same, taking him in, memorizing the shape of him, trying to breathe. Trying to slow the moment down. Trying to stay right in it.

"In my drawer, behind you, there's a . . ."

She shook her head. "I got tested, last week. I trust you."

"Me too," he said. "You sure, though? It's no big deal. I—"

"I'm sure," she said, and then she kissed him, she kissed him like she had nothing left to lose, and his arms were wrapped around her, and his tongue was twisting into hers, and she could taste his heartbeat in her lungs, and she could not remember being anywhere but here, or doing anything but this, or being anyone's but his, and his hands were everywhere, they were all over her, they were skimming the bare skin on her shoulders, they were circling the faint little stretch marks on the sides of her stomach, they were sliding down every link and bump and bone in her slinking spine, they were showing her all the things they'd never had a chance to say—they were tracing her wrist at the bar of that holiday party, they were tasting her lips on the cold, hard floor of that copy room, they were tearing themselves off the frame of that hotel door, throwing her against the wall, telling her to open her eyes, telling her to burn it all down, telling her it wasn't too late to start all over, to turn back time.

"Nicole," he said, and she was just nodding, she was just kissing him, she was just pulling him closer, and she could feel him, she could finally, finally feel him, he was right there, right at the edge of her, looking into her eyes, whispering into her neck, and her skin was hot and her heart was loud and the space between them was nothing now, and he was pushing himself into her, and she was helping him do it, inch by inch, slow and easy and hard, and the room was a blur, a whirl, two quick, deep breaths—her gasp, his groan—and it was effortless. He fit her perfectly.

"Oh my god."

"Holy fucking shit."

Nicole pressed her fingers against her eyelids. Logan laughed into her mouth.

Hips rolled. Hands wandered.

Mouths hung open. Bodies hovered, tangled, and turned.

Time twisted, and they were everywhere.

"I can't believe you're here," Logan said, his mouth glued to hers. They were sitting on the edge of his bed, clinging to each other—her legs locked around his waist, his arms fixed around the small of her back, her hands sealed to his shoulders, his chest, his face. Sweat was dripping down his brow. Nicole was licking it off her lips.

"In your requisite IKEA bed?"

"Yes, Nicole, in my shitty bed. In my arms. In my life."

"Me neither," she said.

And then, smiling, she pushed him down onto his back, tightened her legs around his hips, and nudged him toward the top of his mattress. He shoved a couple of pillows behind his neck as she clamped her hands onto his headboard, as he touched her, kissed her, talked to her, and she was telling him what she wanted, she was showing him what she needed, and he was listening, he was figuring her out, and she bore into him and he bent into her and her body began to beg for it, brace for it—to clench, to clamor, to tremble.

Her eyes floated.

Her lips parted.

"I'm . . . I'm going to come, I think."

"Fuck," he said. "Okay, good. That's— that's great."

She laughed, then sunk deeper into him, and the pleasure—already peaking, but no, not yet, she wasn't even halfway there—began to build, began to grow, stretching from her curling toes to her tightening calves to her roaring ribs to her throbbing throat. It swept across her whole body—a long, lush, perfect tug; a rusty, delirious ache that grew stronger and stronger until she couldn't take it anymore, until she was pounding her fist onto his headboard, until she was hitting his shoulder, until she was falling apart, and he was holding her close, so careful to change nothing, so careful to stay right there, and Nicole—eyes closed, mouth moving—thought, for the first time in a long time, that maybe she would like to die.

"Nicole," he said. "Look at me."

And Nicole, unraveling in his hands, didn't even put up a fight. She simply opened her eyes. And there it was—that look. Two and a half years later, it was exactly the same. Except this time, it didn't hurt a bit. This time, there was nothing to misinterpret or repress or explain away. There was nothing to run from. It was just him, looking right through her. It was just her, looking right back. And when she touched his face, when she glued her open mouth to his lips and called out his name, his jaw slackened and his eyes scrunched and his body shuddered and his lips softened and Nicole—light as air—kissed him, kissed him, kissed him.

And then, after, they lay there, laughing. Because it was ridiculous, wasn't it? But it was also the truth. That they'd done it—and that it had been perfect.

And when they'd finally caught their breaths, a few minutes before she'd climbed back on top of him to see if maybe he'd like to give the whole thing another go, she tucked her buzzing, satisfied, decidedly unbroken body under his arm and kissed his chest.

"I'm so glad we waited," she said.

"Yeah," he said. "Me too."

45

Pillow Talk

By midnight, Nicole and Logan were sitting on his kitchen counter in their underwear, legs tangled, eating frostbitten chocolate ice cream off the same spoon.

"So," Logan said, "about the next thirty-six hours . . ."

"Let me guess. Constant banging, with short breaks to acquire falafel, check the AL West standings, and pass out on your couch?"

Logan snatched back the pint, then kissed her shoulder as his free hand tugged down the neck of a decade-old, perfectly soft T-shirt he'd tossed her way. "Stealing someone's words is a crime, Nicole. Punishable by . . ."

"It's sex, isn't it?"

Logan, mouth still nuzzled into her neck, confirmed Nicole's suspicion. She slid a hand up his leg.

"I know your pitch is Thursday," she said, "so feel free to disappear. Val and I have to finalize our next episode, anyway."

He smiled. "Anything new to report?"

Nicole shook her head. Response to the podcast over the past twenty-four hours had been mostly positive, but those first impressions didn't mean much. Data from their next few recordings, when the conversations truly began to broaden, would provide a little more insight, but it would take time—months, really—to see if they had something special on their hands.

"Honestly, I'm trying not to stress over the analytics yet. I just want it to be good. I just want people to hear it and feel something."

Logan cocked his head. "Is this the same director of business affairs who demanded she personally triple-check the pricing tables on my decks because, and I quote, 'everyone knows graphic designers can't be trusted around an accounting comma'?"

She glared at him. He pulled her between his knees and told her how proud of herself she should be, how good he thought the interview was, and how sexy he found her vocal fry. She told him to go to hell, then stole back the spoon.

"Okay, but seriously," he said, scooting closer. "Thursday, I'll be done in Malibu by one or two at the latest. And then I was thinking, maybe we could just . . . keep doing this all weekend? It's supposed to be superhot out. We could just go to the beach, swim? Or we could leave town, if you wanted? Find somewhere with a pool, or—"

She kissed him.

"Here," she said. "I like it here."

"Yeah?" he said, looking around a bit. Empty walls, warping hardwood, a floor lamp that doubled as a coatrack. "If Quentin fires me, maybe I'll just get an interior design certificate or something. Scale some of this genius, you know? Art is so important."

Nicole rolled her eyes. "Quentin's not going to fire you."

"Oh no, he might. As soon as my flight landed this morning, he screamed at me for an hour from some boat off the South of France. Told me he'd been meditating on it, and that he didn't really give a shit what I pitched anymore, because if I didn't close the deal, I was going to be out of a job. So, yeah. That was fun."

"Wait, that's crazy—even for him. Has he gone completely nuts?"

"Uh, yes?"

They both chuckled. It wasn't funny. But also, it kind of was.

"And you're not freaking out?"

He shrugged between a couple of half-melted spoonfuls. "I mean, I probably should be. But honestly, I'm not afraid to bet on myself. Maybe that's just me being an idiot. Or maybe I'm just numb to all the pressure by now. But at this point, it's kind of like you said. All I can do is show up and try to make the people in that room feel something."

Nicole circled his kneecap. "You ever practice or anything? What you're going to say?"

"Yeah, actually. The night before, I kind of obsess over every page in the deck, make sure everything's perfect. Lock myself in my office or the business center of my hotel or wherever I am . . ."

Nicole nodded. That much, she remembered.

"Then," he said, "I come home or go up to my room and I talk it through. I wander around and think about how I'll connect the dots. I get comfortable with it. Turn the whole thing into one simple story, then try to tell it just right."

"You done that yet?"

"I have not."

She drew her knees to her chest. "Then pitch me."

"No way," he said, his cheeks—maybe for the second or third time ever—turning a little pink. Nicole, all of a sudden, wanted to kiss them. "That's like showing you my first-grade yearbook! What if I had a bowl cut? That's not for you to see!"

"Please?" She tugged his arm. "I want to hear you work your magic! And you know how much I love celebrity-owned tequilas that are three times as expensive as they should be. They have so much . . . heritage. They're so . . . Canadian."

"It's a good product, I'll have you know."

"Then come on," she said, bopping his forearm with the back

of the spoon. "Pitch me. Prove to me, after all this time, your job's real. Show me what else one-half of the winningest policy debate team Issaquah High School has ever seen can do with that mouth of his."

His upper lip quirked. "Did you google me, Nicole? After I specifically asked you not to?"

Nicole shrugged. He shook his head. Both of them were beaming.

"Puh-lease?" she said.

"Fine," he said. "I'll do it. But when I'm done, you're making me a grilled cheese. A giant one. And after that, I'm going to fuck you. Like, really fuck you. Probably on this very counter. And not particularly nicely either."

She inhaled sharply, then kicked him off the counter. "Deal. Now come on, get to work. Sell me some booze."

He laughed. And then he handed her what was left of their pint and pitched her. And then, because he was a man of his word, he did all the other things he'd promised too.

Plus a little extra, just because.

46

Quick Pitch

It was late Wednesday night when Nicole—hunched over her desk—finally finished editing next week's episode. She rubbed her eyes, exported the audio file over to Valerie for review, then collapsed into her office chair and reached for her phone. Her bare feet, digging into her rug as she typed.

> You were incredible earlier, by the way.

A few seconds later, he responded.

> That? In my office? That was nothing. I was stressed. Pressed for time. Undernourished. And these stupid standing desks can't hold any weight.

She laughed.

> I meant your pitch, moron. In your kitchen.

> Oh.

> Forget Quentin. You don't need him. You don't need anybody.

> I really think you could do your own thing. I think you should go for it. You're really, really good.

Bubbles for a while. Then finally, this:

> Thank you.

Nicole stared at it. She read it one, two, three more times.

> No funny comeback?

Now, he responded at once. Two little messages, sent in rapid succession.

> Nope.

> Just thank you.

47

Labor Day Weekend

They spent the next four days on Logan's side of town, doing nothing but jumping into the ocean, watching old movies, and screwing like absolute animals. They slept in. They rode their bikes along the boardwalk. They watched the Mariners utterly derail their season in a single, unspeakable series. They retrieved Nero from his large, air-conditioned (and, according to Logan, "definitely-fucking-haunted") home and relocated him to Logan's ghostless-but-sweltering town house, favorite tennis balls and broken-in dog bed and all.

It was late Saturday afternoon when the long weekend's blistering heat wave peaked on the coast at ninety-nine degrees. Sufficiently fried from the relentless, late-summer sun, they wandered home from the too-crowded beach in search of a freezing cold shower and a nice, long nap. Instead, they wound up lying on the cool, cracked tile of Logan's downstairs bathroom, eating coconut Popsicles and staring at each other, wet bathing suits glued to their salt-softened, sandy skin.

Nicole took a long, last lick of her bar, then inched a little closer to him. "What were you like," she said, "growing up?"

Logan's eyes crinkled. He was easily two shades tanner and three shades blonder than he'd been on Tuesday. "Oh, you know. Fucking nuts."

"Yeah? Tell me."

He scooted a little closer, pushing the hair out of his eyes. "Honestly," he said, "for as long as I can remember, it was complete chaos. There were only four years between Alex and Matty and me, and from day one, we were all absolute hurricanes. My mom was desperate for a girl. Still is too, since Matty and Alex ended up having four boys between them. Apparently, after Matty was born, she even begged my dad to give it one more try. But deep down, I'm pretty sure they knew they'd just get another one of us. And that our house would probably implode, just from the entropy of it all."

Nicole laughed. "Were you three close?"

"Yeah, super," he said. "We all shared a room until Alex left for college too. We had these bunk beds—two of them. Matty and I shared: me on top, him on bottom. Alex got to have his own, because he was the oldest. When we were little, my mom had turned our basement into a playroom, and it sort of devolved into this arcade-science-experiment-extreme-sports-death-zone. I mean, the place was absolutely disgusting. *Duck Hunt*. Nerf guns. Dirty socks everywhere. By the time we were in elementary school, she'd just throw us in there with a tray of snacks and hope for the best."

"That sounds like a pretty fun childhood to me."

"Oh, trust me, it was. We'd tie sheets from the rafters and swing from them. Jump from the loft onto blowup mattresses in the foyer. Tee golf balls off each other's foreheads." He brought her hand to his face, then ran her finger over a tiny scar just beneath his right eyebrow. "That's how I got this."

"Very sexy," she said, inching even closer as she traced it a second time. A few new freckles dusted the bridge of his nose. "Like an em dash. I approve. You should keep it."

He shook his head, laughing. "Anyway, eventually, Alex started to grow out of it, to calm down a little. But not me. Not Matty. All we wanted to do was play. We once broke two windows in a single weekend. Spent half the summer weeding our neighbors' front lawns trying to pay my parents back. We didn't care. Made a game of that too. Anything was better than being in a classroom, you know? School was really hard for us. We just couldn't sit still. Especially me. We both have ADHD, but mine's way worse, and—"

"Wait, you do? I didn't know that."

"Oh, yeah, big-time," he said, dropping his hand to her leg. He poked her knee with his old Popsicle stick a few times, smirking. "Was that not superobvious to you?"

Nicole shook her head.

"It's actually how Dave and I became friends," he said. "In second grade, when I was diagnosed, he was my counselor-assigned study buddy. He was this little genius boy, and I was the class clown. They made him sit with me, help me pay attention, that kind of stuff. He tapped my shoulder if I started staring off into space. Came and got me if I wandered across the classroom midgeography lesson to flip through a book about baby salamanders or whatever.

"Within a month, we were inseparable. He'd come sleep over on school nights and help me do my math homework at the kitchen table while my mom graded papers, and then we'd play with slime or watch *Star Wars* or stay up all night trying to beat some video game. That changed everything for me—having a friend who took school that seriously. That, and the medicine. And, once they knew what to do, my parents were really good about getting us on a schedule and never making us feel stupid, even if we were struggling in class or bouncing off the walls or forgetting our backpacks all the time.

"Because the whole thing was kind of humiliating, you know? Like, the diagnosis and all that. You're just a kid, right? I felt normal, always had. And then, all of a sudden, this doctor who'd tricked me into playing with all the cool toys in her weird office for ten weeks was telling me in nice, small words that something inside my brain wasn't quite right, and I was just the last to know."

Nicole understood that feeling exactly. She took a moment to look at him, to consider him in another way. "I had no idea you ever struggled. I mean, with anything, honestly. You've always seemed so relaxed to me. So happy, so easygoing. So confident."

"Yeah," he said. "I get that a lot."

She slipped her hand onto his wrist. "I'm so sorry if anyone ever made you feel dumb or different or anything like that. Including me. You have to know, Logan, I never meant to . . . When I would tease you, I never . . ."

"Hey," he said, putting his arms around her. "This is not some huge, big thing. Not for me, anyway. Not anymore. It's just, my brain's a little different, that's all. I get obsessed with things. I hyperfocus. I'll run a marathon without music, but forget to open my mail. I'll memorize an entire encyclopedia article about muskrats, then lose my car keys three times in an afternoon. I'll stay up all night doing a ten-thousand-piece puzzle of Niagara Falls, but will not, under any circumstances, put away my laundry. It's just who I am. It's how I'm built."

"I like all those things about you."

"I know," he said, pulling her a little closer.

Nicole took a deep breath. "Every time I called you weird or stupid or anything like that, I was only teasing. I didn't know how else to talk to you. I didn't know what else to do about . . ."

His lips found hers.

She closed her eyes. He kissed her softly, then peeled back the strap of her bathing suit, sliding his forefingers along her sand-speckled tan line while his teeth took slow, small bites of her parted lips. Her chest was rising. Her hips, heightening.

"About this?" he said.

"Yeah," she said, inching down his trunks between quick, shallow breaths while he pulled her thigh over his hip and began working the thin, damp fabric of her top with his thumbs. When her head tipped back and her nipples pinched, he twisted her flat against the tile, yanked down her skin-clinging bottoms, and slammed himself inside of her. She was soaking wet. "About this."

He groaned, kissing her.

"Nothing," he said, "gets me harder." His left hand was clamped onto his vanity; his right, cradling her head. She was panting, breathless, pinned there, covered in sand and salt and summer, just taking him. "Than you giving me a hard time."

"Yeah?"

"I mean it." Another gasp. Another groan. "The way you talk to me . . ."

"Yeah?"

"Yeah," he said, while he literally fucked her senseless on his bathroom floor. "Don't you ever stop."

⁂

Nicole couldn't sleep.

It was Sunday night. Monday, really, by this point. Maybe two or three in the morning, but who could say for sure? She'd been in and out of sleep for hours, drifting between semiconsciousness and whatever dream she'd found herself spinning through now as she lay in Logan Milgram's arms—in Logan Milgram's bed—for the fourth, fifth, sixth night in a row, listening to her mind draw blanks.

She untangled her body from his, so careful not to rouse him, so careful not to break the spell or disturb the soft, sleepy haze that had settled over the place like dust. His room was hushed and tired but not quite dark. Opalescent, almost. Smooth and shadowy; backlit by a smear of silver beaming off the full moon and the milky, flickering glow of a streetlight playing coy behind a barely rustling palm tree.

Beyond that, everything was still.

Unmoving.

Maybe it was the heat. Maybe it was the silence. Or maybe it was, quite simply, that Nicole did not want their weekend to end. That she knew, deep down, sleep would somehow steal those last few hours of summer from them. That, with her eyes closed, the season would fly by. That, like everything else, it would slip away.

And so she reached for him. To trace the lines of his shoulders. To feel him at peace. To remember him this way—here, in this moment, twisted in his own ridiculous sheets, a mess of blond and tan and muscle and calm. A full-grown man who, somehow, belonged to no one. Who seemed to walk through this world completely untethered, free to go anywhere, to do anything, to throw his arms around anyone. And yet, here he was—hers. Hers, in tangles, dozily pulling her back into him again and again, then dreamily drifting deeper into sleep.

And so she charted him.

His collarbone.

His biceps.

The tendons along his triceps, his forearms, his wrists.

Every inch of him, a map. Something to explore. Something to make sense of. Something to capture, to commit to memory, to preserve before the slow, cruel film of time began to wrap itself around the moment, blurring its details, flattening its heartbeat, filing it away.

She could have studied him forever like this—here, at home, at rest. But eventually, he opened his eyes.

"Hi," she said.

"Hi," he said, pulling her into him. "Are you watching me sleep again? Because—"

"How could you be all alone?"

Logan's brow furrowed. "Huh? You're right here."

"No," she said. "I mean you. I don't understand. I never understood. How you even made it to thirty without . . . Why didn't you ever find anyone?"

He shrugged, then ran a few fingers through her hair. Nicole, still tracing him, shook her head.

"Who was the girl in Wisconsin, Logan?"

He pushed his lips together, then exhaled. "Kara Cohen."

Nicole's throat was dry. "Why didn't you go? Why didn't you follow her?"

"Because," he said, "she didn't want me to."

"Wh-what? What happened? Why not?"

"She wasn't ready. We started dating the end of freshman year. We had all the same friends. Everything just clicked. Then, six years later, I was working in Boston and she was finishing up law school in Madison. She got this job at the DA's office over in

Milwaukee, which was not the plan, but I offered to move anyway. I probably begged, to be honest. I was a kid, not even twenty-five. I was naive—wanted what my parents had, wanted it to be easy. But she wasn't ready to settle down. And you can't really argue with that, you know? You can't make someone else sure."

"Did you want to marry her?"

"Yeah," he said.

"Oh," she said.

"Oh?"

"Yes. Oh."

"Nicole Speyer, are you . . . jealous? Of a woman who dumped me fifteen years ago?"

Nicole threw the sheet over her face and squawked. Logan found her underneath it.

"That's very cute," he said. "You're very cute. But trust me, I've moved on. I went to her wedding last summer. Played Frisbee with her husband at her Sunday brunch and everything. Believe me, I'm good."

Nicole nodded. "What was she like?"

"Brunette. Midwestern. Jewish . . ."

Nicole raised an eyebrow.

"Smart as a whip. Great ass. Dog named after some fucking emperor."

"Logan!" She climbed on top of him, laughing. He grinned with delight. "I'm trying to get to know you! Screw you!"

"Again?" he said, his hand already halfway up her shirt. "I mean, if you insist . . ."

48

Fall

Summer burned on. Labor Day came and went, and still, temperatures rose. The days stayed long. The sun stayed hot. The dusk stayed pink.

During the week, Nicole and Valerie threw themselves into the podcast. They talked to women on years-long waiting lists to adopt, women who'd had children and regretted it, women who'd frozen their eggs in a mad dash to preserve their fertility only days before they'd begun chemotherapy, stunned and confused and, sometimes, not even fifteen years old. They focused on good storytelling above all else, but by early November—when Nicole flew to Virginia for Valerie's anatomy scan—they were beginning to lay the groundwork for growth.

Logan closed the big tequila deal, which kept the agency flush, but somehow left Quentin more impulsive—and more meddlesome—than ever before. Logan took a half-dozen calls with a top-notch recruiter, went on a handful of interviews, and—at Nicole's urging—met with an old creative director friend a few times to dream up an agency of his own, but nothing really changed. Between his *Dungeons & Dragons* games, his last-minute, Quentin-mandated trips to Monterey and London, and his regularly scheduled business travel, Logan was essentially gone four nights a week. This, of course, sucked, but was good for Nicole's productivity and even better for her mastery of modern-era phone sex, which, it turned out, was not only a completely necessary comedy of errors, but unbelievably intimate and hot as hell.

When Logan would get home on Friday evenings—tired and hungry and grinning, ear to ear—he and Nicole would order takeout, tear off each other's clothes, then fall asleep by ten or eleven, tops. He'd wake up early, head out for his long run, then spend the afternoon with his friends while Nicole caught up with Mari, flew through a new book, or went on a run of her own. On Saturday nights, they'd go out on a proper date—Nicole in some little dress, Logan in some button-down—and explore Los Angeles. They tried every little place on every last list in every neighborhood they possibly could: Los Feliz, Larchmont Village, Little Ethiopia. They'd linger, they'd drive around, get a drink here, listen to music there. They were, for those five or six hours each week, tourists in their own town: uncovering it, reclaiming it, making it theirs. And then, on Sundays, they'd stay in the South Bay. They'd sleep in, then walk to their little beach and read and swim and eat whatever lunch Nicole had packed for them with their toes wiggling in the hot white sand, then dust off their shins and shake out their towels and—sun setting—head home.

There was no big talk.

There was no discussion of the future.

There was no plan to make a plan, no date circled on the calendar.

Even the mirror selfies of Valerie's growing belly; the quickly deleted, I-still-love-you emails from Gabe; and the barrage of too-nice baby gifts Nicole's mother-in-law had delivered to Nicole's doorstep every single day couldn't break the summer's spell.

But eventually, the season began to turn. The days grew shorter and shorter. The sleeves on Nicole's little date-night dresses, longer and longer. And before they knew it, there were pumpkins on porches and cotton cobwebs on clotheslines and the clocks had fallen back and that first November mist had rolled on in, cold and gray and strange.

But it didn't matter.

Because for Nicole and Logan, the navy five o'clock sky and the cool, fog-cloaked streets and the cans of cranberry sauce piled high at the front and center of every last grocery store in town didn't change a thing. Snow could have fallen on Pacific Coast Highway, and they wouldn't have batted an eye. Because for Nicole and Logan, these past few months, time had managed to stand still.

Couldn't it have stayed that way forever?

49

Paper Planes

"Where do you think that one's going?" Logan said, running his fingers through Nicole's hair as another engine roared through the night sky. They were lying on a fleece blanket in this tiny park off Sepulveda Boulevard where—apparently—people went to watch planes take off, entirely on purpose.

"Hmm." She rolled into him a little closer, her nose smooshed against his navy windbreaker. He'd been away all week—New York, then Chicago for a Friday morning meeting, then Ann Arbor for twenty-four hours to see his college friends and catch the football game against Penn State. She'd only picked him up from the airport thirty minutes ago. "Denver? Oakland?"

He propped himself up on his elbows. He was still in his Michigan cap. "The whole point of this exercise is to use your imagination. Stop picking reasonable destinations. Pick Madagascar! Pick the Galapagos!"

"But you can't fly to those places from LA."

"And an octopus can't up and crack a cold case, can he now? And yet, here I am, reading your weird books, eating your strange food."

"People loved that book, okay? It's very moving!" Nicole climbed on top of him, finding his lips. Another plane took off—destination, unimportant. "And heaven forbid you eat a vegetable."

He laughed, then kissed her again.

He kissed her for longer than he needed to.

When he finally pulled away, he sat up, secured her legs around his hips and pressed his forehead against hers. And for half a second—less, even—she swore she saw him wince.

"God, did I miss you," he said.

She nodded, then pressed her fingers to his lips, already wondering if she'd imagined it. That grimace. That frown.

But no—she was sure.

"What's on your mind?" she said. It wasn't the first time she'd seen him a little off tonight. When she pulled up to the curb at LAX, just before she caught his eye, he'd been staring off into space; his gaze, pained. And sure, that first moment she could write off. He was tired; it'd been a long week. But Logan, frowning? Twice? That just wasn't him. "You seemed upset earlier too."

He clenched his jaw for a second, then smiled. "It's nothing," he said. "Just work stuff. Just a superlong week, that's all. I'm really happy to be home."

Nicole pushed the hair out of his eyes, then dropped her hand to his jaw. He'd turned down two solid job offers already. Smaller agencies, but good ones—single-office shops focused on working with LA-based brands. Less travel, less pressure. And then there was the business plan he and Erika had ironed out over the past couple of months, sitting in his office, collecting dust. Every time they met, Logan would call, absolutely spinning over the idea of starting his own thing. But by the time he fought traffic home, by the time they were eating dinner on his couch, he'd have grown mum about the whole plan, muttering that it was too stressful, that he didn't want to take the risk, that something better would come along soon.

"I know you want to cruise through New Year's," she said. "But there's always going to be another reason to stick around. You can't put this off forever. You're miserable. Quentin's not going to change."

He closed his eyes.

"It's not that simple," he said. "It's . . ."

She looked up at him, waiting.

He looked right back, serious as she'd ever seen him.

Then he took a deep breath and shook out his shoulders.

"You know what?" He pushed his palms against hers. "Fuck it. It doesn't even matter. It's just a job. I'm here. You're here. And we're good, right?"

"Yeah," she said, nodding, scrapping the rest of her speech. The same one she'd delivered to him a dozen times since September. The one where she asked him why he was torturing himself. Why he was traveling to Europe twice a month to build a team he'd never even manage. Why he was so inexplicably resistant to doing the one thing that had always seemed to come so naturally to him: betting on himself. But there was no sense in pushing him any further. After all, it was his career, not hers. And he knew what he was doing. "We're so good."

He grinned and pulled her closer. "I talked about you for twenty-four hours straight, by the way. My friends can't wait to meet you."

One of Logan's roommates from college was getting married next weekend in Mexico. Logan had first mentioned the wedding to Nicole in September, but all of a sudden, it was here. Time was funny like that. Slow and steady. A bit of a drag. Fast as a whip.

"That so?"

"Yep." He slipped his hands beneath her sweatshirt, his fingers finding the bare skin just above the waist of her jeans. "And I'm an excellent wedding date, I'll have you know. I offer three key services: dress zipping, coconut shrimp hoarding, and impractical shoe remediation via piggyback rides to and from the hotel. And if you get me drunk enough, who knows? I might even sleep with you."

"Oh, wow," she said, coming to a stand, then tugging him toward the jam-packed In-N-Out glowing across the street. At the time, a quick burger seemed like a perfectly good idea. "Sex? With me? Not over FaceTime? How generous. Buy me dinner, and I'll consider it."

⌒

They stood in line, thumbing through Logan's phone, looking at flights and toying with the idea of leaving for Mexico a couple of days early. Maybe stretching the trip into more of an all-week thing before they went their separate ways for Thanksgiving. After all, Logan's travel schedule was paused until after the holiday, and since Valerie's father was coming to see the boys, she and Nicole had recorded a few episodes ahead of time.

"I have to pee," Nicole said, once they'd changed their tickets. "Just make sure they put as many pickles as—"

"Humanly possible on there, and ketchup and mustard instead."

She laughed, walking away. "Oh, and a—"

"Massive Diet Coke?" He waved her off. "I'm not new here."

Nicole smiled back, then floated into the restroom, where both stalls were full. With zero else to do, she messed around on her phone. Nothing of interest, really. A few new comments on this week's podcast. A missed call from Mari. Some infighting within Nicole's family's group text about Ethan's latest girlfriend's highly concerning desire to put apples in stuffing. Paige, who couldn't even eat four-fifths of what was on the menu, replied with three rows of red flag emojis, then added that it was a free country, she supposed.

Nicole laughed, then fired off a text to Logan.

> Wait, I think I do want fries. Did you already order? Can we just share?

Three seconds later, this:

> Sorry, honeymoon's over. You may have two.

She rolled her eyes, bit her lip, and—fully prepared to enter negotiations—typed out, **Blow job?** She was about to hit send when she heard a too-sweet, too-familiar voice call out her name.

"Nicole? I thought that was you out there."

Nicole's stomach somersaulted. Standing at the sink was Alexis McMahon—Kyle's wife. Gabe's boss's wife. What the hell was Alexis McMahon doing anywhere south of Wilshire Boulevard? And at the LAX In-N-Out, on a Saturday, at ten thirty at night, no less?

"Alexis, hi . . ." Nicole's voice was wobbling. She steadied it at once. "What are you doing here?"

"Hunter had this twelve-hour coding boot camp in Playa. He didn't like the food."

"Oh," Nicole said. "That sounds really good for him."

Boy, did she not miss this shit. Weighing out her every last word. Letting her whole social life revolve around her husband's ambitions. Trying to remember what she'd worn to dinner last month, so she didn't dare show up to some fancy restaurant in the same little dress a second time. Reminding herself to only voice opinions on things that did not matter because one tiny misstep was enough to leave her and Gabe on the outside, looking in. Straining to make small talk with a bunch of women who were technically so nice, so smart, and so lovely—yet left her feeling like a paper doll.

"We've missed you, all the girls have," Alexis said, drying her hands. She was draped in a chestnut-colored cashmere coat, and her smile was blinding. "I'm sorry I haven't reached out. Harper and Sophie are almost always at the barn, or at a show, and Kyle's just swamped at the office. It's been crazy since we got home from Colorado. You know, with the new school year and all."

The new school year? It was November. Nicole had no idea what Alexis was talking about, and she didn't care. Nicole didn't want anything from Alexis. Not now, and not ever. All she wanted was to get out of this conversation, out of this bathroom, and out of this restaurant—fast.

"Of course," Nicole said, inching backward toward the door. "I know how it is. You have so much on your plate."

"We're all here for you, Nicole. Anything you need." A pause. A glance. A purse of the lips. The howling, tempered silence of two women married to the same damn man. "No matter what you decide."

"Thanks, Alexis. That means a lot," Nicole said, before rushing out the door, straight through the lobby, past a very confused Logan, and right toward the park across the street, where she finally took a big, deep breath of the crisp fall air and wondered just how much of her new life Alexis had seen and whether—assuming it was everything—she was going to do anything about it.

50

Quite Desperately

"You okay?" Logan said, wandering into his bedroom, brushing his teeth as Nicole crawled under the covers. To the right of the dresser, Nero circled a pile of laundry, then plopped himself in the center with a satisfied sigh. "You've barely said a word since we drove home. I bought you two dollars' worth of aspartame, and you didn't even touch it."

Nicole nodded, head on pillow. "I think my period's coming early or something. I'm just really tired."

"Okay," he said, tapping on the doorframe a couple of times. "I'll probably go downstairs and finish my show, then. Let me know if you want some company."

She nodded again, said good night, then watched him walk away.

One step . . .

Two steps . . .

For the first time ever, she wanted him as far away as possible. That instinct—that push—gutted her. This absurd, wonderful, irresistible man. And he couldn't have left her alone fast enough. And just when she was ready to close her eyes and fall apart into his pillowcase for nobody else to see, he turned around.

"Nicole, listen." He sat down on the edge of his bed, searching for her legs under the covers and then circling his hand around her ankle. She raised her head and tried to smile. "You know you can tell me anything, right? That we can talk about all the hard stuff whenever you're ready?"

"I know," she said.

He breathed out. "It's time, I think. We need a plan, okay?"

She nodded but said nothing. Logan, for a moment, pressed his lips into a thin line. And then he said, "I mean it," kissed her forehead, and walked out the door.

He'd left it wide open.

But for the next couple of hours, as Nicole lay there, tossing and turning, listening to the sounds of whatever ten-part Korean War documentary was floating up Logan's stairs, she knew she couldn't tell him a goddamn thing.

She couldn't tell him that the sound of Alexis's voice had ripped open every last wound she hoped might stay scabbed over forever. That each cold, inevitable truth she'd buried had rushed to the surface and filled her lungs with hot, thick panic. That tonight, the clock had struck midnight a hundred times. That, suddenly, March felt imminent. That, back at the diner, when she'd fallen into his arms instead of driving away, she'd gone completely off script. That, when they'd first agreed to take things slow, nine months had seemed like a lifetime. But four? Four months was nothing.

That she was twenty weeks from bringing home a baby, and she still didn't have the courage to set up the nursery, let alone have that long-overdue conversation with Logan about how the hell they were going to do this, or if he really wanted to. That motherhood, now, was catching her by surprise. That, on the nights Logan was in town, she fell asleep in his arms barely thinking about it at all. What it stood for. How hard it might be. How real and close it was. How much it might change her life.

That even if she and Logan stayed together, she would still, in a million ways, lose him and what they had and the way things were right now. That, no matter what, they would lose that magic—that easiness. That she had wasted those years of selfishness, of staying up until four in the morning, building furniture and eating cold pizza and talking about the future, on someone else.

That despite an autumn of cordial-enough estrangement from Gabe and the fact that she'd been gallivanting around Los Angeles with some other guy, she had never meant to put herself in a position where she'd have to worry about what her husband might hear when he rolled into his office Monday morning.

And that, more than anything, she had never, ever meant to fall in love with Logan Milgram.

Which she had.

Quite desperately.

In a way she wasn't sure she'd ever be able to shake.

51

That's Wonderful, Nicole

April, Two Years Ago

Nicole was working quietly in the back of an empty conference room—the office's bustling floor too noisy for her to focus—when she heard a soft knock on the glass door. Standing there, smiling tentatively with two beers in hand, was Logan.

She swallowed, then nodded him inside.

"Hey," he said, sliding one of the bottles across the lacquered table, then dropping his free hand to the top of a rolling chair. Late April beamed through the windows, bright and blue. "Mari told me you were probably hiding in here. We just closed Volvo. Wanted to say thanks for all your last-minute work on that. I know it was a tough one."

She looked up at him and smiled. Since New York, things between her and Logan had been a lot like this. Transactional. Unremarkable. Totally stiff and foreign and all wrong.

"No worries. That's great news."

"Yeah," he said. "I think everyone's going to duck out early—go get a few drinks or whatever. A couple of the guys in accounts just booked a bunch of tables at this place on the water, I think right by you. You should come."

Nicole rubbed her wrist, then eyed the thick stack of paperwork in front of her. "I have to get through all these before I go. And I already have dinner plans. But thank you. And congratulations."

"Fair enough." He nodded at the beer he'd brought her. "Want me to open that, at least? If you're going to be stuck here, might as well have fun doing it."

"Oh, they're just casting contracts," she said as he walked toward her and twisted off her bottle cap with his keys. His hand was inches from hers. For a split second, her muscles clenched and her eyes closed. "But, uh, someone's got to read them."

He nodded, taking a seat on a nearby credenza, stretching a random pad of Post-it notes into an accordion while Nicole highlighted a concerning addendum in two different colors, scribbled down a question for legal, then flagged the page with a sticky tab.

A moment passed.

Nobody said a word.

"You're totally getting Brie's job," he said, eventually. "Every time I talk to her, she's insistent. Nobody here wants to post externally. It's just a formality. You're going to be great."

"Thanks," she said, reaching for a third highlighter.

And then, more silence.

Logan exhaled, then slid off the counter.

"Well, I'll leave you to it." He held out his beer. "Cheers."

She picked up her bottle and tilted it toward his. When their drinks clinked, he glanced at her, then took another sip. Nicole wrinkled her nose, then set hers down.

"You want something else?" he said. "I think there's a Riesling in the back of the fridge."

"No, it's . . . I'm just not drinking, is all."

He looked at her.

She looked at him.

He tilted his head, eyes searching.

She nodded slowly, lips tightening.

And something, somewhere, changed. It was hard to explain, really. It was just this tiny, imperceptible little shift.

Like a piece of ticker tape, quietly settling.

Like an inhale, softly ending.

Like a door, finally closing.

"Wow," he said, scratching his throat. Then, a smile. A nod. "That's wonderful, Nicole."

And it was, wasn't it? That first loss—as hard as it'd been to accept—had been a fluke. Bad things happen. Sometimes, for no reason, they just happen. But they don't happen twice. And this time around, everything was going to be different. This time, everything was going to fall right back into place.

"Can you maybe not mention it to anyone?" she said. "I really want the job. I don't want anything to change. I'm going to keep working after, and . . ."

"Of course." He took a long swig of his beer, then reached for the door. "I'll see you Monday."

52

Sunday Morning

"It's around here somewhere," Nicole said, rummaging through a stack of mail on her kitchen island—shaking—while Gabe stood in front of the refrigerator, keys in hand. A few hours ago, she'd awoken in Logan's bed to a silenced phone flooded with missed calls and text messages. It wasn't until Logan was lacing up his sneakers for his day-late, hangover-delayed long run that she'd finally mustered up the courage to unlock her screen. All Gabe had wanted from her was a lousy piece of mail.

"No worries," he said, running his hand over an empty calendar on the wall. The same one that used to be full of scribbles, full of the biggest details of the little life they'd built together. *Nic hysteroscopy. Gabe Pebble Beach.* Those types of things. "Take your time."

Nicole nodded, still sifting, until she finally pulled out an over-size envelope, walked over to her husband, and placed it in his hands. His wedding band, still on. His face, still soft. If Alexis had seen anything, if she'd said anything to Kyle about last night, Gabe hadn't heard it yet. Nicole still had time. But she had to tell him. She had to tell him today.

"Sorry," she said. "I should've texted you yesterday when I signed for it. I got distracted."

"Really, it's okay." Gabe peeled open the envelope and peeked inside. It'd been overnighted from Switzerland. Some work thing he needed to sign, have notarized, then send back to a fancy bank in Zurich before end of business, Monday. "I know you had company."

Her stomach fell to the floor. "What?"

"Your brother?" Gabe said. "I'm sure the rest of your family hates me by now, but Ethan and I still talk sometimes. Surprised he didn't text or anything."

Nicole stared at him, nodding.

"I don't actually care, Nic," he said before she'd managed to coax a single word out. "It's no big deal. I was just talking to Kyle on the way over here—he was up my ass about the loan docs. Mentioned Alexis saw you at the LAX In-N-Out with some guy in a Michigan hat."

Nicole, finally, let out a breath. This wasn't going to hold up, but it did give her time. A few days, maybe even a week, to figure out exactly what to do. Exactly what to say.

"Yeah," she said. "Quick trip, I guess."

Gabe shrugged. "Anyway, sorry again. Guess my assistant had the wrong weekend address on file. I really didn't mean to bother you."

Nicole was quiet for a moment.

"Actually," she said, "it's kind of nice to see you like this."

He laughed. "What? Like, calm?"

"Yeah," she said, chuckling too. "Calm."

He nodded, then scratched his forearm with the edge of the envelope and closed his eyes. Finally, he clamped his hands onto the marble and leaned forward.

"I miss you, baby," he said. "I miss you so much."

"Gabe . . ."

"Can we just talk? Please? It doesn't have to be right now. But soon, we really should. These past few months—on our anniversary, on my birthday—I just missed you. I know you needed space.

And you deserved it. But I'm changing, I swear. I'm hardly drinking. I'm playing tennis every morning. I think about you all the time. It's never been so clear to me, how much I love you. You and the baby and . . ." He looked around the house, then scrunched his face and stared at her. "I want all of this, Colie. I want to come home."

Nicole bit down on her tongue, then unlatched the dishwasher. "I'm sorry," she said. "I haven't changed my mind."

Gabe nodded, studying the floor as Nicole carefully positioned a single mug on the top rack. After a minute of silence, he rocked himself back from the counter and clicked his tongue.

"So," he said. "Is my mom really sending you a package a day?"

"Yeah. I've been putting it all in the garage. It's a total mess."

"Want me to take a hack at it? I can bring everything upstairs. Break down the boxes, whatever you need."

"Really, it's fine," she said. "I'll get to it over Christmas. Go get your stuff signed."

"Please let me do this one thing, all right? It won't take long. Notary's not free until noon, anyway."

Nicole opened the door to the garage.

"Okay, sure," she said. "Let me find the box cutter."

ൟ

An hour later, Gabe was lying on his back in their upstairs guest bedroom, his bare feet sticking out from beneath an almost-assembled crib as he tightened its last leg into the sturdy maple frame.

"Give it a little shake, okay?" he said to Nicole, who was standing in the doorway, holding four indistinguishable thingamabobs. At her feet, his teeming toolbox. "Make sure it's good?"

She nodded, then rocked the crib a few times. It wobbled. Gabe grunted, then disappeared another couple of inches underneath the slats, muttering for one of his wrenches.

"You're going to have to be more specific," Nicole said, staring at the options in her grip. She'd opened the windows to air the space out, and fall—cool, clean, and bright—had filled the room. Birds were chirping. The sun was shining. It was, oddly, kind of perfect. "I have no idea what you're talking about."

Gabe laughed, sliding out from under the crib. He wiped the sweat off his brow, then stood up and reached into the palm of her hand. But when his fingers touched her skin, Nicole flinched.

"Sorry." He pulled back. "I didn't mean to, uh . . ."

Nicole shook her head, almost chuckling. She was being ridiculous, wasn't she? Putting up these walls, when all Gabe had done so far today—for the last couple of months, really—was suit up and show up and stay relatively quiet. Sure, he still sent rambling emails, but no more than once or twice a week, and always at perfectly reasonable hours. He didn't call. He didn't scream. He didn't bang on the front door in the middle of the night.

Maybe she'd been wrong about him. Maybe they could actually do this.

Be friends.

Coparent.

Find peace.

Nicole slid against the crib and sat down, knees to chest, while Gabe got back to tightening every last nut and bolt.

"I didn't mean it, you know," she said. "That night at your hotel, when I said you were going to be a shitty dad."

Gabe set down his wrench and tipped his head against the

crib's matte-finished frame. A soft breeze swept through the room. Somewhere, a wind chime rustled. It took Nicole a second to remember it was theirs. That they'd installed it, together.

"It's okay," he said. "I probably will be. Runs in the family."

"Don't say that. It doesn't have to be that way."

He shrugged, nodding as Nicole flexed her toes onto the hardwood. And then, for a minute, they both closed their eyes.

"I still can't believe it," he said. "That it actually worked. That we're finally going to have a kid."

"I know." Nicole's jaw was tight. Her chest ached. "I was so ready to stop. After that last round of IVF, I knew I was done. I just didn't know how to tell you. I didn't know how to admit I couldn't keep going. That, in the end, all that pain was going to have been for nothing."

Gabe turned to face her.

She'd forgotten, already, how handsome he was. How normal and decent and real he could be when nobody else was watching. When there was nothing to prove, no one to impress. She'd forgotten, already, that at some point, she had cracked him. That they'd cracked each other. That some speck of their story, some smidgen of it, must have been real. That she had loved him. And that she had wanted this moment with him—this very Sunday morning—more than anything.

"I'm sorry," he said. "I'm so sorry. For all of it. For everything I've put you through. Everything I've put us through."

Nicole nodded. This was the nearest they'd ever been to closure. The moment was right there, floating in front of them—close enough to twist around her fingers. A soft, healthy end. Some strange new beginning. All she had to do was say the words. *Listen,*

Gabe. I'm seeing someone. They were right there, waiting for her, bittersweet and true on the tip of her tongue.

But when she opened her lips to speak, nothing came out. She couldn't make a sound. So she scrunched her face and fiddled with a stripped screw instead.

"You want a cup of coffee or something?" she said.

"Yeah, sure," he said, before disappearing beneath the crib while Nicole headed downstairs to put on a pot of coffee and try to think of another way to tell her husband she was never, ever coming back. She was rummaging through her freezer, searching for a box of biscotti she'd thrown in there a few weeks ago, when Gabe called out from upstairs.

"Hey, Colie? Can you bring a flathead screwdriver when you come up?"

She hollered back, face still in the freezer. "Why isn't it in your toolbox? Where is it?"

"Shit drawer, probably! Can you just check for me?"

She groaned, then yanked open the drawer just to the left of their fridge. It was teeming with gift cards and postage stamps and pens that had run out of ink. Every last divider and tiny acrylic container, purely decorative now.

Nicole still kept the house pretty neat. Sure, back in August, when things were really heating up with Logan and the podcast was brand-new, the place had become a bit of a mess. But life had stabilized since then. She cleaned up after herself. It was just, sometimes, things fell by the wayside. Particularly when they were out of sight.

"Can't find it!"

"Try the other shit drawer! In the garage!"

She groaned again, and then, just when she'd begun to head toward the garage, the doorbell rang. For the first time in a decade, she hoped to god it was Cynthia Speyer, stopping by to pick her apart. But when Nicole opened the front door, it wasn't her mother-in-law standing there. It was her boyfriend, dripping in sweat, holding a grease-stained cardboard box and two giant coffees.

He was wearing a Michigan hat.

53

That's On You

"Logan, I—"

"It's a carrot cake donut!" he said, wiping his forehead with the sleeve of his shirt, then stepping into the foyer and handing her their coffees. "I've never seen one before, my whole life. They're from that new bakery downtown, you been yet? The one with the green sign? I saw it on the specials board when I ran by, so I circled back after and . . ."

He put his free hand on her waist.

Nicole nearly jumped.

"Wh-what's wrong?" he said.

"Listen, um . . ." She eyed Gabe's car parked across the street. This morning, Nicole had left hers in the middle of the driveway after telling Logan, who was halfway out his front door, that she needed to take care of a few things back at her place after she dropped Nero at the groomer. "I—"

"Colie? Who's at the door? You find that flathead yet? I need it!"

Logan's face fell at once. His glow—gone. He knew exactly whose voice he'd heard, calling out from the landing. But before Nicole could begin to explain herself—to either of these men—Gabe had already made it halfway down the stairs. Nicole's heart was pounding between her ears. And Logan was just standing there, his mouth open and his arms slack.

"Holy shit," Gabe said, every last dot connecting in the drop of his voice. He charged down the final few steps—his hands, fists; the tendons in his neck, tight. "It's you! You're the fucking guy!"

Logan dumped the pastry box onto the console. "Hey, man, I—"

"How long?" Gabe said, and then it all happened so fast. Gabe's hands were on the neck of Logan's shirt, pinning Logan—chin up, chest out—against the wall while Nicole was screaming, spinning, telling Gabe to stop, to calm down, to let go. Logan didn't flinch. "How long have you been fucking my wife?"

"Come on," Logan said, sweeping Gabe's fists off his shoulders. "Don't do this. Don't—"

"Answer the fucking question!"

"I would've never laid a finger on—"

"Bullshit! Every time I saw you, you were staring at her! You think I'm some idiot? You think I didn't notice?"

Logan blew out a breath. "You're the one who let her get away, man. That's on you."

Gabe howled, rushing Logan a second time.

"Gabe! Stop it!" Nicole sprung between them. Her hands were on Gabe's chest, holding him back while Logan begged her to get out of the way. She didn't listen. "He didn't do anything!"

Gabe's eyes went wide. "Didn't do anything? Are you kidding me? What, he's just here to bring you breakfast? You guys just get burgers in the middle of the night as old colleagues? Explain it to me, Nicole! Tell me I've got this all wrong."

"I don't have to tell you anything! My life is none of your business!"

Gabe laughed. His face, red. His knuckles, cracking. He tipped his chin toward Logan, who was standing there, inhaling, exhaling, and trying to keep an eye on Nicole.

"How long, dude? Since she first got that job? Four years? You screwing her the whole time? Or just trying to?"

"Nobody here needs this," Logan said. "Not you. Not me. And certainly not Nicole."

Gabe, snickering, stepped forward another inch. Logan breathed out, then locked eyes with Nicole.

"Get your keys," he said to her quietly but firmly. Nicole nodded, then fumbled through the tray on the console table. They had already taken two steps toward the door when Gabe grabbed Logan by the elbow and yanked him back around.

"The fuck are you going?"

"I'm not going to stand here and do this with you," Logan said. "It's ridiculous."

"What, are you some fucking yoga teacher now? Why the hell are you so calm? Colie fucking you six times a day or something? Nothing like that first year with her, huh? All you have to do is read her stupid books, tell her she's pretty, and she'll let you do anything. Fucking beg for it. Best year of my—"

"Shut up!" Nicole said, lunging toward Gabe as Logan—jaw clenched—held her back, one hand clamped onto her shoulder, the other sealed around her wrist. "I fucking hate you!"

"You," Logan said, herding a still-shouting, still-thrashing Nicole behind his body so he was face-to-face with Gabe, "are even worse than I thought you were."

"Yeah? Well, at least I know it! What kind of man are you? You're the one screwing someone else's wife. This, right here, is our house.

Upstairs—our bed. Our baby's crib! Last time I checked, nobody's served me divorce papers. Nobody's—"

"That's bullshit, Gabe!" Nicole said. "That's bullshit, and you know it!"

Gabe's eyes bulged. "Oh god, Nicole. They should give you a fucking Oscar. I mean, really. You are so, so good. The show you put on for me these past few months. Your girl power podcast. Telling me to go to Colorado, telling me to go take care of myself. I've been living in a hotel room, getting wasted, thinking I ruined your life. Thinking I ruined my unborn child's life. You let me fall apart! Why? So you could fuck some loser from your shitty old job in peace? What, were you trying to make me jealous? Or could you not even stand to be alone for a single second? Had to go and get yourself a new husband to cry to every night? Had to—"

"Gabe," Logan said. "Come on. Stop—"

"Fuck you!" Nicole, who'd slipped out of Logan's hold, was inches from Gabe now. Her lungs, burning. Her arms, shooting down her sides. "I hate you! You have taken everything from me! What is your problem!?"

"My problem!? You're my fucking problem! You're worse than me! So I fucked a bunch of women. Big deal! Everybody cheats! But you know what I never did, Nicole?" He stared at her. "I never stopped loving you!"

For a moment, there was silence.

Total, complete stillness.

Gabe's hands were clamped on the top of his head.

Nicole's arms were clasped around her shrinking body.

When her crushed gaze finally met Logan's eyes, she couldn't make a sound. He mouthed that she was okay, that everything was okay, and held out his hand. Shaking, she took a step closer to him and dropped her hand into his. He squeezed her palm one, two, three times, then slipped in front of her and whispered to please drive over to his place, that he would meet her there. She shook her head and stayed right next to him. Gabe—who'd been watching the whole thing—took a step back, jaw slack.

"Holy shit, Colie. You're in way over your head, aren't you?"

"I never want to see you again. I mean it."

"Yeah? What do you want, then? To just live in my house and spend my money and ruin my life? While everyone else feels sorry for you? While you lie to my face? While you look me in the eye and tell me you don't want to know our baby's gender because you suddenly love surprises so much? What, you just want all the attention, all the coddling, every last thing on your terms, while I foot the bill? You know what that makes you? You're a smart girl, but let me give you a little hint, okay? It makes you a—"

"That's enough!" Logan's eyes had narrowed. His mouth was twitching. His hands were closed, quivering fists at his sides. Nicole, by now, had collapsed onto the bottom step of her stairwell, put her head in her hands, and begun to rock back and forth. "Don't say another word!"

Gabe sniggered again; his stare, wild. "Man, she's got you good, doesn't she? Enjoy it while it lasts, dude. She still crazy in the mornings? She still do that thing with—"

"You need to leave, Gabe. Now."

"You can't throw me out of my own house!"

"I don't give a shit," Logan said, his chest rising and falling. His knuckles, by now, white. "Get the hell out."

Gabe wiped his mouth with the back of his hand and grinned. Suddenly, he was breathing easy. The coolness of it all sent a shudder down Nicole's spine. She didn't know him. She didn't know him at all.

"You know what? I'll go. Leave you two lovebirds to it. But let me ask you something, man to man, uh . . ." Gabe looked straight at him. "Sorry, I don't think I ever caught your name."

"Logan."

Gabe sneered. "Logan, that's right. Logan from work. How could I forget? Tell me, Logan from work. You still fuck her if she's pregnant with my kid?"

54

The Pavement

Gabe was gone.

The driveway was quiet.

It was just Nicole and Logan, standing there, counting the cracks in the concrete beneath their feet.

All of a sudden, they could see them.

All of a sudden, they were everywhere.

"Are you okay?" he said, pulling her into him.

"No," she said, drying her face with the sleeve of her sweatshirt. "I'm so sorry. I was about to tell him. He came for this thing for work, we were talking about the baby. I'd been so scared to tell him about us. But the things he said, they're not true. It's just, it's all so complicated. It's such a disaster, all of it."

"It's okay," he said. "I'm right here. I'm not mad. I believe you."

She closed her eyes.

"I don't know how to do this. I don't know if I can do this."

"What?" His arms had fallen by his sides. Nicole, all of a sudden, was lonelier than she could ever remember. "Can't do what?"

"This. Us. All of it. Any of it." Her heart was cold. Numb. Surely, it was breaking. But she couldn't feel a thing. "You have to understand. My life's just a mess right now."

He stared at her, frowning.

"Nicole," he said. "It's my life too."

55

Tough Love

"Holy shit, Nicole."

"I know," she said.

Nicole was curled up in a ball at the foot of her bed, falling apart. And for the past hour, her best friend had just stood there, watching her do it. Nicole had spilled everything. And when there was nothing left to say, no more questions to answer or memories to unfurl, Mari sat down next to Nicole, reached for one of Nero's abandoned tennis balls, and carefully exhaled.

"I think Gabe has a point," she said.

"What?" Nicole stared at her. "What do you mean?"

"Listen, I'm on your team. I'm just saying, he's calling you guys out on this bizarro technicality. He's saying, Logan doesn't get to have you if things had played out in this other, more reasonable way. But here's the thing—they didn't. It's like asking Gabe if he still screws that same particular dog walker if you guys already had two kids in the house—and no Nero. You're both trying to make this black and white, but it's not. And I know you didn't start this war. But honestly, so what if you had? Do you really want to go back to the way things were?"

"No, it's just . . ."

Mari set down the tennis ball and shook her head. "This thing with Logan . . . I never thought, in a million years, that it would end up like this. I knew, after you came clean about the baby, that you guys were in way over your heads. But even then, I thought you were going to maybe date him for a few months, that's all. That night, when I dragged you to his house, I just wanted you to do something for yourself. To have some fun. To realize there was a whole world out there besides Gabe and trying to have a baby and all that. But there is so much you never told me. I had no idea that you . . ."

Nicole held her breath and braced for it.

"How long have you loved him, Nicole?"

She closed her eyes. She didn't know the answer. She'd loved him since September, that much was clear. She'd been sure of it, that Labor Day Weekend in his bedroom, when the only thing she wanted was to stop time, to slow their summer down. And a couple of weeks before that, back in August—that night in the ocean, shivering in his steady arms—she must've been close. She must've, in some way, already understood there was no turning back. But before that? Before that night at his door? When she tried to chart her heartlines, when she tried to make sense of the mess she'd made, her memories went haywire. They played back differently—influenced, distorted. Falling in love could do that. Make you see things a bit more clearly. Make you see things you missed the first time around. Maybe even make you see things that were never really there at all.

"I loved Gabe," she said. "I loved my husband, okay?"

Mari sat there, nodding. "You can tell me the truth, I promise."

"That is the truth!" Nicole rose to her feet and began to pace. "I loved him! I loved Gabe! I picked the life I had planned out. I made a commitment to him, and I kept it! And now I'm worse than him? I'm the one tearing us apart? He ruined everything! Does nobody remember that? That he's been cheating on me for ten fucking years? That I went through hell to give him a baby, and he lied to me every step of the way?"

Mari stood up and placed her hand on Nicole's wrist. Nicole hurled it right off.

"No! It's not fair! It's not fucking fair! Nobody understands what he put me through! What he let me throw away for him! I am so tired of making excuses for him. Why does everyone want me to forgive him? Is it because I'm barren? Because his dad never gave a shit about him? Because his mom's a cold, heartless bitch? Do people just not know what to do with themselves when a thirty-eight-year-old, Ivy League–educated pretty boy who's never flown coach doesn't get a second chance at the life served to him on a silver platter? Do people really still hate women that much? That I have to explain why I wanted out? That I have to defend why I didn't want to sit around and fix him?"

Mari threw her hands on her head. "Nicole! You cannot be the victim forever!"

"Why the fuck not!"

"Because you don't get to have it all, okay! None of us do! That's part of the deal! That's being a woman! You will always be leaving something on the table! No choice you make will ever be the right one to the people who don't give a shit about you! So I'm going to ask you the same thing you asked me when I got cold feet about leaving Lucas, because when it comes down to it, nothing else matters. Do you want to be happy or right?"

"I don't know, okay!" Nicole was spinning. "I don't know!"

"I mean, Jesus, Nic. I love you so much, and I am so on your side, but would you just get out of your own way for once? Do you really want your old life back? Do you really want to be that small again? How many more years are you going to spend letting Gabe call the shots?"

"No, I don't know, I . . ."

"I mean, fine. If that's what you want, go and get it. There's a million reasons to stay. I'm sure you guys could make it work. Take him up on that offer and go start over in New York. Or stay right here and sweep all this shit under the rug. People do it all the time. You know that better than anyone."

Nicole slumped onto the edge of her mattress. Mari, who'd been circling the room, came to a stop and looked right at Nicole.

"Say Gabe never cheats," she said. "Or you just never find out. You take the right flight out of Virginia or your phone never breaks and you never know who you married. There's no Logan. You never see him again. He's just your old colleague who maybe had a little thing for you. You're home with Gabe and your beautiful kid, and there's no Logan. He's nobody. He's just some guy from work. Is that what you want?"

Nicole was quiet.

She was quiet for a long, long time.

"Are you happier? If Gabe never cheats? If you had that first baby, no problem? If you're a saint? If you get every little thing you thought you wanted?"

Nicole put her head in her hands.

"No," she said.

"Then you better go fix this, Nicole. Right now."

56

Through the Fog

Minutes later, Nicole was banging on Logan's front door.

A few lights were on upstairs, and through the screen of his cracked-open kitchen window, the murmur of some retro video game clawed at her quaking heart. Clearly, he was home. But for the first time she could ever remember, he'd closed the door—and locked it.

"Logan! It's me! Please, can we talk?"

No answer. She tried again and again and again.

"Logan, please? I'm so sorry! I—"

Finally, the door opened. But staring back at her wasn't Logan. It was Dave, arms crossed and lips tight. A video game controller, clutched in his hand.

"Logan's in the shower," he said, pulling the door closed. "I'll tell him you stopped by."

"Wait!" Nicole threw her fingers onto the splintering frame. "I just want to talk to him, okay? I made a mistake. He won't pick up my calls. Please, you don't understand."

Dave glanced over his shoulder down Logan's hallway, then stepped outside and shut the door behind him. His hand, still on the knob.

"I think you should go," he said.

Nicole folded her arms across her elbows and frowned. "Why do you hate me so much?"

Dave exhaled slowly, then dropped his grip.

"I don't hate you, Nicole," he said. "It's just, Logan's the closest thing I've ever had to a brother. Since we were kids, we've looked out for each other—you know that. And you know he's got this giant heart, and that he sees the best in everybody. But with you, it's so much more than that. With you, he doesn't think. He never has. So it's nothing personal, okay? I'm just tired of watching him get crushed. Put yourself in my shoes for a minute. Would you sign off on that? Would you want someone like that to keep coming in and out of your best friend's life? Your sister's life?"

Nicole winced. "I didn't . . . I don't . . ." She sat down on the top of the stoop and stared into the crisp noon sky, then craned her neck to face him. "How much do you know?"

"Everything," he said.

"About this summer? About my life? Or about . . . about before?"

He tilted his head. Nicole nodded—barely, slowly—then closed her eyes.

"I'm crazy about him," she said. "You have to know that. I'm not doing this for nothing. I'm not going to hurt him, ever again."

"Listen," he said, taking a seat beside her, then setting down the video game controller. "I know you've been given kind of a raw deal. And I feel for you, I really do. But I just don't see how you guys are going to do this. I know you guys are happy—I've never seen him this happy. I'll give you that. But you know what else I see? Two people who never got the timing right. Two people whose lives are headed in completely different directions, who both know, deep down, exactly how this is going to end."

"I'm sorry," she said. "But I can't just walk away. You can understand that, right?"

Dave shook his head. "He's going to be forty next summer. He's forty, and you're still married, and you're having a baby in, what, four months? Don't you see where I'm coming from? He had this whole life before you showed up. Plans and goals and things that mattered to him—all of it, in motion. Then, out of nowhere, you appear and poof, gone. What happens to all that now? When are you guys going to talk about that? Where does he fit into this world of yours? Where do you fit into his? How are you guys going to do this? How are you going to raise this kid?"

"I don't know," she said. Hands trembling, she rose to her feet. "But I have to try."

↬

Nicole knocked softly on the closed door to Logan's upstairs bathroom, then stepped inside without bothering to wait for the reply that never came. Steam—hot, thick, and tired—filled the room, cloaking every surface: the sweating walls, the clouded mirrors, the rickety panes of fogged-up glass that kept Nicole from laying eyes on the only thing in this world she wanted to see. The shower kept running. The steam kept swirling. Nicole's aching heart kept racing.

"Logan, I'm so sorry."

Silence.

"Please, can we just talk?"

More quiet. She took a step closer, her whole body shaking. Her heart, finally, breaking. Not quite sure what it might do next, if he didn't say something. If he didn't let her make this right.

"You can't do this to me anymore," he said after a minute. His voice was stripped, but still so, so him. Logan, but joyless. "You can't let me in, then throw me out. You can't look at me the way you do, then just run away when things get hard. I don't deserve it. It doesn't work for me. Not anymore."

"I know." Nicole shriveled onto the tile floor and ran her finger along a cracking grout line. She pushed her head against the wall and tried not to cry. "I'm sorry."

He exhaled. "All this stuff between you and Gabe, it's none of my business. I can live with that. I know what I signed up for. But have you really not filed for divorce? Because one minute, everything's perfect, and the next thing I know, your husband's telling me that you're still a family, and you're saying you can't do this. And I trust you, I really do, but you have to reassure me on this one. You have to tell me that your marriage is over."

"I can't get a divorce," she said.

"What?"

"I have to wait. It could be years. I could lose custody of the baby. The surrogacy laws in Virginia, they're really complicated. If I leave him now, then my name might not be on my child's birth certificate, and there's nothing I can do about it. Because I can't even get pregnant right. Because my husband owns me. Because my life is so small, doctors and attorneys and judges and other people's mothers get to tell me how to live it. And for way too long, I've just listened. And I never told you any of this because . . ."

Nicole had untied her shoes, peeled off her socks. Slid off her jeans, her underwear, everything. She stepped into the shower, shivering. Logan's arms were crossed and his shoulders, drooped.

". . . because it's humiliating. Because I wanted you to give me a chance. Because I didn't need to give you a hundred more reasons why I wasn't worth the trouble. And because you've always looked at me like I was perfect, and the truth is, I'm not even close."

He shut his eyes. Water, still falling. Steam, still swirling. She stood there, a foot from him, in pieces. Waiting for him to do something, to say something. To reach out and hold her. Kiss her. Forgive her. Tell her everything was okay. Instead, he took a long, strained inhale, then placed two fingers on her wrist. Nicole held her breath as he opened his eyes.

"What is happening to you is beyond fucked-up," he said. "I can't imagine how trapped you feel. But this is the kind of stuff I need to know. This is the kind of stuff we really need to start talking about."

"I wanted to, I swear. But I'm pathetic, okay? I'm terrified and I'm ashamed and I'm angry. And I'm scared that when you really get to know me, when we finally talk about the future, you're going to realize that I'm nothing special. That I'm just damaged goods."

He flinched. "What have I ever done," he said, "to make you think I needed you to be anything other than exactly who you are?"

"I . . . I don't know."

"You are pushing me away. It has to stop."

She nodded, taking a step closer. And then, through the fog, she began to trace him. Like muscle memory, her fingers were back on his chest, charting him, studying him, slipping across his skin, over and over again, until finally, he exhaled. Until finally, he relaxed. He softened his shoulders, leaned toward her, and dropped his hands around the small of her back. She buried her head into his chest and counted the beats of his heart as he pushed his nose into her neck. She counted them like she had in the parking lot of that diner—like she wasn't sure how many more of them she had left.

"Listen to me," he said. "Whatever story you've got in your head, you have it upside down. All those years, I just wanted to buy you a drink. Take you to dinner, make you laugh, talk to you for as long as I possibly could, then do it again and again until I knew every annoying, horrible, deal-breaking thing about you. All I wanted was a chance to do this. And I'd rather fight with you ten times a day than go back to the way things were. I wanted you off that pedestal more than anything. So stop clinging to it, okay? We don't need it anymore."

"But that first night, in your room . . . You told me I was perfect a million times. You—"

"Because I'm crazy about you! Because you are perfect *for me*! Because you are everything I have ever wanted!" He pulled her closer; his eyes, stressed and strained.

Nicole's whole body ached. This was exactly where she wanted to be. This was exactly what she wanted to hear. Why was it so hard to just stand there and believe him? To take him for his word? To spit out the big, scary thing that had become clearer and clearer to her with every passing day?

"Tell me you know that," he said. "Tell me you know how good this is."

"I know. I really do know."

"I don't have a time machine, Nicole. I can't give you the do-over you want. Can't give you back your twenties, or make it so you never left New York, never married Gabe, never left your job. Can't fix the hell that you went through, or the doctors or lawyers or people you loved who let you down. But I can be here with you now.

And I can tell you with every bone in my body that I am absolutely, one hundred percent all in. That I am not scared. That I would pick whatever absurd thing we've got over anything else, every single time." He cupped her face. "Can you?"

Nicole hesitated. She'd tried to hide it, but she'd paused, and she'd taken a step back, and Logan had seen it. He'd seen it all.

"Nic?" he said again. "Can you?"

She closed her eyes. She was shuddering. She gulped the lump in her throat away.

"I don't think I want more children," she said. "I can't do it again—fight my body. Spend three, four, five more years like that. I'm finally happy. I'm finally almost okay. Almost myself again, and . . ." Another swallow. She opened her eyes. "If you want that, I would understand. I wouldn't be hurt. But we shouldn't do this anymore. If you want something else for your life, we have to stop this now."

"I know," he said. "This isn't a surprise to me, Nicole. I saw you then, and I see you now. And it's okay. I'm okay. I want this. I want you."

She breathed. "Are you sure?"

"I'm so sure. Besides, kids hate me. It's just this energy I give off—I'm too serious."

She laughed through a frown. "It's not a joke, Logan. I really am done. If you're not sure, we shouldn't be together."

He dropped his forehead against hers. "You," he said, "are the one thing I'm sure about."

Her lips curled into a smile. A stupid, giant, painfully reflexive smile. She stepped into him, and he pulled her completely into his arms.

"Come to Seattle," he said. "After you go home for Thanksgiving. Come for the weekend—come meet my family. And then we can figure the rest of this out. We can make a plan for you and what you want for the baby. For me and my work stuff. For everything, okay?"

Nicole nodded. Their bodies were pressed against each other's, and water was falling everywhere.

"Are there any more secrets we need to get out in the open before I kiss you?" he said.

Nicole smirked. "Only that I've kind of always wanted to meet your mom."

"I know," he said, laughing, kissing her, twisting his hands into her hair, sliding them down her soap-slicked spine, then lifting her hips until she was tangled around him, lips parted, nodding. Her inner thighs, coaxing him into her, begging for him. Begging for contact. He turned off the water, then carried her into his room and laid her down on his unmade bed, dripping wet. When he finally slid inside of her, hard and soft and all hers, Nicole began to cry.

"I don't want to lose you," she said. "I can't lose you again."

He pulled her closer. She could taste her tears on his lips.

"You won't."

57

Goodbye

May, Two Years Ago

Nicole's knuckles grazed the glass pane of Logan Milgram's corner office, then mustered up a single, soft knock. He'd been sitting there, AirPods in, knees to chest, the gum soles of his Reeboks tapping against the dark blue cushion of his always-swiveling office chair. His eyes were on his computer screen, and half a stale break room croissant was dangling from his mouth. His hair, as disheveled as expected for half past four on a Monday.

He issued Nicole a cordial smile, nodded her inside, mouthed *Quentin, sorry,* with an obligatory minicringe, then tipped his head toward the couch behind him. Nicole had a seat and, while Logan finished his call, took a few seconds to study the place. The mess of paperwork and random pens and chocolate-covered pretzels on his desk. The stacks of years-old *Adweeks* piled high atop his filing cabinet. The wall-mounted whiteboard calendar where his team's travel schedule for the next six weeks was neatly recorded in color-coded handwriting that definitely wasn't his. The plastic vat of animal crackers he sometimes used as an ottoman.

After begrudgingly agreeing to get on the next flight to Monterey, Logan hung up the phone and spun his chair around.

His right arm was in a brace.

"What can I do for—"

"What's wrong with your hand?"

"I'm, uh, having this problem with the tendon in my thumb."

"Oh, wow," she said. "How'd that happen?"

He scratched his jaw, half chuckling. A year ago, Nicole would've spent thirty minutes guessing how he'd gotten himself into this predicament. Today, she simply waited for an answer.

"Between you and me, I may have taken last week off to hang out with my nephews, but they all got hand, foot, and mouth. Huge outbreak, apparently. We were supposed to go to *Daniel Tiger Live* and everything. Anyway, I ended up playing a hundred hours of video games at my parents' house instead. By Saturday, the swelling in my wrist was so bad, I couldn't even open a can of soda. My mom had to drive me to urgent care. So, yeah, that's what happened. That's how I, a thirty-six-year-old man, spent my PTO."

Nicole laughed. She couldn't help it. The jolt of energy—for half a second—almost made her forget what had happened over the past few days. What she'd decided. What she was doing here. It was the first time she'd felt even close to normal since Thursday.

"What's *Daniel Tiger Live*?" she said.

"Oh, don't worry. You'll find out soon enough."

Nicole's eyes scrunched closed.

Logan's face fell at once.

"I'm sorry," he said, wincing. "I don't know why I said that. I wasn't thinking, I . . ."

"It's fine. It's actually why I'm here. I wanted to come and talk to you."

"Do you want to take time off? You can talk to Emily about that, for sure. If you take medical leave, you're protected. You'll still have Brie's job lined up, she's not leaving until July . . ."

Nicole shook her head.

"I'm not going to take the job," she said as Logan flinched. Her voice was wobbling and her hands were wrung together in her lap. "Today's my last day."

"Nicole . . ."

"Please," she said. "I can't do it all. I need to focus. I need to not be so stressed."

Logan rubbed his throat, nodding. "Of course."

Nicole took another look around—the case of Gatorade under his desk, the Mariners' schedule pasted on his wall, the fish bowl on his coffee table teeming with crumpled-up Post-it notes he was not yet prepared to throw away. Slowly, she came to a stand.

"You should try reading," she said.

"I read," he said.

"I know. But now you've got an extra hundred hours a week, and only one opposable thumb."

He smirked, but barely. "You got any ideas?"

"Yeah, I'll . . . I'll make you a list. I can leave it on your desk tonight, if you want? I know you're heading out soon."

"Oh, okay, wow. Sure. That'd be great." He stood from his chair. "I guess this is goodbye, then."

He held out his good hand. Nicole stared at it.

Logan, mouth twitching, shrugged his shoulders and smiled weakly.

"It's been a pleasure, Missouri."

There it was—that tug, that ache.

"Yeah," she said. "It sure has."

And then she mustered up some semblance of a too-slow, too-long, all-wrong handshake, swallowed a mess of words she did not know how to say, and began to walk away.

"Hey, Nicole?"

She turned around, heart racing.

But what could he possibly do? What could he possibly say? They were work friends. They were colleagues. That was it. That was all.

"I hope you get everything you want," he said.

"You too," she said.

And then she issued him one last half smile, took a deep breath, and quietly closed his door.

58

Cancun

The next few days were magic.

In Mexico, everything was hot and thick and bright: the soft white sand; the turquoise sea; the balmy, salty breeze. Time slowed down again, but this go-around, it felt different. It felt safe. It felt real. They'd sleep till ten, then crack the slider open and sip too-hot coffee as the late morning sun stretched into their hotel room and warmed their braided bodies. Logan ran on the beach. Nicole found a midday yoga class she only half hated. They met up for lazy, poolside lunches that consisted of little more than chips and guacamole and several embarrassingly large frozen margaritas, because if not now, when? They read, they talked, they took those dreamy, sunburnt hotel-robe naps—the ones that felt like forever, like a soft, cozy, slightly delirious hug. And then, as the sun began to dip around six each evening, they'd slide back out of bed, slip into their dinner clothes, and venture outside of the hotel zone to tackle another must-try restaurant on Mari's cousin's college roommate's tourist-trap-free guide to Cancun. They ate tamales stuffed with chaya and octopus, massive cobs of elote, and hot pink tortillas filled with grilled cactus, then washed it all down with local mezcal infinitely better than the crap Logan was selling back in LA.

It was Thursday—their last night before all Logan's friends started rolling into town—when Logan, working his way through a particularly exceptional slice of tres leches cake, stared right at Nicole.

"What?" she said, the back of her fork cold and sweet against her tongue. Her foot, halfway up his shin.

"Nothing," he said, his hand finding her bare knee. "Just really, really happy."

"Yeah?"

"Yeah," he said.

"Me too," she said. "Ridiculously, stupidly happy."

∽

They took the long way to the welcome party—a winding, delightfully lush path of faded stepping stones that connected their hotel room on the edge of the property to the resort's largest pool. Above them, the sunset smeared billowy strokes of gold and peach. Nicole, after three outfit changes, had settled on a ditsy floral slip dress. Logan, a chambray button-down rolled up past his elbows.

"You all right?" he said, pulling a rogue palm frond out of their way.

"Yeah, for sure." She ducked under his arm. "Just a little nervous, that's all."

"My friends are going to love you, okay? Trust me, half these people are from Grand Rapids, Michigan. They're even nicer than me."

"I know, I just feel like a liar. Like I can't tell anyone here who I am or what I do or what my life really looks like."

"You could," he said. "And maybe a few people would think it was weird for, like, three minutes. And then they'd get to know you, and they'd think you were great, and also that you were literally 3D-printed for me, and they wouldn't care."

"3D-printed for you, huh? How romantic. You should pitch that to Hallmark."

"I'm serious, okay?" he said, pinching her waist, then pushing open the pool gate. Music, already swirling. "There's nothing to be afraid of. We don't need to tell anyone anything, at least not yet, but whenever you're ready, we'll do it together, and it's going to be completely fine. I promise."

Nicole nodded, closing the gate behind them, then weaving her fingers into his. String lights stretched over a now-pristine pool deck where lounge chairs had been wiped down, laid flat, restored to order. Guests in sundresses and metallic sandals and freshly pressed chinos talked and laughed and clinked their glasses, their voices blending into one stressless echo. To the left of the buffet, a handful of kids—they must have been nieces and nephews; children of cousins—played a shrieking-but-harmless game of sunset hide-and-seek. And at a high-top in the far-right corner, a group of laughing women around Logan's age sipped their drinks as a curly blonde scrolled animatedly through her phone. Logan followed Nicole's line of sight.

"Which one is Kara?" she said.

He looked at Nicole, then scanned the crowd. "I don't think she's here," he said. "But seriously, you don't need to worry about her. I mean that."

"It's not really about you. It's about me. I just don't want to be blindsided, that's all." She dug her fingers into his back pocket and smirked. "Also, I need to make sure I'm hotter than her. That's just ex-girlfriend 101."

"Really? Because your husband is literally the most beautiful man I've ever seen."

"Nah," Nicole said. "I'd 3D-print you in a heartbeat."

"Stop it," he said, pulling her into him, kissing her, then tugging her toward the center of the party. "You're making me blush."

Logan's friends were lovely. They were also, as promised, virtually all attorneys.

She met Mila and Dev and Jake. She met Carlos and Graham and Kimmy. She met the bride and the groom and the bride's very anxious mother and the groom's very long-winded father. Liquor flowed. Laughter flew. Within ninety minutes, she'd met everyone, really, except Kara—whose jury selection had apparently run long, forcing her and her husband to fly out tomorrow instead.

With the night still young, she and Logan's crew—now rounding out a very drunk two dozen—had galloped to a cantina a few blocks away where the alcohol was overpriced and the air was heavy and sweet. Nicole finished Logan's drinks, and with his hand resting on her waist, tipsily finished his sentences. She made small talk about beach wave best practices and Saint Louis–style barbecue and how, it turned out, Logan had been a groomsman a predictably adorable fourteen times—and that the only thing keeping him out of this weekend's bridal party was Benny's four brothers. And by the time they were shutting down the place at three o'clock in the morning, Nicole knew every last detail of Logan's annual camping trip to Tahquamenon Falls, how he'd been banned from his dorm's common room for microwaving a plastic tub of peanut butter, and how—according to Nicole's new favorite person, Hannah Meyers—Logan had, in a drunken haze, crawled into some random guy's bed freshman year, decided he seemed nice enough, then stayed through lunch the next day. Obviously, Logan had been a groomsman of his too.

"I can't believe you went to Kevin's wedding with some other girl!"

Nicole said, climbing onto Logan's back, giggling as they crossed the street and two of Benny's brothers whooped behind them.

"I can't believe you married some other guy!"

"Rookie mistake! Will try not to do it again!"

And by the time they were stumbling through the hallway of their hotel, hands all over each other, Nicole didn't even care anymore. What anyone thought, what Kara Cohen was up to, how bad her own hair looked in this humidity. Because the minute she closed the door behind them, the man of her dreams was pulling her into bed, peeling off her dress, then attacking her with the beak of a towel-swan while she quacked between fits of laughter.

"How are you even real?" he said.

"CAD model," she said as she climbed on top of him, slowly kissed his jaw, and then—when he least expected it—quacked again. He smacked her in the face with a pillow, then hit the lights. "Fresh off the printer."

59

Wedding Day

Logan, settling into a white folding chair, squinted as the slanting afternoon sun gleamed into his eyes, then put his hand on Nicole's back and passed her a flute of champagne.

"Sorry about that," he said. Somehow, he'd gotten caught up fixing the frozen lock screen on Benny's great-uncle's phone. Seven minutes into what had devolved into a full-on technology lesson, Nicole slipped away to save them two decent seats. "You have my sunglasses, right?"

"Yeah," Nicole said, grabbing them from her bag while he took a long sip of his drink, then leaned into her. His jaw, scraping against the shoulder of her dress—shocking coral and skintight, with a slit up to her thigh and bows for straps.

"You good?" he said.

Nicole nodded, smiling as the music started and a few stragglers scurried to their seats. The truth was, she'd expected the weekend to gnaw at her, to remind her over and over again that her marriage had been real. That her decade with Gabe wasn't something she could repress or reverse or run from forever.

But no. She was fine.

She was Logan's, and she was absolutely fine.

"Thank you," she said, dropping her head onto his shoulder as the ceremony began. As Benny, his brothers, and four corresponding, very shimmery bridesmaids glided barefoot down the aisle. As two comically rigid ring bearers and a grape-juice-soaked flower girl two years too young for the task followed not far behind.

"For what?"

"For everything."

"You're welcome," he said as they stood and turned and watched the beaming, gleaming bride sob her whole way down a petal-dusted swath of sand.

Logan squeezed Nicole's hand. Nicole, eyes wet, squeezed right back.

❦

Logan was a fantastic wedding date.

He was also, quite predictably, a very enthusiastic dancer. All evening, between dinner and father-daughter foxtrots and five-too-many drunken toasts, Logan was dragging a laughing, eye-rolling, hands-all-over-her-man Nicole into the center of the party; his shirt untucked, his tie loose, his forehead glistening. The night, loud and bright and buzzing. They exchanged numbers with the bride's cousin who lived in Studio City, they managed to teach Benny's great-uncle how to FaceTime, and then—because Nicole had decided that watching Logan play Genius Bar in well-tailored pants was somehow the sexiest thing she'd ever seen—they ducked into the photo booth and made out like teenagers for two minutes straight, silly hats and mustaches-on-sticks and all.

About thirty minutes after the cake had been cut, Logan—by now downright drenched in sweat—had gotten caught up talking Big Ten football with an old friend on the still-crowded dance floor. Nicole had kissed her shouting-over-the-music, never-not-moving boyfriend right on the lips, then floated toward the bar to grab them another couple of beers before the night wound down.

She was shifting from heel to heel, trying to keep the pressure off her aching feet, waiting for her drinks when a woman—brunette, cute as a button, a zillion months pregnant—slipped next to her, ordered a club soda with lime, and smiled warmly.

"You must be Nicole," she said.

Nicole's throat went dry. "I, um . . . yeah. Are you—"

"I'm Kara. It's really good to meet you. I've heard a thousand amazing things about you."

Nicole nodded. She could not stop staring at Kara's stomach.

"Y-you too," she said as the bartender slid them their drinks. Another deep breath, and she was fine. She could do this. "Did you just get in? I heard you had to change your trip last minute."

"We barely made it in time for dessert. The only flight I could get today changed planes in Dallas, and we ended up diverted to Springfield, where I don't think I've been since I went to Jewish sleepaway camp in the Ozarks when I was, like, ten and—"

"Wait," Nicole said. "I went to Jewish sleepaway camp in the Ozarks."

"Did you really? Which one?"

They confirmed the camp. It was, indeed, the same.

"This is objectively very funny, right?" Kara said as Logan, from across the dance floor, spotted the women midchuckle. He waved at Kara, then tilted his head, bit his lip, and stared right at Nicole as the party, in that moment, blurred around him. Kara, glowing, took in the whole thing. "I mean, I was this close to being a counselor there when I was nineteen. I backed out at the last second for this internship in DC. And you're what, in your early thirties?

I could've had to check you for lice. You could've been my camper. Can you imagine?"

"While you were dating Logan?" Nicole said, laughing. Kara was lovely. All that panic, and she was great. "You could've written him to say, this uptight child from Saint Louis won't stop washing her hair because she's afraid of getting lice a second time, and it's just making everything worse, because they prefer a clean scalp. And never known it was me. It's legitimately very funny."

Kara smiled again.

"You're fun," she said. "You sure you guys wouldn't want to make the move? We're all nearby, do all the things—Fourth of July on the lake with everyone's kids, that kind of stuff. And houses are still affordable, at least in the suburbs. Plenty of space for all the boring stuff Logan's always wanted: two-point-five kids, a Labrador in the backyard, a thirty percent larger Subaru . . ."

Nicole stared at her.

Everything, spinning.

Everything, falling apart.

"M-move back to Missouri?" Nicole said.

"No," Kara said. "To Chicago. For the new job."

60

The Gulf

The ocean was dark and loud. And for the past ten minutes, Nicole had been standing there, fists clenched, staring straight into it.

"Nicole? Where have you been? I—"

She whirled around. "Take the fucking job, Logan."

"What? No . . . I'm not—"

"It's Carson & Allen, right? Chief sales officer? I called Mari. She said they cleaned house this summer, that they've been assembling some dream team to run the place, shake things up, bring in cool brands. That they're giving out relocation packages and stock options left and right. I think you should do it. I think you should go. I think—"

"Stop it, Nic. Let me explain. I'm not—"

"No! You're a fucking liar! All this time, you had me believing I was the one that could never be honest, who could never let you in! Why didn't you tell me you wanted to move when I was baring my soul to you in your shower? Why'd I have to hear that from your—surprise—super-fucking-pregnant college sweetheart? Why'd I spend the last three months talking to you about some business you were never going to start? Why'd I spend all those nights falling asleep to the sound of your voice while you were in Chicago, planning your new, perfect life? Why'd Kara have to be the one to tell me you wanted—"

"Because I don't want it! Listen to me, okay? I'm going to turn it down! This is what I wanted to talk to you about in Seattle, I swear! I'm sorry Kara told you. That shouldn't have happened. My college friends, they all knew this summer, when there was no you, and then last weekend, when I saw everyone for the game, I told them I was staying in California. I thought I'd have told you by now, but then we had our fight, and I just wanted things to be easy for a few days. I just wanted—"

"Then why the hell would you keep interviewing for it! Why would you hide it from me? And why'd you tell me you didn't—"

"Because I was done in LA!" He pushed the hair off his forehead. He was still drenched in sweat. "Before you showed up, I really was done. I was so fucking lonely! I needed to try something new—to just start over. And then you came along, and everything changed. I didn't want to scare you away. I didn't want to put the brakes on something that hadn't even started yet. And neither did you, remember? You withheld information too. Your baby! Your divorce!"

"You know everything now! I put all my cards on the table. You told me you were all in! That you—"

"I was! I am! But fuck, Nicole, what was I supposed to do? What if I didn't get the job? I didn't want to push you to define us—not that soon, anyway. Not under pressure. Not for maybe nothing. I wanted you, and I wanted the job, and I was afraid I was going to end up with nothing. That's the truth, okay? I didn't know what to do. I was never really sure you were going to stay. I was never really sure if you could do this. If it wasn't just all too much, too hard, too soon."

She looked at him, frowning. "I think you should take it, then. If it's that great, if you wanted it that badly. If the only reason you're—"

"You're not listening to me. I choose you! I choose this! Don't make this something that it's not."

"You need to take the job, Logan. It's perfect for you. I can't hold you back. I can't be the reason you don't—"

"No!"

"Yes! You can't stay! I won't let you!"

He stared at her. "Then why'd you show up at my door?"

"Wh-what?"

"Why'd you show up, then? This summer? What was going through your head when you decided that was a good idea?"

She closed her eyes. "I don't . . . I don't know. But it doesn't matter. It can't matter, because—"

"No! It does matter! I will take responsibility for what happened at work. I fell for a married woman, and that's on me. Fine! But Nicole, I was forgetting you. I let you go. I had almost forgotten you. And then you showed up at my door, what, two hours after your marriage fell apart? Was it even two? Was it?"

"I . . . I don't know."

"Right, you don't even know! What, was this a game to you? Show up at my door, see if maybe I could put you back together again? Oh, stupid Logan, he's so in love with me, maybe he'll make me laugh, maybe he'll take me upstairs, fuck my pain away! Is that what you wanted? Is that why you came to see me?"

Nicole's arms fell to her sides. "You were in love with me? That night?"

"Yes! I've loved you the whole time, Nicole! I've loved you for years! I could never figure out how to make it stop!"

And there it was. That tug. That ache.

Louder than ever before.

Now, unmistakable.

It had been him.

It had been this.

The whole time, it had been this.

Some other life, desperate to unfold.

Some other story, dying to be told.

"Why didn't you tell me? You could have told me!"

"Tell you!? You can't be serious!"

"In New York! You could have said something!" She tried to breathe. "You could have told me. Everything could have been different!"

"Yeah, and then what? What good possibly comes of that?"

"I don't know, okay? I wish I'd known! I couldn't read your mind!"

He yanked at the roots of his hair, sputtering in half circles. "Do you have any idea what it was like, loving you? Every day, all I wanted to do was talk to you. Walk by your desk. Make you laugh. I couldn't get enough. I never wanted it to end. I went on these dates—oh god, I must have gone on a hundred dates between Danielle and Andrea—and I could barely hear a word anyone said. Staring at these women, trying to nod and smile and ask questions, see if maybe I got to know them a little better, stayed out a little later, kissed them a little longer, I could forget you. Because it must've just been an obsession, right? Another hyperfixation of mine. Surely nothing I felt was real. I just needed to find someone to replace you, and then I could erase you from my mind. But I couldn't do it. I couldn't let the idea of you go.

"And then, when you finally left, I thought, I cannot waste another minute of my life loving someone who's never going to be mine. So here's what I did. I split the South Bay in two. I drew a line between our towns. I didn't go into Manhattan Beach for anything, no matter what. It was a stupid plan, it didn't even make sense, but I did it. I ran south and only south—and down by the water, on the bike path, because I knew you'd never run there, that the concrete gave you shin splints. I got a new bagel place, a new auto shop, a new dry cleaner. I downright refused to take PCH. It defied all logic, and I didn't give a shit—anything was better than risking running into you.

"Oh, and your car! Your car! I spent two years having a heart attack every time I saw a navy X5, and guess what? It's white now! The wrong car, and my heart skipped a beat every single time. I didn't know what I wanted more, for it to be some stranger, or for it to be you. To get to see you again. To find out whether you were happy. Whether you'd ever had that baby. I didn't know what to do. I didn't—"

"You should have told me!"

"I couldn't tell you! Not then. You were married! You were trying to have a baby with somebody else! But then you showed up at my door that night and . . . I thought you loved me."

"Wh-what?"

"Come on, Nicole," he said. "Why'd you show up, then? Why'd you do it? If it wasn't that, why'd you come and find me? Why'd you start this? Why'd you do this to me?"

"I just wanted a chance to get to know you! That's all I ever wanted, okay? Just to find out who you really were!"

"Well, congratulations! Now you know!"

And then, for a moment, there was silence.

Logan, spinning, hands on his head.

Nicole, shaking, head in her hands.

The five feet between them, a gulf.

Everything else, crumbling.

"Logan," she said. "I'm sorry, okay? I'm really sorry. But this can't work. This isn't going to work. We can't be together."

"Why not!"

She threw her arms out wide. "Because you want kids, that's why! Kara told me! You told me it didn't matter to you! You made a joke out of it, let me believe I could have you, that we could have this! And then Kara starts talking about you and your imaginary babies and your picket fence dreams like it was the most obvious thing in the world. Like it was nothing. Like I could give you everything you've always wanted, whenever we decided. Like I could give you a normal, perfect life! And I can't! I'm barren, remember? My body doesn't work!"

"Yes, it does! I don't care!"

Nicole shook her head. "Right now you don't, because I'm shiny and new, but that'll fade. And sooner than you think, you're going to wake up and want the things that make settling down worth it. You won't want to make concessions. You'll want your own kids. You'll—"

"I want you!"

"You don't," she said. "You just don't know it yet."

"That's not true! I don't expect anything from you, but for you to be all in!"

"No!" She stomped her bare foot in the sand. "This is what you do, Logan! You talk this big game about going after what you want, and then you don't do it, and then you're miserable! You're doing it with Quentin, and you're doing it with this new job, and now you're going to do it with me. Just fucking do what you want! Hurt people! Go live the life you want!"

"Listen to me! What I want is you!"

"It's too late! It could have been you!"

"I don't have a time machine, Nicole!"

"If you loved me, why didn't you stop me? It should've been you! We could've had everything!"

"*Stop you?* Are you serious? Have you ever thought about what would've happened if I'd actually done that? If I'd actually told you? It would've been a disaster. You weren't going to leave. You weren't going to—"

"You don't know that! You don't know what I would've done!"

He took a step closer, then exhaled. "It wouldn't have changed a thing. And that's okay. It really is okay."

Nicole tried to breathe. "I want a whole mess of you, running around. That's the truth. I want a hundred of you at my feet, tugging on my arm, little and blond and driving me crazy . . ." Her chest howled. "God, you deserve that. I can't take that from you."

"Stop it," he said. "Don't push me away over this."

"You're so perfect, Logan. You're my favorite person in the whole world. Any girl would be lucky to have you. Go to Chicago, okay? Please, take the job. Start a family. Go coach some Little League. Please, just go."

"No! Tell me I can love your kid, and I'm there!"

"Don't you get it? Didn't you see Kara tonight? Didn't you hear Nadia's dad, telling her and Benny to go make him a grandkid before it was too late, while everyone else just laughed? I'm the punch line! Don't you see that? Nobody ever picks me. If you knew the day you met me that my body was broken, you would've never even looked my way."

"You're wrong! You don't get to decide that for me! I don't give a shit about your uterus! The only thing about your medical records that matters to me is that they've caused you pain. That's it, all right? I am not going to change my mind about you! You were made for me. It had to be this way. And that's okay. I promise, it's okay. We can do this. I know we can."

She looked at him. She saw it all flash before her eyes.

It was Logan, sitting on her filing cabinet, laughing at her massive diamond ring.

It was Logan, letting her off the hook when she blurted out she'd like to meet his mother.

It was Logan, staring at her at that holiday party.

It was Logan, pulling his hand off hers on the copy room floor.

It was Logan, making her smile in the middle of her first miscarriage.

It was Logan, walking away in New York when he could have thrown her against the wall.

It was Logan, nodding softly when she told him she was pregnant again.

It was Logan, clenching his jaw as she said goodbye.

And it was Logan, opening the creaking door to his cluttered town house, pouring her a cup of coffee, keeping his distance, saying all the right things. Taking her running, telling her he was sorry things had been so hard, that he had nowhere to be but sitting on the sand, right next to her. Letting her scream at him on her stoop, then making her laugh until everything felt simple and good and easy again. Reading her silly books, buying her coffee, dragging her to the Tar Pits. Watching her stupid movies, feeding her junk food, letting her foot find his under that blanket first. Asking for permission to kiss her that morning in his car. Slowing her down. Driving her home after she couldn't sleep with him. Sitting in that diner, barely flinching when she told him the biggest secret she'd ever buried, then just holding her pain. Pulling her in for a hug in that parking lot, expecting nothing—always, always expecting nothing. Peeling her off him in the passenger seat of her car, setting ground rules, insisting she be sure. Pushing her to stop with the self-pity, to restart the podcast, to ask Valerie, to build something she was proud of. Carrying her up his stairs, inching off her clothes, letting her fall apart in his arms, begging her to open her eyes. Telling her husband to fuck off, telling her she'd always been worth the trouble, telling her he'd choose whatever the hell it was they had above anything else, every single time. Taking her back over and over again, asking for nothing in return, except for her to be all in. Except for her to be here now.

And she knew all that. She knew it. That he was the most precious thing she'd ever known. That she would never, ever find a love like this again. And that she had to do it. She had to let him go.

"Nicole," he said, staring at her. She could barely look at him. "Say something. Don't push me away over this. I love you. I've always been here. I'll always be here. I'm not going to change my mind about you. You're it for me. I want a life with you. Please."

She closed her eyes, and that was it.

A whole summer of heartbreaks, leading her here, to this last and final blow.

"I could never," she said, "waste you on me."

61

Strangers

The hotel room was a crime scene.

Everywhere, proof that they had loved each other here.

The next morning, at the airport, was even worse. Nicole got out of the taxi, then stood at the curb, motionless and crooked and numb, as Logan helped her with her suitcase, pressed his lips together as she whispered thank you, and disappeared into the crowd.

Just like that, it was over.

Their summer, shattered.

Their story, finished.

He was gone.

They were strangers.

62

Kirkwood, Missouri

"Nic, honey?" Nicole's mother said, setting a few bags of groceries onto the granite countertop. "Are you all right? How was your flight?"

It was Sunday afternoon, and Nicole was sitting at her parents' kitchen table in a giant sweatshirt, staring off into space. Her tangled waves were still full of hair spray and her swollen face was still streaked with mascara.

"It was fine. I'm fine."

Her mother looked at her. "Why don't you go take a shower and clean yourself up before dinner? Ethan's on his way back from the airport with Paige, and your dad will be home soon."

Nicole closed her eyes. She couldn't shower. Soon enough, she'd have to do it. She'd have to wash him off her skin. But not yet. For now, he was still all over her. For a few more hours, he was still hers.

"I will before bed," Nicole said. "I'm going to crash early, I think."

Nicole's mother nodded, rinsing a colander of potatoes in the sink. She stopped the water, bundled the spuds in a kitchen towel, then sat down across from Nicole and slid her a paring knife. For maybe five minutes, they sat in silence, peeling potatoes.

"Hey, Mom?"

"Yeah?"

A flash of childhood: A creaking door, her father's footsteps. A shouting match, a stifled sob. And then, breakfast. Everything, the same. Waffles and strawberries and too-sweet syrup. Her mother, pouring two cups of coffee. Her mother, mashing a banana for Ethan with a spoon. Her father, showered, dressed for work, kissing his wife goodbye, and walking right back out the door.

"Why didn't you ever leave him?" she said.

Nicole's mother took a long and careful breath, then reached for another potato. "I loved your father. I still do. Marriage is complicated. You know that."

Nicole nodded, then dug her blade into a pesky, blackened sprout. Her jaw, aching. "I thought I could change him," she said. "When I met Gabe, I thought if he loved me enough, if I did everything right, I could change him. I think I was trying to prove you wrong."

Her mother wiped her eyes. "They don't change, sweetheart. You just get stronger."

Nicole stared at her. And then—when she mindlessly slashed the palm of her hand wide open; when blood began to drip down her shaking arm and onto the cool glass of the table, smearing her tidy pile of potato skins; when she finally took a long, hard look at the mess she'd made—she locked eyes with her mother again and promptly burst into tears.

※

Nicole raked a plastic spoon over her already-melting shaved ice. Strawberry with whipped cream, rainbow sprinkles, and a smattering of Nerds. It was absolutely disgusting in the best possible way—and, in a matter of seconds, had sent her into another fit of hysterics.

"All right," Paige said from the driver's seat. They were sitting in their mother's car—the heat running, the radio humming. Paige had taken one look at Nicole's bandaged hand, bloodshot eyes, and tearstained face, then dragged her straight out the door before their mother could warn them to be home in time for dinner. "What the hell is going on with you? Is this about Gabe? Did something happen?"

Nicole didn't know how to put what she was feeling into words. How could she explain that some turquoise hut nestled inside Kirkwood Park was exactly the kind of bonkers Saint Louis institution her ex-boyfriend, whom she'd never even mentioned to her sister, would've loved? That he'd have wanted to come here three times a day until he'd tried every flavor on the menu, even if it meant combining banana and cherry cola and wedding cake?

She couldn't. And so instead, she stabbed her virtually untouched double scoop again and closed her eyes.

"I fucked up so bad, Paige. With, um . . . with Logan."

Paige's mouth fell open. "Wait, like work Logan? I thought you never even texted him back? I thought that was just a Mari-induced drunken escapade?"

Nicole shook her head. And then, after begging Paige to please, please not judge her, she spilled everything—and she didn't start in July either. She went back to the very beginning, over four years ago, when her and Logan's friendly, rapid-fire rapport had started becoming the highlight of her workdays. Nicole didn't skip a single detail: not the strange way he sometimes looked at her, or how they couldn't help but finish each other's sentences, or how everything felt a little flat and gray and wrong the weeks he was traveling. How, every time the office door swung open, a tiny part of her would look up and hope it was him, chipper and ridiculous and ready to give her a hard time. How she kind of wished he'd tell her where he was going and for how long and why, even though she knew that was completely insane—and that all the information she needed, business-wise, was right on his giant team calendar. How those last few months before she finally quit, whenever they were alone together—when she and Gabe were fighting constantly, when he barely batted an eye as she slipped past him in the house—there was always the teeniest voice in her head, questioning everything. And how, at the end of the day, she had chalked it up to a work crush. A stupid, noisy, nothing little work crush—a flicker of intrusive thoughts; a few too-fast flutters of her already-decided heart. The kind of crush that would surely disappear the second she was stupid enough to act on it. Which—of course—she never, ever was.

And that Logan had been right. That, deep down, in a way she was only now beginning to understand, she must've always known. And that she'd hurt him. She'd really, really hurt him.

And by the time Nicole was done talking, she and Paige were both in tears—and an hour late to a dinner neither of them intended to eat.

"Mom can deal," Paige said. "She's been literally the least supportive person throughout all this."

"I think it's hard for her, with Dad."

"Well, fuck Dad too."

Nicole shook her head, tightening the gauze of her bandage. "My whole life," she said, "ever since we were old enough to figure out what was going on, I judged Mom for staying. I thought it was just kind of pathetic, you know? That we all had to pretend we were this big, happy family. And then when I found out about Gabe, I was even more furious."

"Because you knew how it felt?"

"Yeah. Because it hurt so bad. Because he made me feel like such an idiot. All of a sudden, I got it. That Mom had to fall asleep next to Dad every night, knowing where he'd been, pretending it didn't matter. Pretending she could just take something like that on the chin."

Paige turned on the defroster. Her and Nicole's forgotten desserts idled on the dash. "I mean, who knows what Mom was thinking? She's never exactly been an open book."

"But that's the thing," Nicole said. "I think I get it now. I think I know why she kept taking him back. At least at the very beginning. She was scared. We were so little. She must have been so, so scared. And then, eventually, she just got used to it. It just became her life."

"But you're not Mom, Nic. That's not your story."

"I know that. Trust me, I know that. But I'm terrified. I don't know if I can do this by myself. I've never done anything alone. My whole life, since I was fifteen, I've had some boyfriend, somebody."

"Of course you can do this," Paige said. "Look at what you went through to have a child. You're amazing."

"I don't think going through hell to have a baby makes you any more likely to be a good mother. And I've got nothing to give this kid, anyway. I don't have a job. I don't have a life. The house—it's Gabe's. I signed a prenup. It's California, so it's not like I'll get nothing, but I let this happen. I stopped working, knowing what I'd signed."

"You're wrong, okay? You're not alone. You have me. There's an office in Venice, I'm sure I could do six months down there. Or I can take leave, come be with you when the baby's born. And you'll have Mari. You'll get a job, and you'll figure this out."

"Mari?" Nicole laughed through a few tears. "Mari won't even hold a baby. She thinks they're contagious."

"She'll hold your baby. I promise."

Nicole dried her eyes, then pressed her face against the window. Saint Louis was cold and wet and twinkling.

"We would have been okay," Paige said. "You realize that, right?"

Nicole was quiet.

"I'm not saying divorce is no big deal. Of course it is. But Mom could've left. She could've found someone who wanted to wake up next to her, or just decided she wasn't going to do this with someone who'd hurt her over and over again, and I really believe we would have been okay."

63

Thanksgiving

Nicole rolled over on her parents' sofa and pulled a throw blanket over her aching body. After a relatively uneventful Thanksgiving dinner, only she and Paige were home. Nicole's parents had gone to a neighbor's for a drink. Ethan had brought his girlfriend to a post–football game bonfire with his high school friends. And Nicole and Paige, as usual, had opted to loaf around in their sweatpants, consuming as much BBC-adjacent media as humanly possible.

"You sure you don't want a slice?" Paige said, flopping onto the other side of the couch, a giant hunk of butterless, eggless, lifeless pumpkin pie peeking out from the rim of her navy cereal bowl. Through the open kitchen door, the dishwasher hummed. "I swear it's good."

Nicole shook her head.

"You have to eat something eventually, Nic. It's been days."

"I can't."

Paige plunked her bowl on the coffee table. "You really love him, don't you?"

Nicole pulled the blanket past her nose and closed her eyes. "So, so much."

"Then why don't you just—"

"I don't want to talk about it anymore, okay? Please. It doesn't matter. It's over."

Nicole had been trying her best to keep it together. Trying to make it through her days being helpful and tidy and quiet. Trying to simmer cranberry sauce and cap mushrooms and make sure her father didn't die while deep-frying the turkey. Trying to make it through another minute without thinking about Logan, or where he was, or what he was doing or drinking or rambling about, or what he might've told his mother when forced to explain why Nicole wasn't coming to meet her anymore. Whether he was in as much pain as she was. Whether it hurt when he walked or slept or tried to speak. Whether, when he closed his eyes, all he saw was the two of them, clinging to each other in his bedroom—the rest of the world, quiet; the rest of the world, streaks.

"Okay," Paige said, reaching for the remote by Nicole's ankle. "I was thinking maybe we do *Persuasion* first? The one with the blond Captain Wentworth? God, why do I always forget his name? Rupert something-something?"

Nicole shrunk a little farther into the couch. Paige drew her eyebrows together.

"Why are you doing this to yourself? If you love him, why not just tell him? If he knows everything, and he still loves you, then why not at least try? Why not just say you're sorry?"

"Because I need to love my kid, okay? It's time for me to love my kid."

Paige nodded, then handed Nicole the remote and told her to pick whatever she wanted—depressed person's choice. Nicole, for a minute, poked through a few thumbnails on the flat-screen, then slowly sat herself up.

"Actually," she said, "would you maybe walk with me over to Duffy's? There's something I need to do."

Duffy's—dark and musty—was a time capsule. Nothing had changed. Not the mahogany paneling, the fake plants dangling from the drop ceilings, or the scores of Saint Louis Blues swag hastily framed onto those tobacco-stained brick walls.

Nicole shivered, then slid onto an empty barstool. It was early, but in a few hours, the place would fill. And even now, ten years to the day, she could still see herself right there, backed up against that booth in the corner, hand tucked into the pocket of her new boyfriend's blue jeans.

It had been Gabe's first trip to Saint Louis, and his hands were wrapped around her waist, and some dreadful cover band was playing an acoustic riff on REO Speedwagon's "Keep on Loving You," and he was twirling her around and around, and in that moment, Nicole knew it. That it was never, ever going to get better than this. That she'd do anything to make this last. That she'd do anything to make him hers.

She remembered it all so perfectly.

How it sounded when he'd said it for the first time, when he whispered "I love you" in her ear. How she'd kissed him and—heart on fire—said it right back, and he shook his head and said, "I mean it. I think I'm going to love you forever." How she'd raised an eyebrow and whispered back, "Forever's a long time." How he'd pulled her closer and said, "You don't think I can do it?" How she'd looked right at him and said, "Nope." How he'd kissed her again—this time, hard—then ran his hands up her rib cage, his beer bottle clanking against her arching hip, and said, "You want to let me try?" and Nicole bit her lip and said, "I'd like that," and never, ever looked back.

And now, a decade later, knowing exactly how their story would end, Nicole breathed the memory in, closed her eyes, and finally let it go.

When she glanced up, a stocky bartender in a flannel overshirt and a Cardinals cap was wiping down the counter, eyeing her bandaged hand.

"You all right there?"

"Oh, um, yeah. Sorry."

"You're Mike Hausman's girl, right? The one in LA?"

Nicole nodded.

"First one's on me. What can I get you?"

"Jack and Coke, please."

Some things never changed.

༄

"Valerie? Sorry to bother you so late . . ."

"That's okay!" Valerie was, amazingly, untangling Christmas lights at ten o'clock, Eastern Time—the rest of her family seemingly fast asleep. Second-trimester energy or something like that. "How was your Thanksgiving? Wait, where are you? It sounds loud. Have you been crying?"

A sniffle, and then a nod. "I'm in the bathroom of this dive bar by my parents' house, thinking about divorcing my husband."

"Oh my gosh. I'm so sorry."

Nicole leaned back against the stall. Of all the things she'd pushed aside, of all the things she'd tried to pretend weren't happening, none had scraped at her soul quite like this.

"Hey, Val?"

"Yeah?"

"Is it a boy or a girl?"

"Oh, okay. Wow. Are you sure you want to know? I really thought you wanted to be surprised."

"Not anymore," Nicole said. "I want to be prepared."

Valerie smiled. "You're going to have a daughter, Nicole. It's a girl."

Tears streamed down Nicole's face.

A girl? A girl!

She was going to have a little girl!

"You all right?" Valerie said.

"Yeah," Nicole said, nodding. And she was, wasn't she? She really was. "I just don't know what to say. I don't even know how to begin to thank you."

64

The Prince of Manhattan Beach

With her stomach in knots, Nicole knocked on the freshly painted door of an unremarkable Brentwood apartment, then held her breath as the familiar sound of her husband's footsteps padded toward her.

"Hi," Gabe said, smiling weakly as he pushed the door wide open. It was the Saturday after Thanksgiving, and twelve o'clock on the dot, just like they'd agreed. "Come on in."

Nicole exhaled, then stepped inside. Everywhere, boxes—proof of a strange, new life. On the coffee table, a half-eaten bowl of cereal, a couple of receipts, his keys. Strewn across the quartz countertops, a few bananas, a handful of take-out menus, a stack of mail.

Gabe stared at her hand. "What happened to you? Are you okay?"

"I sort of peeled a potato while experiencing feelings. I'm fine."

Gabe chuckled. Nicole did too. And then she re-remembered why she was here and wiped the smile off her face.

"Can we maybe sit down?" she said.

"Yeah, yes. Of course. Do you want some coffee? You hungry at all, or . . . ?"

Nicole shook her head, then took a seat at his kitchen table—small, white, round. Today's *Financial Times*, already rumpled and read.

"So listen," she said, stacking a couple of coasters with their mates. Gabe was sitting at the edge of his seat, rocking back and forth. "I wanted to—"

"Before you say it, can I go first?"

Nicole shrugged.

"My whole life," Gabe said, "I've been surrounded by men who do whatever they want, take whatever they want, get whatever they want. And for as long as I can remember, that's what I wanted too. That's what being a man looked like to me. Money and girls and . . . and then I met you, and you saw right through it. You laughed in my face when I tried to act cool. You kicked me in the shin when I said something douchey. You made me sing in the car and rank my favorite cheeses and admit that I hated my father. You climbed on top of me when I tried to put up walls. And suddenly it all made sense, this reason to give the rest of it up. To just try and be a decent guy. To try to love you the way I'd promised to love you. But I couldn't do it. I tried, but I just couldn't. And that day at the house, I couldn't stand the idea that another guy got it right. And it looked like he had. Fuck, it looked like he loved you—like you'd finally found a good one. And when I realized it, I couldn't stand it, the idea that I'd really lost you. That I deserved to lose you. That you were going to be better off without me."

"I, um . . ." Nicole wrinkled her nose, then carefully exhaled. "The things you said to me were not okay. That can't happen."

"I know," he said.

"When we have the baby, that can't happen. We can't fight like we've been fighting. We have to do better than our parents. Especially if things are going to be a little different."

He gulped. Nicole bit down on her tongue, then dug into her

purse, pulled out a small turquoise box and slid it across the table. Gabe frowned, then ran his fingers along the curved, velvet edges.

"I'm going to file for divorce as soon as the baby's born," she said. "The day the birth certificate is amended, I'm going to serve you. I don't want to fight. I'm sure it's going to be complicated. Let's try to keep our stuff as simple as we can."

"Colie, I—"

"I will raise the baby with you. I will stay right here in LA. We will do everything we can together, if you want. But we need a therapist. We need to figure this stuff out. My lawyer recommended someone down the street from your office, so maybe we do that. Just let me know what days and times you're usually open and I'll set it up."

He nodded, still tracing the ring box. His gaze, low.

"I'm going to move in with Mari after the holidays, at least until I find a place that makes sense for me. It's expensive here, but I'll figure it out. If you want to move back into the house, it's yours. If not, you can rent it out or sell it or whatever you want—our lawyers can figure that out. I'm going to get a full-time job, probably a few months after the baby is born, and I'm looking for something temporary now. I can't wait until we settle—it just doesn't work for me. We can talk about childcare. I'm already on a few daycare waitlists, which I thought would be good because she'll be an only, but we can figure that out together. Nanny or whatever you think, we can discuss. I'm open."

Gabe stared at her. "Sh-she?"

Nicole nodded, smiling.

"A girl?" he said. "Really?"

"Yeah. I talked to Valerie. We're having a daughter."

Gabe's eyes, which were the slightest bit damp, had lit up. "Holy shit," he said. "I'm going to be dad to a little girl?"

"Yeah," she said. "You are."

And then, for a minute, they just sat there, looking at their hands. Looking at each other.

"I've been thinking about her name a lot," Nicole said. "I know your parents like to do ones that start with 'G,' so maybe we just keep the tradition going. Maybe Gemma or Grace or something like that?"

"Yeah," he said. "That sounds good."

Nicole smiled, then stood up from her chair. "Well, I guess that's it, then. Text me some good times for the therapist. And come get your wine before Mari drinks it all."

He chuckled, shaking his head. "Can I at least walk you to your car?"

Nicole nodded, and off they went, making stiff-but-serviceable small talk about Gabe's nieces and nephews, his dad's virtual golf lessons, and the reemergence of that strange-but-harmless dark patch on Nero's hind paw.

When they'd arrived at her car a couple of blocks away, Nicole felt older, but lighter. She'd always known she'd go. She'd never wanted to stay. But it was one thing to imagine it done, and another to actually say the words when she was utterly, entirely calm. To walk away from a man she'd given every ounce of herself to, even if it meant going it alone.

But she'd done it.

She'd really done it.

"Hey, Colie?" he said, just as she was reaching for her car door.

"Yeah?"

"That first year was real," he said. "I swear, it was real. I'm sorry I let you down. I'm sorry I couldn't do it forever."

Nicole just stood there, nodding, remembering them tangled in a king-size bed, the winter sun a dot rising over Greenwich Village as he'd put his head on her chest and—voice cracked—told her she was the first real friend he'd ever had, and Nicole, lying there, thought somehow, this beautiful, broken boy was probably telling her the truth. That probably, she was.

"It's okay," she said, biting back tears. "Nobody ever taught us how."

And then, something strange happened. Nicole pulled her stiff, shaking, not-particularly-soon-to-be-ex-husband into her arms, closed her eyes, and held him tight as Los Angeles, crisp and blue, carried on.

"Grace," he said as he finally pulled back, rubbing his eyes. "I think I like Grace."

"Me too," Nicole said. "It's perfect."

65

Winter

It wasn't easy, forgetting Logan Milgram.

November drifted into December—the coldest California had seen in a decade—and still, he was everywhere. But Nicole put one foot in front of the other. She cleaned out the closets, touched up a few scuffs along the stairwell, tossed a couple dozen paperbacks into a box for the library.

There was a certain peace—the quiet, tired kind; the kind you earn—in her days now. She walked Nero not for hours, but with intention: thirty minutes, twice a day, morning and night. She cooked. She decluttered. She took every infant care class offered within five miles of her home, asked all the right questions, took copious notes.

She found a contract job. Remote, twenty-five hours a week—nothing fancy. A script editor for a podcast network out of Buffalo. It was lonely work, but she loved it. She'd sit in her office and look for little breaks in someone else's experience, for opportunities to tell someone else's story a tiny bit better. It wasn't a fancy publishing house, but it was hers.

She and Valerie reserved a few hours a day to work on the podcast, whose reach had grown tenfold over the past couple of months. It was the highlight of Nicole's week, chipping away at ugly truths with single mothers, widowed mothers, mothers who'd transitioned. All this, of course, while she and Valerie prepared for the arrival of Nicole's little girl, a moment that was finally beginning to feel real.

But no matter what she did, or where she was, or how busy she kept her hands or her brain or her body, he was there. Every day, she'd check the boxes. Take care of whatever unfinished business had fallen before her. Look for apartments. Send Gabe some annoying article on coparenting. Figure out how to lock down health insurance for a baby born out of state to another woman in a random hospital at an indeterminate date and time, a task that—despite eight years of experience coordinating exceptionally tedious logistical minutiae—made her want to gouge her eyes out.

Still, it didn't matter. Happy. Sad. Busy. Bored. Packing up the house. Calling her parents. Pummeling the absolute shit out of a punching bag while a sweat-drenched, neon-sports-bra-donning Mari cheered her on. No matter what she did, he was there. And every night, as she crawled into bed, she'd reach for him. For his hand. For the phone. She'd remember the way it felt to listen to his voice, listen to him breathe. Listen to him laugh. Listen to him love her.

She'd try to get lost in a novel, lost in a narrative, lost in literally any tale but their own. Thriller, mystery, downright erotica—it didn't matter. Nothing worked. They'd written a love story, and she saw him in every word. And there wasn't a line of prose on this planet another author could've ever penned that'd be dense or dreamy or dreadful enough to drown out their own.

She had loved him.

He had been the love of her life.

And there wasn't a goddamn thing she could do to change that.

Thirty-Three

"Okay," Mari said, talking over Nicole and Valerie's chatter as she ran her hand across the menu. They were at Nicole's birthday dinner—the final night of a girls' weekend Valerie had flown out to California for. The festivities had gone, all things considered, exceptionally well. "I think we get the citrus salad, broccolini, and maybe two pastas and a pizza? Or two pizzas? How hungry are you guys?"

"I'm seven months pregnant," Valerie said, rifling through the breadbasket. "I could eat all that myself."

"I'm easy," Nicole said. "Whatever you guys want."

"Love it when Nic claims to be chill," a voice said from behind the table. Paige plopped herself down in the booth next to Nicole, then dropped her head onto her sister's shoulder. "Considering she's literally the least chill person I've ever met."

"Wait, why are . . . ? Aren't you supposed to be in Portland with Nina?"

"Yeah, well, Mari called me last night and told me to get my butt on a plane. Asked me what kind of awful human being would miss her sister's thirty-third birthday?"

"Uh, any human being? It's a total throwaway birthday."

Paige chuckled, then turned to Valerie, told her how happy she was to meet her, and instantly began rambling about how she couldn't wait to meet her niece, how she was pretty sure her ovaries had just turned on, how she'd just started seeing someone, how she was very confused and probably just midcycle and could someone please get her a drink. Valerie, glowing, laughed right along with her.

"They make a good old-fashioned here," Mari said as she inched the cocktail menu toward Paige. "And this fun twist on an Aperol spritz, but with tequila and habaneros. Always appreciate tequila at an Italian restaurant. Although it's that celebrity-backed, hardly Mexican crap, which you know is total bullshit, and now the billboards are everywhere, and I think PS is going to win an award for it, and"—Nicole's face, for a split second, had fallen, and Mari saw it—"you know what, I think we need at least three pizzas now. Squash blossom? Mushroom? Bianca? Paige, the Bianca, I think you can eat . . ."

Paige was staring at a dinner roll.

Nicole was staring at her cuticles.

Mari was staring at the menu, still talking about pizza.

And Valerie was just sitting there, extremely pregnant, staring back at them.

"What'd I miss?" Valerie said.

"Nothing," Nicole said. "I vote zucchini blossom, since we already have a—"

"Can someone just tell me what's going on? Please?"

Paige nodded at Nicole. Mari reached for Nicole's wrist and gave her a squeeze. And Nicole—pulse pounding—took a deep breath, then began tearing a hunk of ciabatta to absolute shreds.

"Earlier this summer," she said, "when I first found out about Gabe, back when I thought the transfer would never work, I reconnected with this guy from my old job. Nothing ever happened between us. We were friends, you know? Work friends."

Valerie nodded. Mari and Paige sat in silence, looking on. The server stopped by to take their order, but Mari shooed him away.

"Things got out of hand. After the first ultrasound, I realized I could never forgive Gabe. That I didn't even want to. I think—well, I know—that the infertility stuff, it's not what broke our marriage. And it wasn't his years of cheating either. I mean, it was all too much, but I don't think that's why I couldn't take him back."

"Then why not?" Valerie said.

"Because," Nicole said, "I think my marriage had been over for a long time. For years, there was this emptiness that I felt inside, this disconnection I felt from the world around me, and I'd just assumed it was the baby. That motherhood would make everything click. That a baby would make me feel whole, make my life mean something again, make the world I was building with Gabe make sense the way it used to. And by the time I realized what had actually happened, you were already pregnant and . . . I was already falling in love with someone else."

Valerie burst into tears.

Nicole put her head in her hands.

"I'm so sorry. It was an accident. It was supposed to be this stupid little thing. It got so out of control. Every minute I spent with him, I felt so good. And then whenever I talked to you, I felt so bad. I felt like I was betraying you and this baby and everything we worked so hard for. But it's over now, I promise. It's been over for months. I chose the baby. I chose being a good mother. And I am so, so sorry."

Valerie, drying her eyes, was quiet for a minute.

Nicole pushed her breadcrumbs into a tiny pile.

And then, finally, Valerie said this:

"Why would you ever think I wouldn't want you to fall in love again?"

Nicole stared at her. "Because I wanted to be the kind of person you were proud to make a mother. I wanted you to really believe it, that I deserved this. I already put all that on the line, walking out on my marriage. Not even bothering to try and repair it. I wanted to be the kind of mother you are to your boys. I went through hell to be a mom, I . . ."

"Nicole, no. You've got this all wrong."

"I don't, though. I want to be the kind of mother your mom was to you. I want to do this one thing perfectly. It's the least I can do, after everything I've put you through." Nicole glanced at Valerie's stomach. "After everything I'm going to put her through."

"Listen to me," Valerie said. "I love you. You are one of the best friends I've ever had. I think God brought us together for a reason. And I have no doubt in my mind that when you meet your little girl, you're going to put her first. But to think you believe that motherhood is some kind of punishment, that you need to pay for what you've been through, that your kid is going to have a better life because you turned your back on love . . . I think you know better. I think you're just scared. And I think you're making a huge mistake."

Nicole's eyes welled.

Valerie grabbed her hand.

"What's his name?"

"Logan."

"Where is he now?"

"Twenty blocks from here," Nicole said. "Or Chicago. Probably Chicago. I don't know."

"You have to find him."

Nicole shook her head. "It's more than that. It's more than you thinking I'm a good mother. That's not the only reason why it ended. That's not really something I could even see until he was gone. He wants kids. He says he doesn't need them, but it's not true. He did, at least before we were together, and he'd be the most incredible father, and he's either going to leave, or he's going to stay and hate me for it, or I'll hate me for it, and I . . . I'm just done fighting my body. IVF is wonderful, it's a miracle, I'm so grateful for it, but I don't want to go back to that chapter of my life. And adoption, it's not just this solution, you know? It's a whole other journey—and a huge responsibility. I don't want to bring my kid into the world, and then get so wrapped up in having the next one I forget to love the one I've got. And Logan, he deserves his own children. He should have that. He should have it be easy, and—"

"Are you fucking kidding me?" Paige said.

"Wh-what?"

"I mean, goddamnit, Nicole. Listen to yourself. This man loves you, he's told you that he's all in, that he understands you're done, that he'll do whatever's best for you, that you're enough, that loving your kid is enough, and that's still not good enough for you? Because you think he needs biological children? Because you think it's your job to give that to him?"

"Well, yeah, I—"

"What do you think is going to happen when I fall in love? If I want kids? You think the same damn thing isn't going to happen to me? That I'm not going to have to build a family that looks a little different? Or do you not even think about me? About anyone who isn't experiencing the exact same struggle as you? About anyone who doesn't happen to have a zillion dollars to solve their problems?

I mean, you have this podcast, so I know you know better. What happened to you was horrible, okay? But you are not the first fucking person on this planet to go to war with your body."

"I don't think that. I . . ."

But she did think that, didn't she? How else would she have gotten through the past few years? She'd been in survival mode, and she'd lost perspective. You don't go through what she went through and wake up thinking about anybody other than yourself. But those days were over—they were long gone. And here she was, clinging to that same old story.

She was full of shit, wasn't she? Every inch of her armor, scar tissue. Trauma, thick and ugly, holding her back, forcing her hand. Telling her what to do, who to love, when to run.

"Paige, I'm so sorry," Nicole said. "I never—"

"If he says he picks you, let him pick you. If that makes you feel guilty, then do the fucking work. Because this happens to people like me every single day. This is the price we pay for love."

Nicole stared at her sister, heart racing.

Had it really been this simple all along?

What had she done?

And how was she ever going to make it right?

67

Not Without a Fight

She leaped out of the passenger seat.

She raced up his steps.

She threw her knuckles onto his front door.

But already, it was clear. His blinds were too drawn. His mailbox, too full. The take-out menu dangling from his doorknob, too old, too weathered, too wet.

"Ring the bell, Nicole!"

For a single, impossible second, she turned around and stared at her hope-filled friends where Mari's car was idling in the driveway. And then, without a word, she slumped against his front door, heart in a million pieces. She had told him to go. She had given him no reason to stay. And here she was, believing he'd have stuck around. Believing he'd have waited for her.

"Nic?" Paige's head poked out the back window. "What's going on? You didn't even try!"

Nicole shook her head. "He's not here."

"Did you try calling him?" Valerie said. "Maybe he's just traveling!"

Nicole shrugged, then slowly pulled out her phone. After a minute, finally, she forced herself to trace his name, press her finger to the glass, and let it ring. Her heart, skipping a thousand beats at the thought of his voice on the other end of the line, of how he might sound or what he might say. When it went straight to voicemail—the very instant the quiet hum of that same old recording began—

she hung up. She wasn't ready to hear that version of him. That always-on, fun-and-games, sell-you-anything version of him that was for everybody and anybody. Some standard-issue version of him that wasn't just for her.

"Keep trying!" Paige said as Nicole lifelessly dialed one, two, three more times. But by her fifth attempt, Nicole had dropped her phone to the concrete. Mari, who'd been quiet for a while now, got out of the car and carefully walked up his steps.

"Did he take the job?" Nicole said.

"I don't know," Mari said, wiping away the mist on his shuttered kitchen window, attempting to peer through a nothing little crack in the blinds. "I know he was at PS before Christmas—and I just checked online too—but that doesn't really mean anything, especially with all the holidays. Carson just announced their new CEO last week, so it could be a week or two before they name the rest of the big hires. I don't know what his next move is. I don't know what he may have worked out with Quentin, or what he has or hasn't told his team. Maybe he's just on a plane and his phone's off. Maybe he's been on a work trip, and he'll be home in an hour. I just don't know, Nic."

Nicole hung her head. Mari looked around.

"Which neighbor's nicer, one or three?"

"Uh, three," Nicole said. "Definitely three."

"They hear you guys have weird sex all the time?"

Nicole nodded, wincing.

"Good," Mari said, already banging on the unit's front door. But as it swung open, as Mari's shoulders slumped and her neck bowed and her arms stiffened, Nicole understood.

Mari sat down next to Nicole, tipped her head back against no-longer-Logan's front door, and stared into the cold January night. Nicole, knees to chest, closed her eyes.

She had loved this place. She had loved it, all cracked screens and clacking cupboards and creaking floorboards. She had fallen in love with him here. She had changed her life here. She had learned to tell the truth here. It had been the only place, as her world fell apart, where she'd felt safe and good and worth something. And now, it was gone. Erased. Eviscerated. The backbone of their perfect summer, snatched away like it was never theirs at all. It had been home, hadn't it? It had—for those four months of magic—been her home. And now, it was just sitting there, empty, waiting to belong to someone new. She'd never get another chance to watch him float across the hardwood in a pair of crew socks, grinning as he answered his wide-open front door. She'd never get another chance to watch him toss her a beer from his fridge, or pretend not to know how to operate a toaster, or lift her laughing body around his, set her down on his kitchen counter, kiss her for twenty minutes straight, then tell her all about his day.

He was gone.

He was gone, and only because she'd demanded he go.

"Listen to me," Mari said. "You're going to get him back. You're going to fix this. You're going to find a way. That man loves you. He's going to understand. And if it's too late, if he's gone, if he doesn't want to forgive you, if he doesn't want you to fly to Chicago every other weekend for the next eighteen years of your lives, then you're still going to be okay. No matter what, you're going to be okay. But you need to fight for him. If you give up now, it's over. You need to find a way to make this right. And whatever you decide to say, however you decide to say it, it needs to be good. It needs to be really fucking good."

Nicole frowned. "I guess I could call Dave? Or I bet his parents are listed, I bet we could find them. Or his brothers, or Benny, or . . ."

But that was when Valerie shoved her head out the window.

"The podcast!" she said, eyes wide. "Put it on the freaking podcast!"

68

It Was You

"I have spent my whole life trying to be perfect," Nicole said, sitting at Mari's kitchen table, trembling as the live stream button blinked on her laptop's screen. The rest of her crew was banished to Mari's bedroom. "I don't totally know why. First child syndrome? Just really liking things to be neat and organized? I don't know if it even matters, if it's even relevant. But growing up, there was always this part of me that thought if I made straight A's, if my hair was always combed, if my room was always clean, maybe everything else would be okay.

"Then I got older, and things started getting messier. It's not so easy, you know, being perfect once you start drinking, start making mistakes, start getting your heart stomped on by stupid Webster Groves boys. Once the rejection letters from the fancy colleges everyone expected you to get into start to pile up on your parents' kitchen counter. How could I be perfect if I never got off the wait list at Columbia? How could I be perfect if I couldn't get a single publishing house to let me work in their mail room? How could I be perfect if my own body wouldn't do the one thing I really wanted it to? The one thing I was so sure it was made to do?

"I don't know . . . I guess the truth is, I thought being perfect would give me control. I thought that when things got difficult, I just needed to try harder, do more, be better. But that's not what happened, at least these past few years. My perfectionism gutted all the good in my life. It came for my marriage, and then, when that crumbled, it came for me. I know I haven't talked about that here, that it probably seems like Gabe just disappeared, but it's not that simple. Because the truth is, every decision I've ever made—probably up until the night of July eleventh—has been in pursuit of perfection.

"And so, this summer, when I reconnected with an old friend, I didn't understand that I was full of poison. That I hated myself and my body and the decisions I'd made so, so much for not being perfect that I had no idea how to love anyone else. And by the time I realized I was absolutely head over heels for this person, I didn't know how to show it. I didn't know how to tell him. And I didn't know how to believe I deserved that kind of love in return."

She hugged her arms around her elbows and exhaled.

"Logan . . . I know that after the shit I pulled in November, you probably never want to hear from me again, that I'm only making things worse, that I'm only making this harder. And I know you probably think I've only ever thought of myself, but the truth is, I have always hung on every word you've said.

"I know you dressed up as Ken Griffey Junior for five Halloweens in a row, and you would've kept doing it forever, but your mom paid you twenty bucks to be literally anything else, and that was that. I know you Subscribe & Save so you never run out of peanut butter, but things have gotten out of hand, and now you have four cases of Skippy in your closet and two more at your office, and you keep forgetting to cancel the subscription, so the problem just keeps getting worse. I know you have fifty-six thousand two hundred and eighty-three unread emails on your phone, or at least you did the last time I saw it, but that the number makes perfect sense to you, and that you're on top of what's coming in, so what's the big deal, anyway?

"I know your favorite flavor of ice cream is literally any ice cream, that favorite ice creams are a social construct that cause undue familial strife. That you like living in a sleepy little beach town because it's close to your office and the airport and you spend all week traveling to big, fancy cities, so why not come home to a place where there's no traffic and the tacos are cheap and the air is clean and there's nothing to do but take it easy, anyway? I know that your dad's insurance agency was, for some reason, a sponsor of the Issaquah Salmon Days festival, which—if we're being completely honest here, and I guess we are—I would really like you to take me to. I know that every *D&D* character you've ever played is chaotic good. That you can guess every flavor jelly bean with your eyes closed. That Ichiro Suzuki is the true hit king.

"I know you run because it makes your brain feel better, because it grounds you, because it's how you make the rest of your day make sense. And I know that after you finish a marathon, you like to weep in the bathtub and eat cold rotisserie chicken straight out of the carton, because I watched you do it, because you made me feed it to you, and it was absolutely horrific, and somehow, it made me love you a million times more. I know that your childhood was so bonkers it nearly put your mother into an early grave. I know that you're the least competent cook I've ever met, and the best wedding date I've ever had. I know that *Dwarf Fortress* is the most complex computer game ever engineered, and I know that you're so, so good at your job, and that your brain is absolutely incredible, and that, more than anything, you're the greatest man I've ever known.

"And I know, above all else, that I love you. I love you, Logan.

I really, really do. And I know I had no business showing up at your door—not then, and not tonight, and probably not ever again, but I wouldn't take it back. I wouldn't change a thing. I had to know how great you were. I had a feeling that you were going to be the man of my dreams, okay? That's why I showed up. That's the answer to your question. I had a hunch that it was you. I had a hunch, and I was right.

"I was made for you, Logan Milgram. 3D-printed. You're all I see, all the time. Every night, when I close my eyes, it's you. In the morning, you. And I don't know how I missed it before, but I swear to god, I'll never miss it again.

"I want to love you forever. I want you to get on my nerves. I want to want to fucking kill you. I love your stupid face and your stupid hair and your stupid jokes and I love how you have always seen the best in me, and I love every single inch of our impossible, absurd, definitely-in-need-of-an-editor love story.

"The things I was scared of, the sacrifices I wouldn't let you make—I was an idiot. I didn't know how to be loved like that. I had so much growing up to do. You were right, and I was wrong. I was the kid. I was the baby. I want to build a life with you—and the hard stuff, we can figure out together. I can do that. I swear, I can do that. And I don't care anymore that it won't be perfect. That it won't be just so. That it won't look exactly like I thought it would when I was little. I don't care if it's the biggest mess anyone this side of the Missouri River has ever seen. It'll be ours, and we will find our way.

"We can do this. I know we can. And if the offer still stands, I'm all in. Right here, right now. Wherever you are, whatever you've decided, I want you. I want us. I want this. Logan, it was always you, okay? It was always you. I just didn't know it yet."

69

Some Other Story

The Pacific, cold and misty, stared back at her.

Five hours had passed, and nothing.

The once-exploding phone in her back pocket, now set to silent with only one exception. She'd heard from her very confused mother, her suddenly not-so-tight-lipped mother-in-law, even her goddamn high school English teacher. The podcast had spread like wildfire, but from Logan—from the only person on this planet who mattered right now—there was nothing.

There was radio silence.

And so, a couple of hours ago, when the soaring high of telling the whole world just how much she loved him had begun to fade, Nicole grabbed her jacket and slipped out of Mari's apartment to get some air. Instead, she'd found herself wandering the fog-cloaked streets of his old town, retracing their every step, retelling their entire story, remembering what it had felt like—for that perfect summer—to have known a love that real. She had, like a ghost, taken in every inch of the two-square-mile city. The damp, cold mulch of their running path; the shadowy stretch of Pier Avenue that played host to their favorite pastry shops and sandwich spots; the sleeping silhouette of their diner's corner booth, its plastic salt-and-pepper shakers neatly awaiting someone new.

And now, as she stood alone on their beach, as the surf broke and the tide surged and the winter whirled, she inched closer to the coastline, cupped her hands into the icy foam of the frigid shore, and washed away her tears until the salt no longer stung her face and the cold no longer numbed her fingers.

She had put all her cards on the table.

She had put up a hell of a fight.

But before that, she had let him go.

She had pushed him two thousand miles away.

And—adrenaline, gone—she understood.

Not every love could last forever.

Not every mistake could be washed away.

And so, shoes and socks in hand, she dragged her shivering body back up the hill, past the hastily parked cars and the buzzing bars, past the sleeping bookstores and the faded ice cream parlors, until she was turning onto Highland Avenue, until she was turning onto Mari's street, colder and older and ready—finally ready—to call Dave, to face the facts, to wait until Logan's name appeared in bold on a press release written six states away, then begin to turn the page on the love she'd let go to waste. But as Mari's building came into view—thick pink stucco; fading Spanish tile; the light from her living room window, soft and warm and beckoning her to come back home and heal her broken heart—Nicole couldn't help but laugh.

Because none of it mattered.

Because Logan Milgram was sitting right there on the sidewalk in a pair of faded blue jeans, grinning like an idiot, arms wrapped around his bent knees.

"I heard a rumor you loved me!"

"It's true! You're my Captain Wentworth! 'You pierce my soul!'"

He laughed, pushing himself up off the concrete, wiping his palms on the front of his jeans as she threw her arms around his neck and he slid his hands around her waist. But when she tried to find his lips, he held her back, gleaming.

"You, Nicole Speyer, have sent me on quite the wild goose chase."

"Did you take the job? Where do you—"

"Next time you go big, remember to go small."

"Did you move to Chicago? Did you—"

"When I landed, like, ninety minutes ago," he said, thumbing the waist of her jeans, "I had ten thousand notifications. People found me on LinkedIn. People found me on Facebook. I didn't even know I still had that. The messaging app is separate, it was very noisy, I—"

"You were flying home?" Her heart leaped out of her throat. "You live here?"

He nodded, smiling, touching her. "I live here. I live in Culver. I just got back from a meeting in Nashville. I did it—I started my own thing. When you were gone and I had nothing left to lose, it was so clear to me that you were right, that I wanted something that was all mine. And what was holding me back wasn't some job of a lifetime in Chicago, and it wasn't even you. It was this idea that you'd only love me if I was stable, if I made things easy and simple for you. That our relationship could only work if I never let you down, never made things harder. That you wouldn't love me if I started a business that failed, especially while you had a new baby, while you were trying to figure out life without Gabe, if I wasn't always putting your needs first and that's on me. You never asked me to do any of that or give those things up, and I should've gone for it while I still had you. I should've bet on myself while you were still mine. And on a semirelated note, Erika and I just signed a three-year lease for this office space on Jefferson, so I officially have zero dollars to my name."

"Did you really? I'm so proud of you. I'm so happy," Nicole said, pulling him closer, pushing her forehead against his. He smirked, then pressed her arms to her sides.

"Patience, Missouri. Not until I finish my story, all right?"

Nicole rolled her eyes, then gestured for him to carry on.

"So," he said, "turns out my sister-in-law listens to your podcast. Matty's wife, I told you, she did IVF last year too. Anyway, she's calling, she's freaking out, she's just put it all together, that you're the Nicole I was crying about over Thanksgiving. I've got texts from literally everyone at PS—I've got clients calling, which, thanks for that, by the way. Brilliant workaround for my nonsolicitation. I set up four meetings on the way here. Anyway, I've got half my mom's book club calling, someone from the *Issaquah Reporter* calling. Everyone, sending me the link. Everyone, telling me it's the cutest thing they've ever heard. So then I listen to your show on the tarmac. Very well done. A little stalkery, but I'll allow it. Anyway, now I'm crying on the plane—thanks for that too—and also about ready to murder someone, because you know LAX, and it's taking forever for them to find an open gate, and I'm desperate to come and see you, and you know how it takes forever to get a car, so I call Dave and beg him to come get me and—"

"Dave? Dave hates me."

Logan twirled Nicole around and pointed to a royal blue Prius idling across the street. At once, Dave glanced up from his glowing phone and really, truly smiled. Nicole smiled back, shouting that she was sorry, he was right, and she would babysit his kids until the end of time. And then, shaking his head, he gave her a strange little salute and drove away.

"Okay, okay," she said, turning back to Logan, retracing him. His arms, his shoulders, his jaw. Everything, the same. Everything, different. "Then what?"

"So then, we're sitting at the gate with the seat belt sign on for, like, a lifetime, and I'm really starting to lose it, so I tell the flight attendant, 'Hey, this girl, this woman, she loves me. It's her birthday, and she loves me. I have to get off this plane.'"

"And they let you?"

"No! They told me to sit the fuck down!"

"This story is really long. Can you consolidate just this once? I really want to kiss—"

He pushed his index finger against her lips. "This is the deal, Nicole. You talked a big game on that podcast of yours. This is your prize. You begged for this. This is your life now."

She glared at him, laughing. He pulled her closer, smirking.

"So finally, I'm off the plane and Dave finds me, which is a whole other sidequest, and then we rush back to my new apartment because I had something I wanted to bring you. Then we speed back to my old place, because you said you were at my door, but you weren't there. So then we race over to your house, ring the bell. Some lovely family that appears to be idly rich has moved in—great people, very cute dog, gave me a Popsicle—and they said they didn't know where you moved, but they gave me your realtor's number, so I called her, but she was at a boot camp, and once she realized I didn't want to buy a house, she seemed a little annoyed, so that was a dead end. And that's when I realized I should call Mari, that—"

"Why didn't you call me? This story makes no sense."

"Because I wanted to go big! Because I wanted to surprise you! Come on!"

Nicole pulled him in tighter, burrowing her face into his sweatshirt, breathing him in as he talked and talked and talked.

"So then," he said, "finally, on the third try, Mari picks up. Apparently, she missed my first two calls because she was too busy planning you a sad retreat to the coast of Portugal or something. Anyway, she says you're living with her, that you got a job you really like, that—"

"Logan, you have to shut up. You have to get to the point. When I said I wanted to want to kill you, I did not mean immediately. I meant eventually. Like, when I'm fifty."

"You know what, Nicole?"

"What?"

He lifted her off the ground, twirled her in a circle, and pulled her in so tight her heart nearly burst. "You're lucky."

"Oh yeah? Why's that?"

"Because I'm a very nice guy."

"That right?"

"That's right. I'm going to forgive you for telling me to shut up. I'm going to kiss you for, like, forever. And then, after that, you're going to bring me up to Mari's, and I'm going to meet all your noisy friends, and then I'm going to eat all of Mari's food, and then, when that's done, I'm going to take you home and start making up for lost time."

Nicole hooked her fingers into his belt loop. "Plan approved. But those noisy friends are . . . it's my sister. And Valerie. They're both here."

"The baby's here? I get to meet the baby!?"

"I mean, you can't actually meet the baby yet. She's inside Valerie. That's typically how—"

"It's a girl? You're having a girl!?"

Nicole nodded, tears in her eyes.

"I'm so happy for you!" he said. "Can we call my mom? Can we please FaceTime my mom?"

"After we bang, yes. Like, tomorrow morning, okay? We can get on a plane. We can go meet her. Then we can fly to Saint Louis, meet my parents, get it all done in a day. You still have a zillion miles, right?"

Logan grinned, finding her face. Their lips nearly locked.

"Ah!" He pulled away. "I almost forgot. I got you something."

He opened his workbag and handed her the most horrendously wrapped, six-inch-by-six-inch rhombus of a package she'd seen in her thirty-three years of life.

"I assume you'll handle the wrapping from this point forward," Logan said as she peeled back the crinkled, cut-all-wrong, confetti-patterned paper he'd taped directly onto the gift itself. "But if not, that's fine. We'll just be party bag people. I'm good with that."

Nicole laughed, pulling the last few scraps away. It was a book—a board book. *Goodnight Mr. Darcy*.

"Logan, I—"

"Damnit! You've already read it, haven't you? I can get you something else. I can—"

She kissed him.

She kissed him for a long, long time.

"I love you," she said, arms around his neck. "You are such a fucking moron, and I love you. Nothing you say makes any sense. This summer—it was the best, worst thing that could've ever happened to me. I am so unbelievably lucky. You are a complete and utter bonehead. The king of the dingbats. I still cannot believe how much I ended up loving you."

"Sweetest words I've ever heard," he said, kissing her again.

And then, laughing, he carried her up the stairs to Mari's apartment while she tugged on the neck of his sweatshirt, continued to tear him to absolute shreds, and looked into his eyes and told him she loved him over and over again.

Looked into his eyes and saw some other life, starting to unfold.

Saw some other story, finally ready to be told.

EPILOGUE

May, Two Years Later

There was no alarm.

There was no waking up slow.

There was only Gracie Hausman Speyer, screaming into the monitor before the clock had struck six.

"Mammmmmmmaaaaaa!"

Nicole rolled over and groaned, then yanked her phone off the charger, threw on a sweatshirt, and wandered into her daughter's room. Standing in the crib, glaring at her mother, was three feet of full-blown toddler—brown pigtails, ink-blue eyes, and a terribly matted, plush octopus dangling from her cute little fist.

"Gracie, baby, why are you awake? It's so early. It's too early."

"I'm hungry!" She put her less-pudgy-by-the-day arms in the air. "Uppy?"

Nicole chuckled, then pulled Gracie into her arms and padded down the creaking hardwood into a fairly tidy kitchen where an open jar of peanut butter sat on the tile countertop, giant spoon plunked in it. Nicole rolled her eyes, then tossed the utensil in the sink and screwed the lid back on the container. She started the coffee, then flung a frozen waffle in the toaster while Gracie—now in the living room, chasing a not-particularly-pleased Nero around the coffee table—squealed with delight.

By quarter to eight, Nicole and Gracie had read six board books, completed three puzzles, built one architecturally insignificant castle out of magnetic tiles, and watched the same episode of *Peppa Pig* twice. After setting Gracie up with a few crayons and smushing flat a second helping of blueberries for her very fruit-motivated offspring, Nicole collapsed onto the couch. She was in the middle of texting Valerie a few thoughts about next week's recording when her phone buzzed.

> Outside. Need help.

She secured Gracie behind her baby gate, then stepped outside, where Gabe was standing on the porch with a tray of smoked salmon in one hand and a Gabe-size, definitely not-Nicole-approved teddy bear in the other.

"Uh, what is that?"

"This? It's a bear! It's from Costco!"

Nicole shook her head, laughing, then grabbed a bag of bagels from the back seat of Gabe's new car. She held the front door open for him as he slipped across the threshold, arms full.

"Daddy!"

"Is that my little girl!?" Gabe crouched over the playpen as Gracie, shrieking at the sight of her new plush companion, leapt straight into his arms. "Those pajamas are so fun! Are they new? Look at you! You're so cool!"

Nicole smiled. They'd been working on telling Gracie things like that. Things besides *you're so pretty* or *you're so smart*. Gabe and Nicole were always working on something or another. Mostly, though, on making sure Gracie knew that she was loved and wanted and the center of their universe, even if her story had been a little different from the start.

The front door opened.

"Nic? Is Gabe here? That his new car out front?"

"Hey, man," Gabe said, outstretching his hand while Gracie bounced on his hip. Logan wiped his palm on the front of his shorts, then shook Gabe's hand with a smirk.

"That's, uh, quite a bear you've brought us."

Gabe gave Nero a little scratch as he passed by, tail wagging. "Couldn't help myself. I got her one for my place too."

"I get it. I ordered her this ball pit thing last month and then, after we put Gracie down for her nap, Nicole looked at me with a straight face and suggested we keep it in my trunk when we weren't using it."

"She ask it like a question? Like it was your idea? Or was it more of a—"

"Well, isn't this just adorable," Nicole said. "You two, bonding over how annoying I am."

Gabe laughed as Logan, grinning, walked over to Nicole and wrapped his sweat-drenched body around hers until she was smiling, then smooshed his flushed, salty face into her neck until she was shrieking, squirming, shoving him away.

"Sorry, Nic." He pinched her waist before wandering into the kitchen to pour himself a cup of coffee. "It's just . . . you're so annoying."

She glared at him, then at Gabe, as Gracie—now laughing too, because it must've seemed like the thing to do—wriggled out of Gabe's arms and into Logan's lap where he'd just taken a seat at the kitchen table. Gabe sat down across from them as Nicole grabbed a few plates and Logan tore open the bag of bagels. And then, like they always did on Saturday mornings, rain or shine, good week or bad, Gabe's place or Nicole and Logan's, the three of them sat around and ate breakfast and let Gracie leap from lap to lap, soaking up all the attention—and all the strawberry cream cheese—she possibly could.

And then, around noon, when Gracie had gone home with her dad for the weekend and Nicole and Logan had crawled into their half-made bed to try and sleep off another long week, Nicole rolled herself into Logan's arms, pulled the comforter past their shoulders, and closed her tired eyes.

A second later, they flung open.

"Logan," she said, sitting up, nudging him awake. He stared at her—eyes sleepy, adjusting, confused. "What'd you write on that sheet of paper?"

"Wh-what?"

"The day you first kissed me. When I asked you what you'd do to me if I went to the Tar Pits without you? I forgot all about it. I just remembered."

He rubbed his eyes again, then smirked. "I already did it."

"You did? When? That night after the Grand Canyon? Or that time after the salmon festival? Oh, or after I watched the entirety of King Felix's perfect game in that bathing suit you like?"

He shook his head, laughing.

"No, Nicole," he said, pulling her into his arms and drifting back to sleep. "Last October. When I married you."

Acknowledgments

I've wanted to write a novel my entire life. But for years, the stories I started went nowhere. I didn't have anything interesting to say. Then, at twenty-seven, my husband and I started trying to have a baby. I went through everything Nicole went through and more—if I'd given Nicole my entire fertility history, it would've read as unbelievable—and still, nothing worked. A month before my thirtieth birthday, my doctors finally called it: I could not carry children.

At that point, we moved on to gestational surrogacy—a complicated arrangement and an enormous privilege. But that didn't work either. In fact, after the second transfer, my doctor suggested it was time to stop treatment altogether. Like Nicole and Gabe, my husband and I decided to throw a Hail Mary, mostly out of love for our carrier, Ashley, and respect for the three-attempt contract we'd signed. Nine months later, my daughter was born.

To this day, I refuse to believe that the final transfer worked for any other reason than *it just did*. I did not deserve motherhood any more or less than any other human on this planet who desires it. I was fortunate enough to try over and over again until, one day, it simply worked.

But when I realized I was finally going to become a mother, the pain of infertility did not magically wash away. Like Nicole in that ultrasound scene, hearing my child's heartbeat for the first time may have lifted some of the panic, but it did not erase the years of anguish. The pain had festered, and I'd been changed. In relentless pursuit of parenthood, I'd become someone I didn't recognize.

But in my darkest of days, long before we'd met Ashley, when I was sleeping fourteen hours a night, spending my savings on fertility treatments that seemed to work on everyone but me, and sticking around a job I did not love because I was always "nine months away from motherhood," I also knew that, finally, I'd found a story worth writing.

But my experience, in and of itself, was not enough to fill a book. Growing smaller and smaller in a world I'd built for myself with a certain vision in mind was interesting, sure, but it wasn't four-hundred-pages interesting. I needed conflict. I needed my husband to fuck our dog walker. I needed an undeniable, fresh-out-of-the-slammer connection I'd never had a chance to explore. And I needed for all these events—the transfer, discovering the affair, reconnecting with "that guy" from work—to happen within hours of each other . . . before my unnamed protagonist could think better of it.

And that, in essence, was how *The Best Worst Thing* was born. It began as an exploration of my trauma, and then, as Nicole and Logan and the rest of this cast came to life, I disappeared from the story—and the book began to write itself.

There are a million ways for your body to let you down, but there are even more ways to fall in love. We are so much more than what our organs can or cannot do, and we were put on this Earth, above all else, to love. It has been one of the highlights of my life to watch Nicole—and myself—uncover that truth, one page at a time.

And now, without further rambling, are the people who made this book possible.

Ashley Lowe, you made me a mother and showed me a kindness I did not know existed. You changed my life in so many ways. I love you.

ACKNOWLEDGMENTS

My agent, Sabrina Taitz. Thank you for believing in my voice—and for making my dreams come true. Also, for not letting me go on sub with a 431-page manuscript. I hope we get to do this forever.

My editor, Shannon Plackis. You get it, and you get me, and you are so good at giving feedback that it's legitimately terrifying. You're also maybe the only woman on this planet who's more down bad for Logan than I am. The minute we got on that call, I knew it had to be you. Thank you for taking a chance on me.

My husband, Ryan. Thank you for picking up the slack when I decided to spend eighteen months writing a book nobody asked for. Thank you for being my toughest critic and biggest fan. You're a Logan, and I love you. Thank you for asking me to get a bagel after class sophomore year and then never letting me go. And also, for line editing earlier versions of this book twice.

My daughter, Leila. I love you, peanut. Why are you reading this? You cannot read this book until 2037. It's for adults!

My best friend, Aylin Cook. You absolute angel. You listened to me talk about fake people for years, hyped my horrifically bad first draft, and made me believe I could do something impossible, and then, my god, I did. I love you. You have changed my life over and over and over again.

My beta readers: Jill Burriss, Casey Bryan, Helen Okie, Rick Okie, and Rosine Okie. My writing bestie, Elizabeth Richardson. Bridget Costello. Kelani Nicholas. My father, Robert Kramer, and my sister, Lisa Kramer. Kerianne Steinberg. Andrew Kenward, for listening to me yap about how I was going to write a book for twenty years and then, when I finally did, telling me exactly what to do next.

Everyone at Avon, William Morrow, and HarperCollins who

said yes to this story and helped bring it into the world: Yeon Kim, Marie Vitale, Deanna Bailey, Jessica Lyons, May Chen, Tessa Woodward, Jennifer Hart, and Liate Stehlik.

Everyone at William Morris Endeavor, for everything you do behind the scenes. Cashen Conroy, Karolina Kaim, Alicia Everett, and Lauren Rogoff.

Lastly, my mother, Judy Kramer. You're the mom who made me Rice Krispies Treats when I broke my arm on Bike Day. I don't even remember it hurting now. I just remember being really, really happy. I miss you so much. Thank you for everything. Don't worry, I'll find a way to hack into your Facebook and make sure all your friends know I wrote a book.

Oh, and to any human whose body has ever let them down. I hope you find your silver lining. I'd like to think that, most times, when we're ready to look, it's already there.

Discussion Questions

1. When the story opens, it's clear that Nicole's life has grown impossibly small in pursuit of motherhood. Has there been a situation where you've felt disproportionately frozen, stuck, or small? How did it feel when others got the things you wanted or the things you were too afraid, distracted, or numb to go after yourself?

2. Mari's drunken suggestion to knock on Logan's door mere hours after Nicole's marriage falls apart is objectively bonkers. Would you have gone to see your Logan? What would you have done that night if you were in Nicole's shoes?

3. Nicole, for years, knew something was wrong in her marriage. Do you blame her for sticking with the life she had planned out with Gabe? Was there an earlier point in the timeline where you felt Nicole could've changed her life—or where you personally might've done something differently?

4. Nicole leans heavily on Mari, Paige, and Valerie in the final chapters of this story. Who are the friends who've changed your life, and how were they there for you at your lowest?

5. Logan serves as a steady, patient mirror for Nicole, who has so much growing up to do. Have you had a partner or friend who saw the best in you when you could barely see yourself? How did that kind of love change you and the way you saw the world?

6. Nicole's experiences with infertility and infidelity affect every area of her life, including her confidence, self-worth, and sex drive. We see her reclaim her body and learn to trust again, little by little, throughout this story. Have you ever been in a situation where your body or someone you trusted betrayed you? How did those wounds change you, and how did you begin to heal?

Author photo courtesy of the author

LAUREN OKIE studied English and American Literature at NYU. When she's not exploring old traumas or blocking sex scenes on the backs of grocery lists, Lauren works as a copywriter. Originally from Miami, she lives with her husband and daughter in Hermosa Beach, California. This is her debut novel.

Instagram: @laurenokieauthor

DREAM CARS

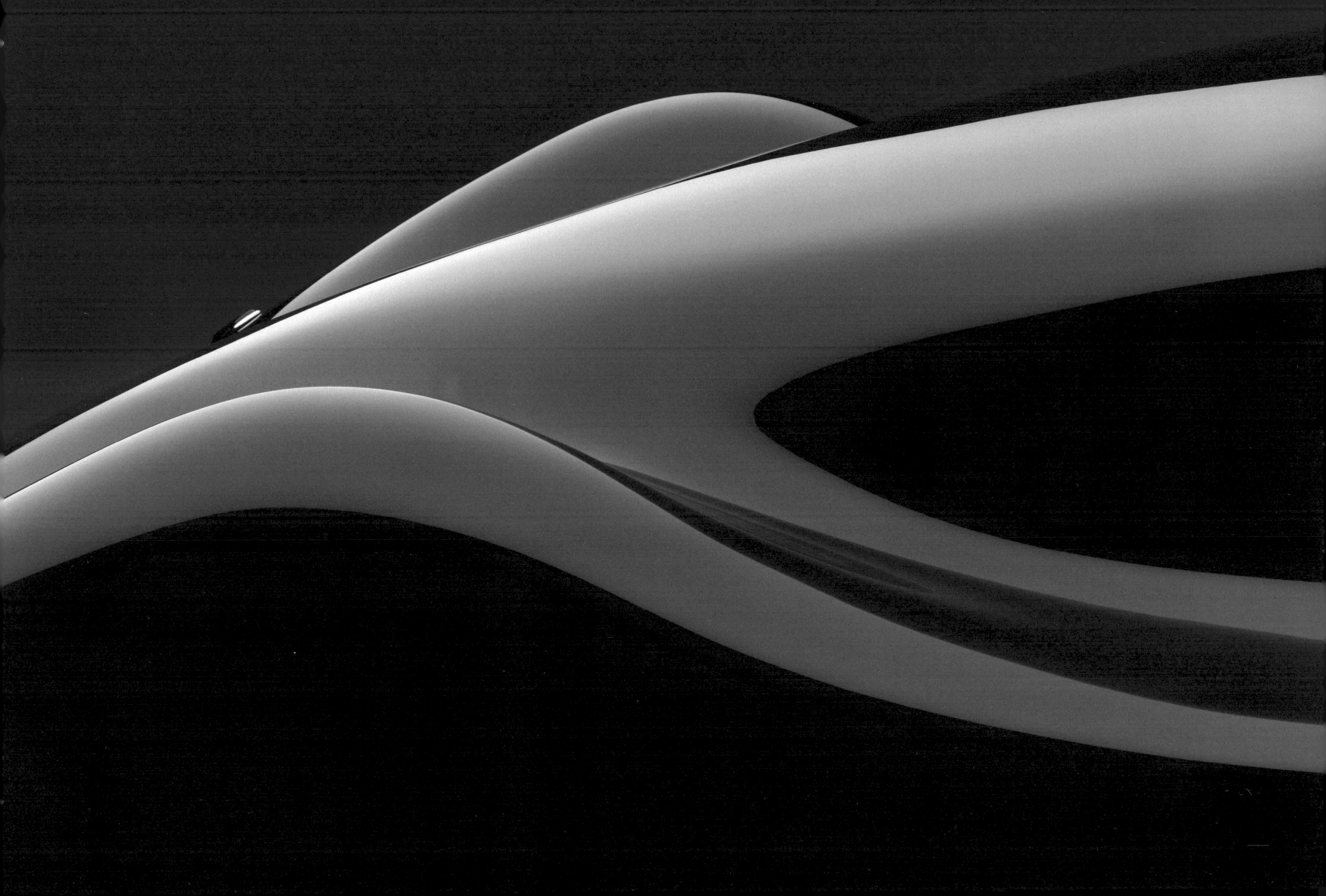

DREAM CARS
INNOVATIVE DESIGN, VISIONARY IDEAS

SARAH SCHLEUNING

KEN GROSS

HIGH MUSEUM OF ART, ATLANTA

Skira Rizzoli
NEW YORK

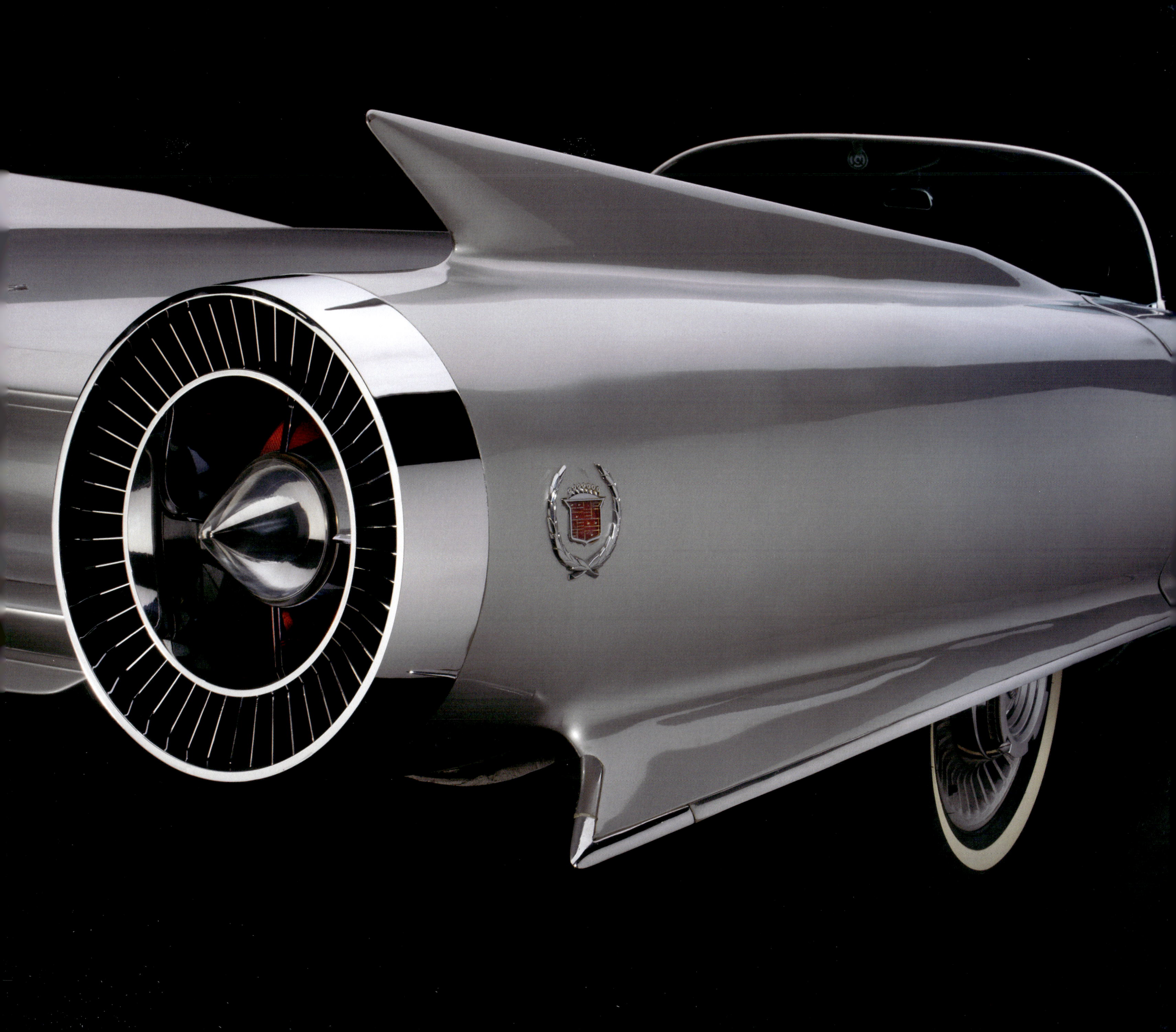

140 TEMP 200
100 215
80 120 160
40 OIL PRESSURE 200
20 40 60 80 100 120 140 160
MILES

Curator's Acknowledgments   6
SARAH SCHLEUNING

Director's Foreword   9
MICHAEL E. SHAPIRO

Sponsor's Statement   11

Dream Cars: Innovative Design, Visionary Ideas   13
SARAH SCHLEUNING

THE AUTOMOBILES
KEN GROSS

1934 Voisin *C-25 Aérodyne*   42
1934 Edsel Ford *Model 40 Special Speedster*   46
1935 Bugatti *Type 57S Compétition Coupé Aerolithe*   50
1936 Stout *Scarab*   56
1941 Chrysler *Thunderbolt*   60
1942 Paul Arzens *L'Œuf électrique*   66
1947 Norman Timbs *Special*   70
1948 Panhard *Dynavia*   76
1948 *Tasco*   82
1951 General Motors *Le Sabre XP-8*   88
1953 General Motors *Firebird I XP-21*   92
1954 Alfa Romeo (Bertone) *Berlinetta Aerodinamica Tecnica 7 (B.A.T. 7)*   96
1955 Chrysler (Ghia) *Streamline X "Gilda"*   100
1956 Buick *Centurion XP-301*   104
1959 Cadillac *Cyclone XP-74*   110
1970 Ferrari (Pininfarina) *512 S Modulo*   116
1970 Lancia (Bertone) *Stratos HF Zero*   122
2001 BMW *GINA Light Visionary Model*   126

Selected Bibliography   133

Checklist of the Exhibition   136

Image Credits   141

NOTE TO THE READER The following format is used to reference each automobile. The year the automobile was made is first. Following the marque (or individual designer), parentheses are used for coachbuilders when not fabricated by the marque. Finally, the car's title is italicized, as is customary for a work of art.

Curator's Acknowledgments

The initial concept for this exhibition was American "dream cars" of the 1950s, first proposed by automotive expert Ken Gross to Michael E. Shapiro, the High's Nancy and Holcombe Green, Jr., Director, in late 2010, shortly before my arrival at the High Museum of Art in May 2011. In consultation with Ken, I expanded the scope of the exhibition to include European and American concept cars from 1933 to today. I am grateful to have been entrusted with curating and expanding the project through the perspective of design history. *Dream Cars* is a visionary exploration of design and innovation through the lens of the automobile, with a dynamic range of examples, including many of the originally proposed dream cars. I extend my gratitude to Michael E. Shapiro and Director of Collections and Exhibitions David Brenneman for their support and for the opportunity to craft this project. I also would like to thank Ken Gross, consulting curator for the exhibition, who helped us navigate the automotive waters and kindly shared his expertise and enthusiasm for the material.

For their support and participation, Ken Gross and I would like to thank the lenders to the exhibition, who graciously agreed to share their vehicles with our visitors. My gratitude goes to Merle and Peter Mullin and the Mullin Automotive Museum Foundation, and Susan Bendrick (1934 Voisin *C-25 Aérodyne*); Kathleen Stiso Mullins, Megan Callewaert, and the Edsel and Eleanor Ford House (1934 Edsel Ford *Model 40 Special Speedster*); Christopher Ohrstrom (1935 Bugatti *Type 57 Compétition Coupé Aerolithe*); Larry Smith (1936 Stout *Scarab*); Roger Willbanks (1941 Chrysler *Thunderbolt*); Serge Chambaud, Tony Basset, Aminata Zerbo, and the Musée des Arts et Métiers, (1942 Paul Arzens *L'Œuf électrique*, owning institution); Gary and Diane Cerveny (1947 Norman Timbs *Special*); Richard Keller, Emmanuel Bacquet, Martin Biju-Duval, and the Cité de l'Automobile—Collection Schlumpf (1942 Paul Arzens *L'Œuf électrique*, displaying institution); Laura Brinkman, Aaron Warkentin, and The Auburn Cord Duesenberg Automobile Museum (1948 *Tasco*); Edward T. Welburn, David Barnas, Greg Wallace, Dave Patterson, Mike Erdodi, and General Motors and the GM Heritage Center (1951 General Motors *Le Sabre XP-8*, 1953 General Motors *Firebird I XP-21*, 1959 Cadillac *Cyclone XP-74*, and 1953 *Firebird I XP-21 scale model*); Scott Grundfor and Kathleen Redmond (1955 Chrysler [Ghia] *Streamline X "Gilda"* and 1954 *Sculpture in Motion*); Tim Shickles, Jeremy Dimick, and the Sloan Museum (1956 Buick *Centurion XP-301*); Silvana Appendino and Collezione Pininfarina (1970 Ferrari [Pininfarina] *512 S Modulo*); XJ Wang Collection (1970 Lancia [Bertone] *Stratos HF Zero*); Dirk Arnold, Stacy Morris, Wayne Shulte, Liz DeSantis, and BMW of North America, Klaus Kutscher and BMW Classic and BMW Museum Munich (2001 BMW *GINA Light Visionary Model*); Detlev von Platen and The Porsche Museum Stuttgart, and Bernd Harling of Porsche Cars North America (2010 Porsche *918 Spyder Concept Car*); Paolo Martin (1970 Ferrari [Pininfarina] *512 S Modulo* original sketches); Jean S. and Frederic A. Sharf and Mark Wallison (Carl Renner works on paper); Brett Snyder (eight assorted works on paper); Carl Solway and Carl Solway Gallery (1981 *Dymaxion* patent); and Cathy Henderson, Helen Baer, Sonja Reid, and The Harry Ransom Center at The University of Texas at Austin (Norman Bel Geddes works on paper).

Many people at the High were instrumental in bringing this project to fruition. I am especially thankful to Berry Lowden Perkins, decorative arts and design curatorial assistant, for all that she brings on a daily basis: her high degree of professionalism, detailed loan and research assistance, communications between the moving parts, and overall diligence in keeping this project on track from its inception. Research Assistant Melissa Maichele also deserves special recognition for her tireless dedication to this project and superb research on the vehicles, designers, and overall history of car design. I am greatly indebted to both of these individuals.

Other departments at the High played an important role in the realization of this project. My thanks go to the following: Exhibitions (Amy Simon, Jim Waters, Larry Miller, Leslie Petsoff, and Maria Kelly), Creative Services (Angela Jaeger, Rachel Bohan, Ewan Green, John Paul Floyd, and Heather Medlock), Registrar and

Rights and Reproduction (Frances Francis, Becky Parker, Paula Haymon, and Laurie Kind), Education (Virginia Shearer, Julia Forbes, Lisa Hooten, Erin Dougherty, Nicole Cromartie, and Deanna Clark), Development (Woodie Wisebram, Susan Aspinwall, Ruth Richardson, Anika Madden, Matthew Tanner, and Ashleigh Hagan), Finance (Rhonda Matheison and Amy Arant), Marketing and Public Relations (Kristen Delaney, Lisa Simon, Felicia Edlin, and Marci Tate), Web (Adam Fenton), Operations and Facilities (Philip Verre and Kevin Streiter), Preparators (Gene Clifton, Cayse Cheatam, Edward Hill, Brian Kelly, Caroline Prinzivalli, and Thomas Sapp), and the entire Security team. I also extend my thanks to Curator of Photography Brett Abbott for his aid in photography research, decorative arts and design departmental interns Indigo Gordon and Kimber Lawson for their contributions, and Toni Pentecouteau and Elizabeth Riccardi for their assistance.

Grateful acknowledgment must be extended to those individuals from around the world who have helped us piece together this exhibition detail by detail. For their willingness to offer information, instruction, expertise, time, and assistance to our cause, I extend my gratitude to Andrea Gollin; Brett Snyder; Dr. Thomas Mao; Archivists Larry Kinsel and Christo Datani at the GM Archives; Archivist Jon Bill at the Auburn Cord Duesenberg Automobile Museum; David Grainger, Thomas Douglas, and Marida Son at The Guild of Automotive Restorers; Adam Lovell, curator of collections at the Detroit Historical Society; David Morys and Libby Oakley at The Bugatti Trust; Danielle Szostak-Viers at Chrysler Historical Services; Paige K. Plant at the Detroit Public Library; Miles Collier, Scott George, and Mark Patrick at The Collier Collection; Marco Fazio at Automobilismo Storico Alfa Romeo Centro Documentazione, Leslie Kendall at the Petersen Automotive Museum; Hampton C. Wayt; Bruce Meyer; Chris Bangle; The National Automobile Museum; Don Williams, Tim McGrane, and the Blackhawk Museum and Collection (1954 Alfa Romeo [Bertone] *Berlinetta Aerodinamica Tecnica [B.A.T. 7]*); Jean-Michel Collart, Hervé Charpentier, and the Musée de l'Aventure Peugeot (1948 Panhard *Dynavia*, owning institution); Sotheby's Museum Services; Andrew Reilly; and Amy Christie and Meghan McGrail at RM Auctions. Special thanks go out to Webb Farrer at Webb Farrer Automotive Management Company Inc. for his expertise and guidance in handling these automotive masterworks, as well as to Michael Furman, Peter Harholdt, Michel Zumbrunn, and Urs Schmid for the principal photography used in the catalogue, and to Steve Petrovich, Shooterz LLC; Joe Wiecha; General Motors; and BMW for the photography of the 1934 Edsel Ford *Model 40 Special Speedster*, 1935 Bugatti *Type 57S Compétition Coupé Aerolithe*, 1956 Buick *Centurion XP-301*, and 2001 BMW *GINA Light Visionary Model*, respectively.

Lastly, a special thank you to Michael, Zuzu, and Vaughn.

Sarah Schleuning
CURATOR OF DECORATIVE ARTS AND DESIGN
HIGH MUSEUM OF ART

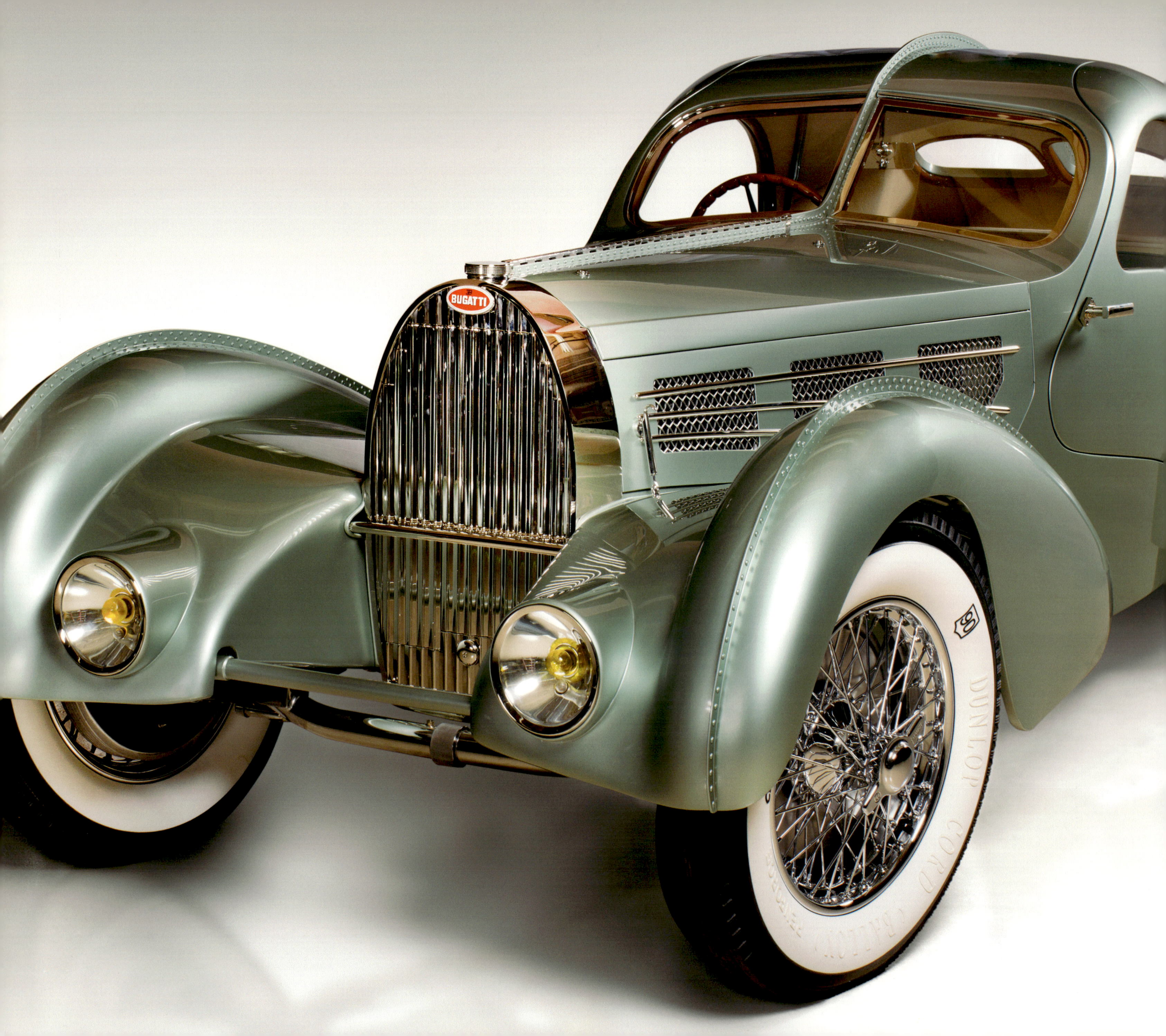
BUGATTI
DUNLOP CORD

Director's Foreword

The automobile has transformed the world in which we live. Everyone has a memory involving these highly evolved, mobile objects that are as diverse as the people who drive them. The automobile has touched each of our lives in some way or another, be it nostalgic memories from a family road trip, the freedom of driving for the first time as a teenager, or perhaps just dreaming of owning a particular car as a signifier of style and success.

From its earliest beginnings as a horseless carriage to the highly innovative designs produced by today's most advanced studios, the story of the automobile is one of innovation, fantasy, and progress, of individuality and freedom. The very idea of a carriage that could move without a horse once was unfathomable. The notion of a motor car equipped with a roof that could retract at the push of a button once was futuristic. And the idea of a car with skin made of fabric is still deemed unbelievable except to those who have seen it. The possibilities for the automobile have advanced far beyond what Henry Ford could have dreamed when the standardized, mass-produced "Tin Lizzie" *Model T* was mobilizing Americans by the millions and changing the landscape of the world a century ago.

It is this element of innovative fantasy that captured my imagination for this exhibition at the High Museum of Art. Following our successful 2010 exhibition *The Allure of the Automobile: Driving in Style, 1930–1965*, we wanted to further explore the automobile as a source of design inspiration. Under the expert tutelage of Sarah Schleuning, our curator of decorative arts and design, and with guidance from consulting curator Ken Gross, *Dream Cars: Innovative Design, Visionary Ideas* delves into the role the automobile plays in shaping ideas of the future and expanding the notion of what is possible. It features eighteen of the most innovative cars of their time, along with sketches, patents, and models by automotive design visionaries. These cars paved the way for future automotive progress and mesmerized the public. Displayed together for the first time in Atlanta, each of these cars is extraordinary in its own way, the brainchild of an industry studio team, or perhaps even one man's individual dream. Some were made out of desire for personal use; others were designed out of competing studios' desire to best their rival. Some are on display here in the United States for the first time. Some exist only in sketches or legend. But all of them are remarkable, rare, and reflect the creative visions of the future for the designers who dreamed them into reality.

We are indebted to the lenders, both public and private, who graciously agreed to share their treasures. The exhibition is made possible by Presenting Sponsor Porsche Cars North America, Inc. We gratefully acknowledge *AutoTrader*, *AutoTrader Classics*, Manheim, WSB-TV, *The Atlanta Journal-Constitution*, and WSB News Talk Radio for their generous support. Additional support for this exhibition is provided by the National Endowment for the Arts.

I hope you enjoy taking this road trip with us.

Michael E. Shapiro
NANCY AND HOLCOMBE T. GREEN, JR., DIRECTOR
HIGH MUSEUM OF ART

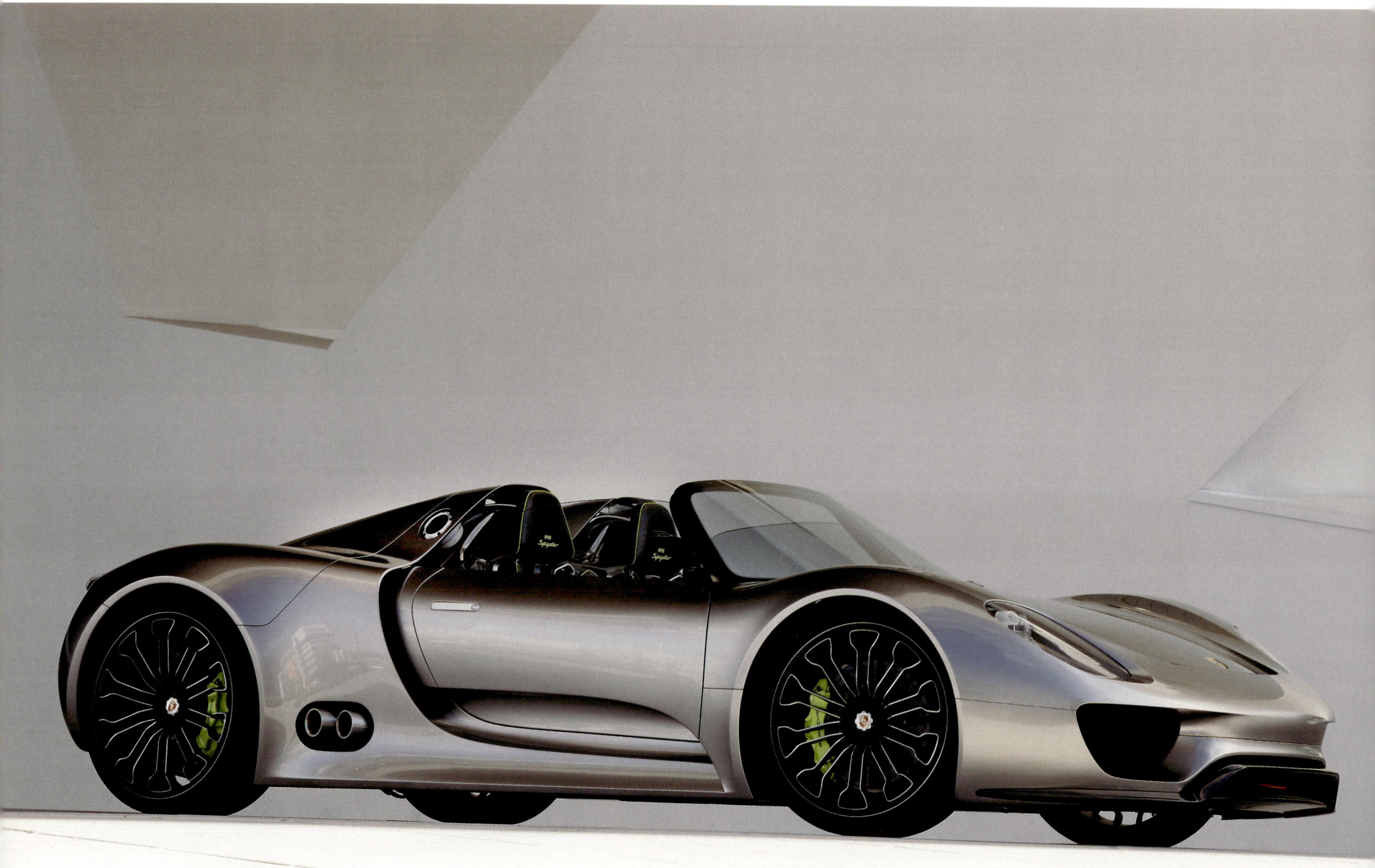

Sponsor's Statement

Design has always been one of the main drivers of man's fascination with automobiles. Designers are by virtue of their profession committed to think boldly, to produce objects that not only are pleasing to the eye but also illuminate a path into an exciting future. Design encompasses more than just looks; good design gets its justification from a distinct element of functionality. And it must be coupled with equally novel and daring technological elements in order to become relevant.

Since its beginning in 1948, Porsche has succeeded in introducing cutting-edge design solutions combined with ever more progressive engineering prowess. Through the decades, all of our sports cars kept their brand identity by adhering to the distinct Porsche design language, while each new model looked new and fresh, adhering to our founder's design credo, "form follows function." And while our designers and engineers were busy developing cars for the road—and did not often indulge in the creation of concept cars over the years—we are gratified that many of these machines became the objects of dreams for generations of car aficionados.

Porsche Cars North America is proud to sponsor *Dream Cars: Innovative Design, Visionary Ideas* after our successful partnership with the High Museum of Art in 2010 in *The Allure of the Automobile: Driving in Style, 1930–1965*. The reason for our engagement is twofold. For one, we identify greatly with the sentiment of the Museum's leadership that automobiles can, in fact, be works of art. The cars on display in this exhibition and the fascinating stories behind them are compelling proof that this belief is correct.

In addition—and equally important—is our company's obligation to give back to the community we call home and where we currently are building our own headquarters, including an Experience Center and a test track. As a corporate citizen of Atlanta, we strive to pay our share in helping to keep this great city's cultural fabric attractive and vibrant. This is why we have embraced wholeheartedly the opportunity to support an exhibition as has never before been staged in this country. Indeed, what better way for a company that knows a thing or two about dream cars than to join the High in realizing a showcase of the same name?

Of course, we are proud to show off our 2010 concept car, the Porsche *918 Spyder*, which epitomizes what a future super sports car can offer, namely fascinating design paired with technological capabilities that combine extreme performance with utmost frugality and environmental friendliness. And, as such, it fits right in with the boldest concepts on display.

We congratulate the High Museum of Art for this exquisite collection of dream cars and hope that its many visitors will enjoy a few hours that are both memorable and educational.

Detlev von Platen
PRESIDENT AND CEO

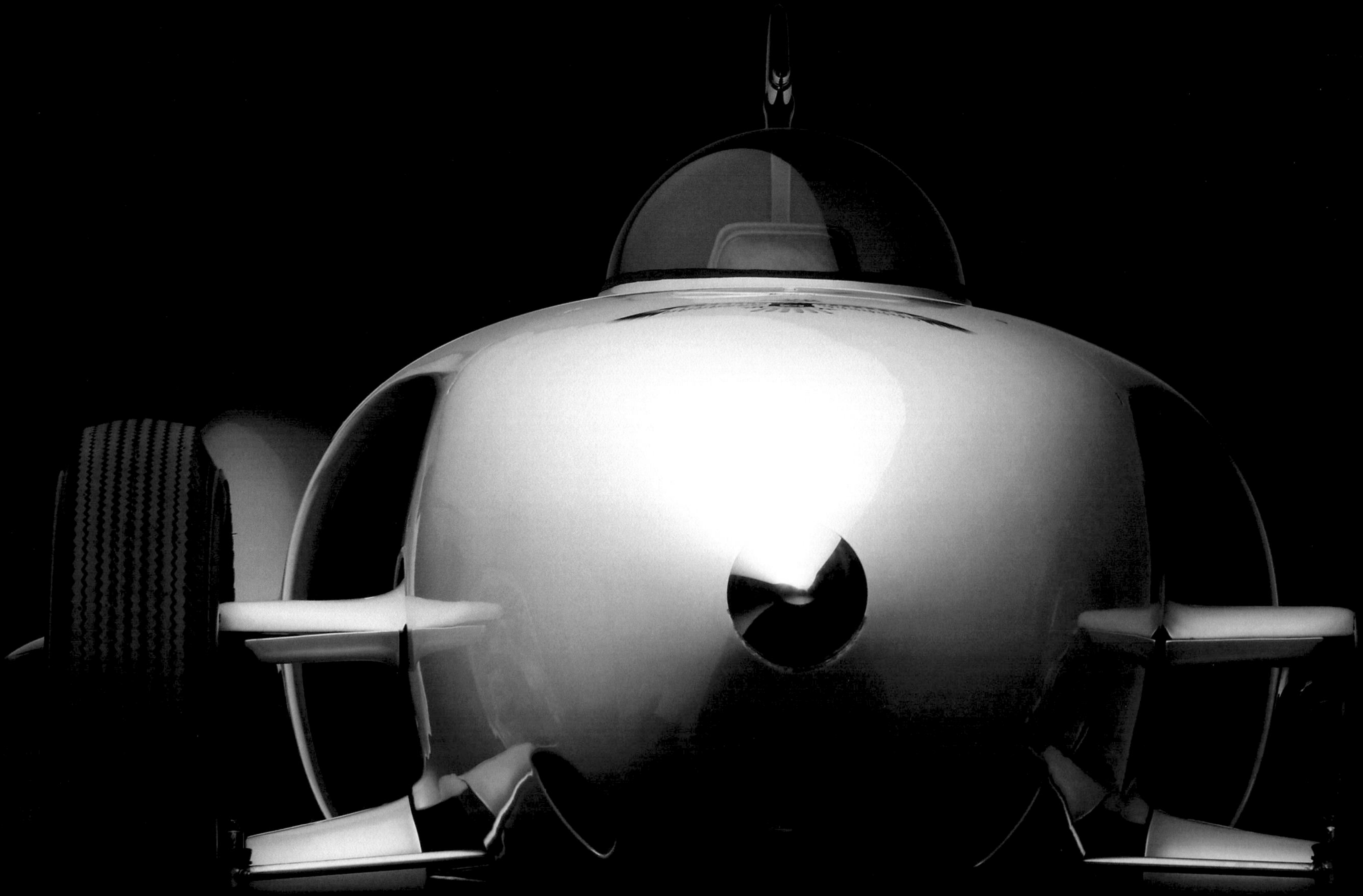

DREAM CARS
INNOVATIVE DESIGN, VISIONARY IDEAS

SARAH SCHLEUNING

... [We] dream of cars that will float and fly, or run on energy from a laser beam, or travel close to the ground without wheels. Such research may border on the fantastic, but so did the idea of a carriage going about the country without a horse.

—*THE FORD BOOK OF STYLING*, 1963[1]

The car moves us from place to place, taking us where we want to go, providing physical freedom that previously was unfathomable and challenging our perceptions of what is possible. As the automobile evolved from curiosity to daily necessity, its form advanced from the elevated, boxy, utilitarian shapes of the early twentieth century—for example, the Ford Motor Company's *Model T*—to the highly designed objects we know today. Innovations in automotive design owe much to the tradition of the concept car, which has continually challenged the status quo and generated both subtle and monumental changes to the ways cars look, function, and inspire.

The transition to motorized transportation is of course linked to the development of the internal combustion engine dating from Karl Benz (one of the pioneering founders of Mercedes-Benz) in 1886. Early on, automakers primarily focused on the inner workings of the machine, with design driven by practical concerns such as a hood protecting the engine. The first car bodies were adapted from horse-drawn carriages, and it took several decades for automotive design to shed its references to the past and develop its own visual language. Coupled with technological advances, the development of the field of industrial design, the rise of advertising, and the growing importance of the consumer, this design evolution led to a broader, more democratized market. New products such as the automobile needed to define themselves by more than just function. The 1938 General Motors brochure *Modes and Motors* explained to the public how the field was changing:

> For art in industry is comparatively new. Only in recent years has the interest of the manufacturer and user alike been expanded from the mere question of "Does it work?" to include "How should it look?" and "Why should it look that way?" Appearance and style have assumed equal importance with utility, price and operation. The artist and the engineer have joined hands to the end that articles of everyday use may be beautiful as well as useful.[2]

The form, style, and beauty of the automobile became just as important as its internal workings. Within a relatively short period of time, people's perception of the car shifted entirely. Originally viewed as a miraculous machine, the car became a projection of the style, values, and status of its owner; automotive design thus became "fashioned by function."[3] While individual concept cars are perhaps not as widely known as some of the iconic luxury automobiles—Rolls-Royce, Hispano-Suiza, or Delahaye—the role they played in automotive and design history (and, to a lesser and differing degree, in its present) was vital. The experimental, concept, or "dream car," as it became known in the early 1950s, is a unique chapter of the history of the automobile. The "dream" represented by these cars was that of future possibilities and pushing the limits of imagination and design, not that of a life of riches and excess. Concept cars were not objects the public could purchase, but rather the testing ground for innovations that might find expression in automobiles produced decades later.

Innovative Automotive Visions

Concept cars long have been a dynamic, actionable way for automakers, custom coachbuilders, and independent designers to showcase and demonstrate forward-thinking automotive design concepts. Imagine an egg-shaped electric car, a three-wheeled automobile with a built-in shopping cart, or a jet fighter rolling down the highway. All of these were among the ideas dreamed up by designers and are included in the selection of concept cars considered in the exhibition *Dream Cars: Innovative Design, Visionary Ideas* and this companion publication. Chosen from hundreds of concepts produced between 1933 and the present day, the visions for these cars are exciting to behold, especially in the context of more conventional contemporary models. Like most concept cars, those examined here were never intended for series production; they all are either singular or, if they made it to the production phase, single-digit production cars meant to explore new frontiers in design, technology, and style. The designers' and automobile companies' objectives were to point the way to the future, to test styling ideas, to predict and experiment with new technology, and, in the end, to dazzle the public and impress the competition. For the creation of these cars, in most cases practicality was not a consideration.

Under the leadership of automotive design legend Harley J. Earl, General Motors was the first to refer to concept cars as "dream cars" in a press release issued February 2, 1953, for the Detroit opening of GM's Motorama. This label quickly caught on and henceforth was used throughout GM publicity materials and soon by other car companies. Earl oversaw the groundbreaking styling department of General Motors from its inception in 1927 (initially called the Art and Colour Section, and later known as the Styling Section) until his retirement in 1959. While concept cars existed before Earl's tenure, those he developed for the Motorama expositions, which ran under various names from 1949 to 1961, introduced a new level of aspiration as well as public involvement. While the notion of dream cars—and even the very words—often evokes nostalgia for the American concept cars specific to the 1950s and 1960s with their prominent tail fins, boat-sized proportions, and bullet-shaped cones (known as Dagmars, coined after a buxom Hollywood starlet), the term is now universal.

Following GM's example, the other major automobile companies quickly established their own design studios. After an initial effort in the 1930s, Ford Motor Company founded its Advanced Styling division in 1948.[4] Its function and role as a maker of dream cars is explored in a 1957 publication:

> . . . a treasure house of ideas for both the immediate and the distant future. . . . Special projects are carried out, such as the creation of "dream cars," used often to test the reaction of the public to new ideas and also to help the product line studio stylists in their never-ending search for new themes and new features.[5]

The dream car, in short, was the embodiment of a better tomorrow.

Concept cars highlighted and advanced the creative possibilities of the automobile, as stylists were free to be inventive and engineers could stretch their imaginations. Often, many advanced attributes were combined in a single stunning show car that, for its day, was considered a technical marvel. But concept cars were much more than novelties; they were experiments. They left their mark not only through the impressive visuals evidenced in these pages, but on future generations of cars and car enthusiasts. General Motors' Styling Section noted, "Out of the merger of art, science and industry have come new techniques that have within themselves the ability to create an entirely new pattern and setting for the life of the world."[6] Ponder the rearview cameras, electrically powered windows, and curved windshields of today's cars. Initially introduced decades ago in concept cars and considered outlandish in their time, all are now standard elements in series production cars.

To produce an automobile, especially a fully functioning one, took significant time and resources. Cars designed for their conceptual value—rather than financial or practical reasons—significantly increased cost. Individuals driven more by vision than practicality, by dream rather than bottom line, created the cars discussed here; some worked under the auspices of automotive coachbuilders such as Carrozzeria Bertone or automobile makers such as General Motors, while others were independent. As the concept cars reflect, the designers' visions were quite varied. Some sought new technological solutions and alternatives such as electric or turbine engines; others found inspiration in different modes of modern transportation, including rockets, jets, and hovercraft. Ongoing scientific advances in aeronautics and aerodynamics beginning in the early twentieth century inspired new shapes that reduced wind resistance and evoked a progressive future.

One such concept car, the three-wheeled *L'Œuf électrique* ("electric egg"), was created by French artist, industrial designer, and engineer Paul Arzens in 1942 as a singular car for his personal use (fig. 1 and pp. 66–69). As its name suggests, the car was shaped like an egg, and it served as a convenient city car in Paris. Designed under the duress of the German occupation of the city during World War II, *L'Œuf* creatively responded to the period's shortages of petrol and other materials. Other cars were designed as generators of new ideas and potential products for future consumers; for example, General Motors hailed its 1951 *Le Sabre XP-8* show car as "a mobile experiment, a flexible project"[7] in its promotional material (fig. 2). This car and other like concept cars were intended to whet the public's appetite for features to come—in the case of the *Le Sabre*, seats that could be heated and interior moisture sensors that triggered the convertible top to close. These experimental cars positioned a company publicly as an innovator and a leader in the field, allowing designers, engineers, and scientists the freedom to create cars of the future—or, as they suggested, "today's fancies can be tomorrow's facts."[8, 9]

FIG. 1 *L'Œuf électrique* in front of the Eiffel Tower, Paris, 1950. Photographed by Arzens's friend Robert Doisneau.

FIG. 2 Brochure for General Motors *Le Sabre XP-8*, 1951.

The Early Dream Cars

The Buick *Y-Job*, designed in 1938 by Harley J. Earl—the US automotive industry's first styling chief—is often considered the seminal concept car. Completed in 1939, Earl created the dashing *Y-Job* as a one-off for his personal use. He drove it daily and considered it his first "laboratory on wheels," a phrase he used frequently years later to describe the ideology behind the GM concept cars. The *Y-Job* predicted many automotive styling features to come, including the low-slung, curvilinear profile; streamlined, wraparound bumpers; and the prevalence of power-operated functions, from retractable convertible tops to disappearing headlamps. The wide, horizontal front grille with thin, vertical slats became a hallmark of future Buicks for decades. Publicity photos of Earl with his car released in 1940 (fig. 3) helped increase the popularity not only of the *Y-Job* but of Earl himself, who became a company vice president that same year.

The 1941 Chrysler *Thunderbolt* (see pp. 60–65) was one of the early concept cars that competed with the Buick *Y-Job*. Its production was rushed so it would be ready for the October 1940 New York International Auto Show. Designed by Alex Tremulis, who originally worked for Earl, it was marketed as "The 'hit' of the New York Show" and the "the Car of the Future" (fig. 4). The car also was heavily promoted as having been created in a wind tunnel to educate the public about aerodynamics and streamlining as "the source of modern, so-called functional styling."[10] The wind tunnel testing provided scientific studies of how the car's shape dealt with continuous airflow and led to refinements that minimized resistance. Five examples of the *Thunderbolt* were produced, each in distinctive colors and accented with a small chrome thunderbolt on each door. The *Thunderbolt* was the first American car to feature an electrically operated retractable hardtop and disappearing headlamps (fig. 5). They were controlled by push buttons on the dashboard, which was leather-covered and featured round, etched Lucite dials. The car was made of modern materials: a predominantly aluminum body (with a steel hood and deck lid) and a chromium band encircling the entire base of the car, including front and rear fender skirts to cover the wheels. The brochure *Chrysler's Thunderbolt and*

FIG. 3 Harley Earl behind the wheel of the Buick *Y-Job*, 1940.

FIG. 4 Promotional postcard sent out by Chrysler dealerships advertising the 1941 *Thunderbolt*.

FIG. 5 The *Thunderbolt*'s retractable hardtop.

Newport: New Milestones in Airflow Designs boasts of this car as being "fashioned by function": "When you look at this beautiful Chrysler Thunderbolt, you are seeing far more than a magnificent motor car . . . you see a forecast of future car styling . . . you see a new milepost in the history of aerodynamics and functional design."[11] The *Thunderbolts* were publicized in part by a 1940–1941 promotional tour around the United States, after which the cars were sold to wealthy consumers.

While these are only two examples of many, the multiple stylistic innovations evidenced in the *Y-Job* and the *Thunderbolt* demonstrate how the concept car functioned as both an idea laboratory and a generator of dreams. These cars were not only functionally innovative but visually appealing as well, due to the increasing focus on the look of industrial objects. But style was not driven purely by aesthetic concerns—there was a strong marketing component in the push to continually advance the way cars looked and functioned. Like all other major industries in the 1930s, automobile companies embraced the notion of "planned obsolescence." New styles, colors, and features were introduced every year; to be truly modern, the consumer needed to have the latest and greatest advances in the field—a phenomenon that is alive and well today. One needs only to consider the frenzy surrounding the launch of each successive iPhone model as an example.

Early French Aesthetic Influences

The French dominated the design vocabulary of the early twentieth century, culminating in the 1925 Paris *Exposition internationale des arts décoratifs et industriels modernes*, which showcased the most modern design of the time, referred to as Moderne style, or what we have come to know as Art Deco.[12] Times were bleak by the late 1920s and people craved inspiration and optimism. World War I, the 1929 stock market crash, and the ensuing depression in the United States, which had worldwide repercussions, left people hoping for a better future as they entertained escapist fantasies about an ideal modern world. Just as they wanted to put the past behind them, people also wanted to move on from the visual modes of the time. Consequently, in industrial design—and, by extension, automotive design—the more angular forms of the 1910s and 1920s gradually were replaced by Machine Age curvilinear forms coming from the United States.

The cars of this period produced by French aeronautic and automobile designer and maker Gabriel Voisin mirrored the evolution of these influences. Voisin found success designing cars with long, angular Moderne-inspired lines. A 1925 *Vogue* cover (fig. 6) features a fashion illustration by Georges Lepape that depicts a couture model draped possessively over a Voisin, with

GEORGES LEPAPE/VOGUE © CONDÉ NAST 1925

FIG. 6 *Vogue* magazine cover drawn by Georges Lepape, 1925.

DREAM CARS 17

the marque's signature winged hood ornament—called the *cocotte*, or "little hen"—featured prominently. Voisin's cars were considered a sign of modernism and luxury and were owned by many of the period's greatest celebrities, including Harry Houdini, Rudolph Valentino, and Josephine Baker. Even the Swiss architect Le Corbusier often featured his own Voisin automobile in photographs of his modern buildings (fig. 7), by implication pronouncing both to be the best of modern design.

Voisin was not interested in bowing to popular aesthetics, particularly the American streamlined design or the Streamline Moderne style of the late 1920s and early 1930s. However, as the French automotive industry declined after the 1929 stock market crash and Voisin's own business struggled with bankruptcy, he introduced a new form with the *C-25 Aérodyne* (pp. 42–45) at the 1934 Paris *Salon de l'Automobile* (fig. 8). This was his "concept" of the new modern look distinguished by curvilinear shapes. Gone were the long, angular lines, which were replaced by elongated, double-arching forms and teardrop-shaped fenders. The remnants of Voisin's early angular designs were apparent only in the *cocotte* (fig. 9) and the jazzy, geometric-patterned interior upholstery fabric (see p. 43).

Voisin's shift in aesthetic influence marks a subtle decline in French dominance as tastemaker, although both he and France continued to play a role in automotive design, most notably with mini-cars in the late 1940s and 1950s. But after World War II, Italy, Germany, and the United States began to exert a greater influence on the industry as a whole, especially in the way of innovative automotive visions.

The Science of Styling: Aerodynamics and Streamlining

One of the most significant influences on automotive design during the 1920s and 1930s was aerodynamics, particularly the science of streamlining, which became very important in the 1930s. Not only was there a desire for cars to be faster, they needed to appear speedy as well. But it was not just automobiles; everything was

FIG. 7 Le Corbusier's Voisin *C7-10 HP* in front of Ville Stein, ca. 1928.

FIG. 8 *C-25 Aérodyne* at the *Salon de l'Automobile*, Paris, 1934.

FACING PAGE FIG. 9 Gabriel Voisin's signature hood ornament, the *cocotte*.

18 DREAM CARS

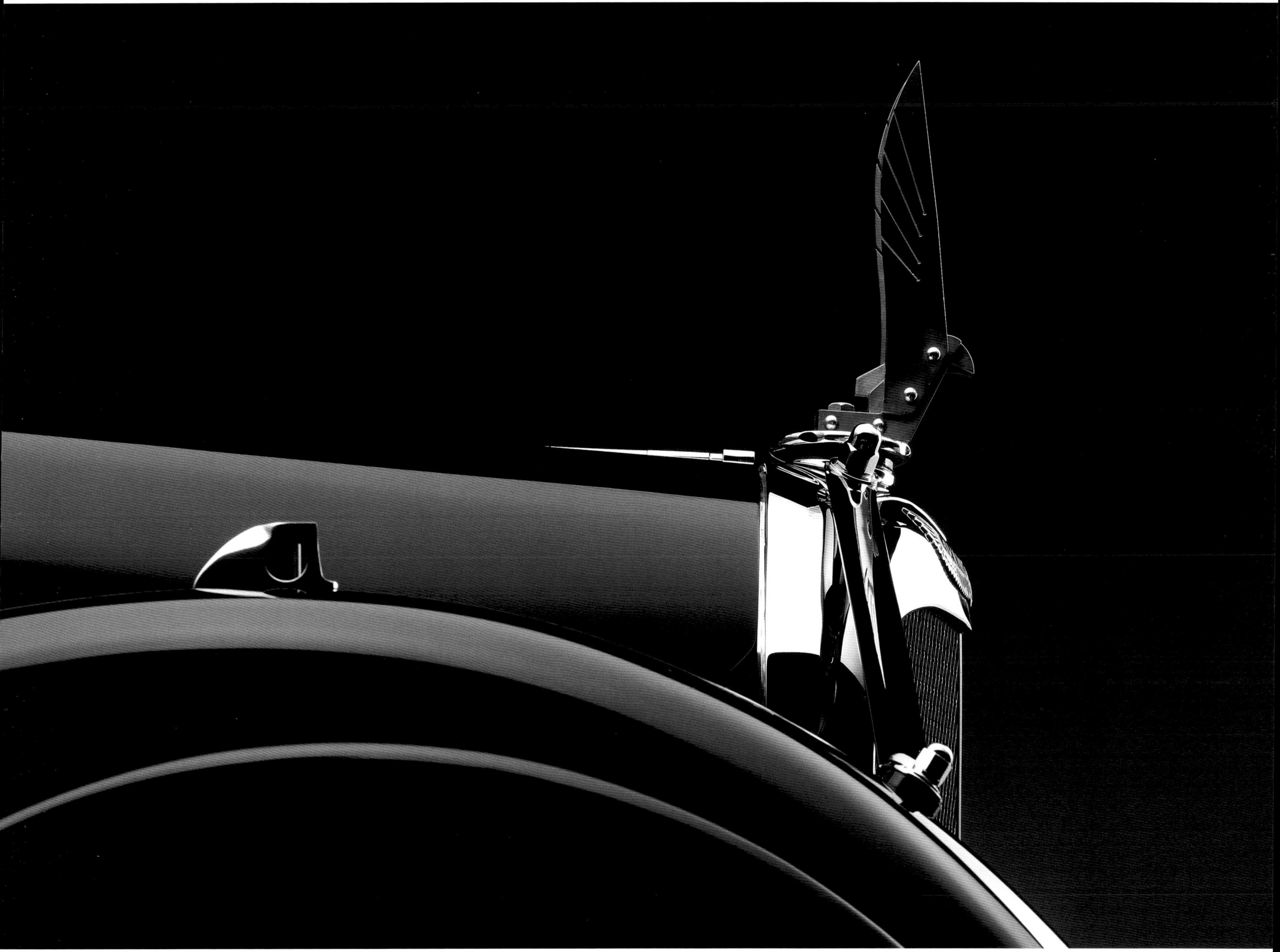

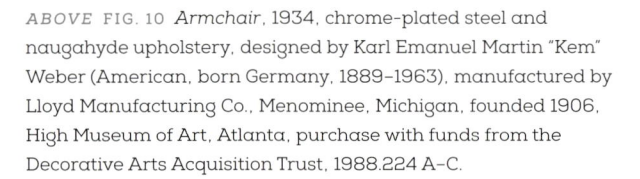

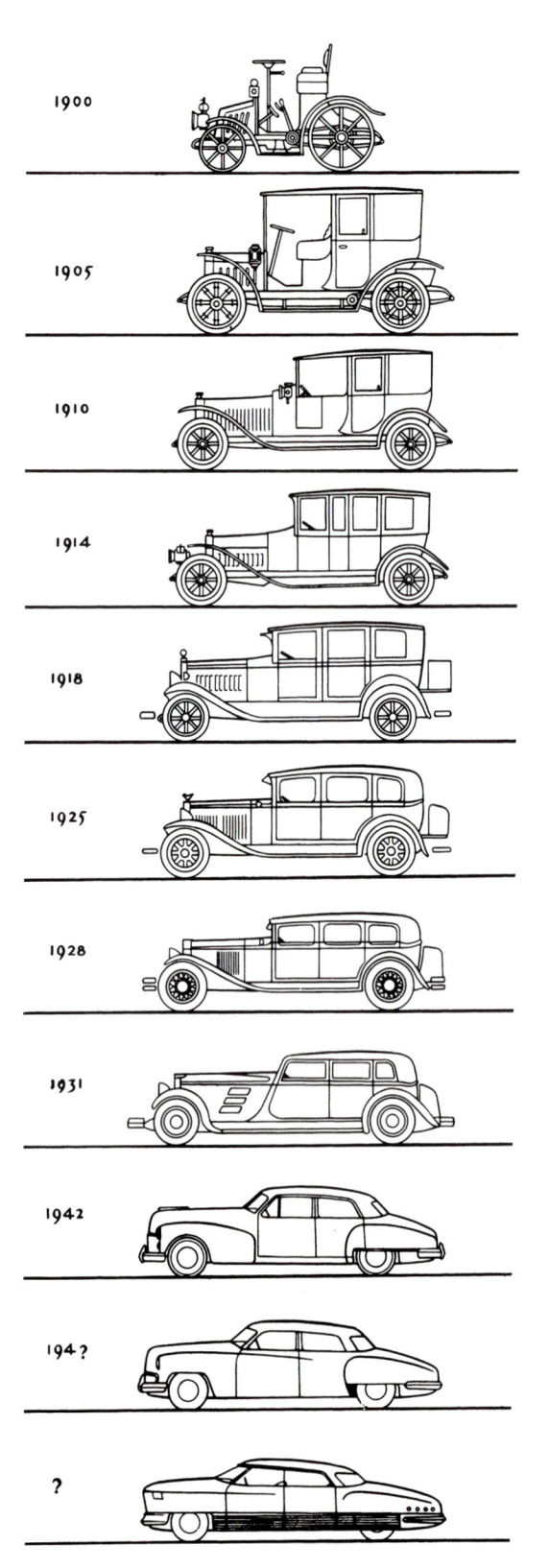

being streamlined, from ships and trains to chairs (fig. 10) and even pencil sharpeners. It became so ubiquitous that in 1933 industrial designer Raymond Loewy produced numerous visual charts to document the evolution of design with the influence of streamlining, including a profile of cars from 1900 to 1942 and beyond (fig. 11).

This was the era of the industrial designer, a time in which the designer of utilitarian objects began to enjoy greater cachet, especially when marketing products to the public. Individuals such as Loewy, Earl, and Russel Wright became known entities. Their signature styling became a selling point. In Earl's introduction to *Styling: The Look of Things*, he defined the stylist within this context:

> During the past twenty-five years, a new kind of creative person has appeared on the American industrial scene taking his place alongside the engineer, production expert, and scientist. Called industrial designer, or Stylist, depending on the custom of his particular business, his influence has grown so that he now controls the appearance of practically every product and convenience we use.
>
> His is the task of making these useful things beautiful, not in the sense of applying superficial surface ornamentation, but in developing a form of beauty exactly suited to the purpose—a form of beauty evolved from within.[13]

The stylist and industrial designer were making more than just objects; they were creating beautiful, functional works to be admired and consumed.

Another notable industrial designer of the period, Norman Bel Geddes, created designs for several cars in the streamlined style. His sketches for *Motor Car Number 9* (ca. 1933)[14] show a teardrop body, both with and without fins, on eight small wheels encased in their own teardrop fenders (figs. 12 and 13). The teardrop epitomizes the shape touted in scientific journals and articles of the day—and in Loewy's own streamlining chart—as the most aerodynamic form (fig. 14).

ABOVE FIG. 10 *Armchair*, 1934, chrome-plated steel and naugahyde upholstery, designed by Karl Emanuel Martin "Kem" Weber (American, born Germany, 1889–1963), manufactured by Lloyd Manufacturing Co., Menominee, Michigan, founded 1906, High Museum of Art, Atlanta, purchase with funds from the Decorative Arts Acquisition Trust, 1988.224 A–C.

RIGHT FIG. 11 Chart illustrating the changing shape of the automobile, by Raymond Loewy, 1933. Reproduced in Donald J. Bush, *The Streamlined Decade* (New York: Braziller, 1975).

20　DREAM CARS

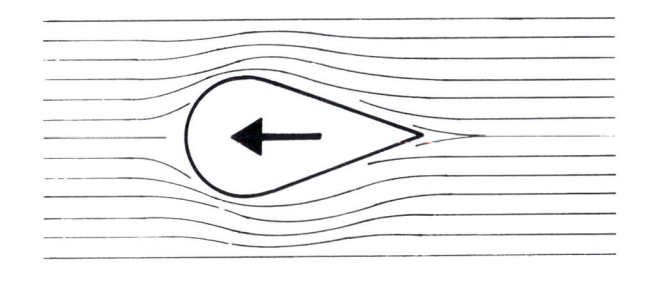

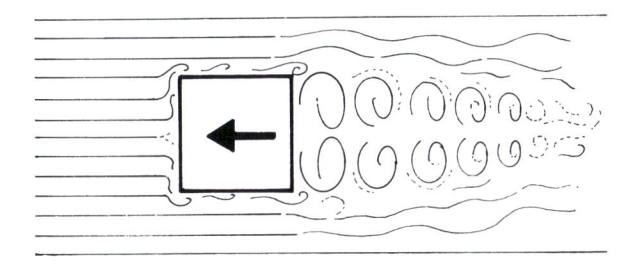

The teardrop shape is also evident in the 1948 Panhard *Dynavia* (see pp. 76-81). The design of *Motor Car Number 9* represents a teardrop in profile, while the body of the *Dynavia* is a tapering teardrop shape that is best appreciated from a bird's-eye view (fig. 15). The car has no angles or sharp edges. One feature that helped minimize wind resistance was the snub-nosed front, which combined a single headlamp, a bumper, and a rounded intake grille to help maintain the ovoid front form. Despite its diminutive stature, low profile, curved front, and pointed tail, the *Dynavia* could seat four and afforded expansive panoramic views. Panhard's French designer Louis Bionier also looked to nature—the shapes of birds and fish—as a source of inspiration for perfect aerodynamic forms.

Tensions gradually developed within the boundaries of streamlining, and in particular its true purpose. Some viewed streamlined design as a response to scientific information on aerodynamics—in other words, streamlining that supported forms such as rounded animals or bullet shapes, because those contours were more wind-resistant and efficient, as seen in automobiles such as the aptly named Stout *Scarab* (pp. 56–59). On the other hand was a more popularized version of streamlining, one that overrode science in favor of drama and overall aesthetic appeal, such as the fluted speed lines that wrapped around the Chrysler *Thunderbolt*.

FIG. 12 Drawing of *Motor Car Number 9* with fins, by Norman Bel Geddes, ca. 1933.

FIG. 13 Photograph of *Motor Car Number 9* model, without fins, by Norman Bel Geddes, ca. 1933.

FIG. 14 Diagram illustrating the principles of streamlining, by Raymond Loewy, ca. 1933. Reproduced in Donald J. Bush, *The Streamlined Decade* (New York: Braziller, 1975).

FIG. 15 A bird's-eye view of the teardrop-shaped 1948 Panhard *Dynavia*.

DREAM CARS 21

While the shape of the *Dynavia* was firmly rooted in scientific ideas of the most efficient, aerodynamic forms, the popular appeal of streamlined design stemmed from curvilinear shapes, shiny modern materials—chrome, tubular steel, vitrolite—and speed lines. In essence, an object's appeal was based on any design features that made it look like it was hurtling through space. In 1933 GM conducted a survey addressing the specific question of scientific versus popular streamlining. The results confirmed that it was the appearance of speed that mattered most to the consumer rather than actual speed performance.[15] In the end, it was the consumer who wielded the most power. While concept cars by nature offered more license and freedom to design, they were still driven by what would appeal to the public.

The Design Process

"Every step in designing an automobile is really a compromise between human imagination and human ingenuity—between what *might* be done and what *can* be done now," stated GM's Styling Section.[16] The design of dream cars—their style, presentation, and innate appeal—was the main focus of their conceptualization, although form had to work in tandem with function. Some concept cars built upon previous ideas, such as refining and expanding a bubble top or a wraparound fender, while others explored new ideas. As imaginative and often outlandish as some of the ideas were, all were carefully considered and meticulously developed. The design phase began with the stylists proposing variations of ideas, usually through numerous drawings. According to a GM publication, "An average of 1,500 separate sketches are prepared in the process of arriving at one finished design."[17]

Between 1908 and 1927 car ownership in the United States increased dramatically, from fewer than two hundred thousand to more than twenty million.[18] As demand grew, so, too, did the desire for diversity and progress in design, with the hope of new shapes, styles, colors, and gadgets. The evolution of automotive design in the early twentieth century is integrally linked, influenced by, and influential in a web of related factors—not only the growing appreciation for design, in which styling and aesthetic qualities became as important as the technology, but also the rise of advertising and marketing, which signified the importance of creating desire and perceived need for objects such as cars, and the development of a significant consumer market.

The increasing premium placed on design was registered by the automobile companies. GM, the largest company, was a leader in car design and the first company to have an in-house automotive styling studio. Its Art and Colour Section (established in 1927 and renamed the Styling Section in 1937 at Earl's insistence) championed the design attributes of a car as equivalent to its engineering feats. The department helped codify many of the steps that are still used in the process of designing a car, including the adoption of color renderings, full-scale drawings, and three-dimensional clay models. Earl quickly learned that he needed to maintain creative control over each car's progression, because after they passed through the Art and Colour Section, production engineers would develop the vehicles further, possibly eliminating some of the design aesthetic. In 1929 Earl requested that he have final approval on all vehicles after the production engineering changes were made, which he was granted.[19] In the meantime, the studio grew rapidly, from ten people when it started to three hundred staff members by 1940, including designers, clay modelers, and metalworkers. The studio was a powerful, image-shaping department and a key factor in the representation and sales success of GM and its role as a tastemaker in the mid-twentieth century.

Designing concept cars allowed designers and stylists to dream big. At the initial stage, that of conceptual renderings, design was not tethered to issues of production, cost, or marketing; however, when developing the look and feel of concept cars, the styling needed to match the technological features, otherwise the public lost interest. Ford's Advanced Styling division defined the special role of its "advanced stylists" as those who specifically worked on cars of the future:

FIG. 16 The General Motors *Firebird I XP-21* on display at the Waldorf-Astoria Hotel for the 1954 Motorama.

FIG. 17 The *GM XP-33 Dart Two-Seat Showcar*, concept sketch by Carl Renner, 1954.

FIG. 18 The *GM XP-33 Dart Two-Seat Showcar*, concept sketch by Carl Renner, 1954.

FIG. 19 The *GM XP-33 Dart Two-Seat Showcar*, concept sketch by Carl Renner, 1954.

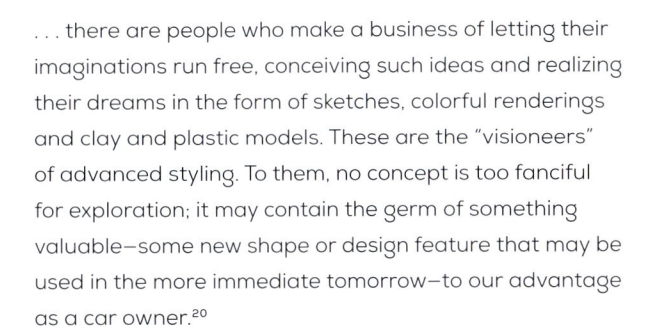

. . . there are people who make a business of letting their imaginations run free, conceiving such ideas and realizing their dreams in the form of sketches, colorful renderings and clay and plastic models. These are the "visioneers" of advanced styling. To them, no concept is too fanciful for exploration; it may contain the germ of something valuable—some new shape or design feature that may be used in the more immediate tomorrow—to our advantage as a car owner.[20]

The duties of a "stylist," "visioneer," or whatever title was appropriated for these designers ranged from the mundane (creating hundreds of variations of a futuristic headlamp) to the fantastic (levitating cars on automated highways). Some were company men, staying within the large automotive corporate structure, while others took their unique bent for futuristic vision to other arenas. Hired as a junior designer in 1945, Carl Renner worked as a stylist at GM for thirty-five years. After his success in designing the Chevrolet *Corvette Nomad* concept station wagon (also known as the Waldorf *Nomad*), one of the showstopper dream cars at GM's 1954 Motorama, Renner caught the eye of Harley Earl himself. Earl requested that Renner become part of a special styling division whose main focus was to create the next show-stopper for the 1955 Motorama. Renner described the assignment as follows:

> Mr. Earl wanted a new idea. He wanted me to come up with a new theme. So the first part of the project was just finding the direction to go in. I knew I had to give him choices.
>
> I went in all areas—coupes, sedans, rocket cars, single bubble, double bubble, way-out levitation cars and sports cars.[21]

Renner began to work on concept sketches for several of the dream cars for the 1955 Motoroma. He also was asked to create multiple drawings to build on the success of the *Firebird XP-21*, or the *Firebird I*, as it is now known (fig. 16 and pp. 92–95). The sketches, titled *Dart* or *XP-33* and done at Earl's behest, showed a two-seater version of the *Firebird* (figs. 17–19). These rough drawings illustrate different wheel treatments and small design changes but maintain the basic look and spirit of the rolling rocket aesthetic of the *Firebird I*.

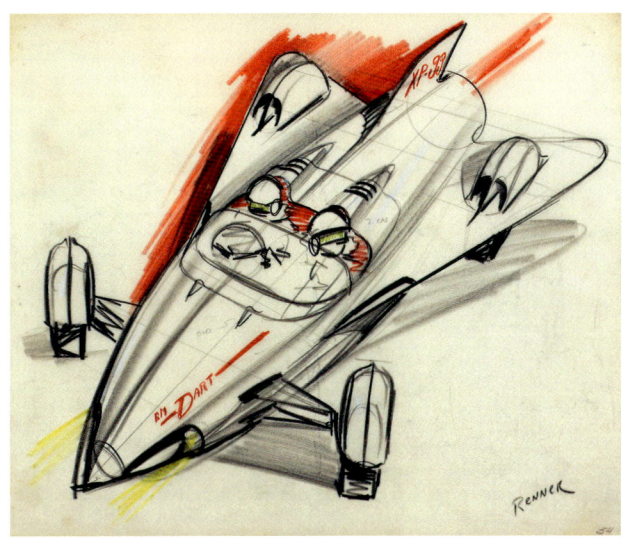

DREAM CARS 23

Renner worked on many types of drawings, from these dynamic sketches to large presentation drawings (fig. 20). Each GM studio had a large area where larger scale drawings, usually done on black canson paper, could be mounted. The wall moved up and down, allowing the drawings to be seen and studied from various angles (fig. 21). One drawing by Renner that survives celebrated the 250th anniversary of the founding of Detroit by Antoine de la Mothe Cadillac. Renner depicted a full-scale (76 × 242 inches) Cadillac convertible concept car, which looked like an updated, 1950s version of Earl's *Y-Job* with elements of the *XP-300* and *Le Sabre XP-8* as well. The dramatic image shows the car racing through Detroit at night, with a cone-shaped red traffic light mirroring the shape of the Dagmars on the front bumper (fig. 22).

Famed designer Syd Mead's career path was quite different from Renner's. Mead, who refers to himself as a "visual futurist," started in the industry in 1959 at Ford Motor Company's Advanced Styling studio, where he worked for two years on several projects, including the two-wheeled concept car *Gyron* (fig. 23). In the early 1960s, he created a series of conceptual illustrations of futuristic automobiles for US Steel that was meant to

FIG. 20 Presentation drawing of the Chevrolet convertible concept car, by Carl Renner, 1952. This large-scale illustration measures 69 × 94 inches.

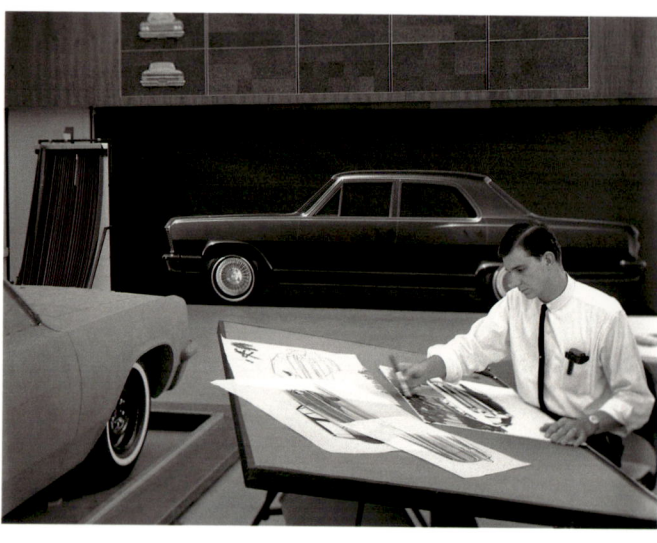

FIG. 21 A General Motors designer at work in the Chevrolet Studio, 1963.

FIG. 22 Life-size rendering of the Cadillac convertible concept car (76 × 242 inches), celebrating the 250th anniversary of Detroit, by Carl Renner, 1951.

24 DREAM CARS

inspire designers and engineers to think of new ways to use steel. Visually related to the *Gyron* is Mead's rendering in this series of the *Gyroscopically Stabilized Two-wheel Car* (fig. 24). The wedge-shaped vehicle is complete with a futuristic background dramatically colored for maximum impact. Known today primarily for his work on classic science fiction films including *Blade Runner*, *Tron*, and *Aliens*, Mead's relatively brief time as a designer of concept cars was a product of his deep engagement with visions of the future, which continues through the present day (as of this writing, he is in his eighties and continues to design actively). His design philosophy is, "There are more people in the world who make things than there are people who think of things to make."[22] Mead's interest is not in what can be achieved, but rather how to inspire people to consider new, fantastical possibilities.

Interestingly, the drawings by many of these influential and innovative stylists are as rare as the concept cars themselves. Many of the works simply were not preserved by the companies, and in most cases the stylists were not permitted to keep copies for themselves, although some did—often by smuggling the drawings out of the studios in creative ways or stealthily retrieving discarded sketches from the trash. The survival rate of completed concept cars is similar to that of the drawings. Of course, a high percentage of concept cars existed on paper only, never making it through the full production process.

Many of the visionary prototypes that were created did not survive in physical form, although often their legacy (and even their legend) remains. The Bugatti *Type 57S Compétition Coupé Aerolithe* (French for "meteor") is a prime example of a car that is so wrapped in its own mystique that recently it was faithfully re-created over a span of five years based only on a handful of historical photographs, known specifications and factory records, and an oil painting done by a Bugatti engineer named Reister in spring of 1935 and presented to Jean Bugatti as a gift (fig. 25). Considered the precursor to the better-known Bugatti *Atlantic*, the *Aerolithe* (fig. 26 and pp. 50–55) was unveiled at the 1935 Paris *Salon de l'Automobile* under its original name *Type 57 Coupé*

FIG. 23 Photograph of the Ford *Gyron* on display.

FIG. 24 *Gyroscopically Stabilized Two-wheel Car*, illustration by Syd Mead, ca. 1960. © OBLAGON, INC. / Photo by Mike Jensen

FIG. 25 Painting of the Bugatti *Type 57S Compétition Coupé Aerolithe*, 1935.

FIG. 26 The Bugatti *Type 57S Compétition Coupé Aerolithe* on display at the *Salon de l'Automobile*, Paris, 1935.

DREAM CARS 25

Spécial, and disappeared shortly thereafter. Conjecture is that it was dismantled for parts, some of which were then used in the production *Atlantics*.

Another concept car that has survived only in legend is the 1956 Chrysler *Norseman* (fig. 27). After a year of designing at Chrysler Corporation Engineering Division, the *Norseman*'s scale model was shipped from Detroit to Italy for Carrozzeria Ghia to fabricate. After another year and a half of fabrication, the finished concept car boasted an arched cantilever roof; narrow A-pillars; a power-operated, retractable sunroof (twelve square feet of glass) over the back seat; and "a sharply sloping hood, upswept tail fins, and a covered, smooth underbody for aerodynamic efficiency." As its press release noted, it "incorporated more structural, chassis, electrical, and styling innovations than any other idea car ever designed by Chrysler."[23] The Norseman was loaded onto an Italian ship to return to the United States for its dramatic unveiling; unfortunately, the ocean liner was the doomed SS *Andrea Doria*, which sank on July 25, 1956. The *Norseman* remains trapped in the ship's hold on the ocean floor, entrenched in concept car legend, existing only in a few rare photographs, renderings, and automotive lore.

There were, in essence, two types of concept cars: the fantastical and those that were exercises in the future of automotive design. In some cases, the renderings also reveal new directions in the automotive audience and markets of their time. For example, the 1964 GM *Runabout* (fig. 28), introduced at the 1964 New York World's Fair, was a three-wheeled, fully electronic automobile complete with a built-in shopping cart. It was one of the early cars that targeted modern, urban women. The *Runabout* represented a time in the United States when people were moving out of the cities and into suburbs, where single-family homes had carports and garages waiting to be filled, and women were asserting their need for independence, especially with transportation. The completed version of this experimental car, like so many others, no longer exists; our experience of it today is only through photographs and renderings.

FIG. 27 Design drawing of the 1956 Chrysler *Norseman*, by C. C. Voss, 1953.

FIG. 28 Design drawing of the 1964 General Motors *Runabout*, by Wayne Cherry, 1964.

From Two Dimensions to Three

As GM's promotional material explains, "Through the preliminary stages of design development miniature scale models provide a ready means of translating the idea and sketches of the artist into three-dimensional forms."[24] Scale models, typically made of clay, could be altered continually as curves were rounded or fins were extended (fig. 29). Other models were made of different materials, at various scales, and ultimately for a range of purposes, from design reviews to presentations (fig. 30) to wind tunnel testing. Even with today's technological advances—including rapid prototyping, CAD drawings, and 3-D printing—the more traditional modeling methods are still in use. In designing the 2010 Porsche *918 Spyder Concept Car* (p. 10), "groundbreaking overall technical concept and innovative detail solutions would demand equally new formal approaches for both exterior and interior," according to Porsche's head of styling Michael Mauer.[25] The styling studio implemented the latest technology alongside more tested methods such as clay models and scale drawings to create the forward-thinking hybrid sports car.

In addition to being integral to the process, the models themselves underwent certain developments of their own. In 1948 designer and engineer Gordon Buehrig was working on the design for the automobile known as the *Tasco* (see pp. 82–87), which stands for The American Sports Car Company (the car and company shared the same name). One of the interesting but ultimately unsuccessful design elements in the *Tasco* was its front fenders, which turned with the wheels, leading to an original use of materials. Buehrig experimented with molded fiberglass to help make the fenders functional. He also used the relatively new vacuum-forming process to create small 3-D models from a then new material, ABS plastic, an innovation that saved both time and money (fig. 31).

One year later Buehrig was hired by Ford's design department, and he brought with him his interest in the method of vacuum-forming plastic for models. He was given the opportunity to demonstrate how inexpensive this approach was and how greatly it aided the design process. Ford Motor Company became the first automobile manufacturer to use this technique in its design process. It was simple, cost-effective, and allowed designers to review and access structural, engineering, and design processes before advancing to the next stage of production.[26] Although Buehrig viewed the *Tasco* as a failure overall because it never reached production, he believed that every project, however flawed, provided learning experiences. He summed up his work on the *Tasco* with this sentiment: "While I have always regretted the losses it sustained, the fun of working on it and some of the concepts it fostered which later saw volume production make up for much of my regret over the car."[27]

Scale models were also used as part of wind tunnel testing. In the early 1950s Chrysler wanted to change its image, so it partnered with Carrozzeria Ghia (considered "consultants") to work on several projects, including the 1955 concept car *Streamline X*, or, as its designer

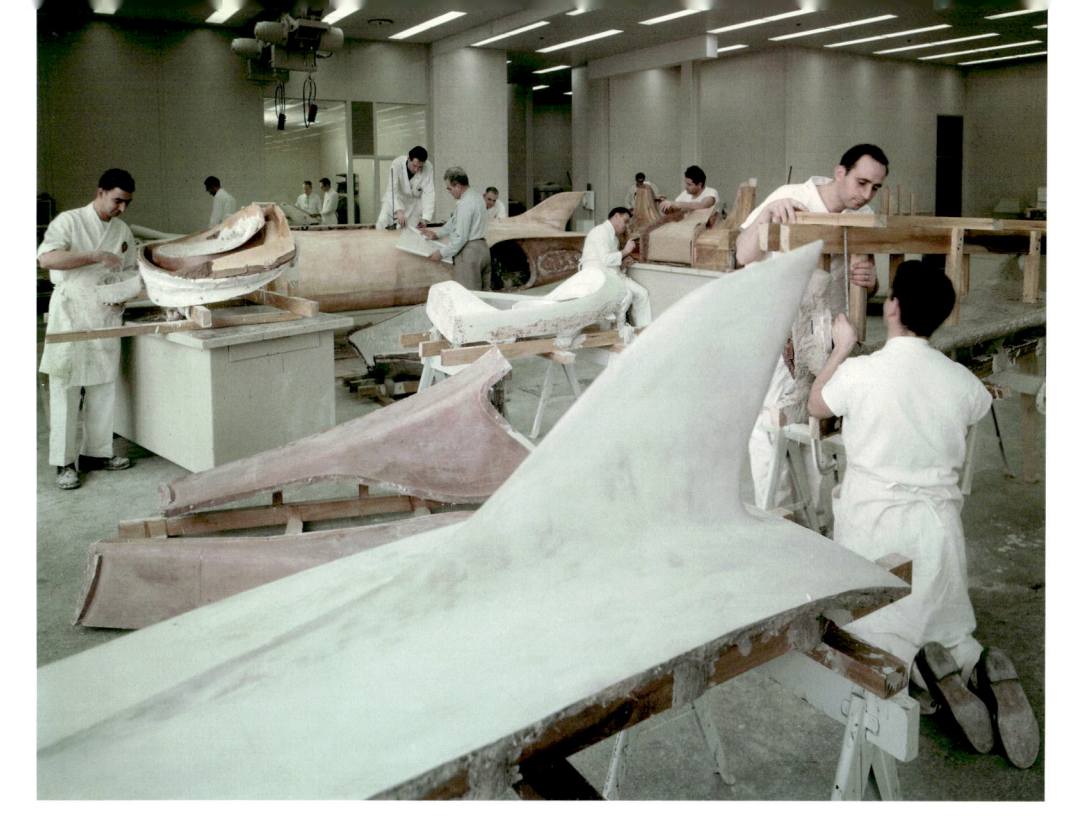

FIG. 29 Designers modeling fins at the General Motors studio.

FIG. 30 Harley Earl with a model of the 1953 General Motors *Firebird I XP-21*.

FIG. 31 Gordon Buehrig with a model of the 1948 *Tasco*.

DREAM CARS 27

Giovanni Savonuzzi nicknamed it, *Gilda* (fig. 32 and pp. 100–103), after Rita Hayworth's sleek title character in the film noir of the same name (fig. 33). A one-fifth-scale plasticine model of the *Gilda* was made especially for wind tunnel testing at the Polytechnic University of Turin (fig. 34). It had small holes in the surface that were filled with black ink, which was fed through tubing at the rear. These holes were placed strategically on the model's surface and the ink would be blown by the wind along the body to indicate airflow over that surface (fig. 35). These studies and tests helped to determine the effectiveness and efficiency of the car's design and illustrated the marriage of the scientific aspects of aerodynamics with the aesthetics and styling of streamlining.

Like conceptual drawings, models sometimes served as the genesis of an idea. The small model *Sculpture in Motion* (fig. 36) made by Virgil Exner, Sr., who joined Chrysler's Advanced Styling group in 1949 and later became their first vice president of styling, is believed to be the inspiration for Savonuzzi's sleek design for the *Gilda*. The model was placed on Exner's desk to display the kind of aerodynamic designs he wanted to see on Chrysler's design drawing boards in the future. This model is also believed to be the genesis of "Forward Look," a major design theme implemented by Exner from 1955 to 1961 that incorporated prominent fins as part of the attempt to modernize Chrysler's image.

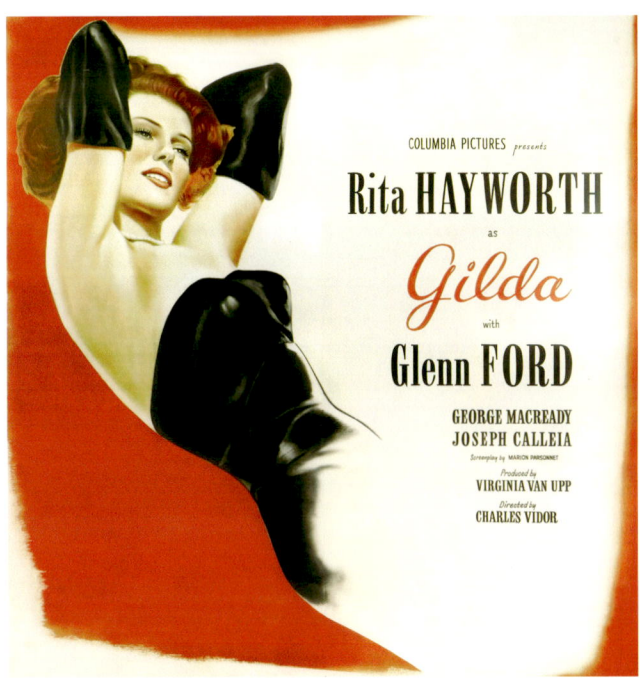

FIG. 32 The Chrysler (Ghia) *Streamline X "Gilda"* on display, 1955.

FIG. 33 A Columbia Pictures movie poster for the 1946 film *Gilda*, starring Rita Hayworth.

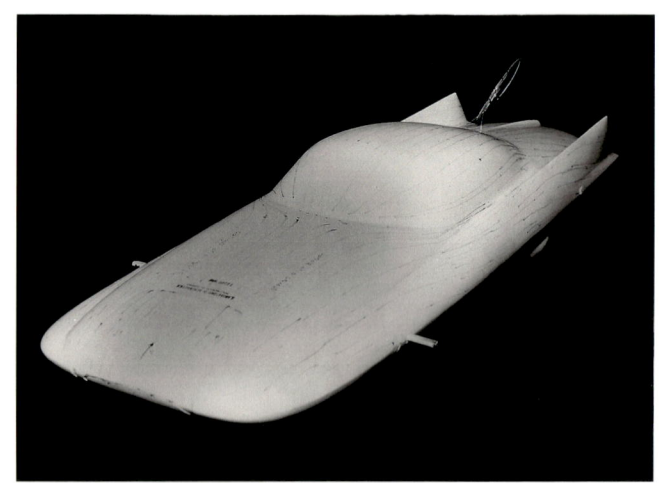

FIG. 34 The *Gilda* model in the wind tunnel at the Polytechnic University of Turin.

FIG. 35 Ink lines demonstrate airflow over the body of the *Gilda* model.

The Speed of Design

Designing a car from start to finish typically took several years and represented a sizable financial investment. Extremely small production runs, as was the case with some concept cars, increased the cost per car even more. According to a July 22, 1951, article in the *New York Times* reviewing the *Le Sabre XP-8*:

> The timeline of the project reveals the amount of time and effort involved: July, 1946, ideas & sketches begun; October, 1948, full-sized drawings started; December, 1948, clay models begun; August, 1949, first part for actual car begun; December, 1949, plaster model underway; March, 1950, first engine run; July 17, 1951, completed car demonstrated at press preview conference [GM's] proving grounds.[28]

This timeline represents not only the various stages of design but also how long the process could take within the large automobile companies. In contrast, it was less systematic for industrial designers or others working outside of the big companies.

It was not unusual for private individuals to create and build their own cars. Some used kits or based their work on parts of other cars with their own unique modifications and designs. Many of these individuals were simply hobbyists or enthusiasts, while others were serious designers working to create new and better visions for the future through improved transportation design. The 1947 Norman Timbs *Special* is a case in point.

Norman E. Timbs was a mechanical engineer who had worked on several larger projects, including the Tucker 48 *Torpedo*. In 1947 he created for his personal use the Timbs *Special* (see pp. 70–75), a visually arresting automobile that epitomized grace and speed. The car articulated the ideas of streamlining and wind resistance with its elongated, curvilinear forms and seemingly single-form body. It had no doors and the two-piece body was fabricated from aluminum. To create this form, Timbs started with drawings, followed by quarter-scale clay models, and then a full-scale wooden body buck (fig. 37) from which the aluminum panels were shaped and welded together.

The car graced the October 1949 cover of *Motor Trend* magazine (fig. 38) and was accompanied by a short article, "Home-Made Streamliner," a title that emphasized that the car was made largely by Timbs himself rather than a coachbuilder or an automobile maker. The article included images and referred to this stunning vehicle as "a little workbench project" but went on to say that it took Timbs more than two and a half years to complete the car, and it cost him around $10,000—far from the accessible hobbyist project indicated by the article's title. The piece concluded by quoting some "pedestrians" who referred to the car as resembling a whale or a turtle, yet "all agree they'd like to own the 'critter' themselves."[29]

ABOVE LEFT FIG. 36 *Sculpture in Motion*, a model by Virgil Exner, Sr., 1954.

ABOVE RIGHT FIG. 37 Norman Timbs stands next to the full-scale body buck of the 1947 Norman Timbs *Special*; he holds a scale model of the car.

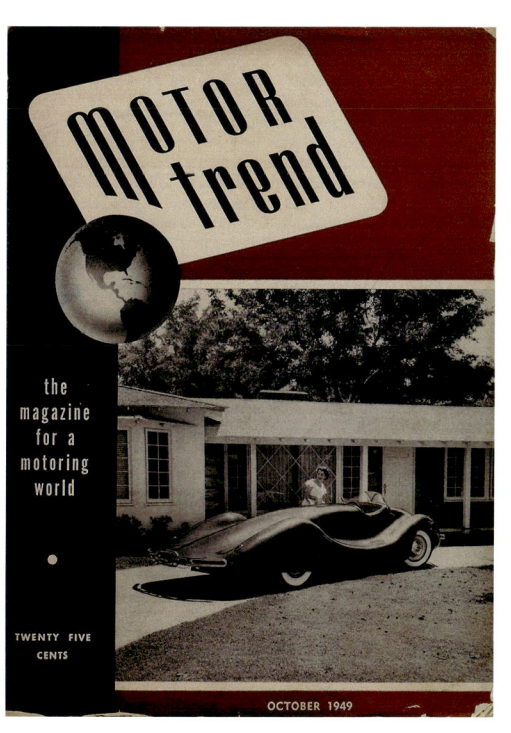

FIG. 38 Cover of *Motor Trend* magazine featuring the 1947 Norman Timbs *Special*, October 1949.

DREAM CARS 29

FIG. 39 Advertisement for the 1936 Stout *Scarab* from *Fortune* magazine, 1935.

David versus Goliath

The 1936 Stout *Scarab* was another of these animal-like cars, its form often described as beetle-shaped. Designed by William Bushnell Stout and hand produced in single-digit numbers by Stout Engineering Laboratories—and later by Stout Motor Car Company of Detroit, Michigan—the *Scarab* was notable for several innovative features. In its desire to be modern, the company positioned the car as looking to nature for its inspiration. Its rear-mounted engine, unusual in that era, afforded more room in the front. "The Scarab designers have taken a tip from Mother Nature, who, recognizing the law of 'survival of the fittest,' has placed the eyes of all animals at the front—not mid-way between the legs in the side of the body."[30]

When Stout was looking to generate excitement and find more investors for the *Scarab*, he placed a bold ad in *Fortune* magazine in 1935 that positioned him and his car as a story of David versus the Goliaths of the car industry. The ad was titled *A Challenge and A Prophecy* (fig. 39); it stated:

> . . . the Scarab rear-engine motor car comes as a friendly but direct challenge to the necessary conservatism of the big-production motor car manufacturers. The Scarab expresses Vision vs. Conservatism; Functional Design vs. Traditional Design; Individuality vs. Standardization; Fine Craftsmanship vs. Mass Production. . . .
>
> THE PROPHECY: The new Scarab will set all future styles in motor cars. The following features now exclusive to the Scarab, will be adopted by all makes of fine cars within three years.[31]

Stout's goal with the *Scarab* was to create a virtual living room on wheels. It could seat up to seven passengers and used modern materials in innovative ways, including an aluminum body, a tubular steel frame, and lace-wood sidewalls that were easy to wipe down. Stout rejected the "coffin-like fabric" of the past for modern, easy-to-clean upholstery. A lowered floorpan gave an extra five inches of headroom, and the lack of running boards added to the usable interior space as well. This car was in essence a precursor to the minivan of today,

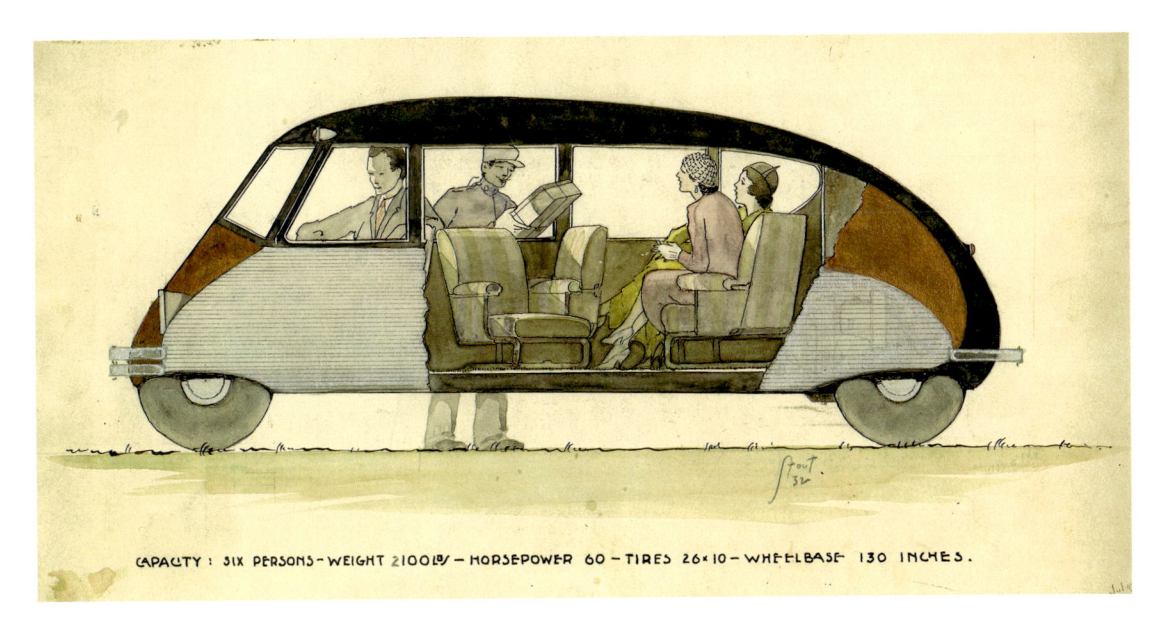

FIG. 40 Technical drawing of the Stout *Scarab* partially cut away to show the interior and passengers, by William Stout, 1932.

FIG. 41 Buckminster Fuller's *Motor Vehicle-Dymaxion Car*, United States Patent Office no. 2,101,057, from the portfolio *Inventions: Twelve Around One*, 1981, a collaboration by Chuck Byrne, published by Carl Solway Gallery, Cincinnati, Ohio.

but with convertible furniture. The front passenger seat could rotate fully, the back seat became a couch, and a table folded out for playing cards or holding drinks (fig. 40). Stout's brochure *Let's Build a Modern Motor Car* claimed, "The movable chairs never leave the floor and a glass of liquid on the card table spills not a drop even on a rough gravel road at speeds of 50 miles an hour or more."[32] Although Stout was correct in that many features soon would become adopted on production cars, estimates are that there were only between six and nine *Scarabs* ever made—each one unique and affordable primarily to the most affluent families—instead of his original, overly ambitious dream of one hundred production *Scarabs*. The legacy of the *Scarab* is the success of Stout's ideas and innovations rather than the car itself.

The Future Past

The Stout *Scarab* was part of a larger trend, as the idea of creating people-movers or cars that could hold several passengers in a streamlined body was prevalent in the 1930s. Even before Stout's car, however, in 1933 the American architect and designer Buckminster Fuller created the *Dymaxion* car (fig. 41) as part of a visionary plan to improve humanity by nurturing it through technology, design, and materials. *Dymaxion* was a name

DREAM CARS 31

Fuller assigned to several of his inventions to signify the cohesion of his vision of a better tomorrow. The car, of which only three were made, was designed in collaboration with aircraft and yacht designer William Starling Burgess, but Fuller patented the design in 1937. A three-wheeled car with a wraparound windshield, the *Dymaxion* could transport eleven passengers. Like Stout, Timbs, Bel Geddes, and Arzens, Fuller worked outside the parameters of the large car companies in the United States and Europe. Although these innovative designers largely worked independently, much of their work received attention. Their visions helped stimulate the public's interest and pushed the automotive industry to explore new ideas—some that ultimately were realized by the mainstream car companies and some that were not.

The 1942 *L'Œuf électrique* was one of the era's most innovative cars. Its creator, Paul Arzens, designed locomotives for the Société Nationale des Chemins de fer Français (French National Railway Company) after World War II. Before being placed on their payroll in 1947, however, he designed unusual automobiles for himself without regard for market trends or catering to clientele tastes. The opposite of a large minivan-type car, *L'Œuf électrique* was an electric, three-wheeled bubble car made of aluminum and Plexiglas (fig. 42 and pp. 66–69) and was designed as Arzens's personal urban mini-car. Equipped with nothing more than a single pedal and a steering wheel, *L'Œuf* was a seemingly simple car that had a tremendous impact, including the distinction of being the world's first bubble car, with its three-quarters Plexiglas dome enclosure. It was in many ways a precursor to the electric smart car and, due to France's wartime petrol shortage, it was decades ahead of the current demand for eco-friendly cars. *L'Œuf* was streamlined and extremely functional—it could travel more than sixty miles on one charge with speeds up to 37 mph.[33] This unique, visionary vehicle proves that necessity and ingenuity do indeed produce some of the greatest innovations.

The production of mini-cars was heavily encouraged after the war, especially in France. With resources and materials scarce and industry in tatters, the French government implemented a postwar five-year plan that encouraged the development of economy cars. Even Voisin entered this market in the late 1940s with a mini-car called the *Biscooter*[34] (fig. 43), which was dramatically different in style from his large, pre-war luxury cars, including his *Aérodyne*. As its name implied, the *Biscooter* was about the size of two motor scooters.

This new direction in automotive design, though evident as early as 1945, was especially apparent in the cars introduced at the Paris *Salon de l'Automobile* in the late 1940s (including *L'Œuf électrique* and the Panhard *Dynavia* at the 1946 and 1948 *Salons*, respectively). A 1945 article in the *Wall Street Journal* discussed this trend:

> "Strange automobiles" are being prepared for the French market, and people who have seen them in Paris describe them as "glass eggs or soap bubbles" . . .
>
> One is an electric car which can average 24 miles an hour, weighs about 150 pounds empty and is 7 feet long (an average American car is just over 16 feet long). This car was designed by Paul Arzens who believes that when made in quantity it may replace the bicycle.[35]

International Automobile Shows and World's Fairs

Though they had been influential for decades, in the postwar era automobile shows became an increasingly important way to generate business and restore confidence in the various car design and manufacturing industries, especially for European companies. International motor shows—held annually in cities such as Paris, New York, Turin, Geneva, and Detroit—long have been a significant way to introduce the latest cars, especially concept cars (in various stages of design). World's Fairs also proved to be effective platforms for introducing new ideas on an international stage. Founded in 1898 and

FIG. 42 Paul Arzens in his *L'Œuf électrique* in front of the Eiffel Tower, Paris, 1944, photographed by Robert Doisneau.

FIG. 43 Gabriel Voisin as a passenger in his *Biscooter* (*Biscúter*), Barcelona, ca. 1953.

held biennially, the Paris *Salon de l'Automobile* is considered the oldest automobile show. The first recognized automobile show in the United States was held in New York City at Madison Square Garden in 1900. This long-standing tradition continues today, as these venues provide the ideal arena to both broadcast the newest automotive innovations and position designers, companies, and countries as leaders in design, technology, and engineering.

When cars such as the Voisin *C-25 Aérodyne* (Paris, 1936; see pp. 42–45), the Buick *Centurion XP-301* (1956 Motorama circuit; see pp. 104–109), and the Ferrari (Pininfarina) *512 S Modulo* (Geneva, 1970; see pp. 116–121) were introduced at a show, they were photographed and written about by the media and assessed by colleagues, enthusiasts, and the general public. The Motoramas and international automobile shows were among the many—and often most successful—ways to showcase, promote, and challenge the public as well as push competitors to create the next best things. Some concept cars were created specifically to be exhibited at these shows and were never seen elsewhere; they were sold, reworked, moved into storage, or destroyed, as they were no longer needed.

The presentation of and reaction to the Alfa Romeo *B.A.T. 5*, *7*, and *9* concept cars illustrate how much influence these automobile shows exerted. Carrozzeria Bertone (established by famed automobile designer and maker Nuccio Bertone) was contacted by Alfa Romeo for a collaborative project based on studies of air drag coefficients. Under Nuccio Bertone's leadership, renowned designer Franco Scaglione created the prototypes or proposals known as the *B.A.T.s* (short for *Berlinetta Aerodinamica Tecnica*) 5, 7, and 9. They were introduced at the *Salone dell'automobile di Torino*—in 1953, 1954, and 1955, respectively—as a way to inspire and stimulate business for both companies and for postwar Italy. The cars were studies in the sculptural grandeur of design, taking aerodynamics and styling to a glorious extreme, seen most dramatically in the *B.A.T. 7*'s rolling, curved fins, which combined the two great symbols of the power of flight: the rugged, aggressive prowess of a jetliner and the fragile elegance of a bird's wing (fig. 44 and pp. 96–99). The *B.A.T.s* made a lasting impression; according to Geoff Wardle, director of advanced mobility research at the Art Center College of Design, "They had a subliminal influence on future vehicle designs."[36]

At the 1970 *Salone dell'automobile di Torino*, Carrozzeria Bertone unveiled yet another grand concept car, the Lancia (Bertone) *Stratos HF Zero* (see pp. 122–125). Nuccio Bertone wanted to call it *Stratolimite*, referring to the limits of the stratosphere, but it quickly became known by its in-house name, *Zero*. Gone were the dramatic curves and soaring references to flight, now replaced by the extreme wedge, low to the ground and slicing through the air at extreme speeds. As a preview of the 1971 Los Angeles Auto Expo in the *Los Angeles Times* described it, "When Bertone builds a prototype, it's original. Original—as in Stratos: one door in the front, full-width headlamps and hydraulically articulated driveshaft are a few of its innovative features along with styling that speaks for itself."[37] A mere thirty-three inches high, the car was a visual tour de force (fig. 45). There was an ongoing battle of the extreme wedge at the time—the shape was featured in several key concept cars, including Bertone's earlier 1968 Alfa Romeo *Carabo* (fig. 46), and there was a competitive race to produce the car that was of the lowest height. The *Zero* debuted only months after another wedge concept car, the 1970 Ferrari (Pininfarina) *512 S Modulo* (see pp. 116–121), debuted in Geneva at thirty-seven inches.

FIG. 44 The Alfa Romeo *Berlinetta Aerodinamica Tecnica 7 (B.A.T. 7)* on display.

FIG. 45 Lancia (Bertone) *Stratos HF Zero* drawing attention in traffic, ca. 1970.

FIG. 46 A model posing with the 1968 Alfa Romeo *Carabo*.

DREAM CARS 33

The *Modulo*'s designs began in 1967 by Italian designer and Pininfarina S.p.A head of styling Paolo Martin. When the finished car was finally unveiled at the 1970 *Salon international de l'automobile Genève* it was black; by the time of the *Salone dell'automobile di Torino* it was repainted white, its originally intended color. It garnered a great deal of attention and won twenty-two international design awards for what was labeled a "pure formal research, in its intentional geometricity."[38] The prototype was selected to represent the best of Italian coachbuilding at the 1970 Osaka World's Fair (called the 1970 Expo). The *Modulo*'s success was attributed to Martin's sculptural approach to design, and it was seen as ushering in "a whole new [a]esthetic in sports car concepts."[39]

The *Modulo*'s innovations included its two overlapping body shells joined by a waistline band that encircled its width (fig. 47), and its low-slung, trapezoidal shape, which positioned the two seats in the center of the car, with the console—which featured bowling-ball-inspired orbs—in line with the wheels (see p. 118). Access to the passenger compartment was gained by sliding the entire cupola, including the windshield, along special guides (fig. 48). This groundbreaking car was all about style and the look of the new, which was in keeping with the design climate of the period, according to Sergio Pininfarina, chairman of Pininfarina. When asked if creativity in Italy was affected by postwar turmoil, he said, "I don't see any direct connection between creativity and the political situation in Italy since the war. . . . I feel that design and style are becoming of greater and greater importance these days. It is more and more important to be different, to look new, to have a personality in cars."[40]

Concept cars are still introduced at these international events today. However, it is increasingly rare for them truly to be "dream cars" or sketches of fantastical ideas and innovations meant to be enjoyed as a promise of the future. Today's concept cars are instead largely market-driven, more previews of design to come rather than explorations of often unrealistic (though imaginative) possibilities. Many, such as the forward-thinking Porsche *918 Spyder* (see p. 10), are closer to prototypes for upcoming production cars than concept cars in the

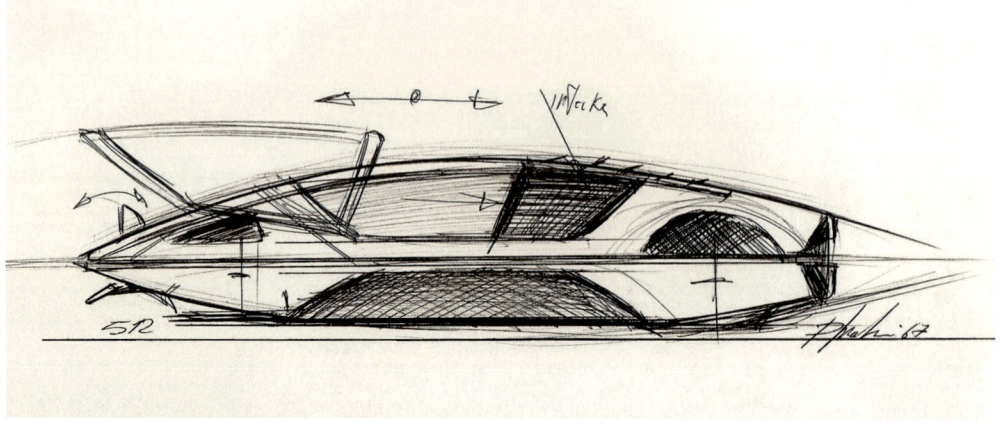

FIG. 47 Illustration of the Ferrari (Pininfarina) *512 S Modulo*, by Paolo Martin, 1970.

FIG. 48 Design sketch of the 1970 Ferrari (Pininfarina) *512 S Modulo*, by Paolo Martin, 1967.

traditional sense. The 2001 BMW *GINA Light Visionary Model* (fig. 49 and pp. 126–131), however, is a strong example of a contemporary concept car that is both fantastic and consumer-driven. First designed in 2001 by then chief of design Christopher Bangle, a press release states:

> All ideas that the GINA Light Visionary Model presents are derived from the needs and demands of customers concerning the aesthetic and functional characteristics of their car and their desire to express individuality and lifestyle ... With this model, BMW Group Design initiates a fundamental discourse about the characteristics that will affect the development of cars in the future. It is therefore fundamentally different from [contemporary] concept cars, which reflect what is expected of them by implementing as many elements as possible in a future production model. In contrast, the GINA Light Visionary Model is a vision of future cars and serves as an object of research.[41]

The *GINA Light Visionary Model* was a shape-shifting car made of tensile fabric stretched over a movable frame of aluminum and flexible carbon fiber. The fabric comprised two layers: an under layer of wire mesh and an outer layer of polyurethane-coated Lycra that was resistant to water, heat, and cold. The name *GINA* (for "Geometry and functions in 'N' Adaptations," with "N" referring to "infinite") refers to a philosophy meant not only to give designers and engineers creative freedom but also to allow them to consider consumers' needs and desires in dramatic new ways, anticipating the future for them. When needed, the front headlights would be exposed and the taillights would shine through the fabric (see p. 131). With the driver seated in the car, the instruments and steering wheel would adjust to the optimal position for that individual; when not in use they rested in a central position. According to the promotional material, the *GINA Light Visionary Model*'s "reduction of the essentials and adaptation to the needs of the driver enhance the emotional impact of the vehicle, fulfilling a key goal of the GINA philosophy."[42]

FIG. 49 The BMW *GINA Light Visionary Model*, 2001.

FIG. 50 At the 1951 General Motors Preview, models display gowns designed by Harley Earl to coordinate with the newest GM cars. From left to right: Frances Mercer, Oldsmobile; Betty McLaughlin, Cadillac; Harley Earl, designer; Judith Ford, Chevrolet; and Suzi Brewster, Buick.

FIG. 51 The spectacle of the 1956 GM Motorama, featuring the *Firebird II*.

FIG. 52 From left to right: Alfa Romeo *B.A.T. 5* (1953), *B.A.T. 7* (1954), and *B.A.T. 9* (1955).

Motoramas and the Dream Cars

Even more than the automobile shows, GM's touring Motoramas served to whet the public's desire with new colors, forms, and technological advances. There were eight traveling Motoramas held between 1949 and 1961; they offered GM an exclusive way to showcase their cars as well as other products of the future.

Beginning on the heels of World War II, the grand GM expositions offered optimism—a vision of future prosperity. The Motorama concept grew out of the yearly industrial luncheons typically held at New York's Waldorf Astoria Hotel in conjunction with the New York Auto Show beginning in 1931. Initially these events were private, for industry only. In the aftermath of the war, the first large-scale event was held in the same place in 1949, but this time it was open to the public. It was not until 1953, with the introduction of the Buick *Wildcat I*, Chevrolet *Corvette* concept car, and other dazzling

36 DREAM CARS

dream cars, that the Motorama became the full-blown spectacle it is remembered as today. The shows typically would start in New York, and then tour to several key cities, including Boston, Chicago, Dallas, Los Angeles, Miami, and San Francisco. There were dancing girls, rotating platforms, large-scale graphics, build-outs, and cutting-edge consumer products—1956, for example, featured the popular *Kitchen of Tomorrow* exhibit by Frigidaire, then owned by GM. Earl often designed the outfits for the women who stood with the cars so that they would match the details of the automobile (fig. 50). It was a well-orchestrated extravaganza (fig. 51) designed to underscore GM's leadership and entice people to buy production cars, which also were on display.

Like the Italian *B.A.T.s 5, 7,* and *9* (fig. 52), the *Firebirds I, II,* and *III* (fig. 53), came to symbolize the era's obsession with outer space and air travel. These cars represent a specific time and place—the drama, excitement, and fascination surrounding jet aircraft, as well as the race to effectively use the turbine engine as a practical alternative for cars. The *Firebirds* maintained a close visual connection to the jet plane itself, as was most evident in the initial design (pp. 92–95). Earl claimed the *Firebird I XP-21* was directly related to the Douglas F4D Skyray and reminisced about how he ripped the image of the plane out of a magazine and decided that his next great dream car (after the success of the General Motors *Le Sabre*) would be the rolling airplane.[43] With its "needle" nose, delta swept-back wings, vertical tail fin, and plastic cockpit bubble top, "The first impression one gets of the Firebird is that it is a jet fighter on four wheels—an impression that prevails even while the car is standing still."[44]

The *Firebirds II* and *III* were introduced at subsequent Motoramas (1956 and 1959, respectively). In GM's booklet *Imagination in Motion—Firebird III*, the distinction is made between the three versions: ". . . the Firebird I for high performance, then the Firebird II for futuristic family car design and now the Firebird III that refines the outstanding features of both."[45] This intentional connection to the jet plane—complete with cockpit, wings, and tail fin features—also alerted the public to the fact that this technology, specifically the turbine engine and the futuristic automated highways featured in the *Firebirds II* and *III*, were visions of the future and not necessarily attainable or marketable in the next few years.

Just as the *Firebirds* represented the fantasy of a futuristic landscape, other concept cars introduced at Motoramas showcased wondrous new innovations that would make the world safer. At the 1956 Motorama, the Buick *Centurion XP-301* (fig. 54 and pp. 104–109) featured a rear-mounted camera with a wide-angle lens and a 4 × 6-inch view screen embedded in the dashboard (see p. 109). With its bubble top and panoramic wraparound windshield, no rearview mirror was necessary; the camera's view was clear at night. GM designer Chuck Jordan (who later became vice president of design) wanted a holistically forward-thinking car— in essence, he "wanted an interior that went with the exterior."[46] The back-up camera is now a fairly standard feature in many cars, but a half-century ago it was an amazing, almost unimaginable possibility.

Three years later, when the futuristic and visually stunning Cadillac *Cyclone XP-74* (fig. 55 and pp. 110–115) was introduced for the automobile show circuit, the *New York Times* noted key safety features in the article "Radar Device in Test Car by G.M. Warns Driver of Road Hazards."[47] Originally designed for the 1959 Motorama but delayed to debut at the first Daytona 500 instead, the car featured proximity-sensing radar units, housed in the large twin nose cones, that scanned the road electronically and warned the driver audibly and visually of objects in its path. The *Cyclone* was equipped with other fantastic gadgets among its many innovations, including a panoramic bubble top that retracted fully when the doors opened or closed. An intercom system

FIG. 53 General Motors' *Firebird* series. From left to right: *Firebird I* (1954), *Firebird II* (1956), and *Firebird III* (1959).

FIG. 54 Promotional photograph of the Buick *Centurion XP-301*, 1956.

FIG. 55 A model demonstrating the retractable bubble top and sliding doors of the 1959 Cadillac *Cyclone XP-74*, shown with the original fins.

allowed passengers to speak to those outside of the car without having to open the full canopy. The thirty-eighth experimental car produced by GM and the last under Harley Earl, the *Cyclone* is considered somewhat unfinished, as Earl retired during its production. Originally painted pearlescent white with a steel blue interior, by 1960 it was repainted—possibly the metallic silver color it is today. The tail fins were drastically cut down and other features were refined when a new head of design, Bill Mitchell, took over for Earl.

The 1961 Motorama was the last. The high costs and time associated with designing such extravagant dream cars had taken its toll, and the *Firebird III* was the only concept car exhibited at the last two Motoramas in 1959 and 1961. Advertising via the relatively new medium of television produced far more effective results and reached a wider audience with less money, time, and effort. Combined with Earl's retirement in 1959, the decade of the Motorama was eclipsed by burgeoning advertising methods and a new era for GM styling under Mitchell's leadership.

The Future Now

The essence and elements of these concept cars live on, even if the cars themselves do not. Their legacy as a whole ultimately is much greater than individual features of automotive design. Dream cars fired the imagination of the car-buying public, generated excitement about the possibilities of future technology, and inspired many individuals to dedicate their careers to the field. Many major figures in the automotive and design worlds were captivated by these concept cars. While the list is long, among those who have identified a direct correlation between concept cars and their career choice is Edward T. Welburn, GM's current vice president of global design, who saw the Cadillac *Cyclone XP-74* in 1960 when it toured cities in major automobile shows; it inspired him to become an automotive designer. As a young boy growing up in the Midwest, former BMW chief of design Chris Bangle was inspired by the extreme wedges of Bertone's concept cars: "I am a child of those Bertone cars, particularly the Carabo [see fig. 33],"

he said. "Discovering its photo for the first time in a library book in Wausau, Wisconsin, marked the moment I discovered auto design."[48]

These cars offer us, the contemporary audience, a glimpse into the future past; they show us what was dreamed possible and believed to be desired by the public. Many of the designs foreshadowed what is now commonplace—the mini-car, the minivan, electric and push-button controls, and the rearview camera. Other concept cars represent ideas that remain fantastical— cars that open where the hood normally is located or cars that have an intercom system to the outside world. Many have become legends, whether the physical body of the vehicle survived or not. But all represent a version of the future—fantastical, practical, safer, faster, sleeker— that offers different types of dreams to the individuals who coveted, ruminated about, and desired what was presented. The concept car represents a transition and arguable dominance of style over engineering. The aesthetics and stylistic "magic" must capture the imagination as a futurist vision; otherwise, regardless of the technological advances, the concepts will fail to be perceived as innovative automotive visions. Today, these concept cars of yesterday continue to provide sparks of possibility and glimpses of a future tomorrow.

NOTES

1 Ford Motor Company, *The Ford Book of Styling*, 68.

2 General Motors Corporation, *Modes and Motors*, 2.

3 Chrysler Corporation, *Chrysler's Thunderbolt and Newport*, 4.

4 Edsel Ford had a styling studio under E. T. "Bob" Gregorie in the early 1930s.

5 Ford Motor Company, *Styling at Ford Motor Company*, 8.

6 General Motors Corporation, *Modes and Motors*, i.

7 General Motors Corporation, *General Motors Le Sabre: An "Experimental Laboratory On Wheels,"* 4.

8 Ibid., 1.

9 When discussing individual cars and projects, this essay focuses on design innovations and development. For a more in-depth discussion of the automobiles and their technical advances—engines, chassis, etc.—please refer to Ken Gross's individual entries in the *Automobiles* section of this catalogue.

10 "Streamlining Reaches Heights in Chrysler's 'Thunderbolt,'" *Christian Science Monitor*, November 8, 1940, 12.

11 Chrysler Corporation, *Chrysler's Thunderbolt and Newport*, 2.

12 The term "Art Deco" was coined in the late 1960s as a reference for the new, streamlined classicism, with geometric and symmetric compositions. "Moderne" is how the style was referred to in its time period.

13 General Motors Corporation, *Styling: The Look of Things*, 2.

14 Bel Geddes numbered his car designs in succession regardless of whether he was working for a client or not, because for him they represented a continuous study of forms, design, and function.

15 Stein, *The Art and Colour of General Motors*, 51.

16 General Motors Corporation, *Modes and Motors*, 18.

17 Ibid., 16.

18 Lamonaca, *Styled for the Road*, 13.

19 Stein, *The Art and Colour of General Motors*, 48.

20 Ford Motor Company, *Styling at Ford Motor Company*, 38.

21 Sharf, *Carl Renner*, 15.

22 Syd Mead, Inc., "Biography," http://sydmead.com/v/11/biography/ (accessed July 19, 2012).

23 Chrysler Corporation, "Chrysler 'Idea' Car Lost," July 26, 1956.

24 General Motors Corporation, *Modes and Motors*, 21.

25 Interview with Michael Mauer, Porsche's head of styling, n.d.

26 Farrell and Farrell, *Ford Design Department*, 217.

27 Buehrig and Jackson, *Rolling Sculpture*, 130.

28 Pierce, "Le Sabre," July 22, 1951.

29 "Home-Made Streamliner," *Motor Trend*, October 1949.

30 Stout Motor Car Corporation, *Let's Build a Modern Motor Car*, 7.

31 "A Challenge and a Prophecy," *Fortune*, 1935.

32 Stout Motor Car Corporation, *Let's Build a Modern Motor Car*, 12.

33 Bobbitt, *Bubblecars and Microcars*, 36–37.

34 The *Biscooter* was later called the *Biscúter* when it was successfully marketed in Spain.

35 "Strange Automobiles," *Wall Street Journal*, June 6, 1945.

36 Phil Patton, "After 53 Years of Beauty Sleep, the BAT is Back," *New York Times*, March 23, 2008, http://www.nytimes.com/2008/03/23/automobiles/collectibles/23BAT (accessed July 19, 2012).

37 "Prototype of Bertone Original," *Los Angeles Times*, May 30, 1971.

38 Pininfarina, "Ferrari Modulo," http://www.pininfarina.com/en/ferrari_modulo/# (accessed July 19, 2012).

39 Ingraham, "Auto Show to Feature Exotic Cars," March 28, 1970.

40 Dole, "Pininfarina," July 15, 1981.

41 BMW Group, "BMW GINA Light Visionary Model," June 10, 2008.

42 BMW Group, "The Future of Beauty," March 31, 2009.

43 Temple, *GM's Motorama*, 136.

44 "XP-21 Firebird Lures Crowds to Motorama," *Los Angeles Times*, March 7, 1954.

45 General Motors Corporation, *Imagination in Motion*, 2.

46 Temple, *GM's Motorama*, 103.

47 "Radar Device in Test Car by G.M.," *New York Times*, February 21, 1959.

48 Phil Patton, "Wedges of Influence From Bertone," *New York Times*, May 1, 2011, http://www.nytimes.com/2011/05/01/automobiles/01BERTONE.html (accessed July 19, 2012).

THE AUTOMOBILES

KEN GROSS

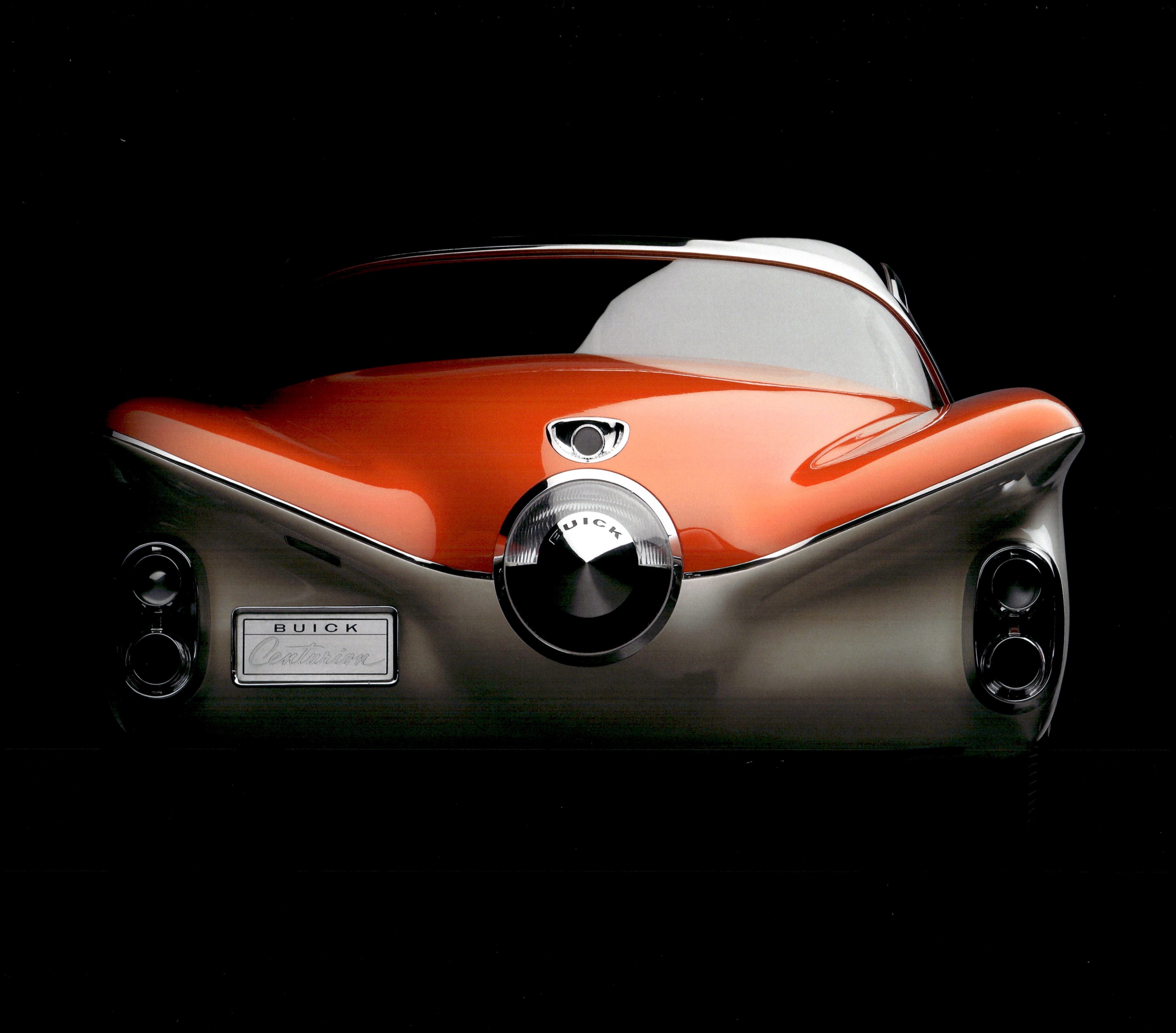
BUICK
BUICK
Centurion

1934 Voisin C-25 Aérodyne

Pioneering French aeronautical engineer Gabriel Voisin was a brilliant eccentric whose profound knowledge of aircraft production contributed to the Allied victory in World War I. Flush with profits when the war ended, Voisin turned to automobile manufacturing—in the words of designer Robert Cumberford, "sometimes with amazing results."[1] The aircraft-like shape, integral construction, and distinctive styling of Voisin cars combined French disregard for convention with a brilliant adaptation of aeronautical principles to the challenge of ground transportation. But Voisin's undeniably unique approach to automobile design did not result in high sales. Voisin authority Richard Adatto wrote, "Voisins were relatively expensive and lacked broad appeal. Gabriel Voisin's solution, typical of the man, was not to follow the crowd."[2]

Streamlining polarized the automotive industry worldwide in the 1930s. Many automakers embraced it—to the detriment of sales for some, as conservative buyers were reluctant to move from familiar upright designs to more curvaceous cars. Overall sales had fallen to just 150 units and Gabriel Voisin badly needed a success. He hoped that his new *C-25 Aérodyne* would appeal to the luxury grand touring market. Its styling was completely original; resembling an aircraft without wings, with its sharply defined lines the *C-25* had "the profile of an aircraft wing . . . outlined by two large, perfect curves, one underlying the roof, the other virtually following the beltline. The effect was that of a curvature at the lower end of the side windows, the rainbow-like arch completing its journey at the base of the radiator."[3]

Like so many early streamlined cars, the *C-25* retained its manufacturer's distinctive and prominent radiator grille, which was topped with Voisin's winged badge and a tall, stylized Moderne motif that resembled the wings of a giant bird. There also was a Jules Verne–inspired quality to the design; Adatto compared the porthole openings in the roof to "the look of a bathyscaphe."[4] At the push of a button, the power sunroof silently slid rearward along the outermost roof rails. It was operated by a small two-cylinder auxiliary suction motor that used engine vacuum, so the roof could only be retracted when the *C-25*'s 2.9-liter, 6-cylinder, 90-hp sleeve valve engine was running. Sleeve valve engines used slotted cylinder sleeves in lieu of conventional poppet valves. They were silent in operation, but the tradeoff was that they required a great deal of lubrication. Voisin surely liked the quietness of sleeve valve operation, but the cars emitted a thin haze of noxious blue smoke whenever they were driven.

Inside the cockpit, four individual seats accommodated as many passengers. The rear seatbacks could be folded flat for additional cargo capacity. The seats were covered in a wild, geometric-patterned cloth that, while attractive, was unlike anything seen on another car of that era—except, of course, another Voisin model.

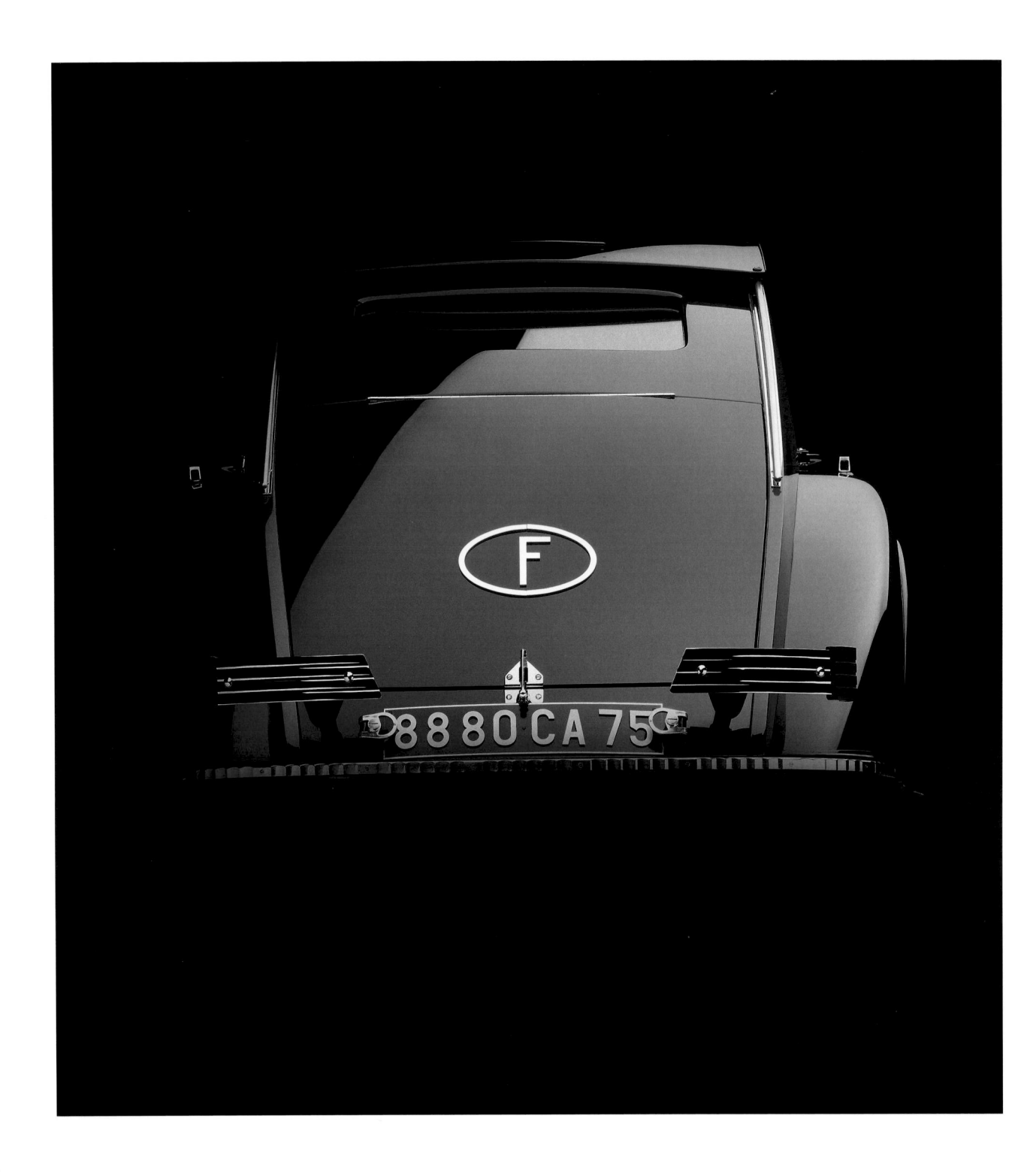

Although the *C-25* received a great deal of notice due to its startling shape, the buying public's response was underwhelming. That did not dissuade Gabriel Voisin, however; he subsequently produced a two-seater sports model—the angular and elegant *C-27* coupe—and then returned to the Paris *Salon de l'Automobile* in 1936 with an updated version of the *Aérodyne*. On the new car, the front fender lines were reshaped and the fenders themselves were lowered, but these changes were not enough; *Aérodyne* production ceased early in 1937. Only six examples were built, four of which are known to survive. Toward the end of production, the engine output was raised to 103-hp at a lazy 3,100 rpm, and the car's top speed was about 60 mph.

Constantly experimenting with new ideas, Voisin followed the *C-25* and *C-27* with the *C-28 Clarière*. Its engine was now an aluminum-block, 3.3-liter, twin-carburetor, 110-hp affair that could turn over 4,000 rpm. It was paired with a Cotal 4-speed electromagnetic pre-selector gearbox, with its operating switch located under the steering wheel; the lever to engage reverse was still on the floor. In the intensely competitive Depression era, a Voisin like this, then priced at more than 90,000 French francs, was considerably more expensive than a Bugatti *Type 57 Galibier* sedan, capable of more than 100 mph, and while the *C-25* was a radical-looking design, it did not offer nearly as much performance.

Ahead of his time, Gabriel Voisin's aim to adapt aircraft styling and advanced technology to automotive design was admirable, and it presaged General Motors' rocket-inspired *Firebird* series by twenty years. This *C-25 Aérodyne* won Best in Class and the coveted Best of Show award at the 2011 Pebble Beach Concours d'Elegance.

LOANED BY MERLE AND PETER MULLIN, BRENTWOOD, CALIFORNIA.

PHOTOGRAPHED BY MICHAEL FURMAN.

1 Cumberford, *Auto Legends*, 121.

2 Adatto, *Sensuous Steel*, 58.

3 Mullin Automotive Museum, *Vitesse-Élégance*, 100.

4 Ibid., 101.

8880 CA 75

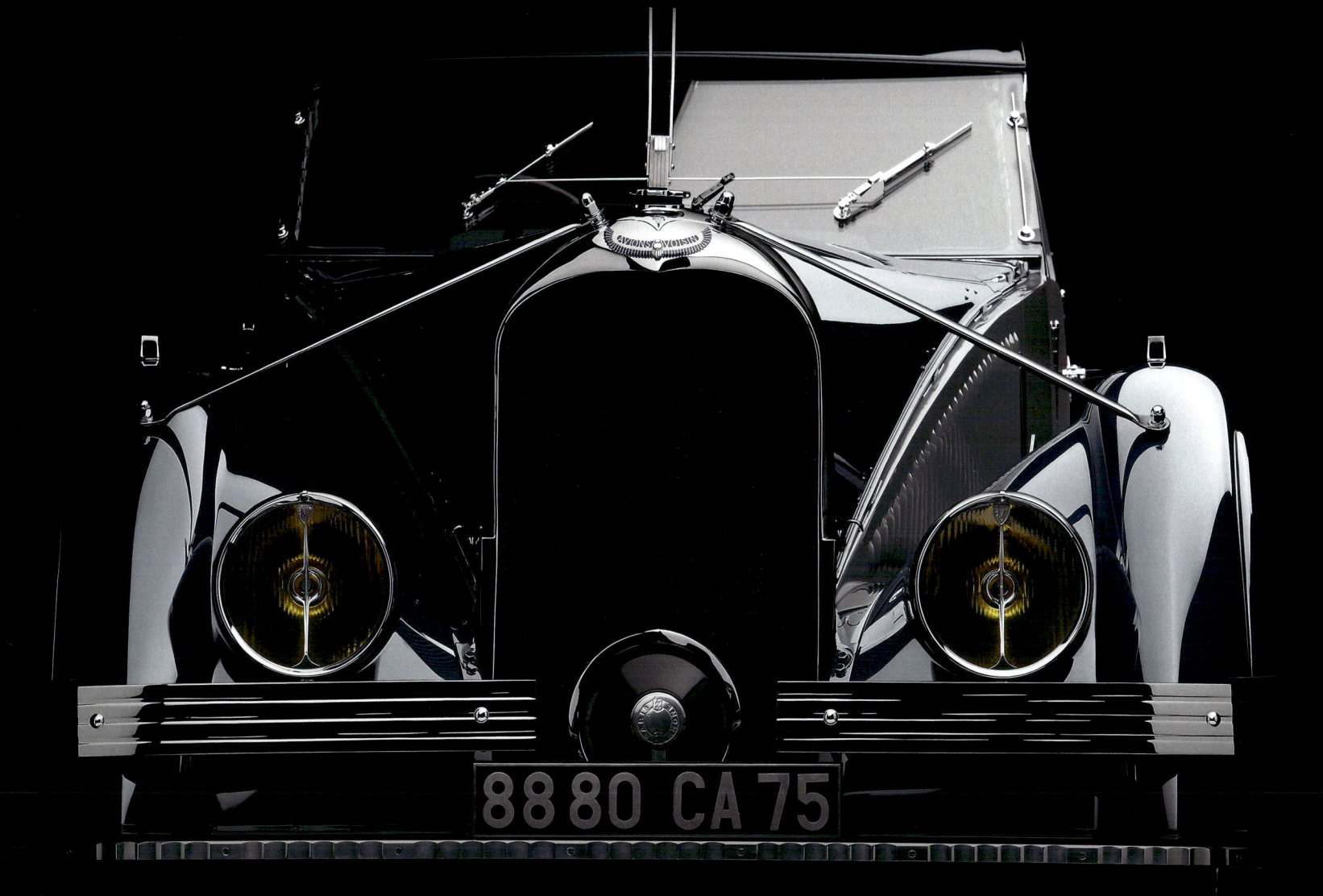

1934 Edsel Ford Model 40 Special Speedster

In 1932 Edsel B. Ford, president of Ford Motor Company, asked his styling chief, Eugene T. "Bob" Gregorie, to build a racy, boat-tail roadster on a Ford chassis of the same year. Two years later in 1934, desiring an even more dramatic personal runabout, Ford commissioned what he called a "continental" roadster that could have limited production potential. Gregorie sketched a few alternatives and built a 1/25th-scale model, which he tested in a small wind tunnel. Because of its 1934 Ford— a.k.a. *Model 40*—origins, the car became known as the *Model 40 Special Speedster*.

Assisted by Ford Aircraft Division personnel, Gregorie and his team fabricated a two-passenger, taper-tailed body with cut-down door openings fashioned from high-quality sheet aluminum and mounted over a custom-welded, tubular aluminum structural framework. This sleek automobile resembles the 1935 Miller-Ford Indianapolis 500 two-man race cars, but it was designed and built prior to their construction.

Specially designed cycle wings turned with the car's Kelsey-Hayes wire wheels. The bodywork followed the

stylist Jim Farrell, he "liked the way it handled and was generally pleased with its design."[1]

The *Speedster*'s long, low proportions were unlike anything Ford Motor Company had ever built. The car was garaged on Ford's estate at Gaukler Pointe from 1934 to 1940, during which time Ford and Gregorie concluded that it was too radical for series production.

A narrow pair of vee-ed grilles limited the flow of cooling air, so the *Speedster* had a tendency to overheat. Gregorie shortened the upper grilles and fabricated a horizontal grille for improved cooling. A 1/10th-scale model was made prior to this work being done, and a photograph dated March 21, 1940, includes a notation from Edsel Ford that reads, "the form is very good, but wonder if the two grilles shouldn't join? E. B. F."[2]

After Edsel Ford died in May 1943, the *Speedster*, valued at $200, was sold to a man in Atlanta who then shipped it to Los Angeles in 1947 and placed it in storage. In the May 1948 issue of *Road & Track*, a classified ad from Coachcraft of Hollywood offered the car for $2,500. In 1952 it appeared in an issue of *Auto Sport Review* photographed with an aspiring actress named Lynn Bari. In 1957 the car was transported back to Georgia, and in January 1958 it was for sale at Garrard Imports in Pensacola, Florida.[3] Bill Warner discovered the *Speedster* languishing in Lakeland, Florida. He later sold it at auction to mega-collector John O'Quinn. After O'Quinn's untimely death in an automobile accident, it was purchased by the Edsel and Eleanor Ford Estate and meticulously restored. Stunningly modern in its time, the freshly restored *Speedster* debuted at the Pebble Beach Concours d'Elegance in August 2011.

LOANED BY THE EDSEL AND ELEANOR FORD HOUSE, GROSSE POINTE SHORES, MICHIGAN.

PHOTOGRAPHY BY STEVE PETROVICH, SHOOTERZ LLC/ COURTESY OF THE EDSEL AND ELEANOR FORD HOUSE.

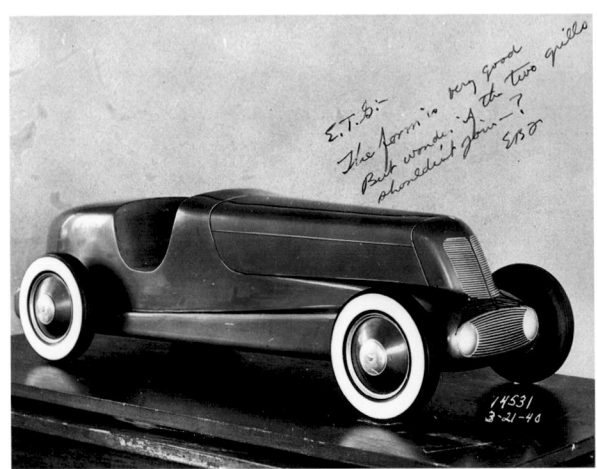

best aircraft practice, being light and very strong. It was originally painted Pearl Essence Gunmetal Dark, with complementary gray leather. An engine-turned panel incorporated period Lincoln instruments—the highest-quality instruments available at the time. The *Speedster* weighed approximately 2,100 pounds. Its original engine was a 75-bhp, *Model 40* flathead V-8, with straight exhausts. Custom touches included a shapely alligator-style hood with louvered side panels, the angle of which subtly matched that of the radiator grille and the windscreen. The *Speedster* had an engine-turned firewall; low-mounted, faired-in headlights; an enclosed radiator with a concealed cap; a starter button on the instrument panel; minimal chrome trim; and no running boards—all features that would not appear on production Fords for years to come. Edsel Ford received his new roadster on September 21, 1934, and, according to former Ford

1 Farrell, *Ford Design Department*, 21.
2 Photos courtesy of the Edsel and Eleanor Ford House.
3 Gross, *History: The Life and Owners of the 1934 Model 40 Special Speedster*.

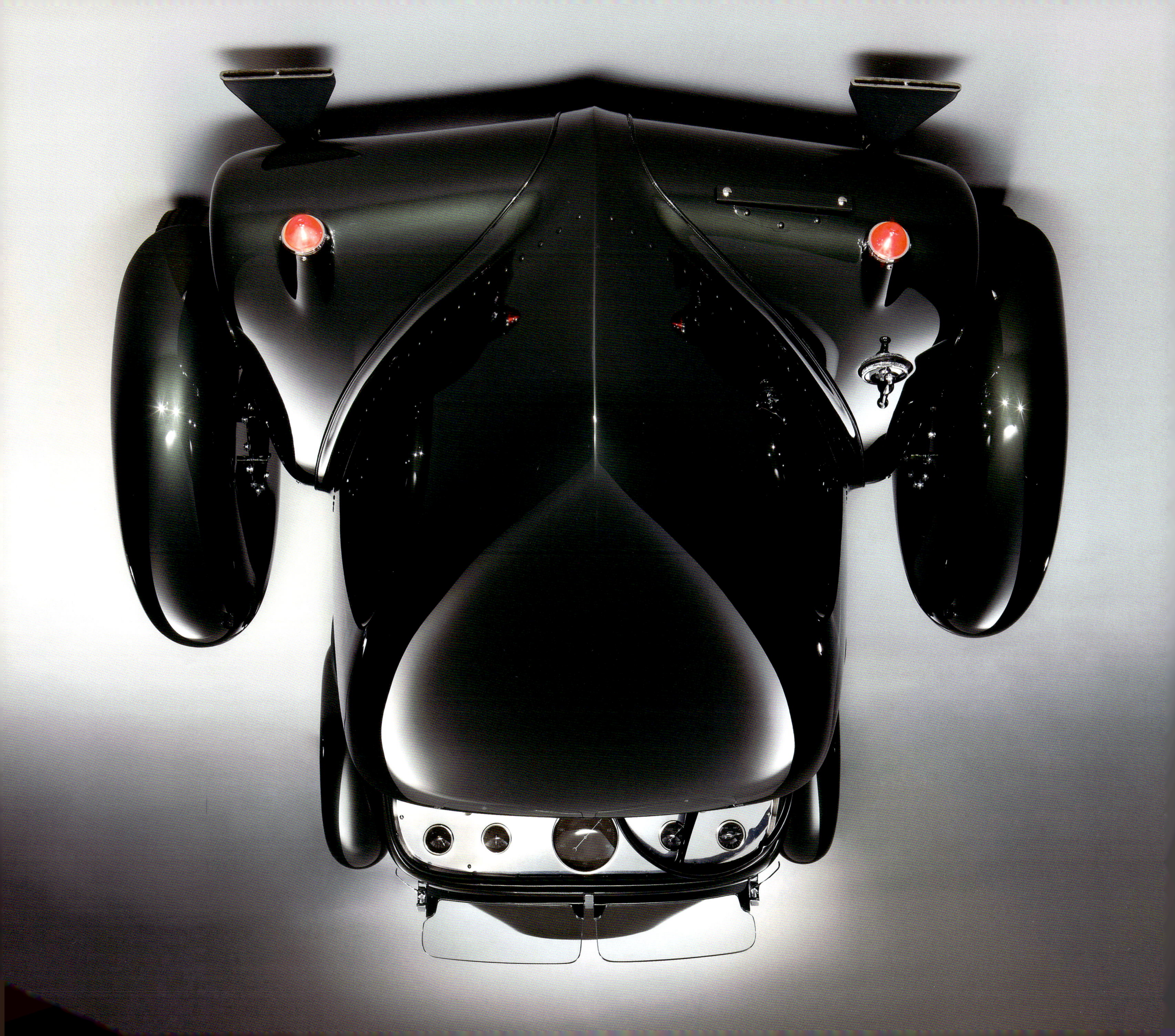

1935 Bugatti Type 57S Compétition Coupé Aerolithe

The *Type 57S Compétition Coupé Aérolithe* was arguably the most sensational show car of the mid-1930s, and the fact that it was a Bugatti should be no surprise. Ettore Bugatti, a trained engineer with an artistic soul, was born into a remarkable Italian family of artists. His father Carlo created intricate, eclectic Art Nouveau furniture, and his aptly named younger brother Rembrandt was a renowned sculptor of animals. Ettore and his family—including his son Jean, who later became a highly imaginative automobile designer in his own right—lived regally on a lavish estate in Alsace-Lorraine near their factory in eastern France. From 1911 to 1939 Bugatti only produced about twelve thousand automobiles, ranging from fast sports and touring cars to successful racing models and even regal limousines. Bugatti's cars were technically complex, often temperamental, very expensive, and hauntingly beautiful. Ettore experimented with aerodynamics and the use of exotic lightweight metals such as magnesium. Known as "Le Patron" ("the Boss"), he favored technology such as overhead camshaft, multi-valve engines and self-adjusting de Ram shock absorbers. But he could be conservative as well. Bugatti eschewed supercharging at first and clung to cable-operated brakes long after hydraulics had proved superior.

Due to France's high tariffs and restricted trade policy, the Great Depression was slow to impact the country, but by the early 1930s the luxury automobile market had dwindled. Ettore and Jean knew that a special new model was needed to help their company survive. The *Type 57*, introduced in 1934, was that car. Its styling was contemporary, and custom coachwork was available for those with means. To maximize the *Type 57*'s impact, Bugatti introduced a streamlined sports model at the back-to-back 1935 Paris and London automobile shows. Initially called the *Type 57S Coupé Spécial* (some sources call this car the *Compétition Coupé*) but more popularly known as the *Aérolithe* (French for "meteor"), the avant-garde speedster was beautifully curved from every side. Its flowing architecture was a marked contrast to the ubiquitous square-rigged cars of the era. The *Aérolithe* rode on a prototype low-slung *Type 57S* ("S" for Sport) chassis, with gondola-shaped frame-rails that tapered rearward for an aerodynamic appearance. The engine was a normally aspirated 3.3-liter, DOHC straight-8.

Bugatti's competitors also experimented with low-volume aerodynamic models, including the sinister-looking Mercedes-Benz *500K/540K Autobahn-Kurier* and Talbot-Lago's voluptuous teardrop coupes, but nothing on European roads in that era was as outrageous as the *Aérolithe*. It was an overnight design sensation, but orders for copies were scarce. Perhaps Bugatti's sleek coupe was considered too radical.

Adding to its problems, the show car was fabricated from Electron, an expensive magnesium and aluminum alloy. The metal proved difficult to weld, so Jean, assisted by head draftsman Joseph Walter, united the major sections using rivets. A spine-like center rib divided the svelte body, a theme repeated in its teardrop-shaped fenders. The doors cut into the roof, opened forward, "suicide-style," and stopped at the midpoint of the body—a sensuous design, but one that made access a challenge. Marque experts believe Bugatti built two *Aérolithe* prototypes, but they did not exist at the same time.

After touring the European continental show circuit, the cars were dismantled and some parts were used to build an updated, more civilized version of the *Aérolithe* called the *Atlantic*.[1] Production *Type 57 Atlantics* were hand-fabricated in aluminum. The rivets were no longer needed, but they looked exotic, so the illusion of a riveted spine was retained. Close-coupled, cramped, poorly ventilated, and rather impractical, the lithe, lightweight coupe was an enthusiast's delight. Only four examples were built, of which three survive.[2]

An avid horseman, "Le Patron" was convinced automobile competition improved the breed, as it did with thoroughbred racing. For this purpose, a *Type 57* on an ultra-low "S" chassis was fitted with streamlined open coachwork. The factory proudly advertised its successes, which included averaging 135.45 mph for one hour, 123.8 mph for 2,000 miles, and 124.6 mph for 2,485 miles. A *Type 57* won the 24 Hours of Le Mans in 1937.

Using the lines of the *Aérolithe*-inspired *Atlantic*, Jean Bugatti later designed the *Atalante*, a slightly larger, more comfortable production Grand Tourer on the *Type 57* chassis. Substantially more successful than

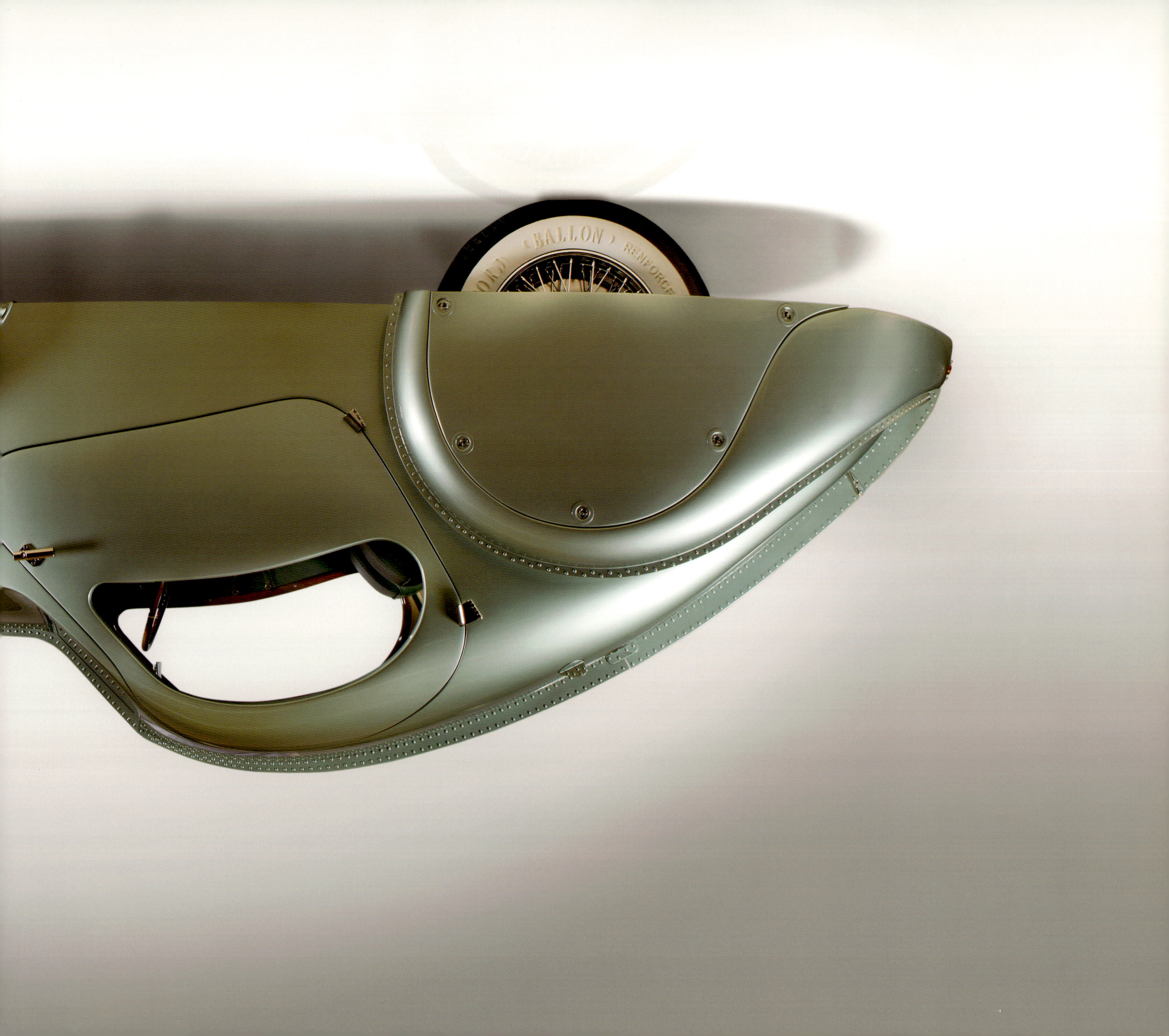
BALLON

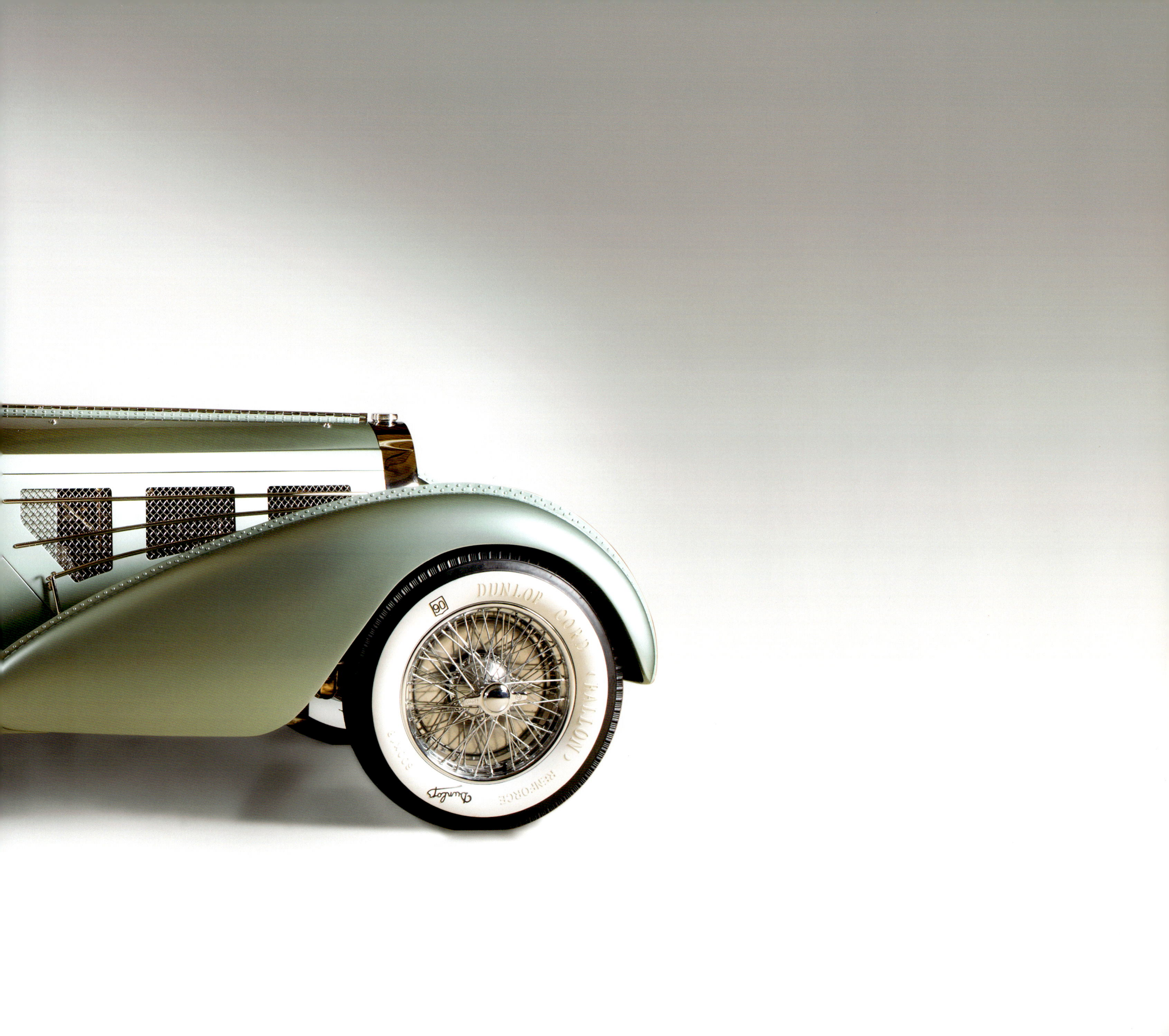
DUNLOP
90

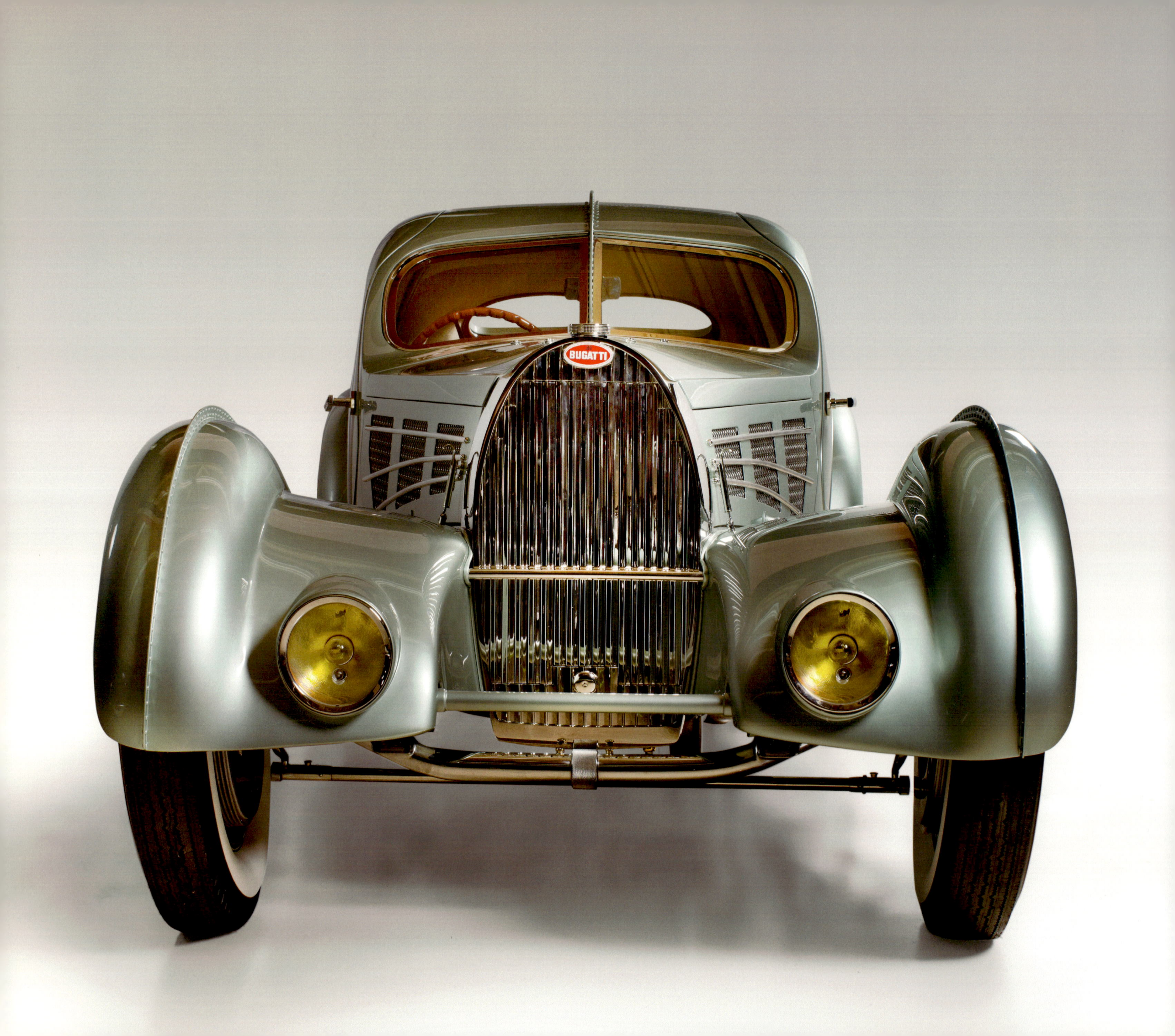
BUGATTI

the *Aerolithe* or the *Atlantic*, about forty *Atalantes* were built on the standard *Type 57* and the sporting *Type 57S* chassis (in this case, the "S" also stands for *surbaissé*, meaning "low-slung") before World War II halted all production.

This *Aerolithe* re-creation was built by David Grainger at the Guild of Automotive Restorers in Bradford, Ontario. Starting with the earliest surviving *Type 57* frame, no. 57104, Grainger and his team obtained sheets of magnesium alloy, and then developed a technique to form the body panels and weld them together using a process that would have been used in 1935. The crème de menthe finish was taken from a painting of the original *Aerolithe* done by a Bugatti engineer named Reister (see p. 25, fig. 25). Every detail was meticulously duplicated, including the double-sided Dunlop tires. The result has been welcomed in Bugatti circles and was featured in *Bugantics*, the Bugatti Owner's Club quarterly publication.[3]

LOANED BY CHRISTOPHER OHRSTROM, THE PLAINS, VIRGINIA.

PHOTOGRAPHY BY JOE WIECHA.

1. Simon and Kruta, *The Bugatti Type 57S*, 36–38.
2. Matthews, *Bugatti Yesterday and Today*, 14–20.
3. Grainger, "Aerolithe," 14–21.

1936 Stout Scarab

William Bushnell Stout, who in 1921 founded *Aerial Age*, the country's first aviation magazine, was an accomplished technical journalist and engineer. His design for the lightweight *Imp* cyclecar—a small, two-seater class of small cars popular before World War I, many of which were tandems—for the Scripps-Booth Company led to a sales management job at Packard, and then to a position as chief engineer in Packard's fledgling aircraft division. Stout's advanced work on internally braced, cantilever-winged aircraft pioneered the development of all-metal airplanes and led to the Stout Air Sedan, the first all-metal commercial aircraft in the United States. After Henry Ford purchased Stout Engineering in 1924, Stout's 3-AT aircraft design evolved into the sturdy Ford Tri-Motor. In 1929 Stout Air Services, a Midwest-based passenger airline, was purchased by United Air Lines.

Drawing on his extensive aeronautical background, Stout began creating a radical sedan concept in the early 1930s. He believed the use of aircraft construction techniques would result in a futuristic car that would be faster and more economical than a conventional automobile. He envisioned a smooth, slightly tapered, and, for its era, startling shape. A tubular frame, covered with aluminum panels, surrounded the *Scarab*'s rear-mounted flathead V-8 engine. A Ford three-speed transmission with a custom transfer case and a six-row chain powered the rear wheels. In what has since become modern practice but was innovative at the time, the wheels were located at the corners of the vehicle. At a time when almost all American vehicles had rigid axles with leaf springs, the *Scarab*'s front independent coil spring suspension design provided a smoother, quieter ride, anticipating today's MacPherson strut setup. (With a MacPherson strut, a shock absorber and a coil spring are combined in one unit with a steering pivot or kingpin.) The rear suspension was composed of twin transverse leaf springs, providing good traction and ease of handling.

The *Scarab*'s roomy passenger compartment was positioned within the car's wheelbase. Access to the interior was provided through a single, central door on the right side, and there was a narrow front door on the left for the driver. The driver's seat and a wide rear bench seat

1936 STOUT *SCARAB* 57

were fixed, but other seats could be repositioned so that the front could accommodate three across, or moved so that passengers could sit around a small table. This unusual configuration anticipated the first minivan. The interior was trimmed in wood, the headliner was varnished wicker, and the seats were accentuated with chrome rails and finished in leather.

The *Scarab*'s distinctive turtle-shell styling reflected a Moderne influence, beginning with decorative "moustaches" below the split windshield, including the unusually shaped headlamps covered with thin grilles, and culminating in fan-shaped vertical fluting, which framed elegant cooling grilles. The V-8 engine was reverse-mounted, with its cooling fan in the rear. The *Scarab*'s smooth envelope body enclosed the wheels and contributed to its quiet operation. The name was a none-too-subtle underscoring of the sedan's pleasant, beetle-like shape. Several toy manufacturers even copied the *Scarab* design for tin toys.

The Stout *Scarab* was a radically different vehicle than its contemporaries. At $5,000 it also was quite expensive, and the Depression-wracked buying public did not recognize its many advantages. A few designers, however—most notably John Tjaarda, with his *Sterkenburg* experimental car; Czechoslovakia's Hans Ledwinka, with the air-cooled, rear-engine Tatra; and Ferdinand Porsche, whose design study for a "people's car" became Germany's Volkswagen—all worked on similar configurations. With modifications, Tjaarda's concept became the streamlined Lincoln-Zephyr; Ledwinka's and Porsche's designs also saw volume production. But it is believed that only six *Scarabs* were built, though some sources say nine.

A few of Stout's investors purchased *Scarabs*, including William K. Wrigley, the chewing gum magnate, and Willard Dow of the Dow Chemical Company. Other owners included tire company owner Harvey Firestone, Robert Stranahan of the Champion Spark Plug Company, and radio host Major Edward Bowes. *Scarab* number five was shipped to France for the editor of *Le Temps*, a prominent Paris newspaper; in the early 1950s it was offered for sale on a Parisian used car lot. This *Scarab* was acquired by Larry Smith, an American collector, and painstakingly restored. It has since been shown at many prominent Concours d'Elegance.

With its aerodynamic shape and reconfigurable interior, the *Scarab* was well ahead of its time as an early forerunner of the minivan.

LOANED BY LARRY SMITH, PONTIAC, MICHIGAN.

PHOTOGRAPHY BY MICHAEL FURMAN.

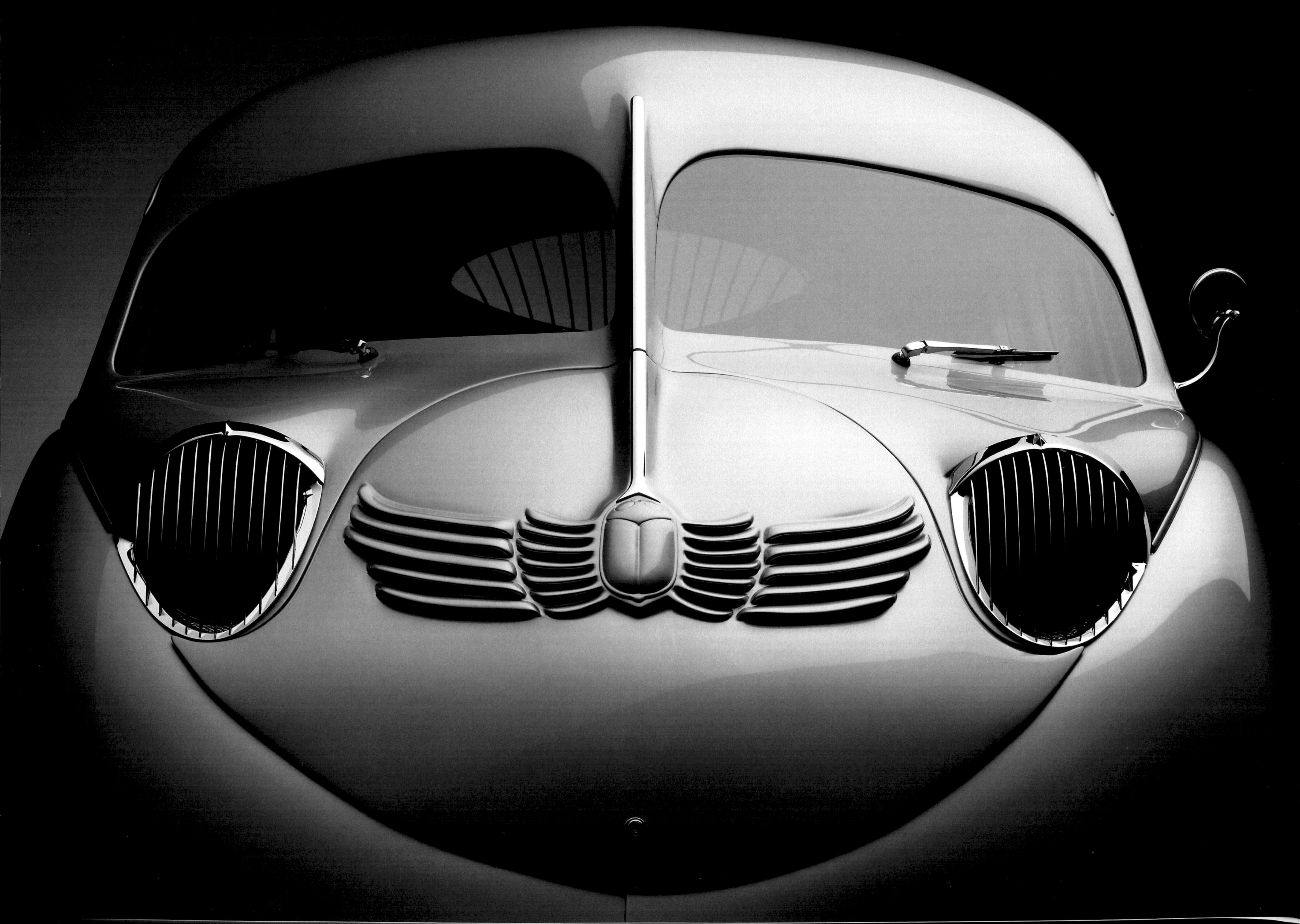

1941 Chrysler *Thunderbolt*

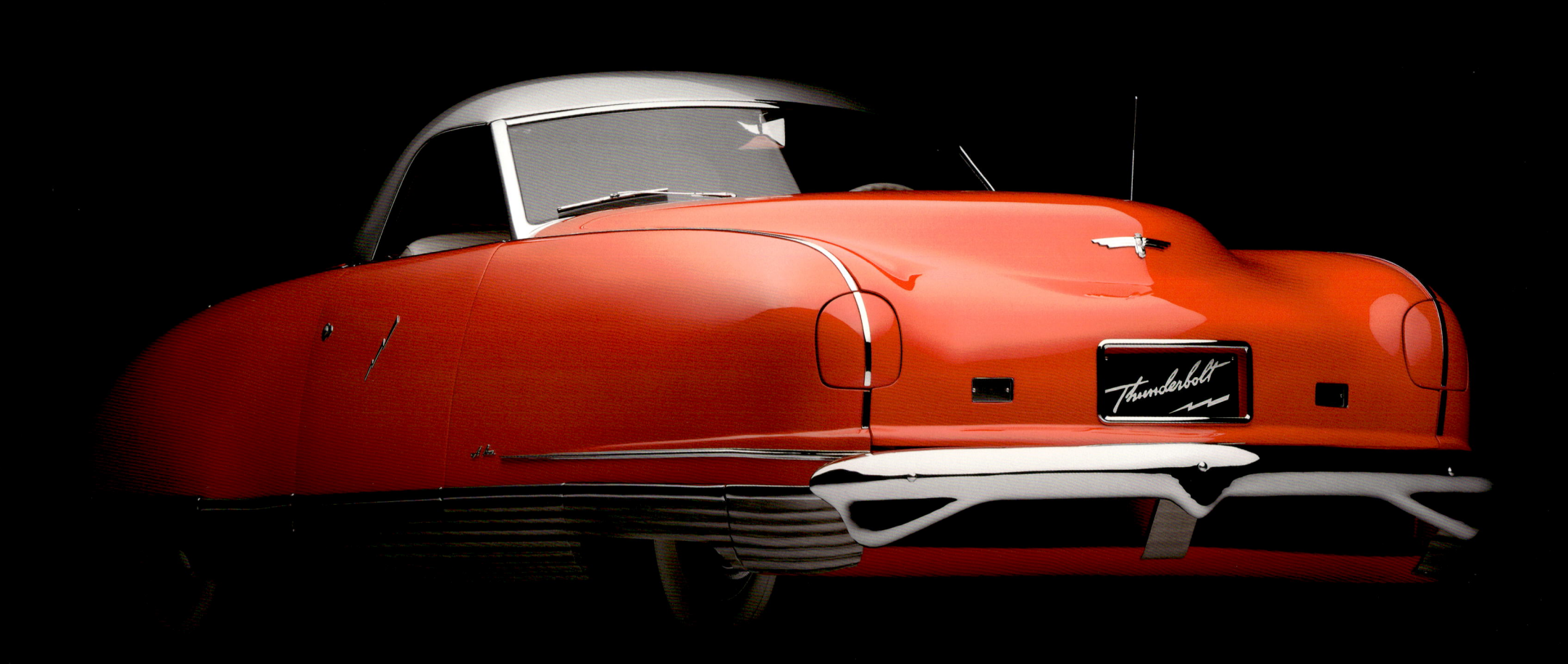

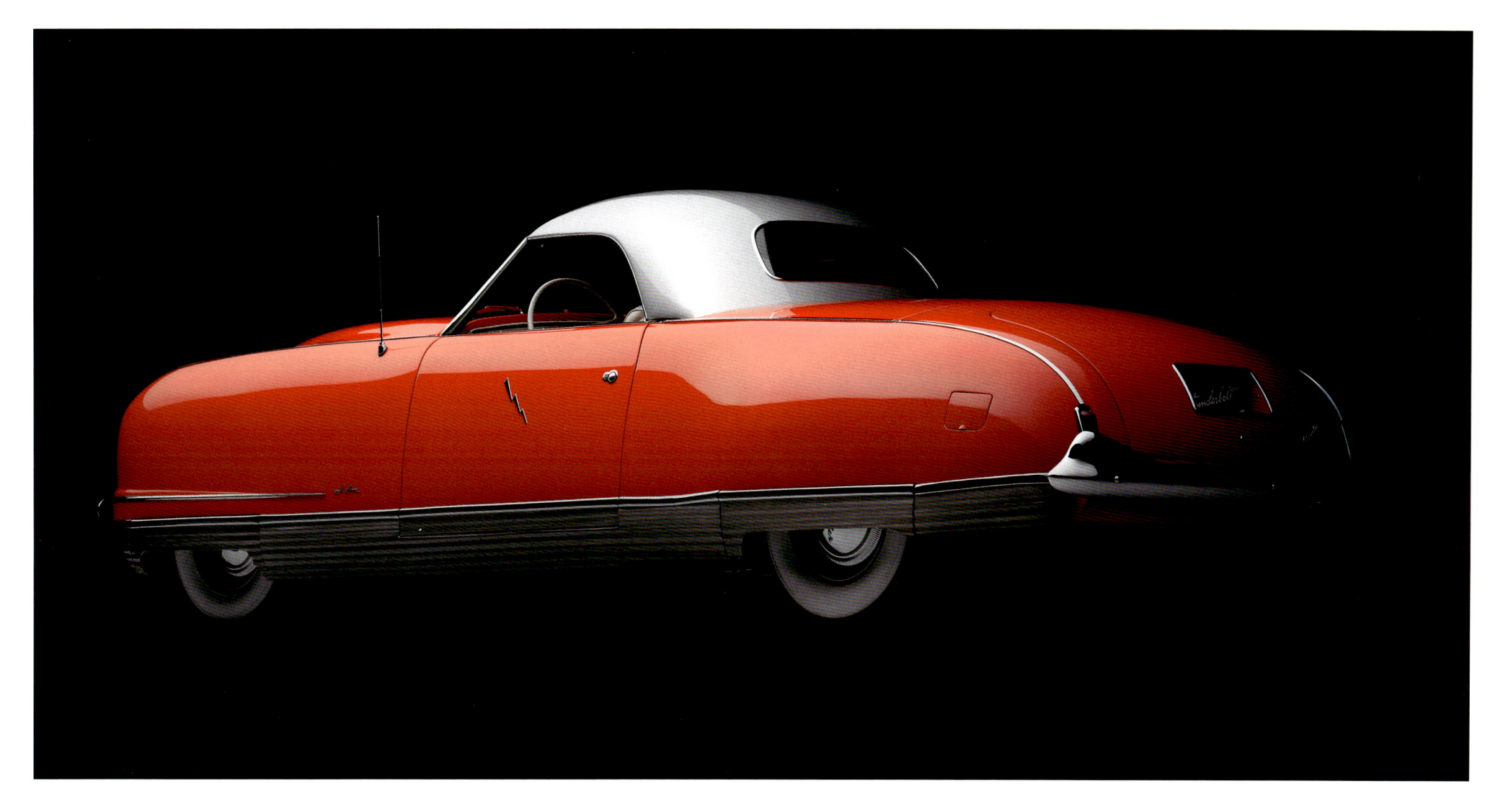

Visitors to the New York International Auto Show in October 1940 were thunderstruck when they gazed upon two sleek convertibles displayed on the Chrysler stand. Five years earlier, Chrysler's then radical *Airflows* had failed to move a sufficient number of buyers into a brave new realm of streamlined design. Undeterred, the company briefly dialed back its peek into the future, only to present an even more dramatic approach in Gotham, dazzling the public with a hint of what could be.

With the *Thunderbolt* roadster and its four-door companion, the *Newport* phaeton, Chrysler offered a distinctly futuristic alternative to conventional models, and discreetly let it be known that while these show cars were display pieces, customers of means could purchase a car of their dreams after they had been displayed around the country. Chrysler confidently touted the *Thunderbolt* as "The Car of the Future" (see p. 16, fig. 4). Sporting a smooth, aerodynamic body shell; hidden headlights; enclosed wheels; and a retractable one-piece metal hardtop, the roadster was devoid of superfluous ornamentation, with the exception of a single, jagged lightning bolt on each door. It stood apart from everything else on the road, hinting that tomorrow's Chryslers would leave their angular, upright, and more prosaic rivals in the dust.

As if the audacious *Thunderbolt* two-seater were not enough, its companion, the four-door *Newport* phaeton, teased all who saw it. With its elegantly stretched

1941 CHRYSLER *THUNDERBOLT* 61

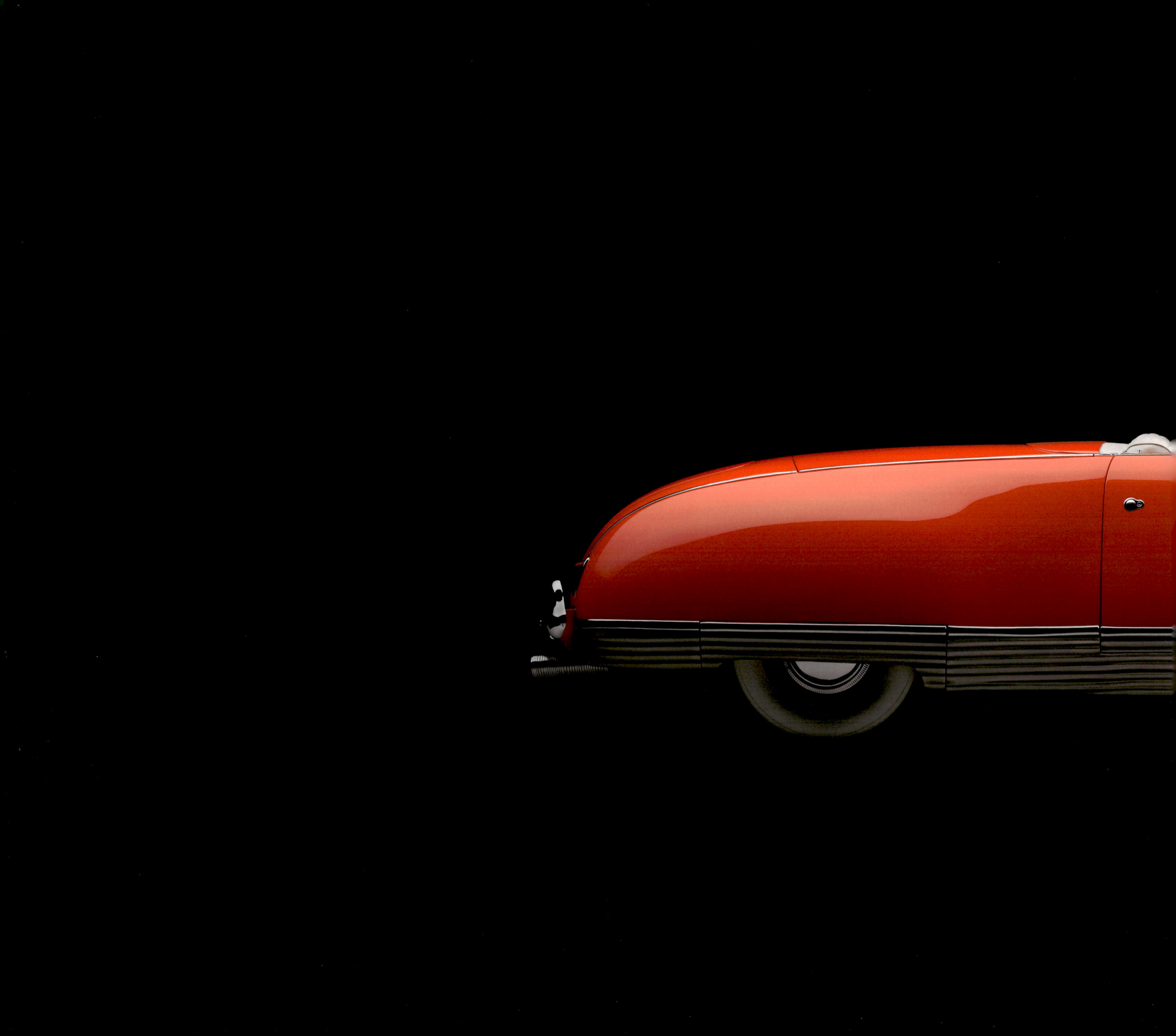

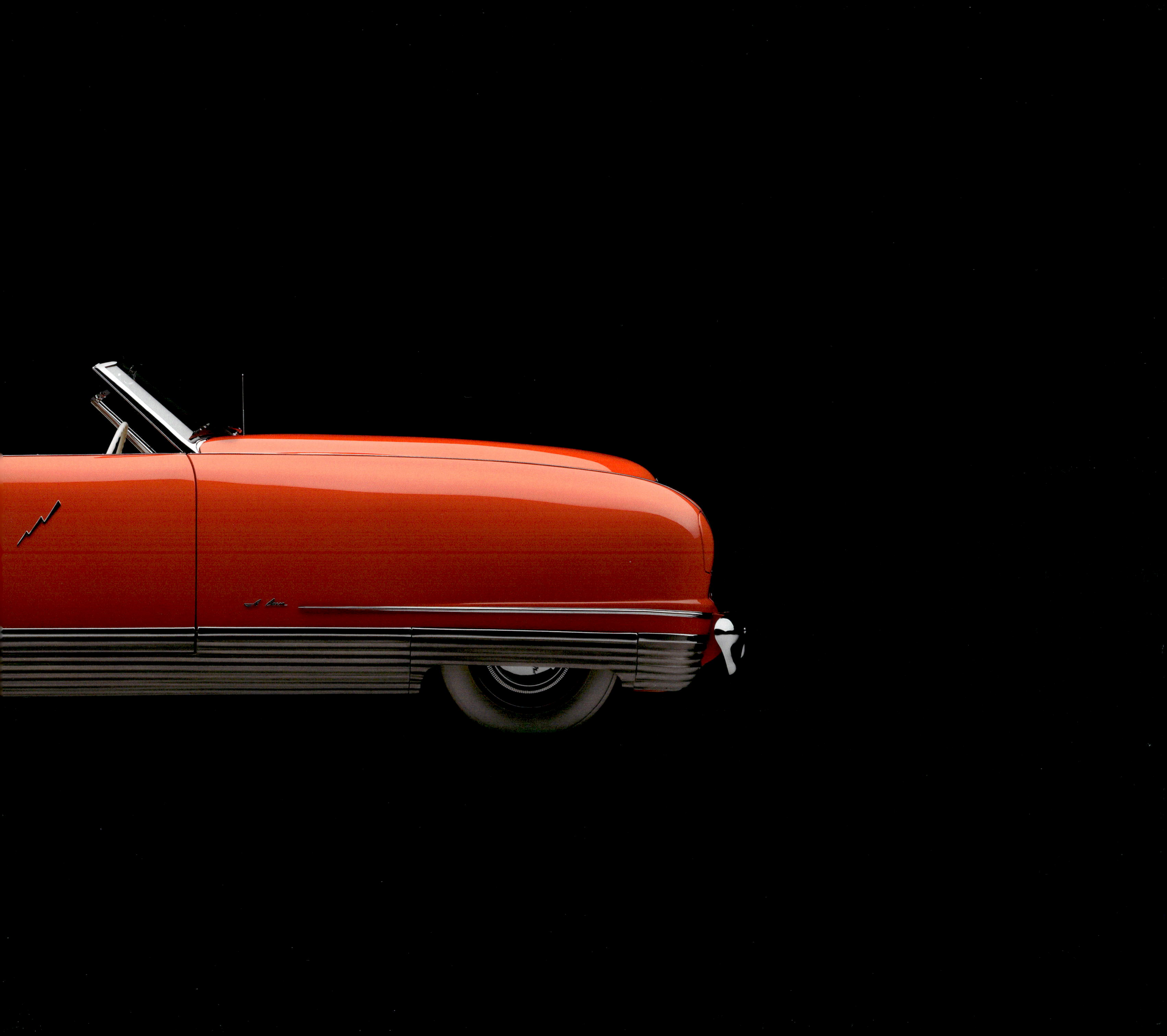

proportions, twin leather-lined passenger compartments, artfully dipped doors, and fold-down windshields, the *Newport* was reminiscent of the classic dual cowl phaetons popular with well-to-do consumers until the mid-1930s; it was, in fact, a last attempt to save this retro design concept. Named for the Rhode Island enclave that was home to extravagant summer "cottages" for the wealthy, the *Newport* epitomized, in the words of noted automobile historian Beverly Rae Kimes, "retro design, 1940s style!"[1]

Adding to the cachet of the *Thunderbolt* and *Newport*, the show cars were built by LeBaron, formerly a noted independent custom coachbuilder, now operating as an in-house affiliate of the Briggs Manufacturing Company. In addition to supplying completed production car bodies for makes such as Ford, Packard, and Chrysler, Briggs also offered an independent design consultancy for its clientele. Chief designer for the two dream cars was LeBaron's Ralph Roberts, who had been responsible for some of the most elegant custom-bodied creations of the classic era. Roberts's co-designer on the project at Briggs was the talented young stylist Alex Tremulis.

The first sketches of the *Thunderbolt*, developed in 1939, intrigued not only the Chrysler Corporation's ultraconservative president, Kaufman Thuma "K. T." Keller, but also David Wallace, who ran the Chrysler Division. Conventional wisdom held that Chrysler had gone too far with its *Airflow* notion. Tremulis astutely suggested that these cars should be touted as "new milestones in Airflow design,"[2] publicly hinting that had it not been for the 1934 *Airflows*, Chrysler styling might not have evolved into these bold, futuristic shapes. After approving development of both concepts, Chrysler brass insisted they be ready for the 1940 automobile show season, in time to debut in New York.

LeBaron employed traditional techniques for limited manufacturing. Aluminum body panels were stretched over wooden framing; the *Thunderbolt*'s full-width hood, which flowed uninterrupted from the base of the windshield to the slender front bumper, and its broad deck lid were both steel, as was the folding, one-piece steel top—a feature designed and patented by Roberts that had never before been seen on an American car. Underscoring the *Thunderbolt*'s sleek shape, its curved, one-piece windshield was devoid of vent-wings; the side windows were operated hydraulically; and the doors were push-button-actuated. Inside, a full bench seat accommodated three passengers. The Moderne design theme extended to the lettering on the instrument dials, with slender white characters set against a light gray background and accented by a bright red needle.

Fluted, anodized aluminum lower body side trim ran continuously from front to rear. Removable fender skirts covered the wheels, which were inset in front so they could turn. Wind tunnel experiments proved that the shrouded wheels were aerodynamically effective, but other than the postwar Nash *Airflyte*, rival manufacturers (and Chrysler) eschewed this feature. The engine was Chrysler's 140-hp, 323.5-cid straight 8, coupled to an experimental fluid drive, semiautomatic overdrive transmission.

Priced at $8,250 each, eight *Thunderbolts* were planned; only five were built, of which four survive. These dramatically modern cars were well received, but their high price tag was a deterrent. The onset of World War II meant that while a few of the *Thunderbolt*'s many advanced features found their way onto production DeSotos and Chryslers, these unique show cars were not replicated when hostilities ceased. The present owner saw this same *Thunderbolt* as a young boy when it was displayed at a Chrysler dealership, and was determined some day to own it.

LOANED BY ROGER WILLBANKS, DENVER, COLORADO.

PHOTOGRAPHY BY MICHAEL FURMAN.

1 Boyce, "1941 Chrysler Thunderbolt," in *Curves of Steel*, 58–59.
2 Ibid., 49.

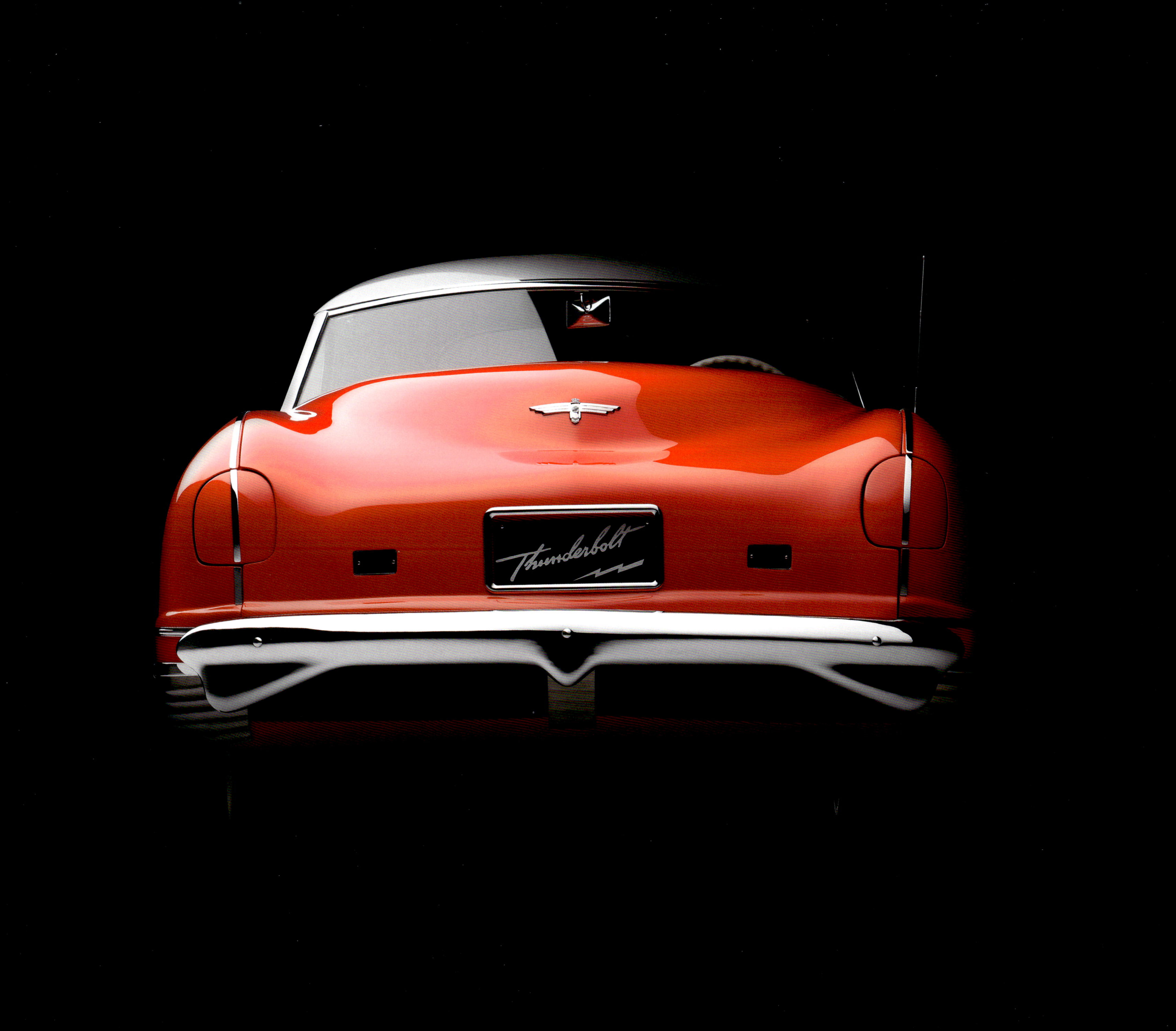
Thunderbolt

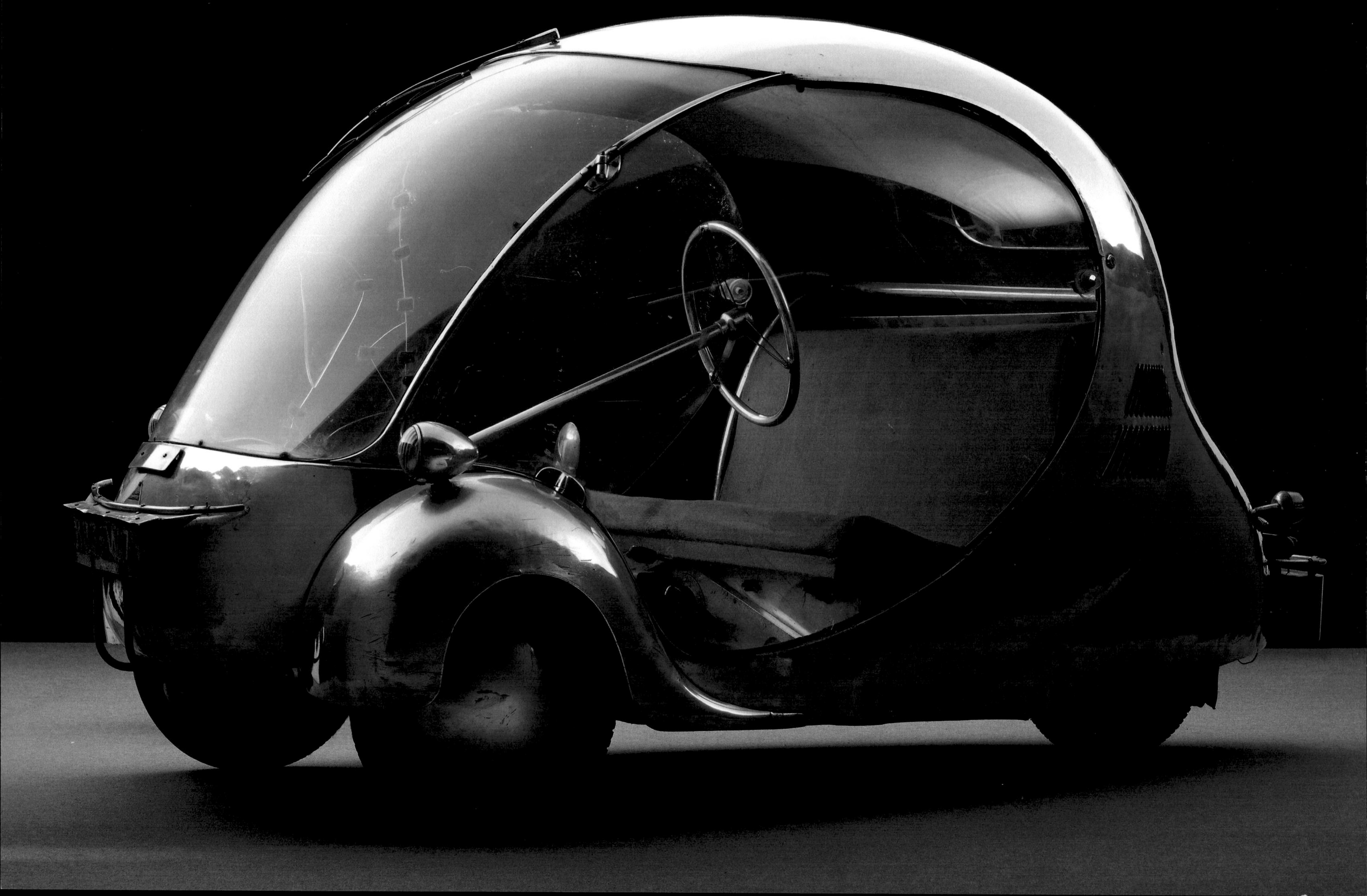

In the early days of the automobile, steam- and battery-powered cars vied with internal combustion engine automobiles for popularity. Before the advent of the self-starter, when all gasoline-fueled cars needed to be hand-cranked, electric cars were popular with female motorists, as they were relatively simple to operate and the batteries could be recharged overnight in a home garage—not to mention that their fifty- to sixty-mile range was quite sufficient for city use. Steam cars were notoriously hard to start as well, because firing the boiler was a complicated procedure that took skill and time. Thus the electric starter catapulted internal combustion engines into the lead. Emissions issues were not yet a concern and fuel was still cheap, so by the end of the 1930s in the United States, electric vehicles had virtually disappeared, except for industrial use. After the onset of World War II, the US government rationed gasoline, but as no new passenger cars were being constructed, Americans simply drove fewer miles with their pre-war cars. Overseas in German-occupied France, fuel was severely rationed, leading to ingenious solutions. People converted their gasoline-powered cars to coal gas or natural gas, and a few home-built battery-powered cars emerged. And one Frenchman developed a small, battery-powered prototype car that was decades ahead of its time.

Paul Arzens was an accomplished and commercially successful artist, sculptor, and later a noted designer of railroad locomotives. He studied art at Paris's École des Beaux-Arts and became a sufficiently successful painter, which allowed him to pursue his interest in engineering and industrial design. In 1935 Arzens designed and built a functional 6-speed transmission, which he installed in a vintage Chrysler. Efforts to interest Peugeot in the design were unsuccessful. Peugeot was planning to use Cotal pre-selector 4-speed semi-automatic gearboxes, so they had no need for Arzens's invention.[1]

Undaunted, Arzens built a dramatic-looking cabriolet on an old Buick chassis in 1938. The two-seater body was streamlined, with a long hood, sweeping fenders, slab sides, and a panoramic, wraparound Plexiglas windshield. The headlights were integrated into the grille. Painted gray and seen by many, the car was nicknamed *La Baleine* ("the whale"), and its advanced styling foreshadowed that of sports cars of the 1950s and 1960s. After the German invasion of France in 1940, when fuel for civilian use was in short supply, Arzens developed a smaller version of *La Baleine* on a vintage Fiat chassis. Instead of an internal combustion engine, however, there was a 10-hp electric motor and accumulator batteries. Arzens claimed his electric "whale" had a range of 125 miles at about 40 mph.[2]

In 1942 Arzens released another innovative electric vehicle that proved to be remarkably ahead of its time. His newest prototype consisted of a clear Plexiglas sphere mounted on a lightweight aluminum chassis, with three tiny wheels. It was instantly christened *L'Œuf* ("the egg"). The body weighed 132 pounds, and with a small electric motor added, the weight rose to 198 pounds; with batteries on board, *L'Œuf électrique* ("the electric egg") weighed 770 pounds. Arzens claimed an approximate sixty-mile range at 44 mph. Even with two passengers, if the speed dropped to 37 mph, the car's range remained consistent.[3]

Arzens received a good deal of notoriety in wartime Paris when he drove his near-spherical bubble car. His design preceded the postwar mini-car trend by several years. *L'Œuf électrique* never went into production and the prototype, which survives today, remains one of a kind. Looking at *L'Œuf* today, with the exception of crash safety considerations, it was a clever approach to low-cost, lightweight, fuel-efficient transportation. But its materials, Plexiglas and aluminum—highly sought for the aircraft industry—ensured that copies would not be built in occupied France.[4]

After the war Arzens developed *La Carosse*, a lightweight, 125-cc, easy-to-produce "everyman's" car with flat sheet-metal panels and a simple tubular chassis that was intended for mass production but ultimately was not marketed. He later worked for the French National Railway Company (SNCF), where he designed the famous BB and CC locomotives, which were widely used in France through the 1970s.

L'Œuf électrique remains a fascinating mobility solution. It must have captivated onlookers in Paris, providing a brief moment of amusement and marvel in a war-torn and oppressed era. Arzens was always an artist and his designs reflected his bold imagination.

LOANED BY THE MUSÉE DES ARTS ET MÉTIERS, PARIS, FRANCE.
PHOTOGRAPHY BY MICHEL ZUMBRUNN AND URS SCHMID.

1   Bellu, "Toutes Les Voitures Françaises," 52.
2   Ibid.
3   Ibid.
4   Georgano, *The Beaulieu Encyclopedia of the Automobile*, 79.

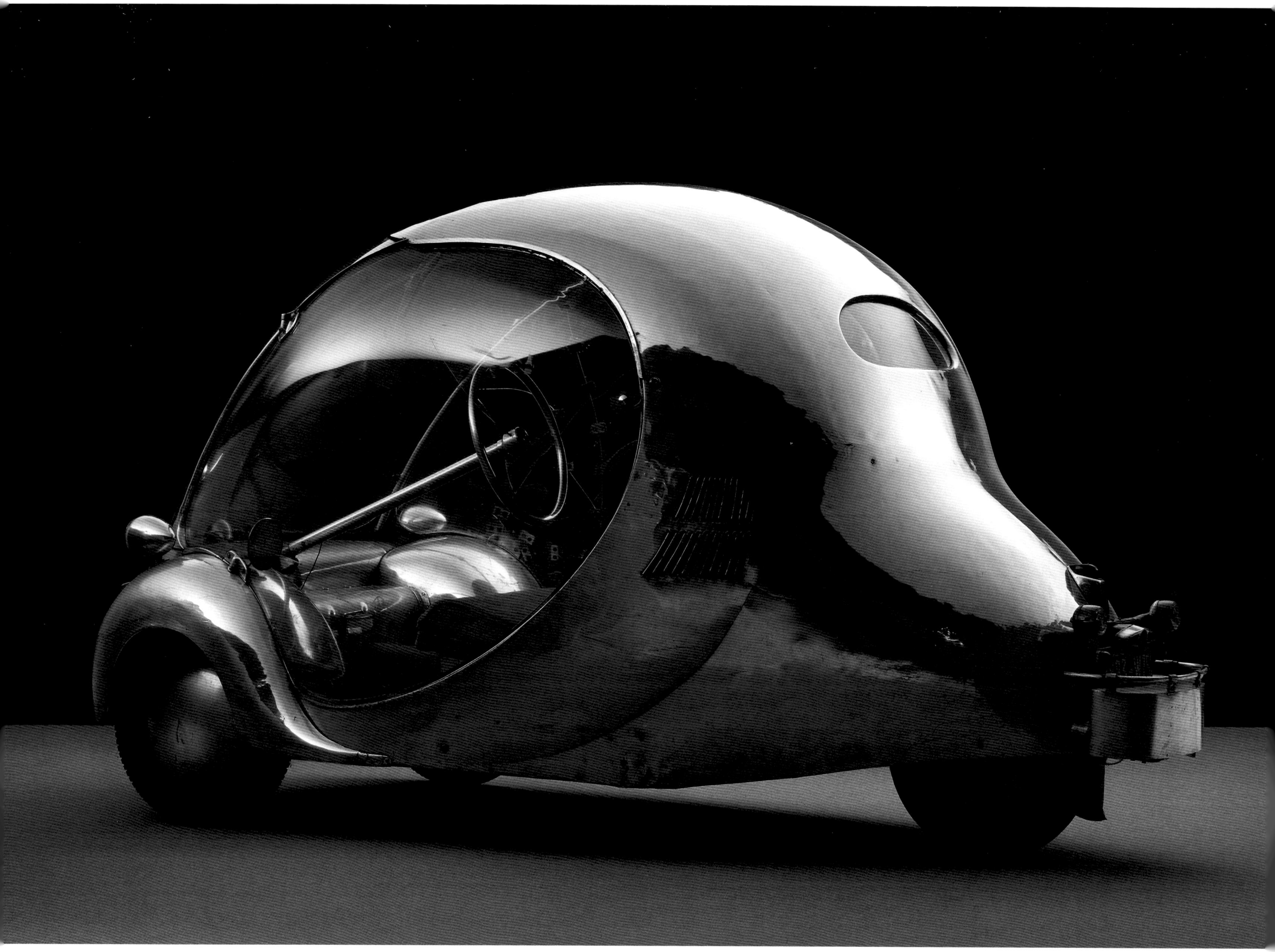

1947 Norman Timbs Special

A mechanical engineer who had earlier designed the 1947/1948/1949 Indy 500–winning *Blue Crown Specials* driven by Bill Holland and Mauri Rose, Norman Timbs worked for Preston Tucker on the highly advanced Tucker *48 Torpedo*, and then built his own road-going car—the dream car of one very talented engineer. Featured on the cover of *Motor Trend* in October 1949 (see p. 29), the sleek, seductive shape of Timbs's rear-engine special was a stunning contrast to the era's bulky, boxy domestic cars.

Using language typical of the 1940s, *Motor Trend* called the Norman Timbs *Special* "an unusually streamlined maroon job"[1] and stated that the car took three years to construct. Its hand-fashioned aluminum body is believed to have been fabricated by noted Los Angeles race car builder Emil Diedt, who worked at California Metalcrafters for a time. Timbs then worked with professional race car builders to help him with the extensively modified chassis. Overall, the Timbs *Special* was built for a reported $8,000—a large sum at the time, considering that a 1949 Cadillac convertible sold new for $3,497.

Timbs's radical roadster had fully skirted fadeaway fenders, a close-coupled cockpit without doors, a raked and split windshield, and twin tailpipes. Since early issues of *Motor Trend* had sepia covers with black-and-white illustrations, readers could not appreciate the Timbs *Special*'s deep, Titian red finish, speckled with 14-karat-gold flake, but they must have been stopped in their tracks by its futuristic appearance. It also boasted a rear-engine configuration, which was unusual for a large car in the postwar era.

1947 NORMAN TIMBS *SPECIAL*

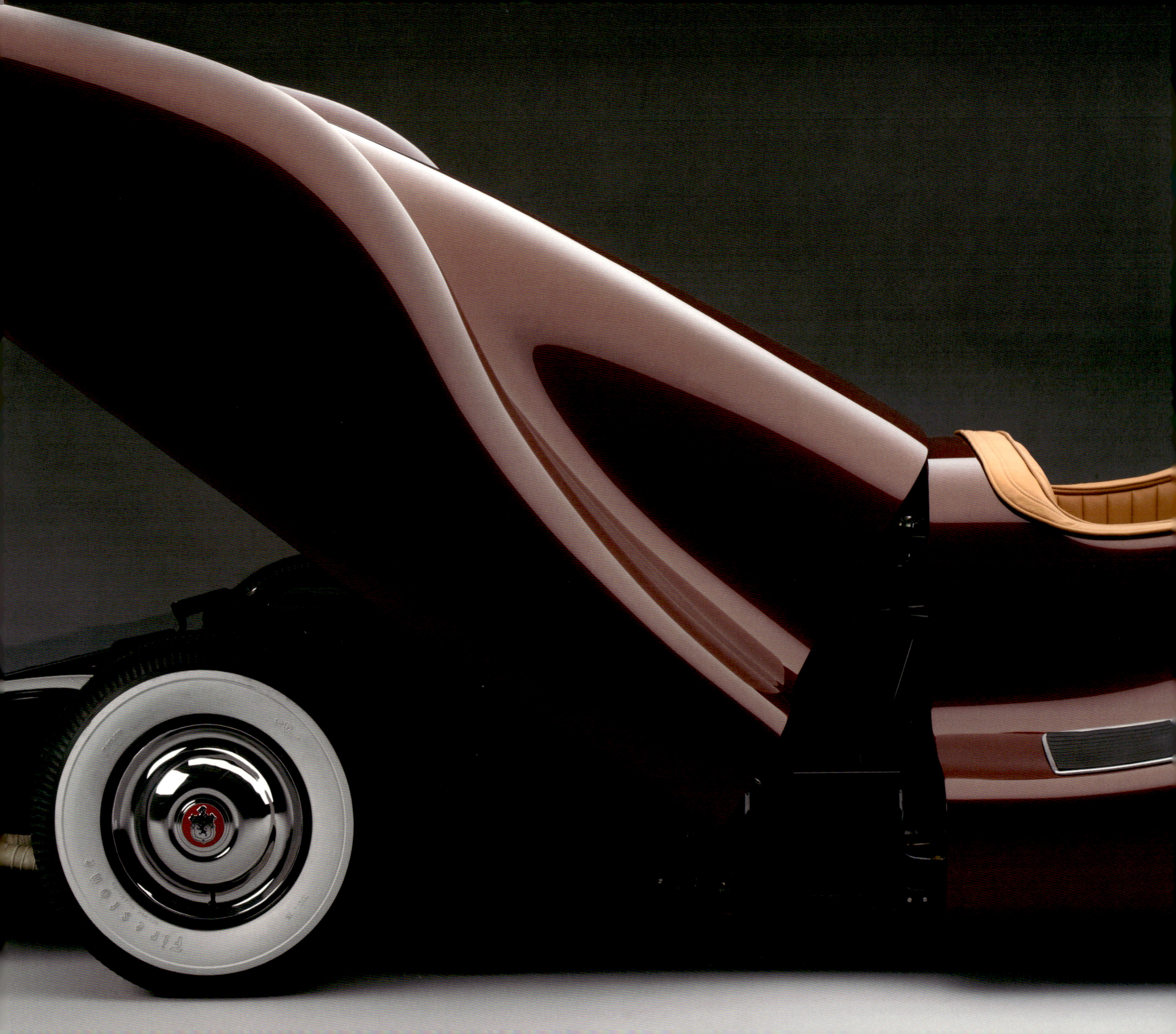
Firestone

The roadster's massive aluminum tail hinged just behind the cockpit like a giant clamshell. It opened hydraulically to reveal a 1947 Buick straight-8 engine fitted with factory-optional dual carburetors. Timbs had ordered the power plant directly from a Los Angeles–based Buick dealer. The long straight-8 was located almost in the center of the car's unique chassis, and a spare wheel was mounted directly behind it. Designed by Timbs using race car practice, the chassis consisted of 4-inch-diameter chrome-moly tubing that was capped at the ends and pressurized by a small air compressor, allegedly to help stiffen the frame and supply air for the air horns. The solid front axle was a conventional Ford I-beam. The rear suspension consisted of a custom-made, Timbs-designed independent swing axle comprising a Packard center section with modified Ford axle bells. The snug cockpit, which was accessible via step plates on each side, resembled that of a high-powered luxury speedboat. There was a wood-trimmed, three-spoke accessory wheel; a column-mounted Ford shift lever; and, as the pièce de résistance, the cockpit, dash surrounds, door panels, and seat were resplendent in tan leather. No top was ever fitted.

The entire front end was a single curvaceous form, with an ovoid chromed grille reminiscent of a then contemporary Italian Cisitalia, flanked by a pair of low-mounted, inset headlights that were in turn framed

1947 NORMAN TIMBS *SPECIAL* 73

by a plated nerf (bumper) bar, which echoed the shape of a similar two-plane bar on the rear. The radiator was mounted behind the grille. There was no hood opening; there were no doors. A full belly pan aided aerodynamic efficiency. The only visible cut line was the thin, vertical break behind the cockpit that separated the extended tail section. At first glance, the entire car appeared to be molded in one continuous form. The overall effect was startling. For 1949, when most production models were relatively tall, boxy, and dripping with chrome, the Timbs *Special* must have resembled a car from outer space.

Timbs himself drove the car, but not a great deal. His son Norman Timbs, Jr., said that his father "was very proud of it, and he compiled an elaborate scrapbook about the car. But it was so futuristic-looking, he couldn't drive it anywhere without people constantly stopping and staring at it. It happened so often, he got tired of it."[2] Timbs eventually decided to sell his roadster. Calling it a "two-seater sports," he advertised it in *Road & Track* in February 1950 for $7,500.[3] The ad ran a photo of Timbs towering over his low-slung two-seater. The copy claimed the car was "capable of over 100-mph," and stated that it "had been driven less than 5,000 miles."[4]

The present owner bought the car in decrepit shape and commissioned a major restoration; it had been stored outside in the California high desert for many years, and had even been used in a movie. A remarkable survivor, the Timbs *Special* won first place in the Sports Custom Class at the 2012 Pebble Beach Concours d'Elegance. Radical, sleek, rear-engined, and startlingly aerodynamic for its era, the Norman Timbs *Special* continues to delight all who see it.

LOANED BY GARY AND DIANE CERVENY, MALIBU, CALIFORNIA.

PHOTOGRAPHY BY PETER HARHOLDT.

---

[1] *Motor Trend*, "Custom Car," October 1949, 20.

[2] Norman Timbs, Jr., in a telephone conversation with the author, February 2010.

[3] *Road & Track*, vol. 1, no. 8, February 1950, classified advertisement, 29.

[4] Ibid.

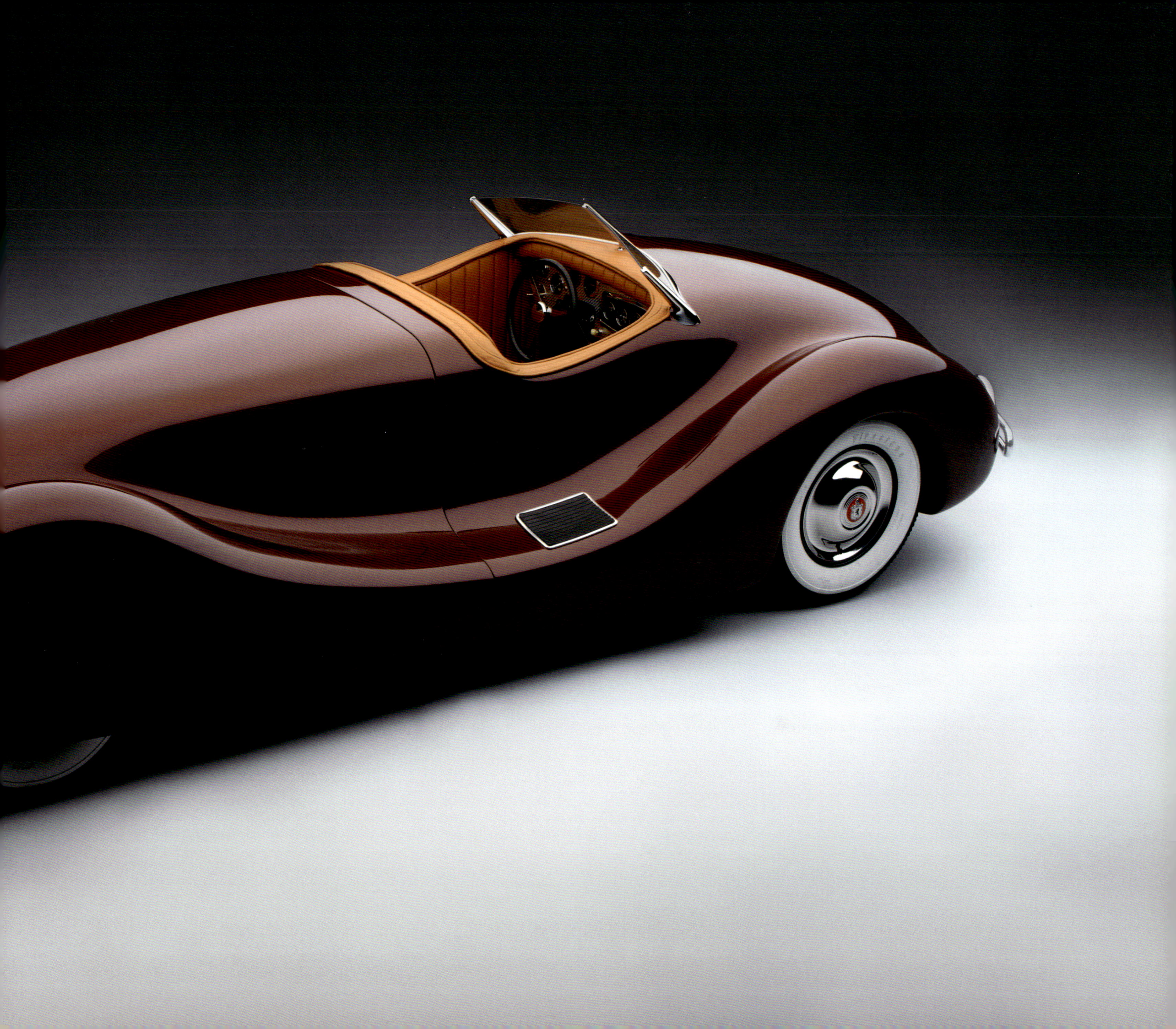

1948 Panhard Dynavia

The French pioneer automaker Panhard and Levassor began building cars in the nineteenth century and was one of world's earliest successful automobile manufacturers. By the 1930s, even as war clouds threatened Europe, the firm looked into the future to produce a dramatically modern car that captured considerable attention thanks to its advanced styling and innovative passenger seating configuration.

With the release of its new *Panoramique* line (panoramic vision sedans) in 1936, Panhard and Levassor offered then radical, semi-streamlined unibody cars in Moderne style. Early examples featured an unusual central driving position. Later models offered thin windshield supports, which framed a pair of small glass windows for better visibility; Panhard and Levassor called the effect "binocular vision." Softly curved fenders covered all four wheels, the roof was gently rounded, and fluted, wing-like louvers vented the engine compartment, complementing the overall design. The *Panoramique*'s elegantly slanted radiator grille suggested a shield, and this shape was matched by the outline of the headlights. Technically, the *Panoramique* was a marvel, featuring torsion bar suspension, dual-circuit hydraulic brakes, and an underslung worm-drive rear axle.[1]

During World War II, Panhard and Levassor's factory built military tanks for the French Army and later produced tank parts, along with wood and charcoal gas generators for the occupying Germans. When the war ended, the company—now simply called Panhard—faced a choice. Overcoming the objections of Paul Panhard, who had managed the company since 1916, and at the insistence of his son Jean, the company's technical director, Panhard ceased production of luxury cars, electing instead to produce the *Dyna* series. Jean's vision for Panhard was to produce economy cars with personality. Automotive writer Serge Bellu poetically noted, "The hopes that were sketchily born after the liberation of France encouraged certain enlightened spirits to conceive motor cars that were, to a greater or lesser degree, revolutionary."[2]

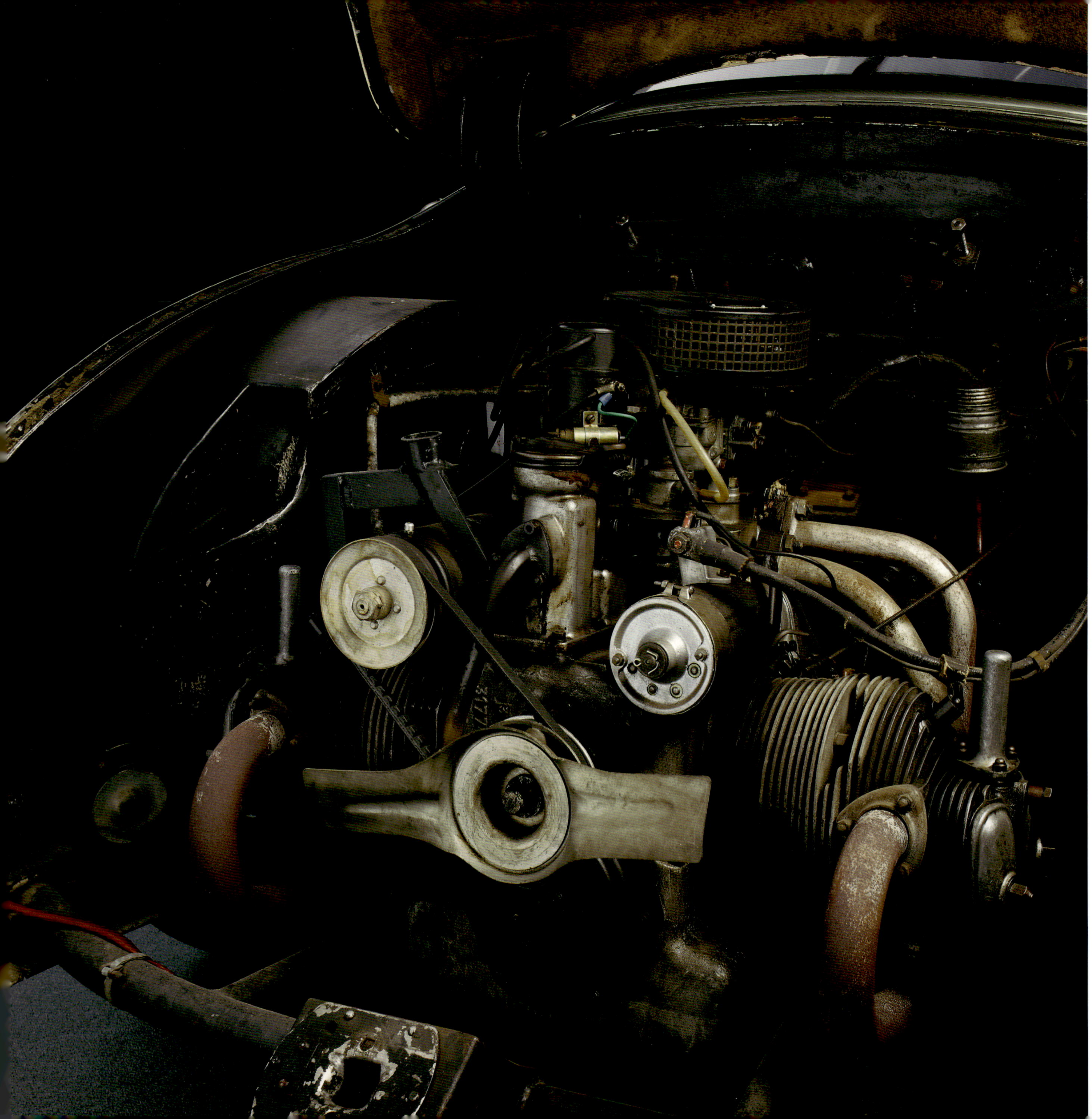
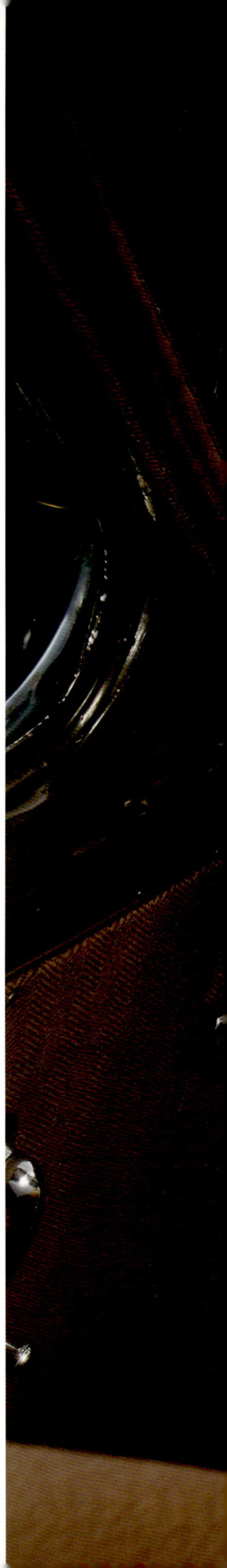

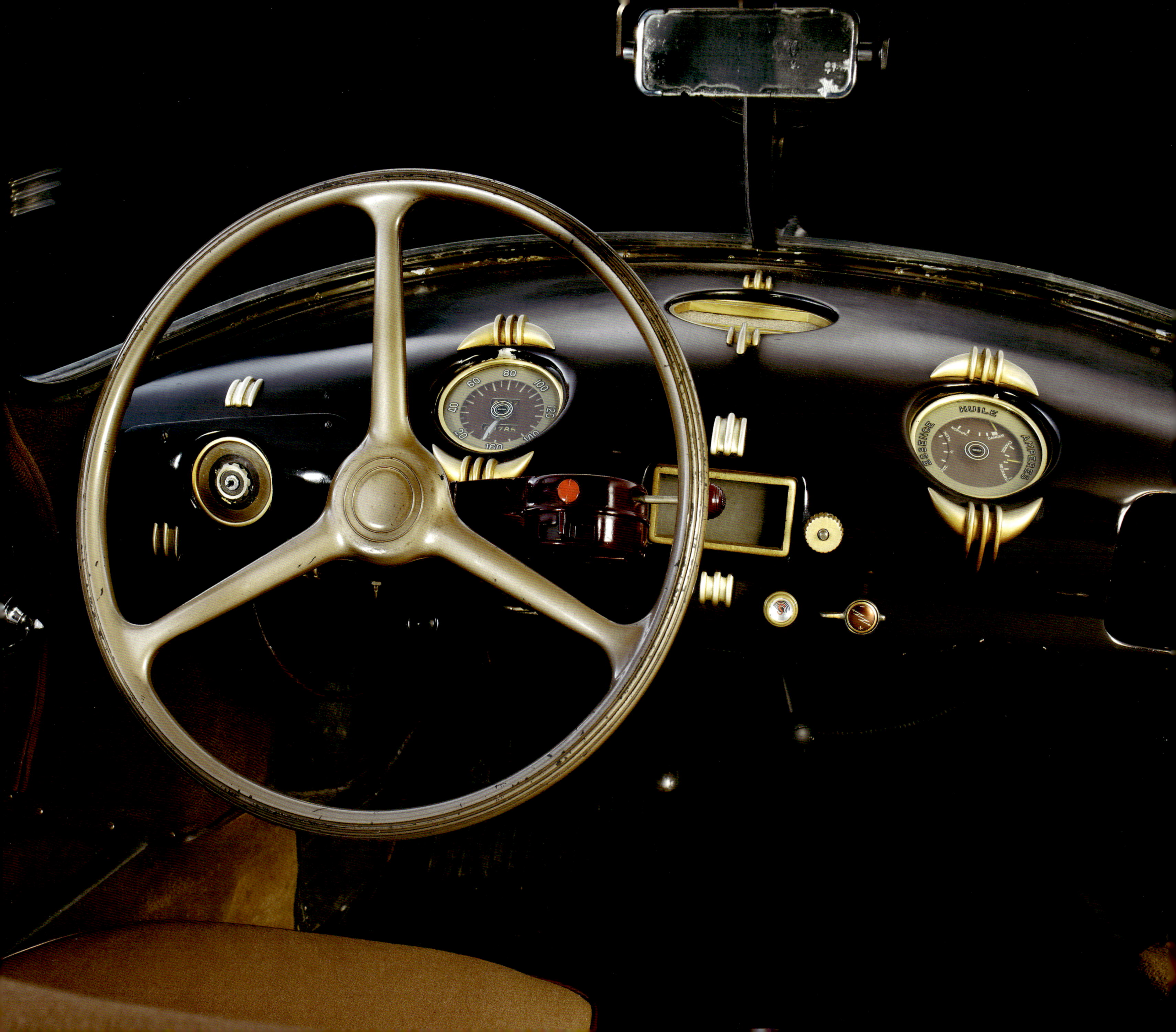
HUILE
ESSENCE
AMPERES

One of those dreamers was Panhard's chief designer, Louis Bionier, who had been responsible for the dramatic shapes of his company's cars since 1921. Bionier reportedly studied the shapes of fish and birds to envision the look of cars to come, and then devised an aerodynamic concept car that became the basis for future production Panhards. Bionier experimented with a car shaped like an airplane as early as 1943; that idea became the basis for his new car. The resulting show car was called *Dynavia*. A highlight of the 1948 Paris *Salon de l'Automobile*, it was built on a relatively short wheelbase platform, with long overhangs. Automotive stylists—and French *carrosseries*, in particular—were fascinated with the teardrop (*goutte de l'eau*) shape, believing it to be the ideal aerodynamic form. The *Dynavia*'s sleek body was an ovoid form, with a rounded front and a sharply defined backbone that led to a distinctly pointed rear.[3]

Inside, the instrument panel was perfectly rounded, matching the lower curve of the windshield. Without compromising the overall teardrop shape, the designers ensured there was room inside for four passengers, while the expansive windows and thin pillars permitted nearly panoramic visibility. Despite the simplicity of the teardrop form, styling details included several overly ornamental elements. Bellu wryly commented that they included, "most notably, the front end treatment which in one over-wrought assemblage took in the headlamps, the bumpers and the grille for the air intake."[4]

The *Dynavia* took its small 28-hp, 610-cc flat-twin engine from the Panhard *Dyna*, which had been introduced in 1946. Despite its low output, the *Dynavia*'s top speed was a commendable 87.8 mph, with 57.7 mpg. Its secret was its streamlined shape and light weight at just 1,865 pounds. Wind tunnel tests on a model *Dynavia* at the Institut Aerotechnique at the École Spéciale Militaire de Saint-Cyr reportedly resulted in a remarkable 0.171Cd (drag coefficient). Tests of the full-size show car in operational trim resulted in an excellent 0.26Cd. (By comparison, today's Mercedes-Benz *CLA*, the most aerodynamically efficient small sedan currently available, has a 0.22Cd.) On the *Dynavia*, weight was saved due to the extensive use of alloys, including Duralinox (durable aluminum alloy).[5]

Panhard built two *Dynavia* concept cars and enough parts for a third car. One of the *Dynavias*, however, was sold to an individual in Switzerland and subsequently wrecked in a road accident. The production *Dyna-54*, which borrowed some of the *Dynavia*'s streamlined shape but with bumpers and lights added to make it more suitable for the road, was introduced in 1953. The car was widened to seat three passengers abreast, front and rear. Its unit-construction body was made entirely of lightweight Duralinox.

Plans were made to expand the *Dyna* line with even more innovative models, but Citroen's purchase of forty-five percent of Panhard in April 1955 and its unwillingness to produce the *Dyna Junior* marked the beginning of the end for Panhard. Many *Dynavia*-influenced practices, such as the extensive use of aluminum alloys, were changed and cheapened as Citroen re-engineered the bodies in steel and attempted to mass-produce Panhard cars. Citroen then decided to use the Panhard manufacturing facilities to build more military vehicles and phase out the Panhard name. Car production ceased in July 1967.[6]

COURTESY OF THE MUSÉE DE L'AVENTURE PEUGEOT, SOCHAUX, FRANCE.

PHOTOGRAPHY BY MICHEL ZUMBRUNN AND URS SCHMID.

[1] Mullin Automotive Museum, *Vitesse-Élégance*, 220–224.
[2] Georgano, *The Beaulieu Encyclopedia*, 1188–1189.
[3] Ibid., 1189.
[4] Bellu, *500 Fantastic Cars*, 18–19.
[5] Ibid., 19.
[6] Georgano, *The Beaulieu Encyclopedia*, 1190.

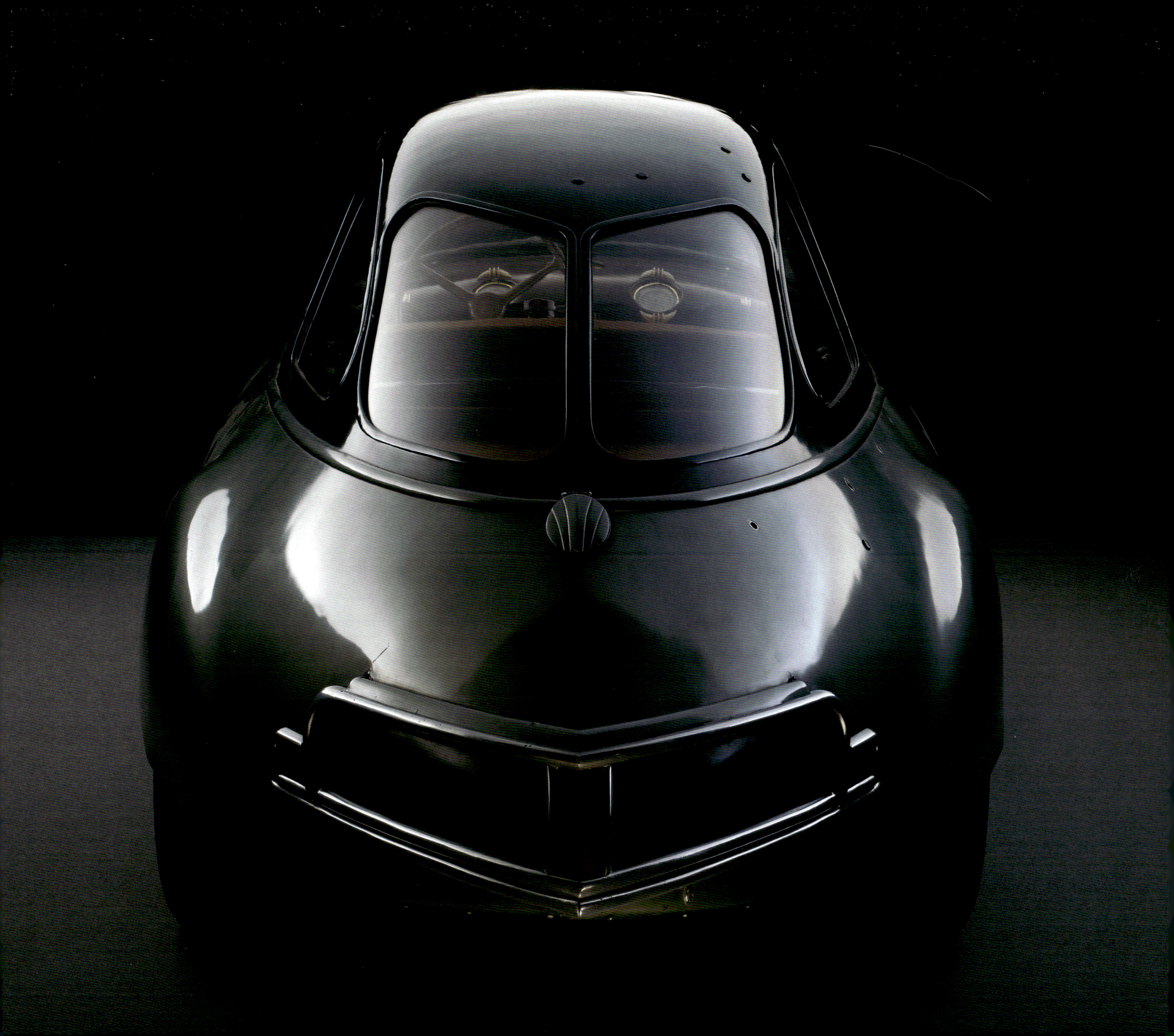

1948 *Tasco*

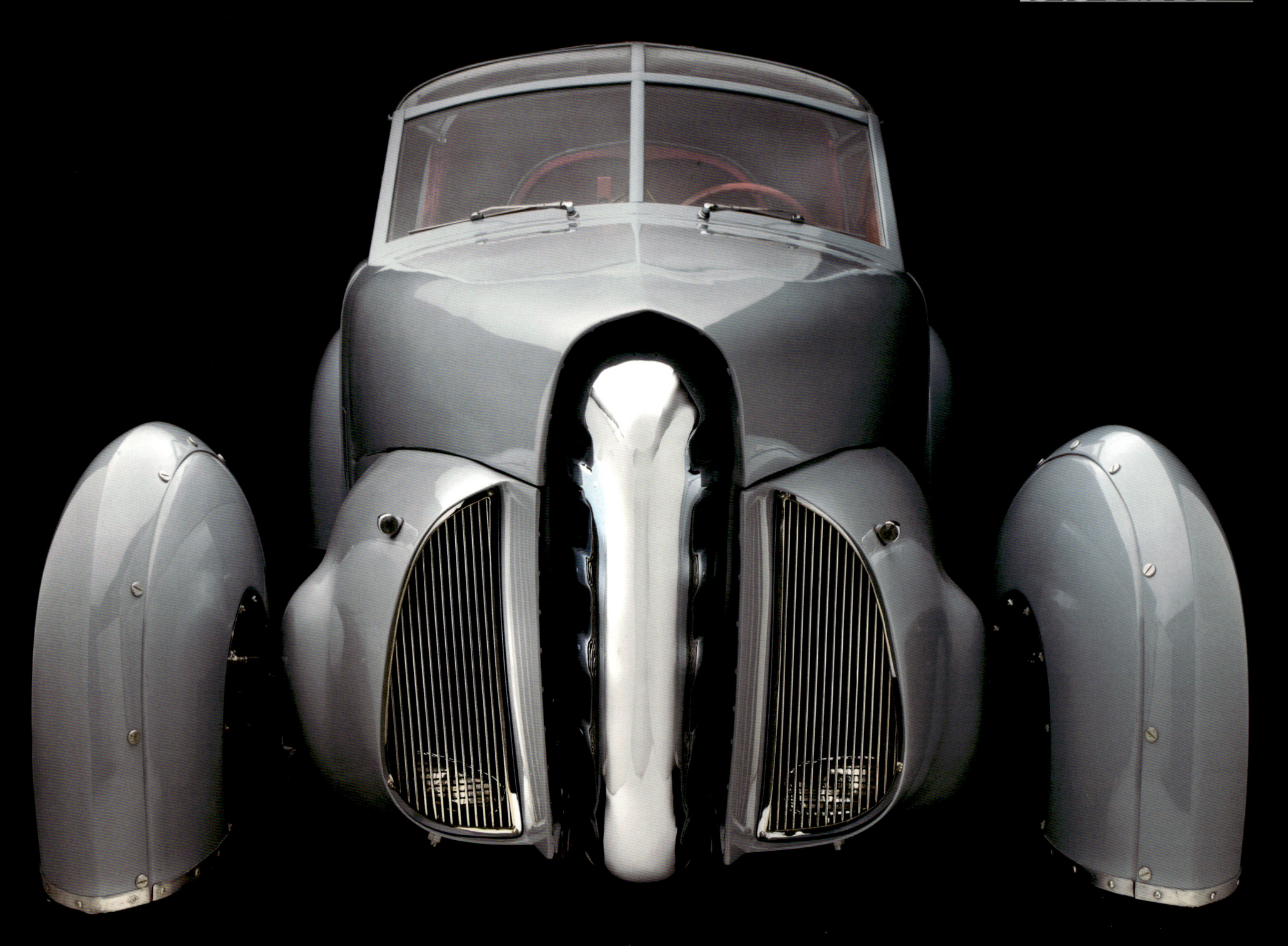

Renowned automotive stylist Gordon Buehrig designed the radical Cord 810/812, the Auburn 851 *Speedster*, and many Duesenberg bodies. Brilliant as they were, all three Indiana companies succumbed to the Depression. Working at Studebaker in 1948, Buehrig became intrigued with a letter from Russ Sceli, a Bugatti enthusiast who envisioned a postwar American sports car.

The time seemed fortuitous. Domestic automakers were still turning out what were fundamentally pre-war designs. Sceli and his colleagues wanted a domestic sports model that would be suitable for the Sports Car Club of America (SCCA) competition. They called their dream car *The American Sports Car*, or *Tasco*. Looking at affordable European entries such as Jaguar and Morgan, a group of ten investors (including Buehrig himself) each put up $5,000 to get the project started, envisioning what Buehrig called "a king-size MG"—a reference to the British sports car manufacturer MG Car Company Limited—with an American chassis and power plant. Ever the visionary, Buehrig eschewed drafty open roadsters and felt that sports car enthusiasts would soon want enclosed coupes. He drew a parallel with the private aircraft industry, where open-cockpit planes had given way to closed cabins after Charles Lindbergh's historic Paris flight. Buehrig envisioned a transparent cabin with a new type of canopy top.

Russ Sceli liked the idea of fully enclosed front fenders that would be attached to the brake backing plates and turn with the front wheels. Buehrig built a one-quarter-scale model from a new material, ABS (acrylonitrile butadiene styrene) vacuum-formable plastic, in late 1948, and work soon began on a full-size prototype. The talented Studebaker design engineer Dale Cosper modified a contemporary Mercury frame with added tubular cross-members for rigidity—although Buehrig regretted that his team did not wait one more year for a new 1949 Ford chassis with independent front suspension. A Mercury flathead V-8 engine was equipped with dual carburetors and twin exhausts. To offset the un-sprung weight of the Tasco's shapely fiberglass fenders, Dow Chemical Company was tapped to build wheels of magnesium. They were strong and light, but very expensive.

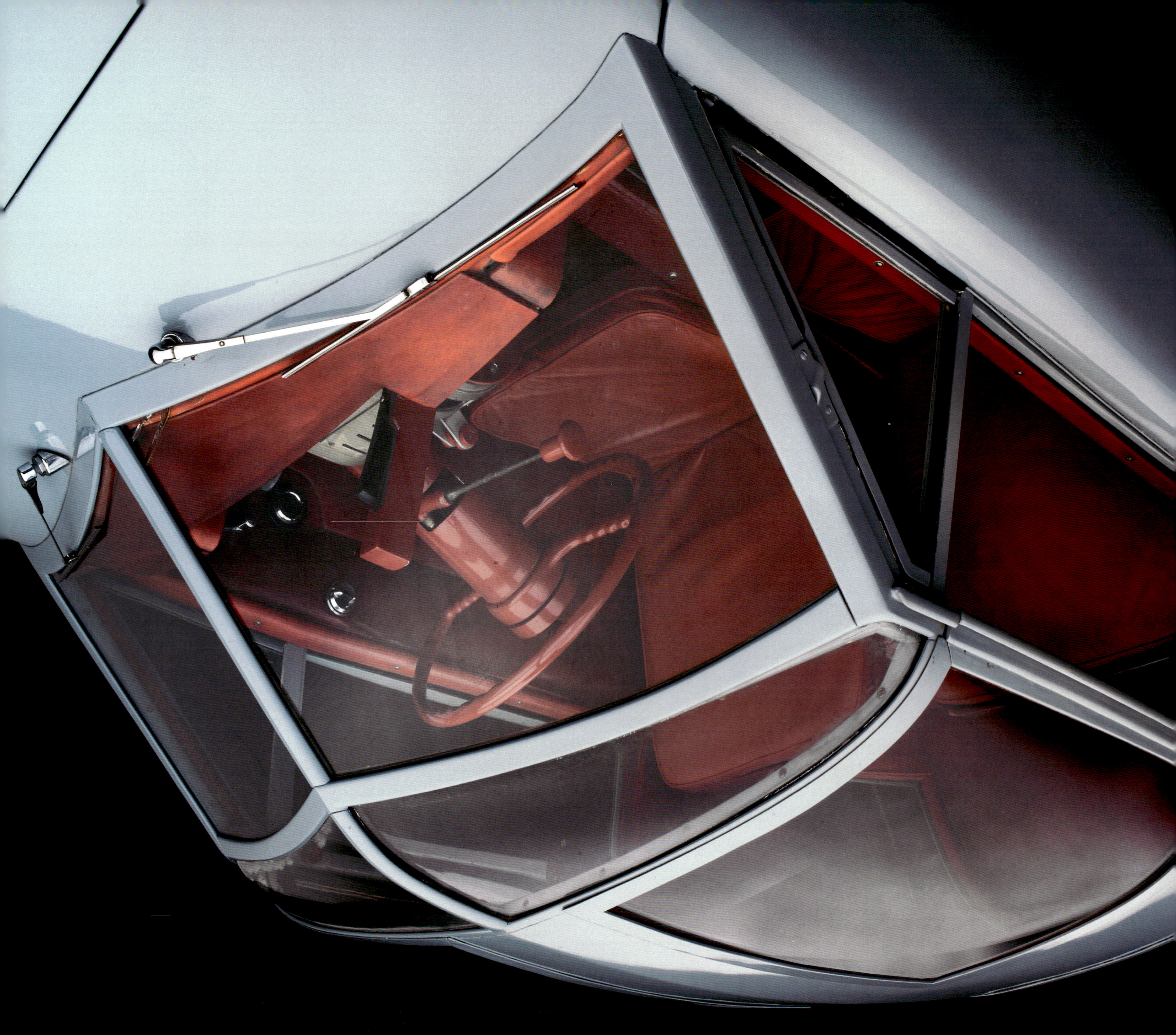

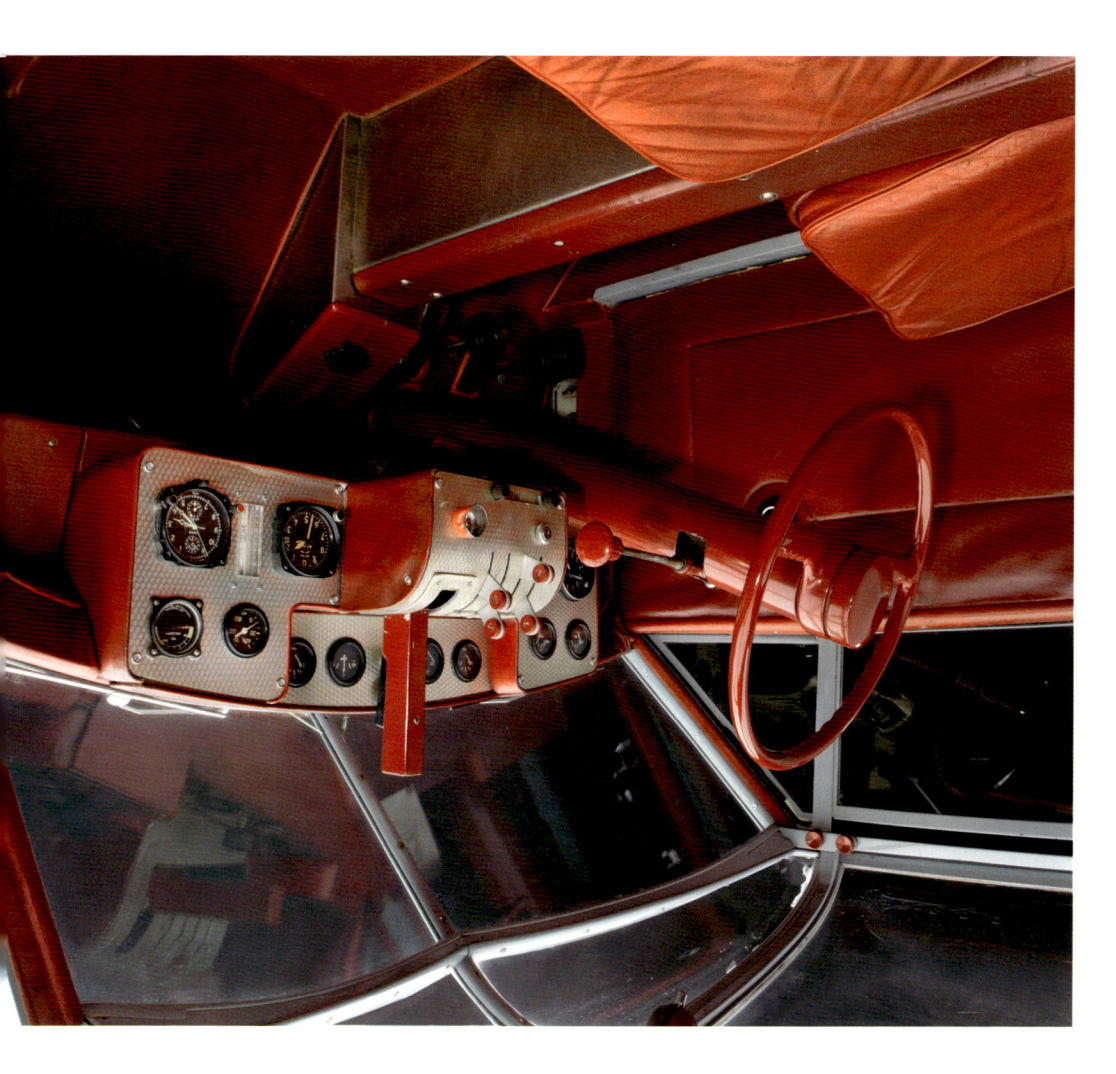

Buehrig and model builder Vic Simney drove the bare chassis to Rosemont, Pennsylvania, where the respected classic coachbuilder Derham Body Company fabricated the new body. The Tasco's clever T-top roof design, with its removable panels, was the first of its kind. Visibility above and to both sides was excellent, much like sitting in a two-seater aircraft. The instrument panel was positioned high in front of the driver, with the steering wheel mounted close to it. Military-style gauges with black-on-white faces and a row of toggle switches mimicked aircraft practice and were unlike those of any road-going vehicle up to that time. There were two gas tanks with a switch that allowed the driver to transfer from one to the other. The driveshaft was enclosed in stainless steel housing and covered with leather. It encased the wiring and fuel lines—likely the first time a driveshaft tunnel had become a design feature. A small, acrylic, bubble-like rear window that resembled the tail gunner's position on a World War II bomber housed the rear license plate. The engine was a Mercury flathead V-8 fitted with Ardun overhead valve cylinder heads.

Thinking that aircraft manufacturers would be looking for something to build in the postwar era, Buehrig showed the prototype to Ercoupe in Baltimore, Maryland; Beech in Wichita, Kansas. He also tried to interest Dick Kraffe, president of the Lincoln Division of Ford Motor Company, but Kraffe declined. By that time, however, the Tasco team had exhausted their funds and the project was stillborn.

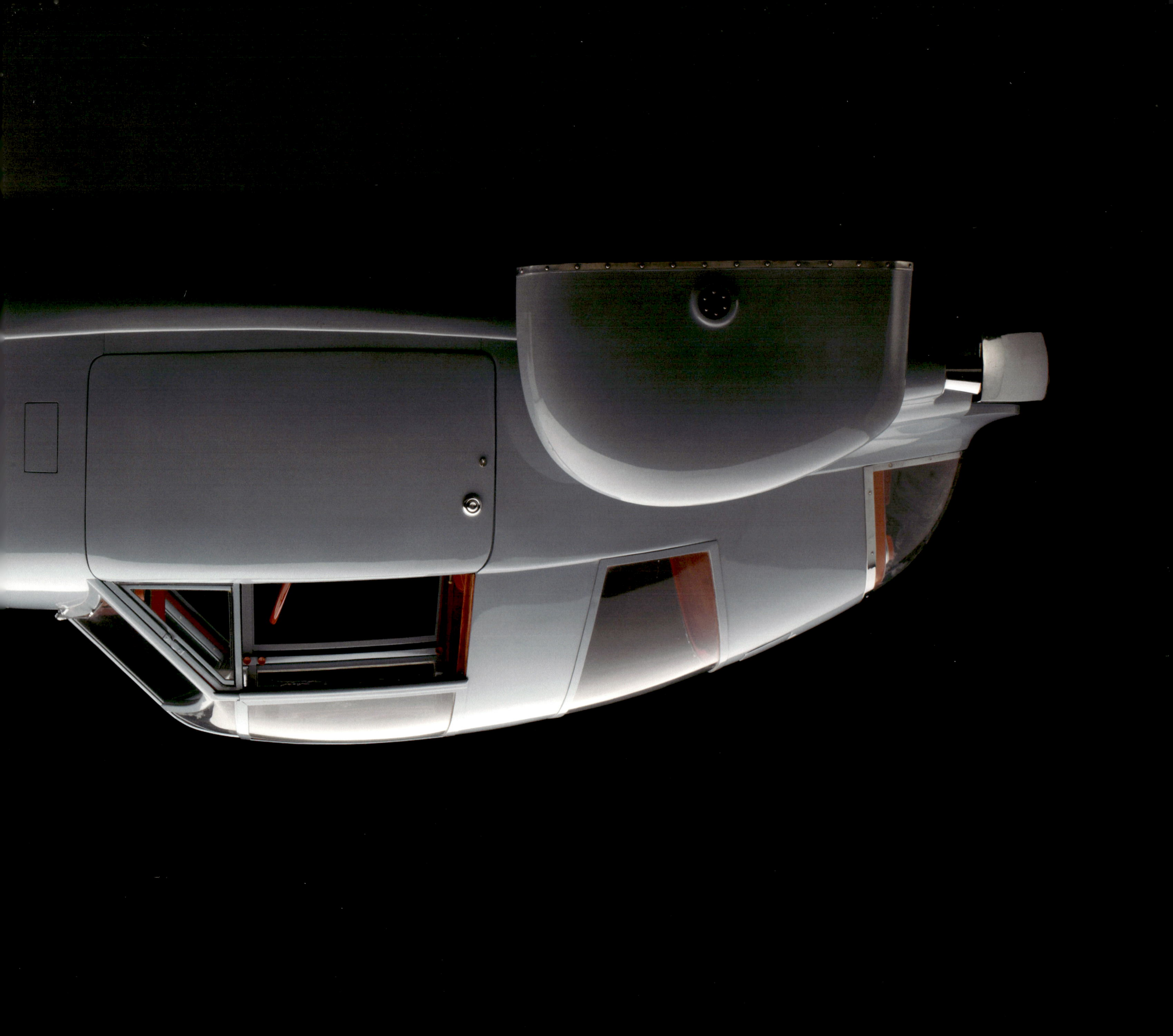

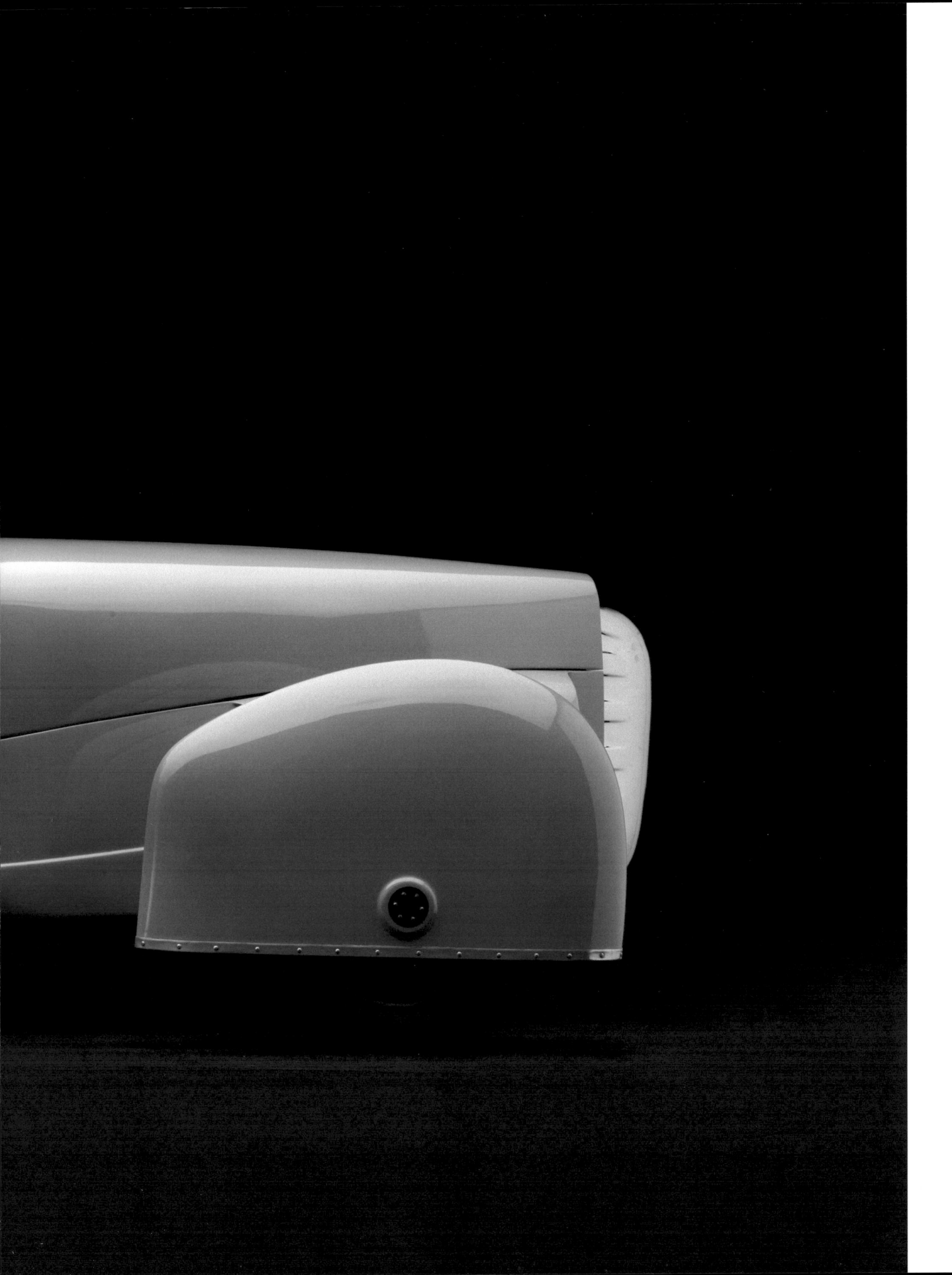

Buehrig had patented the *Tasco*'s novel design features in 1946, and he held the right to his invention for the allowable seventeen years. In 1949 he joined Ford Motor Company as the head of one of its design studios; two years later he was awarded another patent, this one for a lift-off top with removable panels and a built-in structural member that doubled as a rollover bar. He tried to sell this top design successively to Ford, Chrysler, and General Motors—and even to a European supplier—but to no avail. After designing one of his tops, this time equipped with transparent roof panels, to fit his own 1955 *Thunderbird*, Buehrig gave up trying to market the *Tasco*'s pioneering top design. In late 1967 he was surprised to see that General Motors had built its new 1968 *Corvette* with a two-piece Targa lift-off top, which closely resembled his earlier invention. Although Buehrig initially wanted to sue GM for patent infringement, he was advised to accept a settlement. He had felt that his top design would be, in his words, "the convertible of the future, because air conditioning makes the ragtop literally passé."[1] Ahead of its time, the T-top *Tasco*, with its aerodynamic, moveable fenders, surely inspired the 1968 *Corvette*. Vacuum-formed ABS models would soon become common practice in automotive design. Buehrig is best remembered for his work for Auburn, Cord, and Duesenberg; his curious *Tasco* is all but forgotten.

LOANED BY THE AUBURN CORD DUESENBERG AUTOMOBILE MUSEUM, AUBURN, INDIANA.

PHOTOGRAPHY BY PETER HARHOLDT.

---

1 Buehrig and Jackson, *Rolling Sculpture*, 129.

1951 General Motors *Le Sabre XP-8*

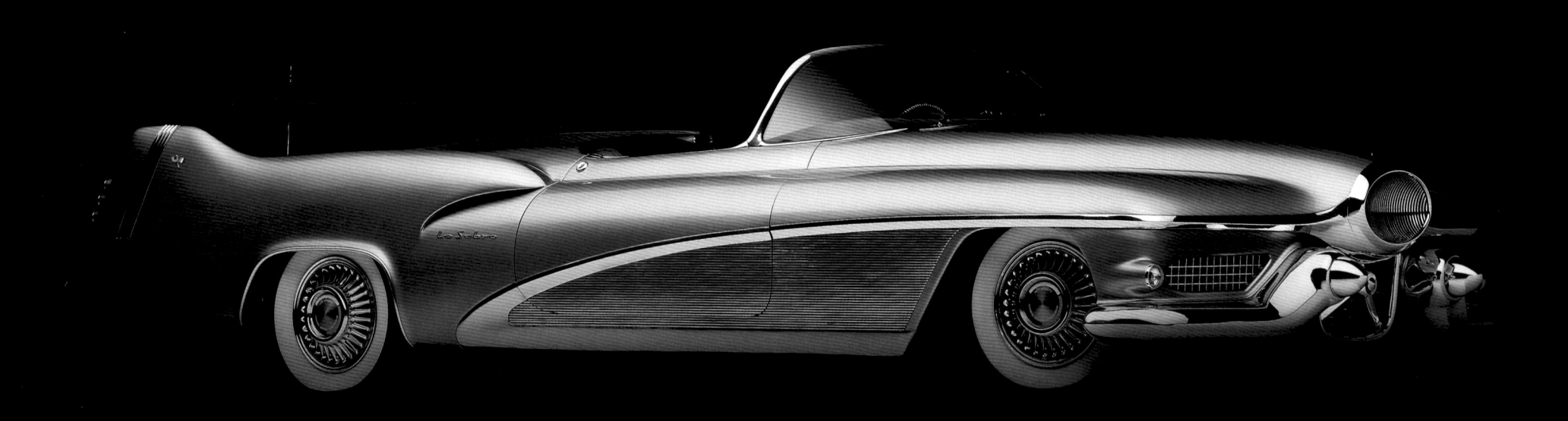

Before the tenure of General Motors' legendary design chief Harley J. Earl, automotive styling was an engineering responsibilty; design was considered frivolous. Over the course of his long career, Earl laid down basic precepts, many of which continue to influence automotive styling today. He initiated aesthetic rules but would break them if results were sufficiently dramatic. According to renowned automotive writer Michael Lamm, "Earl believed mightily in entertaining the spectator during the entire trip around the car."[1] He convinced GM management under Alfred P. Sloan that frequent, style-driven model changes—or "planned obsolescence"—resulted in steady sales increases.

Earl understood and harnessed the play of light on sheet metal forms and chrome trim. He had his designers carefully calculate and plan shadows and reflections, advancing the science of surface development. So it stood to reason that Earl, who never shied from publicity, would create his own unique roadster, partly to dazzle the public but also to indicate future GM styling direction. The result was his 1938 Buick *Y-Job*—thought to be the first true concept car and the pioneer of dream cars—which was designed to inspire all who saw it but was never intended for production. It served for years as his personal transportation—a none-too-subtle reminder that GM's styling chief was a creative genius.

After World War II, Earl and his prolific designers were ready with stunning show cars inspired by jet aircraft, rockets, yachts, and speedboats—and Earl himself needed a new head-turning personal car to replace his now obsolete *Y-Job*. The result was the *XP-8*, better known as the 1951 *Le Sabre*, a dazzling, high-tech rocket sled on wheels that rendered everything on the road immediately passé.

The *Le Sabre*'s radically low-slung roadster body was made of exotic materials: sheet and honeycomb aluminum, several large magnesium castings, and fiberglass. It was very expensive to build. Sources say the cost was between $500,000 and $1,000,000; the equivalent today would be ten times those figures.[2] The *Le Sabre*'s fashionable tinted wraparound (panoramic) windshield, which became a distinctive GM feature that would appear in later production cars, at first rattled glass supplier Libby-Owens-Ford because it was so difficult to execute.[3] The car's hidden headlights were concealed behind an oval grille that resembled a jet air intake, which was matched with a similar round outlet at the base of a triangular trunk. Stylishly flat fenders tapered rearward into a pair of jaunty fins that topped a wide bumper with twin exhaust outlets. The engine was a 335-hp, Roots-type supercharged 215-cid V-8 with an aluminum block and hemi-heads with a then high 10:1 compression ratio. It could operate on gasoline or methanol, fed independently to each of two carburetors from either of two fuel cells hidden in the rear fenders. The Le Sabre's transaxle, another radical departure, was a modified Buick Dynaflow automatic torque converter transmission combined with a de Dion independent rear end. It helped maintain a low silhouette and improved weight distribution. Small-diameter, 13-inch wheels— used to help lower the chassis—incorporated twin three-inch-wide brake shoes in each drum.

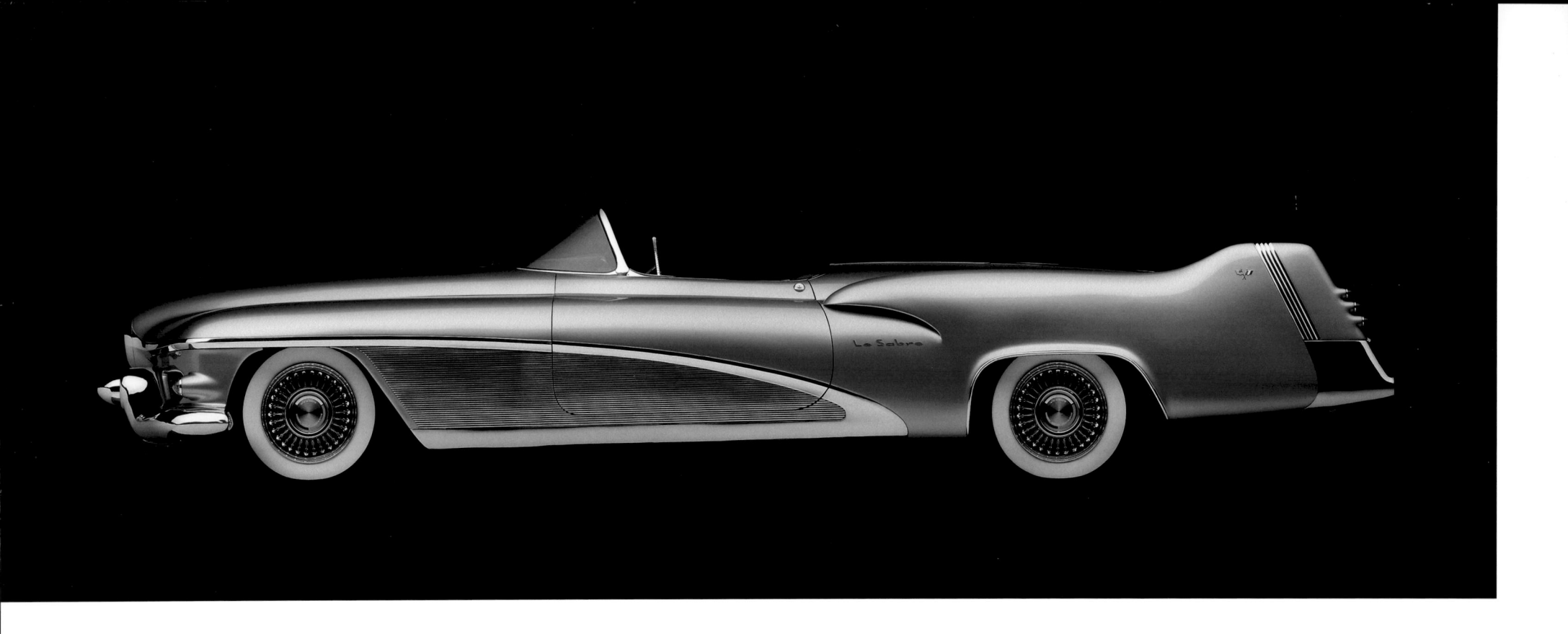

Other advanced features included a rain sensor, which could activate the retractable power top; electric jacks in all four corners; gullwing bumpers with protruding front bumper extensions, called "Dagmars" after a popular busty, blonde movie starlet; a panel full of aircraft-style instruments, including a digital speedometer, a compass, and an altimeter; electrically heated seats; and 12-volt electrics, in an era when most cars were still 6-volt.

A rolling laboratory of engineering and design features, the Le Sabre was first shown at the 1953 Motorama. It later toured the world, impressing all who saw it, including President Dwight D. Eisenhower, who went for a ride in the car with its creator. Earl personally drove the Le Sabre thousands of miles, overtly reminding all who saw him that they were viewing the nation's leading automobile design chief happily ensconced in his element.

LOANED BY THE GM HERITAGE CENTER, WARREN, MICHIGAN.

PHOTOGRAPHY BY MICHAEL FURMAN.

1 Lamm and Holls, *A Century of Automotive Style*, 97.
2 Temple, *GM's Motorama*, 22.
3 Ibid., 23.

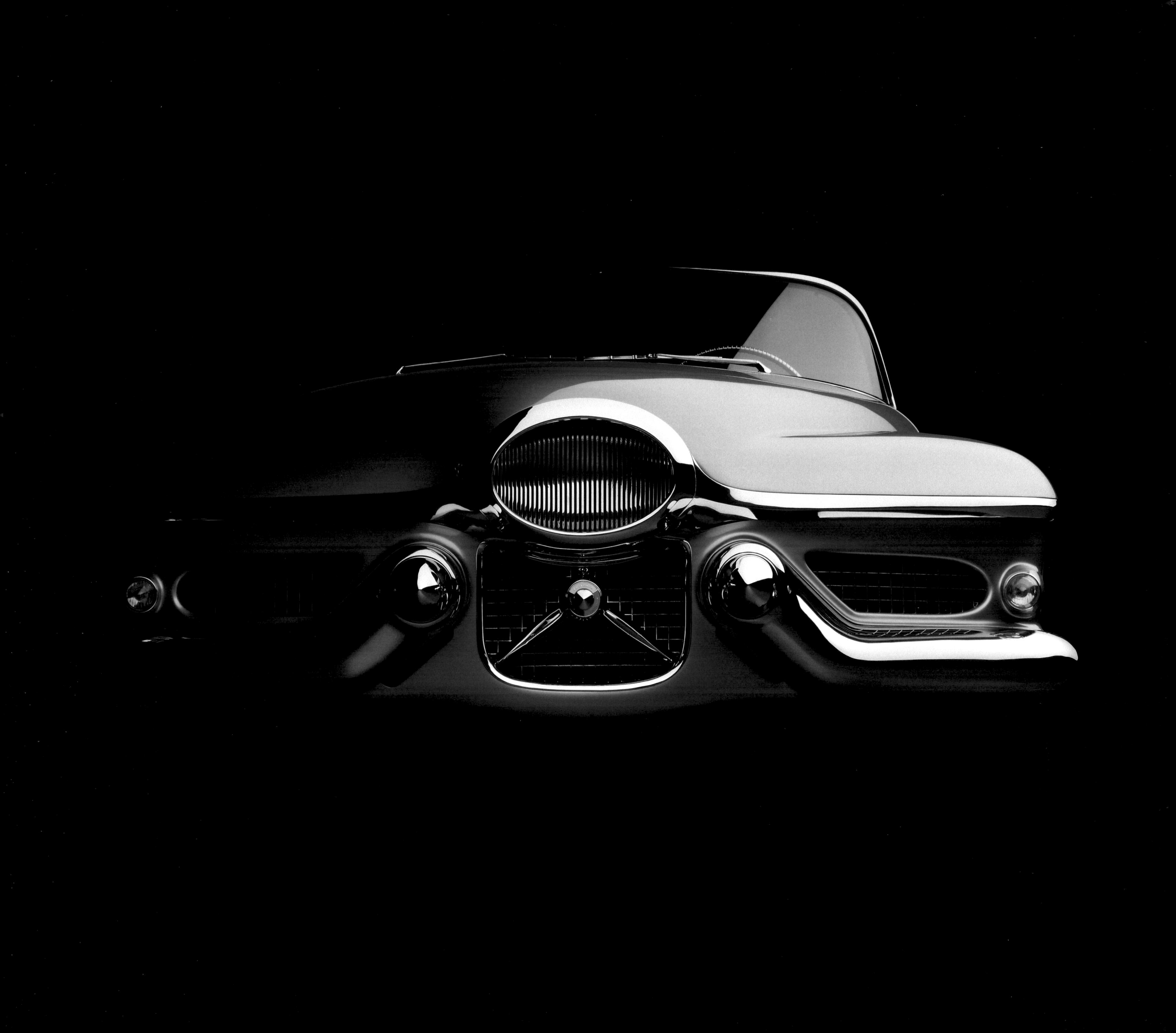

1953 General Motors *Firebird I XP-21*

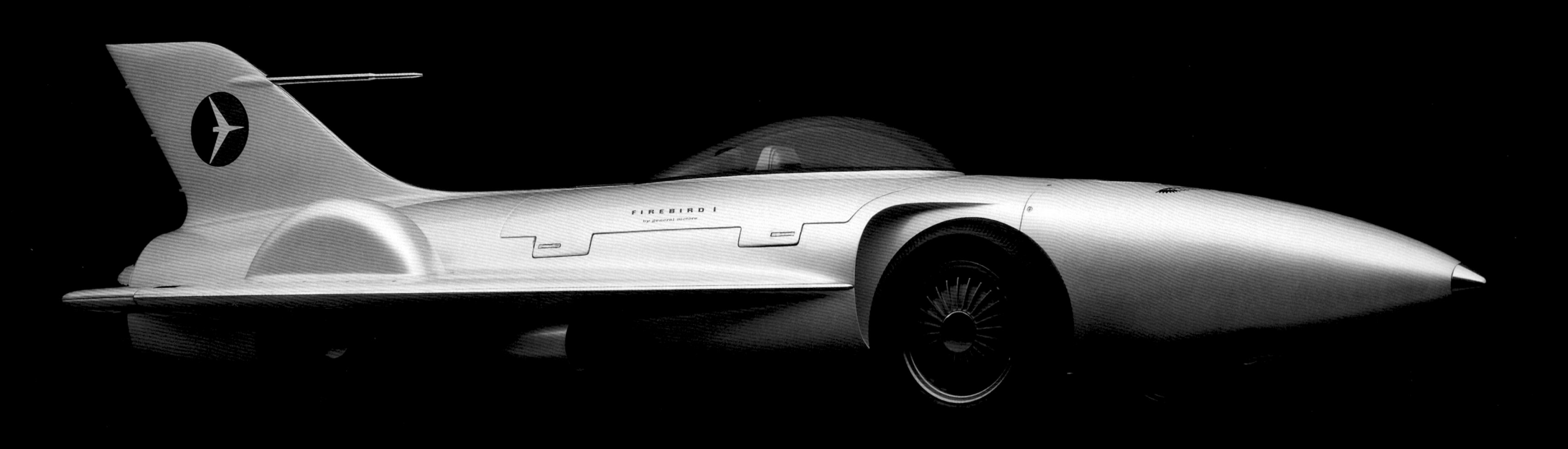

General Motors sought to demonstrate its technical leadership by producing concept vehicles for automobile shows they held across the country from 1949 to 1961. The lavish GM Motoramas featured dream cars from each of the company's divisions, along with experimental models designed to pique the public's curiosity and point the way toward future vehicles. The *XP-21*, better known as the *Firebird I*, was the first gas turbine-powered automobile ever built and tested in the United States; it was essentially a wingless jet plane for the road. When the *Firebird I* was displayed at the 1954 Motorama at the Waldorf-Astoria Hotel in New York City, GM made it clear that the dream car was a design study that would never go on sale to the public. It was created strictly to determine the feasibility of the gas turbine for use in future GM vehicles.

The *Firebird I* concept initiated in GM's styling department, not in engineering. Design chief Harley J. Earl was intrigued with the gas turbine power plant and felt that it lent itself to a design that resembled the era's jet aircraft. Steven Bayley wrote, "Earl liked aircraft because they conformed to his ideas about cars looking longer and lower."[1] Inspired by the Douglas F4D Skyray delta-winged interceptor, the *Firebird I* featured truncated wings that were curved to replicate the shape of those on Navy fighter planes. Although the *Firebird I*'s then lofty power output—370-hp at 26,000 rpm—and its estimated 200-mph top speed were intriguing, the question remained as to whether the gas turbine engine could provide efficient, economical performance.

Several years earlier, the General Motors Research Laboratories Division under Charles McCuen had developed turbine engines for use in trucks and buses. GM's GT-302 turbine resembled a small-scale version of the engine of a jet aircraft, which is propelled via exhaust expulsion; the *Firebird I*'s two-part turbine arrangement consisted of a Whirlfire gasifier that funneled exhaust gas through a power turbine to drive the rear wheels. Large 11-inch, finned aluminum brake drums were located on the outside of the wheels, rather than inside, for faster brake cooling. The trailing edges of the *Firebird I*'s wings incorporated split brake flaps, extending above and below the wings, activated by steering wheel–mounted switches.

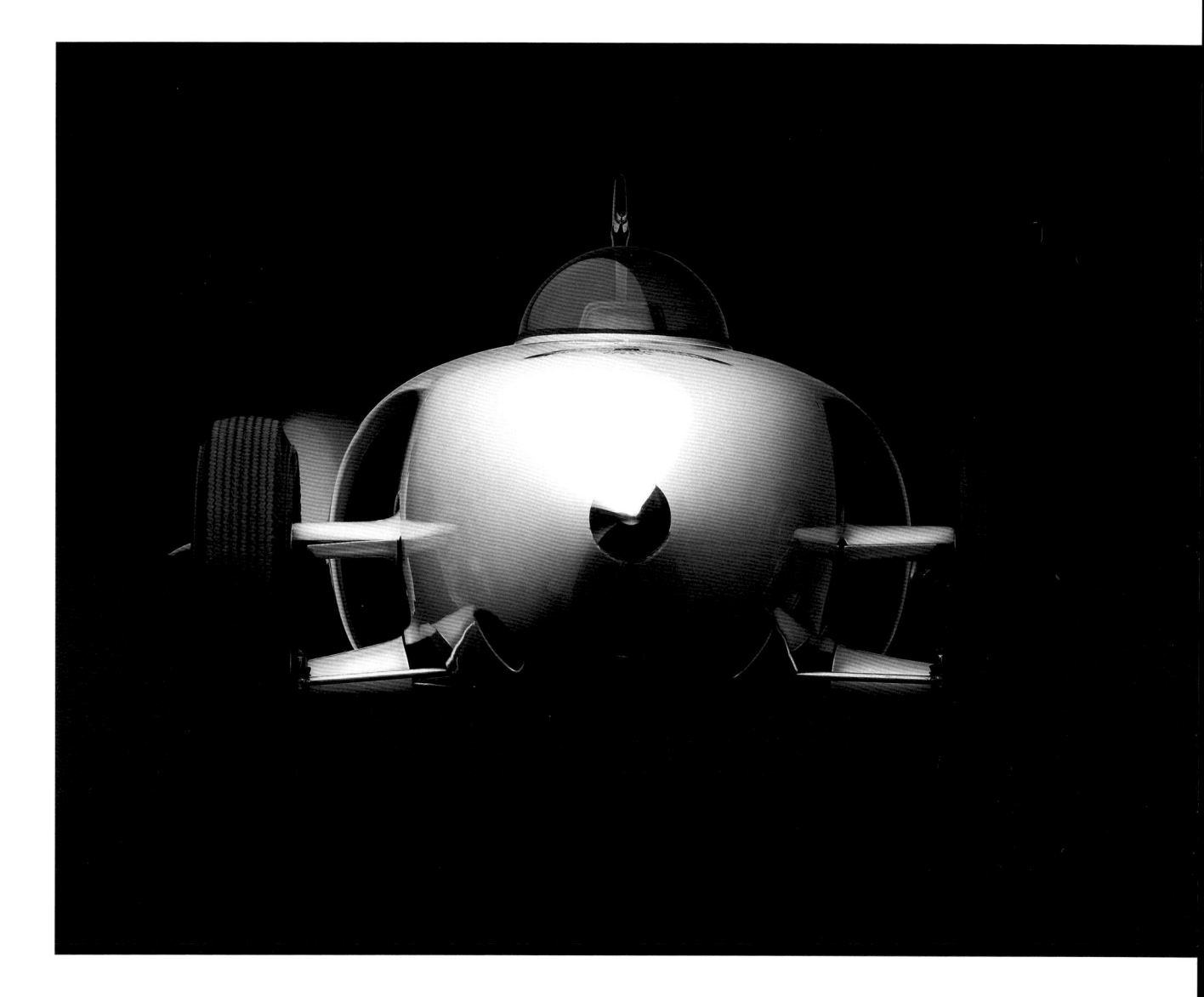

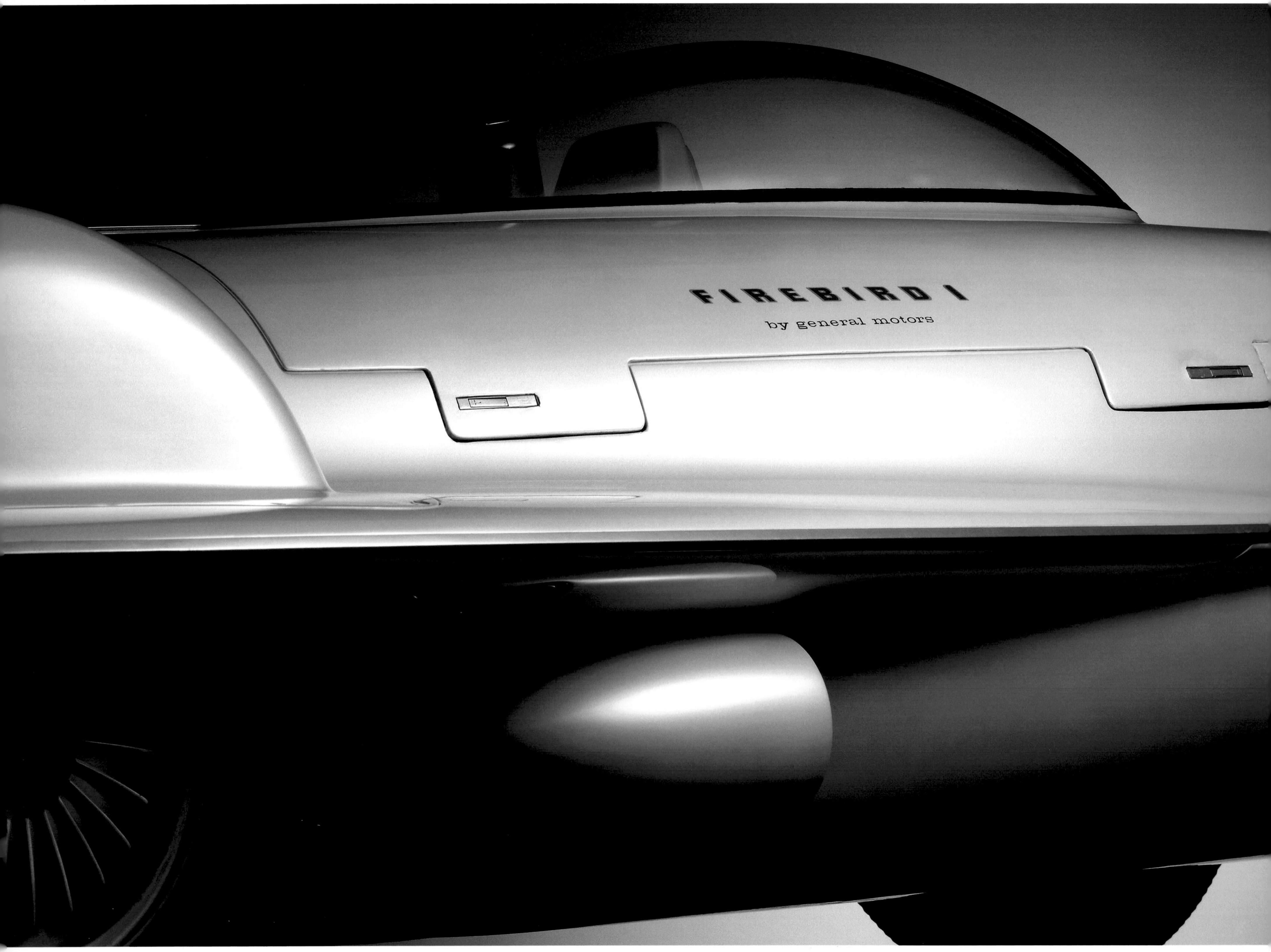
FIREBIRD I
by general motors

The suspension consisted of double wishbones in front and an independent de Dion rear end with two single-leaf springs.[2]

The 2,500-pound experimental jet car's radical styling was refined in wind tunnel tests at the California Institute of Technology. Engineers had to ensure that the *Firebird I*'s small vestigial wings had an inherent negative angle of attack so that the automobile would not actually take off. The rocket car's high speed capability provided an opportunity to test aerodynamics for land-based vehicles. Its tall tail fin was thought to be necessary for stability at high speeds. The large central tailpipe, which accentuated the car's aircraft-like appearance, had to be functional, because a turbine emits a great deal of spent air and exhaust heat. After an Arizona proving grounds accident with Charles McCuen behind the wheel, the *Firebird I* was tested by three-time Indy 500 winner Mauri Rose, but never at its top speed. In the April 1954 issue of *Motor Life*, Rose said, "The car wanted to behave. It wanted to keep going straight ahead. It was perfectly stable."[3]

The *Firebird I* was never considered for production. Besides its radical, impractical single-seater design, its jet engine was simply too loud by automobile standards, and exhaust temperature at the tailpipe was 1,000 degrees Fahrenheit. More importantly, its low fuel economy was unacceptable. There were no EPA emissions standards in 1954, but had they existed the *Firebird I* surely would have failed. The sleek, low speedster, with its towering single tail fin, was a Motorama sensation nonetheless. Visitors marveled at the notion of a jet plane for street driving, fascinated with what they imagined was clearly the car of the future.

GM would go on to create two more turbine-powered dream cars: the four-passenger *Firebird II*, which was designed to be self-guided on an electronic highway, and the multi-winged *Firebird III*. These glimpses into the future captivated audiences but were a technological dead end. As a result, GM never built a production turbine-powered automobile.

LOANED BY THE GM HERITAGE CENTER, WARREN, MICHIGAN.

PHOTOGRAPHY BY MICHAEL FURMAN.

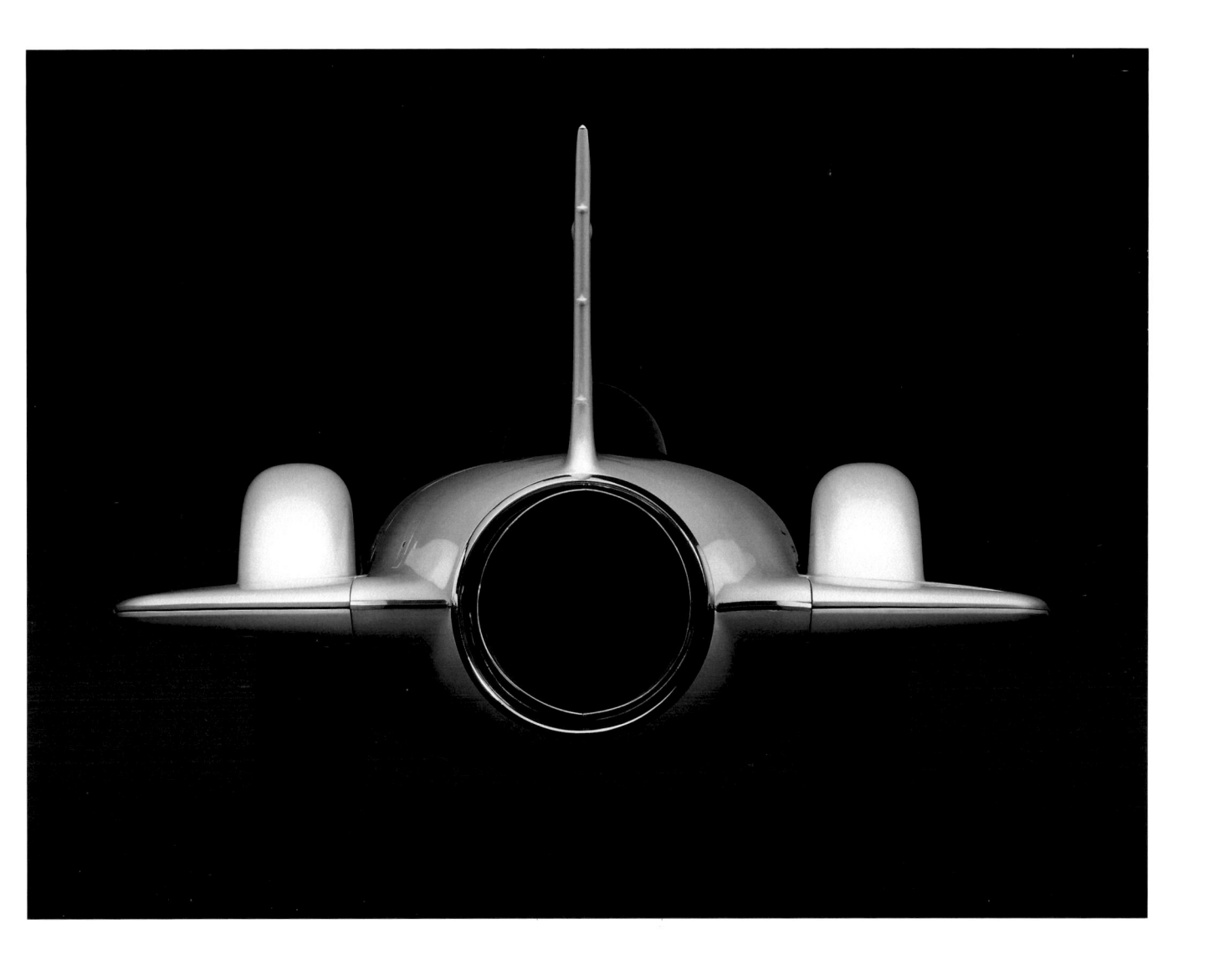

1 Bayley, *Harley Earl*, 99–100.

2 Temple, *GM's Motorama*, 136–137.

3 Ibid., 140.

1954 Alfa Romeo (Bertone)
Berlinetta Aerodinamica Tecnica 7 (B.A.T. 7)

While the renaissance of automotive styling began in Italy in the late 1940s with cars such as Pininfarina's lovely Cisitalia *202* coupe and the Maserati *A61500*, Carrozzeria Bertone was responsible for three of the most memorable concept cars ever conceived. Giuseppe "Nuccio" Bertone and his talented chief designer Franco Scaglione—whom Winston Goodfellow called "an artist with sheet metal"[1]—were intrigued with the possibility of creating visually stunning, aerodynamically efficient sports coupes with the lowest possible drag coefficient (Cd). The resulting cars, which used the Alfa Romeo *1900* chassis and were influenced by the newly emerging jet aircraft industry, were named *B.A.T.*, for *Berlinetta Aerodinamica Tecnica*. The name *BAT*, as it was popularly written, was particularly fitting because the cars' imaginative tail fin treatments were reminiscent of stylized bat wings. In the words of Alfa Romeo authority Joe Benson, "The BAT acronym was so appropriate that it couldn't have been accidental."[2]

From 1953 to 1955 Bertone sequentially presented the *B.A.T. 5*, *B.A.T. 7*, and *B.A.T. 9* coupes (see p. 36) at the annual *Salone dell'automobile di Torino*, introducing one new dream car each year. The *B.A.T. 5* was the first. To minimize its Cd and eliminate as many air vortices as possible, its curvaceous aluminum body featured a round, protruding nose section flanked by two large air openings that resembled jet air intakes. The front and rear wheels were completely enclosed to reduce the resistance created by the turning wheels. The *B.A.T. 5*'s low, wide panoramic windshield and slanted side windows, which were raked at a steep, forty-five-degree angle, were joined to a nearly flat roof that seamlessly tapered into a split rear window, with a slender divider separating a pair of elegantly tapered tail fins. The *B.A.T. 5*'s 75-hp twin-cam engine, light weight (2,400 pounds), and near-perfect aerodynamics—its Cd was 0.23—permitted a 120-mph top speed, reportedly with excellent stability at high speeds.

For 1954, the *B.A.T. 7*'s design built upon its predecessor's styling cues. Bertone and Scaglione had closely studied aircraft wing profiles, which resulted in longer, more dramatically curved tail fins for their newest show car. Scaglione lowered the *B.A.T. 7*'s nose and reworked the flanking air intakes for even more aerodynamic

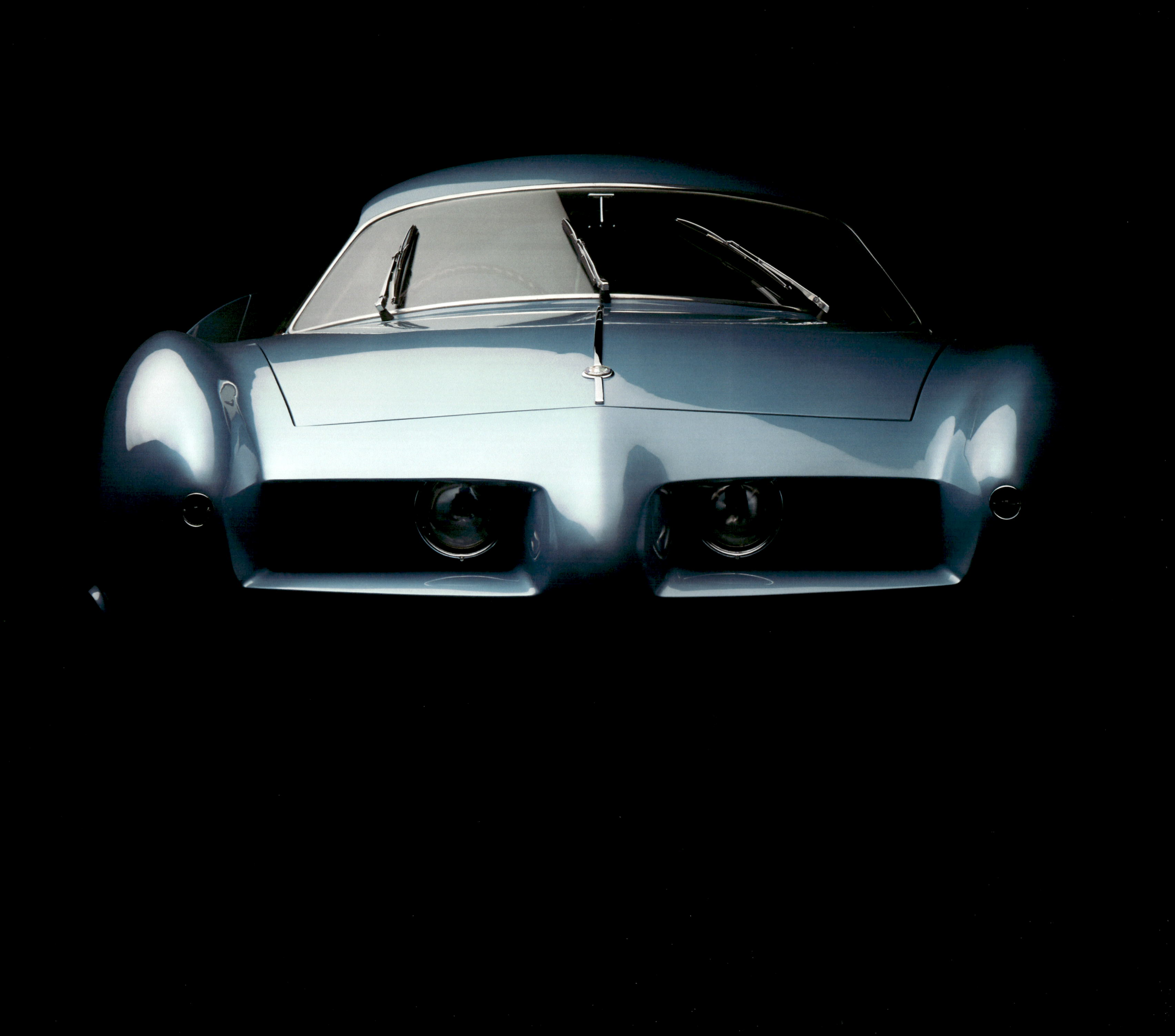

efficiency. The center spine arched like a finned flying buttress before smoothly joining the rounded tail section. Many people consider the B.A.T. 7 to be the most dramatic example of the wild Bertone trio. The changes to the original design resulted in a reduced Cd of just 0.19, which proved to be the lowest number achieved with the three prototypes. Automotive writer Serge Bellu noted:

> A true "dream car" in the sense in which this was meant in the 1950s, B.A.T. 7 swung between lyricism and naivety, with its frankly simplistic detailing borrowed from the world of aviation, its over-the-top fins, and its air intakes suggesting the power of a jet engine. Thanks to the talent of Franco Scaglione, the language became poetic, the scrolls of the rear contracting as if they were the wings of a giant bird.[3]

The third car in this celebrated midcentury trio of Bertone coupes was the B.A.T. 9. With this iteration, an attempt was made to both eliminate some of the earlier cars' more exaggerated styling elements and integrate contemporary Alfa Romeo design cues. The air intakes were reduced in size, an almost conventional-looking Alfa Romeo vertical grille was fitted, and the tail fins were smaller and more angular than the shapely appendages on the first two cars. The B.A.T. 9 is still stunning, suggesting that had Alfa Romeo elected to duplicate it for production, the design exercise would have been practical and of great assistance. Instead of producing the B.A.T. 9, however, Bertone created the limited-edition *Sprint Speciale* series for Alfa Romeo from 1957 to 1962, using styling cues from all three B.A.T. prototypes. Thanks to its refined aerodynamics, acquired from the B.A.T. experiments, the production *Sprint Speciale* could top 124 mph with a 1,300-cc Alfa Romeo *Giulietta* engine.

So innovative was the B.A.T. series that its design remains influential to this day. In Geneva in 2008 Carrozzeria Bertone presented the B.A.T. 11, a new successor to the 1950s series. Based on a new Alfa Romeo *8C Competizione* chassis, the B.A.T. 11 displayed many of the early show cars' design elements, but in thoroughly modern form, with sleeker, more integrated lines and curves. It proved to be a one-of-a-kind exercise and]was not put into production.

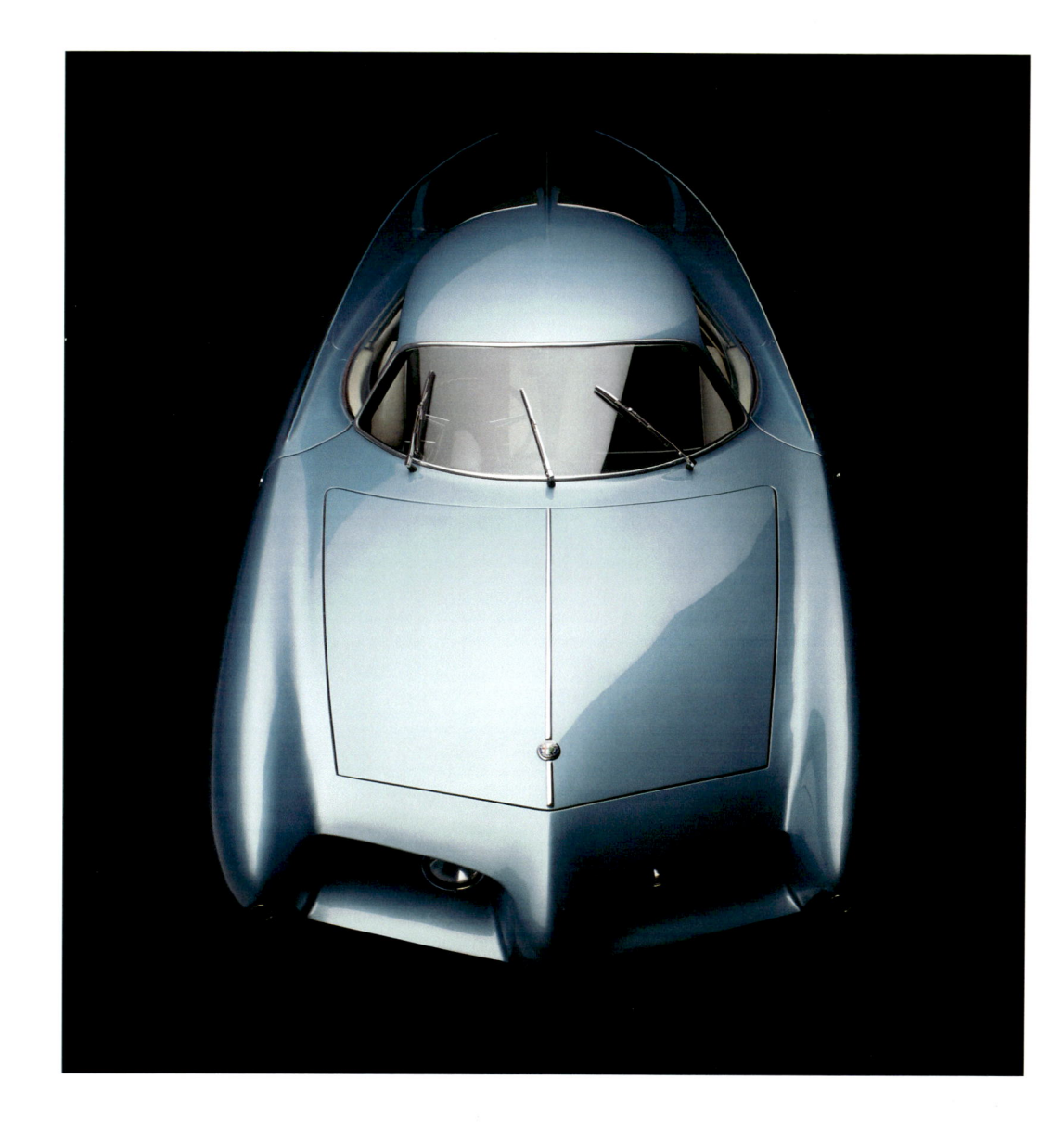

The original three B.A.T. 5, 7, and 9 concept cars are still exciting to see. While Larry Edsall wryly commented that the *BAT* analogy "took the motorcar into a frightening fictional universe," he praised their creator, saying, "With the B.A.T.s, Bertone joined the aristocracy of the styling world."[4]

COURTESY OF DON WILLIAMS AND THE BLACKHAWK COLLECTION, DANVILLE, CALIFORNIA.

PHOTOGRAPHY BY MICHAEL FURMAN.

1 Goodfellow, *Italian Sports Cars*, 53.
2 Benson, *The Illustrated Alfa Romeo Buyers Guide*, 160.
3 Bellu, *500 Fantastic Cars*, 27.
4 Edsall, *Concept Cars*, 49–50.

1955 Chrysler (Ghia) Streamline X "Gilda"

In the exuberant postwar era, automotive design was heavily influenced by jet aircraft styling. Cadillac's tail fins appeared in 1948 and other makes soon followed; by the mid-1950s, sharply pointed appendages on automobile rear fenders were ubiquitous. Chrysler's renowned styling chief Virgil Exner was determined to prove that aerodynamic design was not risky in the marketplace—after the devastating war years, consumers were eager to embrace the design cues of the future—and that tail fins could be functional on passenger cars.

Exner directed Italy's Carrozzeria Ghia designers under Luigi Segre to produce a plan for a hypothetically ideal, wedged-shape coupe. They built a half-scale model with fins that could be altered and measured progressively for wind tunnel testing at the Polytechnic University of Turin (Politecnico di Torino). Dr. Giovanni Savonuzzi, Ghia's brilliant technical director, determined that the model's tapered tail fins improved directional stability in crosswinds at high speeds.[1] For the 1955 *Salone dell'automobile di Torino*, Ghia then built a full-scale mockup with an interior but no engine, and called it the *Gilda*, after a 1946 film noir starring Rita Hayworth (see p. 28). Savonuzzi's daughter Alberta recalled that her father was influenced by an ad for the movie that described Hayworth as a "super-sexy bomb." "When he read that description," she said, "the name Gilda stuck with him. He couldn't resist calling the car that."[2] Painted a startling pairing of silver and orange, with arrow-shaped door handles that accentuated the show car's slippery shape, the *Gilda* was a big hit in Turin, where it was presented as "shaped by the wind."[3] Originally, the show car was to have been fitted with a 1,500-cc OSCA four-cylinder gasoline engine, which, in theory, would have permitted a top speed of 140 mph. It even appeared on *Motor Trend*'s September 1955 issue with

1955 CHRYSLER (GHIA) *STREAMLINE X* "GILDA"

the headline, "The Engine-less Ghia X, 'X' for Chrysler's Gas Turbine?," presaging the first Chrysler turbine car, which was produced almost a decade later in 1963.[4]

Exner then ordered a running full-size, four-passenger, two-door prototype called the *Dart* to be built on a 129-inch-wheelbase Chrysler *Imperial* chassis, using information learned from the *Gilda* exercise. Tested for more than 100,000 miles with a companion four-door model, the two prototypes validated a paper that Exner presented in 1957, claiming legitimate advantages for tail fins as aerodynamic aids on passenger car bodies and earning Chrysler respect for what had become a popular styling trend. The *Gilda* show car inspired the futuristic *Dart* and influenced Chrysler's entire 1957 "Forward Look" styling theme.[5]

The highly respected restorer Scott Grundfor purchased the *Gilda* more than twenty years ago and installed a gas turbine power plant—a development that he feels could have been implemented when the car was first designed. For a low-slung, edgy car that looks like a wingless jet aircraft, the gas turbine power plant, with its characteristically shrill jet engine whine, is the perfect complement to the *Gilda*. So far ahead of its time, the stunning Chrysler (Ghia) *Streamline X "Gilda,"* now almost sixty years old, still attracts appreciative spectators who think it is a much younger car. It has inspired many famous designers as well, including former head of Mercedes-Benz styling Bruno Sacco and the late Strother MacMinn, one of the United States' most influential designers and teachers, who called it "one of the 10 most significant showcars ever built."[6]

LOANED BY SCOTT GRUNDFOR AND KATHLEEN REDMOND, ARROYO GRANDE, CALIFORNIA.

PHOTOGRAPHY BY MICHAEL FURMAN.

1   Lamm, *Road & Track, Show Cars*, 58.

2   Goodfellow, "Ghia's Gilda," 64–71.

3   Jessica Donaldson, "1955 Ghia Gilda Concept," Concept Carz, http://www.conceptcarz.com/vehicle/z5599/Ghia-Gilda-Concept.aspx (accessed July 18, 2013).

4   Ibid.

5   Grist, *Virgil Exner, Visioneer*, 98–101.

6   Goodfellow, "Ghia's Gilda," 70.

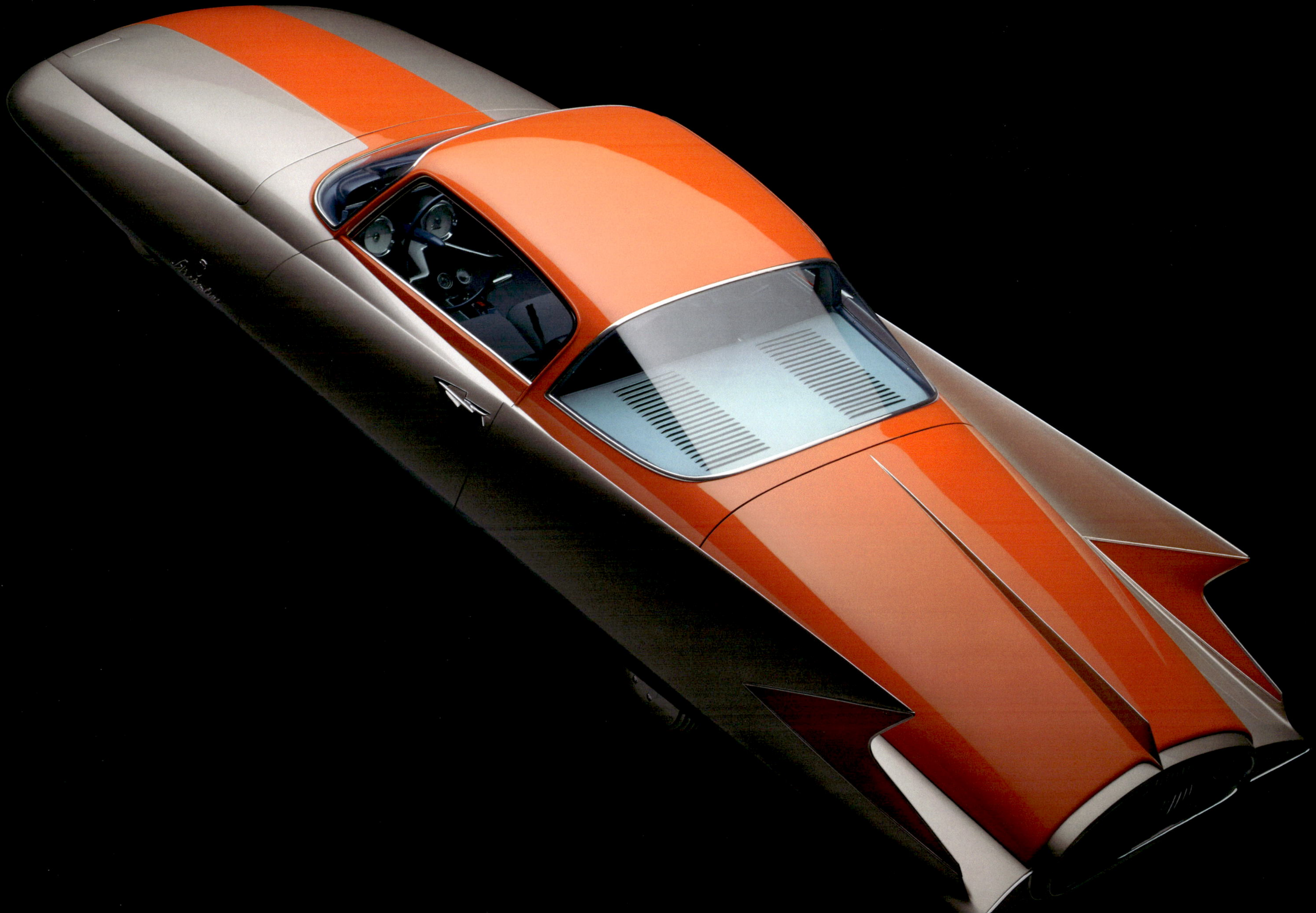

1956 Buick Centurion XP-301

Buick Division of General Motors was an active participant in all of the GM Motoramas. In earlier years Buick's flashy *Wildcat* roadster concept cars had been widely admired, but in 1956 Buick presented a radically different approach on a 118-inch wheelbase: a low, 53^{11}/$_{16}$-inch-high, futuristic 2+2 hardtop coupe (a term used by designers and engineers to signify a pillar-less two-door, four passenger car) with a fiberglass body. It was called the *Centurion*. Its many advanced features included a panoramic windshield—popularly known as a wraparound—an expansive, completely transparent bubble top, and a sweeping, 1951 *Roadmaster Riviera* coupe-style "Sweepspear." A chrome-plated strip that began above the front wheel, curved down just before the rear wheel, and then curved back to the taillight, the "Sweepspear" would soon become a Buick trademark. It also featured fully radiused wheel openings, dramatic wing-type fenders, and a searing hot Elektron Red and Bright White two-tone finish that accentuated the coupe's bold form.

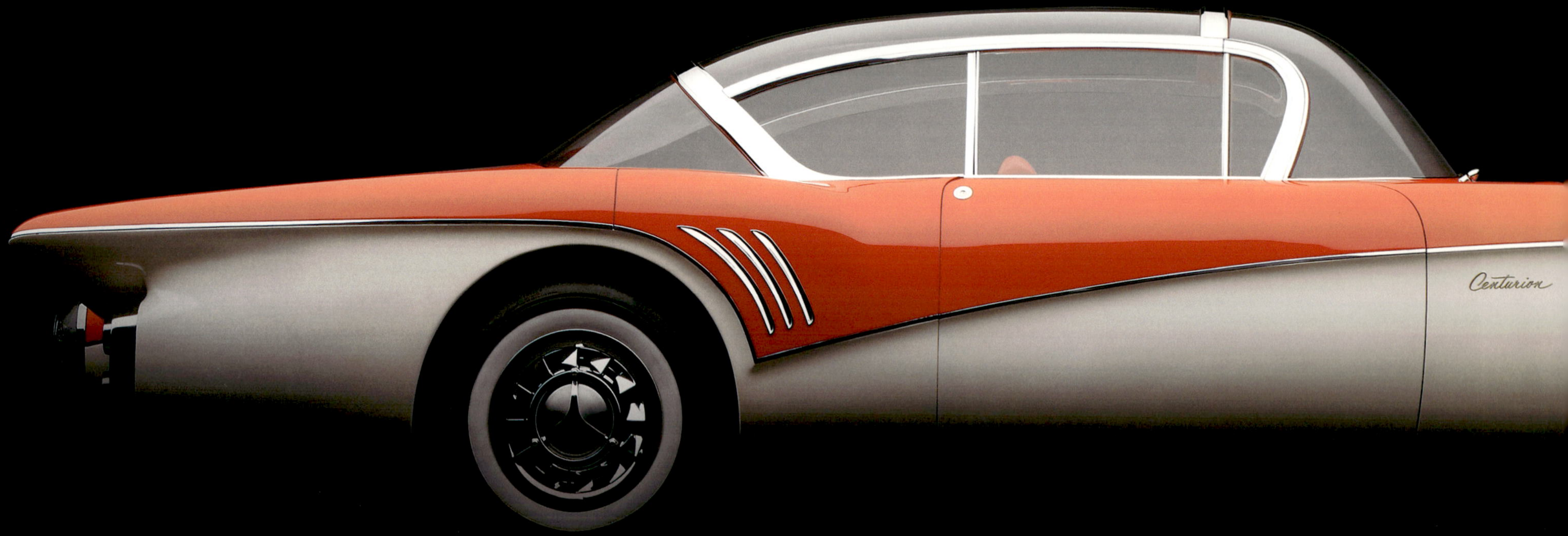
Centurion

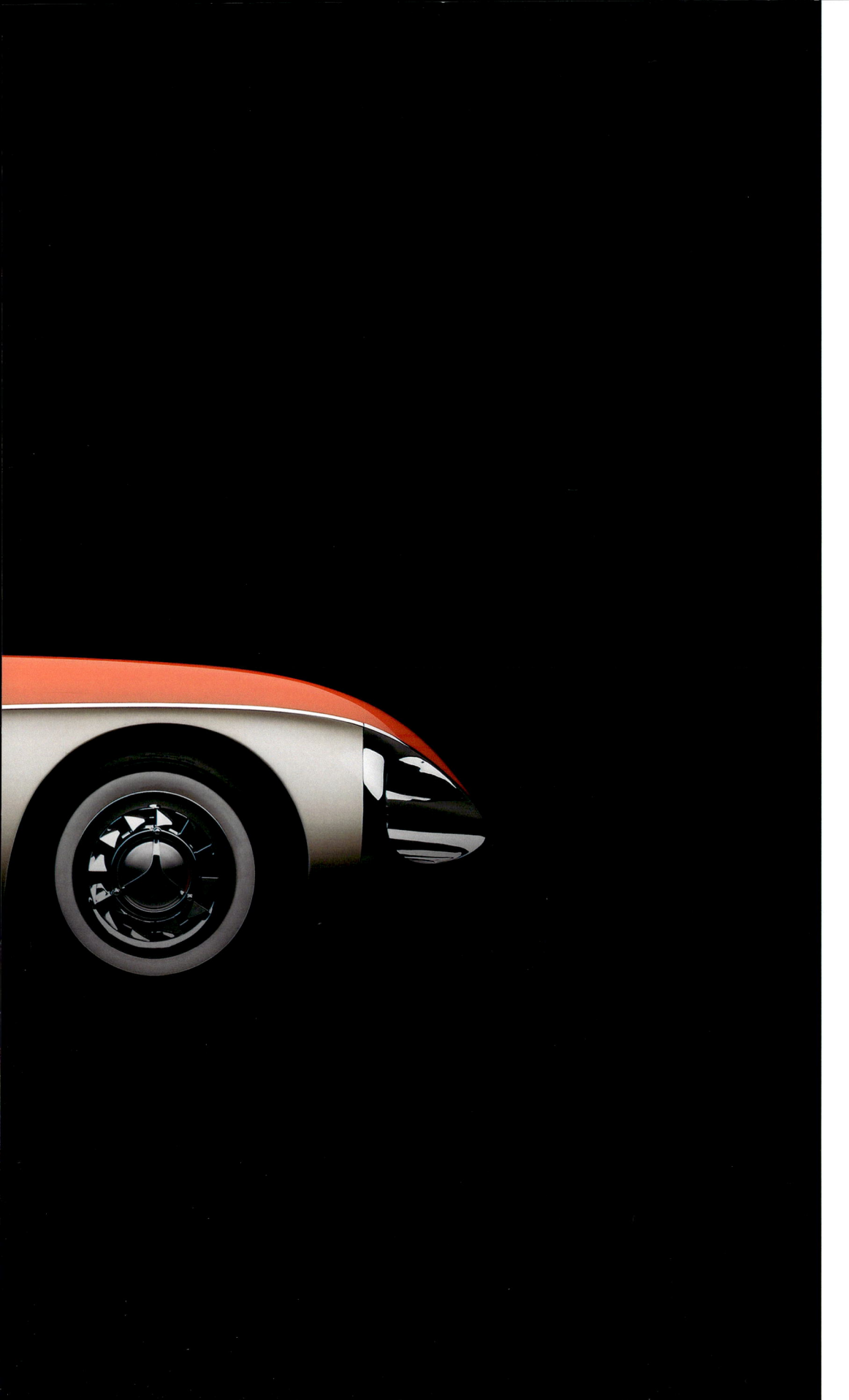

The *Centurion*'s front fenders swept forward to enclose its deeply recessed headlights, and dipped down in a distinctive, shark-like fashion. With the exception of twin air scoops that directed outside air to passengers, the fender line was continuously straight from front to back and the tail tapered to a point that resembled the exhaust outlet of a jet aircraft. A pointed "Dagmar" protrusion in the tail cone housed the brake and reverse lights. On either side of the car, wide rear fenders flowed outward horizontally like the wings of a giant gull. There were no bumpers, but a thin chrome band that circled all the protrusions ostensibly protected the inset headlights and the hull-like rear. Twin exhausts, round parking lights, and directional signals were housed in oval pods located under the artfully flared rear. The license plate was mounted asymmetrically to the left of the tail cone. Curiously, Buick's trademark "Ventiports" (portholes) were not included in this styling exercise.

GM's official designation for this Buick concept car was *XP-301* but it was quickly named the *Centurion*, possibly as an extension of the division's popular *Century* series. The *Centurion*'s aircraft-inspired Elektron Red interior sported four individual bucket seats with wide, horizontal pleats; individual headrests; and retractable seatbelts. When each door was opened, an electrical switch actuated the front seats, which then moved forward or backward on rails as needed, allowing easier access to and egress from the front or rear seats. The steering wheel was mounted aircraft-style on the wide, flat arm of a chromed column that cantilevered out of the dash and extended over the central flow-through console. Push buttons actuated the variable-pitch Dynaflow automatic transmission. The hood sloped toward the front, where it was hinged with the integral grille, and opened forward, away from the car's windshield. The engine was a modified 322-cid Buick OHV V-8 with many chromed accessories and four side-draft, two-barrel carburetors, which helped to achieve the low hoodline. It reportedly developed 325-hp.

There were no rearview mirrors, inside or out, to disturb the clean lines of the *Centurion*. Instead, a revolutionary patented, functional TV camera, positioned above the tail cone, registered the traffic behind the car on a 4 × 6-inch interior screen that was located in the center of the dash. The closed-circuit TV camera, supplied by University Broadcasting System, reportedly weighed six pounds and was designed to be shock-resistant so that changes in the road surface would not interfere with the image on the screen. Chuck Jordan, who went on to become head of GM Design, recalled that he and his team quickly decided that the cantilever steering arm (which is no longer in the *Centurion*) and the rear-facing camera would be part of the package. Management, he said, "wanted an interior that went with the exterior."[1] Also included were a digital clock and a freestanding speedometer, which used a stationary indicator and a revolving dial.

Transparent roofs, electrical seating, digital clocks, rear-mounted cameras, and many other advances in the *Centurion* are commonplace today, but they were considered wildly futuristic for their time. Many of the *Centurion*'s advanced features found their way onto production Chevrolets and Buicks as early as 1969; the pointed tail became a hallmark of Buick's third-generation 1971 *Riviera* coupe. Others did not appear for decades. Buick ultimately used the *Centurion* nameplate on production cars from 1971 to 1973.

LOANED BY THE SLOAN MUSEUM, FLINT, MICHIGAN.
EXTERIOR PHOTOGRAPHY BY MICHAEL FURMAN.
INTERIOR PHOTOGRAPHY COURTESY GENERAL MOTORS.

1 Temple, *GM's Motorama*, 103.

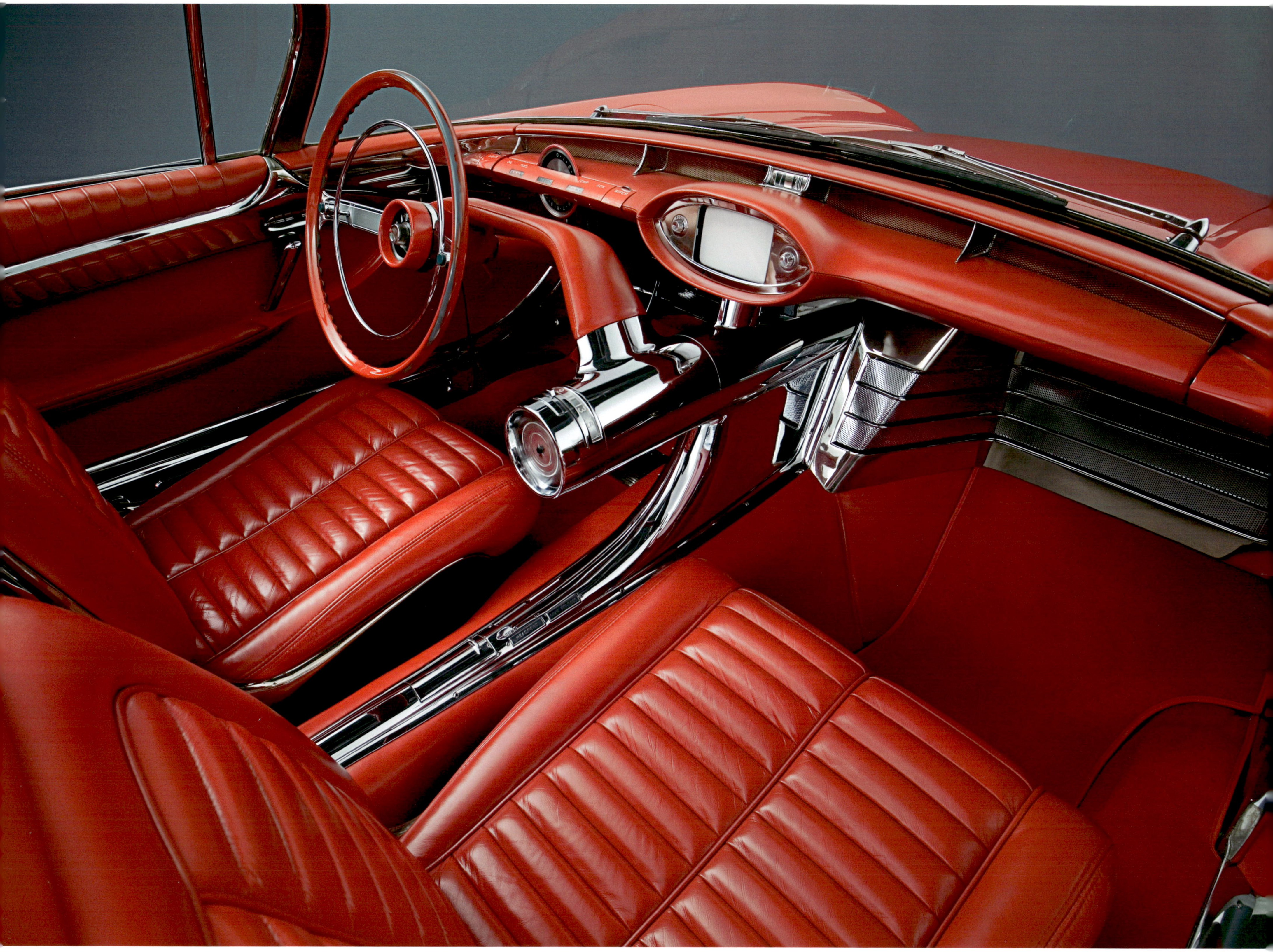

1959 Cadillac Cyclone XP-74

Harley J. Earl's concept cars for General Motors culminated with this last effort, which was introduced just as the now legendary Earl retired. With its soaring bubble canopy, sweeping fenders, sharp vestigial fins, and afterburner-style taillight housings—all jetcraft-like components—the Cadillac *Cyclone XP-74* extended Earl's aircraft-for-the-street philosophy with a design that continues to inspire appreciative looks more than fifty years after its creation.

Earl was an inspired visionary but not a designer. He would tell his art staff what he wanted, and then progressively direct their efforts as they created a series of line drawings, followed by skillfully airbrushed renderings, until their often surreal images matched or even exceeded Earl's initial ideas. Carl Renner—who was simultaneously working on the new *Corvette*—is credited with the basic design for the *Cyclone*. It was not shown at GM's 1959 Motorama and was instead revealed to the public in February 1959, when it starred at the Grand Opening of the Daytona Speedway.[1] Costly, extravagant, and complex to execute, GM's lavish traveling Motoramas were coming to an end, but the automaker still wanted to dazzle the public with the audacity of its dream cars. The jam-packed new NASCAR showpiece was the perfect venue.

Viewed today, the *Cyclone* remains radical; in 1959, it was considered out of this world. Its ominously pointy black nose cones, which flanked the wide Cadillac "egg-crate" grille, were the newest iteration of the previously seen "Dagmar" bumper guards. Quad headlamps were cleverly tucked up in the grillework and could be flipped up to function. Under the wide hood scoop was a powerful 325-hp, 390-cid Cadillac V-8. Originally destined for a fuel-injection system, the power plant was equipped with a low-profile Carter AFB 4-bbl carburetor, bracketed by a cross-flow aluminum radiator with twin fans, and a three-speed, rear-mounted GM Hydra-Matic transmission incorporating a two-speed rear axle that could double the floor-shifted automatic's gear ratios from three to six, though it was not functional.[2] The *Cyclone* also was the first car to feature now standard Saginaw rotary valve power steering.

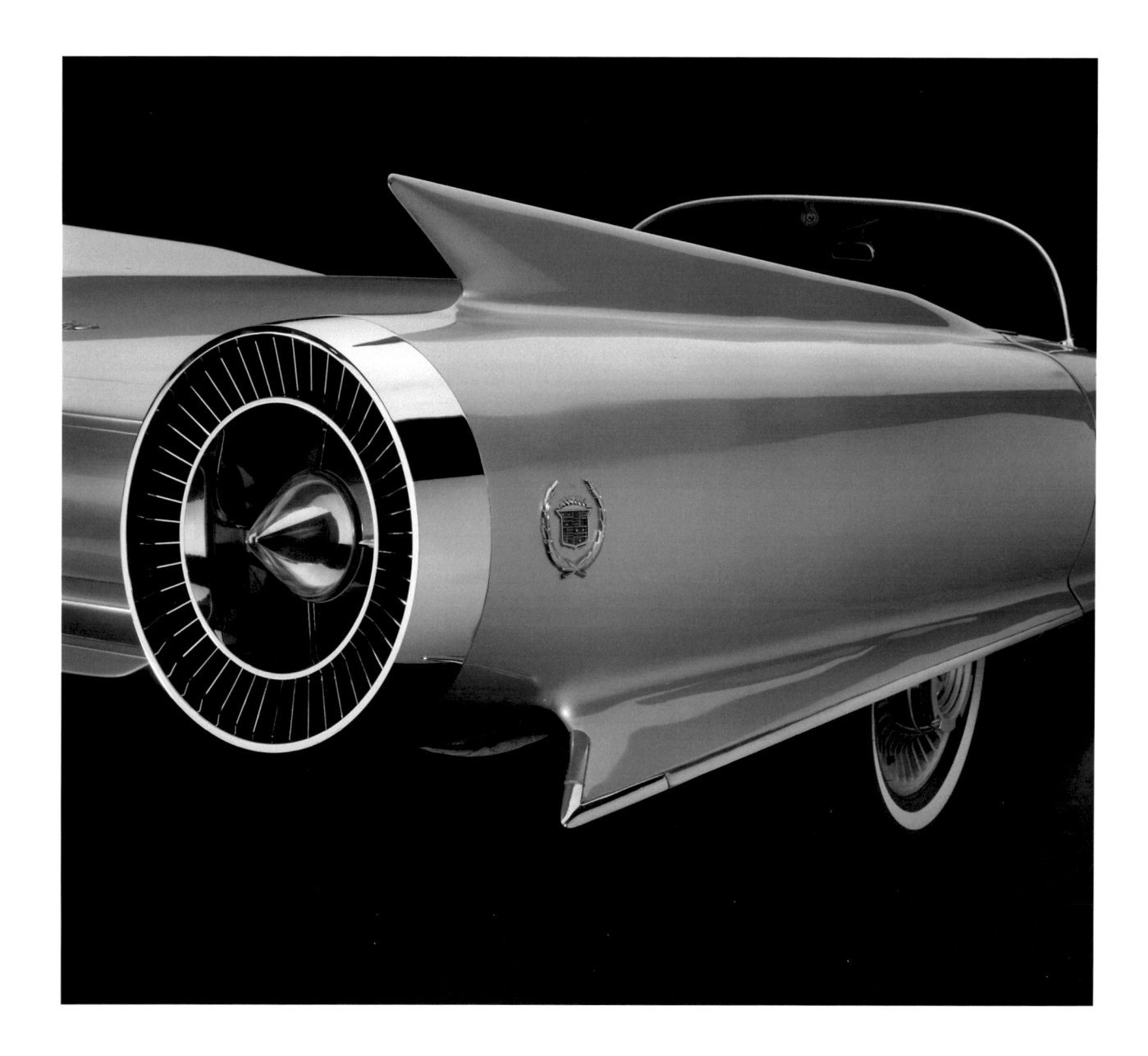

1959 CADILLAC *CYCLONE XP-74* 111

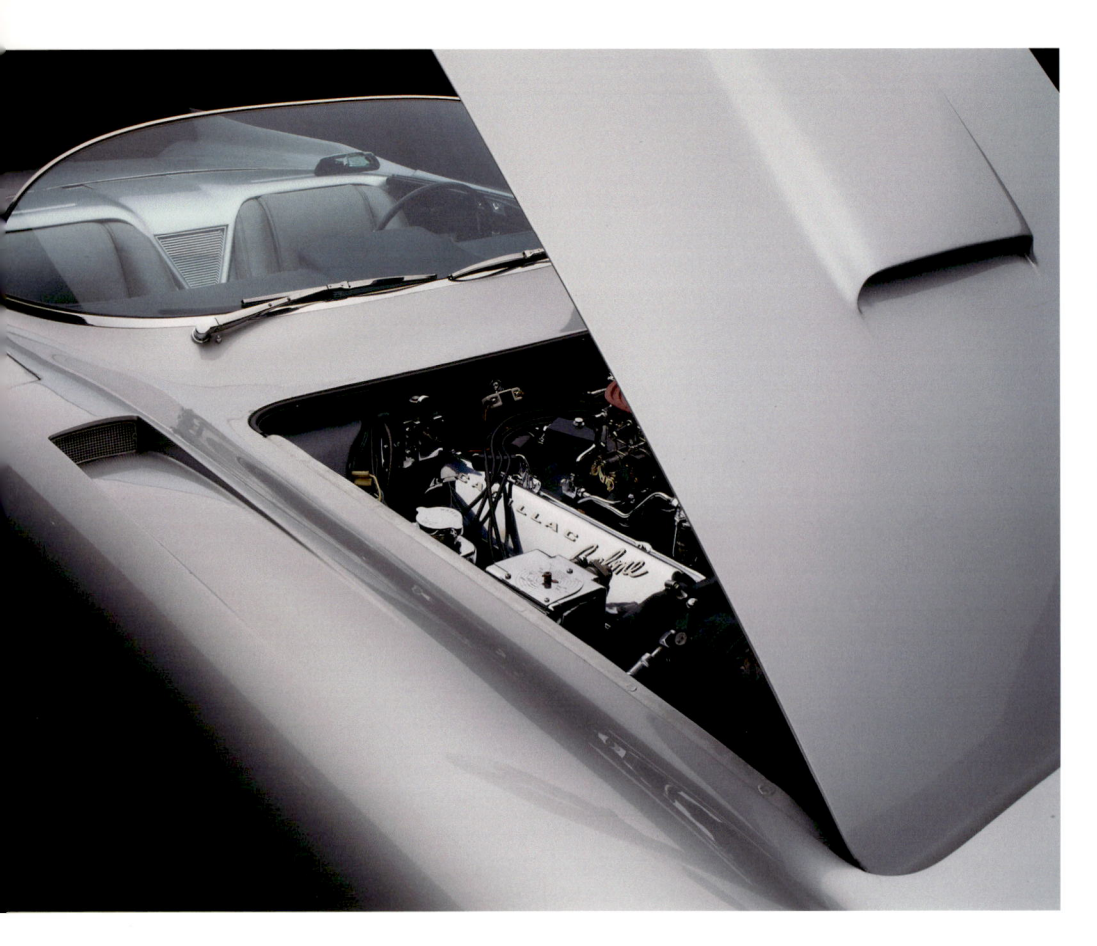

The doors slide rearward like those on a modern minivan. The curvaceous Plexiglas jet-fighter bubble top, which tilts and stows completely beneath the flat deck lid, was configured to elevate automatically if a hint of rain was detected. The prominent nose cones contained innovative proximity sensors designed to respond to complimentary sensors that would be buried in a highway of the future, so as to prevent crashes and even permit hands-free driving. The notion of the autonomous car, imagined a half-century ago, is only now becoming a reality; the *Cyclone* was well ahead of its time in demonstrating how a self-guided automobile could look. The *XP-74*'s creators anticipated this modern development, even if they lacked the sophisticated software and hardware package to make it a reality.

Inside, behind the panoramic windshield, was an engine-turned dash with a sextet of instrument dials, including a 0-to-8,000 RPM tachometer, a 200-mph speedometer, a manifold pressure gauge, a handsome Breitling electric clock, proximity- and stopping distance-sensing gauges for the nose cone sensors, and a horizontal gauge for the radar-sensing crash avoidance system. The *Cyclone* was also equipped with a complete climate-control system.

Built and presented in three phases—and rushed to its first appearance—the *Cyclone* initially appeared with higher, shark-like tail fins (see p. 37, fig. 55), reminiscent of the 1959 Cadillac's high-watermark design, but it lacked the proximity sensors and a functional transaxle. It may have had air suspension initially, but the present suspension consists of independent control arms and coil spings in front and a swing axle and coil springs in the rear. For its second phase, completed after the Daytona debut by William L. "Bill" Mitchell, Earl's equally flamboyant successor, the *Cyclone* was transfomed from

112   1959 CADILLAC *CYCLONE* XP-74

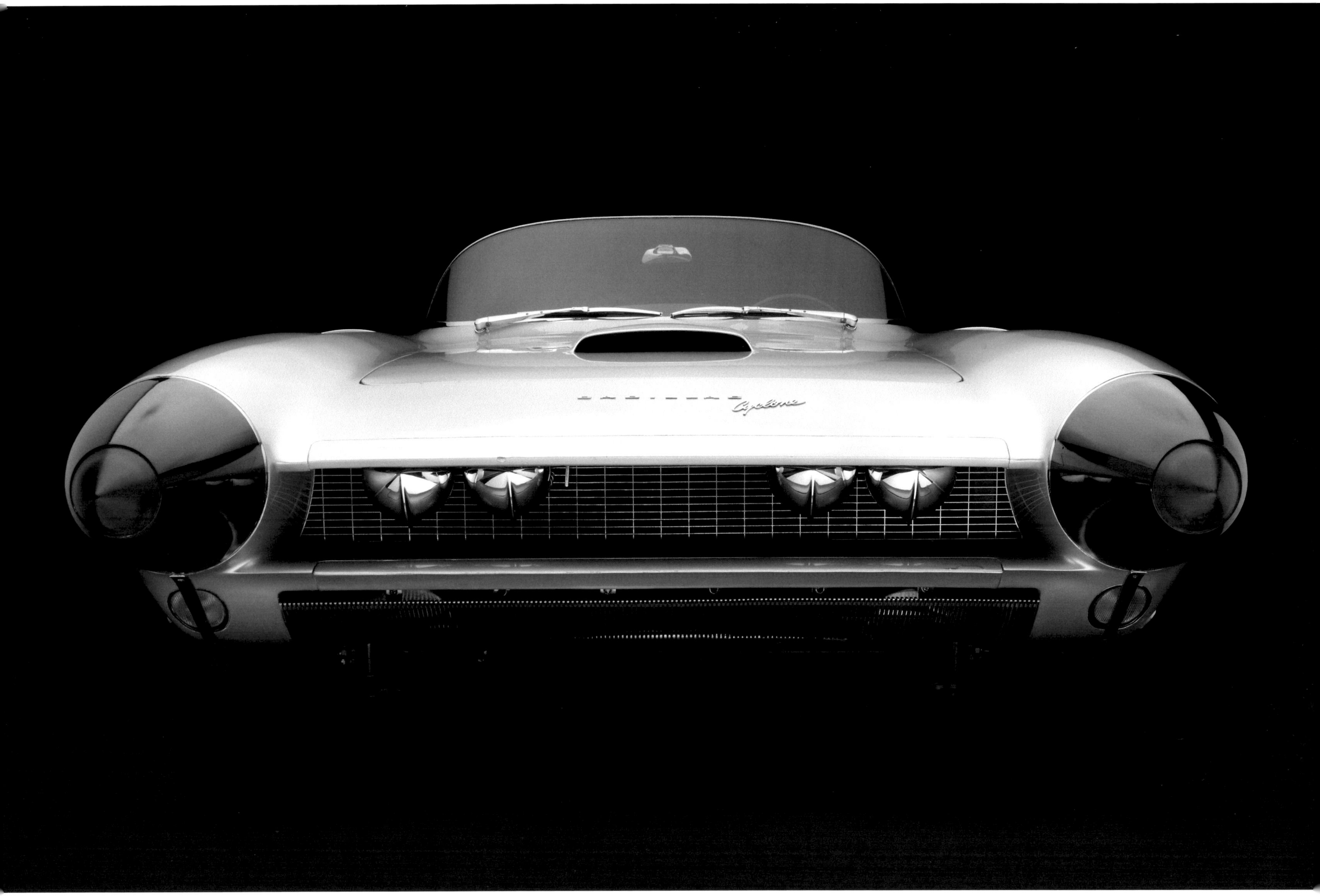
Cyclone

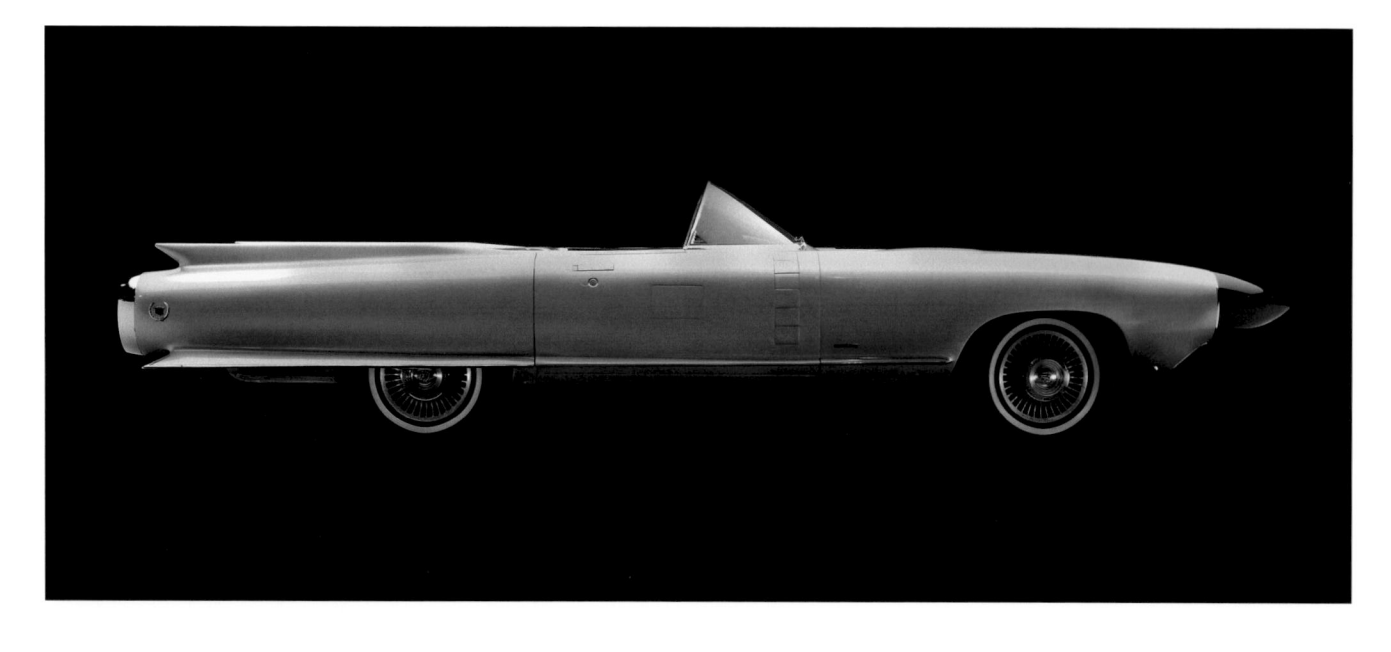

its original white finish, replete with prominent "GM Air Transport" logos, to an almost irridescent silver pearlescent lucite. Mitchell wanted to replace the tall tail fins, but that would have to wait until the next phase.[3] This second version also included a new rear-mounted locking mechanism for the cockpit canopy. Delco Electronics, a GM subsidiary, installed the radar sensors in the nose cones. While Earl would not have restyled an exisiting show car, Mitchell did so, possibly because of cost considerations. It was considerably less expensive to update an existing dream car than to create a new "property," as these show cars were known.

For the New York World's Fair in April 1964, the *Cyclone*'s tail fins were lowered and flattened to their present configuration. Its sharply flared side skeg fins had already appeared on production Cadillacs. Phase-three modifications also included updated thin-vaned wheels and redesigned knock-off hubs.[4] The *Cyclone* appeared in a few Canadian automobile shows in 1966 and 1967. Although some Motorama cars were destroyed when their usefulness had been deemed sufficient, the *XP-74* —Harley Earl's final dream car—survives as a rolling postscript to the glorious Motorama era.

LOANED BY THE GM HERITAGE CENTER, WARREN, MICHIGAN.
PHOTOGRAPHY BY PETER HARHOLDT.

1   Temple, *GM's Motorama*, 150.
2   Lassa, "Inspiration Point," 24-28.
3   Ibid., 30-31.
4   Berghoff, *The GM Motorama*, 90-91.

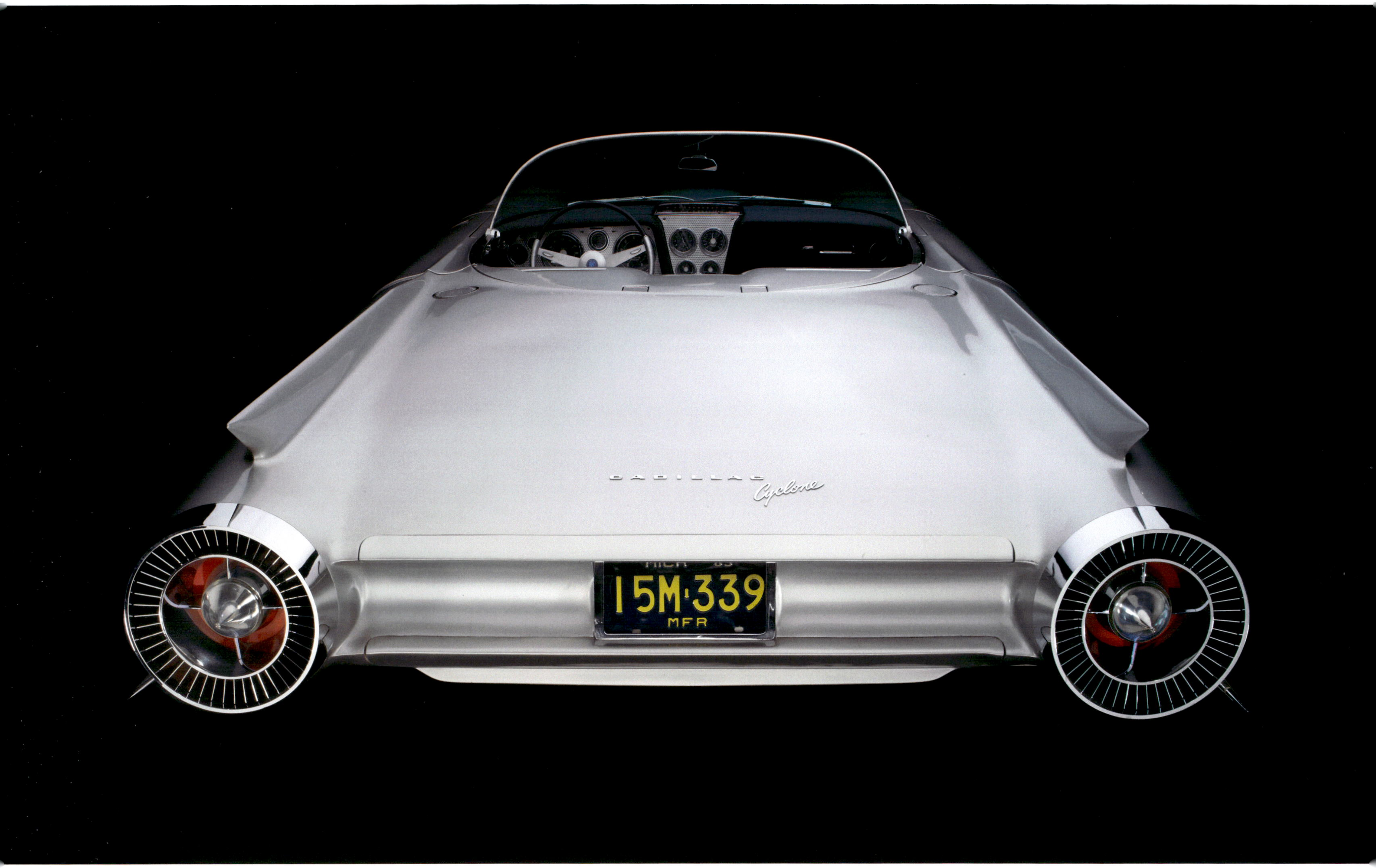
CADILLAC
Cyclone
15M·339
MFR

1970 Ferrari (Pininfarina) 512 S Modulo

In 1969 the FIA (Fédération Internationale de l'Automobile)—the ever-unpredictable French motoring organization that governed European racing competition—established a new 5-liter Sport category formula, but with a twist: manufacturers were required to build at least twenty-five examples of a new race car or they were not allowed to compete. Germany's Porsche, who had never offered a road-going production 5-liter model, surprised the automotive world with a large-displacement 5-liter race car, the *917*. The Italians countered with the Ferrari *512 S* (for 5 liters and 12 cylinders) competition *berlinetta* (Italian for "racing coupe").

Looking to maintain their advantage and squelch any further effort from Porsche, Ferrari gave a new *512 S* chassis to its longtime coachbuilder Carrozzeria Pininfarina, and they undoubtedly were delighted with the outcome: a low-slung, wedge-shaped *berlinetta* show car called the Pininfarina *Speciale*. Resplendent in bright yellow, it appeared at the 1969 *Salone dell'automobile di Torino* even before the racing *512 S* began to compete. The *Speciale* was drivable but it was too radical a body style for use in competition, and there had been only one built. Meanwhile, at endurance races such as the grueling 24 Hours of Le Mans, Ferrari and Porsche would race head to head with their new 5-liter cars. Ferrari's *512 S* had the initial advantage because the Porsche *917* featured such a radical design that its aerodynamics took a long time to perfect, but it would prove its worth eventually and win Le Mans.

Meanwhile, Ferrari and Pininfarina had other plans. Using another *512 S* chassis, Pininfarina created what is still thought to be the wildest-looking concept car ever

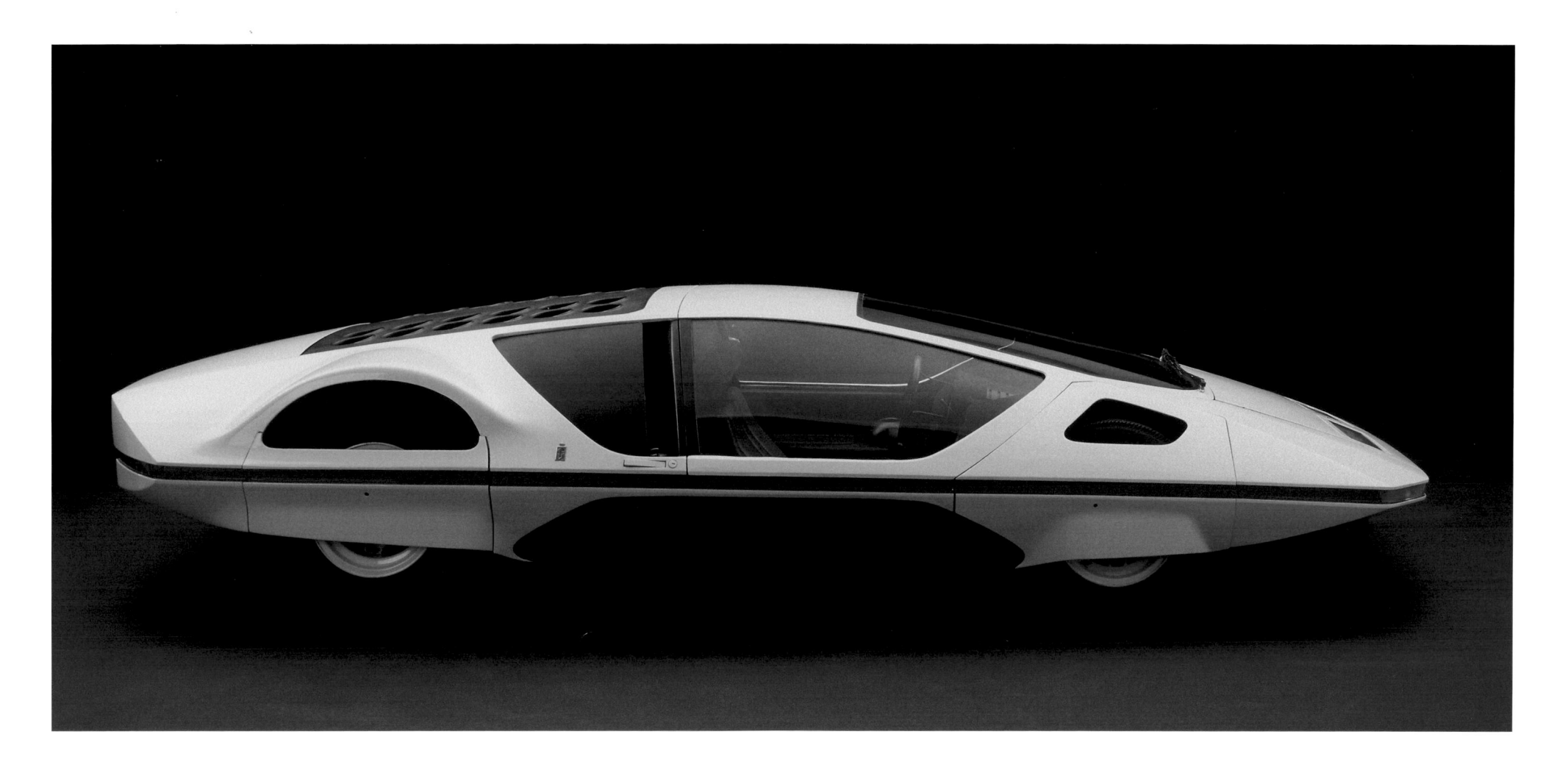

1970 FERRARI (PININFARINA) *512 S MODULO*

created. In March 1970 at the *Salon international de l'automobile de Genève*, Italy's most successful *carrozzeria* rolled out a stunning new concept car called the *Modulo* (Italian for "module"), designed by Paolo Martin. The modular, even graphic division of the surface gave the car its name. *Road & Track*'s Jonathan Thompson wrote, "if ever an automobile deserved to be called a UFO, the Modulo was it."[1] Automotive designers refer to the angle of the side windows and upper section of a car as the "tumblehome." On the *Modulo*, this angle was so severe that the flared wheel fairings for the 15-inch Campagnolo 5-spoke alloy wheels were, in fact, an extension of the roof. In the rear, probably to allow for brake cooling and avoid heat buildup, these fairings were ventilated with a rounded opening on each side; in the front, they were cut away with a triangular-shaped opening. Aerodynamic front skirts limited front wheel travel and were flared out rearward so that the wheels could actually turn in a small radius.

Although it rode on a *512 S* chassis, the Pininfarina *Modulo* was actually wider than the race car that inspired it, because its body panels extended outward and draped over the wheels. At just thirty-seven inches high, it was one of the lowest full-size show cars ever built. The basic body structure consisted of a framework of steel tubing with aluminum panels. Taking the wedge shape to a new extreme, the *Modulo*'s wide, narrowly shaped grille and front end extended rearward across the front of the car and directly into an immense windshield, which flowed from the nose of the car all the way back into the roofline, and then tapered to a bluff rear. The slanted windscreen was raked at an almost impossible angle.

The *Modulo*'s 550-hp, 4-cam 4,933-cc V-12 engine's longitudinal mid-ship location occupied all of the space behind the cockpit, so there was no back window. The running gear comprised a 5-speed gearbox, independent A-arm suspension, rack-and-pinion steering, and Girling disc brakes. Pininfarina used opaque white panels (originally these were painted black) to break up the painted surface. The rocker panels were white as well, and they were angled at each end to match the shape of the windows.[2]

118   1970 FERRARI (PININFARINA) *512 S MODULO*

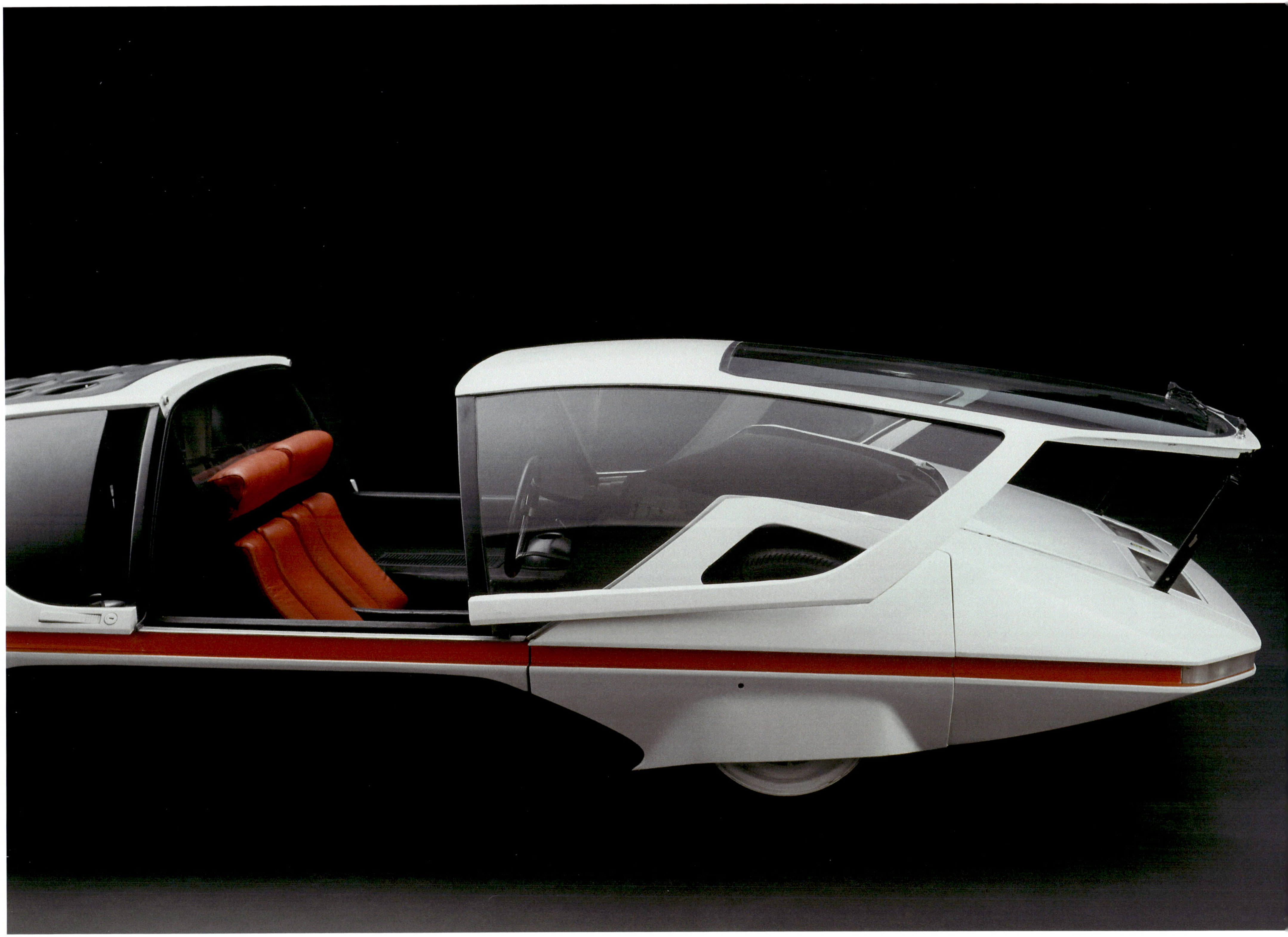

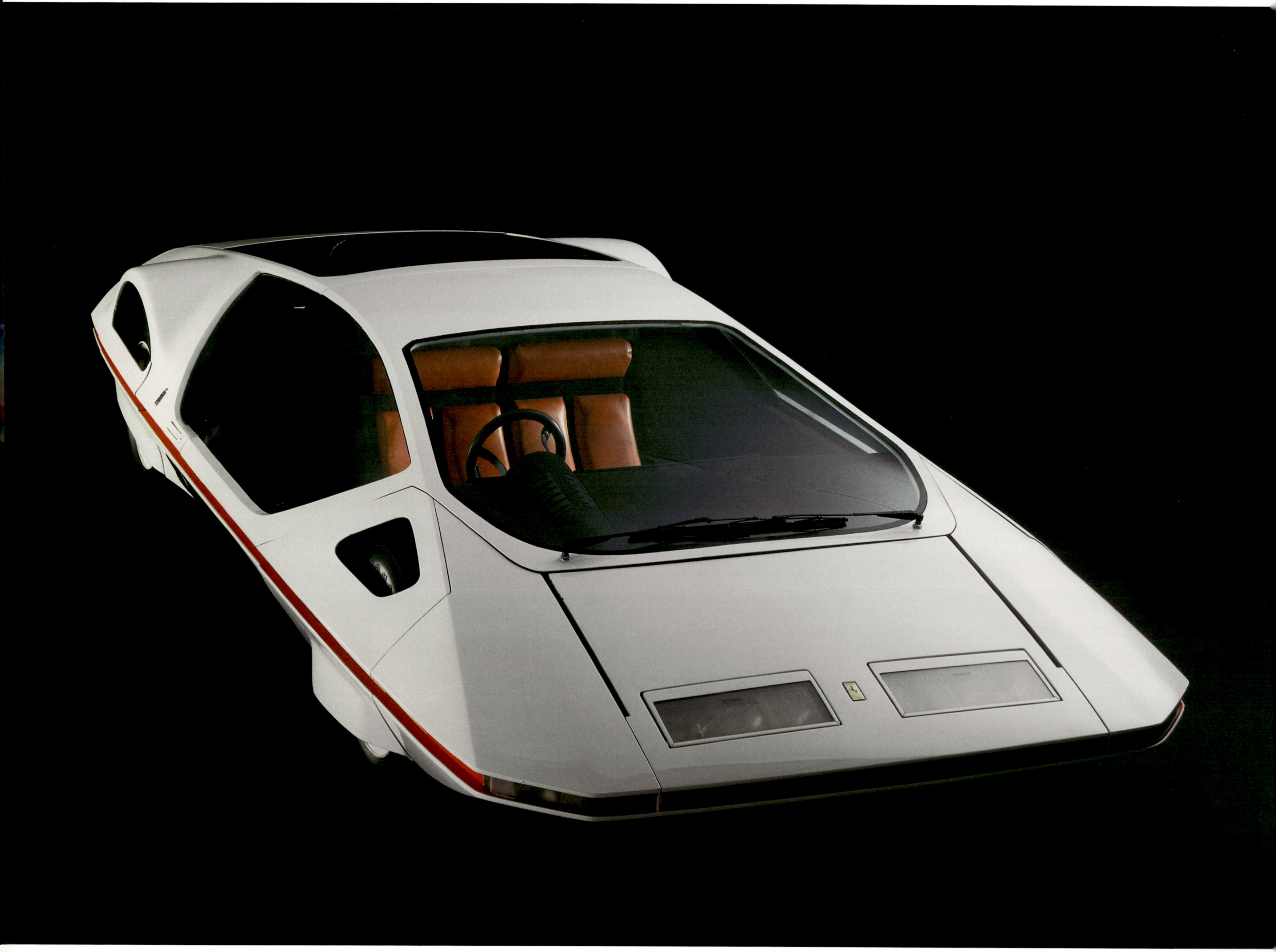

Surely by intention, the *Modulo* bore no resemblance to anything else on the road. Astonishingly low and flat, its width was a mere eighty inches. Forward vision was distorted due to the oblique angle of the windshield, which was fitted with a single large, articulated pantograph-style wiper, in the unlikely event that this bizarre coupe ever ventured out in inclement weather. The windshield and front side windows were joined in an assembly that could be moved forward, thanks to cockpit rails and front-mounted struts, to allow access to the interior. The steering wheel, like those of the *512 S* race cars, was located on the right side, along with the gear shift. The leather-covered seats were plain and simple, as was the instrument panel.

After debuting in Geneva as black, the *Modulo* was repainted its originally intended white to tour the many subsequent automobile shows, including the 1970 Osaka World's Fair, for which it was selected to represent the best of Italian coachbuilding. It appeared at the *Carrozzeria Italiana* exhibition at the Art Center College of Design in Pasadena, California, in 1981 and was shown again three years later at the Los Angeles Auto Show. Jonathan Thompson commented, "If it looked Orwellian in 1970, it still does today. Technology, going in different, more productive directions, has not caught up with it."[3] It could be said that Pininfarina's vision of the future with the *Modulo* was so radical that no one dared (or could) copy it. Thus it remains one of a kind.

LOANED BY COLLEZIONE PININFARINA, CAMBIANO, TURIN, ITALY.

PHOTOGRAPHY BY MICHEL ZUMBRUNN.

---

[1] Thompson, "Still Futuristic After All These Years," 89.

[2] Ibid., 88–89.

[3] Ibid., 90.

1970 Lancia (Bertone) *Stratos HF Zero*

Pininfarina and Bertone were two of Italy's best-recognized and most successful postwar *carrozzerie* and, as such, they often competed for commissions. In the intense competition to win Enzo Ferrari's business, Pininfarina triumphed. They became the Maranello firm's principal supplier after Bertone's angular, stubby design for the Ferrari *308GT4* in 1973 was not updated for its 1975 successor, the *308GTB*. The *308* Pininfarina commission was a breakthrough; it heralded a long line of curvaceous, Pininfarina-styled Ferrari coupes and spiders. But the Torinese *carrozzerie* continued their competition, using the *Salon international de l'automobile de Genève*, the *Salone dell'automobile di Torino*, and other major international expositions to debut outrageous concept cars, principally to impress the public and entice automakers into choosing one of them over the other.

Pininfarina's spectacular show car efforts for Ferrari in the late 1960s and early 1970s—the 1968 *250 P5 Berlinetta Speciale*, the 1969 *512 S Berlinetta Speciale*, and, most dramatically, the ultra-low *512 S Modulo*—received considerable international acclaim. Under the direction of famed automobile designer Giuseppe "Nuccio" Bertone, Carrozzeria Bertone countered with the 1967 Lamborghini *Marzal*—the first wedge-shaped Supercar concept—the 1968 Alfa Romeo *Carabo* (see p. 33), the 1968 Bizzarrini *Manta*, and the 1969 Alfa Romeo *Iguana*. He went a step further at Turin in 1970 with the Lancia *Stratos HF Zero*, designed by Marcello Gandini. Reportedly, Nuccio Bertone had intended to call this strikingly low car *Stratolimite*, referring to the limit of the stratosphere, but soon it became known by its internal nickname, *Zero*.[1]

To directly challenge Pininfarina, whose designs (excepting the *Modulo*) tended to be alluringly curvaceous, Bertone produced a very low, sharply chiseled coupe that appeared to have been carved out of a solid block of bronze. Design experts have commented that the *Stratos HF Zero* was a significant step between the 1968 Alfa Romeo *Carabo* and the production 1974 Lamborghini *Countach*, which popularized the wedge-shaped, angular look seen in many high-performance sports cars. Nothing about it was conventional, save for it having wheels in all four corners. From the thin strip

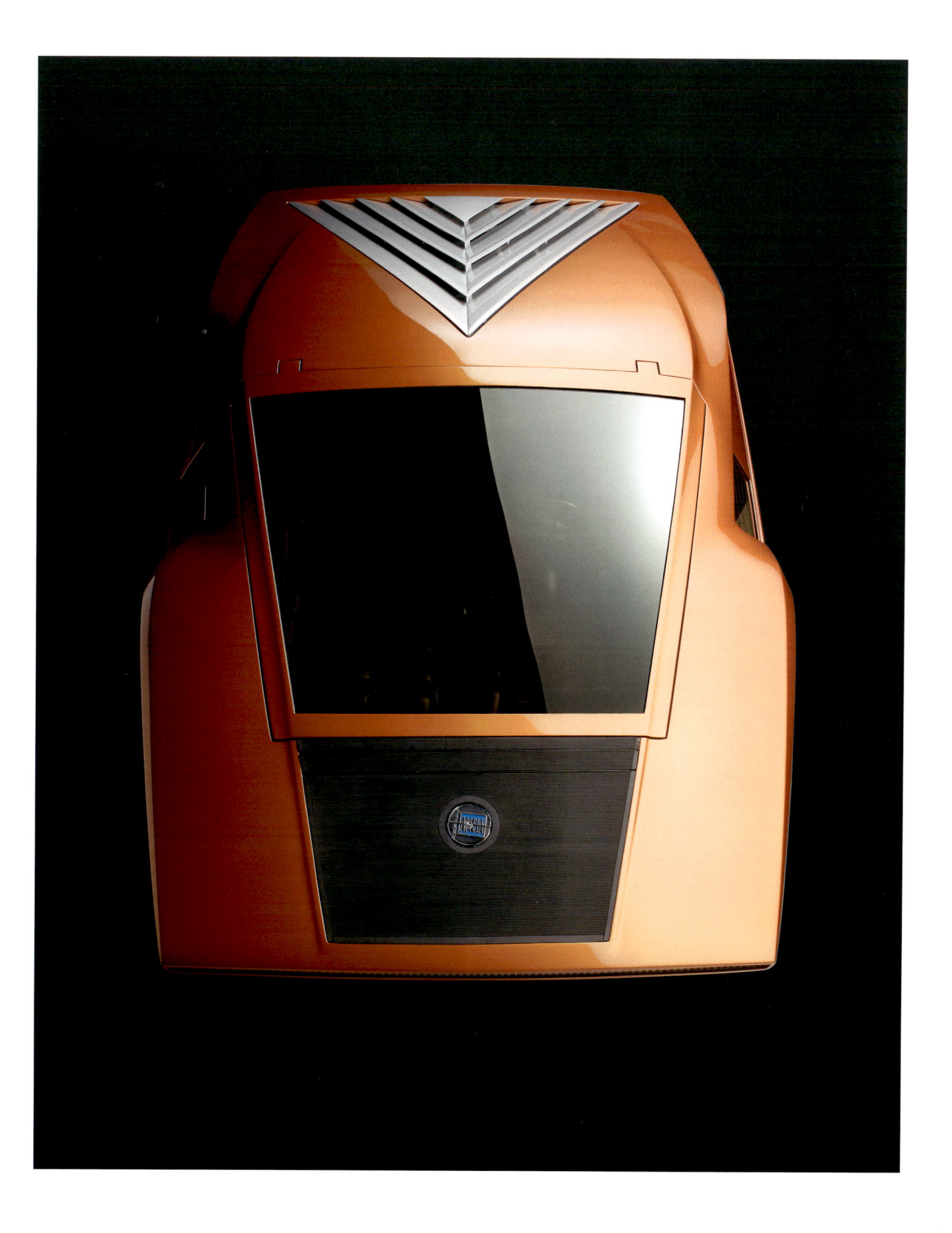

1970 LANCIA (BERTONE) *STRATOS HF ZERO* 123

headlights to the backlit (with eighty-four tiny bulbs) taillights, the Zero presaged many modern dream cars. Even now it looks futuristic. Eugenio Pagliano, responsible for interior design at Carrozzeria Bertone, said the the firm's concept was to see how low a car it could successfully build.[2]

Bertone certainly succeeded. While the the Ferrari 512 S Modulo was 36 13/16 inches high, the Zero was just 33 inches. Gandini told Italian journalist Ginacarlo Perini:

> The very first Stratos was designed as freely as the Autobianchi Runabout, and it reached the aim for which it was intended—to establish a bridge between Lancia and Bertone. Having seen the Zero, Lancia asked us to come up with an idea for a new sports car that would go rallying in the world championships.[3]

When the radical design was completed, Carrozzeria Bertone cleverly assembled the Stratos HF Zero from existing Lancia components. Once the height target was established and construction began, a 1.6-liter Fulvia V-4 engine and its front suspension were obtained, without Lancia's knowledge, from a wrecked Fulvia. The front suspension consisted of a pair of short MacPherson struts; the rear suspension, a double-wishbone/coil spring setup, formerly was the Fulvia's front suspension. A 45-liter fuel tank was positioned alongside the engine, and a pair of electric fans facilitated cooling. Winston Goodfellow wrote, "Bertone noted he made the car without Lancia's knowledge for fear they would negatively react to its audacious design."[4]

Complimenting the Zero's dramatically low stance and aiding its unconventional nature, the cockpit was positioned as far forward as possible, with the twin seats positioned between the front wheels. The steering column could be moved forward to provide room to access the cabin. At the same time, a hydraulic mechanism opened the wide Perspex windscreen, which served as the car's single door. A rubber mat at the bottom of the windshield was the step, and a pop-up wiper was hidden beneath the windshield. Inside, occupants could see directly ahead and above—and little else. The instrument panel was offset on the left of the wheel arch. Italian manufacturer Gallino-Hellebore was responsible for the creation of the unusual and acrobatic steering wheel. There was even room for a spare tire and a small suitcase.

The Zero received a great deal of positive critical acclaim, particularly from other designers. In 1987, Renault Design executive Serge Van Hove, who worked with Gandini, wrote in the Italian magazine Auto & Design, "'What Gandini cares about more than anything else, what makes him unique, is the dreaming.' Match that to Nuccio Bertone's ability to transform dreams into reality, and you have the unrepeatable Stratos Zero."[5]

The cost of building the Zero was reportedly just 40 million lire (about $450,000 in 1970); a new Lancia Fulvia 1.6 Rally coupe was then 2.25 million lire. Some of the Zero's design elements would reach production cars eventually; for example, the squared "chocolate bar" pattern of the seats would appear later on the Lamborghini Countach. In 1971 Quattroruote's editor drove the show car from Milan's beltway into the center of the city to the world-famous Duomo cathedral—a feat that took a brave driver, as the Zero was arguably low enough to be driven under a semi-trailer. Later it was revealed that Bertone himself had driven the Zero on public roads to Lancia's offices, dazzling all who saw it, and marveling when he drove it under the closed entrance barriers at Lancia's racing department. (The result of that momentous meeting was the radical and now highly collectible Lancia Stratos rally car.) Although the production Lancia Stratos—with its mid-mounted Fiat/Ferrari V-6 engine—did not closely resemble the Zero, the edgy, all-wheel-drive race car probably would not have been built were it not for the influence of the inimitable Zero.

LOANED BY XJ WANG COLLECTION, NEW YORK, NEW YORK.

PHOTOGRAPHY BY MICHAEL FURMAN.

1 Edsall, Concept Cars, 62–64.
2 Eugenio Pagliano, Villa d'Este Auction, RM Auctions catalogue, May 21, 2011.
3 Ibid.
4 Goodfellow, Italian Sports Cars, 106–108.
5 Michael Robinson quoting Serge Van Hove, Villa d'Este Auction, RM Auctions catalogue, May 21, 2011.

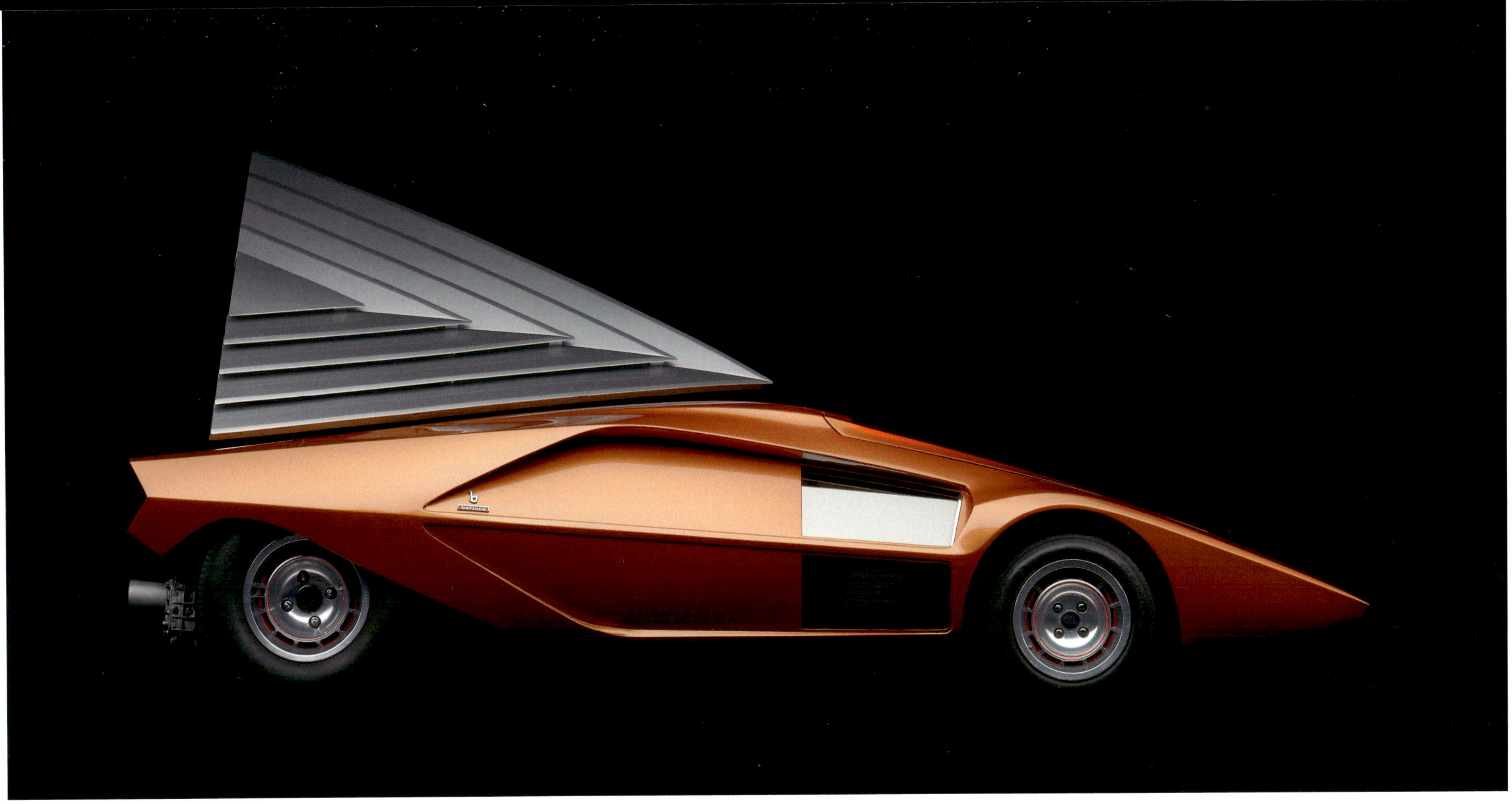

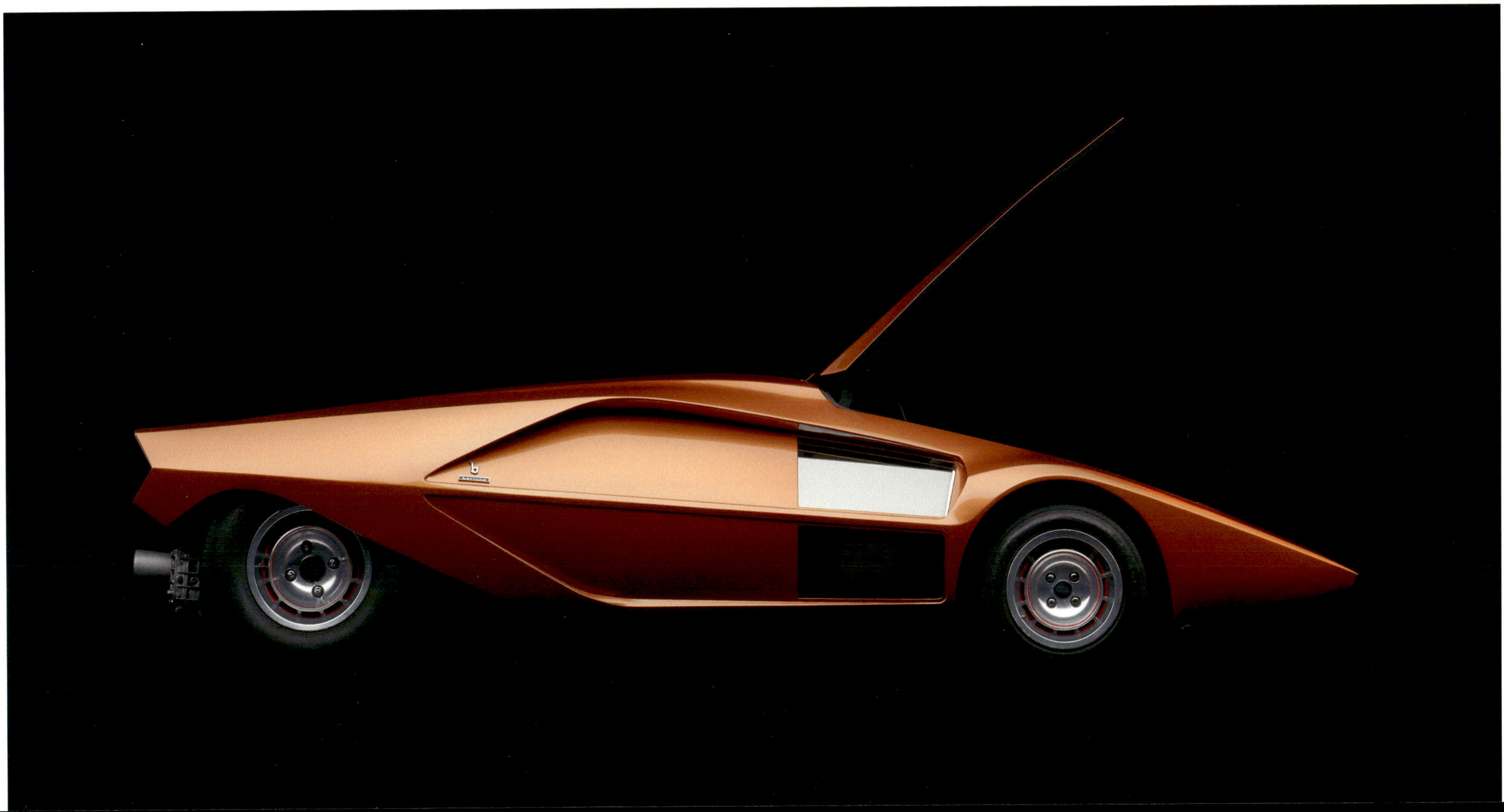

2001 BMW GINA Light Visionary Model

BMW's peripatetic chief of design Christopher Bangle was talented, creative, sometimes controversial, often polarizing, and known for his unconventional thinking. BMW's board of management promoted Bangle in 1992 to be the company's first American-born head of design, because they felt the Germany-based automaker's styling had become bland and predictable. The board wanted BMW, whose sporting cars were always well respected, to be perceived stylistically as a more modern carmaker. Under Bangle's tenure BMW design became more edgy, unpredictable, and the talk of the industry. His so-called flame surfacing required production engineers to develop new techniques in order to execute the complex curves and oblique angles in sheet metal that Bangle and his designers wanted. Under Bangle's leadership, looking to the past but remaining mindful of the future, BMW's concept cars broke new ground and led to design and manufacturing solutions that advanced the brand's capability and appeal—all while increasing sales.

One example of this was the *GINA Light Visionary Model*, which was first designed 2001 as an internal study and was not shown publicly until June 2008. The acronym *GINA* stands for "Geometry and functions In 'N' Adaptations," with "N" representing the mathematical symbol for an infinite number. In a promotional video released by BMW AG, Bangle explained that the *GINA* project permitted the company's Designworks subsidiary in California and his Munich-based design team "to challenge existing principles and design processes." Bangle says he questioned designers and engineers about the construction of a car's body, asking, "Does it have to be made of metal?"[1]

The result was an advanced water-resistant, translucent textile-bodied concept car with a virtually seamless fabric exterior skin—polyurethane-coated Spandex—that could change elements of its shape according to exterior conditions and speed, or at the driver's demand. The fabric was stretched over a frame made of thin aluminum wire, with flexible carbon fiber struts used in critical junctures where movement was required. The shape of the frame was controlled by electric and hydraulic actuators; for example, at first glance the GINA did not appear to have headlights or taillights, but the headlights were cleverly hidden behind a crease in the bodywork that opened like an eyelid. When switched on, the taillights and center brake light glowed through the translucent fabric skin, which was permeable to light but was not transparent. The deployable rear spoiler could "grow" taller to increase down force, enhancing tire grip at high speeds. The rocker panels lowered and widened to improve the GINA's aerodynamics. These stretched fabric elements returned to their normal position when they were not needed to enhance the car's aerodynamics or perform other functions.[2]

The GINA's instrument panel was covered in a gray neoprene cloth material. All the controls, including the steering wheel and other functional elements, remained hidden until the driver pushed the "start" button, at which time the wheel deployed and the headrest rose from the seat. Equally fascinating is the way the smooth fabric skin on the butterfly-style doors symmetrically wrinkled when the doors were opened. Integrated zip fasteners provided access to the oil filler, radiator cap, and windshield washer fluid reservoir. The GINA had just four panels: the hood, the two side panels, and the rear trunk section.

With the GINA project, Bangle wanted his designers to re-examine the principles under which new cars are constructed and to take advantage of advances in materials and construction methods. Author Larry Edsall explained, "The challenge wasn't simply to design a new concept car, but to pursue new concepts for car construction," and quoted Bangle, who said, "This is an industry that needs to understand that it can excite customers in other ways than with price and rebates."

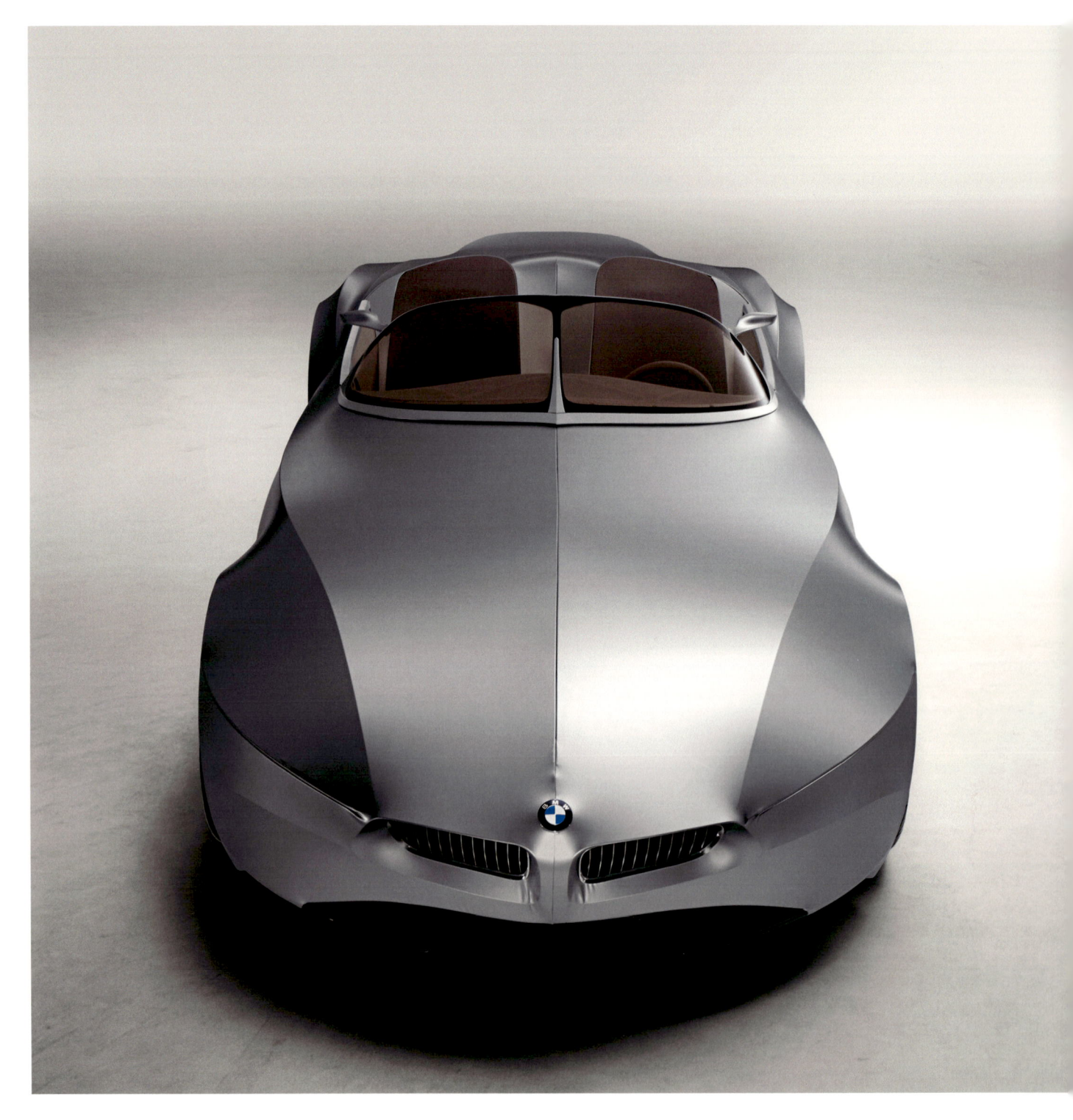

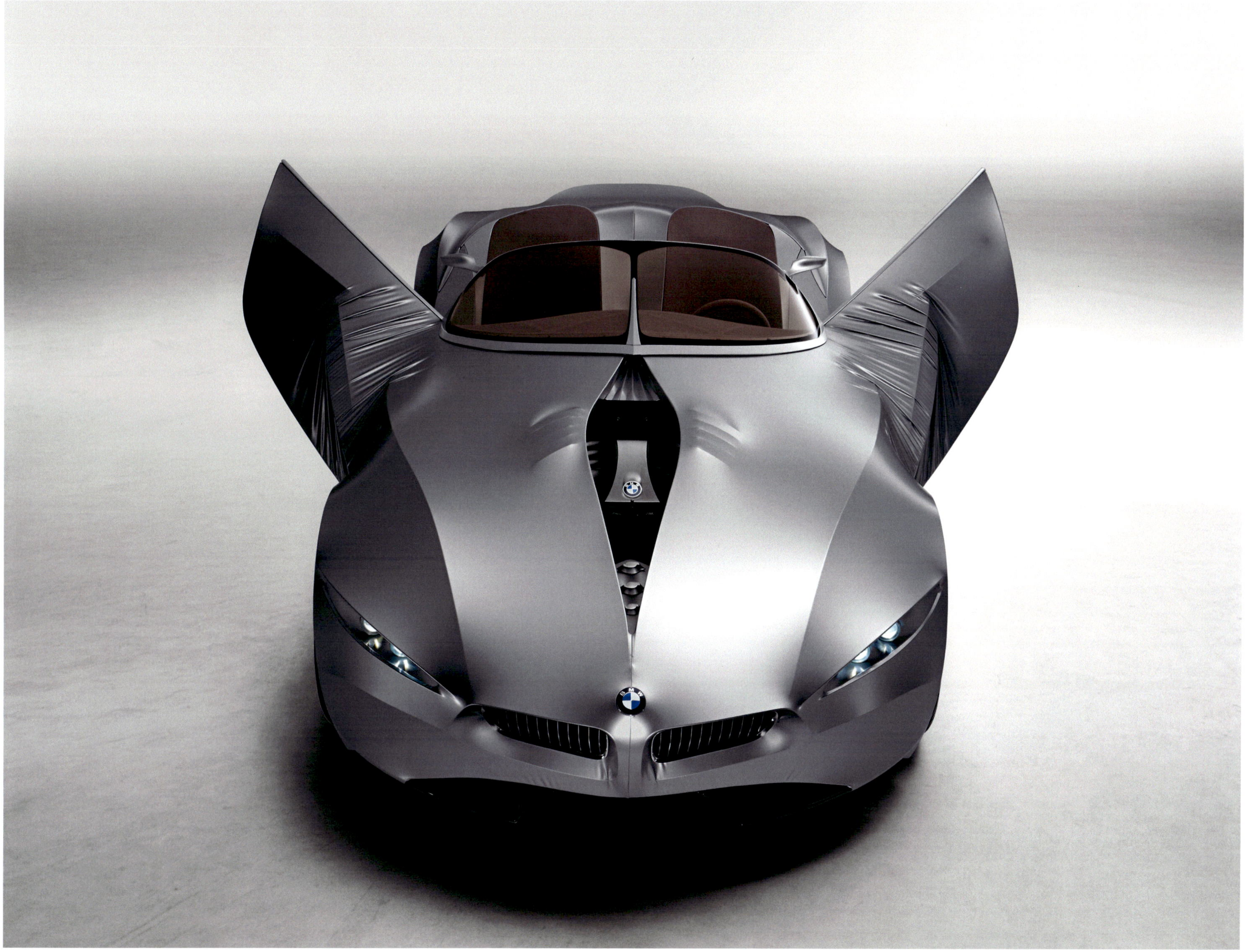

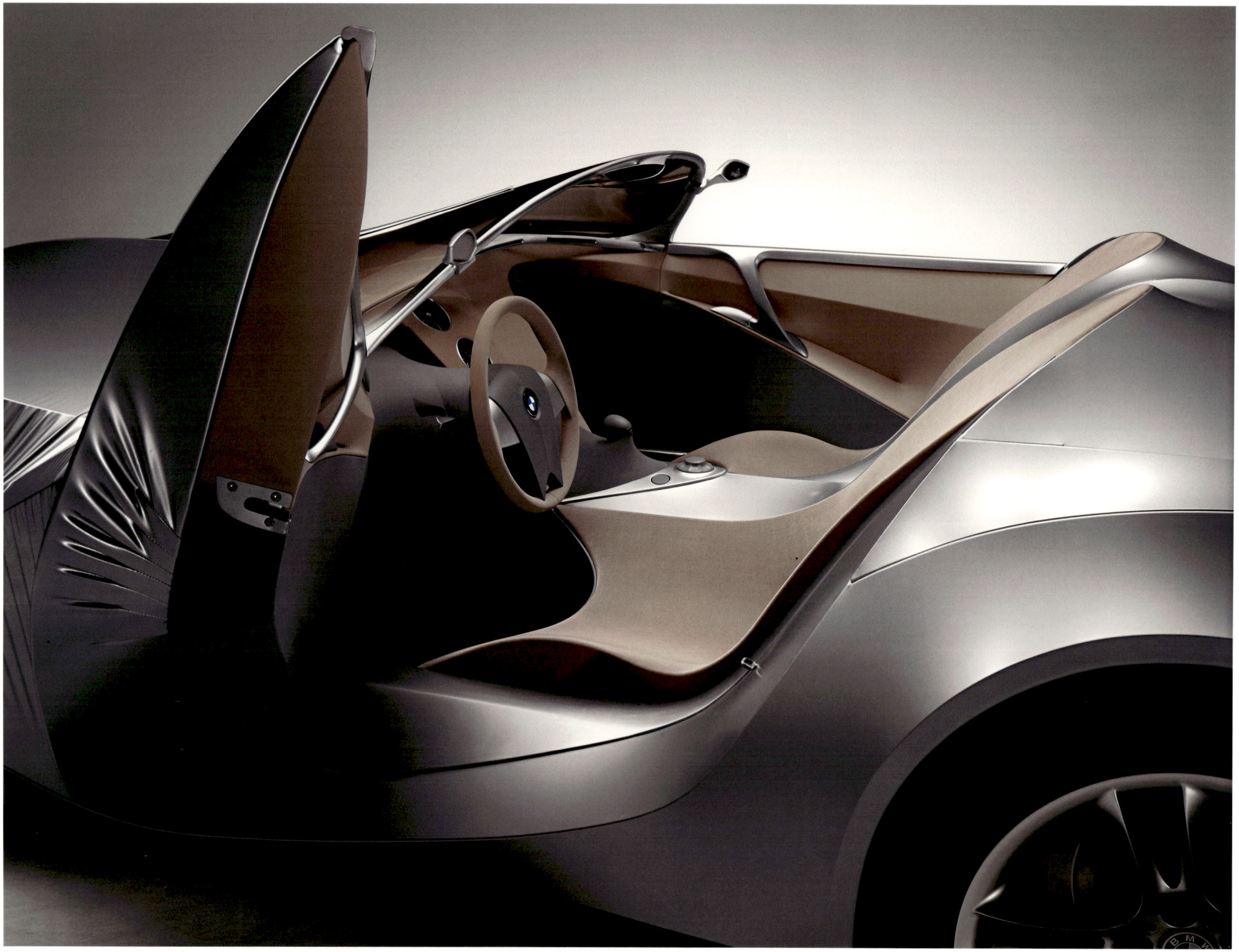

Bangle and his management team discussed the *GINA* program two years before the completion of the *Light Visionary Model*, saying, "The way we make cars is so expensive, and the investment hurdles are so high that the industry is terrified to do anything beyond what it knows will work. I say we have to look at how to get rid of those barriers . . . so every decision you make isn't a million dollar gamble."[3]

Unlike many designers in the past who focused principally on car styling and preferred to let the engineers and production people worry about execution, Bangle looked at the car manufacturing process in its entirety: "Car designers today should be spending their time understanding how cars are made and then get those hurdles down, because then they can do great designs, because the risk factor is completely different. That's what the GINA was all about for us."[4] The *GINA* program helped BMW to develop both rapid manufacturing and digital tooling techniques, and to use a robot-guided steel embossing process to create the hoods for the BMW *Z4M Roadster* and the *M-Coupe*. The *GINA* exercise forced BMW to become more flexible, not just in changing car construction materials but in terms of its future investment and tooling directions as well. "It helped us think about things differently. The materials led the way," Bangle said. "It's thinking context over dogma."[5] The *GINA* did not become a production model, but some of its styling cues have surfaced in modified form. Chris Bangle left BMW in 2009 and now has his own design consulting firm.

LOANED BY THE BMW MUSEUM, MUNICH, GERMANY.

PHOTOGRAPHY COURTESY OF BMW. © BMW AG.

---

1 "Chris Bangle on the BMW GINA Concept," YouTube, June 12, 2008, http://www.youtube.com/watch?v=sSJfrQV6LLI (accessed August 29, 2013).

2 Edsall, *Concept Cars*, 234–238.

3 Ibid., 234.

4 Ibid., 234–235.

5 "Chris Bangle on the BMW GINA Concept," YouTube, June 12, 2008.

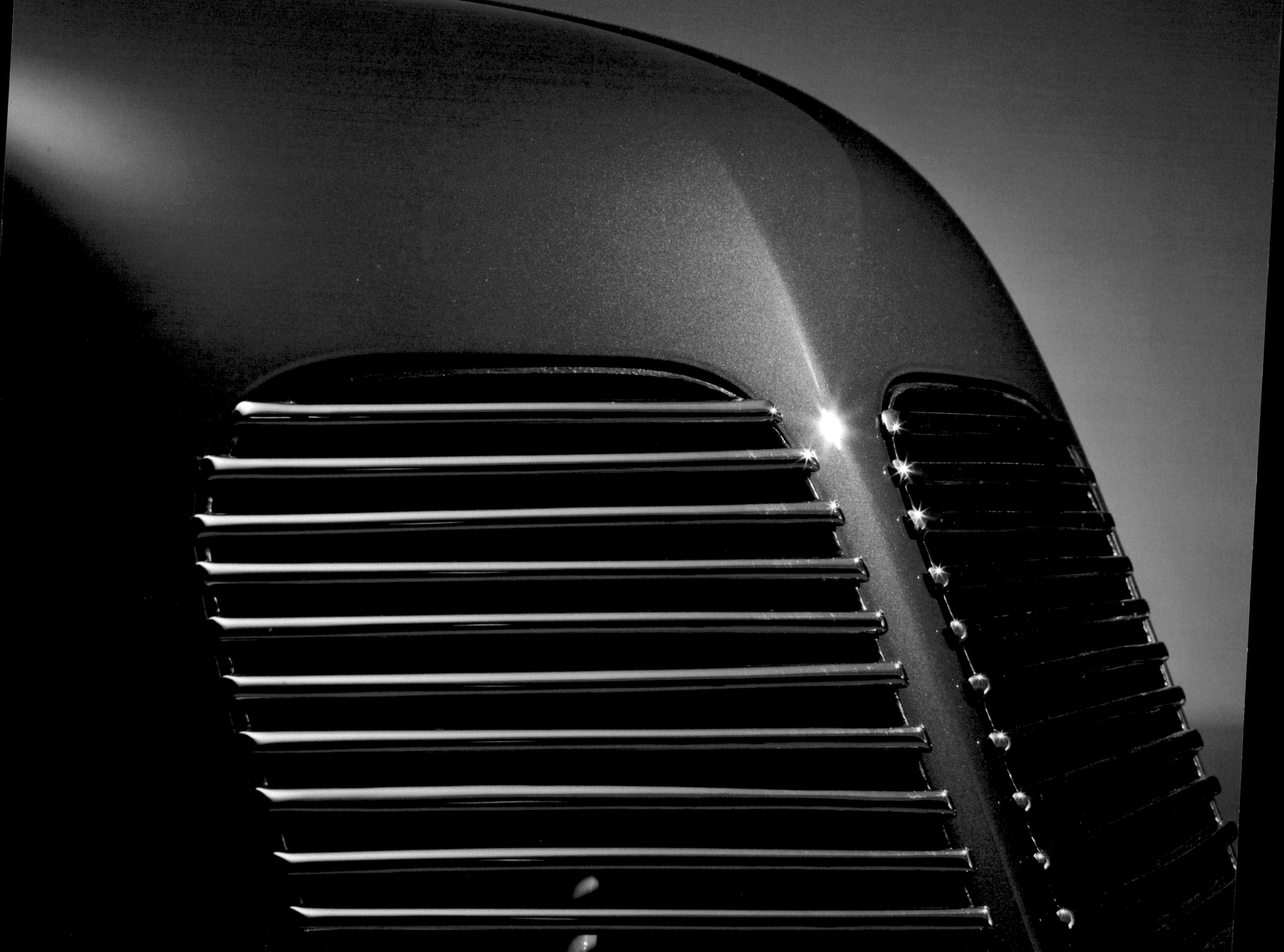

Selected Bibliography

ARTICLES AND EPHEMERA

Bellu, René. "Toutes Les Voitures Françaises, 1940–46: Les Années Sans Salon." Special issue, *Automobilia: L'Histoire Automobile en France*, no. 26 (2003).

Christian Science Monitor. "Streamlining Reaches Heights in Chrysler's 'Thunderbolt,'" November 8, 1940.

Chrysler Corporation. *Chrysler's Thunderbolt and Newport: New Milestones in Airflow Designs*. Auburn Hills, MI: Chrysler Corporation, ca. 1941.

Dole, Charles E. "Pininfarina: Along with Other Italian Design Firms, It Shapes Many of the Cars the World Drives." *Christian Science Monitor*, July 15, 1981.

Exner, V. M. *Styling and Aerodynamics*. Detroit: Society of Automotive Engineers, 1957.

Ford Motor Company. *The Ford Book of Styling: A History and Interpretation of Automotive Design*. Dearborn, MI: Ford Motor Company, 1963.

———. *Styling at Ford Motor Company*. Dearborn, MI: Ford Motor Company, 1957.

Fortune. "The Scarab: A Challenge and a Prophecy," advertisement, 1935.

General Motors Corporation. *General Motors Le Sabre: An "Experimental Laboratory on Wheels."* Detroit: General Motors Corporation, 1951.

———. *Imagination in Motion: Firebird III*. Detroit: General Motors Corporation, 1958.

———. *Modes and Motors*. Detroit: General Motors Corporation, 1938.

———. *Styling: The Look of Things*. Detroit: General Motors Corporation, 1955.

———. *The XP-21 Firebird: General Motors' Newest Experiment on Wheels*. Detroit: General Motors Corporation, ca. 1954.

Goodfellow, Winston. "Ghia's Gilda." *Motor Trend Classic*, Fall 2012.

Grainger, David. "Aerolithe." *Bugantics*, Spring 2013.

Gross, Ken. *History: The Life and Owners of the 1934 Model 40 Special Speedster*. Gross Pointe Shores, MI: The Edsel and Eleanor Ford House, 2012.

Ingraham, Joseph C. "Auto Show to Feature Exotic Cars of Futuristic Design: 'Mini' also to be on Display at Coliseum Next Saturday." *New York Times*, March 28, 1970.

Lamm, John, ed. *Road & Track, Show Cars*, 1984.

Lamm, Michael. "Edsel Ford's Hot Rods." *Special-Interest Autos*, November–December 1970.

Lassa, Todd. "Inspiration Point." *Motor Trend Classic*, Summer 2011.

Los Angeles Times. "Prototype of Bertone Original, as in Stratos," May 30, 1971.

———. "XP-21 Firebird Lures Crowds to Motorama," March 7, 1954.

Motor Trend: The Magazine for a Motoring World. "Home-Made Streamliner," October 1949.

New York Times. "Radar Device in Test Car by G. M. Warns Driver of Road Hazards," February 21, 1959.

Pierce, Bert. "Le Sabre: Future Models Will Benefit From Devices in General Motors Experimental Car." *New York Times*, July 22, 1951, Automobiles.

RM Auctions. *Villa d'Este Auction*. May 20, 2011.

The Stout Motor Car Corporation. *Let's Build a Modern Motor Car*. Dearborn, MI: The Stout Motor Car Corporation, ca. 1935.

Thompson, Jonathan. "Still Futuristic After All These Years." Special Issue, *Road and Track Presents Show Cars, The World's Most Exciting Automotive Fantasies*, 1985.

Wall Street Journal. "French Designer Working on 'Strange Automobiles,'" June 6, 1945.

BOOKS

Adatto, Richard. *Sensuous Steel: The Art Deco Automobile*. St. Paul, MN: Stance & Speed, 2013.

Albrecht, Donald, ed. *Norman Bel Geddes Designs America*. Austin: Harry Ransom Center, The University of Texas at Austin, 2012.

Bayley, Steven. *Harley Earl*. London: Trefoil Publications, 1990.

Bellu, Serge. *500 Fantastic Cars: A Century of the World's Concept Cars*. Translated by Jon Pressnell. Somerset, UK: Haynes Publishing, 2003.

Benson, Joe. *The Illustrated Alfa Romeo Buyers Guide*. Osceola, WI: Motorbooks International, 1983.

Berghoff, Bruce. *The GM Motorama: Dream Cars of the Fifties*. Osceola, WI: Motorbooks International, 1995.

Bobbitt, Malcolm. *Bubblecars and Microcars*. Ramsbury, UK: The Crowood Press Ltd., 2003.

Buehrig, Gordon M. and William S. Jackson. *Rolling Sculpture: A Designer and His Work*. Newfoundland, NJ: Haessner Publishing Inc., 1975.

Bush, Donald J. *The Streamlined Decade*. New York: George Braziller, 1975.

Chapman, Giles, ed. *Car: The Definitive Visual History of the Automobile*. New York: DK Publishing, 2011.

Cumberford, Robert. *Auto Legends: Classics of Style and Design*. London: Merrill, 2004.

Dominguez, Henry. *Edsel Ford and E. T. Gregorie: The Remarkable Design Team and Their Classic Fords of the 1930s and 1940s.* Warrendale, PA: Society of Automotive Engineers, 1999.

Edsall, Larry. *Concept Cars: From the 1930s to the Present.* 2nd ed. New York: Barnes & Noble Inc. by arrangement with White Star S.p.A., 2006.

———. *Concept Cars: From the 1930s to the Present.* 3rd ed. New York: White Star Publishers, 2009.

Farrell, Jim and Cheryl Farrell. *Ford Design Department: Concept & Showcars, 1932–1961.* Roseburg, OR: Jim and Cheryl Farrell, 1999.

Fetherston, David and Tony Thacker. *Chrysler Concept Cars: 1940–1970.* North Branch, MN: CarTech, 2007.

Foster, Norman. *Dymaxion Car: Buckminster Fuller.* London: Ivorypress, 2010.

Georgano, Nick, ed. *The Beaulieu Encyclopedia of the Automobile.* 3 vols. London: Routledge, 2000.

Goodfellow, Winston S. *Italian Sports Cars.* Osceola, WI: Motorbooks International, 2000.

Grist, Peter. *Virgil Exner, Visioneer: The Official Biography of Virgil M. Exner, Designer Extraordinaire.* Dorchester, UK: Veloce Publishing, 2007.

Kimes, Beverly Rae and Winston S. Goodfellow. *Speed, Style and Beauty: Cars from the Ralph Lauren Collection.* Boston, MA: MFA Publications, 2005.

Lamm, Michael and David Holls. *A Century of Automotive Style: 100 Years of American Car Design.* Stockton, CA: Lamm-Morada Publishing Company Inc., 1996.

Lamonaca, Marianne, ed. *Styled for the Road: The Art of Automobile Design, 1908–1948.* Miami Beach: The Wolfsonian–Florida International University, 2009.

Matthews, L. G., Jr. *Bugatti Yesterday and Today: The Atlantic and Other Articles.* Paris: Éditions SPE Barthélémy, 2004.

Mullin Automotive Museum. *Vitesse-Élégance: French Expression of Flight and Motion.* Philadelphia, PA: Coachbuilt Press, 2012.

Sharf, Frederic A. *American Automobile Art, 1945–1970: Drawings from the Great Age of American Car Design.* Newbury, MA: Newburyport Press, 2007.

———. *Carl Renner: 1950s GM Dream Car Creator.* Brookline, MA: Larz Anderson Auto Museum, 2011.

———. *Future Retro: Drawings from the Great Age of American Automobiles.* Boston, MA: MFA Publications, 2005.

Simon, Bernhard and Julius Kruta. *The Bugatti Type 57S.* Munster: Verlagshaus Monsenstein und Vannerdar, 2003.

Sparke, Penny. *A Century of Car Design.* Hauppauge, NY: Barron's Educational Series, Inc., 2002.

Stein, Jonathan A., ed. *Curves of Steel: Streamlined Automobile Design at Phoenix Art Museum.* Philadelphia, PA: Coachbuilt Press, 2007.

———. *The Art and Colour of General Motors.* Philadelphia, PA: Coachbuilt Press, 2008.

Temple, David W. *GM's Motorama: The Glamorous Show Cars of a Cultural Phenomenon.* Edited by Dennis Adler. St. Paul, MN: Motorbooks, 2006.

Voisin, Gabriel. *My Thousand and One Cars.* Translated by D. R. A. Winstone. Coopersfield, UK: Faustroll, 2012.

Wayt, Hampton C. *Driving Through Futures Past: Mid-20th Century Automotive Design.* Aiken, SC: Kythe Publishing Co., 2006.

Wollen, Peter and Joe Kerr, eds. *Autopia: Cars and Culture.* London: Reaktion Books Ltd., 2002.

Checklist of the Exhibition

AUTOMOBILES

Voisin *C-25 Aérodyne*, 1934

Gabriel Voisin (French, 1880–1973), designer
Avions Voisin, French, 1905–1946, fabricator
72 × 78 × 216 inches; 3,500 pounds
Courtesy of Merle and Peter Mullin, Brentwood, California

Edsel Ford *Model 40 Special Speedster*, 1934

Edsel Ford (American, 1893–1943), designer
Eugene T. "Bob" Gregorie (American, 1908–2002), designer
Ford Aircraft Division, American, 1924–1936, fabricator
56½ × 70 × 172 inches; 2,300 pounds
Courtesy of the Edsel and Eleanor Ford House, Grosse Pointe Shores, Michigan

Bugatti *Type 57S Compétition Coupé Aerolithe* (re-creation of 1935 original), 2007–2013

Jean Bugatti (French, born Italy, 1909–1939), designer
Joseph Walter (Nationality and life dates unknown), designer
The Guild of Automotive Restorers, Canadian, founded 1990, fabricator
72 × 72 × 204 inches; 2,550 pounds
Courtesy of Christopher Ohrstrom, The Plains, Virginia

Stout *Scarab*, 1936

William Stout (American, 1880–1956), designer
Stout Motor Car Company, American, 1934–1942, fabricator
70 × 70 × 192 inches; 2,500 pounds
Courtesy of Larry Smith, Pontiac, Michigan

Chrysler *Thunderbolt*, 1941

Ralph Roberts (American, life dates unknown), designer
Alex Tremulis (American, 1914–1991), designer
Briggs Body Works, American, 1909–1954, fabricator
Chrysler Corporation, American, founded 1925, manufacturer
53 × 84 × 216 inches; approximately 3,795 pounds
Courtesy of Roger Willbanks, Denver, Colorado

Paul Arzens *L'Œuf électrique*, 1942

Paul Arzens (French, 1903–1990), designer and fabricator
35$\frac{7}{16}$ × 36$\frac{5}{8}$ × 59$\frac{3}{16}$ inches; 319$\frac{11}{16}$ pounds
Courtesy of Musée des Arts et Métiers, Paris, France

Norman Timbs *Special*, 1947

Norman Timbs (American, 1917–1993), designer
Attributed to Emil Diedt (Nationality and life dates unknown), fabricator
47 × 78 × 216 inches; 2,200 pounds
Courtesy of Gary and Diane Cerveny, Malibu, California

Tasco, 1948

Gordon Buehrig (American, 1904–1990), designer
Derham Body Company, American, 1887–1971, fabricator
58 × 69 × 186 inches; 2,800 pounds
Courtesy of the Auburn Cord Duesenberg Automobile Museum, Auburn, Indiana

General Motors *Le Sabre XP-8*, 1951

Harley J. Earl (American, 1893–1969) and GM Styling Section staff, designers
General Motors Corporation, American, founded 1908, manufacturer
50 × 76½ × 201⅞ inches; 3,800 pounds
Courtesy of GM Heritage Center, Warren, Michigan

General Motors *Firebird I XP-21*, 1953

Harley J. Earl (American, 1893–1969), designer
Robert F. "Bob" McLean (American, life dates unknown), and GM Styling Section staff, designers
General Motors Corporation, American, founded 1908, manufacturer
51 × 80 × 223 inches; 2,440 pounds
Courtesy of GM Heritage Center, Warren, Michigan

Chrysler (Ghia) *Streamline X "Gilda,"* 1955

Giovanni Savonuzzi (Italian, 1911–1987), designer
Virgil M. Exner, Sr. (American, 1909–1973), designer
Carrozzeria Ghia S.p.A., Italian, founded 1915, fabricator
Collaboration with Chrysler Corporation, American, founded 1925
45 × 42 × 204 inches; 1,200 pounds
Courtesy of Scott Grundfor and Kathleen Redmond, Arroyo Grande, California

Buick *Centurion XP-301*, 1956

Harley J. Earl (American, 1893–1969), designer
Charles "Chuck" Jordan (American, 1927–2010), designer
General Motors Corporation, American, founded 1908, manufacturer
54 × 73 × 216 inches; approximately 2,210 pounds
Courtesy of Sloan Museum, Flint, Michigan

Cadillac *Cyclone XP-74*, 1959

Harley J. Earl (American, 1893–1969), designer
Carl Renner (American, 1923–2001), designer
General Motors Corporation, American, founded 1908, fabricator
44 × 76½ × 196 inches; 4,629 pounds
Courtesy of GM Heritage Center, Warren, Michigan

Ferrari (Pininfarina) *512 S Modulo*, 1970

Paolo Martin (Italian, born 1943), designer
Pininfarina, Italian, founded 1930, fabricator
Collaboration with Ferrari S.p.A., Italian, founded 1947
36$\frac{13}{16}$ × 80$\frac{5}{16}$ × 176$\frac{3}{8}$ inches; 1,322$\frac{13}{16}$ pounds
Courtesy of Collezione Pininfarina, Cambiano, Turin, Italy

Lancia (Bertone) *Stratos HF Zero*, 1970

Marcello Gandini (Italian, born 1938), designer
Gruppo Bertone, Italian, founded 1912, fabricator
Lancia Automobiles S.p.A., Italian, founded 1906, producer
33$\frac{1}{16}$ × 73$\frac{5}{8}$ × 151$\frac{9}{16}$ inches
XJ Wang Collection, New York, New York

BMW *GINA Light Visionary Model*, 2001
Christopher Bangle (American, born 1956), designer
Bayerische Motoren Werke (BMW), German, founded 1916, manufacturer
46⁷⁄₁₆ × 79¹⁵⁄₁₆ × 173¼ inches; 3,373 pounds
Courtesy of BMW Museum, Munich, Germany

Porsche *918 Spyder Concept Car*, 2010
Michael Mauer (German, born 1962) and Porsche Design Studio, designers
Porsche Automobil Holding SE, German, founded 1931, manufacturer
45⅞ × 76⅜ × 182¹³⁄₁₆ inches; 3,685 pounds
Courtesy of Porsche Museum, Stuttgart, Germany

MODELS

General Motors Firebird I XP-21 Scale Model, 1953
Fiberglass, metal components, and rubber wheels
Harley J. Earl (American, 1893–1969), designer
Robert F. "Bob" McLean (American, life dates unknown) and GM Styling Section staff, designers
27 × 30 × 84 inches
Courtesy of GM Heritage Center, Warren, Michigan

Sculpture in Motion, 1954
Clay, epoxy resin, and nitrocellulose lacquer
Virgil M. Exner, Sr. (American, 1909–1973), designer
26 × 9 × 4 inches
Courtesy of Scott Grundfor and Kathleen Redmond, Arroyo Grande, California

WORKS ON PAPER

Norman Bel Geddes
American, 1893–1958
Motor Car Number 9 blueprint, ca. 1932
Blueprint on colored paper
19¾ × 29⅞ inches
Courtesy Edith Lutyens and Norman Bel Geddes Foundation/Harry Ransom Center, The University of Texas at Austin

Norman Bel Geddes
American, 1893–1958
Motor Car Number 9 composite sketch, ca. 1932
Charcoal on paper
10¾ × 8⅜ inches
Courtesy Edith Lutyens and Norman Bel Geddes Foundation/Harry Ransom Center, The University of Texas at Austin

Norman Bel Geddes
American, 1893–1958
Motor Car Number 9 drawing, ca. 1932
Charcoal on paper
8⅜ × 10¾ inches
Courtesy Edith Lutyens and Norman Bel Geddes Foundation/Harry Ransom Center, The University of Texas at Austin

Norman Bel Geddes
American, 1893–1958
Motor Car Number 9 drawing, ca. 1932
Charcoal on paper
8⅜ × 10¾ inches
Courtesy Edith Lutyens and Norman Bel Geddes Foundation/Harry Ransom Center, The University of Texas at Austin

Unknown Photographer
Photograph of Motor Car Number 9 model (designed by Norman Bel Geddes), ca. 1932
Gelatin silver print
4¼ × 5 inches
Courtesy Edith Lutyens and Norman Bel Geddes Foundation/Harry Ransom Center, The University of Texas at Austin

Foehl
Nationality and life dates unknown
Untitled (People Mover), ca. 1935
Gouache on colored paper, enhanced by chalk, colored pencil, and ink wash
17 × 27½ inches
Brett Snyder Collection

Arthur "Art" Ross
American, 1913–1981
Dual Pontoon Buick, 1940
Airbrush and pastel on colored paper
30 × 39 inches
Brett Snyder Collection

George S. Lawson
American, 1907–1987
Futuristic Bus, 1946
Gouache on colored paper
24 × 29 inches
Collection of Jean S. and Frederic A. Sharf

George S. Lawson
American, 1907–1987
Futuristic Vehicle and Trailer, 1946
Gouache on colored paper
13 × 32 inches
Collection of Jean S. and Frederic A. Sharf

Carl Renner
American, 1923–2001
Cadillac Convertible Concept Car, 1951
Water-based media on black paper
76 × 242 inches
Collection of Jean S. and Frederic A. Sharf

Carl Renner
American, 1923–2001
Chevrolet Convertible Concept Car, 1952
Water-based media on black paper
69 × 94 inches
Collection of Jean S. and Frederic A. Sharf

Carl Renner
American, 1923–2001
GM XP-33 Dart Two-Seat Show Car, ca. 1954
Colored pencil on tracing paper
21 × 24 inches
Collection of Jean S. and Frederic A. Sharf

Carl Renner
American, 1923–2001
GM XP-33 Le Sabre Dart, ca. 1954
Colored pencil on tracing paper
21 × 24 inches
Collection of Jean S. and Frederic A. Sharf

Carl Renner
American, 1923–2001
GM XP-33 Le Sabre Dart, ca. 1954
Colored pencil on tracing paper
21 × 24 inches
Collection of Jean S. and Frederic A. Sharf

George W. Walker
American, 1896–1993
Untitled (Two Views of a Concept Car), ca. 1957
Gouache enhanced by chalk, colored pencil, and ink wash
36 × 51 inches
Brett Snyder Collection

Peter W. Wozena
American, 1918–2006
Proposal for Cadillac, 1957
Watercolor enhanced by ink and colored and graphite pencils
21 × 25 inches
Brett Snyder Collection

Wayne R. Vieira
American, life dates unknown
Untitled, ca. 1958
Gouache enhanced by chalk, colored pencil, and ink wash
30 × 36 inches
Brett Snyder Collection

Syd Mead
American, born 1933
Untitled (Gyroscopically Stabilized Two-wheel Car), ca. 1960
Gouache enhanced by chalk, colored pencil, and ink wash
29 × 40½ inches
Brett Snyder Collection

Wayne Cherry
American, born 1937
"Runabout" Design Concept, ca. 1964
Gouache enhanced by chalk, colored pencil, and ink wash
19 × 30 inches
Brett Snyder Collection

Paolo Martin
Italian, born 1943
Ferrari Modulo design illustration, 1967
Mixed-media work on paper
Dimensions unknown
Courtesy of Paolo Martin

Paolo Martin
Italian, born 1943
Ferrari Modulo design sketch, ca. 1970
Mixed-media work on paper
Dimensions unknown
Courtesy of Paolo Martin

Alan Young
American, life dates unknown
Untitled (Futuristic Rendering of Wedge-shaped Car), 1977
Gouache enhanced by chalk, colored pencil, and ink wash
26 × 34 inches
Brett Snyder Collection

Buckminster Fuller
American, 1895–1983
Chuck Byrne
American, born 1943
Patent: Motor Vehicle–Dymaxion Car, 1981
Screenprint in white ink on clear polyester film overlaid on screenprint
30 × 40 inches
Courtesy Carl Solway Gallery, Cincinnati, Ohio

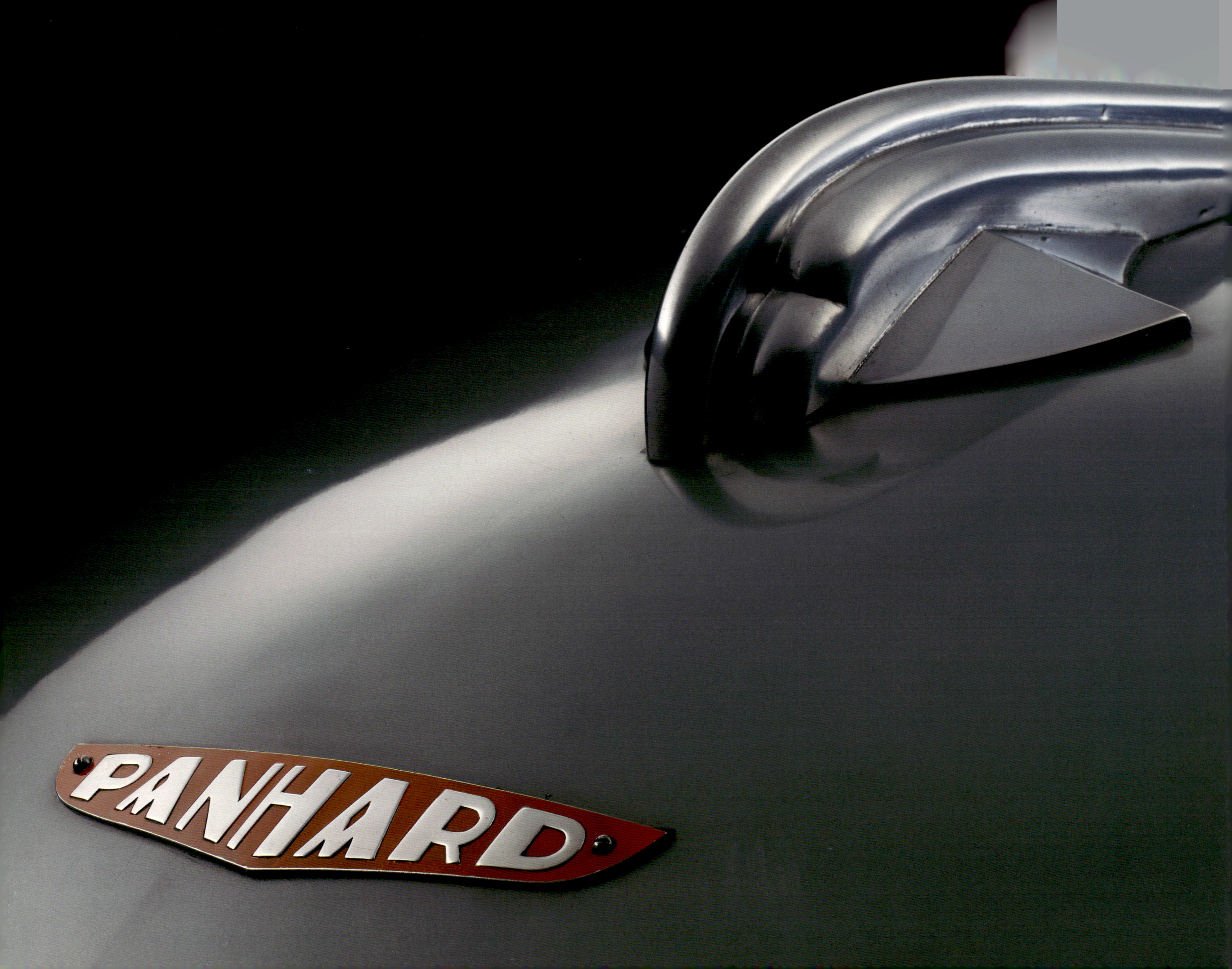
PANHARD

Image Credits

© Robert Doisneau/Rapho: figs. 1, 42

Courtesy of General Motors, from the Brett Snyder Collection: fig. 2

Courtesy General Motors: figs. 3, 16, 21, 29, 30, 51, 53

Courtesy Chrysler Group LLC: fig. 4

Courtesy of Brett Snyder: figs. 5, 32, 50, 55

Georges Lepape/Vogue © Condé Nast 1925: fig. 6

© Fondation Le Corbusier/ARS, 2013: fig. 7

Courtesy of the Free Library of Philadelphia: fig. 8

Photo by Michael Furman: figs. 9, 36

Photo by Michael McKelvey: fig. 10

Courtesy Edith Lutyens and Norman Bel Geddes Foundation/Harry Ransom Center, The University of Texas at Austin: figs. 12, 13

Courtesy of Jean S. and Frederic A. Sharf, photo by Mark Wallison: figs. 17–20, 22

Courtesy of FordImages.com: fig. 23

Brett Snyder Collection; photo by Mike Jensen: figs. 24, 28

Courtesy of the Guild of Automotive Restorers: fig. 25

© The Bugatti Trust: fig. 26

Courtesy of Brett Snyder, from the Bill Brownlie Collection: fig. 27

Courtesy of the Auburn Cord Duesenberg Automobile Museum, Auburn, Indiana: fig. 31

© Photofest: fig. 33

Courtesy of Scott Grundfor: fig. 34

Ken Gross Archives: fig. 37

Courtesy of *Motor Trend* magazine, source Interlink Companies, and Ken Gross Archives: fig. 38

Courtesy of Scott Grundfor and Brett Snyder: fig. 35

Courtesy Detroit Historical Society: figs. 39, 40

Courtesy Carl Solway Gallery, Cincinnati, Ohio: fig. 41

Voiture Minimum: Le Corbusier and the Automobile, p. 46: fig. 43

Alfa Romeo Automobilismo Storico, Centro Documentazione (Arese, Milano): figs. 44, 52

No credit: fig. 45

Photo by Giorgio Lotti/Mondadori/Getty Images: fig. 46

Courtesy of Paolo Martin: figs. 47, 48

Photo by Steve Jackson: fig. 49

Courtesy Sloan Collection: fig. 54

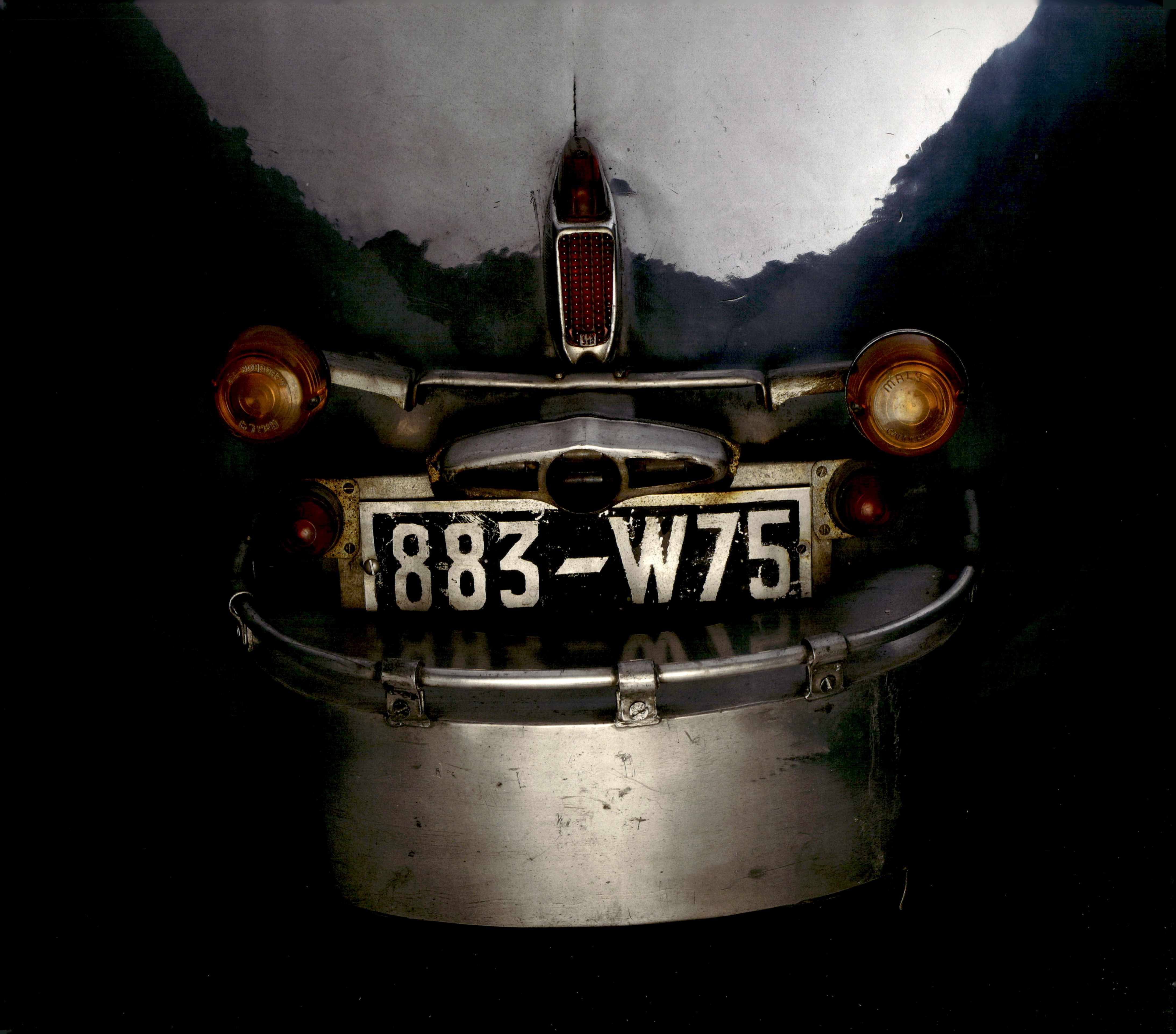
883-W75

Dream Cars: Innovative Design, Visionary Ideas,
is organized by the High Museum of Art, Atlanta.

PRESENTING SPONSOR

PORSCHE

LEAD SPONSORS   CONTRIBUTING SPONSORS   ADDITIONAL SUPPORT PROVIDED BY

AutoTrader.com   AutoTrader Classics   Manheim   WSB-TV 2 ATLANTA   The Atlanta Journal-Constitution   AM 750 WSB NEWS TALK RADIO   DELTA   NAPA   ART WORKS

Published on the occasion of the exhibition
Dream Cars: Innovative Design, Visionary Ideas
May 21–September 7, 2014.

Copyright © 2014 High Museum of Art, Atlanta

All rights reserved. No part of this publication may be reproduced or transmitted in any form or by any means, electronic or mechanical, including photocopy, recording, or any information storage or retrieval system, without permission in writing from the publisher.

Library of Congress Cataloging-in-Publication Data
—Schleuning, Sarah.
 Dream cars : innovative design, visionary ideas / Sarah Schleunung, Ken Gross.
     pages cm
 Includes bibliographical references and index.
 ISBN 978-0-8478-4263-6 (hardback)
1. Experimental automobiles--Exhibitions. 2. Antique and classic cars--Exhibitions. 3. Automobiles--Drawings--Exhibitions. 4. Product design--Exhibitions. 5. High Museum of Art--Catalogs. I. Gross, Ken, 1941- II. High Museum of Art. III. Title.
 TL7.U62A85 2014
 629.222--dc23   2014000794

2014 2015 2016 2017 / 10 9 8 7 6 5 4 3 2 1

Angela Jaeger, Senior Manager of Creative Services
Heather Medlock, Print Production Coordinator
Rachel Bohan, Associate Editor
Ewan Green, Graphic Designer

First published in the United States of America in 2014 by

High Museum of Art
1280 Peachtree Street, N.E.
Atlanta, Georgia 30309
www.high.org

in association with

Skira Rizzoli Publications, Inc.
300 Park Avenue South
New York, NY 10010
www.rizzoliusa.com

Produced by Marquand Books, Inc., Seattle
www.marquand.com

Edited by Rachel Bohan
Designed and typeset by Susan E. Kelly
Typeset in Nexa and Nexa Slab
Proofread by Ted Gilley
Color management by iocolor, Seattle
Printed and bound in China by Arton Color Printing Co., Ltd.

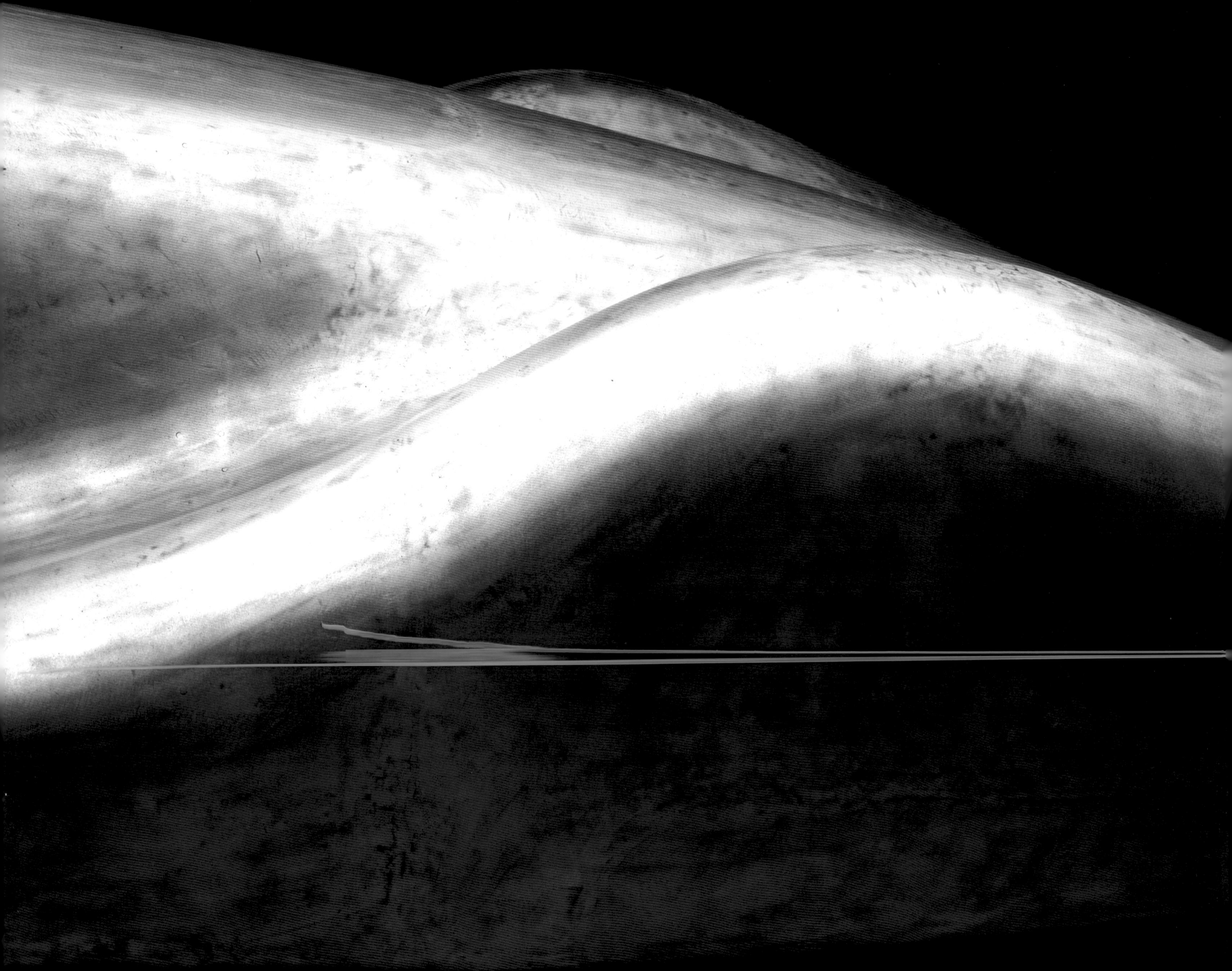

CW01276191

LE MANS 1990-99

For Eva

© Quentin Spurring 2014 (text and statistics)

All rights reserved. No part of this publication may be reproduced or stored in a retrieval system or transmitted, in any form or by any means, electronic, mechanical, photocopying, recording or otherwise, without prior permission in writing from Evro Publishing.

Published in July 2014

Officially licensed by the Automobile Club de l'Ouest

ISBN 978-0-9928209-1-6

Published by Evro Publishing
Westrow House, Holwell, Sherborne, Dorset DT9 5LF
www.evropublishing.com

Printed and bound in the UK by Gomer Press Limited,
Llandysul Enterprise Park, Llandysul, Ceredigion SA44 4JL

Edited by Mark Hughes
Designed by Richard Parsons

Author's acknowledgements
The author acknowledges the commitment of the Automobile Club de l'Ouest to this project, and is especially obliged to Hervé Guyomard and Stéphanie Lopé for their invaluable help in the ACO Archives. Among many other individuals who have assisted, exceptional contributions have been made to the photographic content of this and other volumes in the series by Tim Wright and Kathy Ager at LAT Photographic, and by Jens Torner in Porsche's *Historisches Archiv*.

Jacket illustrations
The front cover depicts the factory-entered Porsche 911 GT1-98 of Allan McNish, Stéphane Ortelli and Laurent Aïello on its way to victory in the 1998 race. The start that year is shown opposite, with Martin Brundle's Toyota vying for the lead with Bernd Schneider's Mercedes-Benz. On the spread overleaf is a view of the Tertre Rouge corner looking back from the start of the Mulsanne straight (part of the old trunk road south to Tours) during the 1995 race. On the back cover, from top left, are four more of the decade's winning cars: the Nielsen/Cobb/Brundle Jaguar XJR12-LM (1990), the Herbert/Weidler/Gachot Mazda 787B (1991), the Brabham/Hélary/Bouchut Peugeot 905B (1993) and the Lehto/Sekiya/Dalmas McLaren F1 GTR (1995).

LE MANS

THE OFFICIAL HISTORY OF THE WORLD'S GREATEST MOTOR RACE

1990-99

24 HEURES DU MANS

Quentin Spurring

CONTENTS

INTRODUCTION	**6**
1990 SEVENTH HEAVEN FOR JAGUAR	**14**
1991 MAZDA FIRST FOR JAPAN	**54**
1992 A HOME WIN FOR PEUGEOT	**86**
1993 PEUGEOT CLOSES OUT THE PODIUM	**114**
1994 PORSCHE PULLS A FAST ONE	**146**
1995 McLAREN STARS ON A NEW STAGE	**184**
1996 OLD FOES JOIN FORCES	**222**
1997 JOEST'S REPEAT PERFORMANCE	**260**
1998 PORSCHE'S GT COMES GOOD	**296**
1999 HIGH FIVES IN GERMANY	**330**
1990-99 STATISTICS	**366**
BIBLIOGRAPHY	**379**
INDEX	**380**

LE MANS 7.5t EN TRANSIT

ANGERS
ARNAGE
LA FLÈCHE
Z.I. Sud

CHARTRES PARIS

ALENÇON LAVAL
LA FERTÉ-BERNARD

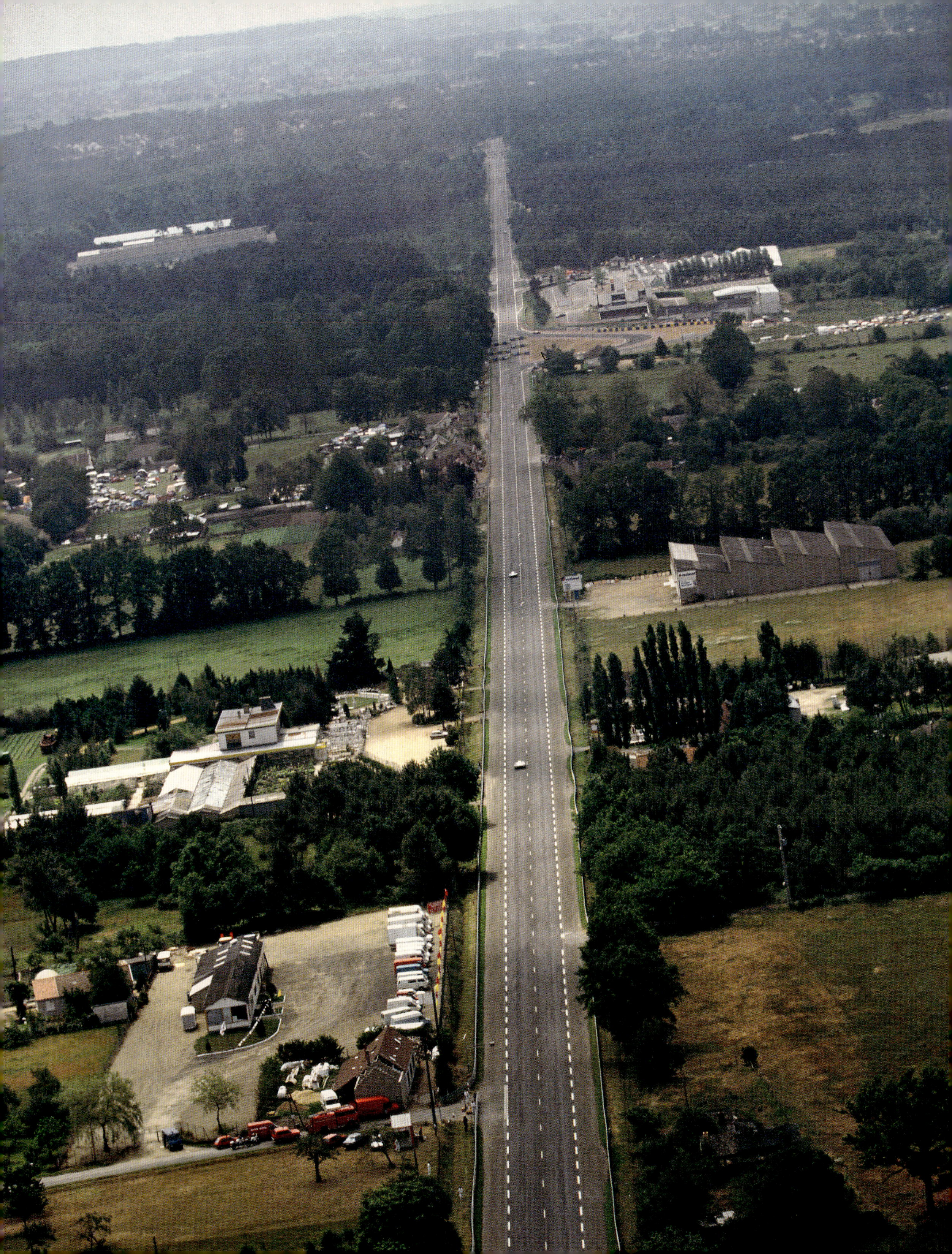

INTRODUCTION
TO ROCK BOTTOM AND BACK AGAIN

The reputation of the world's greatest motor race came under threat at the start of the extraordinary decade covered by this book, but desire to win the handsome Le Mans 24 Hours trophy was undiminished. The unique status of the race saved the day, along with pragmatism and judicious invention on the part of the organizing body, the Automobile Club de l'Ouest.

This decade was difficult for the ACO, and inevitably characterized by unstable technical regulations. Yet, before it ended, the race had been contested by full-on factory teams representing no fewer than 15 automobile manufacturers – Tier 1 companies Audi, BMW, Chrysler, Honda, Jaguar, Mazda, Mercedes-Benz, Nissan, Peugeot, Porsche and Toyota, plus the smaller enterprises of Lotus, Marcos, McLaren and Panoz.

This was a dramatic reverse. The ACO and its regional partners – the Département de la Sarthe, the Région des Pays de la Loire, the Communauté Urbaine du Mans, and the Ville du Mans – had owned and managed the event and its venue since 1985, and had enjoyed unprecedented manufacturer participation in 1988-89. How quickly things can change!

In 1990, the syndicate lost a central component of the Le Mans mystique – the world-famous, 3.5-mile Mulsanne straight. As shown at left, it had to be chicaned after being declared 'dangerous' by the Fédération Internationale du Sport Automobile during its cynical political manipulation, intended to force the Le Mans syndicate to toe its commercial line. And then, in 1992, FISA's ill-conceived new sportscar racing regulations caused the smallest Le Mans field for 60 years…

This had all started in 1988, when FISA had allowed the key stakeholder in Formula 1 new powers in all European-based professional motorsport. At that time, the successful Group C 'fuel formula' had taken sportscar racing (and Le Mans) to dizzy heights, with seven mainstream manufacturers directly involved. Yet FISA's recently appointed VP in charge of promotions, working with the president of its Manufacturers Commission, had resolved to replace Group C with a new formula for high-end sports-racing cars. Bernie Ecclestone and Max Mosley had specified lightweight (750kg) racing coupés powered by the naturally aspirated, 3.5-litre engines that were to be introduced in Formula 1 the following year. And FISA – the motorsport arm of the Fédération Internationale de l'Automobile (FIA) – had adopted this as its premier category.

The new FIA Sportscar class undermined the professional sportscar racing community, which regarded it as a thinly disguised move to herd them towards Grand Prix racing: that same year, only two manufacturers were engaged in Formula 1, both low-volume producers.

Pending the full adoption of the new rules, in 1990-91, Le Mans was won by prototypes of the Group C genre – a Jaguar, then a Mazda that became the first Japanese (and rotary-engined) winner. Then FISA manipulated the regulations so as to favour its new, 750-kilo, ground-effect FIA Sportscars. These were fantastic racing cars, thrilling to watch (and to drive). But they were 'sprint' cars, and prohibitively expensive for all but a handful of manufacturers. Peugeot espoused the concept and managed to win Le Mans in 1992 and 1993 – when the much-vaunted new Sportscar World Championship had already been cancelled for lack of entries.

The FIA blithely declared that GT-type cars were the future for endurance racing. But the ACO – still facing a serious shortage of suitable cars – understood that manufacturers would always want to

LE MANS

CHALLENGE ECOENERGIE

An Index of Energy Efficiency competition had been staged within the context of the Le Mans 24 Hours since 1959, but it was only organized in the first two races of this decade: a Group C2 Spice-Cosworth won in 1990, and a Category 2 Sauber-Mercedes in 1991. The contest was intended to focus the minds of engineers to using as little fuel as possible while deploying sufficient power to win their classes. In 1992, the 'Challenge Ecoenergie' was regarded as irrelevant to the FIA's new sportscar racing class.

The parameters that were applied in the Index competition were devised by the ACO in association with the Jeune Chambre Economique du Mans. Each individual car was given fuel consumption targets against projected average speeds, and the results were calculated using the following formula:

$$CE = \frac{QR}{Q}$$

where CE was the car's index score (*Coefficient d'Equivalence*), QR was the consumption target corresponding with its average speed (including pitstops), and Q was the actual fuel consumption it had achieved.

The period over which the parameters were measured was from the start of the race until the last fuel stop before the start of the 23rd hour, when the average speed calculation was made. The winner was the car achieving the greatest improvement on its target at that point (although it had to go on to qualify as a finisher).

ENTRY LISTS

The entry lists for the annual Le Mans 24 Hours are living things, changing constantly after publication of the acceptances (normally during April), before and after any Prequalifying sessions, and occasionally even during the scrutineering process at the start of race week. Inevitably, some teams withdraw, and are replaced by others whose entries had either been refused or had failed to prequalify. Some entrants will need to change their cars, entries will be taken over by other teams, and so forth. These factors account for apparently missing race numbers, and explains why some of the numbers in the final list might not correspond with others in the same class.

With a few exceptions where late no-shows might be of particular interest, the entry lists in this book generally show the cars that were expected by the scrutineers. If a car listed is shown without a tyre supplier or a weight, for example, it was not presented for technical inspection, and took no part in the event.

win Le Mans with purpose-designed prototypes. Its technical team set out to give GT-type racecars and prototypes a level playing field.

To this end, it began to evolve a concoction of variable parameters for application to any type of car – weights, fuel cell capacities, engine air-inlet restrictors, turbocharger 'boost' pressures, tyre widths. This system would prove to be very workable. It resulted in an over-subscribed entry list as early as 1994 (and the first 'Prequalifying' sessions 12 months later), and was expertly developed over subsequent years. It would become crucial to the outcomes at Le Mans far into the future.

It did not foresee, however, an undesirable effect of the FIA's ill-conceived new 'Grand Touring' regulations. When the new GT1 class came into being in 1994, the entry included independently produced racing versions of Bugatti, Chrysler, Ferrari, Porsche and Venturi road cars. These all satisfied 'the spirit of the regulations'. But the fastest of them was more than 12 seconds slower round the lap than Porsche's 'Dauer 962LM' – nothing but a racing sports-prototype with road car type approval, taking full advantage of a lax homologation rule specifying the production of a single equivalent road car. The ACO could find no way to exclude this outrageous deviant, and a 'Dauer' won the race.

Porsche's 'reverse-engineering' methodology was prohibited as soon as possible, but the homologation rule was not rewritten,

1990-99

so its example was soon followed by other manufacturers with brand-new cars.

The car that exacerbated the situation was the McLaren F1 GTR. It was based on a genuine roadgoing 'supercar' but it was a mid-engined, advanced-composites monocoque with competition-standard chassis, powertrain, suspension, braking and aerodynamic systems. Porsche knew that it could not compete with the McLaren using the rear-engined configuration and pressed-steel monocoque of its 911-series road car. It initiated the Dauer project believing that the McLaren would contest Le Mans in 1994, but it didn't appear until 1995. It then won a very wet race outright.

This was the year in which GT1 should have blossomed. In the knowledge that it was no longer allowed to reverse-engineer a sports-prototype, seven manufacturers were committed to GT1 with production-based cars. The McLaren beat them all easily.

In 1996, Porsche responded with a mid-engined GT1 car, defeated the McLaren – but lost the race to a Porsche-engined prototype. In 1997, when McLaren turned the tables on Porsche but the overall win fell to the very same prototype, the GT1 Porsche had only the front-end of the production model. And Nissan produced a totally new GT1 sports-prototype coupé, with brand styling cues. So did Mercedes-Benz.

Inevitably, someone was going to go the whole hog. In 1998,

TO ROCK BOTTOM AND BACK AGAIN 9

Toyota came with a full-race prototype masquerading unashamedly as a GT car, with no brand styling whatsoever. The GT-One should have won both the next two races, but unluckily failed to do so. In 1998, Porsche's GT1 project finally delivered. In 1999, when the ACO was finally able to stop this nonsense by merging the GT1 and Le Mans Prototype categories, the victor was an honest, open-cockpit spyder from BMW – the sixth manufacturer to win Le Mans in this decade.

The trend throughout the 1990s was towards racing cars, produced by multi-faceted and multi-talented engineering teams, that could be thrashed for 24 hours. Rapid developments in mechanical and aerodynamic grip, fuel efficiency and new materials maintained the original ethos of this race, dating back to its inception in 1923, as the ultimate proving ground for the automobile industry. Over time, 205mph (330kph) on the emasculated *Ligne Droite* evolved as a lowered top-speed target of compromise aerodynamic designs, and this was achieved (and sometimes exceeded) pretty much by all the front-running cars.

Le Mans remained a genuinely international event. A remarkable total of 622 drivers from 32 countries participated in the 1990s. Sadly, there was a fatality: that of young French *comingman* Sébastien Enjolras, whose WR-Peugeot crashed during a Prequalifying session in 1997.

People enter the Le Mans 24 Hours not through any sense of danger, but because it is very, very difficult – supremely demanding on man and machine, a unique test of driving, management, strategic and engineering competence. This never changed. Throughout the 1990s, as in previous decades in its history, the 24-hour race required the competing cars to cover more racing miles over a single weekend than an entire Grand Prix season.

It is no wonder that the satisfaction gained even by finishing Le Mans can be seen on the faces of the people who do so for weeks afterwards – the drivers, of course, but also the designers, race engineers, mechanics, managers, team principals and everyone else involved. The joy of winning endures for the rest of their lives. Despite everything that was thrown at it in the early 1990s, this remained the greatest race in the world.

1990-99

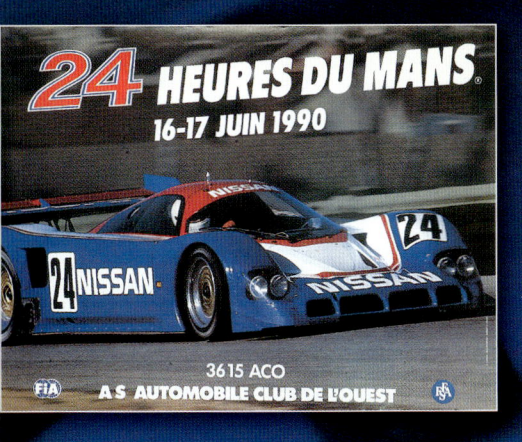

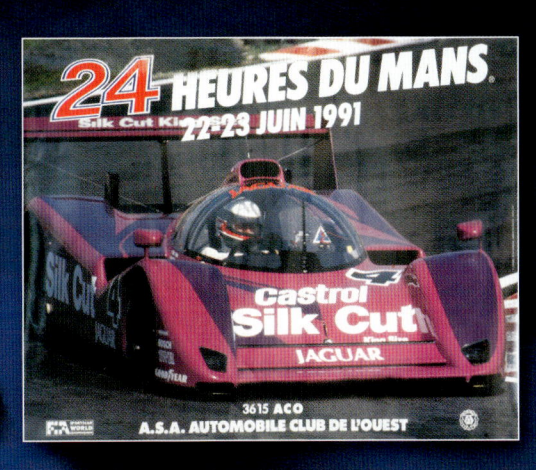

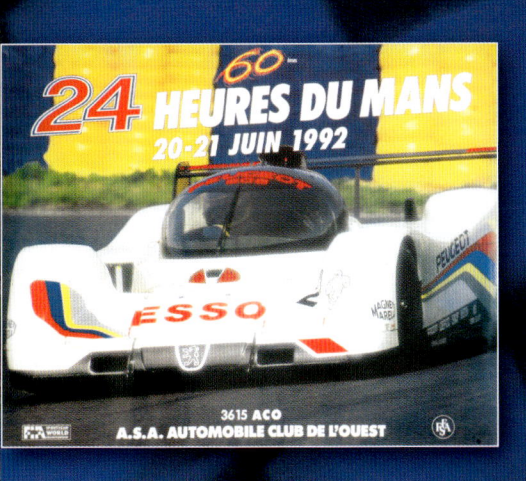

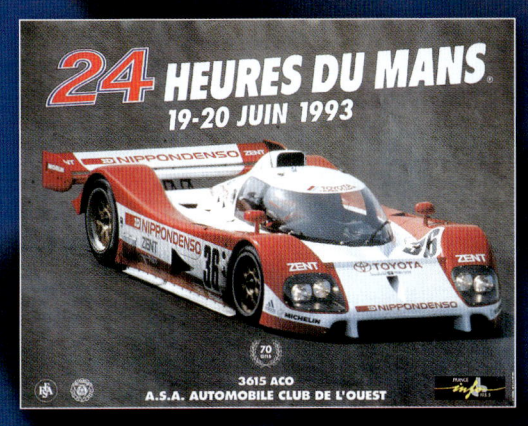

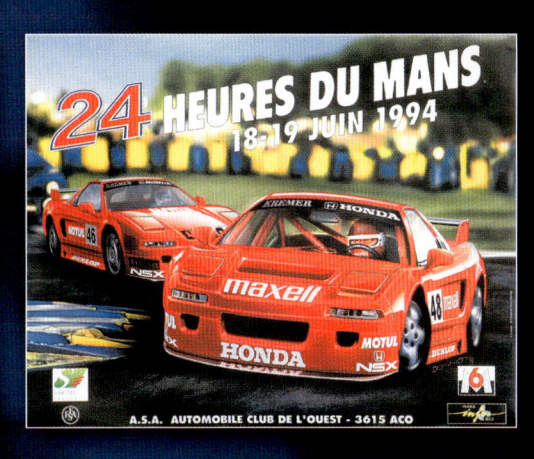

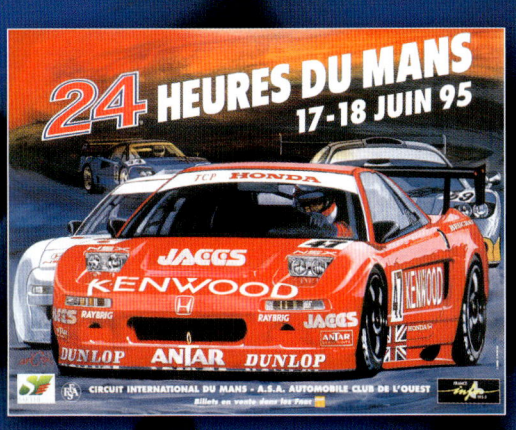

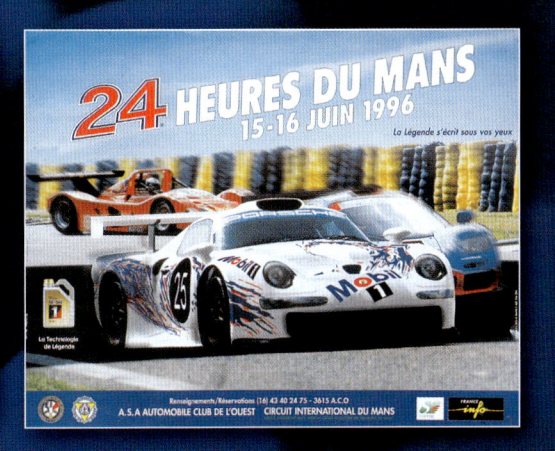

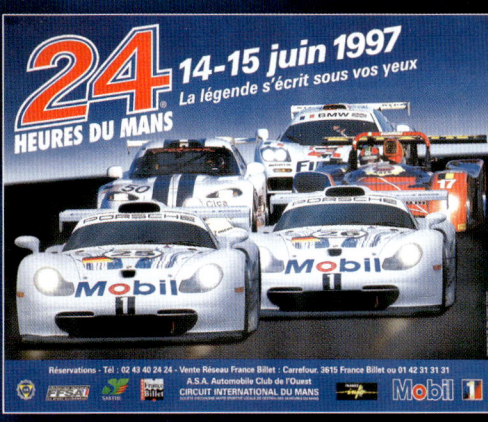

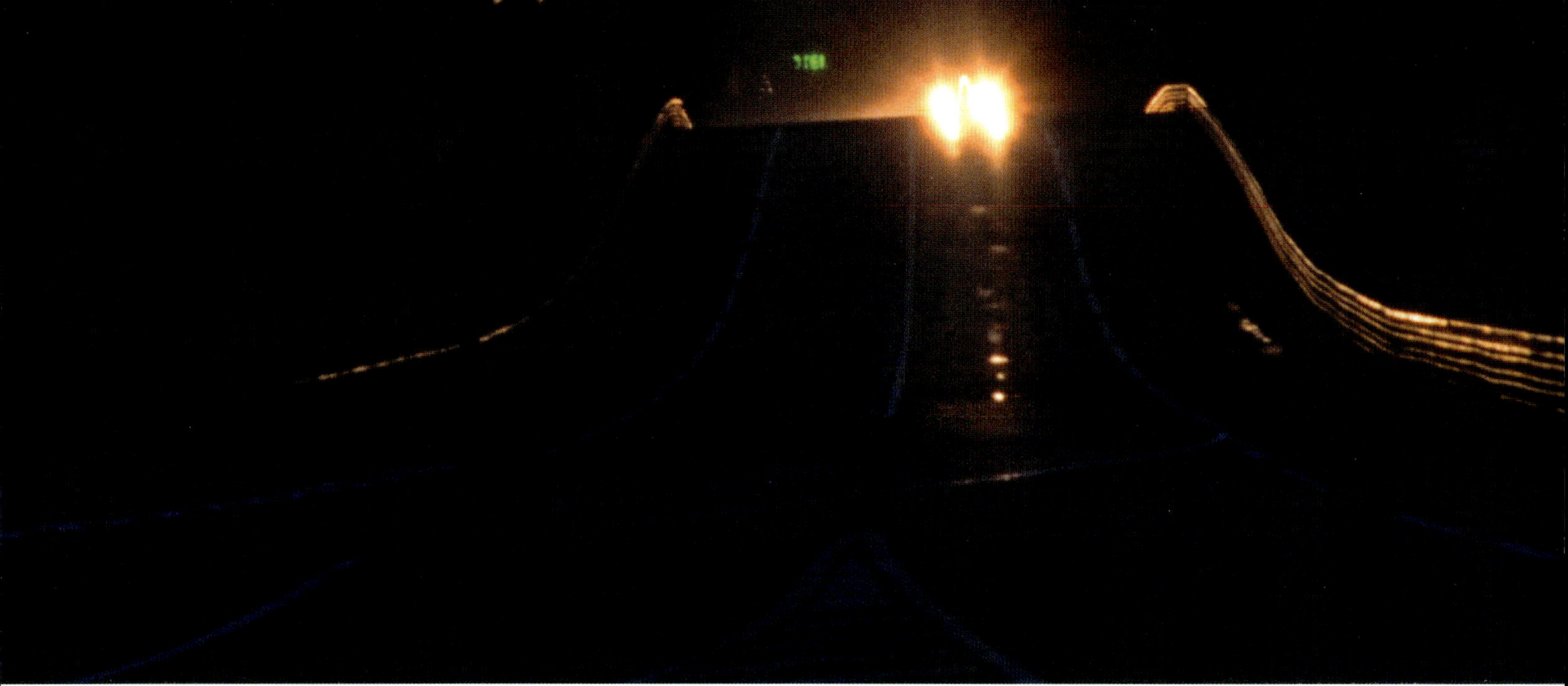

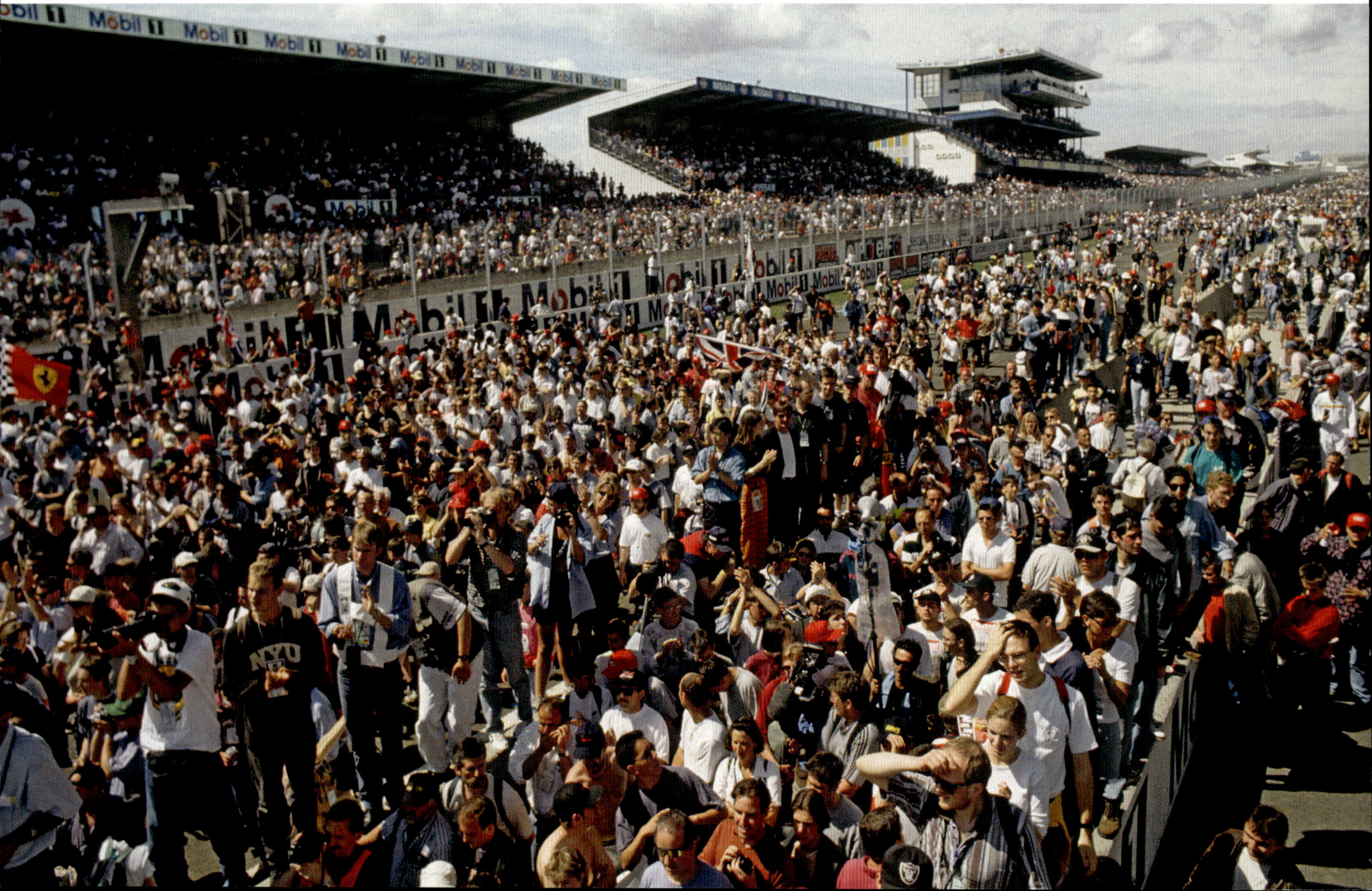
Mobil 1
NYU

1990-99

CIRCUIT DE LA SARTHE

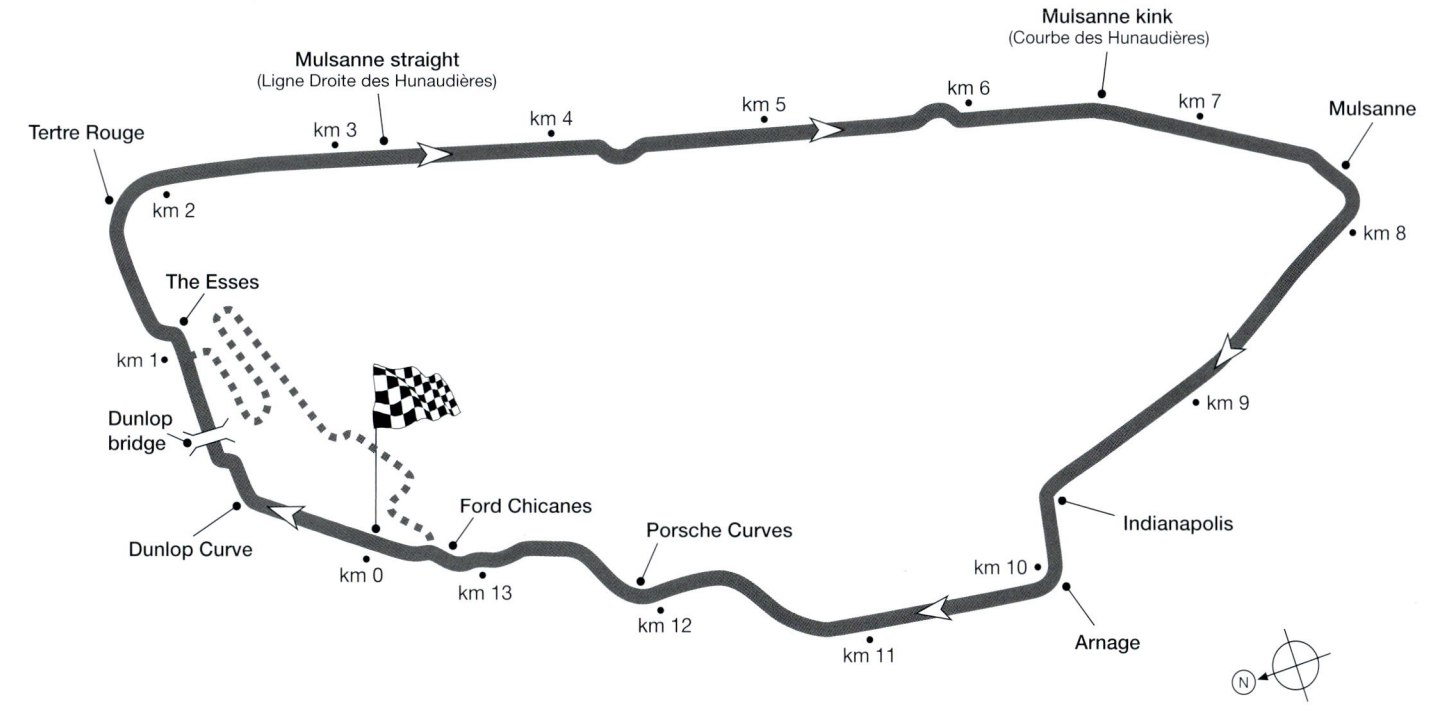

CIRCUIT LENGTH
1990-96 8.451 miles (13.600km)

1997-99 8.454 miles (13.605km)

LAP RECORDS (RACE)
1990-96 3m27.470s,
146.624mph (235.986kph),
Eddie Irvine,
Toyota TS010, 1993

1997-99 3m35.032s,
141.537mph (227.771kph),
Ukyo Katayama,
Toyota GT-One, 1999

RACE AND INDEX WINNERS

Year	Coupe Annuelle à la Distance	Indice Energétique
1990	Jaguar XJR12-LM John Nielsen (DK) Price Cobb (USA) Martin Brundle (GB)	Spice SE88C Robbie Stirling (CDN) James Shead (GB) Ross Hyett (GB)
1991	Mazda 787B Johnny Herbert (GB) Volker Weidler (D) Bertrand Gachot (F)	Sauber-Mercedes C11 Michael Schumacher (D) Karl Wendlinger (D) Fritz Kreutzpointner (D)
1992	Peugeot 905B Mark Blundell (GB) Derek Warwick (GB) Yannick Dalmas (F)	
1993	Peugeot 905B Geoff Brabham (AUS) Eric Hélary (F) Christophe Bouchut (F)	
1994	Dauer 962LM Mauro Baldi (I) Yannick Dalmas (F) Hurley Haywood (USA)	
1995	McLaren F1 GTR JJ Lehto (SF) Yannick Dalmas (F) Masanori Sekiya (J)	
1996	TWR-Porsche WSC95 Davy Jones (USA) Alex Wurz (A) Manuel Reuter (D)	
1997	TWR-Porsche WSC95 Michele Alboreto (I) Stefan Johansson (S) Tom Kristensen (DK)	
1998	Porsche 911 GT1-98 Allan McNish (GB) Laurent Aiello (F) Stéphane Ortelli (F)	
1999	BMW V12 LMR Pierluigi Martini (I) Yannick Dalmas (F) Jo Winkelhock (D)	

TO ROCK BOTTOM AND BACK AGAIN

LE MANS

1990
SEVENTH HEAVEN FOR JAGUAR

LE MANS

RACE INFORMATION

RACE DATE
16-17 June

RACE No
58

CIRCUIT LENGTH
8.451 miles/13.600km

HONORARY STARTER
Raymond Ravenel
President, Organisation
Internationale des Constructeurs
d'Automobiles (OICA)

MARQUES (ON GRID)

ADA	1
ALD	1
Cougar	3
Jaguar	4
Lancia	1
Mazda	3
Nissan	6
Porsche	18
Spice	7
Tiga	1
Toyota	3

STARTERS/FINISHERS
48/28

WINNERS

OVERALL
Jaguar

INDEX OF ENERGY EFFICIENCY
Spice

ENTRY LIST

No	Car	Entrant (nat)	cc	Engine	Tyres	Weight (kg)	Class
1	Jaguar XJR-12LM	Silk Cut Jaguar (GB)	6995	HE V12	Goodyear	931	C1
2	Jaguar XJR-12LM	Silk Cut Jaguar (GB)	6995	HE V12	Goodyear	938	C1
3	Jaguar XJR-12LM	Silk Cut Jaguar (GB)	6995	HE V12	Goodyear	953	C1
4	Jaguar XJR-12LM	Silk Cut Jaguar (GB)	6995	HE V12	Goodyear	949	C1
6	Porsche 962C	Joest Porsche Racing (D)	2994tc	F6	Goodyear	923	C1
7	Porsche 962C	Joest Porsche Racing (D)	2994tc	F6	Michelin	920	C1
8	Porsche 962C	Joest Porsche Racing (D)	2994tc	F6	Michelin	N/A	C1
9	Porsche 962C	Joest Porsche Racing (D)	2994tc	F6	Michelin	913	C1
10	Porsche 962C-K6	Porsche Kremer Racing (D)	2994tc	F6	Yokohama	922	C1
11	Porsche 962C-K6	Porsche Kremer Racing (D)	2994tc	F6	Yokohama	937	C1
12	Cougar C24S	Courage Compétition (F)	2994tc	Porsche F6	Goodyear	914	C1
13	Cougar C24S	Courage Compétition (F)	2994tc	Porsche F6	Goodyear	898	C1
14	Porsche 962C GTI	Richard Lloyd Racing (GB)	2994tc	F6	-	-	C1
15	Porsche 962C	Brun Motorsport (CH)	2994tc	F6	Yokohama	942	C1
16	Porsche 962C	Repsol Brun Motorsport (CH)	2994tc	F6	Yokohama	909	C1
16T	Porsche 962C	Repsol Brun Motorsport (CH)	3164tc	F6	Yokohama	N/A	C1
18	Porsche 962C	Team Davey (GB)	2994tc	F6	-	-	C1
19	Porsche 962C	Team Davey (GB)	2994tc	F6	Dunlop	921	C1
20	Porsche 962C	Team Davey (GB)	2994tc	F6	Dunlop	850	C1
21	Spice SE90C	Spice Engineering (GB)	3494	Cosworth DFR V8	Goodyear	783	C1/3.5
23	Nissan R90CP	Nissan Motorsports International (J)	3496tc	VRH35Z V8	Dunlop	936	C1
23T	Nissan R90CP	Nissan Motorsports International (J)	3496tc	VRH35Z V8	Dunlop	N/A	C1
24	Nissan R90CK	Nissan Motorsports Europe (GB)	3496tc	VRH35Z V8	Dunlop	904	C1
24T	Nissan R90CK	Nissan Motorsports Europe (GB)	3496tc	VRH35Z V8	Dunlop	N/A	C1
25	Nissan R90CK	Nissan Motorsports Europe (GB)	3496tc	VRH35Z V8	Dunlop	906	C1
26	Porsche 962C	Primagaz Compétition (F) Obermaier Racing (D)	2994tc	F6	Goodyear	937	C1
27	Porsche 962C	Primagaz Compétition (F) Obermaier Racing (D)	2994tc	F6	Goodyear	925	C1
30	Spice SE90C	GP Motorsport (GB)	3494	Cosworth DFR V8	Dunlop	N/A	C1/3.5
33	Porsche 962C	Team Schuppan Takefuji (GB)	2994tc	F6	Dunlop	910	C1
36	Toyota 90C-V	Toyota Team TOMS (J)	3169tc	R32V V8	Bridgestone	941	C1
37	Toyota 90C-V	Toyota Team TOMS (J)	3169tc	R32V V8	Bridgestone	939	C1
37T	Toyota 90C-V	Toyota Team TOMS (J)	3169tc	R32V V8	Bridgestone	N/A	C1
38	Toyota 90C-V	Toyota Team TOMS (J)	3169tc	R32V V8	Goodyear	947	C1
38T	Toyota 90C-V	Toyota Team TOMS (J)	3169tc	R32V V8	Goodyear	N/A	C1
42	Nissan R89C	Courage Compétition (F)	3496tc	VRH35Z V8	-	-	C1
43	Porsche 962C GTI	Italya Sports Richard Lloyd Racing (GB)	2994tc	F6	Goodyear	935	C1
44	Porsche 962C	Italya Sports Richard Lloyd Racing (GB)	2994tc	F6	Goodyear	922	C1
45	Porsche 962C	Alpha Racing Team (J)	2994tc	F6	Yokohama	919	C1
54	Lancia LC2 SP90	Mussato Action Car (I)	3050tc	Ferrari V8	Dunlop	907	C1
55	Porsche 962C	Team Schuppan Omron (GB)	2994tc	F6	Dunlop	924	C1
59	Eagle 700	Paul Canary/Eagle Performance Racing (USA)	10176	Chevrolet V8	Goodyear	N/A	C1
61	Norma M6	ASA Armagnac Bigorre (F)	3500	MGN W12	Avon	N/A	C1/3.5
63	Porsche 962C	Trust Racing Team (J)	2994tc	F6	Dunlop	913	C1
82	Nissan R89C	Courage Compétition (F)	3496tc	VRH35Z V8	Goodyear	943	C1
83	Nissan R90CK	Nissan Performance Technology (USA)	3496tc	VRH35Z V8	Goodyear	985	C1
84	Nissan R90CK	Nissan Performance Technology (USA)	3496tc	VRH35Z V8	Goodyear	951	C1
85	Nissan R89C	Team Le Mans (J)	3496tc	VRH35Z V8	Yokohama	929	C1
102	Spice SE89C	Graff Racing (F)	3298	Cosworth DFL V8	Goodyear	766	C2
103	Spice SE88C	Team Mako (GB)	3298	Cosworth DFL V8	Goodyear	781	C2
105	ADA 02B	ADA Engineering (GB)	3298	Cosworth DFL V8	Goodyear	759	C2
106	ALD C289	Automobiles Louis Descartes (F)	3298	Cosworth DFL V8	Dunlop	824	C2
107	Spice SE87C	Pierre-Alain Lombardi (CH)	3298	Cosworth DFL V8	Goodyear	812	C2
110	Argo JM19C	Argo Cars (GB)	3298	Cosworth DFL V8	Goodyear	813	C2
113	Cougar C20B	Etablissements Chéreau (F)	2826tc	Porsche F6	Goodyear	963	C2
116	Spice SE89C	PC Automotive (GB)	3298	Cosworth DFL V8	Goodyear	759	C2
128	Spice SE90C	Chamberlain Engineering (GB)	3955	Cosworth DFL V8	Goodyear	777	C2
131	Spice SE87C	GP Motorsport (GB)	3955	Cosworth DFL V8	Goodyear	782	C2
132	Tiga GC286/9	GP Motorsport (GB)	3955	Cosworth DFL V8	Avon	821	C2
201	Mazda 787	Mazdaspeed (J)	2616r	R26B 4R	Dunlop	831	GTP
201T	Mazda 787	Mazdaspeed (J)	2616r	R26B 4R	Dunlop	N/A	GTP
202	Mazda 787	Mazdaspeed (J)	2616r	R26B 4R	Dunlop	834	GTP
203	Mazda 767B	Mazdaspeed (J)	2616r	13J-MM 4R	Dunlop	852	GTP
230	Porsche 962 GS	Momo Gebhardt Racing (D)	2994tc	F6	Goodyear	954	GTP

1990

ENTRY

Never mind that Group C was doomed: this entry was on a par with those of the late 1980s. There were only three new FIA Sportscars, but a tremendous total of 41 passed through scrutineering in the old Group C1 division (including 20 Porsches), 11 in C2, and four in IMSA GTP. Mercedes-Benz, the 1989 winner, chose not to enter this non-championship event. But official teams were here from Jaguar, Mazda, Nissan, Porsche and Toyota. Alongside 15 factory entries, seven cars were operated by specialist constructors ADA, ALD, Argo, Courage, Norma and Spice.

The atmosphere in the paddock reflected a big Japanese presence. There were 19 Japanese-made cars, 15 drivers, seven teams from the national championship, and many sponsors.

QUALIFYING

Of the three Japanese manufacturers, Nissan was pushing the hardest. Its publicity images seemed to be everywhere in La Sarthe, and the promotion was strengthened when one of its cars went fastest on the first day. But Geoff Brabham's time was obliterated on the Thursday: with a very special engine in another Nissan, Mark Blundell went more than six seconds faster…

Oscar Larrauri lined up in a remarkable second place with a Brun Motorsport Porsche in front of the Nissans qualified by Masahiro Hasemi, Brabham and Kenneth Acheson. Hans-Joachim Stuck was next after his quasi-works Joest Porsche team mate, Jonathan Palmer, had emerged almost unhurt from a 200mph accident on the first day. Three 'atmo' Jaguars and Geoff Lees's Toyota completed the top 10.

RACE

The start was given under the hottest sun of the week and in front of 235,000 people. It happened without Acheson's Nissan, which parked up near the end of the pace lap with a broken transmission. Julian Bailey (from pole) and Larrauri set the early pace. Inside three laps, they were 10 seconds clear of Hasemi, who already had his mirrors full of four howling Jaguars. Then, amazingly, Larrauri took the lead. And kept it through the first fuel stops.

Blundell, having taken over from Bailey, regained the advantage during the second hour, and third driver Gianfranco Brancatelli kept the car in front as the short-tail Brun Porsche faded in the hands of Larrauri's slower co-drivers. With the *langheck* Joest Porsches in deep trouble with their traction, the top six were all Nissan and Jaguar.

At around 8pm, Brancatelli's leading Nissan collided with Aguri Suzuki's lapped Toyota in the fifth-gear approach to the Dunlop curves. The Toyota was wrecked against the barrier there, but the Nissan made it all the way round to pit-lane with a damaged nose and a puncture. Its attempted comeback would end in a transmission failure early on Sunday.

This accident left the race under dispute between Brabham's US-operated Nissan, co-driven by Derek Daly and Chip Robinson, and the Jaguars of Martin Brundle/Alain Ferté/David Leslie and John Nielsen/Price Cobb. The first of these XJRs was then delayed by a water leak, and the NPTI Nissan's lead went firm at 10:40pm when the other was set back by a change of brake pads.

Soon after midnight, the race was run under full-course caution for 14 minutes after a collision between Fabio Magnani's Lancia and Masanori Sekiya's Toyota on the high-speed run towards Indianapolis. The older Group C car was pitched violently over the barriers, but somehow its driver was not seriously injured.

The NPTI Nissan led for more than four hours, until 2:15am, when its own planned pad change put it into a long duel with the Nielsen/Cobb Jaguar. This was the situation at half-time, with the XJR of Jan Lammers/Andy Wallace/Franz Konrad third, and the Brun Porsche still hanging in there.

The fastest car through the night was the delayed XJR of Brundle/Ferté/Leslie. It recovered fifth place, only to be retired just before 7am with a water pump failure. Brundle was switched to the race-leading Jaguar to assist Nielsen in his heroic efforts to compensate for Cobb's dehydration problem, and to cope with a troublesome gearbox.

At 8.45am, the second-placed NPTI Nissan was retired with a fuel leak, and the pressure came off the Jaguar. Cobb could manage only one more shift, but the skill and experience of Nielsen and Brundle kept the V12 car in front. The XJR stripped its fourth gear and went without it to the chequer.

Soon after dawn, an 'off' by Konrad in the first new chicane had cost the Lammers Jaguar more than 10 minutes in repairs, but it completed a 1-2 for the manufacturer thanks to the dreadful luck of Brun Motorsport. Larrauri, overcome by exhaustion, did not drive between daybreak and 1pm, but Jesús Pareja and Walter Brun were able to protect second position. With barely 10 minutes remaining, the engine broke down.

So the best-placed Porsche was the Alpha team's super-reliable 962C, raced onto the podium by Tiff Needell/Anthony Reid/David Sears, ahead of Stuck's Joest entry, co-driven by Derek Bell and Frank Jelinski. Mazda picked up its expected GTP victory, but down in 20th position, only one place ahead of PC Automotive's C2-winning Spice-Cosworth.

SEVENTH HEAVEN FOR JAGUAR

LE MANS

ORGANISATION

As in 1989, the 1990 sportscar racing season was defined as "transitional" ahead of the full implementation of new technical regulations in 1991. Existing Group C hardware could still be raced alongside the new 750-kilo, F1-engined FIA Sportscars, but the latter had precedence in every way. Such was the inherent unsuitability of their 'sprint' engines for long-distance racing, and such the declared desire for TV marketability, that FISA reduced the 1990 race distances to 300 miles (with the single exception of Le Mans).

Clearly, this new formula threatened the viability of the historic 24 Hours. And it came with a series of unwelcome demands of all event promoters, undermining their established TV, timekeeping and other contracts so as to favour the governing body. In the autumn of 1989, negotiations between FISA and the *Syndicat Mixte* at Le Mans turned into a public row, fuelled by the intransigence of the president of both FISA and the broader FIA.

The intensely polemical Jean-Marie Balestre deviously introduced the 5.7km (3.5-mile) Mulsanne straight – part of the very soul of the 24 Hours – as a negotiating lever. Coincidentally, the Le Mans circuit licence was due to expire on 31 December 1989, and he threatened to insist on the installation of chicanes as a condition of its renewal. But Balestre offered the straight (and undertook to provide 60 entries) if the Le Mans syndicate assigned the TV rights to the FIA, and accepted its accreditation and timekeeping arrangements. The syndicate also had to commit to building a completely new pits and paddock complex, which was much needed anyway.

The syndicate agreed to these terms. But now a dispute arose over the duration of the contract. In return for committing to substantial capital investment, the syndicate needed a long-term deal, whereas the FIA insisted on a three-year agreement.

In December 1989, Balestre used the famous *Ligne Droite* to force the issue. He asked the World Motor Sport Council to approve a new rule, limiting the length of any straight, on any circuit, to 2km (1.2 miles). There were two kinks in the Mulsanne straight, but even the distance between them was 3.7km (2.3 miles).

Balestre reminded the WMSC delegates that a WM-Peugeot and a Sauber-Mercedes had recently exceeded 250mph (400kph) on the straight. He told them that, by voting against the new rule, they would effectively assume personal responsibility for any future fatality. The WMSC passed the measure unanimously. For all Balestre's protestations about "safety", it was clearly a political ploy, and a spiteful one at that.

The syndicate called a press conference in Paris at which the ACO president, Raymond Gouloumes, was supported by a national senator, two local MPs, and the mayor of Le Mans. They declared that, through the French ministry of sport, they would try to remove the 'sporting power' for the 24 Hours from FISA, so that their race could go ahead on an independent basis and with the straight intact.

There was a major problem with this strategy. As recently as April 1988, in Paris, the Tribunal de Grand Instance – the highest court in France – had made a ruling that put FISA beyond challenge. Convened to judge a separate matter, the court had concluded that FISA was "the sole organizer of International [motorsport] events" and had added: "No other party can substitute its judgement in safety matters."

It spelled the end of the globally famous Mulsanne straight. In future, chicanes would make the race more arduous for the drivers, and exact more punishing mechanical tolls from brakes, gearboxes, engines and tyres. The new chicanes drastically changed the setup parameters that had traditionally been required to win Le Mans. The untried circuit not only had two extra corners, but five (instead of the previous three) heavy braking points.

Land was acquired and work on the first chicane (pictured on pages 14-15) was sponsored by Nissan and Playstation, and on the second (below left and right) by Michelin. Together they added 65 metres to the lap distance, taking it to 8.451 miles (13.600km). In addition, a twisty new pit-lane entrance was created alongside the Virage Ford chicane. The protracted negotiations meant that the works began late and were not completed until February, a month after FISA's deadline, so the race was excluded from the championship.

FISA still compelled the ACO to admit any new-style FIA Sportscars that were ready. Although free of any fuel restriction, and at least 150kg lighter in weight, they would be merged into the Group C1 division. The non-championship status allowed the ACO to offer a temporary reprieve to otherwise redundant C2 cars.

The regulations covering the existing Group C coupés were unchanged from 1989. FISA would have hampered C1 cars with a 1000kg weight if Le Mans had been part of the championship, but now the numbers were as before: 900kg for C1 cars, 750kg for C2s. The respective total fuel allocations here were 2550 and 1815 litres, with maximum on-board fuel tankage of 100 litres in both classes. Cars in the IMSA GTP division, which were allowed to carry 120 litres in the USA, also had to be fitted here with 100-litre cells, and raced with the same fuel allocation as C1. The racing weights of GTP cars were established on a sliding scale according to engine swept volumes.

The ACO retained its proven timetable and sporting regulations. Scrutineering took place on the Monday and Tuesday of race week in the Quinconces des Jacobins, a big square in the shadow of the St Julien cathedral in the city centre. Qualifying sessions were held on the Wednesday and Thursday evenings, comprising two and a half hours in daylight, followed by an hour's break, and two more hours in darkness. All the drivers had to set qualifying times in the daylight and also to complete three timed laps in the dark.

The teams were now allowed to qualify drivers in T-cars. Any driver failing to achieve a lap-time within 120 percent of the average of the three fastest overall faced exclusion (although the ACO retained discretion to admit non-qualifiers).

The Friday was devoted to preparing the qualified cars for a 30-minute Saturday morning warm-up session, and the start at 4pm. A maximum of three drivers was allowed to race each car, and a minimum of two. Drivers were allowed to switch cars within the same team. No individual was allowed in the cockpit for more than 14 hours in total, or to drive a shift lasting more than four hours, while a break of at least 60 minutes had to be taken between shifts.

No more than four mechanics could be working on a car at any given moment in the pits (excluding specialist technicians from component suppliers). Engines had to be shut down during refuelling, and restarted using an on-board starter motor. Wheel changes could only be carried out after refuelling had been completed. An 80kph (50mph) speed limit was enforced in pit-lane. If a car stopped out on the circuit, only its driver was allowed to work on it, using only spare parts and tools carried on board, and no fuel could be added.

The night-time (during which all cars had to have fully functioning lights) was defined as between 9pm and 4:30am, and indicated by a purple light above the pit-lane.

To be classified as a finisher, a car had to pass under the chequered flag under its own power, and to cover at least 70pc of the distance covered by the winner. The distance covered by each car at the precise 24-hour mark was measured as whole laps completed plus a distance calculated on the basis of its average speed on the preceding lap.

The ACO retained its Index of Thermal Efficiency competition, encouraging development of fuel-efficient engines.

The race director was again Marcel Martin (pictured with the chequered flag), who served until 2000 in charge of 1300 volunteer flag marshals, 130 pit-lane marshals, and 50 other trackside officials. In addition to its technical inspection, media, catering and other staff, the ACO also supplied 120 doctors and 400 other first-aid personnel at every race.

SEVENTH HEAVEN FOR JAGUAR 19

LE MANS

A DOUBLE ONE-TWO

Jaguar's 1988-winning team returned in force, and went home to Oxfordshire with a terrific 1-2 – for the second time this season in a 24-hour race. The winning car (above) was raced by John Nielsen, Price Cobb and (on Sunday) Martin Brundle. It picked up the lead shortly before half-time and, despite gearbox and braking issues, finished four laps ahead of another XJR-12 driven by Jan Lammers, Andy Wallace and Franz Konrad.

The winning drivers are pictured on the podium, with Cobb at left, and Nielsen the precariously balanced centre of attention after a heroic individual performance. In February, the same three had shared the second-placed XJR-12 at Daytona, coincidentally four laps *behind* Lammers, Wallace and Davy Jones.

Tom Walkinshaw Racing's new FIA Sportscar scored a 1-2 at Silverstone in May, but the team did not enter its turbo V6 'sprint' car. Instead, four XJR-12s were assembled in its Kidlington factory specially for this year's race, two of them all-new. TWR's Allan Scott further enhanced the power curve of his 7-litre racing version of the production-based, 24-valve V12, so that it was strong from only 3500rpm. The Zytek-managed 'atmo' engine was still rated at 750bhp at 7000rpm. The five-speed March IndyCar/sportscar gearbox was modified to reduce temperatures. The 12LM also had heavier cast-iron brake discs with more cooling vanes. The winning car, deployed by TWR's Indiana-based IMSA GTP team under Tony Dowe and Ian Reed, had a different (and less effective) braking setup, and also shorter gears than the others.

LE MANS 24 HOURS 1990–99

1990

The 12LM specification was complicated by the team's switch from Dunlop crossply to bigger-diameter Goodyear radial tyres. These required revisions to the suspension geometry and the rear bodywork, which was a component of a much-altered aerodynamic package, devised by Tony Southgate and Alastair McQueen. McQueen spent much of March in the Imperial College wind-tunnel in London in devising a package giving 60pc more downforce for only 20pc more drag. The completed cars were run in a comparative test at Silverstone and then taken to the full-size tunnel at MIRA to ensure they were as identical as possible, so that the drivers' setup programmes could apply to all of them.

In qualifying, the 'atmo' quartet was caught by the ACO's speed trap at between 212 (342) and 220mph (354kph) – as much as 20mph slower than the 9LM had been 12 months before, without the chicanes. Jones emerged with the fastest XJR time (seventh) with the car he shared with Michel Ferté and Luis Perez-Sala, which was engineered by Ken Page. Immediately behind was Brundle, sharing with Alain Ferté and David Leslie and engineered by McQueen. Ninth overall was Nielsen with a re-imported car operated by Dave Benbow of TWR Inc, which had run the successful XJRs at Daytona. The fourth Jaguar was circumspectly qualified 17th by Lammers, engineered by Steve Farrell.

There turned out to be severe bumps in the track surface in the new chicanes. In Wednesday qualifying, the bumps worked loose a nut on Brundle's car, stopping him out on the circuit with no electrics, and a similar problem afflicted Sala on Thursday. The chicanes took more physical effort from the drivers, and Le Mans was no longer feasible with only two. TWR manipulated its squad in case of problems during the race. Sala qualified four seconds off the pace, and was stood down, leaving Jones/Ferté unaccompanied. Similarly Salazar was held in reserve, so that Nielsen/Cobb started on their own.

The four Jaguars were swiftly into their stride. Brundle led the pursuit of the leading turbocars, with Nielsen, the hard-charging Lammers and Jones just behind. Brundle/Ferté/Leslie hit the front before dusk. But at around 9pm, their water temperature started to climb. The cooling system was purged but the problem recurred after only six more laps. The next time, it took only five laps to recur, so water was clearly escaping somewhere. Finally, a pin-hole was found in the swirl pot, caused by material fatigue. While 10 minutes was invested in changing the pot, a broken windscreen was also replaced. After the car had resumed, a mechanic realized that, in the rush, he hadn't properly tightened one of the hose unions. Another stop was needed and the upshot of all this was that the car slipped to 14th.

Very hard driving overnight, when the car was the fastest by far, recovered fourth position. But at 6:50am, Ferté pitted in a cloud of steam. The water pump drivebelt had come adrift. The crew tried to put the belt back on, only to discover that the pump bearing had failed. End of race.

Walkinshaw and TM Roger Silman switched Brundle to TWR Inc's Nielsen/Cobb XJR, which had been leading the race since about 2:30am. Salazar, the 'reserve' in this car, was sent to join Jones/Ferté.

The US-based team had the upper hand in a long duel with its great IMSA rivals, NPTI and Nissan. Nielsen had valiantly been doing the bulk of the work because Cobb had become dehydrated and was struggling with physical exhaustion; he could do only one more stint before the end of the race. A planned pad-change and Nielsen-Brundle handover at 11:30am was extended when a piston jammed in the right-front brake caliper. The crew replaced the red-hot caliper in only six minutes, but it was almost enough to lose the lead to the Brun Porsche. The car had to be nursed over the rest of Sunday with increasingly dodgy brakes and a defective fourth gear. But otherwise it stayed strong to the end, and Walkinshaw ensured that Nielsen was in its cockpit when it reached the flag.

The Lammers/Wallace/Konrad Jaguar completed the 1-2 after the late retirement of the Brun Porsche. A delay during a Saturday evening pad change was caused by a manufacturing error that had omitted the bleed-hole relieving pressure from a brake fluid reservoir. However this XJR established itself in fourth position. It then lost a little time just after 2am when Lammers was punted over the gravel at the first new chicane when lapping Jacques Laffite's Porsche. Three hours later, Konrad crashed into the tyre wall at the same corner, damaging the tub, the nose section, the windscreen and a door. The sturdy Jaguar was fit to continue after only 10 minutes in pit-lane. A fired-up Lammers resumed in seventh place but the car was disputing fourth position with the best of the Joest Porsches by mid-morning.

After running on the lead lap throughout Saturday, the Jones/Ferté/Salazar XJR (pictured overleaf) was hampered by a sticking throttle either side of midnight. Eight minutes were lost, but worse was to follow. Just after daybreak, the combined effect of the bumps and the higher front downforce led to a structural failure of the bond between the nosebox and

SEVENTH HEAVEN FOR JAGUAR 21

LE MANS

the tub. The mechanics riveted the box back in place, but unfortunately one of them drilled a rivet hole through the monocoque and into a fluid reservoir, which had to be replaced. Then the engine started to misfire, then finally to lose oil pressure. One of the drivers had missed fourth gear, sending the RPM beyond 8500 before the rev-limiter could catch it. A weakened spring caused the V12 to drop a valve soon after noon.

It detracted little from the manufacturer's seventh Le Mans success.

BODY BLOW FOR BRUN

The hard-luck story of this Le Mans was all about Brun Motorsport. The Swiss-owned, German-based team produced by far the best performances with a Porsche all week. But it ended in tears virtually within sight of the flag, when the 962C was running second, quite unchallenged.

In qualifying, race engineers Rudi Walch and Roy Giddins put Oscar Larrauri in his regular FIA car, a standard, 1989-built aluminium monocoque from Gerd Schmidt's Porsche Kundensport operation. Like the Porsches operated by the Alpha and Kremer teams, this was prepared in short-tail configuration on the recommendation of Yokohama, which was supplying radial tyres for the first time here, and was cautious about very high speeds. Nevertheless the team had a high-boost, 3.2-litre qualifying engine, specially assembled by Alwin Springer's Andial company in Santa Ana, California, and making as much as 900bhp at 8000rpm on 2.5-bar inlet manifold pressure. The gifted 'Popi' responded with a tremendous time in the third session, and only missed out on pole position when NISMO sent out Mark Blundell in the fourth, with an even more powerful engine.

On Friday, Brun's crew fettled its new 962C for the race with a 3-litre, 760bhp flat-six from the factory. On Saturday, Larrauri was involved in a startline accident in the Renault 21 support race, and his harness bruised his ribs. Then he startled everyone (especially the Nissan drivers) by taking the lead of the 24 Hours on the fourth lap. And holding it…

The Brun Porsche was less strong when Larrauri handed it to Jesús Pareja, and then lost a little more pace when team owner Walter Brun took over. Yet it stayed in contention into the night and, at half-distance, was racing in fourth position, only one lap down.

At this point, Larrauri was sick in the cockpit, a legacy of the Renault accident. He was stood down for the rest of the morning. But Pareja and Brun rose to the occasion: the 962C was only two laps behind the leader at 9am. After losing a lap replacing a flat battery, the car then survived Pareja's collision with Jacques Laffite's Joest Porsche at the Ford chicane. It kept second place through the morning, closing to within a lap of the leading Jaguar when it encountered a brake problem. Larrauri tried one more stint, but was still unwell. It was obvious, anyway, that the faster Jaguar could not be caught.

In the final hour, a loose screw on an engine oil-line began to leak lubricant. With 17 minutes to run, Walch saw the oil pressure dive on the telemetry, and radioed Pareja to slow the car. Smoking heavily (pictured), it crept as far as Mulsanne corner. That was where the engine seized.

Brun's other entry was a one-year-old honeycomb/carbon 'clone' chassis from John Thompson's TC Prototypes company in Northampton, and was raced by Harald Huysman, Massimo Sigala and Bernard Santal. It failed to improve the mood of Brun's desperately disappointed team manager, Peter Reinisch. All three drivers struggled with the brakes, resulting in several off-track excursions, and the 3-litre engine was on its last legs on Sunday afternoon. Pictured at right, the car finished 10th.

The team's fantastic Le Mans performance came at a time when its owner was distracted by the problems of the EuroBrun F1 project, in which he had been the funding partner since 1988. The EuroBruns had been struggling to qualify and, in October 1990, the team closed its doors. Walter Brun's losses were substantial and he found himself struggling to stay in high-level motorsport.

SEVENTH HEAVEN FOR JAGUAR 23

LE MANS

NISSAN'S INFAMOUS FIVE

The transmissions of five powerful Group C1 cars, operated here by Nissan's well-endowed motorsport divisions in Japan, England and the USA, were traumatized by their turbo V8 engines. Only two of the works cars finished, the better-placed fifth in the hands of Nissan's 'superstar' veterans, Kazuyoshi Hoshino and Masahiro Hasemi, co-driven by Toshio Suzuki (below).

Nissan was now flying high in sportscar racing internationally. This was the fifth full year of its in-house Nissan Motorsports (NISMO) operation in Japan. Nissan Motorsports Europe (NME) had been formed to build and race Group C cars the previous season. And Nissan's American subsidiary was dominating Jaguar and Porsche in IMSA's GTP category with Electramotive's evolution of Lola chassis.

For 1989, NME had also chosen Lola Cars as the chassis partner in its Group C project, using the 3.5-litre, DOHC, VRH35Z V8 first seen at Le Mans in 1988. Produced by a team at Nissan Central Laboratories led by Yoshimasa Hayashi, and equipped with two IHI turbos and a JECS management system, this mighty engine was installed fully stressed behind the advanced composites monocoque, and made 800bhp at 7600rpm on race settings, transmitted through a Hewland VGC gearbox. The R89C had proved to be fast but fragile; NME's three cars had failed to finish Le Mans.

This June, no fewer than nine C1 cars were here, including a T-car each for NISMO and NME, and two private entries. There were five R90CK evolutions of the 1989 specification, featuring a range of upgrades on Lola's stiffer T90/10 platform. These included a narrower transmission casing, allowing wider air tunnels, and a carbon-carbon braking system (the first at Le Mans). After Lola's work in the Cranfield wind-tunnel, aerodynamic refinements included a reduced nose with smaller air intakes, a longer raked windscreen and lowered sidepod surfaces.

Meanwhile, in Yasuharu Namba's recently commissioned NISMO engineering centre in Oppama, aerodynamicist Yoshi Suzuka had developed his own lower-downforce evolution of the previous design for use in Japan. Two of these R90CP cars were here, one of them a reworked 1989 chassis in use as a T-car. Each had a higher nose, flattened towards the wheel-arches, a reprofiled underbody, low-line sidepods, and a lower rear wing with endplates attaching to the wheel-arches. NISMO operated the CPs under the direction of Sam Machida and Kazuyoshi Mizuno.

NME directors Howard Marsden and Tetsu Ikuzawa had two CKs and a T-car, managed by Dave Price and Ian Sanders. Over the previous winter, Don Devendorf's Electramotive had been evolved into the manufacturer's Nissan Performance Technology Inc (NPTI) behemoth in

24 LE MANS 24 HOURS 1990–99

1990

Vista, California, and two CKs were entered for NPTI and operated by a US-based crew. Trevor Harris was running the engineering functions alongside Ray Mallock, who had directed the pre-season European test programme. They opted to race both the NPTI cars with ferrous brakes.

NPTI's spirits were high. It had recently completed a new, twin-turbo V6 GTP car, the NPT90, designed by Harris and Suzuka, and it won for the first time at Mid-Ohio a couple of days before the team left for France. Then NPTI's 1988-89 IMSA champion, Geoff Brabham, went fastest on the first day of qualifying with the newest CK.

Brabham's time was obliterated the next day. Ikuzawa had asked NISMO to bring along a special qualifying engine that had shown more than 1000bhp on the bench in Hayashi's race engine division in Yokosuka. This was installed in NME's T-car, and Price invited Mark Blundell and Julian Bailey to toss a coin. Blundell was the winner of the wild ride.

At dusk on Thursday, he went out on Dunlop's qualifying tyres, but all that power spun the rear wheels in fourth gear and soon chewed them to shreds. He had to switch onto race rubber. On his hot lap, Blundell heard an order on his helmet radio from his race engineer, Bob Bell, to back off because the engine was 'overboosting'. He was enjoying the grunt so much, he ripped out the radio lead. The ACO's speed trap did not pick up his maximum velocity. Afterwards, the team established that a jammed wastegate valve had caused the engine output to peak at 1128bhp, and that the top speed had been a shade under 237mph (380kph). The fastest recorded speed there was 227mph (366kph) by Hasemi's CP, which was qualified more than six seconds slower. It was the first Le Mans pole for a Japanese manufacturer, and 24-year-old Blundell was the youngest driver to

secure one. NISMO was so impressed that it later took a piston out of the engine and had it mounted for him as a memento.

Three of the other Nissans qualified 3-4-5 but Kenneth Acheson stopped one of NME's cars near the end of the pace lap, with its CWP glowing red-hot. Race engineer John Travis and his NISMO colleagues later found that gears in the transmission oil pump had failed after being over-heat-treated, and that one had been damaged during a clumsy clutch replacement after the morning warm-up session.

Pictured above, Bailey led the first three laps before giving way to Oscar Larrauri's hard-driven Brun Porsche, but the pole position Nissan soon had the lead back – until just after 8pm, when third driver Gianfranco Brancatelli came up to lap Aguri Suzuki's Toyota, and was squeezed into a major accident entering the Dunlop curves. The Toyota was wrecked but 'Branca' made it all the way round to the pits for a new nose and front tyres. The comeback was hampered by a couple of punctures but, soon after midnight, the CK was back on the lead lap. Then Brancatelli was stopped at Indianapolis by a broken gear selector link. He found a gear and crawled all the way to the pits, continued after a seven-minute stop, and returned the car to Bailey an hour later. As Bailey made his way up pit-lane, part of the damaged fourth gear locked the second-gear selector. Rolled back to its pit, the car spent 17 minutes at rest while the NME crew tried to fix the gearbox – but on his first lap back out, Bailey stopped out in the countryside with no drive. During pit-car radio discussions, the battery went flat, and stopped the engine.

At this stage, Nissan was still leading the race with Brabham's NPTI entry, which was race-managed here by Mallock, and co-driven by Chip Robinson and Derek Daly. However this CK had come under growing pressure from the winning Jaguar. A scheduled brake pad change

SEVENTH HEAVEN FOR JAGUAR 25

LE MANS

by NPTI brought the contenders together, leading to a terrific duel between the rival IMSA teams that endured through the rest of the night and well into the morning. The Nissan (above) was hardly delayed by a pit-lane flash-fire at 7am and the battle was not resolved until 8:45am, when Daly pitted with a leaking fuel cell. A new cell had been fitted for the race after the original had delaminated, but had not been properly secured; it had split after chafing against its retaining bolts. A replacement cell also split when NPTI's crew was fitting it. After losing two hours, the car was retired.

NPTI's other CK, race-engineered by John Christie, was now many laps behind. After being delayed early on by a water leak, Bob Earl lost a wheel as he sped past the pits, and had to cover a very slow lap back to pit-lane. At 7:40pm, Steve Millen pitted with the water leak unsustainable, and the crew had to devote almost two hours to a coolant pipe repair. Later Michael Roe pitted with damaged front bodywork. Millen set the lap record for the revised circuit in trying to catch up, but at 1:30pm another tormented gearbox intervened. The car lost second gear and eventually finished 17th after a broken left-rear suspension damper mount bolt had cost it more than half an hour.

After Hasemi's fine qualifying lap, during which he had collided with Roberto Ravaglia's Toyota in the second chicane, NISMO opted for a steady race pace just under the CP's potential. It was running fifth just before 9pm when Suzuki lost 10 minutes while the crew fixed a front brake problem. The three drivers retrieved fourth position soon after dawn but, at 7:40am, a rear suspension damper broke up after 15 hours of chafing against its twin. The CP also encountered its own gearbox malfunction, leaving it with only first and fifth gears. It struggled to finish a lap ahead of the best Toyota, and claim the Japanese bragging rights.

Later a CP achieved NISMO's first All-Japan victory at Fuji, and further successes delivered the title to Hasemi and Anders Olofsson. In October, Nissan's board bowed to financial pressures and canned the FIA programme with NME, but NISMO upgraded its CP for successful title defences in both 1991 and 1992. Meantime the IMSA domination by NPTI and Brabham was maintained in 1990-91 but, in 1992, after winning the Daytona 24 Hours with an upgraded CK, the team was finally beaten by AAR's Eagle-Toyotas. The 225 staff in Vista then produced an all-new 3.5-litre V12 FIA Sportscar for NISMO. The P35 was aimed at a début in 1993, but Nissan's fast-declining financial position led to its cancellation. NPTI closed its doors that March.

THE PORSCHE ON THE PODIUM

The best-placed Porsche at the chequer, after an amazingly reliable run from start to finish, was the 3-litre, short-tail 962C entered by Alpha Racing Team out of Japan. Pictured below shaping up for Tertre Rouge, it came home third, as strong as it had started.

Yataka Nanikawa had formed this team over the previous winter to contest his national championship with a new, aluminium-hulled 'customer' Porsche, prepared by Tomei Engineering in Gotemba, and driven in the series by Derek Bell and Tiff Needell. It was Needell who observed that the long straight at Fuji International Speedway was about the same length as each of the newly created segments of the Mulsanne straight at Le Mans. Nanikawa invested in extensive setup testing there in preparation for the team's venture to France. TM Takahiro Hori lost Bell to Joest Racing's works team for the big race, so Needell was joined by fellow Britons David Sears and race débutant Anthony Reid.

The sole mechanical problem all weekend for the mechanics under Gary Cummings was a difficult pad change. And the only on-track drama occurred when Reid was slipstreaming a group of cars on the Mulsanne straight, and something (probably a wing mirror) detached from one of them, and struck the windscreen. Later a glass splinter flaked off the screen and lodged in Reid's eye, and he made an early pitstop to have it carefully removed.

Alpha's exceptional performance was in contrast with those of most of the private Porsche teams in this race, which were nothing better than midfield runners.

TROUBLE WITH TRACTION

In the absence of Mercedes-Benz, Porsche saw the chance of a seventh victory for its iconic Group C racecar, in its ninth season of competition. The company came with a full-on factory project, but returned to Stuttgart disappointed.

Porsche had pulled its factory Group C team after the 1988 Le Mans. However, its position changed after Joest Racing's stunning WSPC victory over the dominant Sauber-Mercedes at Dijon in mid-1989. A group of race engineers, led by technical director Norbert Singer, persuaded the management to work with Joest on resumed development of the 962C. Subsequently Porsche had actively supported several privateers here in 1989, but now effectively adopted Joest as its exclusive works team. Four new 962Cs (still with aluminium monocoques) were assembled in the Weissach factory for Reinhold Joest's programme.

Despite the new chicanes, Singer decided on low-line tails for straightline speed and fuel-saving. Working in Porsche's wind tunnel at Weissach, he devised a *langheck* package offering 10pc more downforce relative to the 1989 setup. The speed turned out to be an impressive 227mph (365kph) – but the team's new Michelin tyres were incompatible with the aero. Joest's drivers struggled for grip all week. Hans-Joachim Stuck's race engineer, Roland Kussmaul, equipped him with a 3.2-litre qualifying engine assembled in Joest's workshop near Abtsteinach, east of Mannheim, by the team's own engine wizard, Michel Demont. It made more than 820bhp at 8300rpm on 2.3-bar 'boost', but all that power went up in tyre smoke. Joest's fastest qualifier was three seconds down on Oscar Larrauri's short-tail Brun Porsche. And only three of the works quartet started the race after a violent accident in first qualifying which, like the awesome top speed of the pole position Nissan, cast serious doubt on any 'safety' benefit deriving from the new chicanes.

Jonathan Palmer had just set the third fastest time when, flat in fifth between the new chicanes, his car suddenly veered left. A split-second later, it struck the barrier at 200mph (320kph) with the left-front. It spun round and hit with the right-rear, flew across the track for 100 metres, landed on its wheels, and careened along the three-tier barrier almost to the second chicane. The 962C was wrecked but the shocked driver escaped with a broken thumb and bruising. The team suspected that a tyre had picked up a puncture on stones thrown onto the track surface in the first chicane.

Stuck was under contract to race an Audi in two DTM touring car events at the Nürburgring on Saturday afternoon, so Frank Jelinski started his car, now fitted with a 3-litre motor. From sixth on the grid, it faded into the midfield, still lacking grip. When Stuck returned from Germany, and took over the car from Derek Bell at 5:40pm, he found himself running 14th.

There were several spins on Saturday evening, and fresh pads were often needed in Brembo's cast-iron braking assembles, which were also new to the team. But in the cool of the night (above), the car came onto the front-running pace. It ascended the order dramatically in

LE MANS 24 HOURS 1990–99

the early hours of Sunday and emerged in third place at 10am. However the track was now warming up again and, before noon, the car was repassed by the Lammers Jaguar. Shortly afterwards, Bell was in pit-lane with a broken turbo, and the crew had to take a hacksaw to get it off. It was 18 minutes before Stuck could resume. That eventual fourth place was poor reward.

After Palmer's accident, Bob Wollek was switched to another 3-litre Joest 962C (right), joining Stanley Dickens and Louis Krages (*aka* 'John Winter') in place of the unlucky Will Hoy. Wollek had the same experience as his team mates, fighting for traction when the track surface was warm. Under the race management of Wolfgang Bühren, Wollek brilliantly bullied the car into seventh position during the cool night, but then threw it away with a spin in the first chicane at 9:50am. After an 18-minute stop for a new tail section and other repairs, the car finished eighth.

Joest's other 962C (below) was operated as a 'satellite' entry, managed by 'Siggi' Brunn and Hans-Dieter Dechent, and engineered by Gerhard and Peter Munch. It was driven by Henri Pescarolo, Jean-Louis Ricci and Jacques Laffite. Like Stuck, Laffite had a DTM contract, in his case with BMW, and he actually won one of the Saturday races on the Nürburgring before flying back to Le Mans with his team mate (and Mercedes DTM driver Alain Cudini).

The rest of Laffite's weekend was packed with incident. After a spin by Ricci at Arnage, Laffite went off at Indianapolis and, in the small hours, collided with Jan Lammers's Jaguar in the first chicane, almost taking out both cars. Three laps passed while he was getting out of the gravel trap there. Shortly after 7am, a Laffite-Pescarolo handover was extended to 13 minutes by a faulty clutch. Finally, just before 9:30am, Laffite clipped Jesús Pareja's Brun Porsche in the Ford chicane. Pescarolo's landmark 24th Le Mans ended with 14th position.

SEVENTH HEAVEN FOR JAGUAR

LE MANS

FOUR IN A ROW

Of all the Japanese manufacturers, Mazda had shown the firmest commitment to the 24 Hours, having entered its rotary-engined racecars every year since 1980. The decade had closed with a hat-trick of wins in the IMSA GTP division that had been meaningful only in Mazda's advertising department. Time was now running out for Mazda to win outright. FISA's upcoming regulation changes would make rotaries ineligible in sportscar racing, so Takayoshi Ohashi's Mazdaspeed expanded its programme this year and fielded three new 787 cars in GTP (including a T-car), backed up by a 767B.

The new 787 was an evolution of Nigel Stroud's designs raced in 1988-89, but the 13J engine was now replaced by the new R26B. A clean-sheet design by Mazdaspeed's engine team under Kunio Matsuura, it featured continuously variable-length air intake trumpets controlled by a Nippon Denso electronic management system, again with a peripheral-port injection system but now with three sparkplugs per rotor, instead of two. The new quad-rotor engine was more compact, lighter and more fuel-efficient, and could be raced safely with about 700bhp at 9000rpm – a 70bhp improvement on the 13J. Furthermore it had a wider torque band, and provided much better throttle response. The new engine again drove through Porsche's five-speed gearbox.

As before, Stroud's hulls were built in a carbon/Kevlar weave by Advanced Composites in the UK, and shipped out to Hiroshima for Mazdaspeed to assemble the cars. Chassis modifications included a single radiator built into the nose section, with a 'Gurney' flap attached to its cooling air exit duct to increase front downforce. The radiator ducting in the sides of the 767B was deleted and the 787, retaining its low-line rear wing here, was neater aerodynamically despite big engine bay, exhaust and brake cooling intakes in the rear flanks.

Mazdaspeed débuted the 787 in April

1990

1990 at Fuji and then completed a second car, and took them both to Europe for almost 3000 miles of track-testing at Silverstone and Estoril. Alan Docking was hired as the team manager, and six-times race winner Jacky Ickx as a consultant.

The 787s were lapped more than six seconds faster than the 767B. However the durability disappeared on Saturday. In the car shared with Stefan Johansson and David Kennedy (right), Pierre Dieudonné was leading the division just before 9pm when he pitted with a seizing rear wheel hub, at the cost of 15 minutes. This handed the class lead to the Momo Porsche, until it retired at 2am. An hour later, after another hub replacement, Kennedy parked the car with a terminal engine failure.

The other 787 is pictured top left. This car was spun here by Bertrand Gachot at 6:30pm, taking damage to the bodywork and windscreen that cost 15 minutes in the nearby pits. A fuel-feed malfunction prevented any meaningful recovery by Johnny Herbert or Volker Weidler from this setback and, at 10:30pm, Gachot went off again in the same corner, this time savaging the rear wing and costing another 15 minutes. After Herbert had pitted for 10 minutes with detached bodywork, an electrical failure just before half-time left the car without lights. It resumed after a 53-minute repair, but the wiring harness had overheated fatally.

So it was that the GTP victory fell to the Japanese-driven 767B (pictured making its way up pit-lane), but not without dramas of their own for Yojiro Terada, Takashi Yorino and Yoshimi Katayama. These included a braking problem that needed the system to be purged, a rear hub failure and a broken driveshaft even before 7:30am. That was when the car needed a gearbox rebuild; 90 minutes passed while spare parts were cannibalized from the parked 787s.

It was Mazda's fourth successive class win, but hardly a triumphant one. The very last chance for a rotary would come in 1991…

SEVENTH HEAVEN FOR JAGUAR 31

LE MANS

MOMO MENACES MAZDA

Giampiero Moretti's Porsche 962 (above) was the first to contest the GTP division at Le Mans and it gave Mazdaspeed a most unwelcome new challenger.

The Milanese founder of the Momo wheels brand fed his passion and promoted his business via IMSA GTP programmes in partnership with Electrodyne founder Chester 'Ched' Vincentz, his American agent, punctuated by occasional forays back to Europe. In 1989, he embarked on a transatlantic association with former Group C2 constructor Gebhardt Motorsport in Sinsheim, Germany.

Their one-year-old Porsche 962, built on an ex-Brun TC Prototypes monocoque, was wrecked in the Daytona 24 Hours when a burst tyre sent Derek Bell sliding on his roof for 500 metres. A replacement tub was made by Floridian engineer John Shapiro in Fort Lauderdale, with bodywork drawn by Fritz Gebhardt. The reborn Porsche was then raced by Bell/Moretti to fourth place at Road Atlanta before being shipped to France, where Bell (busy with Joest Porsche) was replaced by former C2 star Nick Adams and Günther Gebhardt, the brother of Fritz, who was here as the team manager.

Although the new Mazdas were clearly faster, Adams qualified the Porsche heavyweight only half a second slower than the older 767B, and the Porsche was good enough in the race to take the lead of the category as soon as the Japanese cars faltered. It led GTP for more than six hours but a broken CWP struck it down at 2am.

1990

NOT SPICY ENOUGH

Spice Engineering's new Group C1/3.5 racecar (below) looked the part but lacked the performance and durability to mount a viable challenge. Mechanical frailty in the race left it 18th at the finish.

In 1989, Gordon Spice's company had become the first brand-name constructor to produce a 750-kilo FIA Sportscar, based on the carbon/aluminium honeycomb monocoque of its successful line of FIA C2/IMSA Lights racecars, but wider and longer, and with swoopier bodywork. The team had contested the WSPC with a single car and had run two at Le Mans, both of which had been stopped by engine failures. For this season Graham Humphrys and Dave Kelly updated their design and a new works car was built in Spice's Brackley factory, alongside duplicates to the orders of customers Dave Prewitt and Charles Zwolsman.

Powered by a Cosworth DFR prepared by John Nicholson, the works C1/3.5 car was crewed here by Tim Harvey and Fermin Velez, its regular SWC drivers, joined by Chris Hodgetts. Managed by Jeff Hazell and race-engineered by Mike Franklin, they had just broken into the top 20 at 8:45pm when a detached exhaust cost 30 minutes in the pits. A recovery was thwarted shortly before half-time by a 45-minute repair to a broken gearlever, followed by a 25-minute delay while the crew purged the cooling system after a hose-clip failure. Gearbox and exhaust problems continued through Sunday.

Prewitt's new C1/3.5 Spice (right) failed to qualify. Using a Cosworth DFR prepared by Terry Hoyle, and under the management of Roy Baker, the Silverstone-based GP Motorsport entry was driven by Pierre de Thoisy, who had covered only nine laps on Wednesday when the engine broke down. Quirin Bovy did only two laps the next evening before the replacement DFR also failed.

Zwolsman, a Dutch drug trafficker, was out on parole after being jailed in 1988 for leading a gang that had smuggled 160,000lb of Moroccan hashish into the Netherlands. His motor racing ambitions were lower. He decided against running his new SE90C in the unrestricted 750kg class, fitted a 3.9-litre DFL, and entered it as a C2 car.

SEVENTH HEAVEN FOR JAGUAR

LE MANS

PIPER CALLS THE TUNE

The last ever winner of the Group C2 category at Le Mans was PC Automotive's Spice SE89C, driven by team co-owner Richard Piper with Olindo Iacobelli and Mike Youles, and powered by a 3.3-litre Cosworth DFL supplied by John Nicholson. Pictured (above) ahead of its Cougar class rival in the Virage Ford, it had come perilously close to being eliminated by someone else's accident.

This was a sweet success for Piper's Greenwich-based team, which had bought this car new in 1989, but had been compelled by budget shortfall to scratch its Le Mans entry. The drivers kept the car in touch with the class-leading Spices of the Graff and Lombardi teams on Saturday afternoon, despite a spin by Youles at Indianapolis. When they were both delayed, it emerged in the lead at 10:45pm.

An hour later, Piper startled Patric Capon, his partner and team manager, by appearing in pit-lane with a detached rear wing and a busted suspension rocker. Piper had been clipped by Hideki Okada's spinning Kremer Porsche in the Nissan chicane. The team fitted a spare aerofoil but did not have the suspension part. Fortunately one was loaned by a generous rival, Dudley Wood. Fitting it cost only 13 minutes, and put the car into an on-track duel with the Zwolsman/Chamberlain SE90C that endured for more than three hours. After its faster rival had been delayed, the white SE89C went on to win with ease, despite needing three new batteries. Its winning margin was a whopping 13 laps.

Charles Zwolsman's higher-specification, 3.9-litre Nicholson-engined SE90C (left), operated by Hugh Chamberlain's team out of Buntingford, England, started as the C2 favourite but failed to finish. The owner, co-driven by Philippe de Henning and Robin Donovan, was delayed for 14 minutes early on by a suspension failure. The drivers recovered well and Henning was battling for the lead at 3:30am when a gearbox breakage sent him to pit-lane and a 45-minute repair. There was no way back but the drivers tried, anyway, and their fate was undeserved: a cruel engine failure at 12:15pm.

The category was led into the twilight by Pierre-Alain Lombardi's Swiss-entered SE87C (top right), powered by a DFL sourced from Heini

LE MANS 24 HOURS 1990–99

1990

Mader. But just after 10:30pm, Denis Morin pitted for a gearbox rebuild that consumed more than an hour. Later braking and ignition problems caused further delays and, at about 6:50am, Lombardi lost braking power altogether at the Nissan chicane, and crashed.

The SE89C fielded by Jean-Philippe Grand and François Feyman (Graff Racing), which had won the 1989 Index of Energy Efficiency, was also a contender. Pictured in the pits, this car was race-prepared near Le Mans by former Rondeau mechanics at Lucien Monté's Synergie company, and was fitted with a 3.3-litre DFL built by Alan Smith. Xavier Lapeyre was contesting the class lead with Morin at 10:30pm when the engine would not restart after a fuel stop. The crew had to replace much of the wiring, at the cost of two hours. Persistence eventually retrieved a distant second place in the division.

The C2 'pole' was claimed by Robbie Stirling with Team Mako's Nicholson-engined, 3.9-litre Spice (below). This was the ex-works 1988 C2 championship-winning chassis with which Don Shead's team from Sevenoaks had finished second in C2 the previous June. Co-driver Ross Hyett was afflicted soon after the start by fuel vaporisation, which put the car at the back of the field. It never recovered: John McNeil's unfortunate crew had to undertake no fewer than three gearbox rebuilds. However, the car was credited with the win in the Index of Energy Efficiency competition with the only positive score, followed by three more Spice-Cosworths.

GP Motorsport operated Dudley Wood's SE87C in C2 alongside its C1/3.5 entry, with a 3.9 DFL built by Terry Hoyle. It went the distance, but Wood and his co-drivers had to cope with persistently malfunctioning fuel-injection and ignition systems, and were further delayed by a gearbox repair.

SEVENTH HEAVEN FOR JAGUAR

TTT TORMENTS

Toyota mounted its biggest effort yet to win Le Mans, but its only surviving car (above), raced by Geoff Lees, Hitoshi Ogawa and Masanori Sekiya, finished sixth.

Having laid the groundwork for its Le Mans campaigns in collaborations with racing specialists Sigma Advanced Racing Developments, Dome Company and Tachi Oiwa Motor Sports, Toyota had first contested this race in 1987 after absorbing TOMS as its official racing division, and recruiting Dome's chief designer, Masahiro Ohkuni. Working alongside Toyota Racing Developments, the existing motorsports engineering division in Yokohama, the Toyota Team TOMS factory in Gotemba had produced the company's first advanced composites Group C racecar in 1988, fitted with a turbo four-cylinder engine. Toyota had finally come onto the pace in 1989 with the introduction of TRD's turbo V8 powertrain, developed by a team led by Tsutomu Tomita.

Toyota entered three race cars and two T-cars for this race, all powered by the robust, 3.2-litre R32V engine. Having since improved the valvegear, lubrication and ignition systems, TRD preferred this more fuel-efficient option here to the 3.6-litre version that was now being used (with little success) by TOMS GB in WSPC races. TRD had also produced a new six-speed gearbox as a component of a much-revised rear end, in which the CWP was raised to improve transmission durability.

Meanwhile TTT had employed a rolling-road wind tunnel for the first time, and was claiming a 20pc increase in downforce for zero drag penalty. The 90CV was a big improvement over the previous models and had débuted in February by winning a 500km All-Japan race at Fuji, driven by Ogawa/Sekiya.

At this time Toyota was ramping up its IMSA programme with Dan Gurney's AAR Eagle team (which landed its first victory at Topeka in May) as well as contesting the WSPC via TOMS GB. However, two of the cars were operated here by TTT, the other by Shin Kato's SARD team, which was racing a works-supported 89C-V in Japan, and returned to Le Mans for the first time since 1978.

The 3.2-litre 90CV Le Mans package was tested in February over more than 3000 miles at Phillip Island in Australia, then over 3000 and 1800 miles in separate trials on Toyota's Shibetsu proving ground. Once in France, TM Hiroshi Fushida had no desire for big-boost heroics in qualifying this time. Lees qualified 10th but soon found his race compromised by a fuel vaporisation problem. The TOMS crew tried switching pumps but the fault persisted and was only cured in the cool of the evening.

Just after midnight, the Toyota emerged virtually unmarked from Sekiya's sideswipe collision with Fabio Magnani's Lancia on the very fast run to Indianapolis, which destroyed the Lancia and caused a full-course yellow. Lees/Ogawa/Sekiya steadily gained places through the rest of the night but, just before 9am, they lost seven minutes when a broken hose clip on

1990

the charge plumbing between the turbo and its intercooler caused an air leak. As Sunday warmed up, the fuel vaporisation returned and the drivers struggled with it all the way to the finish, which they reached with 85 litres of fuel unused. Sixth place was Toyota's best Le Mans result, but it could have been so much better.

The Toyotas were never on the pace of the Nissans and Jaguars. In the car he shared with Johnny Dumfries and Roberto Ravaglia, Aguri Suzuki was being lapped at 8:20pm when he collided on the approach to the Dunlop chicane with Gianfranco Brancatelli's race-leading Nissan. Heavy contact sent the Toyota smashing rearwards into the barrier on the left side of the track (moving it two metres), and it took heavy damage. The marshals there swiftly extinguished a small turbo fire and extricated the Larrousse F1 driver from the cockpit, with nothing more serious than bruising.

The third Toyota (above) was raced by the regular drivers of SARD's Higashimachi-based 89CV. Pierre-Henri Raphanel pitted after only 20 minutes with a braking problem. Early in the second hour, he hit the guardrail at Mulsanne corner, wiping off the nose section. Repairing the front-end damage and fixing the brakes properly took 27 minutes. Roland Ratzenberger went well during the night but Naoki Nagasaka pitted at 9:45am with a misfire. Team manager Keith Greene's SARD crew changed much of the ignition system and sent him out once more but, at 10:30, he stopped at Indianapolis with the engine dead.

SEVENTH HEAVEN FOR JAGUAR 37

LE MANS

NO LUCK FOR KREMER

Although benefiting from the Porsche Kundensport operation with special status as such long-serving customers, Köln Porsche dealers Erwin and Manfred Kremer no longer enjoyed factory support at the level of Joest Racing, but they remained series regulars in the WSPC with their much-modified 'K6' Porsches. The Köln-based team's squad was boosted here by Ligier F1 driver Philippe Alliot, who was switched to Kremer from Joest's factory team after Jonathan Palmer's accident on Wednesday evening.

The very quick Sarel van der Merwe was teamed with Kunimitsu Takahashi and Hideki Okada and qualified their car almost at the head of the second-division Porsches. Pictured left, it was racing solidly in the top dozen at 7:20pm when the engine died as Merwe exited Mulsanne corner, owing to an electrical fault. Merwe emerged, removed the engine cover, and worked on the car until he found a spark. But it was 8pm when he arrived back in pit-lane for a proper repair and a fresh battery. Takahashi resumed in 40th position.

Only eight places had been regained by midnight, when Okada spun into the gravel in the Nissan chicane, clipping the rear wing off the C2 class-leading Spice as he did so. Back in the pits, repairs to the Porsche's rear end cost another 40 minutes. The crestfallen drivers persevered but for little reward. Shortly before 1pm, the gearbox broke as Merwe arrived at the end of the Mulsanne straight. No proper repair was possible and the car sat in the pits for the duration, until the crew found a gear for Merwe to rejoin a few minutes before the end to qualify as a finisher.

Alliot shared the team's other honeycomb TCP chassis with Bernard de Dryver and Patrick Gonin as a late replacement for Thierry Salvador, whose racing licence was revoked after being issued in error. Salvador was sponsoring the car (left) and had commissioned a livery design from artist Peter Klasen, themed on industrial warning notices including 'High Explosive' on the engine cover. This car lost 15 minutes early on Saturday evening for replacement of a detached left-side door, and at 10:40pm Alliot spun into the barrier exiting the Nissan chicane, at the cost of 43 minutes for rear-end repairs. The car had recovered well before noon on Sunday, when a 67-minute stop was needed to replace a rear hub. Dryver crossed the finish line in 16th place.

1990

DEEDS OF COURAGE

Yves Courage had embarked in 1982 on a mission to emulate Jean Rondeau, his fellow Le Mans resident, by winning the great race with a car of his own manufacture, but his best result to date had been third overall in 1987 with the Porsche-engined Cougar C20. This year, with public funding via the Département de la Sarthe administration, he entered a pair of similarly powered, aluminium-honeycomb 'C24S' cars, one being an updated, one-year-old C22 chassis, the other a new car.

In premises near the circuit, Courage engineers Alain Touchais and Jean-Claude Rose converted the 1989 specification to comply with the latest rules and to improve the aero balance by reducing the front overhang and extending the rear. After a series of engine failures in the early-season WSPC events, Courage equipped the older chassis with a twin-turbo, 3-litre flat-six cooled by a mixture of air and water, a set-up that had been discarded by Porsche Motorsport. The team believed the older design to be more durable but it meant adding NACA ducts for air-cooling and relocating a number of engine ancillaries, including the turbochargers and intercoolers. And it was all to no avail: the engine blew up long before it was dark.

After a circumspect qualifying under team manager Jacques Bouquet, the new Cougar (pictured), fitted with the fully water-cooled 3-litre, made solid progress through the field. It raced through the night contesting 12th place with the Team Schuppan Porsche and one of the Joest cars. Well driven by Lionel Robert, Michel Trollé and Pascal Fabre, it stayed strong all the way to the finish, delayed only by a spin by Trollé, a change of battery and minor gear selection problems. Fabre almost caught Geoff Lees's sixth-placed Toyota at the flag.

SEVENTH HEAVEN FOR JAGUAR 39

LE MANS

INFERNO IN THE FOREST

Italian entrant Gianni Mussato brought his ex-works Lancia LC2 Group C car (above) – and wished he hadn't.

Mussato had acquired two spare aluminium monocoques and a stock of parts from Lancia Corse, and had assembled this car to undertake a full WSPC season in 1989. It had failed to finish a race, and had not qualified at Le Mans after a turbo fire. This was its only outing of 1990, fitted with a 3050cc version of the Ferrari-sourced V8 making more than 800bhp with two KKK turbochargers, and an Abarth/Hewland transmission.

The car lost 45 minutes to a gearbox malfunction early in the race, and an hour to a turbo failure soon after dark. Fabio Magnani was racing in last place at 12:45am when he had a misunderstanding with Masanori Sekiya on the flat-out section between Mulsanne and Indianapolis. The passing Toyota tapped the Lancia and it took off at 180mph (290kph), hurtling over the two-tier barrier and through some bushes and saplings, and catching fire before this horrible accident stopped. Thankfully Magnani managed to scramble out of the cabin before the ruptured, half-full fuel cell exploded, and he escaped with minor burns, cuts and a bruised elbow.

The car was less fortunate: it ended up as an ugly blob of twisted metal, as seen on the left.

1990

IN THE PINK

Consistently one of Porsche's best Group C privateers of the previous decade with its own honeycomb chassis, drawn by Nigel Stroud, Silverstone-based Richard Lloyd Racing entered three 962Cs this year, but arrived with only two (pictured before the start). Team manager Ian Dawson was in charge of RLR's own regular honeycomb car and a new one from Porsche – the first chassis the team had bought from the factory for six years (on the left in the photograph). Both were presented in the pink livery of Italya Sports (Joest's 1989 sponsor) and fitted with 3-litre engines. They were qualified by Manuel Reuter and John Watson respectively as the fifth and eighth fastest Porsches.

The honeycomb car raced in the top dozen until Reuter's second shift was hampered by the Goodyear tyres turning on the rims. Later Reuter complained of inconsistent brakes and, after the crew had devoted 10 minutes to fixing the problem, he left the night driving to JJ Lehto and James Weaver. After another short delay due to a clutch problem, they saw the dawn in 16th place, but then a burst rear tyre tested Weaver's reflexes on the Mulsanne straight. He brought the car under control but the flailing rubber smashed through the bodywork and tore the wastegate off a turbocharger. As he arrived in pit-lane, the spilled oil caught fire.

The new car also went well early on in Watson's hands but, at 6:30pm, Allen Berg pitted with a seized wheelbearing, which cost 10 minutes.

Later Bruno Giacomelli shared Reuter's experiences with the tyres and brakes and the car lost another 15 minutes in two pitstops before it was dark. Finally the drivers found consistent pace and steadily picked off cars ahead, emerging in 15th place soon after dawn in spite of frequent pad changes (eight in total). They finished just outside the top 10.

SEVENTH HEAVEN FOR JAGUAR 41

LE MANS

NISSAN'S PRIVATEERS

Backing up the factory-entered Nissans were two privately operated, one-year-old R89Cs, one entered by Yves Courage's team out of its Le Mans raceshop, the other by Tomoo Hanawa's Team Le Mans from Hiroo, near Tokyo. Like the works cars, they were hampered by weak transmissions, and only the Courage car of Alain Cudini, Hervé Regout and Costas Los (below) finished.

Race-managed by Mike Phillips, this R89C lost a lot of qualifying time after a blown tyre had sent Los up the escape road at the entrance to the Porsche curves, but Regout made good progress early in the race, picking up 14 positions before 6pm. That was when a broken rear wing support caused the first of many delays: a braking malfunction, a lost road wheel, electrical problems and crucially a 75-minute gearbox rebuild left the car in 22nd position at the end. Of the drivers, Los was the most frustrated: he was nursing a sore foot that had been run over by a Cougar from the adjacent pit.

'Tom' Hanawa's car was hampered by transmission problems throughout qualifying and over much of the weekend, and the engine added to the woes by developing an elusive misfire on Saturday evening. After a 10-minute stop, Takao Wada resumed with a new ignition box. But a more serious, 73-minute delay came in the small hours while the gearbox was repaired (again). Finally, the failure of the new ignition system killed the engine, stranding Anders Olofsson on the Mulsanne straight in the cold light of dawn.

MIXED FORTUNES

Obermaier Racing's Porsches from Reutlingen, Germany, had generally been Group C midfielders, although one had scored a fortuitous second place in the 1987 Le Mans. This season Hans Obermaier and Jürgen Oppermann had invested in two new honeycomb/carbon chassis from TCP, and were seeing a marked improvement in their team's WSPC performance.

One of the new cars was prepared for Oppermann to race with Harald Grohs and Marc Duez. Like Brun Motorsport, Obermaier brought a qualifying engine from Andial in California, and Grohs used it to good effect despite being the very first driver to sample the beach at the first new chicane. The team adopted a conservative strategy for the race but was undone by incidents involving Oppermann, who collided at 8:25pm with George Fouché's Trust 962C, damaging the rear end, and had several spins. Nevertheless Grohs and Duez were moving up the order nicely when the gearbox broke at 2:45am.

Jürgen Lässig put the team's other long-tail Porsche (above) into the sand at the second Mulsanne chicane on only the second lap of the race, but it wasn't there long, and went really well thereafter. Reliability sent Lässig, Pierre Yver and Otto Altenbach all the way to ninth place.

FIRST-TIME TRUST

The faster of the Japanese-entered Porsches in qualifying – indeed, the third fastest Porsche overall – was the 3-litre Trust Racing car (right) with which George Fouché prevailed by a tenth of a second in a duel with Kremer's Sarel van der Merwe for the honour of being the fastest Springbok in France.

Based in Chiba City and run by Yasuo Toyota and Masamitsu Hayakawa, this team had traded its previous RLR-built Porsches for a brand-new car from Porsche Kundensport. Trust, a front-runner in Japan, was on début here, but team manager Gen Suzuki had high hopes of a strong weekend with the 3-litre 962C. They were soon dashed by repeated stops to secure the front bodywork and Fouché's minor collision at Indianapolis with Oppermann's Porsche.

Fouché and Steven Andskär soldiered on from 41st position and had retrieved 14th place by breakfast-time, only to lose eight minutes with a clutch malfunction. After more delays with a detached door and a suspension damper, they allowed Shunji Kasuya (the 1989 C2 class winner here) a single shift in the car early on Sunday afternoon, and finished 13th.

SEVENTH HEAVEN FOR JAGUAR 43

LE MANS

THE OLD FIRM

Having retired from the cockpit in April 1983, Le Mans winner Vern Schuppan was now intent on running his own team, a series regular in Japan. Schuppan renewed old partnerships this year. He recruited former JW Automotive director John Horsman and Howden Ganley, the co-founder of Tiga Race Cars in High Wycombe, where Team Schuppan had its UK headquarters. Schuppan and Ganley had been team mates not only in F1 with BRM back in 1972, but also in sportscar racing with JW's 1973 Mirage team.

The week did not start well. Both the 962Cs broke their engines on Wednesday, and the team's new 'customer' chassis, driven by Hurley Haywood/Rickard Rydell/Wayne Taylor, lost more track time the next day when the wiring loom had to be replaced. Come Saturday, and their problem was now inconsistent brakes, leading to three pad changes and a system purge before midnight, followed a couple of hours later by a right-rear caliper replacement. After rejoining (left), Taylor was in the final stage of a triple-shift when a turbo exhaust broke, at the cost of an hour back in the pits. The drivers staged quite a recovery after dawn and, despite three more pad changes, converted 20th position to 12th.

The sister car was built on one of the team's own carbon-composite 'clone' tubs, made by Advanced Composites. Eje Elgh, Tomas Mezera and Thomas Danielsson were also set back by an exhaust pipe failure just before dark, costing them 42 minutes – and it happened again at 5am, causing a similar delay. They struggled even more than their team mates with their brakes, needing nine pad changes over the weekend, but finished 15th.

DAMAGED GOODS

Philippe Farjon, who had won C2 in 1989 with his Cougar C20LM (*née* C12), brought the four-year-old car to defend its title, even though it had been listed for sale in a Montlhéry auction catalogue two weeks after the race. Again prepared by Jean-Claude Thibault, and fitted with a mixed-cooling, 2.8-litre Porsche engine, the overweight Cougar (left) was raced this time by its owner with Jean Messaoudi. It never featured. And it was probably just as well that it was Farjon who crashed it out of the race, shortly before 7pm…

44 LE MANS 24 HOURS 1990–99

1990

PHILOSOPHICAL DESCARTES

Automobiles Louis Descartes had contested every Le Mans since 1985 with its neat coupés and its workshop in Levallois, near Paris, had produced its first carbon/honeycomb tub in 1989. After doing nine races that season in the Group C2 category, the C289 was reworked over the winter with new braking assemblies, a revised cooling system and epoxy/Kevlar bodywork. Fitted with a 3.3-litre Cosworth DFL, the C289 was hopelessly outclassed in the C1 class of the WSPC, but could again be entered at Le Mans as a C2 car.

François Migault had the ALD among the class leaders early on but, towards the end of his second shift, the team had to devote 50 minutes to a gearbox rebuild. Jacques Heuclin resumed but, at 7:45pm, the gearbox broke again and he stopped near the Virage Ford.

Louis Descartes was never fazed by such setbacks. He just set about building a new racecar.

SEVENTH HEAVEN FOR JAGUAR 45

LE MANS

TAIL-END TIGA

The last of British entrant Roy Baker's little fleet of Tiga Group C2 cars (left) returned for its final Le Mans, and made the finish after a fraught weekend.

Baker had run this chassis here before. His 'Pink Panther' car from 1988, it had been extensively updated the following season and had since been sold to Alistair Fenwick, who was now racing it in British national events under the management of Malcolm Swetman. Fenwick obtained an entry via the GP Motorsport team, now run by Baker with its co-founder, Dave Prewitt, which also had its Spice here.

Powered by a 3.9-litre, 460bhp DFL built by Terry Hoyle, the Tiga was afflicted from the start by ignition problems. These briefly stranded Craig Simmiss out at Arnage, and later at Indianapolis, and persisted until Sunday morning. The car was also delayed by a malfunctioning fuel pump but struggled to the end as the last classified finisher.

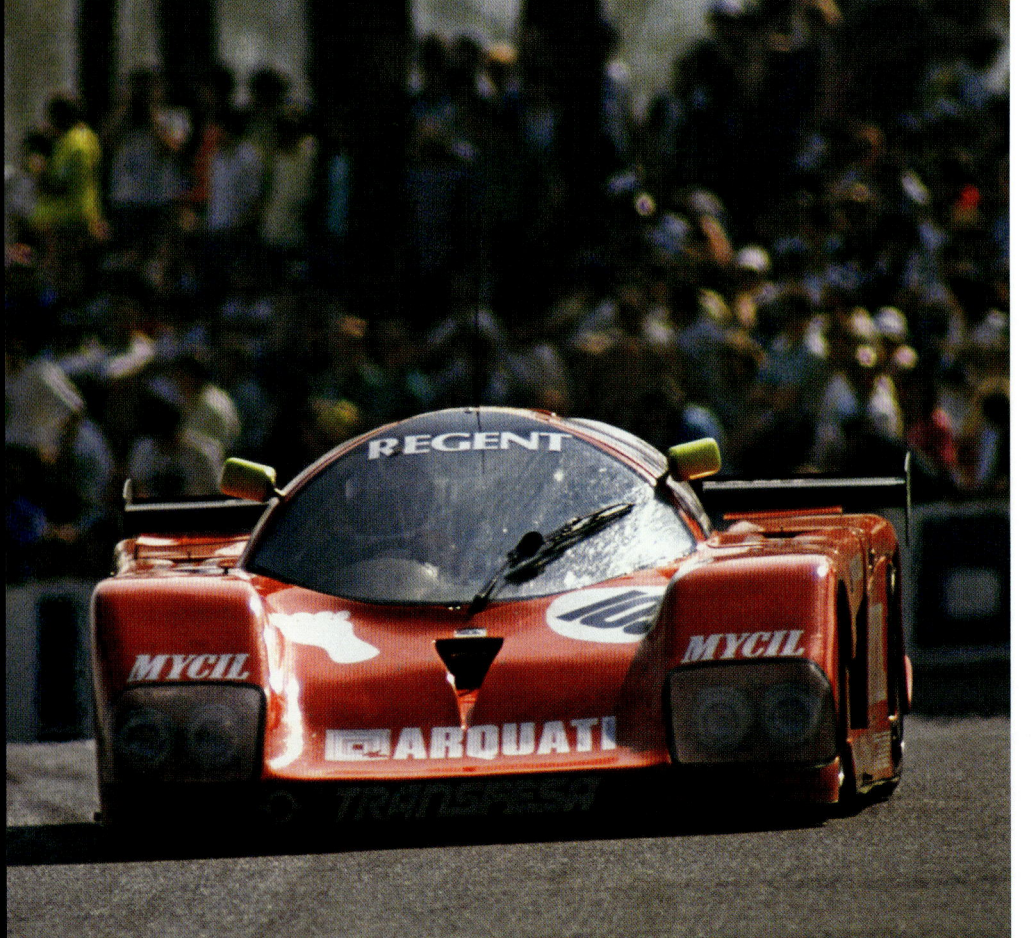

ADA BIDS ADIEU

The tiny ADA Engineering company, run by Ian Harrower and Chris Crawford in Chiswick, London, returned to give its '02B' Group C2 car a final Le Mans outing.

The ADA 02B was an evolution of the Gebhardt design with which the team had won Group C2 here in 1986, substantially reworked by Crawford and Richard Divila and powered by a 3.3-litre Cosworth DFL V8 prepared by John Nicholson. It had been badly damaged at Kyalami at the end of 1987 but was later rebuilt and raced in the 1989 Le Mans. Since then Crawford had further developed the underbody and the suspension systems and the team was contesting the British C2 series. It arrived at Le Mans after winning at Thruxton in May.

Driven by Harrower with John Sheldon and Jerry Mahony, the ADA was handicapped by fuel pump problems for much of Saturday, and lost 20 minutes shortly before dark after the failure of the rear-right suspension wishbone mount. Just after half-time, the wishbone on the other side also broke. After rejoining, Mahony tried to cope with evil handling and had a spin at Tertre Rouge before yet another suspension failure pitched him onto the beach at the Dunlop curves and out of the race.

In September, the ADA won another British C2 race at Donington, finishing as the runner-up in the series.

WHEELS FALLING OFF

British entrant Tim Lee Davey's previous forays to Le Mans with Tiga racecars had been conspicuously underfinanced but, in its second season with Porsches, his team was benefiting from a working relationship with Team Schuppan. In the second half of the 1989 season, Maidstone-based Team Davey had retubbed its 962C with a Schuppan/Advanced Composites monocoque. It was entered here alongside a similar, brand-new chassis.

The new car (pictured during night duty) was literally finished in the paddock, and missed scrutineering, but the ACO generously arranged a Wednesday inspection. It finally took to the circuit on Thursday, and qualified in last place. Inevitably, the weekend brought a range of mechanical setbacks, starting with a faulty turbo that cost 20 minutes on Saturday evening. An hour into the darkness, a road wheel came off as Davey was speeding between the Mulsanne chicanes. He caught the car and got back to the pits, but it took several stops to resolve a problem with the locking mechanism. Later a suspension damper had to be replaced, and a water leak caused another delay. On Sunday afternoon, Le Mans veteran Max Cohen-Olivar was switched from the sister car to co-drive Giovanni Lavaggi to the finish, in 19th place.

Starting the older, 3-litre car, Olivar had felt a vibration in the Porsche curves less than half an hour into the race, and had fortunately been heading for the pits when the left-front wheel came off – with the locking pin still in place. Later Katsunori Iketani was delayed by 80 minutes while TLD's crew replaced a driveshaft and the left-front suspension assembly. Just after dawn, replacing the left-front wheelbearing cost another 35 minutes. The team owner swapped places with Olivar just after 11am, and was soon sharing his dismay when the mechanics had to spend 90 minutes rebuilding the left-front suspension for a second time. The car was classified, although 98 laps behind the winners.

LE MANS

ARGO NOUGHT

One of two cars built this season for Interserie entrant Hans Wittwer, this Group C2 Argo JM19C (above) represented Jo Marquart's Norfolk constructor at its fifth consecutive Le Mans. The Argo's aluminium hull was fitted with enclosed rear bodywork and a 3.3-litre, Nicholson-built Cosworth DFL. Under the team management of Gordon Horn, who had run Martin Schanche's very quick Argos here, the car was driven by three Le Mans rookies. The most experienced, Ian Khan, showed that the car was more than quick enough to qualify, but Californian lawyer Mike Dow and French hillclimber Anne Baverey were 20 seconds slower.

BALLED EAGLE

The only American entry in this race was a three-year-old Corvette GTP (left), originally built by Lola Cars as a works GM Motorsport IMSA GTP car. It failed to qualify.

This particular short-tail Corvette GTP (or Lola T710) was the last such car made and had been raced three times in 1988 by Peerless Racing, one of the works General Motors teams. GM had then cancelled Chevrolet's IMSA programme, which had delivered two GTP victories in four seasons. The car had been purchased by Peerless, which entered only three more races in 1989 before selling it on to Dennis Kazmerowski

1990

in New Jersey. Kazmerowski teamed up for a Le Mans project with Californian Paul Canary. They were joined by Jim Brucker and team manager Jay Drake and, with the help of Joe Schubeck's Eagle Engine company, set up Eagle Performance Racing in Santa Barbara. The team principals evidently believed the 24 Hours could be won by – grunt. The aluminium honeycomb hull was modified to take a monster, 10.2-litre Chevrolet 'big-block' V8. Schubeck had conceived this brute for drag racing and offshore powerboat applications, and rated it at 900bhp at only 5500rpm, driving through a Hewland VGC transaxle.

The re-engined 'Eagle 700' was underfinanced and testing had been confined to a few laps on the Willow Springs circuit in California. In Wednesday qualifying, the engine overheated and the car completed its single flying lap smoking heavily. The next day, it covered two laps before the alternator stopped working and shut off the electronic ignition, stranding the car out in the country for the duration. Only Canary set a time – 86 seconds slower than the qualifying cut-off.

TOO CLEVER BY HALF

One of the most intriguing cars here was the one-off Norma M6 (above), a C1/3.5 project equipped with a W12 engine designed for Formula 1. Sadly the naturally aspirated MGN W12 would never run properly on either of the qualifying days. Much to the frustration of textile entrepreneur and former privateer Sauber owner Noël del Bello, who had helped to finance the project and was to have driven, the Norma failed even to get out on the circuit.

The unique engine was designed and built by Guy Nègre, who had been an engineer in the Renault Sport F1 engine department for six years before 1978, when he had set up his own aircraft engine development company in Vinon-sur-Verdon, in Provence. The Moteurs Guy Nègre W12 seemed to offer as much power as a V12 with better packaging. The drawback was complexity. The engine had three cylinder banks forming two 60deg vees, and its compactness was further enhanced by the innovative use of rotary valvetrains in place of camshafts, to allow a high compression ratio and more RPM. This system caused serious sealing problems. The AGS team ran the engine in a test chassis in the summer of 1989, but that was as close as it came to a Grand Prix.

Nègre joined forces for this Le Mans with Norbert Santos and Marc Doucet, the founders of Norma Auto Concept, a small sports-prototype constructor in St Pé de Bigorre, in the Pyrénées. Santos had contested three French hillclimb series with his previous Norma M5 sports-racer, but had little circuit racing experience.

The refusal of the W12 to run cleanly was the final nail in its coffin. It was never seen again, and neither was the Norma M6 chassis.

SEVENTH HEAVEN FOR JAGUAR 49

LE MANS

24 HEURES DU MANS
16-17 JUIN 1990

3615 ACO
A S AUTOMOBILE CLUB DE L'OUEST

1990

HOURLY RACE POSITIONS

Start	Time	Car	No	Drivers	1	2	3	4	5	6	7	8	9	10	11	12	13	14	15	16	17	18	19	20	21	22	23	24
1	3:27.02	Nissan R90CK	24	Blundell/Bailey/Brancatelli	2	1	1	3	6	7	6	6	11	16	27	DNF												
2	3:33.06	Porsche 962C	16	Larrauri/Pareja/Brun	1	3	7	7	4	2	2	3	2	3	3	4	3	3	3	2	2	2	2	2	2	2	2	DNF
3	3:33.17	Nissan R90CP	23	Hoshino/Hasemi/Suzuki	8	8	8	5	10	9	7	7	5	5	5	5	5	4	4	8	5	6	5	6	5	5	5	5
4	3:33.28	Nissan R90CK	83	Brabham/Robinson/Daly	5	4	3	6	1	3	1	1	1	1	2	2	2	2	2	3	DNF							
5	3:35.76	Nissan R90CK	25	Acheson/Donnelly/Grouillard	DNS																							
6	3:36.08	Porsche 962C	7	Bell/Stuck/Jelinski	16	14	13	11	9	8	9	9	6	6	8	8	7	6	5	4	3	3	3	4	6	6	6	4
7	3:36.10	Jaguar XJR-12LM *	4	Jones/M.Ferté/Salazar	7	7	6	4	5	4	3	5	8	7	6	6	10	9	9	8	12	11	11	DNF				
8	3:36.55	Jaguar XJR-12LM	1	Brundle/A.Ferté/Leslie	3	2	2	1	2	1	12	11	10	8	7	7	6	5	DNF									
9	3:37.00	Jaguar XJR-12LM **	3	Nielsen/Cobb/Brundle	4	5	4	2	3	5	5	2	3	2	1	1	1	1	1	1	1	1	1	1	1	1	1	1
10	3:37.13	Toyota 90C-V	36	Lees/Sekiya/Ogawa	11	24	15	18	17	16	16	15	12	12	11	11	10	9	9	8	7	7	7	6				
11	3:38.28	Porsche 962C	63	Fouché/Andskär/Kasuya	30	40	41	36	31	31	27	26	25	23	18	19	19	17	14	16	15	15	16	16	14	14	14	13
12	3:38.39	Porsche 962C-K6	10	Merwe/Takahashi/Okada	13	12	11	40	37	35	34	32	37	36	33	28	27	26	24	23	21	19	19	18	22	25	24	
13	3:38.67	Porsche 962C	9	Wollek/Dickens/Krages	9	9	10	9	11	12	10	10	9	10	10	10	9	9	8	7	7	7	7	8	8	9	9	8
14	3:38.72	Porsche 962C GTI	43	Reuter/Lehto/Weaver	10	11	12	17	16	17	17	17	17	18	16	16	16	DNF										
15	3:38.74	Toyota 90C-V	37	Suzuki/Dumfries/Ravaglia	12	16	19	12	DNF																			
16	3:39.38	Porsche 962C	26	Grohs/Duez/Oppermann	20	27	21	21	25	22	19	18	18	17	DNF													
17	3:39.76	Toyota 90C-V	38	Raphanel/Ratzenberger/Nagasaka	41	46	42	41	36	34	33	30	28	24	19	20	21	19	18	16	18	DNF						
18	3:39.78	Jaguar XJR-12LM	2	Lammers/Wallace/Konrad	6	6	5	8	7	6	4	4	4	4	3	4	7	4	6	4	4	4	3	3	3	2		
	3:40.24	Porsche 962C	8	Palmer/Wollek/Alliot	DNS																							
19	3:40.27	Porsche 962C-K6	11	Alliot/Dryver/Gonin	23	23	30	26	21	19	25	31	30	28	24	23	23	20	17	14	14	14	14	17	17	17	16	
20	3:41.32	Porsche 962C	45	Needell/Reid/Sears	15	10	9	10	8	10	8	8	7	9	9	8	7	6	6	5	6	5	6	5	4	4	3	
21	3:42.73	Porsche 962C	44	Watson/Giacomelli/Berg	14	13	26	28	32	29	29	27	27	25	22	21	20	18	15	15	13	13	13	12	12	12	11	
22	3:43.04	Mazda 787	202	Herbert/Weidler/Gachot	29	26	40	37	38	36	37	34	33	33	32	34	37	DNF										
23	3:43.35	Mazda 787	201	Johansson/Kennedy/Dieudonné	31	30	23	20	22	25	24	24	22	21	21	DNF												
24	3:43.40	Nissan R89C	85	Wada/Olofsson/Sala	19	43	38	29	24	21	22	23	27	23	22	22	23	DNF										
25	3:44.28	Nissan R90CK	84	Millen/Roe/Earl	21	34	29	35	42	44	42	40	39	38	35	32	30	29	26	26	23	22	20	20	19	18	18	17
26	3:44.34	Cougar C24S	13	Fabre/Trollé/Robert	24	19	17	14	13	13	14	14	14	13	12	13	12	15	11	10	8	9	9	8	8	7		
27	3:45.44	Porsche 962C	33	Haywood/Taylor/Rydell	17	17	16	16	12	15	12	13	13	11	14	12	16	12	9	17	16	15	15	13	13	13	12	
28	3:45.57	Porsche 962C	27	Lässig/Yver/Altenbach	36	29	24	22	18	14	15	15	16	15	15	14	13	11	12	11	11	10	10	10	10	10	10	9
29	3:45.66	Nissan R89C	82	Regout/Cudini/Los	22	15	28	25	23	22	23	29	30	25	24	24	21	19	19	19	22	25	24	23	22			
30	3:45.77	Porsche 962C	6	Pescarolo/Laffite/Ricci	18	25	14	13	15	11	11	9	12	12	13	11	14	13	13	20	19	17	17	15	15	14		
31	3:46.03	Porsche 962C	55	Elgh/Danielsson/Mezera	26	20	18	15	14	33	30	28	26	20	18	18	24	22	21	20	18	16	16	16	15			
32	3:47.75	Spice SE90C	21	Velez/Harvey/Hodgetts	28	22	22	19	27	28	26	25	24	22	30	31	28	27	25	24	23	21	21	19	19	18		
33	3:47.92	Porsche 962C	15	Huysman/Sigala/Santal	25	21	35	30	26	24	20	19	21	19	17	17	15	16	19	12	12	12	12	11	11	10		
34	3:49.45	Mazda 767B	203	Terada/Yorino/Katayama	27	25	20	23	20	23	21	20	29	26	25	22	22	21	26	26	23	22	20					
35	3:49.96	Porsche 962 GS	230	Adams/Moretti/Gebhardt	32	28	25	24	19	18	20	19	20	DNF														
36	3:50.69	Spice SE88C	103	Stirling/Shead/Hyett	47	45	43	42	39	39	38	37	36	39	38	35	33	30	30	29	28	28	27	26	25			
37	3:54.56	Lancia LC2 SP90	54	Monti/Magnani/Hepworth	45	48	47	43	40	40	40	42	44	DNF														
38	3:57.49	Spice SE87C	107	Lombardi/Morin/Lesseps	33	32	31	31	28	26	31	38	38	37	36	33	32	31	DNF									
39	3:59.34	Spice SE89C	102	Lapeyre/Grand/Maisonneuve	38	35	32	32	29	27	35	39	42	41	39	37	36	34	29	28	27	27	26	24	23			
40	3:59.54	Cougar C24S	12	Thuner/Pessiot/Iannetta	37	31	27	27	DNF																			
41	4:00.07	Porsche 962C	19	Olivar/Iketani/Davey	46	39	46	47	44	43	41	41	40	40	37	35	34	35	31	31	30	29	28	28	26			
42	4:00.55	Cougar C20S	113	Farjon/Messaoudi	42	41	39	DNF																				
43	4:02.59	Spice SE87C	131	Jones/Wood/Hynes	40	36	44	45	41	43	44	41	42	40	38	38	36	33	32	32	31	30	30	29	27			
44	4:03.03	ALD C289	106	Migault/Tremblay/Heuclin	44	44	48	46	45	DNF																		
45	4:04.09	Spice SE90C	128	Henning/Zwolsman/Donovan	35	33	37	38	34	38	36	33	32	32	28	29	31	30	28	28	26	26	25	24	25	27	27	DNF
46	4:04.73	Spice SE89C	116	Piper/Iacobelli/Youles	39	37	33	33	30	28	29	31	29	28	26	25	23	24	25	24	22	20	20	21				
47	4:10.46	Tiga GC286/9	132	Simmiss/Fenwick/Postan	48	47	45	44	43	42	44	43	43	41	39	39	37	32	31	31	29	30	30	28				
48	4:13.64	ADA 02B	105	Harrower/Sheldon/Mahony	43	42	34	34	35	37	39	36	35	34	30	33	32	DNF										
49	4:14.90	Porsche 962C	20	Davey/Lavaggi/Olivar	34	38	36	39	35	32	32	35	34	34	31	27	29	28	27	27	24	23	21	21	20	21	21	19
DNQ	4:17.69	Argo JM19C	110	Khan/Baverey/Dow	DNS																							
DNQ	4:20.93	Spice SE90C	30	Thoisy/Bovy/Egoskue	DNS																							
DNQ	5:39.02	Eagle 700	59	Canary/Kazmerowski/Vegher	DNS																							
DNQ	No time	Norma M6	61	Bello/Santos/Boccard	DNS																							

DNF Did not finish   **DNQ** Did not qualify   **DSQ** Disqualified   **FS** Failed scrutineering   **NC** Not classified as a finisher   **RES** Reserve not required

* Car No4 also qualified by Luis Pérez-Sala (E)   ** Car No3 also qualified by Eliseo Salazar (RCH)

SEVENTH HEAVEN FOR JAGUAR

LE MANS

RACE RESULTS

Pos	Car	No	Drivers			Laps	Km	Miles	FIA Class	DNF
1	Jaguar XJR-12LM	3	John Nielsen (DK)	Price Cobb (USA)	Martin Brundle (GB)	359	4882.40	3033.78	C1	
2	Jaguar XJR-12LM	2	Jan Lammers (NL)	Andy Wallace (GB)	Franz Konrad (A)	355	4828.00	2999.97	C1	
DNF	Porsche 962C	16	Oscar Larrauri (RA)	Jesús Pareja (E)	Walter Brun (CH)	353			C1	Engine
3	Porsche 962C	45	Tiff Needell (GB)	Anthony Reid (GB)	David Sears (GB)	352	4787.20	2974.62	C1	
4	Porsche 962C	7	Derek Bell (GB)	Hans-Joachim Stuck (D)	Frank Jelinski (D)	350	4760.00	2957.72	C1	
5	Nissan R90CP	23	Masahiro Hasemi (J)	Kazuyoshi Hoshino (J)	Toshio Suzuki (J)	348	4732.80	2940.82	C1	
6	Toyota 90C-V	36	Geoff Lees (GB)	Masanori Sekiya (J)	Hitoshi Ogawa (J)	347	4719.20	2932.37	C1	
7	Cougar C24S	13	Pascal Fabre (F)	Michel Trollé (F)	Lionel Robert (F)	347	4719.20	2932.37	C1	
8	Porsche 962C	9	Bob Wollek (F)	Stanley Dickens (S)	'John Winter' (Louis Krages) (D)	346	4705.60	2923.92	C1	
9	Porsche 962C	27	Jürgen Lässig (D)	Pierre Yver (F)	Otto Altenbach (D)	341	4637.60	2881.67	C1	
10	Porsche 962C	15	Harald Huysman (N)	Massimo Sigala (I)	Bernard Santal (CH)	335	4556.00	2830.96	C1	
11	Porsche 962C	44	John Watson (GB)	Bruno Giacomelli (I)	Allen Berg (CDN)	335	4556.00	2830.96	C1	
12	Porsche 962C	33	Hurley Haywood (USA)	Wayne Taylor (ZA)	Rickard Rydell (S)	332	4515.20	2805.61	C1	
13	Porsche 962C	63	George Fouché (ZA)	Steven Andskär (S)	Shunji Kasuya (J)	330	4488.00	2788.71	C1	
14	Porsche 962C	6	Henri Pescarolo (F)	Jacques Laffite (F)	Jean-Louis Ricci (F)	328	4460.80	2771.81	C1	
15	Porsche 962C	55	Eje Elgh (S)	Thomas Danielsson (S)	Tomas Mezera (AUS)	326	4433.60	2754.91	C1	
16	Porsche 962C-K6	11	Philippe Alliot (F)	Bernard de Dryver (B)	Patrick Gonin (F)	319	4338.40	2695.75	C1	
17	Nissan R90CK	84	Steve Millen (NZ)	Michael Roe (IRL)	Bob Earl (USA)	311	4229.60	2628.15	C1	
18	Spice SE90C	21	Fermin Velez (SP)	Tim Harvey (GB)	Chris Hodgetts (GB)	308	4188.80	2602.79	C1	
19	Porsche 962C	20	Tim Lee Davey (GB)	Giovanni Lavaggi (I)	Max Cohen-Olivar (MOR)	306	4161.60	2585.89	C1	
20	Mazda 767B	203	Yojiro Terada (J)	Takashi Yorino (J)	Yoshimi Katayama (J)	304	4134.40	2568.99	GTP	
21	Spice SE89C	116	Richard Piper (GB)	Olindo Iacobelli (USA)	Mike Youles (GB)	304	4134.40	2568.99	C2	
22	Nissan R89C	82	Hervé Regout (B)	Alain Cudini (F)	Costas Los (GR)	300	4080.00	2535.19	C1	
23	Spice SE89C	102	Xavier Lapeyre (F)	Jean-Philippe Grand (F)	Michel Maisonneuve (F)	291	3957.60	2459.13	C2	
DNF	Jaguar XJR-12LM	4	Davy Jones (USA)	Michel Ferté (F)	Eliseo Salazar (RCH)	282			C1	Engine
24	Porsche 962C-K6	10	Kunimitsu Takahashi (J)	Sarel van der Merwe (ZA)	Hideki Okada (J)	279	3794.40	2357.73	C1	
25	Spice SE88C	103	Robbie Stirling (CDN)	James Shead (GB)	Ross Hyett (GB)	274	3726.40	2315.47	C2	
26	Porsche 962C	19	Max Cohen-Olivar (MOR)	Katsunori Iketani (J)	Tim Lee Davey (GB)	261	3549.60	2205.61	C1	
27	Spice SE87C	131	Richard Jones (GB)	Dudley Wood (GB)	Stephen Hynes (USA)	260	3536.00	2197.16	C2	
28	Tiga GC286/9	132	Alistair Fenwick (GB)	Alex Postan (GB)	Craig Simmiss (NZ)	254	3454.40	2146.46	C2	
DNF	Spice SE90C	128	Philippe de Henning (F)	Charles Zwolsman (NL)	Robin Donovan (GB)	254			C2	Engine
DNF	Nissan R90CK	83	Geoff Brabham (AUS)	Chip Robinson (USA)	Derek Daly (IRL)	251			C1	Fuel cell
DNF	Toyota 90C-V	38	Pierre-Henri Raphanel (F)	Roland Ratzenberger (A)	Naoki Nagasaka (J)	241			C1	Electrics (ignition)
DNF	Jaguar XJR-12LM	1	Alain Ferté (F)	David Leslie (GB)	Martin Brundle (GB)	220			C1	Engine (water pump)
DNF	Nissan R89C	85	Takao Wada (J)	Anders Olofsson (S)	Maurizio Sandro Sala (BR)	182			C1	Electrics (ignition)
DNF	Porsche 962C GTI	43	Manuel Reuter (D)	JJ Lehto (SF)	James Weaver (GB)	181			C1	Tyre, fire
DNF	Spice SE87C	107	Pierre-Alain Lombardi (F)	Denis Morin (F)	Ferdinand de Lesseps (F)	170			C2	Accident
DNF	ADA 02B	105	Ian Harrower (GB)	John Sheldon (GB)	Jerry Mahony (GB)	164			C2	Suspension
DNF	Mazda 787	201	Stefan Johansson (S)	David Kennedy (IRL)	Pierre Dieudonné (B)	148			GTP	Engine (oil leak)
DNF	Mazda 787	202	Johnny Herbert (GB)	Volker Weidler (D)	Bertrand Gachot (F)	147			GTP	Electrics (overheating)
DNF	Nissan R90CK	24	Mark Blundell (GB)	Julian Bailey (GB)	Gianfranco Brancatelli (I)	142			C1	Transmission (gearbox)
DNF	Porsche 962C	26	Harald Grohs (D)	Marc Duez (B)	Jürgen Oppermann (D)	140			C1	Transmission (gearbox)
DNF	Porsche 962 GS	230	Nick Adams (GB)	Giampiero Moretti (I)	Günther Gebhardt (D)	138			GTP	Transmission (gearbox)
DNF	Lancia LC2 SP90	54	Massimo Monti (I)	Fabio Magnani (I)	Andy Hepworth (GB)	86			C1	Accident
DNF	Toyota 90C-V	37	Aguri Suzuki (J)	Johnny Dumfries (GB)	Roberto Ravaglia (I)	64			C1	Accident
DNF	Cougar C24S	12	Bernard Thuner (CH)	Pascal Pessiot (F)	Alain Iannetta (F)	57			C1	Engine
DNF	Cougar C20S	113	Philippe Farjon (F)	Jean Messaoudi (F)		43			C2	Accident
DNF	ALD C289	106	François Migault (F)	Gérard Tremblay (F)	Jacques Heuclin (F)	36			C2	Transmission (gearbox)
DNS	Nissan R90CK	25	Kenneth Acheson (IRL)	Martin Donnelly (GB)	Olivier Grouillard (F)	0			C1	Transmission (CWP, pace lap)
DNS	Porsche 962C	8	Jonathan Palmer (GB)	Bob Wollek (F)	Philippe Alliot (F)	-			C1	Accident in qualifying
DNQ	Argo JM19C	110	*Ian Khan (GB)*	Anne Baverey (F)	Michael Dow (USA)	-			C2	
DNQ	Spice SE90C	30	*Pierre de Thoisy (F)*	Quirin Bovy (D)	Francesco Egoskue (E)	-			C1	
DNQ	Eagle 700	59	*Paul Canary (USA)*	Dennis Kazmerowski (USA)	David Vegher (USA)	-			C1	
DNQ	Norma M6	61	*Noël del Bello (F)*	Norbert Santos (F)	Daniel Boccard (F)	-			C1	

DNF Did not finish **DNS** Did not start **DNS** Disqualified **FS** Failed scrutineering **RES** Reserve not required **NC** Not classified as a finisher **WD** Withdrawn Drivers in italics did not race the cars specified

1990

CLASS WINNERS

FIA Class	Starters	Finishers	First	No	Drivers	kph	mph	
Group C1	34	22	Jaguar XJR-12LM	3	Nielsen/Cobb/Brundle	204.04	126.79	Record
Group C2	10	5	Spice SE89C	116	Piper/Iacobelli/Youles	172.25	107.04	Record
GTP	4	1	Mazda 767B	203	Terada/Yorino/Katayama	172.25	107.04	Record
Totals	48	28						REVISED CIRCUIT

INDEX OF ENERGY EFFICIENCY

Pos	Car	No	Drivers	Score
1	Spice SE88C	103	Stirling/Shead/Hyett	3.198
2	Spice SE87C	131	Jones/Wood/Hynes	-1.672
3	Spice SE89C	102	Lapeyre/Grand/Maisonneuve	-3.182
4	Spice SE90C	21	Velez/Harvey/Hodgetts	-4.085
5	Porsche 962C	33	Haywood/Taylor/Rydell	-4.548
6	Porsche 962C	9	Wollek/Dickens/Krages	-5.278
7	Porsche 962C	44	Watson/Giacomelli/Berg	-5.595
8	Porsche 962C	7	Bell/Stuck/Jelinski	-5.660
9	Nissan R90CK	84	Millen/Roe/Earl	-5.684
10	Porsche 962C	11	Alliot/Dryver/Gonin	-5.815
&c				

FIA WORLD SPORTS-PROTOTYPE CHAMPIONSHIP

Race	Winner	Drivers
Suzuka (J) 300 miles	Sauber-Mercedes C9	Schlesser/Baldi
Monza (I) 300 miles	Mercedes-Benz C11	Schlesser/Baldi
Silverstone (GB) 300 miles	Jaguar XJR-11	Brundle/A.Ferté
Spa-Francorchamps (B) 300 miles	Mercedes-Benz C11	Mass/Wendlinger
Dijon-Prénois (F) 300 miles	Mercedes-Benz C11	Schlesser/Baldi
Nürburgring (D) 300 miles	Mercedes-Benz C11	Schlesser/Baldi
Donington Park (GB) 300 miles	Mercedes-Benz C11	Schlesser/Baldi
Montréal (CDN) 166 miles *	Mercedes-Benz C11	Schlesser/Baldi
Mexico City (MEX) 300 miles	Mercedes-Benz C11	Mass/Schumacher

* Red-flagged race

FINAL CHAMPIONSHIP POINTS

Final Positions	Team	Points
TEAMS		
1	Team Sauber Mercedes (CH)	67.5
2	Silk Cut Jaguar (GB)	30
3	Nissan Motorsport (J)	26
4	Spice Engineering (GB)	13
5	Joest Racing (D)	8.5
6	Porsche Kremer Racing (D)	5.5
7	Brun Motorsport (CH)	4
8	Richard Lloyd Racing (GB)	3
=	Toyota Team TOMS (J)	3
DRIVERS		
1	Jean-Louis Schlesser (F)	49.5
=	Mauro Baldi (I)	49.5
3	Jochen Mass (D)	48
4	Andy Wallace (GB)	25
5	Jan Lammers (NL)	21
=	Michael Schumacher (D)	21
=	Karl Wendlinger (A)	21
8	Martin Brundle (GB)	19
9	Julian Bailey (GB)	18
10	Mark Blundell (GB)	16
&c		

SEVENTH HEAVEN FOR JAGUAR

LE MANS

1991
MAZDA FIRST FOR JAPAN

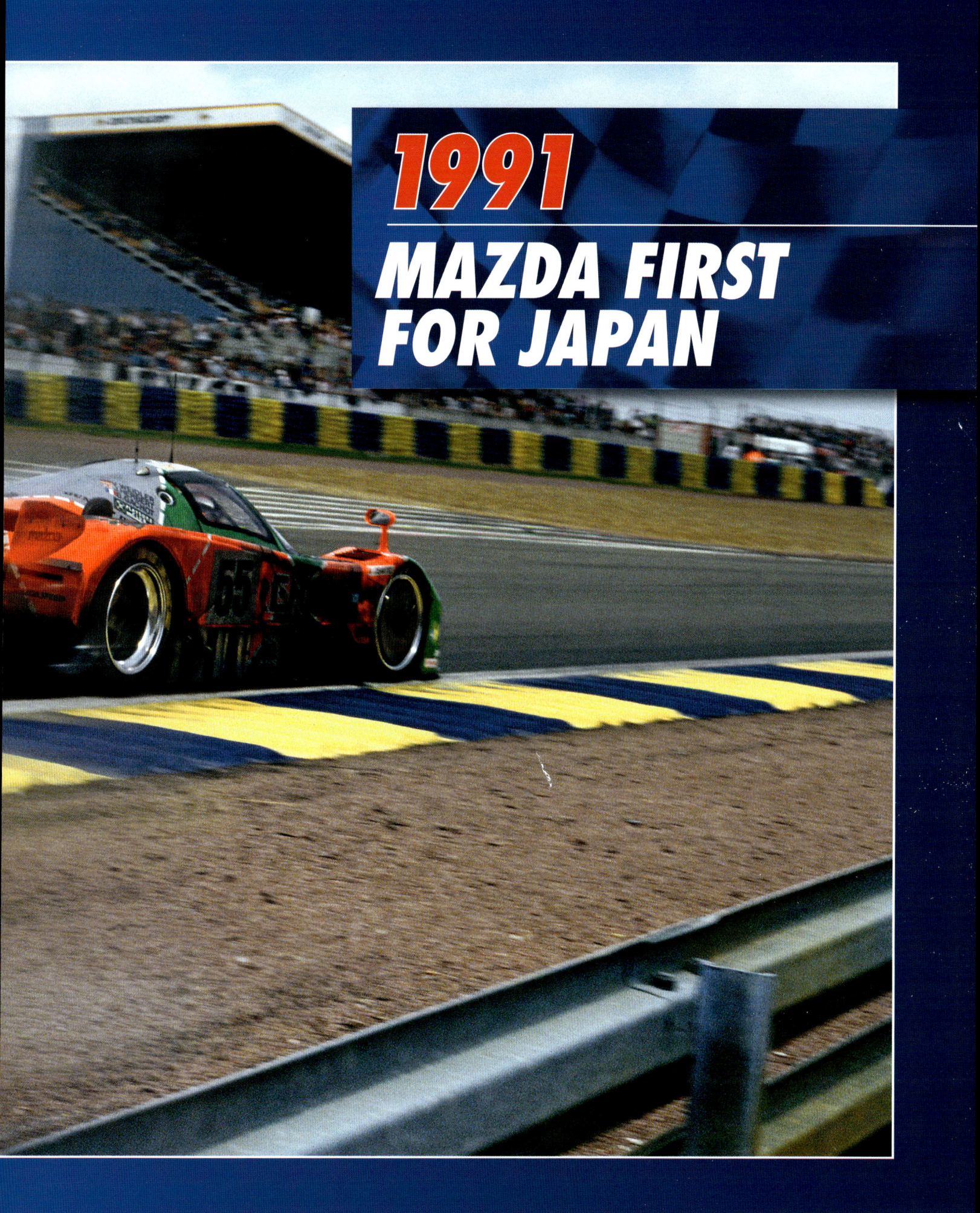

LE MANS

RACE INFORMATION

RACE DATE
22-23 June

RACE No
59

CIRCUIT LENGTH
8.451 miles/13.600km

HONORARY STARTER
Hélène Blanc
Prefect, Département de la Sarthe

MARQUES (ON GRID)
ALD	1
Cougar	3
Jaguar	4
Lancia	1
Mazda	3
Peugeot	2
Porsche	13
ROC	1
Sauber-Mercedes	3
Spice	7

STARTERS/FINISHERS
38/12

WINNERS

OVERALL
Mazda

INDEX OF ENERGY EFFICIENCY
Sauber-Mercedes

ENTRY LIST

No	Car	Entrant (nat)	cc	Engine	Tyres	Weight (kg)	Class
1	Sauber-Mercedes C11	Team Sauber Mercedes (CH)	4973	M.119 V8	Goodyear	1010	Cat 2
2	Sauber-Mercedes C291	Team Sauber Mercedes (CH)	3492	M.291 F12	Goodyear	N/A	Cat 1
3	Jaguar XJR-14	Silk Cut Jaguar (GB)	3493	Cosworth HB V8	Goodyear	N/A	Cat 1
4	Jaguar XJR-14	Silk Cut Jaguar (GB)	3493	Cosworth HB V8	Goodyear	763	Cat 1
5	Peugeot 905	Peugeot Talbot Sport (F)	3499	SA35-A1 V10	Michelin	794	Cat 1
5T	Peugeot 905	Peugeot Talbot Sport (F)	3499	SA35-A1 V10	Michelin	N/A	Cat 1
6	Peugeot 905	Peugeot Talbot Sport (F)	3499	SA35-A1 V10	Michelin	786	Cat 1
6T	Peugeot 905	Peugeot Talbot Sport (F)	3499	SA35-A1 V10	Michelin	N/A	Cat 1
7	ALD C91	Louis Descartes (F)	3494	Cosworth DFR V8	Goodyear	814	Cat 2
8	Spice SE90C	Euro Racing (NL)	3494	Cosworth DFZ V8	Goodyear	805	Cat 1
8T	Spice SE90C	Euro Racing (NL)	3494	Cosworth DFZ V8	Goodyear	N/A	Cat 1
11	Porsche 962C-K6	Porsche Kremer Racing (D)	3164tc	F6	Yokohama	1002	Cat 2
11T	Porsche 962C-K6	Porsche Kremer Racing (D)	3164tc	F6	Yokohama	N/A	Cat 2
12	Cougar C26S	Courage Compétition (F)	2994tc	Porsche F6	Goodyear	1010	Cat 2
13	Cougar C26S	Courage Compétition (F)	2826tc	Porsche F6	Goodyear	1019	Cat 2
14	Porsche 962C	Salamin Primagaz (CH)	3164tc	F6	Goodyear	1019	Cat 2
15	Lancia LC2	Veneto Equipe (I)	3050tc	Ferrari V8	Dunlop	1076	Cat 2
16	Porsche 962C	Repsol Brun Motorsport (CH)	3164tc	F6	Yokohama	1007	Cat 2
17	Porsche 962C	Repsol Brun Motorsport (CH)	3164tc	F6	Yokohama	1007	Cat 2
18	Mazda 787B	Mazdaspeed (J)	2616r	R26B 4R	Dunlop	850	Cat 2
18T	Mazda 787	Mazdaspeed (J)	2616r	R26B 4R	Dunlop	N/A	Cat 2
21	Porsche 962C	Konrad Motorsport (D)	3164tc	F6	Yokohama	995	Cat 2
31	Sauber-Mercedes C11	Team Sauber Mercedes (CH)	4973	M.119 V8	Goodyear	1008	Cat 2
32	Sauber-Mercedes C11	Team Sauber Mercedes (CH)	4973	M.119 V8	Goodyear	1010	Cat 2
32T	Sauber-Mercedes C11	Team Sauber Mercedes (CH)	4973	M.119 V8	Goodyear	N/A	Cat 2
33	Jaguar XJR-12LM	Silk Cut Jaguar (GB)	7400	HE V12	Goodyear	1023	Cat 2
34	Jaguar XJR-12LM	Silk Cut Jaguar (GB)	7400	HE V12	Goodyear	1023	Cat 2
35	Jaguar XJR-12LM	Silk Cut Jaguar (GB)	7400	HE V12	Goodyear	1029	Cat 2
36	Jaguar XJR-12LM	TWR (GB) Suntec Jaguar (J)	7400	HE V12	Goodyear	1029	Cat 2
37	ROC 002	Louis Descartes/ROC Compétition (F)	3493	Cosworth DFR V8	Goodyear	847	Cat 1
38	Spice SE90C	Louis Descartes/Berkeley Team London (GB)	3494	Cosworth DFZ V8	–	–8	Cat 1
39	Spice SE89C	Louis Descartes/Graff Racing (F)	3494	Cosworth DFZ V8	Goodyear	784	Cat 1
40	Spice SE90C	Euro Racing/AO Racing (NL)	3494	Cosworth DFZ V8	Dunlop	773	Cat 1
40T	Spice SE90C	Euro Racing/AO Racing (NL)	3494	Cosworth DFZ V8	Dunlop	N/A	Cat 1
41	Spice SE90C	Euro Racing/Team Fedco (J)	3494	Cosworth DFZ V8	Goodyear	787	Cat 1
42	Spice SE88P	Euro Racing/Classic Racing (USA)	3200tc	Ferrari 308C V8	Goodyear	1010	Cat 2
43	Spice SE89C	Euro Racing/PC Automotive (GB)	3494	Cosworth DFZ V8	Goodyear	786	Cat 1
44	Spice SE89C	Euro Racing/Chamberlain Engineering (GB)	3494	Cosworth DFZ V8	Goodyear	817	Cat 1
45	Spice SE89C	Euro Racing/Chamberlain Engineering (GB)	3494	Cosworth DFZ V8	Goodyear	812	Cat 1
46	Porsche 962C-K6	Porsche Kremer Racing (D)	3164tc	F6	Yokohama	1004	Cat 2
47	Cougar C26S	Courage Compétition (F)	2994tc	Porsche F6	Goodyear	1004	Cat 2
48	Cougar C24S	Courage Compétition (F)	2994tc	Porsche F6	Goodyear	N/A	Cat 2
49	Porsche 962C	Courage Compétition (F) Trust Racing Team (J)	3164tc	F6	Dunlop	1020	Cat 2
50	Porsche 962C	Courage Compétition/Alméras Freres (F)	2994tc	F6	Goodyear	1043	Cat 2
51	Porsche 962C	Salamin Primagaz (CH) Obermaier Racing (D)	3164tc	F6	Goodyear	1044	Cat 2
52	Porsche 962C	Salamin Primagaz (CH) Team Schuppan (GB)	2994tc	F6	Dunlop	1016	Cat 2
53	Porsche 962C	Salamin Primagaz (CH) Team Schuppan (GB)	2994tc	F6	Dunlop	1026	Cat 2
53T	Porsche 962C	Salamin Primagaz (CH) Team Schuppan (GB)	2994tc	F6	Dunlop	N/A	Cat 2
54	Porsche 962C	Salamin Primagaz (CH) Team Davey (GB)	2994tc	F6	Dunlop	N/A	Cat 2
55	Mazda 787B	Mazdaspeed (J)	2616r	R26B 4R	Dunlop	845	Cat 2
56	Mazda 787B	Mazdaspeed (J)	2616r	R26B 4R	Dunlop	850	Cat 2
57	Porsche 962C	Konrad Motorsport/Joest Porsche Racing (D)	3164tc	F6	Goodyear	1017	Cat 2
58	Porsche 962C	Konrad Motorsport/Joest Porsche Racing (D)	3164tc	F6	Goodyear	1020	Cat 2
59	Porsche 962C	Konrad Motorsport/Joest Porsche Racing (D)	2994tc	F6	Goodyear	1020	Cat 2

LE MANS 24 HOURS 1990–99

1991

ENTRY

The uncertainties in the weeks before this race [see panel] bordered on the absurd when FISA found itself with only 17 cars registered for its new Sportscar World Championship, but under contract with the ACO to provide 40. After much negotiation, a way was found to admit non-registered cars, and eventually 46 (plus eight T-cars) went through scrutineering: 14 in Category 1, and 32 in Category 2, from which the winner would surely come.

Jaguar, Mercedes-Benz and Peugeot all brought their new 'sprint' cars, but only the French team had to race them. Four Jaguars faced three Sauber-Mercedes, three Mazdas and the two 750-kilo Peugeots. Porsche again assisted its customer Group C teams, especially Joest, Brun and Kremer. ALD, Courage, ROC and Spice were the racing specialists and brought the number of 'works' entries to 25.

QUALIFYING

As if to add to the absurdity of the situation, FISA had ruled that the first 10 positions on every SWC grid were to be reserved for its F1-engined cars. The effect at Le Mans was that the fastest qualifier, a Group C Sauber-Mercedes, lined up 11th, having lapped almost 40 seconds faster than the 10th placed Spice-Cosworth.

A Category 1 car was actually fastest in the Wednesday sessions. Andy Wallace's Jaguar XJR-14 set the time on a damp track before rain ruined the rest of the evening. The next day, in dry conditions, Jean-Louis Schlesser was fastest for Mercedes. Wallace was seven-tenths slower, and it was decided not to race the relatively fragile 14, anyway.

The other two Saubers were also among the fastest five, driven by Karl Wendlinger and Jonathan Palmer, but their times were beaten by Philippe Alliot in one of the Peugeots. Qualified third and eighth, the Peugeots monopolised the front row, but the smart money was on the old-style Saubers and Jaguars. Mazdaspeed and its drivers inscrutably kept their powder dry for race day…

LE MANS

ORGANISATION

In September 1990, the Le Mans syndicate began a total demolition and rebuild of the pits and paddock complex. Imposing new facilities, costing more than £12 million, made this one of the best equipped racing venues in the world. A 2900-seat grandstand, the race control centre, the media centre and corporate hospitality suites were constructed above 48 fully equipped pits, each 15m long and 5m wide (five times the area of the pits built in 1956), and with its own washroom. The FIA circuit licence now allowed only 48 starters. The width of the startline straightaway was increased to 12m, there was a 3m wide race management zone for the teams, and the new pit-lane was 15m wide. The new facilities made redundant the famous, ramshackle signalling pits on the exit of Mulsanne corner.

On the course itself, the turns at Indianapolis and Arnage were slightly modified to provide extra run-off, and the Mulsanne chicanes resurfaced to eliminate bumps that had caused problems the previous June.

These works were started as soon as FISA had signed a five-year contract with the ACO to include the 24 Hours in the new Sportscar World Championship (SWC). The *Syndicat Mixte* acceded to FISA's demands over TV and other commercial rights, timekeeping and other processes. In return, FISA offered five years of stability – an undertaking that would prove to be risible.

FISA promised worldwide TV promotion for the new series and reduced the standard SWC race distance by 10 percent. Yet, as in 1990, so few FIA Sportscar projects were initiated that it again declared the 1991 season 'transitional' and readmitted Group C1/GTP hardware. FIA Sportscars were to be classified in FISA's Category 1, the C1 and GTP entries in Category 2. The C1s were to be constrained by the same fuel regulations as before (2550 litres here), but were now hit with a 1000kg minimum weight. FISA applied no weight penalty to the rotary-engined Mazdas that had been dominating the GTP division – an astonishing mistake.

The C1/GTP concession gave the deluded FIA and FISA president, Jean-Marie Balestre, the confidence to commit to providing the ACO with at least 50 cars. But when, in March 1991 (only three weeks before the opening event at Suzuka), FISA published the SWC entry list, it contained only 17. The Category 1 FIA Sportscars were five, representing Jaguar, Mercedes-Benz and Peugeot, plus an ALD and a Spice.

Clearly, it was impossible for FISA to honour its contract. Although the ACO accepted a reduction in FISA's commitment, to 40 cars, the governing body came under pressure from event promoters to allow non-registered teams to compete in SWC races, even on a one-off basis. And at the end of March, FISA announced that such a waiver would be applied at Le Mans (and at two non-European events).

RACE

Only 11 of the 38 cars that actually started were FIA Sportscars, but at least Peugeot put on a show for a while. Keke Rosberg led to the first pitstops, with the pole position 905 in second place – until a fuel spillage caused a flash-fire in the pits. Many extinguishers smothered the flames before anyone was hurt, and the car continued after a clean-up. Soon the other 905 was also in trouble, with a misfire, and several pitstops cost it almost an hour. Both the Peugeots were out before Saturday was done, Alliot's with a broken engine, Rosberg's with a busted gear linkage.

Mercedes held down a 1-2-3 for much of the evening after the best of its 'Junior' team drivers, Michael Schumacher, had raced into the lead. The Jaguars were nowhere: surprising everyone, the thirsty V12s could not approach the lap times of the Saubers (and even some of the Porsches) and stay on the fuel schedule.

Just before 8pm, newly into the 'junior' Sauber-Mercedes, Karl Wendlinger lost control as he braked for the Dunlop curves on cold tyres. The C11 smacked the tyre wall there but lost only six minutes while Wendlinger drove all the way round to pit-lane for a new nose and rear wing. It slipped to ninth, but the silver 1-2-3 was regained before nightfall.

It was at that point that the best of the relatively lightweight Mazdas appeared in the top four, driven by Johnny Herbert with Volker Weidler and Bertrand Gachot. It was two laps down on the leading Sauber, in which Schlesser was co-driven by Jochen Mass and Alain Ferté. But, such was Mazda's

1991

The eligibility rules could not be changed without the unanimous agreement of the registered teams, but they were not even consulted. Jaguar and Mercedes, in particular, were furious that Nissan, which (like Toyota) had opted out of the SWC in view of the 100kg weight penalty in Group C1, could now enter them for Le Mans without doing the rest of the series.

A week later, after a hastily convened meeting in Paris with Tom Walkinshaw (representing TWR Jaguar), Jochen Neerpasch (Mercedes-Benz), Jean Todt (Peugeot), Bernie Ecclestone and Max Mosley, Balestre agreed to a temporary solution: non-registered cars would be admitted at Le Mans, but they had to be entered by a registered SWC entrant, and powered by the same engines used by that entrant. Teams racing FIA Sportscars had to enter at least one for the 24 Hours, but the change gave them the option of actually racing Group C cars instead. And it thwarted Nissan, which had been preparing a three-car Group C assault.

The relieved ACO extended its entry deadline to mid-May and, among the teams, deals were cut straight away. Konrad Motorsport nominally entered three Joest-owned Porsches as well as its own single car; Salamin Primagaz four Porsches alongside its two cars; Courage Compétition two Porsches with its four Porsche-engined Cougars; Euro Racing seven Spice-Cosworths with its own two; and Louis Descartes two Spices and a ROC with his ALD. The eventual outcome was just about adequate for the 24 Hours, with 46 cars.

This year the organizing committee cut the 30 minutes from the first qualifying session on each evening that it had added the year before, leaving the teams with four hours of track time on both Wednesday and Thursday, finishing at midnight.

On the Friday evening, a lavish *Son et Lumière* display (right), with fireworks and parades, celebrated the inauguration of the new pits complex.

reputation for durability, Sauber's men knew that it would surely pounce if any silver car faltered.

At 1:50am, one of them did. Palmer pitted with a severe handling imbalance, caused by a damaged underbody after Stanley Dickens had earlier run over some debris on the track. Repairs consumed 35 minutes. At 4:50am, the second-placed 'junior' Sauber was in the pits with a damaged gearbox, and lost 33 minutes.

Now the Mazda was contesting second place with the best of the Jaguars.

At 7:15am, Dickens stopped with his engine cooked, missing its water pump drivebelt. Throughout the morning, the Schlesser/Mass/Ferté Sauber effortlessly maintained a three-lap advantage over the Mazda. But then, at 12:50pm, Ferté was summoned to the pits when Sauber's on-board telemetry warned of an overheating engine. Another thrown belt!

Fifteen minutes later, the Mazda howled past Sauber's feverishly busy mechanics for a third time, and into the lead. When the C11 was retired, Weidler looked over his shoulder – and there was no one there. Fuel-starved Jaguars were now running second, third and fourth, but the best of them was now two laps behind. The 'junior' Sauber, still overheating, was no threat, either.

Herbert, who drove the Mazda for the last two hours, collapsed as he parked up, and was in the medical centre while his co-drivers celebrated on the podium. It was the only sign of weakness over the entire weekend as Mazda became the first Japanese manufacturer to win Le Mans. Team Fedco's Spice put the icing on the cake for Japan as the only Category 1 finisher.

MAZDA FIRST FOR JAPAN 59

LE MANS

MADE TO MEASURE

Mazda dismayed Nissan and Toyota by becoming the first Japanese company to win Le Mans (and the first manufacturer with a non-piston engine). The successful car (below), raced by Johnny Herbert, Volker Weidler and Bertrand Gachot, hardly missed a beat. Its victory was facilitated by an administrative blunder that allowed Mazdaspeed to produce the ideal car for this year's regulatory conditions.

In imposing weight handicaps on all potential challengers to its new F1-engined Sportscars, FISA proposed 1000kg as the Group C minimum, but only 830kg for the rotary-engined, GTP-category Mazdas in the SWC 'sprint' races (which Mazda was contesting with a single entry). However 50kg was added for Le Mans. Mazdaspeed director Takayoshi Ohashi lobbied FISA through March and April, claiming he could not build a viable racecar weighing 880kg.

The regulations were finally confirmed at the end of April. At his desk in Hiroshima, Ohashi read them several times. And, yes, they confirmed that the Mazdas could race at Le Mans at 830kg – pretty much their racing weight here 12 months before. Ohashi kept very, very quiet. He set about preparing his team to win outright with three new cars.

Lacklustre performances by the 787 at Monza and Silverstone caused no alarm among Mazda's rivals, but the B-evolution of Nigel Stroud's design was a much better car. It had slightly increased wheelbase and track dimensions, and Stroud's work in the MIRA wind tunnel lengthened the rear overhang and minimized drag caused by bigger cooling ducts for new carbon-carbon brakes. Bigger-diameter wheels required reworked suspension geometry. Kunio Matsuura's powertrain developments focused on fuel efficiency and included a substantial increase in torque, although the quad-rotor engine's output was unchanged at 700bhp at 9000rpm.

The team retained Jacky Ickx as a consultant. Ickx had contested the previous year's Dakar rally-raid with a Lada Samara run by the ORECA team. Mazdaspeed went with his suggestion of enlisting the help of Hugues de Chaunac's organization to run the cars out of its new facility at Signes, near the Paul Ricard circuit. ORECA conducted a long-distance test there with a development evolution of the 787 in early March, and returned in April with a definitive 787B. In the interim, a 787B had débuted in the WSPC race at Suzuka, finishing sixth.

ORECA operated a 787 at Monza on the same day as a 787B was

LE MANS 24 HOURS 1990–99

1991

MAZDA FIRST FOR JAPAN 61

next raced in an All-Japan event at Fuji, and did so again at Silverstone while the specification was finalized for Le Mans. The heaviest Mazda at ACO scrutineering weighed a whopping 152kg less than the lightest C1 car (a Kremer team Porsche). The Mazdas could easily match their lap times of 12 months previously, while the C1 Porsches and Jaguars were now more than seven seconds slower. However, Ohashi was rightly dismayed by the pace of the C1 Sauber-Mercedes, which had not been here in 1990.

Weidler started the fastest of the Mazdas for its first (and only) motor race, and Herbert broke into the top 10 early in the second hour. By night-time, the car was contesting fourth place with one of the Jaguars, behind a Mercedes 1-2-3.

As two of the silver cars were delayed, the Mazda moved into third place at half-time, and second position an hour later as the Jaguar drivers saved fuel. The Mazda offered no threat to the leading Sauber throughout Sunday morning but, shortly before 1pm, the leader was in pit-lane with a terminal engine failure. Three laps later, a disbelieving Weidler found himself leading the race. He completed a double-shift and handed the car back to Herbert for another double-shift to the finish.

On emerging from the cockpit, Herbert collapsed into the arms of his father. He had had no sleep at all during the 24 Hours, and had complained of a stomach upset. He was taken to the medical centre and missed the podium ceremony, during which many of Mazda's personnel wept openly. Herbert had raced the car for 8h7m, Weidler for 8h19m and Gachot for 6h42m, the remaining 50 minutes having been consumed by 28 scheduled pitstops.

If the team's standout driver was physically spent, the car itself was just fine. Its only delays had been caused by two brake pad changes and one disc change (all pre-planned), two replacement nose sections, and a blown headlamp bulb. Back in Japan, the 787B was stripped down in front of the media, and nothing was found that would have prevented it from completing another 24-hour race.

David Kennedy, Stefan Johansson and Maurizio Sandro Sala raced the sister car (above) to sixth place, having lost a couple of positions either side of 9am when their crew had to spend 16 minutes replacing an overheating driveshaft. This car was fitted with a lower fifth gear ratio than the others, meaning that it used less fuel, but was 20kph (12mph) slower in a straight line.

Yojiro Terada, Takashi Yorino and Pierre Dieudonné ended the weekend two places further down the field with the third 787B. Using ferrous front brakes, they went through pads faster than the others, and were also delayed on Sunday by a puncture and a faulty gearshift mechanism.

1991

LEFT TO STARVE

As it made its way to the podium, Mazda's winning entourage was warmly applauded by many in the professional sportscar racing community, and none more generously than Tom Walkinshaw. This must have been difficult: that pesky rotary was the only obstacle between him and a 1-2-3 result for his Jaguars. No way had the XJR drivers been able to take the fight to the much lighter Mazda while living within their fuel budget. They had been reduced to hoping the Mazda would break. It hadn't.

TWR defended its title with more than 100 personnel and six cars. Two new XJR-12 chassis were produced, while the one that had carried No1 the previous June was updated. In addition, the upgraded XJR-9 that had raced here as No4 in 1990 was rebuilt after a crash at Daytona in February, and was entered for Suntec, the sponsor of TWR's new Japanese championship team.

The SWC rules demanded that any team with an FIA Sportscar had to enter it here, even if it intended actually to race an old-style Group C car, so TWR's road convoy also bore two of its new 750kg racers. Mischief came into TWR's mind – to thwart Peugeot's ambitions for pole position.

The work of the team's new chief designer, Ross Brawn, assisted by John Piper, the XJR-14 was powered by a Jaguar-badged version of Cosworth's F1 Ford HB V8, making 650bhp at 11,500rpm. After ceding victory to Peugeot at Suzuka, TWR had won the next rounds of the SWC at Monza and Silverstone with these very effective 'sprint' cars.

Pictured overleaf at scrutineering, only one XJR-14 was deployed in qualifying. On Wednesday, on a track surface still damp from late-afternoon rain, Andy Wallace only got in one flying lap on slick tyres, but it was good enough for the overnight pole. The next day, all but the first 40 minutes of qualifying was dry, but Wallace's best effort was spoiled when, as he was about to pass team-mate Bob Wollek's XJR-12 in the kink before Indianapolis, its right-rear tyre burst. Wallace had to brake the XJR-14, and admire Wollek's brilliant car control as he kept it out of the wall. Ultimately Wallace was beaten by six-tenths by Jean-Louis Schlesser's Group C Sauber. When TWR announced on Friday that it would not start the XJR-14, Peugeot had the front row to itself.

The 1991 evolution of the XJR-12 incorporated a range of revisions drawn by Alastair McQueen, including a slightly longer nose with a reshaped intake and a spoiler to increase front loading. The braking system was upgraded, with thicker iron discs and carbon-metallic pads. Allan Scott's race engine team had now taken the V12 out to 7.4-litres for a little more power and a higher torque output, and the new package was thoroughly tested at Paul Ricard at the end of May.

MAZDA FIRST FOR JAPAN

LE MANS

Davy Jones/Michel Ferté/Raul Boesel 'raced' into second place at the finish, two laps down on the Mazda. Their XJR-12 stayed mechanically sound throughout and, soon after 10pm, they found themselves in a duel with the Mazda that endured all night. Come Sunday morning, McQueen, race-engineering this car, had to order the drivers to conserve fuel. They were helpless as the rotary rival pulled further and further ahead.

The recruitment of Wollek was a coup for TWR. Taking over after a single-shift by Teo Fabi, just before 5pm, Wollek lost time in a spin at Mulsanne corner but, although race engineer Steve Farrell never allowed his drivers to overspend their fuel allocation, the car (below) emerged in fourth place soon after dawn. At 5:45am, Kenneth Acheson struck a stone-deaf rabbit, whose instant demise caused a pitstop for a new nose, but the delay was minimal. Later a fractured exhaust pipe merely made the engine sound horrible, although the escaping gas gave each of the drivers a headache in turn.

Two laps behind, fourth place fell to the XJR that had been the fastest for most of the race (botom right). Derek Warwick had just gained third place at 9:25pm when he spun into the gravel at Indianapolis, the result of the engine cutting out under braking. He lost four minutes, and more time an hour later in the escape road at the Nissan chicane, for the same reason. The car had recovered from ninth to fourth when, at 2:30am, its engine died at Arnage. Warwick emerged and, taking instructions from race engineer John McLoughlin on his radio, found a detached fuel pump lead. The crew fitted a new

64 LE MANS 24 HOURS 1990–99

pump in the pits and the loss amounted to 13 minutes. After Wallace had slid onto the beach at the first new chicane at 5:15am, losing three laps while marshals hauled out the car, not even John Nielsen, the hero of 1990, could retrieve the situation. At 1:40pm, Warwick went off again, this time at the Dunlop chicane, but lost no more places.

The team's only non-finisher was the Japanese-backed entry, whose drivers had a relentlessly torrid time. The new TWR Suntec team was running an XJR-11 turbo in the JSPC for Mauro Martini/Jeff Krosnoff, who were partnered on their Le Mans débuts by David Leslie. This year's IMSA schedule ruled out a hands-on involvement by TWR's US-based team, whose car had won 12 months before, except for Dave Benbow, who was brought over to race-engineer the Suntec XJR – and had a nightmare weekend.

The setbacks began at 6pm when the engine stopped at the Nissan chicane, due to a faulty fuel pump switch. It took Martini 45 minutes to bypass the switch, restart the engine and get back to pit-lane. Only three laps after rejoining the race, he dropped a wheel heavily over the kerbing of the same corner, and the impact yanked a wishbone mount out of the tub. Repairing the hull and fitting new suspension took more than two hours. The car ran well enough through the night but at breakfast-time Krosnoff crashed at Tertre Rouge. The mechanics toiled for almost an hour to replace the left-rear suspension and the engine cover, and fitted a spare rear wing (above). Krosnoff resumed, but a few minutes later the car lost drive, and stopped at Arnage. Krosnoff tried in vain to find a gear before hitching a lift to pit-lane on a spectator's motorbike.

TWR went on to secure both the SWC Teams and Drivers titles (with Fabi). An XJR-14 was then released to Suntec, and Fabi/David Brabham trounced Toyota, Nissan and Mazda in the JSPC finale at Sugo. The team only ever built one more XJR-12, which finished second to an NPTI Nissan at Daytona in 1992.

MAZDA FIRST FOR JAPAN 65

THREE BLUNTED STARS

Mazda winning this race was less surprising than Mercedes-Benz losing it. The Sauber C11 Group C cars were by far the best here, but the German-Swiss factory team managed to transform an unopposed 1-2-3 at midnight (below) to a fifth place at the finish.

This was the fourth season in which Peter Sauber's distinctive coupés had been the cars to beat as official representatives of the Mercedes brand. Mercedes had first won Le Mans in 1989, when the C9 had taken seven of eight WSPC races. The team had not entered the non-championship 24 Hours in 1990, but the C11 had successfully defended both titles by winning eight of nine events. The C11 was now being superseded by the V12 C291 FIA Sportscar, but it was still a superb long-distance racecar. It was no surprise when the team, for the sake of appearances, completed only two laps with a C291, slow enough not to qualify.

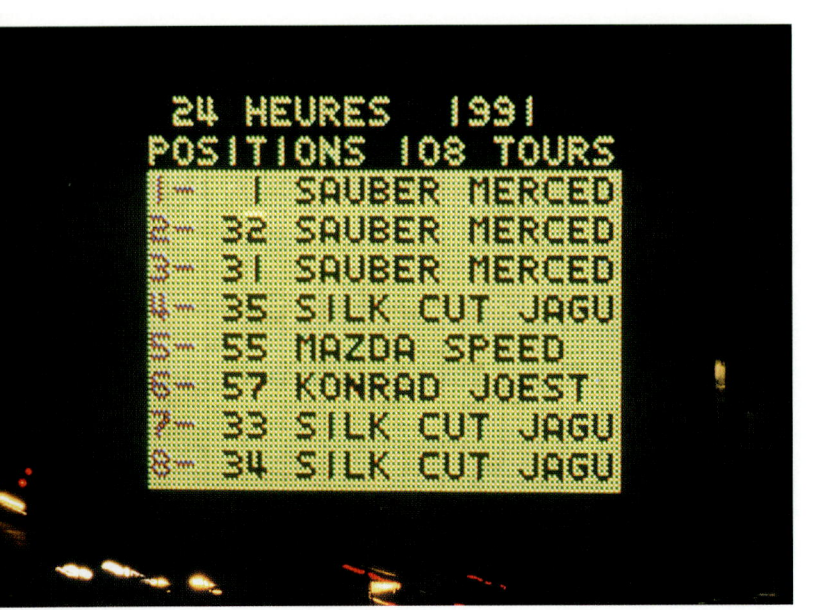

The C11 was an evolution of Leo Ress's Group C design first seen in 1985, now with an advanced composites monocoque bearing the Mercedes M.119 powertrain, the most effective ever raced in the fuel-formula era. The all-aluminium, 5-litre, 32-valve turbo V8 was the successor of the production-based M.117 which, long before the manufacturer's overt involvement, had been discreetly developed for Sauber's project with two KKK turbochargers by Willi Müller and Gert Withalm. They were also responsible for the racing version of the M.119, working within Hermann Hiereth's now 150-strong Motorsport Project Group in the factory at Unterturkheim, on the outskirts of Stuttgart. The 1991 version was 6kg lighter and came with the latest Bosch Motronic MP1.8 fuel-injection system. The Mulsanne chicanes had made this more of a power circuit than ever, and the V8 could safely take 2.4-bar 'boost', making more than 850bhp. It could be raced to the fuel with about 720bhp at 7000rpm at 1.8-bar, also putting tremendous torque through a purpose-designed, five-speed transmission.

The 1991 C11 had a strengthened gearbox, a carbon braking system, and an aero package including a revised nose (improving airflow to the new brakes) and a lowered engine cover and rear aerofoil. Ress was race-engineering the No1 car for Jean-Louis Schlesser, the 1989-90 World

1991

Champion, and sent him out on soft Goodyears to set the fastest time on Thursday evening. 'Schless' went too early: the track was still damp in places, and he drove his best lap a little later, on race rubber. It was more than four seconds slower than Mark Blundell's mega-lap for Nissan 12 months before, but good enough to see off even the 750kg Sportscars of Jaguar and Peugeot. Mercedes Junior Team youngster Karl Wendlinger and Jonathan Palmer were fourth and fifth fastest with the other C11s.

Schlesser (pictured exiting Tertre Rouge) was content to allow the Peugeots their moments of glory on Saturday afternoon, and Mercedes did not hit the front until the second shifts. Michael Schumacher was the first to take the lead with the Junior car (above), followed by Jochen Mass with Schlesser's. Soon Palmer made it a silver 1-2-3.

Just after 8pm, taking over the Junior C11 from Fritz Kreutzpointner, Wendlinger left the pits just as Schlesser came past and, in his anxiety, spun the car on its cold tyres in the Dunlop curve. It smacked the tyre wall there with both ends, but Wendlinger made it back to pit-lane for a fresh nose section and rear wing, at a cost of only six minutes at rest.

Schlesser/Mass/Alain Ferté led effortlessly into the night, with Palmer/Stanley Dickens/Kurt Thiim behind them, and the Juniors third. At 1:50am, Palmer pitted, complaining that the car was wandering beyond his control when it exceeded 180mph: the underbody had been damaged when Dickens had run over some debris on the track in the previous shift. The repairs consumed 36 minutes and the car was never the same again: it turned out that the debris had also damaged an engine mount. Eventually it failed, and took with it a suspension link. Dickens pitted to retire the car at 7:15am.

At this juncture, the No1 Mercedes was still the fastest car in the race – and the most fuel-efficient. After 15 hours of racing, it had averaged 138mph and 49.8 litres/100km of fuel. The equivalent numbers for the Mazda that would win the race were 133 and 52.6, for the best-placed Jaguar 132 and 54.4. The silver car was that good.

But now it was alone in the lead because, during the night, the hard-driving Juniors had been delayed by a gearbox breakage that had left Wendlinger jammed in fourth. Race engineer Reinhard Lechner's crew had needed two stops to rectify the problem, costing more than half an hour.

And the leading C11 was leaking water, and starting to overheat. Ress ordered his drivers to take it easy. At 12:50pm, No1 had been leading for almost 17 hours, but the telemetry showed the temperatures soaring. The water pump had thrown its drivebelt – a problem that, just over an hour earlier, had delayed the Juniors for another 12 minutes. All efforts to restart the engine failed until 1:30pm, long after the Mazda had assumed the lead. And Ferté returned to pit-lane to retire the car after covering a single, smoky lap.

When Kreutzpointner took over from Schumacher to drive the last hour, the surviving C11 was also overheating, and he lost fourth place to a Jaguar with minutes to go. Victory in the Index of Energy Efficiency was small consolation.

This was not the way to end the Le Mans participation of these mighty cars. In December, Mercedes-Benz Motorsport spiked its Sportscar programme, which was employing about 150 powertrain people in Stuttgart and 70 at Sauber's factory in Hinwil, near Zurich.

MAZDA FIRST FOR JAPAN | 67

SPRINT CAR NAMED 'DESIRE'

Three factory teams built 750kg FIA Sportscars for this season, but only Peugeot raced them here. Unlike Jaguar and Mercedes, Peugeot did not possess a Group C racer, so had no choice. And the 905s had not yet been developed for long-distance work: both were parked before it was even dark.

After many years of rallying, Peugeot widened its ambitions in November 1988 by embarking on this all-French 'works' sports-racing project – the first since the Le Mans-winning Renault of 1978. Peugeot's historic lion logo had first been seen at Le Mans way back in 1926 but the manufacturer had never returned, although some technical support had been provided through its back door to the little WM team during the 1980s.

The 905 was produced in the expansive Peugeot Talbot Sport factory in Vélizy, near Paris, in the 10th year of its direction by Jean Todt. His team had won World Rally Championships in 1985-86 but lacked experience in track racing. However, its technical director since 1984 had been André de Cortanze, the former designer of Renault's Le Mans sports-prototypes and F1 cars. Cortanze was tasked with forming a chassis group for the 905 project, working with an engine group under Jean-Pierre Boudy, who had been a key member of the team behind Renault's successful turbo V6 race engines. The aerodynamic development was entrusted to the Aérodyne consultancy in Paris under Robert Choulet, whose long list of credits included Le Mans cars for CD, Matra, Porsche and Alfa Romeo.

Todt approached Dassault (the manufacturer of Rafale and Mirage airplanes in nearby Saint-Cloud) to put Cortanze's monocoque design into advanced composites. The chassis bore Boudy's all-aluminium 'monobloc' SA35 engine, an 80deg, 40-valve V10, fully stressed, with mid-mounted radiators. Peugeot conservatively rated the output of the Magneti-Marelli managed V10 at 600bhp at 12,000rpm. An innovative transaxle split the gearbox either side of the CWP, with first and second gears forward, third to sixth behind; this enhanced weight distribution and set the CWP high enough to allow horizontal driveshafts. Like the new Jaguar and Mercedes, the Peugeot was equipped with carbon brakes from the outset.

Choulet's wind-tunnel work evolved a low-line body including a tiny cockpit with a high-curvature screen, a front splitter, an F1-style 'Coke-bottle' rear end, sculpted, upsweeping sidepods, and a wide, monoplane rear aerofoil mounted to the gearbox.

The 905 was launched at a patriotic media event at Magny-Cours in July 1990 and was raced in the series-closing WSPC events in Montréal and Mexico City, driven by Keke Rosberg/Jean-Pierre Jabouille. After a major winter test programme, the car won the opening round of that year's inaugural SWC series at Suzuka, where Mauro Baldi/Philippe Alliot defeated a Sauber-Mercedes. Less successful performances followed at Monza and Silverstone.

Todt made no secret that his engineers were embarking on their Le Mans learning curve, armed with two race cars and two T-cars.

1991

The race cars were equipped with engines configured for reduced RPM (11,000) with revised valvegear, induction and ignition systems, some of the titanium components replaced with steel versions, a strengthened gearbox, and bigger brakes. Meanwhile Choulet's team evolved a lower-downforce, 'long-tail' aero set-up (with headlights).

The Peugeots started from the front row even though neither Alliot nor Yannick Dalmas managed a traffic-free lap, and were outqualified by Jean-Louis Schlesser's Group C Sauber. After his T-car's oil tank had sprung a leak, Rosberg, co-driving Dalmas here, had shunted their race car in the second chicane.

The Peugeots looked very fine at the front of the race (pictured at the Esses). Alliot led only until he missed a shift on the second lap, and was passed by the former F1 champion. And disaster struck the second-placed 905 (below) in its very first fuel stop. As Alliot vacated the cockpit for Jabouille, fuel spilled onto a hot exhaust and, in an instant, fire erupted at the back of the car, on the tarmac beneath it – and on Jabouille's racing suit. The crew frantically extinguished the flames before anyone was injured. After a quick clean-up, Jabouille was on his way in less than four minutes. But, 45 minutes later, he parked out at Indianapolis with a broken engine.

Meanwhile, as he handed the sister car to Dalmas, Rosberg warned his team mate that its engine was cutting out in third gear. It got worse, and Dalmas pitted out of the lead at 5:10pm. A brief inspection failed to locate the problem and he returned after one more lap, and this time the crew spent 35 minutes replacing the ignition box and wiring (the car is pictured leaving the pit). The Peugeot then went very well until 9:10pm, when Pierre-Henri Raphanel was back in pit-lane with a gearbox breakage. The repair took half an hour and, two laps after rejoining, Rosberg stopped it on the Mulsanne straight, unable to get a gear.

Later in the SWC, Rosberg/Dalmas won two more races for Peugeot at Magny-Cours and Mexico City, but Todt's team was beaten by Jaguar to the championship.

MAZDA FIRST FOR JAPAN 69

ANOTHER LEASE OF LIFE

Porsche Motorsport was now engaged in Formula 1 as the Footwork team's engine supplier but its director, Helmut Flegl, made it clear that it had no resources to deploy its new 'atmo' V12 in an FIA Sportscar project. For the last time, however, 962Cs again provided the backbone of the Le Mans entry, 13 such cars starting the race. Typically, the best result was secured by Joest Racing – but this year that result was seventh place for former works drivers Hans-Joachim Stuck, Derek Bell and Frank Jelinski (pictured in the pits).

Reinhold Joest had not entered the inaugural SWC. Having begun the new season with an emphatic victory over a GTP Nissan in the Daytona 24 Hours, he was one of the Porsche entrants who had suddenly boosted the grids of the German-based Interserie championship. But he seized the chance to race two cars here under the flag of Konrad Motorsport.

The Joest Porsches were returned to short-tail configuration this year, an in-house design with a new rear aerofoil and a wider nose section, creating more front-end downforce and accommodating wider Goodyear radials. Stuck and Bernd Schneider used 3.2-litre engines to get into the top 10 in qualifying, when a spare car was driven by Jürgen Barth. With 3-litre motors for the weekend, Stuck and Schneider raced in the top six early on, but both cars faded when brought back onto the fuel schedule during the evening.

After Louis Krages had relieved Schneider and Henri Pescarolo in a single shift at dusk, their Blaupunkt-sponsored car (below left) remained solid through the night but, soon after dawn, it was retired out of sixth place with an incurable gearbox oil leak. A little later, the engine in the FAT car began to lose water. The team managed to keep it running all the way from there to the finish, but this involved nine deeply frustrating pitstops just to add coolant. The car had been on schedule to finish fourth, but ended up 15 laps behind the winner.

QUADRUPLED COURAGE

Much encouraged by the strong performance of one of his Porsche turbo engined Group C cars in 1990, Yves Courage put together a four-car team this year. Only three started, and only one was classified as a finisher.

Three Cougars bore the latest C26S designation but only two were new this season. These were built on the latest honeycomb tubs by Alain Touchais and Jean-Claude Rose, again fitted with carbon/Kevlar bodywork drawn by Marcel Hubert, similar to the older designs but with a revised nose section (taking cooling air more effectively to the intercoolers), new wheel-arches and a smaller, more adjustable rear aerofoil. The suspension

1991

geometry was redesigned to rid the cars of an understeer characteristic and to handle the 50kg of ballast that was imposed by this year's weight regulation. All three C26s were equipped with Porsche's 3-litre powertrain.

The team's focus was on a brand-new car (right) driven by Johnny Dumfries, reigning All-Japan champion Anders Olofsson and Thomas Danielsson, under the management of Mike Phillips. However, these quick drivers were hampered by an elusive ignition fault almost throughout qualifying (and a broken fuel pump) and, to their dismay, the 'pinking' problem returned on Saturday afternoon. Soon the engine overheated and the car was parked at 7pm.

Lionel Robert, François Migault and Jean-Daniel Raulet were allocated the other new C26 (above), which had already been raced at Monza and Silverstone, and was run by Dominique Méliand, the director of a factory-backed Suzuki 24-hour motorcycle racing team. Migault had a harmless spin at Arnage at sundown but the car was strong all night. On Sunday morning, there were brief delays with a split radiator hose and a battery problem, but it was a fuel pump failure, which stranded Robert on the Mulsanne straight for a while, that prevented a points-scoring finish in the top 10.

The team had reworked as a C26 the C24 that had finished seventh in 1990, and it was raced by Michel Trollé, Claude Bourbonnais and Marco Brand. Their car manager, former Spice entrant John McNeil, had a nightmare weekend. The car was damaged in the gravel at Indianapolis and Tertre Rouge after two of three spins by Bourbonnais. It was also delayed by ongoing braking problems, a front suspension failure, a split oil radiator, a broken gearshift mechanism, and finally a water leak. Trollé drove it under the chequered flag, but it was not classified.

The fourth Cougar was the 1989 chassis that had failed to finish in 1990, similarly upgraded but equipped with the less powerful, air- and

MAZDA FIRST FOR JAPAN 71

LE MANS

water-cooled, 2.8-litre engine. Chris Hodgetts had done enough to get it into the race when, on Thursday evening, race engineer Jean-Claude Thibault did not take fully into account the weight reduction resulting from switching to dry-weather tyres on lighter rims. In a random spot-check on the ACO's weighbridge, the car was found to be 8kg underweight, and excluded.

CLEAN SWEEP FOR JAPAN

The much-vaunted Category 1 division for F1-engined FIA Sportscars, racing without fuel restriction, produced one solitary finisher. But a class win is a class win. Pictured below, the successful Spice SE90C officially represented the new owner of the British sports-racing marque, so both the class winners in this race were Japanese-entered cars.

FISA's interventions in the sportscar racing market had made it an uncertain place to do business. After Lamborghini had cancelled a V12 project with Spice Engineering, company principals Gordon Spice and Ray Bellm called in the receivers in January 1991. Ernst & Young offered Spice as a going concern, including the Spice USA business. In March, the assets were acquired by Fedco, a Japanese corporation that owned the American importer of Bitter Automobil, the German sportscar maker. A new company, Spice Prototype Automobiles, was formed to maintain production in the Brackley factory, where four new cars were built for the new season (eight fewer than in 1990).

No 'works' entry was registered for the inaugural SWC series. However, an entry was filed by Dutch customer Charles Zwolsman's Euro Racing team, which ordered two new chassis and had quasi-works status. Euro Racing's SWC registration gave no fewer than seven other Spices access to the Le Mans paddock, most of them former C2 cars masquerading as FIA Sportscars, with Cosworth DFZ engines.

Zwolsman brought both his SE90Cs to this race, deploying one as a T-car. Managed for Spice by Mike Franklin, the race car (pictured right, ahead of the ROC) was equipped with a 550bhp DFZ, prepared by John Nicholson with modified exhausts. It also had a bigger clutch and brakes, and a six-speed Hewland gearbox with Williams F1 internals.

Cor Euser qualified the car well but Zwolsman wanted to drive the opening shift on Saturday, and it had slipped to the midfield before Euser could get his hands back on it. After a single shift by Tim Harvey, and a better performance by Zwolsman, the car emerged from the decimation among the other Category 1 cars to lead the class, five laps down on the overall lead. Euser was running 14th when a fuel leak suddenly caused a vigorous engine bay fire on the approach to the Virage Ford. He hurriedly parked against the wall in the pit access lane, and vacated the cockpit real quick as a fire marshal ran up with an extinguisher. End of race.

Of the other two 1991-built Spice SE90Cs, one was shipped to Doug Peterson at Comptech for a new IMSA Lights programme with Honda's Acura brand (and won the division first time out at Daytona, ahead of Manufacturers titles in 1991-92-93). The other was ordered by Obermaier Racing for an FIA campaign. On completion of its acquisition of the Spice business, Fedco repurchased Hans Obermaier's car for a Japanese programme that began with a DNF at Fuji in early May. For a Le Mans foray on the Euro Racing ticket, its drivers, Kiyoshi Misaki and Hisashi Yokoshima, were race rookies, but were joined by Naoki Nagasaka, who had driven SARD's Toyota here the previous June.

Under the management of Masata Ishizuka, these three ended the race in 12th and last position. Their mostly solid weekend was spoiled by delays caused by a broken water radiator, a front puncture, problems with the starter electrics, and Yokoshima's spin in the Dunlop chicane. But they went home to Japan with the Category 1 trophy.

As the season continued, it became clear that the Japanese takeover was not the rescue deal it had seemed. The Fedco Spice was only raced once more in Japan, in the July event at Fuji. Investment funding dried up. Just before Christmas, engineering director Graham Humphrys and managing director Jeff Hazell both quit. Soon the company's remaining assets were acquired for their Allard J2X project by Chris Humberstone, Costas Los and Jean-Louis Ricci, who were joining forces with Comptech in the USA.

ROC RENAISSANCE

A pleasant surprise this year was the reappearance of Fred Stalder's Racing Organisation Course team, previously a regular 2-litre Group 6 front-runner with beautifully prepared Chevrons and its own ROC engines. Stalder was tiring of running Audis in the French *Supertourisme* class and saw the new FIA Sportscar category as a chance to advance his ambitions to become a constructor.

This project had originally been conceived in Lausanne, Switzerland, as the Cheetah G606, the latest in the short line of Chuck Graemiger's Group C cars. Cheetah had been inactive since 1986 and lacked the funds to build it. Late in 1989, funding was offered by Swiss businessman Jean-François Fert, whose Saco company was involved in the FIRST F3000 team. Ultimately a car was built by a consortium comprising Saco, Graemiger and ROC.

Track-testing of the 'SGR-001' prototype did not begin until February 1991. It was based on an advanced composites tub, made by Anglia Composites in the UK, to which was grafted a Cosworth DFR prepared by Heini Mader and a Hewland transmission. The carbon/Kevlar body was drawn by French aerodynamicist Robert Choulet.

The first car disappointed in testing at Paul Ricard and as a consequence Fert pulled out. Stalder's team took over the project in its Annemasse HQ, extensively reworking the bodywork, suspension and brakes. Having built an F2 single-seater back in 1980, Stalder named the finished product the ROC 002. It arrived in the paddock lacking track time – and 97kg overweight.

Pascal Fabre and Bernard Thuner were to have been co-driven by Patrick Bardinon, but he failed to get the required licence. In the early laps, Fabre (pictured above behind the Zwolsman Spice) actually led the other 750-kilo Cosworth cars for a few laps, but a driveshaft coupling broke at 6:40pm, and the crew under Guy Falquet found the differential damaged beyond repair.

Stalder intended to continue in the SWC under Louis Descartes's entry, but lack of budget meant the ROC 002 only appeared at Magny-Cours.

LE MANS

'POPI' BLOSSOMS AGAIN

Two of Porsche's established privateer teams had taken FISA's hook on the new 750kg class (a claim of worldwide TV coverage), and had swallowed the whole line – including the sinker (the crippling costs of the hardware). They had embarked on their own FIA Sportscar projects, neither of which was race-ready before Le Mans.

One of these was Brun Motorsport. Two weeks before Le Mans, the last 962C ever to emerge from the Porsche factory was delivered to the team in Gundelfingen, near Freiburg. It was deployed here for Oscar Larrauri, Jesús Pareja and Walter Brun himself – Porsche's stars of 1990.

Just like 12 months before, Larrauri emerged from qualifying with the fastest Porsche lap, and was one of the early front-runners on Saturday. 'Popi' appeared in third place inside the opening 10 laps, from 14th on the grid. Such aggressive pace was beyond any weight-handicapped Porsche for very long and, during the evening, the fuel schedule went out of the window anyway. The engine began to lose oil, and the drivers were reduced to short stints so that lubricant could be added every half-hour. And then, at about 9:30pm, an unscheduled stop cost 23 minutes: the rear suspension failed, overloaded by a 1007-kilo vehicle weight. The car (left) never did recover from these setbacks. More delays followed – major braking problems, a faulty gearshift, a spin apiece by the three drivers. Pareja drove it under the chequer in 10th position.

The sister car (the 962C that had so nearly finished second the year before) had a steady race in the hands of Harald Huysman, Robbie Stirling and Bernard Santal before blowing a head gasket soon after 1am.

The team showed its own 750kg Brun C1 in the paddock and débuted it in the following SWC event at the Nürburgring. Powered by the Judd EV V8 from the same supplier that had engined the now-defunct EuroBrun F1 team, the car failed to start that race, and did not finish at Magny-Cours, Mexico City and Autopolis. This second expensive project again ravaged Brun Motorsport's finances and the team (the winner of the 1986 WSPC) did not survive into 1992.

74 LE MANS 24 HOURS 1990–99

1991

KREMER GAMERS

The Kremer brothers registered their modified Porsches for the SWC and assembled two new 3.2-litre cars to their latest K6 specification, one on a TCP carbon/honeycomb monocoque, the other on a factory-supplied aluminium hull, while keeping a 1990 chassis as a T-car.

Harri Toivonen crashed the carbon car (left) on his out-lap on Thursday evening but Manuel Reuter put of lot of 'boost' through the T-car's 3-litre engine and qualified so well that Kremer joined Brun in putting a car ahead of both the Joest Porsches. With the race car repaired, Reuter was running seventh just before 8pm when a four-minute stop to replace a faulty fuel sensor was enough to lose four positions. Less than an hour later, this year's extra vehicle weight led to a rear suspension failure that cost Toivonen 22 minutes and put the car right out of contention. Reuter/Toivonen/JJ Lehto did their best to stage a recovery but were thwarted by their engine's excessive consumption of both water and oil. They finished ninth.

After a solid opening shift in the sister car by Gregor Foitek, the team made the mistake of relieving him with Manuel Lopez, instead of Tiff Needell. Starting his eighth lap, the Mexican lost control exiting the Dunlop chicane and spun into the right-side barrier under the footbridge there, damaging the rear suspension and wing support. He set off on the long drive back to the pits, but too quickly, and the car understeered into the gravel in the Esses (top). Marshals hauled it behind the barrier and it was posted as the first retirement.

MAZDA FIRST FOR JAPAN 75

LE MANS

BAD FOR KONRAD

SWC entrant Franz Konrad did not risk his own, unraced 750kg Sportscar here and, after selling Le Mans tickets for the three Joest Porsches, operated only his TCP honeycomb 962C (left), fitted with a 3.2 engine and carbon/Kevlar bodywork with a distinctive, short-tail rear end, drawn for the Gütersloh team by Frank Bombien. The team owner was co-driven by Anthony Reid and Pierre-Alain Lombardi but their run ended just after dark with a broken engine.

Like the Brun C1, Konrad Motorsport's KM-011 Sportscar began its brief career with a DNQ at the following WSC meeting, at the Nürburgring. Powered by Chrysler's F1 Lamborghini V12, the car started the last three WSC races but finished only an Interserie event. It finished another Interserie early in 1991, but then the team ran out of funds.

SCHUPPAN FALLS SHORT

Team Schuppan interrupted its Japanese campaign to run two Porsches assembled on its Advanced Composites hulls, each with custom bodywork, with a 1990 aluminium chassis from Stuttgart in reserve. Vern Schuppan used his unexpected presence here to show his new roadgoing 962CR 'supercar' in the paddock.

Roland Ratzenberger, Will Hoy and Eje Elgh were assigned a carbon car that had been re-engineered by Australian former F1 designer Ralph Bellamy, and had débuted as a Team Salamin entry at Silverstone in May. Bellamy's aero package was similar to one he had used on two Dauer Racing GTP Porsches that had showed well in the Daytona 24 Hours, including a big rear aerofoil centrally mounted to the gearbox. The car (pictured leading its stablemate) was on the verge of the top dozen when the left-side turbocharger began malfunctioning soon after midnight, and soon had to be replaced, at the cost of 50 minutes. All three drivers charged hard through the rest of the night but their recovery was halted by a blown head gasket an hour or so after daybreak.

The team's other carbon chassis was equipped with radical aerodynamics drawn by Max Boxstrom, the former Ecosse C2 and Aston Martin AMR-1 designer. The package comprised short-tail bodywork, dramatically lowered and rounded, with a remote, low-line rear wing, and a full-length underbody. Unfortunately the design was all theory and no practice, and it didn't work. James Weaver, Hurley Haywood and Wayne Taylor all found the car undriveable in the opening qualifying session. After Vern Schuppan himself had sampled it, it was discarded and the drivers switched to the standard aluminium car.

1991

This developed an oil leak early in the race morning warm-up, and then the driver's door detached itself during the formation lap, and Weaver peeled into the pits. Fixing the hinges cost 10 minutes and it was just the first of a catalogue of problems. A water leak, a cracked windscreen, an inoperative gearbox oil cooler and an ongoing struggle with the door hinges combined to put the car 27 laps behind the leaders at midnight, and the situation went from bad to worse with increasingly serious braking problems. The car made it to the end but was unclassified.

For the second year running, Tim Lee Davey's Schuppan-hulled Porsche missed scrutineering and was finished in the paddock, using a powertrain hastily hired from the Obermaier team. This time, less than 40 minutes was available for the drivers to qualify a completely unsorted car. It wasn't enough.

DOUBLE WHAMMY

Long-time Porsche entrant Hans Obermaier had intended to switch to a Spice-Cosworth for 1991, but in April resold his new car to Fedco, Spice's new owner, for its Japanese programme. However, Obermaier came to Le Mans on Antoine Salamin's ticket, bringing a Porsche that had not been raced that season (above right).

Jürgen Oppermann was to have driven this one-year-old 'customer' 962C with Jürgen Lässig and Pierre Yver, as he had 12 months before, but fell ill just before the race. He was replaced by Otto Altenbach, who survived a sideswipe collision an hour into the race with Michael Schumacher's race-leading Sauber-Mercedes under braking for the Virage Ford. Later Altenbach went off at the Nissan chicane, losing 12 minutes to repairs just after nightfall. Otherwise the car had a consistent run, typical of Obermaier's approach. The reward was 12th position at 8am, but that was when the brakes failed at Indianapolis, and Lässig crashed out of the race.

The Obermaier Porsche raced in the Primagaz colours of long-time Le Mans enthusiast Jacques Petitjean, as did Salamin's own car (pictured in the pits). The Swiss-based architect, who had filed Le Mans entries for a 962C in 1988-89 but had not been able to fulfil them, was now attempting a full SWC season out of the Alpine village of Noes, near Montreux. Salamin's 1990 'customer' chassis was another fitted over the winter with a composite body made in Bonn, by Frank Bombien. The team owner and regular WSC co-driver Max Cohen-Olivar were joined by eight-times French hillclimb champion Marcel Tarrès. Their weekend ended at around 11pm, when the engine blew a head gasket.

MAZDA FIRST FOR JAPAN 77

LE MANS

TRUSTING IN TWO

Before signing up to the SWC, Yves Courage did a deal with Trust Racing whereby the Japanese team would contest the opening round at Suzuka as a Courage Compétition entry and, in return, would also use Courage's ticket at Le Mans. Trust's one-year-old customer Porsche (left) was raced here by team regulars George Fouché/Steven Andskär, who formed one of only three two-man driving crews in this race.

Now in short-tail configuration, with a 3.2 engine sourced from Andial in California, the 962C developed an ignition problem during the evening that cost 10 minutes in the pits. Strong driving through the night recovered 10th position but then a gearbox rebuild was needed just after dawn. This consumed more than 80 minutes but, even so, the car was heading for 12th place when the differential failed with only 45 minutes remaining.

The Alméras brothers also entered their Porsche via Courage. Pictured below, their car was a TCP honeycomb chassis formerly raced by the Kremer and Leyton House teams, now fitted with a short-tail, carbon/Kevlar body produced in their raceshop in Montpellier. The little team had to rush to get the mothballed 962C race-ready but just had time to test it on Goodyear's southern France test track at Miréval, a few miles down the road. Jacques Alméras was caught out during the evening when being passed by a Brun Porsche at the first Mulsanne chicane, and destruction-tested a tyre wall there. Amazingly, the car was undamaged and was on its way again after a four-minute delay. Back in pit-lane, Jacques had to face the wrath of his brother. But the situation was reversed at nightfall when Jean-Marie crashed out of the race, and at the same location.

1991

MIXED SPICES

There were nine Spices at this year's race meeting, but only seven qualified – and, surprisingly, only the Fedco SE90C finished.

Another Japanese entrant, Tsunemasa Aoshima had taken delivery of an SE90C during the summer of 1990 for a JSPC campaign, and was contesting his domestic series again this year with an all-female driving squad: former World Endurance Championship race winner Desiré Wilson and 1989 Spice USA works driver Lyn St James. For Le Mans, they were to have been co-driven by F3 racer Tomiko Yoshikawa, who had put the ladies' team together on behalf of Sumitomo Rubber Industries (Dunlop Japan). But Yoshikawa could not get the required licence in time and, in her place, recruited French Indy Lights driver Cathy Muller.

The ladies' week started badly. Their pink car was late out of the paddock for Wednesday qualifying and, after only four laps, it was crashed by Wilson at Tertre Rouge. The front of the tub was badly damaged, so the team arranged to hire a spare SE90C that had been brought here by GP Motorsport to serve as a parts depot for the US-entered Spice-Ferrari. It took the whole of Thursday to switch the team's DFZ powertrain and bodywork from the crashed car to the borrowed one, and then only Wilson really had time to get under the qualification cut-off. St James and Muller missed the mark but the stewards used their discretion to admit them to the race.

They didn't last very long. After a couple of delays caused by bodywork fixing problems, Wilson hit the barrier at the Dunlop chicane at 8:40pm. She only made it as far as Tertre Rouge before stopping the car.

PC Automotive returned with the SE89C that had won C2 the previous June, now upgraded for the DFZ/Hewland powertrain (below). This time team owner Richard Piper and Olindo Iacobelli were co-driven by Jean-Louis Ricci. Their weekend was ruined at 9:45pm when the gearbox casing suddenly shattered. The crew had to invest 108 minutes in repairs before other problems, including flat batteries, combined to prevent a meaningful recovery. The car was still around at the finish, but was unclassified.

Hugh Chamberlain's team entered both its Spice SE89Cs – and,

MAZDA FIRST FOR JAPAN 79

LE MANS

at daybreak, retired them from the race within minutes of each other. The one raced by Nick Adams, Robin Donovan and Richard Jones (above) lost 25 minutes to electrical faults, and 80 minutes to a clutch replacement, before the electronics played up again and stranded Donovan out at Tertre Rouge. The sister car was the 1989 C2 championship winner, re-engineered in 1990 by Wuit Huidekoper with a narrower cockpit and a wider rear track, allowing bigger air tunnels.

Driven by John Sheldon and Ferdinand de Lesseps (and for a single shift by Charles Rickett), it succumbed to electronic glitches that had plagued it almost throughout.

Of two Spices entered via Louis Descartes, Graff Racing's SE89C (below) had a strong run until half-time in the hands of Xavier Lapeyre, Jean-Philippe Grand and Michel Maisonneuve. At that stage, this car was leading the Fedco Spice by four laps. But then its DFZ began popping and banging – and, after the crew had replaced the sparkplugs, the battery and other devices, refused to restart.

GP Motorsport's three-year-old IMSA charge was the only US-entered car in this race. An ex-works/Pontiac spare chassis, it had been reworked as a 1000-kilo C1 car by a new team, Classic Racing, and fitted with an oversize, twin-turbo V8 Ferrari 308 engine. The team's only motor broke on Wednesday after Justin Bell had driven five shakedown laps. Having loaned a spare chassis to AO Racing, Dave Prewitt's team tried to qualify Shunji Kasuya via the Japanese team, but he could not achieve an adequate time – and it was Saturday morning before the repaired V8 was running once more. Classic and GPM presented the stewards with a petition signed by the other teams, but were refused a place on the grid.

The drivers of the Berkeley team's ex-works SE90C could not produce valid licences and were refused entry.

80 LE MANS 24 HOURS 1990–99

1991

THE LAST LANCIA

The last Lancia to race at Le Mans (at the time of writing) went for 24 hours, on and off, but was never going to cover enough distance to be classified.

This year Gianni Mussato found a buyer for his surviving LC2 in the Durango Italian F3 team, founded in Viacenza by Ivone Pinton and Enrico Magro, which was also contesting that year's British F3000 series. Durango created a sportscar offshoot, Veneto Equipe, which was managed by Stefano Zanco. It began testing the Lancia at Misano in February and registered for the SWC, but came to France after a DNF at Suzuka and a DNQ at Monza.

Luigi Giorgio's qualifying time was too slow but the ACO used its discretion to allow him to co-drive Almo Coppelli, who was in pit-lane after only two racing laps with a broken windscreen. He was soon back with one of the ground-effect tunnels detached. These stops consumed 96 minutes and, as in 1990, a Mussato-built Lancia spent the Saturday evening in last place.

In fact, the LC2 seemed to divide its time pretty equally on the track and in the pits. As well as ongoing problems with the screen, the Durango crew had to deal with a fuel leak, a broken turbo, suspension damper failures, and a broken gearlever. Electrical problems in the small hours put the car even further behind. Then it needed a new fuel pump, and finally new gear pinions.

After a DNF at the Nürburgring and a DNQ at Magny-Cours, the team was disbanded and Durango concentrated on F3000. In January 1992, Mussato told FISA he was building an FIA Cup racecar, but the project did not materialize.

THE LAST 'WORKS' ALD

Louis Descartes's Parisian team contested Le Mans for the last time this year, and again its weekend was halted by a broken gearbox.

Over the winter, ALD engineer Benôit Hueere had built up a second carbon monocoque with revised suspension geometry and carbon brakes. Cosworth DFR engines, assembled by Langford & Peck, were purchased from the Ligier F1 team, and ambitious little ALD embarked on a full SWC season as a 3.5-litre Sportscar entry.

After Patrick Gonin's opening stints had been interrupted by problems with the engine management electronics, Philippe de Henning was struck by a right-rear suspension failure at Mulsanne corner. He struggled back to pit-lane (right), where the ALD spent the best part of three hours. Then the transmission broke – and Luigi Taverna had not even been in the car.

MAZDA FIRST FOR JAPAN

LE MANS

24 HEURES DU MANS
22-23 JUIN 1991
Castrol
Silk Cut
JAGUAR
3615 ACO
A.S.A. AUTOMOBILE CLUB DE L'OUEST

1991

HOURLY RACE POSITIONS

Qual	Time	Start	Car	No	Drivers	1	2	3	4	5	6	7	8	9	10	11	12	13	14	15	16	17	18	19	20	21	22	23	24
1	3:31.270	11	Sauber-Mercedes C11	1	Schlesser/Mass/Ferté	5	2	2	2	2	1	1	1	1	1	1	1	1	1	1	1	1	1	1	1	1	DNF		
2	3:31.912		Jaguar XJR-14	4	Wallace	DNS																							
3	3:35.058	1	Peugeot 905	5	Baldi/Alliot/Jabouille	15	33	35	36	36	DNF																		
4	3:35.265	12	Sauber-Mercedes C11	31	Schumacher/Wendlinger/Kreutzpointner	4	1	1	1	6	3	3	3	3	2	2	2	4	8	7	7	6	5	5	6	6	4	4	5
5	3:35.957	13	Sauber-Mercedes C11	32	Palmer/Dickens/Thiim	7	4	3	3	1	2	2	2	9	12	11	10	9	9	DNF									
6	3:36.114	14	Porsche 962C	17	Larrauri/Pareja/Brun	3	3	6	5	3	19	19	16	13	13	14	13	11	11	10	11	11	11	11	11	10	10	10	10
7	3:36.848	15	Porsche 962C-K6	11	Reuter/Toivonen/Lehto	8	7	7	11	21	24	22	19	18	16	16	16	15	12	13	11	10	10	10	10	10	9	9	9
8	3:38.886	2	Peugeot 905	6	Rosberg/Dalmas/Raphanel	1	35	33	28	27	28	29	DNF																
9	3:40.526	16	Porsche 962C	58	Bell/Stuck/Jelinski	6	6	4	6	8	7	10	7	10	10	7	7	7	6	5	6	6	7	8	8	8	7	7	7
10	3:40.548	17	Porsche 962C	57	Pescarolo/Schneider/Krages	2	11	9	8	7	5	6	8	7	6	5	6	8	DNF										
11	3:43.496	18	Jaguar XJR-12LM	35	Jones/Boesel/Ferté	10	8	8	9	10	6	4	5	4	3	4	3	3	3	3	2	3	3	3	3	3	2	2	2
12	3:43.503	19	Mazda 787B	55	Herbert/Weidler/Gachot	11	9	10	7	5	4	5	4	5	4	3	4	2	2	2	3	2	2	2	2	2	1	1	1
13	3:44.315	20	Cougar C26S	12	Migault/Robert/Raulet	19	18	18	15	13	12	12	15	14	14	13	14	13	12	13	12	12	12	12	12	12	11	11	11
14	3:45.214	21	Porsche 962C	21	Konrad/Reid/Lombardi	24	26	22	18	18	17	17	DNF																
15	3:45.740	3	Spice SE90C	8	Euser/Zwolsman/Harvey	23	17	14	13	14	DNF																		
16	3:46.181	22	Porsche 962C	49	Fouché/Andskär	13	12	16	22	20	18	16	12	12	11	10	10	12	17	17	15	14	14	14	14	13	12	12	DNF
17	3:46.641	23	Mazda 787B	18	Johansson/Kennedy/Sala	12	10	11	10	9	10	9	9	8	7	8	8	7	6	6	5	4	5	5	5	7	7	6	6
18	3:47.875	24	Jaguar XJR-12LM	33	Warwick/Nielsen/Wallace	9	5	5	4	4	9	7	6	6	5	9	9	9	7	8	8	6	6	6	5	5	5	5	4
19	3:48.519	25	Porsche 962C-K6	46	Needell/Foitek/Lopez	18	36	36	37	37	DNF																		
20	3:48.664	26	Cougar C26S	13	Dumfries/Olofsson/Danielsson	26	19	17	31	32	DNF																		
21	3:49.748	27	Jaguar XJR-12LM	34	Wollek/Fabi/Acheson	21	13	12	12	11	8	8	10	9	8	6	5	5	4	4	4	4	4	4	4	4	3	3	3
22	3:49.867	28	Jaguar XJR-12LM	36	Leslie/Martini/Krosnoff	14	24	34	34	35	31	30	27	25	24	23	23	23	21	21	19	18	DNF						
23	3:50.098	29	Porsche 962C	16	Huysman/Stirling/Santal	16	14	15	14	12	11	11	11	11	DNF														
24	3:50.161	30	Mazda 787B	56	Terada/Dieudonné/Yorino	27	22	21	19	17	13	13	14	13	12	11	12	11	10	10	9	9	9	9	9	9	8	8	8
25	3:52.882	31	Porsche 962C	51	Lässig/Yver/Altenbach	22	20	19	16	15	16	18	17	15	15	15	16	14	14	12	DNF								
26	3:53.833	4	Spice SE90C	41	Misaki/Yokoshima/Nagasaka	20	16	13	17	16	15	14	18	20	18	24	19	18	16	15	14	13	13	13	13	13	13	13	12
27	3:54.480	32	Cougar C26S	47	Trollé/Bourbonnais/Brand	17	15	30	29	28	26	25	22	21	20	20	20	19	18	19	18	15	15	15	15	14	15	15	NC
28	3:55.446	5	ROC 002	37	Fabre/Thuner	30	23	29	33	33	DNF																		
29	3:55.706	33	Porsche 962C	53	Weaver/Haywood/Taylor	36	34	32	30	30	27	26	23	22	21	20	21	21	19	17	16	16	16	16	15	14	NC		
30	3:56.790	34	Porsche 962C	50	Alméras/Alméras/Thoisy	31	25	24	23	21	23	DNF																	
31	3:57.132	35	Lancia LC2 SP91	15	Coppelli/Giorgio	38	38	37	35	34	30	31	28	27	26	25	26	25	22	22	20	19	18	18	18	17	17	NC	
32	3:57.298	6	Spice SE89C	39	Grand/Lapeyre/Maisonneuve	25	28	28	26	25	22	21	20	19	17	17	17	20	DNF										
33	3:59.343	7	ALD C91	7	Henning/Taverna/Gonin	37	37	38	38	32	32	29	28	27	DNF														
34	3:59.674	36	Porsche 962C	14	Salamin/Cohen-Olivar/Tarres	34	27	23	21	22	20	20	21	DNF															
35	4:01.761	37	Porsche 962C	52	Elgh/Ratzenberger/Hoy	33	21	20	20	19	14	15	13	15	19	18	18	17	15	16	DNF								
36	4:02.519	8	Spice SE89C	43	Piper/Iacobelli/Ricci	29	29	25	25	24	27	25	23	23	22	22	22	22	20	20	18	17	17	17	17	16	16	NC	
37	4:05.839		Porsche 962C	59	Barth	DNS																							
38	4:06.578	9	Spice SE89C	45	Adams/Donovan/Jones	35	31	26	24	26	23	24	24	24	22	22	24	24	DNF										
39	4:10.607	10	Spice SE89C	44	Sheldon/Lesseps/Rickett	32	30	27	27	29	28	26	26	25	25	26	DNF												
40	4:11.781	38	Spice SE90C	40	Wilson/St James/Muller	28	32	31	32	31	DNF																		
41	4:14.499	DSQ	Cougar C24S	48	Hodgetts/Hepworth/Lecerf	DNS																							
42	4:18.611	DNQ	Porsche 962C	54	Iketani/Stermitz	DNS																							
43	5:09.145	DNQ	Spice SE88P	42	Bell/Kasuya/Scapini	DNS																							
44	6:55.969	DNQ	Sauber-Mercedes C291	2	Kreutzpointner	DNS																							
	No time	FS	Spice SE90C	38		-																							

DNF Did not finish   **DNQ** Did not qualify   **DSQ** Disqualified   **FS** Failed scrutineering   **NC** Not classified as a finisher   **RES** Reserve not required

LE MANS

RACE RESULTS

Pos	Car	No	Drivers			Laps	Km	Miles	FIA Class	DNF
1	Mazda 787B	55	Johnny Herbert (GB)	Volker Weidler (D)	Bertrand Gachot (F)	362	4922.81	3058.89	Cat 2	
2	Jaguar XJR-12LM	35	Davy Jones (USA)	Raul Boesel (BR)	Michel Ferté (F)	360	4896.00	3042.23	Cat 2	
3	Jaguar XJR-12LM	34	Bob Wollek (F)	Teo Fabi (I)	Kenneth Acheson (GB)	358	4868.80	3025.33	Cat 2	
4	Jaguar XJR-12LM	33	Derek Warwick (GB)	John Nielsen (DK)	Andy Wallace (GB)	356	4841.60	3008.42	Cat 2	
5	Sauber-Mercedes C11	31	Michael Schumacher (D)	Karl Wendlinger (A)	Fritz Kreutzpointner (D)	355	4828.00	2999.97	Cat 2	
6	Mazda 787B	18	Stefan Johansson (S)	David Kennedy (IRL)	Maurizio Sandro Sala (BR)	355	4828.00	2999.97	Cat 2	
7	Porsche 962C	58	Derek Bell (GB)	Hans-Joachim Stuck (D)	Frank Jelinski (D)	347	4719.20	2932.37	Cat 2	
8	Mazda 787B	56	Yojiro Terada (J)	Pierre Dieudonné (B)	Takashi Yorino (J)	346	4705.60	2923.92	Cat 2	
9	Porsche 962C-K6	11	Manuel Reuter (D)	JJ Lehto (SF)	Harri Toivonen (SF)	343	4664.80	2898.57	Cat 2	
10	Porsche 962C	17	Oscar Larrauri (RA)	Jesús Pareja (E)	Walter Brun (CH)	338	4596.80	2856.31	Cat 2	
11	Cougar C26S	12	François Migault (F)	Lionel Robert (F)	Jean-Daniel Raulet (F)	331	4501.60	2797.16	Cat 2	
12	Spice SE90C	41	Kiyoshi Misaki (J)	Hisashi Yokoshima (J)	Naoki Nagasaka (J)	326	4433.60	2754.91	Cat 1	
NC	Porsche 962C	53	Hurley Haywood (USA)	James Weaver (GB)	Wayne Taylor (ZA)	316	4297.60	2670.40	Cat 2	Insufficient distance
NC	Cougar C26S	47	Michel Trollé (F)	Claude Bourbonnais (CDN)	Marco Brand (I)	293	3984.80	2476.04	Cat 2	Insufficient distance
NC	Spice SE89C	43	Richard Piper (GB)	Olindo Iacobelli (USA)	Jean-Louis Ricci (F)	280	3808.00	2366.18	Cat 1	Insufficient distance
NC	Lancia LC2 SP91	15	Almo Coppelli (I)	Luigi Giorgio (I)		111	1509.60	938.02	Cat 2	Insufficient distance
DNF	Porsche 962C	49	George Fouché (ZA)	Steven Andskär (S)		316			Cat 2	Transmission (differential)
DNF	Sauber-Mercedes C11	1	Jean-Louis Schlesser (F)	Jochen Mass (D)	Alain Ferté (F)	319			Cat 2	Engine (overheating)
DNF	Jaguar XJR-12LM	36	David Leslie (GB)	Mauro Martini (I)	Jeff Krosnoff (USA)	183			Cat 2	Transmission
DNF	Porsche 962C	51	Jürgen Lässig (D)	Pierre Yver (F)	Otto Altenbach (D)	232			Cat 2	Suspension
DNF	Sauber-Mercedes C11	32	Jonathan Palmer (GB)	Stanley Dickens (S)	Kurt Thiim (DK)	223			Cat 2	Engine mount
DNF	Porsche 962C	52	Eje Elgh (S)	Will Hoy (GB)	Roland Ratzenberger (A)	202			Cat 2	Engine (head gasket)
DNF	Porsche 962C	57	Henri Pescarolo (F)	Bernd Schneider (D)	'John Winter' (Louis Krages) (D)	197			Cat 2	Transmission (gearbox)
DNF	Spice SE89C	45	Nick Adams (GB)	Robin Donovan (GB)	Richard Jones (GB)	128			Cat 1	Electrics
DNF	Spice SE89C	39	Jean-Philippe Grand (F)	Xavier Lapeyre (F)	Michel Maisonneuve (F)	163			Cat 1	Engine
DNF	Spice SE89C	44	John Sheldon (GB)	Ferdinand de Lesseps (F)	Charles Rickett (GB)	85			Cat 1	Electrics
DNF	Porsche 962C	16	Harald Huysman (N)	Robbie Stirling (CDN)	Bernard Santal (CH)	138			Cat 2	Engine (head gasket)
DNF	Porsche 962C	14	Antoine Salamin (CH)	Max Cohen-Olivar (MOR)	Marcel Tarres (F)	101			Cat 2	Engine (overheating)
DNF	Porsche 962C	21	Franz Konrad (A)	Anthony Reid (GB)	Pierre-Alain Lombardi (CH)	98			Cat 2	Engine
DNF	Porsche 962C	50	Jacques Alméras (F)	Jean-Marie Alméras (F)	Pierre de Thoisy (F)	86			Cat 2	Accident
DNF	Peugeot 905	6	Keke Rosberg (SF)	Yannick Dalmas (F)	Pierre-Henri Raphanel (F)	68			Cat 1	Transmission (gearbox)
DNF	Spice SE90C	8	Cor Euser (NL)	Tim Harvey (GB)	Charles Zwolsman (NL)	72			Cat 1	Fire
DNF	Spice SE90C	40	Desiré Wilson (ZA)	Lyn St James (USA)	Cathy Muller (F)	47			Cat 1	Accident
DNF	ALD C91	7	Philippe de Henning (F)	Luigi Taverna (I)	Patrick Gonin (F)	16			Cat 2	Transmission (gearbox)
DNF	Cougar C26S	13	Johnny Dumfries (GB)	Anders Olofsson (S)	Thomas Danielsson (S)	45			Cat 2	Engine
DNF	ROC 002	37	Bernard Thuner (CH)	Pascal Fabre (F)		38			Cat 1	Transmission (differential)
DNF	Peugeot 905	5	Jean-Pierre Jabouille (F)	Philippe Alliot (F)	*Mauro Baldi (I)*	22			Cat 1	Engine
DNF	Porsche 962C-K6	46	Gregor Foitek (CH)	Tomas Lopez (MEX)	*Tiff Needell (GB)*	18			Cat 2	Accident (steering damage)
DNQ	Porsche 962C	54	*Katsunori Iketani (J)*	*Mercedes Stermitz (A)*					Cat 2	
DNQ	Spice SE88P	42	*Justin Bell (GB)*	*Shunji Kasoya (J)*	*Franco Scapini (I)*				Cat 2	
DNS	Sauber-Mercedes C291	2	*Fritz Kreutzpointner (D)*						Cat 1	Withdrawn
DNS	Jaguar XJR-14	4	*Andy Wallace (GB)*						Cat 1	Withdrawn
DNS	Porsche 962C	59	*Jürgen Barth (D)*						Cat 2	Withdrawn
FS	Cougar C24S	48	Chris Hodgetts (GB)	Andrew Hepworth (GB)	Thierry Lecerf (F)				Cat 2	Failed scrutineering (weight)

DNF Did not finish   **DNS** Did not start   **DSQ** Disqualified   **FS** Failed scrutineering   **RES** Reserve not required   **NC** Not classified as a finisher   **WD** Withdrawn   Drivers in italics did not race the cars specified

1991

CLASS WINNERS

FIA Class	Starters	Finishers	First	No	Drivers	kph	mph	
Category 1	10	1	Spice SE90C	41	Misaki/Tokoshima/Nagasaka	184.75	114.80	Record
Category 2	28	11	Mazda 787B	55	Herbert/Weidler/Gachot	205.13	127.47	Record
Totals	38	12						

INDEX OF ENERGY EFFICIENCY

Pos	Car	No	Drivers	Score
1	Sauber-Mercedes C11	31	Schumacher/Wendlinger/Kreutzpointner	-1.412
2	Mazda 787B	55	Herbert/Weidler/Gachot	-6.269
3	Jaguar XJR-12LM	34	Wollek/Fabi/Acheson	-6.839
4	Porsche 962C	17	Larrauri/Pareja/Brun	-7.145
5	Porsche 962C-K6	11	Reuter/Lehto/Toivonen	-7.414
6	Jaguar XJR-12LM	35	Jones/Boesel/Ferté	-7.627
7	Mazda 787B	18	Johansson/Kennedy/Sandro Sala	-8.045
8	Jaguar XJR-12LM	33	Warwick/Nielsen/Wallace	-8.198
9	Porsche 962C	58	Bell/Stuck/Jelinski	-10.223
10	Mazda 787B	56	Terada/Dieudonné/Yorino	-13.244
&c				

FIA SPORTSCAR WORLD CHAMPIONSHIP

Race	Winner	Drivers
Suzuka (J) 270 miles	Peugeot 905	Baldi/Alliot
Monza (I) 270 miles	Jaguar XJR-14	Warwick/Brundle
Silverstone (GB) 270 miles	Jaguar XJR-14	Warwick/T.Fabi
Le Mans (F) 24 hours	**Mazda 787B**	**Herbert/Weidler/Gachot**
Nürburgring (D) 270 miles	Jaguar XJR-14	Warwick/D.Brabham
Magny-Cours (F) 270 miles	Peugeot 905B	Rosberg/Dalmas
Mexico City (MEX) 270 miles	Peugeot 905B	Rosberg/Dalmas
Autopolis (J) 270 miles	Mercedes-Benz C291	Schumacher/Wendlinger

FINAL CHAMPIONSHIP POINTS

Final Positions	Team	Points
TEAMS		
1	Silk Cut Jaguar (GB)	108
2	Peugeot Talbot Sport (F)	79
3	Team Sauber Mercedes (CH)	70
4	Euro Racing (NL)	54
5	Mazdaspeed (J)	47
6	Porsche Kremer Racing (D)	43
7	Courage Compétition (F)	28
8	Swiss Team Salamin (CH)	26
9	Brun Motorsport (CH)	22
10	Konrad Motorsport (D)	6
DRIVERS		
1	Teo Fabi (I)	86
2	Derek Warwick (GB)	79
3	Mauro Baldi (I)	69
=	Philippe Alliot (F)	69
5	Cor Euser (NL	54
6	Charles Zwolsman (NL)	46
7	Jean-Louis Schlesser (F)	45
=	Jochen Mass (D)	45
9	Michael Schumacher (D)	43
=	Manuel Reuter (D)	43
&c		

MAZDA FIRST FOR JAPAN

LE MANS

1992
A HOME WIN FOR PEUGEOT

LE MANS

RACE INFORMATION

RACE DATE
20-21 June

RACE No
60

CIRCUIT LENGTH
8.451 miles/13.600km

HONORARY STARTER
Prince Albert of Monaco

MARQUES (ON GRID)

BRM	1
Cougar	3
Debora	1
Lola	2
Mazda	2
Peugeot	4
Porsche	5
Spice	3
Tiga	1
Toyota	5
WR	1

STARTERS/FINISHERS
28/14

WINNERS

OVERALL
Peugeot

ENTRY LIST

No	Car	Entrant (nat)	cc	Engine	Tyres	Weight (kg)	Class
1	Peugeot 905B Evo1B	Peugeot Talbot Sport (F)	3499	SA35-A2 V10	Michelin	809	Cat 1
1T	Peugeot 905B Evo1B	Peugeot Talbot Sport (F)	3499	SA35-A2 V10	Michelin	N/A	Cat 1
2	Peugeot 905B Evo1B	Peugeot Talbot Sport (F)	3499	SA35-A2 V10	Michelin	787	Cat 1
2T	Peugeot 905B Evo1B	Peugeot Talbot Sport (F)	3499	SA35-A2 V10	Michelin	N/A	Cat 1
3	Lola T92/10	Euro Racing (NL)	3497	Judd GV10	Michelin	817	Cat 1
4	Lola T92/10	Euro Racing (NL)	3497	Judd GV10	Michelin	790	Cat 1
5	Mazda MXR-01	Mazdaspeed (J)	3497	Mazda MV10	Michelin	779	Cat 1
5T	Mazda MXR-01	Mazdaspeed (J)	3497	Mazda MV10	Michelin	N/A	Cat 1
6	Mazda MXR-01	Mazdaspeed (J)	3497	Mazda MV10	Michelin	778	Cat 1
6T	Mazda MXR-01	Mazdaspeed (J)	3497	Mazda MV10	Michelin	N/A	Cat 1
7	Toyota TS010	Toyota Team TOMS (J)	3497	RV10	Goodyear	812	Cat 1
7T	Toyota TS010	Toyota Team TOMS (J)	3497	RV10	Goodyear	N/A	Cat 1
8	Toyota TS010	Toyota Team TOMS (J)	3497	RV10	Goodyear	799	Cat 1
9	BRM P351	BRM Motorsport (GB)	3491	290 V12	Goodyear	800	Cat 1
10	BRM P351	BRM Motorsport (GB)	3491	290 V12	–	–	Cat 1
11	Konrad KM-011	Konrad Motorsport (D)	3465	Lamborghini 3512 V12	–	–	Cat 1
12	Jaguar XJR-14	RM Motorsport (GB)	3493	Cosworth HB V8	–	–	Cat 1
14	Jaguar XJR-14	RM Motorsport (GB)	3493	Cosworth HB V8	–	–	Cat 1
21	Spice SE90C	Action Formula with Bernard de Dryver (B)	3494	Cosworth DFR V8	Goodyear	808	Cat 1 Cup
22	Spice SE89C	Euro Racing/Chamberlain Engineering (GB)	3494	Cosworth DFZ V8	Goodyear	801	Cat 1 Cup
23	Jaguar XJR12-LM	Gee Pee Motorsport (CH)	7400	HE V12	–	–	Cat 2
27	Spice SE90C	RM Motorsport (GB)	3494	Cosworth DFZ V8	–	–	Cat 1 Cup
28	Jaguar XJR-14	RM Motorsport (GB)	3493	Cosworth HB V8	–	–	Cat 1
29	Tiga GC288/9	Team SCI (I)	3298	Cosworth DFL V8	Goodyear	813	Cat 1 Cup
30	Spice SE90C	Team TDR (GB)	3494	Cosworth DFR V8	Dunlop	829	Cat 1
31	Peugeot 905B Evo1B	Peugeot Talbot Sport (F)	3499	SA35-A2 V10	Michelin	788	Cat 1
31T	Peugeot 905B Evo1B	Peugeot Talbot Sport (F)	3499	SA35-A2 V10	Michelin	N/A	Cat 1
33	Toyota TS010	Toyota Team TOMS (J)	3497	RV10	Goodyear	810	Cat 1
34	Toyota 92C-V	Toyota Kitz Racing with SARD (J)	3576tc	RV36 V8	Bridgestone	915	Cat 2
35	Toyota 92C-V	Trust Racing Team (J)	3576tc	RV36 V8	Dunlop	911	Cat 2
36	Spice SE89C	Euro Racing/Chamberlain Engineering (GB)	3494	Cosworth DFZ V8	Goodyear	810	Cat 1 Cup
38	Jaguar XJR-17	Gee Pee Motorsport (CH) Chamberlain Engineering (GB)	3498	JV6	–	–	Cat 1
51	Porsche 962C-K6	Porsche Kremer Racing (D)	3164tc	F6	Yokohama	945	Cat 3
51T	Porsche 962C-K6	Porsche Kremer Racing (D)	2994tc	F6	Yokohama	N/A	Cat 3
52	Porsche 962C-K6	Porsche Kremer Racing (D)	2994tc	F6	Yokohama	945	Cat 3
53	Porsche 962C-GTI	ADA Engineering (GB)	2994tc	F6	Goodyear	909	Cat 3
54	Cougar C28LM	Courage Compétition (F)	2994tc	Porsche F6	Goodyear	920	Cat 3
55	Cougar C28LM	Courage Compétition (F)	2994tc	Porsche F6	Goodyear	953	Cat 3
56	Cougar C28LM	Courage Compétition (F)	2994tc	Porsche F6	Goodyear	938	Cat 3
57	WR 905 Spyder	Welter Racing (F)	1930	Peugeot Mi16 S4	–	–	Cat 4
58	WR 905 Spyder	Welter Racing (F)	1930	Peugeot Mi16 S4	Michelin	534	Cat 4
59	Norma M7	Noël del Bello Racing (F)	2959	Alfa Romeo 164QF V6	–	–	Cat 4
60	ALD C289/90	Team MP Racing (F)	3000	Peugeot PRV V6	Michelin	840	Cat 2
61	Debora SP92	Didier Bonnet Racing (F)	2959	Alfa Romeo 164QF V6	Pirelli	665	Cat 4
62	Pro-Sport 3000	Martin Crass Racing (GB)	3412	Cosworth FBE V6	–	–	Cat 4
63	Pro-Sport 3000	Don Farthing Racing (GB)	3412	Cosworth FBE V6	–	–	Cat 4
64	Pro-Sport 3000	Pro-Sport Engineering (GB)	3412	Cosworth FBE V6	–	–	Cat 4
65	Pro-Sport 3000	Pro-Sport Engineering (GB)	3412	Cosworth FBE V6	–	–	Cat 4
66	Orion 905 Spyder	Eric Bellefroid (F)	1930	Peugeot Mi16 S4	Michelin	595	Cat 4
67	Porsche 962C	Obermaier Racing (D) Primagaz Compétition (F)	2994tc	F6	Goodyear	1039	Cat 3
68	Porsche 962C	Team Alméras Chotard (F)	2994tc	F6	Goodyear	990	Cat 3
68T	Porsche 962C	Team Alméras Chotard (F)	2994tc	F6	Goodyear	N/A	Cat 3

1992

ENTRY

The ACO extended the entry deadline for the 60th Le Mans 24 Hours until only four weeks before the race, when it mailed 44 acceptances. But many of these were mirages: only 30 cars (plus eight T-cars) arrived for scrutineering. The Sportscar World Championship now being a precarious reality, 22 of these 38 were 3.5-litre 'atmos': six Peugeots, four Mazdas and four Toyotas from the manufacturer teams, plus four Spices, two quasi-works Lolas, a Tiga and a BRM revival project.

FISA's waiver allowing former Group C cars produced only two Toyotas and an ALD in Category 2, and five Porsches and three Cougars in Category 3. Category 4 was supposed to make up the numbers, but only two Peugeot Spiders and a Coupe Alfa Debora showed up.

QUALIFYING

Peugeot put on a show of real strength in the twilight of a sunny Wednesday, when Philippe Alliot defied team orders to back off an overheating engine to complete an astonishing lap almost six seconds faster than Mark Blundell's heroic 1990 performance for Nissan. These FIA Sportscars were that good. Equipped with Michelin's qualifying tyres and Esso's malodorous, special-brew F1 fuel, Alliot went almost 14 seconds faster than his artificial 1991 pole. Derek Warwick crashed in trying to usurp him but, on Thursday, Yannick Dalmas put his repaired 905 on the front row.

The other teams shrugged and concentrated on their race preparations. Geoff Lees, Jan Lammers and Pierre-Henri Raphanel used Toyota's T-car to qualify 3-4-5, ahead of the third Peugeot and the best of the Mazdas.

RACE

When a Spice and the ALD failed to make it through qualifying, the grid was reduced to a paltry 28 – the smallest Le Mans field since 1932. The event lacked Jaguars (for the first time since 1983), and clashed with the football World Cup in Spain. These factors and a sudden change in the weather reduced the race day crowd to 176,000, the majority braving the rain in expectation of a Peugeot victory.

A HOME WIN FOR PEUGEOT

LE MANS

ORGANISATION

In October 1991, when Max Mosley defeated Jean-Marie Balestre to win the presidency of FISA, the western world was in the grip of financial recession. A few weeks later, the FISA Sportscar Commission recommended the cancellation of the 1992 SWC, due to the ongoing shortage of F1-engined Sportscars and the reluctance of the event promoters to pay the sanctioning fees that were now demanded. Jaguar and Mercedes-Benz cancelled their programmes.

Before the Commission's advice could be formally taken by the World Motor Sport Council, the remaining stakeholders in the series got together and a whole series of crisis meetings was held. Finally, in January 1992, the WMSC voted to ratify a championship once more after Mosley and Bernie Ecclestone had somehow persuaded Mazda, Peugeot and Toyota to underwrite it, to the tune of US$600,000 per car.

Only these three companies remained with factory teams, accounting for five of only 13 Sportscars that were registered for the series. FISA had defined a new, less expensive class for so-called FIA Cup cars, with 3.5-litre engines rev-limited to 9500rpm, and ferrous (instead of carbon) braking systems. Eight such cars were registered, bringing the total to 21 – woefully insufficient for Le Mans.

The solution agreed by FISA and the ACO this time was again to define a Category 2 for 1990-specification Group C cars, as long as they were badged for a marque that had been registered for the SWC. These would include old-style Jaguars, Toyotas and Spices (and rotary-engined Mazdas), but not Porsches. So a special dispensation was made for Porsche, said FISA: "On account of the contribution made by this make to the World Championships and to Le Mans over many years." This was later extended to include the French-made Cougars. These Porsche-engined cars were grouped separately in the ACO's Category 3. Only the Category 1 cars could score SWC points.

Owners of the old 'fuel formula' racecars could now revert to the 900kg minimum weight, but FISA hampered them instead with a reduced, 2140-litre fuel allowance. This implied a performance reduction of almost 20 percent so the teams concerned, led by TWR Jaguar, petitioned FISA for the previous 2550 litres. FISA agreed but subject to the unanimous agreement of the registered SWC teams – and Peugeot and Toyota vetoed the move.

The ACO again extended its entry deadline, but it was still not enough. So the organizers created Category 4 for low-budget sports-racing cars built for National championships in Europe, such as the French Peugeot 905 Spider and Coupe Alfa Romeo series, and British Pro-Sport 3000s. The ACO would eliminate dangerous performance differentials by taking the average of the four best lap times in each of the four divisions, and excluding any car unable to qualify within 130 percent of that figure.

Eventually, the ACO scraped together 44 cars – but 14 of these failed to show up. The long-established but no longer relevant Index of Energy Efficiency contest was suspended this year.

As for the spectators, they would have found the distractions of the famous fairground (pictured) a little stronger this June…

1992

Like Alliot and Dalmas, they had reckoned without the defending champions. Peugeot maintained its 1-2 for only five laps before giving way to an impressive wet-weather charge for Mazda by Volker Weidler. In dreadful visibility, Weidler even built up a 12-second lead before the first fuel stops.

The race effectively lost two of the favourites at 5:30pm. Lees, racing in fourth place, was blinded by a wall of spray at the start of the Mulsanne straight, and backed off in fourth gear. The Toyota was struck hard by Alain Ferté's Peugeot and both cars suffered a lot of damage. Somehow they made it back to the pits, and eventually resumed racing near the back – and each headed for a DNF.

Meanwhile Warwick had taken over from Dalmas and had retaken the lead from the Mazda, now driven by Johnny Herbert. Jean-Pierre Jabouille was third in the pole position 905, with the two healthy Toyotas next on much less effective rain tyres. It stayed that way until 9:15pm, when Jabouille passed the Mazda's slowest driver, Bertrand Gachot, to restore the French 1-2.

As night fell, the Mazda's windscreen misted up badly. It had to stop twice for new screens to be fitted, and fell two laps behind the leading Peugeots. When, at around 2am, Alliot spun into the gravel at Indianapolis, the delay cost two laps, but he stayed in second place.

The rain finally eased and – much to Toyota's relief – the track surface was already drying out when dawn broke.

Soon after 6am, Alliot was in the gravel again, this time at the first Mulsanne chicane. The Mazda regained second place, but then a gear linkage repair cost it 10 minutes in the pits. The conditions were much improved for the Toyotas, and a smooth run by Raphanel/Kenneth Acheson/Masanori Sekiya was now rewarded with second position.

But Warwick/Dalmas/Blundell had a cushion of almost five laps. There was ample time to fit a new battery and ignition box when the electrics played up shortly before 9am. That was the only delay, and the car ran out the winner by three laps. It had been 66 years since Peugeot had first entered the race.

The Toyota edged out the Alliot/Jabouille/Mauro Baldi Peugeot for second place by a lap. Maurizio Sandro Sala was drafted into the front-running Mazda after Yojiro Terada had crashed the sister car during the night, but it lost the use of three gear ratios, and finished a distant fourth.

The other Toyota TS010 climbed as high as third on Sunday morning, but was hampered by a misfire and a faulty clutch, and faded to eighth. Consequently fifth position was claimed by Trust Racing's Group C Toyota, raced well by Stefan Johansson/George Fouché/Stefan Andskär after a long delay with a gearbox problem.

Another turbo V8 Toyota was the faster, but had to have a new gearbox fitted on Sunday morning. Both were led for much of the race by the Cougar-Porsche of veterans Bob Wollek/Henri Pescarolo/Jean-Louis Ricci, which rounded out the top six at the end, winning Category 3.

One of the Category 4 Peugeots survived to the finish, but it was not classified after a range of mechanical problems.

A HOME WIN FOR PEUGEOT

LE MANS

PRIDE OF THE LION

Jean Todt's hard-worked, 120-strong Peugeot team was rewarded with an emphatic Le Mans victory in difficult conditions with its latest car (above), driven by Mark Blundell, Derek Warwick and Yannick Dalmas.

The 905 Evo 1-*bis* was built on the same carbon hull as its predecessor but big changes, evolved during and after the 1991 SWC season, were made to Robert Choulet's ground-effect aerodynamics. A stubby nose, substantially lowered between the wheel-arches, contained tightly packaged suspension assemblies and ducts feeding air to the front brakes. More ducts either side of the reworked 'bubble' cockpit cooled the water radiators, now sited in shapely sidepods outboard of the big venturi. Rear brake cooling was now by air scoops protruding above a lowered engine cover, and a massive, bi-plane rear wing with deep endplates was carried further aft.

For Le Mans, Jean-Pierre Boudy's high-revving V10 now made an extra 20bhp at reduced RPM in an endurance specification that included the beefier, early 1991-specification cylinder block, steel (instead of titanium) camshafts, and different pistons, valvegear and electronics. Taking into account Peugeot's computer simulations of 18,000 shifts over the course of 24 hours, the transmission was also strengthened.

The team did a 24-hour test run in May at Paul Ricard, where two artificial chicanes were erected on the Mistrale straight to simulate those on the Mulsanne. Come race week, and the new Peugeot turned out to be no less than 14 seconds faster round the lap than its predecessor – and more than four seconds faster than the new Toyota.

These latest, wide-bodied 750-kilo FIA Sportscars could generate more downforce than any racing car in history. Although capable of well over 200mph, they could pull more than 4G in most corners. On Wednesday, Philippe Alliot secured pole position with a lap almost six seconds faster than Mark Blundell's 1990 record. The Peugeot was that good.

The team used three T-cars in the dry qualifying sessions, transferring the set-ups to three brand-new race cars which, for the most part, stayed in their garages. Warwick crashed his T-car in trying to pass a backmarker in the Nissan chicane on Wednesday but, 24 hours later, Dalmas put it on the front row. Karl Wendlinger's efforts in the third Peugeot were thwarted by an electrical failure on the first day, and a shunt in the same chicane on the second, and he wound up sixth.

After 90 minutes in which the Peugeots vied for the early advantage with the Mazda and the Toyotas, Wendlinger's car became the first French casualty. Co-driver Alain Ferté was disputing fourth place with Geoff Lees's Toyota when, as they backed off in fourth gear for Tertre

A HOME WIN FOR PEUGEOT

LE MANS

Rouge, both men were suddenly blinded by spray from a car ahead. They collided and the two cars ended up parked against the barrier on the left side of the track. Both drivers got out to inspect the damage, and decided they could make it all the way to pit-lane, Ferté peering through a smashed windscreen after contact with the Toyota's rear wing, and struggling with the left-front wheel folded over the crunched nose. The repairs cost 40 minutes.

Meanwhile Dalmas had taken the lead. Warwick and then Blundell continued his good work in the rain and their car, race-engineered by Tim Wright, was never headed again. There was a scare with a malfunctioning ignition system at breakfast time, which cost 12 minutes in two stops while the crew investigated and then replaced the black box and the battery. Otherwise, in contrast with its closest rivals, the car ran strongly to the finish, and completed six more laps than the second-placed Toyota.

Alliot might have secured pole position, but he let down his co-drivers, Mauro Baldi and Jean-Pierre Jabouille. They established their 905 (above) in second place but slipped two laps behind their team mates at around 2am, when Alliot was caught out by a power steering failure and slithered onto the beach at Indianapolis, causing a further five-minute delay while the front bodywork was replaced. Four hours later, Alliot spent four minutes on another beach, this time at the first chicane; he returned to pit-lane for rear body panel replacements and a new airbox. Alliot was mistakenly released from the pitstop with the driver's door missing, which led to a protest from Toyota, and another stop. At 6:45am, Alliot went off at Arnage: more bodywork repairs, another five minutes. Finally, at 10am, an Alliot-Baldi handover stretched to 10 minutes while a broken gear selector was replaced. The car finished a battered third, seven laps behind the winner.

The shunted Peugeot recovered from 21st to eighth position during the night but, at 7:45am, Eric van der Poele stopped on the Mulsanne straight with a terminal engine failure.

94 LE MANS 24 HOURS 1990–99

1992

THE TOYOTA SPLIT

A little dent in French pride was made by Toyota, the other front-runner in this race, when one of its three new FIA Sportscars split the two best Peugeots at the finish, after an outstanding individual performance by Kenneth Acheson, ably supported by Masanori Sekiya and Pierre-Henri Raphanel.

The TS010 was the first racing Toyota not designed by a Japanese engineer, and was mostly raced out of a new factory in England. Since 1987, Nobuhide Tachi's Toyota-affiliated TOMS company had operated a European offshoot under Glenn Waters and Dave Sims in Norfolk premises housing a competition engine shop and Waters's successful F3 team. In 1990, needing a European base for the FIA Sportscar and other projects, Toyota financed a 40,000sq.ft factory for TOMS GB in nearby Hingham. Waters was in the process of moving in when he put Toyota Racing Developments in touch with Tony Southgate, who was leaving TWR after designing its Le Mans-winning Jaguars. Southgate agreed to coordinate the overall design of the all-new TS010, taking specific responsibility for the aero development in London in the Imperial College wind tunnel. He would work for the next three years with TRD's Yokohama-based chief designer, Kazuharu Hatoya, under project manager Haruhiko Saito.

The TS010's full-width advanced composites monocoque, made by Toray Industries in Tokyo, achieved massive torsional rigidity, although the engine was mounted semi-stressed. This all-aluminium, 20-valve, 72deg V10 was produced under the leadership of Tsutomu Tomita at Toyota's Engine Research & Advanced Engineering facility in Shizuoka. Controlled by Toyota's Nippon Denso electronics, it revved to 11,200rpm, making about 660bhp. Tomita was responsible for the entire powertrain including the six-speed gearbox, an inboard, longitudinal unit designed by Nobuaki Katayama. The whole car, including the double wishbone/pushrod suspensions, was superbly engineered, to aircraft tolerances, but the gearbox proved to be fragile in testing.

Southgate worked with Rob Dominy and Geoff Kingston on the carbon/Kevlar body, for which downforce was the keyword. This was generated by wide venturi and an F1-type double rear wing with the bottom section acting as an airflow extension of a very low engine cover. The wing was balanced by a variable-length splitter beneath the nose-mounted water radiator. The aero was also helped by a new freedom in the rules to use polycarbonates for the windshield which, as on the Peugeot, allowed a 'bubble' shaped cockpit.

The prototype TS010 was shaken down in April 1991 and a second car was finished later in the summer. The car was first raced in the Autopolis round of the SWC in Japan that October.

TOMS GB recruited well for the 1992 season, notably by hiring former TWR Jaguar technician Alastair McQueen as chief engineer. The team tested in the New Year at Phillip Island, in Australia, and returned ready to face what it hoped would be substantial opposition in the SWC. However, there were still not enough of these cars – and they were still

A HOME WIN FOR PEUGEOT

LE MANS

unreliable. When a TS010 driven by Geoff Lees/Hitoshi Ogawa won the 270-mile, 11-car opening round of the 1992 SWC, at Monza in April, it was the only car running at the finish!

Peugeot avenged that defeat at Silverstone in May. Two weeks later, Ogawa lost his life in an F3000 race at Suzuka, casting a dark cloud over Toyota's final Le Mans preparations.

TOMS GB built up four chassis for France, one of which was put to very full use as a T-car despite briefly catching fire from an unsecured filler cap on Wednesday just as David Brabham, luckily, was passing the fire point at Mulsanne corner. The rules now allowed the T-car to be used to establish grid positions and, fitted with a 'sprint' engine, it was thrashed on Thursday in turn by Lees, Jan Lammers and Raphanel to take third, fourth and fifth places. The same drivers (Lees and Lammers in brand-new chassis) engaged their race cars with the Peugeots and one of the Mazdas from the outset on Saturday afternoon.

The first to stumble was Lees, 90 minutes into the race, when he collided with Alain Ferté's Peugeot at Tertre Rouge. Eventually Lees made it back to pit-lane with a crunched nose, missing his rear bodywork and with the left-rear wheel far out of line (above left). The car spent 58 minutes being repaired.

It got worse. In Brabham's second shift after taking over, he was caught out on oil dropped at Indianapolis, and the car skipped across the wet beach and into the tyre wall there. It had to be towed out by a rescue vehicle and, back in the pits, a further 45 minutes had to be invested in right-front suspension and bodywork repairs before Ukyo Katayama could resume. The three struggled all night with the handling of the battered car, and finally departed the race when the engine broke down at 7:45am.

Meanwhile the other Toyotas had embarked on their own battle for fourth place in the rain, swapping the position often, but losing about half a lap to the leading Peugeots every hour. The duel endured all night and, soon after dawn, its subject became second position. The matter was settled soon after 8am. Andy Wallace contrived to keep his car (pictured in the pits) out of the wall when his right-rear tyre burst on the flat-in-sixth, 200mph run ahead of Indianapolis but, after a pitstop, the engine developed a misfire and Teo Fabi was soon in pit-lane with an inoperative clutch. A replacement had to be fitted and it was 47 minutes before Fabi grimly went back racing, towards an eighth-place finish with Wallace and Lammers, who drove the fastest lap of the race in his frustration.

Unlike their team mates, Acheson/Sekiya/Raphanel had started the race without tyre warmers, which had caused a couple of harmless spins by Raphanel on cold rubber (bottom left). Their second place came under threat in the late stages from one of the Peugeots but, despite a noisy misfire caused by an untraceable electronics glitch, Acheson – the only Toyota driver who had raced consistently on the Peugeots' pace – held on to it by a lap.

The TS010 could not repeat its Monza win in the SWC but, at the end of the season, Lees and Lammers won All-Japan races at Fuji and Mine, adding to points gained earlier by the Group C 92C-Vs and beating Nissan and Mazda to the Manufacturers title.

A HOME WIN FOR PEUGEOT 97

LE MANS

TOYOTA'S CLASS VICTORY

Toyota Team TOMS belted and braced its trio of FIA Sportscars by actively supporting a pair of 92C-V Group C coupés, which were the only finishers in the ACO's Category 2.

These cars were two of four new evolutions of the 90C-V that had been built by Toyota Racing Developments for that season's All-Japan championship, each with the bigger, 3.6-litre, twin-turbo, 32-valve 'RC36' V8 engine and aero upgrades by Tony Southgate.

The class winner was entered by Trust Racing from Chiba City, which had run Porsches in the Japanese series since its formation in 1985, having formerly sponsored the Nova team. Trust had raced a 'customer' 962C here in 1990-91 but it was maybe unsurprising that Yasuo Toyota, given his surname, had finally switched his team to the Japanese manufacturer in 1992. Trust's car had to undergo repairs on Friday after Steven Andskär had crashed at Indianapolis the previous evening (below), but it went well in the race until Stefan Johansson was stranded out on the circuit at midnight by a gearshift breakage. Eventually he managed to find a gear and made it back to the pits for repairs and the car continued to finish fifth after a forceful final shift by George Fouché.

The 92C-V entered by Shin Kato's SARD team from Higashimachi (left) was very strong all Saturday and entered the night in sixth position. But then Eje Elgh and Roland Ratzenberger in turn spoiled the run

1992

by pitting with damaged nose sections. At half-time, Eddie Irvine was afflicted by a clutch problem that took 24 minutes to fix in pit-lane. Four hours later, an even longer stop was needed to replace the gearbox and one of the turbos, and the car finished ninth, alarming its drivers by jumping out of gear.

COUGAR CONQUERS PORSCHE

Le Mans constructor Yves Courage again raced three of his 3-litre Cougar-Porsches, designated C28LM after another round of mechanical and aerodynamic upgrades, and this time finished the weekend as a very fine class winner thanks to the car of Le Mans super-veterans Bob Wollek and Henri Pescarolo with Jean-Louis Ricci (below). They finished sixth overall, roundly defeating the Porsche 962Cs that shared the class.

The successful Cougar was another honeycomb monocoque, new this year. Marcel Hubert's main aerodynamic changes were a longer engine cover, with a low-line rear wing located outboard of the tail, and NACA ducts for ventilating the cockpit and cooling the rear brakes (instead of unsightly snorkels). The revised specification looked much neater and was also applied to recycled chassis that had started life as a C24 in 1990 and a C26 in 1991. All three cars had newly modified transmission mountings following disappointments in the 24-hour race at Daytona.

Wollek was here for a 22nd time, 'Pesca' for a 26th, and car manager Dominique Méliand allowed Ricci only four single shifts during the race. The car stayed very strong and they reached the top six long before dark, and then embarked on the rainy night battling with a Mazda and one of the Group C Toyotas. Soon after midnight, to everyone's astonishment, Pescarolo slid off the track at Indianapolis. The car was beached on the rumble strip there with its rear wheels in the gravel, and had to be hauled clear by a 4x4 rescue vehicle.

The incident and a 10-minute pitstop that followed cost two positions, but preceded a fighting comeback. Early on Sunday afternoon, the car was running fifth. It lost the position to the other 92C-V when Méliand ordered a routine brake-pad change at 2:25pm, but Wollek brilliantly took it back. A tense battle was unresolved until 15 minutes before the end, when George Fouché overtook Wollek on the pits straight. But the Cougar finished a lap ahead of the Kremers' best-placed Porsche, and three other 962s ended up even further behind.

Lionel Robert, Pascal Fabre and Marco Brand, directed by Jacques Bouquet, had problems with the front bodywork and a puncture, but also looked in good shape as night fell. But then Brand was caught out by the wet track, and crashed out of the race in the Esses.

Jean-François Yvon, Denis Morin and Tomas Saldana drove the oldest of the Cougars in the midfield on Saturday but lost 10 laps to a gearshift malfunction. They were running 12th when their engine broke down just before half-time.

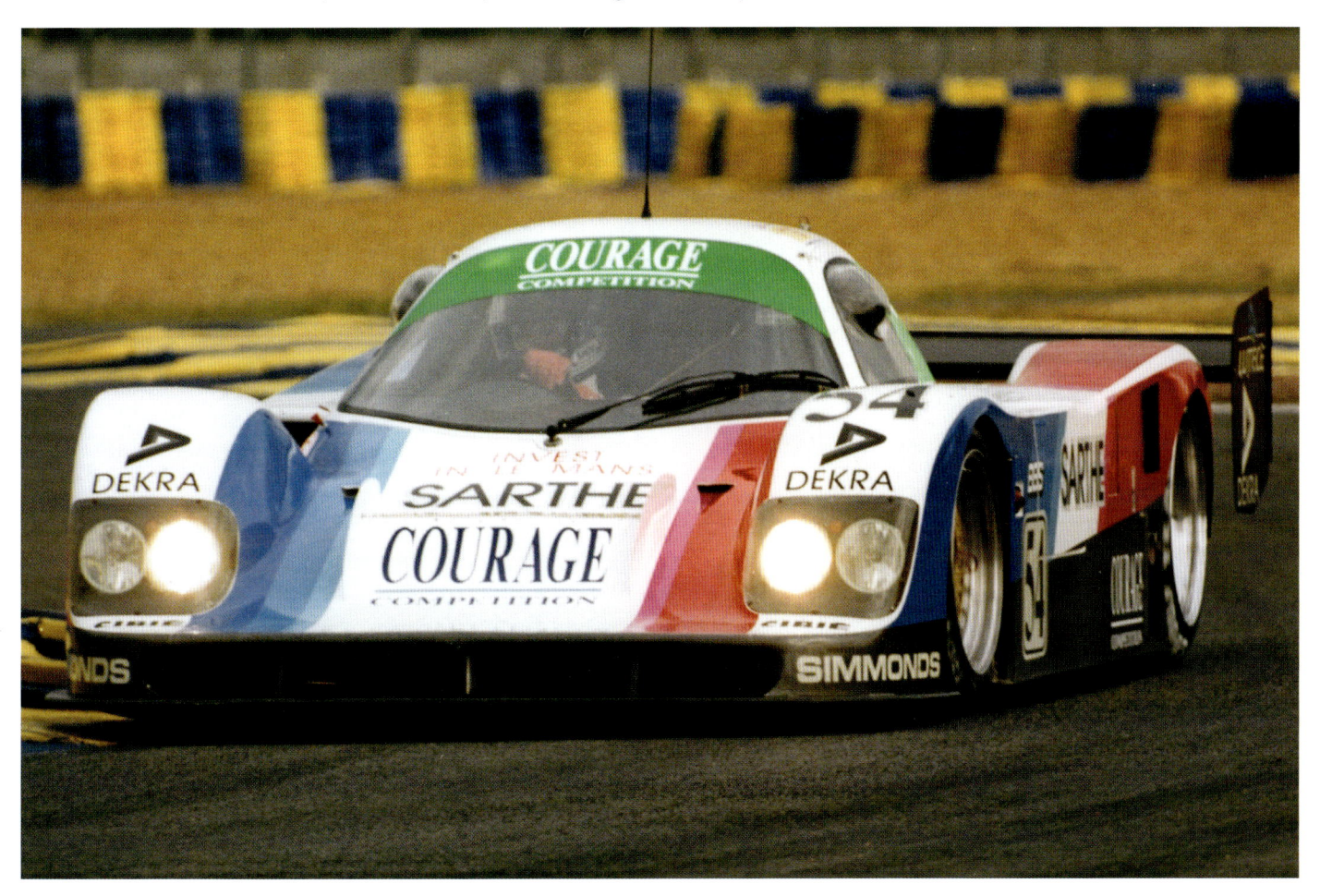

A HOME WIN FOR PEUGEOT

LE MANS

FIVE TO THE RESCUE

Porsche's 956/962C series had often provided the backbone of the entry for a decade, and this year's field would have been even thinner had it not been for five 3-litre 962Cs. While these cars were back at a 900kg minimum weight, they were severely hampered by a reduced fuel allocation, but four of them finished.

The Kremer brothers brought three of their TCP-hulled K6 variants (including a spare) and Manuel Reuter qualified the 3.2-litre car (above) in eighth place. Gianni Lavaggi had a spin in the Virage Ford at dusk and the car needed three fresh batteries during the night, but Reuter and 'Super' John Nielsen (who did three triple shifts) enjoyed a long battle on Sunday with one of the Cougars. Eventually they lost the contest, and finished seventh. Reuter went on to win the 1992 Interserie title with the Kremers' spyder 'K7' racecar.

The other K6 (left), raced by Almo Coppelli with Robin Donovan and Charles Rickett, lost chunks of time to starter motor and clutch replacements and could do no better than 11th.

Like the Kremers, Hans Obermaier was now concentrating on the Interserie. However, he returned to France with the TCP chassis that had been crashed out of the 1991 race by Jürgen Lässig, who again reprised his partnership with Otto Altenbach

100 LE MANS 24 HOURS 1990–99

and Primagaz concessionaire Pierre Yver. This time, driving the heaviest car in the race (top right), they finished 10th after a spin by Lässig cost 10 minutes while the nose and tail sections were replaced.

London-based ADA Engineering had seen no market incentive to move up from Group C2 as a constructor, but founders Ian Harrower and Chris Crawford were racers through and through. They purchased from Richard Lloyd's GTI Engineering enough components to assemble a fifth special-bodied, honeycomb-hulled 962-GTI (bottom). Harrower persuaded five-times winner Derek Bell to race it here alongside his son, Justin, and Tiff Needell. The car ran well until brake problems intervened. Crawford had preferred ferrous to carbon brakes for this project but could not have foreseen porosity in the calipers. This caused such lengthy delays that the car lost 45 laps to the leaders even before half-time. Later it seemed irrelevant when the gearlever came off in Justin's hand. The drivers were relieved when the chequered flag flew, finding them in 12th place.

The only Porsche not to finish was the Alméras brothers' high-tail TCP chassis (right), which had twice been crashed during the 1991 race. A last-minute entry after a sponsorship intervention by Rennes industrialist Jacques Chotard, the car had already lost time with ignition problems when, at around midnight in the Esses, it was crashed again – not by either of its owners this time, but by Max Cohen-Olivar, in his 20th Le Mans.

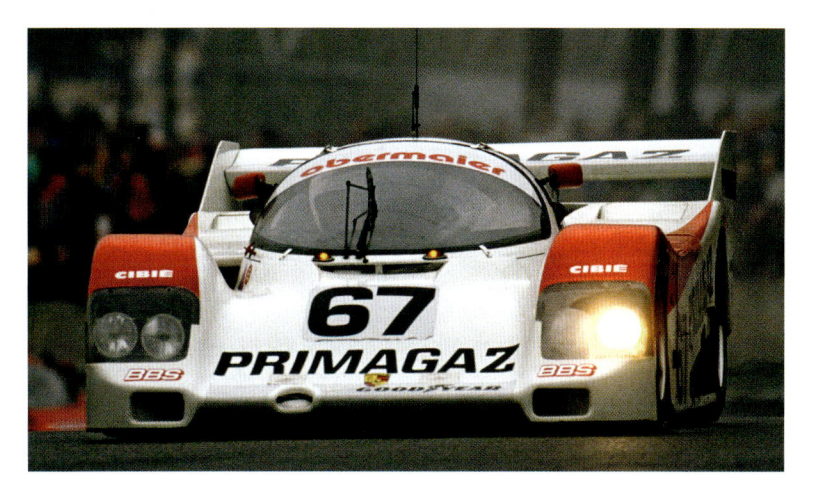

A HOME WIN FOR PEUGEOT 101

LE MANS

TITLE DEFENDERS

Mazdaspeed defended its Le Mans title with two new FIA Sportscars, powered by V10 piston engines, one of which finished fourth in the hands of the same drivers who had won the previous year (below).

The new regulations made Mazda's rotary ineligible, and the company had no suitable power unit. Late that season, the board directors in Japan – for reasons that might have escaped them 12 months later – voted not to rest on their laurels, but to continue with new hardware. While a new rotary GTP contender was designed for the American programme, one-car teams of new-style 750-kilo cars were put together for both the SWC and the All-Japan series. For this purpose, Mazdaspeed ordered Jaguar XJR-14 advanced-composites monocoques from the TWR Group's Astec company and, back in Hiroshima, fitted them with modified F1 engines from John Judd's Engine Developments in Rugby.

Astec had to modify Ross Brawn's hull design (for the Ford HB V8) to take the longer Judd V10, locating the rear bulkhead inset further forward. Mazdaspeed's long-serving technical consultant, Nigel Stroud, oversaw the MXR-01 project and the many modifications needed to make an endurance car from a chassis and a powertrain both created for 'sprint' racing. Five chassis were assembled in Japan, two for use only as test cars for Le Mans.

The main durability focus was on the powertrain. The Judd GV10, first used in Grand Prix racing in 1991, was given the full treatment by the Mazda R&D division as soon as the first unit was delivered that November. Mazda experimented extensively with altered cam profiles and other valvegear components, and with the inlet and exhaust lengths. The eventual MV10 version was a very different specification from the GV10 used in this race by EuroRacing's Lolas, although Mazda retained the Zytek electronic systems. The MV10 produced its peak power of 600bhp at 10,800 instead of 13,000rpm. Mazda engineers also strengthened the pinions and shift mechanisms in the transverse, six-speed, Hewland-based transmission.

Mazdaspeed arrived fresh from a second place in the SWC race at Silverstone (its best finish in the whole series) with two race cars and the two test chassis. The team was dismayed to find that, at 201mph (324kph), the MRX-01 was significantly slower at the fastest points of the circuit than the Peugeot (218mph) and the Toyota (215). To counter this, the team fitted one of the cars on Wednesday with a 13,000rpm, 660bhp qualifying version of its MV10 and Volker Weidler went fifth fastest, only to be demoted two positions on Thursday. Meanwhile, on the other MXR-01, the team removed the rear wing's lower tier so that the wing could be mounted very low (bottom right). This car was qualified 10th by Maurizio Sandro Sala.

Before the start, Mazda Motor chairman Kenichi Yamamoto

1992

presented ACO president Michel Cosson with a replica of the 1991-winning 787B for the Le Mans museum, and six 323GTs kitted out as course cars. With that ceremony done, it began to rain steadily.

Weidler loved this, and so did his car. From the start, it monstered the similarly tyred Peugeots, hitting the front on the sixth lap. The orange-and-green Mazda led the race beyond the first fuel stops but the Peugeots could go further on the fuel, and Johnny Herbert was demoted to second place after taking over the car. Third driver Bertrand Gachot soon slipped to third place behind another Peugeot and, as the ambient temperature fell after nightfall, the Mazda needed two quick stops when the acrylic windscreen misted up. It stayed competitive all night and regained second place soon after dawn, but soon fell back to third again at 7:30am when Gachot pitted for 10 minutes with a troublesome gearshift. In the drier track conditions of Sunday, the Mazda was finally caught by two Toyotas, which had struggled on their rain tyres. At the finish, it was a fighting fourth – with first, third and sixth gears inoperative.

Sala's MRX-01, co-driven by Mazda men Yojiro Terada and Takashi Yorino, was raced with prudence, rather than panache, until 1:15pm, when sixth-placed Terada was caught out by a small river on the entrance to the Porsche curves, and hit the barrier. From mid-morning, a rested Sala was used instead of Gachot in the surviving car.

Mazda axed the MRX programme at the end of the season.

A HOME WIN FOR PEUGEOT   103

LOW LOLAS

A return to Le Mans by Eric Broadley's Lola Cars did not go well. Both its new FIA Sportscars were struck by gearbox failures and only the one pictured above made the finish.

Having spent recent years building GTP and Group C racing cars for Chevrolet and Nissan, Lola Cars ended the 1991 season without a manufacturer contract, and embarked in Huntingdon on its first Lola-branded 'customer' sports-prototype for eight years. The new T92/10 was designed by a group led initially by Wiet Huidekoper, and subsequently by former Spice technical director Graham Humphrys.

The very rigid honeycomb/carbon monocoque, made in-house by Lola Composites, included more complex shapes than had ever been attempted before. The carbon/Kevlar body had a much smaller windscreen and cockpit roof section than Lola's recent projects but, like the Nissans, incorporated two large air intakes on the nose that served both aerodynamic and cooling functions. The sidepods were sculpted low between the wheel-arches and combined with a lowline engine cover to enhance the surface airflows to a high, biplane rear aerofoil with deep endplates. The F1-based 3.5-litre 'atmo' engine, supplied by John Judd, was a compact, 72deg V10 equipped with valvegear that reduced crankshaft speeds by 2000rpm relative to the Grand Prix version. With Zytek and Magneti Marelli electronic fuel-injection and ignition systems, the GV10 engine made 600bhp at 10,800rpm, driving through Lola's six-speed gearbox.

The first cars were ordered by Holland-based Charles Zwolsman's Euro Racing team to replace its Spice-Cosworth. Zwolsman warmed up for his SWC campaign by winning an Interserie race at Mugello but, in both the opening rounds of the new FIA series at Monza and Silverstone, the Lolas encountered big gearbox problems. They came to Le Mans with strengthened transmissions and reworked rear suspensions. Under the team management of Roy Baker and engineering direction of Mike Franklin, they were entered for Heinz-Harald Frentzen with Shunji Kasuya and Hideshi Matsuda, and by Cor Euser with Jesús Pareja and the team owner.

In qualifying, Euser and Frentzen had to run-in the new gearboxes and the team concentrated on race settings, both cars giving away 15-20mph in top speed to the Peugeots and Toyotas. It came as a real surprise when Frentzen went fastest of all in the race morning warm-up session, under steady rain.

Euser's car was in gearbox trouble pretty much from the outset, and he pitted at 5:35pm for a replacement, at a cost of almost 40 minutes. At 8:35pm, Pareja spun into the gravel at one of the Mulsanne straight chicanes and, having extricated the car, parked it at Indianapolis with no drive.

At this moment, the other car was in pit-lane, undergoing its own 40-minute gearbox replacement. Zwolsman asked Matsuda to stand down and took his place in the sister car. Franklin used Frentzen to the maximum permitted, but Zwolsman was off the pace and any slim hope of a recovery was lost at 6am, when Kasuya crashed the car and the crew had to spend 40 minutes rebuilding the front end. Seven hours later, Franklin had to use Kasuya again – and he crashed again at Arnage, with the same result. The drivers were also hampered by a rear wheelbearing failure and by braking problems, and finished 13th with the gearbox on its last legs.

Eight days after the race, Zwolsman was stopped by Dutch traffic police for speeding. In court, the judge found that he had violated the terms of his parole, and he was sent back to prison to serve out the rest of his sentence

1992

for drug smuggling and money laundering. Euro Racing was dissolved in September and the Lolas were sold to collectors by the Dutch government. A third T92/10 was raced by McNeil Engineering in the Interserie until 2001, winning five times.

TRAUMATIC REBIRTH

An ambitious project to revive British Racing Motors, the defunct former F1 marque, was announced in January 1990. Its initial target was to build the second sports-racing car to bear the BRM logo, and the first to race at Le Mans. Both objectives were achieved, but without distinction, and this interesting project was short-lived.

In 1989 John Owen of the Rubery Owen company, the owner of the BRM trademark, decided to cooperate when approached by John Mangoletsi to approve an all-new BRM racing car alongside a roadgoing 'supercar'. Mangoletsi hired former Zakspeed, March, Maurer and Chevron engineer Paul Brown to design the FIA Sportscar with Chris Norris. Supplied by a group of 15 subcontractors, the P351 was assembled in Mangoletsi's Airflow Management design consultancy HQ in Congleton, Cheshire, on an advanced composites tub fabricated by Courtaulds. It was powered by a 3.5-litre V12 engineered by Terry Hoyle and Graham Dale-Jones, based on the architecture of the old 70deg Weslake V12, and driving through a six-speed Xtrac gearbox with a bespoke casing. A supercharged, 4-litre V12 was to power the P401 road car.

Former GRID co-owner Ian Dawson was recruited as the team manager and the first driver to sign up was Harri Toivonen. He was joined by Wayne Taylor in May 1992 when the P351 finally débuted at Silverstone, where it ran into electrical problems in qualifying, and then suffered an oil-pump failure during the race morning warm-up that prevented it from starting.

Mangoletsi's team, then, arrived at Le Mans with an unraced car that had only 75 minutes of track time under its belt. And it was parked all day Wednesday, missing special gearbox bolts that had not been delivered. On Thursday, a gearbox bearing failed after Taylor had done only six laps…

Dawson tried to persuade the stewards to allow Toivonen and Richard Jones to qualify in the Saturday morning warm-up, but was refused – although, under the SWC rules, Taylor was allowed to start. He did so from the pit-lane and went well, picking off slower cars and emerging in 17th position before stopping for fuel. But the test run was halted when a broken gear selector caused a spin in the Virage Ford. Eventually Taylor found a gear and crept into the pits, but the BRM's weekend was done.

The P351 was later raced in an IMSA event at Watkins Glen, where it succumbed to an electrical failure after only five laps. The team returned to Europe and entered the next SWC race at Donington Park, but never appeared. Later Rubery Owen terminated the agreement with Mangoletsi but authorised Dawson to take over the P351 programme from his base at Silverstone, if he could find sponsorship for 1993. But Europe was now firmly in the grip of a financial recession, and no money was to be had.

A HOME WIN FOR PEUGEOT

LE MANS

CHAMBERLAIN'S FIA CUP

Amidst the decline and fall of the British sports-racing brand, in a shrunken market for its products, there were only four Spice-Cosworths this year, all configured as FIA Cup entries. Hugh Chamberlain entered both the Spices he had run here in 1991, and this time both went the distance. But the only classified finisher, in 14th and last position, was the SE89C pictured above in the pits, powered by a Nicholson-built Cosworth DFZ, and driven by PC Automotive team founder Richard Piper with Olindo Iacobelli and Ferdinand de Lesseps.

The FIA Cup division was led throughout the first half of the race by the Spice SE90C that the works team had raced here as a C1/3.5 entry in 1990 (below). Now owned by Bernard de Dryver's newly formed Action Formula team in Brussels, it was equipped with a DFR engine prepared at Merlin Developments by former Cosworth engineer Bruce Stevens. Raced by John Sheldon, Luigi Taverna and Alessandro Gini, under the management of Marc Wouters, it had a solid run into the night, despite Sheldon's spin in the Dunlop chicane. But then persistent fuel-injection problems intervened, causing unpredictable throttle response. Soon after daybreak, this fault caught out Sheldon at the Esses, and he skittered into the gravel there. The stalled engine would not restart.

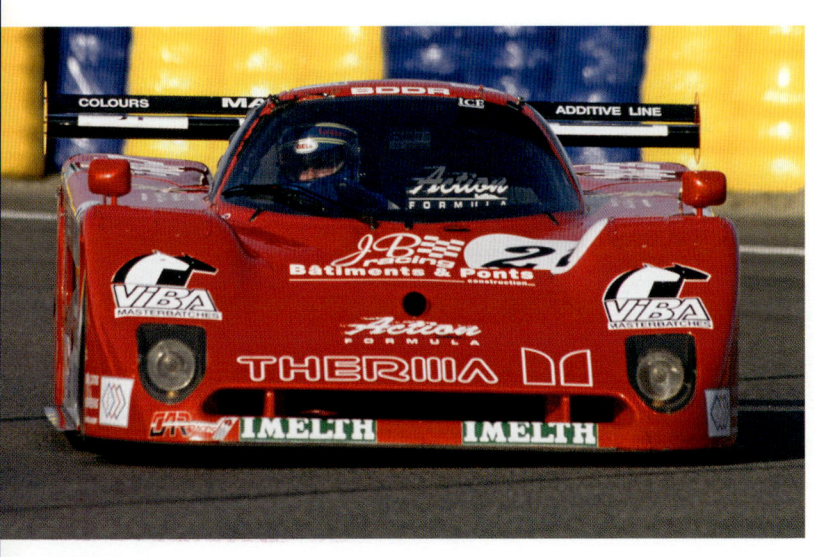

The race strategy of the class-winning drivers had an early setback when Iacobelli ran off the track at about 6pm, and lost time in pit-lane while rear-end damage was repaired and a new wing fitted. A couple of hours later, the crew had to install a new gearbox, putting the car 10 laps behind the class-leading Action Formula Spice (and three laps behind the second-placed Tiga). However, both its rivals were gone soon after daybreak, and Piper finished the race strongly after late alarms caused by malfunctioning engine electronics.

Lesseps had been in the same Spice when it had won the FIA Cup class at Monza and Silverstone, and would go on to win the title with a perfect, undefeated record.

Pictured at top right, Chamberlain's wide-track SE89C was now equipped with a DFZ prepared by Brian Hart, and was raced by three Japanese F3 drivers, all Le Mans rookies. Jun Harada and Kenta Shimamura were co-driven by Tomiko Yoshikawa, who had lacked the licence she had needed to race the AO Racing Spice 12 months before. Shimamura pitted after less than an hour's racing with an ignition problem that was not resolved until the crew had fitted a third electronics control

LE MANS 24 HOURS 1990-99

box. Later the seat mounting broke and, after it had been fixed, the engine took a while to restart. Shimamura damaged the car off the track – twice – and was stranded at Tertre Rouge for a long while with broken suspension. At half-time, the car had covered only 52 laps and was much too far behind to retrieve classification. A gearbox breakage on Sunday afternoon added to the misery, but at least Harada finished the race.

The fourth Spice did not make the race – a familiar tale for its owner, Tim Lee Davey. He had formed TDR, a new team in Allington, Kent, to operate the SE90C that GP Motorsport had loaned to AO Racing here 12 months before. As usual, Davey was embarrassingly short of funds, and did not nominate any drivers until selling seats in the paddock to François Migault, Chris Hodgetts and Thierry Lecerf. But then legal problems parked the car all day Wednesday. All three men qualified the next day but, on Friday, Migault's exasperated sponsors pulled out. The car reappeared in TDR's pit before the start of the race, but it was put back in the transporter after a couple of hours there.

TIGA BOWS OUT

The last Tiga to race at Le Mans was this C2 car (right) entered by the Italian-owned Berkeley Team, which had been evolved from Rome-based Kelmar Racing by Ranieri Randaccio, Vito Veninata and Stefano Sebastiani. The last-named, who raced as 'Stingbrace', was the manager of the Berkeley Hotel in London.

This team had been refused admission 12 months before because its Spice-DFZ had turned up late for scrutineering. Berkeley had raced the Spice in the FIA Cup class in the opening Monza and Silverstone rounds of the SWC, and the Tiga in the first two rounds of the Interserie at Mugello and Nürburgring. The Spice had been plagued by gearbox problems, so the trusty Tiga was preferred for this race. Bought new by Kelmar in 1988, it had been updated the following year to the GC289 specification (with a part-carbon monocoque and modified bodywork) and was powered by a 3.3-litre Nicholson Cosworth DFL.

The Tiga was qualified 25th but, before dark, emerged through the drizzle in 16th position, despite a spin by Veninata in one of the Mulsanne chicanes. Soon before midnight, however, the car needed a new clutch, and lost almost 90 minutes. Ironically, it was a gearbox failure that parked the Tiga a couple of hours later. Perhaps they should have brought their Spice...

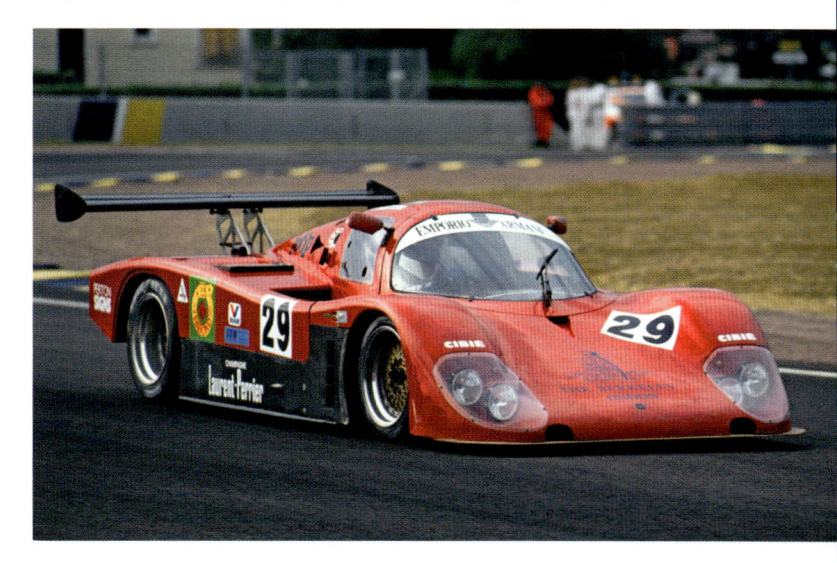

A HOME WIN FOR PEUGEOT 107

LE MANS

A WELCOME COMEBACK

A Le Mans comeback was made this year by the former WM team, now known as WR after the departure of Michel Meunier in 1989 (to concentrate on building engines at Peugeot Talbot Sport). WR was run by Gérard Welter with his wife, Rachel, out of the former WM raceshop in Thorigny-sur-Marne, east of Paris. Welter, the styling director of Peugeot, had retained the link to the manufacturer that had contributed to the tremendous public popularity of WM through the previous decade. He was running 905 Spyders in Peugeot's new national series and, when the ACO declared such cars eligible for this year's 24 Hours to boost the entry, his form was swiftly in the post.

Peugeot had conceived this open-chassis championship in 1990, when it had led the Welters to recreate a race team by asking them to produce the prototype 905 Spyder, a spaceframe reinforced by aluminium honeycomb panels. The 'spec' engine for the centre-seat sports-racers was the 1930cc, 16-valve four-cylinder of the 405 Mi16 road car, making 220bhp at 8000rpm and driving through a Hewland gearbox. Now Martini, Mygale, Norma, ORECA, Orion and Van Diemen had joined the fray.

Welter and his part-time mechanics had to modify their neat racecar by fitting an alternator, bodywork with headlights, a 70-litre fuel cell under the seat with an external filler and vent-valve, and other additions for endurance racing. The team arrived with three engines specially prepared by Alain Guéhennec and the WR was much faster than the other 905 Spyder that started. But the specification was not up to the job: Pierre Petit, Patrick Gonin and Didier Artzet were stopped at nightfall by broken suspension, having already been delayed by a malfunctioning cooling system and a wheelbearing failure.

LE MANS 24 HOURS 1990–99

1992

NO STARS IN ORION
Alongside WR's Peugeot 905 Spyder in Category 4, Eric Bellefroid entered an Orion (bottom left) with a reinforced spaceframe that had been substantially reworked for Le Mans by former ORECA F3 engineer Jacky Renaud and Jacky Carmignon. Reckoning they had done enough to rename it 'RenCar', they had added not only an alternator, a bigger fuel cell and carbon/Kevlar bodywork with lights, but also stronger suspension, a more effective cooling system, and a dry-sump lubrication system for the Hewland gearbox. As reward for all this work they reached the finish, but way too far back to be classified as a finisher.

Somehow, Bellefroid persuaded the ACO to allow alarmingly inexperienced drivers in his car, among whom, believe it or not, only Marc Alexander had any actual racing background. More able drivers were spared the dangers of meeting Bellefroid's drivers on the track throughout the early evening, for that was when the RenCar was in the pits for an engine top-end rebuild due to a blown head gasket. However, it rejoined and kept going to the bitter end. Other problems – including a rear suspension repair on Sunday afternoon – were irrelevant because the Orion was never going to cover sufficient distance.

DEBORA ON DÉBUT
Having failed to qualify his ALD here in 1989, Didier Bonnet ordered a car from Tiga, which abruptly went out of business. So he built the first of his own sports-prototypes the following year using the name 'Debora' (from the letters of Didier Bonnet Racing). The first two cars were used mostly for speed hillclimb events but this year Bonnet kitted out a new aluminium monocoque he had fabricated in his Besançon workshop for the French national Coupe Alfa Romeo series. The immaculately presented little car had pushrod suspension systems, a neat glassfibre body, and the 3-litre V6 from the 164 Quadrifoglio road car, controlled by Bosch Motronic electronics and sending 220bhp to a five-speed Hewland FT200 gearbox.

Pictured above, facing the wrong way at the Virage Ford, the SP92 was not designed for endurance racing and only just scraped through qualifying with a temperamental clutch. After taking it over from Bonnet and Gérard Tremblay, racing politician Jacques Heuclin (a member of the *Assemblée Nationale*) spun off the track at Mulsanne corner when the clutch packed up altogether, and parked the car.

ALD MISSES THE CUT
The tragic death of 39-year-old Louis Descartes in a road accident, in December 1991, inevitably caused his racing team to be disbanded. However, his ALD marque was briefly at this Le Mans. Marc Pachot Racing, which had entered a Lucchini-Alfa Romeo, instead decided to hire the ALD C289 that had raced here in 1990.

Now owned by Joël Couesson, the car had been fitted with a 3-litre 'PRV' V6, race-prepared to make about 300bhp by Auto Robert Vinegra in Bordeaux, and a Hewland DGB transmission. It was 60kg underweight at scrutineering and, ballasted to 900kg, it was hopelessly uncompetitive against the Toyotas in its class.

The French touring car team secured Le Mans veteran Raymond Touroul to co-drive its two rookies but a broken gearbox on Wednesday and an engine failure on Thursday made qualifying impossible – and the car's lap-times were disallowed, anyway, when it was still underweight in post-qualifying inspection.

A HOME WIN FOR PEUGEOT

LE MANS

24 HEURES DU MANS
20-21 JUIN 1992
60èmes

3615 ACO
A.S.A. AUTOMOBILE CLUB DE L'OUEST

1992

HOURLY RACE POSITIONS

Start	Time	Car	No	Drivers	1	2	3	4	5	6	7	8	9	10	11	12	13	14	15	16	17	18	19	20	21	22	23	24
1	3:21.209	Peugeot 905B Evo1B	2	Baldi/Alliot/Jabouille	3	3	3	3	3	2	2	2	2	2	2	2	2	2	5	3	2	3	3	3	3	3	3	3
2	3:22.512	Peugeot 905B Evo1B	1	Warwick/Blundell/Dalmas	2	1	1	1	1	1	1	1	1	1	1	1	1	1	1	1	1	1	1	1	1	1	1	1
3	3:26.411	Toyota TS010	7	Lees/Brabham/Katayama	5	21	24	24	23	20	19	18	17	17	16	14	12	12	11	DNF								
4	3:27.711	Toyota TS010	8	Lammers/Wallace/Fabi	6	4	4	5	4	4	5	5	4	4	4	4	5	3	4	5	8	8	8	8	9	8	8	
5	3:29.300	Toyota TS010	33	Sekiya/Raphanel/Acheson	8	5	5	4	5	5	4	4	5	5	5	5	4	2	2	3	2	2	2	2	2	2	2	
6	3:31.250	Peugeot 905B Evo1B	31	Wendlinger/Poele/A.Ferté	4	20	21	19	16	14	13	11	11	10	10	9	8	8	8	10	DNF							
7	3:34.329	Mazda MRX-R01	5	Herbert/Weidler/Gachot/Sala	1	2	2	2	2	3	3	3	3	3	3	3	3	3	4	5	4	4	4	4	4	4	4	4
8	3:36.317	Porsche 962C-K6	51	Nielsen/Reuter/Lavaggi	11	6	8	10	9	9	9	9	9	8	8	8	7	7	7	7	7	6	6	6	6	7	7	7
9	3:37.109	Lola T92/10	3	Euser/Pareja	23	24	22	22	22	DNF																		
10	3:38.930	Mazda MRX-R01	6	Sala/Yorino/Terada	14	9	9	8	8	8	8	7	6	12	DNF													
11	3:39.850	Toyota 92C-V	34	Irvine/Ratzenberger/Elgh	7	7	6	7	7	6	7	8	7	6	6	9	9	9	8	9	9	9	9	9	9	8	9	9
12	3:40.207	Lola T92/10 *	4	Frentzen/Kasuya/Zwolsman	9	12	11	9	12	15	15	15	15	13	11	11	13	12	12	12	13	13	13	13	13			
13	3:44.248	Cougar C28LM	54	Wollek/Pescarolo/Ricci	10	8	7	6	6	7	6	6	8	7	7	7	6	6	6	6	5	5	5	5	5	6	6	
14	3:44.888	Cougar C28LM	55	Fabre/Robert/Brand	12	11	10	12	11	DNF																		
15	3:44.944	Toyota 92C-V	35	Johansson/Fouché/Andskär	13	10	12	11	10	10	10	10	9	9	10	10	10	9	8	7	7	7	7	6	5	5		
16	3:47.723	Porsche 962C	67	Altenbach/Lässig/Yver	17	14	13	14	12	11	11	12	12	11	14	15	15	14	14	12	11	11	11	11	11	10	11	10
17	3:51.150	Porsche 962C-GTI	53	Bell/Bell/Needell	15	13	14	13	19	19	20	20	18	18	17	16	16	16	13	14	13	13	12	12	12	11	12	12
18	3:52.538	Porsche 962C-K6	52	Coppelli/Donovan/Rickett	20	18	17	17	15	17	16	16	16	16	15	13	13	13	12	11	11	10	10	10	10	10	10	11
19	3:55.765	Cougar C28LM	56	Saldana/Morin/Yvon	16	15	16	16	14	13	14	14	14	14	12	DNF												
20	3:57.455	Porsche 962C	68	Alméras/Alméras/Cohen-Olivar	19	17	18	18	18	18	17	DNF																
21	3:58.595	Spice SE90C	21	Taverna/Gini/Sheldon	18	16	15	15	13	12	13	13	13	11	12	14	15	DNF										
22	4:00.014	Spice SE89C	22	Piper/Iacobelli/Lesseps	21	23	20	21	21	21	21	19	19	18	17	17	17	16	15	14	14	14	14	14	14	14	14	14
23	4:03.186	BRM P351	9	Taylor	24	27	26	26	26	DNF																		
24	4:05.538	Spice SE89C	36	Harada/Shimamura/Yoshikawa	27	25	23	23	25	24	22	22	21	21	20	19	18	18	17	16	15	15	15	15	15	15	15	NC
	4:09.296	Spice SE90C	30	Hodgetts/Migault/Lecerf	DNS																							
25	4:12.665	Tiga GC288/9	29	Randaccio/Veninata/Sebastiani	25	19	19	20	20	16	17	19	20	20	19	18	DNF											
26	4:28.693	WR 905 Spyder	58	Gonin/Artzet/Petit	22	26	25	25	24	23	DNF																	
27	4:46.715	Orion 905 Spyder	66	Breuer/Alexandre/Vita	28	28	27	27	25	23	23	22	22	21	20	19	19	18	17	16	16	16	16	16	16	16	16	NC
28	4:49.019	Debora SP92	61	Bonnet/Tremblay/Heuclin	26	22	DNF																					
DSQ	5:06.789	ALD C290	60	Touroul/Caradec/Pachot	DNS																							

DNF Did not finish **DNQ** Did not qualify **DSQ** Disqualified **FS** Failed scrutineering **NC** Not classified as a finisher **RES** Reserve not required * Car No4 also qualified by Hideshi Matsuda (J)

A HOME WIN FOR PEUGEOT 111

LE MANS

RACE RESULTS

Pos	Car	No	Drivers			Laps	Km	Miles	FIA Class	DNF
1	Peugeot 905B Evo1B	1	Derek Warwick (GB)	Mark Blundell (GB)	Yannick Dalmas (F)	352	4787.20	2974.62	Cat 1	
2	Toyota TS010	33	Masanori Sekiya (J)	Pierre-Henri Raphanel (F)	Kenneth Acheson (GB)	346	4705.60	2923.92	Cat 1	
3	Peugeot 905B Evo1B	2	Mauro Baldi (I)	Philippe Alliot (F)	Jean-Pierre Jabouille (F)	345	4692.00	2915.47	Cat 1	
4	Mazda MRX-R01 *	5	Johnny Herbert (GB)	Volker Weidler (D)	Bertrand Gachot (B)	336	4569.60	2839.41	Cat 1	
5	Toyota 92C-V	35	Stefan Johansson (S)	George Fouché (ZA)	Steven Andskär (S)	336	4569.60	2839.41	Cat 2	
6	Cougar C28LM	54	Bob Wollek (F)	Henri Pescarolo (F)	Jean-Louis Ricci (F)	335	4556.00	2830.96	Cat 3	
7	Porsche 962C-K6	51	John Nielsen (DK)	Manuel Reuter (D)	Giovanni Lavaggi (I)	334	4542.40	2822.51	Cat 3	
8	Toyota TS010	8	Jan Lammers (NL)	Andy Wallace (GB)	Teo Fabi (I)	331	4501.60	2797.16	Cat 1	
9	Toyota 92C-V	34	Eddie Irvine (IRL)	Roland Ratzenberger (A)	Eje Elgh (S)	321	4365.60	2712.65	Cat 2	
10	Porsche 962C	67	Otto Altenbach (D)	Jürgen Lässig (D)	Pierre Yver (F)	297	4039.20	2509.84	Cat 3	
11	Porsche 962C-K6	52	Almo Coppelli (I)	Robin Donovan (GB)	Charles Rickett (GB)	297	4039.20	2509.84	Cat 3	
12	Porsche 962C-GTI	53	Derek Bell (GB)	Justin Bell (GB)	Tiff Needell (GB)	284	3862.40	2399.98	Cat 3	
13	Lola T92/10	4	Heinz-Harald Frentzen (D)	Shunji Kasuya (J)	Charles Zwolsman (NL)	271	3685.60	2290.12	Cat 1	
14	Spice SE89C	22	Richard Piper (GB)	Olindo Iacobelli (USA)	Ferdinand de Lesseps (F)	258	3508.80	2180.26	Cat 1	
DNF	Peugeot 905B Evo1B	31	Karl Wendlinger (A)	Eric van der Poele (B)	Alain Ferté (F)	208			Cat 1	Engine
DNF	Toyota TS010	7	Geoff Lees (GB)	David Brabham (AUS)	Ukyo Katayama (J)	192			Cat 1	Engine
NC	Spice SE89C	36	Jun Harada (J)	Kenja Shimamura (J)	Tomiko Yoshikawa (J)	160	2176.00	1352.10	Cat 1	Insufficient distance
DNF	Spice SE90C	21	Luigi Taverna (I)	Alessandro Gini (I)	John Sheldon (GB)	150			Cat 1	Electrics
DNF	Cougar C28LM	56	Tomas Saldana (E)	Denis Morin (F)	Jean-François Yvon (F)	142			Cat 3	Engine
DNF	Mazda MRX-R01	6	Maurizio Sandro Sala (BR)	Takashi Yorino (J)	Yojiro Terada (J)	124			Cat 1	Accident
DNF	Tiga GC288/9	29	Ranieri Randaccio (I)	'Stingbrace' (Stefano Sebastiani) (I)	Vito Veninata (I)	101			Cat 1	Transmission (gearbox)
DNF	Porsche 962C	68	Jean-Marie Alméras (F)	Jacques Alméras (F)	Max Cohen-Olivar (MOR)	85			Cat 3	Accident
NC	Orion 905 Spyder	66	Walter Breuer (F)	Marc Alexandre (F)	Frank de Vita (F)	78	1060.80	659.15	Cat 4	Insufficient distance
DNF	Cougar C28LM	55	Pascal Fabre (F)	Lionel Robert (F)	Marco Brand (I)	77			Cat 3	Accident
DNF	Lola T92/10	3	Jesús Pareja (E)	Cor Euser (NL)	Charles Zwolsman (NL)	50			Cat 1	Transmission (gearbox)
DNF	WR 905 Spyder	58	Patrick Gonin (F)	Didier Artzet (F)	Pierre Petit (F)	42			Cat 4	Suspension
DNF	Debora SP92	61	Didier Bonnet (F)	Gérard Tremblay (F)	Jacques Heuclin (F)	25			Cat 4	Transmission (clutch)
DNF	BRM P351	9	Wayne Taylor (ZA)	Harri Toivonen (SF)	Richard Jones (GB)	20			Cat 1	Fire
DNQ	ALD C290	60	Raymond Touroul (F)	Didier Caradec (F)	Marc Pachot (F)	-			Cat 2	
WD	Spice SE90C	30	Chris Hodgetts (GB)	François Migault (F)	Thierry Lecerf (F)				Cat 1	Failed scrutineering (weight)

DNF Did not finish **DNS** Did not start **DSQ** Disqualified **FS** Failed scrutineering **RES** Reserve not required **NC** Not classified as a finisher **WD** Withdrawn Drivers in italics did not race the cars specified
* Car No5 also raced by Maurizio Sandro Sala (BR)   ** Car No4 also qualified by Hideshi Matsuda (J)

112 LE MANS 24 HOURS 1990–99

1992

CLASS WINNERS

FIA Class	Starters	Finishers	First	No	Drivers	kph	mph	
Category 1	15	7	Peugeot 905B	1	Warwick/Blundell/Dalmas	199.46	123.94	
Category 2	2	2	Toyota 92C-V	35	Johansson/Fouché/Andskär	190.42	118.33	
Category 3	8	5	Cougar C28LM	54	Wollek/Pescarolo/Ricci	189.83	117.96	Record
Category 4	3	0	–	–	–	–	–	
Totals	28	14						

FIA SPORTSCAR WORLD CHAMPIONSHIP

Race	Winner	Drivers
Monza (I) 500km	Toyota TS010	Lees/Ogawa
Silverstone (GB) 500km	Peugeot 905B	Warwick/Dalmas
Le Mans (F) 24 hours	Peugeot 905B	Warwick/Dalmas/Blundell
Donington Park (GB) 500km	Peugeot 905B	Baldi/Alliot
Suzuka (J) 1000km	Peugeot 905B	Warwick/Dalmas
Magny-Cours (F) 500km	Peugeot 905B	Baldi/Alliot

FINAL CHAMPIONSHIP POINTS

Final Positions	Team	Points
TEAMS		
1	Peugeot Talbot Sport (F)	115
2	Toyota Team TOMS (J)	74
3	Mazdaspeed (J)	39
4	Chamberlain Engineering (GB)	36
5	Euro Racing (NL)	26
6	Team SCI	17
&c		
DRIVERS		
1	Derek Warwick (GB)	98
=	Yannick Dalmas (F)	98
3	Mauro Baldi (I)	64
=	Philippe Alliot (F)	64
5	Geoff Lees (GB)	59
6	Jan Lammers (NL)	35
7	Ferdinand de Lesseps (F)	34
8	Maurizio Sandro Sala (BR)	29
9	Johnny Herbert (GB)	25
10	David Brabham (AUS)	22
&c		
FIA CUP TEAMS		
1	Chamberlain Engineering (GB)	100
2	Team SCI (I)	45
3	GSR (D)	15
FIA CUP DRIVERS		
1	Ferdinand de Lesseps (F)	100
2	Ranieri Randaccio (I)	45
3	Will Hoy (GB)	40
=	Nick Aams (GB)	40
&c		

A HOME WIN FOR PEUGEOT

LE MANS

1993
PEUGEOT CLOSES OUT THE PODIUM

LE MANS

RACE INFORMATION

RACE DATE
19-20 June

RACE No
61

CIRCUIT LENGTH
8.451 miles/13.600km

HONORARY STARTER
René Monory
President, French Senate

MARQUES (ON GRID)
Courage	3
Debora	1
Jaguar	3
Lotus	2
Lucchini	1
Peugeot	3
Porsche	18
SHS/Sehcar	1
Spice	2
Toyota	5
Venturi	7
WR	1

STARTERS/FINISHERS
47/30

WINNERS

OVERALL
Peugeot

ENTRY LIST

No	Car	Entrant (nat)	cc	Engine	Tyres	Weight (kg)	Class
1	Peugeot 905 Evo1C	Peugeot Talbot Sport (F)	3499	SA35 V10	Michelin	809	Cat 1
2	Peugeot 905 Evo1C	Peugeot Talbot Sport (F)	3499	SA35 V10	Michelin	760	Cat 1
2R	Peugeot 905 Evo1C	Peugeot Talbot Sport (F)	3499	SA35 V10	Michelin	N/A	Cat 1
3	Peugeot 905 Evo1C	Peugeot Talbot Sport (F)	3499	SA35 V10	Michelin	785	Cat 1
7	Allard J2X	Jean-Louis Ricci (F)	3494	Cosworth DFR V8	–	–	Cat 1
10	Porsche 962C-K6	Porsche Kremer Racing (D)	2994tc	F6	Dunlop	935	Cat 2
11	Porsche 962C-K6	Porsche Kremer Racing (D)	2994tc	F6	Dunlop	944	Cat 2
12	Courage C30LM	Courage Compétition (F)	2994tc	Porsche F6	Goodyear	946	Cat 2
13	Courage C30LM	Courage Compétition (F)	2994tc	Porsche F6	Goodyear	938	Cat 2
14	Courage C30LM	Courage Compétition (F)	2994tc	Porsche F6	Goodyear	939	Cat 2
15	Porsche 962C-K6	Porsche Kremer Racing (D)	2994tc	F6	Dunlop	926	Cat 2
17	Porsche 962C	Joest Porsche Racing (D)	2994tc	F6	Goodyear	930	Cat 2
18	Porsche 962C	Joest Porsche Racing (D)	2994tc	F6	Goodyear	911	Cat 2
21	Porsche 962C	Obermaier Racing (D)	2994tc	F6	Goodyear	927	Cat 2
21R	Porsche 962C	Obermaier Racing (D)	2994tc	F6	Goodyear	N/A	Cat 2
22	Toyota 93C-V	SARD Company (J)	3576tc	RV36 V8	Dunlop	924	Cat 2
23	Porsche 962C	Team Guy Chotard (F)	2994tc	935/76 F6	Goodyear	989	Cat 2
24	Spice SE89C	Graff Racing (F)	3298	Cosworth DFL V8	Goodyear	787	Cat 2
25	Toyota 93C-V	Trust Racing Team (J)	3576tc	RV36 V8	Dunlop	911	Cat 2
26	Spice SE90C	GP Motorsport (GB)	3494	Cosworth DFZ V8	–	–	Cat 2
27	Spice SE89C	Chamberlain Engineering (GB)	3494	Cosworth DFZ V8	Goodyear	807	Cat 2
28	SHS C6	Roland Bassaler (F)	3453	BMW M88 S6	Goodyear	958	Cat 2
33	WR LM92/3	Welter Racing (F)	1998tc	Peugeot 405T16 S4	Michelin	658	Cat 3
34	Debora SP93	Didier Bonnet Racing (F)	2959	Alfa Romeo 164QF V6	Pirelli	637	Cat 3
35	Lucchini SP91	Sport & Imagine (I)	2959	Alfa Romeo 164QF V6	Pirelli	659	Cat 3
36	Toyota TS010	Toyota Team TOMS (J)	3497	RV10	Michelin	769	Cat 1
37	Toyota TS010	Toyota Team TOMS (J)	3497	RV10	Michelin	776	Cat 1
37R	Toyota TS010	Toyota Team TOMS (J)	3497	RV10	Michelin	N/A	Cat 1
38	Toyota TS010	Toyota Team TOMS (J)	3497	RV10	Michelin	763	Cat 1
40	Porsche 911 Carrera RSR	Obermaier Racing (D)	3756	F6	Pirelli	1203	Cat 4
41	Porsche 911 Carrera 2 Cup	Obermaier Racing (D)	3600	F6	Pirelli	1147	Cat 4
44	Lotus Esprit Sport 300	Lotus Sport/Chamberlain Engineering (GB)	2174tc	907 S4	Dunlop	1079	Cat 4
45	Lotus Esprit Sport 300	Lotus Sport/Chamberlain Engineering (GB)	2174tc	907 S4	Dunlop	1086	Cat 4
46	Porsche 911 Turbo S LM	Le Mans Porsche Team (D)	3160tc	F6	Goodyear	1054	Cat 4
47	Porsche 911 Carrera RSR	Monaco Média International (F)	3756	F6	Pirelli	1097	Cat 4
48	Porsche 911 Carrera 2 Cup	Team Paduwa (B)	3600	F6	Dunlop	1098	Cat 4
49	Porsche 911 Carrera 2	Team Paduwa (B)	3600	F6	Dunlop	1105	Cat 4
50	Jaguar XJ220C	TWR Jaguar Racing (GB)	3498tc	V6	Dunlop	1123	Cat 4
51	Jaguar XJ220C	TWR Jaguar Racing (GB)	3498tc	V6	Dunlop	1125	Cat 4
52	Jaguar XJ220C	TWR Jaguar Racing (GB)	3498tc	V6	Dunlop	1125	Cat 4
55	Venturi 500LM	Riccardo Agusta (I)	2975tc	PRV V6	Dunlop	1135	Cat 4
56	Venturi 500LM	Stéphane Ratel (F)	2975tc	PRV V6	Dunlop	1075	Cat 4
57	Venturi 500LM	Toison d'Or (B)	2975tc	PRV V6	Dunlop	1168	Cat 4
58	Porsche 911 Carrera RSR	Roock Racing International (D)	3756	F6	–	–	Cat 4
59	Porsche 911 Carrera RSR	Roock Racing International (D)	3756	F6	–	–	Cat 4
62	Porsche 911 Carrera RSR	Konrad Motorsport (D)	3756	F6	Yokohama	1133	Cat 4
63	BMW M5 E34	Ed Arnold Racing (USA)	3535	S38B36 S6	–	–	Cat 4
65	Porsche 911 Carrera RSR	Heico Dienstleistungen (D)	3756	F6	Yokohama	1127	Cat 4
66	Porsche 911 Carrera RS	Muhlbauer Motorsport (D)	3600	F6	Pirelli	1094	Cat 4
67	Porsche 911 Carrera 2 Cup	FAR Derkaum (D)	3600	F6	–	–	Cat 4
70	Venturi 500LM	Eric Graham (F)	2975tc	PRV V6	Dunlop	1139	Cat 4
71	Venturi 500LM	Jacadi Racing (F)	2975tc	PRV V6	Dunlop	1075	Cat 4
72	Ferrari 348 LM	Simpson Engineering (GB)	3446	V8	Pirelli	1115	Cat 4
74	Ford Mustang	John Graham (CDN)	–	V8	–	–	Cat 4
75	Chevrolet Corvette C4	Bob Jankel (GB)	6665sc	Chevrolet V8	–	–	Cat 4
76	Porsche 911 Carrera 2 Cup	Cartronic Motorsport (CH)	3600	F6	Pirelli	1113	Cat 4
77	Porsche 911 Carrera RSR	Scuderia Chicco d'Oro (CH)	3756	F6	Pirelli	1133	Cat 4
78	Porsche 911 Carrera RSR	Jack Leconte (F)	3756	F6	Goodyear	1134	Cat 4
91	Venturi 500LM	Alain Lamouille (F)	2975tc	PRV V6	Dunlop	1129	Cat 4
92	Venturi 500LM	BBA Compétition (F)	2975tc	PRV V6	Dunlop	1130	Cat 4
99	MiG H100	Georgia Automotive MiG Tako (GA)	3500tc	Motori Moderni V12	Pirelli	1072	Cat 4

1993

ENTRY

When the ACO revised its entry parameters, in March, it had only 21 cars, four weeks before entries closed. But Group C and especially GT teams responded swiftly, and the list closed 58-strong. In mid-May, the Test Day was reintroduced on the full circuit, and 32 cars participated. Come race week, there were eight no-shows, but clearly Le Mans was back on the right track.

Peugeot and Toyota now had Category 1 to themselves, and each entered three cars. The owners of a couple of Spice-Cosworths opted to run them in Category 2 alongside seven Group C Porsches, three Courages, two Toyotas and an old SHS-Sauber.

Category 3 held only three cars, but the return of the GT class was a great success. Category 4 held a dozen Porsches (including a works entry), seven Venturis, three TWR-built Jaguars, two Lotus Esprits, the first Ferrari to appear at Le Mans since 1984, and a Russian-entered MiG.

QUALIFYING

The six FIA Sportscars dominated a sunny race week, all timed within seven seconds of each other this time. Philippe Alliot was the fastest driver, thus landing a hat-trick of pole positions.

Alliot's best lap, driven on Wednesday, was hampered by traffic, and almost three seconds off his 1992 pole. So he fitted another set of qualifying tyres and tried again – only to crash in the Porsche curves, smiting the barrier there broadside at almost 125mph (200kph). The monocoque was trashed. Team principal Jean Todt ordered the mechanics furtively to assemble a replacement car on a spare monocoque overnight, but called an end to hot laps.

In view of this, Eddie Irvine's Toyota was equipped with a special engine on Thursday for a crack at pole position, but he spun at Mulsanne corner. Irvine's Wednesday time remained good for the front row ahead of Thierry Boutsen (Peugeot), Geoff Lees (Toyota), Pierre-Henri Raphanel (Toyota) and Christophe Bouchut (Peugeot).

RACE

With 48 survivors of qualifying, and GT cars restoring variety, the circuit on Saturday morning seemed much like it had before FISA's ill-judged interventions – except that, despite the warm weather, the sub-standard fields of 1991-92 had reduced the crowd to 110,000. Their enthusiasm was only slightly diminished during the warm-up session, which was red-flagged when the only Ferrari was clipped into the wall by Irvine's passing Toyota.

Alliot and Irvine took off together from the front row, and the Toyota had the lead when the Peugeot locked up and almost spun at Mulsanne corner on the eighth lap. Irvine led for two shifts but his second fuel stop was a slow one. Mauro Baldi, having taken over the

PEUGEOT CLOSES OUT THE PODIUM 117

LE MANS

ORGANISATION

The 1992 FIA Sportscar World Championship had generally provided event promoters (and the paying public) with fewer than a dozen cars. At Monza, only one had finished the race… Once again, FISA's Sportscar Commission recommended its cancellation, and this time objections were few. In October 1992, the World Motor Sport Council formally killed off the series.

No replacement was offered to the sportscar racing community. There would be no FIA championship for 1993 – indeed, no international series of any kind. An attempt to create one, instigated by British entrant Gordon Spice and others, was ruthlessly stamped out.

Spectacular, but super-expensive, the F1-engined cars from Jaguar, Mazda, Mercedes, Peugeot and Toyota had never offered a viable alternative to Group C. Aston Martin and Nissan had initiated programmes but had not pursued them, and neither had Porsche. ALD, BRM, Lola, ROC and Spice had built cars and had raced them at Le Mans, but those from financially strapped Allard, Brun and Konrad had not appeared in the 24 Hours. March and other specialists had developed concepts but had found no customers.

Bernie Ecclestone was not too disappointed. As early as 1994, the Peugeot and Mercedes race engines would be in Formula 1. Mission accomplished, some said – and Jaguar and Toyota would soon follow.

Late in 1992, it was the ACO under its president, Michel Cosson, that began the process of recovering from this débâcle by creating a new 'Le Mans Prototype' category. The LMP cars would be flat-bottom, open-cockpit spyders with central seats, powered by either series-production engines or restricted race engines. Early in 1993, having also lost factory support (Jaguar, Mazda and Nissan), IMSA announced a new 'World Sports Car' category as a replacement for the GTP and Lights coupés. The new WSC sports-racers were also to be flat-bottom spyders but with two seats, and naturally aspirated 'stockblock' engines up to 5000cc.

The ACO was now free to welcome to Le Mans whatever cars it chose. The immediate problem was that FISA's follies over the previous three years had not only reduced the number of suitable cars, but also the number of teams that would have operated them. The

1993

All-Japan championship also collapsed, and Mazda quit high-end motorsport within a fortnight of the cancellation of the SWC. However, several former Group C teams had taken their outdated hardware to independent championships, such as the Interserie, which had been boasting grids of more than 40.

The ACO again defined four categories in which it would offer entries. Category 1 was for the remaining FIA Sportscars of Peugeot and Toyota. Category 2 was for Group C hardware racing to the current IMSA GTP or 1990 FIA rulebook – without fuel restrictions. Instead, air-inlet restrictors had to be fitted on the engines.

Such restrictors were also introduced to equalize performance in Categories 3 and 4. The former accommodated cars based on IMSA's forthcoming 'World Sports Car' regulations, but with production-based motors of 3000cc, or former F3000 engines. Category 4 was reserved for the ACO's own interpretation of the 'global' GT regulations that were currently being formulated.

In August 1992, FISA had outlined rules for a new 'silhouette' GT racing class that it hoped would yield more cars for its struggling SWC series. Eligible cars would retain the production shapes but could be equipped with the 3.5-litre F1 powertrains. The ongoing uncertainty about the future of the SWC itself had ensured that this potentially very expensive new formula was seen as ridiculous. Meanwhile national motorsport bodies were coming up with different GT regulations. FISA had therefore begun negotiations with the ACO, IMSA and JAF (the Japanese national body) with a view to achieving a worldwide formula. For now, the ACO could accept modified series-production GTs and cars from established National championships.

A new rule stipulated that teams must qualify the cars they intended to race. They could run reserve cars (numbered with an R-suffix), but these could only be deployed in case of accident damage to the specified race cars, and would have to start from the back of the grid. No more silly games with T-cars…

This year the ACO revived the Test Day, last held in 1987. The public roadways were closed and the venue prepared so that 32 cars could be tested on the full circuit in mid-May.

pole position 905, recovered the advantage, but all five other factory cars remained close behind.

That changed just before 6:30pm, when Raphanel pitted the third-placed Toyota with an electronics misfire that took several stops to cure. Half an hour later, Peugeot also lost a contender when the leading 905 lost 35 minutes when an oil-line fractured after a trip over high kerbing.

Lees's Toyota hit the front but, after a spectacular skirmish lasting five laps, Boutsen's Peugeot overtook. Co-driven by Yannick Dalmas and Teo Fabi, it held down a narrow lead over the rest of the evening. Lees's TS010, never far behind, was closing in again when co-driver Juan Fangio III was punted from behind by Yojiro Terada's Lotus GT car, just before 11pm. Rear-end repairs consumed 35 minutes and left Boutsen's 905 at the head of a Peugeot 1-2, a lap in front of Bouchut/Eric Hélary/Geoff Brabham. An oil-smeared windscreen delayed the Toyota of Irvine/Toshio Suzuki/Masanori Sekiya and it was another lap down in third place as they raced into the night.

At 3:25am, Fabi pitted the leading Peugeot with smoke in the cockpit from a short-circuit. It was fixed in five minutes, but that was enough to cede the lead to the sister car.

Electrical problems also hampered Irvine's TS010 and strengthened Peugeot's grip on the race, but the outcome of the duel between its two front-running cars was anyone's guess. They raced only seconds apart for several hours. When, just before 7am, Hélary's rear wing was damaged by flying debris, 90 seconds was lost fitting a new one, and Dalmas regained the lead. But less than two hours later, Boutsen lost a lap with a fractured exhaust, and Bouchut was back in front.

When its battery functioned properly, the best-placed Toyota was very fast, and Irvine broke the track record during the morning as he clawed back a lap. However a clutch failure intervened decisively just after noon, and a rear-end replacement cost 34 minutes. A similar job was needed on Lees's Toyota and, on Raphanel's sister car, another transmission failure had been terminal. Instead of a late Japanese challenge, we had a Peugeot 1-2-3 after a recovery by the pole-position 905.

A small consolation for Toyota came with a 1-2 in the Group C division, while Peugeot's weekend was completed by a victory for WR in Category 3. The GT class was very well won by a Jaguar – but later the XJ220C was disqualified, handing the spoils to a Porsche.

PEUGEOT CLOSES OUT THE PODIUM 119

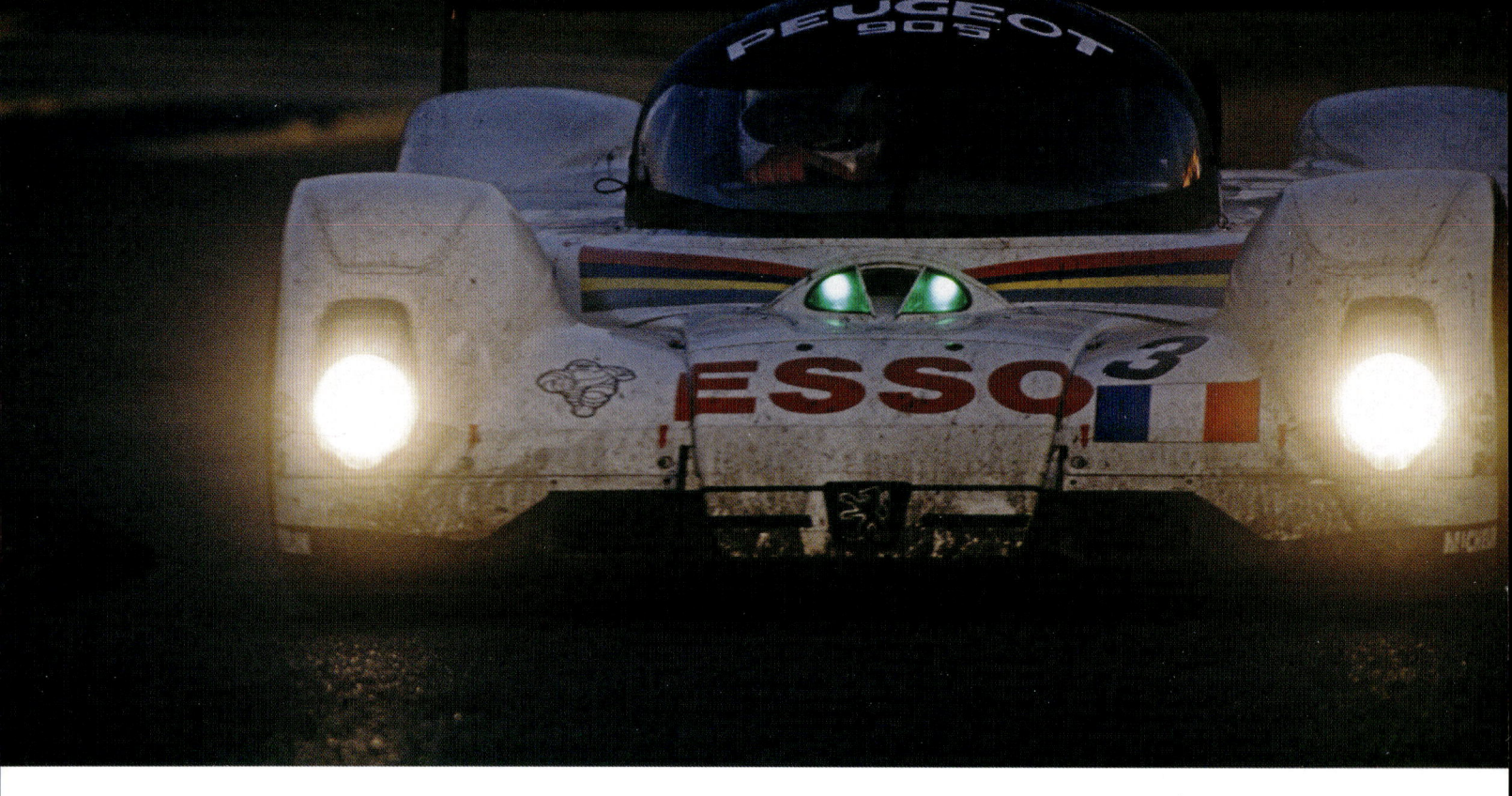

THE LION ROARS LOUDER

The career of the Peugeot 905 ended with Le Mans glory – a 1-2-3 led by the car raced by Geoff Brabham/Christophe Bouchut/Eric Hélary, pictured above and below.

Before the cancellation of the SWC in October 1992, Peugeot had been well advanced with an aerodynamically radical evolution of its 905, and had tested the Evo 2.2 at Magny-Cours. It was never raced. When a defence of its Le Mans title became the only item on its 1993 schedule, Jean Todt's team instead updated its existing chassis to a C-specification, using elements of the Evo 2.2 rear end, including a new, transverse Xtrac sequential-shift gearbox taking revised suspension geometry, and traction control. The team shared the Paul Ricard circuit in early May with Toyota Motorsport for test runs, and then took two cars to the revived Test Day, when they went 1-4, with the Toyotas 2-3.

In race week, Philippe Alliot, making a second pitch for pole position on Wednesday evening, lost control in the double-left section of the Porsche curves, taken flat in fourth. The 905 hit the wall at an oblique angle, in an impact that was registered at 122mph (197kph) by the team's telemetry. The wreck was brought back to the paddock on a flat-bed truck with the front suspension punched into the monocoque. Alliot and co-drivers Mauro Baldi and Jean-Pierre Jabouille resumed their set-up work with their reserve car which, everyone assumed, would have to start the race from the back of the grid.

Miraculously, however, their race car reappeared on Thursday. Really? It was obvious to everyone that a replacement car had been assembled on a spare monocoque. Trouble was, no one could prove anything of the sort – especially as the car was not even at the circuit during Friday. The team claimed it was in its HQ at Vélizy, being checked on the computerized set-up equipment there.

So the lap time Alliot had set before the crash stood, and it proved good enough for the pole when Eddie Irvine's Thursday effort for

LE MANS 24 HOURS 1990–99

1993

PEUGEOT CLOSES OUT THE PODIUM

LE MANS

Toyota was thwarted by traffic. Thierry Boutsen went third fastest with the 1992-winning chassis (above), also with a sprint-specification powertrain, while Bouchut was sixth in the other 905, on qualifying rubber but with the endurance engine.

Alliot led the first seven laps before outbraking himself at Mulsanne corner, clouting a kerb and ceding the advantage to Irvine's Toyota. After the first fuel stops, however, Baldi was back in the lead. The car was still in front just after 7pm when Alliot pitted, trailing smoke: an oil union, damaged on that kerb at Mulsanne corner, had come apart. The loss was 35 minutes. The drivers could never hope to make up an eight-lap deficit. And 21 hours later, after brief delays early on Sunday afternoon with an exhaust problem and a detached door, they had made no inroads into it.

Bouchut had had to stop to have his windscreen cleaned after it had been smeared with oil from Alliot's car, but Boutsen, sharing with Teo Fabi and Yannick Dalmas, continued the battle with the Toyotas towards nightfall. Bouchut, Brabham and Hélary (who had won the Peugeot 905 Spyder support race on race morning) fell a lap behind, having decided to run a steady race until nightfall, and only then to charge.

When both the Japanese cars were delayed, it left a French 1-2.

The Peugeots went onto the same lap at 2:35am, when Fabi pitted with a loose wire sparking behind the dashboard. Less than an hour later, the 905s swapped the lead when Fabi's problem worsened, the cockpit filled with smoke, and he pitted for five minutes while the wiring was properly fixed.

The Peugeots stayed close enough through the night twice to swap places again at around dawn, when they underwent planned brake disc changes. The lead changed again just before 7am when tyre debris thrown up by another car damaged Hélary's rear wing, and a fresh one was needed. And it changed yet again at 8:50am, when Boutsen was in the pits for five minutes with a broken exhaust.

It was the last lead change. With just under six hours remaining, Todt ordered the drivers to hold station. In any case, Fabi was delayed for another five minutes just after midday by another exhaust problem, and slipped two laps behind his team mates. The leaders could later invest one of those laps in checking their own exhaust system, while Toyota's problems allowed the pole-position 905 to retrieve third place.

This turned out to be the manufacturer's last Le Mans for 14 years. The management had already decided to quit sportscar racing for Formula 1. Not with Todt, however. Immediately after the race, he left Peugeot to direct the Scuderia Ferrari.

LE MANS 24 HOURS 1990-99

1993

HEADS ROLL AT TOYOTA

Toyota Team TOMS had done the 1992 Le Mans with suspect gearboxes in its new TS010 Sportscars, and had experienced no problems with them. This year, with the transmissions strengthened, all three of its cars had to have new gearboxes fitted during the race. This ruined an intense battle with the Peugeots. The best Toyota at the finish (above) was a distant fourth behind the French 1-2-3, driven by Eddie Irvine/Toshio Suzuki/Masanori Sekiya.

Chief designer Tony Southgate honed the aerodynamics of the TS010 for this race, and reworked the front suspension to eliminate 'roll'. The changes were evaluated by Geoff Lees on the Snetterton circuit near TOMS GB's Hingham HQ. In Japan, meanwhile, Tsutomu Tomita's powertrain team upgraded the V10 and strengthened the gear linkage in an effort to cope with 90 gearshifts on every lap of the Circuit de la Sarthe. Three new chassis were completed and, in an unlikely collaboration in March, Toyota shared the Paul Ricard circuit with Peugeot to run the latest cars. At the Test Day, the top four were Peugeot-Toyota-Toyota-Peugeot.

The new TS010s returned for race week along with the chassis that had finished second 12 months before, now in use as a spare. The upgrades produced only a small lap-time improvement but the team asked Irvine to make a pitch for pole position on Thursday with a 'sprint' version of the engine. Frustrated by traffic, he spoiled his hot lap by locking up and spinning at Mulsanne corner, and relied on his Wednesday time to qualify second, with Lees and Pierre-Henri Raphanel fourth and fifth. In the race morning warm-up, Irvine clipped Robin Smith's Ferrari 348 LM as he passed it in the Porsche curves, sending it heavily into the wall.

In the race, a fully refocused Irvine monstered Philippe Alliot's Peugeot for seven laps before taking the lead. He held it through the rest of a double-shift, but the TS010 faded in the hands of Suzuki as all six FIA Sportscars stayed close together. Just after 7pm, Sekiya pitted out of fourth place with an oiled windscreen, arriving as the team was working on Raphanel's sister car. Sekiya added to the confusion by also demanding that his drinks bottle was properly secured, and this apparently innocuous incident ended up costing the best part of two laps…

When Sunday dawned, Irvine and his Japanese partners found themselves as Toyota's only men still with any chance of victory, although now three laps down on the leader. Despite having to fit a new battery in almost every fuel stop, they raced in third place for 13 hours and, when Irvine was in the cockpit, he was often the fastest driver out there. At 10:15am, a Sekiya-Irvine handover was extended to almost 10 minutes while the water radiator was cleared to cure overheating, and suddenly

PEUGEOT CLOSES OUT THE PODIUM | 123

LE MANS

the Toyota was five laps behind. It finally lost third place just after midday when it needed a fresh gearbox. The car slipped to sixth behind the Group C Toyotas, but overhauled them both in the final couple of hours to finish fourth.

Raphanel's TS010 (above) was the first to fall out of the lead battle, at 6:30pm. It was pitted out of third place with a misfire, rejoined, and then returned for a new black box, at the total cost of 40 minutes. Andy Wallace and Kenneth Acheson set out to stage a recovery but, at 2am, Wallace felt his gearbox seizing up, and had to pit for a replacement, at the cost of another 30 minutes. The new gearbox only lasted five hours: at 7:45am, Wallace lost drive as he entered the Dunlop curves, and coasted to a stop with the rear end covered in oil.

The third Toyota (pictured leaving its pit) also had a turn leading the race on Saturday evening until, after a crowd-pleasing battle, Lees was displaced by Thierry Boutsen's Peugeot. This TS010 entered the night in second place with Jan Lammers struggling with a loosened gearshift in the cockpit, and using one hand to tighten a screw every time he was on a straight. Nevertheless, he managed to close in again on the leading Peugeot. In the next shift, Juan Fangio II was all set to make another bid for the lead when he was hit from behind by Yojiro Terada's locked-up Lotus after passing it on entry to the second Mulsanne chicane. The TS010 arrived in the pits with its rear wing absent and the rear bodywork and underbody in tatters, which took 35 minutes to fix. On his out-lap from this setback, Lees had trouble with his gearshift, and pitted again. He rejoined in 10th place.

Tremendous driving by all three men, all undertaking triple shifts, recovered fourth position before midday. An hour later, Fangio pitted with a useless gearbox. This replacement also took half an hour, and the car finished eighth.

Afterwards, heads rolled in Tomita's powertrain engineering department. It was a bad way for Toyota – the only manufacturer, incidentally, to remain fully committed to the Group C 'fuel-formula' and 750-kilo concepts throughout the period 1982-93 – to close its TS010 project.

A month after Le Mans, Toyota acquired all the shares in Anderson Motor Sports, which had been building and operating its successful rally cars. It established Toyota Motorsport GmbH in Köln and located all its European-based competition programmes there.

124 LE MANS 24 HOURS 1990–99

1993

ANOTHER TOYOTA 1-2

As in 1992, Category 2 resulted in a 1-2 for Toyota with the same two cars, but this time SARD turned the tables on Trust Racing. The class-winning car (below) was raced for Shin Kato's team, on the 20th anniversary of its Le Mans début, by Roland Ratzenberger, Mauro Martini and Naoki Nagasaki.

Although now known as '93C-V', these sturdy cars had changed little over the previous 12 months save for further aerodynamic fine-tuning. Unlike the 1992 Le Mans, this race pitted the Group C Toyotas directly against eight Porsche 962Cs and the Porsche-engined Courages. The Toyota drivers did not try to match the lap times of their rivals in qualifying but soundly defeated them over the weekend through consistent, competitive race pace and very solid mechanical reliability.

After a mighty opening shift by Ratzenberger, Martini relieved one of the Joest Porsches of the class lead soon after 5pm, and the SARD Toyota was never headed again. Nagasaki was only allowed in the cockpit for three single shifts as this irresistible force marched towards fifth overall, highlighted by Ratzenberger's exceptional night driving.

George Fouché and Steven Andskär again handled Trust's Toyota (right). With Eje Elgh sharing driving duties this time, they finished sixth, five laps behind after a couple of niggling delays, but three laps clear of the nearest Porsche.

PEUGEOT CLOSES OUT THE PODIUM 125

LE MANS

A VICTORY SNATCHED AWAY

Sir Jack Brabham saw two sons on the top steps of Le Mans podiums this year, and left the circuit a very happy man. This new Jaguar XJ220C (above) secured a handsome victory in the GT category, driven by David Brabham/John Nielsen/David Coulthard. But a month after the race, the winning car was excluded from the results.

The XJ220 was based on a mid-engined, four-wheel-drive V12 concept devised in 1988 by Jaguar's engineering director, Jim Randle. When the model was put into production four years later, the 4WD had been deleted to save weight, and so had the V12. The replacement engine, the twin-turbo V6 that had been used in TWR's XJR-10/11 Group C and GTP sports-prototypes, was Jaguar's first with forced induction. Jaguar commissioned TWR to build XJ220s to order in a factory in Bloxham, near Banbury. A new company, Project XJ220 Ltd, was purpose-formed and Jaguar seconded Mike Moreton as the project leader, and Richard Owen as the chief designer. The XJ220 was the first road car to exploit underbody airflows to generate downforce.

A racing version was always planned, but it was finished before the FIA had finalized its future GT regulations. The car was unveiled at the Autosport show in January 1993 with its bonded aluminium honeycomb hull clad with a carbon/Kevlar body panels (in place of aluminium), a front splitter, wider sills, an adjustable rear wing, state-of-the-art racing brake and pushrod suspension systems, and the race version of the V6. This all-aluminium engine, originally designed by David Wood for the Austin Metro 6R4 Group B rally car, was lightly blown by twin Garrett T3 turbos to make 540bhp at 7000rpm, driving through a five-speed gearbox coupled with the rear transaxle of the FFD-Ricardo 4WD system from the concept car. The first XJ220C was shaken down at Silverstone in February by David Leslie, and later easily won a British GT race at Silverstone, in the hands of Win Percy.

At this juncture, TWR had raced further updated XJR12D prototypes at Daytona, but Tom Walkinshaw convinced Jaguar that, in view of the air-inlet restriction now specified for the V12, the new GT car should be entered for Le Mans instead. At first, the XJ220C had been declared ineligible because it complied with rules that were technically not yet in force. However, TWR had found a way into Category 4 via IMSA's unused 'GT International' regulations.

A week after Percy's Silverstone win, TWR team manager Roger Silman took two cars to the Le Mans Test Day. Jay Cochran and Brabham set the 13th and 14th fastest lap times overall – but they were 12 seconds slower than Hans Stuck in the new Porsche 911 Turbo S LM. Intensive testing followed, including long runs at Pembrey.

Brabham qualified second in the category on Thursday, now only 1.3 seconds behind Stuck's works Porsche. Brabham did this 24 hours after the car had been dropped off its jacks onto his foot, which was badly bruised. It was put on a bag of frozen peas whenever it wasn't in use.

The ACO's chief steward caused consternation in the TWR camp on Thursday morning. Alain Bertaut said the cars should be fitted with the catalytic converters that were standard equipment on the roadgoing XJK220. These had been deleted in the racing specification and it was far too late to do anything about it. At Silman's request, IMSA's Amos Johnson sent a fax confirming that the XJ220C did comply with the American rules. However, Johnson's boss, Mark Raffauf, was at Le Mans and contradicted this opinion. Eventually TWR lodged an appeal with the ACO, and the cars started under waiver.

The race began badly when Armin Hahne parked the car he shared with Leslie and Percy with a blown head gasket, having raced for only half an hour. But when the works Porsche was delayed, and later crashed, the other cars took command of the class. Brabham/Nielsen/Coulthard led comfortably until 2:50am, when a ruptured fuel cell intervened. The XJ220C was at rest for 73 minutes and the sister car (top right), driven by Cochran/Andreas Fuchs/Paul Belmondo, took over the lead. Four other Category 4 cars also went ahead before Coulthard could rejoin the race.

At dawn, Fuchs had a blown tyre, which put him backwards into the wall. Repairs to the bodywork and some of the kit in the engine bay took only 18 minutes but, when Belmondo resumed, it turned out the cooling system had been damaged and the turbo V6 soon overheated.

LE MANS 24 HOURS 1990–99

The surviving Jaguar finally caught and passed the class-leading Larbre Porsche at lunchtime, and went on to win Category 4 by two laps. Three weeks later, ahead of the appeal hearing, TWR raced an XJ220C as an International GT entry in an IMSA event at Elkhart Lake, and it won the class driven by Cochran/Davy Jones – without catalytic converters. Back in France the following week, however, TWR's Le Mans appeal was thrown out. The question of the Jaguar's legality did not arise: although the team had filed its appeal to the race organizers correctly, it had not submitted a separate appeal to the FFSA, the French national body, within the time allowed. Oxfordshire residents noticed that the air above them turned an unusually vivid blue for several days.

NO GIANT-KILLING TODAY

Porsche had high hopes that its latest GT racing project (right) would cause an upset at Le Mans, as so many new Carreras had in the past. But the car was eliminated on Saturday evening by a silly accident.

Porsche decided in November 1992 to develop a new car to take advantage of the opportunities opening up in GT racing. The 964-series 911 Turbo S, launched at the 1992 Geneva show, was used as the base car for the one-off Turbo S Le Mans GT. It was equipped in Weissach with a smaller (3.2-litre) version of the air-cooled, twin-turbo 3.6 engine used in the road car, making 480bhp at 6000rpm, and driving through the company's five-speed racing gearbox. An adjustable rear aerofoil was added on top of the road car's standard wing, with a deep spoiler at the front. A cooling air inlet was added near the top of each rear wheel-arch, the arches being much wider in order to house 12-inch wide Goodyear racing tyres and big brake assemblies, controlled by an ABS developed by Bosch.

PEUGEOT CLOSES OUT THE PODIUM

The Turbo S LM won its class and finished seventh overall on début in the Sebring 12 Hours in March, operated for Porsche by Brumos Racing and driven by Hans-Joachim Stuck, Hurley Haywood and Walter Röhrl. It was run in the Le Mans Test Day by Joest Racing before returning for race week in the charge of a reformed factory team under Peter Falk and Norbert Singer, using the same three drivers.

Stuck qualified the 190mph (305kph) car on the GT pole, outpacing the best of TWR's Jaguars by more than a second. Come Saturday afternoon, and Stuck led the class comfortably, acutely embarrassing the drivers of some of the prototypes. But almost 20 minutes was lost early in the second hour when the mechanics had to fix a sticking throttle.

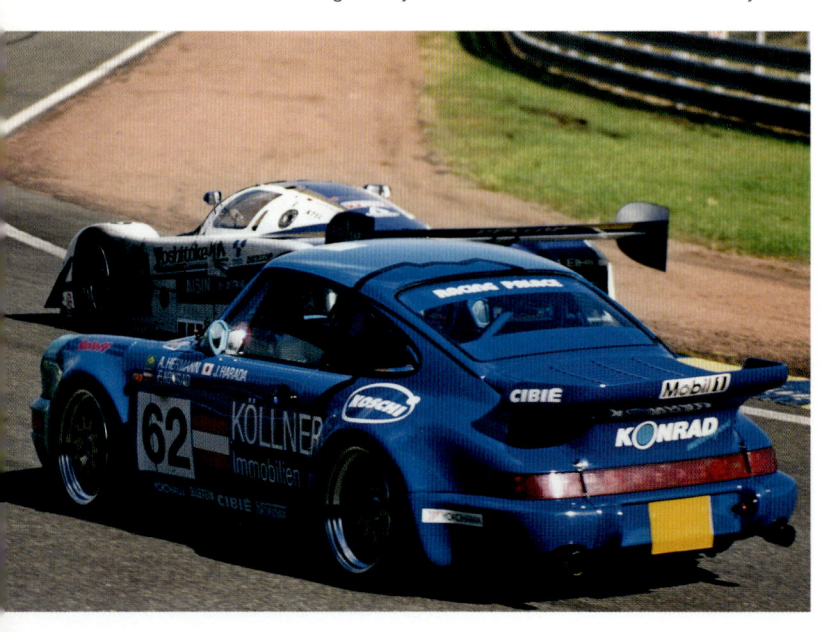

Five hours later, at 10pm, the Porsche drivers had taken back two of the five laps lost to the leading Jaguar. In the twilight, Röhrl was going hard into the first chicane when he smacked into the back of Gérard Tremblay's black Debora prototype, which had been obscured from his sight by a slower 911 Carrera. A sharp collision damaged the Turbo's right-front corner and split the oil cooler, spilling lubricant onto the track surface, which caused several other cars to spin. Röhrl only made it as far as the Porsche curves before the oil-starved engine seized, and he parked up on a grass verge.

The Turbo S LM was raced in 1994 by Larbre Compétition, and it finished second overall at Daytona before winning its class in all four BPR Global GT races contested, using a 3.6-litre flat-six based on the newly introduced 993-series motor. The car was also raced occasionally by Obermaier Racing in 1995 before being retired.

PRIVATE ARMY CALL-UP

The reintroduction of a GT category was welcomed enthusiastically by owners of Porsche's off-the-shelf, 911-based racers. Ten made this year's grid, including six of the latest Carrera RSR models, equipped with 964 Turbo-style bodywork, a large fixed rear aerofoil, and the naturally aspirated, 3.8-litre M64/04 engine making about 330bhp. The Category 4 winner was an RSR (above) entered by Jean-Pierre

128 LE MANS 24 HOURS 1990–99

Jarier's Monaco Média International team, and operated by Larbre Compétition. Raced by Porsche's own Jürgen Barth with Dominique Dupuy and Joël Gouhier, it finished two laps behind the Jaguar that was subsequently disqualified.

This reliable Porsche was clearly the fastest of the German-built private entries. It was good enough to lead the division for more than six hours after the retirement of the leading Jaguar, but did not have the pace to resist the other British car on Sunday morning when it recovered after its mid-race delay.

Three laps behind in second place, and making it a 1-2 for Jack Leconte's Larbre team after a similarly sound race, was the RSR driven by the team owner with Jesús Pareja and Pierre de Thoisy (right). The RSRs of other teams – Heico (below), Chicco d'Oro and Konrad Motorsport (bottom left) – filled the next three positions in the class.

Obermaier Racing fielded two GT cars alongside its Group C Porsche. Philippe Olczyk won the one-make Venturi support race on Saturday morning but, in the main event, the engine of his RSR spent much of Sunday on only four cylinders, and it finished many laps down. The team's Carrera 2 Cup version non-started after being crashed in qualifying by Sergio Brambilla.

Two more 3.6-litre Cup variations of the 911 theme, entered by Jean-Paul Libert and Enzo Calderari, were eliminated from the race by accidents.

PEUGEOT CLOSES OUT THE PODIUM 129

LE MANS

BACK IN THE MIDFIELD

Over the winter, Ford in Detroit stopped Yves Courage using the 'Cougar' name, which was trademarked for a Mercury road car. Thus three 'Courage' racecars were entered for the team's attempt once more to beat the Porsche 962s, and to avenge its late-race defeat 12 months previously by a Group C Toyota of the type that, this year, shared the class. It didn't happen.

The local constructor continued to recycle his aluminium honeycomb monocoques to produce three 'C30' racecars, each again fitted with the 3-litre Porsche 935/76 powertrain and with detail suspension and bodywork upgrades.

The team's heroes of 1992, Bob Wollek and Henri Pescarolo, had gone over to the enemy (Joest Porsche), but Derek Bell was recruited instead. He shared one car with Pascal Fabre and Lionel Robert, who qualified it in 11th position, three seconds clear of Pierre Yver in the sister car co-driven by Jean-Louis Ricci and Jean-François Yvon. The team decided to save time in the pits by attempting three racing shifts on each set of tyres.

After four hours, Bell was running seventh, in among the fastest of the Porsches, when he went off at the second Mulsanne chicane on Goodyears nearing the end of their third shift. The Courage had to be towed out of the gravel by a rescue vehicle and, in the process, lost six places, slipping behind the sister car.

A dogged battle was joined, and lasted all night. Both Courages reverted to two shifts per tyre set and were solidly dependable. It was almost 15 hours before these positions were reversed, soon after 11am. Bell/Robert/Fabre (left) finished 10th, their team mates (below) one position and four laps behind after late-race problems with the rear wing mountings.

After a tentative run, the third Courage failed to finish. Soon after midnight, Alessandro Gini suffered a blown tyre on the short straight linking Indianapolis and Arnage, and woke up a couple of thousand mesmerized spectators there (some of them sober) by spinning tail-first into the barrier.

1993

GASPING FOR AIR

Obermaier Racing's Porsche 962C inflicted a notable defeat of the bigger Joest and Kremer teams in this race, but these old warhorses were only competing with each other. This was the first time the former Group C coupés were allowed to race with no limit on fuel usage, and four Porsche privateers optimistically responded by entering a fleet of seven 962Cs. In an effort to compensate for the new air-inlet restrictors, Porsche's motorsport engineers had worked with colleagues at Bosch to tweak the Motronic 1.7 engine control systems, but outputs were reduced to less than 600bhp, rendering the 900kg Porsches uncompetitive.

The fastest were two *langheck* cars from Joest Racing. Manuel Reuter qualified seventh with one of the chassis that had been used by the team when it had last raced here in 1991 and that was again driven by Louis Krages, alongside Frank Jelinski. Krages ('John Winter') all but ran out of fuel on Saturday evening, at the cost of more than a lap, and later another lap was lost to a water leak. However, Reuter and Jelinski, sharing the night driving, had the car solidly inside the top 10, and lost only one position when the alternator threw its belt soon after dawn. Pictured below, the car survived a broken brake caliper at 10am but, 90 minutes later, an engine failure spelled retirement.

Bob Wollek was only eight-tenths slower than Reuter in qualifying with the sister car. This chassis, which had crashed heavily here in 1990 while qualifying for its maiden event, had been repaired for a while but had never actually been raced. Wollek shared it with his fellow race veteran Henri Pescarolo and débutant Ronny Meixner, who had won the GT class at Daytona in January with a 911 Carrera 2, sponsored by the works Cigarette offshore powerboat racing team. An early delay, caused by a faulty clutch, was soon followed by another, the result of a spin by Meixner (above). On Sunday morning, this car also threw its alternator drivebelt, and a brake problem cost more time. It finished a lacklustre ninth. Late that summer, 51-year-old 'Pesca' consoled himself by winning the French helicopter championship.

PEUGEOT CLOSES OUT THE PODIUM 131

LE MANS

132 LE MANS 24 HOURS 1990-99

1993

These setbacks for Joest Racing handed the marque contest between the Porsches to Hans Obermaier's short-tail 962C, managed here by Alain Duclot. This was the first such car to be raced at Le Mans with a carbon-carbon braking system, and its impact on performance could be measured by the fact that amateur Otto Altenbach was less than a second slower than Wollek in qualifying. After an exceptionally trouble-free race, interrupted only by a precautionary disc change at 7:40am, Altenbach finished seventh with Jürgen Oppermann and Loris Kessel, four laps ahead of Wollek's Joest car.

The Kremer brothers fielded three of its K6 racecars, and brought two to the chequer. The non-finisher was the team's fastest qualifier, an aluminium-chassis car in the hands of Almo Coppelli. He was in pit-lane after only one lap of the race with soft brakes, which took four minutes to fix. Co-drivers Steve Fossett and Robin Donovan did well to haul the car back into the top 15 but, at about 8am, Coppelli ran out of fuel. He tried to get back to the pits on the starter motor, but in doing so he drained the battery (top right).

The carbon-hulled K6 that had finished seventh here 12 months before had an eventful week. On Wednesday, Giovanni Lavaggi crashed when leaving the pits on cold tyres, and the car was under repair in the paddock throughout Thursday. Co-driven by Jürgen Lässig and Wayne Taylor, it went well on Saturday but lost 12 minutes to an exhaust system replacement shortly before 2am. Later a flat battery and cracked brake discs caused more delays, and late on Sunday morning Lavaggi found himself on three wheels when the left-rear fell off in the Porsche curves.

Pictured at bottom left, the car finished 12th. Lässig and Lavaggi retreated to the Interserie and the latter went on to win a second title for the team's open-cockpit 'Kremer K7'.

Driving the aluminium Kremer chassis that had finished 11th in 1992, Tomas Saldana was lucky to stay on the road on Thursday evening when a front brake disc shattered while he was charging through the right-hand kink before Indianapolis. In the race, Saldana, François Migault and Andy Evans (pictured in the pits) had a solid night but were hampered by overheating soon after dawn. They spent all of Sunday grimly holding 13th position, nursing a fragile gearbox.

PEUGEOT CLOSES OUT THE PODIUM 133

LE MANS

The ex-Momo/Gebhardt Porsche 962 that had contested the IMSA category here in 1990, but had not been raced since the 1991 Sebring 12 Hours, was entered by its new owner, Guy Chotard. Pictured at left, this car had been deployed at the 1992 Le Mans as a spare chassis by the Alméras brothers, with sponsorship from refrigeration industrialist Jacques Chotard. It was driven at the Test Day by Didier Caradec, Alain Sturm and none other than Jean-Pierre Beltoise, the former Grand Prix winner who had raced Porsche Carrera Cup cars with Caradec in 1991-92. However Beltoise was unwell in race week and stood down for Denis Morin. Beltoise stayed on as the team's adviser and saw the car race impeccably, except for a brief delay soon after dark when its nose section had to be replaced. It was the slowest of the Porsches, but finished 14th.

A CLASS WINNER AGAIN

One more taste of Le Mans, and Gérard Welter was completely hooked again. And this year his Parisian team emerged as a class winner when it won the three-car Category 3 division with an upgraded version of its centre-seat WR-Peugeot spyder (below left).

The new WR, an aluminium honeycomb monocoque, was fitted with a version of Peugeot Sport's blown, 2-litre 405T16 rally-raid engine, making 725bhp at 7000rpm with a single Garrett turbo and Magneti Marelli fuel injection, and driving through a Hewland DGB transmission. The bodywork was a single piece of carbon/Kevlar material and the car weighed just 658kg.

Thus equipped, Patrick Gonin was able to qualify no less than 34 seconds faster than the 1992 'atmo' car. Gonin finished third with his WR in the Peugeot 905 Spyder support race on Saturday morning, and then, with Bernard Santal and Alain Lamouille, raced the top 20 all afternoon, far ahead of the class rivals. But in the twilight the car ran into wheelbearing problems that dropped it way down the field, and two laps behind the Debora.

Dawn had broken before the WR had regained the lead. Despite brake-fade problems, it was extending its advantage when it was delayed again shortly before 10am because the crew had to invest 28 minutes in replacing a driveshaft. At 2:50pm, when the Debora blew its engine, the WR was trailing it by three laps.

1993

TOUCHING DISTANCE...

This year Didier Bonnet built two honeycomb-hulled Coupe Alfa sports-racers and used the first SP93 for another crack at Le Mans, registered as a WSC entry with the series-production 3-litre Alfa Romeo V6. The 230bhp SP93 went almost 20 seconds faster at the Test Day than the hampered SP92 had managed, and finished up 18th among the 31 participants.

Yvan Muller/Georges Tessier/Gérard Tremblay were delayed by a few niggling problems early in the race, and Tremblay spun and damaged the rear wing at nightfall. But then the Debora (right) went really well. A throttle pedal repair cost a couple of positions, just after dawn. Nevertheless, Muller was leading the WM-Peugeot by three laps, and had a class win almost in the bag, when he parked up with a broken engine with only 70 minutes remaining.

Debora went on to win that year's Coupe Alfa.

LAST-PLACED RUNNER-UP

Last place – second in Category 3 – was the prized possession of this Italian Coppa Alfa Romeo sports-racer (below right), in which 'Gigi' Taverna, Fabio Magnani and Roberto Ragazzi were surprised to make it all the way to the finish.

An aluminium monocoque with a carbon/Kevlar body, the Lucchini SP91 was the seventh sports-racing design from Lucchini Corse, an extension of an engineering company founded by Giorgio Lucchini in Porto Mantovano in 1980. Like most of the previous models, it was powered by the 3-litre V6 from the 164 Quadrifoglio road car, putting only 230bhp through a five-speed Hewland transaxle. The car was operated by Taverna and Pino Sanua, whose Technoracing team had run Alba and Olmas Group C2 coupés in the 1980s.

The Lucchini was 15 seconds slower in qualifying than the similarly powered Debora, and years behind the WR-Peugeot. In the race, it never gave its crew a moment's peace. They had to deal with a split water hose, fuel pressure problems, a detached alternator drivebelt, three suspension failures, faulty headlights and other electrical malfunctions. Finally, on Sunday afternoon, a broken fuel pump took 90 minutes to get at and replace.

PEUGEOT CLOSES OUT THE PODIUM

LE MANS

BOILING ON DÉBUT

Hugh Chamberlain's team took on the Porsches and Jaguars in the GT category with a pair of works Lotus Esprit 300 racecars, both of which succumbed to blown head gaskets on their turbo four-cylinder engines.

The Esprit 300 was the latest version of a model that had been in production since 1976, and restyled a decade later by Peter Stevens. First shown as a concept at the 1992 Birmingham show, it was aimed at capitalizing on American racing successes. Lotus Cars had built 'X180R' Esprits for the SCCA World Challenge series of 1990-91, and had won regularly with 'Doc' Bundy, David Murry and others. For 1992-94, the turbocharged cars had been switched to the IMSA Supercar series, and Bundy had dominated the 1992 championship. IMSA had then penalized the Esprit and it became less effective. To promote the brand and particularly a limited-edition Esprit 300 road car, Lotus decided to deploy a revised racing specification in this year's Le Mans.

The Lotus engineering team improved the torsional stiffness of the Series 4 (X180) bodyshell by adding an engine bay cross-brace, a bonded-in roof panel, a modified front crossmember and backbone, and (for racing) a steel rollcage. The additional weight was offset by the extensive use of composite materials. A front airdam with integral brake cooling ducts was added, and a new rear wing. The front and rear track dimensions were increased and the wheel-arches enlarged to fit wider road wheels and bigger brakes, while the suspension systems were fitted with stiffer springs and dampers. The S4's 2174cc, DOHC engine was equipped with bigger inlet valves and a hybrid Garrett T3/T4 turbocharger with an uprated charge-cooler, making 302bhp at 6400rpm in the Esprit 300 road car. A non-catalyst exhaust system, larger fuel-injectors, higher 'boost' and other modifications increased the output to 400bhp at 7000rpm in the racing version, driving through a five-speed Hewland DGZ gearbox.

In view of the imminent demise of the iconic Team Lotus F1 operation, the Le Mans project was timely for Lotus Cars, which had not competed in European sportscar racing with a factory team for 26 years. Chamberlain Engineering won the contract to operate the cars, but the relationship got off to a poor start when Lotus slipped behind schedule, and missed the Test Day in mid-May. In fact, the cars were only finished the day before scrutineering. All manner of teething problems (including detached body panels) surfaced during qualifying, but Chamberlain contrived to get his cars into the race.

Race veteran Yojiro Terada, co-driving Thorkild Thyrring and Peter Hardman, pitted only 15 minutes after the start to adjust the gear linkage and fix loose body panels, at a cost of 20 minutes. More problems with the bodywork followed on both cars, and Richard Piper arrived in pit-lane missing the entire front section of the car he

136 LE MANS 24 HOURS 1990–99

shared with Olindo Iacobelli and Ferdinand de Lesseps (bottom left). Loosened connections also vexed both cars but the big problem was overheating while the cars were at rest and being refuelled.

Terada's car, which had already been damaged when it was cuffed by Eddie Irvine's passing Toyota, ran into the back of Juan Fangio's similar TS010. However, it was the overheating that eventually did for the Esprits. Terada's blew its head gasket at 1:20am and, after surviving the night, Piper's followed suit at 7:15am.

VENTURI ADVENTURERS

The ACO bolstered this field with a seven-car flotilla of new Venturi 'supercars', developed from the manufacturer's one-make racing specification, and mostly driven for adventure by wealthy amateurs. These '500LM' cars had never been raced before and could not match the customer Porsches in Category 4. However five finished, the best-placed (right) in the hands of Riccardo Agusta, Paolo Mondini and Onofrio Russo.

The first Venturi was a concept shown at the 1984 Paris show by engineer Claude Poiraud and stylist Gérard Godfroy. In 1985, businessman Hervé Boulan bought into the venture and formed MVS (Manufacture des Voitures de Sport) to make the cars. The first prototype was produced in the Rondeau factory at Champagné, near Le Mans.

Jean Rondeau had wound up his sportscar racing team at the end of 1983, but was engaging his facilities and staff in engineering consultancy work. After Rondeau's fatal road accident in December 1985, technical director Philippe Beloou and Lucien Rose took on the business as Méca Auto Système. Beloou evolved Poiraud's steel tube/box-section chassis to take a mid-mounted Renault Alpine GTA powertrain, with the turbo V6 'PRV' engine installed longitudinally and the five-speed gearbox aft of the rear axle, and double-wishbone front suspension with a multi-link set-up at the rear. Godfroy's body shape was developed by aerodynamics consultant Robert Choulet in the Eiffel wind tunnel in Paris. MVS went into production in 1987 with

PEUGEOT CLOSES OUT THE PODIUM 137

LE MANS

the GRP-bodied Venturi 200 in its own factory, near Nantes. The very first customer, that May, happened to be Raymond Gouloumes, the president of the ACO, and 50 cars were sold over the next six months.

In 1989, MVS was purchased by Primwest Holdings, a French-controlled offshore investment fund. Boulan was replaced as the CEO by Xavier de la Chapelle, who changed the company's name back to Venturi and commissioned a new factory at Couëron, another Nantes suburb. In 1992, Poiraud fell out with the new management, and left.

That year it was decided to promote the brand through motorsport, and Venturi bought a majority stake in Gérard Larrousse's F1 team. Stéphane Ratel was recruited to set up the Venturi Compétition division and to run 'arrive-and-drive' events, based on 30 race-prepared '400 Trophée' cars, all maintained by the factory. The company sold its 65 percent stake in Larrousse at the end of 1992, but Ratel's Venturi Trophée series continued and became a catalyst for the BPR Global GT championship in 1994.

The one-make racing car was evolved by Méca, working with Synergie in nearby Changé under two more former Rondeau employees, Lucien Monté and Philippe Bône. Much of this specification was to be used for the new 400 GT. The first road car ever offered with carbon-carbon brakes, this 180mph supercar was an evolution of Venturi's previous models, with a 3-litre PRV engine equipped with two Garrett turbochargers by Philippe Missakian's EIA Moteurs company at Nanterre, in suburban Paris, and a Sadev-modified transmission. Ahead of road car production, a carbon/Kevlar bodied '400 GTR' version was built for racing homologation and was used as the base for the 500bhp 500LM, the first Venturi racing car offered for sale to customers.

The first such was 'Rocky' Agusta, a scion of the Italian helicopter and motorcycle dynasty, who was swiftly followed by Alan Lamouille, Eric Graham, Jean-Luc Maury-Laribière's BBA Compétition team, and Thomas Hamelle and Yann Bialgue at Jacadi Racing. Ratel himself and Toison d'Or ('Golden Fleece', a team set up to run a 500LM in this one race) also entered cars.

Jacadi's Venturi was a focus of media attention because it was raced by French TV star Christophe Déchavanne with former Grand Prix hero Jacques Laffite, who was Venturi's fastest man in qualifying. However, this car's engine expired with only four hours remaining. In the dead car park, it joined Ratel's 500LM (above), which had been crashed very heavily by Claude Brana at 1am, but its driver was thankfully uninjured. Marc Duez, afflicted with a left-rear suspension problem on the Toison d'Or entry, sat out most of the final hour before starting its engine to take the chequered flag.

1993

LAST OF THE SPICES

The latest reprieve for Group C hardware enabled Graff Racing's Spice SE89C (below), last raced here in 1991, to contest Le Mans for a fourth and final time. The Chinon-based car was fitted with a 3.3-litre Cosworth DFL prepared by Alan Smith. Its French rookie drivers had a solid weekend until shortly after 6am, when a gearbox problem cost six positions, but it continued to finish 20th.

Hugh Chamberlain also took the opportunity to revive his 1992 FIA Cup-winning SE89C, also for a fourth Le Mans outing. His team operated the ageing, Nicholson DFZ-engined sports-prototype (right) alongside the 'works' Lotus Esprits. Driven this time by Nick Adams/Hervé Regout/Andy Petery, this car was substantially faster than Graff's and was racing well inside the top 20 on Saturday evening, but engine problems intervened. The car survived the night but blue smoke spelled the end soon after dawn.

PEUGEOT CLOSES OUT THE PODIUM   139

LE MANS

A BLAST FROM THE PAST

The exceptional circumstances surrounding this year's entry parameters allowed French entrant Roland Bassaler to resurrect his amazing Group C Sehcar-BMW (above) and run it in Category 2.

First raced here 10 years before as an SHS (née Sauber) C6, this veteran had been purchased by the Laval BMW dealer from Brun Motorsport ahead of Le Mans in 1985, when it had finished fourth in C2. It had undergone many painstaking transformations for the races in 1986-88, but had not finished again. Bassaler had not been able to bring himself to part with it, but had not expected to get the chance to give it another outing here. He hurried to mail his entry form and to get the car prepared by Lucien Monté's Synergie company in Changé, near Le Mans.

The 'atmo' straight-six BMW M88 only made about 450bhp and the aluminium-monocoque C6 was weighty, but it made the cut. It was hampered by overheating and gearbox problems and, during the night, its rear lights failed. But it was still strong at 7am, when it was crashed out of the race by Jean-Louis Capette.

MIG GROUNDED

An example of the first GT car with an advanced composites chassis structure failed to qualify due to engine installation problems.

The MiG M100 (below) started life as a failed 'supercar' project by former racer Fulvio Ballabio. As an extension of his Marine Monte Carlo boat-building business, the Monaco resident had formed Monte Carlo Automobiles in 1985 and had built and raced an F3000 single-seater. Two years later, he engaged former F1 constructor Guglielmo Bellasi to design the MCA road car, which was the first ever to be produced with a carbon composite monocoque and body. An engine contract was secured with Lamborghini, and Ballabio tested the first MCA Centenaire (named to mark the 100th anniversary of the Automobile Club de Monaco) at Imola late in 1989. The project was supported by the Monaco administration, including Prince Rainier, but only five cars were produced in MCA's factory in the Fontvieille harbour area. These included a version with a removable top, called the 'Beau Rivage', which was exhibited at the 1992 Los Angeles Auto Show. By the end of 1992, the project was moribund. Ballabio agreed when another Monaco resident, Georgian businessman Aleksandr Marianashvili, suggested that the cars could be manufactured in Tbilisi under the name MiG, an acronym of Migrelia Georgia (after a region in the west of the country). This Le Mans entry was intended to kickstart the joint venture.

The MiG M100 was the Beau Rivage, now fitted with a coupé body and a rear wing, and prepared for racing in Giampiero 'Peo' Consonni's workshop in Muggiò, near Monza. Equipped with a 5.5-litre Lamborghini V12, it was operated at the Le Mans Test Day in May 1993 by Supercars, an Italian F3 team, under the supervision of Gianfranco Bonomi di Leidi.

Consonni drove the car with Pierre Honegger. Neither was able to lap in less than five minutes and the team went home dispirited. A subsequent test at Monza yielded performance increases but it was decided that the car needed much more power. A deal was done with Carlo Chiti's Motori Moderni company to fit the 3.5-litre replacement for Subaru's F1 engine. Chiti equipped the unraced V12 with two turbochargers and Consonni installed it with a five-speed Porsche gearbox. There was no time for track-testing…

Over two days of qualifying, only Consonni managed to complete a flying lap, and that was more down to luck than judgement. The engine was located on rubber mounts and the flex in the drivetrain was so bad that the drivers never knew which gear they were engaging. Eventually the clutch disintegrated catastrophically.

That November, back with the Lamborghini engine, the car was raced in the Vallelunga 6 Hours, and finished. However, Marianashvili could not raise the finance to produce more cars and, in 1995, leased the rights to Georges Blain of Aixam, the French specialist vehicle maker, which had recently created its Méga brand. Blain commissioned SERA-CD to redesign the car, sourced V12 engines from Mercedes-Benz, and renamed it the Méga Monte Carlo. GT1 and GT2 racing versions were planned, but again the project came to nothing. Almost two decades later, Ballabio would revive the 1993 Le Mans chassis as the Audi-powered 'Montecarlo/BRC GT W12 Monofuel GPL'. The first all-carbon GT car also became the first to be raced with natural gas fuelling its engine.

NO COMEBACK FOR ALLARD

This extraordinary 'batmobile' (above) is the one-off Allard J2X-C, one of the handful of FIA Sportscars – produced by independent constructors – that appeared at the Test Day but did not make the race.

Former Brun Technics engineer Chris Humberstone gained permission to use the name from Alan Allard, the son of Sidney Allard, who had sometimes caused a stir with his eponymous cars at Le Mans in the 1950s. Humberstone gained finance from Costas Los and former Spice Engineering shareholder Jean-Louis Ricci. Ahead of acquiring the remaining assets of Spice at the end of 1991, they recruited Hayden Burvill and Brun aerodynamicist John Iley to complete the design of the high-downforce J2X, using a Cosworth DFR powertrain. The car was built in Basingstoke and shaken down at Pembrey before being taken to the USA at the end of 1992 for tests at Mid-Ohio, Talladega and Road Atlanta, run in conjunction with the Comptech IMSA Lights Spice team. The Allard principals came close to attracting Honda to the project but, when the manufacturer decided to go IndyCar racing, they soon ran out of funds.

Early in 1993, the project was purchased at auction by Robs Lamplough (for 10 percent of its build cost). He entered it for Le Mans and hired veteran Allard engineer Gordon Friend to prepare it in his workshop in Hungerford. There was no time for any shakedown before the Test Day, and the J2X-C showed an inherent unsuitability for high-speed circuits. Friend took off as much downforce as possible, but Lamplough could not exceed 172mph (277kph). There being no time for the required aero redesign, he scratched the entry. The Allard's only race came in July at Laguna Seca, where Lamplough finished ninth. With the demise of the FIA Sportscar concept, the car had no future.

LE MANS

24 HEURES DU MANS
19-20 JUIN 1993

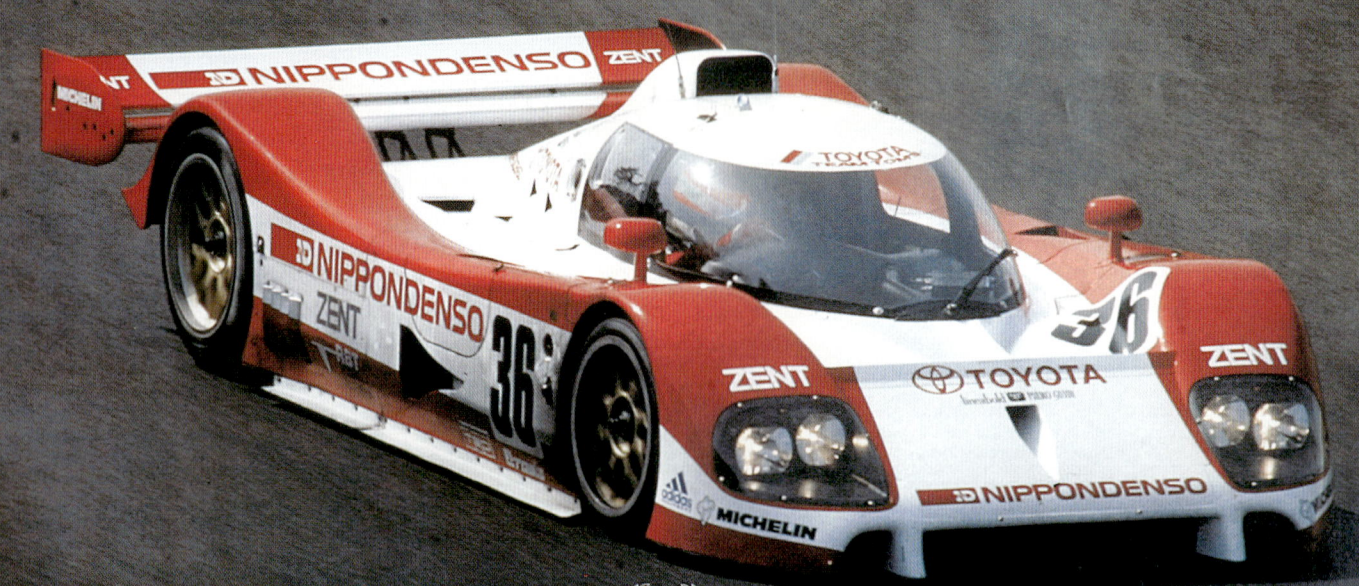

70 ans

3615 ACO
A.S.A. AUTOMOBILE CLUB DE L'OUEST

1993

HOURLY RACE POSITIONS

Start	Time	Car	No	Drivers	1	2	3	4	5	6	7	8	9	10	11	12	13	14	15	16	17	18	19	20	21	22	23	24
1	3:24.94	Peugeot 905 Evo1C	2	Alliot/Baldi/Jabouille	2	1	1	15	14	13	10	9	7	6	5	5	5	4	4	4	4	4	4	4	3	3	3	3
2	3:26.14	Toyota TS010	36	Irvine/Suzuki/Sekiya	1	2	2	4	4	4	4	3	3	3	3	3	3	3	3	3	3	3	3	6	5	5	4
3	3:27.23	Peugeot 905 Evo1C	1	Boutsen/Dalmas/Fabi	3	4	3	2	1	1	1	1	1	1	1	2	2	2	2	1	2	2	2	2	2	2	2	2
4	3:28.21	Toyota TS010	38	Lees/Lammers/Fangio	5	5	4	1	2	2	3	10	10	10	9	10	10	9	6	6	6	6	5	5	4	9	9	8
5	3:31.55	Toyota TS010	37	Acheson/Wallace/Raphanel	4	3	16	24	35	29	24	20	18	17	18	17	16	16	15	DNF								
6	3:32.08	Peugeot 905 Evo1C	3	Brabham/Hélary/Bouchut	6	6	5	3	3	3	2	2	2	2	2	1	1	1	1	2	1	1	1	1	1	1	1	1
7	3:37.63	Porsche 962C	17	Jelinski/Reuter/Krages	7	9	7	8	9	9	8	8	9	9	10	9	9	10	9	8	9	8	9	DNF				
8	3:38.40	Porsche 962C	18	Wollek/Pescarolo/Meixner	9	8	11	10	8	8	9	7	8	7	8	8	6	7	10	9	8	10	10	9	9	8	8	9
9	3:39.37	Porsche 962C	21	Altenbach/Oppermann/Kessel	10	10	8	6	6	7	6	6	7	7	7	7	7	8	8	10	10	9	8	8	7	7	7
10	3:42.22	Toyota 93C-V	22	Ratzenberger/Martini/Nagasaka	8	7	6	5	5	5	5	4	4	4	4	4	4	5	5	5	5	5	6	5	4	4	5	5
11	3:42.59	Courage C30LM	14	Bell/Robert/Fabre	12	12	10	7	13	14	14	14	13	12	12	12	12	12	12	12	12	12	11	10	10	10	10
12	3:44.37	Toyota 93C-V	25	Fouché/Elgh/Andskär	11	11	9	9	7	6	7	5	5	5	6	6	8	6	7	7	7	7	7	7	6	6	6
13	3:45.81	Courage C30LM	13	Yver/Ricci/Yvon	13	13	12	11	11	10	12	11	12	11	11	11	11	11	11	11	11	11	12	11	11	11	11
14	3:47.25	Porsche 962C-K6	15	Coppelli/Donovan/Fossett	31	21	20	16	15	16	16	16	15	15	15	15	15	15	16	15	DNF							
15	3:50.16	Porsche 962C-K6	10	Lässig/Lavaggi/Taylor	14	14	13	12	10	11	11	14	14	14	14	14	14	14	14	14	14	14	14	12	12	12	12
16	3:54.09	Porsche 962C-K6	11	Migault/Evans/Saldana	21	15	14	13	12	13	13	13	13	13	13	13	13	13	13	13	13	13	13	13	13	13	13
17	3:54.97	WR LM92/3	33	Gonin/Santal/Lamouille	18	20	19	17	19	35	36	36	36	34	34	34	33	32	29	29	26	26	29	27	25	27	27	24
18	4:01.08	Spice SE89C	27	Adams/Regout/Petery	23	19	18	20	37	42	43	43	43	39	40	40	40	40	39	DNF								
19	4:01.68	Courage C30LM	12	Yoshikawa/Moran/Gini	17	17	21	19	18	18	18	26	DNF															
20	4:05.45	Porsche 962C	23	Morin/Caradec/Sturm	25	23	22	21	20	19	19	19	19	19	19	18	18	17	17	16	15	15	14	14	14	14
21	4:06.51	Porsche 911 Turbo S LM	46	Stuck/Röhrl/Haywood	15	40	33	26	21	20	DNF																	
22	4:07.88	Jaguar XJ220C	50	Nielsen/Brabham/Coulthard	16	16	15	14	16	15	15	15	16	16	16	24	25	24	22	19	17	17	17	16	15	15	15	DSQ
23	4:09.32	Spice SE89C	24	Bouvet/Balandras/Miot	27	32	38	29	27	25	22	22	20	21	21	20	19	20	26	26	25	25	22	21	21	21	20
24	4:10.50	Jaguar XJ220C	52	Belmondo/Cochran/Fuchs	19	18	17	18	17	17	17	17	18	17	16	17	18	DNF										
25	4:11.71	Jaguar XJ220C	51	Percy/Leslie/Hahne	46	DNF																						
26	4:18.27	Debora SP93	34	Muller/Tremblay/Tessier	28	30	31	37	31	37	34	34	34	32	31	31	31	33	31	28	28	26	24	24	25	DNF
27	4:19.67	Venturi 500LM	71	Laffite/Maisonneuve/Déchavanne	22	37	39	38	33	35	38	38	36	37	37	37	36	33	32	32	31	30	DNF			
28	4:21.77	Venturi 500LM	57	Duez/Bachelart/Verellen	20	22	23	40	39	32	30	29	27	26	26	26	26	24	23	22	24	28	28	28	26	25
29	4:22.96	Porsche 911 Carrera RSR	47	Barth/Gouhier/Dupuy	24	24	24	22	22	21	20	21	20	20	19	20	19	19	18	17	16	16	15	16	16	16	15
30	4:24.54	SHS C6	28	Bassaler/Bourdais/Capette	40	38	40	41	36	39	35	35	35	35	35	34	34	33	34	DNF					
31	4:26.60	Venturi 500LM	70	Witmeur/Neugarten/Tropenat	41	33	29	30	26	26	26	30	29	28	28	27	27	27	28	30	30	30	29	29	28	27
32	4:26.61	Venturi 500LM	55	Russo/Agusta/Mondini	30	31	32	33	33	29	28	30	29	28	29	29	29	30	27	27	27	25	26	25	24	23
33	4:29.74	Porsche 911 Carrera RSR	78	Pareja/Leconte/Thoisy	26	25	25	23	23	23	21	23	22	22	22	22	21	21	19	18	18	18	17	17	17	16
34	4:31.08	Porsche 911 Carrera RSR	77	Haldi/Haberthur/Margueron	29	27	27	25	25	22	23	24	23	23	23	23	22	23	22	21	21	20	20	19	19	19	18
35	4:31.44	Lotus Esprit Sport 300	44	Piper/Iacobelli/Lesseps	33	41	37	36	36	34	32	32	32	32	32	33	35	35	34	DNF					
36	4:32.41	Venturi 500LM	92	Laribière/Krine/Camus	42	39	36	34	34	39	37	40	39	37	37	36	36	36	36	35	32	31	31	32	31	31	29
37	4:33.78	Lucchini SP91	35	Magnani/Taverna/Ragazzi	43	44	45	45	45	42	41	40	42	39	39	39	39	38	36	34	34	33	32	32	32	30
38	4:33.90	Porsche 911 Carrera 2	49	Ilien/Gadal/Robin	37	36	41	39	41	38	33	33	33	33	33	33	32	32	31	30	29	29	28	27	26	29	26
39	4:33.97	Porsche 911 Carrera 2 Cup	76	Calderari/Pagotto/Bryner	32	26	26	27	30	40	DNF														
40	4:34.46	Porsche 911 Carrera RSR	65	Richter/Ebeling/Wlazik	39	28	28	28	24	24	25	25	24	24	24	23	22	23	20	19	20	18	18	18	17
41	4:34.72	Venturi 500LM	56	Los/Badrutt/Brana	47	45	44	43	43	43	40	39	42	DNF												
42	4:35.63	Porsche 911 Carrera RSR	62	Konrad/Harada/Hermann	34	29	30	31	28	27	27	25	25	25	25	24	25	23	22	21	21	21	20	20	20	20	19
43	4:36.42	Porsche 911 Carrera 2 Cup	48	Grohs/Theys/Libert	44	DNF																				
44	4:39.54	Venturi 500LM	91	Roussel/Sezionale/Rohée	35	42	43	44	44	41	42	41	38	38	38	38	37	35	33	33	33	30	30	30	28
45	4:40.08	Lotus Esprit Sport 300	45	Terada/Thyrring/Hardman	45	43	42	42	47	38	37	37	DNF												
46	4:41.77	Porsche 911 Carrera RS	66	Spreng/Angelastri/Müller	36	35	35	32	29	28	29	28	28	27	27	27	28	28	27	24	23	25	23	23	23	21
47	4:42.11	Porsche 911 Carrera RSR	40	Olczyk/Prechtl/Dillmann	38	34	34	35	32	31	31	31	30	29	30	30	29	30	28	25	24	24	23	22	22	22
	4:44.57	Ferrari 348 LM	72	Smith/Sebastiani/Ota	DNS
	4:50.73	Porsche 911 Carrera 2 Cup	41	Grassi/Brambilla/Mastropietro	DNS
DNQ	5:59.15	MiG M100	99	Honegger/Consonni/Renault	DNS

DNF Did not finish **DNQ** Did not qualify **DSQ** Disqualified **FS** Failed scrutineering **NC** Not classified as a finisher **RES** Reserve not required

PEUGEOT CLOSES OUT THE PODIUM 143

LE MANS

RACE RESULTS

Pos	Car	No	Drivers			Laps	Km	Miles	FIA Class	DNF
1	Peugeot 905 Evo1C	3	Geoff Brabham (AUS)	Eric Hélary (F)	Christophe Bouchut (F)	375	5100.00	3168.99	Cat 1	
2	Peugeot 905 Evo1C	1	Thierry Boutsen (B)	Yannick Dalmas (F)	Teo Fabi (I)	374	5086.40	3160.54	Cat 1	
3	Peugeot 905 Evo1C	2	Philippe Alliot (F)	Mauro Baldi (I)	Jean-Pierre Jabouille (F)	367	4991.20	3101.38	Cat 1	
4	Toyota TS010	36	Eddie Irvine (IRL)	Toshio Suzuki (J)	Masanori Sekiya (J)	364	4950.40	3076.03	Cat 1	
5	Toyota 93C-V	22	Roland Ratzenberger (A)	Mauro Martini (I)	Naoki Nagasaka (J)	363	4936.80	3067.58	Cat 2	
6	Toyota 93C-V	25	George Fouché (ZA)	Eje Elgh (S)	Steven Andskär (S)	358	4868.80	3025.33	Cat 2	
7	Porsche 962C	21	Otto Altenbach (D)	Jürgen Oppermann (D)	Loris Kessel (CH)	355	4828.00	2999.97	Cat 2	
8	Toyota TS010	38	Geoff Lees (GB)	Jan Lammers (NL)	Juan Manuel Fangio II (RA)	353	4800.80	2983.07	Cat 1	
9	Porsche 962C	18	Bob Wollek (F)	Henri Pescarolo (F)	Ronny Meixner (USA)	351	4773.60	2966.17	Cat 2	
10	Courage C30LM	14	Derek Bell (GB)	Lionel Robert (F)	Pascal Fabre (F)	347	4719.20	2932.37	Cat 2	
11	Courage C30LM	13	Pierre Yver (F)	Jean-Louis Ricci (F)	Jean-François Yvon (F)	343	4664.80	2898.57	Cat 2	
12	Porsche 962C-K6	10	Jürgen Lässig (D)	Giovanni Lavaggi (I)	Wayne Taylor (ZA)	328	4460.80	2771.81	Cat 2	
13	Porsche 962C-K6	11	François Migault (F)	Andy Evans (USA)	Tomas Saldana (E)	316	4297.60	2670.40	Cat 2	
14	Porsche 962C	23	Denis Morin (F)	Didier Caradec (F)	Alain Sturm (F)	308	4188.80	2602.79	Cat 2	
DSQ	Jaguar XJ220C	50	John Nielsen (DK)	David Brabham (AUS)	David Coulthard (GB)	306	4161.60	2585.89	Cat 4	Exhaust system
15	Porsche 911 Carrera RSR	47	Jürgen Barth (D)	Joël Gouhier (F)	Dominique Dupuy (F)	304	4134.40	2568.99	Cat 4	
16	Porsche 911 Carrera RSR	78	Jesús Pareja (E)	Jack Leconte (F)	Pierre de Thoisy (F)	301	4093.60	2543.64	Cat 4	
17	Porsche 911 Carrera RSR	65	Ulrich Richter (D)	Dirk-Reiner Ebeling (D)	Karl-Heinz Wlazik (D)	299	4066.40	2526.74	Cat 4	
18	Porsche 911 Carrera RSR	77	Claude Haldi (CH)	Olivier Haberthur (CH)	Charles Margueron (CH)	299	4066.40	2526.74	Cat 4	
19	Porsche 911 Carrera RSR	62	Franz Konrad (A)	Jun Harada (J)	Antonio de Azevedo Hermann (BR)	293	3984.80	2476.04	Cat 4	
20	Spice SE88C	24	Jean-Bernard Bouvet (F)	Richard Balandras (F)	Bruno Miot (F)	288	3916.80	2433.78	Cat 2	
DNF	Porsche 962C	17	Frank Jelinski (D)	Manuel Reuter (D)	'John Winter' (Louis Krages) (D)	282			Cat 2	Engine
21	Porsche 911 Carrera RS	66	Gustl Spreng (D)	Sandro Angelastri (CH)	Fritz Müller (D)	276	3753.60	2332.37	Cat 4	
22	Porsche 911 Carrera RSR	40	Philippe Olczyk (B)	Josef Prechtl (D)	Gérard Dillmann (F)	274	3726.40	2315.47	Cat 4	
23	Venturi 500LM	55	Onofrio Russo (I)	Ricardo 'Rocky' Agusta (I)	Paolo Mondini (I)	274	3726.40	2315.47	Cat 4	
24	WR LM92/3	33	Patrick Gonin (F)	Bernard Santal (CH)	Alain Lamouille (F)	268	3644.80	2264.77	Cat 3	
25	Venturi 500LM	57	Marc Duez (B)	Eric Bachelart (B)	Philip Verellen (B)	267	3631.20	2256.32	Cat 4	
26	Porsche 911 Carrera 2	49	Bruno Ilien (F)	Alain Gadal (F)	Bernard Robin (F)	266	3617.60	2247.87	Cat 4	
27	Venturi 500LM	70	Pascal Witmeur (B)	Michel Neugarten (B)	Jacques Tropenat (F)	262	3563.20	2214.07	Cat 4	
DNF	Debora SP93	34	Yvan Muller (F)	Gérard Tremblay (F)	Georges Tessier (F)	259			Cat 3	Engine
28	Venturi 500LM	91	Patrice Roussel (F)	Edouard Sezionale (F)	Hervé Rohée (F)	246	3345.60	2078.86	Cat 4	
29	Venturi 500LM	92	Jean-Luc Maury-Laribière (F)	Michel Krine (F)	Patrick Camus (F)	243	3304.80	2053.50	Cat 4	
30	Lucchini SP91	35	Fabio Magnani (I)	Luigi Taverna (I)	Roberto Ragazzi (I)	221	3005.60	1867.59	Cat 3	
DNF	Toyota TS010	37	Kenneth Acheson (GB)	Andy Wallace (GB)	Pierre-Henri Raphanel (F)	212			Cat 1	Transmission (gearbox)
DNF	Venturi 500LM	71	Jacques Laffite (F)	Michel Maisonneuve (F)	Christophe Déchavanne (F)	210			Cat 4	Engine
DNF	Porsche 962C-K6	15	Almo Coppelli (I)	Robin Donovan (GB)	Steve Fossett (USA)	204			Cat 2	Out of fuel
DNF	Jaguar XJ220C	52	Paul Belmondo (F)	Jay Cochran (USA)	Andreas Fuchs (D)	176			Cat 4	Engine (head gasket)
DNF	SHS C6	28	Roland Bassaler (F)	Patrick Bourdais (F)	Jean-Louis Capette (F)	166			Cat 2	Accident
DNF	Lotus Esprit Sport 300	44	Richard Piper (GB)	Olindo Iacobelli (USA)	Ferdinand de Lesseps (F)	162			Cat 4	Engine (head gasket)
DNF	Spice SE89C	27	Nick Adams (GB)	Hervé Regout (B)	Andy Petery (USA)	137			Cat 2	Engine
DNF	Courage C30LM	12	Tomiko Yoshikawa (J)	Carlos Moran (SAL)	Alessandro Gini (I)	108			Cat 2	Tyre/accident
DNF	Lotus Esprit Sport 300	45	Yojiro Terada (J)	Thorkild Thyrring (DK)	Peter Hardman (GB)	92			Cat 4	Engine (head gasket)
DNF	Venturi 500LM	56	Costas Los (GR)	Johannes Badrutt (USA)	Claude Brana (F)	80			Cat 4	Accident
DNF	Porsche 911 Turbo S LM	46	Hans-Joachim Stuck (D)	Walter Röhrl (D)	Hurley Haywood (USA)	79			Cat 4	Accident damage/engine
DNF	Porsche 911 Carrera 2 Cup	76	Enzo Calderari (CH)	Luigino Pagotto (I)	Lilian Bryner (CH)	64			Cat 4	Accident
DNF	Porsche 911 Carrera 2 Cup	48	Harald Grohs (D)	Didier Theys (B)	Jean-Paul Libert (B)	8			Cat 4	Accident damage/engine
DNF	Jaguar XJ220C	51	Armin Hahne (D)	Win Percy (GB)	David Leslie (GB)	6			Cat 4	Engine (head gasket)
DNS	Porsche 911 Carrera 2 Cup	41	Ruggero Grassi (I)	Sergio Brambilla (I)	Renato Federico Mastropietro (I)				Cat 4	Accident in qualifying
DNS	Ferrari 348 LM	72	Robin Smith (GB)	'Stingbrace' (Stefano Sebastiani) (I)	Tetsuya Ota (J)				Cat 4	Accident in warm-up
DNQ	MiG M100	99	Pierre Honegger (USA)	Giampiero 'Peo' Consonni (I)	Philippe Renault (F)				Cat 4	

DNF Did not finish   **DNS** Did not start   **DSQ** Disqualified   **FS** Failed scrutineering   **RES** Reserve not required   **NC** Not classified as a finisher   **WD** Withdrawn   Drivers in italics did not race the cars specified

CLASS WINNERS

FIA Class	Starters	Finishers	First	No	Drivers	kph	mph	
Category 1	6	5	Peugeot 905 Evo 1C	3	Brabham/Hélary/Boucht	212.50	132.05	Record
Category 2	15	10	Toyota 93C-V	22	Ratzenberger/Martini/Nagasaka	206.88	128.56	Record
Category 3	3	2	WR LM92/3	33	Gonin/Santal/Lamouille	152.23	94.60	
Category 4	23	13	Porsche 911 Carrera RSR	47	Barth/Gouhier/Dupuy	172.46	107.17	Record
Totals	47	30						

TEST DAY – 16 MAY 1993

Pos	Car	Drivers	Time
1	Peugeot 905 Evo1C	Alliot/Baldi	3:29.08
2	Toyota TS010	Lees/Lammers/Fangio II	3:30.86
3	Toyota TS010	Wallace/Acheson/Irvine	3:33.88
4	Peugeot 905 Evo1C	Dalmas/Boutsen	3:34.13
5	Porsche 962C	Wollek/Jelinski/Krages	3:37.14
6	Courage C30LM	Robert/Moran	3:41.49
7	Porsche 962C	Wollek/Pescarolo	3:44.54
8	Porsche 962C	Altenbach/Oppermann	3:47.37
9	Porsche 962C-K6	Saldaña/Donovan/Lavaggi	3:48.78
10	Courage C30LM	Gini/Yvon	3:55.31
&c	32 participants		

LE MANS

1994
PORSCHE PULLS A FAST ONE

LE MANS

RACE INFORMATION

RACE DATE
19-20 June

RACE No
62

CIRCUIT LENGTH
8.451 miles/13.600km

HONORARY STARTER
Charles Pasqua
French Minister of State

MARQUES (ON GRID)

Marque	No
ALD	1
Alpa	1
Alpine	1
Bugatti	1
Chevrolet	1
Courage	3
Dauer-Porsche	2
De Tomaso	1
Debora	1
Dodge	2
Ferrari	4
Harrier	1
Honda	3
Kremer-Porsche	1
Lotus	2
Mazda	1
Nissan	2
Porsche	11
Toyota	2
Venturi	5
WR	2

STARTERS/FINISHERS
48/18

WINNERS

OVERALL
Dauer-Porsche

ENTRY LIST

No	Car	Entrant (nat)	cc	Engine	Tyres	Weight (kg)	Class
1	Toyota 94C-V	Toyota Team SARD (J)	3576tc	R36V V10	Dunlop	967	LM-P1/C90
2	Courage C32LM	Courage Compétition (F)	2994tc	Porsche F6	Michelin	959	LM-P1/C90
3	Courage C32LM	Courage Compétition (F)	2994tc	Porsche F6	Michelin	978	LM-P1/C90
4	Toyota 94C-V	Nisso Trust Racing Team (J)	3576tc	R36V V10	Dunlop	969	LM-P1/C90
5	Kremer K8	Gulf Oil Racing (GB)	2994tc	Porsche F6	Dunlop	947	LM-P1/C90
6	Porsche 962C-GTI	ADA Engineering (GB) Team Nippon (J)	2994tc	F6	Goodyear	961	LM-P1/C90
7	ALD C06	Stealth Engineering/SBF (F)	3453	BMW M88 S6	Goodyear	900	LM-P1/C90
9	Courage C32LM	Courage Compétition (F)	2994tc	Porsche F6	Michelin	973	LM-P1/C90
14	Spice HC94	Brix Racing (USA)	5031	Oldsmobile V8	–	–	IMSA WSC
15	Spice SE90C	Scream Eagles Racing (USA)	3968	Lexus 1UZ-FE V8	–	–	IMSA WSC
20	Debora LM-P294	Didier Bonnet (F)	2959	Alfa Romeo 164QF V6	Pirelli	659	LM-P2
21	WR LM93	Welter Racing (F)	1905tc	Peugeot 405-Raid S4	Michelin	652	LM-P2
22	WR LM94	Welter Racing (F)	1905tc	Peugeot 405-Raid S4	Michelin	652	LM-P2
29	Ferrari F40	Bo Strandell (S) Obermaier Racing (D)	2998tc	F120 V8	Pirelli	1087	LM-GT1
30	Venturi 600LM	BBA Sport et Compétition (F)	2975tc	PRV V6	Dunlop	1135	LM-GT1
31	Venturi 600LM	Agusta Racing Team (I)	2975tc	PRV V6	Dunlop	1100	LM-GT1
33	Porsche 911 Turbo	Konrad Motorsport (D) Patrick Neve Racing (B)	3600tc	F6	Pirelli	1120	LM-GT1
34	Bugatti EB-110S	Michel Hommel (F)	3499tc	V12	Michelin	1370	LM-GT1
35	Dauer 962LM	Le Mans Porsche Team (D)	2994tc	Porsche F6	Goodyear	1025	LM-GT1
35R	Dauer 962LM	Le Mans Porsche Team (D)	2994tc	Porsche F6	Goodyear	N/A	LM-GT1
36	Dauer 962LM	Le Mans Porsche Team (D)	2994tc	Porsche F6	Goodyear	1016	LM-GT1
37	De Tomaso Pantera	ADA Engineering (GB)	4952	Ford 302 V8	Goodyear	1131	LM-GT1
38	Venturi 600LM	Jacadi Racing (F)	2975tc	PRV V6	Michelin	1122	LM-GT1
39	Venturi 600LM	Jacadi Racing (F)	2975tc	PRV V6	Michelin	1114	LM-GT1
40	Dodge Viper R/T10	Rent-a-Car Racing (F) Luigi Racing (B)	7997	SRT/10 V10	Michelin	1340	LM-GT1
41	Dodge Viper R/T10	Rent-a-Car Racing (F) Luigi Racing (B)	7997	SRT/10 V10	Michelin	1345	LM-GT1
45	Porsche 911 Carrera RSR	Heico Service (D)	3756	F6	Pirelli	1132	LM-GT2
46	Honda NSX	Kremer Honda Racing (D)	2977	V6	Dunlop	1043	LM-GT2
47	Honda NSX	Kremer Honda Racing (D)	2977	V6	Yokohama	1061	LM-GT2
48	Honda NSX	Kremer Honda Racing (D)	2977	V6	Dunlop	1126	LM-GT2
48T	Honda NSX	Kremer Honda Racing (D)	2977	V6	Dunlop	N?A	LM-GT2
49	Porsche 911 Carrera RSR	Larbre Compétition/Porsche Alméras (F)	3756	F6	Pirelli	1063	LM-GT2
50	Porsche 911 Carrera RSR	Larbre Compétition (F)	3756	F6	Michelin	1090	LM-GT2
51	Callaway Corvette SuperNatural	Callaway Competition (D/USA)	6243	Chevrolet LT1 V8	Yokohama	1169	LM-GT2
52	Porsche 911 Carrera RSR	Larbre Compétition (F)	3756	F6	Michelin	1075	LM-GT2
53	Lotus Esprit S300	Scuderia Fabio Magnani (I)	2174tc	907 S4	Pirelli	1109	LM-GT2
54	Porsche 911 Carrera Cup	Ecurie Biennoise (CH)	3756	F6	Pirelli	1096	LM-GT2
55	Ferrari 348 LM	Simpson Engineering (GB)	3446	F119 V8	Yokohama	1129	LM-GT2
56	Porsche 911 Turbo	Scuderia Chicco d'Oro (CH)	3600tc	F6	Goodyear	1130	LM-GT2
57	Ferrari 348 GT Competizione	Repsol Ferrari España (E)	3405	F119 V8	Pirelli	1187	LM-GT2
58	Porsche 968 RS Turbo	Seikel Motorsport (D)	2990tc	S4	Yokohama	1212	LM-GT2
59	Porsche 911 Carrera RSR	Konrad Motorsport (D)	3756	F6	Pirelli	1102	LM-GT2
60	Alpine A610	Legeay Sports Mécanique (F)	2975tc	Renault PRV V6	Michelin	1181	LM-GT2
61	Lotus Esprit S300	Lotus Sport/Chamberlain Engineering (GB)	2174tc	907 S4	Michelin	1130	LM-GT2
62	Lotus Esprit S300	Lotus Sport/Chamberlain Engineering (GB)	2174tc	907 S4	Michelin	1120	LM-GT2
63	Harrier LR9 Spyder	Chamberlain Engineering (GB)	1996tc	Cosworth BDG S4	Dunlop	833	LM-P2
64	Ferrari 348 GT Competizione	Repsol Ferrari Club Italia (I)	3405	F119 V8	Pirelli	1152	LM-GT2
65	Venturi 400GTR	Agusta Racing Team (I)	2975tc	PRV V6	Michelin	1151	LM-GT2
66	Porsche 911 Carrera RSR	Erik Henriksen (N) Bristow Racing (GB)	3756	F6	Goodyear	1058	LM-GT2
74	Mazda RX-7	Team Art Nature (J)	2616r	13J 4R	Dunlop	1079	IMSA GTS
75	Nissan 300ZX	Clayton Cunningham Racing (USA)	2960tc	VG30S V6	Yokohama	1206	IMSA GTS
76	Nissan 300ZX	Clayton Cunningham Racing (USA)	2960tc	VG30S V6	Yokohama	1181	IMSA GTS
Reserves							
8	Alpa LM	Roland Bassaler (F)	3494	Cosworth DFZ V8	Goodyear	945	LM-P1/C90
13	Courage C41	Courage Compétition (F)	4500	Chevrolet V8	–	–	IMSA WSC
16	Argo JM19C	Pegasus Racing (USA)	3453	BMW M88 S6	–	–	IMSA WSC
42	Porsche 911 Carrera RSR	Gustl Spreng Racing (D)	3756	F6	–	–	LM-GT2
43	Venturi 600LM	JCB Racing (F)	2975tc	PRV V6	–	–	LM-GT1 *
44	Venturi 600LM	BBA Sport et Compétition (F)	2975tc	PRV V6	–	–	LM-GT1 *
67	Porsche 911 Carrera 2	Patrick Boirdon (F)	3756	F6	–	–	LM-GT2
68	Venturi 400GTR	Agusta Racing Team (I)	2975tc	PRV V6	Dunlop	1074	LM-GT2
69	Porsche 911 Carrera RSR	Guy Chotard (F)	3756	F6	–	–	LM-GT2 *
70	Porsche 911 Carrera RSR	Mühlbauer Motorsport (D)	3756	F6	–	–	LM-GT2
71	Porsche 911 Carrera RSR	Konrad Motorsport (D)	3756	F6	–	–	LM-GT2

* Car Nos 43, 44 and 69 were refused scrutineering because the ACO lacked pit-garage space to accommodate them

1994

ENTRY

The new GT initiatives yielded for the ACO a bumper post-bag containing 83 applications. A selection committee happily reconvened and invited 50 cars to qualify for 48 starting places, also nominating a number of reserves. Only a third were purpose-designed for racing: nine former Group C cars, four LM-P2s, two IMSA WSC cars (which were soon withdrawn) and three IMSA 'silhouettes'. In contrast, there were 15 GT1 cars, and 25 GT2s. The Test Day in early May was attended by 36 cars.

This entry was big and varied, but there were only two overt factory projects: by Honda and Lotus in GT2 partnerships with the Kremer and Chamberlain teams respectively. However, Porsche's competition department was here in force with outrageous so-called GT cars based on the 962C, which were nominally entered by Jochen Dauer, and operated by Joest Racing. Toyota assisted the SARD and Trust teams with their Group C hardware.

QUALIFYING

With about 50 percent less downforce than before, and extra weight, the former Group C cars were twitchy in the turns and their lap times rose by at least 10 seconds. In the opening session on Wednesday, Patrick Gonin took advantage with his nimble WR-Peugeot single-seater and, in trying to oust him from the top spot, Lionel Robert crashed his Courage in the Porsche curves. In the second session, however, Alain Ferté secured a first Le Mans pole position for the local team and, the next evening, Derek Bell went second fastest with the Kremers' K8 spyder, consigning the WR to the second row. Mauro Martini wrestled SARD's Toyota into fourth place ahead of Hans-Joachim Stuck, whose best lap with Porsche's heavy, narrow-tyred Dauer LM was fully 20 seconds outside Oscar Larrauri's 1990 qualifying record for a 962C.

PORSCHE PULLS A FAST ONE 149

LE MANS

ORGANISATION

FISA had made it clear that it now regarded GT racing as the future. The potential was recognized by Jürgen Barth, who had been running a one-make series in Germany for Porsche, and by Patrick Peter and Stéphane Ratel, who had been promoting a similar series in France for the owners of Venturi 'supercars'. They joined forces for 1994 to create the 'BPR' organization and developed their respective championships into an international series, open to all makes. BPR promoted eight events, six in Europe and two in Asia, further stimulating activity in the GT racing sector.

Meanwhile, steps towards reviving the concept of the purpose-designed sports-racing car were also taken this year on both sides of the Atlantic, led by the ACO in Europe, and by IMSA in the USA as it adopted its new 'World Sports Car' category. The ACO understood that teams would always want to race prototypes at Le Mans, but resolved to give GT-type racecars an equal chance of winning. Extending Barth's ideas for the new BPR series, the ACO's technical committee under Alain Bertaut began to evolve a concoction of parameters applying to all cars, initially involving maximum fuel cell volumes, engine air-inlet restrictors of various diameters, minimum weights, and maximum dimensions for the wheel/tyre assemblies. This system would prove to be very workable. It would be crucial to the outcomes of Le Mans this year and in the future.

FISA began to implement a common rules structure for GT cars that had been agreed in principle with the ACO, IMSA and JAF (the Japanese body) at Daytona in January 1993. These rules also specified vehicle weights, fuel tankage and air-inlet restrictors to create a handicap system. FISA's new regulations defined a GT racecar as: "A Grand Touring car recognized by FISA as a *bona fide* road car on sale to the general public and registered for road use in at least two of the following countries: Britain, France, Germany, Japan and the United States." There were 12-month production requirements of 25 cars in GT1, and 200 in GT2. Crucially, even though the whole idea was to make the racing more affordable, the rules allowed a manufacturer to apply for provisional GT1 homologation even at the planning stage.

Effectively, therefore, type approval for a single car was sufficient to race it.

FISA's GT regulations were long in gestation, and the ACO could not wait for them to be finalized because its 1994 competitors needed sufficient notice. The ACO, which had commenced litigation against the FIA for breaching its contract to supply sufficient cars in 1992-93, went ahead and published its own LM-GT1 and LM-GT2 regulations in September. When FISA's regulations were finally approved by the World Motor Sport Council the following month, they were different from the ACO's in many detail areas.

The inherent performance advantages of the purpose-made LMP cars – such as chassis stiffness, aerodynamic proficiency, and suspension and braking capability – were taken into account in defining the ACO rules. The 1000kg GT1 and 1050kg GT2 cars were allowed 50 percent bigger (120-litre) fuel cells. The tyre widths were limited to 14 inches in GT1, and 12 inches in GT2.

Meanwhile the ACO's Le Mans Prototype class was altered to cater for 1990-specification Group C hardware, but such cars had to be converted to open-cockpit spyders with unsculpted underfloors. Turbocharged LM-P1 cars had to weigh at least 950kg, and 'atmos' 900kg. The 620kg LM-P2 class was reserved for the former LMP cars with central seats and production-based engines. Both LMP classes were permitted fuel tankage of 80 litres. Tyre widths were limited to 16 inches in P1, and 12 inches in P2.

No IMSA WSC sports-racers were entered this year, but the ACO offered places to US-based cars complying with IMSA's newly formulated GT Supreme regulations (formerly GTO). In France, the minimum weight in GTS was 1000kg, racing with 100-litre fuel cells on 16-inch wide tyres.

Horsepower in all five classes was controlled by means of air-inlet restrictors, defined according to swept volumes, induction systems and the number of valves per cylinder. The target outputs were 550bhp in P1 (a reduction of at least 150bhp), 400bhp in P2, 650bhp in GT1, 450bhp in GT2, and 650bhp in GTS.

These intriguing new Le Mans regulations caused considerable head-scratching among entrants. For example, the wear rates of the tyres allocated to their cars also became critical – especially in view of the ban on changing tyres during the refuelling process, which meant that every new set of wheels cost extra time.

However, the rule that would lead to lasting controversy was FISA's ill-conceived concession in allowing race-prepared examples of one-off GT road cars. And it started straight away. Porsche studied the rules, built and successfully registered a roadgoing 962C, declared it a GT car, and readied racing versions for the month of June.

The October 1993 meeting of the WMSC also approved Max Mosley's defeat of Jean-Marie Balestre in the FIA presidential election. Mosley's first act was to disband FISA as a separate entity, putting world motorsport under direct FIA management.

The ACO's lawsuit against the FIA was heard by the Tribunal de Grande Instance in Paris. The TGI found for the ACO and awarded damages of FF800,000 (about £95,000). This litigation cleared the air for greatly extended collaboration between the ACO and the governing body in the future.

RACE

Bell's Kremer led at first, but Ferté's Courage and the Dauer LM of Mauro Baldi soon overtook. The biggest advantage of the GT1 cars over the prototypes – their 50 percent bigger fuel tankage – came into play almost immediately. Before the end of the opening hour. Stuck (charging after a first-lap spin) and Baldi were running 1-2 for Porsche. The WR-Peugeots were in pit-lane and the Kremer and the Courages were fading, the latter struggling for grip on hard tyres. Instead, the closest pursuit came from the two Group C Toyotas.

At the end of his opening shift with Baldi's Dauer LM, Yannick Dalmas failed to deploy his reserve fuel tank, and the engine died in the pit entrance road. Willing marshals pushed him to his crew at the bottom of pit-lane. The sister car was more seriously delayed when its left-rear tyre blew as Danny Sullivan was in the Virage Ford, and he had to drive a complete lap for a replacement, at the cost of 11 minutes. These incidents and a strong double-shift by Eddie Irvine put the SARD Toyota into the lead, and the similar Trust Toyota onto the tail of the second-placed Dauer LM.

As dusk approached, the SARD Toyota fell back with the first of three stops for replacement brake discs and pads, but the Trust entry had overhauled the Dauer LM and Bob Wollek now led the race. SARD's delay resulted in a second Toyota-Porsche duel as Stuck's car retrieved fourth position, but it was becoming clear that the Japanese cars held the upper hand. Meanwhile the Courage drivers could fit softer tyres in the cooler evening and were coming back into contention.

The Toyotas went 1-2 as darkness fell, and Hurley Haywood had to limp to pit-lane with a driveshaft problem, losing 12 minutes. This briefly promoted Ferté to third place, but the Courage comeback was short-lived. The sister car soon broke its engine, and a similar failure accounted for Ferté's car before half-time.

Just before 5am, Stefan Andskär pitted the leading Toyota with a severe rear-end vibration. The Trust crew traced the problem to the differential, and had to invest almost an hour in replacing it. Now the SARD Toyota was again the race leader, with the two Dauer LMs in apparently vain pursuit.

Stuck's car suffered another delay just before dawn after the headlights failed when Thierry Boutsen was moving at more than 160mph (260kph). A stop for a new nose section sent it down to third place behind the recovering sister car. Then a front-wheel problem left Boutsen three laps down on the leaders.

The SARD Toyota was clearly faster than the Dauer LMs, and seemed to be home-free. Krosnoff was almost cruising when, only 90 minutes from the finish, a weld suddenly broke in his gear linkage. The 94C-V rolled to a stop just before the pits and the driver emerged, jammed the gearbox into third gear, got back in and restarted. Back in pit-lane, another 13 minutes was lost fixing the linkage.

The Baldi/Dalmas/Haywood Dauer LM was long gone when Irvine took over the Toyota and set about chasing down Boutsen for second place. He finally made it through at the end of the penultimate lap. Boutsen scattered flag-waving marshals as he twice attempted to repass, but he was held at bay all the way to the flag. The ACO's manipulation of the technical regulations had made this a fascinating race from start to finish.

PORSCHE PULLS A FAST ONE | 151

LE MANS

PORSCHE'S LUCKY 13

The production of a single road car with type approval was all Porsche needed to make two Le Mans racers that amounted to Group C 962Cs on narrow tyres. As it happened, this exploitation of the rulebook produced a race that riveted onlookers for 24 hours. It delivered Porsche's 13th victory here, Hurley Haywood's third, Yannick Dalmas's second, and Mauro Baldi's first. The two Dauer LM-GTs are pictured in pit-lane before the race, with the team and the road car.

During 1993, Porsche Motorsport became convinced that McLaren would come racing the following season with its mid-engined 'F1' supercar. The engineers in Weissach had a close look at a McLaren F1 after inviting Thomas Bscher to make a social visit with his road car, and realized that a racing version would beat any rear-engined Porsche. There was no time to create a mid-engined evolution of the 911 for 1994. But a thought occurred to chief engineer Norbert Singer…

Singer's help in producing a roadgoing version of the 962 had recently been sought by Jochen Dauer. The former Porsche 935 racer had turned team owner in 1987 after purchasing Porsche 962s from John Fitzpatrick Racing and with these he had won the 1988 Interserie title. Now he wanted to build road-legal versions. Porsche's director of R&D, Horst Marchart, had disapproved of Dauer's plans, and had discouraged the race team from any involvement. But what if Dauer's project could be used to defeat McLaren at Le Mans?

When Singer and competitions director Max Welti made the suggestion to Marchart, they expected to be shouted at. Instead, Marchart left the meeting and gained board approval.

Dauer had engaged Dutch engineer Wuit Huidekoper for the road car conversion, and had shown a prototype 'Dauer 962' at the Frankfurt show. The aluminium chassis was fitted with carbon/Kevlar bodywork reshaped by Achim Storz to widen the cabin, and made by CTS Composites. A small front compartment accommodated 'luggage'. It retained the racecar's double wishbone suspensions, its ride height being raised by hydraulic units (easily removed for racing). It was equipped with catalytic converters and ABS brakes, as well as cabin trim, sound-proofing, air-conditioning and road-legal lights and mirrors.

Huidekoper and Singer collaborated on the Le Mans project. The 'Dauer LM-GT' had to have a flat bottom, so they reworked the front shape to restore some downforce, and perfected long-tail bodywork in the Weissach wind tunnel. Minimum weight had to be 1000kg, or 100kg more than the original 962C racecar (and 50kg more than that year's P1/C90 prototypes). The interior was stripped but the ducting for the air-conditioning was repositioned to cool the brakes. The car was restricted to 12.5-inch wide rear tyres (instead of 14.5 in P1/C90) but could have a 120-litre fuel cell, against 80. This was a double-edged sword: with full fuel loads, the weight differential would be even greater. With the GT1 air-inlet and 'boost' restrictions, the 3-litre, twin-turbo 962C engine sent 620bhp at 8000rpm through Porsche's all-synchro, five-speed gearbox.

Three 'Dauers' were built in Weissach and the model was

homologated by the German highway authorities in March 1994 – with a long-tail body. In April, Singer showed one to the ACO's chief steward, Alain Bertaut. Again Singer expected to be shouted at, and this time he was right. Bertaut had never seen a project so far outside 'the spirit of the regulations'.

Singer challenged Bertaut to show him the rule that banned the new car. He could not. But he did say that the car needed bumpers. When Singer said he regarded the rear wing as the bumper, Bertaut missed the joke. It took a letter from the national transport ministry to convince him that German road cars did not need bumpers. Finally he agreed to admit the Dauer LM-GT to the 1994 Le Mans – but never again. Ahead of the Test Day, Porsche undertook a 30-hour test at Magny-Cours, and more testing on Goodyear's circuit at Miréval.

As it transpired, Porsche had been wrong about McLaren: no F1 was entered this year. The GT opposition would be easily dominated.

Porsche recruited a team to operate the cars at Le Mans, where the test hack was used as a spare for two new chassis. Singer calculated that they should need 24 pitstops to complete the race, against 30 by the P1/C90 prototypes. Even so, they had no real expectation that they could win outright – not even when Hans-Joachim Stuck went through the speed trap at 204mph (328kph), the fastest of all. Stuck did not match a startling lap time at the Test Day, but qualified fifth. Baldi was seventh in the sister car, and they were more than 12 seconds faster round the lap than the best Ferrari and Venturi sharing the LM-GT1 class.

From the start of the race, the variations in fuel capacity came into sharp focus: the Dauers could cover 13 or even 15 laps between stops, the P1/C90 cars only 11 or 12. When the prototypes went for fuel, Stuck led the race from Baldi until they were relieved by Danny Sullivan and Dalmas.

Dalmas finished his shift too close on the fuel, and only just made it to the pit with the help of marshals. Then Sullivan lost his left-rear tyre exiting the first part of the Virage Ford, spun onto the verge there, and had to creep an entire lap back to pit-lane, at the cost of 11 minutes.

Dalmas retained second place (behind the SARD Toyota) but, at dusk, the last of the grease in the car's left-side driveshaft gaiter came out, and Haywood had to pit for the shaft to be replaced. The penalty was almost 12 minutes.

The Dauers were now racing fourth and sixth but their recoveries were under way, despite a wild trip by Stuck over the gravel at the second Mulsanne chicane, leading to a stop for a new nose section. At half-time, they were third and fourth. That was when the lights went out on Thierry Boutsen. Speeding at more than 160mph (260kph) between the Esses and Tertre Rouge, he had the presence of mind to toggle the headlights switch off and on – and they lit up again just before he arrived at the corner. Nevertheless, he made an immediate stop for another fresh nose section.

Later Boutsen hooked a kerb in the second chicane and broke a front wheel toe-link, causing another delay in the pits. Boutsen trashed a set

PORSCHE PULLS A FAST ONE   153

of tyres in trying to make up the time and pitted ahead of schedule – at the same moment as the other car was making a routine stop. The Dauers were now second and third but, in the confusion, the Toyota extended its lead. And Singer was increasingly concerned about the driveshaft lubrication.

The greasing problem, which was now affecting both cars, had not surfaced in testing, but was put down to the close proximity of the exhaust pipes. While the cars were in the pits for service, Singer could smell the overheated driveshafts. But he was also beginning to smell an outright victory. He made the instinctive decision not to make precautionary driveshaft replacements.

It turned out well: it was the Toyota that was delayed by a mechanical problem. With only 90 minutes remaining, Baldi/Dalmas/Haywood hit the front, and stayed there. And it could so easily have been a Dauer-Porsche 1-2. Only one lap remained when Boutsen, on worn tyres, was overhauled by the recovering Toyota. Try as he might, he could not repass.

After the race, Jochen Dauer triumphantly produced 'Dauer Porsche Wins Le Mans' T-shirts, and handed them to Singer, Marchart and Porsche's CEO, Wendelin Wiedeking, who had flown into Le Mans at lunchtime after hearing that the cars were doing so well. Dauer Sportwagen in Nuremberg capitalized on the success by selling a dozen 962 road cars.

1994

ANGUISH FOR TOYOTA

A long-hoped Le Mans victory was cruelly snatched from Toyota only 90 minutes from the finish by a broken gear linkage on the SARD team's quasi-works Group C coupé (below). It continued to finish second thanks to Eddie Irvine's raw aggression, which prevented a Dauer-Porsche 1-2. His co-drivers were Jeff Krosnoff and Mauro Martini, but the bodywork bore a fourth name – that of Roland Ratzenberger, who had been due to drive this car but was killed in qualifying for the San Marino Grand Prix in May, the day before Ayrton Senna also lost his life.

These very Toyotas had soundly beaten 11 Porsche-powered prototypes to the category win in 1993, so there was every reason to hope for the outright victory this year, when turbo Group C cars were the front-runners once more. The All-Japan championship had gone the same way as the SWC at the end of 1992, so winning Le Mans was the sole objective when both the Toyotas (two-year-old cars, and evolutions of a six-year-old design) were again upgraded by Toyota Racing Developments.

Tsutomu Tomita's powertrain department produced stronger components for the gearboxes and the 3.6-litre twin-turbo engines, which had to be fitted this year with smaller air restrictors. However, the main focus was on the aero in TRD's wind tunnel in Yokohama, both to comply with the latest regulations and to claw back some of the downforce that was lost because of them. The former involved extending the flat bottom to the rear axle line and bringing the trailing edge of the low-mounted rear wing into line with the back of the engine cover. The SARD car, which benefited from the fullest factory support, also had reshaped bodywork, with the tail stepped down aft of the wheel-arches, reprofiled sidepods and a lowered nose section.

The Le Mans Test Day was missed, but both these '94C-V' cars were tested at Fuji (with its super-long straight) before being air-freighted to France. Top speed was about 8mph slower than that of the Porsches and Courages, the engines of which had larger air restrictors, but the Japanese cars compensated with better acceleration through superior torque. There was nothing to choose between the lap times. Martini qualified SARD's car fourth, ahead of both Dauers. The Trust team lost much of Wednesday to electronic engine management issues but the next day George Fouché qualified eighth.

Come the race, however, and it soon emerged that the Dauers could go much further between fuel stops. The Toyota drivers had to race their rugged cars very hard – yet it was the Dauers that faltered in the early stages.

A combative double-shift by Irvine kept the SARD Toyota in

PORSCHE PULLS A FAST ONE 155

LE MANS

contention and, despite a big spin by Martini in the Dunlop chicane, it led the race for more than two hours on Saturday evening, until the Trust car took over while it underwent an unscheduled brake pad change. Co-driven as usual by Steven Andskär and Bob Wollek (out for revenge after being overlooked by Porsche), Fouché went a whole lap ahead when Krosnoff soon had to stop again for new brake discs. But the Toyotas went into the night running 1-2.

They contested the lead with each other and one of the recovering Dauers, until the Trust entry lost the best part of an hour soon after dawn. Andskär pitted from the lead with a rear-end vibration. Two more stops were needed before the crew realized that it was not caused by a loose oil catch-tank, nor the rear wing. Eventually it was wheeled into its garage for a fresh gearbox and differential.

The SARD car took over, and it led the next nine hours. With two hours remaining, it was leading by 42 seconds. Surely, this time, Toyota would win the race…

Not so. Half an hour later, Krosnoff stopped next to the pit entrance lane with no drive: a weld in the gear linkage had broken. He got out and managed to engage third gear on the gearbox, and went to the pits for a repair that took 13 minutes.

Irvine's reduced target on rejoining was Thierry Boutsen's second-placed Dauer, which was only 15 seconds up the road, and on worn tyres. Irvine caught up with two laps remaining, forcing his way past when Boutsen was baulked by backmarkers. Boutsen tried hard to get back, but Irvine was having none of it.

Afterwards, of course, Toyota was the party most aggrieved by Porsche's cynical interpretation of the GT1 rules.

FRONT-ENGINED CONTENDER

This purposeful, US-developed Nissan 300ZX 'silhouette' racer (right) disappointed a team with ambitions to win overall, but won the GTS category by a huge margin in finishing fifth.

The Z31-specification 300ZX, which had been raced successfully in America since 1984, had been replaced by the Z32 in 1989, when Nissan tasked Electramotive, its IMSA GTP team, to develop a Z32-shaped GTO racecar. Trevor Harris based it on a chrome-molybdenum steel tube frame, and it was equipped by John Caldwell with a twin-turbo version of a new DOHC V6, driving through a Hewland VGC transmission. Racing suspension and braking systems completed the mechanical package, which was fitted with a five-piece carbon/Kevlar body set.

Operated for Nissan by Cunningham Racing, the 300ZX turbo project became increasingly competitive against works-backed GTO cars from Audi, Ford, Toyota and Mazda until, in 1992, Nissan won the first

GTS 'silhouette' title, with Steve Millen. Come 1993, and the 300ZX represented Nissan's premier American racing programme, but it was narrowly beaten to the championship by the Ford Mustang. This year, with the V6 now approaching 700bhp at 7500rpm on its Garrett turbochargers, it gained its revenge.

In fact, Clayton Cunningham's team came to France hopeful of a hat-trick in the world's most famous endurance races, its classy 300ZX turbo having outlasted faster prototypes to win both the Daytona 24 Hours and the Sebring 12 Hours. This opened up an intriguing possibility: the first Le Mans victory by a front-engined car since the Ferrari 330LM in 1962. Among the drivers here were Millen, who had raced the winning Nissan in both the Floridian classics after recovering from a big crash at Watkins Glen the previous June, and Paul Gentilozzi, who had won at Daytona.

As it turned out, the Nissan heavyweights could not begin to live with the prototypes on the big straights here. The team had overestimated the downforce needed for this race, and could not dial out crippling drag. The top speed was an inadequate 184mph (296kph) and Millen did well to qualify the Sebring-winning car in the top 10.

Another problem was that the V6 showed a tendency to throw drive belts, which happened both during the week and at the weekend. Gentilozzi, Eric van der Poele and Shunji Kasuya were lucky even to start the Daytona-winning car (right) after it abruptly caught fire on the run to Indianapolis during the race morning warm-up. Their crew performed miracles to get the car ready to race, but they retired during the fourth hour with a disabled ignition system.

Driving the seventh chassis built, Millen/Johnny O'Connell/John Morton also lost an engine belt, which caused a delay while a camshaft was replaced, but were headed for fourth place when they dropped a position at Sunday lunchtime with a gearbox problem. Fifth overall and the category win represented a great result.

Back home, the team completed the GTS season with a 1-2 in the championship with Millen and O'Connell, leading IMSA to declare Nissan's powerful twin-turbo V6 ineligible in 1995. Instead, the 300ZX was equipped with a V8 with which it won its class for the third time at Sebring.

PORSCHE PULLS A FAST ONE | 157

LE MANS

THE SPYDER STRATAGEM

Köln Porsche dealers Erwin and Manfred Kremer had chosen not to build an FIA Sportscar when the rules changed in 1992. Instead, the brothers had switched their modified Porsche 962C-K6 cars to the Interserie championship, with annual diversions to Le Mans. They had also produced single-seat 'K7' spyder versions of the 962, for which Achim Stroth's engineers in Köln replaced the chassis torsional stiffness that disappeared with the roof with a sturdier rollover bar, a steel crossbar at the front and two longitudinal bars, and formed a small cockpit opening of a strong carbonfibre structure. K7 spyders had won the Interserie in 1992 with Manuel Reuter, and again in 1993 with Giovanni Lavaggi. For this season, they decided to produce a similar car complying with the ACO's LM-P1 regulations. Kremer had run a pair of K7s at Le Mans at the 1993 Test Day but the ACO had declared them ineligible.

Stroth and his engineers in Köln created the first K8 by converting an aluminium-hulled K7, undergoing the complex task of changing it into a flat-bottom car. In addition, the tail had to be lengthened with the wing above the bodywork, a two-seat configuration restored, and a small windshield added. The bodywork was made in Nuremberg by Sepp and Roy Korytko in Kevlar-reinforced carbonfibre after tests in Ford Deutschland's wind tunnel.

Just as the first K8 was nearing completion, Kremer Racing secured the deal to operate the factory GT2 Hondas. This threw the future of the K8 into doubt but then the Kremers took a call from Stuart Radnofsky of the Project 100 sports marketing agency. He was seeking a P1 car for a 'Return of a Legend' promotion at Le Mans with Gulf Oil UK, based around five-times race winner Derek Bell. The Kremers readily agreed to supply their unraced K8, and Stroth commissioned UK-based Kiwi Graham Lorimer to operate it. Lorimer had been running an F3000 team out of premises in High Wycombe, where the K8 underwent final race preparation and acquired its Gulf livery.

A setback at the Test Day: Bell could do no better than 14th, the K8 producing far too much downforce, tending to detach its floor, and fracturing the turbo mounts on the engine. It was sent back to SRK in Nuremberg for a new floor and aero modifications, and Lorimer's team found the car much better in an extended test at Most, in the Czech Republic. Back at Le Mans, Bell qualified it second on the grid on Thursday.

Sharing the only open-cockpit P1 racer in the field with Jürgen Lässig and Robin Donovan, Bell gamely wound up the turbos on the 3-litre motor at the rolling start to snatch a 'legendary' moment and lead the field to the Dunlop chicane. However, the Kremer soon faded on unsuitable Dunlop tyres. Things improved when Lorimer sourced different compounds from Dunlop Japan's representative, but Bell had three unscheduled stops in the twilight with a severe vibration, cured by replacing the rear wing. At one point, the throttle stuck open as Bell was in the high-speed, right-hand sweep preceding Indianapolis, and it took all his skill to keep the car out of the wall. Progress was further hampered by a black flag during the night that sent the same driver to another three pitstops to replace faulty tail-lights, but the débutant K8 stayed strong through the rest of Sunday, and finished sixth.

COURAGES FADE FROM POLE

Yves Courage had every reason to hope for outright victory this year, but his two fastest cars went out with engine failures, and the third finished 34 laps behind the winners.

Courage entered his new IMSA World Sports Car project alongside two Group C coupés, but shelved the C41 a month before the race when his engineers ran out of time to prepare the car. It was replaced by a third 'C32LM', hastily assembled on a 1993 spare monocoque.

The 1994 regulations hit Group C entrants with further big reductions in engine output and downforce, and Courage's recycled C30 chassis were substantially modified in an effort to compensate. Marcel Hubert drew a new, integral flat bottom and a longer, low-line tail, with the wing mounted above it. Among other changes, the suspension geometry was redesigned for better compatibility with Michelin tyres, being used by Courage for the first time.

Having driven the fastest lap on the Test Day with one C32LM, Lionel Robert promptly climbed aboard another and went second fastest. In race week, Robert missed out on pole position after clanging the barrier with the left-rear of his car on Wednesday, but Alain Ferté stepped up to the plate with the newest chassis (pictured), although car manager

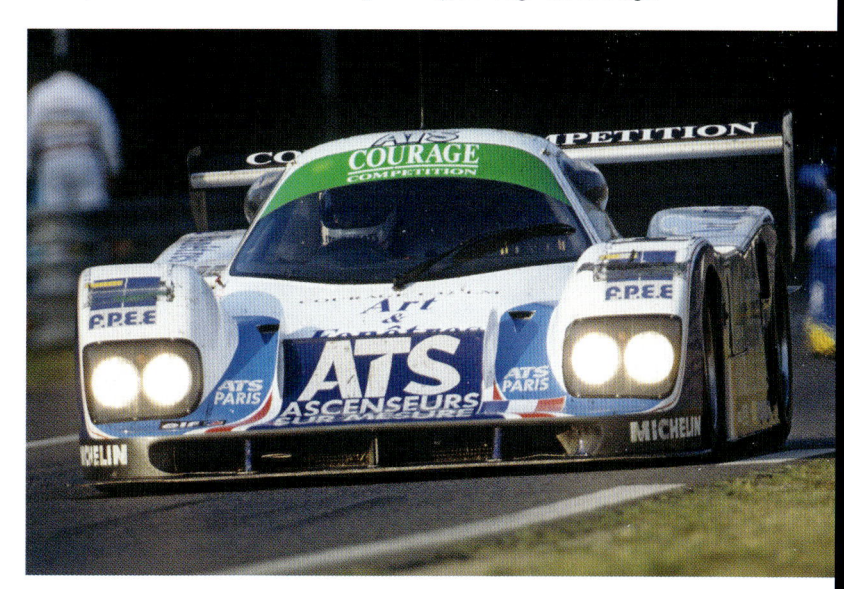

PORSCHE PULLS A FAST ONE

LE MANS

Pascal Fabre, and race-managed by Paolo Catone, was running fifth at 11:30pm when its engine failed. On the stroke of 2pm, the same thing happened to Ferté, Henri Pescarolo and Franck Lagorce, who were running fourth.

These were factory-supplied engines, whereas Mike Phillips's third C32LM was equipped with a Courage-assembled motor. This car (below) was punted off the track on the first racing lap when Jean-Louis Ricci collided with Hervé Regout's WR-Peugeot in the Porsche curves. It was later driven into gravel traps by Philippe Olczyk (at 2am at Tertre Rouge) and by Andy Evans (12 hours later at one of the Mulsanne chicanes). However, apart from a 15-minute delay while a new starter motor was fitted, the car was reliable, and recovered seventh place.

Dominique Méliand delayed his hot lap until 11:30pm. This promising pace disappeared come race day. In an attempt to counter the ability of the Dauer-Porsches to make fewer stops, Michelin supplied exceptionally durable tyres, intended to last through multiple driving shifts. The Courages had already lost a lot of downforce, and the hard tyres also left the drivers struggling for mechanical grip. Two of the cars stayed strong through Saturday evening, but they could not live with the Dauers and Toyotas. Robert's C32LM, co-driven by Perre-Henri Raphanel and

WR ON THE PACE

After such an encouraging Le Mans foray in 1993, WR entered two distinctive single-seat sports-racers in the LM-P2 category, but both were parked just before half-time.

The 1993 car had been re-engineered by Vincent Soulignac with revised suspension rocker arms, a reprofiled rear aerofoil and other upgrades. To reduce its costs, the team changed to a 1905cc turbo Peugeot engine with an almost standard cylinder head and valvegear, but the specified air restrictors allowed comparable output (400bhp) and maintained the car's advantageous power-to-weight ratio. Top speed was increased to almost 190mph (305kph) and Patrick Gonin found more than two seconds in lap time compared with 12 months previously. He caused a tremendous stir on Wednesday by holding the provisional pole position after the first session, ahead of star drivers in much more powerful cars.

Gonin was bumped down to third in the second Thursday session, but was ready to go again on Thursday, only to be thwarted by a problem with the clutch thrust bearing. This led to the failure of Marc Rostan to qualify, so Gonin and Pierre Petit had to do the race unaccompanied. The team completed a second chassis (top) just in time to shake it down in the qualifying sessions; Hervé Regout put it 10th on the grid.

Gonin went fastest in the race morning warm-up but, alas, both WRs slipped to the back of the field during the first hour of racing. Regout collided heavily with Jean-Louis Ricci's Courage as they sped through the Porsche curves for the first time. After a 20-minute repair, he was stuck out on the circuit at 5:35pm by an electrical failure. Regout managed to restart the engine and, after another 20-minute pitstop, Jean-François Yvon resumed – only to return after a single lap. The crew took 50 minutes to fit a new fuel rail. The oil pump failure that stopped the car at 12:50am came as a relief.

The older car was also lucky to race beyond the opening shift: Gonin ran it out of fuel an Indianapolis on his in-lap. Gérard Welter despatched a couple of mechanics to advise Gonin and, when the engine had cooled, the reserve tank suddenly functioned. At 7:30pm, Petit pitted with an oil leak that took more than 90 minutes to fix, ending any remaining hope of a good result. The car was finally eliminated when the engine bay suddenly erupted in flames out at Arnage, and Petit beat a hasty exit.

LARBRE MAKES IT A DOUBLE

Seven Porsche 911 Carreras contested the GT2 division, each powered by the naturally aspirated, 3.8-litre M64/04 flat-six. Larbre Compétition operated three of these cars and delivered a GT double for the manufacturer with Jesús Pareja/Dominique Dupuy/Carlos Palau (below).

Porsche had introduced the Type 993 evolution of its 911-series model range (the last with the air-cooled engines) towards the end of

PORSCHE PULLS A FAST ONE 161

LE MANS

1993, but had yet to offer its racing customers the 911 GT2 derivative, and all these Carreras were the 964-series shape.

Pareja/Dupuy/Palau had an almost perfect weekend. They stalked the fastest GT2 car, the Callaway Corvette, and stayed close enough to take the lead of the class during its extended pitstops. When the Corvette ran out of fuel, they found themselves without challenge and cruised the RSR into eighth position overall. It was Larbre's second consecutive GT2 success here.

Second in the class, after a similarly trouble-free weekend, was the 911 Carrera Cup of Enzo Calderari's Ecurie Biennoise team (left). A new car based in Bienne, Switzerland, and prepared by Stadler Motorsport, it finished far ahead of Konrad Motorsport's RSR (below), which was 10th overall despite losing over half an hour to a gearbox rebuild on Saturday night.

These were the only Carreras to finish. Erik Henriksen's RSR, operated by Peter Bowden's RSR Motorsport, was quick but lost its engine before Saturday afternoon was done. Engine failure before dark also parked Dirk-Reiner Ebeling's Heico team entry (top right), which had finished third in 1993.

Larbre's other entries were both eliminated by accidents. The one raced by team owner Jack Leconte with Pierre Yver/Jean-Luc Chéreau

LE MANS 24 HOURS 1990–99

was crashed at 9:15pm when Chéreau, trying to get out of the way of a Toyota at the entrance to the Porsche curves, hit the barrier and also took out Richard Piper's Lotus. Ninety minutes later, after only two shifts by Jacques Laffite in the Alméras brothers' car (right), Jean-Marie Alméras went off at Tertre Rouge, and the impact with the barrier broke a driveshaft.

Also entered in GT2 was a 3.6-litre Porsche 911 Turbo owned by Cornelio Valsangiacomo, the Swiss importer of the Chicco d'Oro coffee brand. The Carrera RSR that had finished fourth in GT here the previous June, it had been newly re-engined in St Sulpice, near Lausanne, by Haberthur Racing under Guido Haberthur and his son, Olivier, who was among the drivers. The car never featured in the race before blowing a turbocharger soon after dark.

THE MORAL GT1 WINNER

The Dodge brand was here for the first time since 1976, when a NASCAR Charger saloon had broken its engine on the very first lap. This year's two Viper GT1 cars were more robust. Their participation was a totally private venture, and getting them both to the finish was a real achievement for everyone involved. In fact, the Viper raced by René Arnoux, Justin Bell and Bertrand Balas (bottom right) was the moral class winner, beaten only by the two Dauer LMs.

Produced since 1991 by Chrysler's Dodge division in Detroit, the Viper was built on a tubular steel frame enclosed with sheet aluminium. At its heart was an extraordinary 8-litre engine, based on the pushrod, two-valve Chrysler LA that was used to power trucks. The stock cast-iron, 90deg V10 was far too heavy for a passenger application, so Chrysler commissioned its Lamborghini subsidiary to recast the block and heads

PORSCHE PULLS A FAST ONE 163

LE MANS

in aluminium. Even so, it weighed 323kg, making 400bhp at 4600rpm in the 150mph road car, and driving through a sturdy, six-speed Borg-Warner T56 gearbox.

GT1 racing potential in the Viper was seen by Gilles Gaignault, the communications director of a Parisian car hire company. However, he failed to interest Chrysler Corporation, nor its French importer. With Michel Arnaud and Robert Chazal, he therefore formed Rent A Car Racing in Vitry, ordered three cars, and had them converted by racing specialists.

Méca Auto Système, run by ex-Rondeau engineers Philippe Beloou and Jean-Claude Thibault in Jean Rondeau's former factory in Champagné, collaborated on the project with Synergie, Lucien Monté's race preparation specialist in Changé. Méca fitted a rollcage, took out as much weight as it could in the time available, designed and fabricated double-wishbone suspensions, and upgraded the brakes. Meanwhile Multiplast in Vannes produced carbon/Kevlar bodies in place of the standard glassfibre panels. Synergie assembled the cars when the powertrains returned from Luigi Cimarosti's Luigi Racing Team in Liège, which reworked the engines and their electronic fuel-injection systems to make 550bhp at 5700rpm, and produced a new set of gear ratios for the transmission. One car was finished in time for the Test Day in early May, and a second after a two-day test at Zolder.

Despite the loss of 160kg relative to the road car, weight remained a big problem. In qualifying, the faster of the 1340kg Vipers was almost half a minute slower than the much lighter Ferrari that set the (genuine) GT1 pace. Arnoux improved on his best Test Day lap time and went almost 10 seconds faster than Philippe Gache (who had skipped Wednesday qualifying to witness the birth of his baby) in the sister car, which lost a whole lot of track time to engine problems.

After surviving a scrape with the Porsche 968, the Arnoux/Bell/Balas Viper defied expectations and was pretty strong all weekend. It lost time while the brake hydraulics were purged, a broken driveshaft UJ replaced and a detached seat secured, but finished 12th overall.

Gache/François Migault/Denis Morin lost almost 90 minutes on Saturday evening while their crew fitted a new gearbox, which then sprang an oil leak, costing another 25 minutes. They never recovered. Gache damaged the front end against the barrier just after half-time, but the big problem was engine oil pump failures. The yellow car's fourth pump broke a few minutes before the end and Gache was unable to complete the final lap in the time allowed, so the final disappointment of a frustrating week was non-classification.

RACR tried to prequalify one of these Vipers for Le Mans 1995, but it missed the cut.

CAVALLINO COMEBACK

The latest regulations had the happy effect of attracting four Ferrari GT racing cars back to Le Mans, for the first time in 10 years. The fastest was this F40 (facing page), competing in the GT1 category.

1994

The F40 marked the 40th anniversary of Enzo Ferrari's company and was the last model made in Modena before his death in 1988. It was the direct successor of the 288 GTO, an Evoluzione version of which had been developed for Group B competition in 1985, but never raced. Like the GTO, it was based on a tubular steel frame but with a bonded carbon composite floorpan, front bulkhead, dashboard and door sills, and a carbon/aluminium honeycomb structure between the engine and the cabin. The Pininfarina-designed body was made by Scaglietti in a carbonfibre/Kevlar/Nomex weave. The quad-cam, 3-litre V8, fitted with two IHI turbochargers, was again mid-mounted longitudinally with a five-speed gearbox, and made about 480bhp at low 'boost' in the 200mph roadgoing 'supercar'.

The first competition version, the F40 LM, was developed for Ferrari during 1988 by Michelotto in Padua, and was equipped with upgraded double-wishbone suspension, a front splitter, rear diffusers, an adjustable rear wing and additional NACA ducts for increased cooling capacity. A new Weber-Marelli management system and other upgrades to the F120 V8 increased its output to 720bhp at 8100rpm. The prototype LM was first track-tested late in 1988 but it was October 1989 before Ferrari France's team became the first to race one, when Jean Alesi finished third in an IMSA GTO event at Laguna Seca behind works Audi Quattros. The team continued in the USA in 1990 with two cars and top drivers, but won no races.

This F40 was reworked to the LM specification for gentleman driver Luciano della Noce, who campaigned it as a Team Ennea entry in the 1993 Italian GT championship. This season della Noce engaged Swedish entrant Bo Strandell to run the car in the new BPR series, and recruited Anders Olofsson as his co-driver. The F40 was fully competitive in the opening events at Jarama, Dijon and Montlhéry, but unreliable. Then Strandell arranged to take over a Le Mans entry by Hans Obermaier, and the factory helped by supplying endurance-specification 3-litre engines.

In qualifying, Olofsson drove the fastest lap with a genuine GT1 car, ahead of a Venturi and the Bugatti. He began the race with spins at Tertre Rouge and in the Porsche curves, but soon established the Ferrari inside the top 10. After single shifts by Sandro Angelastri and della Noce, Olofsson was stopped at Tertre Rouge at 7:45pm by an electronics glitch. It took him almost 90 minutes to get the V8 restarted and, only 20 minutes after Angelastri had rejoined, it happened again.

The following month, Olofsson and della Noce won the four-hour BPR race at Vallelunga with this much-used racecar.

FERRARIS IN GT2

This field included three GT2 racing versions of the Ferrari 348, and one of them finished fourth in the class behind three Porsches.

Produced between 1989-95, the 348 was a pressed-steel monocoque with a mid-mounted, longitudinal engine (the 3.4-litre, DOHC F119 V8) and a five-speed transverse gearbox. Michelotto produced a Challenge version for a one-make series in 1993 and used some of the specification for a much-lightened Competizione evolution that was offered to customers the same year, equipped with powertrain upgrades and the F40 braking system. Two Competiziones were entered for Le Mans by the Ferrari Club Italia, a federation of almost 500 owner clubs in Italy which, until entering

PORSCHE PULLS A FAST ONE | 165

the Italian Supercar series in 1992 and organizing the 348 Challenge the following season, had prepared Historic racing cars for owners. The team was directed by Franco Meiners and the cars were engineered by FCI's Elio Imberti in premises adjacent to Ferrari's Fiorano test circuit.

Former Brun Porsche star Oscar Larrauri qualified one of these 370bhp Ferraris third in GT2 behind a Corvette and splitting the works Hondas. In the race, 'Popi' (below left) was well-placed when, after a single shift, he handed the car over to Fabio Mancini. The engine broke down in the Virage Ford shortly before Mancini finished his shift.

FCI's other Competizione (below right) was raced by Alfonso d'Orleans Bourbon (a cousin of the king of Spain) and his compatriots, Tomas Saldana and Andres Vilarino. They had a steady and mostly reliable run into 11th overall, interrupted only by a fuel cell problem in the twilight that took 45 minutes to fix.

A third Ferrari 348 was Robin Simpson-Smith's car (pictured above with a Venturi and a Nissan ZX), returning to Le Mans after being punted into the wall by a passing Toyota during the warm-up preceding the 1993 race. In the interim, Simpson Engineering had greatly revised the car in its Gloucestershire base. The team had enlarged and modified the V8 to make about 450bhp, relocated it further forward to make room for a Hewland

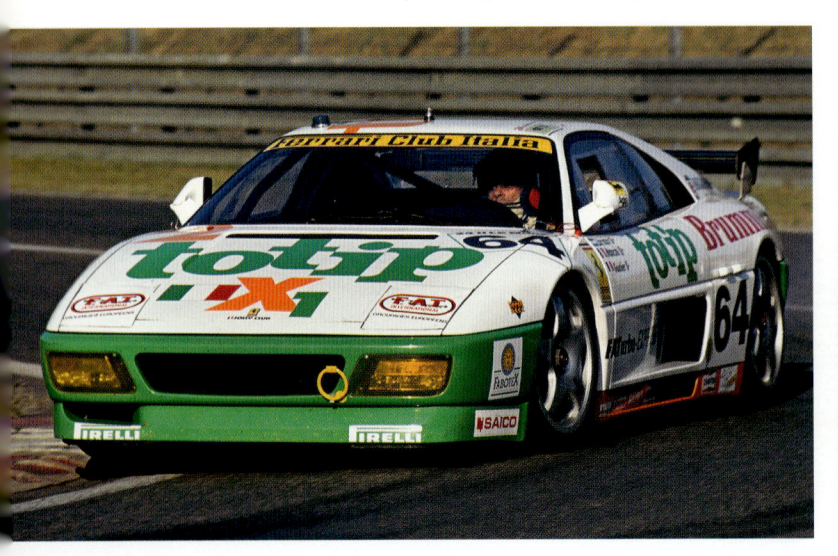

166 LE MANS 24 HOURS 1990–99

1994

DGZ racing gearbox, commissioned F1 designer Sergio Rinland to redraw the rear suspension geometry, fitted AP Racing brakes, and saved weight by making the front spoiler, the doors and the engine cover in Kevlar-reinforced carbonfibre. Smith called the revised car '348 LM' and shook it down in the Silverstone opening round of the British GT series. Having put a big sign on the rear fender – 'IRVINE KEEP CLEAR' – he entered it here for himself, 'Stingbrace' (Stefano Sebastiani) and Tetsuya Ota.

Within an hour of the start, they were having a nightmare with the gearbox. After three rebuilds, Ota was finally stranded out on the Mulsanne straight in the small hours.

THE ARRIVAL OF HONDA

This entry was greatly enhanced by the Le Mans début of Honda, with three GT2 cars. All finished the race. They were beaten in the class by three Porsches, a Ferrari and an Alpine, but the 100 percent finish had been Honda's first objective, so everyone hoped that this was the start of the next big thing from Japan.

Having quit F1 in 1992, after 10 successful seasons yielding six Constructors championships and five Drivers titles, Honda was now evaluating both IndyCar and sportscar racing for its future high-profile motorsport programmes. This project for the mid-engined NSX (first produced in 1990) started life as a two-car campaign in the German-based 1993 ADAC GT Cup series by Seikel Motorsport, which had developed the Civic for European touring car racing in the late 1980s. The cars had shown well with drivers John Nielsen and Armin Hahne, and the latter had won a round at Zolder. Ahead of this season, Honda Motor Europe commissioned TC Prototypes to design and build proper racing NSXs, and offered the Kremer brothers a one-year contract to prepare and operate them.

John Thompson's TCP company in Northampton was made responsible for the chassis, suspension and aerodynamics. Its project designer was Geoff Kingston, whose CV included the TWR-Jaguar Group C projects and a spell at TOMS GB. To reinforce the Honda's extruded aluminium bodyshell, Kingston added a carbon-composite inner monocoque incorporating carbon side beams, an aluminium-honeycomb floor panel, and a steel rollcage. He reinforced the mounting points of the double-wishbone suspension systems, which had been track-developed for Honda by Ayrton Senna, among others. The body shape, refined in the Imperial College wind tunnel in London, provided an improvement of almost 25 percent in downforce over the 1993 NSX racecar. The steering and the ferrous braking systems (with ABS) were also upgraded.

The preparation of the 3-litre, 24-valve V6 was undertaken at the Honda Tochi Centre, which was preparing cars for the All-Japan GT and Touring Car series. The RX306-E4 engine was specifically developed for the NSX, featuring Honda's variable valve timing and valve-lift electronic control (VTEC) systems. Making 380bhp at 8200rpm with the specified

PORSCHE PULLS A FAST ONE

LE MANS

four NSXs to race week, one as a spare. The team under Achim Stroth was supported by 20 Honda personnel, led by Ken Hashimoto. The lightweight cars went through the ACO speed trap at 174mph (280kph) – not fast enough to mount a realistic challenge for the class.

Hahne was very racy in the early race action, but his car, co-driven by Christophe Bouchut and Bertrand Gachot, was then delayed by a broken gear linkage. An oil pump problem followed, and later a breakage inside the gearbox, but this was the best-placed Honda at the end.

Pictured below, the car shared by Philippe Favre with former Porsche 962C driver Hideki Okada and Honda's NSX Driving School instructor, Kazuo Shimuzu, also encountered gearbox problems, and was then set back by an oil leak. After another delay, caused by a faulty gearshift mechanism, it finished 17 laps behind its stablemate.

The third Honda (left) was Japanese-operated by Team Kunimitsu, and driven by team owner Kunimitsu Takahashi with Keiichi Tsuchiya and Akira Iida. They began well but, after three hours, the car needed a fresh starter motor and battery, which cost 35 minutes. It was just the beginning of their woes: two broken driveshafts, a 140-minute gearbox rebuild and a hub-carrier failure all conspired to leave them another 18 laps down.

GT2 restrictors, it was transversely mounted with a strengthened version of Hewland's six-speed, sequential-shift HP2000 Touring Car gearbox.

Hahne warmed up for Le Mans by racing one of the new cars to ADAC GT podiums either side of the Test Day. Formerly an apparently permanent Porsche customer, Köln-based Kremer Racing then brought

The honourable Honda executives both at the track and in Tokyo were happy that all their cars finished, but appalled by the shameless behaviour of Porsche with its race-winning 'Dauer LM'. They wanted to race genuine production-based GT cars…

LE MANS 24 HOURS 1990–99

1994

ALPINE-RENAULT RETURNS

The founder of Alpine, Jean Rédélé, was among 200 Alpine and Renault staff and guests who came to Le Mans to witness the return of the 1978-winning marque. They saw Benjamin Roy, Jean-Claude Police and Luc Galmard drive a consistent race with this GT2 racing version of the A610 (above) and finish fifth in class. The A610 was Alpine's 1991 evolution of the GTA V6 Turbo, with which the Renault group had run heavily promoted one-make series during the 1980s, but this car was a one-off project by a Sarthois tuning specialist. Patrick Legeay had founded Legeay Sports Mécanique in 1980 to upgrade Renaults for the road and to race them and had been successful in the national Coupe R5 Alpine Elf series and the European Cup for the R5 Turbo, then racing the R21 Turbo and the Alpine GTA V6. Based in the village of Teloché, in the rural outskirts of Le Mans, the company now employed 10 people, marketing an upgrade kit for the A610 road car, and preparing Renaults for motorsport clients.

Late in 1993, Legeay won the support of Alpine, which was preparing to mark its 40th anniversary, for a single-car Le Mans programme. In January 1994, he took delivery of a specially prepared steel backbone frame, 35kg lighter than standard, from the Dieppe factory. His crew assembled the car to the GT2 regulations with its own version of the 'PRV' 3-litre V6, with two valves per cylinder (racing against the 24-valve PRVs in the Venturis). Making 430bhp at 6400rpm with two Garrett T3 turbochargers, it drove through a Hewland gearbox with Sadev internals.

Although there were brief delays in the race, caused by a broken exhaust and a faulty gearshift, and the brakes proved to be inadequate, the performance of this untested car was a tribute to Legeay's preparation. He resolved to do even better in 1995.

A new car was built, but a proper Le Mans budget was not secured, and the team missed Prequalifying. The new car was raced in the Paris 1000 BPR event at Montlhéry, but the commercial failure of the A610 had damaged Legeay's business, which was taken over by Jean-Michel Roy (Benjamin's father). The A610 had already been discontinued when Roy and Legeay had a final fling with the GT2 version in March 1996, racing it in the BPR event at Paul Ricard. Alpine's Dieppe factory was switched to the Renault Sport Spider – the car with which Legeay Sports would attempt a recovery.

A PROMISING REVIVAL

In making the first Le Mans appearance by the marque since its victory in 1939, the unique racing Bugatti EB110 SS delivered one of the big surprises of the week. It was racing as high as sixth overall on Sunday morning before turbocharger problems intervened. Sadly it failed to see the finish after being crashed out with less than an hour remaining.

Bugatti had ceased production in 1947 on the death of its founder, but in 1989 Italian entrepreneur Romano Artioli and others acquired the rights to the name, and formed a new company to build a mid-engined 'supercar'. Artioli built a new factory in Campogalliano, north of Modena, and hired former Lancia Stratos and Lamborghini Countach designer Marcello Gandini to draw the new car. The high-specification E110B was unveiled in 1991 on the 110th anniversary of Ettore Bugatti's birth.

In 1993, famed Ferrari engineer Mauro Forghieri joined Bugatti as its technical director, but this racing project, initiated by French publisher Michel Hommell, had no overt factory involvement. The base car was the Sport Stradale version, introduced in 1992. The SS had a more

PORSCHE PULLS A FAST ONE | 169

LE MANS

powerful evolution of Bugatti's all-alloy, 60-valve V12 with four small IHI turbochargers, which drove all four wheels through a six-speed gearbox. As standard, the 3499cc SS engine made more than 600bhp at 8250rpm, offering any intrepid owner a top speed of 216mph (348kph) and the protection of an advanced composites chassis, made by Aérospatiale.

Hommel commissioned the racing car from Le Mans-based specialists Méca and Synergie. The main visible changes to the standard specification were a reduced ride height and modifications to the aluminium bodywork to accommodate larger (18-inch diameter) wheels. Bugatti had homologated an anti-lock carbon braking system and, for racing, this needed extra ventilation, which was built into redesigned suspension uprights. A nose splitter increased downforce. Otherwise much of the work was focused on weight reduction, and almost 300kg was saved relative to the road car – although much of this returned in the shape of the mandatory steel rollcage. Few engine modifications were needed, apart from competition-standard forged pistons and revisions to the fuel system. The weighty (400kg) V12 offered about 640bhp at 7500rpm.

The Bugatti was literally finished in the paddock at the Test Day, but 1993 Le Mans winner Eric Hélary climbed aboard, took it by the throat, and drove the fastest lap by any GT car except a Dauer. Come race week, and a more circumspect Hélary was four seconds slower, lining up 17th.

Only an hour before the race, Beloou's crew discovered a fuel leak. The only timely solution came out of a tube labelled 'Araldite'. Until the adhesive had completely dried, the first couple of shifts had to be driven with the fuel tank half full, but later the well-driven Bugatti made real progress. Hélary, Alain Cudini and Jean-Christophe Bouillon arrived in the top 10 before midnight. They chased down the Larbre team's Porsche through the darkness, and this became the best-placed genuine GT car before 7am.

During the morning, however, all four turbos had to be replaced, one of them twice, and the Bugatti fell far behind. The final disappointment came less than an hour from the end, when Bouillon suddenly swerved to the left and struck the barrier on the Mulsanne straight. A tyre failure was blamed.

The SS was later repaired but was never raced again, instead being retired to Hommell's Manoir de l'Automobile museum in Loheac. Its performance might have encouraged Bugatti to go racing but, in 1995, the manufacturer entered administration. The brand was acquired by the VW Group in 1998 but, in the meantime, the receiver had sold the incomplete EB110 cars and the parts inventory to Dauer Sportwagen in Nuremberg. Over the next decade, the company behind the car that won the 1994 Le Mans would produce only six special-edition 'Dauer EB110' cars, before itself closing its doors in 2008.

1994

SUPER! BUT OUT OF GAS...

An American entrant immediately attracted to the GT1 concept was Reeves Callaway, whose previous Le Mans involvement had been confined to building Group C V8 engines for the Aston Martin AMR-1 in 1989. Callaway was known for his twin-turbo Chevrolet Corvette road smokers. However, his current project was a naturally aspirated version of the Corvette ZR-1, known as the 'SuperNatural', powered by either of the manufacturer's recently introduced all-aluminium V8 engines, the two-valve LT1 or the overhead-cam, four-valve LT5.

Callaway's engines were assembled on new castings in his factory in Old Lyme, Connecticut, to make 475bhp at 6200rpm in the SuperNatural road car. The engines were dry-sumped and fitted with forged steel cranks and pistons, titanium valves, electronic fuel injection and new exhaust systems. Callaway Advanced Technologies also fitted a six-speed ZF manual gearbox and uprated wishbone suspension, braking and control systems.

In 1993, Callaway's European distributor, Ernst Wöhr, entered a SuperNatural in Germany's inaugural ADAC GT series. Callaway helped with race-developed engines and special bodywork for the sheet-reinforced tubular frame, which was drawn by CAT's aerodynamicist, Paul Deutschman. The car was competitive, driven by Boris Said and others, and Callaway set up a European racing division in Leingarten, north of Stuttgart. Soon Callaway Competition GmbH, led by Mike Zoner, employed 17 people and was working on a Le Mans GT2 project.

The car aimed at June 1994 was three months in the making at Leingarten, where the team had composites facilities as well as a fabrication shop. Deutschman's bodywork, including a front diffuser and biplane rear wing, was made in carbon/Kevlar but the weight-saving was negated by a steel rollcage, produced with the German specialist, Hellman. The engine, a 6.2-litre LT1 built for durability, made only 450bhp with the GT2-size air restrictor.

However, the SuperNatural (below) – the first Corvette to contest Le Mans since the Greenwood brothers' extravagant 'Batmobile' in 1976 – turned out to be capable of 187mph (301kph). And Said startled everyone present by landing the GT2 'pole'.

In the race, Said and co-drivers Frank Jelinski and Michel Maisonneuve engaged with the quick Larbre Porsche in a battle that took both cars into the top 10 overall before midnight. At 2:50am, Maisonneuve ran the Corvette out of gasoline in the Porsche curves. A mechanic was sent out with a fuel churn and the car eventually continued, but the ACO's retribution soon followed.

The car later gained three top-four finishes overall from four starts in BPR races, winning the class at Vallelunga and Spa.

PORSCHE PULLS A FAST ONE   171

LOTUS THREE-WHEELERS

Since the 1993 Le Mans, LotusSport and Chamberlain Engineering had completed a lot of work to consolidate the works Lotus Esprit 300s, and they had been raced only in the Suzuka 1000 and in a British GT race at Silverstone. This year the team embarked on a 17-race programme with properly tested GT2 cars, equipped with engine and brake system upgrades. Before the Le Mans Test Day, one of them took Thorkild Thyrring to three British GT victories. And then, at the test, Andreas Fuchs and new team consultant David Kennedy were very competitive, and Fuchs caused a stir when he went fastest in the GT2 class.

Fuchs, sharing his car in race week with Thyrring and Klaus Zwart, did not repeat this feat in qualifying proper. In the race, he stopped at Arnage at 6pm when a sudden stub-axle failure caused his left-rear wheel to come off (above). Fuchs tried in vain to persuade the marshals there to allow him an attempt to reach the pits on three wheels.

While this argument was still going on, Richard Piper, Peter Hardman and Olindo Iacobelli began to make progress with the sister car (left). Before it was dark, however, Piper was involved in a minor accident with Jean-Luc Chéreau's Carrera RSR in the Porsche curves and the right-front wheel of the Lotus was deranged. Again, the driver felt sure

172 LE MANS 24 HOURS 1990–99

1994

he could get back to pit-lane, but was not allowed to do so by the safety-conscious marshals.

A third Esprit 300, a road car modified in Verona by Fabio Magnani for an Italian GT campaign by the AutoXpo team, failed to qualify due to persistent clutch failures.

PANTHER POUNCES BACK

ADA Engineering's Ian Harrower and Chris Crawford studied the GT1 regulations and looked for something to race that would be inexpensive, uncomplicated, light in weight, durable, and equipped with a robust, mid-mounted powertrain. They came up with the De Tomaso Pantera. Although no such car had been raced for eight years, and the Modena factory had produced its last Pantera two years before, they were even able to interest the UK importer, Emilia Concessionaires. The car that resulted was the first Pantera to race at Le Mans since 1979.

Emilia sourced a car and ADA uprated it to designs by Crawford, Paul Barker and freelance consultant Richard Divila. The pressed-steel monocoque with carbon/Kevlar panels, originally engineered by Gian Paolo Dallara, was equipped with a steel rollcage and frame to carry an endurance-specification 5-litre Ford 'stockblock' V8, prepared in San Antonio, Texas, by Lozano Bros. With the Le Mans air restrictor, it produced about 500bhp at 6800rpm via a four-barrel Holley carburettor, driving through a five-speed Toyota Eagle Mk3 GTP (née March) gearbox. A double-wishbone suspension system, racing brakes and a rear aerofoil completed the conversion just in time for ADA to shake down the car at Snetterton before leaving for France.

Pictured above, the Pantera had a top speed of 176mph (284kph) and was driven by Phil Andrews, Dominic Chappell and Jonathan Baker. On the opening lap of the race, Chappell put the car deep into the gravel at the first Mulsanne chicane. In extricating it with a winch, the marshals damaged the gearbox, breaking off the reverse idler, which then caused more internal damage. Eventually the team had to repair the gearbox but, after almost four hours in pit-lane, the Pantera continued. There were further delays with a broken water pump and electrical malfunctions, but the car was strong at the end, albeit unclassified.

ADA later did a couple of races in the British GT championship, which the Pantera then dominated in 1995, driven by Thorkild Thyrring. It was again entered at Le Mans in 1996, but failed to prequalify.

PORSCHE PULLS A FAST ONE

LE MANS

NO PRETENCE HERE

There was a genuine Porsche 962C in this race: ADA Engineering returned with the 962C-GTI it had raced here two years before with the Bell family. In its raceshop in Brentford, west London, the team rebuilt the 3-litre, aluminium-honeycomb chassis to comply with the P1/C90 rules with a flat bottom, added a sloping, low-line engine cover, and entered it alongside its De Tomaso Pantera.

ADA operated the Porsche for 'Team Nippon', a group formed and funded by Masahiko Kondo. The Japanese pop star and F3 racer was partnered on début by Jun Harada (who drove the Porsche on the Test Day) and Tomiko Yoshikawa.

Harada qualified the car well and, although Yoshikawa and Kondo took turns in damaging its front bodywork, the 962C reached the top dozen before midnight. But then Yoshikawa was stranded on the Mulsanne straight with no lights, and stayed there until dawn. Six hours after rejoining the race, Harada pitted with a blown head gasket. The car was parked for almost six hours, but was fired up just before the end so that Yoshikawa could take it to the flag – and experience a repeat of the failure to be classified as a finisher with a Spice in 1992.

ONE LAST SPIN…

In 1990-91, Mazda North America's IMSA GTO programme yielded eight victories for a team of RX-7 'silhouette' racecars, built and operated by Jim Downing in Atlanta, Georgia. Mazda shelved the programme at the end of 1991 to concentrate on a new rotary GTP racecar, and the cars were shipped to Japan. They were noticed there by Yojiro Terada…

Now a veteran of 14 Le Mans starts, Terada could not get it into his head that Mazda rotary engines were no longer competing in France every June. When the ACO opened up this race to IMSA GTS (formerly GTO) cars, 'Terada-san' enthusiastically asked Mazdaspeed to loan him one of the ex-Downing RX-7s. Mazda's motorsport division was sceptical, but agreed after a GTS Nissan had won overall at Daytona and Sebring, and supplied a couple of quad-rotor 13J engines.

The GTO Mazda RX-7, designed by Lee Dykstra (who also drew MNA's 1992 RX-792P prototype), was a steel spaceframe with aluminium and carbonfibre panel reinforcements, fitted with racing suspension, braking and steering systems. Downing's unrestricted engines had been capable of 600bhp at 8500rpm, driving through a five-speed Hewland transmission,

174 LE MANS 24 HOURS 1990-99

1994

but Terada had to make do with less than 500bhp.

Co-driven by Franck Fréon/Pierre de Thoisy, the Mazda was viciously unstable on the big straights in qualifying, and was 20 seconds slower than the Cunningham team's much more powerful Nissan. The drivers spent the whole of Thursday's sessions sorting out the problem. In the race, the car was solid until 10:15pm, when 10 minutes had to be invested in fixing its lights. However, serious delays followed to repair the throttle assembly, a smashed windscreen, a suspension failure and a jammed differential. The old RX-7 finished a battered 15th overall, a very distant second in its class.

Later Terada invited the same co-drivers to race the car in the Suzuka 1000. They led the race at one point, but had to be content with the GTS win.

A REAL GT1 PORSCHE

Porsche discreetly strengthened its bid for an LM-GT1 class win by asking customers not to honour their entries with potential challengers. Jack Leconte of Larbre Compétition reluctantly agreed to scratch the ex-works 1993 Porsche Turbo S LM, which had finished second overall in this year's Daytona 24 Hours. This left only one genuine GT1 Porsche, a 911 Turbo powered by the M64/81 engine, and entered by Konrad Motorsport with Patrick Neve Racing. Pictured above right, it was good enough to spend Saturday well inside the top dozen overall, but broke its engine soon after 11pm.

A DEBORA DÉBÂCLE

For 1994, one of the Coupe Alfa Debora SP93s was updated into the LMP294, conforming with the P2 regulations and with upgrades for endurance racing including an extended engine cover, a smaller rear wing, and a revised flat bottom reaching to the front splitter. The car (right) was fitted with a more powerful, 250bhp V6, and revised rear suspension geometry to improve traction.

Bernard Santal stopped the Debora at the end of its second lap with a major oil leak, and Didier Bonnet's crew had to dismantle and rebuild the top of the engine, which took almost two hours. Restored to the race in a solid last position, the car had just reached the top 30 when rookie Pascal Dro crashed it at 1:25am.

This car was not raced again until it reappeared briefly in a 1998 Interserie event at Most.

PORSCHE PULLS A FAST ONE 175

Le Mans

SBF-ALD-BMW-DNF

The 14th and final Le Mans appearance by an ALD came his year. SBF Team – formed by engineer Jean-Paul Saved, driver Sylvain Boulay and sponsor Christian Fourquemin – arranged an entry in the P1/C90 category for the ALD 06 (left) by taking over a slot vacated by Stealth Engineering, which was to have raced a Porsche.

The 06 was the constructor's last aluminium monocoque racecar, built in 1989, and was powered by the BMW M88 straight-six. The team was able to get it smack on the minimum weight for the class, and the five-year-old, 450bhp car was well suited to this year's regulations. The ALD made up ground steadily after a slow start. It went well during the night and was in 23rd position when the engine broke down, just before half-time.

VENTURI ON THE PACE

This new Venturi 600LM (below left) produced a surprise on Thursday when Michel Ferté was the second fastest driver in a genuine GT1 car. On Saturday, he was racing inside the top 10 overall when engine problems intervened.

Venturi Compétition in Nantes extensively reworked its 'customer' racing specification over the winter of 1993-94. Bodywork revisions included a more rounded nose, incorporating bigger cooling air intakes for bigger carbon-carbon brakes and for the cabin, and a wider tail to accommodate wider tyres, with a redesigned wing. Meanwhile EIA Moteurs upgraded the pistons, camshaft and valvegear of the 3-litre, 24-valve PRV V6, fitted bigger turbochargers, and greatly improved the electronic fuel injection and ignition systems. The 1994 EIA engine offered a 20 percent power hike, to 620bhp at 7000rpm, and the gearbox was fitted with reinforced pinions to compensate.

The new specification transformed performance. Either side of the Test Day, Venturi 600LMs defeated several Porsche 911 turbos to win the Dijon and Montlhéry rounds of the new International GT Endurance series (forerunner of the BPR championship), raced by the Jacadi and JCB teams respectively.

Jacadi's two cars and one car each from Agusta Racing and BBA Compétition gained firm entries for Le Mans, but Jean-Claude Basso's 600LM was listed as a reserve, and was not brought to race week. In qualifying, Ferté

1994

graphically showed the 600LM's new capabilities by beating Jacques Laffite's best 500LM lap time from 1993 by almost 12 seconds. On the other hand, Jacadi's other car suffered a catastrophic engine failure; only Ferdinand de Lesseps was able to qualify, and it was excluded.

Ferté and Michel Neugarten (Jacadi's Dijon winners) were joined here by Olivier Grouillard, who took over the car after Ferté's hard-charging opening shift had taken it into 10th overall. Within 20 minutes, Grouillard pitted with a broken turbo, which cost 25 minutes and as many positions. At 12:30am, the car was back in the pits with broken valvegear. After a three-hour repair, an unwilling Grouillard resumed, but soon parked the car. The following month, Ferté/Neugarten returned to winning form in the GT Endurance series, claiming victory in the Spa 4 Hours.

Jean-Luc Laribière's BBA Compétition 600LM (backed by the 'Betty's Band A' radio station) was presented as an 'art car' by co-driver Hervé Poulain, along the lines of BMWs he had raced here previously. The artist, Arman (Armand Fernandez), called it 'The Reptile'. It went the duration but lost a chunk of time on Sunday morning with a broken gear selector, and then the V6 lost compression on two cylinders. Pictured above right, it was parked in pit-lane for five hours until 10 minutes before the end, when its owner started what was left of the engine and popped and banged under the chequered flag. He had no hope of being classified.

'Rocky' Agusta embarked on the race with a big spin at Tertre Rouge and then his car was twice delayed by a malfunctioning starter motor, and later by problems with the gearshift and a turbo. Just before 3am, Almo Coppelli had to evacuate the cabin when a detached oil line set the engine bay on fire.

Agusta's team also raced two lower-specification Venturi 400 Trophy cars in GT2. Both made it to the finish, but the one raced by Stéphane Ratel (right) had been in pit-lane between 6pm and almost 4am while the crew had undertaken a comprehensive engine rebuild. It was involved in several incidents on Sunday, including a collision with Jeff Krosnoff's leading Toyota, and missed out on classification by 77 laps. Its stablemate lost two hours on Sunday morning to a gearbox rebuild that probably cost it a finish in the top 10.

PORSCHE PULLS A FAST ONE 177

LE MANS

A PORSCHE RARITY

The already varied GT2 category featured this very rare racing Porsche 968 (above), but it did not see Sunday.

The front-engined 944-series was replaced by the 968 in 1992. A turbocharged model was included and, in 1993, Porsche offered motorsport customers lightened racing versions. The 968 Turbo RS was powered by the 3-litre, four-cylinder, SOHC engine with a single turbo, making 350bhp at 5400rpm. Porsche prepared for 100 orders but demand was low and only four were ever produced.

The original works prototype was loaned to Joest Racing and raced by Manuel Reuter in two rounds of the 1993 German national ADAC GT series. Thomas Bscher then acquired it, had it painted yellow, and entrusted it to Peter Seikel's team. Seikel Motorsport in Freigericht, east of Frankfurt, had successfully specialized in touring car racing, but agreed to operate the car in this year's BPR series alongside a Carrera RSR. Bscher arranged for 1990 Le Mans winner John Nielsen to co-drive him and Lindsay Owen-Jones, and they raced at Dijon and Montlhéry before Le Mans. Nielsen (driving here) produced a respectable qualifying time, but the car was crashed out of the race by Owen-Jones soon after 11pm.

After racing this car at Vallelunga and Spa, Bscher sold it into the USA, and it raced in the 1995 Daytona 24 Hours.

HARRIER BOMBS

This quirky car (below) is the one-off Harrier LR9 Spyder, a second Le Mans project by its British constructor, Lester Ray, operated here by Chamberlain Engineering. Epsom-based Harrier, which had failed to qualify its Mazda-engined C Junior racecar here back in 1983, had built a concept roadgoing coupé in 1991, fitted with a mid-mounted 3-litre Alfa Romeo 164 powertrain. This LR9 coupé had been reworked for racing over the winter of 1993-94 and had been entered for Le Mans ahead of its début in a British GT race at Silverstone in March. The spyder therefore startled the ACO's technical inspectors, who were expecting the coupé configured as a GT2 car, but couldn't find the roof. The officials (and the persuasive Hugh Chamberlain) thought it would be churlish to send the

LE MANS 24 HOURS 1990–99

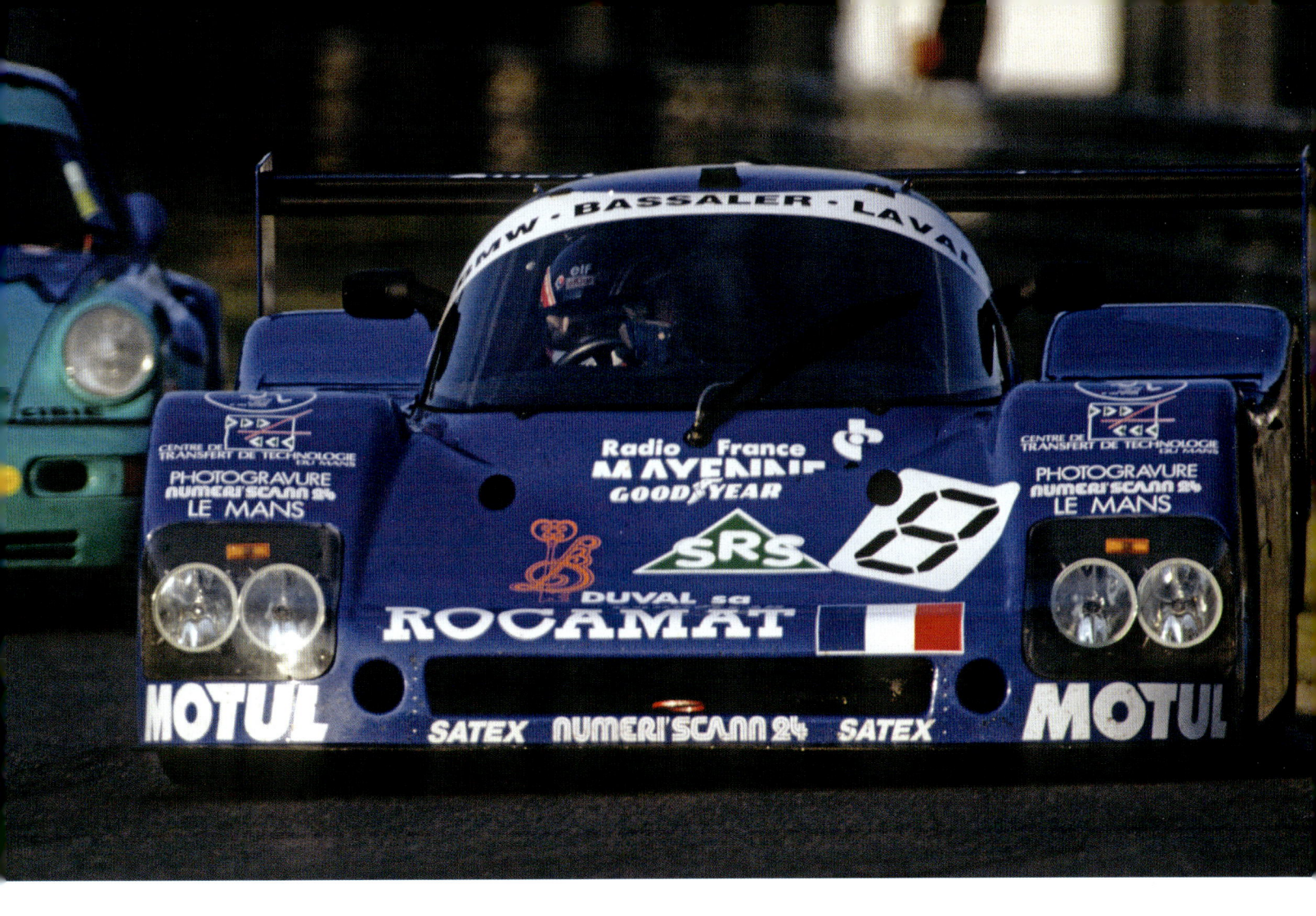

team back to Surrey. Their solution was to redefine the spyder as an LM-P2 (and therefore to pit it against the Debora, which was 174kg lighter).

The HR9 was an aluminium-reinforced steel tubeframe with a glassfibre body. The spyder version was powered by a 2-litre, 350bhp Cosworth BDG prepared by saloon car racing ace Dave Brodie, with a Hewland DG300 transmission. The car, which was shaken down on the MIRA test track before coming to France, was fitted with state-of-the-art digital electronics by Charles Bailey's Astratech company.

Brodie drove the LR9 here with Rob Wilson and William Hewland. They had an exciting time with the unsorted car on Wednesday but it was getting better the next day when Hewland crashed near the start of the Porsche curves, savaging the right-front corner against the wall there. The car was repaired during Friday – or so the team believed. After the Debora had been delayed within minutes of the start, Brodie and Wilson took turns at leading the P2 class! But then the right-front suspension collapsed when Hewland was back in the car, at 7:20pm. Chamberlain's crew invested four hours in another repair, but it happened again soon after Wilson had resumed.

Harrier LR9 coupés won eight races in the British GT series in the period 1995-97, driven by Win Percy, but Ray's cars never returned to Le Mans.

NEW NAME, OLD STAGER

Roland Bassaler seized another chance to race his 1982-vintage Sehcar SHS C6 (above) and sent it to Automobiles Lucien Philippe Associés for four weeks of upgrade work, which proved to be so extensive that Bassaler agreed to change its name. ALPA was a collaboration between two race preparation specialists in suburban Le Mans villages, Méca in Champagné and Synergie in Changé. They had been producing Alpa Formule Renault single-seaters and undertook the upgrade of the C6 on the understanding that two of their promising young drivers, Nicolas Minassian and Olivier Couvreur, would get to drive it in the 24 Hours.

The work was fitted in after ALPA had converted the Bugatti and Dodge Viper GT1 cars that contested this race. The main task was to replace the production-based BMW M88 straight-six with a racing Cosworth DFZ V8, prepared by Heini Mader, which provided a 100bhp hike in power. The car's suspension, braking and cooling systems were also modified, and the engine cover was redesigned, with a rear aerofoil with deep endplates.

The young rookies certainly raised eyebrows in qualifying. Although the team lost hours of track time to an overheating gearbox, Minassian lapped 14 seconds faster than the chassis had gone in 1993 with the BMW engine, and Couvreur was only a tenth slower. Saturday, however, was different.

The first shift, by Patrick Bourdais, went without incident, but Minassian finished the next without the rear wing. A whole catalogue of woes followed: gear-selection problems, a cracked windscreen, a broken engine mounting, an electrical short circuit that filled Bourdais's cockpit with smoke, an ignition failure – all these and other problems preceded the car's eventual demise with a seized wheelbearing.

Bassaler finally put his 12-year-old racing car out to grass.

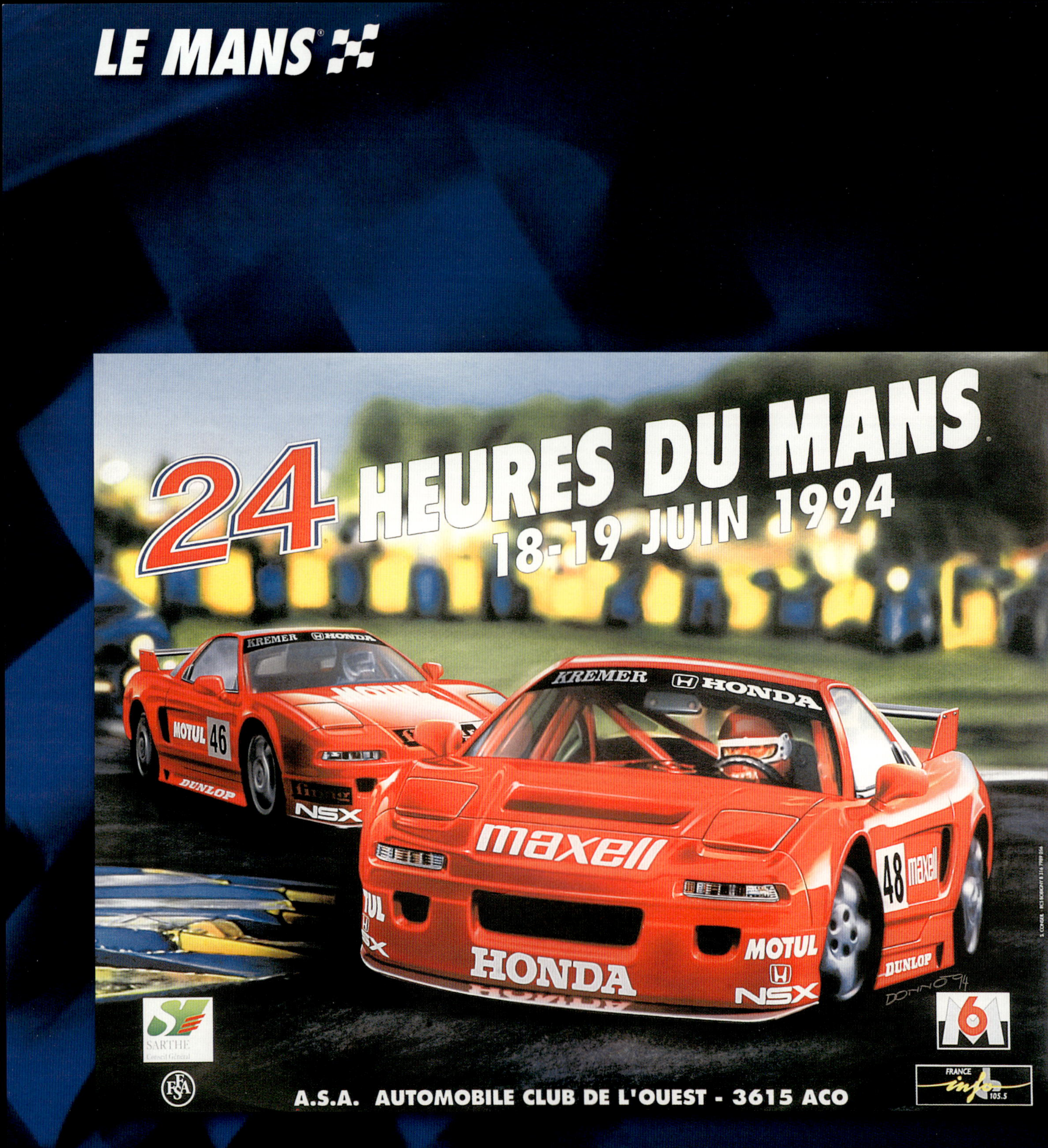
LE MANS
24 HEURES DU MANS
18-19 JUIN 1994
KREMER HONDA
MOTUL 46
DUNLOP
NSX
maxell
48 maxell
MOTUL
HONDA
NSX
DUNLOP
DONNO 94
SARTHE
Conseil Général
FFSA
A.S.A. AUTOMOBILE CLUB DE L'OUEST - 3615 ACO
M6
FRANCE info 105.5

1994

HOURLY RACE POSITIONS

Start	Time	Car	No	Drivers	1	2	3	4	5	6	7	8	9	10	11	12	13	14	15	16	17	18	19	20	21	22	23	24
1	3:51.05	Courage C32LM	2	Pescarolo/A.Ferté/Lagorce	4	5	4	5	6	3	4	4	4	4	DNF													
2	3:51.75	Kremer K8	5	Bell/Donovan/Lässig	9	8	8	8	8	8	12	9	7	7	6	8	8	8	7	7	6	6	6	6	6	6	6	6
3	3:52.58	WR LM93	21	Gonin/Petit *	40	38	26	31	33	29	29	28	24	23	DNF													
4	3:53.01	Toyota 94C-V	1	Irvine/Martini/Krosnoff	2	3	1	1	3	2	2	1	3	2	2	2	1	1	1	1	1	1	1	1	1	1	3	2
5	3:53.71	Dauer 962LM	35	Stuck/Boutsen/Sullivan	1	1	6	6	4	4	3	3	2	3	3	3	3	2	2	3	3	3	3	3	3	3	2	3
6	3:54.25	Courage C32LM	3	Raphanel/Fabre/Robert	6	6	5	4	5	5	5	7	DNF															
7	3:54.85	Dauer 962LM	36	Baldi/Dalmas/Haywood	5	2	2	2	2	6	6	5	5	5	4	4	4	3	3	2	2	2	2	2	2	2	1	1
8	3:55.02	Toyota 94C-V	4	Wollek/Fouché/Andskär	3	4	3	3	1	1	1	2	1	1	1	1	1	5	5	5	5	5	5	5	5	4	4	4
9	3:57.09	Nissan 300ZX	75	Millen/Morton/O'Connell	7	7	7	7	7	7	7	6	6	5	5	4	4	4	4	4	4	4	4	5	5	5	5	
10	3:59.94	WR LM94	22	Regout/Yvon/Libert	41	41	44	39	35	31	32	30	28	29	DNF													
11	4:04.26	Courage C32LM	9	Ricci/Evans/Olczyk	43	37	22	26	20	22	18	15	11	10	11	10	10	9	9	8	8	8	7	7	7	7	7	7
12	4:04.31	Nissan 300ZX	76	Poele/Gentilozzi/Kasuya	8	28	41	DNF																				
13	4:07.05	Porsche 962C-GTI	6	Harada/Yoshikawa/Kondo	35	22	17	13	14	14	13	12	14	19	21	20	19	18	18	18	18	18	22	21	22	23	23	NC
14	4:07.10	Ferrari F40	29	Olofsson/Angelastri/Angelelli	13	10	9	15	32	33	34	36	DNF															
15	4:07.99	Venturi 600LM	38	Grouillard/M.Ferté/Neugarten	10	35	34	30	23	20	17	16	16	22	22	24	DNF											
16	4:10.68	Alpa LM	8	Minassian/Bourdais/Couvreur	25	40	39	37	40	38	36	35	33	31	28	27	DNF											
17	4:16.94	Bugatti EB110 SS	34	Cudini/Hélary/Boullion	22	25	20	17	13	13	8	10	10	9	8	7	7	7	6	10	12	13	15	18	18	20	17	DNF
18	4:17.21	Callaway Corvette SuperNatural	51	Jelinski/Said/Maisonneuve	12	11	14	9	11	9	9	11	9	11	10	15	18	DNF										
19	4:17.71	Porsche 911 Turbo	33	Konrad/Hermann/Sommer	11	9	12	11	10	12	11	18	20	DNF														
20	4:17.74	Mazda RX-7	74	Terada/Fréon/Thoisy	26	17	16	12	12	11	14	14	12	14	17	18	15	15	15	17	17	17	16	15	14	14	14	15
21	4:18.80	Honda NSX	48	Hahne/Bouchut/Gachot	14	18	27	23	24	24	23	22	18	18	19	20	19	19	19	19	18	17	17	15	15	15	15	14
22	4:22.68	Ferrari 348 GT Competizione	64	Larrauri/Mancini/Gouhier	21	34	43	44	DNF																			
23	4:23.75	Honda NSX	47	Takahashi/Tsuchiya/Iida	24	20	19	32	30	25	25	27	27	28	22	22	22	22	22	22	22	21	22	21	21	21	21	18
24	4:24.64	De Tomaso Pantera	37	Andrews/Chappell/Baker	45	44	42	43	44	41	39	37	34	32	27	26	24	23	23	23	23	23	23	23	23	23	22	NC
25	4:25.76	Porsche 911 Carrera RSR	66	Bellm/Nuttall/Rickett	15	14	32	DNF																				
26	4:26.09	Porsche 911 Carrera RSR	52	Pareja/Dupuy/Palau	16	12	10	10	9	10	10	8	8	8	7	6	6	6	8	6	7	7	8	8	8	8	8	8
27	4:26.46	Porsche 911 Carrera Cup	54	Calderari/Bryner/Mastropietro	19	19	18	18	18	15	15	13	13	12	9	9	9	10	10	9	9	9	9	9	9	9	9	9
28	4:26.63	Ferrari 348 GT Competizione	57	Bourbon/Saldana/Vilarino	29	27	23	24	22	25	27	26	23	21	19	17	16	17	15	15	14	12	11	11	11	11	11	11
29	4:27.05	Porsche 911 Carrera RSR	50	Yver/Leconte/Chereau	17	15	15	16	15	DNF																		
30	4:27.30	Debora LMP294	20	Santal/Tessier/Dro	48	48	48	46	42	37	35	34	32	30	DNF													
31	4:27.56	Porsche 911 Carrera RSR	49	Laffite/Alméras/Alméras	20	23	21	20	17	17	16	19	25	DNF														
32	4:28.35	Honda NSX	46	Favre/Okada/Shimizu	47	45	46	38	36	32	31	32	29	25	23	23	23	20	20	20	20	20	19	19	19	17	16	16
33	4:28.37	Porsche 911 Carrera RSR	45	Richter/Wlazik/Ebeling	23	16	13	14	29	DNF																		
34	4:28.53	Alpine A610	60	Roy/Galmard/Police	28	30	28	25	28	27	26	24	21	20	16	16	17	16	16	16	15	14	13	13	13	13	13	13
35	4:28.78	Venturi 600LM	31	Coppelli/Agusta/Krine	32	26	37	33	31	28	28	29	26	24	20	21	DNF											
36	4:29.48	ALD C289	7	Lacaud/Boulay/Robin	42	43	38	35	34	30	30	31	30	26	25	DNF												
37	4:31.00	Porsche 911 Turbo	56	Haberthur/Goueslard/Vuillaume	46	42	35	36	38	35	37	DNF																
38	4:31.92	Venturi 600LM	30	Laribière/Chauvin/Poulain	37	32	30	28	21	18	19	17	15	13	12	11	11	11	11	11	11	11	14	16	16	19	NC	
39	4:32.91	Porsche 968 RS Turbo	58	Nielsen/Bscher/Owen-Jones	34	29	24	21	19	19	21	27	DNF															
40	4:33.35	Ferrari 348 LM	55	Smith/Sebastiani/Ota	36	46	47	45	45	42	41	39	36	34	29	28	DNF											
41	4:33.36	Dodge Viper R/T10	40	Arnoux/Bell/Balas	33	31	25	27	25	21	22	21	17	15	14	13	13	14	14	14	13	12	13	12	12	12	12	12
42	4:33.71	Lotus Esprit S300 Turbo	61	Thyrring/Zwart/Fuchs	27	21	36	40	41	39	DNF																	
43	4:33.85	Porsche 911 Carrera RSR	59	Euser/Huisman/Tomlje	18	13	11	19	16	16	20	22	19	16	13	12	12	12	12	11	10	10	10	10	10	10	10	10
44	4:34.62	Venturi 400GTR	65	Ratel/Hunkeler/Chaufour	31	24	40	42	43	40	40	37	35	30	29	25	24	24	24	24	24	24	24	24	24	24	24	NC
45	4:36.52	Lotus Esprit S300 Turbo	62	Piper/Hardman/Iacobelli	30	33	29	22	26	DNF																		
46	4:37.65	Venturi 400GTR	68	Sirera/Puig/Camp	39	39	31	29	27	23	23	20	18	17	15	14	14	13	13	13	16	17	16	17	18	20	17	
47	4:43.08	Dodge Viper R/T10	41	Migault/Morin/Gache	44	47	45	41	39	34	33	33	31	28	24	22	21	21	21	21	21	21	20	20	20	19	18	NC
48	4:44.15	Harrier LR9 Spyder	63	Wilson/Brodie/Hewland	38	35	33	34	37	36	38	38	35	33	DNF													
DNQ	4:51.38	Venturi 600LM	39	Lesseps/Belmondo/Tropenat	DNS																							
DNQ	5:22.87	Lotus Esprit S300 Turbo	53	Heinkélé/Kuster/Hugenholtz	DNS																							
RES		Venturi 600LM	43	Migault/Basso/Meigemont	-																							
RES		Venturi 600LM	44	Graham/Birbeau/Lécuyer	-																							
RES		Porsche 911 Carrera RSR	69	Gahinet/Caradec/Duigou	-																							

DNF Did not finish **DNQ** Did not qualify **DSQ** Disqualified **FS** Failed scrutineering **NC** Not classified as a finisher **RES** Reserve not required * Car 21 DNQ Marc Rostan (F)

PORSCHE PULLS A FAST ONE 181

LE MANS

RACE RESULTS

Pos	Car	No	Drivers			Laps	Km	Miles	FIA Class	DNF
1	Dauer 962GT-LM	36	Mauro Baldi (I)	Yannick Dalmas (F)	Hurley Haywood (USA)	344	4685.70	2911.55	LM-GT1	
2	Toyota 94C-V	1	Eddie Irvine (IRL)	Mauro Martini (I)	Jeff Krosnoff (USA)	343	4667.57	2900.29	LM-P1/C90	
3	Dauer 962GT-LM	35	Hans-Joachim Stuck (D)	Thierry Boutsen (B)	Danny Sullivan (USA)	343	4667.55	2900.28	LM-GT1	
4	Toyota 94C-V	4	Bob Wollek (F)	George Fouché (ZA)	Steven Andskär (S)	328	4466.40	2775.29	LM-P1/C90	
5	Nissan 300ZX	75	John Morton (USA)	Steve Millen (NZ)	Johnny O'Connell (USA)	317	4314.22	2680.73	IMSA GTS	
6	Kremer K8	5	Derek Bell (GB)	Robin Donovan (GB)	Jürgen Lässig (D)	316	4301.23	2672.66	LM-P1/C90	
7	Courage C32LM	9	Jean-Louis Ricci (F)	Andy Evans (USA)	Philippe Olczyk (B)	310	4219.31	2621.75	LM-P1/C90	
8	Porsche 911 Carrera RSR	52	Jesús Pareja (E)	Dominique Dupuy (F)	Carlos Palau (E)	307	4176.57	2595.20	LM-GT2	
9	Porsche 911 Carrera Cup	54	Enzo Calderari (CH)	Lilian Bryner (CH)	Renato Federico Mastropietro (I)	299	4066.26	2526.65	LM-GT2	
10	Porsche 911 Carrera RSR	59	Cor Euser (NL)	Patrick Huisman (NL)	Matiaz Tomlje (SLO)	295	4011.86	2492.85	LM-GT2	
11	Ferrari 348 GT Competizione	57	Alfonso d'Orleans Bourbon (E)	Tomas Saldana (E)	Andres Vilarino (E)	276	3758.44	2335.38	LM-GT2	
12	Dodge Viper R/T10	40	René Arnoux (F)	Justin Bell (GB)	Bertrand Balas (F)	273	3717.81	2310.14	LM-GT1	
13	Alpine A610	60	Benjamin Roy (F)	Luc Galmard (F)	Jean-Claude Police (F)	272	3698.89	2298.38	LM-GT2	
14	Honda NSX	48	Armin Hahne (D)	Christophe Bouchut (F)	Bertrand Gachot (B)	257	3500.46	2175.08	LM-GT2	
15	Mazda RX-7	74	Yojiro Terada (J)	Franck Fréon (F)	Pierre de Thoisy (F)	250	3405.71	2116.21	IMSA GTS	
16	Honda NSX	46	Philippe Favre (CH)	Hideki Okada (J)	Kazuo Shimizu (J)	240	3262.04	2026.93	LM-GT2	
DNF	Bugatti EB-110S	34	Alain Cudini (F)	Eric Hélary (F)	Jean-Christophe Boullion (F)	230			LM-GT1	Accident
17	Venturi 400GTR	68	Jean-Louis Sirera (F)	Antonio Puig (E)	Xavier Camp (E)	225	3066.10	1905.18	LM-GT2	
NC	Dodge Viper R/T10	41	François Migault (F)	Denis Morin (F)	Philippe Gache (F)	225	3059.87	1901.31	LM-GT1	Last lap too slow
18	Honda NSX	47	Kunimitsu Takahashi (J)	Keiichi Tsuchiya (J)	Akira Iida (J)	222	3020.64	1876.94	LM-GT2	
NC	Venturi 600LM	30	Jean-Luc Maury-Laribière (F)	Bernard Chauvin (F)	Hervé Poulain (F)	221	3007.80	1868.96	LM-GT1	Insufficient distance
NC	De Tomaso Pantera	37	Phil Andrews (GB)	Dominic Chappell (GB)	Jonathan Baker (GB)	210	2865.04	1780.25	LM-GT1	Insufficient distance
NC	Porsche 962C-GTI	6	Jun Harada (J)	Tomiko Yoshikawa (J)	Masahiko Kondo (J)	189	2569.16	1596.40	LM-P1/C90	Insufficient distance
DSQ	Callaway Corvette SuperNatural	51	Frank Jelinski (D)	Boris Said III (USA)	Michel Maisonneuve (F)	142			LM-GT2	Refuelled on circuit
DNF	Courage C32LM	2	Henri Pescarolo (F)	Alain Ferté (F)	Franck Lagorce (F)	142			LM-P1/C90	Engine
NC	Venturi 400GTR	65	Stéphane Ratel (F)	Franz Hunkeler (CH)	Edouard Chaufour (F)	137	1827.21	1135.37	LM-GT2	Insufficient distance
DNF	Venturi 600LM	31	Almo Coppelli (I)	Ricardo 'Rocky' Agusta (I)	Michel Krine (F)	115			LM-GT1	Fire
DNF	Venturi 600LM	38	Olivier Grouillard (F)	Michel Ferté (F)	Michel Neugarten (B)	107			LM-GT1	Engine
DNF	Courage C32LM	3	Pierre-Henri Raphanel (F)	Pascal Fabre (F)	Lionel Robert (F)	107			LM-P1/C90	Engine
DNF	WR LM93	21	Patrick Gonin (F)	Pierre Petit (F)		104			LM-P2	Fire
DNF	Porsche 911 Turbo	33	Franz Konrad (A)	Antonio de Azevedo Hermann (BR)	Mike Sommer (D)	100			LM-GT1	Engine
DNF	ALD C289	7	Dominique Lacaud (F)	Sylvain Boulay (F)	Bernard Robin (F)	96			LM-P1/C90	Engine
DNF	Porsche 911 Carrera RSR	49	Jacques Laffite (F)	Jacques Alméras (F)	Jean-Marie Alméras (F)	94			LM-GT2	Accident
DNF	WR LM94	22	Hervé Regout (B)	Jean-François Yvon (F)	Jean-Paul Libert (B)	86			LM-P2	Suspension
DNF	Porsche 968 RS Turbo	58	John Nielsen (DK)	Thomas Bscher (D)	Lindsay Owen-Jones (GB)	84			LM-GT1	Accident
DNF	Debora LM-P294	20	Bernard Santal (CH)	Georges Tessier (F)	Pascal Dro (F)	79			LM-P2	Accident
DNF	Alpa LM	8	Nicolas Minassian (F)	Patrick Bourdais (F)	Olivier Couvreur (F)	64			LM-P1/C90	Wheel hub-carrier
DNF	Porsche 911 Carrera RSR	50	Pierre Yver (F)	Jack Leconte (F)	Jean-Luc Chereau (F)	62			LM-GT2	Accident
DNF	Lotus Esprit S300 Turbo	62	Richard Piper (GB)	Peter Hardman (GB)	Olindo Iacobelli (USA)	59			LM-GT2	Accident
DNF	Ferrari 348 LM	55	Robin Smith (GB)	'Stingbrace' (Stefano Sebastiani) (I)	Tetsuya Ota (J)	57			LM-GT2	Transmission (gearbox)
DNF	Porsche 911 Carrera RSR	45	Ulrich Richter (D)	Karl-Heinz Wlazik (D)	Dirk-Reiner Ebeling (D)	57			LM-GT2	Engine
DNF	Ferrari F40	29	Anders Olofsson (S)	Sandro Angelastri (CH)	Max Angelelli (I)	51			LM-GT1	Electrics (ignition)
DNF	Harrier LR9 Spyder LM	63	Rob Wilson (NZ)	Dave Brodie (GB)	William Hewland (GB)	45			LM-P2	Suspension
DNF	Porsche 911 Turbo	56	Olivier Haberthur (CH)	Patrice Goueslard (F)	Patrick Vuillaume (F)	42			LM-GT1	Engine (turbocharger)
DNF	Porsche 911 Carrera RSR	66	Ray Bellm (GB)	Harry Nuttall (GB)	Charles Rickett (GB)	38			LM-GT2	Engine
DNF	Lotus Esprit S300 Turbo	61	Thorkild Thyrring (DK)	Klaas Zwart (NL)	Andreas Fuchs (D)	28			LM-GT2	Stub axle/detached wheel
DNF	Nissan 300ZX	76	Eric van de Poele (B)	Paul Gentilozzi (USA)	Shunji Kasuya (J)	25			IMSA GTS	Electrics (ignition)
DNF	Ferrari 348 GT Competizione	64	Oscar Larrauri (RA)	Fabio Mancini (I)	Joël Gouhier (F)	23			LM-GT2	Engine
DNQ	Lotus Esprit S300 Turbo	53	Christian Heinkélé (F)	Guy Kuster (F)	John Hugenholtz (NL)	–			LM-GT2	
DNQ	Venturi 600LM	39	Ferdinand de Lesseps (F)	Paul Belmondo (F)	Jacques Tropenat (F)	–			LM-GT1	
RES	Venturi 600LM	43	François Migault (F)	Jean-Claude Basso (F)	Claude Meigemont (F)				LM-GT1	
RES	Venturi 600LM	44	Eric Graham (F)	François Birbeau (F)	Laurent Lécuyer (CH)				LM-GT1	
RES	Porsche 911 Carrera RSR	69	'Segolen' (André Gahinet) (F)	Didier Caradec (F)	Jean-Louis Le Duigou (F)				LM-GT2	

DNF Did not finish   **DNS** Did not start   **DSQ** Disqualified   **FS** Failed scrutineering   **RES** Reserve not required   **NC** Not classified as a finisher   **WD** Withdrawn   Drivers in italics did not race the cars specified

CLASS WINNERS

FIA Class	Starters	Finishers	First	No	Drivers	kph	mph	
LM-P1/C90	9	4	Toyota 94CV	1	Irvine/Martini/Krosnoff	194.482	120.851	Record
LM-P2	4	0	–	–	–	-	-	
LM-GT1	11	3	Dauer 962LM	36	Baldi/Dalmas/Haywood	195.238	121.321	Record
LM-GT2	21	9	Porsche 911 Carrera RSR	52	Pareja/Dupuy/Palau	174.024	108.133	Record
IMSA GTS	3	2	Nissan 300 ZX	75	Morton/Millen/O'Connell	179.759	111.697	Record
Totals	48	18						

TEST DAY – 8 MAY 1994

Pos	Car	Drivers	Time
1	Courage C32LM	Robert/Fabre/Olcyk	3:47.44
2	Courage C32LM	Robert/Raphanel/Pescarolo	3:51.76
3	Dauer 962LM	Stuck/Boutsen/Baldi/Dalmas	3:52.32
4	WR LM93	Ortelli/Gonin/Yvon	4:00.14
5	Bugatti EB110 SS	Hélary/Malcher	4:12.78
6	Venturi 600LM	M.Ferté/Lécuyer/Tropenat	4:14.32
7	Porsche 911 Turbo S LM	Dupuy	
8	Alpa LM	Couvreur	
9	Porsche 962C-GTI	Harada	
10	Venturi 600LM	Agusta/Taverna	
&c	36 participants		

INTERNATIONAL GT ENDURANCE SERIES

Race	Winner	Drivers
Paul Ricard (F) 4 hours	Porsche 911 Turbo S-LM	Jarier/Pareja/Wollek
Jarama (E) 4 hours	Porsche 911 Turbo S-LM	Jarier/Pareja/Dupuy
Dijon-Prénois (F) 4 hours	Venturi 600LM	Ferté/Neugarten
Linas-Montlhéry (F) 1000km	Venturi 600LM	Pescarolo/Basso
Vallelunga (I) 4 hours	Ferrari F40	Olofsson/Noce
Spa-Francorchamps (B) 4 hours	Venturi 600LM	Ferté/Neugarten
Suzuka (J) 1000km	Porsche 911 Turbo S-LM	Jarier/Pareja/Wollek
Zhuhai (CN) 3 hours	Porsche 911 Turbo S-LM	Jarier/Wollek/Laffite

Non-championship series

PORSCHE PULLS A FAST ONE

LE MANS

1995
McLAREN STARS ON A NEW STAGE

LE MANS

RACE INFORMATION

RACE DATE
17-18 June

RACE No
63

CIRCUIT LENGTH
8.451 miles/13.600km

HONORARY STARTER
Philippe Seguin
President, French National Assembly

MARQUES (ON GRID)

Chevrolet	4
Courage	2
Debora	1
Ferrari	4
Honda	3
Jaguar	2
Kremer-Porsche	2
Kudzu	1
Lister	1
Marcos	2
McLaren	7
Nissan	2
Porsche	10
SARD-Toyota	1
Toyota	1
Venturi	3
WR	2

STARTERS/FINISHERS
48/20

WINNERS

OVERALL
McLaren

ENTRY LIST

No	Car	Entrant (nat)	cc	Engine	Tyres	Weight (kg)	Class
1	Ferrari 333SP	Euromotorsport Racing (USA)	3997	F310E V12	Goodyear	894	LM-WSC *
3	Kremer K8	Kremer Racing (D)	2994tc	Porsche F6	Goodyear	925	LM-WSC *
4	Kremer K8	Kremer Racing (D)	2994tc	Porsche F6	Goodyear	919	LM-WSC
5	Kudzu DG2/3	Mazdaspeed (J) DTR (USA)	1962r	Mazda R20B 3R	Goodyear	820	LM-WSC
6	Norma M14	Norbert Santos (F)	4500	Buick L27 V6	Goodyear	868	LM-WSC
7	Tiga FJ94	Sylvain Boulay (F)	4500	Buick L27 V6	Goodyear	932	LM-WSC
8	WR LM95	Welter Racing (F)	1905sc	Peugeot 405-Raid S4	Michelin	642	LM-P2 *
9	WR LM94/5	Welter Racing (F)	1905sc	Peugeot 405-Raid S4	Michelin	623	LM-P2
10	PRC S94	Vonka Racing Team (CZ)	3000	BMW M88	–	–	LM-P2
11	Courage C41	Courage Compétition (F)	5000	Chevrolet V8	Goodyear	851	LM-WSC *
12	Courage C41	Courage Compétition (F)	5000	Chevrolet V8	Goodyear	899	LM-WSC
13	Courage C34	Courage Compétition (F)	2994tc	Porsche F6	Michelin	901	LM-WSC
14	Debora LMP295	Didier Bonnet (F)	1996tc	Cosworth BDG S4	Michelin	700	LM-P2 *
22	Nissan Skyline GT-R LM	NISMO (J)	2568tc	RB26-DETT S6	Bridgestone	1370	LM-GT1 *
23	Nissan Skyline GT-R LM	NISMO (J)	2568tc	RB26-DETT S6	Bridgestone	1285	LM-GT1
24	McLaren F1 GTR	GTC Gulf Racing (GB)	6064	BMW S70/2 V12	Michelin	1125	LM-GT1 *
25	McLaren F1 GTR	GTC Gulf Racing (GB)	6064	BMW S70/2 V12	Michelin	1135	LM-GT1
26	SARD Toyota MC8-R	SARD Company (J)	3968tc	R40V-T V8	Dunlop	1273	LM-GT1 *
27	Toyota Supra GT-LM	SARD Company (J)	2140tc	3S-GTE S4	Dunlop	1245	LM-GT1 *
28	Toyota Supra GT-LM	Nisso Trust Racing (J)	2140tc	3S-GTE S4	–	–	LM-GT1 *
30	Chevrolet Corvette ZR-1	ZR1 Corvette Team USA (USA)	6243	LT5 DRZ-500 V8	Goodyear	1281	LM-GT1 *
31	Lamborghini Diablo Jota GT1	AIM Team Lamborghini (I)	5709	V12	–	–	LM-GT1 *
34	Ferrari F40 LM	Pilot Aldix Racing (F)	2936tc	F120B V8	Michelin	1061	LM-GT1
36	Porsche 911 GT2 Evo	Larbre Compétition (F)	3600tc	F6	Michelin	1138	LM-GT1 *
37	Porsche 911 GT2 Evo	Larbre Compétition (F)	3600tc	F6	Michelin	1139	LM-GT1 *
40	Ferrari F40 GTE	Ennea Ferrari Club Italia (I)	2998tc	F120B V8	Pirelli	1114	LM-GT1
41	Ferrari F40 GTE	Ennea Ferrari Club Italia (I)	2998tc	F120B V8	Pirelli	1124	LM-GT1
42	McLaren F1 GTR	BBA Compétition (F)	6064	BMW S70/2 V12	Dunlop	1159	LM-GT1
44	Venturi 600S-LM	Société Venturi (F)	2975tc	PRV V6	Michelin	1066	LM-GT1 *
46	Honda NSX GT1	TCP Racing Team Honda (J)	2977tc	RX-306E5 V6	Dunlop	1050	LM-GT1 *
47	Honda NSX GT1	TCP Racing Team Honda (J)	2977tc	RX-306E5 V6	Dunlop	1054	LM-GT1 *
49	McLaren F1 GTR	DPR West Competition (GB)	6064	BMW S70/2 V12	Goodyear	1128	LM-GT1
50	McLaren F1 GTR	Giroix Racing Team Jacadi (F)	6064	BMW S70/2 V12	Michelin	1158	LM-GT1
51	McLaren F1 GTR	DPR Mach One Racing (GB)	6064	BMW S70/2 V12	Goodyear	1130	LM-GT1
52	Lister Storm GTS	Lister Cars (GB)	6996	Jaguar HE V12	Michelin	1270	LM-GT1
54	Porsche 911 BiTurbo	Freisinger Motorsport (D)	3756tc	F6	Goodyear	1166	LM-GT1
57	Jaguar XJ220C	PC Automotive Jaguar (GB)	3498tc	JV6	Dunlop	1170	LM-GT1
58	Jaguar XJ220C	PC Automotive Jaguar (GB)	3498tc	JV6	Dunlop	1171	LM-GT1
59	McLaren F1 GTR	Kokusai Kaihatsu UK (GB)	6064	BMW S70/2 V12	Michelin	1137	LM-GT1
70	Marcos 600LM	Team Marcos (GB)	6243	Chevrolet LT5 V8	Dunlop	1191	LM-GT2 *
71	Marcos 600LM	Team Marcos (GB)	6243	Chevrolet LT5 V8	Dunlop	1167	LM-GT2
73	Callaway Corvette SuperNatural	Callaway Competition (USA)	6243	Chevrolet LT1 V8	BF Goodrich	1233	LM-GT2 *
75	Callaway Corvette SuperNatural	Agusta Racing Team (I/GB)	6243	Chevrolet LT1 V8	Dunlop	1118	LM-GT2
76	Callaway Corvette SuperNatural	Agusta Racing Team (I/GB)	6243	Chevrolet LT1 V8	Dunlop	1118	LM-GT2
77	Porsche 911 GT2	Seikel Motorsport (D)	3600tc	F6	Pirelli	1176	LM-GT2
78	Porsche 911 GT2	Jean-Francois Veroux (F)	3600tc	F6	Goodyear	1169	LM-GT2
79	Porsche 911 GT2	Stadler Motorsport (CH)	3600tc	F6	Pirelli	1177	LM-GT2
81	Porsche 911 GT2	Richard Jones (GB)	3600tc	F6	Goodyear	1175	LM-GT2
82	Porsche 911 GT2	Elf Haberthur Racing (CH)	3600tc	F6	Pirelli	1201	LM-GT2
84	Honda NSX GT	Team Kunimitsu Honda (J)	2977	RX-306E5-IT V6	Yokohama	1055	LM-GT2
91	Porsche 911 GT2	Heico Service (D)	3600tc	F6	Goodyear	1154	LM-GT2
Reserves							
43	Venturi 600LM	BBA Compétition (F)	2975tc	PRV V6	Dunlop	1153	LM-GT1
45	Venturi 600LM	Eric Graham (F)	2975tc	PRV V6	Dunlop	1119	LM-GT1
55	Porsche 911 GT2 Evo	J-C.Miloe/Larbre Compétition (F)	3600tc	F6	Michelin	1180	LM-GT1
88	Ferrari F355 Challenge	Yellow Racing (F)	3496	F129B V12	Michelin	1210	LM-GT2

* Automatic entries (ACO selection). See Non-Prequalifiers table for discarded entries.

1995

ENTRY

The selection committee whittled down 99 applications to 70 and offered guaranteed entries to 20 of them, on an *ad hoc* basis. The remaining 50 were required to prequalify during the Test Day, competing on a class-by-class basis for 34 places in qualifying proper, including four reserves.

Come race week, and most of the 52 cars undergoing the scrutineering process were again GT-type racers: 27 in GT1, and 13 in GT2. There were nine cars in the LM-WSC category, and only three in P2.

Indeed, almost all of an increased manufacturer involvement came in the GT classes, with two works cars from Honda and Nissan, and single entries from new 'supercar' makers Lister and Venturi. Among seven McLarens was the factory's own development car. Jaguar returned with the PC Automotive team, and Toyota was again engaged with SARD. Among the prototypes, Mazda was involved in the Kudzu project, while racing specialists Courage, Debora, Norma and WR operated their own cars. A centre of attention was the first Ferrari prototype here for 23 years, an IMSA WSC racecar for which the factory supplied an engine.

QUALIFYING

Thursday was a great day for the little WR team. Finding six seconds in mechanical and tyre development relative to 1994, William David and Patrick Gonin exploited the light weight of their P2 single-seaters and annexed the front row. The fastest of the three Courage LM-WSC cars was the latest, GM-engined C41 of Eric van der Poele, but it was later disqualified when found to be underweight. So Bob Wollek and Franck Lagorce shared the second row in a French 1-2-3-4, ahead of Thierry Boutsen's 'works' Kremer-Porsche, which had been in a tyre wall on Wednesday.

McLAREN STARS ON A NEW STAGE | 187

LE MANS

ORGANISATION

The most eye-catching alteration to this year's technical regulations was the replacement of the LM-P1/C90 division of 1994 with 'LM-WSC', the ACO's interpretation of IMSA's category. Also this year, the specifications of the engine air-inlet restrictors were linked for the first time to the weights of the cars, as well as their engines: the lighter the car, the less power was available.

For this American season, the ACO had persuaded IMSA to admit prototypes with turbo engines, thereby giving former Group C powertrains another lease of life. A maximum swept volume of 3000cc came with air restrictors. Such LM-WSC cars were now racing against WSC rivals powered by naturally aspirated, production-based engines with IMSA-specified rev limits of 8500rpm for two-valve V8s, and 10,500rpm for four-valve V12s. Minimum weights were set according to the engine volumes and induction systems, and the minimum tyre width was increased to 18 inches. Maximum fuel tankage of 80 litres again applied to all prototypes. LM-P2 was left alone.

LM-GT1 cars could now shed 50 kilos in weight and GT2s no less than 150, the minimum in both classes being set at 900kg. However, the fuel tankage in both GT1 and GT2 was reduced by 20 percent to 100 litres. The maximum tyre widths were unchanged at 14 inches in GT1 and 12 inches in GT2. The controversial 'one-off' rule stayed in GT1, but GT2 cars now had to be based on models that had entered series production before February 1995.

The ACO received so many applications that it decided to add two prefabricated pit garages at the top of pit-lane, and to introduce a Prequalifying process during the Test Day at the end of April. A selection committee listed 20 cars that would be exempted from this process – the first 'automatic entries'.

Also for the first time, a drivers' parade was organized in the Le Mans city centre the evening before the race (above). A big crowd of enthusiastic citizens watched the drivers being taken past in veteran and vintage cars.

The Le Mans Technoparc, built near the circuit to house motorsport specialists and other engineering companies, opened in 1995. Among the first to use premises there were Elf, Méca Auto Système, Synergie Automobile and the short-lived DAMS F1 project.

188 LE MANS 24 HOURS 1990–99

RACE

This was one of the wettest races in Le Mans history. Rain started to fall before it was an hour old, and continued until mid-morning Sunday – and even then there were occasional showers until the chequered flag put an end to everyone's misery.

The WRs were soon under pressure from Wollek's Courage but were running 1-2 when the rain began shortly before 5pm. Then both cars lost time in the pits with faulty oil seals on driveshaft UJs. Later in the evening, under heavy rain, Gonin aquaplaned on the Mulsanne straight and crashed heavily, causing a 45-minute full-course yellow. Gonin was hospitalised with broken ribs.

At the green, those of the 168,000 spectators who remained were surprised to witness the arrival of a fleet of rainworthy McLarens at the front of the race, mixing it with the Courage prototypes until Henri Pescarolo's C41 was terminally starved of fuel by an electrical failure.

Shortly before 8pm, running second and hunting Jochen Mass's McLaren, Mario Andretti crashed Wollek's C36 in the Porsche curves, tripping himself on a pay driver in a Kremer K8. The Courage lost its rear wing and took suspension damage, and 29 minutes passed in pit-lane before Eric Hélary could resume.

This mistake by Andretti left Mass, relatively snug in the cockpit of Dave Price Racing's lead car, at the head of an unexpected McLaren 1-2-3. Philippe Alliot in a GTC entry and Derek Bell in the other DPR entry followed closely.

Soon after dark, Alliot was leading when he was punted off the road in the Porsche curves by a backmarker blinded by his spray. The DPR team went into the night holding the top two positions, Mass co-driving John Nielsen and car owner Thomas Bscher, and Bell his son, Justin, with Andy Wallace. They were now pursued by the factory-supported McLaren of JJ Lehto/Yannick Dalmas/Masanori Sekiya.

Mass was leading by the best part of a lap at 3am, but then he pitted with a badly slipping clutch. The DPR crew took 70 minutes to replace it, but Nielsen drove off the track on his out-lap, and parked with no drive. As the night gave way to a drizzly dawn, Bell/Bell/Wallace were leading from Lehto/Dalmas/Sekiya, and a valiant recovery by Wollek/Andretti/Hélary had yielded third place, although still four laps down. The delayed Courage, Boutsen's Kremer and the Kudzu-Mazda were the only open-cockpit WSC prototypes still racing.

Through the morning, forceful driving by Lehto brought the 'non-works' McLaren close enough to the DPR car to show in the lead during the pitstop sequences, but Bell Sr's hopes of a sixth Le Mans victory stayed intact. Before noon, a strong shift by Wallace put his car a lap ahead again.

It was not to be. At 2pm, Bell was struggling with his gearshift, and the box engaged first gear in the Ford chicane. The car spun through 360deg, and it took a while for Bell to find a gear to get him going again. Later, a routine stop stretched to five minutes, for the same reason.

The 'non-works' McLaren, as grey as the weather, had only to keep going to win the race. With just over an hour remaining, Wollek brilliantly bullied his Courage to within a lap of the leader but, on worn tyres, there was no way he could get any closer. Behind Wallace, more McLarens finished fourth and fifth, just ahead of the Kremer.

One of the factory Hondas won GT2, while a Debora-Cosworth was the only P2 finisher.

LE MANS

A MYTH EXPLODED

Conventional wisdom had it that no manufacturer would win Le Mans at its first attempt. Only Ferrari had ever done it, in 1949. And McLaren's achievement went further. All seven racing versions of the 'F1' in existence started, and displayed remarkable durability and pace in atrocious conditions. F1s were among the fastest cars out there when the rain was at its worst. One was crashed out, another broke its transmission, but the others finished 1-3-4-5, and 13th. The winning F1 GTR (pictured) was raced by JJ Lehto, Yannick Dalmas and Masanori Sekiya.

When McLaren went into production in Woking in 1992 with its innovative three-seat, mid-engined, butterfly-doored sportscar, it had not envisaged racing it. However, designer Gordon Murray had created the ultimate 'supercar', using high-specification structures and running gear developed in the racecar industry. It was stiff, it was light, it had great balance, it had 200mph performance – and it had a flat bottom between the axle lines with a ground-effect rear diffuser.

The F1 was an advanced-composites monocoque, mostly formed of carbonfibre weaves over aluminium-honeycomb core material, with a front bulkhead of magnesium alloy. The carbon/Kevlar body, styled by Peter Stevens and developed in the MIRA wind tunnel and McLaren's own facility, enclosed a cabin in which a central driver's seat was located slightly ahead of a passenger seat on each side.

After Honda had turned him down, McLaren chairman Ron Dennis approached BMW to provide the engine. The manufacturer's accomplished engine chief, Paul Rosche, purpose-designed a compact, lightweight, quad-cam, 6.1-litre, 60deg V12 with variable valve timing, and BMW built, tested and delivered it in only 13 months. It was bolted to lateral chassis extensions and a wide alloy casting, linked to the transmission bellhousing by steel tubes. Controlled by a TAGtronic management system, its output was 625bhp at 7400rpm, driving through a transverse, six-speed McLaren/Getrag gearbox.

In 1994, Dennis was finally persuaded by F1 owners, notably pharmaceuticals entrepreneur Ray Bellm and banker Thomas Bscher, to engineer a GT1 racing version for the 1995 BPR series. Dennis formed McLaren Cars Motorsport and recruited former Spice Engineering managing director Jeff Hazell as the project manager. Murray took the 19th F1 monocoque out of the production line and used it as a prototype to test modifications he designed with Barry Lett, including a non-structural rollcage, an adjustable rear aerofoil, various cooling ducts, and upgraded double-wishbone suspension and braking systems. BMW Motorsport took a close interest and the air-restricted

1995

race version of the 'atmo' V12 was rated at 640bhp at 7500rpm, with the catalytic converters and silencers removed.

After four months of development, six cars were delivered to four racing customers: two to Bscher, two to Bellm and his new racing partner, Lindsay Owen-Jones (who needed another in April to replace a car destroyed at Jarama), and one each to Noël del Bello and Fabien Giroix. The best-driven of these McLarens immediately set the pace in the BPR championship, taking six wins from the first seven four-hour events that preceded Le Mans.

In early May, the prototype completed a 22-hour test at Magny-Cours, evaluating a Le Mans kit and a dry-sump oiling system for the gearbox after several failures. The specification included carbon brakes and, to cool them, NACA ducts in the nose and engine cover. There were modifications to the underbody, extra protection for the radiator inlets, and strengthened lower suspension arms.

The customer teams were dismayed when the unpainted '01R' prototype arrived at Le Mans, attended by several McLaren personnel (including four mechanics). This looked very much like a works entry. McLaren was outraged! The company's line was that this car had been leased to a Japanese-owned company called Kokusai Kaihatsu UK (translation: 'International Development UK'). After a deal with Giroix

McLAREN STARS ON A NEW STAGE | 191

LE MANS

had fallen through, Paul Lanzante, a personal friend of Dennis who was operating a Porsche in the BPR series but had no Le Mans entry, was running the car here. Lanzante Motorsport was also on Le Mans début, but the car was race-engineered by former Spice technical director Graham Humphrys.

The engine of the 'non-works' GTR was over-revved on Thursday, probably because a bent selector rod in the gearbox had damaged the synchros. The crew had to devote Friday to changing the engine and rebuilding the gearbox, and the car was shaken down at 2am on race morning on the adjacent airfield. Another last-minute alarm came with a fuel pump failure on the dummy grid: the car raced throughout with the reserve pump.

After a great opening shift by John Nielsen, the first McLaren driver genuinely to lead the race was his co-driver, Jochen Mass, in the cockpit of one of Bscher's cars (below) operated out of Bookham, Surrey, by David Price. Despite a malfunctioning windscreen wiper, Mass, Nielsen and Bscher himself led on-and-off for more than nine hours. Soon after 3am, however, Mass pitted ahead of schedule, unable to cope any longer with a slipping clutch. After a 70-minute delay, Nielsen drove onto the beach at the second chicane and, with no drive, the car stayed there.

The other DPR-tended F1 (at left, caked in carbon brake dust) was raced by Andy Wallace with father-and-son co-drivers Derek and Justin Bell. Wallace led for a while on Saturday afternoon during a remarkable

LE MANS 24 HOURS 1990–99

triple stint, some of it spent excitingly on slick tyres on a mostly damp track surface. When he finally handed the car to Derek, Price's crew had to spend 12 minutes replacing a broken throttle cable. Derek did a terrific job to claw back both the lost laps and, when the West FM-sponsored sister car had its clutch problem, the yellow Harrods McLaren was right there to take over the lead.

The KK McLaren was now chasing hard. A thoroughly absorbing battle ensued, during which the 'non-works' F1 came close enough to take the lead several times during the fuel-stop sequences. On Sunday morning, more exceptional driving by Wallace established a clear advantage, but then the Harrods F1 had to stop for fresh brake pads. Lehto charged. But 53-year-old Bell showed why he had won this race five times, and matched his lap times – until his transmission started to play up. This caused a 360deg spin in the Virage Ford and later, when he made the car's penultimate fuel stop, a five-minute delay while he found a gear (sixth) to get moving again.

The KK car took over at the front, and for good. Its sole problem was that spray and grit from the track surface were contaminating its external gearshift mechanism, but the crew immersed it in a bath of WD40 lubricant at every pitstop, and it held.

In his final shift, Wallace was hampered by the gear selection problem and could not resist Bob Wollek's Courage WSC racer. After having a car in the lead for 21 hours, the DPR team finished third.

Fourth place fell to one of Bellm's Gulf-liveried McLarens (below), operated out of Cranleigh by GTC Competition under former EMKA Group C constructor Michael Cane. This car started well with a strong double shift by Mark Blundell, but then the team owner crashed in the Porsche curves. The repairs consumed 45 minutes. The Lotus F1 driver and Maurizio Sandro Sala did what

LE MANS

they could to retrieve the situation, and the car reappeared in the top five at half-time.

After Pierre-Henri Raphanel had been delayed early on by a puncture, Philippe Alliot was also quick in the other Gulf car. Just before nightfall, in fact, when the track conditions were at their worst, he passed Mass to take the lead. Forty minutes later, Alliot was clipped from behind in the Porsche curves by a GT2 Porsche he had just overtaken, and punted into the wall.

The French-entered McLarens were not equipped with the full Le Mans kit and raced with ferrous brake discs. Giroix Racing, run by Thierry Lecourt out of a south-eastern Parisian suburb, used a synthetic composite fuel here, based on alcohol distilled from beet. Its owner started but could not fire the engine after his first fuel stop, at a cost of 18 minutes while his crew replaced the starter motor. Olivier Grouillard and Jean-Denis Délétraz eventually hauled the car up to fourth, but finished fifth after a Sunday morning brake change. Bello's F1, run by BBA Compétition from St Ouen, was also delayed early on, by a broken gear selector that cost almost 40 minutes. Marc Sourd, Hervé Poulain and Jean-Luc Maury-Laribière could rise no higher than 13th.

Afterwards the race winner was proudly taken back to Woking, where McLaren continued to deny that it had been a works entry, while the Lanzante team prepared its Porsche for the rest of the BPR series. Nielsen and Bscher went on to clinch the BPR title to conclude McLaren's fantastic maiden season in European sportscar racing.

THE MAIN CHANCE MISSED

The Courage C34 spyder pictured below would surely have won the race had Mario Andretti not allowed himself to be tripped up by a backmarker. The mistake cost Andretti and Bob Wollek a real opportunity finally to complete their illustrious CVs with a Le Mans victory. Neither of these great racing drivers would ever do so, and neither would Yves Courage.

Still based on the original design dating back to the mid-1980s, the C34 was an open-top conversion of the third of the C30 Group C coupés, which had been raced here by Robert/Fabre in 1993-94. Porsche supplied the motors and engineers to oversee them, plus two of the drivers who were to have raced new works WSC cars until the factory shelved the project.

Wollek went fastest in Prequalifying, and headed the Wednesday timesheets with one of Courage's self-prepared engines. For Thursday evening this was replaced by a factory flat-six, which demanded relocation of the turbos and intercoolers. Despite reducing his lap time by five seconds, Wollek slipped to fourth behind the featherweight WR-Peugeots and one of the new Courage-Chevrolets (which was then disqualified).

Race-engineered by Dominique Méliand, Wollek and then Andretti embarked on a purposeful race strategy that found the car handily placed in second position under the evening rain. At 7:45pm came disaster in the left-right ess in the Porsche curves. Andretti came up to lap a Kremer K8 and made a classic Le Mans mistake: he over-estimated the ability of the driver in front. Antonio Hermann braked far earlier than Andretti expected;

he locked up trying to avoid hitting the Kremer, and the Courage spun backwards into the wall, knocking off the rear wing and damaging the right-rear. Andretti hauled the car back into pit-lane, where Méliand's crew laboured for half an hour replacing suspension wishbones and the front and rear bodywork. Eric Hélary rejoined in 28th position, six laps down on the race-leading McLarens.

A tremendous comeback performance, by all three drivers, took back two laps before half-time, and recovered third place. Two more laps were taken back before midday. Going into the final hour, the Courage was only a lap behind and, when the Harrods McLaren was delayed, Wollek found himself in second place once more. He took a whole-hearted tilt at the win but, after his final fuel stop, with a heavier car on worn rubber, he ruefully settled for that position.

DISAPPOINTING ON DÉBUT

The long-delayed début of the Courage C41 World Sports Car was a big letdown. One car was disqualified on Thursday evening, and the other (right) was parked when the race was only two hours old.

Yves Courage decided in 1993 to embark on a WSC project and race it on both sides of the Atlantic, with a view to selling cars to customers. Freelance former Minardi and Peugeot designer Paolo Catone started work in Courage Compétition's Le Mans factory in January 1994. The original intention had been to run the first C41 at Le Mans that June, but this proved to be over-ambitious for this small company.

LE MANS

The C41 was built around a monocoque formed from Aerospatiale-supplied carbonfibre laminates over a honeycomb core, and made in France by Compostiex. The hull was fitted with IMSA's mandatory aluminium rear bulkhead and steel rollhoops. Catone's pushrod suspension systems were made in England by G Force. His bodywork was formed in carbonfibre/Kevlar over Nomex, after more than 200 hours of aero development in the Sardou wind tunnel.

The C41 was designed to take any 'atmo' motor specified by customers. The first chassis was fitted with a 5-litre, 16-valve 'small-block' Chevrolet LT1 V8 prepared by Fritz Kayl's Katech company in Michigan. At IMSA's 8000rpm rev limit, it sent 600bhp to a five-speed longitudinal gearbox supplied by SDC (later known as Intermotion).

The shakedown tests of the C41 were finally carried out on the Le Mans Bugatti circuit in October 1994 and the car was scheduled to début in the 1995 Daytona 24 Hours. For a variety of reasons, however, it was not run in public until the Le Mans Test Day in April 1995, when Eric van der Poele was second fastest behind Bob Wollek in Courage's converted Group C spyder. The team then decided to run two Porsche-engined cars in the race, and only one of the new C41s. However, the team was refused leave to change its entries, and had to scurry to complete a second race-ready C41, for which similar engines were sourced from Comptech in California.

Poele qualified the Comptech C41 third fastest, but the team somehow allowed this car onto the track in final qualifying no less than 17kg underweight, as measured by the ACO's scales at the end of the session. The mistake had arisen from the installation of the aluminium engine instead of the Katech cast-iron block for which the car had been engineered, and a switch from ferrous to carbon-carbon brakes.

The Katech C41 (below), race-engineered by Ricardo Divila, was qualified on the second row by Franck Lagorce, sharing it with the turbo C34. Henri Pescarolo raced in the top six, but Lagorce was halted on the stroke of 6pm by low fuel-pump pressure. A weakened battery, resulting from a failing alternator, was the cause.

THE AMERICAN DREAM

The most notable IMSA WSC project was the Ferrari 333 SP, which brought the manufacturer back to Le Mans with a sports-prototype for the first time since 1973 (right).

Known in Maranello as *Il Sogno Americano* ('the American Dream'), the project resulted from the enthusiasm for IMSA's new class shown by Giampiero Moretti of Momo, his friend Piero Lardi Ferrari (Enzo's son), and Gian Luigi Buitoni, the president of Ferrari North America. The car was designed during 1993 by Mauro Rioli before Tony Southgate was brought on board as a consultant. The car was based on a flat-bottom, carbonfibre/honeycomb monocoque made in Modena by a team led by Giorgio Panini.

1995

The WSC regulations specified that the 'atmo' engine could not displace more than 4000cc and had to be sourced from a production car. Ferrari could use the 4-litre F310E, a 65deg, 60-valve V12 (similar to the Scuderia's contemporary F1 engine) because, in 4.7-litre form, it would power the upcoming F50 road car. With Weber-Marelli fuel injection, it produced about 600bhp in the sportscar racing application and drove through a transverse, five-speed, sequential-shift gearbox. This was designed and made at Dallara Automobili, as were the suspension systems. Dallara was also commissioned to assemble the cars, and its wind tunnel was used by Dialma Zinelli and Giorgio Camaschella to develop the carbon/Kevlar bodywork, featuring a central fin.

The new Ferrari was to be raced only by privateers and the first four cars were allocated to the EuroMotorsport, Momo and Scandia teams. The 333 SP débuted in the third round of the 1994 IMSA series at Road Atlanta, and the first-mentioned teams finished 1-2. In the following round, at Lime Rock, the Italian cars monopolized the podium, and would take three more wins that season, all by Momo.

The 333 SP was conceived as a 'sprint' car and, early in 1995, proved unreliable in the Daytona 24 Hours. But then, with revised bodywork, Scandia managed to win the Sebring 12 Hours.

Antonio Ferrari's Indianapolis-based EuroMotorsport was the first to race a 333 SP at Le Mans; Momo also filed an entry, but missed the deadline… EuroMotorsport went ahead with its entry despite one of its chassis having been written off in Fabrizio Barbazza's career-ending accident at Road Atlanta at the end of April. A spare tub was shipped to Le Mans ahead of the team's arrival, and was built up in the pit garage, where it was equipped with the constructor's endurance racing kit, including a detuned V12 and strengthened gearbox internals. The yellow Ferrari was entrusted to René Arnoux, Jay Cochran and Massimo Sigala.

First in line for scrutineering, it was detained at the first check for an hour while the team and the inspectors argued. The ACO needed to fit its own device (rather than IMSA's) for checking that the 10,500rpm rev limit specified for the Ferrari would not be infringed. The team ultimately had to comply, and the car sat out first qualifying while a Stack recording tachometer, with its flywheel pick-up and reader, was fitted to the V12. On the second evening, Cochran qualified the car a cautious 17th.

Sigala produced a surging early run all the way to third place, but the car stopped out on the track on the seventh lap. The fault was later traced to stone damage to the crankshaft-mounted ignition trigger. After the car had been recovered, and the broken component replaced, the V12 immediately fired up in the garage.

Back across the Atlantic, with four more victories this season, Ferrari won IMSA's Makes title, and Scandia's Fermin Velez the Drivers championship.

McLAREN STARS ON A NEW STAGE 197

LE MANS

HONDA MOVES UP

Although consoled by a GT2 class win, Honda was deeply disappointed in its move up to the GT1 category, which was aimed at this race only. One of its new NSX racecars was retired long before dark and, almost at the same time, the other was crashed so heavily in a rainstorm that the repairs took several hours.

John Thompson's TC Prototypes organization set up its own quasi-works race team to operate these cars, which it had again built on behalf of the factory. TCP's project engineer, Doug Bebb, based the new chassis on the company's neat GT2 car, as run in the 1994 Le Mans by Kremer Racing, which had gone on to win three ADAC GT races. However, Bebb made a fundamental change by turning the transversely mounted 3-litre V6 engine through 90deg. This added to the wheelbase and required redesigned suspension geometry and rear bodywork, but allowed Bebb to use Hewland's six-speed, sequential-shift, inboard-transverse TGT gearbox, in place of the touring car gearbox that had been so fragile in 1994. Other improvements included carbon-carbon brakes. One of the cars bore a Honda-developed engine with two turbochargers, raising the peak power figure of 390bhp at 8000rpm of the naturally aspirated unit to 600bhp at 1.2bar.

Honda's project team, led by Ken Hashimoto and Eiichi Omura, was granted two automatic entries. Philippe Favre attempted to

198 LE MANS 24 HOURS 1990–99

prequalify a third GT1 car, but ran into electrical problems and did not get a flying lap.

After losing track time in qualifying to gearbox problems, the turbo GT1 car (bottom left) went eight seconds faster round the lap than the GT2 version had managed 12 months before. In the race, however, Armin Hahne completed only seven, intermittently driven laps before the team decided not to attempt a clutch replacement.

This decision might have been different had the team known that Favre would soon crash the 'atmo' GT1 Honda (top left) in the rain, incurring damage that took five hours to repair. Hideki Okada and Naoki Hattori used the rest of the race as an extended test session, with no hope of completing enough distance. And an oil leak caused further delay before the finish.

HONDA WINS LE MANS

Team Kunimitsu's one-year-old Honda NSX (above) began to make a big blip on the factory team's radar on Saturday evening. Raced (as in 1994) by Kunimitsu Takahashi, Keiichi Tsuchiya and Akira Iida, it went on to defeat a couple of Corvettes and to outlast all the Porsches, delivering a famous victory in the GT2 class.

The eventual success was unexpected not only because the 3-litre 'atmo' V6 gave away as much as 100bhp to its rivals. The car was in trouble even before the start. A leaking sensor mount in the engine lubrication system caused a flash fire, and Tsuchiya had to join the race from pit-lane. Not long afterwards, the car needed an exhaust system rebuild, and slipped six laps behind the class leaders.

At this juncture, the two works GT1 cars had just run into big trouble, and things were looking bleak for Honda. But the GT2 entry ran like a dream for the rest of the weekend and took full advantage of its low fuel consumption. As rivals faltered, it picked up the class lead soon after 8am and went on to finish eighth overall. The following month, Kunimitsu proved that this had been no fluke by inflicting another GT2 defeat on Porsche in the BPR race at home at Suzuka.

In Prequalifying, another GT2 Honda, entered by former Grand Prix driver Satoru Nakajima, lost chunks of time to a suspension repair, and missed the cut.

WR HITS THE FRONT

One of the most pleasing achievements of Le Mans 1995 was that of Gérard and Rachel Welter's team of volunteers, who not only monopolized the front row of the grid, but led the first hour of the race with their distinctive, central-seat WR-Peugeots.

Mechanically these neat cars were little changed from 1994, although with some strengthened components after 2000km of testing at Paul Ricard. An ignition problem in first qualifying prevented either engine from exceeding 6000rpm and was traced to the incompatibility of new sensors with the Magneti Marelli management system, and they were changed on Thursday morning. Now the drivers of the super-light cars could exploit the full 400bhp. William David's pole position was driven in daylight with the lighter of the carbon/Kevlar bodied cars, and then, in darkness, Patrick Gonin secured the front row. Gonin's car had missed scrutineering because its transporter had been stuck on the *autoroute* from Paris after a traffic accident, but the ACO had helpfully arranged an individual inspection.

McLAREN STARS ON A NEW STAGE | 199

Gonin took the lead at the start (above). On the fourth lap, David was passed by Bob Wollek's Courage before making a quick stop to get his windscreen secured. Even so, the fuel-efficient WRs were running 1-2 at the end of the opening hour.

It was too good to last, of course. In the second hour, Pierre Petit pitted Gonin's car for 16 minutes for a new left-hand driveshaft. The sealing boot on the outer end of the component had split, and the UJ had seized without lubrication. The team improvised additional seals on the other boots, and pitted the sister car for a precautionary change.

The WRs could run four stints on a single set of tyres, which were too hard for the wet conditions. Later, the Safety Cars were deployed for 47 minutes after Gonin had moved off-line in heavy rain to overtake another car between the second Mulsanne chicane and the 'bosse' (the hump), and aquaplaned into a major accident. It took half an hour to extricate him from the inverted car, and he was taken to hospital with minor injuries.

The other WR also went off the road twice but, on each occasion, David was able to reach the pits for repairs. It raced on until late Sunday morning, when the fuel pump packed up.

PLAYING THE GAME

Nissan's factory team returned to Le Mans after a five-year absence, and finished fifth in GT1 with a front-engined car (right) that took 'the spirit of the regulations' to its most literal extreme.

In touring car racing, the Nissan Skyline had become one of the most successful cars of all time, winning many events and National championships in Japan, Australia, Britain and Spain, as well as the blue-riband Internationals at Spa, Bathurst and Macau. In 1993-94, the GT-R version, created by Kazutoshi Mizuno, had dominated Mazda in the first two seasons of the All-Japan GT series, and in 1994 a factory IMSA GTU entry had shown well on début in the Daytona 24 Hours.

This encouraged Nissan to try the GT-R at Le Mans. NISMO brought

200 LE MANS 24 HOURS 1990–99

a pair of upgraded JGTC-specification cars, specially assembled on the road car's pressed-steel monocoque structure. They were powered by new, stronger 'R33' versions of the 2.6-litre, 24-valve straight-sixes, rated at 600bhp at 7600rpm with electronic injection and Garrett turbochargers. Nissan's all-wheel-drive system was not allowed, so the cars were adapted to rear-wheel drive. One GT-R LM had a six-speed Xtrac sequential-shift gearbox, the other a standard five-speed unit, and both were equipped with double-wishbone suspension and carbon brake systems. The carbon-composite body, a little longer and wider than the production version, was developed in NISMO's wind tunnel. The main problem was weight: the lighter of the cars was 130kg heavier than even the ferrous-braked McLarens that shared the class.

The NISMO Le Mans team under Sugawara Takami put its precious, 48-year-old 'superstar', Kazuyoshi Hoshino, with Masahiko Kageyama and Toshio Suzuki in the lighter, six-speed car. The talented Suzuki put on a tremendous charge on Saturday evening that took the GT-R LM to an unlikely seventh overall before dark. It came to naught at 10:50pm, when Kagayama pitted with the one of the gear cogs broken in the sequential 'box. The replacement endured for another 12 hours, until it happened again in the late morning and the car was retired.

The other car (pictured) stayed strong. Hideo Fukuyama, Shunji Kasuya and Masahiko Kondo persevered with a circumspect strategy, designed to finish at any cost. Having suffered minimal mechanical setbacks, they rounded out the top 10, splitting the GT2 Corvettes.

RAIN ON KREMER'S PARADE

After the 1994 Le Mans, the Gulf Kremer K8 was sold back to Kremer Racing, and then on to Franz Konrad. The Kremers completed a second K8, which they ran as a 'works' entry in the 1995 Daytona 24 Hours. Exceeding their wildest dreams, Giovanni Lavaggi, Jürgen Lässig, Marco Werner and Christophe Bouchut won after faster cars had faltered. The team stayed on in Florida for Sebring, but there was no repeat.

A third K8 was built before Le Mans on an all-composite TCP hull, and all three might have been here. Konrad arranged to take over Jan

LE MANS

Vonka's entry (for an LM-P2 PRC) for his K8, with which he had shared victory with Wilson Fittipaldi in the Interlagos 1000 Miles in Brazil in April. The ACO ruled that no change of car was allowed and, instead, Konrad and Antonio Hermann went with the Kremers and shared the Daytona-winning chassis with Lässig. Porsche came to the party and, to partner Bouchut in the new car, supplied Hans-Joachim Stuck and Thierry Boutsen, who had been recruited to race its aborted WSC project. Norbert Singer and other factory team engineers were also on hand to help the Kremers, and both cars were equipped with 3-litre engines from Weissach.

Boutsen qualified fifth but had to start from the pits after a gear selection problem. The team's high hopes were literally dampened when the rain set in: the car turned out to be undriveable on a wet surface. Eventually 12 minutes were invested in fitting softer suspension dampers – to little effect. Then Stuck spun and clipped the barrier on his out-lap from a routine stop, unaware he had been put on intermediate tyres. These dramas sent the car from sixth place to 30th, but the handling was improved considerably a couple of hours later when the crew raised the rear wing and sharpened its angle of attack. A recovery began, and it took the K8 all the way back to sixth place at the end.

The older car (below) also suffered in the rain, and Hermann's excessive caution under braking in the Porsche curves was partly responsible for Mario Andretti's shunt in the second-placed Courage-Porsche. However, Konrad's determination forced the car into the top six at around midnight. The position was thrown away in a number of off-track incidents and later the K8 was afflicted by soaked electrics, which eventually caused its retirement at breakfast time.

PLANTED IN FRANCE

Third place in WSC fell to American driver/constructor Jim Downing's neat Mazda rotary-engined Kudzu (right), co-driven by Yojiro Terada and Franck Fréon. The Kudzu was a quasi-works entry from Mazdaspeed and was invited to this race by the ACO, along with the factory Hondas, Nissans and Toyotas.

Downing had successfully raced Mazda saloons in IMSA series since 1974, all assembled in his workshop in Atlanta, and had moved on to prototypes in 1985, winning the inaugural Camel Lights championship with a Mazda-engined Argo (the first of three consecutive titles). He began to produce his own prototypes in 1988. Downing underlined the Japanese connection by naming them after

LE MANS 24 HOURS 1990–99

1995

a genus of vine from Japan: while working at the US Department of Agriculture during WW2, his father had helped to introduce the fast-growing (and invasive) 'kudzu' plant to southern states for soil erosion control and cattle fodder.

The first three Kudzus were Argo-lookalike Camel Lights coupés, designed by Sam Garret. These 'DG1' sports-racers contested 67 IMSA races between late 1989 and 1993, the first with the twin-rotor Mazda, the others with the Buick V6 (in cars sold to Michael Gue's Essex Racing). Then Garret drew the DG2 to take the Buick and Downing built two, the second for Team Scandia owner Andy Evans. When Mazda offered its triple-rotor engine, Garret designed a spyder evolution and Downing made a sixth monocoque, formed of aluminium honeycomb with carbon-composite structural panels.

First raced in mid-1993, the one-off DG3 won IMSA's inaugural WSC title in 1994 for Wayne Taylor. After a design update by Dave Lynn, it finished third overall in the 1995 Daytona 24 Hours, and was again running third at Sebring in March when 'Butch' Hamlet crashed it as he started the final lap, writing off the chassis against a bridge support.

As this was the car that Downing had entered for Le Mans, he and his crew had to rush to assemble a replacement, using DG3 bodywork and running gear, including carbon brakes, on the team's older DG2 tub. They did a great job to get the car to France six weeks later for Downing to learn the circuit during the Prequalifying weekend.

Full-on support came from Mazdaspeed, which boosted Downing's small team in race week to almost 40, arranged Terada's inclusion, engaged Nigel Stroud as the race engineer, and liveried the car in the same colour scheme as Stroud's 1991-winning Mazda 787B. The 1995 rules restricted the team's engine builder, Rick Engeman, to the triple-rotor R20B engine rather than the more powerful, quad-rotor R26B. Driving through a five-speed March 88T transaxle, and making 465bhp at 8200rpm, it gave away 60-80bhp to the Chevrolet- and Porsche-powered cars that shared the class.

The team lost much of both qualifying days trying to prevent the front end bottoming on the track surface. Only in the race morning warm-up was a failure in the nosebox structure discovered. The crew hurried to fix it, but the car ended up starting the race from pit-lane.

However, durability had been the strongest suit of both previous Kudzu-Mazdas. Amazingly, the car maintained the tradition in this race, deluged, as it was, by about 17 hours of steady rain. The lightweight, low-downforce Kudzu could do three stints on a single set of wet-weather tyres and, after strategically cautious driving on Saturday, it popped up in the top 10 soon after midnight. The car went on to hold down seventh overall throughout the second half, buzzing round like a sewing machine.

It was the first genuine WSC car home, beaten only by two Porsche-powered LM-WSC entries. Mazdaspeed boss Takayoshi Ohashi was delighted, and bought the Kudzu for Mazda's museum.

McLAREN STARS ON A NEW STAGE

LE MANS

COMPETITIVE CORVETTES

Callaway Competition assembled three 'lightweight' GT2 Corvettes over the winter of 1994-95, the first for its own, satellite Callaway Schweiz team, the others to the order of former Venturi owner 'Rocky' Agusta. The new cars, powered by Callaway's version of the Chevrolet LT1 V8 making 480bhp at 6250rpm, were about 60kg lighter than the 1994 racecar, mainly thanks to reinforcing the central structure with steel pressings that were half the production thickness. The 1995 design also incorporated a range of mechanical and aerodynamic refinements.

Callaway accepted the ACO's invitation to enter the 'SuperNatural' that had gone so well the previous June, but his new Schweiz car, a week after a DNF in the Nürburgring BPR race, was crashed heavily in Prequalifying by Enrico Bertaggia. Meanwhile, one of Agusta's cars set the GT2 pace in Almo Coppelli's hands.

Agusta Racing set up a UK base in Brackley, under expert Le Mans team manager Keith Greene. Additional stiffening was built into the frame, the engine and gearbox mountings were strengthened, and the rear wing was relocated. The team did four BPR events before Le Mans, where Greene race-engineered one of the cars. The other was run by Lucien Monté's Synergie company, which had raced the Bugatti here in 1994 and, this year, had prepared a GT1 Aston Martin that narrowly failed to prequalify.

Agusta started qualifying with a six-speed ZF gearbox in one car, and Xtrac's sequential GT unit in the other. After the ZF car suffered two gearbox failures (due to incorrect assembly), it was fitted with an Xtrac transmission on Thursday so that Coppelli could claim the GT2 'pole', and then switched back to another new ZF for the race.

Thorkild Thyrring came under immediate challenge on Saturday from the Stadler team's Porsche but, with Coppelli and Patrick Bourdais co-driving, Agusta's faster car was running second in class and 12th overall at nightfall when it lost 22 minutes replacing the starter motor. At 1am, Thyrring crashed at the first Mulsanne chicane. He got the car back to the pits, but the damage was irreparable.

The Porsche having also just retired, the GT2 lead was now contested by Agusta's Xtrac car (pictured leaving its pit), in the hands of its owner with Robin Donovan and Eugene O'Brien, and Callaway's own entry (top left), driven by Bertaggia with Frank Jelinski and Johnny Unser. Both were racing strongly but under increasing pressure from the Kunimitsu Honda, which could run two and sometimes three laps longer on the fuel. The Corvettes were finally caught on Sunday morning and demoted to second and third in class, with the works car ahead after Agusta's had needed an extra brake pad change.

THE WETTEST WINNERS

For his fourth Le Mans with his Debora sports-prototypes, Didier Bonnet built a new, more powerful P2 *barquette*, based on an aluminium-honeycomb tub designed by former Tiga engineer Roger Rimmer, again fitted with carbon/Kevlar bodywork drawn by Bonnet himself. After the demise of the Coupe Alfa Romeo series, Bonnet switched to the 2-litre Cosworth BDG engine of the Ford Escort Turbo, prepared by FocheAuto to deliver 450bhp at 9000rpm with a single Garrett turbocharger, and driving through a five-speed Hewland FGC gearbox.

Bernard Santal and Patrice Roussel both spun the Debora during the race, and then the car lost 25 minutes for a new radiator to be fitted. Edouard Sezionale was twice stuck out on the circuit with wet electrics, on the second occasion for 45 minutes. But the car survived, and its soaking wet drivers claimed the P2 class victory.

LE MANS

FERRARI HOT IN GT1

The Ferrari F40s alarmed the McLaren teams by qualifying 1-2-3 in the GT1 division, 6-7-8 overall, but only two completed the race, both after delays.

In 1994, two years after the road car had been discontinued, the new BPR championship created a demand for a racing specification for the Ferrari that went further than the F40 LM. Ferrari commissioned Michelotto to create the F40 GT Evoluzione. The aerodynamics were improved in the Fiat wind tunnel, the front and rear track dimensions were increased, the suspension reworked and the gearbox strengthened. Ferrari began to produce 3.5- and later 3.6-litre versions of the twin-turbo V8 with modified exhaust systems, making about 660bhp with the specified air-inlet restrictors.

Luciano della Noce's F40, converted to the GTE specification, was operated here by the Ferrari Club Italia alongside a second car, both with discreet factory support and 3-litre, 620bhp long-distance engines. In addition, Stéphane Ratel's newly formed Pilot Racing team fielded the 3-litre F40 LM with which it was contesting that year's BPR series out of the Le Mans Technoparc. One of the 'lightweight' cars that had been built for the 1990 IMSA series, it was race-prepared there by RF Sport.

These cars had showed competitive form in some of the seven BPR races that preceded Le Mans, and Pilot's car had been the fastest GT1 in Prequalifying in the hands of Michel Ferté. Nevertheless, the steel-braked F40s caused quite a stir in race week when Fabio Mancini, Ferté and Anders Olofsson narrowly outpaced half a dozen McLarens. Olofsson's final qualifying effort was ended by a terrifying, 185mph (300kph) spin when a tyre burst as he shaped up for the Nissan chicane; he calmly got out of the lightly damaged car, strolled to the nearby café, and telephoned his wife in Sweden. In the race, Olofsson's pacy triple shift established a place inside the top 10 but, at 7:50pm, Tetsuya Ota rolled to a halt at Mulsanne corner with a broken gearbox.

Gary Ayles pitted Mancini's GTE (above) after only 35 minutes with an ignition malfunction. The crew spent more than half an hour replacing the battery, the coil and the sparkplugs, but the problem persisted after Massimo Monti had taken the car back on track. By the time it was rectified, the Ferrari was 23 laps behind the leaders – and then a gearbox rebuild consumed another half-hour. It eventually finished 18th after Ayles had tested the gravel trap in the Esses.

After Ferté had been delayed by a punctured tyre on the F40 LM, co-driver Olivier Thévenin was penalized five minutes for overtaking under the full-course yellows. Pictured at right, the car retrieved a top-10

1995

position during the rest of Saturday evening, but a spin by Carlos Palau at dusk damaged the rear bodywork, dropping it to 22nd. Solid night driving recovered eighth position before dawn. However, at 11:35am Ferté was dumped on the beach in the Dunlop curves after an incident with Mark Blundell's McLaren. This delay cost three positions and was followed two hours later by another rear puncture that condemned Thévenin to a 30-minute crawl back to pit-lane, and 12th at the finish. Three weeks later, Ferté/Thévenin raced this LM to victory in the four-hour BPR race at Anderstorp, its only success in the series.

Christian Heinkélé's Yellow Racing team failed to prequalify its Ferrari F355 (right), which had contested GT2 in the BPR races at Ricard and Jarama, but it was later called up to the reserve list. This car – an evolution of the 348 – was prepared by Auvergne Moteurs in Clermont Ferrand to the new-for-1995 Ferrari Challenge specification, with upgraded suspension and braking systems and powertrain modifications including a six-speed transmission. Lucien Guitteny was recruited for race week and went 17 seconds faster than the 380bhp car had managed in Prequalifying, but didn't get to race.

McLAREN STARS ON A NEW STAGE 207

LE MANS

SUFFERING SUPRA

The first appearance by a Toyota Supra racecar outside Japan (above) was a harrowing experience for Shin Kato's quasi-works SARD team.

Prior to coming so close to winning the 1994 Le Mans with an upgraded Group C car, Toyota had decided to continue in sportscar racing under the emerging new regulations and had initiated separate projects for the upcoming LMP and GT1 categories. Toyota Racing Developments based its GT racecar on the front-engined Supra model.

Former Dome engineer Ken-Ichi Mitani was charged with the chassis and suspension design of the Supra, and for the aero development in TRD's full-scale wind tunnel. The selected engine was the proven, 2.1-litre 3S GTE four-cylinder, which had seen extended service both in Group C and – with Eagle – in IMSA GTP. Turbocharged to produce 650bhp at 7500rpm, it was installed in the Supra's steel chassis with Xtrac's six-speed sequential gearbox.

The prototype Supra GT was tested in August 1994 and SARD débuted the car with Jeff Krosnoff at Sugo in September. TRD then assembled LM-specification cars for SARD and Trust to race in the 1995 Le Mans. SARD's GT-LM was damaged by Krosnoff on the Ti circuit in April and, a couple of weeks later, Trust's was wrecked by Thomas Danielsson at Fuji while being shaken down for Le Mans Prequalifying. Only Kato's car made it to race week, for which he renewed with Krosnoff and Mauro Martini (who had raced his 94C-V to second place 12 months before) and signed Marco Apicella.

Krosnoff was very strong in the early stages but the car slipped back when Apicella stopped at 6:20pm for the undertray to be secured. The recovery was thwarted at 9:30pm when the team had to replace the gearbox, which took just under an hour. Throughout the rain thereafter, the drivers struggled manfully with aquaplaning, and they were wide-eyed with exhaustion when the Supra finished 14th.

CLUTCHES OF STRAW

Although Shin Kato's SARD company was actively racing the works Toyota Supra GT, it believed that the mid-engined MR2 was a better bet for the GT1 class and initiated its own project in its Higashimachi workshop, also homologating a single road car. The SARD MC8-R was a lengthened

1995

SW20-series MR2, housing a 4-litre Lexus V8 fitted with two KKK turbos, good for about 600bhp at 6100rpm, sent through a Hewland six-speed gearbox. The car was overweight and this was its first race. It was beset by new-car and other problems. A drooping diffuser in qualifying hindered Kenneth Acheson and Alain Ferté, and team manager Hervé Maréchal realized that the failure of third driver Tomiko Yoshikawa (a Japanese TV celebrity) to qualify made it impossible for the car to complete the race.

Before this consideration came into play, the car (bottom left) started almost 90 minutes late from the pit-lane as a result of a clutch problem during the warm-up. Soon Ferté returned to the pits for another new clutch. Eventually the car consumed the team's stock of spare clutches, and was parked.

AN EXPENSIVE WEEKEND

One of only four privately entered GT1 Porsches finished, after all Larbre Compétition's cars had been eliminated by accidents.

Porsche had long accepted that it could not beat the mid-engined McLaren F1 with its traditional design, which had the mass of the engine behind the rear axle. Pending the arrival of a mid-engined GT1 car, Porsche was pinning its hopes on success in GT2 with its new 'customer' cars. However, it accommodated a few owners wanting a GT1 package, including Jack Leconte's Normandy-based team.

The 'GT2 Evo' specification, devised by Roland Kussmaul, included a taller rear wing assembly with enlarged turbo air inlet ducts, lightened doors, revised arches to take wider tyres, and an improved ABS with bigger brakes. Larbre took delivery of two brand-new cars on the Monday of race week, after Jürgen Barth had shaken them down on Friday at the Weissach test track. They had factory-supplied M64/83 engines, making 600bhp at 7200rpm with a special intake manifold, conrods, pistons and camshaft, and uprated KKK turbos.

Larbre had started the BPR series with three consecutive second places behind McLarens with Jean-Pierre Jarier, Bob Wollek and Christophe Bouchut. With his regular co-drivers released to race prototypes here, Jarier was partnered by Erik Comas and Jesús Pareja. Pictured above, they reached fourth overall before it was dark but at 9:35pm Pareja hit the wall in the Porsche curves. Stéphane Ortelli, Emanuel Collard and Dominique Dupuy stepped up for the team and themselves annexed fourth place, but at 11:10pm Collard was punted out of the race by Andreas Fuchs's GT2 Porsche under braking for Mulsanne corner.

Larbre took over Jean-Claude Miloe's reserve entry to run an older third car, fitted with a lower-specification, 550bhp M64/81 engine prepared in its Caën raceshop, and driven by the team owner with Pierre Yver and refrigerated truck manufacturer Jean-Luc Chéreau. Yver went into the gravel trap at Arnage at 7:45pm; he managed to extricate the damaged car, but it only went as far as the Porsche curves.

The only GT1 Porsche to finish was a 3.8-litre, 720bhp version, built in Karlsruhe by Manfred Freisinger's team with an enlarged M64/04 engine.

McLAREN STARS ON A NEW STAGE

LE MANS

Pictured above, this car, with Wolfgang Kaufmann at the wheel, went off at Arnage in the twilight and then more seriously in the first Mulsanne chicane; he recovered the car and stopped for attention to the rear brakes. The car slipped far down the order, and its recovery was thwarted when a new gearbox had to be fitted late on Sunday morning.

XJ EXPLOITS

This year's Prequalifying sessions included three Jaguar XJ220Cs. One of two new cars with which Hugh Chamberlain was contesting the 1995 BPR Global GT series was afflicted by an elusive misfire and missed the cut, but two ex-works cars entered by Richard Piper's PC Automotive team were sent briskly through to race week by Win Percy (the Jaguar he had driven here in 1993) and Tiff Needell (the ex-Cochran car).

These cars, which had been idle through 1994, had been purchased by PC patron Tony Brooks and were undertaking a BPR season under the engineering management of Chris Crawford and Bob Skene, with their Motronic-controlled, twin-turbo V6 motors reworked by TWR Engines to make 600bhp at 7600rpm. The Jaguars still gave away 40bhp to the McLarens – and 50kg in weight.

Nevertheless, the car shared by Needell, James Weaver and the team owner (top right) made a real impact under the rain on Saturday afternoon and into the night. From 22nd on the grid, it moved into fourth overall behind three McLarens as darkness fell, and held it strongly until shortly before half-time, when the V6 abruptly broke its crankshaft.

In the sister car (left), Bernard Thuner lost a lot of ground to a puncture early in the second hour but, with Percy and Olindo Iacobelli as his co-drivers, retrieved a place in the top 10 before midnight. At 3am, Percy pitted after going off the road, arriving for attention with the front end dragging along the track surface. He resumed after a 50-minute stop but the suspension damage had made the car undriveable, and Crawford's crew gave up on the repair at 7am.

1995

McLAREN STARS ON A NEW STAGE 211

LE MANS

STORM HITS FRANCE

The new Lister Storm GT1 (below) was only raced at Le Mans this season, but certainly made an impression, and not only with the wonderful noise it made.

Starting in 1954, Brian Lister had produced about 50 sports-racing cars that had gained iconic status in British motorsport circles. Lister-Jaguars had been raced at Le Mans in 1959 (when production ceased) and 1963. The marque was revived in 1986 when, with Lister's personal support, Laurence Pearce began to use the name to brand a series of highly modified Jaguar road cars, notably the XJS. In 1991, Pearce resolved to create his own Jaguar-powered, 200mph 'supercar'. His engineering team produced a carbonfibre-reinforced aluminium frame to take a front-mounted, 7-litre V12 and a longitudinal, six-speed Getrag transmission, and fabricated a brutal-looking body, mainly in aluminium alloy. The first Lister Storm was completed in his factory in Leatherhead, Surrey, two years later. The 2+2 Storm was inevitably very expensive, and only four would ever be sold.

Pearce resolved to convert one of the road cars to racing GT1 specification and to promote the brand in the 1995 Le Mans. Fitted with a Zytek-controlled engine (prepared by TWR Engines to make 620bhp at 6500rpm), a Hewland SGT gearbox, a steel rollcage, a carbon/Kevlar body and racing brakes, the car was completed just in time for Geoff Lees to drive it in Prequalifying. The Storm GTS progressed to race week as a reserve, under the direction of former TOMS GB boss Glenn Waters.

Joined by Rupert Keegan and Dominic Chappell, Lees qualified the Storm towards the back of the GT1 class, but splitting the Jaguars. The crew had to scurry to replace a busted gearbox after the race morning warm-up, but this was a promising début until 8:50pm, when Keegan spun into the gravel at one of the Mulsanne chicanes. The clutch was wrecked as the car was extricated.

PORSCHES BEATEN IN GT2

The new-generation, 993-series Porsche 911 GT2 'customer' racecar, introduced this season, won the class 10 times from 12 BPR events, but missed out at Le Mans. The ACO had a big choice in GT2 for this race and only six of the new Porsches took the start. Three were still around 24 hours later – well beaten by the Honda and a couple of Corvettes.

Porsche employed some of the specification of its one-off 1993 Turbo S Le Mans for the new GT2 car, which was equipped with the TAGtronic-controlled, air-cooled, twin-turbo, 3.6-litre M64/81 flat-six. The drive was handled by a six-speed, all-synchro Porsche/Getrag manual gearbox. The front suspension was by MacPherson struts, the rear by a multi-link layout, and weight was reduced by a GRP rear wing and nose, tail and door panels.

Two of these 3.6-litre, 450bhp Porsches had the pace to win the division, but both were crashed. The one prepared by Erwin and Manfred Kremer for a third Le Mans foray by Dirk-Reiner Ebeling's Heico team (above) climbed into seventh place overall before it was dark, but then Tomas Saldana went off in the Porsche curves. Reinach-based Stadler Motorsport, which entered this race on the back of four BPR class wins, also had a fast car (right) and it was sixth overall when Andreas Fuchs punted the back of one of the Larbre team's GT1 Porsches at the end of the Mulsanne straight, putting both cars into the sand.

Rookie Charles Margueron's accident had already eliminated the Haberthur team's other Swiss-entered car (co-driven by Jo Siffert's son, Philippe), and the best finisher of Porsche's more cautiously paced survivors was the GT2 entered by Peter Seikel, fourth in the class ahead of those of Jean-François Veroux (bottom right) and Richard Jones.

Obermaier Racing's GT2 Porsche missed the cut in Prequalifying.

WAKING UP IN WILTSHIRE

A welcome addition to the GT2 class this year was a two-car team from Marcos Cars, the niche sportscar manufacturer in Westbury, Wiltshire. Both were still racing at lunchtime on Sunday but one failed to finish and the other was unclassified.

Marcos had entered the 24 Hours on three occasions in the 1960s and the LM600 was its first Le Mans car since 1967. The front-engined racer was evolved from the LM500s with which Team Marcos had entered the British GT series in 1994, winning a couple of races with Chris Hodgetts. The square-section steel spaceframe was drawn by Colin Denyer and Chris Lawrence with an aluminium floor and honeycomb reinforcement

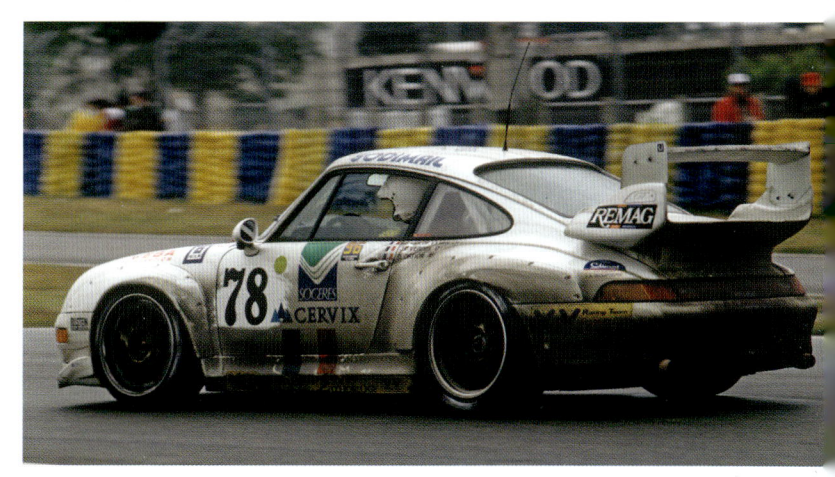

McLAREN STARS ON A NEW STAGE 213

LE MANS

plates. The frame was fitted with MacPherson strut front suspension and a double-wishbone rear layout, and clad in polyester bodywork shaped like Dennis Adams's design for the 1992 Mantara road car. In place of the LM500's Rover V8, the engine outrigger frame carried a 6.3-litre, 32-valve Chevrolet LT5 V8 prepared by Lozano Bros in the USA. Rated at 500bhp at 6250rpm, this drove via a longitudinal Hewland STA five-speed sequential-shift gearbox, attached to the engine by a Marcos-produced bellhousing.

Ahead of Prequalifying, Marcos expanded its works team under Dave Prewitt, and Hodgetts took an LM600 to a maiden victory at Donington. David Leslie then prequalified on the pace of the slower Porsche 911 GT2s.

The Marcos raced by Hodgetts, Cor Euser and Thomas Erdos, race-engineered by Denyer, charged towards the front on Saturday evening. Pictured at left, it was up to 18th overall (fourth in class) before dark, but then Euser was in the escape road at the first Mulsanne chicane, and tapped the tyre wall there. Damage was slight, but soon its driver pitted for a new electronics black box and repairs to the exhaust system, losing almost half an hour. The LM600 was strong again through the night and into the morning, but was stuck out on the circuit at 11:40am by a broken driveshaft UJ.

The other Marcos (above), managed by Roy Baker, was raced by Leslie with François Migault and Chris Marsh, the son of the co-founder of Marcos, Jem Marsh. This car had its gearbox changed after it had leaked oil during the Saturday morning warm-up. An electrical failure stranded Migault out at Tertre Rouge at 6:30pm, but he got out, removed the bonnet, and tried to fashion a temporary repair. Baker sent a couple of mechanics to the scene to offer advice from a discreet distance, and Migault never gave up. Almost three hours later, he miraculously reappeared in pit-lane, where the crew put Leslie back on track in 10 minutes. The car then ran reliably enough to the finish, but was not classified.

Later in the summer, Hodgetts and Erdos (who won at Brands Hatch) were very competitive in British GT, and the GT2 title went to the former.

214 LE MANS 24 HOURS 1990–99

1995

ADIEU TO VENTURI

This year Venturi lost several of its customers but tried to retrieve the situation by preparing and entering a specially configured works car for the first time (below). This 600S-LM showed great form on début, beaten in GT1 qualifying only by one of the McLarens (and the three Ferraris). Driven by Le Mans rookie Jean-Marc Gounon, it went more than 10 seconds faster than the best 600LM had gone 12 months before, lapping well inside four minutes. Alas, its competitiveness did not last long on Saturday.

Venturi Compétition was now under the leadership of Denis Morin, who had raced a variety of cars here in the period 1979-94. He commissioned Méca Système to build a stiffer, lighter, part-carbon chassis and produced an entirely new aerodynamic set-up, packaging the front splitter, the rear diffuser, the wing and other outer surfaces to generate more downforce for similar drag. The brakes were again improved and EIA Moteurs further modified the 3-litre PRV V6 with a new fuelling system and uprated turbos. The modifications were tested at Paul Ricard and on Venturi's private track.

Gounon spent the first two laps in sixth place, the third lap in fifth – and then a water hose came apart. The V6 was seriously overheated, damaging a head gasket. The works mechanics spent two hours rebuilding one cylinder bank and replacing a turbo. Gounon, Paul Belmondo and Arnaud Trévisiol attempted a revival but the 600S-LM had never been out in the rain, and didn't like it. The car was further delayed by niggling problems and, although still running, was not classified as a finisher.

The other Venturis were two-year-old chassis, upgraded to the 600LM specification by BBA Compétition (which hedged its bets with a McLaren in this race) and by Auto Vitesse for Eric Graham. BBA's car was eliminated by an engine-bay fire soon after 6am, and Graham's (above) by an electrical failure after midday.

Although Venturis were raced in National events well into the 2000s, these were the last to race at Le Mans. The following year, BBA failed to get its 600LM (upgraded to the S-specification) through Prequalifying. Venturi was bought by Thai entrepreneur Seree Ravkit but, with dramatically shrinking demand, the company entered administration in January 2000. The remnants were purchased from the receiver by Monegasque Gildo Pallanca Pastor, who saw a future based not on gentleman-racer performance, but on electric engines.

McLAREN STARS ON A NEW STAGE

LE MANS

CANNIBAL CORVETTE

A fourth Chevrolet in this race was over-ambitiously prepared for the GT1 category by Corvette Challenge series entrant Doug Rippie, the man behind the series of high-performance 'Black Widow' Corvette road cars. Rippie built two ZR-1s in Plymouth, Minnesota, using a body shape and single-plane rear wing that had been designed for GM by Bob Riley for IMSA GTO and Trans-Am racing in 1987. The ladder-frame chassis was fitted with Rippie's wishbone suspension systems, and equipped with his take on Chevrolet's 32-valve, 6.3-litre LT5 V8, which had been developed by Lotus Engineering for the ZR-1. Driving through a five-speed Weismann gearbox, Rippie's engines made 575bhp at 6800rpm.

Rippie formed a non-profit corporation, ZR-1 Corvette Team USA, to help finance his Le Mans effort with contributions from America's enthusiastic Corvette community. The team débuted this overweight car at Sebring in March because it was cheaper to enter the 12 Hours than to hire a circuit for testing. It failed to finish, but was invited by the ACO to Le Mans anyway. The underfinanced team was still unable to undertake proper track-testing, and it showed.

The Corvette (left) only just qualified with an engine that had lost compression on several cylinders. It was replaced before the race, but John Paul Jr stopped the car only 15 minutes after the start when the new V8 overheated. It took him half an hour to restart it and get back to the pits. The Corvette spent much of Saturday there while the crew replaced the cylinder heads with those from the practice engine. Against expectations, the cannibalized V8 last until midday Sunday.

NORMA FAILS AGAIN

Having moved on from his Le Mans disappointment in 1990, Norbert Santos built a series of 3-litre Alfa Romeo 164 engined sports-racing cars to contest national circuit races and hillclimbs. A 1992 Le Mans entry for Noël del Bello failed to materialize but, in 1995, Santos reappeared at Le Mans with his latest evolution, the Norma M11, which was powered by a 4.5-litre Buick V6 race-prepared by Jim Ruggles.

The team had done a 1000km test at Nogaro and, on Wednesday, Dominique Lacaud lapped the Norma (left) on the same pace as the Kudzu, but then persistent engine problems intervened. His co-drivers never got into the car.

Despite its Le Mans setbacks, Norma Auto Concept successfully continued to produce branded sports-racing cars for many years.

216 LE MANS 24 HOURS 1990–99

1995

TIGA TRIBULATION

French entrant Sylvan Boulay created a WSC racecar (right) by fitting polyester spyder bodywork to his seven-year-old Tiga GC287 aluminium monocoque, a veteran of three IMSA Lights championships in the USA. Boulay and former ALD engineer Jean-Paul Sauvée converted the car in his Vitré workshop, east of Rennes, retaining its 500bhp, 4.5-litre Buick V6 (built by Jim Ruggles) and Hewland DGB transmission. The three rookies who tried in vain to qualify the 'FJ94' never saw that much power.

A GT1 ASTON MARTIN

One of the marques conspicuously missing from Le Mans in this decade was Aston Martin. Plans to extend its Le Mans programme into the 1990s with the Protech organization had come to nothing with the bankruptcy of Protech early in 1990 and the acquisition of Aston Martin by the Ford Motor Company. The nearest Aston Martin came was with this one-off, independently produced GT1 racecar, which Prequalified as a reserve.

This project was initiated by French publishing millionaire Michel Hommell, who acquired a DB7 shell from the manufacturer and commissioned the build from Lucien Monté's Synergie company in Le Mans. Richard Williams supplied two detuned, 6.3-litre versions of the AMR-1 Group C V8, sending 620bhp to a six-speed ZF transmission. Synergie added carbon/Kevlar body panels and doors but the end product still weighed 1330kg.

The DB7 (right) was finished only just in time for Prequalifying and not even the skills of Eric Hélary and Alain Cudini could overcome the lack of test mileage. Hélary missed the GT1 cut by less than four seconds. The Aston Martin was listed as the third reserve in the class but Hommell was so exasperated that he withdrew the car and put it in his private museum.

The first non-prequalifiers at Le Mans included the VBM, a spaceframe Ford GT40 lookalike built with the backing of former Le Mans driver Michel Elkoubi by French engineers Patrick Bornhauser and Jean-François Metz, which ran into turbo problems on its PRV V6. Ascari Cars, a new British 'supercar' manufacturer, also failed to make the cut with a GT1 racing version of its first FGT road car, built for Dutch customer Klaas Zwart.

McLAREN STARS ON A NEW STAGE 217

LE MANS

24 HEURES DU MANS
17-18 JUIN 95
TCP HONDA
JACCS
KENWOOD
RAYBRIG
ANTAR
DUNLOP
BEUCRAT
HONDA
SARTHE
CIRCUIT INTERNATIONAL DU MANS - A.S.A. AUTOMOBILE CLUB DE L'OUEST
Billets en vente dans les Fnac
FRANCE info 105.5

1995

HOURLY RACE POSITIONS

Prequalifying			Start	Time	Car	No	Drivers	1	2	3	4	5	6	7	8	9	10	11	12	13	14	15	16	17	18	19	20	21	22	23	24
3	3:53.42	David	1	3:46.05	WR LM94/5	9	David/Bouvet/Balandras	1	5	24	30	26	18	16	12	22	16	18	19	17	17	15	13	13	13	19	DNF			
*	3:51.84	Gonin	2	3:48.10	WR LM95	8	Gonin/Petit/Rostan	2	29	28	39	DNF																		
2	3:50.65	Poele	DSQ	3:48.38	Courage C41	12	Poele/Beretta/Tomlje	DNS																						
1	3:49.31	Wollek	3	3:48.76	Courage C34	13	Wollek/Andretti/Hélary	3	4	3	2	25	15	13	8	6	6	5	3	3	3	3	3	3	3	3	3	3	3	2
*			4	3:52.34	Courage C41	11	Pescarolo/Lagorce/Bernard	6	8	39	DNF																			
5	3:57.53	Bouchut	5	3:55.09	Kremer K8	4	Stuck/Boutsen/Bouchut	11	6	29	24	20	13	11	7	5	6	7	6	6	6	6	6	6	6	6	6	6	6	6
6	3:58.11	Olofsson	6	3:55.15	Ferrari F40 GTE	41	Ayles/Monti/Mancini	42	42	41	38	36	34	33	32	30	30	29	29	27	27	24	24	22	22	20	18	19	19	18
4	3:55.51	M.Ferté	7	3:55.69	Ferrari F40 LM	34	M.Ferté/Thévenin/Palau	18	15	12	9	21	14	22	16	14	14	11	11	8	8	8	8	8	8	11	10	12	12	12
10	3:59.23	Olofsson	8	3:56.01	Ferrari F40 GTE	40	Olofsson/Noce/Ota	13	10	16	25	35	35	DNF																
9	3:59.09	Dalmas	9	3:57.18	McLaren F1 GTR	59	Dalmas/Lehto/Sekiya	9	9	5	6	5	4	3	3	3	2	2	2	2	2	1	1	2	2	2	2	1	1
*			10	3:57.64	Venturi 600S-LM	44	Gounon/Belmondo/Trévisiol	46	47	45	44	41	39	37	35	32	32	31	31	29	29	28	27	27	26	25	23	22	21	21	21
*	4:01.37	Blundell	11	3:58.47	McLaren F1 GTR	24	Blundell/Sala/Bellm	7	3	15	35	29	22	14	10	8	7	7	5	5	5	4	4	4	4	4	4	4	4
7	3:58.78	Nielsen	12	3:58.56	McLaren F1 GTR	49	Nielsen/Mass/Bscher	4	2	1	1	2	1	1	1	1	9	DNF												
12	4:00.07	Wallace	13	3:58.80	McLaren F1 GTR	51	Bell/Bell/Wallace	5	1	2	4	3	3	2	2	2	2	1	1	1	1	2	2	1	1	1	1	2	3
8	3:58.79	Raphanel	14	3:59.05	McLaren F1 GTR	25	Alliot/Raphanel/Owen-Jones	8	7	4	3	2	1	10	DNF															
11	4:00.03	Grouillard	15	3:59.66	McLaren F1 GTR	50	Giroix/Deletraz/Grouillard	26	35	27	20	15	10	9	5	7	5	4	4	4	4	§	5	5	5	5	5	5	5
*			16	4:00.02	Kremer K8	3	Lässig/Konrad/Hermann	10	11	7	7	11	9	7	6	15	15	16	14	11	16	19	21	21	DNF				
*			17	4:00.07	Ferrari 333SP	1	Arnoux/Cochran/Sigala	43	44	DNF																				
*			18	4:02.91	Porsche 911 GT2 Evo	37	Collard/Ortelli/Dupuy	22	19	11	10	8	5	4	24	DNF														
*	4:03.83	Downing	19	4:03.07	Kudzu DG2/3	5	Downing/Terada/Fréon	23	20	10	14	16	16	17	11	9	8	8	7	7	7	7	7	7	7	7	7	7	7
17	4:05.23	Sourd	20	4:04.52	McLaren F1 GTR	42	Sourd/Poulain/Maury-Laribière	44	41	38	37	34	32	29	23	23	20	19	17	15	15	13	14	14	15	13	13	13	13
19	4:06.76	Lacaud	DNQ	4:04.89	Norma M14	6	Lacaud/Libert/Dro	DNS																						
16	4:05.14	Dupuy	21	4:05.36	Porsche 911 GT2 Evo	36	Jarier/Comas/Pareja	12	16	6	5	4	DNF																	
14	4:03.63	Needell	22	4:08.67	Jaguar XJ220C	57	Weaver/Needell/Piper	27	13	9	11	6	6	5	4	4	8	8	6	DNF									
26	4:14.57	Coppelli	23	4:09.19	Callaway Corvette	76	Thyrring/Coppelli/Bourdais	25	23	17	15	13	12	24	19	16	28	DNF											
20	4:08.74	Lees	24	4:09.21	Lister Storm GTS	52	Lees/Keegan/Chappell	38	31	34	34	38	DNF																
13	4:03.29	Percy	25	4:09.45	Jaguar XJ220C	58	Percy/Thuner/Iacobelli	14	25	22	19	17	11	12	9	10	10	14	24	25	25	25	DNF						
*			26	4:09.61	Nissan Skyline GT-R LM	23	Hoshino/Suzuki/Kageyama	17	17	14	12	9	7	8	26	24	21	17	16	14	13	18	22	23	23	DNF			
15	4:04.08	Kaufmann	27	4:09.91	Porsche 911 BiTurbo	54	Kaufmann/Ligonnet/Hane	20	12	18	18	14	25	23	21	18	20	18	16	14	14	15	15	14	17	18	19	18	19
*			28	4:10.12	Honda NSX GT1 Turbo	47	Capelli/Hahne/Gachot	43	45	DNF																				
23	4:09.41	Clérico	29	4:10.21	Venturi 600LM	43	Lécuyer/Clérico/Chauvin	40	32	31	29	27	24	21	19	22	21	21	23	23	DNF								
*			30	4:10.36	Toyota Supra GT-LM	27	Krosnoff/Apicella/Martini	16	14	20	16	12	27	32	30	27	26	25	22	21	19	19	16	16	15	14			
*			31	4:11.03	SARD Toyota MC8-R	26	A.Ferté/Acheson	48	46	44	43	42	40	38	36	34	34	33	33	DNF									
29	4:15.37	Calderari	32	4:12.48	Porsche 911 GT2	79	Calderari/Bryner/Fuchs	24	18	8	13	10	8	6	28	DNF													
21	4:08.86	Yver	33	4:13.22	Porsche 911 GT2 Evo	55	Luc/Chéreau/Leconte	32	26	26	33	37	36	35	DNF														
*			34	4:14.43	Nissan Skyline GT-R LM	22	Fukuyama/Kondo/Kasuya	37	24	25	22	22	17	15	13	11	12	10	10	9	9	9	10	11	11	10	11	10	10
24	4:11.24	Lesseps	35	4:15.00	Venturi 600LM	45	Graham/Lesseps/Birbeau	36	37	36	32	32	31	30	29	27	26	25	26	21	21	20	20	20	21	21	DNF		
27	4:14.85	Takahashi	36	4:15.55	Honda NSX GT	84	Takahashi/Tsuchiya/Iida	19	40	37	31	30	26	20	19	16	15	13	11	12	11	9	9	8	8	8	8		
*			37	4:15.88	Callaway Corvette	73	Jelinski/Unser/Bertaggia	31	28	30	26	23	20	18	14	13	12	10	10	11	10	10	9	9	9	9			
25	4:14.09	Santal	38	4:16.01	Debora LMP295	14	Santal/Roussel/Sezionale	29	34	33	27	33	33	31	31	29	29	28	28	26	24	23	22	21	20	19	20	20	20
*			39	4:16.12	Callaway Corvette	75	Donovan/O'Brien/Agusta	30	21	19	15	19	23	20	15	12	11	13	12	11	10	12	12	12	12	11	11		
35	4:21.27	Saldana	40	4:17.10	Porsche 911 GT2	91	Saldana/Castro/Bourbon	28	22	13	8	7	26	DNF															
32	4:17.64	Margueron	41	4:17.33	Porsche 911 GT2	82	Thoisy/Siffert/Margueron	15	43	43	42	DNF																	
*			42	4:18.93	Marcos 600LM	70	Euser/Hodgetts/Erdos	21	30	23	21	18	21	25	22	18	25	27	27	24	26	25	25	25	24	24	DNF		
34	4:21.04	Leslie	43	4:21.13	Marcos 600LM	71	Leslie/Migault/Marsh	41	38	40	40	39	37	34	33	31	30	28	27	26	24	23	22	22	NC				
*			44	4:22.36	Honda NSX GT1	46	Okada/Favre/Hattori	33	39	42	41	40	38	36	34	33	32	32	30	29	28	28	27	26	25	23	23	NC	
33	4:20.48	Adams	45	4:23.24	Porsche 911 GT2	81	Adams/Jones/McQuillan	35	36	35	31	28	27	26	23	21	22	20	20	18	18	18	18	17	17	17			
31	4:17.39	Dickens	46	4:23.35	Porsche 911 GT2	77	Seikel/Kuster/Dolejsi	39	33	32	28	30	29	27	25	24	22	20	18	17	17	14	14	15	15				
18	4:06.22	Jones	DNQ	4:23.57	Tiga FJ94	7	Jones/Massé/Provost	DNS																						
36	4:22.06	Ortion	47	4:24.69	Porsche 911 GT2	78	Vyver/Ortion/Veroux	34	27	21	23	21	19	22	18	17	17	24	21	19	18	16	16	15	15	14	16	16	
*			48	4:27.89	Chevrolet Corvette ZR1	30	Paul/McDougall/Mero	47	48	46	45	43	41	39	37	35	34	34	31	31	30	29	29	28	27	26	24	DNF	
*			RES	4:30.19	Ferrari F355 Challenge	88	Heinkélé/Guitteny/Oborn	-																					

DNF Did not finish **DNQ** Did not qualify **DSQ** Disqualified **FS** Failed scrutineering **NC** Not classified as a finisher **RES** Reserve not required * Automatic entry

LE MANS

RACE RESULTS

Pos	Car	No	Drivers			Laps	Km	Miles	FIA Class	DNF
1	McLaren F1 GTR	59	Yannick Dalmas (F)	JJ Lehto (SF)	Masanori Sekiya (J)	298	4055.800	2520.152	LM-GT1	
2	Courage C34	13	Bob Wollek (F)	Mario Andretti (USA)	Eric Hélary (F)	297	4046.339	2514.274	LM-WSC	
3	McLaren F1 GTR	51	Derek Bell (GB)	Justin Bell (GB)	Andy Wallace (GB)	296	4030.430	2504.388	LM-GT1	
4	McLaren F1 GTR	24	Mark Blundell (GB)	Maurizio Sandro Sala (BR)	Ray Bellm (GB)	291	3966.833	2464.871	LM-GT1	
5	McLaren F1 GTR	50	Olivier Grouillard (F)	Jean-Denis Deletraz (CH)	Fabien Giroix (F)	290	3956.324	2458.341	LM-GT1	
6	Kremer K8	4	Hans-Joachim Stuck (D)	Thierry Boutsen (B)	Christophe Bouchut (F)	289	3939.401	2447.826	LM-WSC	
7	Kudzu DG2/3	5	Jim Downing (USA)	Yojiro Terada (J)	Franck Fréon (F)	282	3846.505	2390.103	LM-WSC	
8	Honda NSX GT	84	Kunimitsu Takahashi (J)	Keiichi Tsuchiya (J)	Akira Iida (J)	275	3746.959	2328.248	LM-GT2	
9	Callaway Corvette SuperNatural	73	Frank Jelinski (D)	Johnny Unser (USA)	Enrico Bertaggia (I)	273	3713.295	2307.330	LM-GT2	
10	Nissan Skyline GT-R LM	22	Hideo Fukuyama (J)	Masahiko Kondo (J)	Shunji Kasuya (J)	271	3695.879	2296.508	LM-GT1	
11	Callaway Corvette SuperNatural	75	Robin Donovan (GB)	Eugene O'Brien (GB)	Ricardo 'Rocky' Agusta (I)	271	3686.061	2290.408	LM-GT2	
12	Ferrari F40 LM	34	Michel Ferté (F)	Olivier Thévenin (F)	Carlos Palau (E)	270	3681.213	2287.395	LM-GT1	
13	McLaren F1 GTR	42	Marc Sourd (F)	Hervé Poulain (F)	Jean-Luc Maury-Laribière (F)	266	3623.945	2251.811	LM-GT1	
14	Toyota Supra GT-LM	27	Jeff Krosnoff (USA)	Marco Apicella (I)	Mauro Martini (I)	264	3597.984	2235.679	LM-GT1	
15	Porsche 911 GT2	77	Peter Seikel (D)	Guy Kuster (F)	Karel Dolejsi (CZ)	263	3585.386	2227.851	LM-GT2	
16	Porsche 911 GT2	78	Eric van de Vyver (F)	Didier Ortion (F)	Jean-François Veroux (F)	262	3570.306	2218.481	LM-GT2	
17	Porsche 911 GT2	81	Nick Adams (GB)	Richard Jones (GB)	Gerard McQuillan (GB)	250	3406.099	2116.448	LM-GT2	
18	Ferrari F40 GTE	41	Gary Ayles (GB)	Massimo Monti (I)	Fabio Mancini (I)	237	3232.396	2008.514	LM-GT1	
19	Porsche 911 BiTurbo	54	Wolfgang Kaufmann (D)	Michel Ligonnet (F)	Yukihiro Hane (J)	229	3124.714	1941.604	LM-GT1	
20	Debora LMP295	14	Bernard Santal (CH)	Patrice Roussel (F)	Edouard Sezionale (F)	222	3027.187	1881.003	LM-P2	
DNF	WR LM94/5	9	William David (F)	Jean-Bernard Bouvet (F)	Richard Balandras (F)	196			LM-P2	Engine (fuel pump)
NC	Venturi 600S-LM	44	Jean-Marc Gounon (F)	Paul Belmondo (F)	Arnaud Trévisiol (F)	193	2624.800	1630.972	LM-GT1	Insufficient distance
NC	Marcos 600LM	71	David Leslie (GB)	François Migault (F)	Chris Marsh (GB)	184	2502.400	1554.916	LM-GT2	Insufficient distance
DNF	Venturi 600LM	45	Eric Graham (F)	Ferdinand de Lesseps (F)	François Birbeau (F)	178			LM-GT1	Electrics
DNF	Kremer K8	3	Franz Konrad (A)	Jürgen Lässig (D)	Antonio de Azevedo Hermann (BR)	163			LM-WSC	Electrics
DNF	Nissan Skyline GT-R LM	23	Kazuyoshi Hoshino (J)	Toshio Suzuki (J)	Masahiko Kageyama (J)	157			LM-GT1	Transmission (gearbox)
DNF	Jaguar XJ220C	57	James Weaver (GB)	Tiff Needell (GB)	Richard Piper (GB)	135			LM-GT1	Engine (crankshaft)
DNF	Marcos 600LM	70	Cor Euser (NL)	Chris Hodgetts (GB)	Thomas Erdos (BR)	133			LM-GT2	Transmission (driveshaft)
DNF	McLaren F1 GTR	49	Jochen Mass (D)	John Nielsen (DK)	Thomas Bscher (D)	131			LM-GT1	Transmission (clutch)
DNF	Venturi 600LM	43	Emmanuel Clérico (F)	Laurent Lécuyer (CH)	Bernard Chauvin (F)	130			LM-GT1	Fire
DNF	Jaguar XJ220C	58	Win Percy (GB)	Bernard Thuner (CH)	Olindo Iacobelli (USA)	123			LM-GT1	Accident damage
NC	Honda NSX GT1	46	Hideki Okada (J)	Philippe Favre (CH)	Naoki Hattori (J)	121	1645.600	1022.526	LM-GT1	Insufficient distance
DNF	Callaway Corvette SuperNatural	76	Thorkild Thyrring (DK)	Almo Coppelli (I)	Patrick Bourdais (F)	96			LM-GT2	Accident
DNF	Porsche 911 GT2 Evo	37	Emmanuel Collard (F)	Stéphane Ortelli (F)	Dominique Dupuy (F)	82			LM-GT1	Accident
DNF	Porsche 911 GT2	79	Enzo Calderari (CH)	Lilian Bryner (CH)	Andreas Fuchs (D)	81			LM-GT2	Accident
DNF	McLaren F1 GTR	25	Pierre-Henri Raphanel (F)	Philippe Alliot (F)	Lindsay Owen-Jones (GB)	77			LM-GT1	Accident
DNF	Porsche 911 GT2 Evo	36	Jean-Pierre Jarier (F)	Erik Comas (F)	Jesús Pareja (E)	64			LM-GT1	Accident
DNF	Porsche 911 GT2	91	Tomas Saldana (E)	Miguel Angel de Castro (E)	Alfonso d'Orleans Bourbon (E)	63			LM-GT2	Accident
DNF	Chevrolet Corvette ZR-1	30	John Paul Jr (USA)	Chris McDougall (CDN)	Jim Meras (USA)	57			LM-GT1	Engine
DNF	Ferrari F40 GTE	40	Anders Olofsson (S)	Luciano Della Noce (I)	Tetsuya Ota (J)	42			LM-GT1	Transmission (gearbox)
DNF	Lister Storm GTS	52	Geoff Lees (GB)	Rupert Keegan (GB)	Dominic Chappell (GB)	40			LM-GT1	Transmission (clutch)
DNF	Porsche 911 GT2 Evo	55	Pierre Yver (F)	Jean-Luc Chéreau (F)	Jack Leconte (F)	40			LM-GT1	Accident
DNF	WR LM95	8	Patrick Gonin (F)	Pierre Petit (F)	Marc Rostan (F)	33			LM-P2	Accident
DNF	Courage C41	11	Henri Pescarolo (F)	Franck Lagorce (F)	Eric Bernard (F)	26			LM-WSC	Electrics (battery)
DNF	SARD Toyota MC8-R	26	Alain Ferté (F)	Kenneth Acheson (GB)		14			LM-GT1	Transmission (clutch)
DNF	Porsche 911 GT2	82	Pierre de Thoisy (F)	Philippe Siffert (CH)	Charles Margueron (CH)	13			LM-GT2	Accident
DNF	Ferrari 333SP	1	Massimo Sigala (I)	René Arnoux (F)	Jay Cochran (USA)	7			LM-WSC	Electrics (ignition)
DNF	Honda NSX GT1	47	Armin Hahne (D)	Ivan Capelli (I)	Bertrand Gachot (B)	7			LM-GT1	Transmission (clutch)
DNQ	Norma M14	6	Dominique Lacaud (F)	Jean-Paul Libert (B)	Pascal Dro (F)	-			LM-WSC	Engine
DNQ	Tiga FJ94	7	John Jones (CDN)	Jean-Marc Massé (F)	François Provost (F)	-			LM-WSC	Engine
RES	Ferrari F355 Challenge	88	Lucien Guitteny (F)	Christian Heinkélé (F)	François Oborn (F)	-			LM-GT2	
DSQ	Courage C41	12	Eric van de Poele (B)	Olivier Beretta (MC)	Matiaz Tomlje (SLO)				LM-WSC	Underweight in qualifying

DNF Did not finish **DNS** Did not start **DNS** Disqualified **FS** Failed scrutineering **RES** Reserve not required **NC** Not classified as a finisher **WD** Withdrawn Drivers in italics did not race the cars specified

1995

CLASS WINNERS

FIA Class	Starters	Finishers	First	No	Drivers	kph	mph	
LM-WSC	6	3	Courage C34	13	Wollek/Andretti/Hélary	168.600	104.763	Record
LM-P2	3	1	Debora LMP295	14	Santal/Roussel/Sezionale	126.133	78.375	Record
LM-GT1	27	10	McLaren F1 GTR	59	Dalmas/Lehto/Sekiya	168.992	105.007	
LM-GT2	12	6	Honda NSX GT	84	Takahashi/Tsuchiya/Iida	156.123	97.010	
Totals	48	20						

NON-PREQUALIFIERS

No	Car	Entrant (Nat)	cc	Engine	Class	Pos	Time
2	Ferrari 333SP	JF America Racing (USA)	3997	F310E V12	WSC	NA	
10	WR LM94	Alain Lebrun (F)	1998	Peugeot S4	LM-P2	45	6:17.89
20	Jaguar XJ220C	Chamberlain Engineering (GB)	3498tc	V6	LM-GT1	30	4:16.27
32	Lamborghini Jota GT1	AIM Team Lamborghini (I)	5709	V12	LM-GT1	NA	
33	Ascari FGT	Ascari Cars (GB)	5752	Ford Windsor V8	LM-GT1	28	4:15.26
35	Aston Martin DB7	Manoir de l'Automobile (F)	3239sc	S6	LM-GT1	WD	4:09.07
48	Honda NSX GT1	Honda Motor (J)	2977	V6	LM-GT2	NT	No time
53	Porsche 911 Biturbo	Obermaier Racing (D)	3600tc	F6	LM-GT1	42	4:38.26
56	Callaway Corvette	Callaway Competition (USA)	6200	Chevrolet LT5 V8	LM-GT2	NA	
61	Dodge Viper	Rent-a-Car Racing Team (F)	7998	V10	LM-GT1	39	4:29.28
74	Callaway Corvette	Callaway Schweiz (CH)	6200	Chevrolet LT5 V8	LM-GT1	41	4:36.45
83	VBM 4000GTC	Jean-Francois Metz (F)	2975tc	PRV V6	LM-GT2	43	4:46.88
85	Honda NSX GT1	Team Nakajima Honda (J)	2977	V6	LM-GT2	37	4:22.75
86	Venturi 400 GTR	Sport Time (E)	2975tc	PRV V6	LM-GT2	38	4:22.90
87	Ferrari F355 Challenge	Patrick Boidron (F)	3496	F129B V8	LM-GT2	44	4:47.23

DSQ Disqualified **NA** Non-arrival **NT** No time set **WD** Withdrawn after Prequalifying

BPR GLOBAL GT ENDURANCE SERIES

Race	Winner	Drivers
Jerez (P) 4 hours	McLaren F1 GTR	Sandro Sala/Bellm
Paul Ricard (F) 4 hours	McLaren F1 GTR	Sandro Sala/Bellm
Monza (I) 4 hours	McLaren F1 GTR	Nielsen/Bscher
Jarama (E) 4 hours	McLaren F1 GTR	Sandro Sala/Bellm
Nürburgring (D) 4 hours	McLaren F1 GTR	Sandro Sala/Bellm
Donington Park (GB) 4 hours	McLaren F1 GTR	Nielsen/Bscher
Montlhéry (F) 1000km	Porsche 911 GT2	Oberndorfer/Hübner
Anderstorp (S) 4 hours	Ferrari F40 LM	Ferté/Thévenin
Suzuka (J) 1000km	McLaren F1 GTR	Sandro Sala/Bellm/Sekiya
Silverstone (GB) 4 hours	McLaren F1 GTR	Wallace/Grouillard
Nogaro (F) 4 hours	McLaren F1 GTR	Wallace/Grouillard
Zhuhai (CN) 3 hours	McLaren F1 GTR	Wallace/Grouillard

FINAL CHAMPIONSHIP POINTS

Final Positions	Driver (Nat)	Points
DRIVERS		
1	John Nielsen (DK)	252
=	Thomas Bscher (D)	252
3	Enzo Calderari (CH)	205
=	Lilian Bryner (CH)	205
5	Ray Bellm (GB)	201
6	Maurizio Sandro Sala (BR)	194
7	Andy Wallace (GB)	145
8	Bob Wollek (F)	124
9	Jean-Pierre Jarier (F)	110
10	Franz Konrad (A)	107
&c		

McLAREN STARS ON A NEW STAGE

LE MANS

1996
OLD FOES JOIN FORCES

LE MANS

RACE INFORMATION

RACE DATE
15-16 June

RACE No
64

CIRCUIT LENGTH
8.451 miles/13.600km

HONORARY STARTER
Alain Delon
Actor

MARQUES (ON GRID)

Chevrolet	1
Chrysler	4
Courage	3
Ferrari	6
Honda	1
Kremer-Porsche	2
Kudzu	1
Lister	1
Marcos	1
McLaren	7
Nissan	2
Porsche	12
Riley&Scott	1
SARD-Toyota	1
Toyota	1
TWR-Porsche	2
WR	2

STARTERS/FINISHERS
48/25

WINNERS

OVERALL
TWR-Porsche

ENTRY LIST

No	Car	Entrant (nat)	cc	Engine	Tyres	Weight (kg)	Class
1	Kremer K8	Kremer Racing (D)	2994tc	Porsche F6	Goodyear	901	LM-P1 *
2	Kremer K8	Kremer Racing (D)	2994tc	Porsche F6	Goodyear	911	LM-P1
3	Courage C36	Courage Compétition (F)	2994tc	Porsche F6	Michelin	906	LM-P1 *
4	Courage C36	Courage Compétition (F)	2994tc	Porsche F6	Michelin	901	LM-P1
5	Courage C36	La Filière Elf (F)	2994tc	Porsche F6	Michelin	896	LM-P1
7	TWR-Porsche WSC95	Joest Racing (D)	2994tc	F6	Goodyear	899	LM-P1
8	TWR-Porsche WSC95	Joest Racing (D)	2994tc	F6	Goodyear	891	LM-P1
9	Debora LMP296	Didier Bonnet (F)	1998tc	Cosworth BDG S4	Michelin	665	LM-P2 *
14	WR LM96	Welter Racing (F)	1999tc	Peugeot 405-Raid S4	Michelin	663	LM-P2
17	Ferrari 333SP	Team Scandia (USA) Racing for Belgium (B)	3997	F310E V12	Pirelli	880	IMSA-WSC
18	Ferrari 333SP	Team Scandia (USA) Rocket Sports Racing (USA)	3997	F310E V12	Pirelli	877	IMSA-WSC
19	Riley & Scott Mk3	Riley & Scott Cars (USA)	3998	Oldsmobile Aurora V8	Pirelli	903	IMSA-WSC
20	Kudzu DLM	Mazdaspeed (J)	1962r	Mazda R20B 3R	Goodyear	732	LM-P2 *
22	Nissan Skyline GT-R LM	NISMO (J)	2795tc	RB26-DETT S6	Bridgestone	1279	LM-GT1 *
23	Nissan Skyline GT-R LM	NISMO (J)	2795tc	RB26-DETT S6	Bridgestone	1285	LM-GT1
25	Porsche 911 GT1	Porsche AG (D)	3164tc	F6	Michelin	1056	LM-GT1
25T	Porsche 911 GT1	Porsche AG (D)	3164tc	F6	Michelin	N/A	LM-GT1
26	Porsche 911 GT1	Porsche AG (D)	3164tc	F6	Michelin	1049	LM-GT1
27	Porsche 911 GT2 Evo	Chereau Sports/Larbre Compétition (F)	3600tc	F6	Michelin	1176	LM-GT1
28	Lister Storm GTL	Newcastle United Lister (GB)	6996	Jaguar HE V12	Michelin	1124	LM-GT1
29	McLaren F1 GTR LM	DPR Mach One Racing (GB)	6064	BMW S70/3 V12	Goodyear	1061	LM-GT1
30	McLaren F1 GTR LM	DPR West Competition (GB)	6064	BMW S70/3 V12	Goodyear	1062	LM-GT1
33	McLaren F1 GTR LM	Gulf Racing (GB)	6064	BMW S70/3 V12	Michelin	1061	LM-GT1
34	McLaren F1 GTR LM	Gulf Racing (GB)	6064	BMW S70/3 V12	Michelin	1059	LM-GT1
37	Porsche 911 GT2 Evo	Konrad Motorsport (D)	3600tc	F6	Michelin	1143	LM-GT1
38	McLaren F1 GTR LM	Team Bigazzi (I)	6064	BMW S70/3 V12	Michelin	1050	LM-GT1
39	McLaren F1 GTR LM	Team Bigazzi (I)	6064	BMW S70/3 V12	Michelin	1052	LM-GT1
44	Ferrari F40 GTE	Igol-Ennea (I)	3600tc	F120B V8	Pirelli	1113	LM-GT1
45	Ferrari F40 GTE	Igol-Ennea (I)	3600tc	F120B V8	Pirelli	1110	LM-GT1
46	SARD Toyota MC8-R	Team Menicon SARD (J)	3968tc	R40V-T V8	Dunlop	1061	LM-GT1
48	Chrysler Viper GTS-R	Canaska Southwind Motorsport (USA)	7986	356/T6 V10	Michelin	1233	LM-GT1
49	Chrysler Viper GTS-R	Canaska Southwind Motorsport (USA)	7986	356/T6 V10	Michelin	1238	LM-GT1
50	Chrysler Viper GTS-R	Viper Team ORECA (F)	7986	356/T6 V10	Michelin	1243	LM-GT1
51	Chrysler Viper GTS-R	Viper Team ORECA (F)	7986	356/T6 V10	Michelin	1231	LM-GT1
52	Chrysler Viper GTS-R	Viper Team ORECA (F)	7986	356/T6 V10	–	–	LM-GT1
53	McLaren F1 GTR LM	Kokusai Kaihatsu Racing (GB)	6064	BMW S70/3 V12	Michelin	1055	LM-GT1 *
55	Porsche 911 GT2 Evo	Roock Racing Team (D)	3600tc	F6	Michelin	1124	LM-GT1
56	Ferrari F40 LM	Ferté Pilot Racing (F)	3500tc	F120B V8	Michelin	1124	LM-GT1 *
57	Toyota Supra LM	Toyota Team SARD (J)	2140tc	3S-GTE S4	Dunlop	1141	LM-GT1 *
59	Ferrari F40 GTE	Ennea Ferrari Club Italia (I)	3500tc	F120B V8	Pirelli	1124	LM-GT1
61	McLaren F1 GTR LM	Franck Muller (NL)	6064	BMW S70/2 V12	–	–	LM-GT1
70	Porsche 911 GT2	Steve O'Rourke (GB)	3600tc	F6	Dunlop	1174	LM-GT2
71	Porsche 911 GT2	New Hardware Parr Motorsport (NZ)	3600tc	F6	Pirelli	1187	LM-GT2
73	Porsche 911 GT2	Elf Haberthur Racing (CH)	3600tc	F6	Dunlop	1166	LM-GT2
74	Callaway Corvette SuperNatural	Agusta Racing Team (I/GB)	6243	Chevrolet LT1 V8	Dunlop	1106	LM-GT2
75	Honda NSX GT	Team Kunimitsu Honda (J)	2977	RX306-E5 V6	Yokohama	1086	LM-GT2 *
77	Porsche 911 GT2	Seikel Motorsport (D)	3600tc	F6	Dunlop	1178	LM-GT2 *
79	Porsche 911 GT2	Roock Racing Team (D)	3600tc	F6	Michelin	1108	LM-GT2
81	Marcos Mantara 600LM	Team Marcos (GB)	6143	Chevrolet LT5 V8	Dunlop	1113	LM-GT2
82	Porsche 911 GT2	Larbre Compétition (F)	3600tc	F6	Michelin	1198	LM-GT2
83	Porsche 911 GT2	New Hardware PARR Motorsport (NZ)	3600tc	F6	Dunlop	1161	LM-GT2
Reserves							
15	WR LM95/6	Welter Racing (F)	1999tc	Peugeot 405-Raid S4	Michelin	691	LM-P2
32	Renault Spider V6 Coupé	Legeay Sports (F)	2975tc	Renault PRV V6	Dunlop	992	LM-GT1
40	Venturi 600LM	BBA Competition (F)	2955tc	PRV V6	Michelin	1132	LM-GT1
72	Porsche 911 GT2	Stadler Motorsport (CH)	3600tc	F6	Pirelli	1165	LM-GT2

* Automatic entries (ACO selection). See Non-Prequalifiers table for discarded entries

1996

ENTRY

Nine manufacturers were directly engaged this year. From 107 applications, the ACO accepted 76 and sent 66 of them through eight hours of Prequalifying at the end of April. As it transpired, 53 cars participated in the race meeting itself, most of them again contesting the GT divisions: 27 in GT1 and 12 in GT2. There were only 14 prototypes: seven P1s, three IMSA-WSC cars and four P2s.

Porsche returned with a controversial new GT1 car, and faced teams representing Chrysler, Lister, McLaren, Nissan and Toyota; the GT2 category was contested by Honda and Marcos. Porsche also contributed to P1 with Joest Racing, while Oldsmobile backed Riley & Scott (R&S) in the WSC class, and Mazda returned with Kudzu in P2. Counting the prototypes of Courage, Debora and WR, 22 cars were operated by their constructors.

QUALIFYING

When less than a second covered the best five P1 cars and the two works GT1 Porsches, it justified a decision by the ACO, stressing its aim of equalizing performance, to form the first 12 rows of the 2x2 starting grid with the fastest prototypes on the left, and GT cars on the right.

Eric van der Poele drove the fastest lap on Wednesday with the Scandia team's Ferrari WSC racer. The time was beaten the next day by Pierluigi Martini with Joest Racing's TWR-Porsche and by Jérome Policand, who almost landed Courage's second pole in three years. 'Davy' Jones in the other TWR-Porsche and Wayne Taylor in the R&S-Oldsmobile were also on the pace.

One of the GT1 Porsches was crashed heavily by Karl Wendlinger just before midnight on Wednesday, but Yannick Dalmas used the repaired car to pip Thierry Boutsen by seven-thousandths and earn a front-row start.

OLD FOES JOIN FORCES 225

LE MANS

ORGANISATION

This year the ACO technical committee added two further interlinked parameters to enhance the flexibility of the formula it used to equalize performance across the board. Engine swept volume and turbocharger inlet manifold pressure ('boost') were added to vehicle weight, fuel tankage, tyre width, and the number and diameter of engine air-inlet restrictors.

The committee again redefined its LM-P1 division, imposing revised bodywork dimensions along the lines of IMSA's WSC class, a minimum weight of 875kg, and maximum swept volumes of 3000cc for forced-induction engines and 5100cc for 'atmos'. The 80-litre fuel cells were retained, and a maximum tyre width of 16 inches restored.

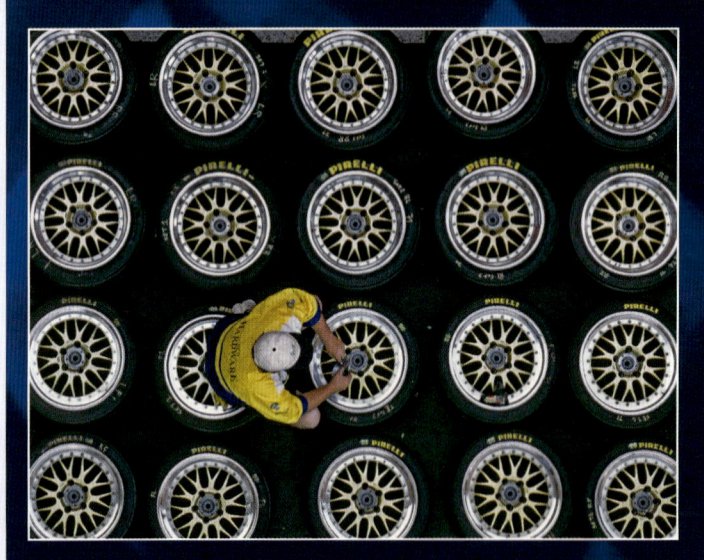

Similar aerodynamic constraints were imposed in P2, and two-seat cars were now admitted. The minimum weight was increased from 620 to 650kg. Turbocharged engines were now limited to 2000cc and four cylinders, and 'atmos' to 3400cc and six cylinders. The fuel cells were reduced from 80 to 62 litres, but the tyre width was increased from 12 to 14 inches.

In addition, the ACO catered separately this year for US-based cars complying with IMSA's 'atmo' WSC regulations.

In LM-GT1, substantial engine modifications were now allowed, but GT2s still had to use series-production motors. The maximum swept volumes in both GT classes were now set at 4000cc for turbos, and 8000cc for 'atmos'. Minimum weights were defined on a scale covering the range 900-1300kg, according to the volume of the engine, its induction system, its number of valves per cylinder, and the diameters of its air-inlet restrictors. GT1 cars were allowed the latest carbon-carbon braking systems but GT2s had to be fitted with ferrous brakes. Fuel tankage remained unchanged at 100 litres in both classes, and tyre widths at 14 inches front and 12 rear.

The ACO's entry selection committee halved the number of cars granted automatic entries to 10. The start was given at 3pm, one hour earlier than normal, to allow the tens of thousands of British spectators at the race to watch on TV a European Cup football match between England and Scotland. The spectator banks opposite the pits were now protected by chain-link safety fencing, as well as a concrete ditch.

This year IMSA was sold to Wall Street financier (and Scandia sportscar team owner) Andy Evans and former Reebok CEO Roberto Muller, and renamed Professional Sports Car Racing (PSCR).

RACE

The 3pm start was taken by 48 cars in bright sunshine, and 168,000 spectators saw Dalmas and Bob Wollek leading the first four laps in team formation with the GT1 Porsches. But they could not resist the TWR-Porsches of Jones and Didier Theys. A fine triple shift by Jones handed Alex Wurz a firm lead when he took over just after 5pm.

The other fancied prototypes were already in trouble. Poele had put his Ferrari into the gravel on the second lap, losing the best part of two laps, while Didier Cottaz had pitted the fastest Courage for 12 minutes with an electronics fault, and the R&S was stymied by excessive fuel consumption.

Joest's neat cars could go fully 12 laps on their 80-litre fuel cells (a lap further than any other prototype) and could run three shifts between tyre changes. The GT1 Porsches, being heavier and on narrower tyres, were slightly outperformed, could do only 13 laps on 100 litres, and needed new rubber in every other daytime stop.

The writing was therefore quickly on the wall – although, with Hans-Joachim Stuck co-driving Boutsen and Wollek, Porsche had a squad good enough to stay in contention. During Saturday evening, Porsche had a 1-2-3-4, in the order P1-GT1-P1-GT1. But Stuck was squeezed over high kerbing while lapping a Courage and, at 9:30pm, the crew had to invest 11 minutes in replacing the underbody. Before the work was done, Dalmas pitted after a spin, at a cost of eight minutes. The Joest team's early 1-2 was restored, with the Jones/Wurz car, co-driven by Manuel Reuter, leading.

From that moment, Porsche's factory team needed similar setbacks to hamper the leading TWR-Porsches. Only one of them suffered. And the second GT1 Porsche was further delayed when first Wendlinger and then Goodyear damaged it in gravel traps.

It was half-distance before Stuck/Wollek/Boutsen could recover second place from Martini/Theys/Michele Alboreto. At that stage, the delayed Policand Courage and WSC Ferrari had retrieved fourth and fifth. However, the Ferrari broke its gearbox and needed a fresh rear end, after which a suspension failure pitched Eric Bachelart into the wall at the Dunlop bridge. And then Alliot crashed the Courage at Tertre Rouge.

1996

Later on Sunday morning, a three-stint charge by Stuck made dramatic inroads into the race leader, such that the GT1 car almost led during the pitstop sequences. But that was as close as the factory team came. Joest's men had a little in hand, and their equipment stayed strong. They won by a lap.

There was only one TWR-Porsche on the podium. At 9:20am, Martini dropped the pole-position car at the first Mulsanne chicane. After a stop for body repairs, Theys resumed in fourth place, but was soon struck by an electronics glitch. Eventually the car recovered third position while Ray Bellm's McLaren, well driven by JJ Lehto and James Weaver, underwent a 90-minute pitstop for a new gearbox. However, a broken driveshaft parked Martini only 40 minutes from the end, leaving the second GT1 Porsche to inherit the position, although Scott Goodyear went off and damaged the car's nose.

Transmission problems plagued several other McLarens, but the marque filled the next three positions. GT2 was dominated by Roock Racing's Porsche, and the Kudzu-Mazda was the only P2 finisher.

OLD FOES JOIN FORCES

MIGHTY MONGREL

The Porsche WSC95 may have looked bland, but it delivered pole position on début for Pierluigi Martini, and victory for Davy Jones, Manuel Reuter and Alex Wurz.

This interesting car was produced by a unique collaboration between Porsche Motorsport and TWR, which had been such fierce rivals in Group C. After a winning season in the 1991 SWC, and a less successful 1992 IMSA campaign, there was only one raceworthy survivor of the three Jaguar XJR-14 ground-effect coupés. The 1991 Nürburgring SWC winner, this was mothballed in the TWR Inc workshops in Valparaiso, Indiana, where Tony Dowe reckoned it could be the basis of a flat-bottom spyder for IMSA's new World Sports Car class. But TWR had no suitable engine. Then, in September 1994, IMSA confirmed that turbochargers would be allowed in WSC the following season. Dowe saw an opportunity for Porsche – which had no suitable chassis. He proposed a marriage of convenience to Alwin Springer at Porsche North America.

Eventually a deal was agreed by Tom Walkinshaw and Porsche Motorsport director Max Welti. Porsche offered powertrains, technical expertise and cash for a short, two-car 1995 WSC programme taking in the 'triple crown' races at Daytona, Sebring and Le Mans.

Ian Reed and TWR's best UK-based mechanic, Dave Fullerton, went ahead with converting the Cosworth V8-powered XJR-14 in Valparaiso, using the existing chassis and a new hull ordered from Astec, the TWR Group's advanced composites specialist. In 1992, TWR had reworked Ross Brawn's design as the Mazda MXR-01, but that had also been a ground-effect FIA Sportscar, and its load-bearing Judd V10 installation was not possible for the 3-litre, water-cooled, twin-turbo Porsche flat-six. As many as 15 engineers and mechanics were flown out from Weissach to get involved in the powertrain-related issues, under the supervision of Norbert Singer.

Reed drew a new aluminium transmission casing to allow Porsche's five-speed gearbox to take some of the chassis loads, while retaining the XJR-14 rear suspension geometry. The conversion also included Reed's sturdy roll-hoop to compensate for the loss of structural rigidity that went with the roof, with a large engine air intake beneath, and a smaller fuel cell. The aero package had to be redrawn in view of the open cockpit and IMSA's ban on ground-effect venturi, nose wings and two-tier rear wings, and air scoops added on the rear wheel-arches to cool the turbo intercoolers.

The first completed car was track-tested at Charlotte in December 1994 by Thierry Boutsen and Scott Goodyear, and was then driven in IMSA's official Daytona test session in January by Bob Wollek and Mario Andretti, going fourth fastest behind two Ferraris and an R&S.

IMSA was convinced that Porsche was sandbagging. And Ferrari's Luca di Montezemolo was bending IMSA's ear with complaints that, since Porsche only intended to race in the enduros, it was unfair

1996

on the privateer Ferrari 333 SP teams doing the whole championship. Ten days before qualifying proper at Daytona, IMSA hit twin-turbo WSC cars with a 100lb (45kg) weight increase and smaller air restrictors, reducing output by 15 percent. Porsche had no time to make the necessary alterations and angrily withdrew from both of the Floridian events. Although the ACO did not change its new LM-WSC regulations, Porsche also pulled the new cars out of Le Mans, and concentrated on its GT1 project.

Here was the ideal scenario for an intervention by the ever-opportunistic Reinhold Joest from his lair in Wald-Michelbach, Germany. Joest's team had not raced its own cars at Le Mans for three years and was now operating Opel Calibra Touring Cars. In February 1996, he persuaded the new Porsche Motorsport director, Herbert Ampferer, to lend him the unraced WSC prototypes for a crack at Le Mans.

In view of the more stringent engine restrictions in the ACO's new P1 regulations, Singer used the wind tunnel at Weissach to evolve a concave form for the nose, a cut-off engine cover and a centrepost-mounted rear wing, the whole generating comparable downforce for less drag. The engine airbox was offset to the left so that the airflow was unobstructed by the driver's head. Joest race engineers Ralf Jüttner and Walter Bühren then worked with Goodyear's technicians during 2100 miles of circuit work on Goodyear's test track at Miréval.

Four of the drivers who had been recruited for the aborted 1995 programme had been reassigned to Porsche's GT1 project, but Joest signed handy replacements. Martini claimed the Le Mans pole with the new chassis, which was race-engineered by Bühren and co-driven

OLD FOES JOIN FORCES

LE MANS

by Michele Alboreto and Didier Theys. The original Jaguar chassis, engineered by Jüttner, was qualified sixth by Jones.

In the race, Theys and Jones only spent four laps behind the works GT-type Porsches before passing them. Three factors combined to establish the black TWR-Porsche in a lead that was real, in the sense that they overcame the handicap of refuelling more often than the GT cars: the pace of the car, the durability of its tyres, and a very strong triple shift by Jones, during which he broke the track record on successive laps.

That lead was maintained by Wurz and Reuter. Apart from a couple of laps in the twilight, these three held a narrow advantage all the way to a planned brake disc/pad replacement at 8:30am. One of the 911 GT1s overtook but, when it pitted for fuel, Jones went back ahead, and the TWR-Porsche was never overtaken again. It was as strong at the finish as it had been 24 hours earlier: a perfect performance, involving less than 51 minutes stationary in the pits.

The sister car (below) raced in the top three until a slide down the order began at 9:20am when Martini, trying to rip off a visor strip, missed his braking point and slithered onto the beach at the Nissan chicane. After a pitstop, Theys was stranded on his out-lap at Mulsanne corner by an engine management glitch. He was able to restart but, 10 minutes later, it happened again at the Mulsanne kink. Theys pitted for a fresh Motronic control box, but the engine stopped again soon after midday as Alboreto was exiting the first chicane. The car was running eighth when, at 2:15pm, Martini was halted for good when an inner driveshaft joint came apart as he drove out of Arnage.

Reinhold Joest did not mind too much. His deal with Porsche stated that, if he won the race, he would get to own the successful car. This made his smile even broader.

230　LE MANS 24 HOURS 1990–99

1996

A NEW DEPARTURE

The controversial mid-engined Porsche 911 GT1s finished second and third overall but demolishing all opposition in the category, including the McLaren F1s, fell short of Porsche's ambitions for the new cars raced by Bob Wollek, Hans-Joachim Stuck and Thierry Boutsen, and by Karl Wendlinger, Yannick Dalmas and Scott Goodyear (leading in the photo below).

Herbert Ampferer, newly installed as the director of Porsche Motorsport, was given the go-ahead for this project immediately after McLaren's victory in the 1995 Le Mans. The initial concept for the first Porsche ever to bear its engine ahead of the transmission and within the wheelbase was drawn by Horst Reitter. Norbert Singer's design team retained the pressed-steel monocoque of the 993-series production 911, but put a wall and a tube frame behind the cockpit bearing the powertrain in a lengthened wheelbase. As rivals swiftly pointed out, the whole rear end, including suspension by reversed upper wishbones with transverse 'coilovers', operated by pushrods and bell-cranks, owed much to the 962 and nothing to the 911.

This was also the first Porsche GT car with a fully water-cooled engine, as used in the later Group C cars. The purpose-designed, 3.2-litre 911 GT1 motor was a 24-valve version of the 'boxer' flat-six, with chain-driven camshafts, two KKK turbochargers, multi-point sequential fuel injection, and a 'coil-at-plug' CD ignition system. Control was by a TAGtronic 3.8 EMS with advanced diagnostics, and peak output under the LM-GT1 restrictions was declared at 590bhp at 7200rpm. The transmission system centred on a new, six-speed sequential-shift gearbox with synchromesh. A carbon ABS braking system completed an impressive mechanical package.

The carbon/Kevlar bodywork design involved Harm Lagaay, Porsche's head of styling, and Tony Hatter, who had drawn the 993-generation road car, before being refined in the Weissach wind tunnel.

The first 911 GT1 was rolled out at Weissach in mid-March 1996, just eight months after first sketches had been made, and was shaken down on the test circuit there by Jürgen Barth. The new car was extensively tested before and after its unpainted public début in Le Mans Prequalifying at the end of April. After durability runs at Weissach, the prototype 911 GT1 ran at Estoril, and an extended test at Paul Ricard included a 24-hour endurance run. During the test programme, covering almost 7000 miles, Michelin was chosen as the tyre supplier over Dunlop, Goodyear and Pirelli.

Porsche built two roadgoing versions during the homologation process, which was completed in April (with EU certification, rather than the German national approval issued for the even more controversial Dauer LM).

Ampferer's reformed factory team suffered an early setback on

Wednesday night when Wendlinger crashed heavily into the wall in front of the old Mulsanne corner signalling pits, destroying the front end of his car. The steel noseframe was one of the few components interchangeable with a roadgoing 911. It was after midnight when Singer telephoned veteran race engineer Werner Hillburger at home in Stuttgart, and persuaded him to leave his bed, return to the factory, collect a new frame, and set out on a three-hour drive to Frankfurt airport, where a chartered aircraft awaited him. It took off at 5:30am on Thursday morning and, a couple of hours later, landed on the airfield adjacent to the circuit. The car was repaired well in time for the second qualifying sessions.

In the race, Dalmas and Wollek led the first four laps in formation, but it soon became clear that the ACO's application of varied performance parameters was giving the TWR-Porsche prototypes a slight edge: 1050kg, 100-litre fuel tankage and narrow tyres was not quite as good over the distance as 900kg, 80-litre tankage and wide tyres. Moreover both the 205mph (330kph) 911 GT1s were delayed at dusk. Stuck was pushed over high kerbing when lapping Philippe Alliot's Courage, and eventually needed an 11-minute stop for a new undertray. Before Boutsen could resume, Dalmas arrived in the adjacent pit with his car's nose full of gravel from the beach at Mulsanne corner, and Goodyear had to wait eight minutes while the crew replaced a front brake caliper.

Wollek/Stuck/Boutsen all raced brilliantly through the night in pursuit of the leading TWR-Porsche, and Stuck actually had the lead briefly at breakfast time before stopping for fuel. But the leaders had performance in hand to respond, and the 911 GT1 was again a lap behind at 3pm.

In the sister car (above), Wendlinger and later Goodyear both emulated Dalmas by spinning into sandtraps, and at half-time they were 12th. They only finished on the podium because of Sunday's attrition.

Later in the season, Porsche decided to offer 911 GT1 'customer' cars for the 1997 season, so the factory team shook up the McLaren and Ferrari owners in the BPR series, winning at Brands Hatch, Spa and Zhuhai.

BACK DOWN TO EARTH

The much-modified 1996 McLaren F1 GTRs were outperformed this year by the Porsche 911 GT1s, and several were hampered by fragile gearboxes. Six GTRs finished, but this time the best-placed was fourth (top right). One of Thomas Bscher's cars, run by David Price Racing, it was co-driven by John Nielsen and Peter Kox.

McLaren Cars Motorsport (MCM) began work in Woking on the next version of its GTR a month after winning the 1995 Le Mans, now collaborating more closely with BMW Motorsport in Munich. Expanded

1996

to 45 people and also working on a BMW Super Touring project, MCM mounted the engine lower in the chassis and upgraded the suspension with new uprights and pick-up mounts. The steering, braking, cooling and electronic control systems were also improved. Aero modifications aimed at better efficiency and adjustability were proven this time in the Activa (formerly Brabham) wind tunnel, and included a large front splitter, front and rear bodywork extensions and new side panels. Weight-saving was prioritized and the 1996 GTR was as much as 70kg lighter.

Meanwhile, Paul Rosche's engine team reacted to this year's reduced air restrictors by increasing the compression ratio of the 48-valve V12, and revising the camshafts, the fuelling, the collector box airflows, and the water and oil pumps. The 1996 engine supplied 600bhp at 7300bhp through a redesigned and lighter transmission system, so power loss was limited to 40bhp.

MCM completed nine new chassis, the first of which served as a works development car. This was taken to Le Mans Prequalifying in April, equipped with an 'LM' endurance kit including a magnesium alloy differential case, an extended roof-mounted engine air ram-inlet, revised sideskirts and 'bubble' headlamp covers. BMW Motorsport decided to enter the arena by commissioning the Bigazzi team, its Italian partner in touring car racing since 1992, to operate a quasi-works team, for which it ordered three new GTRs. Ray Bellm and Lindsay Owen-Jones ordered two, and so did All-Japan GT entrant Kazimuchi Goh. The other went to Fabien Giroix and new partner Franck Muller. Thomas Bscher kept his 1995 chassis but they were updated by DPR to the new specification.

The latest McLarens won the first four rounds of the BPR series ahead of Le Mans. Only seven arrived for race week: BBA Compétition's 1995 car had been crashed by Michel Ligonnet during Prequalifying, and stymied by clutch problems after being hurriedly repaired. The 1996-spec GTR was the fastest of all the McLaren F1 variants that raced at Le Mans, reaching 205mph (330kph).

BMW's cars were entered by Aldo Bigazzi and his son, Paolo, out of their base in San Gimignano, south-west of Florence, and managed by Gabriele Rafanelli. Each needed two gearboxes to complete the race. BMW factory driver Steve Soper drove the fastest GTR lap in qualifying with the car owned by BMW GB, and co-driven by Jacques Laffite and Marc Duez. They raced without major incident until 4:25am, when Duez pitted out of seventh position, stuck in gear. The crew had to invest an hour in replacing the clutch and gearbox. After another delay with a detached exhaust, Soper spun off at Tertre Rouge at 8am, and another 25 minutes went in front-end repairs. These delays were compounded by air-jack failures, and the car finished 11th.

Four times the winner of the Spa 24 Hours, the Bigazzi team also ran a car owned by BMW North America and driven by Danny Sullivan,

OLD FOES JOIN FORCES

LE MANS

Johnny Cecotto and triple F1 World Champion Nelson Piquet (below). They lost sixth place soon after nightfall through a braking problem, and slipped further back after dawn when a radiator had to be replaced. The drivers were making up time during Sunday morning when, like their team mates, they could only watch for an hour while the mechanics replaced their gearbox. The result was eighth position.

Bscher's DPR-operated McLarens, which had been so strong 12 months before, had an unremittingly torrid week, struggling with abominable handling and excessive wear of both brakes and tyres. The DPR mechanics under Ian Sanders lost count of the times they replaced the brake discs and, at one stage, new calipers were needed on the Nielsen/Kox/Bscher entry. On Sunday morning, Kox failed to improve David Price's mood by taking to the escape road in the first Mulsanne chicane – where, a couple of hours later, the car's owner was in a light collision with Pierre-Henri Raphanel's Gulf McLaren, which sent him into the gravel.

In the other DPR McLaren, Derek Bell, Andy Wallace and Olivier Grouillard (who twice went off the road) encountered gear selection and clutch problems to add to their handling difficulties. The drivers had to nurse their car over the final four hours, with only fourth and fifth gears available. Both DPR cars had been outside the top 20 at midnight, so to finish fourth and sixth felt almost like winning.

JJ Lehto was the second fastest GTR driver in qualifying with the GTC-operated car shared with owner Ray Bellm and James Weaver (above left), which was McLaren's best performer by far. Despite JJ's nocturnal visit to the gravel trap at the first chicane, the Gulf F1 led all its stablemates for more than 20 hours. It was running third overall at 10am, but the clutch had already begun playing up. A couple of hours later,

234 LE MANS 24 HOURS 1990–99

it had to be replaced, which took almost 90 minutes. They finished ninth.

Their team mates, Raphanel, David Brabham and Owen-Jones, decided on a conservative race strategy in anticipation of the transmission problems. During the evening, Brabham could not avoid contact in the Virage Ford with Franck Fréon's Mazda, but the car escaped without serious damage. During the night, the GTC crew had to replace first the fuel pump, then the oil pump, and a fractured clutch oil-line. After Raphanel's incident with Bscher, the car finished fifth – with its gearbox on its last legs.

McLaren itself had no use for its automatic entry, gained by winning in 1995, so offered it to Muller and Giroix, whose car was originally on the reserve list. It was therefore entered under the spurious 'Kokusai Kaihatsu Racing' banner. Regular drivers Fabien Giroix and Jean-Denis Délétraz were joined here by Maurizio Sandro Sala, who was driving when a driveshaft broke during Saturday evening. After repairs, the car had just arrived back in the top 20 when the engine broke down 30 minutes before half-time. It was the only McLaren retirement.

Later McLaren had to share BPR victories with Ferrari and Porsche, but Weaver and Bellm clinched a second BPR title for the company. In Japan, Goh's Team Lark won four races and beat the works Nissans and Toyotas to the GT500 championship, while Lanzante Motorsport won the British GT1 title with an ex-GTC 1995 McLaren.

ANOTHER LETDOWN

There was no sign of the WSC Courage C41 this year. The local team raced three C36-Porsches, two entered by Courage Compétition, the other nominally by Elf La Filière, the new motorsport academy in the Le Mans Technoparc. These LM-P1/C90 entries were seen as potential winners, and the one allocated to Mario Andretti, Derek Warwick and Jan Lammers (above) started as one of the hot favourites.

The C36 continued the lineage that began with the first aluminium-honeycomb Group C chassis more than 10 years before. Among Courage's annual upgrades were carbon brakes, which needed revised suspension uprights and bigger cooling ducts. The aerodynamic changes included a fairing on the rollover bar and a reshaped, stiffer rear wing, located lower to offer a small reduction in drag. The new 'boost' restriction reduced the output of Courage's engines (assembled in the Le Mans factory by Jean-Luc Chedorge) to 520bhp, about 80bhp down on 1995.

The fastest Courage in qualifying was the one that had finished second in 1995. Race engineer Alain Clairval put it on soft tyres so that Jérôme Policand could set the second best time on Thursday evening while his team mates scrubbed tyres and ran-in race engines. The car was driven from the start of the race by Didier Cottaz, who had it in fourth place just after 4pm when he ran into electrical problems.

LE MANS

A new black box was fitted in 12 minutes. Later Philippe Alliot had a light collision with Hans Stuck's Porsche GT1, but the Courage (above) made great progress through the night. It was back in fourth place at 6:35am when Alliot crashed spectacularly out of the race in the Esses, blaming a stuck throttle.

Ninety minutes after Cottaz's electrical failure, the same thing happened to Lammers, racing in seventh place. This time the engine cut out altogether, although fortunately at the entrance to the Virage Ford. After the driver spent a chunk of time heroically pushing it to its pit, the car lost 50 more minutes while the crew, under Keith Greene, traced the problem. With another new black box, Warwick joined the race 20 laps behind the leaders, in 45th position, and showed his frustration with an embarrassing spin in the pit-lane entrance road as he completed the shift. It was a long night…

Soon after dawn, more problems occurred. The left-front wheel came off as Lammers approached the pit entrance (lucky again!). At 11am, Andretti ran the car onto the beach at Indianapolis, and repairs in pit-lane cost another 35 minutes. Finally, with less than an hour to go, it was Warwick's turn to lose a wheel, out at Indianapolis. The car was restored to the race and the exasperated drivers finished 13th.

Consequently the La Filière car (left) secured the team's best result – seventh overall, second in class. Directed by Pierre Daveau and Serge Ghezzi, this C36 had a relatively quiet race in the hands of Henri Pescarolo/Franck Lagorce/Emmanuel Collard, save for a one-hour delay for a clutch replacement soon after midnight, after Collard had contrived to bring in the stricken car from the verge at Arnage.

236 LE MANS 24 HOURS 1990–99

1996

SCANDIA SCARLET

Andy Evans's Scandia team interrupted its IMSA campaign to cross the Atlantic with its two Ferrari 333 SP sports-racers, one of which was leased to Pascal Witmeur and entered for his Racing for Belgium children's charity project. One departed the race before it was dark, and the other soon after dawn.

The performance of WSC cars had been restricted here in 1995 by a 10,500rpm rev limit, but now the 4-litre V12 was obliged to breathe through an air-inlet restrictor. Evans recruited Tony Southgate, Ferrari's former 333 SP consultant, to design a new-pattern airbox to compensate, but the engine was more than 60bhp down on its output for IMSA races.

Scandia ran one car with the standard bodywork in Prequalifying but, come race week, both sported new bodies, designed by Southgate and Dialma Zinelli in Dallara's wind tunnel. The wheel-arches were reprofiled to reduce frontal area, surface louvres were deleted, the side panels were modified, and the front splitter was cut back to the nose profile. These modifications and a one-piece rear wing generated less downforce, but the lower drag pushed top speed from 185 to the target 205mph (330kph), and allowed the use of softer tyre compounds.

Having driven both cars in Prequalifying (and set the two best times), Eric van der Poele was fastest again after the first day of qualifying proper. This caused a lot of excitement when the news reached Maranello. The team was strongly urged not to risk the cars on Thursday, but to set them up for the race, run them for three installation laps, and park them. As a result, Poele was pipped to the pole by a TWR-Porsche and a Courage. Yvan Muller, allowed out for six laps on a short lead on Wednesday, qualified 13th with the other 333 SP, shared with Evans himself and Fermin Velez.

Early in the race, the ambient temperature was much higher than at any time during qualifying, and the softer tyres blistered badly. Pirelli had supplied the team with four compounds but the drivers needed the hardest to complete two stints on one set.

On only the second lap, Evans was in the Mulsanne corner gravel trap after swerving to avoid another car, sustaining front-end damage. A fresh radiator and nose were fitted but the car (leading at right) lost four laps in the process. Two hours after rejoining, the Wall Street banker (and new owner of the IMSA series) was still in the cockpit when the engine stopped in the Porsche curves. It had run for 11 laps on the previous stint and still had four litres in

OLD FOES JOIN FORCES

the fuel cell. Evans was approaching the end of his 11th lap on this tank when the V12 ran out...

Scandia's other Ferrari – sponsored here by 1001 Belgian citizens, including entertainment, sporting and royal celebrities – had better fortune for a long while. Poele raced in the leading group until the tyre problem dropped him back. Co-driven by Eric Bachelart and Marc Goossens, the car (above) went much better in the cool of the night. Soon after dawn, the crew completed a gearbox replacement in half an hour, and then Poele broke the lap record several times. The surviving 333 SP was running fifth when Bachelart crashed it on the run down towards the Esses, just before 7am.

Over in America, the 333 SP was being outperformed by the latest R&S sports-racers. Ferrari secured only three victories in the final season of the IMSA series, all by Momo Corse.

ROOCKIE CONQUEST

The GT2 division was well won by Le Mans rookies Ralf Kelleners, Bruno Eichmann and Guy Martinolle, driving for Roock Racing Team, which was also on début here. Pictured at top right, their car led the class throughout and finished four laps clear of its closest challenger in a 1-2 for the Porsche 911 GT2.

This year Porsche's private army provided eight of 11 starters in the category and, after the disappointment of Le Mans 1995, Porsche Motorsport prepared M64/81 engines for seven of them. The ACO allowed these cars slightly bigger air restrictors this time, which translated to a useful 25bhp hike in power, to about 475bhp. The car prepared by Fabian and Michael Roock also benefited from Porsche's Evo upgrades and had as much as 40bhp over the opposition: Kelleners's excellent class 'pole' was more than six seconds faster than the best Porsche GT2 lap from 1995.

The Roock team from Leverkusen moved up this year to the BPR series from the ADAC GT championship and was immediately competitive against the established teams in both GT1 and GT2. After the early departure of the Marcos, its GT2 entry dominated here. The crew had ample time to replace a broken driveshaft at around midday. However, the drivers spent the last 90 minutes with frayed nerves, and with a precariously feathered throttle, after the fractures of two of three bolts securing a turbocharger to its exhaust manifold.

The fancied GT2 teams were also beaten by another newcomer, calling itself 'Le Kiwi Comeback'. Both PARR Motorsport entries bore the names of 1966 winners Chris Amon and Bruce McLaren, and the little team finished second with four-time New Zealand Porsche Cup champion Bill Farmer and his fellow Kiwi Greg Murphy sharing with Robert Nearn. Pictured (bottom right) in the Virage Ford, their car spent less time in the pits than any other except the overall winner.

PARR (founder Paul Robe's full initials) had been set up only 12 months before in Crowhurst to run Farmer's new 911 GT2 in BPR events. This season it entered the Daytona 24 Hours, and the car led the class for a long while with Farmer, Murphy, Nearn and Stéphane Ortelli (on loan

1996

OLD FOES JOIN FORCES

from Porsche). The team then picked up another 911 GT2, owned by three British amateurs, and prequalified both at Le Mans, before running Farmer's car to second place at Montlhéry. After the owners had pulled the second car, Robe did a Le Mans deal with Peter Seikel, whose car was raced by Ortelli with Andy Pilgrim and another Kiwi, Andrew Bagnall. After the last-named had survived a big spin in the Dunlop curves, the car slipped behind the Honda in the division at 7:20am while the PARR crew replaced a turbo (above). It held on to fourth place despite ongoing turbo problems.

Seikel's other Porsche qualified last and finished fifth with a lacklustre performance that included Guy Kuster running out of gasoline, and driving a quarter-mile to his pit on the starter motor. Sixth was Jack Leconte's Larbre car (an 'Evo' version that had raced here in GT1 the previous June), which held second place before a long stop soon after 1am for new turbochargers.

Both the other 911 GT2s departed on Saturday afternoon, Steve O'Rourke's new EMKA car (repaired after Soames Langton's shunt in qualifying) when it broke its engine. The car of the Haberthur brothers, Olivier and Christian (below left), was stranded out in the country by a broken gear linkage. Stadler Motorsport's 911 GT2 was listed as a reserve, and was damaged in an accident in qualifying.

MAZDA WINS AGAIN

Five years after winning outright, Mazdaspeed went home to Hiroshima with another Le Mans trophy when Jim Downing's factory-backed American team was the only finisher in the LM-P2 category with its new Kudzu DLM, driven by Downing with his 1995 partners, Yojiro Terada and Franck Fréon.

Again entered at the ACO's invitation, the DLM was designed by Dave Lynn, and had débuted at Daytona in early February. The six previous Kudzu cars had started out as ground-effect designs, but the DLM was purpose-built for IMSA's flat-bottom WSC rules. The carbon/honeycomb hull had structural improvements aimed at reducing

1996

weight without compromising stiffness, such as a subframe optimized for the low-mounted rotary engine, and an integral rollover fabrication. Lynn devised a new aero package with a splitter ahead of the mandatory flat surface, and cut-outs in the wheel-arches further to increase front downforce without adding drag.

The three-rotor engine was equipped with the team's own intake system, first tried at Sebring in 1995, with in-line injectors offering better fuel flow. This helped a little with an engine now strangled by the ACO air restrictor, and developing about 400bhp at 8500rpm (65bhp less than in 1995). Nevertheless, the DLM was about 90kg lighter than its forerunner, and almost six seconds faster round the Circuit de la Sarthe.

Race-engineered again by Nigel Stroud, with Downing's long-serving engineer, John Greene, the Kudzu survived Fréon's light collision with David Brabham's McLaren in the Virage Ford in the early evening, and ran reliably until 1.30am, when Terada pitted with a punctured oil cooler. This was replaced in a 14-minute stop but, a couple of hours later, a more serious problem arose when a pinion bearing failed in the differential. Downing was able to continue for a while, but gearshifts were inducing high gearbox temperatures. The team had no spare gearbox, so the crew embarked on a rebuild that consumed five hours.

Fréon was eventually rejoined the race at 9:20am. Minor damage was caused two hours later when he spun into the gravel trap at Indianapolis. But the DLM, pictured below with the Larbre team's GT2 Porsche, made it to the finish, 103 laps down – but still a class winner.

NON-VENOMOUS VIPERS

A top-10 finish by the new GT1 Viper GTS-R raced by Price Cobb, Mark Dismore and Shawn Hendricks came as a pleasant surprise for Chrysler Corporation.

After the French privateer effort here of 1994, Chrysler was advised by a British motorsport consultant (who had better remain nameless) that the front-engined, 8-litre V10 Viper could win outright. The manufacturer chose to offer racecars to private entrants, with a range of specifications and technical support. Group director of engineering François Castaing set the Viper Engineering division under Neil Hannemann to work with the Chrysler Technology Center in Auburn Hills, Michigan, on creating a ground-up GT racing car, starting with the steel-tube chassis frame.

This was fully integrated with the rollcage and made more than twice as rigid as the standard structure, with a fully triangulated engine bay outrigger, a strengthened rear frame, and lightweight steel panels beneath the cabin providing reinforcement and the flat bottom. The powertrain was mounted lower, and slightly further rearward. The body was developed in the Reynard wind tunnel in England with a new rear wing and interchangeable underbodies, a cleaner nose, side exhaust sill fairings and the various inlet and cooling ducts. The bodies were then made in carbon/Kevlar by Reynard Composites.

Four race-engine options were based on a lighter version of the pushrod V10 that was new for the 1996 model year. John Caldwell's Caldwell Development company in California fitted a new flywheel, camshaft, valvegear and conrods, and uprated the fuelling, cooling,

OLD FOES JOIN FORCES | 241

LE MANS

oiling, ignition and control systems. The LM-GT1 specification, finalized with the help of Heini Mader in Gland, Switzerland, offered about 690bhp. The V10 drove through a racing clutch and the road car's six-speed Borg-Warner transmission – preferred to racing units because of the high torque output.

The stock double-wishbone suspension geometry was retained but its components were remade in aerospace aluminium alloys and combined with racing uprights, dampers and anti-roll bars. A carbon braking system was offered, the power steering and other control systems were upgraded, and Viper Engineering worked closely with Michelin USA on tyre development.

For 1996, Chrysler supplied cars to two 'official' representatives, Victor Sifton's Toronto-based Canaska-Southwind team in North America, and Hugues de Chaunac's Signes-based ORECA organization in Europe (where the Viper was now branded as a Chrysler, not a Dodge). Three of these cars débuted at Daytona in early February, Canaska ran two at Sebring, and ORECA one in the Jarama BPR race in April. When five cars were brought to Prequalifying, the GTS-R turned out to be about six seconds slower than the new GT1 McLarens and Porsches. ORECA withdrew one of its three cars and, in race week, neither team saw the point of going for lap time.

Eric Hélary drove the fastest Viper lap in qualifying proper, but the other car qualified among the GT2s after a crankshaft breakage, to the dismay of ORECA technical director Arnaud Elizagaray, sporting director Pierre Dieudonné and team manager Philippe Leloup. This car was the only Viper not to finish, falling victim to a piston failure shortly before half-time when miles behind due to earlier starter motor and wheelbearing replacements. Hélary/Olivier Beretta/Philippe Gache (top left) finished 21st after losing 90 minutes to a broken oil pump, and more than an hour during the small hours to electrical malfunctions.

The successful Canaska Viper (above) suffered two broken fuel pumps, and its rear wheelbearings were overheated by the new brakes. TM Charlie Cook had to ask the drivers to nurse the car over the last six hours, with the brake bias balanced towards the front.

Its stablemate (bottom left) finished 23rd. Punctures far from the pits had delayed Alain Cudini and then John Morton before the team owner went off in one of the Mulsanne chicanes soon after dawn, damaging the car but eventually bringing it back to pit-lane for repairs. Later more time was spent replacing a seized rear wheelbearing and then Sifton did it again, this time at Indianapolis.

Later in the summer, ORECA entered four more BPR events, and Canaska contested the IMSA race at Mosport. No meaningful result was gained. By then, the penny had long since dropped, and was rolling down the road towards a GT2 programme in 1997.

OLD FOES JOIN FORCES

LE MANS

TRIPLE WHAMMIED

One year on from an inauspicious début by a Ford-engined Riley & Scott Mk3 in the 1995 Daytona 24 Hours, this Oldsmobile-backed chassis (below) won the race for Doyle Racing in the hands of Scott Sharp/Wayne Taylor/Jim Pace – and followed up with another victory in the Sebring 12 Hours, where Eric van der Poele drove in place of Sharp. The team just had to come to France in a bid for a unique 'triple crown'. Unfortunately a transmission failure at half-time intervened.

Bob Riley and expatriate Briton Mark Scott formed their racing partnership in 1990, building successful Chevrolet-shaped Trans-Am spaceframes (R&S Mk1) for customers. The Mk2 was a road car project, and the Mk3 was the Indianapolis-based company's first sports-racing car. During the 1995 IMSA season, the 'works' Mk3 and two customer cars became persistent thorns in the sides of the rival WSC teams and, with five victories for Dyson Racing, James Weaver ran Fermin Velez's Ferrari very close for the Drivers title.

Designed by Bob Riley, the Mk3 was assembled on a tubular spaceframe with bonded-on advanced-composites panelling. Its carbon/Kevlar bodywork was developed for downforce by aircraft designer John Roncz, using the Lockheed wind tunnel. Above an extended splitter, the nose contained a wide air intake for the radiator with ducts on either side taking airflow to the front brakes. Tall, flat-topped sidepods extended to the full width of the car and the engine airbox was arched by the rollover hoop. The engine cover and rear wheel-arches ended immediately behind the wheels, with an outboard wing mounted on the gearbox. Beneath this bodywork, Riley installed his innovative ('Riley Rocker') suspension systems, with separated springs and dampers.

The Mk3 was designed with an engine bay outrigger to take any stock-block powertrain. This chassis was powered by a 4-litre version of the all-aluminium, 32-valve Oldsmobile V8, as used in 4.5-litre form that year in the manufacturer's very successful Aurora coupés in the IMSA GTS-1 division. Built for Oldsmobile by Fritz Kayl's Katech race engine specialist in Clinton, north of Detroit, the WSC engine was limited by regulation to 10,500rpm and was rated at 550bhp at 9000rpm. The six-speed gearbox was the latest version of the venerable March unit, now supplied under licence by GeaRace.

The 'works' Mk3 came to Le Mans with a near-standard body, and far too much drag. The rear wing was flattened and the splitter shortened. When Taylor went third fastest in Prequalifying, the team hoped these adjustments would be enough, even though the drivers reported that they hardly had to brake for some corners, but merely

1996

to lift off the throttle. Another handicap for the R&S here was the rule obliging WSC cars to fit ferrous brakes – three disc changes would be needed to get through 24 hours.

Taylor started the R&S in seventh position. In the early laps on Saturday, the car turned out to be much heavier on fuel than expected. Race engineer Bill Riley had calculated that, to remain competitive, Sharp/Taylor/Pace would need to run as many as 11 laps between stops, but the car turned out to be half a gallon short of achieving even a 10-lap run. Some consolation came with the revelation that it could run four or five stints on the same set of tyres, so the pitstops were less time-consuming than they might have been. There were just more of them than planned…

Further delays were caused by an exploding valve on a nitrogen bottle at a routine pitstop, and Pace's excursion into the Indianapolis gravel trap, which filled the car with shingle and cracked a brake disc, costing six laps in repairs. Just after nightfall, Taylor also wasted time on a beach. Finally, at 2:35am, running down in 16th position, Pace stopped the Daytona and Sebring winner on the big straight with the CWP broken.

Back home in Indiana, the works/Doyle Racing alliance regrouped to win the next IMSA WSC race at Sears Point, and Taylor went on to clinch the first of a hat-trick of titles for Riley & Scott.

NISSAN OUTGUNNED

The performance of Nissan's GT-R LM racecars (above) had been greatly improved over the winter, but these front-engined saloons, although powerful, were no match for the GT1 Porsches or the latest McLarens. Only one finished the race.

NISMO returned to Japan after its exploratory 1995 GT1 foray and stroked out the heavy, iron-block, twin-turbo engine to 2.8 litres (lifting output to 600bhp despite this year's smaller air inlets), and mounted it lower in the engine bay and a little further rearward. A weight-saving programme through the whole car achieved a 40kg reduction. This time both Nissans were fitted with Inisia-JECS H-pattern gearboxes for the sake of durability. NISMO conducted extended tests on the Aida and Fuji circuits before running the cars in Prequalifying, and checked them out at Magny-Cours being bringing them to race week – when the lap-time gain of all the development turned out to be no less than 10 seconds.

Toshio Suzuki, sharing this time with both Nissan veterans Kazuyoshi Hoshino and Masahiro Hasemi, achieved a victory of sorts by lapping the faster car under four minutes. He went six seconds faster than namesake Aguri Suzuki, who was back here for the first time since his big Toyota crash in 1991, and was co-driven by Masahiko Kondo and Masahiko Kageyama.

OLD FOES JOIN FORCES

LE MANS

The faster car (above) had a terrific weekend, and arrived in the top dozen overall on Sunday morning. Then, at 11:50am, Toshio pitted to report a drivetrain vibration. The crew had to spend 35 minutes replacing the propshaft, and Hasemi drove it under the flag in 15th position. The other GT-R LM was similarly reliable throughout Saturday and all night, only for Aguri to crash in the Esses at 7am, blaming sudden brake failure.

Back in Tokyo, the GT-R LM project was halted, two years into a three-year programme. Although it marketed a special 'LM Limited' edition of the Skyline, Nissan's board was shocked by the purpose-designed Porsche 911 GT1. The company had been made to look naïve. Face had to be saved. NISMO commissioned an advanced GT1 racecar from TWR in England.

FASTER BUT STILL FRAGILE

Four Ferrari F40s contested GT1 but, although a couple could now be lapped much faster than 12 months before, they were not competitive with the latest McLarens and Porsches, and all were parked before half-time.

Michelotto's 1996 F40 GTE specification included an Xtrac six-speed sequential-shift gearbox, carbon-ceramic brake discs and other upgrades. Ferrari Club Italia's Igol-Ennea team (opposite) fitted all the newly available components and fresh livery to the car that had been raced here in 1994-95 (with Carl Rosenblad now co-driving Anders Olofsson and owner Luciano della Noce) and its 1995 F40 (for Eric Bernard/Jean-Marc Gounon/Paul Belmondo). Each was now fitted with the 3.6-litre engine, making 640bhp at 7300rpm.

In qualifying, Gounon beat the best F40 lap times of 1995 by more than three seconds, yet lined up in 16th position. After a cautious start

1996

by Belmondo, and a stronger shift by Gounon, Bernard encountered ignition problems at 4:40pm. The team replaced the black box and the battery and sent him on his way after a 15-minute delay, but the electrical malfunctions persisted and the car was retired at 6:30pm.

Olofsson also went much quicker in qualifying than he had the previous June in Noce's car, which was here for its third Le Mans (and the 32nd of its 39 races altogether). The old warhorse ran strongly and without mishap until 10pm, when Noce parked in the Arnage escape road with a blown engine.

The FCI team also entered a less-modified third GTE (bottom left), fitted with the 3.5-litre V8 and ferrous brakes, in which F40 regular Tetsuya Ota was partnered by Robin Donovan and Piero Nappi. They also had a good run but the first signs of a failing clutch came at dusk. At 2:50am, the clutch came apart, pitching Donovan into a gravel trap.

Stéphane Ratel's blue Pilot F40 LM (right) now also had the 3.5 engine. Nicolas Leboissetier had a spin in the second Mulsanne chicane 40 minutes into his first racing shift at Le Mans, and the much more experienced Michel Ferté later followed his example at Indianapolis. At 10:15pm, Olivier Thévenin pitted with a broken pinion in the gearbox. An hour went by before Leboissetier could set out on another shift – and, when he refuelled, gasoline from the vent bottle spilled onto the left-side exhaust, and the rookie found himself sitting in a fireball that lit up the pit-lane. The flames were quickly extinguished but the car's electrics were burned out.

These were the last F40s to appear at Le Mans. Although Ferrari commissioned Michelotto to produce three GT1 racing variants of the F40's replacement, the composite-hulled, 'atmo' V12 F50, testing during 1996 showed that they would have been uncompetitive with the latest GT1-legal prototypes. They were never raced.

OLD FOES JOIN FORCES 247

LE MANS

A FINAL FLING

Unwilling to invest a mile-high heap of yen in a sham GT1 project, Honda had pulled out of sportscar racing, preferring to dominate the IndyCar series in the United States. However Kunimitsu Takahashi's team, whose dependable 'atmo' NSX had won the 1995 GT2 class here (and later the Tokachi 24 Hours back home), took up its automatic entry for a third crack at Le Mans (above).

This time Team Kunimitsu had the trackside assistance of Seikel Motorsport, which had now operated Honda's official team in European touring car racing for three seasons. Takahashi was co-driven yet again by Keiichi Tsuchiya and Akira Iida, and they again had a very solid weekend, interrupted only by a couple of time-consuming punctures on Saturday evening. However, the Honda was not as competitive on a dry track as it had been in the rain of 1995, and the reward for its reliability this time was third in GT2 behind two Porsches.

Takahashi took his car back home, where he raced it for several more seasons with no more overseas forays.

KREMERS CRASH OUT

Kremer Racing had now returned to the Porsche fold, running GT2 cars in the new BPR series, but the Köln team also assembled a fourth K8 spyder and again entered two such cars at Le Mans. Both were crashed out of the race. This year's smaller air restrictors limited

1996

output to 530bhp, so Achim Stroth and his engineering team lightened the bodywork and took 30kg out of the cars (which were still overweight). Revised ducting to improve the airflow to the turbos, the radiators and the brakes came at a small cost in drag, and these revisions were tested in May on one car at Jarama, and on both at Most.

The new chassis (bottom left), driven by team regulars Christophe Bouchut and Jürgen Lässig with Harri Toivonen, was delayed early on when Lässig was stranded with no drive out at the Esses. It took him more than 20 minutes to find a gear, and a further 18 minutes disappeared in the pits while the linkage was repaired. The car was starting to make progress back up the field when Lässig dropped it in the Porsche curves. He made it back to pit-lane, but the damage was terminal.

What was left of the other K8 (right) was already in the truck. After a strong double shift by George Fouché, this car was spun at the same spot by Steve Fossett, and then crashed heavily at 7:20pm when the engine cover flew off on the super-fast run between Mulsanne and Indianapolis. A helpless Stanley Dickens was pitched into a 190mph accident, involving the barriers on both sides of the track. Mercifully the car did not flip over. The 1989 Le Mans winner emerged wide-eyed but unhurt.

LISTER PROGRESS

Having débuted his Lister Storm GTS in the 1995 Le Mans, Laurence Pearce engaged Tony Southgate to design the essentials of a major upgrade. Southgate concentrated on the front-engined car's tricky weight distribution, moving the big V12 engine six inches further aft in the frame, and locating a transverse Hewland TGT gearbox (first seen on the 1995 Le Mans Hondas) within the rear axle assembly. He also redesigned the front suspension and, to improve turn-in, used big wheels and wide tyres at the front as well as the rear.

Subsequently the upgrade was continued by Geoff Kingston, who started by taking no less than 100kg of weight out of the car. The first revised Storm was taken to Florida for the Daytona 24 Hours, but

OLD FOES JOIN FORCES

LE MANS

Kenneth Acheson was tripped up by a backmarker and pitched into multiple rolls on the infield there.

Back in Leatherhead, only about 20 percent of the wreck was found to be salvageable. Kingston took the opportunity to redesign the monocoque and had it made in aluminium honeycomb and carbon by G Force Composites. The replacement car was about 45kg lighter again, and Geoff Lees went 12 seconds faster at Prequalifying than he had managed with the 1995 car. In race week, the Lister was on the pace of the Ferraris and McLarens.

Lees/Tiff Needell/Anthony Reid raced strongly and were running 13th at 4:45am, when Needell pitted with an inoperative gearbox. It took more than 80 minutes to fit a replacement. Two hours after rejoining, the car lost another 45 minutes to a fractured brake master cylinder, and finished 19th after covering only four laps in the final hour with a sick engine.

Later Lees/Needell later did four BPR Global GT races, but the Storm did not finish again.

IN THE WALL

The centre-seat WR-Peugeots raced for the last time, because the ACO's 1997 regulations would require LMP cars to be two-seaters. Having locked out the front row of the grid 12 months before, the team found new limits on its car's performance: a reduction in air-restrictor diameter, the addition of 30kg to the overall weight of 620kg in 1995, the imposition of a 'boost' limit, and a reduced, 62-litre fuel cell. Although increased in swept volume to 1999cc, the single-turbo engines were about 30bhp down.

These limitations and a big shunt meant that only one of five WRs made it through Prequalifying, and only after a big push in the final minutes by Patrick Gonin with the team's new chassis. William David lost control at Tertre Rouge on a hot lap and hit Bertrand Gachot's ex-works 1994 WR (fitted with a Ssangyong 2-litre turbo), which was parked on the verge and being worked on by two mechanics. One of them was injured, and both cars were badly damaged. Another 1994 chassis, entered by Graff Racing, and Alain Lebrun's 1993 car also failed to prequalify. However,

250 LE MANS 24 HOURS 1990–99

1996

the Welters presented a 1995 chassis at scrutineering as a reserve entry. Gonin qualified the lead car 12th (more than four seconds off the 1995 pole) and, as a result of the Debora's engine failure on race morning, both WRs started.

After a reliable early run, the newer car lost its right-rear wheel on the Mulsanne straight. Pierre Petit three-wheeled back to the pits and continued, but Gonin crashed out on Sunday morning. Its twin (left) was delayed first by a puncture, then a transmission rebuild, and a cooling system repair. It too finished its race in the wall when David went off in the Porsche curves at daybreak.

SUFFERING SUPRA

Toyota returned with a reworked Supra GT1 racecar (above), but it was not competitive with the latest McLarens and Porsches, and was crashed out of the midfield on Sunday morning.

TRD revised the specification of the Supra GT1 over the winter, and built four new cars for works-supported teams to contest the now-booming All-Japan GT series, with smaller, 2-litre versions of the turbocharged, four-cylinder 3S-GTE engines and Hewland gearboxes to comply with JAF's regulations. A fifth Supra was specially built for SARD to operate at Le Mans, again with the 2.1 engine but with an Xtrac six-speed sequential gearbox. The ACO's 1996 regulations limited output to 600bhp at 7000rpm. The Supra weighed nearly 100kg less than in 1995, mainly through the deletion of some rollcage elements and the use of more carbon/Kevlar material in the body, which was much altered after wind-tunnel development.

Masanori Sekiya/Masami Kageyama/Hidetoshi Mitsusada raced without mishap in the midfield until just after half-time, when Mitsusada's spin damaged the underfloor and exhaust system. These were repaired but, at 8:10am, the same driver was clipped by Scott Goodyear's Porsche 911 GT1 in the Porsche curves, lost control and hit the wall.

Although the Toyota Supra would win the 1997 All-Japan GT title for Pedro de la Rosa and Michael Krumm, this was its final appearance at Le Mans: the GT1 goalposts had been moved out of its sights.

Shortly after Le Mans, an all-new Toyota LMP sports-racer was tested in England. Toyota had commissioned the project from TOMS GB in January 1996. Designed by Andy Thorby and Martin Ogilvie, it was a carbonfibre/honeycomb monocoque with the four-cylinder 3S-GTE turbo and an Xtrac transverse gearbox. The first chassis was completed in June and tested at Snetterton. The LMP was aimed at Le Mans 1997, but it never happened.

LE MANS

FINISHING ON SEVEN

After its disappointment in June 1995, the SARD team brought its Toyota MR2-based MC8-R to the finish in the Suzuka 1000 round of the BPR series that August, and built up a second GT1 car (below) over the winter for another Le Mans attempt.

The extensively reworked 1996 MC-8R was no less than 212kg lighter than the previous car, due mainly to a much lighter structure made from thinner-gauge sheet steel. It was also equipped with a 15kg lighter transmission assembly, with a March five-speed gearbox with the oil tank relocated into the bellhousing, while more weight was saved by lighter bodywork.

The lowered racing weight of the car obliged the team to fit smaller air restrictors to the twin-turbo, 4-litre Lexus V8, and 'boost' pressure was also much reduced, limiting the engine to 600bhp at 7000rpm. Prior to Le Mans, the new car completed 1250 miles of track work at Paul Ricard, Snetterton and Le Mans in the Prequalifying sessions, driven by Alain Ferté.

The MC-8R ran consistently for the first six hours, but persistently overheated, which eventually led to a gearbox failure requiring the whole unit to be changed.

This accomplished, the car rejoined the race, only to break a piston. This was isolated and, by keeping to a 5600rpm rev limit and making frequent stops for water, Ferté, Mauro Martini and Pascal Fabre drove the car to the finish, second to last.

GOING DUTCH

Marcos built a third, stiffer 600LM racecar late in 1995 for Cor Euser to set up Team Marcos International in his native Holland, where it was equipped with a DOHC Chevrolet LT5 V8 prepared by Kok Motorsport. Co-driven by Thomas Erdos, it began its season with GT2 pole positions in the BPR events at Paul Ricard and Jarama and, in between, led the class at Monza until mechanical problems intervened. At Prequalifying, Euser again embarrassed the Porsche and Corvette teams by setting the fastest GT2 time. One of the 1995 cars, now owned by Rob Schirle, failed to make the cut even though Win Percy went four seconds faster than Euser had managed the year before.

Euser/Erdos then won GT2 in the Silverstone BPR race, and finished first overall in a British GT event at the same venue. No wonder the team came back to France brimming with confidence.

The yellow Marcos (right) had ignition problems in qualifying but was soon up to third in the class on Saturday, and challenging for the lead. After a single shift by French journalist Pascal Dro, Euser was driving when, just after 6pm, the engine began smoking heavily. The crew added six litres of oil but, on his out-lap, the V8 spewed it all onto the track. It transpired that an electrical fault had shut down a sensor, starving one cylinder of fuel and causing a holed piston.

Over the rest of the summer, Euser continued to get GT2 poles in the BPR series, but won the class only at Zhuhai. Meanwhile Schirle and co-driver Dave Warnock won the GT2 title in the British series.

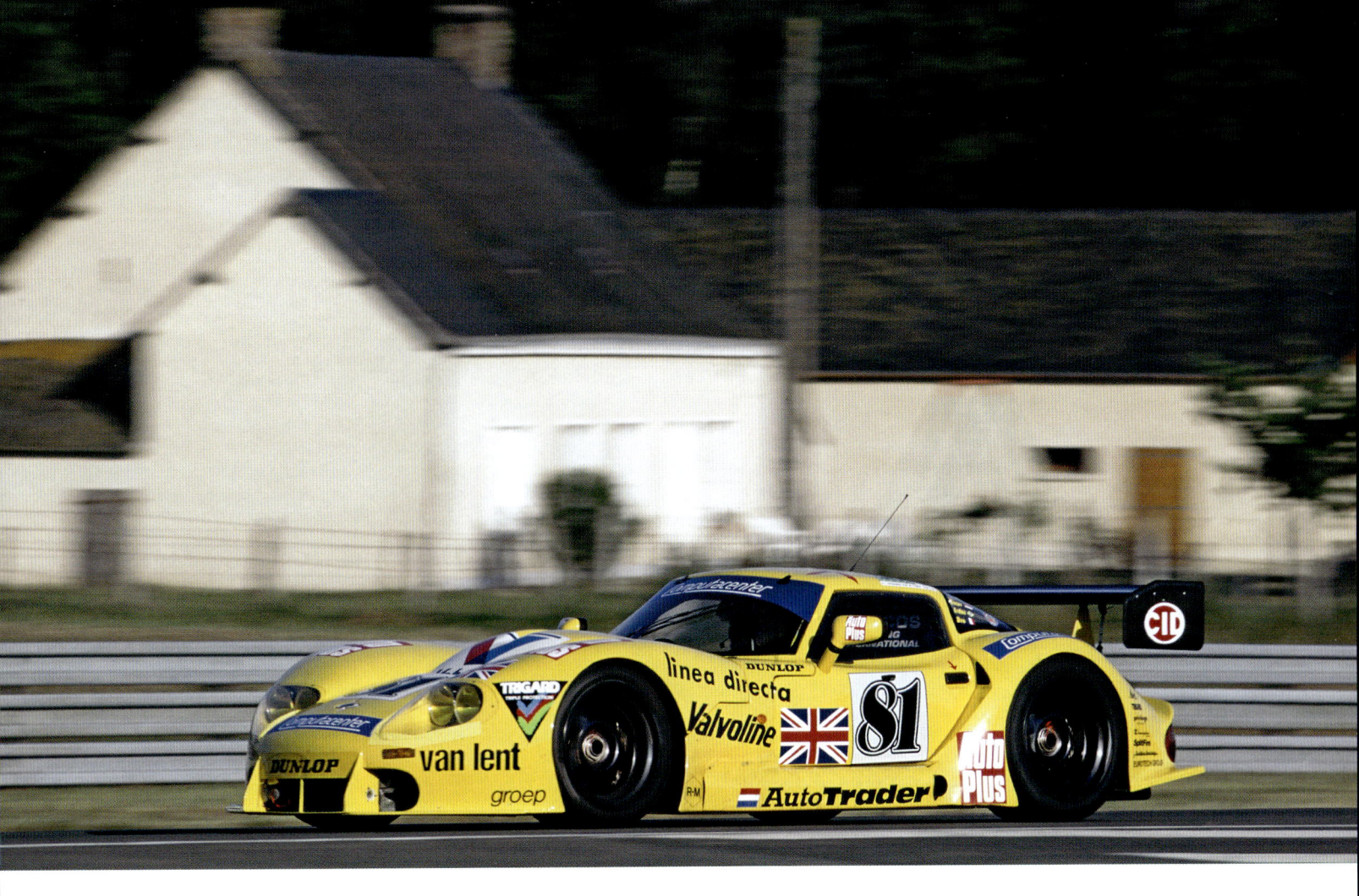

FREQUENT TRAVELLER

This year Callaway Competition entered a purpose-designed GT1 coupé, the front/mid-engined Callaway C7-R. Built in its European racing HQ at Leingarten, this had a carbon-composites monocoque with a ground-effect aero package, and was powered by a 665bhp evolution of Callaway's 'SuperNatural' Chevrolet LT5 V8. Two of these promising cars were brought to Prequalifying. However, one was unfinished, and did not run, while the development prototype, which had been testing for a couple of months, broke its differential and missed the cut.

This season 'Rocky' Agusta's team ran its sole-surviving Callaway Corvette (right) to a lowly finish at Daytona and then Almo Coppelli won the GTS-1 division in the opening round of the SCCA World Challenge in St Petersburg. The next day, the car was flown back to Europe for the first three rounds of the BPR series at Ricard, Monza and Jarama. Back across the Atlantic, Coppelli scored two more class victories at Mosport and Lime Rock, and then the hard-working Corvette returned to England for Le Mans preparations. Its exhausted mechanics were replaced for this race by a Callaway crew.

Coppelli matched his 1995 qualifying time but was beaten to the GT2 'pole' by the Roock team's Porsche. Just after 8pm on Saturday, Coppelli ran over some debris on the Mulsanne straight and burst the left-rear tyre. By the time he reached pit-lane, the flailing rubber had destroyed the rear bodywork and many of the ancillaries in the engine compartment. Two hours were required for repairs, but during that time the crew did not notice a small crack in the gearbox casing. Back on track, an oil leak ruined the transmission, forcing the car's retirement just after half-time.

It continued to criss-cross the Atlantic. It struggled in three more BPR outings but Coppelli did enough in North America to clinch the GTS-1 championship. As for the C7-R, it did not race until the Daytona 24 Hours the following January, and was then made obsolete by rule changes.

LE MANS

OUTDATED CUSTOMERS

Three Porsche 911 GT2 Evos were entered in the GT1 division even though their owners could not hope to compete with the factory team's mid-engined 911 GT1s. The only Evo to reach the end was Jean-Luc Chéreau's, in which Larbre Compétition displayed the owner's lack of ambition by fitting a 475bhp GT2 engine for the weekend, and going for durability. Pictured (above) leading one of the new factory cars into Tertre Rouge, Chéreau, Pierre Yver and Jack Leconte finished miles behind after losing almost two hours replacing blown turbochargers.

Franz Konrad's Gütersloh-based car (pictured at the start of the Mulsanne straight) never featured before midnight, when it was crashed at speed by rookie Wido Roessler while exiting Arnage. Roock Racing's Evo was delayed by an oil leak and a rear suspension failure, both when Jean-Pierre Jarier was driving, and when Jesús Pareja was trying to make up more time lost to a driveshaft breakage, the engine packed up at 11:10pm and he parked at Mulsanne corner.

LE MANS 24 HOURS 1990-99

1996

DEBORA MISSES OUT

Two new Debora LMP296 prototypes were built this year, and the ACO selected one of them to take a bye to race week (right). The Besançon team had to prequalify a second car, and failed to do so despite its ability to lap three seconds faster than the LMP295, thanks to aerodynamic upgrades. The ACO's 1996 regulation changes brought the bodywork rules in P1 and P2 into line, which allowed Didier Bonnet to fit a rear wing overhanging the tail of the car, and high enough above the engine cover to allow it to work properly. On the other hand, the 1996 rules strangled the 2-litre Cosworth turbo engine with a smaller restrictor and lower 'boost', reducing its output to only 360bhp at 8000rpm.

An electronics problem in Wednesday qualifying prevented the LMP296 from running cleanly. This was rectified for the second sessions, but only just long enough for Floridian hotel owner Edouard Sezionale to scrape the car into the race. A blown engine in the Saturday morning warm-up prevented the Debora from taking the start.

LOCAL INTEREST

Legeay Sports, the Renault tuning specialist in Teloché, near Mulsanne corner, returned to its local race with this evolution of the Renault Sport Spider (right), but it prequalified only as a reserve.

The aluminium-chassis, plastic-bodied RS Spider was powered by the 2-litre, 16-valve F7R engine from the Clio Williams road car, installed transversely amidships in unit with the gearbox. Designed by Claude Fior, it went on sale early in 1996. A Cup racing version was offered from the outset, offering 180bhp and a six-speed Sadev transmission with sequential-shift controls. In all, 80 of these racecars would be produced.

Legeay Sports converted a frame from Fior's factory in Nogaro by fitting a longer, coupé body and the 3-litre, twin-turbo PRV V6 powertrain from its Alpine A610 GT2 project. The team had to enter this 500bhp one-off in the GT1 division and it was hampered by its brick-like aerodynamics. Despite the best efforts of Marc Sourd, it was outpaced even by the GT2 Porsches. It came to race week, but was not needed.

OLD FOES JOIN FORCES

LE MANS

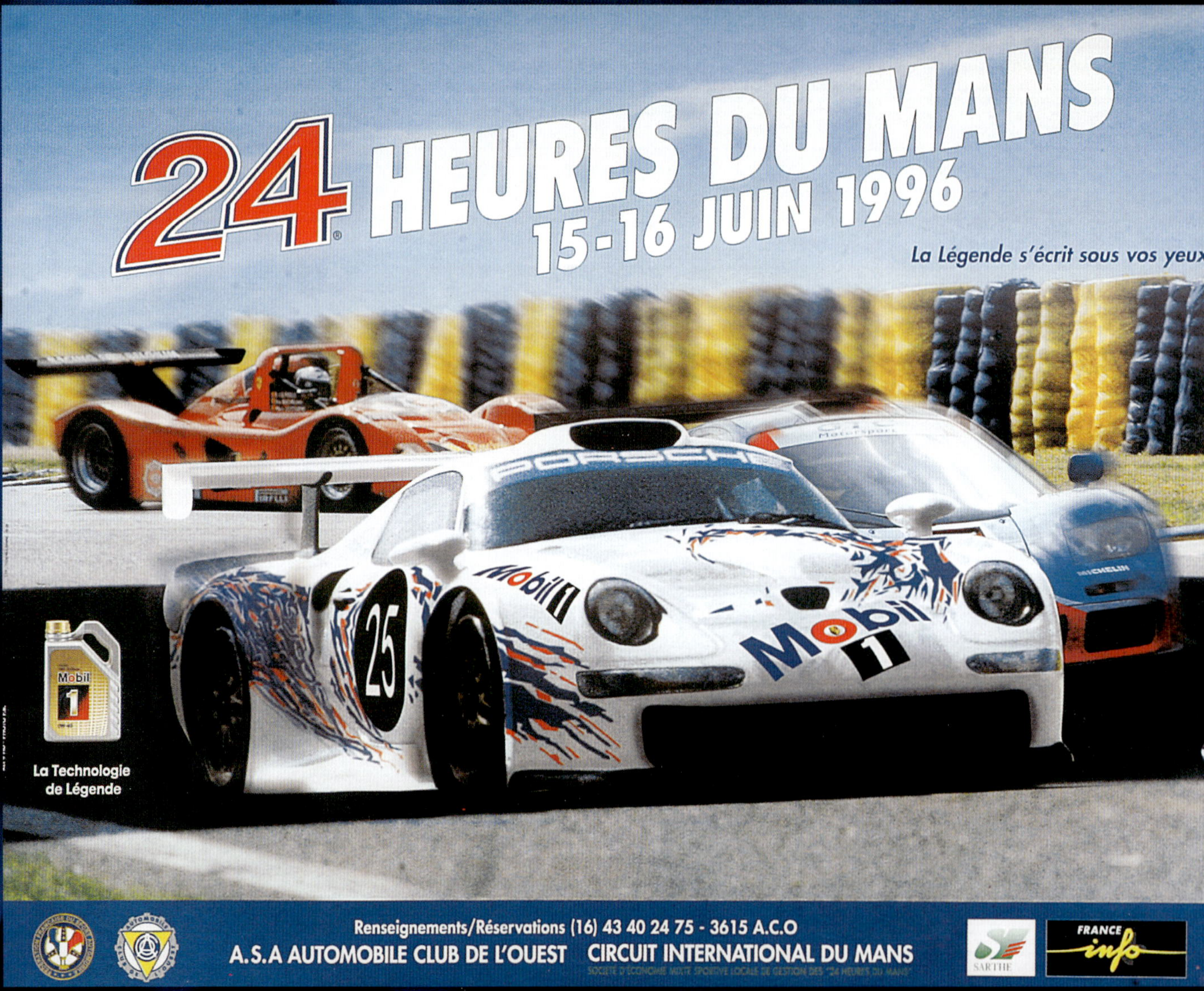

24 HEURES DU MANS
15-16 JUIN 1996
La Légende s'écrit sous vos yeux
PORSCHE
Mobil 1
25
La Technologie de Légende
Renseignements/Réservations (16) 43 40 24 75 - 3615 A.C.O
A.S.A AUTOMOBILE CLUB DE L'OUEST
CIRCUIT INTERNATIONAL DU MANS
SARTHE
FRANCE info

1996

HOURLY RACE POSITIONS

Prequalifying		Start	Time	Car	No	Drivers	1	2	3	4	5	6	7	8	9	10	11	12	13	14	15	16	17	18	19	20	21	22	23	24
5	3:49.623	Martini	1	3:46.682	TWR-Porsche WSC95	8	Alboreto/Martini/Theys	2	2	3	3	3	3	2	2	2	2	3	3	3	3	3	3	3	3	4	4	3	6	8	DNF
*	3:52.297	Policand	3	3:46.792	Courage C36	3	Alliot/Policand/Cottaz	4	33	19	18	14	12	10	9	6	5	4	4	4	4	4	DNF								
1	3:47.795	Poele	5	3:46.838	Ferrari 333SP-LM	17	Poele/Goossens/Bachelart	14	8	10	6	8	7	8	8	5	6	5	6	5	5	10	DNF								
15	3:52.207	Wendlinger	2	3:47.132	Porsche 911 GT1	26	Dalmas/Wendlinger/Goodyear	3	5	4	4	4	4	7	10	8	7	11	9	12	9	7	5	5	5	6	6	4	3	3	3
11	3:50.995	Boutsen	4	3:47.139	Porsche 911 GT1	25	Wollek/Stuck/Boutsen	5	4	2	2	2	2	4	4	3	3	2	2	2	2	2	2	2	2	2	2	2	2	2	2
10	3:50.912	Reuter	7	3:47.383	TWR-Porsche WSC95	7	Jones/Wurz/Reuter	1	1	1	1	1	1	1	1	1	1	1	1	1	1	1	1	1	1	1	1	1	1	1	1
3	3:48.963	Taylor	9	3:47.635	Riley & Scott Mk3	19	Sharp/Taylor/Pace	15	12	6	9	17	17	17	16	16	16	15	19	DNF											
18	3:53.746	Cecotto	6	3:48.530	McLaren F1 GTR LM	38	Soper/Laffite/Duez	9	9	8	10	9	9	6	7	9	9	7	7	7	12	16	12	13	16	15	16	14	14	13	11
4	3:49.441	Lammers	11	3:49.749	Courage C36	4	Andretti/Lammers/Warwick	8	7	18	44	38	37	34	31	28	26	21	18	18	17	14	15	12	10	10	8	16	13	15	13
6	3:50.248	Lehto	8	3:49.951	McLaren F1 GTR LM	33	Weaver/Lehto/Bellm	6	6	5	5	5	5	3	3	4	4	6	5	6	6	5	4	4	4	3	3	7	10	10	9
*			13	3:50.130	Kremer K8	1	Bouchut/Toivonen/Lässig	7	3	33	43	39	38	38	34	31	DNF														
8	3:50.312	Gonin	15	3:50.252	WR LM96	14	Gonin/Petit/Rostan	20	45	44	35	40	39	39	35	34	30	29	27	26	26	23	21	20	21	23	DNF				
2	3:48.608	Poele	17	3:50.849	Ferrari 333SP-LM	18	Evans/Muller/Velez	48	47	48	DNF																				
12	3:51.233	Raphanel	10	3:51.292	McLaren F1 GTR LM	34	Brabham/Raphanel/Owen-Jones	16	14	14	11	11	10	11	11	13	11	10	11	9	8	6	7	6	7	8	7	6	4	5	5
13	3:51.484	Soper	12	3:51.547	McLaren F1 GTR LM	39	Piquet/Sullivan/Cecotto	10	11	7	8	7	8	9	6	11	10	9	8	8	7	8	6	8	8	7	10	9	9	9	8
20	3:56.128	Gounon	14	3:52.072	Ferrari F40 GT Evo	45	Gounon/Bernard/Belmondo	19	46	42	46	DNF																			
7	3:50.272	Lagorce	19	3:52.149	Courage C36	5	Pescarolo/Collard/Lagorce	12	10	9	7	6	6	5	5	7	13	24	20	19	18	17	11	10	12	11	11	9	8	7	7
9	3:50.334	Bouchut	21	3:52.376	Kremer K8	2	Fouché/Dickens/Fossett	13	17	22	29	DNF																			
14	3:51.602	David	25	3:53.954	WR LM95/6	15	David/Enjolras/Trévisiol	17	21	21	19	18	26	23	20	25	32	32	30	29	29	DNF									
*			16	3:54.026	McLaren F1 GTR LM	53	Sala/Giroix/Deletraz	24	16	15	15	33	28	31	28	23	20	19	DNF												
22	3:57.133	Lees	18	3:54.603	Lister Storm GTL	28	Lees/Needell/Reid	18	19	13	14	13	14	16	15	15	13	13	13	13	13	19	18	22	21	19	19	19	18	19
25	3:57.740	Olofsson	20	3:54.730	Ferrari F40 GT Evo	44	Olofsson/Rosenblad/Noce	22	20	16	16	16	15	15	DNF																
16	3:53.171	Nielsen	22	3:55.924	McLaren F1 GTR LM	30	Nielsen/Bscher/Kox	21	15	12	12	10	13	12	12	10	8	8	10	11	10	9	8	7	6	5	5	5	5	4	4
19	3:55.484	Wallace	24	3:56.210	McLaren F1 GTR LM	29	Bell/Wallace/Grouillard	25	13	11	13	12	11	13	13	12	14	12	12	10	11	11	9	9	9	9	9	8	7	6	6
*	3:58.635	M.Ferté	26	3:57.225	Ferrari F40 LM	56	M.Ferté/Thévenin/Leboissetier	23	22	27	20	19	20	32	37	38	DNF														
*	3:57.956	Fréon	23	3:57.336	Kudzu DLM	20	Downing/Terada/Fréon	11	18	17	17	15	16	14	14	14	12	14	14	14	23	27	28	28	28	27	26	26	26	26	25
21	3:57.704	Gache	27	3:59.062	Chrysler Viper GTS-R	50	Hélary/Beretta/Gache	33	26	24	22	41	42	41	38	35	33	33	33	31	31	30	27	25	24	23	23	22	21
29	4:00.420	Jarier	28	3:59.630	Porsche 911 GT2 Evo	55	Jarier/Pareja/Chappell	43	48	46	41	36	35	33	36	37	37	37	DNF												
30	4:01.272	Hasemi	29	3:59.946	Nissan Skyline GT-R LM	23	Hasemi/Hoshino/Suzuki	32	28	26	24	23	19	22	21	19	18	18	17	17	16	15	14	13	13	13	12	16	16	15
23	3:57.549	Cobb	30	4:01.195	Chrysler Viper GTS-R	48	Cobb/Dismore/Hendricks	29	24	20	28	22	22	21	18	18	17	16	16	16	14	12	10	15	14	14	14	11	11	11	10
31	4:02.013	Nappi	31	4:02.550	Ferrari F40 GT Evo	59	Donovan/Nappi/Ota	27	29	28	25	24	29	25	24	33	34	34	32	DNF											
36	4:04.351	Robert	RES	4:03.181	Renault Spider V6 Coupé	32	Sourd/Robert/Daoudi	—																							
28	4:00.416	Cudini	32	4:03.781	Chrysler Viper GTS-R	49	Cudini/Morton/Sifton	37	32	45	36	32	33	30	29	30	31	31	29	28	28	28	25	26	25	24	24	24	23
34	4:02.694	Konrad	33	4:05.148	Porsche 911 GT2 Evo	37	Konrad/Azevedo/Roessler	31	27	25	23	20	21	20	19	DNF															
41	4:08.938	Eichmann	34	4:05.889	Porsche 911 GT2	79	Kelleners/Eichmann/Martinolle	26	23	23	21	21	18	18	17	17	19	17	15	15	15	13	14	11	11	12	12	13	12	12	12
*			35	4:06.184	Nissan Skyline GT-R LM	22	Suzuki/Kageyama/Kondo	35	40	37	32	28	25	24	23	26	23	22	22	22	21	19	16	DNF							
*			36	4:06.532	Toyota Supra LM	57	Sekiya/Mitsusada/Kageyama	30	30	32	27	25	29	30	27	25	25	24	23	24	24	23	DNF								
42	4:09.392	Coppelli	37	4:09.350	Callaway Corvette	74	Coppelli/Agusta/Camus	47	42	41	37	34	40	42	39	36	35	35	35	DNF											
33	4:02.172	A.Ferté	38	4:09.453	SARD Toyota MC8-R	46	A.Ferté/Martini/Fabre	36	34	30	30	27	23	37	40	39	36	36	34	32	32	31	29	27	27	26	25	25	25	25	24
38	4:05.997	Favre	RES	4:09.673	Venturi 600S-LM	40	Clérico/Lécuyer/Maury-Laribière	—																							
47	4:12.599	Evans	39	4:10.204	Porsche 911 GT2	83	Ortelli/Pilgrim/Bagnall	42	38	36	34	31	30	27	27	24	24	23	23	20	20	20	18	17	17	18	18	18	19	17
45	4:10.948	Neugarten	40	4:10.781	Porsche 911 GT2	73	Neugarten/Seiler/Ilien	46	44	39	42	DNF																			
35	4:04.326	Chéreau	41	4:10.848	Porsche 911 GT2 Evo	27	Chéreau/Yver/Leconte	38	37	35	31	29	27	26	25	22	21	27	31	30	29	26	24	23	22	23	23	22
26	3:58.588	Dupuy	42	4:11.014	Chrysler Viper GTS-R	51	McCarthy/Bell/Dupuy	41	36	31	38	42	41	40	41	40	38	38	36	DNF											
40	4:08.931	Euser	43	4:11.660	Marcos Mantara 600LM	81	Euser/Erdos/Dro	28	25	40	45	DNF																			
44	4:10.849	Goueslard	44	4:11.789	Porsche 911 GT2	82	Goueslard/Ahrle/Bourdais	34	31	29	26	26	24	22	22	20	27	26	25	24	22	25	23	22	19	20	21	21	21	20
43	4:10.689	Langton	45	4:12.787	Porsche 911 GT2	70	O'Rourke/Holmes/Langton	44	41	47	DNF																				
46	4:11.367	Ortelli	46	4:12.878	Porsche 911 GT2	71	Murphy/Farmer/Nearn	39	35	34	33	30	31	28	26	21	20	21	21	19	18	17	16	16	15	15	15	14	14
49	4:14.260	Richter		4:14.220	Porsche 911 GT2	72	Calderari/Bryner/Richter	DNS																							
*	4:14.969	Tsuchiya	47	4:18.473	Honda NSX	75	Takahashi/Tsuchiya/Iida	45	39	38	40	35	34	35	32	29	28	29	28	26	25	24	21	18	18	17	17	17	16
*	4:18.174	Seikel	48	4:22.697	Porsche 911 GT2	77	Kuster/Jurasz/Suzuki	40	43	43	39	37	36	36	33	32	29	30	27	27	24	21	21	20	19	20	20	20	18
*			RES	4:33.664	Debora LMP296	9	Lecerf/Basso/Sezionale	DNS																							

DNF Did not finish **DNQ** Did not qualify **DSQ** Disqualified **FS** Failed scrutineering **NC** Not classified as a finisher **RES** Reserve not required * Automatic entry

OLD FOES JOIN FORCES

LE MANS

RACE RESULTS

Pos	Car	No	Drivers			Laps	Km	Miles	FIA Class	DNF
1	TWR-Porsche WSC95	7	Davy Jones (USA)	Alex Wurz (A)	Manuel Reuter (D)	354	4814.400	2991.529	LM-P1/C90	
2	Porsche 911 GT1	25	Hans-Joachim Stuck (D)	Bob Wollek (F)	Thierry Boutsen (B)	353	4800.812	2983.086	LM-GT1	
3	Porsche 911 GT1	26	Karl Wendlinger (A)	Yannick Dalmas (F)	Scott Goodyear (CDN)	341	4637.591	2881.665	LM-GT1	
4	McLaren F1 GTR LM	30	John Nielsen (DK)	Thomas Bscher (D)	Peter Kox (NL)	338	4596.801	2856.320	LM-GT1	
5	McLaren F1 GTR LM	34	David Brabham (AUS)	Pierre-Henri Raphanel (F)	Lindsay Owen-Jones (GB)	335	4556.007	2830.971	LM-GT1	
6	McLaren F1 GTR LM	29	Derek Bell (GB)	Andy Wallace (GB)	Olivier Grouillard (F)	328	4460.794	2771.809	LM-GT1	
7	Courage C36	5	Henri Pescarolo (F)	Emmanuel Collard (F)	Franck Lagorce (F)	327	4447.196	2763.360	LM-P1/C90	
8	McLaren F1 GTR LM	39	Nelson Piquet (BR)	Danny Sullivan (USA)	Johnny Cecotto (YV)	324	4406.403	2738.012	LM-GT1	
9	McLaren F1 GTR LM	33	James Weaver (GB)	JJ Lehto (SF)	Ray Bellm (GB)	323	4392.800	2729.554	LM-GT1	
10	Chrysler Viper GTS-R	48	Price Cobb (USA)	Mark Dismore (USA)	Shawn Hendricks (USA)	320	4352.000	2704.202	LM-GT1	
11	McLaren F1 GTR LM	38	Jacques Laffite (F)	Steve Soper (GB)	Marc Duez (B)	318	4324.805	2687.304	LM-GT1	
12	Porsche 911 GT2	79	Ralf Kelleners (D)	Bruno Eichmann (CH)	Guy Martinolle (F)	317	4311.224	2678.865	LM-GT2	
13	Courage C36	4	Mario Andretti (USA)	Jan Lammers (NL)	Derek Warwick (GB)	315	4284.006	2661.953	LM-P1/C90	
14	Porsche 911 GT2	71	Greg Murphy (NZ)	Bill Farmer (NZ)	Robert Nearn (GB)	313	4256.792	2645.043	LM-GT2	
15	Nissan Skyline GT-R LM	23	Toshio Suzuki (J)	Masahiro Hasemi (J)	Kazuyoshi Hoshino (J)	307	4175.201	2594.345	LM-GT1	
16	Honda NSX GT	75	Kunimitsu Takahashi (J)	Keiichi Tsuchiya (J)	Akira Iida (J)	305	4148.009	2577.448	LM-GT2	
DNF	TWR-Porsche WSC95	8	Michele Alboreto (I)	Pierluigi Martini (I)	Didier Theys (B)	300			LM-P1/C90	Transmission (driveshaft)
17	Porsche 911 GT2	83	Stéphane Ortelli (F)	Andy Pilgrim (USA)	Andrew Bagnall (NZ)	299	4066.389	2526.732	LM-GT2	
18	Porsche 911 GT2	77	Guy Kuster (F)	Manfred Jurasz (A)	Takaji Suzuki (J)	297	4039.208	2509.843	LM-GT2	
19	Lister Storm GTL	28	Geoff Lees (GB)	Tiff Needell (GB)	Anthony Reid (GB)	295	4011.997	2492.935	LM-GT1	
20	Porsche 911 GT2	82	Patrice Goueslard (F)	André Ahrle (F)	Patrick Bourdais (F)	284	3862.407	2399.984	LM-GT2	
21	Chrysler Viper GTS-R	50	Eric Hélary (F)	Olivier Beretta (MC)	Philippe Gache (F)	283	3848.790	2391.523	LM-GT1	
22	Porsche 911 GT2 Evo	27	Jean-Luc Chéreau (F)	Pierre Yver (F)	Jack Leconte (F)	279	3794.412	2357.734	LM-GT1	
23	Chrysler Viper GTS-R	49	Alain Cudini (F)	John Morton (USA)	Victor Sifton (CDN)	269	3658.409	2273.226	LM-GT1	
24	SARD MC8-R	46	Alain Ferté (F)	Mauro Martini (I)	Pascal Fabre (F)	256	3481.606	2163.366	LM-GT1	
25	Kudzu DLM	20	Yojiro Terada (J)	Jim Downing (USA)	Franck Fréon (F)	251	3413.596	2121.106	LM-P2	
DNF	WR LM96	14	Patrick Gonin (F)	Pierre Petit (F)	Marc Rostan (F)	221			LM-P2	Accident
DNF	Courage C36	3	Philippe Alliot (F)	Jérôme Policand (F)	Didier Cottaz (F)	215			LM-P1/C90	Accident
DNF	Nissan Skyline GT-R LM	22	Aguri Suzuki (J)	Masahiko Kageyama (J)	Masahiko Kondo (J)	209			LM-GT1	Accident
DNF	Ferrari 333SP-LM	17	Eric van de Poele (B)	Marc Goossens (B)	Eric Bachelart (B)	208			IMSA-WSC	Accident
DNF	Toyota Supra LM	57	Masanori Sekiya (J)	Hideoshi Mitsusada (J)	Masami Kageyama (J)	205			LM-GT1	Accident
DNF	WR LM95/6	15	William David (F)	Sébastien Enjolras (F)	Arnaud Trévisiol (F)	162			LM-P1/C90	Accident
DNF	Riley & Scott Mk3	19	Scott Sharp (USA)	Wayne Taylor (ZA)	Jim Pace (USA)	157			IMSA-WSC	Transmission (CWP)
DNF	McLaren F1 GTR LM	53	Maurizio Sandro Sala (BR)	Fabien Giroix (F)	Jean-Denis Deletraz (CH)	146			LM-GT1	Engine
DNF	Ferrari F40 GTE	59	Robin Donovan (GB)	Piero Nappi (I)	Tetsuya Ota (J)	129			LM-GT1	Accident
DNF	Callaway Corvette	74	Almo Coppelli (I)	Ricardo 'Rocky' Agusta (I)	Patrick Camus (F)	114			LM-GT2	Transmission (clutch)
DNF	Kremer K8	1	Christophe Bouchut (F)	Harri Toivonen (SF)	Jürgen Lässig (D)	110			LM-P1/C90	Accident
DNF	Porsche 911 GT2 Evo	37	Franz Konrad (A)	Antonio Hermann (BR)	Wido Roessler (D)	107			LM-GT1	Accident
DNF	Ferrari F40 GT Evo	44	Anders Olofsson (S)	Carl Rosenblad (S)	Luciano della Noce (I)	98			LM-GT1	Engine
DNF	Chrysler Viper GTS-R	51	Perry McCarthy (GB)	Justin Bell (GB)	Dominique Dupuy (F)	96			LM-GT1	Engine
DNF	Porsche 911 GT2 Evo	55	Jean-Pierre Jarier (F)	Jesús Pareja (E)	Dominic Chappell (GB)	93			LM-GT1	Engine
DNF	Ferrari F40 LM	56	Michel Ferté (F)	Olivier Thévenin (F)	Nicolas Leboissetier (F)	93			LM-GT1	Fire
DNF	Kremer K8	2	George Fouché (ZA)	Stanley Dickens (S)	Steve Fossett (USA)	58			LM-P1/C90	Accident
DNS	Debora LM-P296	9	Thierry Lecerf (F)	Jean-Claude Basso (F)	Edouard Sezionale (F)	52			LM-P2	
DNF	Porsche 911 GT2	73	Michel Neugarten (B)	Toni Seiler (CH)	Bruno Ilien (F)	46			LM-GT2	Transmission (gearbox)
DNF	Marcos Mantara 600LM	81	Cor Euser (NL)	Thomas Erdos (BR)	Pascal Dro (F)	40			LM-GT2	Engine
DNF	Ferrari F40 GT Evo	45	Jean-Marc Gounon (F)	Eric Bernard (F)	Paul Belmondo (F)	40			LM-GT1	Electrics
DNF	Porsche 911 GT2	70	Steve O'Rourke (GB)	Guy Holmes (GB)	Soames Langton (GB)	32			LM-GT2	Engine
DNF	Ferrari 333SP-LM	18	Andy Evans (USA)	Yvan Muller (F)	Fermin Velez (E)	31			IMSA-WSC	Out of fuel
DNS	Porsche 911 GT2	72	*Enzo Calderari (CH)*	*Lilian Bryner (CH)*	*Ulrich Richter (D)*				LM-GT2	Accident in practice
RES	Renault Sport Spyder	32	*Marc Sourd (F)*	*Lionel Robert (F)*	*Stéphane Daoudi (F)*				LM-P2	
RES	Venturi 600S-LM	40	*Emmanuel Clérico (F)*	*Laurent Lécuyer (CH)*	*Jean-Luc Maury-Laribière (F)*				LM-GT1	

DNF Did not finish   **DNS** Did not start   **DSQ** Disqualified   **FS** Failed scrutineering   **RES** Reserve not required   **NC** Not classified as a finisher   **WD** Withdrawn   Drivers in italics did not race the cars specified

1996

CLASS WINNERS

FIA Class	Starters	Finishers	First	No	Drivers	kph	mph	
LM-P1/C90	8	3	TWR-Porsche WSC95	7	Jones/Wurz/Reuter	200.583	124.636	Record
LM-P2	2	1	Kudzu DLM	20	Downing/Terada/Fréon	142.250	88.390	Record
IMSA-WSC	3	0	–	–	–	–	–	
LM-GT1	25	15	Porsche 911 GT1	25	Wollek/Stuck/Boutsen	200.042	124.300	Record
LM-GT2	10	6	Porsche 911 GT2	79	Kelleners/Eichmann/Martinolle	179.625	111.614	Record
Totals	**48**	**25**						

NON-PREQUALIFIERS

No	Car	Entrant (Nat)	cc	Engine	Class	Pos	Time
10	Debora LMP296	ASA Sequanie (F)	1998tc	Cosworth BDG S4	LM-P2	51	4:14.731
11	WR LM94	Graff Racing (F)	1950tc	Peugeot 405-Raid S4	LM-P2	WD	3:53.295
12	WR LM94	Bertrand Gachot (F)	1999tc	Ssangyong S4	LM-P2	27	3:59.491
16	WR LM93	Alain Lebrun (F)	1950tc	Peugeot 405-Raid S4	LM-P2	59	4:39.003
21	Tiga FJ94	Sylvain Boulay (F)	4500	Buick V6	LM-P2	NA	
24	Nissan Skyline GTR-LM	NISMO (J)	2795tc	RB26-DETT S6	LM-GT1	WD	4:01.960
31	Renault Spider V6 Coupé	Legeay Sports (F)	2975tc	PRV V6	LM-GT1	55	4:20.990
35	Lotus Esprit V8	Lotus Racing Team (GB)	3506tc	T918 V8	LM-GT1	NA	
36	Lotus Esprit V8	Lotus Racing Team (GB)	3506tc	T918 V8	LM-GT1	NA	
41	McLaren F1 GTR	BBA Competition (F)	6064	BMW S70/2 V12	LM-GT1	39	4:06.929
42	Callaway Corvette C7-R	Callaway Competition (USA)	6297	Chevrolet LT5 V8	LM-GT1	48	4:13.869
43	Callaway Corvette C7-R	Callaway Competition (USA)	6297	Chevrolet LT5 V8	LM-GT1	NA	
47	Porsche 911 GT2 Evo	Kremer Racing (D)	3600tc	F6	LM-GT1	37	4:04.880
52	Chrysler Viper GTS-R	Viper Team ORECA (F)	7986	356/T6 V10	LM-GT1	WD	4:31.794
54	Honda NSX	Gary Ward (GB)	2977	J30A4 V6	LM-GT2	NA	
58	McLaren F1 GTR	Larbre Compétition (F)	6064	BMW S70/2 V12	LM-GT1	NA	
60	De Tomaso Pantera	ADA Engineering (GB)	4952	Ford Cleveland V8	LM-GT1	52	4:16.471
62	Bugatti EB110 SS	Monaco Racing Team (F)	3499tc	V12	LM-GT1	56	4:26.288
76	Porsche 911 GT2	Team Jumbo Pao de Acucar (P)	3600tc	F6	LM-GT2	54	4:19.859
78	Porsche 911 GT2	Richard Jones (GB)	3600tc	F6	LM-GT2	53	4:18.210
80	Marcos LM600	Team Marcos (GB)	6143	Chevrolet LT5 V8	LM-GT2	50	4:14.560
84	VBM 4000 GTC	Jean-François Metz (F)	2975tc	PRV V6	LM-GT2	58	4:32.700
85	Ferrari F355	Yellow Racing (F)	3496	F120B V8	LM-GT2	57	4:31.794

DSQ Disqualified   **NA** Non-arrival   **NT** No time set   **WD** Withdrawn after Prequalifying

BPR GLOBAL GT ENDURANCE SERIES

Race	Winner	Drivers
Paul Ricard (F) 4 hours	McLaren F1 GTR	Weaver/Bellm
Monza (I) 4 hours	McLaren F1 GTR	Nielsen/Bscher
Jarama (E) 4 hours	McLaren F1 GTR	Weaver/Bellm
Silverstone (GB) 4 hours	McLaren F1 GTR	Wallace/Grouillard
Nürburgring (D) 4 hours	McLaren F1 GTR	Kox/Bscher
Anderstorp (S) 4 hours	Ferrari F40 GTE	Olofsson/Noce
Suzuka (J) 1000km	McLaren F1 GTR	Weaver/Bellm/Lehto
Brands Hatch (GB) 4 hours	Porsche 911 GT1	Stuck/Boutsen
Spa-Francorchamps (B) 4 hours	Porsche 911 GT1	Stuck/Boutsen
Nogaro (F) 4 hours	McLaren F1 GTR	Weaver/Bellm
Zhuhai (CN) 4 hours	Porsche 911 GT1	Collard/Kelleners

FINAL CHAMPIONSHIP POINTS

Final Positions	Driver (Nat)	Points
DRIVERS		
1	James Weaver (GB)	248
=	Ray Bellm (GB)	248
3	Bruno Eichmann (D)	178
=	Gerd Ruch (D)	178
5	Thomas Bscher (D)	174
6	Anders Olofsson (S)	164
7	Luciano della Noce (I)	164
8	Jean-Marc Gounon (F)	151
=	Eric Bernard (F)	151
=	Paul Belmondo (F)	151
&c		

LE MANS

1997
JOEST'S REPEAT PERFORMANCE

LE MANS

RACE INFORMATION

RACE DATE
14-15 June

RACE No
65

CIRCUIT LENGTH
8.454 miles/13.605km

HONORARY STARTER
Jacques Regis
President, Fédération Française
du Sport Automobile (FFSA)

MARQUES (ON GRID)

Bugatti	1
Chevrolet	1
Chrysler	4
Courage	4
Ferrari	2
Ford	2
Kremer-Porsche	1
Kudzu	1
Lister	2
Lotus	1
Marcos	1
McLaren	5
Nissan	3
Panoz	3
Porsche	16
TWR-Porsche	1

STARTERS/FINISHERS
48/17

WINNERS

OVERALL
TWR-Porsche

ENTRY LIST

No	Car	Entrant (nat)	cc	Engine	Tyres	Weight (kg)	Class
2	WR LM97	Rachel Welter (F)	1998tc	Peugeot 405-Raid S4	–	-	LM-P650 *
3	Ferrari 333 SP	Momo Racing (USA)	3997	F310E V12	Yokohama	890	LM-P875
4	Ferrari 333 SP	Michel Ferté Pilot Racing (F)	3997	F310E V12	Dunlop	892	LM-P875
5	Kremer K8	Kremer Racing (D)	2994tc	Porsche F6	Goodyear	928	LM-P875
6	Kremer K8	Kremer Racing (D)	2994tc	Porsche F6	Goodyear	909	LM-P875
7	TWR-Porsche WSC95	Joest Racing (D)	2994tc	Porsche F6	Goodyear	904	LM-P875 *
8	Courage C36	La Filière ELF (F)	2994tc	Porsche F6	Michelin	916	LM-P875
9	Courage C36	Courage Compétition (F)	2994tc	Porsche F6	Michelin	896	LM-P875
10	Courage C36	Courage Compétition (F)	2994tc	Porsche F6	Michelin	894	LM-P875
13	Courage C41	Courage Compétition (F)	2994tc	Porsche F6	Michelin	895	LM-P875
14	BRM P301	Pacific Racing (GB)	2996tc	Nissan V6	Pirelli	907	LM-P875
15	Kudzu DLM4	Team DTR (USA) Mazdaspeed (J)	2616r	Mazda R26B 4R	Goodyear	908	LM-P875
21	Nissan R390 GT1	NISMO (J) TWR (GB)	3496tc	VRH35 V8	Bridgestone	1041	LM-GT1
22	Nissan R390 GT1	NISMO (J) TWR (GB)	3496tc	VRH35 V8	Bridgestone	1037	LM-GT1
23	Nissan R390 GT1	NISMO (J) TWR (GB)	3496tc	VRH35 V8	Bridgestone	1029	LM-GT1
25	Porsche 911 GT1 Evo	Porsche AG (D)	3164tc	F6	Michelin	1059	LM-GT1 *
26	Porsche 911 GT1 Evo	Porsche AG (D)	3164tc	F6	Michelin	1062	LM-GT1
27	Porsche 911 GT1	BMS Scuderia Italia (I)	3164tc	F6	Pirelli	1063	LM-GT1
28	Porsche 911 GT1	Konrad Motorsport (D)	3164tc	F6	Pirelli	1056	LM-GT1
29	Porsche 911 GT1	JB Racing (F)	3164tc	F6	Michelin	1055	LM-GT1
30	Porsche 911 GT1	Kremer Racing (D)	3164tc	F6	Goodyear	1057	LM-GT1
32	Porsche 911 GT1	Roock Racing International Motorsport (D)	3164tc	F6	Michelin	1066	LM-GT1
33	Porsche 911 GT1	Schübel Engineering (D)	3164tc	F6	Michelin	1061	LM-GT1
39	McLaren F1 GTR	GTC/Gulf Team Davidoff (GB)	5990	BMW S70/3 V12	Michelin	934	LM-GT1 *
40	McLaren F1 GTR	GTC/Gulf Team Davidoff (GB)	5990	BMW S70/3 V12	Michelin	929	LM-GT1
41	McLaren F1 GTR	GTC/Gulf Team Davidoff (GB)	5990	BMW S70/3 V12	Michelin	929	LM-GT1
42	McLaren F1 GTR	BMW Motorsport (D)	5990	BMW S70/3 V12	Michelin	986	LM-GT1
43	McLaren F1 GTR	BMW Motorsport (D)	5990	BMW S70/3 V12	Michelin	967	LM-GT1
44	McLaren F1 GTR	Team Lark (J) Parabolica Motorsport (GB)	5990	BMW S70/3 V12	Michelin	941	LM-GT1
45	Lister Storm GTL	Newcastle United Lister Cars (GB)	6996	Jaguar HE V12	Dunlop	1039	LM-GT1
46	Lister Storm GTL	Newcastle United Lister Cars (GB)	6996	Jaguar HE V12	Dunlop	1047	LM-GT1
49	Lotus Elise GT1	GTI Lotus Racing (GB)	5993	Chevrolet LT5 V8	Michelin	981	LM-GT1
50	Lotus Elise GT1	GTI Lotus Racing (GB)	5993	Chevrolet LT5 V8	Michelin	972	LM-GT1
52	Panoz Esperante GTR-1	DAMS (F)	5950	Ford V8	Michelin	950	LM-GT1
54	Panoz Esperante GTR-1	David Price Racing (GB)	5998	Ford V8	Goodyear	958	LM-GT1
55	Panoz Esperante GTR-1	David Price Racing (GB)	5998	Ford V8	Goodyear	962	LM-GT1
60	Callaway Corvette LM-GT	Agusta Racing Team (I/GB)	5990	Chevrolet LT5 V8	Dunlop	1117	LM-GT2
61	Chrysler Viper GTS-R	Viper Team ORECA (F)	7986	356-T6 V10	Michelin	1163	LM-GT2
62	Chrysler Viper GTS-R	Viper Team ORECA (F)	7986	356-T6 V10	Michelin	1175	LM-GT2
63	Chrysler Viper GTS-R	Viper Team ORECA (F)	7986	356-T6 V10	Michelin	1239	LM-GT2
64	Chrysler Viper GTS-R	Chamberlain Engineering (GB)	7986	356-T6 V10	Goodyear	1274	LM-GT2
66	Saleen Mustang RRR	Saleen-Allen Speedlab (USA)	5900	Ford V8	Dunlop	1259	LM-GT2
67	Saleen Mustang RRR	Saleen-Allen Speedlab (USA)	5900	Ford V8	Dunlop	1259	LM-GT2
70	Marcos Mantara 600LM	Team Marcos Racing International (GB)	5990	Chevrolet LT5 V8	Dunlop	1114	LM-GT2
71	Marcos Mantara 600LM	Team Marcos Racing International (GB)	5990	Chevrolet LT5 V8	Dunlop	1110	LM-GT2
73	Porsche 911 GT2	Roock Racing Team (D)	3600tc	F6	Michelin	1154	LM-GT2 *
74	Porsche 911 GT2	Roock Racing Team (D)	3600tc	F6	Michelin	1193	LM-GT2
75	Porsche 911 GT2	Larbre Compétition (F)	3600tc	F6	Michelin	1166	LM-GT2 *
77	Porsche 911 GT2	Larbre Compétition/Chéreau Sports (F)	3600tc	F6	Michelin	1155	LM-GT2
78	Porsche 911 GT2	Elf Haberthur Racing (CH)	3600tc	F6	Dunlop	1154	LM-GT2
79	Porsche 911 GT2	Konrad Motorsport (D)	3600tc	F6	Pirelli	1110	LM-GT2
80	Porsche 911 GT2	GT Racing Team (CH)	3600tc	F6	Michelin	1152	LM-GT2
84	Porsche 911 GT2	Stadler Motorsport (CH)	3600tc	F6	Pirelli	1154	LM-GT2

* Automatic entries: (2) Prototype class winner 1996 Coupe d'Automne, (7) Prototype class winner 1996 Le Mans, (25) GT1 class winner 1996 Le Mans, (39) winner 1996 Global GT Series, (73) GT2 class winner 1996 Le Mans, (75) GT1 class winner 1996 Coupe d'Automne. See Non-Prequalifiers table for discarded entries

ENTRY

This was when the Le Mans 24 Hours finally completed repairs to its quality and reputation after the FIA's ill-judged interference at the start of the decade. The ACO selection committee was spoiled for choice. It culled 86 applications to 76, and exactly half the cars that made it past Prequalifying and into race week were operated by their constructors. Among these were 10 manufacturer teams, most of them again in GT1.

These represented Chrysler, Lister, Lotus, Marcos, Nissan, Panoz and Porsche; Mercedes-Benz did not enter its new GT1 cars, but BMW Motorsport returned, running two McLarens. Among only 11 prototypes, Porsche again assisted Joest Racing, and Mazda was back with Kudzu. Pacific Racing ran the one-off BRM, now with a Nissan engine, while Courage again fielded its own sports-racers, and Saleen came with two Ford-based GT2 cars.

QUALIFYING

In the end, 63 cars pursued 46 entry slots during the Prequalifying weekend in May: 13 prototypes went for eight slots in their class, 29 GT1s for 22 slots, and 21 GT2s for 16 slots. In addition, the six teams holding byes through to race week took the opportunity to test and to gauge the opposition. The weekend was much soured by the fatal accident of young Sébastien Enjolras, which led WR to withdraw its team.

Fifty-two cars came for race week. This year the ACO did away with reserves, so that the fastest 48 qualified. The teams operating the slowest cars had to forego their normal race-preparation procedures and concentrate just on getting in.

The first man to pitch for pole position was Thierry Boutsen in one of the new factory Porsches, but his time was obliterated on Thursday by a skittish lap by Michele Alboreto with the 1996-winning TWR-Porsche. Boutsen responded with an equally brave improvement, but it was not enough. Eric van der Poele was third fastest with one of TWR's new Nissan GT1 cars, edging out JJ Lehto in one of the BMW-developed McLarens, Emmanuel Collard in the other works Porsche, Martini in BMS Scuderia Italia's Porsche 911 GT1 'customer' car (the best of six here), and Martin Brundle, who had been fastest in Prequalifying in another Nissan.

The fastest prototypes and GT1s shared only the first 10 rows of the grid this time, alternating by class with the prototypes again on the left. Thus the ninth fastest Ferrari 333 SP would start from the second row.

LE MANS

ORGANISATION

At the request of the FIM, the motorcycle racing governing body, the Le Mans syndicate modified the chicane layout at the Dunlop curve before this year's race, and extended the run-off area there. The lap distance was increased by five metres, to 8.454 miles (13.605km).

Apart from minor dimensional adjustments, the teams were relieved to find the technical regulations virtually unchanged, for the first time this decade. GT2 cars were now allowed carbon braking systems if such were fitted to the base road car. As a safety measure, GT1s had to race with white headlights and GT2s with yellow, allowing drivers immediately to see what was behind. Less than a fortnight before race week, the ACO accepted FIA advice that all GT-type cars had to incorporate a space for 'luggage'.

The *ad hoc* selection method used in 1995-96 had been controversial, so specific requirements were defined this time and applied to only six cars (which would become the norm). These were based on results achieved the previous season at Le Mans and associated events (as shown in the Entry List panels). The class-by-class Prequalifying process was extended to two days to accommodate as many as 70 cars competing for 46 places in qualifying proper. Half the field ran on Saturday and the others on Sunday. Lest track conditions differed over the two days, the ACO issued separate results for each day, and the circuit was indeed appreciably faster on the Sunday.

During race week, the World Motor Sport Council approved new GT1 regulations incorporating more stringent controls over cockpit and other dimensions, in an attempt to exclude the increasingly controversial 'specials'. This infuriated Nissan (which had just built a new car) and Toyota (which was almost ready to test one). They asserted that compliance with full European type approval should be sufficient for defining a road car, but to no avail. The ACO responded by confirming that it would not apply the new rules in 1998, when Le Mans would be the only race for these manufacturers.

Meanwhile the 1996 BPR Global GT series had been evolved into a new FIA GT Championship. Separately, a short series of races for prototypes, called the International Sports Racing Series, was organized this year by John Mangoletsi, who had created the BRM FIA Sportscar project six years before. The ISRS would expand in 1998 to eight events (including one on the permanent Le Mans Bugatti circuit) and would develop into the Sports Racing World Cup (SRWC) in 1999, and a revived FIA Sportscar Championship in 2000.

1997

RACE

From the outset, this was a reprise of the 1996 contest between Porsche's GT1 team and Joest Racing with its Porsche-powered prototype. About 170,000 people saw Bob Wollek grab the lead with Boutsen's Porsche but, on the fourth lap, he was usurped by Alboreto. The TWR-Porsche held the advantage for the first couple of hours, but under pressure from both works Porsches, two of the Nissans and BMW's 'works' McLarens.

The non-Porsche opposition wilted. Riccardo Patrese was in the gravel on his first out-lap with Poele's Nissan, while Brundle's sister car needed a new clutch. Neither recovered from these delays; all three Nissans had gearbox oil cooler problems, and these two would be retired soon after half-distance.

No sooner had Steve Soper taken over Lehto's third-placed McLaren-BMW but a split water hose sent him back to pit-lane; this car would recover to seventh before Lehto crashed it at Arnage on Sunday morning.

The factory team established a 1-2 during a circumspect triple shift by Stefan Johansson, who was still learning the TWR-Porsche. Boutsen/Wollek/Hans-Joachim Stuck consolidated by repeatedly making their fuel last for 13 laps, against 12 by team mates Collard/Yannick Dalmas/Ralf Kelleners. Alboreto/Johansson, sharing the TWR-Porsche with Tom Kristensen, could stay on the same lap, but this year they enjoyed no performance advantage over the GT1 Evos. As the privately owned Porsches encountered various mishaps, the only remote opposition to the top three came from the GTC team's McLarens.

Porsche had everything under control through the night and into a dry morning. But at 7:45am came a shock: under pressure from Dalmas, Wollek went off the road at Arnage – and had to park the damaged car in the Porsche curves.

Dalmas took over with two minutes in hand over the TWR-Porsche. The lead was extended to just over a lap during the morning, and endured for six hours. But at 1:45pm, Kelleners hurriedly parked near the start of the Mulsanne straight with the remaining GT1 Evo spectacularly on fire from a transmission oil leak.

Kristensen found himself leading Le Mans with nobody behind him in reach. Joest's TWR-Porsche became only the third car in history to win in consecutive years, one previous such car having been the same team's Porsche 956 in 1984-85 – an extraordinary achievement. It had a lap in hand over the GTC McLaren of Anders Olofsson/Pierre-Henri Raphanel/Jean-Marc Gounon. GTC also lost a car to fire near the end, so third place fell to the BMW Motorsport entry of Eric Hélary/Peter Kox/Roberto Ravaglia.

GT2 was won by the Haberthur team's Swiss-entered Porsche.

JOEST'S REPEAT PERFORMANCE

LE MANS

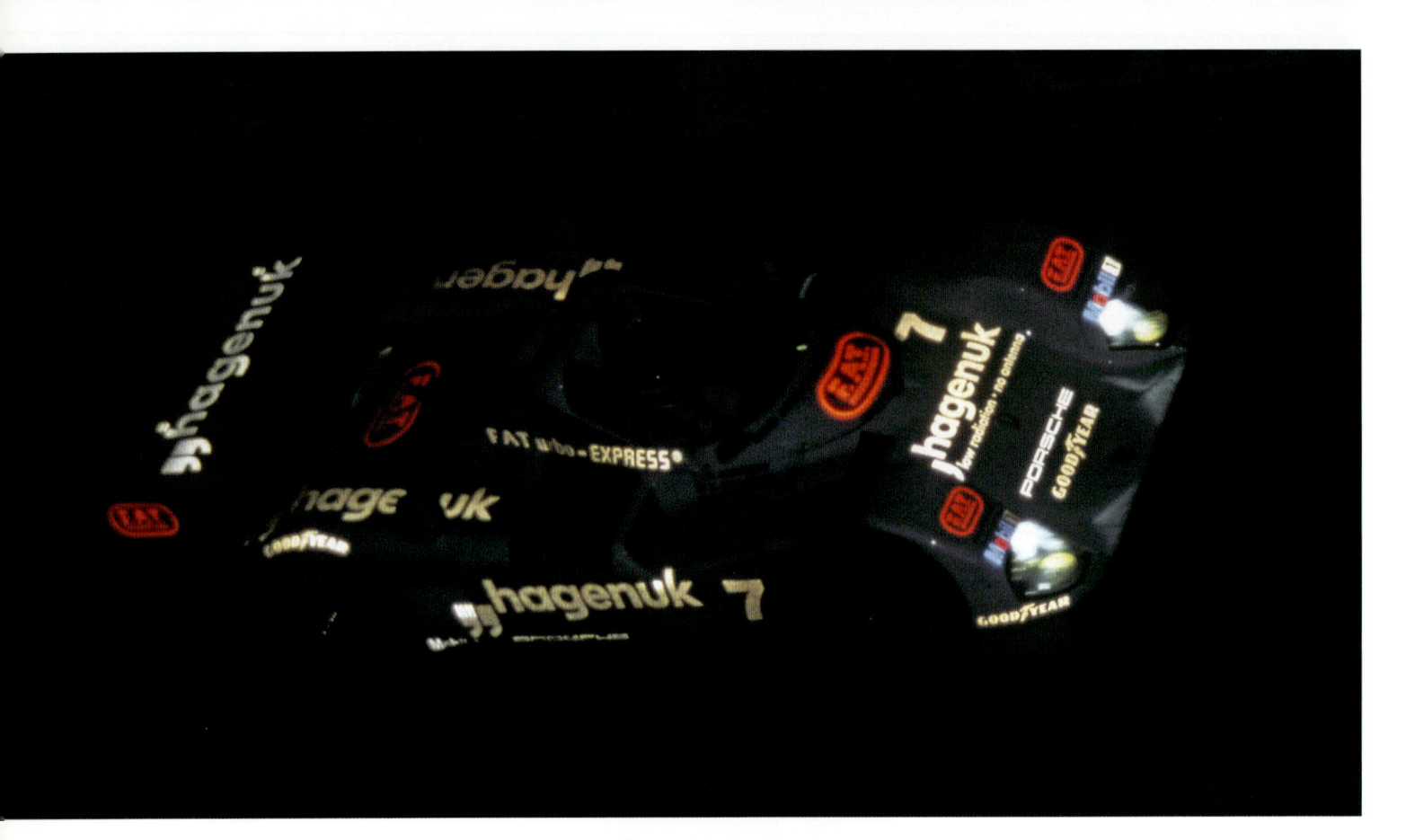

ON THE DOUBLE AGAIN

Joest Racing's remarkable achievement in winning Le Mans in consecutive years with the same car was not unique: the very same team had raced a Porsche 956 to victories here in 1984-85, and the JW team had done it with a Ford GT40 in 1968-69. The unique part was that the TWR-Porsche WSC95 won in both 1996 and 1997 from pole position. It was raced this time by former Ferrari F1 team mates Michele Alboreto and Stefan Johansson with FIA F3000 championship leader Tom Kristensen, on his Le Mans début.

The 1996-winning WSC95 had been taken back in triumph to Reinhold Joest's raceshop east of Mannheim, and the sister car had gone to the Porsche Motorsport HQ near Stuttgart. Neither had been raced again in 1996 but Joest decided to defend his Le Mans victory. Few mechanical upgrades were made, although Joest Racing was invited to join the factory team when it hired the Paul Ricard circuit to test its new-evolution 911 GT1 cars. Although Joest had an automatic entry, the car was again tested in the Prequalifying sessions, when Alboreto was second fastest behind one of the new Nissans.

In qualifying proper, the circuit changes and

266 LE MANS 24 HOURS 1990–99

Goodyear tyre development contributed when Alboreto went more than five seconds quicker than Pierluigi Martini 12 months before, and secured the car's second consecutive pole. Alboreto (above) lost out on the opening lap of the race to Bob Wollek's works Porsche GT1, but moved into the lead after four laps. He drove a triple shift and, after almost 2h18m at the wheel, handed an advantage of almost a minute to Johansson.

However, neither Johansson nor Kristensen could resist the factory GT cars for long. By 8pm, the solo TWR-Porsche had been relegated to third place, and that was where it stayed through the night. Despite solid reliability, and a succession of well-driven triple shifts, Joest's men went a lap down on the leaders at half-distance.

Even when one of the GT1s crashed at about 8am, the team nurtured no hope of another victory. The other was also out of reach, and the deficit was extended to two laps by 11am. But the leading Porsche caught fire shortly before 2pm and, a few minutes later, Kristensen was at the front, en route to his first Le Mans victory. Alboreto took over for the run to the flag, finishing only a lap ahead of the second-placed McLaren.

JOEST'S REPEAT PERFORMANCE 267

LE MANS

CRASH AND BURN

Porsche's evolution 911 GT1 racecars dominated the Le Mans weekend – until Sunday afternoon. Neither finished.

Detail changes, arising from lessons learned in the BPR series, were made to the specification of the 911 GT1 and incorporated into a short production run of 'customer' cars for 1997. The Porsche appeared to be the car to beat this season until the announcement of smaller air restrictors for turbo engines, which caused a 10 percent reduction in top-end power – enough to render the 911 GT1 uncompetitive in the early rounds of the new FIA GT championship. In addition, this year's FIA rules outlawed the car's ABS, adding to braking distances.

After private testing at Weissach by Bob Wollek, a special Le Mans version of the 911 GT1 was first seen at Prequalifying in May. The new evolution retained the same chassis and powertrain as the customer cars, and essentially the same suspension except for revisions to widen the front track. The underbody configuration was also unchanged but, after an intensive wind-tunnel programme, significant changes were made to the upper surfaces. The 1997 configuration had a smoother overall shape, with the rear bodywork swept down closer to the ground plane. The ACO's rules for turbo engines were more lenient than those applied in the early rounds of the FIA series, so the water-cooled, 3.2-litre, twin-turbo flat-six made 590bhp at 7200rpm here.

The factory entries secured second and fifth places on the grid in the hands of Thierry Boutsen and Yannick Dalmas, went 1-2 in the race morning warm-up, and took firm grip of first and second places during the third hour of the race. Wollek/Boutsen/Hans-Joachim Stuck (pictured with the winning prototype) and Dalmas/Ralf Kelleners/Emanuel Collard held station throughout the night. At dawn, a run to a 1-2 finish seemed unstoppable.

At 7:45am, leading Dalmas by just a few seconds, Wollek sent the leading car hard over high kerbing at Arnage, and tore apart a driveline joint. He set off for pit-lane but trickled only as far as the Porsche curves.

The sister car took over and led for the next six hours but, just before 1:45pm, the game was suddenly up for the Porsche factory. Kelleners felt the gearbox tightening and was headed for pit-lane when the whole rear end abruptly caught fire as he crested the Mulsanne '*bosse*'. He managed to stop the blazing car and hurriedly abandoned it.

268 LE MANS 24 HOURS 1990–99

1997

JOEST'S REPEAT PERFORMANCE 269

LE MANS

PICKING UP THE PIECES

The latest McLaren F1 GTRs were faster than the 1996 cars, and more reliable. After the decimation at Porsche, Anders Olofsson, Pierre-Henri Raphanel and Jean-Marc Gounon raced one of the GTC team cars (top right) to a fighting second place, only a lap behind the victorious prototype and winning the LM-GT1 class. And the podium was completed by one of the Schnitzer team's works BMW Motorsport cars (below), in the hands of Peter Kox, Roberto Ravaglia and 1993 Le Mans winner Eric Hélary.

McLaren Cars Motorsport's engineering team under Gordon Murray concentrated over the winter on saving yet more weight and increasing downforce. Weight-saving structural changes were made to the rear of the monocoque, and the new GTR had redesigned and lightened driveline and suspension components. After the dramas of Le Mans 1996, MMC switched to a new Xtrac six-speed sequential-shift gearbox, for which it made a lightweight, magnesium alloy casing.

In Munich, BMW did its bit by taking 25kg out of Paul Rosche's BMW V12 which, in the interests of durability, was given a stroke reduction and a new swept volume of 5990cc. The 1997 race engine was equipped with new conrods and camshafts, a titanium alloy exhaust system and carbonfibre cam covers.

In total, no less than 100kg was saved relative to the 1996 car. It would have been even more, but the GTR now had heavier, longer and slightly wider bodywork. The front and rear overhangs were greatly increased to increase downforce, mainly with a longer diffuser in the extended tail. A small width increase and changes to the suspension geometry allowed wider wheel-arches and track dimensions at both front and rear.

MCM's endurance kit included a reprofiled, single-plane rear wing and other pieces to optimize airflow over and under the car, including the cooling ducts. The BMW Motorsport cars were the only McLarens using a competition version of the road car's ABS (permitted under the ACO rules). Since this required a specially configured front bulkhead, both were new chassis for this race, increasing the Schnitzer team's fleet to four cars. Six others were sold during 1997, four to GTC's Gulf team, and one each to London hedge fund manager David Morrison's new Parabolica Motorsport and Kazimuchi Goh's Team Lark. None of the previous GTRs was upgraded to the 1997 specification, and BBA Compétition's car failed to prequalify.

The addition of ABS to the two Schnitzer cars pushed their weight over 950kg which, with the smaller engines, allowed the use of bigger air restrictors. This enabled the team to configure its V12s to make 605bhp at only 6500rpm. The engines in the lighter GTC and Parabolica GTRs, with their smaller restrictors, produced 600bhp at 7000rpm. The class victory for GTC, which mounted a three-car assault with McLaren's support, came as some consolation for a very expensive week. The team lost two cars to fires, the first in Wednesday qualifying when an oil line fractured and Chris Goodwin had to bale out of the cockpit rapidly. The inferno in the engine bay delaminated the rear chassis bulkhead, and team manager Michael Cane had to withdraw the car. It was a pity, because his other GTRs raced extremely well.

The GTR driven by owner Ray Bellm with Andrew Gilbert-Scott/Masanori Sekiya (pictured in the pits) was in the top six virtually throughout. Although

TOKYO
Ueno Clinic
Gulf
MICHELIN
KENWOOD
MICHELIN
KENWOOD

Ueno Clinic
Gulf
MICHELIN
KENWOOD

it got a four-minute stop-go penalty for speeding in pit-lane, it was headed for fifth place or better with only two hours to go. That was when it suddenly ignited as Gilbert-Scott sped over the Mulsanne 'bosse'. It happened only four laps after a fuel stop, and the rear end was blazing fiercely when the driver finally stopped the car near the fire post at Mulsanne corner.

Gounon had an early scare when he was tapped into a spin by Eric Bernard's Panoz in a traffic jam, emerging unscathed thanks to the quick reactions of Mauro Baldi in the Konrad Porsche. GTC's third car (loaned by McLaren) then had a relatively trouble-free run all the way to second place. Its drivers kept the Porsches constantly under pressure by maintaining a competitive pace while eking out their fuel loads to 14 laps, instead of 12 or 13. Their result was richly deserved.

GTC's performance edged that of BMW's factory team. Now run by Herbert Schnitzer and Karl 'Charly' Lamm at Schnitzer Motorsport in Freilassing, near Munich, it came to Le Mans unbeaten in the first three races of the inaugural FIA GT championship. The fastest McLaren driver in Prequalifying, JJ Lehto did it again in race week, qualifying three seconds faster than the best 1996 GTR time, which had been set by his regular 1997 co-driver, Steve Soper. The car lined up fourth, splitting the factory Porsches. Lehto and Soper, who had won two FIA GT events, were co-driven here by Nelson Piquet. Starting the race with an impressive triple shift, Lehto charged up to third. Soper took over but the V12 immediately overheated, and he came straight back to the pits. Replacing an inaccessible split water line cost the car nine laps. All three drivers now thrashed it, and it was back inside the top 10 well before half-time. Lehto was running seventh at 8:30am, when he spun at Arnage and hit the barrier.

The sister car was troubled by difficult handling throughout the first half, but the problem was alleviated by a switch to a different Michelin compound in the small hours. Hélary/Ravaglia/Kox encountered no more setbacks and raced on to third place, two laps down on the Gulf McLaren.

Goh did not have an entry for his Lark McLaren but did a deal with Morrison, the other new F1 owner, to sponsor his Parabolica entry. The 27th GTR of 28 produced, this car (pictured in the Esses) was prepared in Parabolica's Didcot raceshop, directed by Graham Humphrys and Dave 'Beaky' Sims. Goodwin and Gary Ayles had shaken it down by bullying GT2 hardware in a British GT series race at Silverstone a month before Prequalifying, but they were stood down here to accommodate Goh's men, Keiichi Tsuchiya, Katsumoto Kaneishi and Akihiko Nakaya, who was attempting a comeback after a horrific All-Japan F3000 accident at Suzuka in 1992. Goodwin found a (hot) berth at GTC, and Ayles was recalled when Kaneishi was off the pace in a Paul Ricard test and again at Prequalifying.

In race week, Ayles produced a surprise by qualifying 10th, the second fastest of the five McLarens. And he sprang another by racing among the leaders in the early laps. The car was well inside the top dozen at 9:30pm when (for the second time) Nakaya hooked a kerb on the outside of Tertre Rouge. It spun back across the track and smashed into the right-side barrier.

The homologation requirement compelled McLaren to build a road car with the longtail bodywork; three were produced, going by the name 'F1 GT'. The F1 GTR won only two more FIA GT races that season, and lost the championship to the new Mercedes CLK. McLaren Cars and BMW Motorsport, having neither the budget nor the inclination to produce a full-on GT1 racer, axed their joint programme at the end of the year. BMW already had other plans, involving a different Grand Prix team…

1997

SAVING FACE

Nissan returned to Le Mans with three new, purpose-designed, mid-engined GT1 racecars on a mission to erase its embarrassment over the outclassed Skyline project. The R390 GT1s showed the pace to do just that, but enforced specification changes in race week caused insurmountable overheating problems. The one car that reached the finish (pictured) had been fitted with a replacement gearbox.

The R390s were produced by TWR in England, which also operated them. TWR had undergone big changes since its Group C Jaguar days. Tom Walkinshaw had bought into the Arrows F1 team and had relocated TWR to its Leafield factory. The American operation in Indiana had been closed and its former head, Tony Dowe, was now in Leafield. It was Dowe who secured a two-year GT1 contract with NISMO principal Kunihiko Kakimoto. The deal was not finalized until September 1996, and time constraints were an issue throughout the design and build programme.

TWR set up the Nissan operation in a separate factory at Broadstone, where a staff of 45 was assembled under Roger Silman and the design team was again led by Tony Southgate. The advanced composite monocoque was similar to that of the Jaguar XJR-15, a road car devised for a one-make race series in 1992 that had been Southgate's last project for TWR before joining Toyota. The Nissans were not built on old XJR-15 shells, but on tubs slightly wider and shorter and much stronger, with the sides and roof in a single moulding. An initial run of five was made by Astec. These included a chassis for the single road car homologation process, which was subcontracted out to a group of former Team Lotus engineers in Norfolk.

Le Mans was the only race on Nissan's schedule, so Southgate could optimize the aerodynamics (in the Imperial College wind tunnel) for the specific demands of the circuit. The car had a narrow superstructure ahead of a rear wing canted rearward over a rounded tail, pulling airflow

JOEST'S REPEAT PERFORMANCE

out of a diffuser aft of the flat bottom. Front-end downforce to balance the rear wing was generated by diffusers beneath the nose. The carbon/Kevlar body, incorporating cooling-air ducts for the nose-mounted radiator and side-mounted turbo intercoolers, was given Nissan styling elements drawn by TWR's Ian Callum. The double-wishbone, pushrod suspension was mounted at the rear directly to the transmission casing, and TWR fabricated uprights designed to flow air through the carbon-carbon braking assemblies.

The R390 was powered by a derivative of the robust engine used by Nissan for its own Group C projects over 1988-90. In unrestricted form, it had been good for more than 1000bhp, and had secured pole position for Le Mans in 1990. For its GT1 application seven years later, Nissan and TWR opted to run their racecar to a 1000kg minimum weight, to gain additional air restrictor diameter. Thus the 3.5-litre, 32-valve VRH35L V8, with two IHI turbochargers and JECS electronics, developed 600bhp at 7000rpm. The transverse, six-speed, sequential gearbox was designed and produced by TWR with Xtrac.

In April, the only spare chassis failed the mandatory FIA crash test when the radiator was knocked into the monocoque. After revising the radiator installation, the team consequently had to crash-test one of the actual race cars a week later. It then successfully completed four days of testing at Estoril, covering more than 3700 miles. In Prequalifying, Martin Brundle raised NISMO's hopes sky-high by driving the fastest lap.

Only 10 days before the race, the team was notified of the ACO's insistence that a luggage space was provided on GT1 cars. The only available area on the R390 was beneath the rear cover, and was used to flow air to the gearbox oil cooler. Hasty changes had to be made, including a re-routed exhaust system, and some were completed in the paddock on Tuesday of race week after a final test at Silverstone. The cars were qualified third by Eric van der Poele, seventh by Brundle, and 14th by Erik Comas, amid great concern over high temperatures resulting from the altered gearbox cooling arrangements.

Starting the race with a strong double shift, Poele vied for the lead with the TWR-Porsche and one of the Porsche GT1s before handing over to Aguri Suzuki. The car, race-engineered by Southgate himself, was still in contention at 7pm, when Riccardo Patrese climbed aboard – and the overheated starter motor seized. Pictured in the pits, the car dropped to 33rd position while a replacement was fitted, and then it was further delayed by a stop to replace the gearbox oil cooler after excessive heat had caused the assembly to come apart. When the new starter motor failed at 1:45am, the gearbox was on its last legs, and the car was retired.

Brundle was also very quick early on, but at 6:40pm Jorg Müller pitted his car out of fifth place with the same cooling problems. The R390 lost 25 positions while the gearbox oil cooler was replaced. Run by Steve Farrell, this car was co-driven by Wayne Taylor in place of Mauro Martini, who had been knocked off his trail bike by a car the weekend before the race.

1997

It lasted until 20 minutes after half-time when Müller, struggling with a failing gearbox, crashed and badly mauled the underbody.

The remaining car, driven by Comas with Kazuyoshi Hoshino and Masahiko Kageyama, only made it through to the finish after a new gearbox oil cooler had been fitted at dusk, and a new gearbox in the small hours. They were 12th. It was no consolation that a TWR-built chassis won the race, and TWR set out to reverse Nissan's disappointment in 1998.

ANDRETTI ANGUISH AGAIN

Mario Andretti returned to Courage Compétition for yet another attempt to add a Le Mans victory to his F1 and IndyCar successes, this time with his son, Michael. Co-driven by Olivier Grouillard, they had a wretched weekend that ended prematurely on Sunday morning.

Their 'Stars & Stripes' C36 (right) was delayed in 57-year-old Mario's first shift when a blown fuse took out ignition on one cylinder. It got worse before dark: the car needed a replacement clutch, and dropped completely out of contention. Later all three drivers were hampered by fuel pick-up problems, and the car was shunted several times during their attempts to retrieve a hopeless situation. Following Mario's spin at Tertre Rouge nine hours out from the end, a broken suspension mounting led the team to give up a bad job.

As in 1996, a C36 (below) was entered for the La Filière Elf academy,

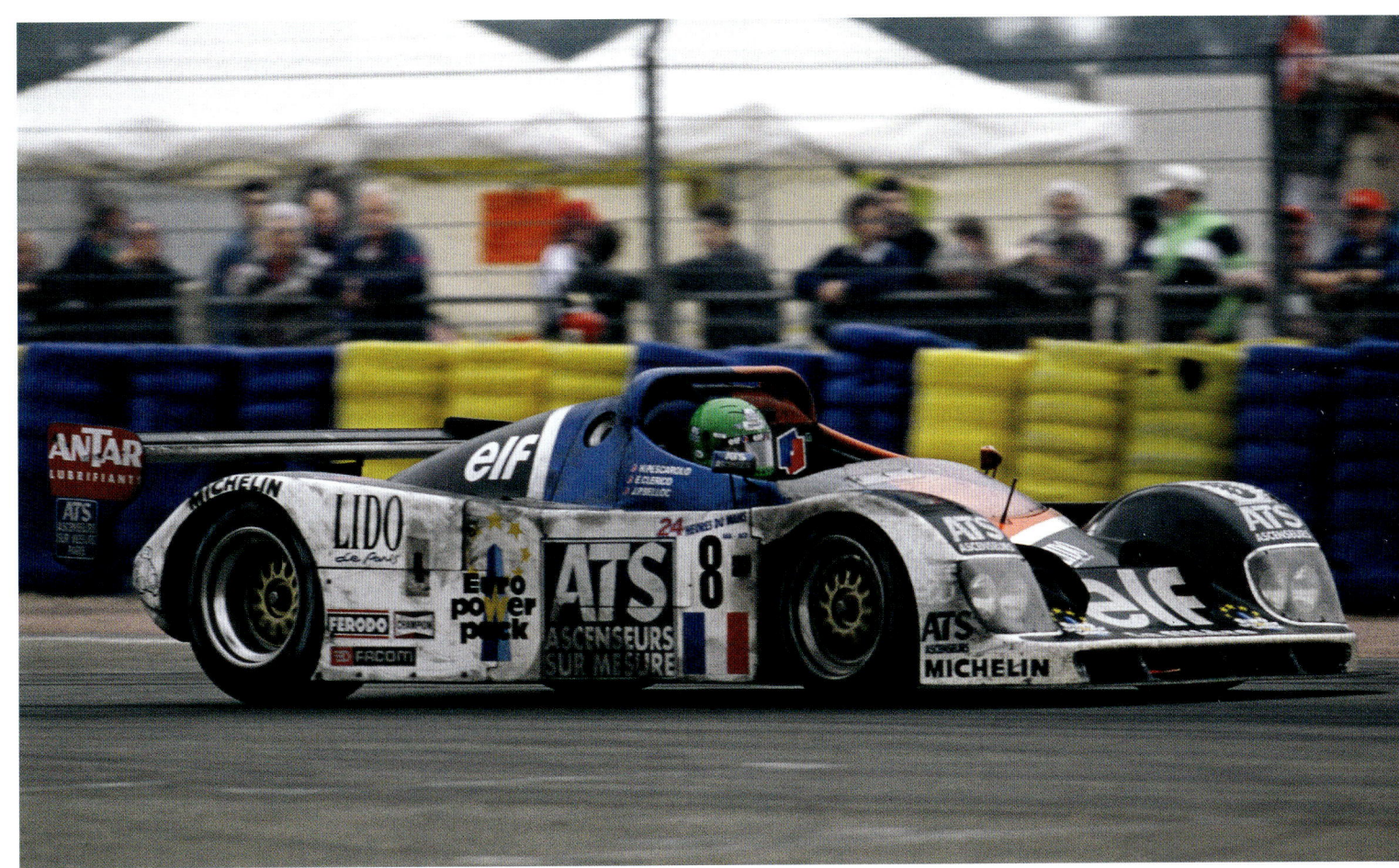

JOEST'S REPEAT PERFORMANCE 275

LE MANS

and this was the best-placed at the end, in seventh place. This car's Porsche flat-six was prepared by Michel Demont at Joest Racing, whereas the Courage entries relied on the team's in-house engine shop. The car had to be extensively repaired on Friday after Emmanuel Clérico had clobbered the pit-wall in Thursday qualifying. Early in the race, first Clérico and then Henri Pescarolo had several spins and, after investing time in changing the suspension dampers, the team realized that the front of the tub had been damaged. The repair consumed more than an hour before Jean-Philippe Belloc took the car back racing. In the circumstances, it had an exceptional run to the finish.

The third C36 also saw the chequered flag, down in 16th place. The car had already lost a lot of time with a malfunctioning throttle mechanism when the fuel cell sprang a leak and had to be replaced a couple of hours into the race. Jean-Louis Ricci, Fredrick Ekblom and Jean-Paul Libert went well after the job was finished, and Ekblom overhauled the Kudzu in the dying minutes.

THREE-WHEEL WINNER

A *schwadron* of eight 3.6-litre Porsche 911 GT2s contested the class and, after both the front-running ORECA Vipers had been crashed, the winner was Elf Haberthur Racing. Raced by Jean-Claude Lagniez, Michel Neugarten and Guy Martinolle, its Porsche was contesting its third Le Mans, and beat Roock Racing's more fancied cars into second and third.

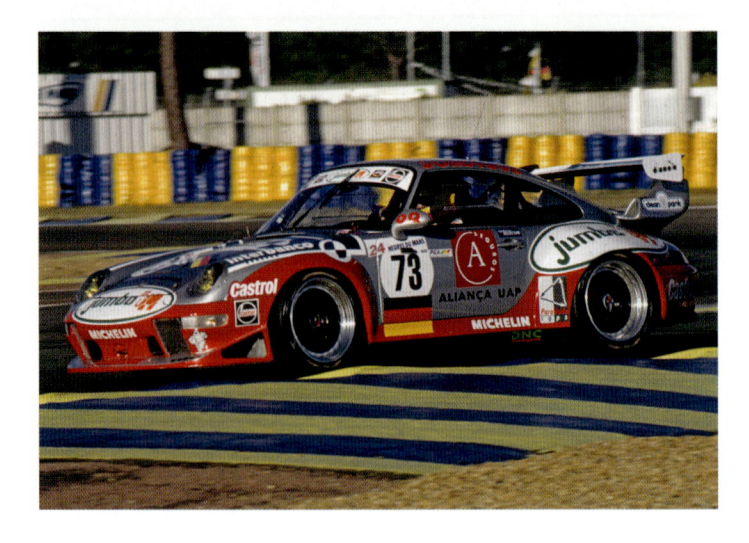

Several of these Porsches came within striking distance of the Vipers as night fell, including the pre-race favourites from the Larbre and Roock teams. However, Larbre lost the car raced by team owner Jack Leconte with Jean-Pierre Jarier and Jean-Luc Chéreau to a transmission failure at nightfall.

Stadler Motorsport entered its car for a third time here (pictured with a Marcos in the Dunlop curve) and Enzo Calderari was the first Porsche driver to take the GT2 lead, but an engine failure stopped the run before half-time. When Patrick Bourdais crashed Larbre's surviving car out of its own third Le Mans, and pitted with major suspension damage, one of Roock's cars (top left) took over as the closest challenger to the leading Viper. In the hands of the Mello-Breyner brothers, it hit the front soon after dawn when the Viper ran into trouble but, after leading for only half an hour, was itself in the pits for 16 minutes with a broken gear selector.

That was when the Haberthur brothers' 911 took the lead. It kept it until 8:50am when, 20 minutes after a routine stop, its left-rear wheel came off as Martinolle negotiated the Virage Ford. Martinolle was able to three-wheel into the adjacent pits (pictured above), and he was on track again after losing only seven minutes there.

The lead was inherited by Bruno Eichmann in Roock's other 911 GT2 (below right), but his bid was soon thwarted by a broken turbo, and later by André Ahrlé's shunt at Indianapolis. The Haberthur car recovered the advantage and held off a charge by Eichmann/Ahrlé/Andy Pilgrim, winning by more than a lap, with the Mello-Breyners a distant third.

Luigi Pagotto's Basel-based 911 was the only other GT2 Porsche to finish. Franz Konrad's 911 GT2 (below left) was retired in the small hours with a broken engine, while Larbre's frustrating weekend ended just before midday when a broken transmission stranded Bourdais in the Porsche curves.

Four more 911 GT2s missed the cut in Prequalifying.

JOEST'S REPEAT PERFORMANCE 277

LE MANS

CRASHES CRAMP CHRYSLER

Chrysler's decision to adapt its Viper GTS-R racecar to contest the GT2 class at Le Mans and in the FIA GT Championship paid off as soon as the 1997 season began. In the big one at Le Mans, however, the fastest Vipers were both crashed out of the lead. The manufacturer's highest finisher was delayed by transmission problems and came home fifth in the category, driven by John Morton, Justin Bell and Pierre Yver (below), who needed a new gearbox and differential to get to the finish.

The Viper was now the focus of a promotion of the Chrysler brand in the European market, and contested only three American races all season. The manufacturer reappointed ORECA as its factory team, now with a brief to develop and assemble the cars, as well as operating them. Over the winter, ORECA's raceshop near the Paul Ricard circuit evolved a lighter version of the chassis, with transmission, suspension, braking and control improvements. Meanwhile, John Caldwell produced a new intake system that allowed the big 'atmo' V10 to run up to 1000rpm faster, countering the effects of the GT2-sized air-inlet restrictor.

ORECA sold two of its 1996 Vipers to former Spice entrant Hugh Chamberlain, replacing them with two new 'lightweight' chassis. The French team won the GT2 category at Hockenheim and Silverstone either side of Le Mans Prequalifying, where one of Chamberlain's entries was eliminated. ORECA drivers Tommy Archer and Philippe Gache headed GT2 in qualifying with lap times more than two seconds faster than their nearest rivals. They continued their dominance in the early race action, until 7:20pm, when Gache/Olivier Beretta/Dominique Dupuy lost 17 minutes to a broken throttle linkage. A couple of hours later, Soheil Ayari put the leading Viper backwards into the wall at the end of the Porsche curves; the car skittered along it for 100 metres, rebounded back onto the track, and caught fire from the ruptured fuel cell.

The sister car (pictured in the Dunlop chicane) regained the class lead as the race entered the night, and held onto it throughout the darkness, running as high as 12th overall and, at one stage, holding a six-lap advantage over its closest rival. At dawn, however, it ran into ignition problems, and lost 40 minutes in two pitstops. It was still six laps behind the Haberthur Porsche at 1:15pm, when Beretta crashed out of the race.

The Chamberlain team's Viper, equipped with a Mader-prepared V10, was the last GT2 car home. The team had to stand down Jari Nurminen when he became unwell on Saturday evening, so John Hugenholtz and Chris Gleason had to do most of the race on their own. They had a long rest soon after dawn while the crew replaced a broken valve spring and fixed a transmission oil leak.

Viper Team ORECA went on to win the GT2 Teams championship, and the Drivers title (for Bell).

MOMO MAKES IT

Giampiero Moretti's Momo Corse team finally made it to Le Mans with a Ferrari 333 SP sports-racer (right) and returned to Miami with a top-six finish by the owner with Max Papis and Didier Theys.

Moretti had bought this car from Andy Evans at the end of the 1996 season (during which it had 'Raced for Belgium' at Le Mans), and it arrived fresh from winning an IMSA race at Lime Rock in May. A second 333 SP in this race (below), purchased by Pilot Racing from the EuroMotorsports team, had not been raced since the 1994 season, at the start of which it had secured Ferrari's first IMSA WSC victory, at Road Atlanta. Both cars were fitted with the original body kit, rather than the low-drag set-up used for Scandia's effort 12 months before. However, the Momo car incorporated a range of detail aero revisions drawn by American freelance consultant Gary Grossenbacher to minimize drag.

LE MANS

Scandia Racing had started this season with second place at Daytona and first at Sebring, but such results were beyond the 333 SP in the biggest long-distance race of the year. In qualifying, Theys went half a second faster than Eric van der Poele had managed the previous year and, early in the race, gained ground that was then lost by Moretti. Strong driving by Papis retrieved the situation but, during the night, the owner again lost positions, and then the crew under Kevin Doran had to replace the alternator. This procedure had to be repeated later in the morning. At the end, the Ferrari had slipped 40 laps behind the winner.

Michel Ferté had run the Pilot Ferrari out of fuel on the Mulsanne straight on Saturday evening, claiming that the reserve tank had failed to function. The blue car was eventually brought back to the paddock and was on hand as a spare parts depot when the Momo team needed a third alternator.

Later in the season, 333 SPs struggled against the new Riley & Scott but won three more IMSA events in America, and the Zolder event in the inaugural ISRS.

THE NOISE WAS NICE…

A 'front-engined' car aimed at winning overall, the Panoz Esperante GTR-1 was one of the most interesting GT racing projects of the decade. Moreover it added an agreeable, throaty V8 rumble at all the venues where it was raced, starting at Sebring in March 1997. On the new American marque's Le Mans début, it was let down by engines that were not up to a 24-hour job, and none of the three cars finished.

Ohio-born Italian-American Don Panoz made his fortune in the pharmaceuticals industry before helping his son, Danny, to become a low-volume sportscar manufacturer. Their first car, the cycle-fendered, aluminium-framed AIV Roadster, went into production in 1997, when Panoz Motorsports was also established at the Road Atlanta circuit in Braselton, Georgia. However, they engaged a British company, Reynard Special Vehicle Projects, to design and build the GTR-1 racecars in Brackley.

RSVP's John Piper led the design team, working with Doug Skinner, Chris Rushforth and aero consultant Nigel Stroud. They set out to produce effectively a two-seat 'formula' car shaped like Luis Romo's styling for the Esperante, which was designer John Leveritt's next series-production Panoz. The racecar was based on a state-of-the-art monocoque, but Danny Panoz insisted that the engine was to be old technology – an all-American stock-block Ford V8, mounted ahead of the cabin. This caused complex problems of vehicle dynamics even though the engine was placed behind the front axle.

Reynard's ongoing IndyCar programme left no capacity to undertake the composites production for the GTR-1, and it was subcontracted to DPS Composites. Late in 1996, when Don Panoz called by the DPS factory at Bookham, he spotted Thomas Bscher's McLaren racecars next door, and asked David Price if he would run two

Panoz 'works' cars in the FIA GT series and at Le Mans. DPR also built and homologated a single roadgoing GTR-1 to satisfy the eligibility rule.

The central section of the honeycomb/carbon monocoque, incorporating the roof structure, had exceptionally high torsional stiffness, but the Ford V8 could not be fully stressed in the hull. It needed tubular steel A-frames, one on each side and a third over the top of the engine. The rear suspension was mounted on the casing of an outboard, longitudinal gearbox, bolted to the rear of the central chassis and also supported by a pair of A-frames. The six-speed gearbox was purpose-designed by Xtrac for the GTR-1 and bore the clutch at its forward end, helping rearward weight bias, reducing the loads on the carbon propshaft, and allowing the transaxle, clutch and alternator to be removed in one unit and replaced in 20 minutes. A similar unitary approach was adopted at the front, where the suspension was mounted on a forward chassis unit using technology tried and tested on Reynard's successful IndyCar single-seaters.

Stroud's aerodynamics were developed in Reynard's wind tunnel. Very tight packaging achieved a small frontal area, and the V8 was fed air via ducting on the underside of the nose, with cooling for two side-mounted water radiators via channels on either side of the front chassis structure. Diffusers under the nose exited into large front wheel openings, through which air was ducted to cool the side-exiting exhaust systems. A diffuser and external aerofoil added rear downforce.

Panoz Cars asked Roush Engines in Livonia, Michigan, to develop an endurance racing version of Ford's 'Windsor' NASCAR motor, a 6-litre pushrod V8. With the ACO-specified air restrictors, Roush claimed 600bhp at 7200rpm. The GTR-1 débuted with a DNF in the Sebring 12 Hours, but then Andy Wallace/'Doc' Bundy won a two-hour race at Road Atlanta.

Two GTR-1s were entered by David Price Racing, a third (the newest chassis, above) by Jean-Paul Driot's DAMS team in Ruaudin, close

JOEST'S REPEAT PERFORMANCE | **281**

to Le Mans. DAMS engineer Claude Galopin took the precaution of shipping its engines to Zytek, which remapped them for its electronic management system. Consequently it was reliable in qualifying and Franck Lagorce claimed a respectable 17th grid position. DPR retained the engines in their original form, and continued to struggle with a very narrow power band and the mapping; the side exhausts constantly emitted flames as raw fuel was burned, adding to the orange gaiety as the drivers applied the carbon-carbon brakes. David Brabham went only 1.6 seconds slower than Lagorce, but Wallace's best time with the other DPR Panoz, another 1.1 seconds down, was not enough to qualify. This car owed its place on the grid to the fire that eliminated one of the GTC team's McLarens.

The DAMS entry, co-driven by Jean-Christophe Boullion and Eric Bernard, had a setback before the race had even started, when Lagorce collided with Kazuyoshi Hoshino's Nissan in the Virage Ford on the parade lap. Lagorce completed the opening lap in the pits, where temporary repairs to the front bodywork consumed more than four minutes. A proper repair was completed later and the car then made solid progress. Shortly before half-time, Lagorce was hunting 12th place when the engine sprang a terminal oil leak.

Both DPR cars lost time in the pits to transmission problems early in the action, but also had enough pace to move back up the order. The one raced by Brabham with Bundy and Perry McCarthy was about to break into the top 10 at 3am, when a catastrophic engine failure on the Mulsanne straight (pictured) came with a fire that sent McCarthy scurrying out of the cockpit. Wallace, James Weaver and 'Butch' Leitzinger had just made the top 10 at 10:15am, when Leitzinger was on the radio to report another broken engine.

Later in the American season, the GTR-1 won at Sears Point and Laguna Seca.

LAST AGAIN

For its 18th participation in the great race, Mazdaspeed was again represented by a Kudzu driven by Jim Downing, Yojiro Terada and Franck Fréon. Downing's team returned to Atlanta with the unwelcome distinction of being the last classified finisher at Le Mans for the second year running.

The latest Kudzu was purpose-built for Mazda's R26B quad-rotor engine, which had won outright here in 1991. Downing had lobbied IMSA for more than two years before the American sanctioning body finally accepted this engine for its WSC class in October 1996, when the 10th Kudzu, the 'DLM4', was designed by Dave Lynn, again working alongside Sam Garret.

The DLM4 monocoque was again made of aluminium-skinned honeycomb, with carbonfibre skins around the cockpit and fuel cell. The wheelbase had to be longer than its predecessor's to accommodate the framework carrying the bigger engine and the GeaRace (formerly March) five-speed gearbox. To use the four-rotor engine at Le Mans, the car was required to run under WSC regulations, limiting the transmission

1997

to five speeds and ruling out carbon brakes. Complying with the LMP875 regulations, the DLM4 was also no less than 176kg heavier than the 1996 Le Mans car.

Mazdaspeed's 1991 engine had been capable of 700bhp in qualifying trim but now IMSA WSC engines were rev-limited according to swept volume, configuration and valvegear. This year the four-valve Ford and Oldsmobile V8s were limited to 10,500rpm, the five-valve Ferrari V12 to 11,500rpm, and the four-rotor Mazda to only 9000rpm. Downing's engine builder, Rick Engeman determined that the added weight and complexity of the variable inlet system that had been used on the 1991 Le Mans engine offered no advantage in WSC, so it was removed. Engeman's R26B made about 560bhp in WSC events, but at Le Mans its air restrictor cost about 70bhp.

As before, a major aerodynamic consideration was the need to cool the engine, which generated more heat than a conventional piston engine of equivalent displacement. The R26B required oversized radiator cores, and big body apertures to provide them with enough airflow. The resulting aerodynamic drag proved to be a major handicap to top speed at Prequalifying. The team planned a last-ditch effort with all the cooling apertures taped up, but this came to naught when the engine oil sump pressurized, blowing out all the oil. The car had to be parked, and missed the cut.

When a reprieve came with the withdrawal of WR after its fatal accident, Downing's team immediately went to work on a huge job list. Lower-drag nose and tail panels were designed and manufactured, and the front and rear suspension systems reworked. The engine was remapped, and a new inlet system produced. The sump problem was cured by fitting a bigger oil tank. In Wednesday qualifying, the revised car tended to 'porpoise' on the faster sections of the track, due to the new nosebox flexing. After this had been reinforced, the car made it into the race on the second evening.

The DLM4 (below) ran well enough until it got dark, but at 10:45pm the front leg of the right-rear lower wishbone failed, overheated by the engine exhaust system. An hour was lost while reinforcing gussets were welded onto the replacement before it was fitted.

At 1:25am, Downing pitted with the nose section damaged, at a cost of 24 minutes. An hour later, replacement of a front suspension damper cost another 16 minutes. Three fuel stops were extended for investigations of a rough engine before it was found that a broken piece of air filter had been sucked into an inlet trumpet.

Later on Sunday, the team saw that the upper suspension mounting bolts were pulling out of the tub. These were drilled out and replaced but, when the car returned to the pits after a single lap, it was discovered that both front dampers had also been broken. A rear wishbone failure, 28 minutes before the end, was the final straw. Even Terada-san's famous smile was missing when he drove the Kudzu under the chequered flag, 98 laps behind the overall and LMP875 class winner.

Back in Georgia, the DLM4 was replaced by the last Kudzu, the four-rotor 'DLY', which raced until the end of the 2002 season, but not at Le Mans.

JOEST'S REPEAT PERFORMANCE 283

LE MANS

UNCOMPETITIVE CUSTOMERS

The reconfigured works Porsche 911 GT1 Evos were backed up by six standard-specification 'customer' cars, but none could prevent a McLaren class win. The best-placed at the finish was the oldest, Horst Schübel's Schwarzenbruck-based entry, pictured at left leading Konrad Motorsport's similar car. It came fifth in the hands of Armin Hahne, Pedro Lamy and Patrice Goueslard. All were held on leashes by team manager John McLoughlin over the first half of the race but a water leak that manifested itself during the night could not be resolved and, instead of mounting a charge on Sunday, the drivers had to nurse the car all the way to the finish.

BMS Scuderia Italia's car (below) came within half a second of the second factory 911 in qualifying. After a couple of seasons running Nissans in the Super Tourenwagen series in Germany, Giuseppe Lucchini's team had signed on as one of the first customers for a 911 GT1. The time was set by one of the Brescia team's former F1 drivers, Pierluigi Martini, who was co-driven by Christian Pescatori in the new FIA GT championship. At Le Mans, they were joined by Brazilian pay-driver Antonio Hermann, who had a couple of spins on Saturday evening. Hermann's second stint ended soon after 1am with a broken gearbox, which took 66 minutes to replace. Nevertheless, eighth position had been recovered when Pescatori crashed at Arnage on Sunday morning, and struggled to pit-lane for suspension repairs, at a cost of another 47 minutes. The late-race retirements left the car eighth once more, but it could have been so much better.

284 LE MANS 24 HOURS 1990-99

Another new 911 GT1 customer was JB Racing, a team formed two years before by Jean-Pierre Jabouille and Jean-Michel Bouresche in Pontault-Combault, south-west of Paris, to contest Porsche Supercup events. Driven by Alain Ferté with Jürgen von Gartzen and Olivier Thévenin, their Porsche (above) held eighth position overall for eight hours. But Thévenin was suddenly hobbled by a blown engine shortly before 8am and stopped the car at a fire post just before the Mulsanne 'bosse', where the marshals quickly extinguished a flash fire.

In the cabin of the Kremer Racing entry (below left), Christophe Bouchut led all the others early in the race. Then Bertrand Gachot was delayed by a broken suspension damper and, soon after dark, the same thing happened to Andy Evans. The car had fallen outside the top 10 when it ran into overheating problems that led to its retirement at breakfast time.

On the warm-up lap Roock Racing's GT1 (below right) was found to have an oil leak, which was fixed on the grid, but Allan McNish lasted only eight laps before hitting the wall at the Porsche curves, losing a wheel. Franz Konrad's car, co-driven by Mauro Baldi and Robert Nearn, was running just outside the top 10 in the small hours when the former Sauber-Mercedes star hit the barrier in the Porsche curves, and it sustained terminal suspension damage.

JOEST'S REPEAT PERFORMANCE 285

LE MANS

SOLO LOTUS

Lotus suffered yet more Le Mans disappointment this year. Having intended to field three of its new Elise GT1 cars, it ended up racing only one (above), and it broke down during the small hours.

The works Lotus Esprit racing project had continued in 1995-96 with an in-house team based in the former Team Lotus HQ in Ketteringham Hall, although without another Le Mans attempt. Among just three races contested in 1995, an Esprit inflicted one of only two defeats on the new Porsche GT2s in the BPR series. In 1996, the team took on a full BPR programme, using GT1 cars engineered by Martin Ogilvie, the former chief designer at Team Lotus, powered by the company's twin-turbo, 3.5-litre V8. They had a poor season, and this year Lotus Racing switched to the new, mid-engined Elise model.

The Elise was drawn by chief engineer Richard Rackham and head of design Julian Thomson. Its base was a lightweight, epoxy-bonded aluminium alloy frame made in Norway by Hydro Aluminium. Ogilvie's longer racing version of the frame incorporated stiffening structures which, with the steel rollcage, made it five times more rigid. A high-downforce aero package of demountable carbonfibre/Kevlar body panels was developed in the MIRA wind tunnel, including a front splitter, a full-width rear wing, and cooling vents for the front-mounted radiator, the carbon brakes and the cabin.

The Elise GT1 was designed to take the engine from the 1996 Esprit V8 but, in January 1997, an FIA rules revision slapped such engines with punitive air restrictors. Instead, Ogilvie turned to the naturally aspirated 6-litre Chevrolet LT5 V8, which had originally been developed by David Whitehead at Lotus Engineering for General Motors for use in the 1990 Corvette ZR-1. The race version of the DOHC engine was good for 575bhp at 7200rpm and drove through a six-speed, transverse Hewland TGT200 sequential gearbox.

The team did not get its definitive race engines until a week before the FIA GT series opener in April at Hockenheim, where all three cars failed to finish. Three weeks later, the two-car works team, managed by Ian Foley and race-engineered by George Howard-Chappell, breezed through Le Mans Prequalifying – although a satellite Elise, operated by FIRST Racing, failed to make it after being crashed by Ratankul Prutirat.

In qualifying proper, one of the Elises was plagued by ill-handling on the first day, and electrical problems and a malfunctioning throttle on the second, and was culled from the GT1 class. Jan Lammers lined up the other car among the slower GT1 McLarens and Porsches and made unimpeded progress during Saturday evening, moving up to 15th place with Mike Hezemans and 'Sandy' Grau. An engine oil pump failure ended the run at 1:15am.

Back in the BPR series, the Elise could not compete with the latest GT1 cars, and Lotus axed the project at season's end.

THE LISTER SISTERS

Having run the 1996 Storm GTS racecar in that year's Daytona 24 Hours, Lister Cars built two new 'GTL' chassis, one for the works team to run in a short FIA GT programme, the other to the order of Jake Ulrich for the British GT series. Designed by Geoff Kingston, they were built on carbonfibre central shells and the only body parts carried over from the previous GTS were the roof panel and the windscreen, now set at a shallower angle to lower the roofline. The big Jaguar V12 was moved even further aft within a lengthened wheelbase, and the fuel cell was relocated behind the driver. Aerodynamic improvements included a diffuser ramp between the rear wheels, a new rear wing mounted on pylons above 'ducktail' rear bodywork, and a longer overhang with diffusers ahead of the front wheels.

Lister was now running its own engine department, under Ian Smith, who saved 20kg of powertrain weight by using aluminium cylinder bore liners and a revised intake system made in carbon-composites. Fuelling and ignition was now controlled by a MoTec engine management system and, with the ACO-specified air restrictors, the 7-litre V12 made 655bhp at 6600rpm. The transverse Hewland TGT six-speed gearbox was equipped with a stronger selector mechanism in a lighter casing and the GTLs were fitted with carbon brakes.

These narrower and more slippery cars were about 100kg lighter than the GTS, and almost 40bhp more powerful. And Geoff Lees found his car to be almost seven seconds faster when he prequalified ninth in GT1. Julian Bailey was slower in the sister car, which was turning a wheel for the first time after being all but written off by its Texan owner in practice for the opening British GT race at Silverstone. The team did a great job in assembling a new car in just over three weeks and, between Prequalifying and race week, Ulrich/Ian Flux won handsomely from pole position at Donington – Lister's first victory for 38 years. Bailey then turned the tables on Lees in the Le Mans qualifying sessions.

After single shifts in the race by Lees and Tiff Needell, George Fouché was on his first flying lap when he spun backwards into the wall at Arnage. The car sustained too much chassis and exhaust damage for immediate repair and had to be retired.

Bailey and then Mark Skaife started strongly in the other GTL (above), but then, when Thomas Erdos was speeding along the Mulsanne straight, it had a major tyre failure that tore up the rear bodywork and wiped out the gearbox oil cooler. The car resumed after repairs, but then encountered a transmission failure. The gearbox was replaced but the clutch was found to be at fault and, while this was being changed, the team discovered damage to the underside of the car that had not been detected earlier. It too was retired.

Although it did not win again, Ulrich's Lister remained competitive in British GT, while the works car did four American events at the end of the season, including the final rounds of the FIA GT series.

FIRST OUT AGAIN

The BRM sports-racing car that had registered the first retirement from the 1992 Le Mans returned this year under new ownership – and repeated the performance (above).

In 1996, the mothballed P351 FIA Sportscar was bought by Keith Wiggins, the owner of Pacific Racing in Norfolk. Pacific had built on successful F3000 programmes by entering F1 in 1993, but had withdrawn after three seasons at that level. Instead, Wiggins steered his team towards the new-for-1997 International Sportscar Racing Series.

Pacific engineer Peter Weston designed the many modifications the coupé BRM needed to comply with the latest regulations, and Wiggins engaged Pilbeam Racing Designs to do the work. Former BRM F1 designer Mike Pilbeam's company (based in Bourne, the old BRM headquarters) converted the car into a spyder, replacing the lost chassis rigidity by adding a sturdy rollover structure. The rearend also had to be modified to replace the former V12 powertrain with a twin-turbo, 3-litre Nissan 300ZX V6 sourced from Clayton Cunningham in the USA, and prepared for this application by Janspeed. The work was completed in November 1996 and Pacific took the car testing at Snetterton in a timely manner.

Now known as the BRM P301, the car débuted at the opening ISRS event at Donington Park, but non-started due to electrical problems. Wiggins and team manager Ian Dawson (reunited with the project) then decided to concentrate their limited resources on Le Mans, where the drivers were Harri Toivonen (who had been entered in the same chassis in 1992), Eliseo Salazar and Jesús Pareja. This time all three drivers qualified, Toivonen the fastest. His race endured for six laps before the engine broke.

The BRM P301 reappeared in 1998 in the ISRS races at Misano and Donington, but again failed miserably in both these events. And that was it for the BRM, a racing project always hampered by lack of funds. Pacific closed its doors long before the season was done.

SALEEN'S SALOONS

A Ford presence at Le Mans, for the first time since a NASCAR Torino had raced in 1976, came in the form of two Mustang-based racecars entered by the Saleen-Allen Speedlab team from New Irvine, near Santa Ana in California.

Steve Saleen had successfully raced Mustangs in the Trans-Am series and had been producing road car conversions since 1984, always promoting them on the race track. He introduced this model, the Saleen SR, in 1994, when he also expanded the race team by going into partnership with racing veteran Bob Bondurant and actor and comedian Tim Allen.

The racing Saleen 'RRR' (a play on an Allen catchphrase) complied with the SCCA's World Challenge regulations, which were broadly similar to the FIA and ACO GT2 rules. It was based on the manufacturer's pressed-steel body monocoque (with Kevlar panels), and designed by a team led by former NPTI engineer Chris Willis. This was not an official factory project, but it did benefit from financial and technical assistance from Ford in Detroit. The Special Vehicle Engineering division advised on suspension design and other aspects of the chassis, and the independent rear suspension was developed by Ford Motorsport.

The naturally aspirated, all-aluminium, two-valve, 5.9-litre Ford V8 was

1997

prepared by McLaren Engines in Livonia, Michigan. Equipped with electronic fuel injection, it produced more than 500bhp at 7000rpm with the specified air restrictors, and drove through an Xtrac six-speed, sequential-shift gearbox. For this race, the team hedged its bets by fitting one car with a five-speed Hewland manual transmission.

The team came to Prequalifying after racing these cars at Daytona and Sebring, and then ran them in the Silverstone round of the FIA GT series in May. Saleen needed a team manager with Le Mans experience and hired former C2 entrant Roy Baker. The Hewland car surprised him and everyone else in qualifying when Price Cobb set the third fastest GT2 lap time. The top-end power was sufficient to take the cars to 197mph (317kph), despite their weight and the brick-like aerodynamics. Rob Schirle was three seconds slower with the Xtrac version (above), in which Historic racer Allen Lloyd failed to qualify.

Both Mustangs were soon in trouble on Saturday. Dave Warnock ran the Xtrac car through a gravel trap and damaged its exhaust system, and then the gearbox malfunctioned. Electrical problems first surfaced soon after Schirle had resumed, and caused the car's retirement in the small hours. Its stablemate, driven by Cobb with the team owner and Carlos Palau, was also delayed by transmission problems but survived the night. Soon after 8am, a wheelbearing failed.

The Saleen-Allen team was disappointed and surprised, because these cars were normally so robust. Schirle bought one of them and formed his Cirtek Motorsport team to contest the British GT series. The other went back to America, where the team clinched its fourth SCCA Manufacturers title.

KREMER TRAUMA

Kremer Racing came to Le Mans after winning the Monza 1000 round of the new ISRS with a K8 driven by John Nielsen and Thomas Bscher, and lined up the same two cars that had raced here 12 months before.

The Monza drivers chose to race Bscher's McLaren at Le Mans, and it was a poor decision: they non-started after a fire on Thursday. That said, the newer of the K8s was also eliminated the same evening: Giovanni Lavaggi was going for a time on his fourth lap when he crashed heavily, and the car took more front-end damage than could be repaired during Friday.

The other K8 (below), driven by Jürgen Lässig with Tomas Saldana and Carl Rosenblad, was qualified way down in 32nd position, but had climbed into the top 15 when its Porsche flat-six blew shortly after 11pm.

JOEST'S REPEAT PERFORMANCE

LE MANS

'ROCKY' ON THE ROCKS

Pictured left, Agusta Racing's three-year-old Callaway Corvette, one of seven US-sourced GT2 cars, was now equipped with further aerodynamic tweaks, much-improved (but still ferrous) brakes, and a 6-litre, 32-valve Chevrolet LT5 V8 – prepared in California by Comptech – for which a modest 450bhp at 6400rpm was claimed.

Almo Coppelli qualified the 'LM-GT' eighth in the class but, during the first two hours of the race, climbed to third behind the ORECA Vipers. At 6:15pm, a misfire brought 'Rocky' Agusta into the pits. The Lanzante Motorsport crew adjusted the ignition timing and sent Agusta on his way. The team owner was trying to stretch his second tank of fuel for one more lap when it ran dry at Indianapolis.

Agusta entered only three FIA GT events this summer before selling the LM-GT into the Belcar endurance series, in which it competed for three more seasons.

MARCOS BOWS OUT

Team Marcos International had two of its Mantara 600LM GT2 cars here, but one failed to qualify and the other (left) went out very early in the race.

The Dutch-owned team's latest, 6-litre Chevrolet LT5 engines were prepared by Kok Motorsport to develop 500bhp at 6250rpm, and the spaceframe cars were among the lightest in the class. But the team had an early setback in qualifying, when the car that had raced here 12 months before suffered a broken rocker. Only the newer chassis made it into the race.

Euser's first fuel stop extended to 13 minutes while the crew fixed the starter motor, and then a misfire turned out to be caused by nothing more than a loose plug lead. At 5:25pm, Harald Becker abandoned the car with a massive engine oil leak.

With the arrival of the Vipers and revitalized Porsches, the quasi-works Marcos was no longer a potent force in the FIA GT championship. The team continued to race in the FIA and Belcar series in 1998-99, but did not enter Le Mans.

EARTHQUAKE VICTIM

The most notable non-prequalifier was this one-off Matrix MPX-1 (above), a spyder conversion of the successful 1990 Nissan NPT90 IMSA GTP racecar. It was built in Los Angeles by Matrix Motor which, after the closure of NPTI in 1993, had rebuilt Nissan GTP cars, notably for Momo Racing. Matrix was relaunched in 1996 by Frenchman 'Lilo' Benzieron and Briton Wayne Hennebury, with the long-term aim of creating a roadgoing 'supercar'. Only eight days before Prequalifying, literally as the team was packing up the car, an earthquake in the Simi Valley damaged its North Hollywood workshop and destroyed bodywork that had been purpose-designed for Le Mans. The car arrived in an untested condition, and incurable braking and other problems thwarted Bernard de Dryver, Robin Donovan and Tim Richardson.

SARD also failed to prequalify two much-lightened Toyota MC8-Rs, now equipped with shorter-stroke versions of the Lexus V8. Olivier Grouillard found no less than 17 seconds in lap time relative to 1996, but the GT1 bar had been raised so high that even this was insufficient.

Eliminated from GT2 was a racing evolution of 'Tony' Gillet's quirky, Belgian-made, front-engined Vertigo road car, built on an aluminium honeycomb/carbon monocoque designed by Charles Vandenbosh. Parisian owner Eric van der Vyver undertook the conversion using a turbocharged, 450bhp Ford Escort RS Cosworth engine, but the 'Vertigo VdeV' owner was way off the pace.

After the 1996 Le Mans, Legeay Sports had partnered with Roy Johnson's RJ Racing team to win national GT races in Britain (with Marc Sourd) and France (with Stéphane Daoudi). Patrick and Mikaël Legeay and their partner, Jean-Luc Roy, entered into a joint venture with Johnson to produce a road car, also equipped with the Safrane turbo V6, in order to homologate the coupé as a GT2 racer in 1997. The chosen name was Helem (the 'H' is silent), a declaration of the group's intentions. The racing season began with a third place at Nogaro but, in Le Mans Prequalifying (below), Sourd and Daoudi were thwarted by a shunt with one car, and engine problems on the other.

In P2, the 1997 evolution of the neat Debora sports-racer was a quicker car and David Dessau lapped close to four minutes but, being grouped with much more powerful LM-P875 racecars, it too missed the cut.

LE MANS®
24®
HEURES DU MANS
14-15 juin 1997
La légende s'écrit sous vos yeux
PORSCHE
Mobil
1
Réservations - Tél : 02 43 40 24 24 - Vente Réseau France Billet : Carrefour. 3615 France Billet ou 01 42 31 31 31
A.S.A. Automobile Club de l'Ouest
CIRCUIT INTERNATIONAL DU MANS
SOCIÉTÉ D'ÉCONOMIE MIXTE SPORTIVE LOCALE DE GESTION DES 24 HEURES DU MANS
FÉDÉRATION FRANÇAISE
FFSA
DU SPORT AUTOMOBILE
SARTHE
RÉSEAU
France Billet
FRANCE info
Mobil 1

1997

HOURLY RACE POSITIONS

Prequalifying		Start	Time	Car	No	Drivers	1	2	3	4	5	6	7	8	9	10	11	12	13	14	15	16	17	18	19	20	21	22	23	24
*	3:43.799	Alboreto	1	3:41.581	TWR-Porsche WSC95	7	Alboreto/Johansson/Kristensen	1	1	3	3	3	3	3	3	2	3	3	4	3	3	3	2	2	2	2	2	2	1	1	1
*	3:50.178	Stuck	2	3:43.363	Porsche 911 GT1 Evo	25	Wollek/Stuck/Boutsen	9	4	2	1	1	1	1	1	1	1	1	1	1	1	1	4	DNF							
16	3:48.905	Poele	4	3:45.324	Nissan R390 GT1	22	Patrese/Poele/Suzuki	2	6	5	33	35	34	32	27	25	25	27	27	DNF											
3	3:45.973	Lehto	6	3:45.402	McLaren F1 GTR	42	Lehto/Soper/Piquet	4	3	22	26	21	18	18	14	12	10	10	9	9	9	9	8	7	DNF						
2	3:44.685	Dalmas	8	3:45.490	Porsche 911 GT1 Evo	26	Dalmas/Collard/Kelleners	3	2	1	2	2	2	2	2	3	2	2	2	2	2	2	1	1	1	1	1	1	4	DNF	
18	3:49.603	Martini	10	3:45.913	Porsche 911 GT1	27	Martini/Pescatori/Hermann	22	17	14	14	15	14	14	12	14	20	18	16	15	13	13	12	9	8	10	10	10	8	8	8
1	3:43.152	Brundle	12	3:46.228	Nissan R390 GT1	21	Brundle/Müller/Taylor	5	5	29	39	38	38	36	34	32	29	25	24	DNF											
20	3:50.055	Bouchut	14	3:46.389	Porsche 911 GT1	30	Bouchut/Evans/Gachot	6	8	8	13	8	9	8	13	16	14	11	11	11	10	12	15	DNF							
4	3:46.005	Theys	3	3:46.431	Ferrari 333SP	3	Moretti/Theys/Papis	7	12	15	12	10	8	12	10	10	9	9	10	10	11	10	10	11	9	8	8	8	6	6	
19	3:49.926	Ayles	4	3:47.108	McLaren F1 GTR	44	Ayles/Nakaya/Tsuchiya	13	14	12	11	11	20	DNF																	
17	3:49.439	McNish	5	3:47.314	Porsche 911 GT1	32	McNish/Wendlinger/Ortelli	46	DNF																						
6	3:46.381	Lamy	6	3:47.428	Porsche 911 GT1	33	Lamy/Hahne/Goueslard	15	13	11	9	13	11	10	7	7	7	7	7	7	7	7	6	6	6	6	6	6	6	4	5
8	3:47.361	Cottaz	7	3:47.662	Courage C41	13	Cottaz/Policand/Goossens	8	10	10	7	7	7	2	19	19	16	14	13	12	12	11	8	7	7	7	7	7	5	4	
11	3:47.704	Comas	8	3:47.745	Nissan R390 GT1	23	Hoshino/Comas/Kageyama	11	15	9	8	9	12	11	9	9	17	24	22	22	20	18	15	14	11	12	13	12	5		
15	3:48.877	Ekblom	9	3:48.011	Courage C36	10	Ekblom/Ricci/Libert	21	21	34	40	40	40	39	37	37	35	32	29	27	27	27	23	22	21	20	20	20	17	16	
5	3:46.381	Kox	10	3:48.057	McLaren F1 GTR	43	Kox/Ravaglia/Hélary	10	7	7	5	6	5	5	6	6	6	6	6	6	5	5	4	4	4	4	4	3	3		
29	3:52.943	Lagorce	11	3:48.123	Panoz Esperante GTR-1	52	Lagorce/Bernard/Boullion	42	31	24	19	20	19	19	17	15	13	13	DNF												
10	3:47.439	A.Ferté	12	3:48.341	Porsche 911 GT1	29	A.Ferté/Gartzen/Thévenin	16	16	13	10	12	10	9	8	8	8	8	8	8	8	8	9	DNF							
7	3:47.190	Gounon	13	3:48.369	McLaren F1 GTR	41	Raphanel/Olofsson/Gounon	12	9	4	4	4	4	4	4	4	4	4	3	4	4	3	3	3	3	3	2	2	2		
13	3:47.814	Lammers	14	3:48.395	Lotus Elise GT1	49	Lammers/Hezemans/Grau	26	25	20	17	17	15	15	16	22	26	DNF													
23	3:50.949	Clérico	15	3:48.651	Courage C36	8	Pescarolo/Belloc/Clérico	35	23	33	38	36	33	30	25	26	24	22	20	19	16	15	14	11	9	8	9	9	7	7	
*	3:53.750	Gilbert-Scott	16	3:48.665	McLaren F1 GTR	39	Gilbert-Scott/Sekiya/Bellm	14	11	6	6	5	6	5	5	5	5	5	5	5	5	6	6	5	5	5	5	5	5	DNF	
14	3:48.559	Nielsen		3:49.330	McLaren F1 GTR	40	Nielsen/Bscher/Goodwin	DNS																							
27	3:52.074	Baldi	28	3:49.465	Porsche 911 GT1	28	Baldi/Konrad/Nearn	23	22	19	16	14	13	13	11	11	12	DNF													
24	3:51.154	Bailey	29	3:49.653	Lister Storm GTL	46	Bailey/Erdos/Skaife	18	18	16	25	37	36	37	35	DNF															
9	3:47.435	Brabham	30	3:49.699	Panoz Esperante GTR-1	55	Brabham/McCarthy/Bundy	17	35	25	20	19	16	16	15	13	11	15	DNF												
12	3:47.771	Lees	31	3:50.398	Lister Storm GTL	45	Lees/Needell/Fouché	25	42	DNF																					
22	3:50.293	Wallace	32	3:50.852	Panoz Esperante GTR-1	54	Wallace/Weaver/Leitzinger	19	19	38	35	32	29	26	28	28	28	23	21	20	17	17	12	10	DNF						
30	3:53.000	M.Ferté	11	3:51.092	Ferrari 333SP	4	M.Ferté/Campos/Nearburg	20	43	44	DNF																				
21	3:50.123	Giroix	DNQ	3:51.373	Lotus Elise GT1	50	Giroix/Deletraz	DNS																							
26	3:51.928	Ma.Andretti	13	3:51.378	Courage C36	9	Andretti/Andretti/Grouillard	32	24	18	29	30	35	33	31	27	27	21	18	17	19	16	19	DNF							
34	3:56.320	Rosenblad	15	3:55.981	Kremer K8	5	Saldana/Rosenblad/Lässig	24	20	17	15	16	17	17	DNF																
37	3:58.663	Fréon	17	3:56.122	Kudzu DLM4	15	Downing/Terada/Fréon	28	33	31	32	31	30	29	32	29	31	28	25	24	24	24	17	19	18	18	18	19	16	17	
35	3:56.479	O'Connell	19	3:56.734	BRM P301	14	Salazar/Toivonen/Pareja	DNF																							
32	3:53.907	Lavaggi	DNQ	3:56.929	Kremer K8	6	Lavaggi/Maury-Laribière/Chauvin	DNS																							
46	4:05.977	Archer	33	4:04.589	Chrysler Viper GTS-R	62	Duez/Archer/Ayari	30	26	21	18	18	DNF																		
41	4:04.615	Beretta	34	4:04.654	Chrysler Viper GTS-R	61	Beretta/Gache/Dupuy	27	27	23	30	26	22	20	18	17	15	12	12	13	20	22	20	16	15	14	14	14	15	DNF	
47	4:07.447	Cobb	35	4:06.922	Saleen Mustang RRR	67	Cobb/Saleen/Palau	34	37	41	42	41	39	38	36	36	34	31	30	28	28	28	DNF								
42	4:04.641	Jarier	36	4:07.137	Porsche 911 GT2	77	Jarier/Chéreau/Leconte	29	32	27	21	22	26	34	DNF																
40	4:04.587	Pilgrim	37	4:07.153	Porsche 911 GT2	74	Ahrle/Pilgrim/Eichmann	31	39	40	37	34	31	28	24	24	23	19	19	18	15	14	13	12	13	13	11	12	10	10	
45	4:05.970	Dupuy	38	4:08.081	Chrysler Viper GTS-R	63	Morton/Bell/Yver	43	44	39	36	33	32	31	30	30	32	30	28	26	25	25	20	18	17	17	17	17	17	14	
53	4:09.520	Schirle	39	4:09.801	Saleen Mustang RRR	66	Schirle/Warnock	33	41	42	43	42	41	40	38	38	DNF														
49	4:08.948	Coppelli	40	4:10.048	Callaway Corvette LM-GT	60	Coppelli/Agusta/Graham	36	28	37	34	DNF																			
51	4:09.114	Calderari	41	4:10.094	Porsche 911 GT2	84	Calderari/Bryner/Zadra	38	29	26	22	23	21	21	26	33	DNF														
*	4:14.212	P.Mello	42	4:10.479	Porsche 911 GT2	73	Mello-Breyner/Mello-Breyner/Mello-Breyner	41	36	32	27	27	25	23	21	20	18	17	14	14	18	17	17	16	15	15	14	11	11		
*	4:19.764	Resende	43	4:10.903	Porsche 911 GT2	75	Bourdais/Kitchak/Reisende	40	38	35	28	28	24	24	29	34	33	29	26	25	26	26	22	21	20	21	DNF				
52	4:09.412	Neugarten	44	4:11.134	Porsche 911 GT2	78	Neugarten/Martinolle/Lagniez	37	30	30	24	24	23	22	20	18	19	16	15	16	14	13	12	12	13	11	9	9			
58	4:10.868	Hürtgen	45	4:11.630	Porsche 911 GT2	80	Hürtgen/Robinson/Price	47	46	43	41	39	37	35	33	31	30	26	23	23	23	23	18	17	16	16	16	13	13		
57	4:10.740	Euser	46	4:11.904	Marcos Mantara 600LM	70	Euser/Becker/Suzuki	45	45	DNF																					
48	4:08.181	Seiler	47	4:11.911	Porsche 911 GT2	79	Seiler/Schumacher/Ligonnet	39	34	28	23	25	28	25	22	21	21	DNF													
56	4:10.498	Nurminen	48	4:12.696	Chrysler Viper GTS-R	64	Hugenholtz/Nurminen/Gleason	44	40	36	31	29	28	27	23	23	22	20	19	21	21	21	16	20	19	19	19	18	15		
50	4:09.080	Haterd	DNQ	4:22.904	Marcos Mantara 600LM	71	Migault/Chappell/Maunoir	DNS																							

DNF Did not finish   **DNQ** Did not qualify   **DSQ** Disqualified   **FS** Failed scrutineering   **NC** Not classified as a finisher   **RES** Reserve not required   ***** Automatic entry

JOEST'S REPEAT PERFORMANCE

LE MANS

RACE RESULTS

Pos	Car	No	Drivers			Laps	Km	Miles	FIA Class	DNF
1	TWR-Porsche WSC95	7	Michele Alboreto (I)	Stefan Johansson (S)	Tom Kristensen (DK)	361	4909.589	3050.671	LM-P875	
2	McLaren F1 GTR	41	Pierre-Henri Raphanel (F)	Anders Olofsson (S)	Jean-Marc Gounon (F)	360	4895.996	3042.225	LM-GT1	
3	McLaren F1 GTR	43	Eric Hélary (F)	Peter Kox (NL)	Roberto Ravaglia (I)	358	4868.810	3025.332	LM-GT1	
4	Courage C41	13	Didier Cottaz (F)	Jérôme Policand (F)	Marc Goossens (B)	336	4569.596	2839.410	LM-P875	
5	Porsche 911 GT1	33	Pedro Lamy (P)	Armin Hahne (D)	Patrice Gouesland (F)	331	4501.599	2797.159	LM-GT1	
DNF	Porsche 911 GT1 Evo	26	Yannick Dalmas (F)	Emmanuel Collard (F)	Ralf Kelleners (D)	327			LM-GT1	Fire
DNF	McLaren F1 GTR	39	Andrew Gilbert-Scott (GB)	Masanori Sekiya (J)	Ray Bellm (GB)	326			LM-GT1	Fire
6	Ferrari 333 SP	3	Giampiero Moretti (I)	Didier Theys (B)	Max Papis (I)	321	4365.603	2712.655	LM-P875	
7	Courage C36	8	Henri Pescarolo (F)	Jean-Philippe Belloc (F)	Emmanuel Clérico (F)	319	4338.409	2695.757	LM-P875	
8	Porsche 911 GT1	27	Pierluigi Martini (I)	Christian Pescatori (I)	Antonio de Azevedo Hermann (BR)	317	4311.197	2678.848	LM-GT1	
9	Porsche 911 GT2	78	Michel Neugarten (B)	Guy Martinolle (F)	Jean-Claude Lagniez (F)	307	4175.212	2594.351	LM-GT2	
10	Porsche 911 GT2	74	Andre Ahrle (D)	Andy Pilgrim (USA)	Bruno Eichmann (CH)	306	4161.594	2585.890	LM-GT2	
11	Porsche 911 GT2	73	Manuel Mello-Breyner (P)	Tomas Mello-Breyner (P)	Pedro Mello-Breyner (P)	295	4004.249	2488.120	LM-GT2	
12	Nissan R390 GT1	23	Kazuyoshi Hoshino (J)	Erik Comas (F)	Masahiko Kageyama (J)	294	3995.157	2482.471	LM-GT1	
13	Porsche 911 GT2	80	Claudia Hürtgen (D)	John Robinson (GB)	Hugh Price (GB)	287	3903.198	2425.330	LM-GT2	
14	Chrysler Viper GTS-R	63	John Morton (USA)	Justin Bell (GB)	Pierre Yver (F)	278	3780.790	2349.269	LM-GT2	
15	Chrysler Viper GTS-R	64	John Hugenholtz (NL)	Jari Nurminen (SF)	Chris Gleason (USA)	269	3658.404	2273.222	LM-GT2	
16	Courage C36	10	Fredrik Ekblom (S)	Jean-Louis Ricci (F)	Jean-Paul Libert (B)	265	3603.999	2239.417	LM-P875	
17	Kudzu DLM4	15	Jim Downing (USA)	Yojiro Terada (J)	Franck Fréon (F)	263	3576.793	2222.512	LM-P875	
DNF	Chrysler Viper GTS-R	61	Olivier Beretta (MC)	Philippe Gache (F)	Dominique Dupuy (F)	263			LM-GT2	Accident
DNF	Porsche 911 GT1 Evo	25	Hans-Joachim Stuck (D)	Bob Wollek (F)	Thierry Boutsen (B)	238			LM-GT1	Accident
DNF	Panoz Esperante GTR-1	54	Andy Wallace (GB)	James Weaver (GB)	Butch Leitzinger (USA)	236			LM-GT1	Engine
DNF	McLaren F1 GTR	42	JJ Lehto (SF)	Steve Soper (GB)	Nelson Piquet (BR)	236			LM-GT1	Accident
DNF	Porsche 911 GT1	29	Alain Ferté (F)	Jürgen von Gartzen (D)	Olivier Thévenin (F)	236			LM-GT1	Engine/fire
DNF	Porsche 911 GT1	30	Christophe Bouchut (F)	Andy Evans (USA)	Bertrand Gachot (B)	207			LM-GT1	Engine (overheating)
DNF	Porsche 911 GT2	75	Patrick Bourdais (F)	Peter Kitchak (USA)	André Lara Resende (BR)	205			LM-GT2	Accident damage
DNF	Courage C36	9	Mario Andretti (USA)	Michael Andretti (USA)	Olivier Grouillard (F)	197			LM-P875	Accident damage
DNF	Panoz Esperante GTR-1	52	Franck Lagorce (F)	Eric Bernard (F)	Jean-Christophe Boullion (F)	149			LM-GT1	Engine (oil pressure)
DNF	Panoz Esperante GTR-1	55	David Brabham (AUS)	Perry McCarthy (GB)	Harry 'Doc' Bundy (USA)	145			LM-GT1	Fire
DNF	Nissan R390 GT1	21	Martin Brundle (GB)	Jörg Müller (D)	Wayne Taylor (ZA)	139			LM-GT1	Transmission (gearbox)
DNF	Porsche 911 GT1	28	Mauro Baldi (I)	Franz Konrad (A)	Robert Nearn (GB)	138			LM-GT1	Accident damage
DNF	Ford Saleen Mustang RRR	67	Price Cobb (USA)	Steve Saleen (USA)	Carlos Palau (E)	133			LM-GT2	Wheel hub-carrier
DNF	Porsche 911 GT2	79	Toni Seiler (CH)	Larry Schumacher (USA)	Michel Ligonnet (F)	126			LM-GT2	Engine
DNF	Nissan R390 GT1	22	Riccardo Patrese (I)	Eric van der Poele (B)	Aguri Suzuki (J)	121			LM-GT1	Transmission (gearbox)
DNF	Lotus Elise GT1	49	Jan Lammers (NL)	Mike Hezemans (NL)	Alexander 'Sandy' Grau (D)	121			LM-GT1	Engine (oil pressure)
DNF	Kremer K8	5	Tomas Saldana (E)	Carl Rosenblad (S)	Jürgen Lässig (D)	103			LM-P875	Engine
DNF	Porsche 911 GT2	84	Enzo Calderari (CH)	Lilian Bryner (CH)	Angelo Zadra (I)	98			LM-GT2	Engine
DNF	McLaren F1 GTR	44	Gary Ayles (GB)	Keiichi Tsuchiya (J)	Akihiko Nakaya (J)	88			LM-GT1	Accident
DNF	Lister Storm GTL	46	Julian Bailey (GB)	Thomas Erdos (BR)	Mark Skaife (AUS)	77			LM-GT1	Transmission (gearbox)
DNF	Porsche 911 GT2	77	Jean-Pierre Jarier (F)	Jean-Luc Chéreau (F)	Jack Leconte (F)	77			LM-GT2	Transmission
DNF	Chrysler Viper GTS-R	62	Marc Duez (B)	Tommy Archer (USA)	Soheil Ayari (F)	76			LM-GT2	Accident
DNF	Callaway Corvette LM-GT	60	Almo Coppelli (I)	Ricardo 'Rocky' Agusta (I)	Eric Graham (F)	45			LM-GT2	Out of fuel
DNF	Ford Saleen Mustang RRR	66	Rob Schirle (GB)	David Warnock (GB)		28			LM-GT2	Electrics
DNF	Lister Storm GTL	45	Geoff Lees (GB)	George Fouché (ZA)	Tiff Needell (GB)	21			LM-GT1	Accident
DNF	Ferrari 333SP	4	Michel Ferté (F)	Adrian Campos (E)	Charles Nearburg (USA)	18			LM-P875	Out of fuel
DNF	Marcos Mantara 600LM	70	Cor Euser (NL)	Harald Becker (D)	Takaji Suzuki (J)	15			LM-GT2	Engine (oil leak)
DNF	Porsche 911 GT1	32	Allan McNish (GB)	Karl Wendlinger (A)	Stéphane Ortelli (F)	8			LM-GT1	Accident
DNF	BRM P301	14	Harri Toivonen (SF)	Eliseo Salazar (RCH)	Jesús Pareja (E)	6			LM-P875	Engine
DNS	Kremer K8	6	Giovanni Lavaggi (I)	Jean-Luc Maury-Laribière (F)	Bernard Chauvin (F)				LM-P875	Accident in qualifying
DNS	McLaren F1 GTR	40	John Nielsen (DK)	Thomas Bscher (D)	Chris Goodwin (GB)				LM-GT1	Fire in qualifying
DNQ	Lotus Elise GT1	50	Fabien Giroix (F)	Jean-Denis Deletraz (CH)					LM-GT1	
DNQ	Marcos Mantara 600LM	71	François Migault (F)	Dominic Chappell (GB)	Henri-Louis Maunoir (F)				LM-GT2	

DNF Did not finish **DNS** Did not start **DSQ** Disqualified **FS** Failed scrutineering **RES** Reserve not required **NC** Not classified as a finisher **WD** Withdrawn Drivers in italics did not race the cars specified

1997

CLASS WINNERS

FIA Class	Starters	Finishers	First	No	Drivers	kph	mph	
LM-P875	10	6	TWR-Porsche WSC95	7	Alboreto/Johansson/Kristensen	204.540	127.096	Record
LM-GT1	22	5	McLaren F1 GTR	41	Raphanel/Olofsson/Gounon	204.000	126.760	Record
LM-GT2	16	6	Porsche 911 GT2	78	Neugarten/Martinolle/Lagniez	173.960	108.094	Record
Totals	48	17						REVISED CIRCUIT

NON-PREQUALIFIERS

No	Car	Entrant (Nat)	cc	Engine	Class	Pos	Time
2	WR LM97	Rachel Welter (F)	1998tc	Peugeot 405-Raid S4	LMP/WSC	WD	4:34.947
12	Debora LMP297	Didier Bonnet (F)	1994tc	Cosworth S4	LMP/WSC	43	4:04.849
16	Matrix MPX-1	Matrix Motor (USA)	2939tc	Nissan VG30ET V6	LMP/WSC	44	4:05.846
17	WR LM97	Alain Lebrun (F)	1905tc	Peugeot 405-Raid S4	LMP/WSC	NT	No time
24	Ferrari F40 GT Evo	Ennea Ferrari Club Italia (I)	3500tc	F120B V8	GT1	NA	
31	Porsche 911 GT1	Société Larbre Compétition (F)	3164tc	F6	GT1	NA	
34	Sard Toyota MC8-R	Team Menicon SARD (J)	3968tc	Toyota 1UZ-FE V8	GT1	31	3:53.315
35	Sard Toyota MC8-R	Team Menicon SARD (J)	3968tc	Toyota 1UZ-FE V8	GT1	28	3:52.334
36	Helem V6	RJ Racing (GB/F)	3040tc	PRV V6	GT1	38	3:59.755
37	Helem V6	RJ Racing (GB/F)	3040tc	PRV V6	GT1	39	4:00.230
38	McLaren F1 GTR	BBA Compétition (F)	5990	BMW S70/3 V12	GT1	33	3:56.032
47	Lotus Elise GT1	GBF UK (GB)	5993	Chevrolet LT5 V8	GT1	NA	
48	Lotus Elise GT1	GBF UK (GB)	5993	Chevrolet LT5 V8	GT1	NA	
51	Lotus Elise GT1	GT1 Team Lotus (GB) Franck Muller (NL)	5993	Chevrolet LT5 V8	GT1	36	3:56.487
53	Panoz Esperante GTR-1	Société DAMS (F)	5950	Ford V8	GT1	WD	3:51.666
65	Chrysler Viper GTS-R	Chamberlain Engineering (GB)	7986	356-T6 V10	GT2	55	4:09.704
68	Saleen Mustang RRR	Saleen Allen Speedlab (USA)	5900	Ford V8	GT2	NA	
69	Gillet Vertigo VdeV	Eric van de Vyver (F)	1993tc	Cosworth YBT S4	GT2	61	4:24.156
72	Marcos Mantara LM600	Team Marcos Racing International (GB)	5997	Chevrolet V8	GT2	NA	
76	Porsche 911 GT2	Bruno Krauss Rennsporttechnik (D)	3600tc	F6	GT2	54	4:09.667
81	Porsche 911 GT2	GT Racing Team (CH)	3600tc	F6	GT2	62	4:59.064
82	Porsche 911 GT2	PARR Motorsport (GB)	3600tc	F6	GT2	NA	
83	Porsche 911 GT2	Gerard McQuillan (GB)	3600tc	F6	GT2	59	4:11.589
85	Porsche 911 GT2	Steve O'Rourke (GB)	3600tc	F6	GT2	60	4:11.954

DSQ Disqualified   **NA** Non-arrival   **NT** No time set   **WD** Withdrawn after Prequalifying

INTERNATIONAL SPORTS RACING SERIES

Race	Winner	Drivers
Donington Park (GB) 320km	TWR-Porsche WSC95	Johansson/Martini
Zolder (B) 200km	Ferrari 333 SP	Theys/Lienhard
Brno (CS) 50km	Centenari M1	Merzario
Jarama (E) 300km	Courage C41	Cottaz/Policand

Non-championship series

FIA GT CHAMPIONSHIP

Race	Winner	Drivers
Hockenheim (D)	McLaren F1 GTR	Soper/Lehto
Silverstone (GB)	McLaren F1 GTR	Ravaglia/Kox
Helsinki (SF)	McLaren F1 GTR	Soper/Lehto
Nürburgring (D)	Mercedes-Benz CLK-GTR	Schneider/Ludwig
Spa-Francorchamps (B)	McLaren F1 GTR	Soper/Lehto
Zeltweg (A)	Mercedes-Benz CLK-GTR	Schneider/Ludwig/Mayländer
Suzuka (J) 1000km	Mercedes-Benz CLK-GTR	Schneider/Nannini/Tiemann
Donington Park (GB)	Mercedes-Benz CLK-GTR	Schneider/Wurz
Mugello (I)	McLaren F1 GTR	Soper/Lehto
Sebring (USA)	Mercedes-Benz CLK-GTR	Schneider/Ludwig
Laguna Seca (USA)	Mercedes-Benz CLK-GTR	Schneider/Ludwig

FINAL CHAMPIONSHIP POINTS

Final Positions	Driver (Nat)	Points
GT1 TEAMS		
1	AMG Mercedes (D)	110
2	BMW Motorsport Schnitzer (D)	85
3	Gulf Team Davidoff (GB)	37
4	Porsche AG (D)	35
5	Roock Racing (D)	8
6	David Price Racing (GB)	4
&c		
GT2 TEAMS		
1	Viper Team ORECA (F)	126
2	Roock Racing (D)	83
3	Konrad Motorsport (D)	15
4	Krauss Motorsport (D)	13
=	Marcos Racing International (GB)	13
6	Karl Augustin (A)	8
&c		
GT1 DRIVERS		
1	Bernd Schneider (D)	72
2	Steve Soper (GB)	59
=	JJ Lehto (SF)	59
4	Klaus Ludwig (D)	51
5	Marcel Tiemann (D)	34
=	Alessandro Nannini (I)	34
&c		
GT2 DRIVERS		
1	Justin Bell (GB)	66
2	Bruno Eichmann (CH)	65
3	Olivier Beretta (NC)	60
=	Philippe Gache (F)	60
5	Claudia Hurtgen (D)	55
6	Ni Amorim (P)	44
&c		

JOEST'S REPEAT PERFORMANCE

LE MANS

1998
PORSCHE'S GT COMES GOOD

LE MANS

RACE INFORMATION

RACE DATE
6-7 June

RACE No
66

CIRCUIT LENGTH
8.454 miles/13.605km

HONORARY STARTER
Bill Campbell
Mayor of Atlanta, Georgia, USA

MARQUES (ON GRID)

BMW	2
Chrysler	5
Courage	4
Debora	1
Ferrari	4
Kremer-Porsche	1
McLaren	2
Mercedes-Benz	2
Nissan	4
Panos	2
Porsche	16
Riley&Scott	1
Toyota	3

STARTERS/FINISHERS
47/23

WINNERS

OVERALL
Porsche

ENTRY LIST

No	Car	Entrant (nat)	cc	Engine	Tyres	Weight (kg)	Class
1	BMW V12 LM	Team BMW Motorsport (D)	5990	S70/3 V12	Michelin	930	LM-P1
2	BMW V12 LM	Team BMW Motorsport (D)	5990	S70/3 V12	Michelin	916	LM-P1
3	Ferrari 333 SP	Momo Racing (USA)	3997	F310E V8	Yokohama	904	LM-P1
5	Ferrari 333 SP-98	JB Racing (F)	3997	F310E V2	Michelin	881	LM-P1
7	Porsche LMP1-98	Porsche AG/Joest Racing (D)	3196tc	F6	Goodyear	890	LM-P1 *
8	Porsche LMP1-98	Porsche AG/Joest Racing (D)	3196tc	F6	Goodyear	889	LM-P1
10	Ferrari 333 SP	Pilot BSM Racing (F)	3997	F310E V12	Dunlop	879	LM-P1
12	Ferrari 333 SP	Doyle-Risi Racing (USA)	3997	F310E V12	Pirelli	917	LM-P1
13	Courage C51	Courage Compétition (F)	3000tc	Nissan VRH-30L V8	Michelin	894	LM-P1
14	Courage C51	Courage Compétition (F)	3000tc	Nissan VRH-30L V8	Michelin	893	LM-P1
15	Courage C36	Courage Compétition/La Filière Elf (F)	2994tc	Porsche F6	Michelin	929	LM-P1
16	Kremer K8	Kremer Racing (D)	2994tc	Porsche F6	Goodyear	924	LM-P1
21	Riley & Scott Mk3	Solution-F/Philippe Gache (F)	5078	Ford V8	Pirelli	919	LM-P1
22	Debora LMP296	Didier Bonnet (F)	3200	BMW M88 S6	Michelin	700	LM-P2
24	Courage C50	Courage Compétition (F) Team AM-PM (J)	2994tc	Porsche F6	Michelin	891	LM-P1 *
25	Porsche 911 GT1-98	Porsche AG (D)	3196tc	F6	Michelin	967	LM-GT1
26	Porsche 911 GT1-98	Porsche AG (D)	3196tc	F6	Michelin	967	LM-GT1
27	Toyota GT-One	Toyota Motorsport (J)	3576tc	R36V V8	Michelin	924	LM-GT1
28	Toyota GT-One	Toyota Motorsport (J)	3576tc	R36V V8	Michelin	920	LM-GT1
29	Toyota GT-One	Toyota Motorsport (J)	3576tc	R36V V8	Michelin	920	LM-GT1
30	Nissan R390 GT1	NISMO (J)	3496tc	VRH 35L V8	Bridgestone	1015	LM-GT1
31	Nissan R390 GT1	NISMO (J)	3496tc	VRH35L V8	Bridgestone	1017	LM-GT1
32	Nissan R390 GT1	NISMO (J)	3496tc	VRH35L V8	Bridgestone	1017	LM-GT1
33	Nissan R390 GT1	NISMO (J)	3496tc	VRH35L V8	Bridgestone	1008	LM-GT1
35	Mercedes-Benz CLK-GTR	AMG Mercedes (D)	6000	M.119 V8	Bridgestone	971	LM-GT1
36	Mercedes-Benz CLK-GTR	AMG Mercedes (D)	6000	M.119 V8	Bridgestone	976	LM-GT1 *
40	McLaren F1 GTR	GTC Gulf Team Davidoff (GB)	5990	BMW S70/3 V12	Pirelli	954	LM-GT1 *
41	McLaren F1 GTR	GTC Gulf Team Davidoff (GB)	5990	BMW S70/3 V12	Goodyear	961	LM-GT1 *
44	Panoz Esperante GTR-1	Panoz Motorsports (USA) DAMS (F)	5999	Ford V8	Michelin	961	LM-GT1
45	Panoz Esperante GTR-1	Panoz Motorsports (USA)	5999	Ford V8	Michelin	962	LM-GT1
50	Chrysler Viper GTS-R	Viper Team ORECA (F)	7986	356-T6 V10	Michelin	1156	LM-GT2
51	Chrysler Viper GTS-R	Viper Team ORECA (F)	7986	356-T6 V10	Michelin	1161	LM-GT2
53	Chrysler Viper GTS-R	Viper Team ORECA (F)	7986	356-T6 V10	Michelin	1181	LM-GT2
55	Chrysler Viper GTS-R	Chamberlain Engineering (GB)	7986	356-T6 V10	Dunlop	1215	LM-GT2
56	Chrysler Viper GTS-R	Chamberlain Engineering (GB)	7986	356-T6 V10	Dunlop	1334	LM-GT2
60	Porsche 911 GT2	Larbre Compétition/ETS Chéreau Sports (F)	3600tc	F6	Michelin	1159	LM-GT2
61	Porsche 911 GT2	Krauss Race Sports International (D)	3600tc	F6	Dunlop	1127	LM-GT2
62	Porsche 911 GT2	CJ Motorsports (USA)	3600tc	F6	Goodyear	1148	LM-GT2
64	Porsche 911 GT2	Roock Racing Team (D)	3600tc	F6	Yokohama	1161	LM-GT2
65	Porsche 911 GT2	Roock Racing Team (D)	3600tc	F6	Yokohama	1058	LM-GT2
67	Porsche 911 GT2	Elf Haberthur Racing (CH)	3600tc	F6	Dunlop	1116	LM-GT2
68	Porsche 911 GT2	Elf Haberthur Racing (CH)	3600tc	F6	Dunlop	1168	LM-GT2 *
69	Porsche 911 GT2	Michel Nourry (F)	3600tc	F6	Goodyear	1155	LM-GT2
70	Porsche 911 GT2	Konrad Motorsport (D)	3600tc	F6	Dunlop	1109	LM-GT2
71	Porsche 911 GT2	Estoril Racing (P)	3600tc	F6	Pirelli	1185	LM-GT2
72	Porsche 911 GT2	Larbre Compétition (F)	3600tc	F6	Michelin	1180	LM-GT2
73	Porsche 911 GT2	Konrad Motorsport (D)	3600tc	F6	Dunlop	1108	LM-GT2
74	Saleen Mustang RRR	Cirtek Motorspirt (GB)	5900	Ford V8	GT2	N/A	LM-GT2

* Automatic entries: (7) Prototype class winner 1997 Le Mans, (24) Prototype class winner 1997 Coupe d'Automne, (36) GT1 class winner 1997 FIA GT Championship, (40) GT1 class winner 1997 Le Mans, (41) GT1 class winner 1997 Coupe d'Automne, (68) GT2 class winner 1997 Le Mans. See Non-Prequalifiers table for discarded entries

1998

ENTRY

This year's entry was dramatically enhanced by the arrival of powerful factory teams deployed by BMW with a new P1 project, by Mercedes-Benz with hardware that was dominating the FIA GT series, and by Toyota with an exotic new GT1 racer. Porsche continued with its GT1 programme and hedged its bets by updating Joest Racing's 1997-98 winning P1 cars. Nissan again fielded its GT1 cars and supplied works engines for Yves Courage's prototypes.

Lotus and Marcos had gone, but ambitious Panoz in GT1 and Chrysler in GT2 continued with their American-sourced, production-based cars. Courage, Kremer and Riley & Scott (R&S) were the specialist constructors in the P1 division, in which there were four Ferrari World Sports Cars. A Debora-BMW was the only P2 on the list, but this was a terrific entry. Including the nine factory teams, no fewer than 27 cars were operated by their manufacturers.

QUALIFYING

The effect of the ACO regulations was that, to be competitive in this race, P1 prototypes had to be much faster than GT1 cars. Qualifying proved that such was not the case: GT1 machinery filled the first five positions on the grid, and eight of the top 10.

PORSCHE'S GT COMES GOOD 299

LE MANS

ORGANISATION

Once again, changes to the technical regulations were mercifully few. The maximum volume of naturally aspirated engines in the LM-P1 class was increased from 5100 to 6000cc, and turbos from 3000 to 4000cc. In LM-P2, six-cylinder 'atmo' engines of up to 3500cc became mandatory.

In the sporting regulations, the ACO reverted to a normal starting grid, with the cars lined up in qualifying order, irrespective of class. The start was given at 2pm, two hours earlier than usual, so as to avoid a TV clash with the French Open tennis tournament in Paris.

The ACO's 400km race in September on the Bugatti circuit, a round of the ISRS, was won by the JB Giesse Ferrari of Emmanuel Collard/Vincenzo Sospiri, which dominated the championship. However the class winners in the 1998 Coupes d'Automne event were no longer guaranteed entries for the 24 Hours the following season. That role passed to an important new race in the United States.

In October, with the ACO's copyright permission, American entrepreneur Don Panoz promoted the first 1000-mile 'Petit Le Mans' sportscar race at Road Atlanta, Georgia. It was a round of the PSCR series and was won by one of Doyle-Risi Racing's Ferraris.

Mercedes, Porsche and Toyota picked up where they had left off at the end of Prequalifying five weeks before, with respectively FIA GT champion Bernd Schneider, Allan McNish and Martin Brundle again their main men. Brundle's Toyota GT-One set the pace in both Wednesday sessions, when the track was still 'green'. The next day, Schneider's CLK beat his best lap time by more than a second. Christophe Bouchut qualified third with the other Mercedes, while McNish was pipped to fourth position by his Porsche team mate, Jorg Müller. The best prototype was Pierluigi Martini's BMW.

RACE

From the pole, Schneider managed to keep Brundle at bay at the 2pm start, but only by means of a brake-locking moment at the first turn. The Toyota went past anyway on the Mulsanne straight. And the Mercedes effort was short-lived: a hydraulics failure left Schneider's engine without lubrication after only 19 laps, and the same thing happened to Bouchut after 31. So was BMW's: broken wheelbearings accounted for both cars before nightfall.

A strong shift by Thierry Boutsen established a Toyota 1-2 in

300 LE MANS 24 HOURS 1990–99

front of a Porsche 3-4, but it only lasted until about 5:30pm, when a braking imbalance on the leading car sent Eric Hélary into a big spin at the Virage Ford. Two pitstops were needed to sort out the problem, at the cost of more than half an hour. At the same time, the third, Japanese-crewed GT-One lost a chunk of time in three stops to resolve a gearshift breakage. The cars resumed respectively in 26th and 19th positions and would never again feature, although Brundle's would reappear in the top 10 before he crashed at the Ford chicane, caught out by a rain shower at dawn.

Boutsen/Geoff Lees/Ralf Kelleners were now leading, and had the situation in hand for Toyota. They were matching the chasing pace of the GT1 Porsches, Müller/Bob Wollek/Uwe Alzen ahead of McNish/Laurent Aïello/Stéphane Ortelli.

But the next blow for Toyota came at 10:40pm, when Lees lost 16 minutes in the pits to gearbox repairs, slipping to seventh. The GT1 Porsches assumed first and second positions. At 1:30am, the first of several rain showers heralded a hard night for all the pit crews. The Porsches traded the lead through the squalls until an outstanding wet-weather shift by McNish took him clear of the sister car.

But the Toyota staged quite a recovery. Just before 6am, caught on slicks under another shower, Müller dropped the leading car at the first chicane on the big straight, and had to limp to pit-lane for front underbody repairs. Ten minutes later, McNish pitted with an overheating engine, caused by a hose failure. As both the GT1 Porsches were at rest, Lees took back the lost laps and, at 6:20am, retrieved the lead. McNish rejoined three laps behind the Toyota, Alzen four.

At 7:50am, it all changed again. The leading GT-One pitted for another new gear cluster, which was fitted by the crew in only 10 minutes. Now the three leaders were on the same lap, the Porsches ahead.

The rest of the morning was dry and delivered a treat for the 185,000 spectators as the contenders went flat-out for the win, taking turns at the front according to their pitstops. Porsche triple-stinted its Michelin tyres in a bid to counter the Toyota's slightly superior pace, but gradually the GT-One gained the upper hand, and put a lap on one of the 911 GT1s. At 12:35pm, Kelleners was more than a minute ahead of McNish, both men with one fuel stop to come. That was when the GT-One's gearbox broke as it exited Mulsanne corner.

McNish covered the remaining 85 minutes without mishap and celebrated Porsche's 16th victory here in a formation finish with Alzen. Three laps behind, Nissan retrieved third place with its consistent, Japanese-driven car after a lacklustre weekend.

After the failure of the Courages, the P1 division fell to Doyle-Risi Racing's US-entered Ferrari. LM-GT2 resulted in a 1-2 for ORECA's works Chrysler Vipers.

THIRD TIME LUCKY

Porsche Motorsport's 911 GT1 racecars finally came good. The car driven by Laurent Aïello, Stéphane Ortelli (holding the camera in the photo below right) and Allan McNish finished precisely a lap ahead of its stablemate, crewed by Bob Wollek/Jörg Müller/Uwe Alzen. It was Porsche's 16th victory in the great race – a 50th birthday present for the company – and the 16th and last overseen by its accomplished motorsport engineering director, Norbert Singer. In view of the arrivals of the Mercedes CLK and Toyota GT-One, Singer and his staff in Weissach replaced the pressed-steel monocoque of the 911 GT1 over the winter with a hull made entirely in carbonfibre and honeycomb material, like the rival designs. The relatively narrow monocoques were made with integral roofs by Lola Composites and the basic structure was similar to that of the Lola T92/10 Group C chassis designed by Wiet Huidekoper, the Dutch engineer who had also played key roles in the GT1 projects since 1995. A main underbody panel extended from the front axle centreline to the trailing edge of the diffuser and the only other separate body panels were a small underbody under the nose, the crash box, the sidepods, the tail, the nose and two doors.

1998

The GT1-98 bore its fuel cell between the seat-back and the rear bulkhead, whereas the 1996-97 cars had retained the standard location in the nose. The cooling and F1-style suspension systems were totally revised, the latter partly to increase adaptability on a car being used in the FIA GT series. Under the ACO's rules, GT1 cars could run without the FIA-regulation underbody 'plank'.

A weight reduction of 25kg in the drivetrain was achieved by using new materials. The mass of the 600bhp flat-six was born by steel frames linking the rear tub bulkhead to a substantial bellhousing forming the oil reservoir (the first such arrangement on any Porsche racecar), to which the outboard, longitudinal gearbox was attached. In qualifying, each car used a six-speed, sequential-shift gearbox that had been introduced late in 1997. However, this had been unreliable in early-season FIA GT events, and was replaced during Friday by the proven synchromesh gearbox.

McNish's GT1-98 was the fastest in the class in May, but Prequalifying delivered a big blow to Porsche's effort: two 1998-specification cars had been allocated to the Zakspeed team, and equipped with Pirelli tyres that turned out to be inadequate. Armin Hahne (below right) was bumped out of race week in the final minutes by the Nova team's semi-works Nissan R390. In qualifying proper, Porsche was beaten to the class pole for the first time in three years: Müller and McNish qualified fourth and fifth, 0.32sec apart.

In the race, the Porsches were outgunned in the early going by two Toyotas. When one of them was delayed in the early evening, the GT1-98s annexed second and third places, but Porsche had to wait until nightfall before the other Toyota slipped up, and it finally secured a 1-2. The team held it throughout the night, during which fine wet-weather driving by McNish took his car clear of its stablemate. But both cars ran into trouble soon after dawn.

First, the second-placed GT1-98 (above right) needed a new front undertray after Müller, caught out by a sudden squall, went off the track at the first Mulsanne chicane. Ten minutes later, McNish pitted with an overheating engine after a hose failure, and the Porsches were in pit-lane together. Each delay cost around 30 minutes, in which time the best Toyota went three laps ahead.

It was not until the 23rd hour, and a transmission failure on the leading GT-One, that the Porsches took a decisive lead. The team was triumphant afterwards, but one of its drivers broke down in tears in the media centre. At 54, the brilliant Bob Wollek realized that this 28th attempt might have been his final opportunity to win the great race.

In 1997-98, Porsche produced 21 variants of the 911 GT1, among which the road cars were offered at a price of DM 1.55 million.

PORSCHE'S GT COMES GOOD 303

ROBBED AGAIN!

The performance by Toyota Team Europe in its first-ever motor race was mightily impressive. A gearbox failure, only 85 minutes out from the finish, prevented an astounding victory with one of its German-built GT-One racecars (pictured below during service), driven by Geoff Lees, Thierry Boutsen and Ralf Kelleners. For Toyota, it was 1994 all over again…

The all-new GT-One (*aka* TS020) was blatantly an out-and-out sports-prototype coupé, designed purely for Le Mans, and homologated by the production of just two roadworthy versions. Its story really started late in 1995. That was when Toyota Motorsport GmbH, the rallying organization in Köln that had won the 1993-94 World Championships, suffered a traumatic reverse. To the huge embarrassment of the Japanese parent company, TMG was caught cheating by the FIA. An unauthorized engineer had devised an illegal turbocharger air intake system (bypassing the mandatory restrictor). Toyota was summarily disqualified from the championship.

Toyota switched its European motorsport budget exclusively to track racing. In mid-1996, it decided to base its operations in its expansive but now under-used facilities in Germany. TOMS GB was wound down, and its LMP project was cancelled. In its place, TMG embarked on this GT1 programme, run by its former rally team under Ove Andersson.

The TS010 FIA Sportscar of 1992-93 had been beaten at Le Mans by the Peugeot 905, designed by André de Cortanze, who was now recruited by TMG as its technical director. Joining in January 1997, Cortanze led the design team for the TS010's spectacular successor. The project design, build and race teams were formed, and the cars designed, built and thoroughly tested, in little more than 12 months.

Cortanze recruited Jean-Claude Martens (formerly with Team Lotus in F1) as the chief designer with responsibility for the composite structures, and Joanna Moss (formerly with Lola Cars) as the chief aerodynamicist. TMG's powertrain chief, former Zakspeed F1 engine designer Norbert Kreyer, was already in place, having been hired for the rally programme, as was Jörg Zander, who designed the transmission casing and the suspension systems.

The GT-One took GT1 engineering to an entirely new level. Its narrow, advanced-composites monocoque, with an integrally moulded roof,

304 | LE MANS 24 HOURS 1990-99

was made in Germany by Dornier Aerospace. It tapered towards the front, where it was slightly raised, so that the driver sat at an angle with his feet elevated.

The complex shape of the tub was an integral part of the aero package, which was finalized by Moss in the Dallara wind tunnel in Italy. Her radical solutions directed airflow under the narrow nose across a broad splitter, and then above and below the leading edge of the mandatory flat bottom. The panels between the nose and the wheel-arches had a wing form, while the straked underside of the nose curved upwards either side of the centre section, and airflow over its upper surface was diverted laterally by the sides of the tub, exiting through big vents behind the front wheels. The side-mounted radiators and the turbo intercoolers were cooled through ducts in the doors. TMG dispensed entirely with Toyota styling cues.

A new, all-aluminium, 32-valve V8 was produced by Kreyer's TMG engine group for use as a fully stressed chassis member. With two Garrett turbos, and purpose-designed Bosch electronic ignition and fuel-injection systems, Kreyer's engine weighed almost 40kg less than Toyota's Group C motor. Its output with the ACO's specified air restrictors and 'boost' limit was 600bhp at 6500rpm. The longitudinally mounted TMG/Xtrac six-speed, sequential-shift gearbox was augmented by a traction-control system.

F1-style pushrod suspension systems were used front and rear and the carbon-carbon braking systems were ABS-assisted. Somehow TTE was able to convince the ACO officials that the car's fuel tank – empty at scrutineering – was allowable as the mandatory luggage space: well, it could, theoretically, hold a suitcase.

After substantial long-distance testing, including a 16-hour run at Spa,

the team made a pole-position bid only with Martin Brundle, on the first evening. He went fastest but was beaten by a Mercedes 24 hours later. Ominously, one car suffered a differential failure on the first evening while the others had gear-selection problems, which were put down to debris in the mechanism. The Toyotas lined up second, seventh and eighth on the grid.

Brundle (top left), racing with the traction control and ABS disengaged, established a solid lead before the end of the first lap. Co-driven by Emmanuel Collard and then Eric Hélary, this GT-One was in front until

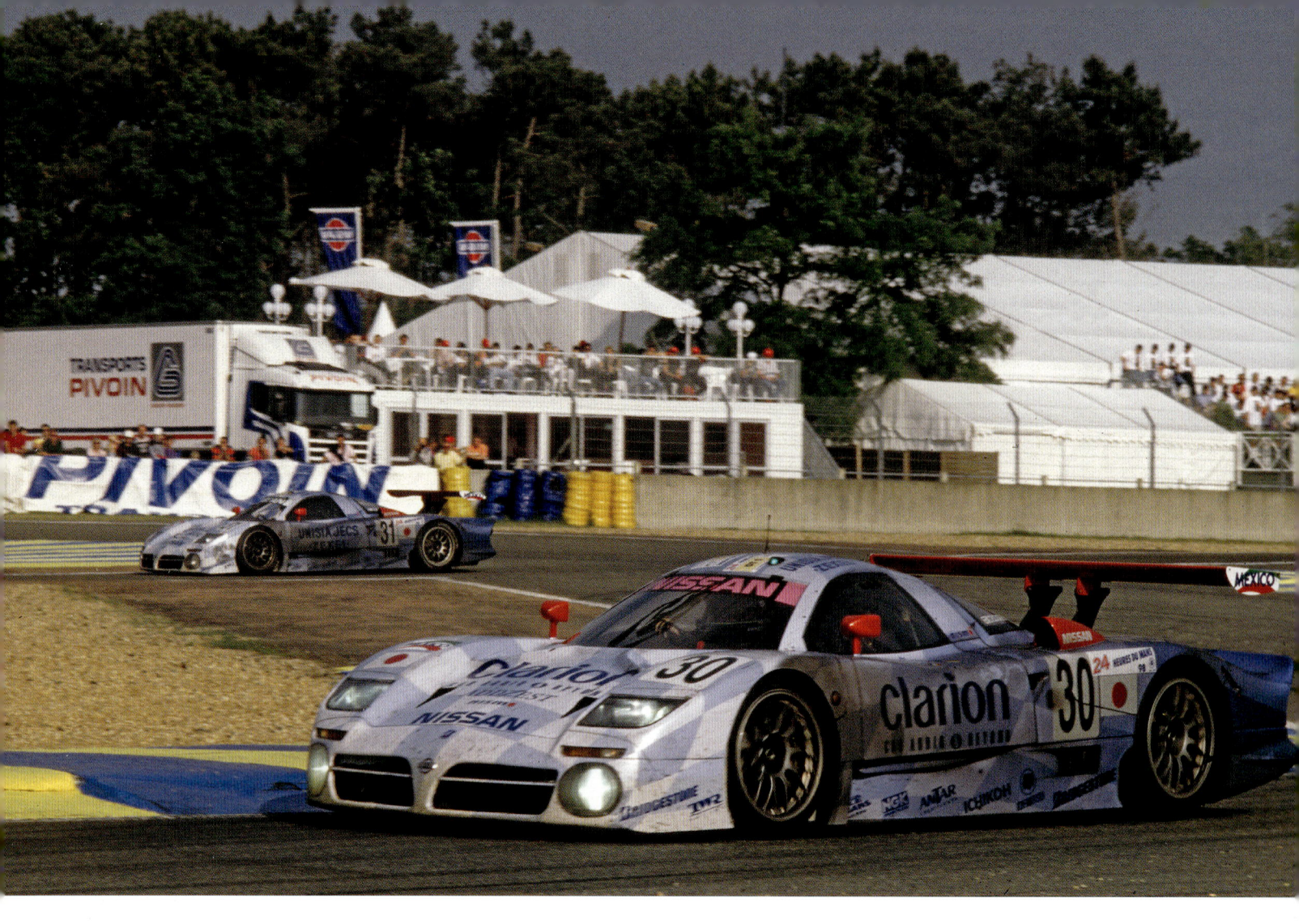

5:25pm, when Hélary ran into the Virage Ford gravel trap. The car lost eight laps having its braking system checked and repaired. It took nine hours, until half-time, to recover a position in the top 10. Three hours later, Brundle crashed out of the race in a squall of rain, also at the Ford chicane.

When Hélary had his braking problem, the sister car of Lees/Boutsen/Kelleners stepped up to the lead, and it held it for the next five hours. At 10:40pm, Lees could cope no longer with a worsening gearshift problem. TTE's crew replaced the gear cluster in less than 16 minutes, but the car slipped to seventh. Eight hours later, at 6am, a terrific recovery performance by all three drivers was rewarded when both the race-leading Porsches hit trouble. The GT-One's advantage was soon extended to three laps. But a second gear-cluster change allowed one of the Porsches to get back on the lead lap and slightly ahead.

At this point, the GT-One still held a distinct advantage: the refuelling sequence meant that it would be in front if and when it reached the finish. Cruelly, just 85 minutes from the end, Kelleners suffered a terminal gearbox failure that prevented him returning to the pits.

The first of the GT-Ones to encounter transmission problems was the 'Japanese' car of Ukyo Katayama/Toshio Suzuki/Keiichi Tsuchiya, when downshifting became difficult during the third hour. A series of pitstops, including one for a gearshift cable replacement (which took 30 minutes) and a 20-minute pause for a fresh gear cluster, left the car 22 laps behind the leader, and dropped it to the tail of the field. The drivers raced on but could finish no higher than ninth.

NISSAN ON THE PODIUM

Nissan and TWR achieved major improvements this year and brought three cars into the top six at the finish. The updated R390 GT1 of Aguri Suzuki, Kazuyoshi Hoshino and Masahiko Kageyama had no significant mechanical setbacks all weekend and finished third – the first Le Mans podium by an all-Japanese driving crew.

NISMO's 1998 programme with TWR again took the R390s only to Le Mans, so this time chief designer Tony Southgate had plenty of time to resolve the issues that had ruined the team's hopes in 1997. Astec built three new monocoques to take a range of upgrades.

The tail section of the bodywork was re-engineered to create the 'luggage space' and the 1998 car had a square, 'flip-up' tail, extended rearward but with the rear wing relocated forward. The underside of the nose was reprofiled and the brake and gearbox cooling systems improved. The bodywork changes were proven in the full-size tunnel at the Nissan Technical Centre in Atsugi, Japan. NISMO also developed the twin-turbo V8 to find more power and better cooling, while Xtrac worked with TWR in redesigning the transverse gearbox.

Southgate also took the time to develop the ideal suspension geometry and fitted the car not only with ABS but also with traction control – technology that had been banned in F1 at the end of the 1997 season. Sourced by TWR from Williams Grand Prix Engineering, the traction-control system was redeveloped for the GT1 application at a cost of £250,000 per car.

1998

The team undertook three 24-hour tests and, at Prequalifying, Erik Comas, Franck Lagorce and Aguri Suzuki all went more than four seconds faster than Martin Brundle had achieved 12 months before. After the grief of June 1997, and all his work over the winter, Southgate's first sighting of the new Toyota sent him apoplectic, because Toyota had persuaded the ACO technical inspectors that the fuel cell could be interpreted as the luggage compartment.

John Nielsen qualified the Nissan he shared with Lagorce and Michael Krumm (left) in 10th place, but the car advanced steadily on Saturday and reached a promising third position just after midnight. Four hours later, a fuel pump electrical failure cost 12 minutes in the pits, and later two pitstops to secure a loose undertray cost another five laps, leaving it in fifth place at the finish.

At dusk, Comas, Jan Lammers and Andrea Montermini (below) lost four laps replacing the left-front suspension upright. Soon after 1am, four more laps disappeared when all four brake discs had to be replaced, but the drivers recovered fifth position on Sunday afternoon. In the final hour, Montermini lost it to a charging Lagorce.

A fourth R390 in this race was the first chassis made (the Patrese car from 1997), now equipped by NISMO with the latest bodywork and powertrain. It was operated by Nova Engineering, Moto Moriwaki's Shizuka-based team that had won six national Group C titles in the 1980s with Porsches. In 1990, Moriwaki had switched camps to Nissan by buying RC89 and RC90 chassis to defend his 1989 All-Japan title, and had subsequently become involved in the Skyline GT-R programme. Surprisingly, this was this accomplished team's début Le Mans. Masami Kageyama and rookies Satoshi Motoyama and Takuya Kurosawa were strong on Saturday and arrived in the top 10 before dark, but at 1:30am Kageyama spun into the wall and damaged the underbody and the left-side turbocharger and intercooler. Repairs consumed 84 minutes and Kurosawa returned to the race in 25th position. A very determined comeback converted this to 10th at the finish.

After Le Mans, TWR began work on an all-new LMP car aimed at extending the deal with Nissan into 1999 and beyond. But Nissan instead turned to G Force for its R391 racecar. TWR was unable to place Tony Southgate's design elsewhere, and the project group was disbanded.

PORSCHE'S GT COMES GOOD 307

LE MANS

P1 FOR FERRARI

In view of the disappointing performance of the Ferrari 333 SP spyders in the 1997 race, it came as a surprise when four such cars were entered this time – but the Doyle-Risi entry (below) emerged with victory in the LM-P1 division, driven by Eric van der Poele, Wayne Taylor and Fermin Velez.

Three of these Ferraris were new cars. The Doyle-Risi and Momo teams had ordered theirs for the USRRC Can-Am and PSCR World Sports Car championships that had replaced the IMSA series in the United States the previous season, while JB Racing was contesting the FIA-sanctioned ISRS series. All were equipped with Michelotto's latest updates.

Aero revisions included a longer nose and more enclosed sidepods than the originals, while running gear updates included larger-diameter wheels with carbon brake systems. The sweet-sounding V12 was fitted with smaller valves, revised combustion chambers, and a modified lubrication system. With the specified P1 air-inlet restrictor, it was rated at 600bhp at 10,500rpm. A new six-speed option was available for the transverse, sequential-shift gearbox.

The Doyle-Risi team had been formed in 1997 as a partnership between Dan Doyle and Giuseppe Risi, the former co-owner of the GRID Group C project of 1982-83 and now a Houston Ferrari dealer. In place of Doyle's successful R&S chassis, they had bought two Ferraris, retaining Poele and Taylor to drive. This one did the Daytona test in January and was then shipped to Europe, where Doyle-Risi joined the Moretti team in setting *tifosi* hearts a-flutter in the non-championship Monza 1000 in March. The following month, the other car established the team's winning credentials at Las Vegas.

Early in its second-ever race, Poele's car lost a road wheel. He crept back to the pits for a replacement, but the cost was five laps. The Ferrari then ran very reliably and, after 18 hours, it became the leading prototype on the demise of the last-surviving Courage C51, and went on to finish eighth overall. At the end of the season, Doyle-Risi's other Ferrari won the inaugural Petit Le Mans race at Road Atlanta.

Giampiero Moretti's car arrived at Le Mans with a chance of a fantastic hat-trick, having won the USRRC's Daytona 24 Hours and the PSCR's Sebring 12 Hours with Moretti, Mauro Baldi and Didier Theys. It finished this race in 14th place, third in class. It lost 10 minutes soon after midnight after Theys had damaged the front splitter, and almost 20 minutes in the small hours after Baldi, caught out on slicks by a rain shower, had spun and savaged the rear wing. After daybreak, the decisive problem came in the form of a broken gearbox, which the crew replaced in 90 minutes.

Jean-Pierre Jabouille and Jean-Michel Bouresche had replaced their Porsche GT1 with another 1998-built 333 SP. It débuted at Paul Ricard in April, and then won at Brno in May in the hands of Vincenzo Sospiri and Emmanuel Collard, who landed a works Toyota drive in this race and was replaced by Jean-Christophe Boullion and Jérôme Policand. Boullion emerged as the fastest Ferrari driver here before JB Racing's qualifying engine split an oil line. The crew rebuilt the entire rear end in less than three hours to get Sospiri qualified.

Come Saturday afternoon, Boullion produced a terrific opening shift that was then almost matched by Sospiri. The JB Ferrari (above) went from 17th on the grid to seventh at the three-hour mark, but 50 minutes later Policand lost four laps for replacement of a wheelbearing. It took nine hours for the drivers to recover seventh place. And it was all for nothing: the car was retired soon after half-time with a gearbox bearing failure. Sospiri, reunited with Collard, went on to win the next five rounds of the ISRS, and the championship.

The fourth 333 SP was Pilot Racing's four-year-old chassis (below), sponsored here by the Le Mans municipality. Team principals Stéphane Ratel and Michel Ferté did not go for Michelotto's update kit, and retained the original engine specification and five-speed transmission, as well as ferrous brakes. Ferté, Pascal Fabre and François Migault had a reliable race until the gearbox broke after 15 hours.

VIPERS STRIKE

The ORECA team made up for the crashes that had stopped its front-running GT2 Vipers the previous June by delivering a dominant 1-2 in the division for Chrysler, led by the car raced by Justin Bell, David Donohue and Luca Drudi (below).

Over the winter, the Viper Engineering and ORECA development teams concentrated on aerodynamics, durability and vehicle weight. Neil Hannemann's Detroit-based project team used Reynard's UK wind tunnel and Lockheed's full-scale tunnel in Marietta, Georgia, and tested the results on Chrysler's proving ground at Chelsea, Michigan, and at Phoenix, Arizona. The most visible change was a revised nose and diffuser, both aiding the underbody aerodynamics and improving airflow to the engine.

Meanwhile, Caldwell Development reduced the engine's oil consumption and improved fuel efficiency, redesigned the fragile exhaust system and the fuelling system, and rectified a problem with cracking inlet ports. These new specifications were all passed on to the Viper production line. A major redesign of the electrical wiring system saved no less than 40kg of weight on its own. ABS was fitted to Hugues de Chaunac's quasi-works ORECA cars, all three of which were new this FIA GT season. They were opposed by two cars operated by Chamberlain Engineering, which did not have ABS or carbon brakes.

In qualifying, ORECA's Vipers were five seconds faster round the lap than the 1997 cars, and Olivier Beretta became the first GT2 driver to lap in less than four minutes as they annexed three of the top four places. However, the team lost the car started by Karl Wendlinger and Marc Duez (above) early on Saturday evening when Patrick Huisman, running second in the class, was stranded in the pit deceleration roadway by an electrical failure that had short-circuited the battery. The crew was not allowed down the road to push it to its pit.

Soon Pedro Lamy was driving the class-leading Viper into the pits with a cracked exhaust manifold, which took 18 minutes to fix. This car soon returned after the gear selector mechanism had broken during a downshift; replacing the gearbox consumed another 22 minutes.

LE MANS 24 HOURS 1990–99

1998

Beretta/Lamy/Tommy Archer recovered manfully from ninth in the class to finish second, five laps behind the third ORECA car, which led GT2 for the duration with an exceptionally reliable run.

Both the Chamberlain entries also went the distance. Gary Ayles, Matt Turner and John Hugenholtz, driving Chamberlain's ex-ORECA 1996 Viper (right), finished sixth in class after losing over an hour to a broken exhaust, while the newer car came in eighth having spent three hours in the pits for a new gearbox and clutch.

Later Viper Team ORECA successfully defended its 1997 FIA GT2 championship, winning a shared Drivers title for Wendlinger and Beretta.

A BRIEF DÉBUT

BMW had tasted Le Mans victory with McLaren in 1995, and had liked it. The company fielded a pair of new, 'atmo' V12-engined Le Mans Prototypes, swiftly developed in collaboration with Williams Grand Prix Engineering as a prelude to a six-season F1 partnership, due to begin in 2000. They were raced here by Team Rafanelli only a year after the manufacturer had opened discussions with Williams. One of them was the fastest LMP in qualifying but, in the race, a critical design error caused the rear wheelbearings to lose lubrication. Both the V12LM racecars were back in their transporter before it was even dark.

This LMP project followed an intervention by BMW's marketing director, Karl-Heinz Kalbfell, who had been dismayed by the arrival of out-and-out racing cars masquerading as modified road cars. These had dead-ended BMW's 'works' programme with McLaren in 1997 and, like any sensible person, Kalbfell saw only confusion and expense in the flawed GT1 concept. Moreover, BMW North America was pressing for a new car with which to contest IMSA's WSC category.

To this end, Rafanelli – one of the manufacturer's successful quasi-works touring car teams (formerly known as Bigazzi) – was tasked with running a Riley & Scott Mk3 in the 1998 ISRS, using works 4-litre V8

PORSCHE'S GT COMES GOOD | 311

LE MANS

engines prepared by Heini Mader. IMSA rules excluded the 6-litre BMW Typ-70 V12 that had been produced for the McLaren F1, a new evolution of which powered the new LMP.

The V12LM was designed by John Russell with Williams and BMW colleagues in dedicated premises at Williams's HQ in Grove, Oxfordshire, starting as late as August 1997. The carbonfibre/honeycomb hull, made by G Force Composites, had a broad forward structure to comply with an LMP regulation specifying a minimum width of 300mm either side of the longitudinal centreline (to provide enough space for both the driver and a nominal passenger). The engine was mounted in steel A-frames and recessed into the rear bulkhead to place its mass forward in the chassis. This also created space for the Xtrac six-speed, sequential-shift, inboard transverse gearbox forward of the rear axle.

For its new application, the 60deg V12 was required to breathe through much smaller air restrictors than had been the case with the McLaren GT1 car. Many revisions were made in Munich to address this, and to reduce the length and the weight of the engine. The latest motor had new camshafts, fuel injectors and exhaust systems, longer inlet trumpets, and a shallower sump that allowed the engine to be lowered and fitted with a smaller flywheel and clutch. One of the last racing projects undertaken by famed BMW Motorsport engineer Paul Rosche, ahead of his retirement later that year, the LMP engine was 22kg lighter than the GT version of 1997. Managed by a TAGtronic 3.12 EMS, it was rated at 550bhp at 6500rpm.

The overall shape of the V12LM was devised by BMW stylist Jan Hettler, before Jason Somerville in Grove was charged with making it work as a racecar. The body was evolved for low drag in Williams's wind tunnel. To keep the frontal area small, a conventional overhead engine airbox was rejected in favour of ram tubes either side of the cockpit, clearing the airflow ahead of a low-mounted rear wing. The radiator cooling air inlet was on the underside between the front wheels – a solution later found to cause problems when the temperature of the track surface was high.

Gabriele Rafanelli's team sent mechanics to Grove to help in assembling the cars but débuted them at Prequalifying with very little test mileage behind them. In race week, Pierluigi Martini and Tom Kristensen lined up sixth and 12th on the grid. And in the first hour Martini charged impressively into third place – only to collide with Olivier Thévenin's Courage soon after taking on fuel. Repairs to the front bodywork took 10 minutes. Martini was climbing back through the field when, at a routine stop during the fourth hour, a wheelbearing was found to have lost its grease.

By this time, the pace and fuel efficiency of Kristensen's sister car (below), co-driven by Hans Stuck and Steve Soper, had come into play, and it was comfortably holding third place. But Soper was called in for his wheelbearings to be checked, and a similar fault was found. A design error in the suspension uprights had resulted in misfitting seals. Both cars were withdrawn on safety grounds.

In October, Rafanelli's V8-powered R&S won the last-ever IMSA series race at Laguna Seca.

A TWO-HOUR COMEBACK

Mercedes-Benz Motorsport returned to Le Mans after a seven-year absence to race two new GT1 racecars, based on the chassis that had taken on the McLaren F1s in 1997, and won six of 11 events in the inaugural FIA GT championship. One started on pole position and led briefly, but the manufacturer's comeback was all over only two hours after the start.

Mercedes contracted out production of these cars to AMG (Hans Werner Aufrecht's organization in Affalterbach, Germany), which had been responsible for the manufacturer's advanced-specification DTM/ITC touring cars until the series imploded late in 1996. Curiously, this was only a second Le Mans attempt by AMG: on its previous visit, back in 1978, the team had failed to qualify a Mercedes 450SLC.

AMG's new evolution of the CLK-GTR was designed very much with Le Mans in mind, and designated 'CLK-LM'. It was substantially new, although outwardly similar to the 1997 racecar, which had been designed after the Mercedes engineers had dissected a McLaren F1 purchased from Fabien Giroix.

The major change in the specification was a switch from the 6-litre V12 of the GTR to a 6-litre V8, derived from the M.119 which, in turbocharged form, had won the 1989 Le Mans in a Group C Sauber. Using the V8, lighter and shorter than the V12, achieved both better weight distribution and a reduction in centre-of-gravity height. With the ACO's specified air restrictors for the 950kg vehicle weight, and controlled by a Bosch Motronic control system, it made 600bhp

LE MANS

at 7000rpm. It drove the LM via the GTR's transverse, six-speed sequential gearbox, produced by Mercedes in conjunction with Xtrac and newly equipped with electro-hydraulic gear selection actuated by steering wheel paddles.

The engine was mounted semi-stressed to the advanced composites tub within a frame support, which cleverly demounted as a single unit with the engine, gearbox and differential housing. The hull was again made in England by DPS Composites and was similar to that of the GTR, but the bodywork was heavily revised. The radiators were relocated from the nose of the GTR to the sidepods of the LM, and fed cooling air by intakes either side of the windscreen and ducts formed in the doors. In addition to moving weight within the wheelbase, this allowed the bonnet line to be lowered between the wheel-arches. The LM was built on the same homologated wheelbase as the GTR but was slightly wider, higher and longer, the tail being extended partly to create the mandatory GT1 'luggage space'. The air inlet below the long nose overhang was now used to supply air to the front brakes, while a roof-mounted scoop fed air to the engine and, as on the GTR, the rear brakes were cooled via NACA ducts in the engine cover.

AMG's chassis design team, led by Gerhard Ungar, added a nostalgic touch by giving the LM gullwing doors, reminiscent of the 1952-winning 300SL. Mercedes strongly believed that its racecars should have brand styling cues and this one, therefore, was given a grille and the three-pointed star emblem.

The GTR's double-wishbone and pullrod-actuated suspension systems were replaced by pushrod layouts, while carbon brakes with ABS completed the package. Prior to Le Mans, the AMG team completed more than 6200 miles of testing, including a 24-hour run at Homestead, sunny Florida. The team came to France after winning the first two rounds of the 1998 FIA GT series with the GTR.

As the reigning FIA GT champion, AMG received one automatic entry, but its second car was required to prequalify in early May, when it went third fastest in GT1. In race week, defending FIA GT champion Bernd Schneider clinched pole position, with Christophe Bouchut third.

Schneider won the sprint away from the start but was soon passed by the best Toyota. At one hour, Schneider was still in second place, Jean-Marc Gounon eighth. But then Schneider suffered an electrical malfunction, leading to power-steering pump failure; the servo drive for the steering pump was common to the oil pump, and an engine failure swiftly followed. Bouchut had the sister car in fifth place before being stopped for the same reason.

AMG returned to the FIA GT championship, and won all remaining eight races, using the LM version in place of the GTR from August onwards. The joint champions were Klaus Ludwig and Ricardo Zonta, who had never even had the chance of racing at Le Mans.

STEADY AS SHE GOES

The McLaren F1 GTR could no longer be a contender, but Michael Cane decided to take up two automatic entries for this year's race, gained through the 1997 class win and another (by John Nielsen/Thomas Bscher) in the Le Mans 4 Hours three months later. The GTC team's two cars, each driven by its amateur owner and two professionals, went through scrutineering in the same 'longtail' specification as they had the previous June, but this time they were 15 seconds off the pace in qualifying. Durability, fuel efficiency and good pit work would have to be GTC's watchwords and they paid dividends. Dawn found the two McLarens in sixth and seventh positions overall, although only one car made the finish.

Bscher went with Emmanuel Pirro and Rinaldo Capello in the GTR that had been damaged by fire in 1997 qualifying here and that he was still campaigning in the FIA GT series. Their run in the black car (right) came to a sudden end when Pirro crashed, soon after 7am.

Former EMKA Group C team owner/driver Steve O'Rourke recruited Tim Sugden and Bill Auberlen to share his latest acquisition, the ex-works/Schnitzer GTR that had been the fastest McLaren in JJ Lehto's hands 12 months before. Pictured above, the car arrived after a win and two second places in the British GT championship (in which O'Rourke/Sugden had won the 1997 GT2 title with a Porsche). Its owner was caught out by a wet track at the Nissan chicane, and spun into the gravel. But it went on to repeat GTC's 1997 feat by spending less time at rest in pit-lane than any other car. The reward was a wildly unexpected fourth place.

It was not such a bad way to end McLaren's involvement with Le Mans, and O'Rourke hosted a huge post-race party to celebrate. And the final hurrah was another British GT title at season's end.

PORSCHE'S GT COMES GOOD 315

LE MANS

ROUND THE CLOCK AT LAST

The longest a Panoz GTR-1 had ever raced was 18 hours, at Daytona earlier in the year, but this works-entered car (below) did the whole 24, David Brabham, Andy Wallace and Jamie Davis finishing seventh.

Reynard's chassis-development programme over the winter included longer bodywork overhangs at both front and rear, separating the aerodynamics from the effect of the wheels and providing more adjustment. Reynard also increased the front and rear track dimensions, redesigned the suspension geometry, and improved chassis stiffness by replacing the steel engine-support frame with carbon plates.

The first Panoz programme in 1997 had been hampered by problems with the oil pressure, cooling, wiring harness and control systems of the Roush-prepared, 6-litre Ford pushrod V8. Even so, Panoz retained both the engine and its supplier this season, while handing responsibility for the engine-management systems to Zytek in England. Roush came up with an improved inlet manifold design and took off some weight by making more use of carbon composite materials for the inlet trumpets and other parts. The big V8 now made 630bhp at 6250rpm.

The Panoz team arrived in France fresh from a 1-2 at Lime Rock in May, and the improved on-track performance was immediately apparent. Georgia-based Panoz Motorsports, now led by former TWR executive Tony Dowe, entered a 1998 car in association with David Price Racing in England, and Brabham used it to find an improvement of almost eight seconds in qualifying relative to the best Panoz lap 12 months before. Brabham started 11th and the drivers improved on that position in the twilight. Just after midnight, when it was running ninth, the car lost 35 minutes while DPR's mechanics traced and resolved a short circuit in the wiring loom by replacing the entire dashboard. But otherwise the car was very solid and went some way to dispel doubts that a pushrod V8 could achieve a competitive finish at Le Mans.

1998

The DAMS team's updated 1997 car (top left), raced by Eric Bernard/Johnny O'Connell/Christophe Tinseau, lost 23 minutes to an early starter motor failure. Later, at 6:50pm, O'Connell was stranded out on the circuit with no gears. He got out, removed the tail section, engaged a gear by kicking the gearbox, and returned to the pits, where the car spent another 43 minutes. The problems persisted and, just after 10pm, the gearbox had to be replaced, at the cost of a further 27 minutes. Finally, just before dawn, 15 minutes went in replacing the front underbody after Bernard slipped off the track during a shower. The car was running 19th just before 11am, when another gearbox failure parked it.

'SPARKY' SPIKED

Panoz Cars became the first constructor to exploit kinetic energy recovery in a high-level racing car when it commissioned Bill Gibson's Zytek company in Repton, England, to incorporate a 'hybrid' system in an Esperante GTR-1 for this year's Le Mans. Unfortunately, the Panoz Q9 did not prequalify due to the failure of the main shaft in the electric motor, leaving driver James Weaver with all the extra weight of the KERS but no electric power to compensate.

The Q9 (below) was produced by a project team led for Reynard by Andy Thorby, and operated by David Price's team. Its KERS used regenerative energy from braking to drive Zytek's purpose-designed, liquid-cooled, permanent-magnet motor-generator, mounted on top of the gearbox, and intended to supply about 120kW (equivalent to 160bhp). However, the technology of the batteries, assembled by Zytek from Varta-manufactured cells and located next to the driver in the air-cooled cabin, was not yet mature enough to reach this potential performance.

Ahead of Prequalifying, track time for the Q9 (nicknamed 'Sparky' by the DPR team) was limited to a shakedown on the MIRA test track and runs on the Le Mans airfield runway, when the KERS had worked just fine. When it mattered, however, the weight penalty of the defunct electric motor, the batteries and the power electronics without hybrid assistance was so big that Weaver had no hope of prequalifying. Typically, he put his abundant talent on the line and gave it his very best shot. Weaver missed the cut by 8.4 seconds but went quicker than a P1 Kremer K8 that made the race, and all the GT2 cars.

It was a pity that the rules offered the ACO no flexibility to give the Q9 a 'wild card' entry, because this innovative car might have advanced the introduction of gasoline-electric Le Mans hybrids by years. Don Panoz has never received enough credit for his vision. He wanted 'Sparky' to whistle at speed, so DPR fitted a reed in a door exit duct.

That October, in Panoz's inaugural Petit Le Mans race at Road Atlanta, Zytek made the electric motor shaft in a stronger material, and 'Sparky' finished third in GT1 (while living up to its nickname by showering an alarmed Weaver with sparks from the battery packs). Panoz spiked the project but Zytek, of course, continued to develop its hybrid system for Le Mans and other applications.

PORSCHE'S GT COMES GOOD 317

LE MANS

NISSAN GETS COURAGE

Courage Compétition arrived with the highest expectations for its two new C51 prototypes, which were equipped by Nissan with works engines. One of them was good enough to lead the P1 division, but neither finished.

The C51 was the first product of an ambitious new Le Mans partnership with the manufacturer, the seeds of which had been sewn when Courage ran a March-Nissan here back in 1989. At its core was an engine supply for Courage in return for chassis expertise in the development of the 1999 Nissan R391. This was a serious effort by Nissan, like Porsche, to give itself a second string to its bow, and to cover the possibility that circumstances (if not the ACO's technical regulations) might favour prototypes over GT1 cars like its own R390.

The VRH-30L engine supplied to Courage was based on the company's Group C power unit, and was developed by NISMO's competition engine division in Omori, a southern suburb of Tokyo. The 32-valve, 3-litre V8 was equipped with two IHI turbochargers and with fuelling and ignition equipment by JECS (now known as Nissan Electronics). Making 540bhp at 6500rpm at only 1.0 bar of 'boost' pressure, the V8 drove through Hewland's new, longitudinally mounted, six-speed, sequential-shift LSG gearbox.

C41 designer Paolo Catone led the engineering team on the C51 project, the build of which began immediately after Le Mans 1997. The new car was based closely on the carbon/honeycomb C41 but the team undertook

LE MANS 24 HOURS 1990-99

many modifications, including bodywork revisions that involved a return to the St Cyr wind tunnel in Paris. New pick-up points were incorporated to revise the pushrod front suspension geometry, and the rear end was entirely reworked to take the Nissan V8. NISMO sent two engineers to all Courage's test sessions and to race week, and Chris Goodwin of Nissan Motorsport Europe was posted to Courage's factory for a period of four months prior to the race. The powertrain installation was undertaken under the direction of Nick Wasyliw, the former Roni F3000 team principal who, with the Intermotion company, had supplied the original gearbox for the C41 project.

Courage became the French constructor with the most Le Mans participations this year, and used his 17-race experience to order Fredrik Ekblom and Didier Cottaz to qualify the C51s with circumspection. Although briefly delayed in a gravel trap, Cottaz's car (facing page, top) had a mechanically reliable and pacy run, and soon moved up the board into a solid top-six position. At half-time, it was leading the prototype division in third overall, and was more than two laps ahead of Nissan's GT1 entries. Given what was to happen among the leading Porsche and Toyota GT1 cars, it could even have popped out into the lead of the race. However, Marc Goossens was delayed for 10 minutes at 4:40am by a throttle cable fault, and the car's promising run was halted four hours later when a gearbox bearing collapsed, the result of an oil delivery problem.

Ekblom's C51 (facing page, bottom) suffered a variety of delays, notably Takeshi Tsuchiya's collision at 3:50pm with a GT2 Porsche, which cost 14 minutes for a new nosebox. In the evening, Patrice Gay pitted for 12 minutes for a fresh left-rear hub carrier. Then, at 10:15pm, there was a brief fire during a refuelling stop. Shortly afterwards, the engine overheated and the head gasket blew on the left-hand cylinder bank. It turned out that a nylon water radiator bleed tube had partially melted in the fire, and had slowly leaked the coolant.

COURAGE'S SURVIVORS

Both Yves Courage's Porsche-powered prototypes were delayed in the race, but they survived to finish in line astern, fourth and fifth in class.

The team had addressed the engine-cooling problems that had spoiled the 3-litre C41's 1997 race by relocating the radiators and modifying the ducting. The installation was subcontracted to Promotion Racing Team under Daniel Vergnes, the new tenant in the former Rondeau workshop in Champagné.

Redesignated as the C50, the modified car (below) was sold before the race to Yukiatsu Akizawa's AM-PM publishing company in Japan. It was badly delayed at the one-hour mark after Olivier Thévenin had collided with Pierluigi Martini's BMW LM. The car lost 51 minutes while

LE MANS

internal damage to the left-hand sidepod was made good, involving a new radiator and hoses. Thévenin, Franck Fréon and Japanese veteran Yojiro Terada recovered into 14th position but lost 38 minutes soon after midday when the brake hydraulics had to be bled and replenished. The C50 was caught by the Momo Ferrari, and Terada lost the place to Dider Theys with minutes remaining.

Meanwhile, the La Filière Elf motorsport academy operated its C36 here for a third successive June. Henri Pescarolo (above) had very quick partners this time in Olivier Grouillard and French F3 championship leader Franck Montagny, making his Le Mans début. They hauled the car into the top dozen before dark, but 'Pesca' slipped back with gearbox problems. Soon after midnight, the team had to devote 97 minutes to repairs, but soldiered on to finish 16th.

THIRD TIME UNLUCKY

Although Herbert Ampferer's programme was focused on victory with the latest GT1-98 racecar, the twice-bitten Porsche Motorsport director hedged his bets by working with the team that had triumphed over his GT projects in both 1996 and 1997. Joest Racing was invited to loan its TWR-built chassis to Weissach, to be raced one more time as a works entry. Joest's now famous sports-racer, along with its sister car (owned by Porsche), gained a factory 3.2-litre engine in place of the Joest-prepared 3-litre with which it had won in 1997, and a range of upgrades.

The car, now called 'Porsche LMP1-98', had a quite different appearance. New front bodywork, with two pronounced concave indentations in the upper surface of the nose section, was designed by Norbert Singer's team. The big offset airbox beneath the rollhoop, which had created turbulence in the airflow to the rear wing, was replaced by a new engine cover and rear wing package. The objective was to improve all-round aerodynamic efficiency, both in downforce and drag, and also enhancing fuel efficiency.

The two cars were also equipped with the same powertrain as the GT1-98 and the synchromesh version of Porsche's new six-speed sequential gearbox. To accommodate the new powertrain, the Joest team under Ralf Jüttner reworked the rear of the monocoque, and altered the load-bearing engine frame. New suspension uprights were also produced. Joest substantially revised the cooling systems, relocating the radiators in the sidepods and modifying the intercooler ducting. The new engine involved a switch from a Bosch to a TAG electronic control system, and Joest also produced an entirely new wiring loom.

In the P1 application, the engine had to be fitted with smaller air restrictors than those on the GT cars and made 530bhp at 7200rpm. In the favour of the prototypes were their vehicle weights, almost 80kg lighter than their 600bhp GT stablemates.

In qualifying, it turned out that the aero changes and the 3.2 engine contributed to a lap-time improvement of only about a second relative to the same car's 1997 pole position. The new bodywork had also made the cars less stable than before, making them a handful for a 24-hour race. The double winner, in which Michele Alboreto and Stefan Johansson were co-driven this time by Yannick Dalmas, was qualified ninth by Alboreto, but Pierre-Henri Raphanel lined up the sister chassis way back in 20th position after a gearbox failure had added to the team's apprehension.

In the race, the fears were justified. Alboreto/Johansson/Dalmas (above) were hampered by a mysterious but temporary loss of pressure in the left-hand turbocharger, but they were racing towards one-third distance in sixth position when the engine abruptly shut down. The flywheel had cracked and, expanding due to centrifugal force, it had broken off the ignition sensor.

The sister car (right) was placed in the top five by Raphanel and James Weaver but, at 4:45am, a rain shower caught out Skip Barber race school instructor David Murry, and he crashed in the Porsche curves, damaging its rear end against a barrier. The car was repaired in a 23-minute pitstop but the rear bodywork flew off as soon as Weaver approached maximum speed on his out-lap, causing a character-building spin at 185mph (300kph). The cover struck the rear wing a hefty blow, and further damaged the wing mounting bolts. The team decided it would be unsafe to continue with the back of the car in this condition.

It was a disappointing end to a short but spectacular career…

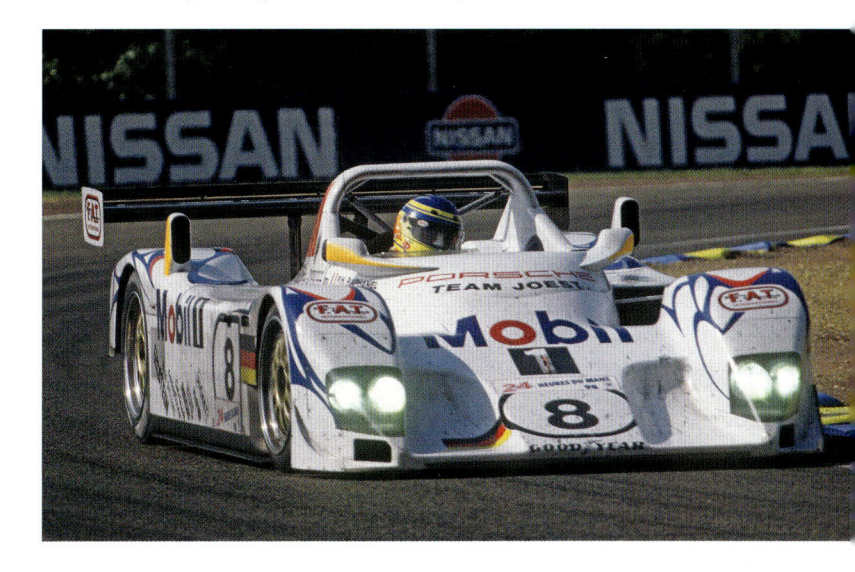

PORSCHE'S GT COMES GOOD 321

LE MANS

K8 SWANSONG

Kremer Racing attempted to prequalify a 'K8 Evo' version of its Porsche spyder, but untested aerodynamic developments made it viciously unstable at high speeds, and it failed to make the cut despite the brave efforts of Enrico Bertaggia. The 'works' team's other car was also almost bumped by Franz Konrad in his own K8, but Almo Coppelli pipped him by 0.008sec. So the Kremers were down to a single entry for their 29th consecutive Le Mans (left).

The K8 was now long past its sell-by date but Coppelli, 'Rocky' Agusta and Xavier Pompidou had a solid weekend. They started 29th and finished 12th, which translated to second in the P1 division – albeit 18 laps behind the class-winning Ferrari.

It was the last appearance of a K8 at Le Mans.

BUSHWHACKED BIKERS

Philippe Gache ordered a Riley & Scott Mk3 (the 15th of the 16 such cars so far produced) for a programme in the ISRS. He raced it here with two rookies – former motorcycle racers Didier de Radiguès and Wayne Gardner, Australia's first 500cc World Champion, in 1987.

This new P1 racer was prepared at Venelles, north of Aix-en-Provence, by Eric Chantriaux's Solution F company, best known for its rally cars, which had built a Trophée Andros ice racing car for Gache the previous winter. The 5-litre, 16-valve Ford V8 was assembled by NASCAR and Trans-Am specialist Kinetic to send 550bhp at 7200rpm to a five-speed GeaRace transmission. The car made its first appearance at Prequalifying, for which it arrived late, and only did three laps…

Going for a time on Thursday, Gache crashed at Tertre Rouge and smashed up the car's right-rear corner. Team manager Thierry Lecourt and race engineer Hugues Baude opted for a cautious approach on Wednesday to bed in the bike racers. Since his retirement from motorcycle racing in 1992, Gardner – 'The Wollongong Whiz' – had raced V8 Supercars in his native Australia and a works TOMS Toyota Supra in Japan, while Radiguès had raced a works-backed BMW 320i to the 1997 Belgian Procar title (winning the Spa 24 Hours with Marc Duez/Eric Hélary). But the R&S prototype (left) was a different experience for both men.

Their race with the repaired R&S went very well until 6:45pm, when Gardner sampled one of the beaches, at a cost of 16 minutes back in the pits. Three hours later, Radiguès pitted with a broken gearbox, which was replaced in 45 minutes. The car was running well again when a piston failure suddenly parked its owner in the small hours.

Later this car had mixed results in the ISRS but ended the season with a victory at Kyalami. In America, 'Butch' Leitzinger won a second consecutive IMSA WSC title with Ford-powered R&S chassis.

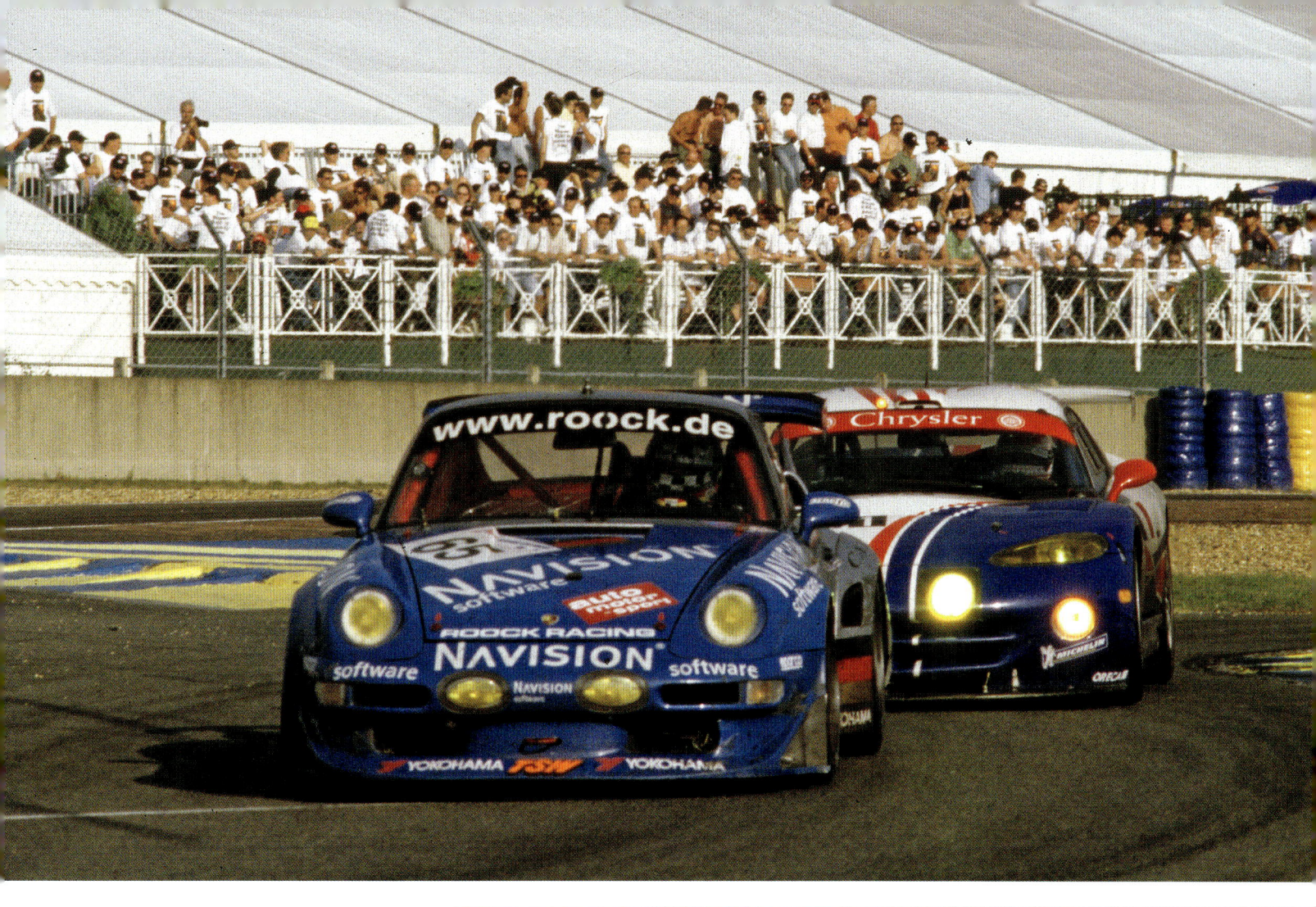

PAIN FOR PORSCHE

Twelve of 18 cars in the GT2 class were Porsches, but numerical superiority was not translated into another class win. All those that finished were delayed and the best-placed – third behind two Vipers – was one of the Roock Racing entries, driven by Michel Ligonnet, Robert Nearn and Claudia Hürtgen. It took the fight to the Vipers (as pictured above) and was racing in second place just after 11am when Hürtgen went to the pits for more than two hours for a new gearbox.

Michel Nourry's débutant team from Verneuil had bought Jack Leconte's old 'Evo' 911 GT2, and entered it for its fourth consecutive Le Mans. It finished fourth in the hands of its new owner, who shared with Jean-Louis Ricci and Thierry Perrier. The other GT2 Porsches to reach the finish were the Roock brothers' second entry and the Haberthur brothers' faithful 1997 class winner (pictured being refuelled), which was also here for a fourth time. The Swiss team's second Porsche departed at breakfast time with its transmission broken.

PORSCHE'S GT COMES GOOD

LE MANS

Two cars jointly entered by Larbre Compétition and Chéreau Sports were fancied for the win and the one pictured above led the Vipers after the start in the hands of Jean-Pierre Jarier, only to fade before succumbing to broken suspension shortly before dawn. The other had a relentlessly unreliable weekend and eventually finished last.

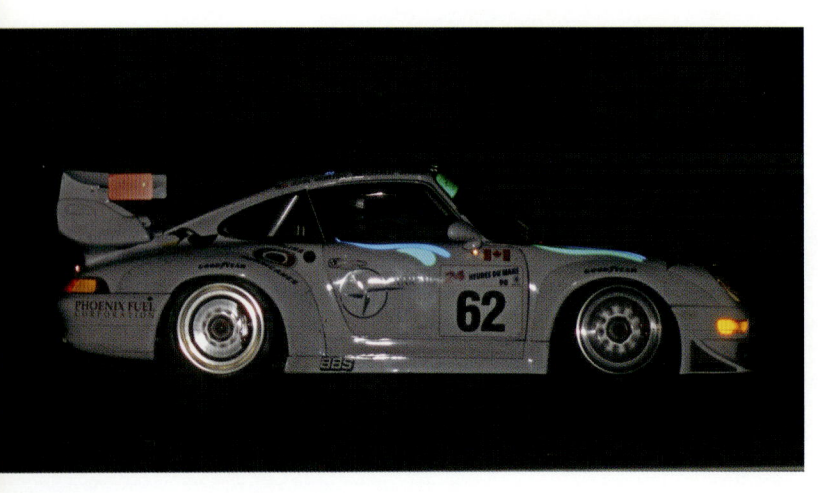

Franz Konrad's team had an even more disappointing race, losing Toni Seiler's car to a piston failure after only two laps, and the other to a nasty accident during the fifth hour. This car had rejoined after losing a chunk of time in pit-lane while a driveshaft assembly was replaced when Nick Ham found himself without brakes at the end of the Mulsanne straight. The speeding Porsche caught in the gravel trap and flipped through a 2.5m-high debris fence into a spectator area. Ham escaped with severe bruising but two spectators were injured by flying debris, neither seriously.

An interesting Porsche GT2 newcomer was that of CJ Motorsports (left), newly formed by Canadian John Graham, based in West Palm Beach, Florida, and run by John Christie and Terry Dale. Graham, Harald Grohs and John Morton lost a lot of time to a broken driveshaft and a bodywork repair, and were trying to recover lost ground when Graham crashed at daybreak.

Of the other new entrants, Bruno Krauss from Fellbach lost his car to an engine failure at nightfall, while Michel Monteiro's Estoril Racing was the unluckiest team, retiring from the race with a broken engine with only 10 minutes remaining.

1998

DEBORA TRIES AGAIN

This year, Didier Bonnet replaced the Cosworth BDG turbo in his Debora P2 car with a Randlinger-prepared BMW straight-six. Controlled by a Bosch Motronic EMS, the M88 engine made 350bhp at 7000rpm and was mated to the same five-speed Hewland FGC gearbox. The Debora was now heavier at 700kg – 50kg over the minimum class limit, but still by far the lightest car in the race. The only P2 car in the field, the Debora was required to run in the May session as part of the GT2 class, rather than with the P1 runners. It therefore made it through to race week in the able hands of Lionel Robert, although it lapped five seconds slower than the LMP297.

Starting from 40th on the grid, Robert, Edouard Sezionale and Pierre Bruneau reached 30th at the end of the first hour before a driveshaft failure sank them back through the field. The car (right) was retired with the gearbox broken shortly before half-time.

HELIMINATION

Baed on the Renault Spider, 'Helem' coupés achieved four podiums from 11 starts in the 1997 French GT series, and RJ Racing brought one of the cars to Le Mans for another prequalifying attempt this year. Engine problems meant its ticket to race week was on the reserve list. The Helem (bottom right) was duly presented at scrutineering, but failed: the team had so modified its rear end that the ACO's chief scrutineer, Daniel Perdrix, regarded it as a different car. Renault soon stepped in to put an end to the Helem venture. Claude Fior, the designer of the Renault Spider, bought the racing hardware, and modified the specification to take a Ferrari V8 (a project that would cease after Fior's death in a microlight accident in 2001).

Roy Johnson's partners in the Helem enterprise, Mikaël and Patrick Legeay, were already engaged with François Migault in creating a new LM-P1 car, based in the Le Mans Technoparc. VN Composite made the Sarta 624 monocoque, which was to have been fitted with a turbo PRV V6 powertrain, but the car was not finished in time for 1998 Prequalifying, and the project was axed.

Another technical inspection casualty at Prequalifying was a Lister Storm. Over the winter Laurence Pearce's team had extensively reworked the rear chassis bulkhead, which involved the removal of the rear window. Like the Helem, the Lister was excluded because the scrutineers regarded it as a new car that had not received type approval. That was the end of Lister's involvement with Le Mans, although the company went on to great success in the British GT series, winning the championship in 1999 and 2001.

PORSCHE'S GT COMES GOOD 325

LE MANS®
24® HEURES DU MANS
6 et 7 JUIN 1998 - Départ 14H00
la légende s'écrit sous vos yeux
CIRCUIT INTERNATIONAL DU MANS
A.S.A. Automobile Club de l'Ouest
FFSA
DataSPort
BILLETTERIE INFORMATIQUE
France Billet
RENSEIGNEMENTS : 02 43 40 24 24 ou MINITEL 3615 ACO
VENTE ACO : 02 43 40 24 75 • VENTE RESEAU FRANCE BILLET/CARREFOUR :
01 42 31 31 31 - MINITEL : 3615 FRANCE BILLET ou magasins Carrefour
France info
Mobil 1

1998

HOURLY RACE POSITIONS

Prequalifying		Start	Time	Car	No	Drivers	1	2	3	4	5	6	7	8	9	10	11	12	13	14	15	16	17	18	19	20	21	22	23	24
3	3:38.057	Schneider	1	3:35.544	Mercedes-Benz CLK-GTR	35	Schneider/Ludwig/Webber	2	DNF																						
2	3:37.696	Brundle	2	3:36.552	Toyota GT-One	28	Brundle/Collard/Hélary	1	1	1	26	24	23	18	17	17	16	14	10	14	14	DNF									
*	3:46.020	Schneider	3	3:36.901	Mercedes-Benz CLK-GTR	36	Bouchut/Gounon/Zonta	8	5	DNF																						
4	3:38.909	Müller	4	3.38.084	Porsche 911 GT1-98	25	Wollek/Müller/Alzen	6	3	3	2	2	2	2	2	1	2	1	2	2	2	2	2	2	4	4	3	3	3	2	2
1	3:37.687	McNish	5	3:38.407	Porsche 911 GT1-98	26	McNish/Ortelli/Aïello	4	4	4	3	3	3	3	3	2	1	2	1	1	1	1	1	2	2	1	2	2	2	1	1
11	3:41.412	Martini	6	3:38.829	BMW V12LM	2	Martini/Winkelhock/Cecotto	9	27	21	42	DNF																			
5	3:39.649	Boutsen	7	3:40.042	Toyota GT-One	29	Lees/Boutsen/Kelleners	3	2	2	1	1	1	1	1	7	7	7	5	4	3	3	3	1	1	2	1	1	1	DNF	
10	3:41.301	Katayama	8	3:40.472	Toyota GT-One	27	T.Suzuki/Katayama/Tsuchiya	5	6	5	19	36	39	37	33	26	25	22	20	19	18	17	17	12	10	10	10	10	10	9	9
21	3:44.720	Alboreto	9	3:40.503	Porsche LMP1-98	7	Alboreto/Johansson/Dalmas	14	14	16	10	8	7	6	DNF																
7	3:40.926	Lagorce	10	3:40.649	Nissan R390 GT1	30	Nielsen/Krumm/Lagorce	13	10	9	4	4	6	4	4	3	3	3	6	6	5	5	5	5	4	5	5	5	5	6	5
12	3:41.667	Brabham	11	3:40.730	Panoz Esperante GTR-1	45	Brabham/Wallace/Davies	15	15	13	12	11	11	8	9	9	16	16	15	13	13	10	9	8	8	8	8	8	7	7	7
19	3:44.528	Kristensen	12	3:41.599	BMW V12LM	1	Stuck/Kristensen/Soper	7	7	6	6	DNF																			
6	3:40.778	Comas	13	3:41.621	Nissan R390 GT1	31	Lammers/Comas/Montermini	12	9	8	5	5	14	13	12	12	9	13	12	10	10	8	7	7	7	7	7	6	5	6	6
8	3:40.927	A.Suzuki	14	3:42.397	Nissan R390 GT1	32	A.Suzuki/Hoshino/Kageyama	18	13	10	9	9	8	7	6	6	6	6	5	4	4	3	4	3	5	4	4	4	3	3	3
23	3:47.397	Ekblom	15	3:43.244	Courage C51	14	Ekblom/Gay/Tsuchiya	20	23	29	23	18	24	21	18	18	DNF														
14	3:43.588	Cottaz	16	3:43.471	Courage C51	13	Cottaz/Goossens/Belloc	19	12	12	8	7	4	5	4	4	4	4	3	4	4	8	DNF								
9	3:41.039	Boullion	17	3:44.458	Ferrari 333 SP-98	5	Boullion/Policand/Sospiri	10	8	7	17	15	13	12	10	10	8	7	9	DNF											
13	3:42.347	Bernard	18	3:44.602	Panoz Esperante GTR-1	44	Bernard/Tinseau/O'Connell	17	18	15	18	33	40	38	36	36	34	34	32	28	28	24	20	19	19	20	DNF				
16	3:43.739	Motoyama	19	3:45.293	Nissan R390 GT1	33	Motoyama/Kurosawa/Kageyama	16	17	14	11	10	9	9	8	8	10	15	14	15	20	18	16	13	12	12	11	10	10		
17	3:43.786	Wollek	20	3:45.452	Porsche LMP1-98	8	Weaver/Raphanel/Murry	11	11	11	7	6	5	7	5	5	5	5	8	7	7	7	DNF								
15	3:43.735	Theys	21	3:45.745	Ferrari 333 SP	3	Baldi/Theys/Moretti	21	16	18	14	12	10	10	11	11	13	12	11	11	12	12	11	15	18	18	17	16	15	14	
18	3:44.442	Poele	22	3:46.289	Ferrari 333 SP	12	Poele/Taylor/Velez	23	26	27	21	19	17	17	16	15	14	13	12	11	11	10	9	9	9	9	9	8	8		
*	3:47.902	Capello	23	3:50.566	McLaren F1 GTR	41	Pirro/Capello/Bscher	24	19	23	20	16	15	15	14	14	12	11	10	9	8	7	DNF								
*	3:51.842	Sugden	24	3:50.863	McLaren F1 GTR	40	Sugden/Auberlen/O'Rourke	9	22	17	13	13	16	14	13	13	11	9	8	8	6	6	6	6	6	6	6	5	4		
24	3:49.061	Grouillard	25	3:51.535	Courage C36	15	Pescarolo/Grouillard/Montagny	25	20	19	15	14	12	15	15	17	17	28	28	25	23	21	19	18	17	18	18	16	16		
28	3:51.818	Gache	26	3:54.274	Riley & Scott Mk3	21	Gache/Gardner/Radiguès	22	21	20	16	17	22	19	23	31	28	27	25	DNF											
*	4:03.371	Terada	27	3:56.658	Courage C50	24	Terada/Fréon/Thévenin	28	45	42	41	40	36	35	32	27	26	26	23	22	20	19	17	17	16	16	15	15	14	14	15
27	3:50.770	M.Ferté	28	3:57.546	Ferrari 333 SP	10	M.Ferté/Migault/Fabre	26	25	28	28	25	25	22	20	22	21	20	19	18	17	15	20	DNF							
30	3:54.617	Coppelli	29	3:57.814	Kremer K8	16	Coppelli/Agusta/Pompidou	27	24	22	25	20	18	20	19	18	18	17	16	16	14	15	14	14	14	14	13	12	12		
33	4:00.120	Beretta	30	3:59.981	Chrysler Viper GTS-R	51	Beretta/Lamy/Archer	33	29	24	22	21	19	26	30	34	30	28	27	25	21	19	18	17	15	16	16	13	13		
35	4:01.921	Wendlinger	31	4:05.006	Chrysler Viper GTS-R	50	Wendlinger/Duez/Huisman	34	30	43	DNF																				
26	3:49.225	Jarier	32	4:05.010	Porsche 911 GT2	60	Jarier/Rosenblad/Donovan	35	34	30	29	26	26	27	25	24	23	23	24	26	31	DNF									
34	4:00.665	Dupuy	33	4:05.648	Chrysler Viper GTS-R	53	Bell/Donohue/Drudi	37	31	26	24	22	21	24	22	20	19	19	18	17	15	16	14	13	11	11	11	12	11		
39	4:04.121	Ham	34	4:06.110	Porsche 911 GT2	70	Konrad/Schumacher/Ham	32	44	44	43	DNF																			
38	4:03.925	Eichmann	35	4:06.205	Porsche 911 GT2	64	Ligonnet/Hürtgen/Nearn	31	28	25	27	23	20	21	21	20	21	20	19	16	14	12	13	13	15	17	17				
37	4:03.380	Goueslard	36	4:06.511	Porsche 911 GT2	72	Goueslard/Chéreau/Yver	36	32	34	39	37	35	39	38	36	36	35	34	31	30	27	25	24	24	24	23	23			
42	4:06.215	Neugarten	37	4:08.326	Porsche 911 GT2	67	Lagniez/Neugarten/Smadja	39	36	32	31	28	27	28	26	25	24	25	26	23	24	22	22	DNF							
43	4:06.608	Amorim	38	4:08.958	Chrysler Viper GTS-R	55	Amorim/Gomes/Mello-Breyner	38	35	31	30	27	28	25	24	23	22	24	22	21	27	25	26	25	25	23	22	21			
45	4:08.246	Maison-neuve	39	4:09.263	Porsche 911 GT2	71	Maisonneuve/Monteiro/Monteiro	41	37	33	32	29	34	32	34	33	32	31	29	27	26	25	24	22	22	22	20	18	DNF		
48	4:09.959	Robert	40	4:09.453	Debora LMP2-96	22	Robert/Sezionale/Bruneau	30	33	41	40	38	37	36	37	37	37	DNF													
40	4:04.618	Ayles	41	4:09.683	Chrysler Viper GTS-R	56	Ayles/Turner/Hugenholtz	45	42	39	34	30	33	29	31	30	35	35	33	33	30	29	26	24	23	23	22	22	19		
44	4:06.814	Grohs	42	4:10.215	Porsche 911 GT2	62	Morton/Grohs/Graham	40	38	36	36	35	34	33	28	29	27	30	31	34	32	DNF									
46	4:09.016	Trunk	43	4:11.606	Porsche 911 GT2	61	Müller/Trunk/Palmberger	46	40	45	38	39	38	40	39	39	DNF														
50	4:14.452	Pilgrim	44	4:11.910	Porsche 911 GT2	65	Schirle/Ahrle/Warnock	43	40	37	37	34	32	30	27	28	29	33	33	31	30	27	25	24	23	26	26	25	24	22	
49	4:10.716	Perrier	45	4:19.476	Porsche 911 GT2	69	Perrier/Nourry/Ricci	42	39	35	33	31	30	29	31	32	31	29	29	29	27	21	20	21	21	21	20	18			
41	4:06.201	Seiler	46	4:20.426	Porsche 911 GT2	73	Seiler/Kitchak/Zadra	47	DNF																						
*	4:23.924	Graham	47	4:23.655	Porsche 911 GT2	68	Poulain/Graham/Maury-Laribière	44	41	38	35	32	31	32	35	34	33	32	30	29	29	26	27	21	20	19	19	19	20		
			FS	No time	Helem V6	58	Gonin/Roy	-																							

DNF Did not finish **DNQ** Did not qualify **DSQ** Disqualified **FS** Failed scrutineering **NC** Not classified as a finisher **RES** Reserve not required * Automatic entry

PORSCHE'S GT COMES GOOD 327

LE MANS

RACE RESULTS

Pos	Car	No	Drivers			Laps	Km	Miles	FIA Class	DNF
1	Porsche 911 GT1-98	26	Allan McNish (GB)	Stéphane Ortelli (F)	Laurent Aïello (F)	351	4783.781	2972.498	LM-GT1	
2	Porsche 911 GT1-98	25	Bob Wollek (F)	Jörg Müller (D)	Uwe Alzen (D)	350	4770.127	2964.014	LM-GT1	
3	Nissan R390 GT1	32	Aguri Suzuki (J)	Kazuyoshi Hoshino (J)	Masahiko Kageyama (J)	347	4721.414	2933.745	LM-GT1	
4	McLaren F1 GTR	40	Tim Sugden (GB)	Bill Auberlen (USA)	Steve O'Rourke (GB)	343	4672.796	2903.535	LM-GT1	
5	Nissan R390 GT1	30	John Nielsen (DK)	Michael Krumm (D)	Franck Lagorce (F)	342	4649.099	2888.811	LM-GT1	
6	Nissan R390 GT1	31	Jan Lammers (NL)	Erik Comas (F)	Andrea Montermini (I)	342	4649.012	2888.757	LM-GT1	
7	Panoz Esperante GTR-1	45	David Brabham (AUS)	Andy Wallace (GB)	Jamie Davies (GB)	335	4562.990	2835.305	LM-GT1	
8	Ferrari 333 SP	12	Eric van der Poele (B)	Fermin Velez (E)	Wayne Taylor (ZA)	332	4516.928	2806.684	LM-P1	
DNF	Toyota GT-One	29	Geoff Lees (GB)	Thierry Boutsen (B)	Ralf Kelleners (D)	330			LM-GT1	Transmission (gearbox)
9	Toyota GT-One	27	Toshio Suzuki (J)	Ukyo Katayama (J)	Keiichi Tsuchiya (J)	326	4443.214	2760.880	LM-GT1	
10	Nissan R390 GT1	33	Satoshi Motoyama (J)	Takuya Kurosawa (J)	Masami Kageyama (J)	319	4337.425	2695.146	LM-GT1	
11	Chrysler Viper GTS-R	53	Justin Bell (GB)	David Donohue (USA)	Luca Drudi (I)	317	4308.193	2676.982	LM-GT2	
12	Kremer K8	16	Almo Coppelli (I)	Ricardo 'Rocky' Agusta (I)	Xavier Pompidou (F)	314	4264.196	2649.643	LM-P1	
13	Chrysler Viper GTS-R	51	Olivier Beretta (MC)	Pedro Lamy (P)	Tommy Archer (USA)	312	4240.199	2634.732	LM-GT2	
14	Ferrari 333 SP	3	Mauro Baldi (I)	Didier Theys (B)	Giampiero Moretti (I)	311	4226.493	2626.216	LM-P1	
15	Courage C50	24	Yojiro Terada (J)	Franck Fréon (F)	Olivier Thévenin (F)	304	4133.121	2568.197	LM-P1	
16	Courage C36	15	Henri Pescarolo (F)	Olivier Grouillard (F)	Franck Montagny (F)	300	4089.012	2540.789	LM-P1	
17	Porsche 911 GT2	64	Michel Ligonnet (F)	Claudia Hürtgen (D)	Robert Nearn (GB)	285	3880.925	2411.490	LM-GT2	
DNF	Porsche 911 GT2	71	Michel Maisonneuve (F)	Manuel Monteiro (P)	Michel Monteiro (P)	277			LM-GT2	Engine
18	Porsche 911 GT2	69	Thierry Perrier (F)	Michel Nourry (F)	Jean-Louis Ricci (F)	276	3761.703	2337.409	LM-GT2	
19	Chrysler Viper GTS-R	56	Gary Ayles (GB)	Matt Turner (USA)	John Hugenholtz (NL)	270	3680.780	2287.126	LM-GT2	
20	Porsche 911 GT2	68	Hervé Poulain (F)	Eric Graham (F)	Jean-Luc Maury-Laribière (F)	268	3642.599	2263.402	LM-GT2	
21	Chrysler Viper GTS-R	55	Ni Amorim (P)	Gonçalo Gomes (P)	Manuel Mello-Breyner (P)	264	3599.133	2236.393	LM-GT2	
22	Porsche 911 GT2	65	Rob Schirle (GB)	André Ahrle (F)	David Warnock (GB)	247	3366.987	2092.145	LM-GT2	
23	Porsche 911 GT2	72	Patrice Goueslard (F)	Jean-Luc Chéreau (F)	Pierre Yver (F)	240	3257.856	2024.334	LM-GT2	
DNF	Panoz Esperante GTR-1	44	Eric Bernard (F)	Christophe Tinseau (F)	Johnny O'Connell (USA)	236			LM-GT1	Transmission (gearbox)
DNF	Courage C51	13	Didier Cottaz (F)	Marc Goossens (B)	Jean-Philippe Belloc (F)	232			LM-P1	Transmission (gearbox)
DNF	McLaren F1 GTR	41	Emanuele Pirro (I)	Rinaldo Capello (I)	Thomas Bscher (D)	228			LM-GT1	Accident damage
DNF	Porsche LMP1-98	8	James Weaver (GB)	Pierre-Henri Raphanel (F)	David Murry (USA)	218			LM-P1	Rear bodywork damage
DNF	Ferrari 333 SP	10	Michel Ferté (F)	François Migault (F)	Pascal Fabre (F)	203			LM-P1	Transmission (gearbox)
DNF	Porsche 911 GT2	67	Jean-Claude Lagniez (F)	Michel Neugarten (B)	David Smadja (F)	198			LM-GT2	Transmission
DNF	Toyota GT-One	28	Martin Brundle (GB)	Emmanuel Collard (F)	Eric Hélary (F)	191			LM-GT1	Accident
DNF	Ferrari 333 SP	5	Jean-Christophe Boullion (F)	Jérôme Policand (F)	Vincenzo Sospiri (I)	187			LM-P1	Transmission (gearbox)
DNF	Porsche 911 GT2	60	Jean-Pierre Jarier (F)	Carl Rosenblad (S)	Robin Donovan (GB)	164			LM-GT2	Suspension
DNF	Porsche 911 GT2	62	John Morton (USA)	Harald Grohs (D)	John Graham (CDN)	164			LM-GT2	Accident
DNF	Riley & Scott Mk3	21	Philippe Gache (F)	Wayne Gardner (AUS)	Didier de Radiguès (B)	155			LM-P1	Engine (piston)
DNF	Courage C51	14	Fredrik Ekblom (S)	Patrice Gay (F)	Takeshi Tsuchiya (J)	126			LM-P1	Engine (overheating)
DNF	Porsche LM-P1 98	7	Michele Alboreto (I)	Stefan Johansson (S)	Yannick Dalmas (F)	107			LM-P1	Electrics
DNF	Debora LMP2-96	22	Lionel Robert (F)	Edouard Sezionale (F)	Pierre Bruneau (F)	106			LM-P2	Transmission (gearbox)
DNF	Porsche 911 GT2	61	Bernhard Müller (D)	Michael Trunk (D)	Ernst Palmberger (D)	71			LM-GT2	Engine
DNF	BMW V12LM	1	Hans-Joachim Stuck (D)	Tom Kristensen (DK)	Steve Soper (GB)	60			LM-P1	Wheelbearing
DNF	BMW V12LM	2	Pierluigi Martini (I)	Joachim Winkelhock (D)	Johnny Cecotto (YV)	43			LM-P1	Wheelbearing
DNF	Mercedes-Benz CLK-GTR	36	Jean-Marc Gounon (F)	Christophe Bouchut (F)	*Ricardo Zonta (BR)*	31			LM-GT1	Engine (oil pump)
DNF	Chrysler Viper GTS-R	50	Karl Wendlinger (A)	Marc Duez (B)	Patrick Huisman (NL)	28			LM-GT2	Electrics
DNF	Porsche 911 GT2	70	Franz Konrad (A)	Larry Schumacher (USA)	Nick Ham (USA)	24			LM-GT2	Accident
DNF	Mercedes-Benz CLK-GTR	35	Bernd Schneider (D)	*Mark Webber (AUS)*	Klaus Ludwig (D)	19			LM-GT1	Engine
DNF	Porsche 911 GT2	73	Toni Seiler (CH)	Peter Kitchak (USA)	Angelo Zadra (I)	2			LM-GT2	Engine (piston)
FS	Helem V6	58	*Benjamin Roy (F)*	Patrick Gonin (F)					LM-GT2	Failed scrutineering

DNF Did not finish   **DNS** Did not start   **DSQ** Disqualified   **FS** Failed scrutineering   **RES** Reserve not required   **NC** Not classified as a finisher   **WD** Withdrawn   Drivers in italics did not race the cars specified

1998

CLASS WINNERS

FIA Class	Starters	Finishers	First	No	Drivers	kph	mph	
LM-P1	14	5	Ferrari 333 SP	12	Poele/Velez/Taylor	199.292	123.834	
LM-P2	1	0	–	–	–	-	-	
LM-GT1	15	9	Porsche 911 GT1	26	McNish/Ortelli/Aiello	188.167	116.921	
LM-GT2	17	9	Chrysler Viper GTS-R	53	Bell/Donohue/Drudi	179.500	111.536	Record
Totals	**47**	**23**						

NON-PREQUALIFIERS

No	Car	Entrant (Nat)	cc	Engine	Class	Pos	Time
4	Ferrari 333 SP-98	La Filière Elf (F)	3997	F310E V12	LM-P1	NA	-
6	Ferrari 333 SP	GTC Motorsport Lanzante (GB)	3997	F310E V12	LM-P1	NA	-
9	Ferrari 333 SP	Pilot BSM Racing (F)	3997	F310E V12	LM-P1	NA	-
11	Ferrari 333 SP-98	Ecurie Biennoise (CH)	3997	F310E V12	LM-P1	NA	-
17	Kremer K8	Kremer Racing (D)	2995tc	Porsche 935/76 F6	LM-P1	36	4:02.163
18	Kremer K8	Konrad Motorsport (D)	3165tc	Porsche 935/76 F6	LM-P1	31	3:54.625
19	WR LMP98	Gérard Welter (F)	1995tc	Peugeot 405-Raid S4	LM-P1	32	3:56.582
20	WR LMP98	Jean-Luc Sonnier Idée Verte (F)	1995tc	Peugeot 405-Raid S4	LM-P1	52	4:48.010
23	Sarta 624	Sarta Project Lukoil (F)	2946tc	Renault PRV V6	LM-P1	NA	-
34	Nissan R390 GT1	NISMO (J)	3496tc	VRH35L V8	GT1	NA	-
37	Lister Storm GTL	Newcastle United Storm (GB)	6996	Jaguar HE V12	GT1	FS	-
38	Porsche 911 GT1-98	Zakspeed Racing (D)	3196tc	F6	GT1	18	3:43.911
39	Porsche 911 GT1-98	Zakspeed Racing (D)	3196tc	F6	GT1	22	3:44.794
42	McLaren F1 GTR	Parabolica Motorsport (GB)	5990	BMW S70/3 V12	GT1	NA	-
43	McLaren F1 GTR	Parabolica Motorsport (GB)	5990	BMW S70/3 V12	GT1	NA	-
46	Panoz GTR-1 Q9	Panoz Motorsports (USA)	5999	Ford V8/Zytek	GT1	29	3:53.199
47	Porsche 911 GT1	Millennium Motorsport (GB)	3164tc	F6	GT1	NA	-
48	Porsche 911 GT1	Larbre Compétition (F)	3164tc	F6	GT1	25	3:49.225
52	Chrysler Viper GTS-R	Viper Team ORECA (F)	7986	356-T6 V10	GT2	NA	-
54	Chrysler Viper GTS-R	Orion Motorsport (GB)	7986	356-T6 V10	GT2	DSQ	-
57	Helem V6	RJ Racing (F)	2975	PRV V6	GT2	FS	-
58	Helem V6	RJ Racing (F)	2975	PRV V6	GT2	51	4:21.604
59	Lotus Esprit V8 Turbo	Pilbeam Racing Designs (GB)	3506tc	T918 V8	GT2	DSQ	-
66	Porsche 911 GT2	Roock Racing Motorsport (D)	3600tc	F6	GT2	53	5:00.367
75	Saleen Mustang	Cirtek Motorspirt (GB)	5900	Ford V8	GT2	47	4:09.895

DSQ Disqualified   **FS** Failed scrutineering   **NA** Non-arrival   **NT** No time set   **WD** Withdrawn after Prequalifying

INTERNATIONAL SPORTS RACING SERIES

Race	Winner	Drivers
Paul Ricard (F) 2h30m	Ferrari 333 SP	Theys/Lienhard
Brno (CS) 400km	Ferrari 333 SP	Collard/Sospiri
Misano (I) 400km	Ferrari 333 SP	Collard/Sospiri
Donington Park (GB) 400km	Ferrari 333 SP	Collard/Sospiri
Anderstorp (S) 400km	Ferrari 333 SP	Collard/Sospiri
Nürburgring (D) 400km	Ferrari 333 SP	Collard/Sospiri
Le Mans Bugatti (F) 400km	Ferrari 333 SP	Collard/Sospiri
Kyalami (ZA) 2h30m	Riley & Scott Mk3	Policand/Formato

FIA GT CHAMPIONSHIP

Race	Winner	Drivers
Oschersleben (D) 500km	Mercedes-Benz CLK-GTR	Ludwig/Zonta
Silverstone (GB) 500km	Mercedes-Benz CLK-GTR	Schneider/Webber
Hockenheim (D) 500km	Mercedes-Benz CLK-GTR	Schneider/Webber
Dijon-Prénois (F) 500km	Mercedes-Benz CLK-GTR	Ludwig/Zonta
Hungaroring (H) 500km	Mercedes-Benz CLK-GTR	Schneider/Webber
Suzuka (J) 1000km	Mercedes-Benz CLK-LM	Schneider/Webber
Donington Park (GB) 500km	Mercedes-Benz CLK-LM	Schneider/Webber
A1-Ring (A) 500km	Mercedes-Benz CLK-LM	Ludwig/Zonta
Hockenheim (D) 500km	Mercedes-Benz CLK-LM	Ludwig/Zonta
Laguna Seca (USA) 500km	Mercedes-Benz CLK-LM	Ludwig/Zonta

FINAL GT CHAMPIONSHIP POINTS

Final Positions	Team/Driver	Points
GT1 TEAMS		
1	AMG Mercedes (D)	146
2	Porsche AG (D)	49
3	Persson Motorsport (D)	24
4	Zakspeed Racing (D)	20
5	DAMS (F)	17
6	GTC Competition (GB)	4
GT2 TEAMS		
1	Viper Team ORECA (F)	130
2	Roock Racing (D)	31
3	Konrad Motorsport (D)	25
4	Elf Haberthur Racing (CH)	15
5	Krauss Motorsport (D)	14
6	Marcos Racing International (GB)	13
&c		
GT1 DRIVERS		
1	Klaus Ludwig (D)	77
=	Ricardo Zonta (BR)	77
3	Bernd Schneider (D)	69
=	Mark Webber (AUS)	69
5	Allan McNish (GB)	27
=	Yannick Dalmas (F)	27
&c		
GT2 DRIVERS		
1	Olivier Beretta (MC)	92
2	Pedro Lamy (P)	92
3	Karl Wendlinger (A)	38
4	Bruno Eichmann (D)	22
5	Justin Bell (GB)	20
6	Franz Konrad (A)	20
&c		

PORSCHE'S GT COMES GOOD

LE MANS

1999
HIGH FIVES IN GERMANY

LE MANS

RACE INFORMATION

RACE DATE
12-13 June

RACE No
67

CIRCUIT LENGTH
8.454 miles/13.605km

HONORARY STARTER
Joan Hall
Minister of Tourism, South Australia

MARQUES (ON GRID)
Audi	4
BMW	4
Chrysler	8
Courage	3
Ferrari	1
Lola	3
Mercedes-Benz	2
Nissan	1
Panoz	2
Porsche	11
Riley&Scott	3
Toyota	3

STARTERS/FINISHERS
45/22

WINNERS

OVERALL
BMW

ENTRY LIST

No	Car	Entrant (nat)	cc	Engine	Tyres	Weight (kg)	Class
1	Toyota GT-One	Toyota Motorsport (J)	3576tc	R36V V8	Michelin	907	LM-GTP
2	Toyota GT-One	Toyota Motorsport (J)	3576tc	R36V V8	Michelin	901	LM-GTP
3	Toyota GT-One	Toyota Motorsport (J)	3576tc	R36V V8	Michelin	900	LM-GTP
4	Mercedes-Benz CLR	AMG Mercedes (D)	5721	GT108C V8	Bridgestone	915	LM-GTP *
5	Mercedes-Benz CLR	AMG Mercedes (D)	5721	GT108C V8	Bridgestone	925	LM-GTP
6	Mercedes-Benz CLR	AMG Mercedes (D)	5721	GT108C V8	Bridgestone	914	LM-GTP
7	Audi R8R	Audi Sport Team Joest (D)	3595tc	V8	Michelin	914	LMP
8	Audi R8R	Audi Sport Team Joest (D)	3595tc	V8	Michelin	921	LMP
9	Audi R8C	Audi Sport UK (GB)	3595tc	V8	Michelin	941	LM-GTP
10	Audi R8C	Audi Sport UK (GB)	3595tc	V8	Michelin	957	LM-GTP
11	Panoz LM-P-1 Roadster S	Panoz Motorsports (USA)	5999	Ford V8	Michelin	902	LMP
12	Panoz LM-P-1 Roadster S	Panoz Motorsports (USA)	5999	Ford V8	Michelin	914	LMP
13	Courage C52	Courage Compétition (F)	3495tc	Nissan VRH35L V8	Bridgestone	914	LMP
14	Courage C50	La Filière Elf/Pescarolo Promotion Racing (F)	2994tc	Porsche F6	Pirelli	910	LMP
15	BMW V12 LMR	BMW Motorsport (D)	5990	S70/3 V12	Michelin	915	LMP
16	BMW V12 LMR	BMW Motorsport (D)	5990	S70/3 V12	-	-	LMP
17	BMW V12 LMR	BMW Motorsport (D)	5990	S70/3 V12	Michelin	914	LMP
18	BMW V12 LM	David Price Racing (GB) Bscher Racing (D)	5990	S70/3 V12	Yokohama	927	LMP
19	BMW V12 LM	David Price Racing (GB) Team Go (J)	5990	S70/3 V12	Michelin	927	LMP
21	Courage C52	NISMO (J)	3495tc	Nissan VRH35L V8	Bridgestone	906	LMP
22	Nissan R391	NISMO (J)	4997	VRH50A V8	Bridgestone	907	LMP
23	Nissan R391	NISMO (J)	4997	VRH50A V8	Bridgestone	916	LMP
24	Riley & Scott LMP99	Autoexe Motorsports (J)	5954	Ford V8	Yokohama	910	LMP
25	Lola B98/10	DAMS (F)	3998	Judd GV4 V10	Pirelli	901	LMP
26	Lola B98/10	Konrad Motorsport (D) Racing for Holland (NL)	5970	Ford V8	Dunlop	912	LMP
27	Lola B98/10	Kremer Racing (D)	5970	Ford V8	Goodyear	910	LMP
29	Ferrari 333 SP	JB Racing (F)	3997	F130E V12	Pirelli	904	LMP
30	Ferrari 333 SP	JB Racing (F)	3997	F130E V12	-	-	LMP
31	Riley & Scott Mk3	Riley & Scott Europe (F)	5954	Ford V8	Pirelli	942	LMP
32	Riley & Scott Mk3	Riley & Scott Europe (F)	5954	Ford V8	Pirelli	965	LMP
50	Chrysler Viper GTS-R	CICA Team ORECA (F)	7986	356-T6 V10	Michelin	1169	LM-GTS
51	Chrysler Viper GTS-R	Viper Team ORECA (F)	7986	356-T6 V10	Michelin	1164	LM-GTS *
52	Chrysler Viper GTS-R	Viper Team ORECA (F)	7986	356-T6 V10	Michelin	1167	LM-GTS *
53	Chrysler Viper GTS-R	Viper Team ORECA (F)	7986	356-T6 V10	Michelin	1166	LM-GTS
54	Chrysler Viper GTS-R	Paul Belmondo Racing (F)	7986	356-T6 V10	Dunlop	1175	LM-GTS
55	Chrysler Viper GTS-R	Paul Belmondo Racing (F)	7986	356-T6 V10	Dunlop	1197	LM-GTS
56	Chrysler Viper GTS-R	Chamberlain Engineering (GB)	7986	356-T6 V10	Michelin	1189	LM-GTS
57	Chrysler Viper GTS-R	Chamberlain Engineering (GB)	7986	356-T6 V10	Michelin	1180	LM-GTS
60	Porsche 911 GT2 (993)	Freisinger Motorsport (D)	3600tc	F6	Dunlop	1120	LM-GTS *
61	Porsche 911 GT2 (993)	Freisinger Motorsport (D)	3600tc	F6	Dunlop	1121	LM-GTS
62	Porsche 911 GT2 (993)	Roock Racing Team (D)	3746tc	F6	Yokohama	1112	LM-GTS
63	Porsche 911 GT2 (993)	Roock Racing Team (D)	3746tc	F6	Yokohama	1103	LM-GTS
64	Porsche 911 GT2 (993)	Konrad Motorsport (D)	3746tc	F6	Dunlop	1109	LM-GTS
65	Porsche 911 GT2 (993)	Larbre Compétition/Chéreau Sports (F)	3600tc	F6	Michelin	1112	LM-GTS
66	Porsche 911 GT2 (993)	Estoril Racing Communication (F)	3600tc	F6	Pirelli	1150	LM-GTS
67	Porsche 911 GT2 (993)	Larbre Compétition (F)	3600tc	F6	Michelin	1111	LM-GTS
80	Porsche 911 GT3 (996)	Champion Racing (USA)	3598	F6	Pirelli	1104	LM-GT *
81	Porsche 911 GT3 (996)	Manthey Racing (D)	3598	F6	Pirelli	1106	LM-GT
83	Porsche 911 RSR (993)	Gerard MacQuillan (GB)	3746	F6	Yokohama	1101	LM-GT
84	Porsche 911 RSR (993)	Perspective Racing (F)	3746	F6	Pirelli	1108	LM-GT

* Automatic entries: (4) GT1 winner 1998 FIA GT Championship, (51) GT2 class winner 1998 Le Mans, (52) GT2 winner 1998 FIA GT Championship, (60) GT2 class winner 1998 Petit Le Mans, (80) GT1 class winner 1998 Petit Le Mans. Porsche did not take up the sixth automatic entry. See Non-Prequalifiers table for discarded entries

ENTRY

Porsche rested on its laurels after its hat-trick, and was effectively replaced by a powerful newcomer in the shape of Audi. This was another tremendous entry, also featuring full-on factory teams from BMW, Mercedes-Benz, Nissan, Panoz and Toyota, alongside 'works' entries from racing specialists Courage, Lola and Riley & Scott. Including Chrysler's Vipers, seven manufacturers were here, contributing 20 of the 48 cars. There were eight GTP entries and 20 LMPs, supported by an eye-catching 16 cars in GTS, and four in GT.

QUALIFYING

Twelve months of intense development reduced the lap times of all the front-running cars by five seconds and more. Even the débutant Audis went under the 1998 pole.

The first session was red-flagged for almost an hour for barrier repairs at Tertre Rouge after Eric van der Poele crashed one of Nissan's new prototypes there. At the restart, no one could touch the Toyota GT-Ones of Martin Brundle and Thierry Boutsen. An impressive run by David Brabham's new Panoz roadster was good enough for third on the first day, but the front-engined car slipped to fifth on Thursday when JJ Lehto and Bernd Schneider came on strong for BMW and Mercedes respectively.

This was a brave performance by Schneider. Mercedes was having a torrid time trying to stop its CLR from taking off in the aerodynamic wakes of other cars. Mark Webber had gone airborne

HIGH FIVES IN GERMANY | 333

LE MANS

ORGANISATION

The most significant among a series of revised technical regulations this year was the abolition of separate GT1 and sports-racing categories. The GT1 class was renamed 'LM-GT Prototype', and those expensive racecars masquerading as production-based cars were integrated in a single class with the open-cockpit LM Prototypes. Full type approval was no longer required and a previous three-year notice period for major technical modifications was cancelled.

All GTP and LMP cars were limited in overall width to 2000mm, while the flat-bottom surface between the front and rear axle centre lines now had to extend over the full width of the car, rather than within the width of the front-track dimension. Traction-control systems and ABS brakes were no longer permitted, even if previously homologated. Maximum tyre widths were imposed of 14 inches for the GTP cars, and 16 inches for LMPs. The LMP minimum weight was increased by 25kg to 900kg to bring it into line with GTP.

Turbocharged engines were limited to 4000cc in both divisions. The largest permitted naturally aspirated swept volumes were 8000cc in GTP, and 6000cc in LMP. The manipulation continued of engine air-inlet restrictor diameters, as it had since 1994.

In addition, the same transmission rules now applied for both GTP and LMP. These limited the gearbox to six forward speeds, and outlawed automatic and semi-automatic operation. Differentials with electronic, pneumatic or hydraulic control mechanisms were also prohibited. There was also a new 'LMP-650' class, but no entries were received.

There were also big changes in the other 'GT' classes. The former GT2 was renamed 'LM-GTS', and only cars with chassis made from metallic materials were permitted. Stressed engine installations were outlawed. A relaxation in air-inlet restrictors and turbocharger 'boost' pressure limits produced a small increase in engine output. A new 'LM-GT' class was introduced for cars in regular production, marketed by a manufacturer recognized by the ACO, and on sale in a major country. The minimum weight was set at 1100kg in both these divisions.

The ACO implemented maximum fuel tankage of 90 litres for all cars, representing a 10-litre reduction for GT-type models, and a 10-litre increase for the prototypes.

Meanwhile, across the Atlantic, Don Panoz acknowledged that the ACO was the organization with the greatest competence to devise and evolve sportscar racing regulations. He gained the ACO's full cooperation and created the inaugural American Le Mans Series, which comprised eight races beginning with the historic Sebring 12 Hours.

This year the *Syndicat Mixte* funded new grandstands next to the ACO offices and further construction work in the retail and catering 'Village' infield of the Dunlop curve – during which site workers unearthed an unexploded, 25-kilo bomb from the Second World War.

In June 1999, the EU commission opened an investigation into the FIA over anti-competitive behaviour in the commercialization of FIA-sanctioned series, the eventual outcome of which would be positive for the ACO and Le Mans.

at 200mph earlier in the evening, ending up on his roof, surprised to be unharmed. Minor suspension and aero adjustments were shown to be inadequate in the race morning warm-up when the hapless Webber flipped again. The team's decision to race its surviving cars was highly controversial.

RACE

Brundle lost no time in confirming that he and his pole-position Toyota were the class of the field. Ahead of the first fuel stops, he outclassed Boutsen, Lehto and Schneider to establish a solid lead – only to be baulked on the way to his pit. The delay dropped him to third behind Schneider and Boutsen and he never led again. A hydraulics glitch robbed the car of its power steering and its paddle gearshift system, and Brundle was 10 laps behind the leaders at dusk when a blown tyre, caused by debris on the track, sent him off the road at the first Mulsanne chicane.

Shortly before this incident, Peter Dumbreck, running fourth for Mercedes, was following Brundle on the fast chute towards Indianapolis when he became a passenger in the third and most frightening of the week's CLR somersaults. This time the car took off and flew over the guardrail and into the forest. Miraculously, again, Dumbreck was unhurt.

Schneider's Mercedes was withdrawn from the race, the lead of which was now hotly contested by Allan McNish in Boutsen's Toyota and Tom Kristensen in Lehto's BMW. The GT-One was a little faster but less fuel-efficient than the V12 LMR, and was losing time in the pitstops, taking longer to restart due to overheating fuel injectors. It made for a riveting duel that lasted all the way to 3:10am.

McNish had broken the lap record, but the BMW was marginally holding the upper hand when Boutsen made a classic Le Mans error. He made a split-second decision to lap a GT2 Porsche just ahead of the heavy braking zone before the Dunlop curves. The vastly superior stopping power of the GT-One left the weighty Porsche nowhere to go. It punted the Toyota heavily into the wall.

Barrier damage, and an oil trail deposited over much of the circuit by the damaged Porsche, caused a 75-minute full-course yellow. The green, at around dawn, found Lehto/Kristensen/Jörg Müller with a three-lap lead over team mates Yannick Dalmas/ Pierluigi Martini/Joachim Winkelhock. The remaining Toyota was third but four laps down after what looked like an overly cautious run by its Japanese drivers. Yet Ukyo Katayama came within 90 seconds of the second-placed BMW just before 8:30am, when Winkelhock spun and pitted for the car to be checked by his crew.

Effortlessly maintaining a four-lap lead, Lehto had the race in the bag when, shortly before midday, a detached roll-bar link suddenly jammed open his throttle as he sped through the Porsche curves, and the BMW smacked into the wall.

Now the 180,000 spectators were buzzing again: two minutes separated the lone survivors of the BMW and Toyota teams. After shifts by Dalmas and Toshio Suzuki, Martini and Katayama took over for the final dash to the chequer.

Both men further lowered the lap record but Toyota's computers were predicting a neck-and-neck finish. The gap was down to 80 seconds with 54 minutes remaining, when Katayama was forced over the kerbs at the first chicane when lapping Thomas Bscher's fifth-placed BMW LM. He had to nurse the GT-One back to the pits with a punctured rear tyre, and it was all over.

The top five finishers were all made in Germany. Third and fourth were Audi's new spyders, displaying durability that would set the standard throughout the following decade. The first six in GTS were all Chrysler Vipers, with the GT-winning, quasi-works Porsche 996 finishing in their midst.

ANGLO-BAVARIAN PERFECTION

After an enduring battle with Toyota, BMW scored a stunning victory with a new version of its V12 LMP car (above), raced by Yannick Dalmas, Pierluigi Martini and Jo Winkelhock, after the sister car (below) had been eliminated by an accident when leading. Like its great rival, McLaren, the Williams Formula 1 business thus added a Le Mans success to its impressive CV.

Graham Humphrys was recruited as the chief designer of the new car, which was again produced by Williams Grand Prix Engineering's engineering group under John Russell, reporting to BMW's Ulrich Schiefer. Through the late summer of 1998, the BMW V12LMs were used for a six-month development programme to test fresh design features and new parts. In the end, the new V12LMR inherited only 68 components from a total of 3500 in the 1998 racecar.

The bodywork design process was reversed so that Jason Somerville's aero team decided upon an optimum package before BMW branding touches were added by McLaren F1 stylist Peter Stevens, with minimal disruption to performance. The LMR not only looked better, but generated more downforce than its predecessor for no increase in drag. A single-seater style rollhoop behind the driver (allowed by an anomaly in the technical regulations) greatly improved airflow to the low-mounted rear wing and gave the car a 'sidecar' appearance accentuated by an offset engine airbox, the inlet for which was on top of the RH sidepod. This configuration was evolved with new cooling arrangements, using air flowing over the upper surface of the nose, rather than from the underside. The airflow under the nose was instead flowed over a splitter beneath a raised footbox, and vented through extractors behind the front wheels (as first seen on the Toyota GT-One).

The carbonfibre/honeycomb monocoque was completely new, with an extra bulkhead to support the rollhoop. G Force being committed to Nissan's GT1 project, the new tubs were made by CTS (formerly Lola Composites). The engine installation, again employing steel A-frames, was further aft in the chassis to improve weight distribution, with a shortened transmission casing.

336 LE MANS 24 HOURS 1990–99

1999

The suspension, steering and braking systems were also redesigned, with the emphasis on simplicity and durability.

The LMR was powered by an upgraded version of the 48-valve V12, developed for better fuel efficiency by Herbert Vögele at BMW Motorsport in Munich under its new engine boss, Werner Laurenz. With the latest Le Mans air restrictors, it now made 580bhp at 6500rpm. The 1998 cars had been overweight but the LMR needed ballast to make the 900kg LMP weight limit.

BMW's racecars were operated this season by Charly Lamm's Team Schnitzer, which had run BMW-backed McLarens in 1997. They débuted in March 1999 when two were entered for the Sebring 12 Hours. One was written off, but the other won the Floridian race in the hands of JJ Lehto, Jörg Muller and Tom Kristensen. The following month, when Gerhard Berger and Mario Theissen started work as the joint directors of BMW Motorsport in Munich, they already had a winning car.

One of three LMRs at Prequalifying appeared in livery created by artist Jenny Holzer, in the tradition of the BMW 'Art Cars', but the team opted to race only two chassis. The LMRs could hit 201mph (324kph) on the Mulsanne straight, but were outpaced by Toyota's GT Prototypes both in Prequalifying and in race week, lining up third and sixth.

On Saturday, however, they caused great disquiet among rivals when they were able to run 14 laps on their first tanks of fuel – at least one more than the opposition. Solid reliability and exemplary pitwork by the Schnitzer crew helped to keep the BMWs in contention throughout the rest of the weekend.

HIGH FIVES IN GERMANY

LE MANS

The Sebring winners, teamed up again, spent much of Saturday evening and almost all night fighting for the lead with one of the Toyotas. It was a captivating contest. But when the Toyota crashed out of second place at 3:10am, Kristensen found himself behind a Safety Car leading the race by three laps from his team mate, Dalmas.

A deserved 1-2 finish was in prospect until the leading car hit trouble at midday. The top of the right-front suspension damper collapsed, causing the car to sag on that corner – which allowed the anti-roll bar lever to over-travel and resulted in the throttle lever jamming wide open. Lehto hit the wall hard in the Porsche curves, escaping the crash with a gashed knee and mild concussion.

The remaining car, race-engineered by Schnitzer's Hans Reiter, stepped up to the lead. Although the last-surviving Toyota closed in during the afternoon, Reiter was sure his drivers had the matter in hand. The Toyota's charge was stopped by a puncture, anyway, and Martini took the BMW under the chequer more than a lap ahead. It was a fourth victory for Dalmas in eight years. The car established an extraordinary record for the least time spent stationary in the pits – just over 33 minutes.

Afterwards the Schnitzer team continued its programme in the inaugural American Le Mans Series. Lehto/Steve Soper won BMW's comeback race at Sears Point and two more later in the summer but, having missed two events to do Le Mans, BMW lost the championship to Panoz. The LMR's career would end the following season with the same result in a series dominated by Audi.

338 LE MANS 24 HOURS 1990–99

LIGHTNING STRIKES THRICE

Toyota undertook a whole lot of preparation for this Le Mans and started as the odds-on favourite but – as in 1994, and again in 1998 – victory was snatched from the Japanese company in late-race drama. This time it was not a mechanical failure but a puncture that intervened with 55 minutes remaining when the GT-One of Toshio Suzuki, Ukyo Katayama and Keiichi Tsuchiya (above) might have been homing in on success at last.

Three new GT-Ones were built for this year's race with upgraded aerodynamics. Downforce was increased through subtle differences in the front-end and tail treatments and a redesigned underwing, while the radiator and intercooler ducting configurations were also new.

After the disasters of 1998, a TMG priority was to strengthen the gearbox internals. The gearbox was housed in a revised magnesium alloy casing, while the shift was changed to steering-wheel levers, while keeping a manual option open. TMG also undertook a weight-saving programme on its 600bhp DOHC V8 engine, revised its exhaust and turbo installations, and improved combustion efficiency and fuel economy.

Other changes were driven by the ACO's latest rules, aimed at equalizing performance in the newly redefined GTP (previously GT1) and LMP classes, such as a 90-litre fuel cell (reduced from 100). The weighty ABS and traction-control systems used in 1998 were now banned, so the 1999 cars were substantially lighter than their already svelte predecessors, allowing even more ballast low down in the chassis to perfect the handling.

In evolving the new specification, the team spent many days running Le Mans simulations and pounding round the Paul Ricard and Barcelona circuits (although a planned 24-hour test at Spa was snowed off). Come Prequalifying in early May, the new cars were a whopping six seconds faster than the 1998 versions. Optimistic rivals attributed some of this gain to the fact that the trackside kerbs had been removed for the ACO's 24-hour motorcycle race, and had not yet been replaced. Before returning for qualifying proper, Toyota took two cars back to Paul Ricard and put 4000 miles on both. With the kerbs reinstalled, they then went even quicker…

Martin Brundle's first pole position here was achieved with the first sub-3m30s lap since the last year of the high-downforce, F1-engined FIA Sportscars; the GT-One was now less than four seconds away from the TS010 of 1993 and reached 217mph (351kph) before Brundle hit the brakes at the first Mulsanne chicane. Thierry Boutsen completed an all-Toyota front row, and Katayama qualified eighth, complaining of traffic on his hot lap.

Both the front-row cars disputed the lead with the BMWs and the Mercedes in the early action. After Brundle's good work had been continued by Emmanuel Collard, Vicenzo Sospiri pitted the pole position GT-One for attention to its power-steering and gearshift hydraulic system, a fluid leak in which had damaged the gearbox internals. The gear cluster was replaced, and the delay cost 24 minutes. Now without power steering and with the manual shift mechanism engaged, the car resumed outside the top 10.

Brundle was making up the lost time when he ran over some debris on the track approaching the first chicane on the Mulsanne straight, and burst a tyre. The GT-One instantly swapped ends and he couldn't keep it out of the barriers. Brundle tried to get back to the pits, but now both rear tyres were flat, and the gearbox was breached by being dragged along the track surface. He only made it as far as Indianapolis.

Boutsen/Allan McNish/Kelleners took up the challenge, but Kelleners was delayed just after 8pm when the steering wheel gearshift malfunctioned. Shortly before half-time, Boutsen was charging in second place, a lap behind the leading BMW, when he made a classic sportscar racing mistake. He made a split-second decision to pass Michel Maisonneuve's GT2 Porsche, rather than follow it all the way through the right-left-right of the Dunlop chicane. The Toyota's carbon-carbon brakes were much too good for the heavier, iron-braked Porsche, and the GT-One was punted very hard into the wall. Repairs to the barriers caused a long full-course yellow, but the consequences were more serious for Boutsen. He broke some vertebrae in his back and was helicoptered to hospital in Paris, where he decided never to race again.

The sole-surviving Toyota moved up to third, but was now four laps behind the leading BMW. Its Japanese drivers had not only been on a circumspect lap-time schedule, but seemed to have taken themselves out of the game by insisting on fresh tyres at every fuel stop, instead of running two shifts per set like all the other front-runners. This alone had accounted for two of the lost laps. Nevertheless, the policy almost paid off on Sunday afternoon when one BMW was delayed, and the other eliminated. The car completed the 23rd hour still a lap behind the leader, but with a fuel stop in its pocket. Katayama was told to go flat-out, and Toyota's computers predicted that it would be too close to call at the finish…

Five minutes later, the new leader had made the first of its two final stops, the gap was down to 80 seconds – and Katayama was baulked by Thomas Bscher's one-year-old BMW LM as he lapped it in the first Mulsanne chicane. The Toyota was forced over one of those high kerbs there. The left-rear tyre was punctured, but it didn't go down until Katayama was on the fast approach to Indianapolis. He caught the car and made it back to pit-lane, but the bid was finished by a four-minute delay.

And that was it for the wonderful Toyota GT-One. The project was terminated after a board decision to enter Formula 1 instead.

AUDI'S GREAT START

After this race, Audi's management executives and racing engineers expressed genuine surprise at the result achieved by their new LMP racecars, which finished third and fourth on the company's Le Mans début. This was Audi's first collaboration with Reinhold Joest's experienced and accomplished team, and all involved hoped it might lead to something big. They had no idea…

Having radically improved its brand image with successful rallying and then touring car projects, this was the company's first competition programme with purpose-built racing cars since the 1930s, when its four-rings logo had been carried by the fabled Auto Union Grand Prix cars. Audi Sport created both an LMP spyder and a GT-type coupé. Having started in mid-1997, the R8R (for 'roadster') LMP programme under project leader Wolfgang-Dieter Appel was much longer-established than the R8C (coupé) GTP, but the powertrain was common to both cars.

Audi Sport's engine group under Ulrich Baretzky chose a turbocharged V8 – the first purpose-built Audi/Auto Union race engine for 60 years. It was designed by Hartmut Diel and produced in the former NSU factory in Neckarsulm. The 3.6-litre, DOHC engine was managed by a Bosch MS2.8 ignition system and blown by twin Garrett turbos. With the air-inlet restrictors specified in the two classes, it made 610bhp in GTP and 550bhp in LMP, both at 7200rpm. And it was very strong from the outset: an early test engine completed a 53-hour Le Mans race simulation without failure on a dynamometer in the Audi Sport base in Ingolstadt.

The engine drove through a six-speed sequential-shift gearbox produced by Audi engineers with Rob Simmonds at Ricardo in England. On the R8R only, gearshifting was by a compressor-driven, pneumatic paddle system on the steering wheel that had originally been made for motorcycles by Erwin Gässner's Mega Line company.

The widely used inboard gearbox configuration generally meant that the whole rear axle had to be removed to make ratio changes. Therefore the rear wing of the R8R was mounted on the bodywork, allowing the axle and gearbox assembly to be changed in a few minutes – a well-kept secret at Audi Sport. In addition, the exhaust primaries were curved over the support frames of the semi-stressed engine, to facilitate engine changes.

A conventional sportscar advanced-composites hull, with the fuel cell between the seat back and the rear bulkhead and sidepod and nosebox attachments, was developed in conjunction with Dallara Automobili, which made the chassis. A key engineer left the R8R design group early in the project and it lost its way as a consequence. At Gian Paolo Dallara's suggestion, Tony Southgate was recruited to help the programme back on track, starting with an extended test behind closed doors at Most, in the Czech Republic.

The initial R8R aerodynamic design had been done by Michael Pfadenhauer in the Swiss National Aircraft tunnel at Emmen, with Fondmetal Technologies in a consultancy role. In January 1999, when Audi Sport commissioned its own wind tunnel in Ingolstaft, it was further developed by Southgate, who took advantage of the deletion in the LPM regulations of a flat-bottom requirement under the front of the monocoque to produce a bigger diffuser, raising the pedals to make space. The tail was lowered to work with the increased front downforce. The nosebox also bore two radiators, while each sidepod flowed air through a turbo intercooler. The R8R was one of the first sports-racing cars equipped with power steering.

The original prototype, which had extensive Audi styling, was revealed in late 1998 and undertook track testing at Hockenheim and elsewhere that led to the development of a 'Step 2' version with Southgate's more purposeful body design. This made its début in the Sebring 12 Hours in March 1999, when two cars were run under the Audi Sport Team Joest banner, and showed their durability by finishing third and fifth. New 'Step 3' racecars were built for Le Mans, incorporating further developments. The engine, transmission and rear suspension were unchanged, but much else of the Sebring specification was improved, and the Le Mans cars were smaller and lower.

The new cars showed satisfactory pace Prequalifying and in race week they were the ninth and 11th fastest qualifiers. Rinaldo Capello was half a second faster than Frank Biela, Audi's multiple touring car champion, who won an ACO trophy as this year's fastest rookie. Joest's team devised a race strategy aimed at holding these positions, seeing what transpired, moving up if practicable, and finishing first time out. However, there was serious concern over the latest 'Step 3' gearboxes. Like their colleagues running the R8Cs, Joest made sure it had several complete rear-end assemblies in its pit garages.

Sure enough, Laurent Aïello had to pit Capello's car (above) out of eighth place just after 7pm for a new gearbox, at the cost of less than 10 minutes behind the pit garage's closed doors. Rival teams had no idea that a gearbox had been replaced so fast. Michele Alboreto helped Aïello and Capello to recover sixth place during the night but, at 6:35am, he stopped for another fresh gearbox. An hour later, he lost 28 minutes to an electrical failure – and then Capello took his turn to break a gearbox. Finally, with 45 minutes remaining, Aïello's reactions were tested when the right-rear tyre went down as he was tanking towards Indianapolis.

All these dramas left the car in a distant fourth place at the end, 14 laps behind the sister car, having spent almost an hour longer stationary in pit-lane.

The podium finish by Biela/Emanuele Pirro/Didier Theys was relatively uneventful, and without a gearbox failure. This R8R unobtrusively ascended into the top five before dark and its only serious problems came with an unscheduled brake-disc change, a broken exhaust pipe, and an electronic engine management glitch that started at 9:25am and cost less than 15 minutes.

Audi's people were delighted. But not one predicted that the four-ring symbol would dominate Le Mans for years to come…

ALTERNATIVE AUDIS

Alongside its R8R prototypes, Audi Sport raced a pair of brand-new GTP coupés, designed and built in England with the same powertrains. Like one of the spyders, both closed-cockpit cars encountered a number of transmission failures. Neither finished.

The green light for the Audi R8C was given as late as September 1998. The project was assigned to Audi Sport UK, headed by Richard Lloyd and team manager John Wickham, and the car was designed and constructed by Racing Technology Norfolk (RTN) in the Hingham factory that Toyota had built for TOMS GB and sold to the VAG Group in July 1998. The design team was led by Peter Elleray, who worked closely on the aero with Audi Sport's technical consultant, Tony Southgate.

The carbonfibre/honeycomb monocoque structure, produced in RTN's in-house composites shop, bore the driver closer to the centre of the car than the R8R. The aero was designed by Southgate using the Emmen wind tunnel in Switzerland. The swoopy coupé body was fitted with gullwing doors and was very different from that of the spyder, with substantially longer front and rear overhangs, and the rear wing mounted on the gearbox. The narrower GTP tyres helped reduce drag and, in the further interests of low frontal area, the roofline was at the minimum height specified for GTP cars with a hump inbuilt to accommodate the driver's helmet.

The powertrain was identical to that of the R8R but the engine specification was altered to accommodate the different air restrictors. The version in the R8C made an extra 50-60bhp, but the GTP was as much as 30kg heavier.

The first R8C was shaken down at Snetterton early in April 1999. In its next track test at Paul Ricard, it encountered cooling airflow deficiencies that had to be addressed by enlarging the inlet in the nose and altering the other ducts. Consequently the R8Cs arrived very short of testing at Prequalifying, one of them after only a shakedown. A number of 'new-car' problems had to be overcome in these sessions before both set lap times good enough to return in June. However, the R8C showed very strong top speed, hitting 217mph (349kph) as it reached the chicane near the café on the Mulsanne straight.

The new, lighter 'Step 3' gearbox was made available to the GTP team only at the beginning of race week, and was therefore totally untried. While a gearbox could easily be changed in 10 minutes on the R8R, the job took half an hour on the R8C. And during qualifying, the revised gearbox proved to be big trouble: manufacturing errors led to shifting problems and several gearbox replacements. After limited track time, the R8Cs started 20th and 23rd, qualified by Andy Wallace and Stéphane Ortelli.

Only 20 minutes into the race, Wallace was in pit-lane for a new gearbox, losing 42 minutes. Against the odds, the replacement lasted eight hours until James Weaver had to stop half an hour after midnight. Perry McCarthy took over but was soon back with a gear-shifting fault. The car (below) was finally halted by a third transmission failure six hours from the finish; this time McCarthy couldn't get back for repairs.

The team's other car was long gone. After an early stop by Ortelli with a detached engine cover, he and Stefan Johansson had made up time but, 45 minutes after climbing into the cockpit, Christian Abt stopped just after Tertre Rouge at 7:50pm with the differential broken.

Afterwards Audi decided to go the LMP route to Le Mans success. However, development of the GTP version continued at RTN and would eventually lead to a Le Mans project for Bentley, VAG's luxury brand – and victory here in 2003.

HIGH FIVES IN GERMANY

LE MANS

MAYHEM AT MERCEDES

The Le Mans cars of the factory Mercedes-Benz team had been parked after only two hours in 1998. This time, they lasted less than five. Between them Mark Webber and Peter Dumbreck survived three terrifying somersaults, two for Webber – in qualifying and in the race morning warm-up – and another for Dumbreck in the race. At that point the surviving car was withdrawn. It was a very uncomfortable reminder for the company of the terrible Le Mans catastrophe back in 1955.

Exotic GT1 cars having been banned from the FIA GT series, AMG set out to design its 1999 GT Prototype as a dedicated Le Mans racecar, built to the 900kg minimum weight. Even so, the Mercedes CLR was mechanically similar to the CLK-LM of 1998 with the notable exception of its engine. This was the 5.7-litre, 32-valve GT108C V8, engineered in Stuttgart by Dietmar Kamczyk. Fitted with smaller air restrictors than the V8 of the 950kg CLK-LM, it made just over 600bhp at 7000rpm.

The lower half of Gerhard Ungar's DPS-manufactured monocoque was unchanged, but the upper section was altered in view of a new homologation rule that called for a load test on the complete cockpit section of a car, whereas previously the rollcage could be tested in isolation. The front section of the CLR's titanium rollcage was formed in carbonfibre composites, reducing mass high up in the chassis. The latest rules also allowed a narrower cockpit that gave the CLR a strikingly different appearance, accentuated by a flatter nose, lowered bodywork between the front and rear wheel-arches, and a lowered tail section.

1999

The aero testing was carried out in the University of Stuttgart wind tunnel, and Fondmetal Technologies was retained as a consultant on the package even though the Italian specialist undertook a similar role on the Audi R8R. The CLR had a shorter wheelbase than its GTP rivals, with longer front and rear overhangs. It had the same overall length as the CLK-LM, but, in the interests of drag reduction, the car was narrower and lower in height.

AMG began design work on the CLR in September 1998, and roll-out was in late February 1999. In the run-up to Prequalifying, the team tested very extensively, in the USA on the road course at Homestead and the high-speed oval at Fontana, and in Europe at Magny-Cours and the Hockenheimring. In all, the test mules covered almost 30,000 miles. Nevertheless, one of the three cars at Prequalifying was damaged when a front suspension link pulled out of the monocoque.

Much worse followed in race week. In Thursday qualifying, on the high-speed section between Mulsanne and Indianapolis corners, Webber was pulling out to pass a slower car on the approach to a brow when the CLR lifted clear of the ground. Then it tipped over at right angles to the track surface, landed on its right side, bounced back onto its wheels, and slammed into the barrier. The monocoque was undamaged and the car was repaired during Friday and made ready for the race, in which the CLRs were due to start from fourth, seventh and 10th positions.

But in the warm-up on Saturday morning, on his out-lap, Webber went airborne again (facing page). This time his car flipped end over end after cresting the Mulsanne 'bosse' (again in the wake of other cars), landed on its roof, and slid all the way to the Mulsanne corner escape road. Again the 21-year-old driver escaped merely with bruising from his harness.

Twin dive-planes (part of the team's wet-weather set-up) were added to the noses of the other CLRs while the team principals discussed whether or not to race. As it transpired, the decision to race might have cost Norbert Haug his job as the director of Mercedes-Benz Motorsport. However, senior-level Daimler-Benz executives had flown in that morning to watch the start. Acting on the advice of AMG's engineering team (and the drivers), they effectively took the decision out of Haug's hands.

Christophe Bouchut started one of the CLRs and, after being relieved

HIGH FIVES IN GERMANY | 345

LE MANS

by Nick Heidfeld, raced it in third place before Dumbreck was given his turn in the cockpit. On his third lap, Dumbreck was in a light collision with Manuel Monteiro's GT2 Porsche in the Virage Ford, but continued in hot pursuit of the second-placed Toyota. Two laps later, he crested the Mulsanne 'bosse' in its wake – and the CLR took off dramatically. It somersaulted through the air at treetop level, and landed on its wheels on the far side of the guardrail in an area from which, as luck would have it, trees had been felled a fortnight earlier. After seeing this shocking incident on the big trackside TV screens, people in the grandstands cheered when Dumbreck – dazed, bruised but otherwise undamaged – got himself out of the wreck.

In the sister car, Bernd Schneider had been very quick early in the race and had emerged in the lead after the first fuel stops, ahead of the Toyotas. The car had slipped back when Pedro Lamy had taken over but, after another aggressive shift by Schneider, Franck Lagorce was running fourth when he was summoned to the pits at 8:45pm for the car to be withdrawn.

The FIA acted swiftly. The governing body asked the French national body for a full report and instructed its Advisory Expert Group, chaired by Prof Sid Watkins, urgently to devise new technical regulations to prevent flat-bottom sports-racing cars going airborne. The fact remained that only AMG Mercedes had got it wrong. The team itself pulled the flawed CLRs from a planned ALMS campaign.

SIX OF THE BEST

Chrysler Vipers impressively filled the top six places in the newly redefined GTS division. The works Viper Team ORECA followed up its GT2 successes in 1997-98 with a 1-2 in the class, and Olivier Beretta/Karl Wendlinger/Dominique Dupuy (pictured below) finished 10th overall.

With the elimination of the GT1 category, the Viper was able to win FIA GT championship events outright. The Viper Engineering, ORECA and Caldwell development engineers stayed with their proven package for the 1999 season, confining themselves to detail upgrades. Additional cross-bracing further stiffened the engine frame. The Reynard wind tunnel in Shrivenham was again used for optimization of the air dam, the rear wing and a shorter diffuser. The engine was remapped to improve low-end acceleration and fuel consumption, the exhausts were shortened, and an oil cooler was added for the Borg-Warner transmission. The ABS (prohibited by the GTS regulations) was removed.

ORECA built three new-specification cars (with carbon brakes) for its own FIA GT programme and, in the series opener at Monza in April, Wendlinger/Beretta duly scored the first overall victory by a Viper in an International race.

Chamberlain Engineering purchased a new car and was running it alongside a late-1998 model in the FIA GT series. Another new chassis was sold to Paul Belmondo's new team under Claude-Yves Gosselin, which also bought a 1998 ORECA team car; these were prepared by Didier Faure in his base near Caën. ORECA sold another 1998 car to

CICA Concessionaires (bottom right) and it was prepared and operated here by Jean-Philippe Grand's Graff Racing team in Changé, near Le Mans. All eight of these Vipers raced in this Le Mans, and there might have been two more: Jean-Luc Maury-Laribière's failed scrutineering at Prequalifying, when the UK-based Brookspeed team's unfinished road car conversion completed only one flying lap.

Viper Team ORECA, now with Pierre Dieudonné added to its management team, took up two automatic entries. In qualifying, Beretta beat his 1998 lap time by more than three seconds to take the GTS pole, ahead of team-mate Marc Duez, Emmanuel Clérico in the older Belmondo chassis (repaired after a big Prequalifyng accident), Jean-Philippe Belloc in the third ORECA car, and Ni Amorim for Chamberlain Engineering.

Beretta/Wendlinger/Dupuy dominated the class from start to finish with an almost perfect run, always with the upper hand over their team mates. The on-track challenge of Duez/Justin Bell/Tommy Archer, already marred by a puncture, evaporated at 10am when Archer went off the track and damaged the gearbox. ORECA's crew replaced the transmission in only 35 minutes – without losing second place.

At noon on Sunday, all eight Vipers were still racing. But then David Donohue stopped the third-placed ORECA car, shared with Belloc and Soheil Ayari, on the Mulsanne straight with a broken engine. Amorim, co-driven by John Hugenholtz and Tony Seiler, picked up third place for Hugh Chamberlain's team, ahead of the Mello-Breyner brothers in the CICA entry. Clérico, Jean-Claude Lagniez and Guy Martinolle (pictured above in the pits) finished fourth for Belmondo after Clérico had had to drive half a lap to pit-lane with the car's right-rear wheel missing.

Chamberlain's second Viper gave team manager Derek Kemp a fraught Saturday evening with persistent electrical problems and pitstops for engine sump and gear-selector replacements. It never recovered, and finished a solid last, 29 laps behind Belmondo's newer car. This had to be repaired twice after being put off the track by its owner on Saturday evening and by Tiago Monteiro on Sunday morning.

Back in the FIA GT championship, the ORECA-built Vipers won all 10 races. Nine of these fell to the works team, and Wendlinger/Beretta were again crowned as the joint champions.

A DÉBUT VICTORY

Porsche's only interest in this race was in supplying an engine for one of the Courage prototypes and watching over a dozen customers racing in the GTS and GT classes. Its eight cars were no match for the Vipers in GTS, but there was no opposition to the four naturally aspirated Porsches in the GT division, which was won by 25 laps by the débutant Manthey Racing team, whose car (above) was raced by Uwe Alzen, Patrick Huisman and Luca Riccitelli.

During 1998, Porsche had replaced its 993-shape 911 passenger car with the totally reworked 996-series, which started to become available this season in a racing version known as the 911 GT3. This was based on the current Supercup specification, with new valve gear for the 3.6-litre M96/77 engine yielding an extra 40bhp at higher RPM, bigger brakes, a modified 'uniball' suspension system, and carbonfibre fenders, doors and engine cover. Porsche's customer competition director, former Le Mans winner Jürgen Barth, used this race effectively to announce that the order book was now open, and was actively supporting the first two customers here.

Olaf Manthey, running his new 911 GT3 out of Rheinbreitbach, south-east of Bonn, enjoyed a great weekend as the car raced almost faultlessly throughout. Having spent only 49 minutes stationary in pit-lane, it finished 13th overall – with four GTS Vipers in its wake.

Pictured in the pits, the other 911 GT3 was entered by Dave Maraj's five-year-old Champion Racing team (from Pompano Beach, Florida), which decided to take up an automatic entry, gained in the inaugural Petit Le Mans race the previous October, for its first foray overseas. Substantial factory support for Maraj included drivers Bob Wollek, Dirk Müller and Bernd Mayländer, but they suffered all weekend: a 40-minute gearbox repair on Saturday evening, rear-end damage caused by a puncture at nightfall, a 50-minute gearbox replacement in the small hours, off-track excursions by Mayländer and Wollek, and finally a seized wheelbearing. They were glad to see the flag.

The other Porsches in LM-GT were relatively slow, 993-shape, 3.75-litre 911 RSRs entered out of Boulogne by Thierry Perrier and out of the Isle of Man by Gerard McQuillan. Both failed to qualify under the 125

1999

percent regulation, but the ACO used its discretion to allow Perrier's car onto the grid. It survived Michel Nourry's moment in one of the Mulsanne straight chicanes to finish another four laps down.

BMW'S BACK-UPS

After being used in late 1998 as test hacks, BMW Motorsport's two V12LM chassis were sold to privateers Thomas Bscher and Kazumichi Goh. Bscher renewed his relationship with David Price, forming Price+Bscher Racing to contest the new ALMS. DPR also prepared the Team Goh car for Le Mans, using BMW Motorsport-prepared, 6-litre V12s similar to those of the factory team.

For the new season Williams engineer Gordon Day (on loan to DPR) retained the chassis, powertrain installation and most of the running gear of the V12LM's post-1998 Le Mans package, as well as the underbody airflows to the radiators. However, aero consultant Peter Stevens heavily revised the upper-surface aerodynamics. Using Williams wind-tunnel data as a baseline, he redeveloped the nose shape and the underwing profile, added underwing strakes, reshaped the front edge of the sidepods, and developed a bigger and more adjustable rear wing. All were made by DPR's sister company, DPS Composites. Meanwhile a 90-litre fuel cell was fitted to comply with the LMP rules.

After testing at Silverstone and Paul Ricard, the package was race-tested in March in the Sebring 12 hours, where Bscher's V12LM was crashed by Steve Soper.

This car (bottom) was again co-driven at Le Mans by Soper, who had raced it here 12 months before, and Bill Auberlen. They ran in the top 10 from the fifth hour onwards. This was despite Auberlen's curious difficulty negotiating the Nissan chicane: he lost time in the gravel there just before dark, and was in the escape road four times during the night, and once again in the morning…

Soper, who drove the maximum 14 hours, put the car in line for a podium finish, but his outstanding individual performance was spoiled by a 45-minute stop for a clutch replacement with four hours to run. In the final hour, Bscher intervened in the outcome of the race when he baulked Ukyo Katayama's second-placed Toyota, and apologetically blamed clutch problems for the manoeuvre. The car finished fifth, only a lap away from the second of the Audis.

The Japanese-owned BMW was 15th fastest in qualifying, fractionally quicker than it had managed as a works entry in 1998, in the hands of Hiro Matsushita, IndyCar driver and heir to the Pioneer fortune. It also had a reliable race after Hiroki Katoh's first-corner collision with Johnny O'Connell's Panoz, but lost time in an extended brake-pad change soon after 2am. The car lasted until 11:15am, when Akihiko Nakaya rolled to a halt on the Mulsanne straight with no drive.

In September, Price+Bscher's BMW finished fourth in an SWC event

LE MANS

on the Nürburgring but, in the ALMS, it secured only two points-scoring finishes. The partnership broke up at the end of the season when DPR committed to a long-term deal with Panoz, but Bscher would run his car at Le Mans one more time the following June.

Team Goh ran its car (above) to third place at the end of the season in the Fuji 1000 and then announced a partnership for 2000 with Dome Company. The Japanese constructor heavily modified the V12LM, but it was never raced again.

COURAGE-NISSAN PROGRESS

Courage Compétition brought three cars to the finish inside the top 10, led in sixth place by the latest Nissan-engined C52 (left) raced by former F1 drivers Alex Caffi, Andrea Montermini and Domenico 'Mimmo' Schiattarella.

The C52 was an evolution of the C51 and the same monocoques were used, but NISMO financed many upgrades, engineered by Paolo Catone and including the entire powertrain from the 1998 Nissan R390 GT1. The twin-turbo VRH35L V8 delivered more power this year for less fuel, with a new camshaft design and other improvements made in Japan. The suspension was reworked to handle a switch from Michelin to Bridgestone tyres, a modified rear diffuser required relocating the rear chassis bulkhead, the nose and cockpit surround were revised, and a smaller rollover structure was fitted. The changes delivered a four-second improvement in lap time relative to 1998.

Race-managed by Mario Cugnola and Chris Goodwin, the three Italians ran strongly but lost 23 minutes in two night-time stops for the brake system to be bled and the left-front wheelbearings to be replaced. Further time was lost at sunrise when the gearshift fell apart in Schiattarella's hand, putting him onto the beach in the Dunlop curve.

The other C52 (above) was entered by NISMO alongside its R391 racecars, but operated by a Courage crew led by Catone. Raced by Fredrik Ekblom/Didier Cottaz/Marc Goossens, it had to have two starter motors replaced over the course of the weekend and, like its stablemate, was hampered by fading brakes. The car was headed for seventh place with 70 minutes remaining when Cottaz was squeezed onto a beach. Hurried repairs back in pit-lane cost 33 minutes and the position.

'PESCA' TAKES HIS BOW

Henri Pescarolo finally discarded the faithful Courage C36 and took over the C50 that had raced here 12 months before. He sourced 3-litre Porsche engines from Michel Demont at Joest Racing, and commissioned Daniel Vergnes's Promotion Racing in Champagné to prepare and operate the Le Filière Elf entry. Before the race, Vergnes had to strengthen the nosebox to pass the latest crash test, and also reworked the rollover structure. Pictured below, the C50 proved dependable all weekend save for a 26-minute delay in the small hours while the crew replaced the left-rear hub carrier. Co-driven by Michel Ferté and Patrice Gay, the indomitable 'Pesca' finished ninth in his record 33rd (and final) Le Mans.

LE MANS

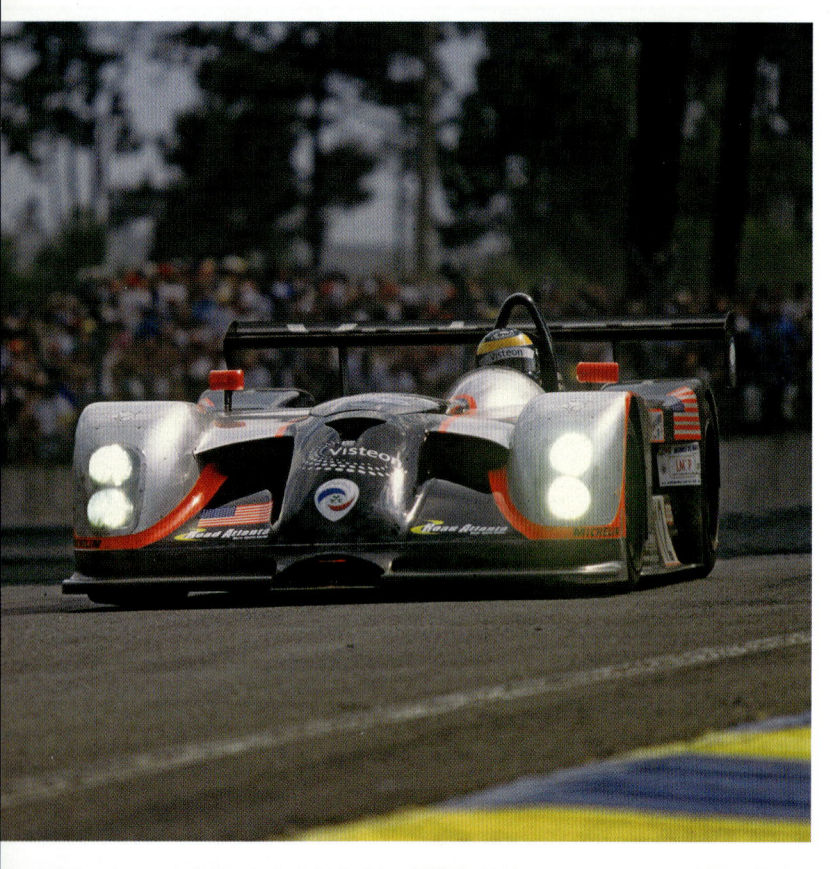

PANOZ AL FRESCO

Panoz Motorsports showed the scale of its ambition this year by taking its unique front/mid-engine philosophy into the LMP category. The Anglo-American enterprise brought both its new cars to the finish, led by David Brabham, Eric Bernard and Robert 'Butch' Leitzinger (below).

The new car was designed by Andy Thorby, who had been recruited by Panoz Motorsports after the 1998 Le Mans to draw a rear/mid-engined Le Mans Prototype, powered by a purpose-produced Cosworth engine. However, this project chafed against the all-American philosophy of Panoz. It was dropped in December and, instead, Thorby and Martin Reed reworked the GT-1 racecar as an LMP.

Working with the C&B Consultants aerodynamics agency in Poole, Thorby developed spyder bodywork in the wind tunnels of the Jordan Formula 1 team and Glasgow University, keeping the car as low as possible and incorporating a single-seater-style rollhoop to minimize interference to the airflow to the rear wing; this configuration was like that of the BMW LMR, although with the driver on the other side of the car. The nose section was reshaped to accommodate both a low-drag set-up for Le Mans and a higher-downforce configuration for the ALMS. The engine air feed was relocated to the upper surface of the nose section, using a NACA duct, and the central duct down on the splitter now fed air to the front brakes.

Thorby retained the central component of the GTR-1 chassis, reinforcing it at DPS Composites to compensate for the absence of

352 **LE MANS 24 HOURS 1990–99**

a roof, but extended the wheelbase and widened the track dimensions. These changes achieved a static front/rear weight distribution similar to those of rear/mid-engined prototypes. New suspension geometry was needed but the GTR-1 upright and hub packages could be retained.

After its experiences with Roush Engines, Panoz Motorsports appointed Robert Yates Engine Development to assemble its 6-litre pushrod Ford V8s. The company in Mooresville, North Carolina, evolved broader torque and power characteristics, at the sacrifice of some top-end performance. Dave Kriska's Yates engine made about 620bhp at 7200rpm with the ACO-specified air-inlet restrictors, and was again run with Zytek electronic control systems. The rear-mounted longitudinal Xtrac six-speed gearbox was retained.

The Panoz LMP débuted in the second race of the inaugural ALMS on its home circuit of Road Atlanta, finishing fifth only a lap behind the winning R&S. A second chassis was then completed for the 'works' team, managed by Tony Fox, to take to Prequalifying. The LMP was built right down to the 900kg weight and David Brabham amazed onlookers with a lap time that was only beaten by one of the Toyotas. Come race week, despite using a higher-RPM qualifying engine, Brabham went 1.8 seconds slower, and lined up fifth.

On Saturday, this Panoz raced strongly into the night, but then the normally robust transmission overheated and two gearbox replacements were needed, the first just after 1am. Ten hours later, the drivers had retrieved sixth position but slipped back again when the team tried replacing the gearbox oil cooler, before fitting another fresh gearbox. Even then, the drivers finished the race with problematical gearshifts.

In the sister car (pictured exiting the Esses), Johnny O'Connell collided with Hiroki Katoh's BMW in the very first corner, and had to pit for the front bodywork to be secured with tape. The car, co-driven by Jan Magnussen/Max Angelelli, was back in the top dozen just after dark, when it developed an oil leak. About 105 minutes was lost in tracing and replacing a split oil pipe. Engine overheating contributed to further unscheduled pitstops, and both O'Connell and Magnussen had a couple of spins.

Despite these setbacks, the cars achieved the first 100 percent finish for the team in three attempts at Le Mans. Later in the summer, the Panoz LMP won ALMS races at Mosport and Portland before Brabham/Wallace/Bernard triumphed in the Petit Le Mans in October.

AN 'ATMO' SURPRISE

Even in June 1998, given the parlous state of Japan's economy and Nissan's own financial situation, it was unclear whether the company would contest the 1999 Le Mans. Nissan's difficulties were well known, and it was already negotiating a bail-out with Renault. Yet there was a defiant final fling at Le Mans, where NISMO fielded a pair of brand-new prototypes with new 'atmo' race engines. One was destroyed in qualifying, but the other (above) was impressive until being sidelined with head gasket failure.

It came as a surprise (certainly to TWR) in late summer 1998 when NISMO principal Kunihiko Kakimoto revealed that an all-new Nissan LMP was being produced in England by G Force Precision Engineering, and that a NISMO design office had been set up near its Fontwell factory on the south coast. G Force had recruited for the project Nigel Stroud, Doug Skinner and Chris Rushforth, all of whom had worked on the Panoz GT1 racecars at Reynard. A core group of 10 designers was evenly split between G Force and NISMO, the latter under chief designer Tsutomu Nagashima. Most of the components making up the R391, including the carbon/honeycomb hulls, were manufactured by G Force Composites on the same premises.

A requirement of NISMO's design brief was a semi-stressed, naturally aspirated engine, in place of the turbocharged motors of the R390 GT1 racecars. NISMO had started development of such a power unit for racing in 1997. The 5-litre VRHSOA engine was a DOHC V8, and was essentially the same as Nissan's concurrent 4-litre, Infiniti-branded Indy Racing League engine. It was fitted at Le Mans with a Nissan Electronics (formerly JECS) management system, making 620bhp at 7000rpm. A magnesium alloy bellhousing casting provided the interface between the engine and the NISMO/Xtrac sequential-shift, six-speed transverse gearbox, an evolution of the 1998 unit produced for the R390.

Stroud was responsible for the aero, and undertook the wind-tunnel testing at MIRA, then at Imperial College in London. A notable feature of the final package was the absence of an overhead airbox for the engine, which was fed by low-level inlets on either side of the cockpit. More inlet ducts cooled the side-mounted water radiators and carbon brake assembles.

The first R391 was built through January 1999 and had its first test at Paul Ricard in late February. Two cars were completed in time for Prequalifying, and proved to be more than three seconds faster round the lap than the R390s.

The team had a big setback in the opening qualifying session on the Wednesday when Eric van der Poele crashed heavily at Tertre Rouge with his throttle jammed wide open. The R391 smacked into the barrier with its left-front, and the impact moved the barrier back more than a metre. The session was red-flagged and marshals took almost an hour to extricate the driver, who had fractured several vertebrae and would spend the next month in traction. The monocoque was damaged beyond repair.

The remaining car, driven by Satoshi Motoyama/Erik Comas/Michael Krumm, qualified 12th and ran well in the early stages, climbing as high as fourth at nightfall despite Krumm's trip onto the beach at one of the Mulsanne chicanes. At 10:20pm, Comas was in the pits for a new nosecone after another incident, and five positions were lost. The run was ended an hour later when a head-gasket failure parked Motoyama on the verge in the Porsche curves.

1999

LOLAS WANTING

Three new Lola prototypes started this race but none finished, although the one pictured above was competitive in the early stages (and not by cutting corners!).

The sharp revival of sportscar racing on both sides of the Atlantic gave Martin Birrane's newly acquired Lola Cars International a market for the first Lola-branded 'customer' sports-racer since 1992, and the Huntingdon company created the B98/10 for a wide variety of engines. The chief designer was former F1 engineer Peter Weston, who started out by modeling the rival Ferrari and R&S prototypes before producing a one-third-scale model of his own car for a four-month programme in the Cranfield Institute wind tunnel. The outer skin of the advanced-composites monocoque also served as the bodywork, which was completed by front splitter/diffuser, floor and tail panel assemblies. Air was ducted to rear-mounted water coolers from the flow around the sides of the cockpit opening. Each monocoque was produced as a generic structure with tubular steel A-frame supports and Lola supplied a dedicated bellhousing for Ford V8, Judd V10 and Porsche flat-six powertrains. The sequential-shift, six-speed transverse gearbox was a sportscar derivative of the one used in Lola's contemporary ChampCar single-seater, originally developed in conjunction with Hewland.

The first car was completed in December 1998 and seven more were sold. The three that came through Le Mans Prequalifying were being raced by the DAMS and Kremer teams in the SRWC, and by Konrad Motorsport in the ALMS. The Konrad car was fitted with an extended tail section, and all three were equipped with rear diffusers that were allowed under the ACO's 1999 rules.

Jean-Paul Driot's DAMS team fitted its car with a 4-litre, 40-valve Judd GV4 engine (evolved from the V10 that had powered Lolas here in 1992), making 620bhp at 10,800rpm. Regular DAMS driver Jean-Marc Gounon had been offered a factory Mercedes drive for this race (which he didn't get to start), so it was Franck Montagny who qualified the black car 12th on the grid. Co-driven by Christophe Tinseau and David Terrien, the DAMS Lola started well, but it was then delayed by starter motor problems, and succumbed to an engine failure after five hours. Later Gounon was back in the Lola when it won the four rounds of this year's SRWC that did not fall to Ferraris.

Erwin Kremer's Lola was equipped with a 6-litre, 16-valve Ford V8, rated at 740bhp at 7400rpm. The Roush-prepared engine developed overheating problems in qualifying and Didier de Radiguès ended up 20th on the grid, co-driven by Tomas Saldana and Grant Orbell. Radiguès had the car in 14th place after the opening hour and, although he later ran it out of fuel at the bottom of pit-lane, it reached 10th before 2am. But then the crew had to spend 66 minutes rebuilding

HIGH FIVES IN GERMANY 355

356 LE MANS 24 HOURS 1990-99

the gearbox. Two laps after rejoining the race, Saldana was back to report that the gearbox had broken again. The car is pictured at bottom left.

Franz Konrad's entry had started the ALMS season with the turbo V8 from the 1997 Lotus Elise GT1 project. After this had overheated badly at Daytona and Sebring, he replaced it here with another Roush-prepared Ford V8. He was not very happy when this also overheated in qualifying, perplexing Roush engineer Tom Albert, who had been sent to oversee the Kremer and Konrad installations. Former race winner Jan Lammers qualified 21st and raced the car as part of the 'Racing for Holland' programme with Tom Coronel and Peter Kox. It was delayed early on by a smoky gearbox oil leak (as pictured at the tail of the group). After dark, it was spun by Kox at Mulsanne corner and then put into the gravel by Coronel at one of the Mulsanne chicanes, causing damage to the rear bodywork and the exhaust system that took 50 minutes to repair. A broken gear selector during the night was followed by a terminal gearbox failure at 8:40am.

THE LAST 333 SP

The ACO had expected at least four Ferrari 333 SPs this year, but only one turned up for race week. The last such car to race at Le Mans, it was parked with a broken engine before it was dark.

The Texan-based Doyle-Risi team decided not to take up two automatic entries, gained through winning the P1 division in the 1998 race and Petit Le Mans later that season. JB Racing did the Prequalifying sessions with two cars, one with the latest Michelotto body kit, the other with a body developed by Jean-Pierre Jabouille in the St Cyr wind tunnel in Paris, featuring an extended engine cover and revisions to the nose section. Both prequalified easily but the team, disappointed with the lap times, decided not to race either.

Instead, it fielded a brand-new 333 SP (the 30th of 41 that would eventually be produced) that had been delivered a couple of weeks after Prequalifying. It arrived for its maiden race after almost a week of testing at Paul Ricard, where it had been equipped with the latest, high-compression version of the V12 and a strengthened gearbox. In qualifying proper, Jérôme Policand went a full two seconds faster than he had managed in either of the older cars the previous month. His best time would have landed pole position in 1997 but, these days, it was good enough only for 13th.

Mauro Baldi started the race but did not complete his double shift because a pinion in the revised gearbox broke after less than an hour. JB's crew spent 75 minutes replacing the transmission. The fruitless efforts of Policand, Baldi and Christian Pescatori to claw back a 22-lap deficit were terminated at dusk by a broken camshaft.

Consolation for JB Racing came at the end of the season as Emmanuel Collard and Vincenzo Sospiri successfully defended their ISRS title in the new Sports-Racing World Cup, securing the second of a hat-trick of championships. However, the five-year-old concept was now uncompetitive with the works Audis and BMWs in the ALMS.

LE MANS

BANG! BANG! BANG!

Three Riley & Scott Mk3 LMP cars contested this race and they were all back in their transporters before half-time with broken engines.

The Indianapolis constructor launched its Series 2 Mk3 this season and immediately returned to Victory Lane with Dyson Racing, winning the Daytona 24 Hours for the third time in four years. The victory by Andy Wallace, 'Butch' Leitzinger and Elliott Forbes-Robinson was followed by another in the third race of the USRRC series at Lime Rock by Wallace/James Weaver – and that was enough for R&S to win the championship, because it was then cancelled due to lack of entries.

The Series 2 chassis was modified in a number of areas, notably with the introduction of an inboard Hewland LSG transverse gearbox in place of the former longitudinal unit. In addition, a new bulkhead was designed for the back of the monocoque, with a recess allowing the powertrain to be moved forward. This required a different fuel cell configuration, and relocating the rear wing support struts to mount on the differential casing. The changes brought the mass of the gear cluster within the car's wheelbase, lowered the height of the car's centre of gravity, saved 10kg of weight, and improved the efficiency of the rear diffuser now permitted in the LMP rules.

In November 1998, R&S had produced 16 of its effective Mk3 racecars, and needed a European sales and service agent. The company appointed Thierry Lecourt and Philippe Gache, who had run a car in that year's ISRS, and set up a satellite base in the Signes industrial park near the Paul Ricard circuit.

Only one of the Le Mans cars was built from scratch to the new specification, to the order of Autoexe Motorsports, a Tokyo-based Japanese enterprise led by Yojiro Terada. Gache's 1998 car and another 'works' entry (an unraced spare IMSA WSC chassis from 1997) were rebuilt with the new kit. The oldest car was built to a 950kg minimum weight (allowing bigger engine air restrictors), the others to 900kg. Solution F, Eric Chantriaux's Provence company that had prepared Gache's R&S, was commissioned to build and service the 6-litre Ford V8 engines, which were equipped with Magneti Marelli electronics. The quoted output in all the cars was 650bhp at 7500rpm.

Franck Fréon was the fastest R&S driver in qualifying with the lightweight Autoexe entry (below), which had previously raced only in the Sebring 12 Hours in March. After early shifts in the race by Fréon and Terada – competing here for the 20th time – Robin Donovan pitted at 6:10pm with an inoperative clutch. Adjustments took 15 minutes and Fréon resumed, but soon the team had to invest 90 minutes in replacing the clutch. The car was well down the order when the engine blew at 2am.

Pictured at right, Gache's Mk3 was afflicted early on by an oil leak that took three hours to fix, and lost its engine four hours after resuming. After a strong triple shift by Marco Apicella, the other R&S Europe entry (above) lost 50 minutes to a broken fuel pump during the evening, before its V8 went the same way as the others at nightfall. It had been its only race.

After Le Mans, Autoexe's R&S competed only in the Fuji 1000 in Japan at season's end, while Gache's car did not finish any SRWC events. Things were better in the United States: Dyson Racing won only once in the ALMS, but consistent results delivered the Drivers title for Forbes-Robinson and Leitzinger.

The genial 'Terada-san', by the way, was one of only four men to start every Le Mans in the decade covered by this book, the others being Henri Pescarolo, Bob Wollek (who finished nine times) and Pierre Yver. His co-driver in the Autoexe R&S, Donovan, would also have started 10 races had the Matrix survived Prequalifying in 1997.

LE MANS

1999

PORSCHE THRASHED

Eight outdated Porsche 911 GT2s had no chance in the GTS division. The fastest in qualifying was seven seconds slower than the Viper on the class 'pole'. The best finisher was 32 laps behind the class winner (and 24 laps behind the new GT-winning Porsche GT3). Pictured at top left, this was Franz Konrad's car that had lasted only two laps 12 months before, driven this time by its owner with Americans Charles Slater and Peter Kitchak. The latter left the track six times during the race, causing delays of varying duration, and his co-drivers also had off-track excursions.

Freisinger Motorsport gained an automatic entry, having won GT2 in the 1998 Petit Le Mans, and lined up two cars. One of them was trashed against the wall in the Porsche curves by Manfred Jurasz at the first opportunity, but the other (following in the photograph) went very well, leaving the other Porsches far behind. Michel Ligonnet/Wolfgang Kaufmann/Ernst Palmberger reached 16th overall before half-time but then a driveshaft failure intervened, and finally the engine broke soon after dawn.

The fastest Porsche in qualifying was one of the Larbre/Chéreau entries (top right), driven by Patrice Goueslard, but the car lost more than five hours to a major rear-end rebuild on Saturday evening after a broken flywheel caused havoc in the engine bay. The car continued after the mechanics' heroics, and took the flag, but was unclassified. Jack Leconte's other car was quick when Jean-Pierre Jarier was driving but broke its engine just after 2am.

The Roock brothers also entered two Porsches, one of which finished (bottom left) after delays caused by a gearbox rebuild, a spin by Claudia Hürtgen into the Dunlop chicane gravel trap, and an engine-bay fire that startled André Ahrlé. The other car received two driveshaft replacements before its engine blew at 10:45am, causing another fire that was quickly extinguished.

The Monteiro brothers' 911 GT2 (right) had already lost a lot of time to an oil leak when Michel was in a sideswipe collision with one of the Mercedes on Saturday evening. Just after 3am, Michel Maisonneuve was relying on a small piece of road for braking at the Dunlop chicane when he suddenly found Thierry Boutsen's Toyota in the way, and could not avoid hitting the GT-One very hard up the rear.

HIGH FIVES IN GERMANY

BMW vient, Toyota vient, Chrysler et Mercedes viennent, Nissan vient et Audi vient.

Et vous, vous venez ?

24 HEURES DU MANS 99
12 et 13 JUIN - 16h00

Ne laissez pas la légende s'écrire sans vous.

HOURLY RACE POSITIONS

Prequalifying		Start	Time	Car	No	Drivers	1	2	3	4	5	6	7	8	9	10	11	12	13	14	15	16	17	18	19	20	21	22	23	24
1	3:31.857	Brundle	1	3:29.930	Toyota GT-One	1	Brundle/Collard/Sospiri	3	4	3	3	12	17	27	32	DNF															
5	3:33.174	Boutsen	2	3:30.801	Toyota GT-One	2	McNish/Boutsen/Kelleners	2	2	1	2	2	2	1	2	2	2	2	8	DNF											
4	3:32.867	Lehto	3	3:31.209	BMW V12 LMR	17	Kristensen/Lehto/Müller	4	1	2	1	1	1	2	1	1	1	1	1	1	1	1	1	1	1	1	1	DNF			
6	3:33.864	Schneider	4	3:31.541	Mercedes-Benz CLR	6	Schneider/Lagorce/Lamy	1	3	4	5	DNF																			
2	3:31.941	Brabham	5	3:33.711	Panoz LM-P-1 Roadster S	12	Brabham/Bernard/Leitzinger	8	7	7	8	5	7	7	7	7	12	9	9	8	8	7	6	6	6	6	9	8	8	8	7
23	3:44.982	Dalmas	6	3:33.931	BMW V12 LMR	15	Dalmas/Martini/Winkelhock	6	6	6	6	3	3	3	3	3	3	3	2	2	2	2	2	2	2	2	2	1	1	1	1
14	3:38.227	Bouchut	7	3:34.138	Mercedes-Benz CLR	5	Heidfeld/Dumbreck/Bouchut	5	5	5	4	9	DNF																		
3	3:32.426	Katayama	8	3:34.755	Toyota GT-One	3	Katayama/T.Suzuki/Tsuchiya	11	10	9	6	6	5	4	4	4	4	4	4	3	3	3	3	3	3	3	3	3	3	2	2
11	3:37.509	Capello	9	3:34.891	Audi R8R	7	Alboreto/Aiello/Capello	9	9	8	15	14	12	11	9	9	8	8	6	6	6	9	8	8	7	6	4	5	4	4
*	3:39.730	Webber		3:35.301	Mercedes-Benz CLR	4	Webber/Gounon/Tiemann	DNS																							
8	3:36.390	Pirro	10	3:35.371	Audi R8R	8	Pirro/Biela/Theys	10	11	12	11	4	5	4	5	5	5	5	3	4	4	4	4	4	4	4	5	4	3	3	3
10	3:36.955	Motoyama	11	3:36.043	Nissan R391	22	Comas/Krumm/Motoyama	7	8	10	7	7	4	9	14	DNF															
12	3:37.600	Tinseau	12	3:36.468	Lola B98/10	25	Montagny/Tinseau/Terrien	13	15	15	26	21	27	DNF																	
15	3:40.573	Policand	13	3:38.468	Ferrari 333 SP	29	Baldi/Pescatori/Policand	29	45	41	39	37	34	DNF																	
19	3:42.831	Kato	14	3:38.478	BMW V12 LM	19	Matsushita/Katoh/Nakaya	21	17	16	14	13	11	11	11	9	15	23	26	27	27	27	26	24	DNF						
22	3:44.350	Goossens	15	3:39.248	Courage C52	21	Cottaz/Goossens/Ekblom	12	11	10	8	6	6	7	7	7	7	7	8	7	7	7	7	6	7	7	8
9	3:36.577	Magnussen	16	3:39.519	Panoz LM-P-1 Roadster S	11	Magnussen/Angelelli/O'Connell	16	19	20	19	17	13	13	26	30	30	27	26	23	22	20	19	17	16	13	13	11	11	11
17	3:41.568	Auberlen	17	3:40.359	BMW V12LM	18	Soper/Bscher/Auberlen	15	13	13	12	10	9	8	8	8	6	6	5	5	5	5	5	5	5	4	5	5
18	3:42.785	Montermini	18	3:40.683	Courage C52	13	Caffi/Montermini/Schiattarella	17	14	13	11	10	10	10	11	10	10	9	9	8	8	8	7	6	6
27	3:48.406	Wallace	19	3:42.155	Audi R8C	10	Weaver/Wallace/McCarthy	45	42	37	35	31	28	26	23	24	29	30	28	25	23	22	25	DNF						
24	3:45.541	Radigues	20	3:42.906	Lola B98/10	27	Saldana/Orbell/Radiguès	14	16	17	16	15	14	15	12	12	10	19	25	28	28	29	DNF							
20	3:43.687	Lammers	21	3:43.973	Lola B98/10	26	Lammers/Kox/Coronel	41	40	33	32	23	22	19	29	27	25	23	20	21	20	19	17	19	24	25	25	24	23	24	DNF
21	3:43.786	Ortelli	22	3:45.202	Audi R8C	9	Johansson/Ortelli/Abt	40	20	19	21	DNF																			
29	3:50.274	Fréon	23	3:45.928	Riley & Scott LMP99	24	Terada/Fréon/Donovan	22	31	39	41	40	39	37	36	34	34	DNF													
26	3:47.996	M.Ferté	24	3:46.658	Courage C50	14	Pescarolo/M.Ferté/Gay	19	18	18	17	16	15	14	13	13	13	14	14	13	13	13	13	13	12	12	10	9	9	9
25	3:47.871	Gache	25	3:47.681	Riley & Scott Mk3	31	Gache/Formato/Thévenin	18	37	42	44	42	41	39	38	DNF															
28	3:48.884	Apicella	26	3:48.391	Riley & Scott Mk3	32	Apicella/Rosenblad/Lewis	20	24	24	23	29	35	35	DNF																
13	3:38.000	Poele		3:49.284	Nissan R391	23	Poele/A.Suzuki/Kageyama	DNS																							
*	3:57.225	Beretta	27	3:56.588	Chrysler Viper GTS-R	51	Wendlinger/Beretta/Dupuy	23	21	21	18	19	16	16	15	14	14	11	12	10	10	10	9	10	10	9	10	10	10
*	3:58.522	Belloc	28	3:57.113	Chrysler Viper GTS-R	52	Archer/Duez/Bell	24	22	22	20	18	18	17	16	15	15	12	11	11	11	11	15	14	12	12	12
33	4:01.875	Clérico	29	3:59.193	Chrysler Viper GTS-R	55	Clérico/Lagniez/Martinolle	34	32	31	27	25	20	20	18	17	17	16	14	14	14	17	16	16	16
31	3:59.361	Wendlinger	30	4:00.869	Chrysler Viper GTS-R	53	Donohue/Belloc/Ayari	25	22	22	20	19	18	18	17	16	16	13	12	12	12	12	11	11	16	DNF				
34	4:01.970	Amorim	31	4:00.984	Chrysler Viper GTS-R	56	Amorim/Hugenholtz/Seiler	26	25	26	24	28	24	24	22	21	21	20	18	16	16	15	15	16	16	14	14
40	4:07.024	Goueslard	32	4:03.498	Porsche 911 GT2 (993)	65	Chéreau/Goueslard/Yver	36	34	40	43	41	40	38	37	35	35	34	34	31	30	30	29	29	28	27	26	25	24	23	NC
43	4:12.072	Jarier	33	4:04.397	Porsche 911 GT2 (993)	67	Jarier/Bourdais/Thoisy	37	28	28	31	26	25	21	20	20	26	30	30	DNF											
32	4:01.480	Erdos	34	4:05.047	Chrysler Viper GTS-R	57	Erdos/Vann/Gläsel	42	44	43	40	38	36	35	34	33	33	33	32	29	28	27	26	24	23	22	22
38	4:04.253	Konrad	35	4:05.290	Porsche 911 GT2 (993)	64	Konrad/Kitchak/Slater	31	36	34	34	30	33	28	25	23	23	22	19	18	18	18	20	23	22	21	20	19	19
35	4:03.827	M.Mello	36	4:05.829	Chrysler Viper GTS-R	50	Mello-Breyner/Mello-Breyner/Mello-Breyner	35	33	32	33	27	26	25	24	22	22	21	17	17	17	16	16	17	17	15	15	15	15
37	4:04.085	Kaufmann	37	4:05.873	Porsche 911 GT2 (993)	61	Palmberger/Kaufmann/Ligonnet	30	29	29	25	22	21	18	17	18	16	21	22	DNF											
39	4:05.094	Belmondo	38	4:06.776	Chrysler Viper GTS-R	54	Belmondo/Monteiro/Rostan	32	30	30	30	32	30	29	27	25	24	22	19	19	19	21	20	19	19	18	17	17	17
41	4:07.207	Haupt	39	4:06.834	Porsche 911 GT2 (993)	63	Haupt/Robinson/Price	44	41	36	37	33	29	30	28	26	25	24	20	21	21	20	19	DNF						
36	4:03.846	Hürtgen	40	4:07.707	Porsche 911 GT2 (993)	62	Hürtgen/Ahrle/Vosse	33	43	45	42	39	37	34	32	32	31	29	26	26	26	25	23	23	22	21	20	20
44	4:12.717	Maisonneuve	41	4:09.709	Porsche 911 GT2 (993)	66	Monteiro/Monteiro/Maisonneuve	39	35	38	38	36	36	33	33	31	31	32	DNF												
42	4:11.629	Alzen	42	4:11.051	Porsche 911 GT3 (996)	81	Alzen/Huisman/Riccitelli	28	27	25	28	24	23	22	19	19	19	18	15	15	14	14	14	15	13	13	13
*	4:14.202	Müller	43	4:13.651	Porsche 911 GT3 (996)	80	Wollek/Mayländer/Müller	27	26	27	29	35	32	32	31	28	28	29	29	27	27	22	22	21	20	20	19	19
*	4:15.623	Iketani	44	4:15.793	Porsche 911 GT2 (993)	60	Lintott/Jurasz/Iketani	38	38	44	DNF																				
45	4:31.666	Perrier	45	4:27.657	Porsche 911 RSR (993)	84	Perrier/Ricci/Nourry	43	39	35	36	34	31	31	30	29	28	28	27	24	24	24	24	22	22	22	21	21	21
46	4:33.326	Neugarten	DNQ	4:31.206	Porsche 911 RSR (993)	83	McQuillan/Neugarten/Gleason	DNS																							

DNF Did not finish **DNQ** Did not qualify **DSQ** Disqualified **FS** Failed scrutineering **NC** Not classified as a finisher **RES** Reserve not required * Automatic entry

LE MANS

RACE RESULTS

Pos	Car	No	Drivers			Laps	Km	Miles	FIA Class	DNF
1	BMW V12 LMR	15	Yannick Dalmas (F)	Pierluigi Martini (I)	Joachim Winkelhock (D)	366	4982.974	3096.271	LMP	
2	Toyota GT-One	3	Ukyo Katayama (J)	Toshio Suzuki (J)	Keiichi Tsuchiya (J)	365	4971.215	3088.964	LM-GTP	
3	Audi R8R	8	Emanuele Pirro (I)	Frank Biela (D)	Didier Theys (B)	361	4911.143	3051.637	LMP	
4	Audi R8R	7	Michele Alboreto (I)	Laurent Aïello (F)	Rinaldo Capello (I)	347	4724.871	2935.893	LMP	
5	BMW V12 LM	18	Steve Soper (GB)	Thomas Bscher (D)	Bill Auberlen (USA)	346	4713.650	2928.921	LMP	
6	Courage C52	13	Alex Caffi (I)	Andrea Montermini (I)	'Mimmo' Schiattarella (I)	343	4660.565	2895.935	LMP	
7	Panoz LM-P-1 Roadster S	12	David Brabham (AUS)	Eric Bernard (F)	'Butch' Leitzinger (USA)	337	4587.348	2850.440	LMP	
8	Courage C52	21	Didier Cottaz (F)	Marc Goossens (B)	Fredrik Ekblom (S)	335	4551.747	2828.319	LMP	
9	Courage C50	14	Henri Pescarolo (F)	Michel Ferté (F)	Patrice Gay (F)	328	4466.596	2775.409	LMP	
10	Chrysler Viper GTS-R	51	Olivier Beretta (MC)	Karl Wendlinger (A)	Dominique Dupuy (F)	326	4439.021	2758.274	LM-GTS	
11	Panoz LM-P-1 Roadster S	11	Jan Magnussen (DK)	Max Angelelli (I)	Johnny O'Connell (USA)	324	4410.482	2740.541	LMP	
12	Chrysler Viper GTS-R	52	Tommy Archer (USA)	Marc Duez (B)	Justin Bell (GB)	319	4343.782	2699.096	LM-GTS	
13	Porsche 911 GT3 (996)	81	Uwe Alzen (D)	Patrick Huisman (NL)	Luca Riccitelli (I)	318	4320.392	2684.562	LM-GT	
14	Chrysler Viper GTS-R	56	Ni Amorim (P)	John Hugenholtz (NL)	Toni Seiler (CH)	315	4283.209	2661.458	LM-GTS	
15	Chrysler Viper GTS-R	50	Manuel Mello-Breyner (P)	Pedro Mello-Breyner (P)	Tomas Mello-Breyner (P)	313	4265.509	2650.459	LM-GTS	
16	Chrysler Viper GTS-R	55	Emmanuel Clérico (F)	Jean-Claude Lagniez (F)	Guy Martinolle (F)	310	4222.664	2623.837	LM-GTS	
DNF	Chrysler Viper GTS-R	53	David Donohue (USA)	Jean-Philippe Belloc (F)	Soheil Ayari (F)	304			LM-GTS	Engine
DNF	BMW V12 LMR	17	Tom Kristensen (DK)	JJ Lehto (SF)	Jörg Müller (D)	304			LMP	Accident
17	Chrysler Viper GTS-R	54	Paul Belmondo (F)	Tiago Monteiro (P)	Marc Rostan (F)	300	4083.442	2537.328	LM-GTS	
18	Porsche 911 GT2	64	Franz Konrad (A)	Peter Kitchak (USA)	Charles Slater (USA)	294	3995.933	2482.953	LM-GTS	
19	Porsche 996 GT3	80	Bob Wollek (F)	Bernd Mayländer (D)	Dirk Müller (D)	293	3980.274	2473.223	LM-GT	
20	Porsche 993 GT2	62	Claudia Hürtgen (D)	Andre Ahrle (D)	Vincent Vosse (B)	291	3956.120	2458.214	LM-GTS	
21	Porsche 993 RSR	84	Thierry Perrier (F)	Jean-Louis Ricci (F)	Michel Nourry (F)	289	3935.378	2445.326	LM-GT	
22	Chrysler Viper GTS-R	57	Thomas Erdos (BR)	Christian Vann (GB)	Christian Gläsel (D)	271	3683.086	2288.559	LM-GTS	
NC	Porsche 911 GT2	65	Jean-Luc Chéreau (F)	Patrice Gouesland (F)	Pierre Yver (F)	240			LM-GTS	Insufficient distance
DNF	Porsche 911 GT2	63	Hubert Haupt (D)	John Robinson (GB)	Hugh Price (GB)	232			LM-GTS	Engine/fire
DNF	BMW V12 LM	19	Hiro Matsushita (J)	Hiroki Katoh (J)	Akihiko Nakaya (J)	223			LMP	Transmission (gearbox)
DNF	Lola B98/10	26	Jan Lammers (NL)	Peter Kox (NL)	Tom Coronel (NL)	213			LMP	Transmission (gearbox)
DNF	Audi R8C	10	James Weaver (GB)	Andy Wallace (GB)	Perry McCarthy (GB)	198			LM-GTP	Transmission (gearbox)
DNF	Toyota GT-One	2	Allan McNish (GB)	Thierry Boutsen (B)	Ralf Kelleners (D)	173			LM-GTP	Accident
DNF	Porsche 911 GT2	61	Ernst Palmberger (D)	Wolfgang Kaufmann (D)	Michel Ligonnet (F)	157			LM-GTS	Engine
DNF	Lola B98/10	27	Tomas Saldana (E)	Grant Orbell (ZA)	Didier de Radiguès (B)	146			LMP	Transmission (gearbox)
DNF	Porsche 911 GT2	67	Jean-Pierre Jarier (F)	Sébastien Bourdais (F)	Pierre de Thoisy (F)	134			LM-GTS	Engine
DNF	Porsche 911 GT2	66	Manuel Monteiro (P)	Michel Monteiro (P)	Michel Maisonneuve (F)	123			LM-GTS	Accident
DNF	Nissan R391	22	Erik Comas (F)	Michael Krumm (D)	Satoshi Motoyama (J)	110			LMP	Engine (head gasket)
DNF	Toyota GT-One	1	Martin Brundle (GB)	Emmanuel Collard (F)	Vincenzo Sospiri (I)	90			LM-GTP	Accident damage
DNF	Lola B98/10	25	Franck Montagny (F)	Christophe Tinseau (F)	David Terrien (F)	77			LMP	Engine
WD	Mercedes-Benz CLR	6	Bernd Schneider (D)	Franck Lagorce (F)	Pedro Lamy (P)	76			LM-GTP	Withdrawn
DNF	Mercedes-Benz CLR	5	Nick Heidfeld (D)	Peter Dumbreck (GB)	Christophe Bouchut (F)	75			LM-GTP	Accident
DNF	Riley & Scott LM-P99	24	Yojiro Terada (J)	Franck Fréon (F)	Robin Donovan (GB)	74			LMP	Engine
DNF	Ferrari 333 SP	29	Mauro Baldi (I)	Christian Pescatori (I)	Jérôme Policand (F)	71			LMP	Engine (camshaft)
DNF	Riley & Scott Mk3	32	Marco Apicella (I)	Carl Rosenblad (S)	Shane Lewis (USA)	67			LMP	Engine
DNF	Audi R8C	9	Stefan Johansson (S)	Stéphane Ortelli (F)	Christian Abt (D)	55			LM-GTP	Transmission (gearbox)
DNF	Riley & Scott Mk3	31	Philippe Gache (F)	Gary Formato (ZA)	Olivier Thévenin (F)	25			LMP	Engine (oil pressure)
DNF	Porsche 911 GT2	60	Raymond Lintott (AUS)	Manfred Jurasz (A)	Katsunori Iketani (J)	24			LM-GTS	Accident
DNS	Mercedes-Benz CLR	4	*Mark Webber (AUS)*	*Jean-Marc Gounon (F)*	*Marcel Tiemann (D)*	-			LM-GTP	Accident in warm-up
DNS	Nissan R391	23	*Aguri Suzuki (J)*	*Masami Kageyama (J)*	*Eric van der Poele (B)*	-			LMP	Accident in qualifying
DNQ	Porsche 993 RSR	83	Gerard McQuillan (GB)	Michel Neugarten (B)	Chris Gleason (USA)	-			LM-GT	

DNF Did not finish **DNS** Did not start **DSQ** Disqualified **FS** Failed scrutineering **RES** Reserve not required **NC** Not classified as a finisher **WD** Withdrawn Drivers in italics did not race the cars specified

1999

CLASS WINNERS

FIA Class	Starters	Finishers	First	No	Drivers	kph	mph	
LM-P	19	9	BMW V12LMR	15	Dalmas/Martini/Winkelhock	206.960	128.599	Record
LM-GTP	7	1	Toyota GT-One	3	Katayama/Suzuki/Tscuchiya	206.000	128.008	Record
LM-GTS	16	9	Chrysler Viper GTS-R	51	Beretta/Wendlinger/Dupuy	184.290	114.518	Record
LM-GT	3	3	Porsche 996 GT3	81	Alzen/Huisman/Riccitelli	179.420	111.492	Record
Totals	45	22						

NON-PREQUALIFIERS

No	Car	Entrant (Nat)	cc	Engine	Class	Pos	Time
4	Ferrari 333 SP-98	La Filière Elf (F)	3997	F310E V12	LM-P1	NA	-
6	Ferrari 333 SP	GTC Motorsport Lanzante (GB)	3997	F310E V12	LM-P1	NA	-
9	Ferrari 333 SP	Pilot BSM Racing (F)	3997	F310E V12	LM-P1	NA	-
11	Ferrari 333 SP-98	Ecurie Biennoise (CH)	3997	F310E V12	LM-P1	NA	-
17	Kremer K8	Kremer Racing (D)	2995tc	Porsche 935/76 F6	LM-P1	36	4:02.163
18	Kremer K8	Konrad Motorsport (D)	3165tc	Porsche 935/76 F6	LM-P1	31	3:54.625
19	WR LMP98	Gérard Welter (F)	1995tc	Peugeot 405-Raid S4	LM-P1	32	3:56.582
20	WR LMP98	Jean-Luc Sonnier Idée Verte (F)	1995tc	Peugeot 405-Raid S4	LM-P1	52	4:48.010
23	Sarta 624	Sarta Project Lukoil (F)	2946tc	Renault PRV V6	LM-P1	NA	-
34	Nissan R390 GT1	NISMO (J)	3496tc	VRH35L V8	GT1	NA	-
37	Lister Storm GTL	Newcastle United Storm (GB)	6996	Jaguar HE V12	GT1	DSQ	-
38	Porsche 911 GT1-98	Zakspeed Racing (D)	3196tc	F6	GT1	18	3:43.911
39	Porsche 911 GT1-98	Zakspeed Racing (D)	3196tc	F6	GT1	22	3:44.794
42	McLaren F1 GTR	Parabolica Motorsport (GB)	5990	BMW S70/3 V12	GT1	NA	-
43	McLaren F1 GTR	Parabolica Motorsport (GB)	5990	BMW S70/3 V12	GT1	NA	-
46	Panoz GTR-1 Q9	Panoz Motorsports (USA)	5999	Ford V8/Zytek	GT1	29	3:53.199
47	Porsche 911 GT1	Millennium Motorsport (GB)	3164tc	F6	GT1	NA	-
48	Porsche 911 GT1	Larbre Compétition (F)	3164tc	F6	GT1	25	3:49.225
52	Chrysler Viper GTS-R	Viper Team ORECA (F)	7986	356-T6 V10	GT2	NA	-
54	Chrysler Viper GTS-R	Orion Motorsport (GB)	7986	356-T6 V10	GT2	DSQ	-
57	Helem V6	RJ Racing (F)	2975	PRV V6	GT2	FS	-
58	Helem V6	RJ Racing (F)	2975	PRV V6	GT2	51	4:21.604
59	Lotus Esprit V8 Turbo	Pilbeam Racing Designs (GB)	3506tc	T918 V8	GT2	DSQ	-
66	Porsche 911 GT2	Roock Racing Motorsport (D)	3600tc	F6	GT2	53	5:00.367
75	Saleen Mustang	Cirtek Motorsport (GB)	5900	Ford V8	GT2	47	4:09.895

DSQ Disqualified   **NA** Non-arrival   **NT** No time set   **WD** Withdrawn after Prequalifying

SPORTS RACING WORLD CUP

Race	Winner	Drivers
Barcelona (E) 2h30m	Ferrari 333 SP	Collard/Sospiri
Monza (I) 500km	Ferrari 333 SP	Collard/Sospiri
Spa-Francorchamps (B) 2h30m	Ferrari 333 SP	Baldi/Redon
Enna-Pergusa (I) 2h30m	Ferrari 333 SP	Pescatori/Moncini
Donington Park (GB) 2h30m	Lola B98/10	Gounon/Bernard
Brno (CS) 2h30m	Lola B98/10	Gounon/Tinseau
Nürburgring (D) 2h30m	Lola B98/10	Gounon/Bernard
Magny-Cours (F) 2h30m	Ferrari 333 SP	Lavaggi/Mazzacane
Kyalami (ZA) 200km	Lola B98/10	Gounon/Bernard

FIA GT CHAMPIONSHIP

Race	Winner	Drivers
Monza (I)	Chrysler Viper GTS-R	Beretta/Wendlinger
Silverstone (GB)	Chrysler Viper GTS-R	Beretta/Wendlinger
Hockenheim (D)	Chrysler Viper GTS-R	Belloc/Dupuy
Hungaroring (H)	Chrysler Viper GTS-R	Belloc/Dupuy
Zolder (B)	Chrysler Viper GTS-R	Beretta/Wendlinger
Oschersleben (D)	Chrysler Viper GTS-R	Beretta/Wendlinger
Donington Park (GB)	Chrysler Viper GTS-R	Beretta/Wendlinger
Homestead (USA)	Chrysler Viper GTS-R	Clérico/Belmondo
Watkins Glen (USA)	Chrysler Viper GTS-R	Belloc/Donohue
Zhuhai (J)	Chrysler Viper GTS-R	Beretta/Wendlinger

FINAL CHAMPIONSHIP POINTS

Final Positions	Team/Driver	Points
TEAMS		
1	JB Giesse Team Ferrari (F)	121
2	BMS Scuderia Italia (I)	107
3	DAMS (F)	80
4	Target 24 (I)	53
5	GLV Brums (I)	51
6	Autosport Racing (I)	48
&c		
SR2 Class Champion	Cauduro Tampolli Team (I)	
DRIVERS		
1	Emmanuel Collard (F)	104
=	Vincenzo Sospiri (I)	104
3	Christian Pescatori (I)	101
4	Emmanuele Moncini (I)	92
5	Mauro Baldi (I)	85
6	Jean-Marc Gounon (F)	80
&c		
SR2 Class Champion	Angelo Lancelotti (I)	

FINAL CHAMPIONSHIP POINTS

Final Positions	Team/Driver	Points
TEAMS		
1	Chrysler Viper Team ORECA (F)	137
2	Chamberlain Motorsport (GB)	40
3	Freisinger Motorsport (D)	23
4	Paul Belmondo Racing (F)	20
5	Konrad Motorsport (D)	13
+	Lister Storm Racing (GB)	13
&c		
DRIVERS		
1	Karl Wendlinger (A)	78
=	Olivier Beretta (MC)	78
3	Jean-Philippe Belloc (F)	53
4	David Donohue (CDN)	25
5	Dominique Dupuy (F)	24
6	Wolfgang Kaufmann (D)	21
=	Christian Gläsel (D)	21
=	Christian Vann (D)	21
&c		

HIGH FIVES IN GERMANY

LE MANS

STATISTICS
DATA FOR THE DECADE

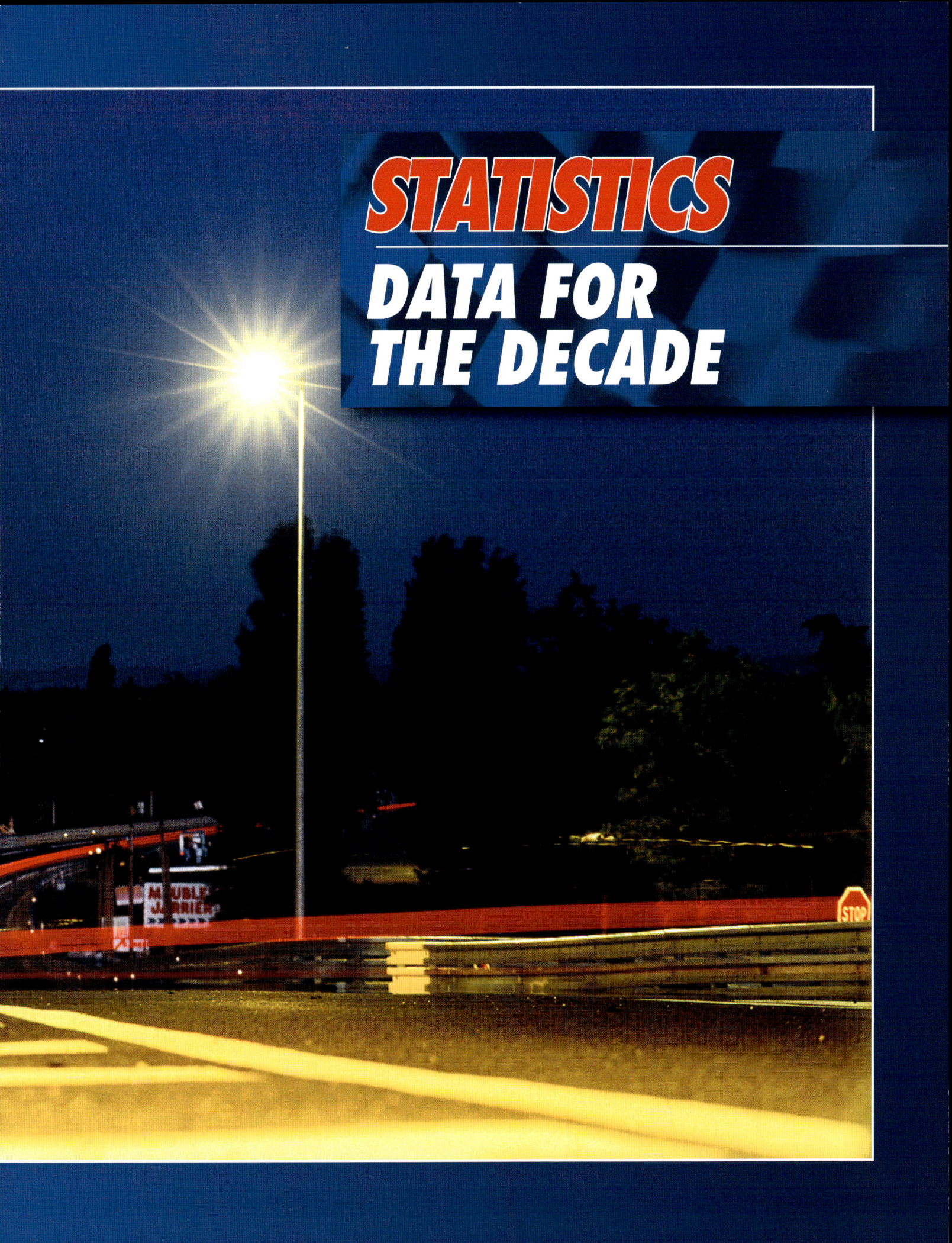

LE MANS

MARQUE RECORDS

STARTS													FINISHES										
Make	1990	1991	1992	1993	1994	1995	1996	1997	1998	1999	Total	%	Total	1990	1991	1992	1993	1994	1995	1996	1997	1998	1999	Make
ADA	1										1	0	0	0										ADA
ALD	1	1			1						3	0	0	0	0			0						ALD
Alpa/Sehcar				1	1						2	0	0					0	0					Alpa/Sehcar
Alpine-Renault					1						1	100	1					1						Alpine-Renault
Audi										4	4	50	2										2	Audi
BMW								2	4		6	33	2									0	2	BMW
BRM			1								1	0				0								BRM
Bugatti					1			1			2	0	0					0			0			Bugatti
Chevrolet					1	4	1	1			7	29	2					0	2	0	0			Chevrolet
Chrysler/Dodge					2		4	4	5	8	23	74	17					1		3	2	4	7	Chrysler/Dodge
Cougar/Courage	3	3	3	3	3	2	3	4	4	3	31	55	17	1	1	1	2	1	1	2	3	2	3	Cougar/Courage
Dauer-Porsche					2						2	100	2					2						Dauer-Porsche
De Tomaso					1						1	0	0					0						De Tomaso
Debora		1	1	1	1			1			5	20	1			0	0	0	1		0			Debora
Ferrari					4	4	6	2	4	1	21	29	6					1	2	0	1	2	0	Ferrari
Ford								2			2	0	0								0			Ford
Harrier					1						1	0	0					0						Harrier
Honda						3	3	1			7	71	5						3	1	1			Honda
Jaguar	4	4		3		2					13	38	5	2	3		0		0					Jaguar
Kremer-Porsche					1	2	2	1	1		7	43	3					1	1	0	0	1		Kremer-Porsche
Kudzu						1	1	1			3	100	3						1	1	1			Kudzu
Lancia	1	1									2	0	0	0	0									Lancia
Lister						1	1	2			4	0	0							0	1	0		Lister
Lola			2							3	5	20	1			1							0	Lola
Lotus			2	2			1				5	0	0			0	0			0				Lotus
Lucchini				1							1	100	1				1							Lucchini
Marcos						2	1	1			4	0	0						0	0	0			Marcos
Mazda	3	3	2		1						9	67	6	1	3	1		1						Mazda
McLaren						7	7	5	2		21	67	14						5	6	2	1		McLaren
Mercedes-Benz		3							2	2	7	14	1		1							0	0	Mercedes-Benz
Nissan	7				2	2	2	3	4	1	21	50	10	2				1	1	1	1	4	0	Nissan
Orion				1							1	0	0				1							Orion
Panoz								3	2	2	7	43	3								0	1	2	Panoz
Peugeot		2	3	3							7	56	5		0	2	3							Peugeot
Porsche	18	13	5	18	11	10	12	16	16	11	130	52	68	15	3	4	13	3	4	8	6	7	5	Porsche
Riley & Scott							1		1	3	5	0	0							0		0	0	Riley & Scott
ROC		1									1	0	0		0									ROC
Spice	7	7	3	2							19	47	9	6	1	1	1							Spice
Tiga	1		1								2	50	1	1		0								Tiga
Toyota	3		5	5	2	2	2		3	3	25	60	15	1		4	4	2	1	1		1	1	Toyota
TWR-Porsche							2	1			3	67	2							1	1			TWR-Porsche
Venturi				7	5	3					15	40	6				5	1	0					Venturi
WR				1	1	2	2	2			8	13	1				0	1	0	0	0			WR
Totals	49	38	28	47	48	48	48	48	47	45	445	47	209	29	12	15	30	18	20	25	17	23	22	Totals
	1990	1991	1992	1993	1994	1995	1996	1997	1998	1999	Total	%	Total	1990	1991	1992	1993	1994	1995	1996	1997	1998	1999	

1990-99

DRIVER RECORDS

Driver		Nat	'90	'91	'92	'93	'94	'95	'96	'97	'98	'99
Christian	ABT	D										DNF
Kenneth	ACHESON	GB	DNF	3	2	DNF		DNF				
Nick	ADAMS	GB	DNF	DNF		DNF		17	NPQ			
Riccardo 'Rocky'	AGUSTA	I				23	DNF	11	DNF	DNF	12	
André	AHRLÉ	F						20	10	22		20
Laurent	AÏELLO	F						PQ		1		4
Michele	ALBORETO	I						DNF	1	DNF		4
Marc	ALEXANDER	F				NC						
Philippe	ALLIOT	F	16	DNF	3	3		DNF	DNF			
Jacques	ALMÉRAS	F		DNF	DNF		DNF					
Jean-Marie	ALMÉRAS	F		DNF	DNF		DNF					
Otto	ALTENBACH	D	9		10	7						
Uwe	ALZEN	D									2	13
Ni	AMORIM	P								21		14
Mario	ANDRETTI	USA						2	13	DNF		
Michael	ANDRETTI	USA								DNF		
Phil	ANDREWS	GB					NC		NPQ	PQ		
Steven	ANDSKÄR	S	13	DNF	5	6	4					
Sandro	ANGELASTRI	CH				21	DNF					
Max	ANGELELLI	I					DNF					11
Marco	APICELLA	I						14			DNF	
Tommy	ARCHER	USA								DNF	13	12
René	ARNOUX	F					12	DNF				
Didier	ARTZET	F			DNF							
Bill	AUBERLEN	USA								4		5
Philippe	AUVRAY	F						NPQ				
Soheil	AYARI	F							PQR	DNF		DNF
Gary	AYLES	GB						18		DNF	19	NPQ
Eric	BACHELART	B				25		DNF				
Johannes	BADRUTT	USA				DNF						
Andrew	BAGNALL	NZ							17			
Julian	BAILEY	GB	DNF						DNF			
Jonathan	BAKER	GB					NC	NPQ				
Richard	BALANDRAS	F				20		DNF				
Bertrand	BALAS	F					12	NPQ				
Mauro	BALDI	I			DNF	3	3	1		DNF	14	DNF
Michael	BARTELS	D								NPQ		
Jürgen	BARTH	D				15		PQ				
Roland	BASSALER	F				DNF						
Jean-Claude	BASSO	F					RES		DNF			
Anne	BAVEREY	F		DNQ								
Harald	BECKER	D								DNF		
Derek	BELL	GB	4	7	12	10	6	3	6			
Justin	BELL	GB		DNQ	12		12	3	DNF	14	11	12
Ray	BELLM	GB					DNF	4	9	DNF		
Noël del	BELLO	F	DNQ									
Jean-Philippe	BELLOC	F								7	DNF	DNF
Paul	BELMONDO	F				DNF	DNQ	NC	DNF			17
Anthony	BELTOISE	F								PQ		
Olivier	BERETTA	MC						FS	21	DNF	13	10
Allen	BERG	CDN	11									
Eric	BERNARD	F						DNF	DNF	DNF	DNF	7
Pierre-François	BERNIGAUD	F						NPQ				
Enrico	BERTAGGIA	I						9	NPQ		NPQ	
Frank	BIELA	D										3
François	BIRBEAU	F					RES	DNF				
Mark	BLUNDELL	GB		DNF	1			4				
Daniel	BOCCARD	F		DNQ								
Raul	BOESEL	BR			2							
Patrick	BOIDRON	F						NPQ				
Didier	BONNET	F				DNF		NPQ				
Patrick	BORNHAUSER	F						NPQ	NPQ			

Driver		Nat	'90	'91	'92	'93	'94	'95	'96	'97	'98	'99
Christophe	BOUCHUT	F				1	14	6	DNF	DNF	DNF	DNF
Sylvain	BOULAY	F					DNF	PQ				
Jean-Christophe	BOULLION	F							DNF		DNF	DNF
Alfonso d'Orleans	BOURBON	E							11	DNF		
Claude	BOURBONNAIS	CDN			NC							
Patrick	BOURDAIS	F				DNF	DNF	DNF	20	DNF	PQ	DNF
Thierry	BOUTSEN	B				2	3	6	2	DNF	DNF	
Jean-Bernard	BOUVET	F				20		DNF			NPQ	
Quirin	BOVY	D	DNQ									
David	BRABHAM	AUS			DNF	DSQ			5	DNF	7	7
Geoff	BRABHAM	AUS	DNF			1						
Sergio	BRAMBILLA	I				DNS						
Claude	BRANA	F				DNF						
Gianfranco	BRANCATELLI	I	DNF									
Marco	BRAND	I		NC	DNF							
Walter	BREUER	F		NC								
David	BRODIE	GB				DNF						
Walter	BRUN	CH	DNF	10								
Martin	BRUNDLE	GB	1						DNF	DNF	DNF	
Pierre	BRUNEAU	F						NPQ	NPQ	DNF		
Lilian	BRYNER	CH			DNF	9	DNF	DNS	DNF			
Thomas	BSCHER	D			DNF	DNF	4	DNS	DNF	5		
Harry 'Doc'	BUNDY	USA					DNF					
Paul	BURDELL	USA				NPQ						
Alex	CAFFI	I										6
Enzo	CALDERARI	CH			DNF	9	DNF	DNS	DNF			
Xavier	CAMP	E				17	NPQ					
Adrian	CAMPOS	E						DNF				
Patrick	CAMUS	F			29		DNF	PQ				
Paul	CANARY	USA	DNQ									
Ivan	CAPELLI	I				DNF						
Rinaldo	CAPELLO	I								DNF	4	
Jean-Louis	CAPETTE	F			DNF							
Didier	CARADEC	F	DNQ	14	RES							
Miguel Angel de	CASTRO	E				DNF						
Johnny	CECOTTO	YV				8	DNF					
Dominic	CHAPPELL	GB			NC	DNF	DNQ					
Edouard	CHAUFOUR	F			NC							
Bernard	CHAUVIN	F			NC	DNS						
Jean-Luc	CHÉREAU	F			DNF	22	DNF	23	NC			
Dave	CLARK	GB							NPQ			
Emmanuel	CLÉRICO	F			DNF	RES	7	PQ	16			
Price	COBB	USA	1			10	DNF					
Jay	COCHRAN	USA			DNF	DNF	NPQ					
Max	COHEN-OLIVAR	MOR	19	DNF	DNF							
Emmanuel	COLLARD	F				DNF	7	DNF	DNF	DNF		
Ben	COLLINS	GB				NPQ						
Erik	COMAS	F			DNF	12	6	DNF				
Giampiero 'Peo'	CONSONNI	I		DNQ								
Almo	COPPELLI	I	NC	11	DNF	DNF	DNF	DNF	12			
Tom	CORONEL	NL									DNF	
Didier	COTTAZ	F					DNF	4	DNF	8		
David	COULTHARD	GB		DSQ								
Olivier	COUVREUR	F			DNF							
Alain	CUDINI	F	22		DNF	NPQ	23					
Yannick	DALMAS	F	DNF	1	2	1	1	3	DNF	DNF	1	
Derek	DALY	IRL	DNF									
Thomas	DANIELSSON	S	15	DNF								
Stéphane	DAOUDI	F				RES	NPQ					
Tim Lee	DAVEY	GB	26									
William	DAVID	F			DNF	DNF						
Jamie	DAVIES	GB						7				

DNF Did not finish **DNQ** Did not qualify **DNS** Did not start **DSQ** Disqualified **FS** Car failed scrutineering **NC** Not classified as a finisher **NPQ** Did not prequalify **RES** Reserve not required for race **WD** Withdrawn
PQ Drove a successful car in Prequalifying but not nominated for race week **PQR** Prequalified as a reserve but not nominated for race week

LE MANS

DRIVER RECORDS CONTINUED

Driver		Nat	'90	'91	'92	'93	'94	'95	'96	'97	'98	'99
Richard	DEAN	GB						NPQ				
Alexandre	DEBANNE	F								NPQ		
Christophe	DÉCHEVANNE	F				DNF						
Didier	DEFOURNY	B							PQ			
Jean-Denis	DELETRAZ	CH						5	DNF	DNF	NPQ	
Stanley	DICKENS	S	8	DNF				PQ	DNF			
Pierre	DIEUDONNÉ	B	DNF	8								
Gérard	DILLMANN	F				22						
Mark	DISMORE	USA							10			
Karel	DOLEJSI	CZ						15				
Martin	DONNELLY	GB	DNF									
David	DONOHUE	USA									11	DNF
Robin	DONOVAN	GB	DNF	DNF	11	DNF	6	11	DNF	NPQ	DNF	DNF
Michael	DOW	USA	DNQ									
Jim	DOWNING	USA						7	25	17		
Pascal	DRO	F					DNF	DNQ	DNF			
Luca	DRUDI	I							NPQ	11	PQ	
Bernard de	DRYVER	B	16						NPQ			
Marc	DUEZ	B	DNF			25			11	DNF	DNF	12
Peter	DUMBRECK	GB										DNF
Johnny	DUMFRIES	GB	DNF	DNF								
Dominique	DUPUY	F				15	8	DNF	DNF	DNF	PQ	10
David	DUSSAU	F							NPQ			
Bob	EARL	USA	17									
Dirk-Reiner	EBELING	D				17	DNF					
Francesco	EGOSKUE	E	DNQ									
Bruno	EICHMANN	CH							12	10	PQ	
Fredrik	EKBLOM	S							16			8
Eje	ELGH	S	15	DNF	9	6						
Sébastien	ENJOLRAS	F							DNF	NPQ		
Thomas	ERDOS	BR						DNF	DNF	DNF	PQ	22
Cor	EUSER	NL		DNF	DNF		10	DNF	DNF	DNF		
Andy	EVANS	USA				13	7		DNF	DNF		
Owen	EVANS	GB							PQ			
Teo	FABI	I		3	8	2						
Pascal	FABRE	F	7	DNF	DNF	10	DNF		24		DNF	
Juan Manuel II	FANGIO	RA				8						
Philippe	FARJON	F	DNF									
Bill	FARMER	NZ					14					
Philippe	FAVRE	CH					16	NC				
Ron	FELLOWS	CDN										PQ
Alistair	FENWICK	GB	28									
Alain	FERTÉ	F	DNF	DNF	DNF		DNF	DNF	24	DNF		
Michel	FERTÉ	F	DNF	2			DNF	12	DNF	DNF	DNF	9
Gregor	FOITEK	CH			DNF							
Gary	FORMATO	ZA										DNF
Steve	FOSSETT	USA				DNF			DNF			
George	FOUCHÉ	ZA	13	DNF	5	6	4			DNF	DNF	
Heinz-Harald	FRENTZEN	D				13						
Franck	FRÉON	F					15	7	25	17	15	DNF
Andreas	FUCHS	D				DNF	DNF	DNF				
Hideo	FUKUYAMA	J						10				
Philippe	GACHE	F					NC		21	DNF	DNF	DNF
Bertrand	GACHOT	F	DNF	1	4			14	DNF	NPQ	DNF	
Alain	GADAL	F					26					
André	GAHINET	F					RES					
Luc	GALMARD	F						13				
Grégoire de	GALZAIN	F										PQ
Wayne	GARDNER	AUS								DNF		
Jürgen von	GARTZEN	D							DNF			PQ
Jean	GAY	F							NPQ			
Patrice	GAY	F									DNF	9

Driver		Nat	'90	'91	'92	'93	'94	'95	'96	'97	'98	'99
Günther	GEBHARDT	D	DNF									
Paul	GENTILOZZI	USA							DNF	PQ		
Bruno	GIACOMELLI	I	11									
Andrew	GILBERT-SCOTT	GB								DNF		
Alessandro	GINI	I				DNF	DNF					
Luigi	GIORGIO	I		NC								
Fabien	GIROIX	F						5	DNF	DNQ	NPQ	
Christian	GLÄSEL	D										22
Chris	GLEASON	USA							NPQ	15		DNQ
Goncalo	GOMES	P									21	
Guillaume	GOMEZ	F								NPQ		NPQ
Patrick	GONIN	F	16	DNF	DNF	24	DNF	DNF	DNF	NPQ	FS	
Chris	GOODWIN	GB								DNS		
Scott	GOODYEAR	CDN							3			
Marc	GOOSSENS	B							DNF	4	DNF	8
Claude-Yves	GOSSELIN	F										PQ
Patrice	GOUESLARD	F					DNF		20	5	23	NC
Joël	GOUHIER	F						15	DNF			
Jean-Marc	GOUNON	F						NC	DNF	2	DNF	DNS
Eric	GRAHAM	F						RES	DNF		DNF	20
John	GRAHAM	CDN									DNF	
Jean-Philippe	GRAND	F	23	DNF								
Ruggero	GRASSI	I				DNS						
Alexander 'Sandy'	GRAU	D								DNF		
Nigel	GREENSALL	GB							NPQ			
Stéphane	GREGOIRE	F							NPQ			
Harald	GROHS	D	DNF			DNF					DNF	
Olivier	GROUILLARD	F		DNF				DNF	5	6	DNF	16
Lucien	GUITTENY	F							DNQ	NPQ		
Olivier	HABERTHUR	CH					18	DNF				
Armin	HAHNE	D					DNF	14	DNF		5	NPQ
Claude	HALDI	CH					18					
Nick	HAM	USA									DNF	
Yukihiro	HANE	J						19				
Jun	HARADA	J			NC	19	NC					
Peter	HARDMAN	GB							DNF	NPQ		
Ian	HARROWER	GB	DNF									
Tim	HARVEY	GB	18		DNF							
Masahiro	HASEMI	J	5						15			
Toon van der	HATERD	NL								PQ		
Naoki	HATTORI	J					NC					
Hubert	HAUPT	D										DNF
Hans	HAUSER	CH						NPQ				
Hurley	HAYWOOD	USA	12	NC		DNF	1					
Nick	HEIDFELD	D										DNF
Christian	HEINKÉLÉ	F						DNQ	DNQ	NPQ		
Eric	HÉLARY	F			1	DNF	2	21	3	DNF		
Shawn	HENDRICKS	USA						10				
Philippe de	HENNING	F	DNF	DNF								
Andrew	HEPWORTH	GB	DNF	FS								
Johnny	HERBERT	GB	DNF	1	4							
Antonio de Azevedo	HERMANN	BR			19	DNF	DNF	DNF	8			
Jacques	HEUCLIN	F	DNF	DNF								
William	HEWLAND	GB				DNF						
Mike	HEZEMANS	NL							DNF			
Chris	HODGETTS	GB	18	FS	DNS			DNF				
Guy	HOLMES	GB							DNF			
Pierre	HONEGGER	USA					DNQ					
Kazuyoshi	HOSHINO	J	5					DNF	15	12	3	
Will	HOY	GB	DNF									
Kurt	HUBER	CH					NPQ					
John	HUGENHOLTZ	NL					DNQ			15	19	14

370 LE MANS 24 HOURS 1990-99

1990-99

Driver		Nat	'90	'91	'92	'93	'94	'95	'96	'97	'98	'99
Patrick	HUISMAN	NL						10			DNF	13
Franz	HUNKELER	CH						NC				
Claudia	HÜRTGEN	D								13	17	20
Harald	HUYSMAN	N	10	DNF								
Ross	HYETT	GB	25									
Stephen	HYNES	USA	27									
Olindo	IACOBELLI	USA	21	NC	14	DNF	DNF	DNF				
Alain	IANNETTA	F	DNF									
Akira	IIDA	J					18	8	16			
Katsunori	IKETANI	J	26	DNQ								DNF
Bruno	ILIEN	F				26			DNF			
Eddie	IRVINE	GB			9	4	2					
Jean-Pierre	JABOUILLE	F		DNF	3	3						
François	JAKUBOWSKI	F							NPQ			
Neil	JAMIESON	CDN						PQ				
Jean-Pierre	JARIER	F					DNF	DNF	DNF	DNF	DNF	
Frank	JELINSKI	D	4	7		DNF	DSQ	9				
Stefan	JOHANSSON	S	DNF	6	5					1	DNF	DNF
Davy	JONES	USA	DNF	2					1			
John	JONES	CDN						DNQ				
Richard	JONES	GB	27	DNF	DNS			17	NPQ			
Manfred	JURASZ	A						18			DNF	
Masahiko	KAGEYAMA	J					DNF	DNF	12	3		
Masami	KAGEYAMA	J						DNF		10	DNS	
Katsumoto	KANEISHO	J							PQ			
Shunji	KASUYA	J	13	DNQ	13		DNF	10				
Ukyo	KATAYAMA	J				DNF				9	2	
Yoshimi	KATAYAMA	J	20									
Hiroki	KATOH	J										DNF
Wolfgang	KAUFMANN	D						19		NPQ		DNF
Dennis	KAZMEROWSKI	USA		DNQ								
Rupert	KEEGAN	GB						DNF				
Ralf	KELLENERS	D							12	DNF	DNF	DNF
David	KENNEDY	IRL	DNF	6								
Loris	KESSEL	CH				7						
Ian	KHAN	GB	DNQ									
Peter	KITCHAK	USA							DNF	DNF	18	
Masahiko	KONDO	J					NC	10	DNF			
Kilian	KONIG	GB										NPQ
Franz	KONRAD	A	2	DNF		19	DNF	DNF	DNF	DNF		18
John van	KOUWEN	NL							PQ			
Peter	KOX	NL							4	3		DNF
Louis	KRAGES	D	8	DNF	DNF							
Fritz	KREUTZPOINTNER	D		5								
Michel	KRINE	F				29	DNF					
Tom	KRISTENSEN	DK							1	DNF	DNF	
Jeff	KROSNOFF	USA		DNF			2	14				
Michael	KRUMM	D								5	DNF	
Takuya	KUROSAWA	J					NPQ			10		
Guy	KUSTER	F				DNQ	15	18				
Dominique	LACAUD	F				DNF	DNQ	NPQ				
Jacques	LAFFITE	F	14			DNF	DNF	11				
François	LAFON	F										PQ
Jean-Claude	LAGNIEZ	F					PQ	9	DNF	16		
Franck	LAGORCE	F				DNF	DNF	7	DNF	5		WD
Jan	LAMMERS	NL	2		8	8		13	DNF	6		DNF
Alain	LAMOUILLE	F				24						
Pedro	LAMY	P							5	13		WD
Soames	LANGTON	GB						DNF				
Xavier	LAPEYRE	F	23	DNF								
André	LARA REISENDE	BR							DNF			

Driver		Nat	'90	'91	'92	'93	'94	'95	'96	'97	'98	'99
Oscar	LARRAURI	RA	DNF	10			DNF					
Jürgen	LÄSSIG	D	9	DNF	10	12	6	DNF	DNF	DNF		
Giovanni	LAVAGGI	I	19		7	12				DNS		
Jean-Louis	LE DUIGOU	F					RES					
Nicolas	LEBOISSETIER	F							DNF		DNS	
Thierry	LECERF	F			FS	DNS			DNS			
Jack	LECONTE	F					16	DNF	DNF	22	DNF	
Laurent	LÉCUYER	CH						RES	DNF	RES		
Geoff	LEES	GB	6		DNF	8		DNF	19	DNF	DNF	
JJ	LEHTO	SF	DNF	9				1	9	DNF		DNF
Robert 'Butch'	LEITZINGER	USA								DNF		7
Patrick	LEMARIE	F						PQ				
David	LESLIE	GB	DNF	DNF		DNF		NC				
Ferdinand de	LESSEPS	F	DNF	DNF	14	DNF	DNQ	DNF				
Shane	LEWIS	USA										DNF
Jean-Paul	LIBERT	B			DNF	DNF	DNQ		16			
Michel	LIGONNET	F					19	NPQ	DNF	17	DNF	
René	LIGONNET	F					PQ					
Ray	LINTOTT	AUS										DNF
Geoff	LISTER	GB								PQ		
Allen	LLOYD	USA								PQ		
Pierre-Alain	LOMBARDI	CH	DNF	DNF								
Tomas	LOPEZ	MEX		DNF								
Costas	LOS	GR	22		DNF							
Klaus	LUDWIG	D								DNF		
Arie	LUYENDIJK	NL						NPQ				
Sascha	MAASSEN	D								NPQ		
Gerard	MACQUILLAN	GB							NPQ			PQR
Fabio	MAGNANI	I	DNF		30							
Jan	MAGNUSSEN	DK										11
Jerry	MAHONY	GB	DNF									
Michel	MAISONNEUVE	F	23	DNF		DNF	DSQ			DNF	DNF	
Akihiko	MAKAYA	J										PQ
Jean-Pierre	MALCHER	F							PQR			
Fabio	MANCINI	I				DNF	18					
Charles	MARGUERON	CH			18		DNF					
Chris	MARSH	GB					NC					
Mauro	MARTINI	I		DNF		5	2	14	24	PQ	PQ	
Pierluigi	MARTINI	I						DNF	8	DNF		1
Guy	MARTINOLLE	F						12	9			16
Jochen	MASS	D		DNF			DNF					
Jean-Marc	MASSÉ	F					DNQ					
Renato	MASTROPIETRO	I			DNS	9						
Franck	MATIFAS	F					NPQ					
Hideshi	MATSUDA	J			13							
Hiro	MATSUSHITA	J										DNF
Henri-Louis	MAUNOIR	F					DNQ					
Jean-Luc	MAURY-LARIBIÈRE	F			29	NC	13	RES	DNS	20		
Bernd	MAYLÄNDER	D										19
Perry	McCARTHY	GB					DNF	DNF	PQ	DNF		
Chris	McDOUGALL	CDN					DNF					
Allan	McNISH	GB						DNF	1	DNF		
Gerard	McQUILLAN	GB					17	NPQ	DNQ			
Claude	MEIGEMONT	F					RES					
Ronny	MEIXNER	USA			9							
Manuel	MELLO-BREYNER	P					NPQ	11	21	15		
Pedro	MELLO-BREYNER	P					NPQ	11		15		
Tomaz	MELLO-BREYNER	P					NPQ	11		15		
Jim	MERAS	USA				DNF						
Sarel van der	MERWE	ZA	24									
Jean	MESSAOUDI	F	DNF									
Jean-François	METZ	F				NPQ	NPQ					

DNF Did not finish **DNQ** Did not qualify **DNS** Did not start **DSQ** Disqualified **FS** Car failed scrutineering **NC** Not classified as a finisher **NPQ** Did not prequalify **RES** Reserve not required for race **WD** Withdrawn
PQ Drove a successful car in Prequalifying but not nominated for race week **PQR** Prequalified as a reserve but not nominated for race week

DATA FOR THE DECADE   371

LE MANS

DRIVER RECORDS CONTINUED

Driver		Nat	'90	'91	'92	'93	'94	'95	'96	'97	'98	'99
Tomas	MEZERA	AUS	15									
François	MIGAULT	F	DNF	11	DNS	13	NC	NC		DNQ	DNF	
Steve	MILLEN	NZ	17				5					
Nicolas	MINASSIAN	F					DNF					
Bruno	MIOT	F				20						
Kiyoshi	MISAKI	J		12								
Hideoshi	MITSUSADA	J							DNF			
Paolo	MONDINI	I				23						
Franck	MONTAGNY	F									16	DNF
Manuel	MONTEIRO	P								DNF	DNF	
Michel	MONTEIRO	P								DNF	DNF	
Tiago	MONTEIRO	P										17
Andrea	MONTERMINI	I									6	6
Massimo	MONTI	I	DNF					18				
Carlos	MORAN	SAL				DNF						
Gianni	MORBIDELLI	I							PQ			
Giampiero	MORETTI	I	DNF						6	14		
Denis	MORIN	F	DNF		DNF	14	NC					
John	MORTON	USA					5	23	14	DNF		
Satoshi	MOTOYAMA	J								10	DNF	
Bernhard	MÜLLER	D							NPQ	DNF		
Cathy	MÜLLER	F		DNF					NPQ			
Dirk	MÜLLER	D										19
Fritz	MÜLLER	D				21						
Jörg	MÜLLER	D							DNF	2		DNF
Yvan	MÜLLER	F				DNF		DNF				
Greg	MURPHY	NZ										
David	MURRY	USA								DNF		
Naoki	NAGASAKA	J	DNF	12		5						
Akihiko	NAKAYA	J							DNF	DNF		
Piero	NAPPI	I							DNF			
Charles	NEARBURG	USA							DNF			
Robert	NEARN	GB						14	DNF	17		
Tiff	NEEDELL	GB	3	DNF	12			DNF	19	DNF		
Bernd	NETZEBAND	D				DNF						
Michel	NEUGARTEN	B			27	DNF		DNF	9	DNF	DNQ	
John	NIELSEN	DK	1	4	7	DSQ	DNF	DNF	4	DNS	5	
Kris	NISSEN	DK						NPQ				
Luciano della	NOCE	I						DNF	DNF			
Michel	NOURRY	F									18	21
Jari	NURMINEN	SF							15			
Harry	NUTTALL	GB					DNF					
François	OBORN	F						DNQ				
Eugène	O'BRIEN	GB						11				
Johnny	O'CONNELL	USA					5		PQ	DNF	11	
Hitoshi	OGAWA	J	6									
Hideki	OKADA	J	24				16	NC				
Philippe	OLCZYK	B				22	7					
Anders	OLOFSSON	S	DNF	DNF		DNF	DNF	DNF	2			
Jürgen	OPPERMANN	D	DNF	DNF		7						
Grant	ORBELL	ZA										DNF
Alfonso de	ORLEANS	E						NPQ	NPQ			
Steve	O'ROURKE	GB						DNF	NPQ	4		
Stéphane	ORTELLI	F						DNF	17	DNF	1	DNF
Didier	ORTION	F						16				
Tetsuya	OTA	J				DNS	DNF	DNF				
Lindsay	OWEN-JONES	GB						DNF	5			
Jim	PACE	USA							DNF			
Marc	PACHOT	F					DNQ					
Luigi	PAGOTTO	I					DNF			PQ		
Carlos	PALAU	E						8	12	DNF		
Gildo	PALLANCA-PASTOR	MC							NPQ			

Driver		Nat	'90	'91	'92	'93	'94	'95	'96	'97	'98	'99
Ernst	PALMBERGER	D									DNF	DNF
Jonathan	PALMER	GB	DNS	DNF								
Max	PAPIS	I								6		
Jesús	PAREJA	E		DNF	10	DNF	16	8	DNF	DNF		
Riccardo	PATRESE	I								DNF		
John Jr	PAUL	USA							DNF	PQ		
Scott	PEELER	USA								NPQ		
Luis	PEREZ-SALA	E	DNS									
Win	PERCY	GB				DNF		DNF	NPQ	NPQ		
Thierry	PERRIER	F									18	21
Henri	PESCAROLO	F	14	DNF	6	9	DNF	DNF	7	7	16	9
Christian	PESCATORI	I								8		DNF
Pascal	PESSIOT	F	DNF									
Andy	PETERY	USA				DNF						
Pierre	PETIT	F			DNF		DNF	DNF				
Andy	PILGRIM	USA								17	10	PQR
Richard	PIPER	GB	21	NC	14	DNF	DNF	DNF				
Nelson	PIQUET	BR							8	DNF		
Emanuele	PIRRO	I									DNF	3
Eric van der	POELE	B		DNF		DNF	FS	DNF	DNF	8	DNS	
Jérôme	POLICAND	F							DNF	4	DNF	DNF
Jean-Claude	POLICE	F				13						
Xavier	POMPIDOU	F									12	
Alex	POSTAN	GB	28									
Hervé	POULAIN	F					NC	13			20	
Josef	PRECHTL	D				22						
Hugh	PRICE	GB							PQ	13		DNF
François	PROVOST	F						DNQ				
Ratanakul	PRUTIRAT	TH							NPQ			
Antonio	PUIG	E						17	NPQ			
Michel	QUINIOU	F									PQ	
Didier de	RADIGUÈS	B									DNF	DNF
Roberto	RAGAZZI	I				30						
Ranieri	RANDACCIO	I			DNF							
Pierre-Henri	RAPHANEL	F	DNF	DNF	2	DNF	DNF	5	2	DNF		
Stéphane	RATEL	F					NC					
Roland	RATZENBERGER	A	DNF	DNF	9	5						
Jean-Daniel	RAULET	F		11								
Roberto	RAVAGLIA	I	DNF							3		
Philippe	RÉGNIER	F					NPQ					
Hervé	REGOUT	B	22			DNF	NPQ					
Anthony	REID	GB	3	DNF			19					
Philippe	RENAULT	F			DNQ							
Manuel	REUTER	D	DNF	9	7	DNF		1				
Jean-Louis	RICCI	F	14	NC	6	11	7		16	18	21	
Luca	RICCITELLI	I									13	
Tim	RICHARDSON	USA						NPQ				
Ulrich	RICHTER	D			17	DNF	DNS	PQ				
Charles	RICKETT	GB		DNF	11	DNF						
Gerold	RIED	D				PQ						
Lionel	ROBERT	F	7	11	DNF	10	DNF	PQ	RES	DNF		
Bernard	ROBIN	F		26	DNF							
Chip	ROBINSON	USA	DNF									
John	ROBINSON	GB						13	DNF			
Michael	ROE	IRL	17									
Wido	ROESSLER	D			DNF							
Hervé	ROHÉE	F	28									
Walter	RÖHRL	D	DNF									
Keijo 'Keke'	ROSBERG	SF	DNF									
Carl	ROSENBLAD	S						DNF	DNF	DNF		
Marc	ROSTAN	F			DNF	DNF	DNF	NPQ	NPQ	17		
Patrice	ROUSSEL	F			28	20						

372 LE MANS 24 HOURS 1990–99

1990-99

Driver		Nat	'90	'91	'92	'93	'94	'95	'96	'97	'98	'99
Benjamin	ROY	F					13			NPQ	FS	
Onofrio	RUSSO	I				23						
Rickard	RYDELL	S	12									
Boris II	SAID	USA						DSQ	NPQ			
Antoine	SALAMIN	CH			DNF							
Eliseo	SALAZAR	RCH	DNF							DNF		
Tomas	SALDAÑA	E				DNF	13	11	DNF	NPQ	DNF	NPQ	DNF
Steve	SALEEN	USA								DNF		
Maurizio	SANDRO SALA	BR	DNF	6	4			4	DNF	NPQ		
Bernard	SANTAL	CH	10	DNF		24	DNF	20				
Norbert	SANTOS	F	DNQ									
Kouji	SATOU	J						NPQ				
Franco	SCAPINI	I		DNQ								
Domenico 'Mimmo'	SCHIATTARELLA	I										6
Bob	SCHIRLE	GB							NPQ	DNF	22	
Jean-Louis	SCHLESSER	F		DNF								
Bernd	SCHNEIDER	D		DNF						DNF	WD	
Larry	SCHUMACHER	USA							DNF	DNF		
Michael	SCHUMACHER	D		5								
John	SCHUMANN	NL							PQ			
David	SEARS	GB	3									
Stefano	SEBASTIANI	I			DNF	DNS	DNF					
Peter	SEIKEL	D						15				
Toni	SEILER	CH						DNF	DNF	DNF	14	
Masanori	SEKIYA	J	6		2	4		1	DNF	DNF		
Oriol	SERVIA	F							NPQ			
Edouard	SEZIONALE	F				28		20	DNS	NPQ	DNF	
Scott	SHARP	USA						DNF				
James	SHEAD	GB	25									
John	SHELDON	GB	DNF	DNF	DNF							
Kenja	SHIMAMURA	J			NC							
Kazuo	SHIMIZU	J					16					
Philippe	SIFFERT	CH						DNF				
Victor	SIFTON	CDN							23			
Massimo	SIGALA	I	10					DNF				
Craig	SIMMISS	NZ	28									
Jean-Louis	SIRERA	F					17					
Mark	SKAIFE	AUS							DNF			
Charles	SLATER	USA										18
David	SMADJA	F								DNF		
Robin	SMITH	GB				DNS	DNF					
Steve	SOPER	GB						11	DNF	DNF	5	
Vincenzo	SOSPIRI	I								DNF	DNF	
Marc	SOURD	F						13	RES	NPQ		
Gustl	SPRENG	D				21						
Lyn	ST JAMES	USA			DNF							
Mercedes	STERMITZ	A			DNQ							
Robbie	STIRLING	CDN	25	DNF								
Hans-Joachim	STUCK	D	4	7		DNF	3	6	2	DNF	DNF	
Alain	STURM	F				14						
Tim	SUGDEN	GB							NPQ	4		
Danny	SULLIVAN	USA					3	8				
Kasikam	SUPHOT	TH							NPQ			
Aguri	SUZUKI	J	DNF					DNF	DNF	3	DNS	
Takaji	SUZUKI	J							18	DNF		
Toshio	SUZUKI	J	5		4		DNF	15		9	2	
Kunimitsu	TAKAHASHI	J	24			18	8	16				
Patrick	TAMBAY	F						NPQ				
Tetsuya	TANAKA	J					NPQ					
Marcel	TARRES	F		DNF				NPQ	NPQ			
Luigi	TAVERNA	I		DNF	DNF	30						
Wayne	TAYLOR	ZA	12	NC	DNF	12			DNF	DNF	8	
Yojiro	TERADA	J	20	8	DNF	DNF	15	7	25	17	15	DNF

Driver		Nat	'90	'91	'92	'93	'94	'95	'96	'97	'98	'99
David	TERRIEN	F								PQR		DNF
Georges	TESSIER	F			DNF	DNF						
Olivier	THÉVENIN	F						12	DNF	DNF	15	DNF
Didier	THEYS	B			DNF				DNF	6	14	3
Kurt	THIIM	DK		DNF								
Pierre de	THOISY	F	DNQ	DNF		16	15	DNF				DNF
Bernard	THUNER	CH	DNF	DNF				DNF				
Thorkild	THYRRING	DK			DNF	DNF	DNF	NPQ				
Marcel	TIEMANN	D										DNS
Christophe	TINSEAU	F								NPQ	DNF	DNF
Harri	TOIVONEN	SF		9	DNS				DNF	DNF		
Matiaz	TOMLJE	SLO					10	FS				
Raymond	TOUROUL	F			DNQ							
Gérard	TREMBLAY	F	DNF		DNF	DNF						
Arnaud	TRÉVISOL	F						NC	DNF			
Michel	TROLLÉ	F	7	NC								
Jacques	TROPENAT	F			27	DNQ						
Michael	TRUNK	D								NPQ	DNF	
Keiichi	TSUCHIYA	J			18	8	16	DNF	9	2		
Takeshi	TSUCHIYA	J							DNF			
Matt	TURNER	USA								19		
Jake	ULRICH	USA							PQ			
Johnny	UNSER	USA					9					
Christian	VANN	GB										22
David	VEGHER	USA	DNQ									
David	VELAY	F							NPQ			
Fermin	VELEZ	SP	18					DNF		8		
Vito	VENINATA	I		DNF								
Philip	VERELLEN	B		25								
Jean-François	VEROUX	F					16					
Andres	VILARINO	E				11						
Frank de	VITA	F		NC								
Vincent	VOSSE	B										20
Patrick	VUILLAUME	F			DNF							
Eric van de	VYVER	F					16	NPQ				
Takao	WADA	J	DNF									
Andy	WALLACE	GB	2	4	8	DNF		3	6	DNF	7	DNF
David	WARNOCK	GB						NPQ	DNF	22		
Derek	WARWICK	GB						13				
John	WATSON	GB	11									
James	WEAVER	GB	DNF	NC		DNF	9		DNF	DNF		
Mark	WEBBER	AUS								DNF	DNS	
Volker	WEIDLER	D	DNF	1	4							
Karl	WENDLINGER	A		5	DNF			3	DNF	DNF	10	
Julian	WESTWOOD	GB										PQR
Desiré	WILSON	ZA		DNF								
Rob	WILSON	NZ			DNF							
Joachim	WINKELHOCK	D							DNF		1	
Pascal	WITMEUR	B		27								
Karl-Heinz	WLAZIK	D		17	DNF							
Bob	WOLLEK	F	8	3	6	9	4	2	2	DNF	2	19
Dudley	WOOD	GB	27									
Alex	WURZ	A					1					
Hisashi	YOKOSHIMA	J	12									
Takashi	YORINO	J	20	8	DNF							
Tomiko	YOSHIKAWA	J		NC	DNF	NC						
Mike	YOULES	GB	21									
Pierre	YVER	F	9	DNF	10	11	DNF	DNF	22	14	23	NC
Jean-François	YVON	F		DNF	11	DNF						
Angelo	ZADRA	I						DNF	DNF			
Ricardo	ZONTA	BR							DNF			
Klaas	ZWART	NL			DNF	NPQ						
Charles	ZWOLSMAN	NL	DNF	DNF	DNF							

DNF Did not finish **DNQ** Did not qualify **DNS** Did not start **DSQ** Disqualified **FS** Car failed scrutineering **NC** Not classified as a finisher **NPQ** Did not prequalify **RES** Reserve not required for race **WD** Withdrawn
PQ Drove a successful car in Prequalifying but not nominated for race week **PQR** Prequalified as a reserve but not nominated for race week

DATA FOR THE DECADE

LE MANS

REASONS FOR RETIREMENTS

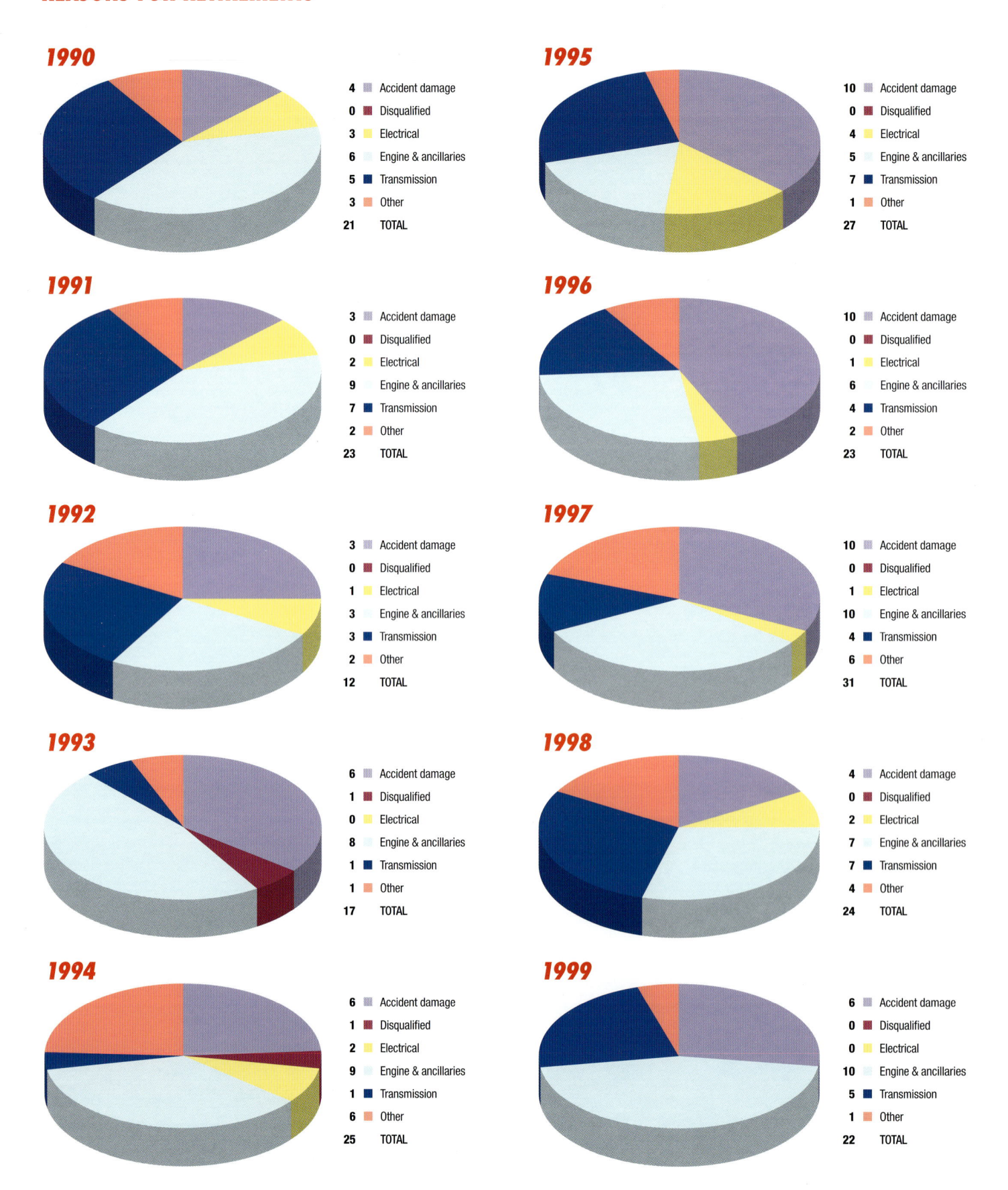

1990
4	Accident damage
0	Disqualified
3	Electrical
6	Engine & ancillaries
5	Transmission
3	Other
21	**TOTAL**

1991
3	Accident damage
0	Disqualified
2	Electrical
9	Engine & ancillaries
7	Transmission
2	Other
23	**TOTAL**

1992
3	Accident damage
0	Disqualified
1	Electrical
3	Engine & ancillaries
3	Transmission
2	Other
12	**TOTAL**

1993
6	Accident damage
1	Disqualified
0	Electrical
8	Engine & ancillaries
1	Transmission
1	Other
17	**TOTAL**

1994
6	Accident damage
1	Disqualified
2	Electrical
9	Engine & ancillaries
1	Transmission
6	Other
25	**TOTAL**

1995
10	Accident damage
0	Disqualified
4	Electrical
5	Engine & ancillaries
7	Transmission
1	Other
27	**TOTAL**

1996
10	Accident damage
0	Disqualified
1	Electrical
6	Engine & ancillaries
4	Transmission
2	Other
23	**TOTAL**

1997
10	Accident damage
0	Disqualified
1	Electrical
10	Engine & ancillaries
4	Transmission
6	Other
31	**TOTAL**

1998
4	Accident damage
0	Disqualified
2	Electrical
7	Engine & ancillaries
7	Transmission
4	Other
24	**TOTAL**

1999
6	Accident damage
0	Disqualified
0	Electrical
10	Engine & ancillaries
5	Transmission
1	Other
22	**TOTAL**

1990-99

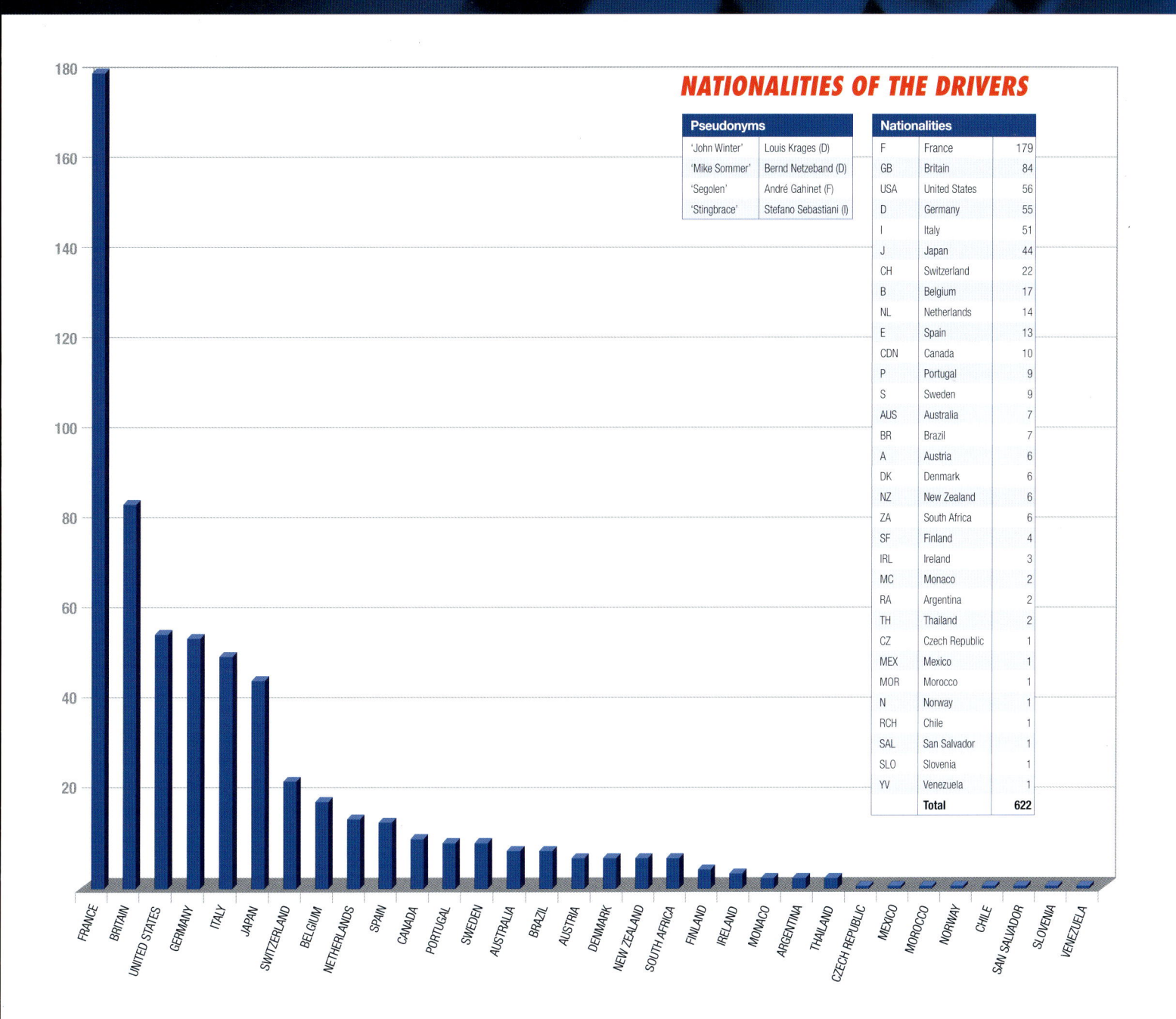

NATIONALITIES OF THE DRIVERS

Pseudonyms	
'John Winter'	Louis Krages (D)
'Mike Sommer'	Bernd Netzeband (D)
'Segolen'	André Gahinet (F)
'Stingbrace'	Stefano Sebastiani (I)

Nationalities		
F	France	179
GB	Britain	84
USA	United States	56
D	Germany	55
I	Italy	51
J	Japan	44
CH	Switzerland	22
B	Belgium	17
NL	Netherlands	14
E	Spain	13
CDN	Canada	10
P	Portugal	9
S	Sweden	9
AUS	Australia	7
BR	Brazil	7
A	Austria	6
DK	Denmark	6
NZ	New Zealand	6
ZA	South Africa	6
SF	Finland	4
IRL	Ireland	3
MC	Monaco	2
RA	Argentina	2
TH	Thailand	2
CZ	Czech Republic	1
MEX	Mexico	1
MOR	Morocco	1
N	Norway	1
RCH	Chile	1
SAL	San Salvador	1
SLO	Slovenia	1
YV	Venezuela	1
	Total	622

WINNING TYRE COMPANIES

Year	1990	1991	1992	1993	1994	1995	1996	1997	1998	1999
Goodyear					■		■	■		
Dunlop		■								
Michelin			■	■		■			■	■

DATA FOR THE DECADE 375

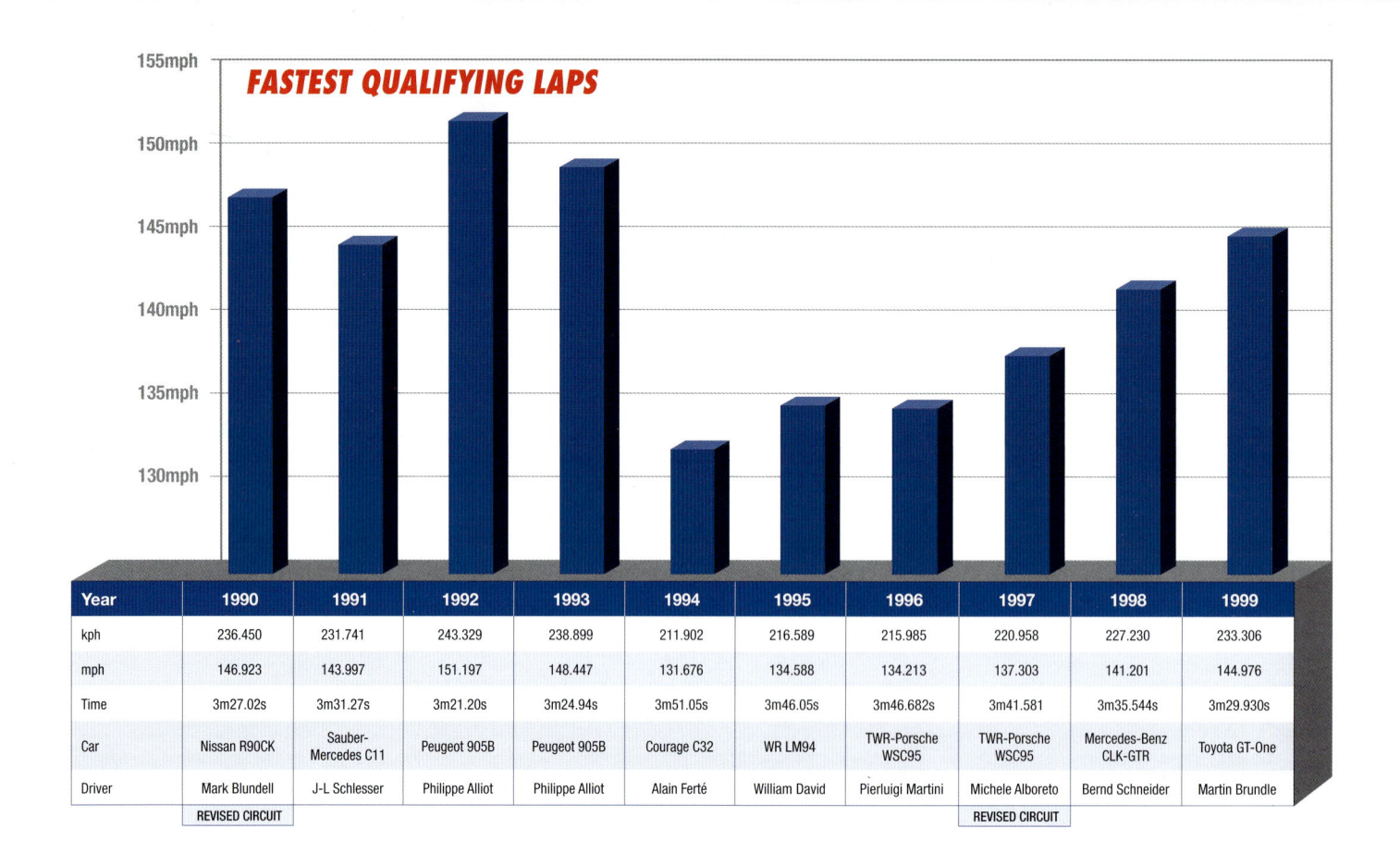

LE MANS

FASTEST QUALIFYING LAPS

Year	1990	1991	1992	1993	1994	1995	1996	1997	1998	1999
kph	236.450	231.741	243.329	238.899	211.902	216.589	215.985	220.958	227.230	233.306
mph	146.923	143.997	151.197	148.447	131.676	134.588	134.213	137.303	141.201	144.976
Time	3m27.02s	3m31.27s	3m21.20s	3m24.94s	3m51.05s	3m46.05s	3m46.682s	3m41.581	3m35.544s	3m29.930s
Car	Nissan R90CK	Sauber-Mercedes C11	Peugeot 905B	Peugeot 905B	Courage C32	WR LM94	TWR-Porsche WSC95	TWR-Porsche WSC95	Mercedes-Benz CLK-GTR	Toyota GT-One
Driver	Mark Blundell	J-L Schlesser	Philippe Alliot	Philippe Alliot	Alain Ferté	William David	Pierluigi Martini	Michele Alboreto	Bernd Schneider	Martin Brundle

1990: REVISED CIRCUIT; 1997: REVISED CIRCUIT

FASTEST RACE LAPS

Year	1990	1991	1992	1993	1994	1995	1996	1997	1998	1999
kph	222.515	227.125	230.622	235.986	210.544	211.573	215.723	217.534	220.812	227.771
mph	138.264	141.135	143.302	146.634	130.832	131.471	134.050	135.176	137.213	141.537
Time	3m40.03s	3m35.564s	3m32.295s	3m27.47s	3m52.54s	3m51.410s	3m46.958s	3m45.068s	3m41.809	3m35.032s
Car	Nissan R90CK	Sauber-Mercedes C11	Toyota TS010	Toyota TS010	Dauer 962LM	WR LM94	Ferrari 333 SP	TWR-Porsche WSC95	Toyota GT-One	Toyota GT-One
Driver	Steve Millen	Michael Schumacher	Jan Lammers	Eddie Irvine	Thierry Boutsen	Patrick Gonin	Eric van der Poele	Tom Kristensen	Martin Brundle	Ukyo Katayama

1990: REVISED CIRCUIT; 1997: REVISED CIRCUIT

LE MANS 24 HOURS 1990–99

1990-99

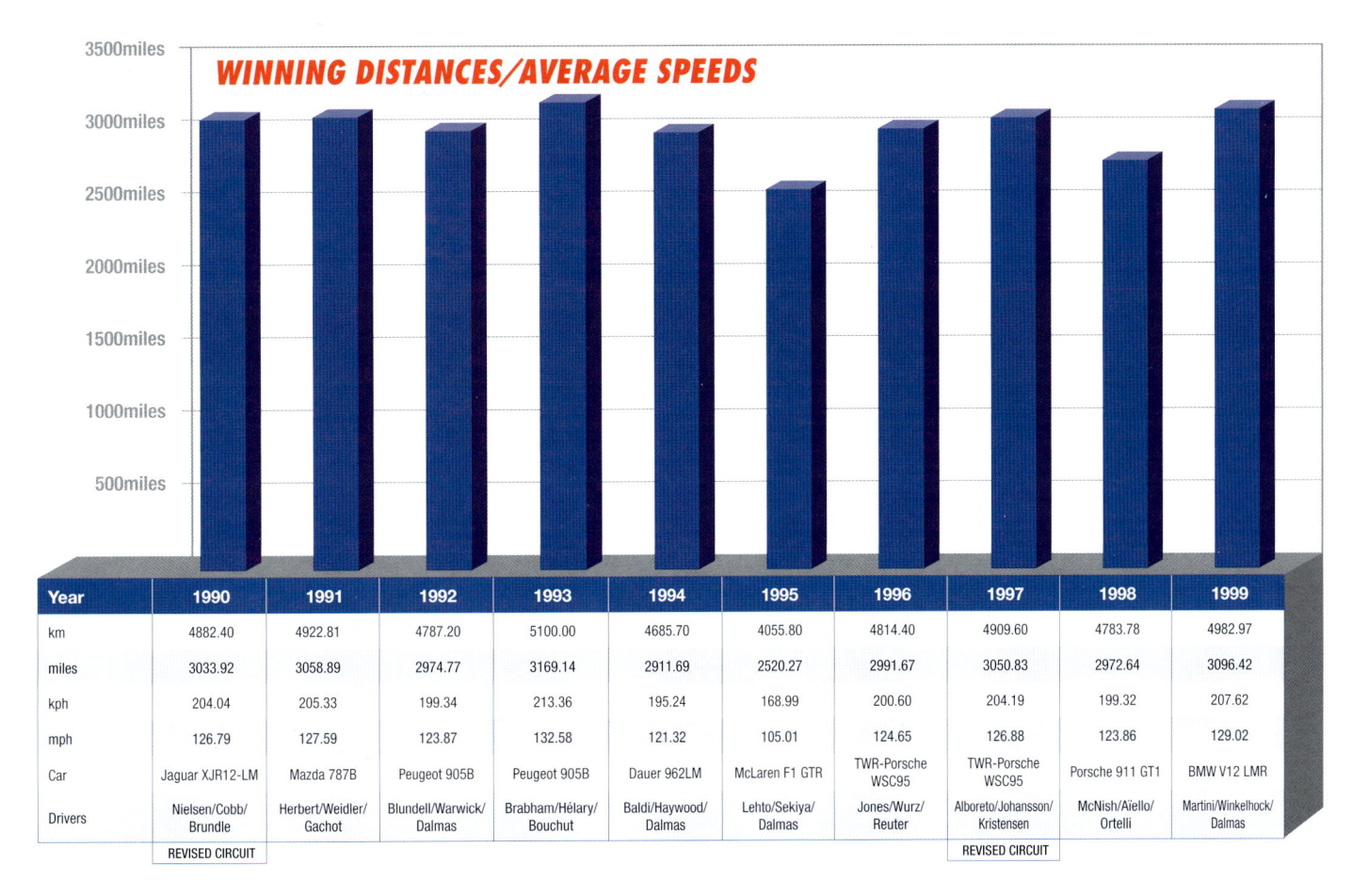

WINNING DISTANCES/AVERAGE SPEEDS

Year	1990	1991	1992	1993	1994	1995	1996	1997	1998	1999
km	4882.40	4922.81	4787.20	5100.00	4685.70	4055.80	4814.40	4909.60	4783.78	4982.97
miles	3033.92	3058.89	2974.77	3169.14	2911.69	2520.27	2991.67	3050.83	2972.64	3096.42
kph	204.04	205.33	199.34	213.36	195.24	168.99	200.60	204.19	199.32	207.62
mph	126.79	127.59	123.87	132.58	121.32	105.01	124.65	126.88	123.86	129.02
Car	Jaguar XJR12-LM	Mazda 787B	Peugeot 905B	Peugeot 905B	Dauer 962LM	McLaren F1 GTR	TWR-Porsche WSC95	TWR-Porsche WSC95	Porsche 911 GT1	BMW V12 LMR
Drivers	Nielsen/Cobb/ Brundle	Herbert/Weidler/ Gachot	Blundell/Warwick/ Dalmas	Brabham/Hélary/ Bouchut	Baldi/Haywood/ Dalmas	Lehto/Sekiya/ Dalmas	Jones/Wurz/ Reuter	Alboreto/Johansson/ Kristensen	McNish/Aïello/ Ortelli	Martini/Winkelhock/ Dalmas

1991: REVISED CIRCUIT
1997: REVISED CIRCUIT

MARGINS OF VICTORY

Year	1990	1991	1992	1993	1994	1995	1996	1997	1998	1999
km	54.40	36.81	81.90	13.59	18.13	9.46	13.40	13.60	13.65	11.76
miles	33.80	22.87	50.89	8.44	11.27	5.88	8.33	8.45	8.48	7.31

DATA FOR THE DECADE

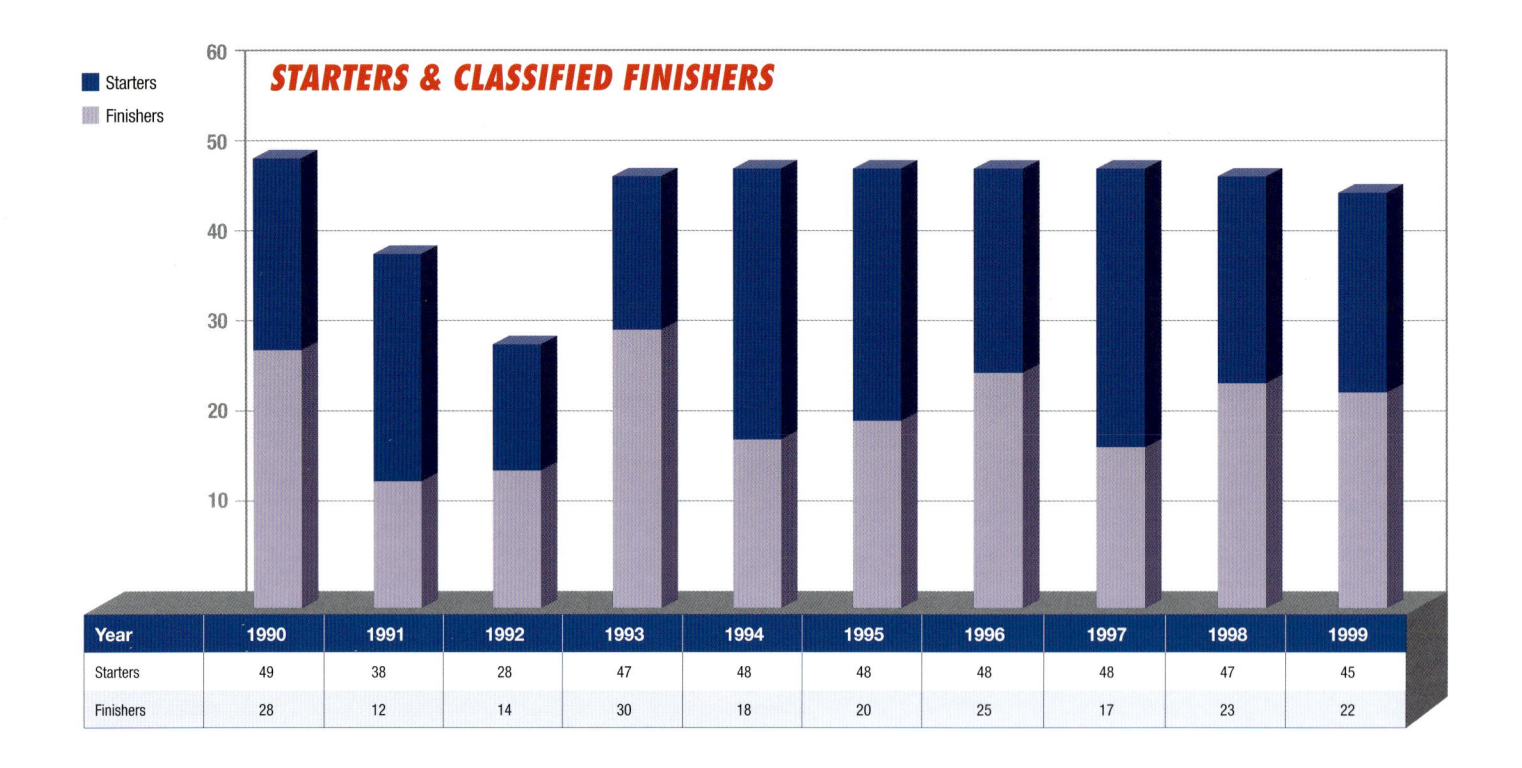

LE MANS

STARTERS & CLASSIFIED FINISHERS

- Starters
- Finishers

Year	1990	1991	1992	1993	1994	1995	1996	1997	1998	1999
Starters	49	38	28	47	48	48	48	48	47	45
Finishers	28	12	14	30	18	20	25	17	23	22

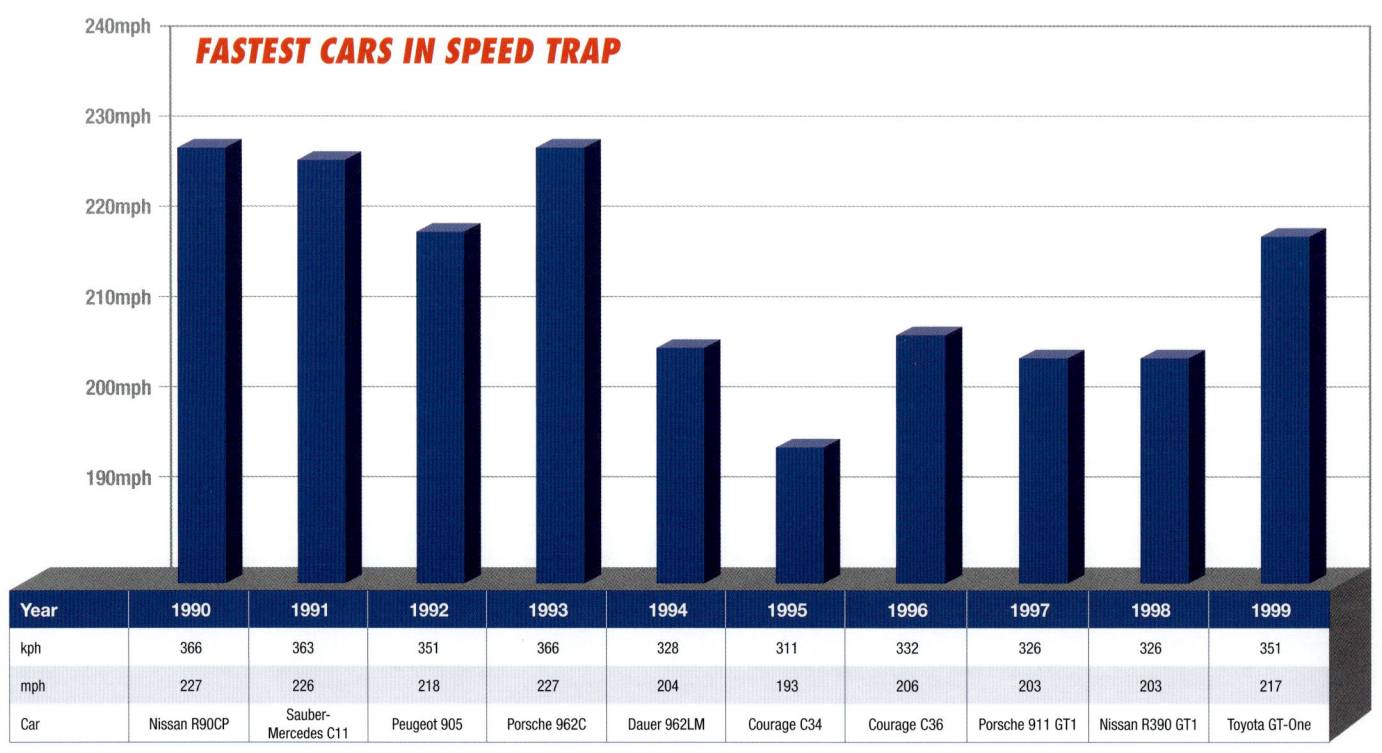

FASTEST CARS IN SPEED TRAP

Year	1990	1991	1992	1993	1994	1995	1996	1997	1998	1999
kph	366	363	351	366	328	311	332	326	326	351
mph	227	226	218	227	204	193	206	203	203	217
Car	Nissan R90CP	Sauber-Mercedes C11	Peugeot 905	Porsche 962C	Dauer 962LM	Courage C34	Courage C36	Porsche 911 GT1	Nissan R390 GT1	Toyota GT-One

NB: The speed trap ahead of the first chicane on the Mulsanne straight was not constantly in operation and some speeds were unrecorded

LE MANS 24 HOURS 1990–99

1990-99

BIBLIOGRAPHY

The author has raided many contemporary reports (among which those by Gary Watkins in *Autosport* and Alan Lis in *Racecar Engineering* were found to be the most reliable and informative) and countless websites for nuggets of information. In addition, the following excellent books are recommended for further reading:

24 HEURES DU MANS: TOME 3 – 1986-2010
By Christian Moity, Jean-Marc Teissèdre and Alain Bienvenue
Editions Le Mans Racing/Vif-Argent (2010)

24:16: AN AUTOBIOGRAPHY
By Norbert Singer with Michael Cotton
Coterie Press (2006)

FROM DRAWING BOARD TO CHEQUERED FLAG
By Tony Southgate
Motor Racing Publications (2010)

LE MANS: A CENTURY OF PASSION
By Michel Bonté, François Hurel & Jean-Luc Ribémon
Automobile Club de l'Ouest (2006)

LE MANS 24 HOURS YEARBOOKS 1990-99
By Christian Moity & Jean-Marc Teissèdre
ACO with Autotechnica (1990), PBS (1991-93), IHM (1994-99)

LIFE OF SPICE
By Gordon Spice
Haynes Publishing (2009)

PORSCHE 956-962
By Ulrich Upietz
Gruppe C Motorsport-Verlag (1993)

PORSCHE: EXCELLENCE WAS EXPECTED
By Karl Ludvigsen
Bentley Publishers (2003)

THE BRITISH AT LE MANS
By Ian Wagstaff
Motor Racing Publications (2006)

THE INTERNATIONAL MOTOR RACING GUIDE
By Peter Higham
David Bull Publishing (2003)

PHOTOGRAPHIC CREDITS

Automobile Club de l'Ouest: 7, 8, 9 (a), 9 (b), 10 (a), 10 (b), 12 (a), 12 (b), 17, 18 (bl), 18 (br), 19, 20 (a), 20 (b), 22, 23 (b), 24, 25, 26, 27, 29 (a), 29 (b), 30 (a), 30 (b), 31 (a), 31 (b), 33 (a), 34 (a), 34 (b), 35 (a), 35 (c), 37 (a), 38 (a), 39 (a), 39 (b), 40 (b), 41 (a), 42 (a), 42 (b), 43 (b), 44 (a), 46 (a), 48 (b), 49, 57, 58, 59 (a), 59 (b), 60, 61 (b), 62, 64 (a), 65 (a), 65 (b), 66 (b), 67, 69 (a), 69 (b), 70 (b), 71 (a), 71 (b), 72 (a), 72 (b), 74 (a), 74 (b), 75 (b), 77 (b), 78 (b), 79 (a), 79 (b), 80 (a), 81 (a), 89, 90 (a), 90 (b), 93 (a), 93 (b), 97, 99, 102, 103 (b), 106 (a), 109, 118, 119, 120 (a), 123, 124 (a), 124 (b), 125 (a), 128 (b), 130 (a), 130 (b), 131 (a), 131 (b), 133 (a), 133 (b), 134 (b), 135 (a), 135 (b), 136, 137 (a), 137 (b), 138, 140 (a), 140 (b), 149 (a), 149 (b), 154 (a), 154 (b), 156, 157 (a), 157 (b), 158 (a), 158 (b), 159 (a), 159 (b), 160 (a), 160 (b), 161 (a), 163 (b), 164, 165, 166 (br), 167, 168 (a), 168 (b), 169, 174 (b), 175 (b), 176 (b), 177 (a), 177 (b), 179, 187 (a), 188 (a), 188 (bl), 188 (br), 190, 192 (a), 192 (b), 193 (a), 193 (b), 194, 195 (a), 196, 199, 200 (b), 201 (b), 202, 203, 204 (b), 205 (b), 207 (a), 208 (a), 208 (b), 209, 211 (a), 211 (b), 213 (b), 214 (a), 214 (b), 215 (a), 215 (b), 217 (a), 225 (a), 225 (b), 226, 227 (a), 227 (b), 229 (a), 230 (b), 233, 234 (a), 234 (b), 236 (a), 239 (b), 241, 242 (a), 242 (b), 243, 246 (a), 246 (b), 247 (a), 249 (b), 254 (a), 255 (a), 260-261, 263, 264 (a), 264 (bl), 264 (br), 265, 266 (a), 266 (b), 271 (b), 273 (a), 274, 276 (a), 276 (b), 277 (bl), 278 (b), 281 (b), 283, 284 (a), 285 (br), 289 (a), 291 (a), 291 (b), 300 (a), 300 (b), 301, 302 (br), 304 (b), 305 (a), 305 (b), 306, 307 (a), 307 (b), 308 (a), 308 (b), 309 (a), 309 (b), 310 (b), 311 (a), 311 (b), 313 (b), 315 (a), 316 (a), 316 (b), 318 (a), 318 (b), 319, 320, 321 (b), 322 (a), 323 (a), 323 (b), 324 (a), 324 (b), 325 (a), 325 (b), 330-331, 333 (a), 333 (b), 334, 335, 336 (a), 337 (a), 337 (b), 338 (a), 338 (b), 339, 340, 341, 342, 343 (a), 344 (a), 345 (a), 345 (b), 346, 347 (a), 347 (b), 350 (a), 350 (b), 351 (a), 351 (b), 352 (a), 352 (b), 353, 354, 355, 356 (a), 357, 358, 359 (a), 359 (b), 360 (a), 361 (a), 379

LAT Photographic: Front cover, 3, 4-5, 6, 14-15, 21, 23 (a), 28, 32, 33 (b), 35 (b), 36, 37 (b), 40 (a), 41 (b), 43 (a), 44 (b), 45, 46 (b), 47, 48 (a), 54-55, 61 (a), 63, 64 (b), 66 (a), 68, 73, 75 (a), 76 (a), 76 (b), 77 (a), 78 (a), 80 (b), 81 (b), 86-87, 91, 92, 94, 95, 96 (a), 96 (b), 98 (a), 98 (b), 100 (b), 101 (a), 101 (c), 103 (a), 104, 105, 106 (b), 107 (a), 107 (b), 108 (a), 108 (b), 114-115, 117, 120 (b), 121 (a), 121 (b), 122, 125 (b), 126, 127 (a), 132 (a), 132 (b), 134 (a), 139 (a), 139 (b), 141, 146-147, 153, 166 (a), 166 (bl), 170, 171, 172 (a), 172 (b), 173, 174 (a), 175 (a), 176 (a), 178 (b), 184-185, 187 (b), 189, 191 (a), 191 (b), 195 (b), 197, 198 (a), 198 (b), 200 (a), 204 (a), 205 (a), 206, 207 (b), 210 (b), 212, 216 (a), 216 (b), 217 (b), 222-223, 228, 229 (b), 230 (a), 237, 238, 244, 245, 247 (b), 248 (a), 250, 251, 252, 253 (a), 253 (b), 255 (b), 267 (b), 269 (a), 270, 271 (a), 272, 273 (b), 275 (a), 277 (a), 278 (a), 279 (a), 279 (b), 280, 281 (a), 282, 285 (a), 286, 287, 288, 290 (a), 290 (b), 296-297, 299 (a), 299 (b), 304 (a), 310 (a), 312, 313 (a), 314, 315 (b), 317, 322 (b), 336 (b), 343 (b), 344 (b), 349, 356 (b), 366-367

Porsche: 38 (b), 70 (a), 100 (a), 101 (b), 127 (b), 128 (a), 129 (a), 129 (b), 151, 152, 153, 161 (b), 162 (a), 162 (b), 163 (a), 163 (c), 178 (a), 201 (a), 210 (al), 210 (ar), 213 (a), 213 (c), 231, 232, 235, 236 (b), 239 (a), 240 (a), 240 (b), 248 (b), 249 (a), 254 (b), 267 (a), 268, 269 (b), 275 (b), 277 (br), 284 (b), 285 (bl), 289 (b), 302 (a), 302 (bl), 303 (a), 303 (b), 321 (a), 348 (a), 348 (b), 360 (b), 361 (b)

KEY (a) above/top, (b) below/bottom, (c) centre

BIBLIOGRAPHY 379

INDEX

AAR Eagle team 26, 36
Abt, Christian 343
Acheson, Kenneth 17, 25, 64, 91, 95, 97, 124, 209, 250
Action Formula 106
ADA Engineering 46, 101, 173–4
02B 46
Adams, Dennis 214
Adams, Nick 32, 80, 139
Advanced Composites 30, 44, 47, 76
Aérodyne 68
Aérospatiale 170, 196
AGS F1 team 49
Agusta, Riccardo 'Rocky' 137–8, 177, 204–5, 253, 290, 322
Agusta Racing team 176, 204–5, 253, 290
Ahrlé, André 277, 361
Aïello, Laurent 13, 301–2, 342
Airflow Management 105
Aixam 141
Akizawa, Yukiatsu 319
Albert, Prince of Monaco 88
Albert, Tom 357
Alboreto, Michele 13, 226, 229–30, 263, 265–7, 321, 342
ALD (Automobiles Louis Descartes) 45, 59, 80, 108, 176
06 176
C289 45, 109
C91 80–1
Alesi, Jean 165
Alexander, Marc 109
Alfa Romeo 109, 135, 205
Allard, Alan 141
Allard, Sidney 141
Allard J2X 73, 141
Allen, Tim 288
Alliot, Philippe 38, 58, 68–9, 89, 91–4, 117, 120, 122, 189, 194, 226, 232, 236
Alméras, Jacques 78, 101, 134, 163
Alméras, Jean-Marie 78, 101, 134, 163
ALPA 179
Alpha Racing Team 17, 27
Alpine-Renault 169, 255
A610 169
Altenbach, Otto 43, 77, 100–1, 133
Alzen, Uwe 301–2, 348
AMG Mercedes 313–14, 344–5
AM-PM Publishing 319
American Le Mans Series 334
Amon, Chris 238
Amorim, Ni 347
Ampferer, Herbert 228, 231–2, 320
Andersson, Ove 304
Anderson Motor Sports 124
Andial 22, 43, 78
Andretti, Mario 189, 194–5, 228, 235–6, 275
Andretti, Michael 275
Andrews, Phil 173
Andskär, Steven 43, 78, 91, 98, 125, 151, 156

Angelastri, Sandro 165
Angelelli, Max 353
Anglia Composites 73
AO Racing 79, 80, 106–7
Aoshima, Tsunemasa 79
Apicella, Marco 208, 359
Appel, Wolfgang-Dieter 340
Archer, Tommy 278, 311, 347
Argo Cars 48
JM19C 48
'Arman' (Armand Fernandez) 177
Arnaud, Michel 164
Arnoux, René 163–4, 197
Arrows F1 team 273
Artioli, Romano 169
Artzet, Didier 108
Ascari Cars FGT 217
Astec 102, 228, 273
Aston Martin 217
DB7 GT1 217
Astratech 179
Auberlen, Bill 315, 349
Audi Sport 333, 335, 340–3
R8C 340-3
R8R 340-2
Audi Sport UK 342
Aufrecht, Hans Werner 313
Autoexe Motorsports 358
AutoXpo 173
Auvergne Motors 207
Auto Vitesse 215
Ayari, Soheil 278, 347
Ayles, Gary 206, 272, 311

Bachelart, Eric 226, 238
Bagnall, Andrew 240
Bailey, Charles 179
Bailey, Julian 17, 25, 287
Baker, Jonathan 173
Baker, Roy 33, 46, 104, 214, 289
Ballabio, Fulvio 140–1
Balas, Bertrand 163–4
Baldi, Mauro 13, 68, 91, 94, 117, 119–20, 122, 151–4, 272, 285, 309, 357
Balestre, Jean-Marie 18, 58, 90, 150
Barbazza, Fabrizio 197
Bardinon, Patrick 73
Baretzky, Ulrich 340
Barker, Paul 173
Barth, Jürgen 70, 129, 150, 209, 231, 348
Bassaler, Roland 140, 179
Basso, Jean-Claude 176
Baude, Hugues 322
Baverey, Anne 48
BBA Compétition 176–7, 194, 215, 233, 270
Bebb, Doug 198
Becker, Harald 290
Bell, Bob 25
Bell, Derek 17, 27–8, 32, 70, 101, 130, 149, 151, 158–9, 189, 192–3, 234
Bell, Justin 80, 101, 163–4, 189, 192–3, 278–9, 310, 347
Bellamy, Ralph 76
Bellasi, Guglielmo 140
Bellefroid, Eric 109
Bellm, Ray 72, 190, 193, 227, 233–4, 270–2
Bello, Noël del 49, 191, 194, 216

Belloc, Jean-Philippe 276, 347
Belmondo, Paul 126, 215, 246–7, 346–7
Beloou, Philippe 137, 164, 170
Beltoise, Jean-Pierre 134
Benbow, Dave 21, 65
Benzieron, 'Lilo' 291
Beretta, Olivier 243, 278, 310–11, 346–7
Berg, Allen 41
Berger, Gerhard 337
Berkeley Team London 80, 107
Bernard, Eric 246–7, 272, 282, 317, 352–3
Bertaggia, Enrico 204–5, 322
Bertaut, Alain 126, 150, 153
Bialgue, Yann 138
Biela, Frank 341–2
Bigazzi, Aldo 233
Bigazzi, Paolo 233
Bigazzi team 233–4
Birrane, Martin 355
Bitter Automobil 72
Blain, Georges 141
Blanc, Hélène 56
Blaupunkt 70
Blundell, Mark 13, 17, 22, 25, 67, 89, 91–2, 94, 193–4
BMS Scuderia Italia 284
BMW 140, 190, 232, 265, 270, 272, 311, 325, 335, 349
BMW Motorsport 232, 270, 311, 336, 349
V12 LM 311–2, 349–50
V12 LMR 336–8
BMW North America 311
Boesel, Raul 64
Bombien, Frank 76–7
Bondurant, Bob 288
Bône, Philippe 138
Bonnet, Didier 109, 135, 175, 205, 255, 325
Bornhauser, Patrick 217
Bouchut, Christophe 13, 117, 119–20, 122, 168, 201–2, 209, 249, 285, 300, 314, 345–6
Boudy, Jean-Pierre 68, 92
Bouillon, Jean-Christophe 170, 282, 309
Boulan, Hervé 137–8
Boulay, Sylvain 176, 217
Bouquet, Jacques 39, 99
Bourbon, Alfonso d'Orleans 166
Bourbonnais, Claude 71
Bourdais, Patrick 179, 205, 276–7
Bouresche, Jean-Michel 285, 309
Boutsen, Thierry 117, 119, 122, 124, 151, 153, 156, 187, 202, 225–8, 231–2, 263, 265, 268, 301, 304, 306, 333–5, 339–40, 361
Bovy, Quirin 33
Bowden, Peter 162
Boxstrom, Max 76
BPR (Barth-Peter-Ratel) 150
Brabham, David 65, 97, 126, 235, 241, 282, 316, 333, 352–3
Brabham, Geoff 13, 17, 25–6, 119–20, 122
Brabham, Sir Jack 126
Brambilla, Sergio 129
Brana, Claude 138

Brancatelli, Gianfranco 17, 25, 37
Brand, Marco 71, 99
Brawn, Ross 63, 102, 228
BRM (British Racing Motors) 105, 288
P351 105
P301 288
Broadley, Eric 104
Brodie, Dave 179
Brooks, Tony 210
Brown, Paul 105
Brucker, Jim 49
Brumos Racing 128
Brun, Walter 17, 22–3, 74
Brun Motorsport 17, 22–3, 29, 43, 74, 140
C91 74
Brundle, Martin 13, 20–1, 263, 265, 274, 300–1, 305–6, 333–4, 339
Bruneau, Pierre 325
Brunn, 'Siggi' 29
Bscher, Thomas 151, 178, 189–92, 194, 232–4, 280, 289, 315, 335, 340, 349–50
Bugatti, Ettore 169
Bugatti 169–70
EB110 SS 169–70, 179
Bühren, Walter 229
Bühren, Wolfgang 29
Buick 216–7
Buitoni, Gian Luigi 196
Bundy, Harry 'Doc' 136, 281–2
Burville, Hayden 141

C&B Consultants 352
Caffi, Alex 350
Calderari, Enzo 129, 162, 276
Caldwell, John 156, 241, 278
Caldwell Development 241, 310, 346
Callaway, Reeves 171
Callaway Advanced Technologies 171
Callaway Competition 171, 204, 253, 290
Callaway Schweiz 204
Callum, Ian 274
Camaschella, Giorgio 197
Campbell, Bill 298
Canary, Paul 49
Canaska-Southwind team 243
Cane, Michael 193, 270, 315
Capello, Rinaldo 315, 341–2
Capette, Jean-Louis 140
Capon, Patric 34
Caradec, Didier 134
Carmignon, Jacky 109
Carrozzeria Pininfarina 165
Carrozzeria Scaglietti 165
Castaing, François 241
Catone, Paolo 195–6, 318, 350
Cecotto, Johnny 234
Challenge Ecoenergie 8, 19, 35, 67, 90
Chamberlain, Hugh 34, 79, 106, 136, 139, 178, 210, 278, 347
Chamberlain Engineering 34, 80, 106–7, 136–7, 139, 172–3, 178–9, 210, 278–9, 310–11, 346–7
Champion Racing 348
Chantriaux, Eric 322, 358
Chapelle, Xavier de la 138

Chappell, Dominic 173, 212
Chaunac, Hugues de 60, 243, 310
Chazal, Robert 164
Chedorge, Jean-Luc 235
Cheetah Cars 73
Chéreau, Jean-Luc 162–3, 209, 254, 276
Chéreau Sports 324, 361
Chevrolet 48, 171, 204, 216, 252, 286, 290
Callaway Corvette C7-R 253
Callaway Corvette SuperNatural GT1 171
Callaway Corvette SuperNatural GT2 204–5, 253, 290
Corvette XR-1 216
Chiti, Carlo 141
Chotard, Guy 134
Chotard, Jacques 101, 134
Choulet, Robert 68–9, 73, 92, 137
Christie, John 26, 324
Chrysler Corporation 163, 241, 278, 310, 335, 346
Chrysler Viper GT1 241–3
Chrysler Viper GT2 278–9, 310–11, 335, 346–7
CICA Concessionaires 346–7
Cimarosti, Luigi 164
Cirtek Motorsport 289
CJ Motorsports 324
Clairval, Alain 235
Classic Racing 79
Clérico, Emmanuel 276, 347
Cobb, Price 13, 20, 241, 289
Cochran, Jay 126–7, 197
Cohen-Olivar, Max 47, 77, 101
Collard, Emmanuel 209, 236, 265, 268, 300, 305, 309, 339, 357
Comas, Erik 209, 274–5, 307, 354
Communauté Urbaine du Mans 7
Compostiex 196
Comptech 73, 141, 196
Consonni, Giampiero 'Peo' 141
Cook, Charlie 243
Coppelli, Almo 81, 100, 133, 177, 204–5, 253, 290, 322
Coronel, Tom 357
Cortanze, André de 68, 304
Corvette 48, 171, 204–5, 216, 253, 290
Cosson, Michel 103, 118
Cosworth Engineering 33, 34–5, 45, 46, 48, 63, 72–3, 79, 81, 106–7, 139, 141, 179, 205, 325
Cottaz, Didier 226, 235–6, 319, 351
Coulthard, David 126
Courage, Yves 39, 42, 70, 78, 99, 130–1, 159, 194–5, 299, 319
Courage Compétition 39, 42, 59, 70, 78, 99, 130, 149, 151, 159, 187, 189, 194, 225, 235, 275, 318, 350
C20 39, 44
C22 39
C24S 39
C26S 70
C28LM 99
C30 130

1990-99

C32LM 159–60
C34 194
C36 235–6, 275–6, 320
C41 159, 195–6, 235
C50 319, 351
C51 318–9
C52 350–1
Couesson, Joël 109
Couvreur, Olivier 179
Cranfield wind tunnel 24, 355
Crawford, Chris 46, 101, 173, 210
CTS Composites 152, 336
Cudini, Alain 42, 170, 217, 243
Cugnola, Mario 351
Cummings, Gary 27
Cunningham, Clayton 157, 288
Cunningham Racing 156–7, 175

Dale, Terry 324
Dale-Jones, Graham 105
Dallara, Gian Paolo 173, 341
Dallara Automobili 197, 305, 341
Dalmas, Yannick 13, 69, 89, 91–2, 94, 119, 122, 151–4, 189–90, 225–6, 231–2, 265, 268, 321, 335–6, 338
Daly, Derek 25–6
DAMS 281–2, 316–7, 355
Danielsson, Thomas 44, 71, 208
Daoudi, Stéphane 291
Dassault 68
Dauer, Jochen 149, 152, 154
Dauer Sportwagen 154, 170
Daveau, Pierre 236
Davey, Tim Lee 47, 77, 107
David, William 187, 199–200, 250–1
David Price Racing (DPR) 189, 192–3, 232–3, 234, 280–2, 316–17, 349–50
Davis, Jamie 316
Dawson, Ian 41, 105, 288
Day, Gordon 349
De Tomaso Pantera GT1 173
Debora 109, 134–5, 175, 205, 255, 291, 325
 LMP294 175
 LMP295 205
 LMP296 255, 325
 LMP297 291
 SP92 109
 SP93 134–5
Déchavanne, Christophe 138
Dechent, Hans-Dieter 29
Délétraz, Jean-Denis 194, 235
Delon, Alain 225
Demont, Michel 28, 276, 351
Dennis, Ron 190–2
Denyer, Colin 213–4
Département de La Sarthe 7, 39
Descartes, Louis 45, 73, 80–1, 109
Dessau, David 291
Deutschman, Paul 171
Devendorf, Don 24
Dickens, Stanley 67, 249
Diel, Hartmut 340
Dieudonné, Pierre 31, 62, 243, 347
Dismore, Mark 241
Divila, Richard 46, 173, 196

Docking, Alan 31
Dodge see Chrysler
Dome Company 36, 350
Dominy, Rob 95
Donohue, David 310, 347
Donovan, Robin 34, 80, 100, 133, 159, 205, 247, 291, 358–9
Doran, Kevin 280
Dornier Aerospace 305
Doucet, Marc 49
Dow, Mike 48
Dowe, Tony 20, 228, 273, 316
Downing, Jim 174, 202–3, 240, 282–3
Doyle, Dan 308
Doyle Racing 244–5
Doyle-Risi Racing 300, 308, 357
DPS Composites 280, 314, 344, 349, 352
Drake, Jay 49
Driot, Jean-Paul 281, 355
Dro, Pascal 175, 252
Drudi, Luca 310
Dryver, Bernard de 38, 106, 291
Duclot, Alain 133
Duez, Marc 43, 138, 233, 310, 322, 347
Dumbreck, Peter 334–5, 344, 346
Dumfries, Johnny 37, 71
Dupuy, Dominique 129, 161–2, 209, 278, 346–7
Durango team 81
Dykstra, Lee 174
Dyson Racing 244, 358

Eagle Performance Racing 49
Earl, Bob 26
Ebeling, Dirk-Reiner 162, 213
Ecclestone, Bernie 7, 59, 90, 118
Ecurie Biennoise 162
EIA Moteurs 138, 215
Eichmann, Bruno 238, 277
Eiffel wind tunnel 137
Ekblom, Fredrick 276, 319, 351
Electramotive 24, 156
Electrodyne 32
Elf La Filière team see
 La Filière Elf
Elgh, Eje 44, 76, 98–9, 125
Elizagaray, Arnaud 243
Elkoubi, Michel 217
Elleray, Peter 342
Emilia Concessionaires 173
EMKA team 240, 315
Emmen Swiss National Aircraft wind tunnel 341, 342
Energy Efficiency competition 8, 19, 35, 67, 90
Engine Developments (Judd) 102, 104, 228, 355
Engeman, Rick 203, 283
Enjolras, Sébastien 10, 263
Ennea team 246–7
Erdos, Thomas 214, 252, 287
Ernst & Young 72
Essex Racing 203
Estoril Racing 324, 361
Euro Racing 59, 72–3, 102, 104–5
EuroBrun F1 team 23
EuroMotorsport 197

Euser, Cor 72, 104, 214, 252, 290
Evans, Andy 133, 160, 203, 237–8, 279, 285

Fabi, Teo 64–5, 97, 119, 122
Fabre, Pascal 39, 73, 99, 130, 160, 194, 252, 309
Falk, Peter 128
Falquet, Guy 73
Fangio, Juan II 119, 124
Farjon, Philippe 44
Farmer, Bill 238
Farrell, Steve 21, 274
FAT Turbo Express 70
Faure, Didier 346
Favre, Philippe 168, 198–9
FCI team 247
Fedco 73, 79–80
Fenwick, Alistair 46
Ferrari 40, 80, 123, 164, 196, 206, 228, 237, 246, 279, 308, 357
 F40 164–5
 F40 GTE 246–7
 F40 LM 206–7, 247
 333 SP 196–7, 237–8, 279–80, 308–9, 357
 348 GT2 165–6
 348 LM 166–7
 355 207
Ferrari Club Italia 165–6, 206–7, 246–7
Ferrari North America 196
Ferrari, Antonio 197
Ferrari, Enzo 165
Ferrari, Piero Lardi 196
Fert, Jean-François 73
Ferté, Alain 17, 21, 58–9, 67, 91–2, 94, 97, 149, 151, 159–60, 209, 252, 285
Ferté, Michel 21, 64, 176–7, 206–7, 247, 280, 309, 351
Feyman, François 35
FFSA (Fédération Française du Sport Automobile) 127, 345
Fiat wind tunnel 206
FIM (Fédération Internationale de Motocyclisme) 264
Fior, Claude 255, 325
FIRST Racing 286
FIA (Fédération Internationale de l'Automobile) 7, 334
 Expert Advisory Group 345
 World Motor Sport Council 18, 90, 150, 264
FISA (Fédération Internationale du Sport Automobile) 7, 18–19, 58, 89–90, 150
 Manufacturers Commission 7
 Sportscar Commission 118
Fittipaldi, Wilson 202
Flegl, Helmut 70
Flux, Ian 287
FocheAuto 205
Foitek, Gregor 75
Foley, Ian 286
Fondmetal Technologies 345
Footwork F1 team 70
Forbes-Robinson, Elliott 358–9
Ford Motor Company 130, 280, 291, 316, 322, 353, 355, 358–9
 Saleen Mustang RRR 288–9
Ford Deutschland wind tunnel 158
Ford Motorsport 288
Forghieri, Mauro 169

Fossett, Steve 133, 249
Fouché, George 43, 78, 91, 98–9, 125, 155–6, 249, 287
Fourquemin, Christian 176
Fox, Tony 353
Franklin, Mike 33, 72, 104
Freisinger, Manfred 209
Freisinger Motorsport 209–10, 361
Frentzen, Heinz-Harald 104
Fréon, Franck 175, 202–3, 235, 240–1, 282, 320, 358–9
Friend, Gordon 141
Fuchs, Andreas 126, 172, 209, 213
Fukuyama, Hideo 201
Fullerton, Dave 228
Fushida, Hiroshi 36

G Force Composites 312, 354
G Force Precision Engineering 196, 307, 353–4
Gache, Philippe 164, 243, 278, 322, 358–9
Gachot, Bertrand 13, 31, 58–62, 91, 103, 168, 250, 285
Gaignault, Gilles 164
Galmard, Luc 169
Galopin, Claude 282
Gandini, Marcello 169
Ganley, Howden 44
Gardner, Wayne 322
Garret, Sam 203, 282
Gartzen, Jürgen von 285
Gässner, Erwin 341
Gay, Patrice 319, 351
Gebhardt, Fritz 32
Gebhardt, Günther 32
Gebhardt Motorsport 32, 46
Gentilozzi, Paul 157
Ghezzi, Serge 236
Giacomelli, Bruno 41
Gibson, Bill 317
Giddins, Roy 22
Gilbert-Scott, Andrew 270–2
Gillet, 'Tony' 291
Gillet Vertigo 291
Gini, Alessandro 106, 130
Giorgio, Luigi 81
Giroix, Fabien 191, 233, 235, 312
Giroix Racing 191–2, 194, 233
Gleason, Chris 279
GM Motorsport 48, 107
Godfroy, Gérard 137
Goh, Kazimuchi 233, 235, 270, 272, 349–50
Gonin, Patrick 38, 81, 108, 134, 149, 160–1, 187, 189, 199–200, 250–1
Goodwin, Chris 270, 272, 351
Goodyear, Scott 226–8, 231, 251
Goossens, Marc 238, 319, 351
Gosselin, Claude-Yves 346
Goueslard, Patrice 284, 361
Gouhier, Joël 129
Gouloumes, Raymond 18, 138
Gounon, Jean-Marc 215, 246–7, 265, 270, 272, 314, 355
GP Motorsport 35, 46, 79, 80
Graemiger, Chuck 73
Graff Racing 34–5, 80, 139, 250, 347
Graham, Eric 138, 215
Graham, John 324

Grand, Jean-Philippe 35, 80, 347
Grau, Alexander 'Sandy' 286
Greene, John 241
Greene, Keith 37, 204, 236
Greenwood brothers 171
Grohs, Harald 43, 324
Grossenbacher, Gary 279
Grouillard, Olivier 177, 194, 234, 275, 291, 320
GTC Competition 193, 234–5, 265, 272, 315
Gue, Michael 203
Guéhennec, Alain 108
Guitteny, Lucien 207
Gulf Oil UK 158
Gurney, Dan 36

Haberthur, Christian 240, 323
Haberthur, Guido 163
Haberthur, Olivier 163, 240, 323
Haberthur Racing 163, 213, 240, 265, 276–7, 323
Hahne, Armin 126, 167–8, 199, 284, 303
Hall, Joan 332
Ham, Nick 324
Hamelle, Thomas 138
Hamlet, 'Butch' 203
Hanawa, Tomoo 42
Hannemann, Neil 241, 310
Harada, Jun 106–7, 174
Hardman, Peter 136–7, 172
Harrier Cars 178
 LR9 Spyder 178–9
Harris, Trevor 25, 156
Harrods 192, 195
Harrower, Ian 46, 101, 173
Hart, Brian 106
Harvey, Tim 33, 72
Hasemi, Masahiro 17, 24, 26, 245
Hashimo, Kazuyoshi 24
Hashimoto, Ken 168, 198
Hatoya, Kazuharu 95
Hatter, Tony 231
Hattori, Naoki 199
Haug, Norbert 345
Hayakawa, Masamitsu 43
Hayashi, Yoshimasa 24–25
Haywood, Hurley 13, 44, 76, 128, 151–2, 154
Hazell, Jeff 33, 73, 190
Heico team 129, 162, 213
Heidfeld, Nick 346
Heinkélé, Christian 207
Hélary, Eric 13, 119–20, 122, 170, 189, 195, 217, 243, 265, 270, 272, 301, 305–6, 322
Helem 291, 325
 V6 291, 325
Hellman 171
Hendricks, Shawn 241
Hennebury, Wayne 291
Henning, Philippe de 34, 81
Henriksen, Erik 162
Herbert, Johnny 13, 31, 58–62, 91, 103
Hermann, Antonio 194, 202, 284
Hettler, Jan 312
Heuclin, Jacques 45, 109
Hewland, William 179
Hezemans, Mike 286
Hiereth, Hermann 66
Hillburger, Werner 232

INDEX 381

Hodgetts, Chris 33, 72, 107, 213–14
Holzer, Jenny 337
Hommell, Michel 169–70, 217
Honda Motor 167, 198, 248
　NSX GT1 198
　NSX GT2 167–8, 199, 248
Honda Tochi Centre 167
Honegger, Pierre 141
Hori, Takahiro 27
Horn, Gordon 48
Horsman, John 44
Hoshino, Kazuyoshi 24, 201, 245, 275, 282, 306
Howard-Chappell, George 286
Hoy, Will 29, 76
Hoyle, Terry 33, 35, 46, 105
Hubert, Marcel 70, 99, 159
Hueere, Benôit 81
Hugenholtz, John 279, 311, 347
Huidekoper, Wuit 80, 104, 152, 302
Huisman, Patrick 310, 348
Humberstone, Chris 73, 141
Humphrys, Graham 33, 73, 104, 192, 272, 336
Hürtgen, Claudia 323, 361
Huysman, Harald 23, 74
Hydro Aluminium 23, 286
Hyett, Ross 13, 35

Iacobelli, Olindo 34, 80, 106, 136–7, 172, 210
Ickx, Jacky 31, 60
Ikuzawa, Tetsu 24
Iida, Akira 168, 199, 248
Iketani, Katsunori 47
Iley, John 141
Imberti, Elio 166
Imperial College wind tunnel 21, 167, 273, 354
IMSA (International Motor Sports Association) 119, 126–7, 149, 226, 228
Index of Energy Efficiency competition 8, 19, 35, 67, 90
Irvine, Eddie 13, 99, 117, 119–20, 122–3, 137, 151, 155–6
Ishizuka, Masata 73
ISRS (International Sports Racing Series) 264

Jabouille, Jean-Pierre 68–9, 91, 94, 120, 122, 285, 309, 357
Jacadi Racing 138, 176–7
JAF (Japan Automobile Federation) 119, 150, 251
Jaguar Cars 20–3, 63–5, 89, 126–7, 210–11
　XJR-12LM 20–2, 63–5
　XJ220C 126–7, 210–11
Jarier, Jean-Pierre 128–9, 209, 254, 276, 324, 361
JB Racing 285, 308, 357
Jelinski, Frank 17, 28, 70, 131, 171, 205
Joest, Reinhold 70, 229–30, 266, 340, 342
Joest Racing 17, 28–9, 70, 128, 131–3, 149, 153, 178, 226–30, 265–7, 276, 320–1, 321, 340–2, 351
Johansson, Stefan 13, 62, 91, 98, 265–7, 321, 343
John Fitzpatrick Racing 152
Johnson, Amos 126

Johnson, Roy 291, 325
Jones, Duane 'Davy' 13, 20–1, 64, 127, 225–6, 228–30
Jones, Richard 80, 105, 213
Jordan wind tunnel 352
Judd, John 102, 104
Jurasz, Manfred 361
Jüttner, Ralf 229–30, 320
JW Automotive 44

Kageyama, Masahiko 201, 245, 251, 275, 306
Kageyama, Masami 307
Kakimoto, Kunihiko 273, 353
Kalbfell, Karl-Heinz 311
Kamczyk, Dietmar 344
Kaneishi, Katsumoto 272
Kasuya, Shunji 43, 80, 104, 157, 201
Katayama, Nobuaki 95
Katayama, Ukyo 13, 97, 306, 335, 339–40, 349
Katayama, Yoshimi 31
Katech 196, 244
Kato, Shin 36, 125, 208–9
Katoh, Hiroki 349, 353
Kaufmann, Wolfgang 210, 361
Kayl, Fritz 196, 244
Kazmerowski, Dennis 48–9
Keegan, Rupert 212
Kelleners, Ralf 238, 265, 268, 301, 304, 306, 339–40
Kelly, Dave 33
Kemp, Derek 347
Kennedy, David 31, 62, 172
Kessel, Louis 133
Khan, Ian 48
Kinetic 322
Kingston, Geoff 95, 167, 249–50, 287
Kitchak, Peter 361
Klasen, Peter 38
Kok Motorsport 252
Kokusai Kaihatsu UK 191, 235
Kondo, Masahiko 174, 201, 245
Konrad, Franz 76, 201–2, 254, 277, 285, 322, 324, 357, 361
Konrad Motorsport 17, 20, 59, 70, 76, 129, 162, 175, 201–2, 254, 277, 284–5, 322, 324, 355–7, 360–1
　KM-011 76
Korytko, Roy 158
Korytko, Sepp 158
Kox, Peter 232, 234, 265, 270, 272, 357
Krages, Louis ('John Winter') 29, 70, 131
Krauss, Bruno 324
Krauss Race Sports International 324
Kremer, Erwin 38, 158, 167, 202, 213, 355
Kremer, Manfred 38, 158, 167, 202, 213
Kremer Racing 34, 38, 43, 75, 100, 131–3, 149, 151, 158–9, 167–8, 187, 201–2, 213, 248–9, 285, 289, 322, 355–7
Kremer K8 see Porsche
Kreutzpointner, Fritz 13, 67
Kreyer, Norbert 304–5
Kriska, Dave 353
Kristensen, Tom 13, 265–7, 312, 335, 337–8

Krosnoff, Jeff 65, 151, 155–6, 177, 208
Krumm, Michael 251, 307, 354
Kudzu 202, 240, 282
　DG2/3 202–3
　DLM 240–1
　DLM4 282–3
Kurosawa, Takuya 307
Kussmaul, Roland 28, 209
Kuster, Guy 240

La Filière Elf 235–6, 275–6, 320, 351
Lacaud, Dominique 216
Laffite, Jacques 22, 29, 138, 163, 177, 233
Lagaay, Harm 231
Lagniez, Jean-Claude 276, 347
Lagorce, Franck 160, 187, 196, 236, 282, 307, 346
Lamborghini 76, 141, 163
Lamm, Karl 'Charly' 272, 337
Lammers, Jan 17, 20–1, 29, 89, 97, 124, 235–6, 286, 307, 357
Lamouille, Alain 134, 138
Lamplough, Robs 141
Lamy, Pedro 284, 310–11, 346
Lancia 40, 81
　LC2 40, 81
Langford & Peck 81
Langton, Soames 240
Lanzante, Paul 192
Lanzante Motorsport 192, 235, 290
Lapeyre, Xavier 35, 80
Larbre Compétition 127–9, 161–3, 175, 209, 213, 240, 241, 254, 276–7, 324, 361
Larrousse, Gérard 138
Larrousse F1 team 138
Lässig, Jürgen 43, 77, 100–1, 133, 159, 201, 249, 289
Laurenz, Werner 337
Larrauri, Oscar 17, 22–3, 25, 28, 74, 149, 166
Lavaggi, Giovanni 47, 100, 133, 158, 201, 289
Lawrence, Chris 213
Le Mans Syndicat Mixte 7, 18, 58, 334
Le Mans Technoparc 188, 235
Leboissetier, Nicolas 247
Lebrun, Alain 250
Lecerf, Thierry 107
Lechner, Reinhard 67
Leconte, Jack 129, 162–3, 175, 209, 240, 254, 276, 323, 361
Lecourt, Thierry 194, 322, 358
Lees, Geoff 17, 36, 39, 89, 91–2, 97, 117, 119, 123–4, 212, 250, 287, 301, 304, 306
Legeay, Mikaël 291, 325
Legeay, Patrick 291, 325
Legeay Sports Mécanique 169, 255, 291, 325
Lehto, JJ 13, 41, 75, 189–90, 193, 227, 234, 263, 265, 272, 333–5, 337–8
Leidi, Gianfranco Bonomi di 141
Leitzinger, Robert 'Butch' 282, 322, 352, 358–9
Leloup, Philippe 243
Leslie, David 17, 21, 65, 126, 214

Lesseps, Ferdinand de 80, 106, 136–7, 177
Lett, Barry 190
Leveritt, John 280
Lexus 291
Libert, Jean-Paul 129, 276
Ligonnet, Michel 233, 323, 361
Lister, Brian 212
Lister Cars 212, 249, 287, 325
　Storm GTS 212, 249–50
　Storm GTL 287, 325
Lloyd, Allen 289
Lloyd, Richard 101, 342
Lola Cars (International) 24, 48, 104, 355
　B98/10 355–7
　T710 (Corvette GTP, Eagle 700) 48
Lola Composites 104, 302
Lombardi, Pierre-Alain 34–5, 76
Lopez, Manuel 75
Lorimer, Graham 158
Los, Costas 42, 73, 141
Lotus Cars 136–7, 172–3, 286
　Esprit 300 GT2 136, 172
　Elise GT1 286
Lotus Engineering 216, 286
LotusSport 172
Lotus Racing 286
Lozano Bros 173, 214
Lucchini, Giorgio 135
Lucchini, Giuseppe 284
Lucchini Corse 135
　SP91 135
Ludwig, Klaus 314
Luigi Racing Team 164
Lynn, Dave 203, 240–1, 282

McCarthy, Perry 282, 343
McLaren, Bruce 238
McLaren cars 9, 189–94, 232–4, 265, 270–2, 315
McLoughlin, John 64, 284
McNeil, John 35, 71
McNish, Allan 13, 285, 300–3, 335, 339–40
McQueen, Alastair 21, 63–4, 95
McQuillan, Gerard 348
Machida, Sam 24
Mader, Heini 34–5, 73, 179, 243, 312
Magnani, Fabio 17, 36, 40, 135, 173
Magnussen, Jan 353
Magro, Enrico 81
Mahony, Jerry 46
Maisonneuve, Michel 80, 171, 340, 361
Mallock, Ray 25
Mancini, Fabio 166, 206
Mangoletsi, John 105, 264
Manoir de l'Automobile museum 170, 217
Manthey, Olaf 348
Manthey Racing 348
Maraj, Dave 348
Marc Pachot Racing 108
Marchart, Horst 152, 154
Marcos Cars 213, 252, 276, 290
　600LM 213–4, 252–3, 290
Maréchal, Hervé 209
Margueron, Charles 213
Marianashvili, Aleksandr 140–1
Marquart, Jo 48
Marsden, Howard 24
Marsh, Chris 214
Marsh, Jem 214

Martens, Jean-Claude 304
Martin, Marcel 19
Martini, Mauro 65, 125, 149, 155, 208, 252, 263, 274–5
Martini, Pierluigi 13, 225–30, 267, 284, 300, 312, 319, 335–6, 338
Martinolle, Guy 238, 276–7, 347
Mass, Jochen 58–9, 67, 189, 192
Matrix Motor 291
　MPX-1 291
Matsuda, Hideshi 104
Matsushita, Hiro 349
Matsuura, Kunio 30, 60
Maury-Laribière, Jean-Luc 138, 177, 194, 347
Mayländer, Bernd 348
Mazda 30, 58, 91, 102, 174, 202, 240, 282
Mazdaspeed 30–1, 57, 60–1, 102–3, 202–3, 282–3
　767B 30–1
　787 30–1, 60–1
　787B 60–1
　MRX-01 102–3, 228
　RX-7 GTO 174
Mazda North America 174
MCA Centenaire Beau Rivage 140
McLaren Cars Motorsport (MCM) 9, 190, 232, 270
　F1 GTR 9, 190, 232–3, 270–1, 315
McLaren Engines 289
McNeil Engineering 105
Méca Auto Système 137, 164, 170, 179, 215
Mega Line 341
Meiners, Franco 166
Meixner, Ronny 131
Méliand, Dominique 71, 99, 160, 194–5
Mello-Breyner, Manuel 277, 347
Mello-Breyner, Pedro 277, 347
Mello-Breyner, Tomas 277, 347
Mercedes-Benz 66, 300, 313, 333, 344
Mercedes-Benz Motorsport 9, 66–7, 300–1, 313–14, 333–5, 344–6
　CLK-GTR 9, 313–4
　CLR 344–6
　Sauber C9 66
　Sauber C11 66–7
　Sauber C291 66
Merwe, Sarel van der 38, 43
Messaoudi, Jean 44
Metz, Jean-François 217
Meunier, Michel 108
Mezera, Tomas 44
MGN (Moteurs Guy Nègre) 49
Michelotto Automobili 165, 206, 245–6, 308–9, 357
MiG (Migrelia Georgia) 140–1
　M100 140–1
Migault, François 45, 71, 107, 133, 164, 214, 309, 325
Millen, Steve 26, 157
Miloe, Jean-Claude 209
Minassian, Nicholas 179
MIRA wind tunnel 21, 190, 286, 354
Misaki, Kiyoshi 73
Missakian, Philippe 138
Mitani, Ken-Ichi 208
Mitsusada, Hidetoshi 251

1990-99

Mizuno, Kazutoshi 24, 200
Momo Corse 32, 197, 279, 291, 308
Monaco Media International 128–9
Mondini, Paolo 137
Monory, René 116
Montagny, Franck 320, 355
Monté, Lucien 138, 140, 164, 204, 217
Monte Carlo Automobiles 140
Monteiro, Manuel 346, 361
Monteiro, Michel 324, 361
Monteiro, Tiago 347
Montermini, Andrea 307, 350
Montezemolo, Luca di 228
Monti, Massimo 206
Moreton, Mike 126
Moretti, Giampiero 32, 196, 279–80, 309
Morin, Denis 35, 99, 134, 164, 215
Moriwaki, Moto 307
Morrison, David 270, 272
Morton, John 157, 243, 278, 324
Mosley, Max 7, 59, 90, 150
Moss, Joanna 304–5
Moteurs Guy Nègre see MGN
Motori Moderni 141
Motorsport Project Group 66
Motoyama, Satoshi 307, 354
Muller, Cathy 79
Müller, Dirk 348
Muller, Franck 233, 235
Müller, Jörg 274–5, 300–3, 335, 337
Müller, Willi 66
Muller, Yvan 135, 237
Munch, Gerhard 29
Munch, Peter 29
Murphy, Greg 238
Murray, Gordon 190, 270
Murry, David 136, 321
Mussato, Gianni 40, 81
MVS (Manufacture des Voitures de Sport) 137

Nagasaka, Naoki 37, 73, 125
Nagashima, Tsutomu 354
Nakajima, Satoru 199
Nakaya, Akihiko 272, 349
Namba, Yasuharu 24
Nanikawa, Yataka 27
Nappi, Piero 247
Nearn, Robert 238, 285, 323
Needell, Tiff 17, 27, 75, 101, 210, 250, 287
Neerpasch, Jochen 59
Nègre, Guy 49
Neugarten, Michel 177, 276
Nicholson, John 33–4, 46, 72
Nielsen, John 13, 20–1, 65, 100, 126, 167, 178, 189, 192, 194, 232, 235, 289, 307
Nippon Denso 30, 95
Nissan 24, 42, 156, 200, 245, 273, 288, 291, 306, 318, 350, 353
 300ZX 156–7
 R390 GT1 9, 273–5, 306–7
 R391 353–4
 R89C 42
 R90CK 24–6
 R90CP 24–6
 Skyline GT-R 200–1
 Skyline GT-R LM 245–6
Nissan Central Laboratories 24

Nissan Motorsports (NISMO) 24–6, 200, 245–6, 273, 306–7, 318–9, 350–1, 353–4
Nissan Motorsports Europe (NME) 24–6, 319
Nissan Performance Technology Inc (NPTI) 24–6, 291
Nissan Technical Centre 306
Noce, Luciano della 165, 206, 246–7
Norma Auto Concept 49, 216
 M5 49
 M6 49
Norris, Chris 105
Nourry, Michel 323, 349
Nova Engineering 307
Nurminen, Jari 279

Obermaier, Hans 43, 73, 77, 100, 133, 165
Obermaier Racing 43, 73, 77, 100–1, 128–9, 131–3, 165, 213
O'Brien, Eugene 205
O'Connell, Johnny 157, 317, 349, 353
Ogawa, Hitoshi 36, 97
Ogilvie, Martin 251, 286
Ohashi, Takayoshi 30, 60, 62, 203
Ohkuni, Masahiro 36
Okada, Hideki 34, 38, 168, 199
Olczyk, Philippe 129, 160
Oldsmobile 244
Olofsson, Anders 26, 42, 71, 165, 206, 246–7, 265, 270
Omura, Eiichi 198
Opel 228
Oppermann, Jürgen 43, 77, 133
Orbell, Grant 355
ORECA 60, 109, 243, 278–9, 310–11, 346–7
Orion (RenCar) 109
O'Rourke, Steve 240, 315
Ortelli, Stéphane 13, 209, 238, 240, 301–2, 343
Ota, Tetsuya 167, 206, 247
Owen, John 105
Owen, Richard 126
Owen-Jones, Lindsay 178, 191, 233, 235

Pace, Jim 244–5
Pacific Racing 288
Page, Ken 21
Pagotto, Luigi 277
Palau, Carlos 161–2, 207, 289
Pallanca Pastor, Gildo 215
Palmberger, Ernst 361
Palmer, Jonathan 17, 28, 38, 67
Panini, Giorgio 196
Panoz, Danny 280
Panoz, Don 280, 300, 317, 334
Panoz Motorsports 280, 316, 333, 352
 Esperante GTR-1 280–1, 316–7
 LM-P-1 Roadster 352–3
 Q9 Hybrid 317
Papis, Max 279–80
Parabolica Motorsport 270, 272
Pareja, Jesús 17, 22–3, 29, 74, 104, 129, 161–2, 209, 254, 288

PARR Motorsport 238–40
Pasqua, Charles 148
Patrese, Riccardo 265, 274
Paul Belmondo Racing 346–7
Paul Jr, John 216
PC Automotive 34, 80, 210–11
Pearce, Laurence 212, 249, 325
Peerless Racing 48
Percy, Win 126, 179, 210, 252
Perdrix, Daniel 325
Perez-Sala, Luis 21
Perrier, Thierry 323, 348–9
Pescarolo, Henri 29, 70, 91, 99, 130–1, 160, 189, 196, 236, 276, 320, 351, 359
Pescatori, Christian 284, 357
Peter, Patrick 150
Peterson, Doug 73
Petery, Andy 139
Petit, Pierre 108, 161, 200, 251
Petitjean, Jacques 77
Petit Le Mans 300
Peugeot Sport 68, 91, 108, 117, 119, 122, 134, 149, 151, 160, 199, 250
 905 68–9
 905 Evo-1B 92–4
 905 Evo-1C 120–2
 905 Evo-2.2 120
Pfadenhauer, Michael 341
Phillips, Mike 42, 71, 160
Pilbeam, Mike 288
Pilbeam Racing Design 288
Pilgrim, Andrew 240, 277
Pilot Racing 206, 247, 279–80, 309
Pinton, Ivone 81
Piper, John 63, 280
Piper, Richard 34, 80, 106, 136–7, 172, 210
Piquet, Nelson 234, 272
Pirro, Emanuele 315, 342
Poele, Eric van der 94, 157, 187, 196, 225–6, 237–8, 244, 263, 265, 274, 308, 354
Poiraud, Claude 137–8
Policand, Jérôme 225, 235, 309, 357
Police, Jean-Claude 169
Pompidou, Xavier 322
Porsche 127–34, 149–54, 161–3, 175, 209, 212–13, 226–32, 238–40, 260–1, 265–9, 276–7, 284–5, 300–3, 320–4, 335, 348–9
 911 GT1 10, 231–2, 268–9, 284–5, 302–3
 911 GT2 212–3, 238–9, 254, 276–7, 323–4, 360–1
 911 GT2 Evo 209, 240, 254
 911 GT3 348–9
 911 Turbo GT1 175
 962C 23, 27, 28–9, 39, 44, 70, 74–7, 99–101, 125, 131–4, 149–50, 158–9, 174
 962GS 32
 964-series 127–9
 968 Turbo RS 178
 993-series 212–3
 Carrera RSR 128–9, 162–3, 348–9
 Dauer 962LM 8–9, 152–4
 Kremer K8 158–9, 201–2, 248–9, 322
 Kremer K8 Evo 322
 LMP1-98 320–1

Turbo S Le Mans 127–8, 175, 212
WSC95 228, 266–7
Porsche Kundensport 22, 38, 43
Porsche Motorsport 39, 70, 152, 228–9, 238, 266, 231, 302–3, 320–1
Porsche North America 228
Poulain, Hervé 177, 194
Prewitt, Dave 33, 46, 80, 214
Price, David 24, 192, 234, 280, 317, 349
Price+Bscher Racing 349–50
Primwest Holdings 138
Project 100 158
Project XJ220 Ltd 126
Promotion Racing Team 319, 351
Protech 217
Prutirat, Ratankul 286
PSCR (Professional Sports Car Racing) 226, 308

Racing for Belgium 237–8, 279
Racing Technology Norfolk 342
Rackham, Richard 286
Radiguès, Didier de 322, 355
Radnofsky, Stuart 158
Rafanelli, Gabriele 233, 312
Raffauf, Mark 126
Ragazzi, Roberto 135
Randaccio, Ranieri 107
Randle, Jim 126
Randlinger 325
Raphanel, Pierre-Henri 37, 69, 89, 91, 95, 97, 117, 119, 123–4, 160, 194, 234–5, 265, 270, 321
Ratel, Stéphane 138, 150, 177, 206, 247, 309
Ratzenberger, Roland 37, 76, 98–9, 125, 155
Raulet, Jean-Daniel 71
Ravaglia, Roberto 26, 37, 265, 270, 272
Ravenel, Raymond 16
Ravkit, Seree 215
Ray, Lester 178
Rédélé, Jean 169
Reed, Ian 20, 228
Reed, Martin 352
Région des Pays de La Loire 7
Regis, Jacques 262
Regout, Hervé 42, 139, 161
Reid, Anthony 17, 27, 76, 250
Reinisch, Peter 23
Reiter, Hans 338
Reitter, Horst 231
Renaud, Jacky 109
Renault 49, 137, 169, 255, 291, 325, 353
 Sport Spider V6 255
RenCar see Orion
Rent A Car Racing 164
Ress, Leo 66–7
Reuter, Manuel 13, 41, 75, 100, 131, 158, 178, 226, 230
Reynard Composites 241
Reynard Special Vehicle Projects (RSVP) 280, 317
Reynard wind tunnel 241, 281, 346
RF Sport 206
Ricardo 341
Ricci, Jean-Louis 29, 73, 80, 91, 99, 130, 141, 160, 276, 323

Riccitelli, Luca 348
Richard Lloyd Racing (RLR) 41, 101
Richardson, Tim 291
Rickett, Charles 80, 100
Riley, Bill 245
Riley, Bob 216, 244
Riley & Scott 244, 311, 322, 358
 R&S Mk3 244–5, 322, 358–9
Riley & Scott Europe 358–9
Rimmer, Roger 205
Rinland, Sergio 167
Rioli, Mauro 196
Rippie, Doug 216
Risi, Giuseppe 308
RJ Racing team 291, 325
Robe, Paul 238–9
Robert, Lionel 39, 71, 99, 130, 149, 159–60, 194, 325
Robert Yates Engine Development 353
Robinson, Chip 25
ROC (Racing Organisation Course) 73
 002 73
Roe, Michael 26
Roessler, Wido 254
Röhrl, Walter 128
Romo, Luis 280
Roncz, Jim 244
Rondeau, Jean 39, 137, 164
Roni F3000 team 319
Roock, Fabian 238, 323, 361
Roock, Michael 238, 323, 361
Roock Racing 238, 254, 276–7, 285, 323, 361
Rosa, Pedro de la 251
Rosberg, Keke 58, 68–9
Rosche, Paul 190, 233, 270, 312
Rose, Jean-Claude 39, 70
Rose, Lucien 137
Rosenblad, Carl 246, 289
Rostan, Marc 161
Roush Engines 281, 316, 353, 355, 357
Roussel, Patrice 205
Rover 214
Roy, Benjamin 169
Roy, Jean-Luc 291
Roy, Jean-Michel 169
RSR Motorsport 162
Rubery Owen 105
Ruggles, Jim 216–7
Rushforth, Chris 280, 354
Russell, John 312, 336
Russo, Onofrio 137
Rydell, Rickard 44

St James, Lyn 79
Said, Boris 171
Saito, Haruhiko 95
Salamin, Antoine 59, 77
Salamin team 59, 77
Salazar, Eliseo 288
Saldana, Tomas 99, 133, 166, 213, 289, 355–7
Saleen, Steve 288–9
Saleen-Allen Speedlab 288–9
Salvador, Thierry 38
Sanders, Ian 24, 234
Sandro Sala, Maurizio 62, 91, 102–3, 193–4, 235
Santal, Bernard 23, 74, 134, 175, 205
Santos, Norbert 49, 216
Sanua, Pino 135

INDEX 383

LE MANS

SARD (Sigma Advanced
  Racing Developments)
  36–7, 98–9, 125, 149, 151,
  155–6, 208–9, 251–2, 291
  MC8-R see Toyota
Sardou wind tunnel 196
Sarta 624 LM-P1 project 325
Sauber, Peter 66
Sauber cars see
  Mercedes-Benz
Sauvée, Jean-Paul 217
Saved, Jean-Paul 176
SBF Team 176
Scaglietti 165
Scandia team 237–8
Schanche, Martin 48
Schiattarella, Domenico
  'Mimmo' 350–1
Schiefer, Ulrich 336
Schirle, Rob 252, 289
Schlesser, Jean-Louis 58–9,
  63, 66–7, 69
Schmidt, Gerd 22
Schneider, Bernd 70, 300,
  314, 333–5, 346
Schnitzer, Herbert 272
Schnitzer Motorsport 270,
  337–8
Schubeck, Joe 49
Schübel, Horst 284
Schübel Engineering 284
Schumacher, Michael 13,
  58, 67
Schuppan, Vern 44, 76
Scott, Allan 20, 63
Scott, Mark 244
Scuderia Chicco d'Oro
  129, 163
Sears, David 17, 27
Sebastiani, Stefano
  ('Stingbrace') 107, 167
Seguin, Philippe 186
Sehcar SHS C6 140, 179
Seikel, Peter 178, 213, 240
Seikel Motorsport 167, 178,
  213, 240, 248
Seiler, Toni 324, 347
Sekiya, Masanori 13, 17, 36,
  40, 91, 95, 97, 119, 123,
  189–90, 251, 270–2
Senna, Ayrton 167
SERA-CD 141
Sezionale, Edouard 205,
  255, 325
Shapiro, John 32
Sharp, Scott 244–5
Shead, Don 35
Shead, James 13
Sheldon, John 46, 80, 106
Shibetsu proving ground 36
Shimamura, Kenta 106–7
Shimuzu, Kazuo 168
Siffert, Jo 213
Siffert, Philippe 213
Sifton, Victor 243
Sigala, Massimo 23, 197
Silman, Roger 21, 126, 273
Simmiss, Craig 46
Simmonds, Rob 341
Simpson Engineering 166
Simpson-Smith, Robin 166–7
Sims, Dave 'Beaky' 95, 272
Singer, Norbert 28, 128,
  152–4, 202, 228–9,
  231–2, 302, 320
Skaife, Mark 287
Skene, Bob 210
Skinner, Doug 280, 354

Slater, Charles 361
Smith, Alan 35, 139
Smith, Ian 287
Smith, Robin 123
Solution F 322, 358–9
Somerville, Jason 312, 336
Soper, Steve 233, 265, 272,
  312, 338, 349
Sospiri, Vincenzo 300, 309,
  339, 357
Soulignac, Vincent 160
Sourd, Marc 194, 255, 291
Southgate, Tony 21, 95, 98,
  123, 196, 237, 249, 273–4,
  306–7, 341–2
Spice, Gordon 33, 72
Spice Engineering 33, 72,
  79, 106
  SE87C 34–5
  SE89C 34–5, 79–80,
    106, 139
  SE90C 32, 72–3, 79–80,
    106–107
Spice Prototype
  Automobiles 72
Spice USA 72
Springer, Alwin 22, 228
SRWC (Sports Racing
  World Cup) 264
Ssangyong 250
Stalder, Fred 73
Stalder Motorsport 162,
  205, 213, 240, 276
St Cyr wind tunnel 319, 357
Stealth Engineering 176
Stevens, Bruce 106
Stevens, Peter 136, 190,
  336, 349
Stirling, Robbie 13, 35, 74
Storz, Achim 152
Strandell, Bo 165
Stroth, Achim 158, 168, 248
Stroud, Nigel 30, 41, 60, 102,
  203, 241, 280–1, 354
Stuck, Hans-Joachim 17, 28,
  70, 126, 128, 149, 151,
  153, 202, 226–7, 231, 265,
  268, 312
Sturm, Alain 134
Sugden, Tim 315
Sullivan, Danny 151, 153,
  233–4
Sumitomo Rubber
  Industries 79
Suzuka, Yoshi 24
Suzuki, Aguri 17, 25, 37,
  245–6, 274, 306–7
Suzuki, Toshio 24, 119, 123,
  201, 245–6, 306, 335, 339
Swetnam, Malcolm 46
Synergie 35, 140, 164, 170,
  179, 217

Tachi, Nobuhide 36, 95
Takahashi, Kunimitsu 38, 168,
  199, 248
Takami, Sugawara 201
Tarrès, Marcel 77
Taverna, Luigi 81, 106, 135
Taylor, Wayne 44, 76, 105,
  133, 203, 225, 244–5,
  274, 308
TC Prototypes (TCP) 23, 43,
  75, 76, 78, 100, 101, 167,
  198, 201
TDR (Tim Davey Racing) 107
Team Alméras Chotard 101
Team Davey 47

Team Ennea 165
Team Goh/Team Lark 233–5,
  270, 272, 349–50
Team Guy Chotard 134
Team Kunimitsu Honda 199,
  205, 248
Team Le Mans 42
Team Mako 35
Team Marcos International
  252, 290
Team Nippon 174
Team Rafanelli 311–12
Team Salamin 76, 77
Team Scandia 197, 237,
  279–80
Team Schnitzer 270, 337–8
Team Schuppan 44, 47, 76
Terada, Yojiro 31, 62, 91,
  103, 119, 124, 136–7,
  174–5, 202–3, 240–1,
  282–3, 320, 358–9
Terrien, David 355
Tessier, Georges 135
Theissen, Mario 337
Thévenin, Olivier 206–7,
  247, 285, 319–20
Theys, Didier 226, 229,
  279–80, 309, 320, 342
Thibault, Jean-Claude 44,
  72, 164
Thiim, Kurt 67
Thoisy, Pierre de 33, 129, 175
Thompson, John 22, 167, 198
Thomson, Julian 286
Thorby, Andy 251, 317, 352–3
Thuner, Bernard 73, 210
Thyrring, Thorkild 136–7,
  172–3, 205
Tiga Race Cars 44, 46, 47,
  107–8, 217
  GC286/9 46
  GC287 217
  GC288/9 107–8
Tinseau, Christophe 317, 355
Todt, Jean 59, 68, 92, 117,
  120, 122
Toivonen, Harri 75, 105,
  249, 288
Tomei Engineering 27
Tomita, Tsutomu 36, 95,
  123, 155
TOMS (Tachi Oiwa Motor
  Sports) 36–7, 95–9, 123,
  251, 304
TOMS GB 95, 123, 212, 251,
  304, 342
Touchais, Alain 39, 70
Touroul, Raymond 109
Toyota, Yasuo 43
Toyota 10, 36, 91, 95, 117,
  119, 122, 149, 151, 155,
  208, 251, 291, 300, 304,
  333, 339
  89CV 36
  90CV 36–7
  92CV 98
  93CV 125
  94CV 155
  SARD MC8-R 208–9,
    252, 291
  Supra GT1 208, 251
  TS010 95–7, 123–4
  TS020 (GT-One) 10, 304–6,
    339–40
Toyota Engine Research &
  Advanced Engineering 95–7
Toyota Motorsport GmbH
  (TMG) 304, 339

Toyota Racing Developments
  (TRD) 36–7, 95–8, 155, 208
Toyota Team Europe (TTE)
  304–6
Toyota Team TOMS (TTT) 36–7,
  95–7, 98, 123–4
Travis, John 25
Tremblay, Gérard 109,
  128, 135
Trévisiol, Arnaud 215
Tribunal de Grand Instance
  18, 150
Trollé, Michel 39, 71
Trust Racing 43, 78, 98, 125,
  149, 151, 155–6, 208
Tsuchiya, Keiichi 168, 199, 248,
  272, 306, 339
Tsuchiya, Takeshi 319
Turner, Matt 311
TWR (Tom Walkinshaw Racing)
  20–1, 63–5, 95, 126–7,
  228–9, 246, 265, 273,
  306–7, 320, 353
TWR Engines 212
TWR Inc 20–3, 228
TWR Suntec 65

Ulrich, Jack 287
Ungar, Gerhard 314, 344
University of Glasgow
  wind tunnel 352
University of Stuttgart wind
  tunnel 345
Unser, Johnny 205
USRRC Can-Am Series 308

Valsangiacomo, Cornelio 163
Vandenbosh, Charles 291
VBM (Voitures Bornhauser
  Metz) 4000GTC 217
Velez, Fermin 33, 197, 237,
  244, 308
Veneto Equipe 81
Veninata, Vito 107
Venturi Compétition 137,
  150, 176, 215
  400 Trophy 177
  500LM 137
  600LM 176, 215
  600S-LM 215
Vergnes, Daniel 319, 351
Veroux, Jean-François 213
Vilariño, Andrés 166
Ville du Mans, 7
Vincentz, Chester 'Ched' 32
Viper Engineering 241,
  310, 346
Viper Team ORECA
  see ORECA
VN Composite 325
Vögele, Herbert 337
Vonka, Jan 201–2
VW Group 170
Vyver, Eric van der 291

Wada, Takao 42
Walch, Rudi 22–23
Walkinshaw, Tom 21, 59, 63,
  126, 228, 273
Wallace, Andy 17, 20, 63,
  65, 97, 124, 189, 192–3,
  234, 281–2, 316, 343,
  353, 358
Warnock, Dave 252, 289
Warwick, Derek 13, 64–5,
  89, 91–2, 94, 235–6
Wasyliw, Nick 319
Waters, Glenn 95, 212

Watkins, Prof Sid 346
Watson, John 41
Weaver, James 41, 76–7,
  210, 227, 234–5, 243,
  282, 317, 321, 343, 358
Webber, Mark 333–4, 344–5
Weidler, Volker 13, 58–62,
  91, 102–3
Welter, Gérard 108, 134, 161,
  199, 251
Welter, Rachel 108, 134,
  199, 251
Welti, Max 152, 228
Wendlinger, Karl 13, 58, 67,
  92, 225, 231–2, 310–11,
  346–7
Werner, Marco 201
West FM 193
Weston, Peter 288, 355
Whitehead, David 286
Wickham, John 342
Wiedeking, Wendelin 154
Wiggins, Keith 288
Williams, Richard 217
Williams Grand Prix Engineering
  306, 311–12, 336–8, 349
Willis, Chris 288
Wilson, Desiré 79
Wilson, Rob 179
Winkelhock, Joachim 13,
  335–6
Withalm, Gert 66
Witmeur, Pascal 237
Wittwer, Hans 48
Wöhr, Ernst 171
Wollek, Bob 28, 63–4, 91, 99,
  130–1, 133, 151, 156, 187,
  189, 193–6, 209, 226, 228,
  231–2, 265, 267–8, 301–3,
  348, 359
Wood, David 126
Wood, Dudley 34–5
WR (Welter Racing) 108,
  119, 134, 149, 151, 160,
  187, 189, 199, 250
  LM92 108
  LM92/3 134
  LM93/4 160–1
  LM94 160–1
  LM94/5 199–200
  LM95 199–200
  LM96 250–1
Wright, Tim 94
Wurz, Alex 13, 226, 228, 230

Yamamoto, Kenichi 102–3
Yellow Racing 207
Yokoshima, Hisashi 73
Yorino, Takashi 31, 62, 103
Yoshikawa, Tomiko 79, 106–7,
  174, 209
Youles, Mike 34
Yver, Pierre 43, 77, 101, 130,
  162–3, 209, 254, 278, 359
Yvon, Jean-François 99,
  130, 161

Zakspeed 303, 304
Zanco, Stefano 81
Zander, Jörg 304
Zinelli, Dialma 197, 237
Zoner, Mike 171
Zonta, Ricardo 314
ZR-1 Corvette Team USA 216
Zwart, Klaas 172, 217
Zwolsman, Charles 33–4,
  72–3, 104–5
Zytek 20, 104, 282, 316–7